Music Education Yearbook 1998/99

Editor: Laura Dollin

Assistant Editor: Karen Harman

Fifteenth Edition

Rhinegold Publishing Limited
241 Shaftesbury Avenue
London WC2H 8EH

Editorial: 0171 333 1761
Book Sales: 0171 333 1721 Advertising: 0171 333 1733
Fax: 0171 333 1769
Email: meyb@rhinegold.co.uk

First published 1998 in Great Britain by
Rhinegold Publishing Limited, 241 Shaftesbury Avenue,
London WC2H 8EH *tel:* 0171 333 1700

Music Education Yearbook
— 1998/99
Fifteenth Edition of
British Music Education Yearbook

British Library Cataloguing in Publication Data.
A catalogue record for this book is available from the British Library.

ISBN 0 946890 77 3
ISSN 1353-8896

Printed in Great Britain by Perfectaprint, Byfleet, Surrey.

Contents

Resources Published in 1997

National and Regional Organisations

Resources for Teachers

Youth Performance

Examinations

Schools

Further and Higher Education

Teacher Training Courses

International Study

Conferences, Recreational and Part-Time Courses

Jazz In Education

Suppliers and Services

Reference

Indexes

Key and Abbreviations

General. The geographical scope of this book covers England, Scotland, Wales, Northern Ireland and the Channel Islands.

Addresses. Postal listing is followed by the telephone, fax, email numbers and website addresses. *Also fax* after a telephone number indicates the number can also be used as a fax line. Conventional address abbreviations are used in all listings and are not included below.

Abbreviations. Abbreviations which appear in only one section of the book are explained in the rubric to the relevant section. Others are listed below, divided according to type.

Musical Performance

Br	brass	hpd	harpsichord
bsn	bassoon	inst	instrument, instrumental
chmbr	chamber	m/class	masterclass
cl	clarinet	mus	music, musical
comp	composition	ob	oboe
c/point	counterpoint	orch	orchestra, orchestral
db	double bass	org	organ
eh	english horn (cor anglais)	perc	percussion
ens	ensemble	perf	performing, performance
fl	flute	picc	piccolo
gui	guitar	pno	piano
hn	horn	sax	saxophone
hp	harp	str	string

Positions

admin	administrator, administration	ed	editor
asst	assistant	hon	honorary
chmn	chairman	mgr	manager, managing
co-ord	co-ordinator	mkt	marketing
cond	conductor		
dir	director		

Other

ABRSM	Associated Board of the Royal Schools of Music	min	minimum
a/v	audio visual	ms(s)	manuscript(s)
c/room	classroom	mus tech	music technology
dept	department	NC	National Curriculum
DfEE	Department for Education and Employment	pa	per annum
educ	education, educational	p/grad	postgraduate
elec	electronic	p/t	part-time
ext	extension	p/wk	per week
FE	further education	RAM	Royal Academy of Music
f/t	full-time	RCM	Royal College of Music
gen	general	snr	senior
gr	grade	tech	technology
GSMD	Guildhall School of Music and Drama	tel	telephone
HE	higher education	t/p	teaching practice
hr	hour	T/T	teacher training
IT	information technology	u/grad	undergraduate
jnr	junior	univ	university
KS	key stage	w/day	week day
LA	local authority	w/end	weekend
LEA	local education authority	wk	week
max	maximum	w/shop	workshop
		WWW	worldwide web
		yr	year

Music Degrees and Diplomas

The following are generally recognised music qualifications. It should be noted that some refer to institutions which are no longer functioning.

University Degrees

AMusM	master of musical arts of Nottingham University
AMusD	doctor of musical arts of Nottingham University
BA	bachelor of arts
Bed	bachelor of education
BHum	bachelor of humanities
BMus	bachelor of music
BPhil	bachelor of philosophy
MA	master of arts
MEd	master of education
MLitt	master of letters
MMus	master of music
MMusRCM	master of music of the Royal College of Music
MPhil	master of philosophy
MusB	bachelor of music
MusBac	bachelor of music
MusD	doctor of music
MusM	master of music
PhD	doctor of philosophy

Diplomas of Graduate Status

Several institutions have the power to grant 'graduate diplomas'. The following selection is of those diplomas most commonly awarded.

Dip Mus Ed (RSAM)	diploma in musical education of the Royal Scottish Academy of Music and Drama
FRCO	fellow of the Royal College of Organists
GBSM	graduate of the Birmingham School of Music
GCLCM (LightMusic)	graduate of the City of Leeds College of Music (Light Music)
GDBM	graduate diploma in Band Musicianship, University of Salford
GDWCMD	graduate diploma of Welsh College of Music and Drama
GGSM	graduate of the Guildhall School of Music and Drama
GLCM	graduate of the London College of Music
GNSM	graduate of the (former) Northern School of Music
GRNCM	graduate of the Royal Northern College of Music
GRSM	graduate of the Royal Schools of Music
GTCL	graduate of Trinity College of Music

Other Diplomas

These are usually awarded for either performing or teaching, and cover a wide range of subjects and instruments. Special qualifications may be additionally designated, eg TD for 'teaching diploma'.

ABCA	associate of the British College of Accordionists
ABSM	associate of the Birmingham School of Music
ADCM	Archbishop's diploma in church music
AGSM	associate of the Guildhall School of Music and Drama
ALCM	associate of the London College of Music
A Mus LCM	associate in general musicianship of the London College of Music
A Mus NCM	associate in theory of music of the National College of Music
A Mus TCL	associate in compositional techniques of Trinity College of Music
ANCM	associate of the National College of Music
ANSM	associate of the (former) Northern School of Music
ARCM	associate of the Royal College of Music
ARCO	associate of the Royal College of Organists
ARCO(CHM)	associate of the Royal College of Organists, choirmaster's diploma
ARMCM	associate of the (former) Royal Manchester College of Music
ARNCM	associate of the Royal Northern College of Music
ATCL	associate of Trinity College of Music
ATSC	associate of the Tonic Sol-Fa College of music
Dip Ed	diploma in education (various institutions)
Dip Mus Ed	diploma in musical education (various institutions)
Dip RAM	recital diploma of the Royal Academy of Music
DipTMus	Scottish music teaching diploma
DPLM	diploma of proficiency in light music of the City of Leeds College of Music
DRSAM	diploma in music of the Royal Scottish Academy of Music and Drama
FLCM	fellow of the London College of Music
FRCO (CHM)	fellow of the Royal College of Organists, choirmaster's diploma
FRMCM	fellow of the (former) Royal Manchester College of Music
FTCL	fellow of Trinity College of Music
FTSC	fellow of the Tonic Sol-Fa College of Music
LBCA	licentiate of the British College of Accordionists
LGSM	licentiate of the Guildhall School of Music and Drama
LLCM	licentiate of the London College of Music
L Mus LCM	licentiate in general musicianship of the London College of Music
L Mus NCM	licentiate in theory of music of the National College of Music
L Mus TCL	licentiate in compositional techniques of Trinity College of Music
L Mus TSC	licentiate in general musicianship of the Tonic Sol-Fa College of Music
LNCM	licentiate of the National College of Music
LRAM	licentiate of the Royal Academy of Music
LRSM	licentiate of the Royal Schools of Music
LTCL	licentiate of Trinity College of Music
LTCL(GMT)	licentiate in general musicianship (teachers) of Trinity College of Music
LTSC	licentiate of the Tonic Sol-Fa College of Music
LWCMD	licentiate of the Welsh College of Music and Drama
PDBM	professional diploma in band musicianship, University of Salford
PDBM(PMR)	professional diploma in band musicianship (popular music with recording), University of Salford
PGCC(Band)	postgraduate higher certificate in band conducting, University of Salford
PPRNCM	professional performer of the Royal Northern College of Music

Honorary Awards

ARCM	associate of the Royal Academy of Music
ARSCM	associate of the Royal School of Church Music
D Mus (Cantuar)	doctor of music, awarded by the Archbishop of Canterbury
FBSM	fellow of the Birmingham School of Music
FGSM	fellow of the Guildhall School of Music and Drama
FNCM	fellow of the National College of Music
FNSM	fellow of the (former) Northern School of Music
FRAM	fellow of the Royal Academy of Music
FRCM	fellow of the Royal College of Music
FRNCM	fellow of the Royal Scottish Academy of Music and Drama
FRSCM	fellow of the Royal School of Church Music
FWCMD	fellow of the Welsh College of Music and Drama Hon
ARAM	honorary associate of the Royal Academy of Music Hon
ARCM	honorary associate of the Royal College of Music Hon
FGSM	honorary fellow of the Guildhall School of Music and Drama Hon
FRAM	honorary fellow of the Royal Academy of Music Hon
FTCL	honorary fellow of Trinity College of Music Hon
FTSC	honorary fellow of the Tonic Sol-Fa College of Music Hon
GDBM	honorary graduate in band musicianship, Salford College of Technology Hon
GSM	honorary member of the Guildhall School of Music and Drama Hon
LCM	honorary member of the London College of Music Hon
RAM	honorary member of the Royal Academy of Music Hon
RCM	honorary member of the Royal College of Music Hon
RSCM	honorary member of the Royal School of Church Music Hon
TSC	honorary member of the Tonic Sol-Fa College of Music

A Year in Music Education

By Leonora Davies

'Music is alive and healthy. Of its nature it is a survivor and committed music teachers will always find ways of enhancing their art, whatever the legal and financial arrangements of the time.' These are the encouraging words of Leon Crickmore, former HMI and now Consultant for Higher Education and Training in Music, providing us with a suitably positive opening for this overview of music education in the last year.

There are many shining lights to illuminate the wealth of activity and progress that is characteristic of another year in music education. OFSTED report that 1996-97 was a good year for music in the curriculum. 'Teaching in Key Stages 1 and 2 remains good and there was markedly more good teaching in Key Stage 3 than in previous years. GCSE numbers were sustained in most schools' claims their most recent publication which documents and disseminates this good practice.

Music education, however, is not just confined to the parameters of the school timetable; there is an increased awareness among musicians who do not necessarily work regularly within education, of the importance of music education at all levels. Provision should be available for people with a wide range of needs and aspirations - for adults, children, amateurs, aspiring professionals and those involved in musics of particular ethnic traditions within the popular and commercial areas, as well as those committed to music within the Western high art tradition.

Through the commitment and influence of organisations such as Music for Youth and the British Federation of Youth Choirs, opportunities for children of all ages to perform in a variety of different contexts continue to flourish.

However we do seem to have arrived at a very particular cross-roads in music education and it is important that the issues are clear. There are those who feel that it is important for the professional voice to be heard above that of the politician. Music in the curriculum and the provision and accessibility of instrumental tuition - the foundation planks central to any music education system - are under grave threat from political recommendation, facing subsequent erosion and possible destruction.

The statutory requirements within the National Curriculum for music have had a positive influence in significantly raising the awareness in teachers across all phases of education of the importance placed on a planned scheme of music-making activities within the curriculum. Of course the provision, the quantity and quality of these activities is patchy, particularly in primary schools, but many of us would support the official OFSTED commentary that there is clear evidence of continuing improvement and that these trends would continue given the opportunity to do so. Nobody is underestimating the importance of literacy and numeracy, but there is now such irrefutable evidence as to the importance of the arts in their contribution not only to children's learning and concentration skills, but also to their holistic education, that any devaluation of the subject within the curriculum can only have a devastating effect in the long-run.

Above all, it is vital that parents and students understand the implications of what is happening and the potential long-term effects on a music education system that has been the pride of this country and the envy of the world, not simply in the quality of its musical achievements, but more importantly also for the access and breadth of opportunity it has given to so many students from different backgrounds.

The threat to instrumental tuition also has a knock-on effect on the provision of bands, instrumental ensembles and orchestras. The Associated Board's research findings published in November 1997 suggest that there has been a severe reduction in the number of children of primary school age who are now learning an instrument. Within the Education Bill presently going through parliament there are suggestions that funding currently held centrally by LEAs for such services as school meals and instrumental provision, must be delegated to the schools themselves for them to use as they deem appropriate. This could mean the demise of centrally organised instrumental schemes in LEAs who often offer support to pupils otherwise unable to afford instrumental tuition. The alarmist slogan of 'Can't pay, can't play' is on the horizon.

I am sure that many in the education profession, as elsewhere, felt that the 2 May 1997 brought a new dawn, full of hope and opportunity and fresh ears to hear and listen. Now many are reeling from government action which apparently de-values music in the curriculum. We appear instead to have a game in which the ball of music education is bounced between the DfEE (Department for Education and Employment) and the DCMS (Department for Culture, Media and Sport).

If there is to be an erosion of music-making within the primary curriculum this will have an inevitable knock-on effect on the secondary curriculum, on further and higher education and the training of future teachers. Perhaps it is time to take a radical look at the conventions of the secondary music timetable. Professor Keith Swanwick suggested in a recent article in the TES that 'Young people [in secondary schools] regard school music as a quaint sub-culture separated from music out in the world.' This is certainly true in some instances, but there are also numerous examples of excellent practice where teachers do manage to juggle all the balls. One of the most positive and musically productive developments referred to at the beginning of this article is the partnership between professional musicians and composers working alongside teaching colleagues. The results of these creative and collaborative projects involving large numbers of pupils have a profound and significant impact on all who are involved.

One of Keith Swanwick's suggestions is that we could consider clustering schools to pool the musical expertise of the teachers themselves. In this way, schools might see themselves more as facilitating agencies than sole providers. 'The division between curriculuar and extra-curricular music would then be eroded and the job of secondary music teachers become realistic'.

There are now a number of specialist schools being set up across the country. Although there has been resistance to this idea amongst the traditionalists in education it may be that for many young people these could be their salvation. Is it too simplistic to contrast the intrinsic qualities of self-discipline and co-operation - not to say imagination and creativity - that are part of arts education with the unproductive, ill-disciplined behaviour that we see all too often in young people without focus or appropriate challenge?

The BRIT School in Croydon is an example of a whole school based on clear objectives and disciplines that come from involvement in the performing arts which are taught as rigorously and seriously as Science and Maths. Not all the students continue with their education in the arts, but as the Principal Clare Venables says, 'Whatever they do, I know that they have been stretched by their time with us and have learned through experience of the joys of collaboration, mutual respect and responsibility. Somewhere in London is a policeman who specialised in drama and dance. For some reason I find that very comforting.'

Lottery money has already had a significant influence on funding for some arts activities and in itself is to be welcomed, but it will not provide long-term answers to the current problems and may divorce some music-making activities from the curriculum altogether.

Viewed positively, these threats to the very foundations of music education have become a subject of substantial political debate both in the media and in newspapers and we must all continue to keep this a high profile issue at this crucial time.

The situation in higher education and initial teacher training is still very confused. The focus on English and Maths in the training of primary teachers will inevitably mean even less time is devoted to training in other specialist subjects. The effects of this in institutions will need to be monitored closely. There is already evidence in the number of students applying to graduate courses that music is a shortage subject, but that must be balanced by recent HMI findings that the quality of training provided by many PGCE courses is of a high standard. Certainly my own experience is that these courses continue to turn out young teachers who are full of enthusiasm and energy, and who have a range of musical and personal skills that are totally appropriate for the modern classroom. This must be encouraging for all of us.

However, there are real issues about the funding support for students wishing to specialise in music at tertiary level. Janet Ritterman, Director of the Royal College of Music believes that 'an arrangement which removes the maintenance grant is likely to deter many of those who under present arrangements would have been able to pursue their studies at tertiary level.'

Despite these potential difficulties there is a wide and exciting range of courses and training opportunities currently available in both initial and continuing music education. Established institutions such as Trinity College of Music offer an MA in Music Education which attracts diverse professionals ranging from teachers to orchestral players; the Associated Board's Professional Development course for Instrumental and Singing Teachers leading to the CT ABRSM award draws increasing numbers and has established itself as a recognised pathway for the instrumental or singing teacher wishing to broaden and deepen their teaching skills.

The Guildhall School of Music continues to offer the Advanced Certificate Course in Performance and Communication Skills and there is a welcome proliferation of courses in Studio music and Music Technology across the country. The Universities of Salford and Leeds offer particular courses in a range of popular musical styles and jazz studies and many of these, along with a number of teacher training courses include some focus on world musics as an integral part of the students' training.

Finally, the influence of IT and the growing use of Internet facilities offer a very exciting and potentially powerful learning tool to schools and institutions in every area of the curriculum, but particularly within Music and Music Technology. The DfEE supported an important project through BECTA (British Educational Communications and Technology Agency) in the development of Teacher Support materials for KS3. The Training Programme will be made available to all schools in the country during the coming year with the possibility of a nationally organised in-service training programme.

The British Music Centre project is a joint venture between the leading music industries trade organisations to create a home for British popular music in London. Projects such as these, along with technological advances and government plans for the National Grid for Learning where creativity and technology could come together, should propel us with some excitement and enthusiasm towards the year 2000.

[I wish to thank the following individuals who were consulted for this article: John Stephens, *Director of Music Education, Trinity College of Music*; Janet Ritterman, *Director, Royal College of Music*; Richard Morris, *Chief Executive, Associated Board of the Royal Schools of Music*; Professor Keith Swanwick, *Professor of Music Education at the Institute of Education*; Leon Crickmore, *Consultant, Higher Education and Training in Music*; Janet Mills, *HMI*].

Leonora Davies is the Chair of the National Association of Music Educators *and an Inspector for Music and Music Services in the London Borough of Haringey.*

Preface and Acknowledgements

It is often said that there is nothing more constant than change. This could not be more true when it comes to music education, and as the new editor of the *Music Education Yearbook* it is my pleasure to introduce you to the 1998/99 edition which, I hope, provides the wealth of information required to keep up with these changes.

First and foremost, those familiar with the book will notice that the layout has been totally redesigned, presenting more defined, user-friendly listings. We have introduced a column structure to clarify the contact details for each entry, as well as bolder section headers for ease of reference.

Also new in this edition is the inclusion of three new sections: *Conferences, World Music* and *Financial Services*. Conferences are a rapidly growing industry and it became clear that many organisations hold regular events that may be of national interest to those working in music education. It also became increasingly apparent that World Music is an area that has developed considerably since its introduction to the National Curriculum, warranting a resources section in the book. The Financial Services section provides a list of accountants and insurance companies who deal particularly with arts and music clients.

A year in music education would not be complete without some administrative shufflings. To ensure that we remain confused for another year, 1st April 1998 saw the remainder of the Local Authority boundary changes take place. The Exam boards have also made significant changes to their structure. As the range of qualifications on offer continues to broaden, the need has arisen to enable both academic and vocational qualifications to operate from within the same organisation. This has led to the launch of OCR by UCLES and the RSA Examinations boards and the Assessment and Qualifications Alliance (AQA) by the Associated Examining Board and City & Guilds. More details on these changes may be found in the *Examinations* sections. The Scottish Exam Board is now known as the Scottish Qualifications Authority.

All in all, with the new design of the book and the significant research required to launch the new sections, the compilation of this edition has been particularly challenging and without the help of numerous organisations and individuals it would not have been possible. Sincere thanks must go to the contributors, Nigel Morgan for compiling the Information Technology chapter with its new website section, Elizabeth Smith of the *International Centre for Research in Music Education* for the Educational Resource Material section and Leonora Davies for taking on the *Year in Education* article. Alan and Elaine Kitcher of *A & E Internet* have been indispensible with their technological expertise, guiding us through the trials and tribulations of a new software package. Closer to home my thanks must go to Sarah Williams who has devoted a great deal of extra time to ensure the smooth running of the schedule, to Robert Holmes for his co-operation on the new sections, and of course to Karen Harman who remained admirably composed when I was far from it, and whose support and integrity have been invaluable.

Laura Dollin
London, April 1998

Editor Laura Dollin **Assistant Editor** Karen Harman **Publishing Manager** Sarah Williams **Head of Advertising Sales** Robert Holmes **Advertising Manager** Hannah Saunders **Advertising Sales** Samantha Clark, Daniel Burman, Stephen Reck **Production Controller** Joanna Moore **Design Manager** Sharon Gallagher **Designers** Steve Talkington, Phil Wingrove, Hallam Bannister **Marketing Manager** Richard Thomas **Book Sales Administrator** Penny Mills **Marketing Director** Keith Diggle **Managing Director** Tony Gamble

National and Regional Organisations

National Education Departments

Department for Education and Employment (DFEE)
Sanctuary Buildings, Great Smith St, London SW1P 3BT
Tel: 0171 925 5000 *Fax:* 0171 925 6000

David Blunkett, Secretary of State for Education and Employment.
The DFEE aims to promote economic growth and personal development by raising standards of educational achievement and skill through the promotion of a competitive, efficient, effective and flexible labour market.

Department for Education for Northern Ireland
Inspectors' Office, Rathgael House, Balloo Rd, Bangor, Co Down BT19 2PR
Tel: 01247 279726 *Fax:* 01247 279721

Roger S Jarvis, inspector (mus).
Education in Northern Ireland is administered centrally by the Department of Education and locally by five Education and Library Boards: Belfast, North Eastern, South Eastern, Southern, and Western (for addresses *see* **Local Music Education** section). The structure of education (school divisions, examinations, higher education, etc) corresponds to that prevailing in England.

Scottish Office Education and Industry Department
Floor 2a, Victoria Quay, Edinburgh EH6 6QQ
Tel: 0131 244 0949 *Fax:* 01382 201767

D G Norris, national specialist, mus.
HM Inspector of Schools Office, Floor 5, Wellgate House, Wellgate, Dundee *Tel:* 01382 224155. The Department (under Donald Dewar, The Secretary of State for Scotland and Brian Wilson, Minister of State for Education) has responsibility for education at all levels in Scotland. The Scottish Office is not affected by legislation affecting education in England and Wales unless similar legislation is applied independently to Scotland. Hence, the changes in the DFEE do not impinge on the SOEID which continues with its own structures and policies as approved by the Minister for Education in Scotland.

Welsh Office Education Department (WOED)
Fourth Floor, Crown Buildings, Cathays Pk, Cardiff CF1 3NQ
Tel: 01222 825111 ext 6082 *Fax:* 01222 826111

Schools Inspectors

The Education (Schools) Act of 1992 established two new non-Ministerial government departments, one in England and the other in Wales, to assume overall responsibility for the inspection of schools. In England, the Office of Her Majesty's chief Inspector of Schools has since become known as OFSTED (Office for Standards in Education). In Wales there is OHMCI (Wales) (Office of Her Majesty's Chief Inspector of Schools in Wales). HM Inspectors also offer independent professional advice, based on inspection to other government departments, LEAs, teachers and others as required.

England

Office for Standards in Education
Government Buildings, Marston Rd, Oxford OX3 0TY
Tel: 01865 247203 *Fax:* 01865 792517

Janet Mills HMI, specialist adviser for mus.

Office for Standards in Education
44-60 Richardshaw La, Pudsey, W Yorks LS28 7RU
Tel: 0113 257 5411 *Fax:* 0113 257 1857

Mrs M M Martin HMI.

Wales

Office of Her Majesty's Chief Inspector of Schools in Wales

Phase 1, Government Buildings, Ty Glas Rd, Llanishen, Cardiff CF4 5FQ
Tel: 01222 761456 ext 5293 *Fax:* 01222 758182

G Adams, HMI for mus.

The Office of Her Majesty's Chief Inspector in Wales was established in September 1992 as a new Department of State. It has the functions of advising the Secretary of State on the quality of education and educational standards in schools in Wales and of overseeing and regulating the new independent inspection system.

Office of Her Majesty's Chief Inspector of Schools in Wales

3rd Floor, Ty Nant, 180 High St, Swansea, W Glamorgan

SA1 5LN
Tel: 01792 463702 *Fax:* 01792 653058

R I Swain, HMI for mus.

Scotland

HM Inspector of Schools Office (Scotland)

HM Inspector of Schools Office, Saughton House, Broomhouse Dr, Edinburgh EH11 3XD
Tel: 0131 244 8426 *Fax:* 0131 244 8424

A Armstrong, HMI for mus.

HM Inspector of Schools Office (Scotland)

Floor 5, Wellgate House, Wellgate, Dundee DD1 2DB
Tel: 01382 224155 *Fax:* 01382 201767
Email: dg_norris@hq.hmis.scotoff.gov.uk

D G Norris, national specialist HMI for mus.

The British Council

The British Council is Britain's principal agent for cultural relations abroad and is an independent, non-political organisation incorporated by Royal Charter and managed by Dr David Drewry, working to a board of management. It provides access to British ideas, talents and experience in education and training, books and periodicals, the English language, the arts, the sciences and technology. The British Council's Music Unit develops the policies and plans for the Council's activities involving British music and musicians overseas.

Press and Public Relations Department
10 Spring Gardens, London SW1A 2BN
Tel: 0171 4878 *Fax:* 0171 389 4971.

Ruth Brander, pres offr.

Music Unit Performing Arts Department
11 Portland Place, London W1N 4EJ
Tel: 0171 389 3080 *Fax:* 0171 389 3057

Julia Rose, head.

Arts Councils

Arts Council of England
14 Great Peter St, London SW1P 3NQ
Tel: 0171 333 0100 *Fax:* 0171 973 6590

Pauline Tambling, dir of education and training.
The Arts Council of England (ACE) actively promotes education and training as fundamental to the development of the nation's cultural life. It is concerned with four key objectives: (1) Advocating lifelong learning and winning the argument for change. ACE advocates that both formal and informal learning opportunities in the arts should be available to all members of society; (2) Creating infrastructures and resources. ACE works in partnership to ensure that there is adequate training provision to support the continued growth and success of Britain's cultural industries. It encourages and supports developments in education and training which meet the needs of artists from culturally diverse backgrounds and those practising in the Disability Arts field; (3) Disseminating knowledge. ACE identifies and promotes good practice. Through the dissemination of information, it seeks to increase awarenesss of the arts and encourage the provision of quality learning opportunities; (4) Funding. In order to achieve its primary objectives, ACE ensures public funds are used effectively and efficiently, and seeks to increase investment in the arts by working co-operatively with other funding agencies. ACE believes that the arts make an important and valuable contribution to our success as a nation, both socially and economically.

Arts Council of Wales
9 Museum Pl, Cardiff CF1 3NX
Tel: 01222 394711 *Fax:* 01222 221447

Emyr Jenkins, chief exec; Lyn Davies, snr mus offr

The Scottish Arts Council
12 Manor Pl, Edinburgh EH3 7DD
Tel: 0131 226 6051 *Fax:* 0131 225 9833

Seona Reid, dir

Arts Council of Northern Ireland
MacNeice House, 77 Malone Rd, Belfast BT9 6AQ
Tel: 01232 385200 *Fax:* 01232 661715

Brian Ferran, chief exec; Philip Hammond, performing arts dir.

Regional Arts Boards

English Regional Arts Boards
5 City Rd, Winchester, Hants SO23 8SD
Tel: 01962 851063 *Fax:* 01962 842033
Email: info.erab@artsfb.org.uk
Website: www.arts.org.uk

Christopher Gordon, chief exec; Carolyn Nixson, asst. The ten Regional Arts Boards in England exist to promote and develop the arts and the audience for the arts in their regions. They provide information, help and guidance to all kinds of arts organisations in their area and in many cases can provide financial assistance. English Regional Arts Boards is the representative body for the ten RABs. Its Winchester secretariat provides project management, services and information for the members and acts on their behalf in appropriate circumstances.

East Midlands Arts Board
Mountfields House, Epinal Way, Loughborough, Leics LE11 0QE
Tel: 01509 218292 *Fax:* 01509 262214
Email: info.ema@artsfb.org.uk

John Buston, chief exec; Penny Hefferan, arts offr, orch mus; Helen Flach, head of perf arts; Karl Chapman, arts offr, contemporary mus. Derbys (excluding the High Peak District), Leics, Northants and Notts. The Board aims to enrich life in the East Midlands by offering the opportunity for everyone to participate in and enjoy the arts.

Eastern Arts Board
Cherry Hinton Hall, Cambridge CB1 4DW
Tel: 01223 215355 *Fax:* 01223 248075
Email: info@eastern-arts.co.uk

Lou Stein, chief exec; Kate Tyrell, mus offr.
Beds, Cambs, Essex, Herts (other than London borough overlap), Lincs, Norfolk, Suffolk.

London Arts Board
3rd Floor, Elme House, 133 Long Acre, London WC2E 9AF
Tel: 0171 240 1313 *Fax:* 0171 240 4580
Email: ame@lonab.demon.co.uk

Trevor Phillips, chmn; Andrew McKenzie, principal mus offr.
Covers the area of 32 boroughs of London and the Corporation of London.

North West Arts Board
Manchester House, 22 Bridge St, Manchester M3 3AB
Tel: 0161 834 6644; 0161 834 9131 *Fax:* 0161 834 6969
Email: nwarts-info@mcr1.poptel.org.uk
Website: www.poptel.org.uk./arts/

Debra King, perf arts offr (mus).
Cheshire, Greater Manchester, High Peak (Derbys), Lancs, Merseyside.

Northern Arts Board
9-10 Osborne Terrace, Jesmond, Newcastle upon Tyne NE2 1NZ
Tel: 0191 281 6334 *Fax:* 0191 281 3276
Email: norab.demon.co.uk

Andrew Dixon, chief exec; Brian Debnam, head of perf arts; Mark Monument, offr for perf arts. Teesside, Cumbria, Durham, Northumberland, Tyne and Wear.

South East Arts
10 Mount Ephraim, Tunbridge Wells, Kent TN4 8AS
Tel: 01892 515210 *Fax:* 01892 549383

Debra Reay, dir perf arts; Jonathan Dabner, mus offr; Felicity Harvest, chief exec.
Kent, Surrey, E and W Sussex.

South West Arts
Bradninch Pl, Gandy St, Exeter EX4 3LS
Tel: 01392 218188 *Fax:* 01392 413554
Email: swarts@mail.zynet.co.uk

Graham Long, chief exec; Nicholas Capaldi, dir of perf arts; Ouvrielle Holmes, Sarah Holmes, perf arts admin. Bath, Bristol, Cornwall, Devon, Dorset (excluding Bournemouth, Poole, Christchurch), Glos, N Somerset, N E Somerset, Somerset, South Glos.

Southern Arts Board
13 St Clement St, Winchester, Hants SO23 9DQ
Tel: 01962 855099 *Fax:* 01962 861186
Email: sarts-info@geo2.poptel.org.uk

Robert Hutchison, chief exec; David Everett, mus offr; Jane Bryant, educ and planning offr.
Berks, Bucks, SE Dorset (Bournemouth, Christchurch and Poole), Hants, IoW, Oxon, Wilts.

West Midlands Arts
82 Granville St, Birmingham B1 2LH
Tel: 0121 631 3121; 0121 693 6878 (lottery info)
Fax: 0121 643 7239
Email: west.midarts@midnet.com
Website: www.arts.org.uk/

Sally Luton, chief exec; Anne Gallacher, planning offr, educ; Val Birchall, mus offr.
Hereford and Worcester, Shrops, Staffs, Stoke-on-Trent, Warwicks, W Midlands.

Yorkshire and Humberside Arts
21 Bond St, Dewsbury, W Yorks WF13 1AX
Tel: 01924 455555 *Fax:* 01924 466522
Email: yharts-info@geo2.poptel.org.uk

Roger Lancaster, chief exec; Jim Beirne, dir of perf arts; Glyn Foley, mus offr.
S Yorks, W Yorks, N Yorks, N Lincs, N E Lincs, E Riding and Hull and York cities.

Local Music Education

In the following list, details of local authority music provision are given for all education authorities in the UK and the Channel Islands. Although many new unitary authorities were created in April 1998, often music education provisions have remained the same. Further details about changes in your area should be obtained by direct contact with your local authority.

Some authorities will have an independent music service that provides a similar service to other education authorities. Conductors of youth ensembles are shown, preceded by an oblique stroke.

The order of this list is Inner London (with the Centre for Young Musicians listed first), Outer London, England (Unitary Authorities, Cities and Towns with Metropolitan Status), England (Counties), Scotland, Wales, Northern Ireland.

Inner London

Centre for Young Musicians
Morley College, 61 Westminster Bridge Rd, London SE1 7HT
Tel: 0171 928 3844 *Fax:* 0171 928 3454
Email: info@cymlondon.demon.co.uk

Stephen Dagg, dir; Oliver Butterworth, head of performance.
Orchestras: London Schools Symphony Orchestra.
Music Centres: The Centre for Young Musicians provides high-calibre, specialist training on all orch insts, rcdr, gui, pno, org and voice for musically gifted children. In addition to expert individual tuition pupils receive a full programme of ens, choral and musicianship training. Classes in jazz, Indian mus, composition, chmbr mus and chmbr orch are available. A-level and pre A-level mus courses are also provided where appropriate. Lunchtime m/classes and recitals. The centre operates on 32 Sats of the academic year and applications are welcome from pupils in f/t education in the state sector. Pupils from all sectors, who wish to continue with their current inst teacher are invited to apply for the new Core Curriculum course as advertised in the prospectus.
Awards: Many pupils from inner London boroughs are supported by their local authority or school. Where this is not the case, parents unable to meet the full fees may be eligible for CYM awards. All other costs are met by the Foundation for Young Musicians. Louis Watt Memorial Competition for inst/vocal performance annually, £400.
Courses: 4-6 day courses held each school holiday (including some summer residential courses). 14 groups: London Schools Symphony Orchestra (longer courses); concert orch; symphonic and concert bands; gui, recorder and str ens; jnr courses for br, w/wind, str, recorder, gui, perc and musicianship. Courses are open to young musicians from all school sectors.

Camden
Camden Music, The Medburn Centre, 136 Chalton St, London NW1 1RX
Tel: 0171 387 1995; 0956 317442 *Fax:* 0171 383 0875

David Hornbrook, inspector for the arts; Peter West, mus co-ord.
Orchestras: Camden youth orch/John Catlow, rcdr ens/Angela Rodriguez, youth choir/Jenny Morgan, jnr choir/Paul Newbury, sinfonia/Richard Martyn and Kerry Heffer, training orch/Paul Newbury.
Music Centres: Camden Saturday Music Centre, Camden School for Girls, Sandall Rd, London NW5.
Courses: A range of primary and secondary in-service courses for teachers.

Corporation of London
Education Dept, PO Box 270, Guildhall, London EC2P 2EJ
Tel: 0171 332 1750 *Fax:* 0171 332 1621
Email: david.smithcity@compus.bt.com

David Smith, city educ offr.
Courses: The Strings Project at the Sir John Cass's Foundation Primary School enables every child in yrs 4-6 to learn the vn. Regular performance opportunities.

5

Greenwich

Education Inspectorate, Peggy Middleton House, 50 Woolwich New Rd, London SE18 6HQ
Tel: 0181 317 5777 *Fax:* 0181 317 5780

Christopher Harrison, inspector for mus.
Orchestras: Major-minor band/Arthur Brookes, Greenwich youth band/Chris Lloyd, Greenwich street band/Kay Charlton.
Music Centres: Greenwich Music Makers incorporates a range of Sat morning and twilight activities, including Junior Music Makers, Greenwich Community Choir, street band, inst tuition and parent-child w/shops. Full details from Miriam Coe at Greenwich Community College *Tel:* 0181 319 8088.
Awards: Greenwich Music Trust, formed in 1993, offers support for musical activities including individual bursaries.
Courses: A full programme of in-service courses is co-ordinated by Greenwich Professional Development Centre *Tel:* 0181 850 5043. Greenwich Music Makers runs holiday mus courses for young people, including an annual summer residential course.

Hackney

Education Dept, Edith Cavell Building, Enfield Rd, London N1 5BA
Tel: 0181 356 5000 ext 7218

Anne Cartwright, mus inspector.
Orchestras: Hackney youth orch and jazz ens/ Nick Ridout.
Music Centres: Centre for Young Musicians *see entry above.* Professional Development Centre, Albion Dr, London E8 4LI *Tel:* 0171 241 5522.
Awards: Helps sponsor children to attend Centre for Young Musicians.
Courses: INSET course published in annual brochure.

Islington

Islington Education Dept, Laycock St, London N1 1TH
Tel: 0171 457 5223 *Fax:* 0171 457 5829

Orchestras: Islington strs group, rcdr ens, fl choir, schools choirs, schools jazz orch, schools renaissance band.
Music Centres: Islington Saturday Music Centre, Laycock Primary School, Laycock St, Islington, London N1. Contact Richard Frostick *tel:* 0171 254 4452.
Courses: Full in-service training programme for teachers.

Kensington and Chelsea

Education Dept, Town Hall, Hornton St, London W8 7NX
Tel: 0171 937 5464 *Fax:* 0171 361 2078

Orchestras: Kensington and Chelsea college orch/Lesley Larkum, philharmonic orch/Roger Gabriel, college wind ens/Derek Carden,

Portobello orch/Richard Gonski.
Music Centres: Centre for Young Musicians *see entry above.* Sat morning school at Hortensia Rd, London SW10 0QS *tel:* 0171 351 7127.
Courses: Courses for adults with children in br, w/wind, str, pno and gui. Kensington and Chelsea College, Wornington Rd, London W10 1QS, mus foundation course (FE).

Lambeth

Education Dept, 234-244 Stockwell Rd, Brixton, London SW9 9SP
Tel: 0171 926 2559

Music Centres: Sat morning 'In Tune' for primary pupils. Subscribing borough to the Centre for Young Musicians *see entry above.*
Courses: In-service training is available through consultancies with a community mus resource centre 'Musicworks'.

Lewisham

Lewisham Education QAD Team, Professional Development Centre, Kilmorie Rd, London SE23 2SP
Tel: 0181 291 5005 *Fax:* 0181 291 6259

Christopher Harrison, gen adviser (mus).
Music Centres: Lewisham Junior Centre for Young Musicians opened in Jan 1997 and provides mus activities for primary age children on Sat mornings. Lewisham provides funding for pupils to attend the Centre for Young Musicians *see entry above.*
Courses: A full programme of support for schools is provided by the Lewisham Education QAD Team. Courses on all aspects of the mus curriculum are organised at Lewisham Professional Development Centre. School-based support is arranged on request and a range of publications is available.

Southwark

Education Dept Inspectorate, 1 Bradenham Close, London SE17 2QA
Tel: 0171 525 5020 *Fax:* 0171 525 5025

Marianne Breedon, visual and perf arts inspector; Tom Deveson, mus advisory teacher.
Courses: Termly courses of mus in the NC, mus for class teachers and planning for mus in schools.

Tower Hamlets

Education Offices, Mulbery Pl, Clove Cres, London E14 2BG
Tel: 0171 364 5000 *Fax:* 0171 364 6421

Monika Maywood, inst services admin.

Tower Hamlets Inspection and Advisory Service

Education Offices, Mulberry Pl, Clove Cres, London E14 2BG
Tel: 0171 364 5000

Diana Warne, inspector for mus.

Orchestras: Tower Hamlets youth and community band/Jonathan Ticher.
Music Centres: Sat mus centre at Bow School, Paton Cl, Fairfield Rd, London E3 2QD *Tel:* 0181 980 0118, Kim Kirk, head of centre.

Wandsworth Borough Council Education Dept
Curriculum and Professional Development Service, Professional Centre, Franciscan Rd, London SW17 8HE
Tel: 0181 682 3759 *Fax:* 0181 682 4016
Email: rcrocker@profcent.edex.co.uk
Website: www.shared.insnet.net/profcent

Roger Crocker, development offr (mus).
Orchestras: SW London area orch started Dec 1996.
Music Centres: Mus support service to schools. Wandsworth Junior Centre for Young Musicians (Sat centre).
Awards: Special mus education at CYM *see entry above* and discretionary awards to Sat mus colleges.
Courses: Music Curriculum Support: nursery, early years, KS1, primary and KS2. Starting points for the generalist teacher; using ethnic insts from Asia and Africa; nursery and early years mus provision; mus technology in the classroom; in-school mus support; developing mus from KS2 to KS3. Music Technology Support: regional mus technology centre for South London. Mus projects: children's opera; opera w/shops with history; mus technology project (vocal); participation in world premiere. CD recording for UNICEF for general release (now available). Also area festivals.

Westminster
Education/Leisure Dept, 4th Floor, Westminster City Hall, Victoria St, London SW1E 6QP
Tel: 0171 641 2543 *Fax:* 0171 641 2281

Deirdre McGrath, dir of educ and leisure dept.
Orchestras: Westminster acts as lead borough for CYM *see entry above* which runs LSSO, symphonic and concert bands, rcdr, gui ens and steel orch.
Music Centres: Foundation mus class at Sat morning centre for pupils aged 7-9. Places available on special mus course at Pimlico School for gifted young musicians.

Outer London

Barking and Dagenham
Music Centre, Adult College, Fanshawe Cres, Dagenham, Essex RM9 5QA
Tel: 0181 593 8257 *Fax:* 0181 595 1395

Sue Sharp, head of community mus educ service.
Orchestras: 4 concert wind bands, orchs and ens (catering for every level of ability), children's choir, young singers, adult choir.
Music Centres: Mus centre (Sat morning, weekday evening) with inst tuition, aural and theory, practical playing, and rehearsal of ens as above and at above address.
Courses: Programme of adult classes, recreational, GCSE and A-level.

Barnet
Music Education Services, Annexe, Educational Services, Friern Barnet La, London N11 3DL
Tel: 0181 359 3111 *Fax:* 0181 359 3105

Andrew Emeny, mgr mus educ services.
Orchestras: Barnet schools symphony orch/David Temple, schools wind orch/James Williams, schools br band/Ben Mason, youth big band/Paul Taylor.
Music Centres: Sat morning mus centres for children aged 4-19 at East Barnet (East Barnet School), Finchley (Moss Hall Junior School) and Hendon (St Marys CE High School). Finchley jnr mus centre on Tue evenings.
Courses: Half-term 2-day jnr w/wind and jnr br.

Bexley
The Bexley Music Centre for Music and Dance, 27 Station Rd, Sidcup, Kent DA15 7EB
Tel: 0181 302 1456 *Fax:* 0181 300 6619

Michael Purton, chief exec; John MacKenzie, centre admin; Jenny Breen, company sec.
Orchestras: Bexley Music Centre symphony orch; various other symphony orchs, str orchs, ens, concert wind bands, choirs, inst groups.
Music Centres: Borough mus centre for adults and children (Sat morning, weekday any time).
Awards: Bursaries (dependent on financial status) for inst lessons available through Bexley London Borough, Hillview Dr, Welling DA16 3RY. For bursaries for centre membership contact the company sec.
Courses: Residential holiday courses; annual course visits abroad, exchange visits abroad and various other courses for most ens and groups.

Brent
Brent Music Service, 2-12 Grange Rd, Willesden, London NW10 2QY
Tel: 0181 937 3484 *Fax:* 0181 937 3401

Paul Fensom, head of service; Karen Hunt, deputy head of service.
Orchestras: Brent youth steel band/Alfred Totesaur, jazz orch/Keith Martin, soul choir/Stephen Cole, br band/Phillip Littlemore, youth mus theatre/Rob Seymour.

Music Centres: Sat morning mus school at Kingsbury High School, Stag La, Kingsbury. Asian mus school at Alperton High School, Ealing Rd, Alperton. Irish mus school at Eaton Grove Community Centre, Rugby Rd, Kingsbury. Under 5's mus w/shops at Willesden Green Library Centre, High Rd, Willesden.
Courses: Various school holiday courses.

Bromley
London Borough of Bromley, Education Dept, Civic Centre, Stockwell Close, Bromley BR1 3UH
Tel: 0181 464 3333 *Fax:* 0181 313 4122

Margaret Ralph, inspector for mus.

Bromley
Bromley Youth Music Trust, Bromley Youth Music Centre, Bromley, Kent BR2 8AA
Tel: 0181 467 1566 *Fax:* 0181 468 7595

Peter Mawson, principal.
Orchestras: Bromley youth symphony orch (plus 3 other orchs), Bromley youth choir, 4 wind bands, str quintets, wind quartets, br ens, secondary school training band (all are trust ens catering for all abilities).
Music Centres: 2 Sat morning mus schools (orch, wind band school). Playing opportunity for all to age 18.
Awards: Grant aid awarded annually to gifted young musicians for tuition with selected teachers and performers.
Courses: 2 non-residential orch, wind band and choral courses organised annually for local children. Chmbr orch and Bromley Youth Concert Band annual tours. Occasional in-service courses for teachers.

Croydon
Davidson Professional Centre, Davidson Rd, Croydon CR0 6DD
Tel: 0181 655 1299

Sarah L Inglis, mus adviser.
Orchestras: Run by Croydon Music Teaching Agency (20 Southbridge Rd, Croydon CR0 1AE *tel:* 0181 681 0909).
Music Centres: Run by Croydon Music Teaching Agency.
Courses: Curriculum courses run at Davidson Professional Centre.

Croydon
Croydon Music Teaching Agency, 20 Southbridge Rd, Croydon, Surrey CR0 1AE
Tel: 0181 681 0909 *Fax:* 0181 686 9489
Email: music@dircon.co.uk
Website: www.dircon.co.uk/music/

Ian Butterworth, dir.
Orchestras: Croydon youth orch/Ian Butterworth

and others, schools wind orch/Gordon Graham, schools sinfonia/Gordon Graham, schools symphonic band/David Rampani, schools steel orch/Ricky de Cairos, fl harmonic/Carolyn Kelly, young musicians orch/Bronia Parry.
Music Centres: Croydon School Music Centre (Sats during term-time and Mon/Tue evenings during term-time). Croydon School Piano Centre (Sats during term-time) for tuition in pno, general musicianship. Croydon Young Musicians (Sats during term-time) for younger inst players. Area band w/shops (Tue/Wed/Fri evenings). Area str w/shops (Tue/Thu evenings).
Courses: Several holiday orch courses pa for inst players of all abilities; band and orch visits abroad every year; annual fl, vc and bass days; programme of w/shops and m/classes. Consultancy service for schools, accredited through Trinity College of Music.

Ealing
Perceval House, 12-14 Uxbridge Rd, London W5 2HL
Tel: 0181 579 2424 *Fax:* 0181 566 3362

Tony Shield, gen inspector, mus.
Orchestras: Ealing youth orch/Mark Gooding, youth wind band/Derek Leach, Featherstone br band/Mike Worthington (regular concerts in and out of borough), youth choir/Paul Ayres, Hanwell children's choir/Philip Wilson.
Music Centres: Ealing jnr mus school (Ceri McInally, dir), Sat during term-time. Complete mus training for primary and secondary pupils: inst tuition, orchs, bands, ens, aural and theory classes.
Awards: Musically talented children sponsored as jnr exhibitioners at RCM, RAM, GSM, TCL and LCM (auditions held annually).
Courses: Youth wind band and youth orch holiday courses; plus many specialist and non-specialist teachers' courses held regularly.

Enfield
Education Dept, PO Box 56 Civic Centre, Silver St, Enfield, Middx EN1 3XQ
Tel: 0181 967 9249 *Fax:* 0181 967 9740

Stephen Block, adviser for mus and perf arts; Susan Granger, head of Enfield arts support service.
Orchestras: Enfield young symphony orch; bands, orchs, and ens for all levels of ability.
Music Centres: Enfield Arts Support Service, Aylward School, Windmill Rd, Edmonton, London N18 1NB, *tel:* 0181 807 8881. Inst tuition, bands, orchs and ens throughout the borough.
Courses: Summer residential youth orch, wind and jazz band courses. INSET courses in primary mus and arts co-ordination; primary class teachers in mus and performing arts; mus with technology, secondary mus; primary and

secondary mus teacher induction courses, INSET courses for inst teachers.

Haringey
Music Centre, PDC, Downhills Park Rd, London N17 6AR
Tel: 0181 829 5033 *Fax:* 0181 365 8253

Leonora Davies, inspector for mus and mus services; Patrick Millard, inst scheme co-ord.
Orchestras: Haringey young musicians/Nicholas Wilks (organised by LEA), jnr str band/Julie Spencer and Sue Hilton, jnr wind band/Jim Tomlinson, borough big band/Jim Tomlinson. Playing days throughout the year organised by mus centre.
Music Centres: Music centre at above address.
Awards: Awards in conjunction with the Tottenham Grammar School Foundation for Haringey school pupils only. Inst scheme for jnr exhibition; fee paying with some LEA support for those unable to pay.
Courses: 5-day orch courses organised during summer term. Half day in-service courses for inst staff each term. Half-term holiday courses for jnr bands and orchs.

Harrow
Harrow Music and Arts Service, Harrow Teachers' Centre, Tudor Rd, Wealdstone, Harrow HA3 5QD
Tel: 0181 424 3855

Kevin Sadler, schools mus & arts service mgr & adviser; Kathy Cubbitt, admin finance offr.
Orchestras: Harrow students' philharmonic orch/Adrian Brown, students' symphonic winds/Mark Gooding, youth choir/Joy Hill, students' steel band/Dexter Joseph, plus 10 other bands and orchs. Contact Mark Gooding *tel:* 0181 420 1519.
Music Centres: Harrow School for Young Musicians, Hatchend High School, Headstone La, Harrow, Middx HA3 6NR. Mark Gooding, dir.
Courses: Inst and vocal teaching service, w/shops in schools. In-service training for mus teachers.

Havering
Directorate of Education and Community Services
Havering Music School, The Walk, Hornchurch, Essex RM11 3TL
Tel: 01708 450313 *Fax:* 01708 620199

Isobel Liebman, principal.
Orchestras: Various inst ens meet in different parts of the borough weekly: vn, va and vc ens (pre-gr 1-2), Havering young str players (gr 1-2), jnr br band (gr 1-4) and wind band (gr 1-4). Many inst ens meet weekly at the mus centre and Havering Sixth Form College. These include fl choir (gr 4 min), cl choir (gr 4 min), youth br band (gr 4 min), sinfonietta strs (gr 3 min), youth orch (gr 6 min). Vocal groups include the young singers and youth choir.

Music Centres: Sat mus centre at Havering Sixth Form College, Wingletye La, Hornchurch. Inst tuition, aural, theory, keyboard, orchs, bands, choirs and ens at all levels. Individual and group lessons.
Courses: W/shops, competitions, festivals, in-service for teachers.

Hillingdon
Hillingdon Music Service, Compass Theatre, Glebe Av, Ickenham, Middx UB10 8PD
Tel: 01895 630155 *Fax:* 01895 623724

Vincent Raven, head of service.
Orchestras: Hillingdon school's symphony orch/Rupert D'Cruze, Hillingdon school's philharmonic orch/John Brennan and Matthew Thomas; school's concert band/Jennifer Steele, girl singers/Jo McNally, br band/Matthew Thomas, jazz band/Melvyn Care. Also other orchs, bands, choirs and chmbr ens.
Music Centres: Address as for Music Service. Ens rehearse at Abbotsfield and Swakeleys schools.
Awards: Individual tuition available for mus centre students.
Courses: Foreign tours for snr ens, residential courses in half-term holidays.

Hounslow
Education Department, Civic Centre, Lampton Rd, Hounslow, Middx TW3 4DN
Tel: 0181 862 5372 *Fax:* 0181 862 5380

Martin Hinckley, general adviser mus/art.

Hounslow
Music Service, De Brome Building, 77 Boundaries Rd, Feltham, Middx TW14 5DT
Tel: 0181 862 6942 *Fax:* 0181 862 6943

Betty Woodbridge, head of mus services.
Orchestras: Hounslow youth orch/Jacques Cohen, youth wind orch/Jim Clow, schools str orch/Rachelle Goldberg, youth perc ens/Martin Pyne, Chiswick area wind band/Tim Turner, Feltham area wind ens/Sally Greaves, Hounslow area str orch/Marion Seymour, Feltham area str orch/Angela Jessop, jnr choir, rock/pop group/Lee Neale.
Music Centres: Music Centre/Adult Community Centre - The Green School for Girls, Busch Corner, Isleworth TW7 5BB *Tel:* 0181 847 1562. Chrissy Parsons, organiser. Day and evening mus classes for youth and adults; widespread opportunities for tuition, playing, ens, w/shops.
Awards: Sat morning activities for musically talented children at The Green School. Entry by audition only. Applications to Rachelle Goldberg, head of specialist mus school, De Brome Building, 77 Boundaries Rd, Feltham, Middx TW14 5DT.

Courses: Inst and composition course, both 1-day w/shops and non-residential holiday courses for ens playing.

Kingston Music Service
37 Fullers Way North, Tolworth Girls' School, Surbiton KT6 7LQ
Tel: 0181 391 9248 *Fax:* 0181 391 5185

Joan Child, head of mus services and mus adviser; Andy Paget, arts co-ord.
Orchestras: Youth sinfonia/James Thomas, youth concert band/Alec Warne, youth concert orch/Martin Stuart, schools training band/Nicole Willis, schools orch/Kate Fairbrother, jnr strs/Kate Fairbrother, gui ens/Steven Chapman and Jeremy Dunning, fl choir/Rhian Clement, young voices/Stephanie Nunn.
Music Centres: Coombe mus centre (Sat morning) open to pupils aged 6-18. Tolworth mus centre (weekday evenings).
Awards: Gifted children supported to attend jnr depts of London conservatoires.
Courses: Regular tours for sinfonia and youth concert band; w/shops for primary children, infant and jnr choral festivals. Programme of in-service training for primary and secondary teachers and for inst teachers.

Merton
Merton Music Foundation, Chaucer Centre, Canterbury Rd, Morden, Surrey SM4 6PX
Tel: 0181 640 5446 *Fax:* 0181 640 6990

John Mander, dir.
Orchestras: Merton youth orch/Martin Stuart, youth concert band/John Mander, youth jazz orch/John Mander, jnr orch, schools orch, schools concert band, 2 str ens, 2 br ens, 2 gui ens, 2 choirs.
Music Centres: Merton Music Foundation at above address.
Awards: Awards and charitable trust funds available to students. Grants available to schools, colleges and arts organisations.
Courses: Courses and tours abroad during Easter and summer holidays. The MMF provides regular INSET for mus teachers, both inst and class (further information from above address). Also provides and co-ordinates professional musicians working in Merton schools. Activities offered range from concerts to composers in residence.

Newham
Education Dept, Broadway House, High St, London E15 1AJ
Tel: 0181 555 5552 ext 42431; 0181 472 9895 *Fax:* 0181 503 0014

David Lister.
Orchestras: Newham schools symphony orch, wind orch, br band (each with jnr orch and

chmbr ens). Regular concerts in borough and major concert halls.
Music Centres: Newham Instrumental Music Service based at Newham Academy of Music, Wakefield St, London E6 1NG *Tel:* 0181 472 9895. Access to tuition via Newham schools. Tuition available in full range of orch and band inst, steel pans, sitar, tabla, harmonium, pno and rcdr. Jean Michel Jarré mus technology studio. Weekly rehearsals for borough orchs, bands and ens.
Awards: London Docklands Development Corporation inst awards.
Courses: Holiday courses. Full programme of INSET for teachers.

Redbridge
Redbridge Music Service, John Savage Centre, Fencepiece Rd, Hainault, Ilford, Essex IG6 2LJ
Tel: 0181 501 3944 *Fax:* 0181 500 3893

Eric Forder, mus service dir.
Music Centres: Redbridge Music School at above address. Sat morning and weekday evenings; inst, aural, theory lessons; 3 orchs, 3 wind bands, br band, 3 choirs, gui ens, rcdr ens, 7 jnr ens.
Courses: Various residential and non-residential w/end and holiday courses for mus school pupils (locally, at Glasbury House, Herefordshire and international tours). In-service training for inst teachers, specialist and non-specialist c/room teachers.

Richmond upon Thames
Education Dept, Regal House, London Rd, Twickenham TW1 3QB
Tel: 0181 891 7557; 0181 941 7258

Mike Walsh, snr inspector; Philip Trumble, dir of Richmond Music Trust.
Orchestras: Richmond youth symphony orch/Peter Currie, youth concert band/Margaret Hodges, jazz orch, jnr concert band.
Music Centres: Weekday evenings and Sat mornings, orch, band, choirs and ens activity at all levels.
Awards: 3 awards annually given by Richmond LEA to Richmond upon Thames resident pupils who show exceptional potential in mus.
Courses: Holiday orch and band courses, chmbr mus courses and jnr mus courses.

Sutton
Sutton Youth Music Service, Wandle Valley School, Welbeck Rd, Carshalton, Surrey SM5 1LP
Tel: 0181 640 8781 *also fax*

Nigel Hiscock, head of service; Lynn Atkins, admin.
Orchestras: Sutton youth symphony orch, young musicians' orch, young musicians' training orch, young musicians' str group, Sutton schools concert bands, perc ens and fl choir.

Music Centres: School mus centre used weekdays for rehearsals.
Courses: Courses and tours abroad and in the UK for orchs, bands and ens.

Waltham Forest
Education Centre, 97 Queen's Rd, Walthamstow, London E17 8QS
Tel: 0181 521 3311 ext 4393 *Fax:* 0181 509 9668

Monique Cremnitz, head of mus service.

Orchestras: Schools orch, intermediate orch, jnr orch, 6 str orchs, 3 br bands, 2 big bands, steel band, snr wind band, concert band, intermediate band and jnr band.
Music Centres: Centrally organised mus school (Sat morning, Mon and Wed evenings), Heathcote School, Normanton Pk, London E4 6ES. Mus theory, ens as above, and chmbr mus.

England (Unitary Authorities, Cities and Towns with Metropolitan Status)

Barnsley
Performing Arts Development Service, Grove St, Barnsley
Tel: 01226 291525

Lesley Hepworth, head of service.
Orchestras: Youth strs/Mary Rafferty, youth guis/Kevin Bolton, youth orch/John Grinnell, metropolitan band/John Grinnell, youth concert band/Roger Scorah, jnr concert band/John Grinnell.
Music Centres: Different venues running activities c/o Performing Arts Development Service, address above.
Awards: Various discretionary awards available.
Courses: Various residential and non-residential courses for orch and band members including occasional tours abroad. Courses for teachers on all aspects of mus and performing arts in education.

Bath and North East Somerset
Music Service, PO Box 25, Riverside, Temple St, Keynsham BS31 1DN
Tel: 01225 395110 *Fax:* 01225 395210

Carole Timms, head of mus service.
Orchestras: West of England schools symphony orchestra/Peter Stark, West of England schools symphonic wind band/Rob Wiffin.
Music Centres: Mendip Music Centre, Thursday 4.30-6.30pm, Bath Society of Young Music Musicians, Saturday 9.15-12 noon.
Courses: West of England schools symphony orch and symphonic wind band, 4 days each in Oct, Feb and Jul.

Birmingham
Education Dept, Martineau Education Centre, Balden Rd, Harborne, Birmingham B3 2EH
Tel: 0121 427 3020/2950 *Fax:* 0121 428 1172

Robert Bunting, schools adviser mus.
Orchestras: Birmingham schools' symphony orch/Peter Bridle, schools' wind orch/John

Wesley-Barker, schools' concert orch/Robert Vivian, schools' chorale/Jeffery Skidmore, br band, jazz ens, community choir, steel band, Asian mus ens. Players drawn from city schools by annual audition (except community choir). Concert trips abroad; w/end and other courses for all city ens as above, plus w/shop opportunities with CBSO.
Music Centres: Music Service, Martineau Education Centre, Balden Rd, Harborne, Birmingham B32 2EH *Tel:* 0121 428 1175 *Fax:* 0121 428 3755. David Perkins, head of mus service.
Awards: Discretionary awards available subject to criteria available from Awards Section, Council House, Birmingham.
Courses: Birmingham Advice and Support Service, Martineau Education Centre, Balden Rd, Birmingham B32 2EH *Tel:* 0121 428 1167. Susan Scarsbrook, teacher adviser co-ord. In-service courses and w/shops provided throughout city. Publications available for purchase. Courses validated by Trinity College of Music. Yearly course programme and resource brochure available on request. Artist in residence co-ordination available via arts education co-ord, Pepita Hanna *Tel:* 0121 425 1177.

Blackburn with Darwen Borough Council
Town Hall, Blackburn BB1 7DY
Tel: 01254 585585

P Watson, chief exec.
On 1 April 1998 Blackburn with Darwen Borough Council became a unitary authority.

Blackpool Borough Council
Municipal Buildings, Town Hall, Blackpool FY1 1AD
Tel: 01253 477477

G E Essex-Crosby, chief exec.
On 1 April 1998 Blackpool Borough Council became a unitary authority.

Bolton

Bolton LEA Music Centre, The Deane School, New York, Bolton BL3 4NG
Tel: 01204 658804 *Fax:* 01204 658830
Email: boltonits@aol.com

Paul Payton, head of mus service.
Orchestras: Youth orch and youth chmbr orch/Paul Payton, jnr youth orch/Mrs C Baxendale, training orch/Mrs A Jackson, youth concert band and youth fl choir/Mrs M Kay, youth wind ens/R Rawson, training wind ens and schools stage band/K Sagar, youth cl choir/Mrs S Scattergood, youth stage band/S Grills, schools br band and youth br band/C Cull, jnr youth choir/S Wilding, youth choir/Mrs J Hampson, youth perc ens/G Watton, beginner rcdr ens and youth rcdr ens/P Pemrick, Rivington jnr str ens and Turton jnr str ens/Mrs J Smith, Deane jnr str ens.
Music Centres: Bolton LEA Music Centre at above address, comprising 21 ens.
Courses: Annual holiday courses for mus centre ens, International Youth Philharmonic (BYO) with twin towns.

Bournemouth *see* Dorset

Bracknell Forest Borough Council

Easthampstead House, Town Square, Bracknell, Berks RG12 1AQ
Tel: 01344 424642 *Fax:* 01344 352810
Email: 113001.2213@compuserve.com
Website: www.bracknell-forest.gov.uk

Allison Fletcher, asst dir of educ; David Marcou, principal, Berks Young Musicians Trust.
Orchestras: Service provided by Berkshire Young Musicians Trust.
Music Centres: South Berkshire Music Centre, c/o Brakenhale School, Rectory La, Bracknell RG12 7AB.
Awards: Refer to BYMT.
Courses: Refer to BYMT.

Bradford

Music Service, Bradford Education, Flockton House, Flockton Rd, Bradford, W Yorks BD4 7RY
Tel: 01274 751934 *Fax:* 01274 390081

Bill Turner, acting mgr.
Orchestras: Bradford youth orch/Peter Mountain, youth br band/Jim Shepherd and Keiron Anderson, str school/Peter Mountain.
Music Centres: Ilkley Music Centre, c/o Bradford and Ilkley Community College, Wells Rd, Ilkley LS29 9JH (Keiron Anderson, head; Sat 9.15am-1pm); Keighley Music Centre, c/o St Annes RC Primary School, North St, Keighley BD21 3AD (Kathleen Bhowmick, head; Wed 6-9pm; Sat 9.15am-12.15pm); McMillan Music Centre, c/o Bradford and Ilkley Community College, McMillan Building, Trinity Rd, Bradford BD5 0JD (John Griffiths, head), Tues 5-8pm;

North Bradford Music Centre, c/o Beckfoot Grammar School, Wagon La, Bingley BD16 1EE (John Abbey, head; Thu 6.30-9pm).

Brighton and Hove Music Service

Edward House, 77 Grand Parade, Brighton BN2 2JA
Tel: 01273 293524 *Fax:* 01273 293611

Peter Chivers, head of mus service.
Orchestras: Brighton and Hove wind orch/Peter Chivers, youth str/Mary Shannon, chmbr orch.
Music Centres: As address for Music Service.
Courses: Various summer schools. Community choir. Teachers' courses.

Bristol

Bristol Schools Music Service, Bristol Education Centre, Sheridan Rd, Horfield, Bristol BS7 0PU
Tel: 0117 931 1111 ext 255 *Fax:* 0117 931 1619

Paul Matthews, mgr.
Orchestras: A joint arrangement with the former Avon county schools orch and wind band, now West of England schools orch and wind band.

Bury

Bury Music Centre, Mersey Dr, Whitefield, Manchester M45 8LN
Tel: 0161 796 9910 *Fax:* 0161 796 5143

Jeffrey Wynn Davies, dir of mus; Paul W Jarvis, head of centre.
Orchestras: Bury youth orch, training orch, 3 br bands; 3 concert bands, str orchs, wind ens, dance band.
Music Centres: Bury Music Centre, Mersey Dr, Whitefield, Manchester. Activities include orchs and ens as above.
Courses: European tours most years. Occasional 'repertoire sessions' for youth orch.

Calderdale

Schools' Music Centre, Wellesley Pk, Highroad Well, Halifax, W Yorks HX2 0BA
Tel: 01422 366456 *Fax:* 01422 347900

Stephen Langdon, head of mus service.
Orchestras: Calderdale youth orch, Calderdale youth wind orch, Calderdale strs, Calderdale youth gui ens (all membership by audition), Halifax jnr and snr orch and gui ens, East Calderdale jnr and snr orchs and gui ens, West Calderdale jnr and snr orchs and gui ens. All ens open to students of school-age.
Music Centres: Halifax Music Centre, 2 branch centres at Rastrick and Hebden Bridge.

Coventry

Performing Arts Service, Leasowes Av, Coventry CV3 6BH
Tel: 01203 692348 *Fax:* 01203 692717

Owen Dutton, head of perf arts service.

Orchestras: City of Coventry youth orch/Brian Chappell. Many varied orchs, bands, ens and groups, catering for all levels of ability.
Music Centres: Coventry Performing Arts Service (address above) offering activities and courses for all abilities and age groups in dance, theatre and mus.
Awards: Sir Charles Barratt and Mary Palmer Foundations annual awards for outstanding students. Courtaulds Music Award.
Courses: Mid-term course for youth orch. Occasional w/end courses, eg str, rock groups, improvisation. Regular INSET opportunities with a different focus, eg world arts, technology, singing, dance, drama.

Darlington
Music Service, Borough Rd, Darlington DL1 1SG
Tel: 01325 380757 *Fax:* 01325 352473

Mr Allen.

Derby
Music Activities, Derby City Education Service, Middleton House, 27 St Mary's Gate, Derby DE1 3NN
Tel: 01332 716886 *Fax:* 01332 716920

Philip King, adviser.
Orchestras: Derbyshire city and county youth orch/Peter Stark (guest cond), wind band/Murray Slater.
Music Centres: Sat morning centre, St Benedict's School, Duffield Rd, Darley Abbey, Derby DE22 1JD *tel:* 01332 558007. Brenda Davies, admin.
Courses: Range of week, day and twilight in-service courses for teachers. Infant and primary festivals.

Doncaster
William Appleby Music Centre, Danum Rd, Doncaster DN4 5HE
Tel: 01302 323556 *Fax:* 01302 323605

Peter R Bear, dir of mus services.
Orchestras: Doncaster youth orch/Peter Bear, membership by audition. 28 other orchs and bands, all insts welcome.
Music Centres: William Appleby Music Centre, Danum Rd, Doncaster, open all week. Organises bands, orchs, ens playing, theory, adult inst lessons, pre-school groups and other activities.
Awards: William Appleby Trust Fund provides small awards to help talented children.
Courses: Mus centre organises residential and non-residential courses in UK and abroad. In-service courses for teachers on various aspects of mus teaching. Termly community orch and band w/shops.

Dudley
Dudley Local Education Authority, Saltwells Education Development Centre, Bowling Green Rd, Dudley, W Midlands DY2 9LY
Tel: 01384 813746 *Fax:* 01384 813801

Clive Kempton, mus inspector; Jan Benbow, advisory teacher.
Orchestras: Youth orchs and ens, area groups, tuition on all orch insts. Choral network includes: youth choir (SATB), youth chorus (SSA), young singers (SS), 6 area choirs. British Federation of Young Choirs special project area.
Music Centres: Dudley Music Centre, Lawnswood Rd, Wordsley, W Midlands *tel:* 01384 813865, Gerald Johnson, head of centre.
Awards: Orchs and ens parent's fees with LEA subsidy. Choirs free membership and open access.
Courses: M/classes, vocal training, c/room work. Tours and special events.

East Riding of Yorkshire
Schools' Music Service, 8 Lord Roberts Rd, Beverley HU17 9BE
Tel: 01482 885646 *Fax:* 01482 885647

Robert Mitchell, arts in educ offr.
Orchestras: East Riding youth orch/Robert Mitchell, wind band/Peter Walker and Sharon Walker, string training orch/Lesley Ward and Margaret Bryan, perc ens/Christopher Bradley.
Music Centres: Longcroft School, Church Rd, Beverley. Also Sat w/shop sessions throughout E Riding.
Awards: Advanced inst/vocal scheme of monthly lessons for pupils with gr 8 distinction. Support for members of NYO and NYC.
Courses: Annual summer school or foreign tour.

Gateshead
Dryden PDC, Evistones Rd, Low Fell, Gateshead, Tyne and Wear NE9 5UR
Tel: 0191 482 4133

J C Treherne, head of mus service.
Orchestras: Gateshead metropolitan orch/J Treherne, 2 jnr training str orchs, vc orch, jnr br group/Matthew Lawson, wind bands, jnr and snr br bands, snr choir, jnr festival chorus (all at county level) plus various other ens playing opportunities at all standards.
Music Centres: A mus centre with wide range of activities including practical playing, mus theory, w/end w/shops, visiting performers, regular concerts, practice facilities, electronic apparatus studios.
Awards: Grants given for performing and teaching courses for students admitted to institutions for higher education.
Courses: Many 1-day 'play-days' organised for

various ens; regular chmbr, orch and choral courses, and many other performance activities. Regular in-service courses for teachers and for snr offrs and advisers of the LEA. Music in the NC, various evenings in designated schools in the Authority, 4-5pm.

Halton Borough Council
Education Department, Grosvenor House, Halton Lea, Runcorn, Cheshire WA7 2WD
Tel: 0151 424 2061 *Fax:* 0151 471 7321

Graham Talbot, dir of educ.

Hartlepool *see* Tees Valley Music Service

Herefordshire
Instrumental Music Service, Herefords Educ and Conference Centre, Blackfriars St, Hereford HR4 9HS
Tel: 01432 354391 *Fax:* 01432 276969

Paul Aldred, head of inst mus service.
Orchestras: Herefordshire young people's orch/Paul Aldred, Herefordshire young people's choir, Herefordshire youth choir, concert band, Saturday Players, Hereford Schools' br group, intermediate orch, training orch, training br band, training w/wind ens, prelim w/wind ens, perc group, theory.
Music Centres: Ross-on-Wye Area Music Centre, John Kyrle High School, Ross-on-Wye, Herefords, Tue 4-5pm; Ledbury Area Music Centre, The John Masefield High School, Ledbury, Herefords, Wed 3.45-8pm.
Awards: At the discretion of the head of service.
Courses: Annual courses for orchs, choirs and bands.

Isle of Wight
Music Service, Directorate of Education, County Hall, Newport, Isle of Wight, PO30 1UD
Tel: 01983 823435 *Fax:* 01983 826099

Neil Courtney, head of inst mus.
Orchestras: County youth orch/Neil Courtney, youth wind band/Grahame Holmes, youth choir/Annette Martin, youth jazz ens/Charlie Ross, and other wind bands and orchs.
Music Centres: County mus centre on Sat mornings in Newport. Wind bands and orchs from elementary to county youth level. Caters for age 10-21.
Awards: Senior county mus award and bursaries by audition.
Courses: Non-residential courses for mus centre groups held during school holidays. Regular programmes of foreign tours and exchanges for snr county groups. In-service courses for specialist and non-specialist mus teachers held regularly.

Kingston upon Hull
Music Support Service, Albemarle Music Centre, Ferensway, Hull HU2 8LZ
Tel: 01482 223941 *Fax:* 01482 320565

Christopher Maynard, dir of perf arts; June Pitts, head of service.
Orchestras: City of Hull youth symphony/Chris Maynard, youth br band/Garry Oglesby, youth symphonic wind band/Niall McEwen and Diana Keech, youth jazz orch/Mike Brown, youth choirs/Carol Campbell-Smith and Catherine Maynard, plus a range of training and jnr orchs and bands rehearsing weekly at the mus centre.

Kirklees
Kirklees Education Advisory Service, The Deighton Centre, Huddersfield HD2 1JP
Email: alan.simmons@geo2.poptel.org.uk

Kirklees
Kirklees Music School, The Oastler Centre, 2nd Floor Co-operative Buildings, 103 New St, Huddersfield HD1 2UA
Tel: 01484 426426 *Fax:* 01484 480490

David Williams, principal.
Orchestras: Kirklees schools' symphony orch/David Williams, youth wind orch/David Williams, Kirklees youth br band/Stuart Fawcett, youth training br band/Stuart Fawcett, schools' training orch/Ralph Barker, chorale/Cath Williams, schools' jazz orch/Simon Mansfield, schools' gui orch/Janet Robinson.
Music Centres: 7 throughout borough, Sat morning and weekday evenings. 20 wind bands, 13 str ens, 4 big bands, 6 gui ens, 2 perc ens, cl choir. Colne Valley Music Centre, c/o Colne Valley High School, Gillroyd La, Linthwaite, Huddersfield; Holme Valley Music Centre, c/o Holmfirth High School, Heys Rd, Holmfirth; Huddersfield Music Centre, The Oastler Centre, 103 New St, Huddersfield; Scissett Music Centre, c/o Scissett Middle School, Wakefield Rd, Scissett, Huddersfield; Batley Music Centre, c/o Batley Boys High School, Field Head, Batley; Dewsbury Music Centre, c/o The Mirfield Free Grammar, Kitson Hill Rd, Mirfield; Cleckheaton Music Centre, c/o Whitcliffe Mount School, Turnsteads Av, Cleckheaton.
Awards: 23 scholarship places and 70 bursary places.
Courses: The Kirklees Music Service Educational Trust has a contract with Kirklees Local Education Authority to provide INSET to specialist and non-specialist teachers, and curriculum support. Undertakes courses and tours at home and abroad.

Knowsley

Training and Conference Centre, Knowsley La, Huyton, Merseyside L36 8HW
Tel: 0151 443 5615/6 *Fax:* 0151 480 4411

Stephen Titchmarsh, head of perf arts services.
Orchestras: Knowsley youth orch/Simon Gay, concert band/Martin Robinson, intermediate choir/Nicola Hutton, jnr choir/Fiona Paton, mus theatre/Stephen Titchmarsh, community orch/Sally Bleasdale, choral society/Alan Free, schools orch/Martin Robinson.
Music Centres: 2 regional mus centres at Kirkby, Prescot (mostly jnr level) and Teachers Centre at above address.
Awards: Mus awards offered.
Courses: Regular annual residential courses, plus numerous teachers courses; school-based inst, w/end and summer orch courses. NC courses in mus, dance, drama. Inst skills for teachers courses.

Leeds

City Council Dept of Education, Music Support Service, The West Park Centre, Spen La, Leeds LS16 5BE
Tel: 0113 230 4074 *Fax:* 0113 230 4073

C P Brackley Jones, head of mus support service and mus adviser.
Orchestras: City of Leeds youth orch/Colin P Brackley Jones, youth concert band/Aubrey Beswick, youth br band/Graham Walker, youth jazz-rock orch/Barry Rickarby, jazz-rock ens, youth training orch, schools' intermediate/jnr concert bands, jnr str orch, jnr br band, youth opera, schools steel band, schools choir.
Music Centres: Rehearsals for ens listed above are held at the West Park Centre. Area mus centres at Guiseley, Horsforth, Wetherby, East Leeds, Scott Hall, Rothwell, South Leeds, Pudsey.
Awards: Financial assistance for residential mus courses.
Courses: Holiday courses held for youth orch and other ens; w/end residential inst courses; also orch concerts, opera w/shops, and activities organised by Leeds Schools Music Association. A variety of in-service courses are offered for inst teachers and teachers in primary, secondary and special schools.

Leicester City Council *see* Leicestershire and Leicester

Liverpool

Education Offices, 14 Sir Thomas St, Liverpool L1 6BJ
Tel: 0151 225 2707 *Fax:* 0151 225 2718

Aelwyn Pugh, inspector for curriculum (with mus); Marie Pinnington, admin offr, mus support service.
Orchestras: Liverpool youth orch.
Music Centres: Sat morning mus school at Greenbank Annexe, Sandown College, Greenbank Rd, Liverpool L18. Evening mus centre: New Heys School, Heath Rd, Liverpool.
Courses: Range of in-service courses for teachers at all levels and at special schools.

Luton

Luton Music Service, Education Dept, Unity House, 111 Stuart St, Luton LU1 5NP
Tel: 01582 548217/548202 *Fax:* 01582 548202/548454

Stephen Beaven, adviser and inspector for mus; Priti Patel, mus admin offr.

Manchester

Music Service, Zion Arts Centre, Stretford Rd, Manchester M15 5ZA
Tel: 0161 226 4411/22 *Fax:* 0161 226 1010

Allan Jones, gen adviser (mus) and head of mus service.
Orchestras: Manchester symphonia/David Wainwright, Mancunian winds/Allan Jones, North symphony orch/Pamela Wainwright, South symphony orch/David Wainwright, North concert band/Malcolm Cockerill, South concert band/David Caine, North br band/Stephen Corbett, boys' choir/Adrian Jessett, girls' choir/Delia Maunder, south swing band/George Galway.
Music Centres: Teaching and ens city-wide for all ages and abilities; Sat mornings and weekday evenings; wind bands, steel bands, choirs, dance/swing bands and other ens; wide range of world mus plus inst tuition and theory.
Awards: None as such; there is open access to advanced mus study centres.
Courses: Full in-service training programme for mus teachers to be found in Inspection and Advisory Service Professional Development Programme.

Medway Council

Compass Centre, Chatham Maritime, Chatham, Kent ME4 4YN
Tel: 01634 727777

R Bolsin, dir of educ.

Middlesbrough *see* Tees Valley Music Service

Milton Keynes Music Service

Stantonbury Campus, Milton Keynes MK14 6BN
Tel: 01908 224250 *Fax:* 01908 225271

Nigel Mainard, head of service; Malcolm Crane, Jenny Brown, mus centre co-ords.
Orchestras: Orchs, bands and ens of all levels, during week and Sat morning.
Music Centres: Rcdr, perc, gui, keyboard,

kindermusik and choir.
Awards: Young musicians award scheme for subsidised inst tuition at mus centre. Annual audition during summer term.
Courses: Residential and non-residential courses for orch, bands, chmbr mus, jazz and musicianship. Tours abroad for mus centre groups. CPD courses in twilight for mus co-ords on schools.

Newcastle upon Tyne
Advisory Service, Education Dept, Civic Centre, Newcastle upon Tyne NE1 8PU
Tel: 0191 232 8520 ext 5391 *Fax:* 0191 211 4983

Steve Halsey, gen adviser mus.
Orchestras: Schools training str orch; jazz orch, schools wind bands at jnr, intermediate and snr levels; youth choir.
Music Centres: Nemco, Pendower Hall EDC, Westgate Rd, Newcastle; Kenton School, Drayton Rd, Newcastle NE3 3RU.
Awards: Applications for assistance are considered by the Education Committee as the need arises.
Courses: End of yr courses organised for all schools orchs/bands (see above). Foreign exchanges for snr groups. Regular programme of in-service courses for teachers.

North East Lincolnshire
Music and Performing Arts, Education Development Service, Springfield Centre, Springwood Cres, Grimsby DN33 3HL
Tel: 01472 323113 *Fax:* 01472 276913

R W Lawrance, education development offr.
Orchestras: Grimsby, Cleethorpes and District youth orch (contact Leo Solomon, 1 Maple Grove, New Waltham, Grimsby DN36 4PU *Tel:* 01472 824463), South Bank youth brass (contact M Blow, 36 Boundary Rd, Grimsby).

North Lincolnshire
Music Support Service, c/o John Leggott College, West Common La, Scunthorpe, N Lincs DN17 1DS
Tel: 01724 297157 *Fax:* 01724 863907

S Fareham, head of service; E Hardy, deputy head of service; S Russell, co-ord.
Orchestras: Scunthorpe and District schools' orch rehearses fortnightly at John Leggott College, W Common La, Scunthorpe DN17 1DS.
Music Centres: John Leggott College, fortnightly.
Courses: Occasional residential orch courses.

North Somerset
North Somerset Music Service, Station Rd, Congresbury BS19 5DX
Tel: 01934 832395 *also fax*

Jan Dobbins, mus service mgr.

North Tyneside
School Services, Stephenson House, Stephenson St, North Shields, Tyne and Wear NE30 1QA
Tel: 0191 200 5025 *Fax:* 0191 200 6091
Email: nteaiu@rmplc.co.uk

Bob Harrison, head of mus service.
Orchestras: Youth orch/J Pearce, youth training orch/T Garbutt, jnr orch/Mrs J Craig, concert wind band/R Harrison, youth training wind band/M Moore and J Flood, rcdr consorts/Mrs H Graham and J Reeve.
Music Centres: All authority based ens meet Sat morning at Linskill Centre, Linskill Terrace, North Shields. Activity centres at local schools.
Courses: Some players attend 1-wk summer course meeting of Northern JPO; holiday courses for most groups. Some players attend the Young Sinfonia.

Nottingham City Council
The Guildhall, Nottingham NG1 4BT
Tel: 0115 915 5555

E F Cantle, chief exec.
Orchestras: On 1 April 1998 Nottingham City Council became a unitary authority.

Oldham
Metropolitan Borough Music Centre, The Lyceum, Union St, Oldham, Lancs OL1 1QG
Tel: 0161 627 2332 *Fax:* 0161 620 0259

Eileen Bentley, dir of mus.
Orchestras: Various orchs, bands and choirs at all levels operating from Oldham Music Centre (address as above).
Music Centres: Oldham Metropolitan Borough Music Centre.
Courses: Frequent non-residential w/end and holiday orch and inst courses, for most snr ens; occasional guest conductor. Also residential summer courses and foreign concert tours.

Peterborough City Council
Town Hall, Bridge St, Peterborough PE1 1PJ
Tel: 01733 563141

W E Samuel, chief exec.
On 1 April 1998 Peterborough City Council became a unitary authority.

Plymouth City Council
Civic Centre, Plymouth PL1 2EW
Tel: 01752 668000

Mrs A Stone, chief exec.
On 1 April 1998 Plymouth City Council became a unitary authority.

The Borough of Poole Council
Civic Centre, Poole, Dorset BH15 2RU
Tel: 01202 633633

J Brooks, chief exec.
On 1 April 1998 the Borough of Poole became a unitary authority.

Portsmouth City Council
Civic Offices, Guildhall Sq, Portsmouth PO1 2AL
Tel: 01705 822251

Nick Gurney, chief exec.

Reading Borough Council
Civic Centre, Reading, Berks RG1 7TD
Tel: 0118 939 0900

Ms J Markham, chief exec.
On 1 April 1998 Reading Borough Council became a unitary authority.

Redcar and Cleveland see Tees Valley Music Service

Rochdale
Music Service, Fieldhouse School, Greenbank Rd, Rochdale OL12 0HZ
Tel: 01706 750288 *Fax:* 01706 656043

Fred Bowker, head of service.

Rotherham
Education Dept, Norfolk House, Walker Pl, Rotherham S65 1AS
Tel: 01709 382121 ext 3698 *Fax:* 01709 839771

Geoffrey Thomas, adviser for mus and perf arts.
Orchestras: For details of mus provision *see* Rotherham Music Service.
Courses: Annual summer course for young musicians.

Rotherham Music Service
Parkhurst Teachers' Centre, Doncaster Rd, Rotherham S65 2BL
Tel: 01709 828191 *Fax:* 01709 379601

Geoffrey Thomas, adviser for mus and perf arts; David Lever, head of mus service.
Orchestras: Rotherham youth orch and young sinfonia/Geoffrey Thomas, David Lever and Nicola Livesey; schools youth br band/Jeremy Wade, intermediate band/Robert Murray and Huw Lewis, schools concert band/Peter Sinclair and Jim Whyte, Chantry band/Joy Crick and Sonia Mellor.
Music Centres: Ens rehearse weekly, br band twice weekly. Sat morning mus centres at Clifton Comprehensive Upper School and Oakwood Comprehensive. Weekly and Sat ens open to all ages. There are str orchs, br and wind bands; also gui, rcdr, choirs, big band and keyboard tuition plus aural and theory study.
Courses: Residential and non-residential courses with local and guest tutors and peripatetic staff for snr ens; also tours. Annual summer holiday courses open to all Rotherham pupils.

Rutland Council
Catmose, Oakham, Rutland LE15 6HP
Tel: 01572 722577

Janice Morphet, chief exec; Carol Chambers, school effectiveness offr, Rutland LEA.
Orchestras: Rutland primary orch/Albert Cortese.

Salford Music Support Service
Education Centre, London St, Salford, Lancs M6 6QT
Tel: 0161 743 4268 *Fax:* 0161 743 4249

Anthony Briggs, inspector for mus and performing arts; Colin Green, head of mus support service.
Orchestras: City youth orch, youth concert band, schools orch, centre strs, introductory orch, Suzuki vn ens, training band, jazz band, fl and cl groups, adult str band, community wind band and choir.
Music Centres: Mus centre at Swinton High School, Sefton Rd, Pendlebury on Mon, Wed and Fri, age 5-adult.
Courses: Biennial tours organised for concert band and youth orch alternately. Residential mus-making courses for younger children and adults.

Sandwell
Dept of Education and Community Services, PO Box 41, Shaftesbury House, 402 High St, W Bromwich, Sandwell, W Midlands B70 9LT
Tel: 0121 569 8502 *Fax:* 0121 569 8518

Richard T Worth, gen adviser; Keith C Watts, head of mus service.
Orchestras: Youth orch/John Dawson, youth concert band/David Swanson, youth br band/eith Watts, training orch/Andrew Crabtree, training concert band/Wesley Kendrick, training br band/Ian Gibbs. All orchs and bands gr 4-8. Sandwell Young Voices/Lynn Allemann.
Music Centres: 2 Sat morning mus centres provide early ens experience; intermediate wind band and intermediate str ens and gui tuition. Causeway Green Music Centre, Sheila Martin (dir); Charlemont Music Centre, Tom Morgan (dir).
Courses: Ingestre Hall Residential Centre offers a variety of w/end and week courses for primary and secondary school groups; band and orch residential courses. Principal: Ms J Blake *Tel:* 01889 270225 *Fax:* 01889 270225.

Sefton

Education Dept, Town Hall, Bootle, Merseyside L20 7AE
Tel: 0151 934 3343

Jacque Emery, gen adviser (mus and RE); Geoffrey Reed, head of mus service.
Orchestras: Sefton youth wind orch/Geoffrey Reed, youth jazz orch/Glenn Waite, youth str orch/Keith Matthews, youth br band/Morris Fogg, youth choir/Pam Horswood.
Music Centres: Central Music Centre, Redgate, Formby, Merseyside L37 4EW *Tel:* 01704 872773.
Courses: Residential courses for all groups, European tours. In-service courses for teachers.

Sheffield Music Services

Bannerdale Centre, Bannerdale Rd, Sheffield S7 2EW
Tel: 0114 250 6860 *Fax:* 0114 250 6862

Peter M Bell, head of mus services.
Orchestras: City of Sheffield youth orch, schools snr orch and 7 feeder orchs, youth festival band/Clive Scott, plus additional feeder band, girls' choir with 4 other choirs/Vivien Pike, cl choir, 3 rcdr consorts/Virginia White and Diane Chamberlain, 2 br bands/Michael Dodd and Andrew Corker.
Music Centres: Central mus centre co-ordinating peripatetic c/room and inst teachers; provision of facilities for the mus ens; Associated Board Examination centre for Sheffield.
Courses: Regular concerts and tours at home and abroad for all top ens; residential w/ends for jnr ens; participation in national festivals.

Slough Borough Council

Town Hall, Bath Rd, Slough SL1 3UQ
Tel: 01753 523881

John Christie, chief educ offr.
Orchestras: Music Services currently provided by Berkshire Young Musicians Trust *see above.*

Solihull

Education Dept, PO Box 20, Council House, Solihull, W Midlands B91 3QU
Tel: 0121 704 6619 *Fax:* 0121 704 8065

Joyce Rothschild, inspector of schools (mus); Tony Veal, head of mus service; Tim Low, head of Sat mus centre.
Orchestras: Solihull youth chmbr orch/Dorothy Berry, youth orch/Michael Beavis, youth jazz orch/Roger Harris, youth wind band/Tony Veal, other wind bands and orchs at jnr and intermediate levels.
Music Centres: 9 mus centres throughout area including Lyndon Music Centre, Daylesford Rd, Solihull, W Midlands B92 8EJ *Tel:* 0121 743 2483. Also Sat morning mus centre for age 8-18 offering wide range of activities at above address.
Awards: Children of school age attending lessons

at a recognised college of mus may reclaim 50% fees from the authority.
Courses: Orchs and bands have annual courses and tours abroad each yr. Residential courses also run for other orchs and bands. Regular in-service courses for teachers.

South Gloucestershire

Music Service, Poole Ct, Poole Court Dr, Yate BS37 5PP
Tel: 01454 313334 *Fax:* 01454 312838

Ian Rogers, head of mus service.
Music Centres: Area mus centres at Filton, Kingswood, Thurnbury and Yate.

South Tyneside

Dept of Education, Town Hall and Civic Centre, S Shields NE33 2RL
Tel: 0191 427 1717; 0191 519 1909 (teachers centre)
Fax: 0191 427 0584

Roger McKone, gen adviser for mus.
Orchestras: Wind band; jnr, snr and intermediate str orchs; plus other ens.
Music Centres: 3 Sat morning mus centres for primary and secondary pupils.
Awards: Discretionary awards available from LEA.
Courses: Many occasional courses available.

Southampton

City of Southampton Music Services, 5th Floor, Frobisher House, Nelson Gate, Southampton SO15 1GX
Tel: 01703 833633 *Fax:* 01703 833324

Philip Litchfield, mus dir and inspector for mus.

Southend-on-Sea Borough Council

Civic Centre, Southend-on-Sea, Essex SS2 6ER
Tel: 01702 215000

D Krawiec, chief exec.
Orchestras: On 1 April 1998, Southend-on-Sea Borough Council became a unitary authority.

Stockport

Music Centre, Dialstone Centre, Lisburne La, Stockport SK2 7LL
Tel: 0161 474 2233 *Fax:* 0161 474 2218

Colin Edwards, advisory teacher.
Orchestras: Stockport schools' snr br band/Colin Duxbury, intermediate br band/Peter Gray, Stagesound, youth orchs/Derrick Margerson and Tamandra Ford, youth choirs/John Pomphrey and Imelda Leah, snr wind band/Huw James, intermediate wind band/Jeremy Sleith.
Music Centres: Main mus centre as above, plus Junior Music Centre, c/o Hazel Grove Primary School, Chapel St, Hazel Grove, Stockport SK7 4JH. Lilian Hardbattle, head of inst teaching; Huw James, head of mus support service.
Courses: Variety of w/end and holiday courses for

young musicians sponsored by mus service. Full range of INSET courses for specialist and non-specialist teachers.

Stockton on Tees *see* Tees Valley Music Service

Stoke-on-Trent
City Music School, Corneville Rd, Bucknall, Stoke-on-Trent ST2 9EY
Tel: 01782 233657/233793/1/6 *Fax:* 01782 233792

Ronald Fargher, principal; Michael Thorley, head of mus in performance; Sue Hallam, mus co-ord.

Sunderland
Advisory Service, Broadway Education Development Centre, Springwell Rd, Sunderland SR4 8NW
Tel: 0191 553 5600 *Fax:* 0191 553 5633

Stephen Auster, mus adviser.
Orchestras: Community ens meeting weekly and for short courses. Chmbr choir for ages 9-14.
Awards: LEA tuition fee remission scheme.
Courses: Community extra-curricular mus programme. Primary, secondary and special mus in-service courses. Mus IT centre.

Swindon
Swindon Music Service, Sanford House, Sanford St, Swindon SN1 1QH
Tel: 01793 463869 *Fax:* 01793 488597

David Barnard, head of service.

Tameside
Instrumental Music Teaching Agency, Education Development Centre, Lakes Rd, Dukinfield, Tameside
Tel: 0161 344 2121 *Fax:* 0161 339 8994

Kelvin Carnaffan, principal adviser; Ray Owen, gen adviser (creative arts); Godfrey Calcutt, head of agency.
Orchestras: Tameside youth orch; intermediate and chmbr orchs, w/wind and br groups; also str, gui (all borough groups).
Music Centres: Stamford High School, Mossley Rd, Ashton under Lyne OL6 9SD. Fri evening and Sat morning. Tuition for all ages.
Courses: Occasional non-residential ens courses; LEA participating member of Greater Manchester Centre for Curriculum Music.

Tees Valley Music Service
The Oakland Centre, Fakenham Av, Middlesbrough TS5 4QQ
Tel: 01642 819903 *Fax:* 01642 852104

David Kendall, head of service; co-ords: John Mackenzie, Hartlepool; Rita Perkins, Middlesbrough; Christine Cope, Stockton on Tees; Joan Ditton, Redcar & Cleveland.
Orchestras: Tees Valley Music Service serves the districts of Middlesbrough, Hartlepool, Stockton on Tees and Redcar and Cleveland. Tees Valley youth orch, youth choir, boys' choir, vc consort, wind orch, br band.
Music Centres: 4 district mus centres including Hartlepool Music Centre, c/o Brierton School, Catcote Rd, Hartlepool; Middlesbrough Music Centre, The Oakland Centre, Fakenham Av, Middlesbrough; Stockton Music Centre, c/o Ian Ramsey School, Greens La, Stockton on Tees; Redcar & Cleveland Music Centre, c/o Rye Hills School, Warwick Rd, Redcar TS10 2EP.
Awards: Preston Simpson scholarship for pupils of gr 5+ and Sterndale scholarship (girls) both by audition for pupils who reside in Hartlepool district.
Courses: In-service courses for all KS.

Telford and Wrekin District Council *see* Shropshire

Thurrock Borough Council
Civic Offices, New Rd, Grays RM17 6SL
Tel: 01375 652652

K Barnes, chief exec.
On 1 April 1998 Thurrock Borough Council became a unitary authority.

Torbay Council
Civic Offices, Castle Circus, Torbay TQ1 3DR
Tel: 01803 296244

K Parr, head, Devon Youth Music.
Orchestras: Activities run in conjunction with Devon Youth Music.

Trafford
Education Dept, PO Box 19, Town Hall, Tatton Rd, Sale M33 1YR
Tel: 0161 912 3060 *Fax:* 0161 912 3059

Martin Flatman, mus adviser; Jane Paton, primary mus support teacher.
Orchestras: Trafford youth orch/Jonathan Brett, youth chmbr orch/Jennifer Merren (gr 3-6), jnr strs/Christine Boardman (gr 1-3).
Music Centres: 2 mus centres at Flixton (Fri evening), Stretford (Sat morning); elementary tuition and ens playing opportunities, and mus theory (primary and secondary age).
Awards: Awards for gifted children to attend RNCM jnr dept.
Courses: Annual residential youth orch course; occasional non-residential day courses.

Wakefield
Manygates Music Centre, Manygates La, Wakefield, W Yorkshire WF2 7DQ
Tel: 01924 303306 *also fax*

Geraldine Gaunt, mus adviser and inspector; Val Jennings, head of inst service.
Orchestras: Wakefield youth symphony orch,

youth wind band, youth symphony wind band, Metropolitan br band, Metropolitan schools band, youth choir, wind band, various orchs, br bands, and other ens at all levels based at mus centres.
Music Centres: Manygates Music Centre (main Wakefield Centre) with Sat morning and weekday evening activities including practical ens playing, bands and theory classes; also other centres at Minsthorpe High School, New College, Pontefract, Southdale Junior School and Wrenthorpe Junior and Infants School.
Courses: Annual youth orch summer course. A whole range of INSET training courses in mus. Based at Manygates Music Centre.

Walsall
The Music Centre, c/o Bloxwich C of E School JMI, High St, Bloxwich, Walsall WS3 3LP
Tel: 01922 491320

Michael Parrott, head of service.
Orchestras: A full range of orchs and bands.
Music Centres: The Music Centre, Forest Community Association, Hawbush Rd, Leamore, Walsall WS3 1AG *Tel:* 01922 492080.
Courses: W/shops and festivals, performance projects, plus in-service courses for teachers.

Warrington Borough Council
Education Dept, Newtown House, Buttermarket St, Warrington WA1 2NH
Tel: 01925 444400

S Broomhead, chief exec.

West Berkshire Borough Council *formerly* Newbury
Education Dept, West St, Newbury, Berks RG14 1BZ
Tel: 01635 519728/519727 *Fax:* 01635 519725

Orchestras: Refer to Berkshire Young Musicians Trust entry below.

Wigan
Metropolitan Wigan Instrumental Teaching Provision, The Professional Development Centre, Park Rd, Hindley, Wigan WN2 3RY
Tel: 01942 255227 *Fax:* 01942 255217

Havilland Willshire, co-ord, MWITP.
Orchestras: Metropolitan youth orch, snr orch, 2 jnr orchs; also jazz orch, br bands, symphonic band, swing band. Wide range of ens, covering all ages and abilities.
Music Centres: Leigh Music Centre and Wigan Music Centre organised centrally by inst teaching provision. Wide range of ens for players of gr 1 standard and above.
Awards: Children may apply for places at

Chetham's School or the RNCM.
Courses: Wide range of non-residential courses for different insts and ens throughout summer. Residential courses for youth orch. Mus tours abroad for snr ens.

Windsor & Maidenhead Royal Borough Council
Town Hall, Maidenhead SL6 1RF
Tel: 01628 796163 *Fax:* 01628 796256

M D Peckham, dir of educ.

Wirral
Dept of Education, Hamilton Education Offices, Conway St, Birkenhead, Merseyside L41 4FD
Tel: 0151 666 4324 *Fax:* 0151 666 4207

David L Straughan, mus inspector.
Orchestras: Wirral schools and intermediate orchs/Philip Chapman, schools and intermediate br band/Alan Milnes, schools concert band/ David Straughan, schools intermediate wind band/Denise Scott, schools big band/David Semans.
Music Centres: 4 Sat morning mus centres at Oldershaw School, Valkyrie Rd, Wallesey; Pensby Boys' School, Irby Rd, Heswall; Bebington High School, Higher Bebington Rd, Bebington; Park High School, Birkenhead.
Awards: PRS composers in educ scheme 1997-8.
Courses: Annual residential courses organised for above groups in the UK and abroad.

Wokingham District Council
Council Offices, Shute End, Wokingham RG40 1BN
Tel: 0118 977 8948 *Fax:* 0118 977 8677

Mrs G Norton, chief exec; Jacky Griffin, dir of educ and cultural services.

Wolverhampton
Wolverhampton Music School, Graiseley Hill, Wolverhampton WV2 4NE
Tel: 01902 312065 *Fax:* 01902 558106

David Woodyer, head of mus service.
Orchestras: Wolverhampton youth orch, 5 orchs, 5 wind bands, br band, jazz orch, early mus group, early years group (all levels of ability catered for in a 'pyramid' system). Asian mus tuition.
Music Centres: Central borough mus school (Sat morning and weekday evenings; rehearsals for ens as above, plus theory study and inst tuition).
Awards: Various awards and bursaries for musically gifted children.
Courses: Regular residential and non-residential holiday courses; annual tours abroad; also regular in-service training for teachers.

York

City of York Schools Advisory Service, White Cross, 150 Haxby Rd, York YO3 7JS
Tel: 01904 673434 *Fax:* 01904 673439
Email: gordon.pearce@york.gov.uk

Gordon Pearce, gen adviser (mus and performing arts); Gill Cooper, mgr of performing arts service.

Orchestras: Symphony orch, concert band, big band, gui, rcdr groups, primary choir, snr choir, str orch, concert orch.
Music Centres: City of York Music Centre, Queen Ann School, Queen Anne's Rd, York (Alison Goffin, head; Sat morning).

England (Counties)

Avon

Orchestras: Avon has been replaced by the unitary authorities of Bristol, South Gloucestershire, North West Somerset and Bath & North East Somerset.

Bedfordshire

County Music Service, Emerald Ct, Pilgrim Centre, 20 Brickhill Dr, Bedford MK41 7PZ
Tel: 01234 213439 *Fax:* 01234 363516

Ian G Smith, county mus offr; John Shayler, Nick Quinn, joint acting mus service mgrs; Ken Storry, curriculum adviser and inspector for mus.
Orchestras: County youth orch/Michael Rose; 2nd youth orch/Ian Smith, 3 other orchs; concert band/Chris Robinson, 2 other bands; 2 youth choirs; youth opera; br band; jazz band; steel band; perc group. Several area bands and orchs.
Music Centres: 5 Sat morning mus schools at Redborne Upper School, Ampthill; Pilgrim House, Brickhill Dr, Bedford; Stratton Upper School, Eagle Farm Rd, Biggleswade; Manshead School, Dunstable Rd, Caddington; Vandyke Upper School, Vandyke Rd, Leighton Buzzard.
Awards: For Sat morning exhibitions at jnr dept of London College of Music.
Courses: Regular courses for orchs, bands, etc, during holidays and half terms in Luton and Bedfordshire, both in UK and abroad plus day courses for various inst groups. Also in-service courses for teachers. *Additional info:* In Apr 1997 Bedfordshire was divided into Luton (a unitary authority) and Bedfordshire.

Berkshire

Education Dept, Shire Hall, Shinfield Pk, Reading, Berks RG2 9XE
Tel: 0118 923 3675 *Fax:* 0118 975 0360

David Congdon, mus inspector.
Courses: Consultancy, advice and a full range of courses are available.

Berkshire Young Musicians Trust

Stoneham Ct, 100 Cockney Hill, Reading, Berks RG30 4EZ
Tel: 0118 901 2350 *Fax:* 0118 901 2351

David Marcou, principal; Lady Solti, Evelyn Glennie OBE, patrons.
Orchestras: Berkshire boys' choir, Berkshire girls' choir/Gillian Dibden, youth br band/Bernard Hazelgrove, gui orch/Colin Arenstein, perc and marimba ens/Andrew Leask, str training orch/Nick Beach, youth wind orch/Charles Henwood, youth choir/Gillian Dibden, youth orch/Robert Roscoe, rcdr ens/Susanna Westmeath.
Music Centres: 4 area mus centres: Central Berkshire, address and tel as above, Simon Salisbury, area head; East Berkshire, c/o Oakfield First School, Imperial Rd, Windsor SL4 3RJ *Tel:* 01753 854598, Graham Sanders, area head; South Berkshire, c/o Brakenhale School, Rectory La, Bracknell RG12 7BA *Tel:* 01344 360036, Robert Priestley, area head; West Berkshire, c/o Shaw House School, Church Rd, Shaw, Newbury RG13 2DU *Tel:* 01635 48814, Nick Beach, area head. All mus centres offer group and individual lessons, bands, choirs, inst general musicianship, jnr w/shops and kindermusik, theory and composition classes.
Awards: Award and scholarship schemes available.
Courses: Residential and non-residential courses: chmbr mus, inst, orch, choral, opera, composition. Many performing opportunities for pupils including tours abroad for county and area groups. Regular staff development days for all staff.

Buckinghamshire

Education Dept, County Hall, Aylesbury, Bucks HP20 1UZ
Tel: 01296 382439 *Fax:* 01296 383948

Helen Blakeman, adviser and head of mus services.
Orchestras: County youth orch/Ian Hooker plus full range of bands, orchs, choirs, ens, kindermusik, jazz and early mus at each area mus centre; steel pans in High Wycombe only. Entry to youth orch by annual audition.
Music Centres: Sat morning and weekday twilight

and evening mus centre activities at: Amersham Music Centre, c/o Woodside School, Mitchell Walk, Amersham HP6 6NW *Tel:* 01494 722291 *also fax*, David Crook, co-ord; Aylesbury Music Centre in Aylesbury and Winslow, c/o Elmhurst Middle School, Dunsham La, Aylesbury HP20 2DB *Tel:* 01296 28941 *also fax*, Hugh Molloy, area hd; High Wycombe Music Centre, c/o Sands Middle School, Mill End Rd, High Wycombe, HP12 4BA *Tel:* 01494 445947 *Fax:* 01494 442773, Malcolm Pollock, area hd.
Awards: County scholarships for subsidised inst tuition at mus centres. Annual auditions, May.
Courses: Sep, Dec and Easter courses for county youth orch; some summer concert tours. County-wide programme of CPD programmes to support class teachers in primary and secondary phase; area mus consortia of secondary mus teachers; some area primary consortia. *Additional Information:* In Apr 1997 Buckinghamshire was divided into Milton Keynes (a unitary authority) and Buckinghamshire.

Cambridgeshire
Education Office, Gazeley House, Princes St, Huntingdon, Cambs PE18 6NS
Tel: 01480 425839 *Fax:* 01480 425804

Frances Williams, gen inspector for mus; Peter Britton, mgr, Cambs inst mus agency.
Orchestras: Cambs county youth orch, various area br and concert bands, orchs, str and other ens, catering for all levels of ability in Cambridge, Huntingdon, Fenland, Peterborough. Also independent Cambs Holiday Orch, Cambs Boys' Choir.
Music Centres: Area mus centre at Fenland Music Centre, March. Also Sat mus schools based at Bottisham, Comberton and Duxford. Cambridge Music School at Chesterton.
Awards: Wilfred Charles Hayden Trust of 1 or more annual awards (by audition) to outstanding children from old admin area of Cambs and Isle of Ely.
Courses: Various internal county courses; also concerts, tours, special events and twinning abroad organised for ens as above. *Additional Information:* In Apr 1998 Cambridgeshire was divided into Peterborough (a unitary authority) and Cambridgeshire.

Cheshire
Cheshire Advisory Service, Hadfield House, County Hall, Chester CH1 1SQ
Tel: 01244 603362 *Fax:* 01244 603813

Mervyn Williams, county mus adviser.
Orchestras: County youth orch, chmbr choir, chmbr orch, boys choir, choir and br band (rehearsals by arrangement); 15 other area bands, orchs (meet weekly).

Music Centres: Inst mus base: Cheshire School of Music, Woodford Lodge, Woodford La West, Winsford, Cheshire CW7 4EH.
Courses: Tours abroad (including USA, Czech Republic, Austria and Japan), regular courses for county and district groups. *Additional Information:* In Apr 1998 Cheshire was divided into Warrington, Halton (unitary authorities) and Cheshire.

Cleveland
Cleveland has been replaced by Middlesbrough, Hartlepool, Stockton-on-Tees and Redcar and Cleveland.

Cornwall
Advisory Service, Pondhu House, Penwinnick Rd, St Austell PL25 5DP, Cornwall
Tel: 01872 327516 *Fax:* 01726 77041

Derek Kitt, county adviser for mus.
Orchestras: Cornwall youth orch/David Frost, youth br band, youth jazz orch, youth wind orch, youth perc ens, youth fl choir, chmbr choir, youth str orch, cl choir.
Music Centres: The Music Service, Percuil Building, Daniell Road Site, Truro TR1 2DA *Tel:* 01872 323476 *Fax:* 01872 225041. John Harries, head of the mus service; Rod Pierce, mgr.
Courses: Annual residential Easter course; 4 residential w/end courses pa; 4-day annual county tour. Three 1-day non-residential in-service courses, with annual 3-day residential course. 2 day in-service residential courses, twilight courses for groups/individual schools; training days for groups of schools/individual schools. Cross-curricular courses with other subjects; joint mus dept and inst service staff courses.

Cumbria
Education Service, 5 Portland Sq, Carlisle CA1 1PU
Tel: 01228 606846 *Fax:* 01228 606920

Noel Bertram, head, schools mus service.
Orchestras: Cumbria youth orch, various regionally-based groups.
Music Centres: Most areas have centres organised locally.
Courses: Residential courses for young instrumentalists.

Derbyshire
Music Activities, Advisory & Inspection Service, Chatsworth Hall, Chesterfield Rd, Matlock DE4 3FW
Tel: 01629 580000 ext 5720 *Fax:* 01629 580350

Philip King, adviser.
Orchestras: Derbyshire City and County youth orch/Peter Stark (guest cond), city and county wind band/Murray Slater.

Music Centres: Bands, orchs and choirs at centres throughout the county, including Chesterfield, SE Derbys, S Derbys, Wirksworth, Bakewell, Buxton and Hope Valley. All funded and organised by parent committees.
Courses: Residential courses and tours organised for many groups, including county intermediate band and orch courses. INSET: range of week, day and twilight courses for teachers; infant and primary festivals. *Additional Information:* In Apr 1997 Derbyshire was divided into Derby (a unitary authority) and Derbyshire.

Devon
Devon Youth Music, County Music Office, Countess Weir School, Lower Weir Rd, Exeter EX2 7BR
Tel: 01392 877493 *Fax:* 01392 876130

Ken Parr, head; Melvyn Batten, deputy head.
Orchestras: County youth and youth concert orch/Melvyn Batten, youth jazz orch/Ken Parr, youth wind orch/Stan Hacking, youth string orch/Shelagh Batten, youth perc ens and bsn ens/Michael Merryweather, cl ens/Marina Kennel.
Music Centres: Centres throughout the county offering inst teaching, ens and other mus opportunities.
Courses: Residential summer school for snr ens and courses throughout the year for other groups. *Additional Information:* In Apr 1998 Devon was divided into Plymouth, Torbay (unitary authorities) and Devon. Joint arrangements will provide inst mus tuition and mus activities.

Devon Curriculum Advice
Expressive Arts Base, Salisbury Rd, Plymouth PL4 8QZ
Tel: 01752 223581 *Fax:* 01752 253537
Email: jforster@www.devon-cc.gov.uk

John Forster, adviser for mus; Noelle Boucherat, adviser for mus.
Orchestras: For inst mus services *see* Devon Youth Music above.
Courses: Programme of courses supporting school teachers in raising the quality of teaching and learning in mus at all key stages. *Additional Information:* In Apr 1998 Devon was divided into Plymouth, Torbay (unitary authorities) and Devon.

Dorset
Music Service, c/o Carter Community School, Blandford Close, Hamworthy, Poole BH15 4BQ
Tel: 01202 678233 *Fax:* 01202 679381

David Kenyon, David Norton, heads of service.
Orchestras: Dorset youth orch, youth wind orch, youth wind sinfonia, youth jazz orch, youth perc ens, youth sinfonia, jnr strs, youth choir, youth gui ens.

Music Centres: Bournemouth Music Centre, Summerbee School, Mallard Rd, Bournemouth (Ieuan Davies, dir); Christchurch Music Centre, Twynham School, Sopers La, Christchurch (Ieuan Davies, dir); Dorchester and Weymouth Music Centre, St Osmunds Middle School, Rothesay Rd, Dorchester, and The Wey Valley School, Dorchester Rd, Weymouth (Walter Brewster, dir); West Dorset Music Centre, St Mary's CE School, Skilling Hill Rd, Bridport (Pat Crawford, dir); Sherborne Music Centre, The Gryphon School, Bristol Rd, Sherborne (Tom Forward, dir).
Courses: Wide range of courses offered through Professional Development Services, County Hall, Dorchester DT1 1XJ *Tel:* 01305 224530. *Additional Information:* In Apr 1997 Dorset was divided into Bournemouth, Poole (unitary authorities) and Dorset.

Durham
County Durham Music Support Service, Music Centre, Darlington Music Centre, Borough Rd, Co Durham DL1 1SG
Tel: 01325 380757 *Fax:* 01325 352473

John Allen, head of service.
Orchestras: County symphony orch and chmbr orch/Tony Oliver, county wind ens/Ray Dales and Steve Down, county br band/Alfred Hind, county youth choir/Alan Woods. 19 other orchs, 11 wind bands, 2 early mus groups (covering all ability levels from beginner through district to county level).
Music Centres: Mus centres and Sat morning schools in various county schools. Mus school organised from above address (alternate Sats, sometimes all day) for age range 7-18, with activities including ens work and sectionals. Mus centre recording studio facilities and mobile digital recording facility.
Awards: LEA grants awarded for recreational courses organised outside county, also to support students to attend BYSO, NJPO, NYO, NYC.
Courses: Annual 3-day courses including orch, 2 wind bands, br band; individual inst clinics and w/shops (2 pa for each inst), 3-4 tours abroad each year; at least 3 concerts performed by each ens. Area mus festivals organised. Also in-service courses for teachers: vocal course, a basic curriculum for non-specialist course, jazz and improvisation course and curriculum support to schools.
Additional Information: In Apr 1997 County Durham was divided into Darlington (a unitary authority) and County Durham.

East Sussex

Advisory, Inspection and Training Service, PO Box 4, County Hall, St Annes Cres, Lewes BN7 1SG
Tel: 01273 481208/481000 *Fax:* 01273 481902

Karen Brock, county mus adviser.

East Sussex

County Music Service, Watergate La, Lewes, E Sussex BN7 1UQ, Lewes BN7 1SG
Tel: 01273 472336 *Fax:* 01273 486396

Roy Wales, dir East Sussex county mus service.
Orchestras: Orchs, bands, ens and choirs based in Lewes, Hastings, Brighton, Eastbourne and Crowborough. County youth orch, concert band, youth choir, children's choir, E Sussex chorus.
Music Centres: 4 regional mus centres in Lewes, Eastbourne, Crowborough and Hastings and 7 area centres.
Courses: Residential and non-residential w/end and holiday courses on an area county basis, specialist mus course for A-level candidates at County Music Centre. Summer school for 3 weeks in Jul. Extensive in-service training programme. Projects with Glyndebourne, London Sinfonietta, Jazz Education Trust. *Additional Information:* In Apr 1997 East Sussex was divided into Brighton & Hove (a unitary authority) and East Sussex.

Essex

Music and Youth Arts, Community Education Service Group, Essex County Council, PO Box 47, County Hall, Victoria Rd South, Chelmsford CM1 1LD
Tel: 01245 436052/436309 *Fax:* 01245 436319

Richard Brittain, asst mgr, mus services; Bella D'Arcy, mgr, youth arts.
Orchestras: 2 county youth orchs/Christopher Adey and Antoine Mitchell.
Music Centres: Peripatetic inst services to schools and young people. Youth arts partnerships.
Courses: 2 courses each for youth orchs, summer school plus tours. Youth Music projects; dance and mus projects; mus technology; recording sessions; youth camps (mus, dance, drama). *Additional Information:* In Apr 1998 Essex was divided into Southend, Thurrock (unitary authorities) and Essex.

Gloucestershire

Colwell Centre for Arts in Education, Derby Rd, Gloucester GL1 4AD
Tel: 01452 330300 *Fax:* 01452 330311

Brian Ley, head of mus service; Richard Ling, head of inst teaching; Brenda Whitwell, mgr.
Orchestras: County youth orch/Charles Peebles, symphonic wind band/Roger Abbott, young jazz orch/Tony Sheppard. Also various area orchs, choirs and jazz ens.
Music Centres: 5 mus centres (Brookfield, Cirencester, Forest of Dean, Nailsworth, Tewkesbury). Age 7-16, all abilities. Orch and band playing, theory and aural classes, ens playing.
Courses: Annual orch summer school also open to players living outside the county. 26 Jul-1 Aug 1998.

Guernsey

Schools Music Service, Education Dept, Grange Rd, St Peter Port, Guernsey GY1 1RQ, CI
Tel: 01481 727797 *Fax:* 01481 717745

John Whomersley, mus organiser.
Orchestras: Guernsey youth orch, concert band, girls choir/Christine Dawber, youth choir, children's choirs, elementary str orchs, training youth orch, elementary and training wind bands, primary groups. Also Channel Islands youth orch/Keith Smith, organised jointly by Guernsey and Jersey Education Departments.
Music Centres: Guernsey Music Centre, Grammar School, Les Varendes, St Andrews and St Peter Port School, Les Ozouets, St Peter Port: training in aural, theory of mus, orchs, bands and ens, support services.
Awards: Awards for attendance on courses, grant aid provision.
Courses: Youth orch and wind band courses locally and abroad, courses with visiting tutors. Channel Islands youth orch course.

Hampshire

Music Service, Hampshire Music Centre, Gordon Rd, Winchester SO23 7DD
Tel: 01962 861502 *Fax:* 01962 863690
Email: edmsmcla@hants.gov.uk

Richard Howlett, head of mus service; Allison Price, deputy head of service.
Orchestras: 40 area and 10 county ens. Hampshire county youth orch/Nicholas Wilks, county youth band/Leighton Rich, youth jazz orch, county youth choir, children's choir.
Awards: Scheme of awards for individual tuition available to children showing outstanding mus ability in annual auditions.

Hereford and Worcester

In April 1998 Hereford and Worcester was divided into Herefordshire (a unitary authority) and Worcestershire.

Hertfordshire

County Music Service, The Education Centre, Butterfly Rd, Wheathampstead AL4 8PY
Tel: 01582 830379 *Fax:* 01582 830383
Email: john.witchell@hcc.gov.uk

John Witchell, head of mus service, county mus adviser.

Orchestras: Hertfordshire county youth orch/John Witchell, youth wind orch/Philip Ellis, schools symphony orch/Rebecca Kelly, county br/Clifford Jones, county youth choir (SATB)/Cathy Heller-Jones, youth jazz ens/Eddie Harvey, classical gui ens/Gillian Bassett, rcdr ens/Annabel Sanders-Hewett, Ace of Herts choir (SSA)/Val Whitlock.

Music Centres: West Hertfordshire Music School, Watford School of Music, Nascot Wood Rd, Watford WD1 3RS, Philip Ellis. North Herts Music School, Highbury House, Highbury Rd, Hitchin SG4 9RU, Meirion Williams. Mid Herts Music School, Sir Frederic Osborn School, Herns Lane, Welwyn Garden City AL7 2AF, Peter Twitchin. East Herts Music Centres, Ingram House, Bishop's College, Churchgate, Cheshunt EN8 9NH, David Boarder and Rebecca Kelly. Dacorum Music Centre, Heath Barn, St John's Rd, Hemel Hempstead HP1 1ND, Angela Gilby. Stevenage Music Centre, Valley Way, Stevenage SG2 9AB, Sylvia Downes. St Albans Music School, Townsend Drive, St Albans AL3 5RL, Jennifer Hopkins.

Courses: 3 pa for county orchs (some residential) plus ens throughout the year. Various teachers courses throughout the year offering wide-ranging skill development and NC support.

Humberside

Humberside has been replaced by the unitary authorities of Kingston upon Hull, East Riding of Yorkshire, North Lincolnshire and North East Lincolnshire.

Isle of Man

Music Centre, Government Buildings, Lord St, Douglas, Isle of Man IM1 1LE
Tel: 01624 686555 *Fax:* 01624 686557

Bernard G F Osborne, head of inst mus service.
Orchestras: Manx youth orch/Bernard Osborne, youth choir/Mr E A Q Davidson; other ens for all playing standards organised through schools.
Music Centres: Ramsey Music School, Ramsey Grammar School; Peel Music School, Queen Elizabeth II High School, Peel; Douglas Music School, Ballakermeen High School, Douglas; all Sat morning, organising ens work, rehearsals of ens as above, various other activities.
Awards: Aid available from internally organised award scheme.
Courses: Manx Youth Choir meets regularly; Manx Youth Orch weekly rehearsals supplemented by residential study courses; in-service courses for teachers.

Jersey

Professional Development Centre, PO Box 142, Jersey JE4 8QJ
Tel: 01534 509491 *Fax:* 01534 509380

Mel Davison, adviser for creative and expressive arts; Colin R Amos, head of inst service.
Orchestras: Jersey youth orch/Gwenda Harris, jnr str orch/Pat Woodsford, intermediate youth orch/Liz Laurens, jnr wind band/Jean Hall, intermediate wind band/Allan Jones, youth wind band/Neil Sawyer, jnr girls' choir/Susan DeGruchy, intermediate girls' choir/Gillian Marquer, snr girls' choir/Elizabeth du Feu, boys' choir/Malcolm Whittell. Also Channel Islands youth orch/Keith Smith.
Music Centres: Island Music Centre: training in theory and opportunities to play in orchs, bands and ens.
Awards: Discretionary grants scheme for children with special mus needs, and for purchase of insts. Competitions for str, w/wind, br and pno.
Courses: Annual youth orch, wind band tours and courses abroad; various other inst w/end and holiday courses at all levels for choirs and insts. C I Music Council (co-ordinates concert tours), Peter Curtis, chmn.

Kent Curriculum Services Agency

South Borough Buildings, Loose Rd, Maidstone, Kent ME15 6TL
Tel: 01622 672202 ext 233 *Fax:* 01622 691412

Derek Blease, county lead consultant for mus.
Courses: OFSTED inspection, Pre-OFSTED inspection, review and advice, post-OFSTED support. Schools and consortium-based support for NC mus implementation. Cross-county INSET courses. Demonstration lessons, w/shops and curriculum support projects. Mus festivals. Mus INSET and w/shops. *Additional Information:* In Apr 1998 Kent was divided into Medway (a unitary authority) and Kent. The services provided by KCSA will remain unchanged.

Kent Music School

Kent Music Centre, The Masters House, College Rd, Maidstone ME15 6YQ
Tel: 01622 691212 *Fax:* 01622 688544
Email: kmsho@cix.compulink.co.uk

Michael Wearne, dir.
Orchestras: Kent county youth orch, schools orch/Alan Vincent, youth wind orch/Alan Hutt, youth symphonic band/Alan Hutt, youth and jnr choirs, youth singers, youth chmbr choir, county jnr singers, youth barbershop/Andrew Larner, youth recorders/Marion Scott, youth jazz orch/Geoff Miller.
Music Centres: Kent centre for young instrumentalists (Sat morning) for musically

talented children at Kent Music Centre, The Master's House, College Rd, Maidstone, Kent ME15 6YQ. Area mus centres.
Awards: Kent Music School Bursary Fund.
Courses: Orch, wind band, choral residential summer mus courses and many non-residential area courses. *Additional Information:* In Apr 1998 Kent was divided into Medway (a unitary authority) and Kent.

Lancashire
Education Dept, County Hall, Fishergate, Preston, Lancs
Tel: 01772 254868

J J Grisdale, head of service.
Orchestras: Lancs students' symphony orch/J Clayton, students' chmbr orch/J Clayton, students' training orch/T Jackson, students' jazz orch/S Grills, students' concert band/G Balson, youth br band/P Read.
Music Centres: Music Service base, Chorley Education Support Centre, Schools Services Division, Weldbank La, Chorley PR7 3NN *Tel:* 01257 234450. Regional mus inspectors based in Preston (M Lormor), Blackburn (M Tomlinson), Rossendale (G Balson).
Awards: Individual awards available to talented mus children for appropriate tuition beyond county boundaries.
Courses: All county ens as above organise regular residential and non-residential courses throughout yr. Symphony orch, concert band and br band have tours abroad. *Additional Information:* In Apr 1998 Lancashire was divided into Blackburn, Blackpool (unitary authorities) and Lancashire.

Leicestershire and Leicester
Arts in Education, Knighton Fields Centre, Herrick Rd, Leicester LE2 6DH
Tel: 0116 270 0850 *Fax:* 0116 270 4928

Peter Baker, service mgr; Russell Parry, head of inst tuition; Catherine Hutchon, head of perf and dance.
Orchestras: Leicestershire schools symphony orch/Russell Parry, symphonic wind band/Andrew Bound; 8 supporting orchs and bands plus youth choirs.
Music Centres: Knighton Fields Centre, Herrick Rd, Leicester LE2 6DH.
Awards: Michael Tippett Bursary for final year students awarded annually.
Courses: In-service courses for teachers both in school and centrally organised. Residential and non-residential courses for orchs, bands, choirs and other student groups. Also a full service for dance and drama. *Additional Information:* In Apr 1997 Leicestershire was divided into Leicester, Rutland (unitary authorities) and Leicestershire.

Lincolnshire
Education and Cultural Services Dept, County Offices, Newland, Lincoln LN1 1YQ
Tel: 01522 552222 ext 3331 *Fax:* 01522 553257

D W Harries, head of mus support service.
Orchestras: Lincolnshire youth symphony orch/Wynne Harries, youth concert orch/Richard Green, youth symphonic wind band/David Dorey, youth concert band/David Chambers.
Music Centres: Lincoln Music Centre, c/o City of Lincoln Community College, Skellingthorpe Rd, Lincoln (M Stockdale); Spalding Music Centre, Neville Av, Spalding (M Horsfall); Sleaford and Grantham Music Centres, c/o Kestevan and Grantham Girls' School, Sandon Rd, Grantham (M Duckels); Grantham County Music School, 339 Harlaxton Rd, Grantham (Mrs R D Parry); Sam Newsom Music Centre, South St, Boston (L Hextall, H Black); Louth, Horncastle and Market Rasen Music Centres, c/o De Aston School, Market Rasen (Mrs P Barber).
Courses: 4 residential inst w/end courses for local children and foreign tours. In-service courses provided by Curriculum and Monitoring Branch of the Education Dept, c/o Horncastle Curriculum Centre, Horncastle College, Horncastle, Lincs.

Norfolk
Centre for the Arts in Education, Bull Close Rd, Norwich NR3 1NG
Tel: 01603 618914 *Fax:* 01603 764419

David Sheppard, mgr arts in educ services.
Orchestras: Norfolk youth orch/guest professional conductor, Norwich students orch/John Burdett, Norwich students concert band/Kevin Hegarty, Norwich students jazz orch/David Amis. 19 additional ens at all levels.
Music Centres: Norwich mus centre: specialised perc studio and tuition; mus technology studio and tuition; gamelan orch in multi-cultural studio with tuition. Private Sat morning schools in West, East and South Norfolk.
Awards: Occasional support given to students for advanced mus courses through access to a Trust Fund; support for members of National Youth Orchestra; occasional support for special events.
Courses: Residential orch courses bi-annually for 200+ players in 4 ens. Occasional course on jazz, gamelan, strs during week and at w/end. In-service courses on mus technology, NC issues and practice.

North Yorkshire
County Music Service, County Hall, Northallerton, N Yorks DL7 8AE
Tel: 01609 780780 ext 2599 *Fax:* 01609 778611

David Morgan, head of inst mus service; David Parkinson, snr mus adviser.

Orchestras: N Yorkshire schools' concert band, schools' symphony orc.

Music Centres: Sat morning mus centres at: Harrogate Granby High School, Avondale Rd, Harrogate, N Yorks HG1 4AR; Aireville School, Gargrave Rd, Skipton, N Yorks BD23 1UQ; Allertonshire School, Brompton Rd, Northallerton, N Yorks DL6 1ED; Scarborough VIth Form College, Sandybed La, Scarborough, N Yorks YO12 5LF; Selby High School, Leeds Rd, Selby, N Yorks YO8 0HT; Whitby Community College, Prospect Hill, Whitby, N Yorks YO21 1LA.

Courses: Annual Easter/summer residential courses for orch and band.

Northamptonshire

Inspection and Advisory Service, John Dryden House, 8-10 The Lakes, Northampton NN4 7DD
Tel: 01604 237083 *Fax:* 01604 236240

David Bray, county mus inspector.

Courses: Advice and consultancy service. In-service training and support in the following areas: general class teachers at pre-school, KS1 and KS2; specialists in all key stages; micro-technology; musical skills for teachers; planning and managing the mus curriculum; assessment; supply and returning teachers; world musics; area carol festivals; area infant/jnr festivals and w/shops; residential enrichment courses for singing, cross-curricular projects, A-level and GCSE; enrichment courses for special schools.

Northamptonshire Music Service

125-129 Kettering Rd, Northampton NN1 4AZ
Tel: 01604 37117; 01604 24103 *Fax:* 01604 603070

Peter Dunkley, head of county mus service.

Orchestras: County youth orch/Peter Dunkley, training orch/Graham Tear, jnr orch/Ruth Allen, concert band/Adele Sellers-Peck, training band/Paul Truman, jnr band/Peter Smalley, youth br band/Rachel Coles, training br band/Peter Smalley, big band/Richard Baker, jazz 2/Ray Meadham, jazz 3/Catrin Roberts, youth choir/David Bray, snr girls choir/Stephen Meakens, girls choir/Davina Kennedy, boys choir/Andrew Moody, str orch/Richard Wright, chmbr orch/David Leech, fl choir/Catrin Roberts, cl choir/John Sharp, folk group/Richard Leigh, gui orch/John Draper, jnr br group/Jo Coventry and various str quartets, etc.

Music Centres: Central Northampton (Kettering Rd) acts as a base for the inst mus team and as rehearsal venue for all county activities. 14 additional regional centres (mainly jnr) which meet on Sat mornings in term-time and aim to build upon children's talents. Admission open to all. For termly fee children can have access to

ens training, general musicianship classes, choirs, nursery mus groups, bands, orchs, perc, chmbr mus, handbells, dance, etc. Centres at: Southfield School, Banbury Rd, Brackley; Kingswood School, Gainsborough Rd, Corby; Daventry Tertiary College, Badby Rd, Daventry; The Ferrers School, Queensway, Higham Ferrers; Guilsborough Primary School, High St, Guilsborough; Tresham College, Windmill Av, Kettering; King's Cliffe Middle School, Nene Valley Centre, Oundle; Prince William School, Herne Rd, Oundle; Northampton, Lings Upper School, Trinity Upper School, Roade School, Duston Middle School; Nicholas Hawksmoor Primary School, Towcester; John Lea School, Doddington Rd, Wellingborough.

Awards: Grants for musically talented children (LA and special trust funded). Youth Music Fellowship provided by BBC Northampton.

Courses: Wide range of courses at all levels. 1-day and residential inst courses during all holidays (including half-term) for orchs, bands, rcdrs and all other ens; term-time residential primary str and rcdr w/shops; orch and band tours abroad. Summer school.

Northumberland

Education Development Centre, Hepscott Pk, Stannington, Morpeth, Northumberland NE61 6NF
Tel: 01670 533000 *Fax:* 01670 533591

Alison Rushby, snr adviser/inspector (mus); Trevor Snowdon, head of mus service; John P Verney, deputy head, mus service.

Orchestras: Northumberland county symphony orch/John P Verney, concert band/Mr J Snowdon, jazz orch/David Hignett, jnr wind band/David Hignett, str orch/Ruth Turner, Alnwick youth orch/Carole Robb, Morpeth first schools orch/Mr A Thompson, Blyth Town Band/Mr R McCluskey.

Music Centres: Berwick Music Centre, c/o Berwick High School.

Nottinghamshire

Arts Support Service, Mandela Centre, Green St, The Meadows, Nottingham NG2 2LA
Tel: 0115 953 5040

John Auty, head of arts support service.

Orchestras: Nottinghamshire Education symphony orch, concert band, brassery, choir.

Music Centres: Sat morning mus w/shops in Rural, Coalfield and Greater Nottingham. Age range 7-19, ens, choral, musicianship.

Awards: Specialist tuition available through m/classes to young people who audition and gain membership of the symphony orch, concert band, brassery or choir. Auditions held annually.

Courses: Inst and mus teaching service throughout the county including the city of

Nottingham. *Additional Information:* In Apr 1998 Nottinghamshire was divided into the City of Nottingham (a unitary authority) and Nottinghamshire.

Oxfordshire

Music Service, Oxford School, Glanville Rd, Oxford OX4 2AU
Tel: 01865 779959 *Fax:* 01865 712438

Richard Hallam, dir and inspector of mus.
Orchestras: Wide variety of orchs and ens.
Music Centres: Central mus school (Oxford), 8 area mus schools and many weekday activities within county.
Courses: Various residential and non-residential county inst courses (during all main school holidays). Touring by orchs at home and overseas. Full range of in-service training for special school teachers, general/specialist primary and specialist secondary teachers.

Shropshire

Shropshire Music Service, Longmeadow, Bayston Hill, Shrewsbury SY3 0NU
Tel: 01743 874145 *Fax:* 01743 872666

Keith Havercroft, county mus adviser; Glenn Pollard, head of mus service.
Orchestras: Shropshire youth orch/R W Wysome, youth concert band/A Atkin, youth br band/D Heywood, training youth orch, training youth concert band, boys' choir, girls' choir, youth choir, 10 area orchs, bands, ens; vc ens, perc ens, fl ens.
Music Centres: County mus school meets fortnightly in Shrewsbury, Sat morning, age 9-21, rehearsal of ens as above. 8 wkly area mus schools (ens work and teaching).
Awards: Financial aid discretionally awarded to gifted children for mus study.
Courses: Residential chmbr mus course, w/end concerto course, m/classes (for in-county students); other orch courses and adult/young people w/end courses as need arises. Widespread overseas tours and exchanges; participation in annual international youth mus festival. Teachers' courses and w/shops for KS1-4 and post-16. *Additional Information:* In Apr 1998 Shropshire was divided into Telford and Wrekin (a unitary authority) and Shropshire. PLEASE SUPPLY INFORMATION ON RECENT AUTHORITY CHANGES WITHIN YOUR COUNTY AND GIVE RELEVANT ADDRESS DETAILS FOR MUSIC DIVISIONS

Somerset

Somerset Music, Education Development Service, The Holway Centre, Keats Rd, Taunton TA1 2JB
Tel: 01823 349350 *Fax:* 01823 349351

Graham Bland, dir of mus.
Orchestras: Somerset county youth orch/Martyn Owen, youth concert band/Keith Thomas, county youth choir/Stephen Knight, county youth training orch/John Jones.
Music Centres: Provision of all-round mus tuition and the opportunity to enjoy mus-making.
Courses: For orchs, bands, choirs and a variety of mus insts.

Staffordshire

County Music Service, Corporation St, Stafford ST16 3LX
Tel: 01785 356505 *Fax:* 01785 356512
Email: graham.standley@staffordshire.gov.uk

Graham Standley, head of mus service, Staffs.
Orchestras: Staffordshire youth orch and youth jazz orch/Graham Standley, youth choir/Alan Chappell, youth wind orch/Frank Wadkin, youth br band/David Godfrey, youth rcdr ens/Terence Carter.
Music Centres: 7 regional mus centres within Staffs: Cannock (S Staff), Jeremy Dutton; Tamworth, Terence Cregan; Burton-upon-Trent (including Uttoxeter), Naomi Turner; Stafford (including Stone), Patrick Park; Lichfield and Rugeley, Terence Carter; Newcastle under Lyme, Quentin Duerden; Moorlands, David Godfrey. School for talented young musicians, Lesley Park.
Awards: Awards for musically talented children.
Courses: Each inst group meets weekly, regular programme of concerts. Short tour abroad for one group annually. Entry by audition. Also in-service courses for specialist/non-specialist primary and secondary teachers. *Additional Information:* In Apr 1997 Staffordshire was divided into Stoke-on-Trent (a unitary authority) and Staffordshire.

Suffolk

County Music Service, Northgate Arts Centre, Sidegate Lane West, Ipswich, Suffolk IP4 3DF
Tel: 01473 281866 *Fax:* 01473 286068

Philip Shaw, county adviser for mus; Pauline Allen, county advisory teacher for mus; David Bramhall, snr county mus tutor.
Orchestras: Suffolk youth orch/P J Shaw, youth sinfonia/P J Shaw, youth wind band/Suzanne Dexter Mills, youth choir/D J Bramhall, young strs/Anna Appleton. Also regional youth orchs, bands and choirs based in Ipswich, Bury St Edmunds and Lowestoft. Also area and district intermediate and jnr orchs, bands and choirs for all levels of ability.
Music Centres: In Ipswich (c/o Northgate Arts Centre, address above); Bungay, Beccles, Lowestoft, Framlingham, Eye (all c/o North Suffolk Professional Development, Lovewell Rd, Lowestoft NR33 0RQ *Tel:* 01502 562250); Sudbury, Haverhill, Bury St Edmunds, Newmarket (all c/o West Suffolk Performing Arts Centre, King Edward VIth Upper School, Grove Rd, Bury St Edmunds IP33 3BH *Tel:* 01284 723105); catering

for all levels, age 5-19. Inst ens, choral singing, musicianship, theory, etc.
Awards: LA support offered where appropriate. Discretionary awards for jnr college, advanced tuition and special mus schools.
Courses: Residential and day courses for county ens including annual festivals and foreign tours, etc. Residential and in-service courses for mus teachers.

Surrey

Surrey Youth Music and Performing Arts, County Music Centre, Westfield Primary School, Bonsey La, Woking GU22 9PR
Tel: 01483 728711 *Fax:* 01483 725980

Keith Willis, head of SYMPA.
Orchestras: County youth orch/Keith Willis and John Forster (Fri evenings), county wind orch/Hugh Craig (Fri evenings), county youth choir/Keith Clark (Wed evenings); also 47 area and county groups throughout the Authority.
Music Centres: 5 based throughout county at Leatherhead, Merstham, Guildford, Staines, Woking. Enquiries to G Allitt, Manager Customer Services, Westfield Primary School, Bonsey La, Westfield, Woking, Surrey GU22 9PR *Tel:* 01483 727634.
Awards: Talented children sponsored to attend

jnr depts of GSMD, RAM, RCM, TCM (min gr 5 distinction at age 11); enquiries to Elizabeth Smith, admin officer at County Music Centre.
Courses: 5-day residential Easter course for orch, wind band, jazz players and choir. Projects with London Sinfonietta, ROH, Academy of St Martin in the Fields, Guildford Philharmonic.

Warwickshire

County Music Service, 22 Northgate St, Warwick CV34 4SR
Tel: 01926 412803 *also fax*

Garry Jones, mus inspector & dir of county mus; Jim Norden, head of inst tuition.
Orchestras: Warwickshire county youth orch/Ray Hutchinson, county wind band/James Norden, county youth chorale/Garry Jones, county youth br/Stephen Cooper, county fl choir/Jan Roddy, county cl choir/Lisa Crompton, county youth chorus/Jeremy Dibb. Also other ens, including county steel pan and rock/pop.
Music Centres: 4 regional mus centres and a developing network of 12 area centres. A wide variety of linked activities including tuition, ens, orch, choirs and bands.
Courses: Mus inspection, development and advice. Numerous local and regional courses. Publications on curriculum, vocal repertoire and extra-curricular mus. Training in school inst and

vocal teaching. Inspection for primary and secondary. 4-day residential courses for young musicians.

West Sussex
Education Dept, Western Area Professional Centre, Stockbridge Rd, Chichester, W Sussex PO19 1RF
Tel: 01243 532970 *Fax:* 01243 531080

David Williams, gen adviser (mus); Christopher Mahy, head of inst teaching service; Michael Sullivan, head of mus awards and performance.
Orchestras: W Sussex youth orch, youth wind orch, str orch, boys' and girls' choirs; also 22 area groups throughout authority.
Music Centres: Crawley Area Music Centre, c/o Hazelwick School, Mill La, Crawley, W Sussex RH10 1SU (R Hinchliffe); Chichester Area Music Centre, c/o WAPC, Stockbridge Rd, Chichester PO19 2EF (Michael Sullivan).
Awards: Jnr mus exhibitions to London conservatoires; award scheme for in-county individual tuition.
Courses: Young inst (str and wind band) courses at Lodge Hill Residential Centre, Watersfield, Nr Pulborough, W Sussex RH20 1LZ. Regular in-service courses for teachers are provided.

Wiltshire Music Service
Education Dept, County Hall, Trowbridge, Wilts BA14 8JB
Tel: 01225 713824 *Fax:* 01225 713876

Phillip Scott, mus service mgr.
Orchestras: Wiltshire and Swindon youth orch, 2 area youth orchs, wind and jazz bands with feeder jnr and intermediate groups.
Music Centres: West Wilts Young Musicians (600 members aged 6-19) at Wilts Music Centre, Ashley Rd, Bradford on Avon; Salisbury Area

Young Musicians (500 members aged 6-19) at St Martins junior school, Shady Bower, Salisbury.
Awards: A number of children are supported to attend mus college jnr depts in London.
Courses: Wiltshire and Swindon youth orch, residential and non-residential courses plus tours abroad. Also regular tours for many ens as well as national festival participation, competitions and exchanges. *Additional Information:* In Apr 1997 Wiltshire was divided into Thamesdown (Swindon) (a unitary authority) and Wiltshire.

Worcestershire Instrumental Music Service
Queen Elizabeth High School, Panniers La, Bromyard HR7 4QS
Tel: 01885 488715 *Fax:* 01885 482499
Email: imshq@worcestershire.gov.uk

Chris Stowell, head of service; Gordon Hartley-Bennett, deputy head of service, br; Robert Marshall, head of N Worcs, str, Lesley Cox, Hilary Harris, joint heads, S Worcs, vocal.
Orchestras: Worcestershire youth symphony orch/Robert Marshall, youth wind orch/Colin Farlow, youth choir/Lesley Cox and Carol Green, intermediate orch/Chris Eldridge, intermediate wind orch/Sarah Ellis.
Music Centres: Music Centres at Kidderminster, Bromsgrove, Evesham, Pershore and Worcester.
Courses: Regular programme of concerts for all ens and mus centres; national festival participation; annual tour abroad for one snr ens; annual residential courses for br, w/wind and str players respectively; 1-day and w/end w/shops; project work in schools; INSET courses available.
Additional Information: In April 1998 Hereford and Worcester was divided into Herefordshire (a unitary authority) and Worcestershire.

Scotland

Aberdeen City
Summerhill Education Centre, Stronsay Dr, Aberdeen AB15 6JA
Tel: 01224 208626 *Fax:* 01224 208674

David Eastwood, asst dir of educ.
Orchestras: 7 orchs.
Music Centres: Aberdeen Music Centre, Summerhill Education Centre, Stronsay Dr, Aberdeen AB15 6JA.

Aberdeenshire Council
Summerhill Education Centre, Stronsay Dr, Aberdeen AB15 6JA
Tel: 01224 208662 *Fax:* 01224 208671

Lloyd Davies, educ offr for mus.
Music Centres: North Aberdeenshire Music Centre at Fraserburgh Academy, Central Aberdeenshire Music Centre at Inverurie Academy and South Aberdeenshire Music Centre at Mackie Academy, Stonehaven.

Angus
Education Development Service, Bruce House, Wellgate, Arbroath DD11 3TE
Tel: 01241 435019

Andrew Ross, co-ord, expressive arts.
Orchestras: Str orchs, wind bands, symphony orch, jazz band.
Music Centres: Angus Music Centre, Montrose Rd, Forfar.
Awards: Arts aid scheme to assist pupils with special tuition and national course participation.
Courses: Residential courses, orch, band and choral.

Argyll and Bute
Education Dept, Argyll House, Alexandra Parade, Dunoon, Argyll PA23 8AJ
Tel: 01369 704000

Ronald M Gould, head of support service.

Orchestras: Kintyre schools' wind band, Cowal schools' wind band, Oban and Lorn schools' wind band, Mid-Argyll schools' wind band, Islay schools' wind band.
Awards: Argyll Trust Fund.
Courses: Various band courses organised. In-service courses for teachers and inst teachers.

Clackmannanshire

Education and Community Service, Educational Development Section, Castle St, Alloa FK10 1EX
Tel: 01259 45000 *Fax:* 01259 452440

Music Centres: Hillfoots Music for Youth, c/o Martin Jones, Alva Academy, Queen St, Alva.
Awards: Clackmannanshire Arts Forum.
Courses: Alloa Community Music Project, Town Hall, Alloa *tel:* 01259 218491.

Dumfries and Galloway

Department for Education, Council Offices, Sun St, Stranraer DG9 7JJ
Tel: 01776 702151 ext 61219 *Fax:* 01776 704819

Davida H Allison, admin assistant.
Orchestras: Regional youth orch and concert band; other orchs and bands.
Music Centres: Area groups rehearse evenings during term-time at Stranraer Academy, McMaster's Rd, Stranraer DG9 8NY; Castle Douglas High School, Dunmuir Rd, Castle Douglas DG7 1LQ; Dumfries High School, Marchmount, Dumfries DG1 1PX.
Awards: Scheme to support musically talented children qualifying for RSAM Sat morning school.
Courses: Children sponsored to attend courses run by Scottish Amateur Music Association. Annual competitive mus festival, end of May (Stranraer). Staff development courses organised and delivered locally on pupil closure days to meet staff's identified needs.

Dundee City

Educational Development Service, Gardyne Rd, Dundee
Tel: 01382 462857 *Fax:* 01382 462862
Email: advisers@educational-development-service.dundeecity.sch.uk

Charles Maynes, co-ord for expressive arts.
Orchestras: 2 symphony orchs, 2 str orchs, 3 wind bands, 2 br bands, traditional fiddle group, jazz/stage band, pipe band, snr and jnr choirs.
Music Centres: 1a West Bell St Dundee; ens rehearse Oct to Easter.
Awards: Pupils subsidised for NYOS and SAMA courses.
Courses: Residential courses for all orchs and bands, normally long w/end. Dundee Schools Festival of Music and Drama every two yrs. Continuous staff development programme.

East Ayrshire

Instrumental Service, James Hamilton Academy, Sutherland Dr, Kilmarnock KA3 7DF
Tel: 01563 543591 *Fax:* 01563 534370

Andrew Keachie, principal teacher of inst service.
Orchestras: Various school orchs, wind bands, jazz bands, br bands including East Ayrshire schools br band and schools choir.
Awards: Children supported for participation in orchs, bands, shows.

East Dunbartonshire

Boclair House, 100 Milngavie Rd, Bearsden, Glasgow G61 2TQ
Tel: 0141 942 9000 *Fax:* 0141 942 6814

Ian Mills, dir of educ; George Kelly, head of inst tuition.
Orchestras: George Kelly.
Awards: Support to pupils attending NYO, NYSOS, NYC.

East Lothian District Council

Council Buildings, Haddington, East Lothian EH41 3HA
Tel: 01620 827576 *Fax:* 01620 827446

Margaret O'Conner, mgr, cultural services.

East Renfrewshire

Eastwood Park, Rouken Glen Rd, Giffnock, East Renfrewshire G46 6UG
Tel: 0141 577 3223 *Fax:* 0141 577 3276

Jillian Carrick, mus co-ord.
Orchestras: East Renfrewshire snr str orch/Michael Calder, snr concert band/Kevin Price.
Music Centres: Several jnr orchs, bands and ens. Williamwood High School, Seres Rd, Clarkston G76 7NS.
Awards: Assistance for pupils gaining places on national courses.
Courses: Several courses at Castle Toward Residential School.

City of Edinburgh

Education Support Services, George IV Bridge, Edinburgh EH1 1UQ
Tel: 0131 469 3387 *Fax:* 0131 469 3100

Colin O'Riordan, principal offr, mus.
Orchestras: 4 orchs, 2 wind bands, 2 jazz orchs, classical gui ens, strathspey and reel society.
Courses: Residential courses for orch, wind band, jazz orch, classical gui ens, electric gui ens. Summer concert series. Extensive in-service provision for school mus and inst staff.

Falkirk Council

Education Service, McLaren House, Haypark, Marchmont Av, Polmont, Falkirk FK2 0NZ
Tel: 01324 506600 *Fax:* 01324 506601
Email: education@falkirkalmac.co.uk

Ann Carnachan, head of educ support; Gillian Thomson, support offr, expressive arts.
Orchestras: Various ens.

Fife

Education Service, Auchterderran Centre, Woodend Rd, Cardenden, Fife KY5 0NE
Tel: 01592 414659 *Fax:* 01592 414641
Email: gwilson@itasdare.demon.co.uk

Graeme Wilson, adviser in mus.
Orchestras: Fife youth orch/G Wilson, youth concert band, youth str orch, youth perc ens, schools wind band, schools str orch, 3 area str orchs, 3 area wind bands, youth gui ens, youth choir, jnr singers.
Courses: Residential weekends for youth orch, concert band, gui ens, youth choir. Annual Easter course for youth str orch and perc ens. INSET courses for teachers and instructors.

Glasgow City Council

Department of Education, Charing Cross Complex, House 1, 20 India St, Glasgow G2 4PF
Tel: 0141 287 8182 *Fax:* 0141 287 8212
Email: rmackie@essglasgow.org.uk

Ronnie Mackie, adviser in creative & aesthetic subjects.
Orchestras: Glasgow schools' symphony orch, primary orch, concert band, str orch, jazz band, pipe band.
Courses: Easter course for str orch, summer course for symphony orch, various w/end courses for other groups. In-service courses for 5-14, Standard grade and Highers.

Highland

The Education Centre, Castle St, Dingwall, Ross-shire IV15 9HU
Tel: 01349 863441 *Fax:* 01349 865637
Email: bert_richardson@hcs.uhi.ac.uk

H C Richardson, mus adviser.
Orchestras: Highland Regional youth orch/H C Richardson and Nigel Boddice, youth choir/ George McPhee. Locally organised wind bands, br bands, pipe bands, str groups and orchs.
Awards: Representation scheme giving support for attendance at approved events (eg NYOS).

Inverclyde Council

Education Services, 105 Dalrymple St, Greenock
Tel: 01475 882828 *Fax:* 01475 726412

Joy Monteith, head of service, libraries, museums; Bernard McLeary, dir of educ services.

Orchestras: Charles Keenan.
Music Centres: Greenock Music Centre, Greenock Academy, Madeira St, Greenock PA16 7XE.

Midlothian

Greenhall Centre, Gowkshill, Gorebridge, Midlothian EH23 4PE
Tel: 01875 825015

David O'Connor, mus organiser.

Moray

Education Department, Council Office, High St, Elgin IV30 1BX
Tel: 01343 543451 *Fax:* 01343 540399

John M Mustard, head of mus instruction services.
Orchestras: Moray concert brass/Glenn Munro, senior orch/John M Mustard.
Music Centres: Moray Music Centre, Education Offices, Academy St, Elgin (John Mustard).

North Ayrshire Council

Cunninghame House, Irvine KA12 8EE
Tel: 01294 324453 *Fax:* 01294 324444

Brian Kerr, head of inst services; Norma McCrone, adviser in arts development.
Orchestras: North Ayrshire schools concert band/Brian Kerr, schools choir/Mae Murray.
Music Centres: Sat morning perc class, Kilwinning Academy.
Awards: Help given towards course fees for national youth orchs, etc.
Courses: Courses for concert band and choir; w/end courses for choirs, orchs, bands; international exchanges.

North Lanarkshire Council

Quality Development Service, Municipal Buildings, Kildonan St, Coatbridge
Tel: 01236 441200

Jim Park, head of inst mus.
Music Centres: Coatbridge High School, Albert St, Coatbridge.

Orkney Islands

Education Dept, Council Offices, Kirkwall, Orkney KW15 1NY
Tel: 01856 873535 ext 2419 *Fax:* 01856 870302

E Holt, gen adviser.
Orchestras: Orkney schools swing band/D Griffith.
Courses: Orkney school inst mus course.

Perthshire and Kinross Council

Education Dept, Blackfriars, Perth PH1 5LU
Tel: 01738 476200 *Fax:* 01738 476210

Len McConnell, head of educ services.

Renfrewshire Council
Education Development Service, South Building, Cotton St, Paisley PA1 1LE
Tel: 0141 887 8212 *Fax:* 0141 887 9142

Anna Paterson, mus organiser.
Orchestras: Orch/Gerard Doherty, 1st concert band/Albert Sloan, 2nd concert band/Andrew Laird, 1st br band/Michael Howie, 2nd br band/Douglas Thomson, choir for secondary pupils/Christine Badger.
Music Centres: Sat mus centres at: Paisley Grammar, Glasgow Rd, Paisley PA1 3RP; St Mirin's High, Ferguslie, Paisley PA1 2QY.
Awards: Grants made to assist with tuition at RSAMD.

Scottish Borders
Education Dept, Council HQ, Newtown St Boswells, Melrose TD6 0SA
Tel: 01835 824000 ext 5483 *Fax:* 01835 822145

Alistair Salmond, adviser in arts.
Orchestras: Intermediate orch/James Letham, jnr orch/Simon Johnston, chmbr ens (Sat morning), regional intermediate choir, regional wind orch/Kevin Price, reserve and training bands, str ens/Barbara Mythen.
Music Centres: Held at Galashiels Academy, Elm Row, Galashiels TD1 3HU.
Awards: Borders Young Musicians awards.
Courses: Various w/end courses.

Shetland Islands
Education Offices, Schlumberger Base, Gremista Industrial Estate, Lerwick, Shetland Islands ZE1 0PX
Tel: 01595 744318 *Fax:* 01595 692810

Gordon Yeaman, educ adviser (expressive arts).
Orchestras: Shetland youth jazz, schools traditional fiddles, schools wind band, schools str orch.

South Lanarkshire
Education Services, Almada St, Hamilton ML3 0AE
Tel: 01698 454545 *Fax:* 01698 454465

Colin Bowen, inst co-ord; Brian Dunabie, adviser in creative and aesthetic subjects.
Orchestras: Lanarkshire orch society/David Kent

Stirling Council
Viewforth, Stirling FK8 2ET
Tel: 01786 443337 *Fax:* 01786 443394

Bob McGowan, educ development offr.
Orchestras: Stirling Council schools snr orch, jnr orch, choirs.
Courses: Mus making w/ends for orchs and choirs.

West Dunbartonshire Council
Quality Development Service, Council Offices, Garshake Rd, Dumbarton G82 3PU
Tel: 01389 737334 *Fax:* 01389 737348

Ellen McBride, quality development adviser; Christine Sinclair, p/t mus instruction.

West Lothian Council
Education Services, Lindsay House, Southbridge St, Bathgate EH48 1TS
Tel: 01506 776137 *Fax:* 01506 776378

Derek Oates, educ offr.
Orchestras: Contact Brian Duguid, arts unit mgr: The Arts Unit, Almondbank Campus, Craigshill, Livingston EH54 5EJ *Tel:* 01506 777585 *Fax:* 01506 777590.

Western Isles Council
Council Offices, Sandwick Rd, Stornoway, Isle of Lewis PA87 2BW
Tel: 01851 703773 *Fax:* 01851 706022

R J Woolford, asst dir of educ and leisure.
Awards: Awards made on an individual basis.

Wales

Blaenau Gwent County Borough Council
c/o Greater Gwent Music Support Service, Melfort Rd, Newport, South Wales NP9 3FP
Tel: 01633 223196 *Fax:* 01633 252051

Alun D Williams, head of service; Brian Mawby, dir of educ.
Orchestras: See Greater Gwent Music Support Service for mus provision organised in collaboration with other authorities. Also Blaenau Gwent county youth br band/Colin Rees, big band/Colin Rees.
Music Centres: Blaenau Gwent Music Centre, Nantyglo Leisure Centre, Nantyglo (Stephen

David, head of centre). Sat morning, wind, br and str ens.
Awards: Advanced tuition mus scheme for talented students.
Courses: Full programme of residential and non-residential courses.

Bridgend County Borough Council
c/o Director of Education, Sunnyside, Bridgend
Tel: 01656 643227 *Fax:* 01656 646966

Kevin Adams, adviser in mus; D M A Hughes, co-ord of inst mus service.
Orchestras: County Borough of Bridgend youth

orch: rehearsals 6-8pm Friday evenings, Ynysawdre Comprehensive School, Heol Yr Ysgol, Tondu, Bridgend. Bridgend, Rhondda-Cynon-Taff, Merthyr Tydfil and Caerphilly orchs combine to form Glamorgan Valleys' youth orch/Kevin Adams; br band/Howard Jones; wind band/David Hughes. *Music Centres:* Fri evenings Sep-Apr.

Caerphilly County Borough Council
Council Offices, Caerphilly Rd, Ystrad Mynach, Hengoed CF82 7EP
Tel: 01443 815588 *Fax:* 01443 816998

Neil Harries, dir of educ and leisure; Keith Ellerington, principal mus offr.
Orchestras: See Caerphilly Music Service for mus provision. Bridgend, Rhondda-Cynon-Taff, Merthyr Tydfil and Caerphilly county borough orchs combine to form Glamorgan Valleys' Youth Orchestra.

City and County of Cardiff
Education Department, County Hall, Atlantic Wharf, Cardiff CF1 5UW
Tel: 01222 872844 *Fax:* 01222 872762
Email: case@rmplc.co.uk

Chris Jones, mus and creative arts adviser.
Orchestras: See Cardiff County and Vale of Glamorgan Music Service for details of joint mus provision.

Cardiff County and Vale of Glamorgan Music Service
The Friary Centre, The Friary, Cardiff CF1 4AA
Tel: 01222 640950/1 *Fax:* 01222 227471

Mostyn Davies, head of mus service.
Orchestras: Cardiff County and Vale of Glamorgan youth orch/Eric Phillips, youth chmbr orch/Eric Phillips, youth wind band/Peter Knight, youth jazz orch 'Jazz News'/Edward John, youth br band/Keith Griffin, symphonic br/Matthew Thistlewood, youth choir/Kelvin Thomas, high schools' orch/Charles Maynard, high schools' wind band/Eric Phillips, high schools' br band/Adrian Dinsmore, high schools' choir/John Wickett, transitional orch/Keith Griffin, intermediate str ens/Penny Hughes, fl ens/Iau Provis, cl ens/David Bordessa, double reed group/Beryl James, transitional br band/Charles Maynard, training br band/Ian Roberts, intermediate br band/David Short, preliminary br band/Gareth Jones, jnr orch/Russell Webb, jnr br band/Shirley Ap Glyn, jnr choir/Georgina Cooper and Jenny Ives, class 3 br band/Sarah Corcoran, class 2 br band/Clive Morris, class 1 br band/Shirley Ap Glyn, perc classes/Rachel Payne.

Cardiganshire (Ceredigion)
Education Office, Marine Terrace, Aberystwyth, Ceredigion SY23 2DE
Tel: 01970 633614 *Fax:* 01970 615348

John H Jones, head of mus service.
Orchestras: Ceredigion orch, str orch, wind band, area training and jnr ens.
Music Centres: Mon, Tue, Wed and Fri evenings at local schools.
Awards: Various awards to support musically talented pupils.
Courses: Annual residential courses for Three Counties (Carmarthenshire, Cardiganshire and Pembrokeshire) youth orch, bands and youth choir.

Carmarthenshire
Griffith Jones Centre, St Clears, Carmarthenshire SA33 4BT
Tel: 01994 231223; 01267 267803 *Fax:* 01994 231255
Email: ewjonescarm@satproj.org.uk

Emyr Wynne Jones, mus adviser; Norman Roberts, head of mus service.
Orchestras: Carmarthenshire youth orch, br band, wind band, choir; area orchs, bands, training ens; rcdr, gui and hp ens. Rock and pop w/shops and jnr choirs.
Music Centres: W/end courses held at Ferryside Residential Centre. Weekly rehearsals at various school venues.
Awards: Various awards to support musically talented children.
Courses: Annual residential courses for the Three Counties (Carmarthenshire, Cardiganshire and Pembrokeshire) youth orch, bands and youth choir. In-service courses for teachers (primary and secondary), curriculum leaders and peripatetic staff.

Conwy County Borough Council
Education Dept, Dinerth Rd, Colwyn Bay LL28 4UL
Tel: 01492 575002 *Fax:* 01492 541311

Julie Meehan, expressive arts development offr.
Orchestras: Jnr and intermediate regional ensembles throughout the county; snr activities by agreement with two inter-county providers. Four Counties orchs, ensembles and choir/Jefferson Thomas. Canolfan Gerdd William Mathias orchs, ensembles and choir/Dennis Williams.
Music Centres: Llandudno, Llandudno Senior, Penrhyn Bay and Llanrwst Music Centres.
Awards: Various throughout the year to support musically talented pupils.
Courses: Various residential regional courses.

Denbighshire County Council

Education Dept, County Hall, Mold CH7 6GR
Tel: 01824 706751 *Fax:* 01824 706780

Orchestras: Denbighshire, Conwy, Flintshire and Wrexham combine to form Four Counties youth choir/Jean Stanley-Jones, youth wind band, youth orch/M C Fallowfield and Gareth Jones, youth br band.

ESIS

Education Support and Inspection Service, G5, Treforest Industrial Estate, Pontypridd CF37 5YL
Tel: 01443 845400 *Fax:* 01443 842639

Orchestras: Looks after visiting teachers of inst mus and various ens for Merthyr Tydfil. Rhondda-Cynon-Taff youth br band/Howard Jones, Rhondda-Cynon-Taff youth orch/Derek Holvey, Merthyr Tydfil youth orch/Sian Jenkins, Bridgend youth orch/Karen Hnyda. Bridgend, Rhondda-Cynon-Taff, Merthyr Tydfil and Caerphilly orchs combine to form Glamorgan Valleys' youth orch and br band/Howard Jones.
Additonal info: ESIS advises and inspects schools in the 4 county boroughs of Bridgend, Rhondda-Cynon-Taff, Merthyr Tydfil and Caerphilly.

Flintshire County Council

County Hall, Mold, Flintshire CH7 6ND
Tel: 01352 704097 *Fax:* 01352 754202

Jean Stanley-Jones, head of mus support service.
Orchestras: Denbighshire, Conwy, Flintshire and Wrexham combine to form Four Counties youth choir/Jean Stanley-Jones, youth wind band, youth orch/M C Fallowfield and Gareth Jones, youth br band.
Music Centres: Mold Alun/Maesgarmon campus, meeting wkly on Fridays.

Greater Gwent Music Support Service

Melfort Rd, Newport, South Wales NP9 3FP
Tel: 01633 223196 *Fax:* 01633 252051

Alun D Williams, county mus adviser and head of service.
Orchestras: Full range of Greater Gwent, County Borough and district ens including Greater Gwent youth orch, string orch, choir, jazz orch, brass band, wind symphonia, big band, trad jazz band.
Music Centres: Newport Music Centre, Brynglas House, Newport: Sat morning weekly, wind, br and str ens, theory (Alun F Williams); Newport (Caerleon) Music Centre, Caerleon Comprehensive School: Sat monthly, str ens (Peter James); Torfaen Music Centre, The Settlement, Pontypool: Mon evening weekly, wind, br and str ens, theory (Geoff Barrett); Blaenau Gwent Music Centre, Nantyglo Comprehensive School, Nantyglo: Sat morning weekly, wind, br and str ens (Stephen David); North Monmouthshire Music Centre, Monmouth Comprehensive School: Sat mornings weekly, wind br and str ens (David Davies); South Monmouthshire Music Centre, Chepstow Comprehensive School: Sat morning weekly, wind, br and str ens (David Davies).
Awards: Advanced mus tuition scheme for talented students.
Courses: A full programme of residential and non-residential courses.

Gwynedd and Anglesey

Schools Music Services, Canolfan Gerdd William Mathias Music Ctr, Gwynedd County Offices, Castle St, Caernarfon, Gwynedd LL55 1SH
Tel: 01286 679025/679976 *Fax:* 01286 672635

Dennis Williams, dir of school mus services.
Orchestras: Snr orch/Gareth Glyn, concert wind band/John Glyn Jones, wind band/Wyn Williams, br band/Gwyn Evans, intermediate str orch/Robbie Leyshon, hp consort/Dafydd Huw Jones, gui ens/Colin Tommis, big band/Paul Roberts, youth choir/John S Davies.
Music Centres: Monthly Sat rehearsals for all groups above at Ysgol Friars' School, Eithinog, Bangor and Gwynedd.
Awards: Discretionary awards for attending national groups. Awards offered by Friends of Gwynedd Youth Music, Anglesey Music Trust and Dr Williams Trust, Dolgellau to local students.
Courses: Annual residential courses for all bi-county mus groups at Normal College, Bangor during Jun and Jul. Other jnr mus courses at various centres within Gwynedd and Ynys, Mon throughout the year.

Merthyr Tydfil County Borough Council

Civic Centre, Castle St, Merthyr Tydfil CF47 8AN
Tel: 01685 725000 *Fax:* 01685 722146

G Meredith, chief exec.
Orchestras: See ESIS entry above. *Additional info:* The Education Directorate is at Ty Keir Hardie, Riverside Ct, Avenue de Clichy, Merthyr Tydfil CF47 8XD *Tel:* 01685 724600 *Fax:* 01685 721965. D Jones, dir of education.

Monmouthshire County Council

c/o Greater Gwent Music Support Service, Melfort Rd, Newport, South Wales NP9 3FP
Tel: 01633 223196 *Fax:* 01633 252051

Alun D Williams, head of service; Joyce Redfearn, chief exec.
Orchestras: See Greater Gwent Music Support Service for mus provision organised in collaboration with other authorities.

Music Centres: North Monmouthshire Music Centre, Monmouth Comprehensive School, Monmouth. David Davies, head of centre; Sat morning, w/wind, br and str ens. South Monmouthshire Music Centre, Chepstow Comprehensive School, Chepstow. David Davies, head of centre; Sat morning, w/wind, br and str ens.
Awards: Advanced mus tuition scheme for talented students.
Courses: Full programme of residential and non-residential courses is available.

Neath and Port Talbot County Borough Council
Civic Centre, Port Talbot SA13 1PJ
Tel: 01639 763333 *Fax:* 01639 763000

Phillip Emanuel, mgr, W Glamorgan mus service.
Orchestras: The mus service for Neath Port Talbot is subject to a joint working agreement with the City and County of Swansea see Swansea for orch details.
Music Centres: 12 mus centres catering for all levels of youth mus.
Awards: Assistance offered to promising students through various scholarships and friends of W Glamorgan Youth Music.
Courses: Residential and non-residential courses and tours.

Newport County Borough Council
c/o Greater Gwent Music Support Service, Melfort Rd, Newport, South Wales NP9 3FP
Tel: 01633 223196 *Fax:* 01633 252051

Alun D Williams, county borough mus and adviser/head of service.
Orchestras: See Greater Gwent Music Support Service for mus provision organised in collaboration with other authorities.
Music Centres: Newport (Brynglas) Music Centre, Brynglas House, Newport (Alun F Williams, head), Sat morning, w/wind, br and str ens, theory; Newport (Caerleon) Music Centre, Caerleon Comprehensive School (Peter James, head), Sat monthly, str ens.
Awards: Advanced tuition mus scheme for talented students.
Courses: Full programme of residential and non-residential courses is available.

Pembrokeshire County Council
County Education Office, St Thomas Green, Haverfordwest SA61 1QZ
Tel: 01437 764551 *Fax:* 01437 769557

Chris Llewellyn, county head of mus service.
Orchestras: Pembrokeshire schools orch/J Rodge, schools training orch/C Llewellyn, schools symphonic wind band, youth choir/John S Davies; 6 area primary school orchs, 2 area br bands.

Music Centres: 9 centres.
Awards: Various awards to support musically talented children.
Courses: Annual course for Pembrokeshire schools orch. Involvement in Three Counties (Carmarthenshire, Cardiganshire and Pembrokeshire) orch, wind band and choir.

Powys Council
Education Dept, Powys County Council, Powys County Hall, Llandrindod Wells, Powys LD1 5LG
Tel: 01597 826422 *Fax:* 01597 826475

M R J Barker, dir of education.

Rhondda Cynon Taff County Borough Council
The Pavilions, Clydach Vale CF40 2XX
Tel: 01443 424000

Simon Thomas, mus service co-ord.
Orchestras: See ESIS entry above. Bridgend, Rhondda-Cynon-Taff, Merthyr Tydfil and Caerphilly orchs combine to form Glamorgan Valleys' youth orch/Jeffrey Francis and br band/Howard Jones.

Swansea County Council
c/o Swansea City Council, Education Dept, County Hall, Swansea SA1 3SN
Tel: 01792 636000 *Fax:* 01792 636642

P Emanuel, mgr, West Glamorgan mus service.
Orchestras: The mus service for the City and County of Swansea is subject to a joint working agreement with Neath Port Talbot. West Glamorgan youth str orch, youth br band, youth wind orch and youth symphony orch.
Music Centres: 12 mus centres catering for all levels of youth mus.
Awards: Assistance offered to promising students through various scholarships and friends of W Glamorgan Youth Music.

Torfaen County Borough Council
Education Service, County Hall, Cwmbran, Torfaen NP4 2WN

M de Val, dir of educ; Alun D Williams, head of service; Alun F Williams, area organiser.
Orchestras: See Greater Gwent Music Support Service for mus provision organised in collaboration with other authorities.
Music Centres: Torfaen Music Centre, The Settlement, Pontypool (Geoff Barrett); Mon evening, w/wind, br and str ens, theory.
Awards: Advanced tuition mus scheme for talented students.
Courses: Full range of residential and non-residential courses is available.

Vale of Glamorgan Council
Education Department, Civic Offices, Holton Rd, Barry
CF63 4RU
Tel: 01446 700111 *Fax:* 01446 701820

Orchestras: See Cardiff County and Vale of
Glamorgan Music Service for details of joint mus
provision.

Wrexham County Borough Council
Education Dept, Roxborough House, Regent St, Wrexham
Tel: 01978 297500

J Thomas, head of mus support service.
Orchestras: Wrexham Music School jnr and snr
orch, jnr and snr wind band, advanced w/wind
ens/Dave Parsonage, str orch, youth choir,
Wrexham Schools br band/John Herbert.
Cross-county groups previously Clwyd have
formed Four Counties youth choir/Jean Stanley
Jones, youth wind band, youth orch/M C
Fallowfield and Gareth Jones, youth br
band/Nigel Seaman.
Music Centres: Wrexham Music School, St Davids
HS, Wrexham, Colin Fisher, dir.

Northern Ireland

Belfast Education and Library Board
Education Dept, 40 Academy St, Belfast BT1 2NQ
Tel: 01232 564000/322435 *Fax:* 01232 331714

Sean McElhatton, adviser, creative and
expressive studies; Robin Hewitt, principal tutor
(school of mus).
Orchestras: Belfast youth orch/Stanley Foreman;
also various str and training orchs, bands,
choirs.
Music Centres: Jnr mus centre and many activities
at Belfast School of Music, 99 Donegall Pass,
Belfast BT7 1DR *Tel:* 01232 322435.
Awards: Annual awards to members of the Belfast
Youth Orchestra and Belfast School of Music.

North-Eastern Education and Library Board
Music Service, County Hall, 182 Galgorm Rd, Ballymena,
Co Antrim BT42 1HN
Tel: 01266 662566/662578 *Fax:* 01266 46071

Eric Boyd, head of mus services.
Orchestras: NE Ulster schools symphony
orch/Eric Boyd, intermediate orch/Noelene
Carslaw, jnr orch/Bill Fergusson, snr wind
band/Alan Hunter, jnr wind band/J Johnston; 4
area str orchs.
Music Centres: Northern (Ballymoney) Music
Centre, 23 Charles St, Ballymoney; Central
(Ballymena) Centre, Ballee High School,
Ballymena; Southern (Newtownabbey) Centre,
Old Monkstown Primary School, Jordanstown
Rd; Western Magherafelt, c/o Music Service.
Aural and theory study, choirs and vocal study,
many ens and inst activities.
Courses: 1-week orch inst course for primary age
range. Teacher training: Consortia training
courses for non-specialist primary teachers in 5
areas. School based in-service courses for
primary teachers on request. Centre-based and
school-based training for post-primary mus
teachers.

South-Eastern Education and Library Board
South Eastern Music Centre, Church Rd, Ballynahinch,
Co Down BT24 8LP
Tel: 01238 562030 *Fax:* 01238 565120

Brian Agus, dir of mus.
Orchestras: SE youth orch/Lawrence Neill; 2
central orch tiers and 2 central concert band
tiers (all fed from 4 district jnr groups and school
ens).
Music Centres: South Eastern Music Centre,
Ballynahinch, plus 4 district centres in Bangor,
Castlereagh, Dounpatrick and Lisburn; rehearsals
of ens as above, gr 5 to diploma theory and aural
training, inst tuition and playing on all band, orch
insts; also pno and chmbr mus activities.

Southern Education and Library Board
SELB Music Service, Bann House, Bridge St, Portadown,
Craigavon BT63 5AE
Tel: 01762 332371 *Fax:* 01762 394525

Eithne Benson, asst educ offr; Martin White, dir
of orch and bands.
Orchestras: S Ulster youth orch/Martin White,
youth band/Uel Faulkner, str orch/Andrew Tohill,
wind ens/Elaine Mills, youth academy/Seamus
Dinsmore, academy band/Denis Rooney. Also 3
area jnr str orchs, 3 area jnr wind bands, 6 area
rcdr, singing and jnr mus groups.
Music Centres: 3 mus centres: Portadown Music
Centre, Bann House, Bridge St, Portadown BT63
5AE (M White); Newry Music Centre, SELB
Multi-Purpose Centre, Downshire Rd, Newry
BT34 1DX (E Mills); Dungannon Music Centre,
SELB Multi-Purpose Centre, Thomas St,
Dungannon BT70 1HW (S Dinsmore). Age 7-21
activities: rcdr, singing, theory, advanced
teaching, exhibitions, mus w/shops, recitals.
Awards: Annual awards to members of orchs,
bands and ens.
Courses: Youth orch and band 1-2 week
residential summer courses, plus special

concerts, tours abroad (including Vienna, Paris, Switzerland, Eire, IoM, and Belgium), Summer school 18-21 Aug (gr 1-8). In-service courses for mus teachers organised for SELB by Mrs M Yeomans, adviser for creative and expressive studies, Southern Education and Library Board, 3 Charlemont Pl, The Mall, Armagh BT61 9AX.

Western Education and Library Board

Music Service, 1 Spillars Place, Omagh, Co Tyrone BT78 1HL
Tel: 01662 244821 ext 145 *Fax:* 01662 246716

Dónal Doherty, mus adviser.

Orchestras: Western youth orch/Dónal Doherty, youth wind band/Bob Quick, intermediate str orch, 3 area str and 2 area wind training orchs.
Music Centres: 3 area mus centres used for advanced teaching after school and orchs at w/end.
Courses: Residential summer courses for wind orch and symphony orch; non-residential w/end courses for training orchs.

RESOURCES PUBLISHED IN 1997

Music Teacher Magazine

Rhinegold Publishing Ltd publishes *Music Teacher* magazine every month. Listed below are the articles that appeared in the magazine from January 1997 to December 1997. The magazine also carries reviews of new books and music in every issue. For details of subscriptions, availability of back numbers or a free sample issue, please contact 0171 333 1720. For editorial enquiries contact 0171 333 1747.

January 1997

Carol A Gartrell
Circular motion (p13)

An appraisal of the implications for primary initial teacher training of DFEE circular 14/93

Diarmid Campbell
Test pieces (p18)

Report on MEG's new GCSE music syllabus.

Tony Cliff
Modular approach (p20)

Reviews of the Yamaha P50-m module, Roland's Sound Canvas SC88 Pro and Twiddly Bits MIDI files

Matthew Greenall
Excellent adventure (p22)

Education programme using music of Gyorgy Ligeti and involving students at GSMD

David Bowman
A-level history and analysis (p24)

Divergent trends in 20th-century music: Cage, Britten and Berio

February 1997

Elizabeth Bray
Class Struggle (p11)

Are music teachers judged more by their extra-curricular work than what they do in the classroom?

Eric Proctor
Scale models (p14)

A method for introducing pupils to practising

scales which will help them to go on to practise them independently

Tony Cliff
Mixing it (p16)

Choosing a mixing desk

Rebecca Agnew
Top brass (p18)

Talking to the competitors and organisers at the National Youth Brass Band Championships

David Bowman
A-level history and analysis (p20)

Music in the late Renaissance: A Gabrieli, Morley and Gesualdo

March 1997

Andrew Stewart
Text best thing (p11)

An investigation of the role of ur-text editions.

Marion Whittow
First time for everything (p15)

The art of giving a new pupil their first lesson.

Tony Cliff
Taking effect (p19)

A look at effects and processors and the creative manipulation of sound.

Madelyn Cohen
The awkward stage (p22)

How the Young Concert Artists Trust helps young musicians with the early stages of their performing career.

David Bowman
A-level history and analysis (p25)

Corelli, Couperin, Bach.

April 1997

Joy Watson
Late call (p11)

Approaches to teaching adult beginners.

Richard Smythe
Up to speed (p14)

Examining the issues of speed and flexibility

Sarah Brown
Compose yourself (p17)

The beneficial effects of encouraging pupils to practise composition.

Tony Cliff
Information overload (p19)

Report on the 1997 Frankfurt Music Fair.

Andrew Stewart
Free for all (p22)

Interview with Owen Murray, professor of the classical accordion at the Royal Academy of Music.

David Bowman
A-level history and analysis (p25)

Lully (An Air from Le Bourgeios Gentilhomme) and Strauss (Horn concerto no 2, op 11).

May 1997

Mary Black
Tuning in (p11)

Dealing with 'out of tune' singers in the classroom.

Andrew Peggie
On file (p14)

A tribute to Music File.

Lucien Jenkins
Reaching the well springs (p16)

David Takeno talks about his pupils and his teachers.

Rebecca Agnew
Off the beaten track (p19)

A look at the wide range of options open to musical school-leavers.

Madelyn Cohen
Blowing hot and cold

Jazz education.

Andrew Stewart
Game plan (p27)

Looking at the courses available at the London College of Music.

Tony Cliff
On track (p30)

Review of the Yamaha MD4 Digital Multi-tracker.

David Bowman
A-level history and analysis

Vocal music in England in the baroque era: Purcell and Handel.

June 1997

Andrew Peggie
Mammoth task (p13)

The 1997 MIA show.

Ella Fourie
Sight unseen (p22)

Arguing for the need to value sight-reading skills.

Andrew Green
Learning on the Job

A look at Trinity College of Music's new MA in Music Education.

Madelyn Cohen
Two's company (p32)

Interview with Steven Doane and Rosie Elliot.

Tony Cliff
Dark skies lighten (p34)

MIDI files.

David Bowman
A-level history and analysis (p37)

The classical sonata principle I.

July 1997

Clare Stevens
Children of our times (p12)

Tackling the challenges of contemporary music with children's choirs.

Coral Davies
Song lines (p15)

Improvised songs used as a link between children's pre-school musical experience and composition.

Sheila Gaskell
Teaching a deaf pupil (p20)

Teaching piano to a deaf pupil.

Tony Cliff
Shelf life (p23)

The John Hornby Skewes and Co Ltd works.

David Bowman
A-level history and analysis (p29)

The classical sonata principle II: Bach and Clementi.

August 1997

Olga Dalli Clews
A piano pupil with median ray electrodactyly (p12)

Teaching a pupil born with a disabled left hand.

Andrew Stewart
Fast and Lucie (p18)

A report on Lucie and Roddie Skeaping's music education shows in schools.

Tony Cliff
Taking the mike (p21)

Microphones.

September 1997

Terry Grimley
Opera and the deaf audience (p12)

English Touring Opera's education and community programme.

Richard Smythe
Mirror image (p15)

Practising using a mirror.

Lesley Page
Fully comprehensive (p17)

Ensuring quality of access in class music teaching.

Tony Cliff
Love of mike (p21)

Guidance on using the microphone technique necessary to produce a high-quality vocal track.

Rebecca Berkeley
Drumming down (p27)

Trying out a range of percussion instruments with young children.

October 1997

David Anderson
Music therapy (p12)

One music teacher's experience of moving into music therapy.

Grenville Hancox
Support system (p15)

Reviews Vivace Practice Studio, accompaniment software.

Rebecca Berkeley
World beaters (p26)

Using percussion instruments at key stage 3.

David Bowman
GCSE analyses (p28)

Haydn: Trumpet concerto (London Examinations)

Julie Nicolaou
Musical kindergartens (p32)

Structured approaches to musical play for the very young.

November 1997

Clare Stevens
The right school (p13)

The different kinds of musical schooling available.

Susan Elkin
Over the water (p18)

Music education in the Republic of Ireland.

Tony Cliff
Wider still and wider (p23)

Sibelius music typesetting software.

Andrew Stewart
Making the grades (p27)

Interviews with the new chief examiner, and the director of music, drama and speech at Trinity College of London.

David Bowman
GCSE analyses (p32)
Bach and Haydn (Northern Ireland CCEA)

Carolyn Baynes
Responding creatively to the troubled child (p36)
Ways of coping with disturbed and disruptive young children.

Caroline Heslop
Dalcroze and Eurhythmics (p40)
Music and dance, the work of Emile Jacques Dalcroze.

December 1997

Fred Redwood
According to plan (p12)
A visit to the Academy of Contemporary Music.

John Watson
The fire sermon (p15)
The music dramas of Alan Ridout.

David Bowman
GCSE analyses (p19)
Vivaldi: Concerto Op 8, no 3 ('Autumn' from The Seasons)

Tony Cliff
Loud and clear (p23)
Public address equipment.

Katy Dyer
Visually-impaired adults (p28)
Teaching keyboards to visually-impaired adults.

Carolyn Baynes
Tobin system (p30)
Candida Tobin's Tiny Steps to Music.

Music Teacher Guides

The following booklets have been published with *Music Teacher* in 1997 and are available separately from Rhinegold Publishing.

Teaching Popular Music
Articles by Rebecca Agnew, Sandra Bradley, Rachel Oakden, Tony Cliff, Antonia Couling, Kevin Stephen, Steve Berry.

Guide to Leisure Courses 1997

Teaching primary music
Articles by Margaret Hope Brown, Sandra Bradley, Rachel Connolly, Clare Stevens, Judith Deeble, Caroline Heslop, Carolyn Warner.

Teaching world musics
Articles by June Boyce Tillman, Malcolm Floyd, Judith Deeble, Solveig McIntosh, Edward Ho, Trevor Wiggins.

Guide to Music Technology
Articles by Norton York, Allen Brown, Julie Gaudin, Brian Roberts, Ken Kessler, Tony Cliff, Judith Deeble.

Notes for the Associated Board Piano Exams
By Susan Higgins

Teaching contemporary music
Articles by Matthew Greenall, Andrew Peggie, Clare Stevens, Roger Thomas, Caroline Heslop, Barry Russell.

Guide to Leisure Courses 1998

British Journal of Music Education

Cambridge University Press at the Edinburgh Building, Shaftesbury Rd, Cambridge CB2 2RU
Tel: 01223 312393 publish the above journal three times per year in March, July and November.

Volume 13 Number 1, March 1996

Janet Mills
Starting at Secondary School p 5.

Christopher Naughton
Thinking Skills in Music Education p 15.

Trevor Wiggins
The World of Music in Education p 21.

Carol Richards and Roy Killen
Preservice Music Teachers: Influences on Lesson Planning p 31.

Patricia Gane
Instrumental Teaching and the National Curriculum: A Possible Partnership? p 49.

Desmond Hunter and Michael Russ
Peer Assessment in Performance Studies p 67.

Volume 13 Number 2, July 1996

Elizabeth Oehrle
Intercultural Education Through Music: Towards a Culture of Tolerance p 95.

Vic Gammon
What is Wrong With School Music? - a response to Malcolm Ross p 101.

Tim Howell
Musical Analysis: Back to Basics? p 123.

Yo Tomita and Graham Barber
New Technology and Piano Study in Higher Education: Getting the Most out of Computer-Controlled Player Pianos p 135.

Charles Byrne
The Use of Pattern and Echo in Developing the Creative Abilities of Secondary School Pupils p 143.

Mike Searby and Tim Ewers
Peer Assessing Composition in Higher Education p 155.

Volume 13 Number 3, November 1996

Angela Major
Reframing Curriculum Design p 183.

Jenny Hughes
'How Strange the Change From Major to Minor': Musical Discourse and Musical Development p 195.

Makoto Nomura
Follow Children's Music!... the Fundamental Idea p 203.

Philip Priest
General Practitioners in Music: Monitoring Musicianship Skills Among Intending Secondary Teachers p 225.

Chris Harrison and Linda Pound
Talking Music: Empowering Children as Musical Communicators p 233.

Christopher Pilsbury and Philomena Alston
Too Fine a Net to Catch the Fish? An Investigation of the Assessment of Composition in GCSE Music p 243.

Julia Winterson

So What's New? A Survey of the Education

Policies of Orchestras and Opera Companies p 259.

Volume 14 Number 1, March 1997

John Paynter

The form of finality: a context for musical education p5.

Charles Plummeridge

The rights and wrongs of school music: a brief comment on Malcolm Ross's paper p23.

Pamela Hurry

A-level Music: a survey of options form music lecturers in higher education p29.

Gordon Cox

'Changing the face of school music': Walford Davies, the gramophone and the radio p45.

Lena Blackford

Musical education in Russian secondary schools p57.

Gary Beauchamp

INITIAL TRAINING + INSET = Confident teachers. A formula for success? p69.

Susan Hallam

The development of memorisation strategies in musicians for education p87.

Volume 14 Number 2, July 1997

Janet Mills

The DfEE/NCET Music/IT Support Project p 109.

Christopher Naughton

Music technology tools and the implications of socio-cognitive research p111.

Ann Colley, Chris Comber and David Hargreaves

What happens to boys and girls in coeducational and single sex schools? P119.

Kevin Rogers

Resourcing music technology in secondary schools p129.

David Bray

CD-Rom in music education p137.

William Salaman

Keyboards in schools p143.

Andy Hunt and Ross Kirk

Technology and music: incompatible subjects? p151.

Gordon Dalgarno

Creating an expressive performance without being able to play a musical instrument p163.

Phil Ellis

The Music of Sound: a new approach for children with severe and profound and multiple learning difficulties p173.

Volume 14 Number 3, November 1997

Keith Swanwick

Assessing Musical Quality in the National Curriculum p205.

Ruth Thomas

The Music National Curriculum: Overcoming a Compromise p217.

Borje Stalhammar

School and Music-school Collaboration in Sweden p237.

Jane W Davidson and Jonathan A Smith

A Case Study of 'Newer Practices' in Music Education at Conservatoire Level p251.

Peter Johnson

Performance as Experience: the problem of assessment criteria p271.

Peter Cope and Hugh Smith

Cultural context in musical instrument learning p283.

International Journal of Music Education

The International Society for Music Education publishes the above Journal twice yearly in May and November *see* **Periodicals.**

Number 27 May 1996

Robert Walker

Music education freed from colonialism: a new praxis.

Huib Schippers

Teaching world music in the Netherlands: towards a model for cultural diversity in music education.

Liora Bresler

Traditions and change across the arts: case studies of arts education.

Estelle Jorgensen

The artist and the pedagogy of hope.

Number 28 November 1996

David Elliot

Consciousness, culture and curriculum.

Keith Swanwick

Music education liberated from new praxis.

Roland Persson

Brilliant performers as teachers: a case study of commonsense teaching in a conservatoire setting.

Margaret Barrett

Children's aesthetic decision-making: an analysis of children's musical discourse as composers.

Number 29 May 1997 (Conference Edition)

Bennett Reimer

Should there be a universal policy of music education?

Richard Letts

Music: universal language between all nations?

Patricia Shehan Campbell

Music, the universal language: fact or fallacy?

Constantijn Koopman

Music as language: an analogy to be pursued with caution.

Kazadi wa Mukuna

The universal language of all times?

Isabel Aretz de Ramon y Rivera

The universal language of all cultures.

Tsuneaki Miyoshi

Music education a comparison between East (Japan) and West.

Inger-Marie Amtmann

Music for the unborn child.

Kjell Skyllstad

Music in conflict management - a multicultural approach.

Marie McCarthy

The role of ISME in the promotion of multicultural music education, 1953-96.

Number 30 November 1997

David Goldsworthy

Teaching gamelan in Australia: some perspectives on cross-cultural music education.

Akosua Addo

Children's idiomatic expressions of cultural knowledge.

Nita Temmerman

An investigation of undergraduate music education curriculum content in primary teacher education programmes in Australia.

Tim Joss

Professional music groups and the community: the Bournemouth Sinfonietta in Romania.

Leon Burton

A discipline of knowledge approach to promoting music as a universal and vital language of all cultures and times.

49

Educational Resource Material

Elizabeth Smith

The following is a list of educational resource material published in 1997. The list is divided as follows:

i)	Books for music teachers and classroom material
ii)	Vocal music, musical plays, operettas and cantatas
iii)	Music for brass
iv)	Music for guitar
v)	Music for keyboard
vi)	Music for percussion
vii)	Music for recorders
viii)	Music for strings
ix)	Music for woodwind
x)	Music for mixed ensembles

Under each of these headings, titles are listed alphabetically by composer/arranger except where it is more applicable to list an entry by title, in which case these entries will be found at the head of each sub-section. All the publications listed are available for reference purposes at the International Centre for Research in Music Education, University of Reading and some may also be held at other resource centres (*see* **Resource Centres**). Further details of book and music publishers, educational recordings and other educational resources can be found in the **Suppliers and Services** section.

Books for Music Teachers and Classroom Material

Music File Series 9 1996/97
Stanley Thornes £64.57 (incl VAT).

Support service for secondary school music teachers.

Adams, Pauline: Sounds Musical
£19.95 (teacher's resource book); £10.50 (pupils' set of 3 books); £19.95 (CD or cassette pack); £69.95 (discount starter pack).

60 practical, progressive units of work based on a rich diversity of musical styles using a wide variety of cross-curricular starting points suitable for Key Stage 2.

Arch, G and Rooke, P: Changes
Studio Music Company £4.50.

7 songs with additional teacher's notes about life in Britain since 1930 suitable for Key Stage 2.

Arch, G and Rooke, P: Dynasty
Studio Music Company £4.50.

7 songs with additional teacher's notes about life in Tudor England suitable for Key Stage 2.

Arch, G and Rooke, P: What a Reign!
Studio Music Company £4.50.

7 songs with additional teacher's notes about life in the Victorian era suitable for Key Stage 2.

Barratt, Carol: School Daze
Novello £3.95.

Songs and topic work about school suitable for Key Stages 2 and 3 from the Totally Topical series.

Brewer, Mike: Kick-start Your Choir
Faber £3.95.

Confidence-boosting strategies for all those who direct a choir.

Cain, Tim: Fanfare 1
Cambridge University Press £4.95 (student's book); £12.95 (CD); £15.95 (teacher's book for Fanfare 1 and 2 combined).

Music course based around a wide selection of musical extracts suitable for Key Stage 2, ages 7-9.

Cain, Tim: Fanfare 2
Cambridge University Press £4.95 (student's book); £12.95 (CD); £15.95 (teacher's book for Fanfare 1 and 2 combined).

Music course based around a wide selection of musical extracts suitable for Key Stage 2, ages 9-11.

Coombes, Douglas: The Ancient Times Songbook
Lindsay Music £14.95 (book and CD).
Songs and information about the Ancient Greeks, Romans and Egyptians suitable for upper Key Stage 1 and Key Stage 2.

Crocker, E and Leavitt, J: Essential Musicianship Book 1 - A Comprehensive Choral Method
Hal Leonard/Music Sales £15.95 (teacher's book); £6.95 (student's book).
A carefully structured programme for developing skills in theory, sight-reading and performance.

Elliott, Katie: The Complete Theory Fun Factory
Boosey & Hawkes £6.75.
Music theory puzzles and games for the early grades.

Gilbert, Jean: European Festivals
Oxford University Press £19.95 (book and CD).
Songs, dances and customs from around Europe with a variety of follow-up activities suitable for Key Stages 2-3.

Killjan, J, O'Hern, M and Rann, L: Essential Repertoire for the Young Choir
Hal Leonard £17.95 (teacher's book: available for mixed voices, tenor/bass or treble); £8.95 (student's book: available for mixed voices, tenor/bass or treble).
A wider variety of songs from different historical periods, countries and cultures, including background information, suggested lesson plans and performance tips.

Lougheed, Judith: Signposts to Music
Oxford University Press £24.50.
Pack of 7 booklets covering all the elements.

Lougheed, Judith: Signposts to Music - Duration
Oxford University Press £3.95.
Games and activities suitable for Key Stages 1-2 for investigating musical elements.

Lougheed, Judith: Signposts to Music - Dynamics
Oxford University Press £3.95.
Games and activities suitable for Key Stages 1-2 for investigating musical elements.

Lougheed, Judith: Signposts to Music - Pitch
Oxford University Press £3.95.
Games and activities suitable for Key Stages 1-2 for investigating musical elements.

Lougheed, Judith: Signposts to Music - Structure
Oxford University Press £3.95.
Games and activities suitable for Key Stages 1-2 for investigating musical elements.

Lougheed, Judith: Signposts to Music - Tempo
Oxford University Press £3.95.
Games and activities suitable for Key Stages 1-2 for investigating musical elements.

Lougheed, Judith: Signposts to Music - Texture
Oxford University Press £3.95.
Games and activities suitable for Key Stages 1-2 for investigating musical elements.

Lougheed, Judith: Signposts to Music - Timbre
Oxford University Press £3.95.
Games and activities suitable for Key Stages 1-2 for investigating musical elements.

Randall, A and Randall, E: Aural in Practice Grade 1
Fentone £8.95 (book and tape).
Key facts and helpful hints for aural tests.

Randall, A and Randall, E: Aural in Practice Grade 2
Fentone £8.95 (book and tape).
Key facts and helpful hints for aural tests.

Randall, A and Randall, E: Aural in Practice Grade 3
Fentone £8.95 (book and tape).
Key facts and helpful hints for aural tests.

Randall, A and Randall, E: Aural in Practice Grade 4
Fentone £9.95 (book and tape).
Key facts and helpful hints for aural tests.

Randall, A. and Randall, E: Aural in Practice Grade 5
Fentone £9.95 (book and tape).
Key facts and helpful hints for aural tests.

Sebba, Jane: Percussion Players - Glock around the Clock 9+
A & C Black £11.99.
An exploration of composing and performing with tuned percussion including a cassette or CD suitable for Key Stage 2.

51

**Sebba, Jane: Percussion Players -
Ring-a-ding-ding 7+**
A & C Black £11.99.

An exploration of composing and performing with tuned percussion including a cassette or CD suitable for Key Stage 2.

**Whettam, Graham: The Chef Who Wanted to
Rule the World**
Meriden Music £2.95 (score); 95p (chorus part).

A classroom music drama for unison voices and percussion.

Vocal Music, Musical Plays, Operettas and Cantatas

A Christmas Celebration
Faber £3.50.

11 carols from Georgian England for SATB choir and organ/piano from the Choral Programme Series.

Folksongs from Africa
Faber £4.95.

A cassette to accompany the book from the Folksongs series suitable for Key Stages 1-3.

Folksongs from India
Faber £4.95.

A cassette to accompany the book from the Folksongs series suitable for Key Stages 1-3.

Passiontide Masterworks
Faber £3.50.

7 songs from the 16th, 17th and 18th centuries for SATB choir and organ/piano from the Choral Programme Series.

Pendragon
Weinberger £10.95 (vocal score); £6.50 (script).

Musical based on the legend of King Arthur suitable for secondary schools, devised by the National Youth Music Theatre.

Shakespeare Song Album
Boosey & Hawkes £15.50.

23 songs to texts by William Shakespeare for voice and piano.

Songbirds: Me
A & C Black £12.50.

Songs for 4-7 year olds, including a cassette or CD containing both sung and accompaniment only versions.

Songbirds: Seasons
A & C Black £12.50.

Songs for 4-7 year olds, including a cassette and accompaniment only versions.

The Giggly, Grumpy, Scary Book
Universal £9.95.

Songs for infants by Diamond, Holdstock, Moses and Sebba, including CD with accompaniments.

Ades, Thomas: Life Story
Faber £8.95.

For soprano and piano based set to text by Tennessee Williams.

Arch, Gwyn (arr): Songs of the City
Faber £2.50.

4 songs for SA(B) choir and piano from the Faber Young Voices series.

Arch, Gwyn (arr): Merry Christmas Everybody!
Faber £3.50.

Christmas pop classics for SSA and piano from the Choral Programme Series.

Barratt, Carol: Six Songs for Singing
Boosey & Hawkes £5.25.

For baritone and piano.

Blake, Howard: All God's Creatures
Faber £7.95.

Song-cycle for children's voices and orchestra or piano.

Britten, Benjamin: Who are these children?
Faber £7.95.

A song cycle for tenor and piano.

Bruckner, A: The Great Unaccompanied Motets
Faber £3.50.

7 motets for unaccompanied SATB choir from the Choral Programme Series.

Campbell, Debbie: Pepys' Show
Golden Apple £6.95 (teacher's book); £3.50 (pupil's book); £5.95 (cassette).

Musical bringing to life events during the lifetime of the diarist Samuel Pepys, suitable for Key Stages 2-3.

Harris, P and Brewer, M: Improve your Sight-Singing! Elementary Level
Faber £3.95.
A complete method for choral and solo singers available for high/medium voice and for low/medium voice either treble or bass clef.

Harris, P and Brewer, M: Improve your Sight-Singing! Intermediate Level
Faber £3.95.
A complete method for choral and solo singers suitable for Grades 4-5 available for high/medium voice and for low/medium voice in either treble or bass clef.

Harvey, Jonathan: How Could the Soul Not Take Flight
Faber £3.95.
For double choir.

Haydn, Joseph: Missa Brevis in F
Faber £12.00 (full score).
For SATB chorus, soprano soloists and orchestra.

Hedger, A and Wainwright, S: A Victorian Christmas Party
Golden Apple £6.95 (teacher's book); £3.50 (pupil's book); £5.95 (cassette).
A festive musical set during the Crimean war, suitable for Key Stage 2.

Hedger, Alison: The Soldier's Christmas
Golden Apple £5.95 (teacher's book); £5.95 (cassette).
A Biblical Nativity seen through the eyes of the Roman soldiers, suitable for Key Stages 1-2.

Hoile, Caroline: Noah
Golden Apple £5.95.
9 songs telling the traditional Bible story with improvised musical percussion and actions suitable for Key Stage 1.

Holdstock, Jan: Footprints on the Moon - Apollo 11
Golden Apple £5.95 (teacher's book); £2.95 (pupil's book); £5.95 (cassette).
The story of the first landing on the moon, told through narration and songs, suitable for Key Stages 2-3.

Holdstock, Jan: In Viking Times
Golden Apple £5.95 (teacher's book); £2.95 (pupil's book); £5.95 (cassette).
A musical with narration and songs, suitable for Key Stages 2-3.

Lyon, David: At Christmastime
Studio Music Company £1.50.
A song for unison or two-part junior voices and piano, or for SA choir and piano.

Lyon, David: Listen to the Bells
Studio Music Company £1.50.
For SA choir and piano.

Matthews, David: Vespers
Faber £9.95.
For mezzo-soprano; tenor soli, chorus and orchestra.

Maxwell Davies, Peter: Seven Summer Songs
Chester £12.95.
A song-cycle for unison voices, piano, recorders and percussion depicting a stay on a farm in the Orkneys, suitable for Key Stage 2.

Porter, Jennifer: Simply Nativity
Golden Apple £5.95.
The traditional Biblical Nativity story with a simple piano part suitable for pre-school and Key Stage 1.

Rathbone, J (arr): Classic Victorian Ballads
Faber £3.50.
5 ballads for SATB choir and piano from the Choral Programme Series.

Rogers & Hammerstein (arr Arch): Hits from South Pacific and Carousel
Faber £2.50.
4 songs for SA(B) choir and piano from the Faber Young Voices series.

Rogers & Hammerstein (arr Arch): Hits from The King and I and Oklahoma
Faber £2.50.
4 songs for SA(B) choir and piano from the Faber Young Voices series.

Rose, P and Conlon, A: Arabica
Weinberger £12.95 (vocal score); £4.50 (vocal part); £3.50 (word book).
A cantata published in association with WWF, suitable for secondary schools, dealing with the issue of fair trade with the third world.

Somervell, Arthur: A Shropshire Lad
Boosey & Hawkes £8.75.
Settings of 10 poems by A E Housman for voice and piano.

Weber, Carol Maria von: Mass in Eb
Faber £17.50 (full score).
For SATB chorus, soloists and orchestra.

Wilson, Sheila: Rock the Boat
Golden Apple £6.95 (teacher's book); £2.50 (pupil's book); £5.95 (cassette).

A rock musical based on the story of Noah, suitable for Key Stages 2-3.

Winter, R and Arch, G (arr): Smash Hits for Christmas!
Faber £2.50.

3 Christmas songs for SA(B) choir and piano from the Faber Young Voices series.

Music for Brass

Barratt, Carol: Bravo Trombone!
Boosey & Hawkes £8.25.

More than 20 pieces for trombone and piano.

Barratt, Carol: Bravo Trumpet!
Boosey & Hawkes £8.25.

More than 20 pieces for trumpet and piano.

Bernstein, L (arr Elliot): Leonard Bernstein for horn
Boosey & Hawkes £8.25.

A selection of pieces for advanced students.

Bernstein, L (arr Elliot): Leonard Bernstein for trombone
Boosey & Hawkes £8.25,

A selection of pieces for advanced students.

Bernstein, L (arr Elliot): Leonard Bernstein for trumpet
Boosey & Hawkes £8.25.

A selection of pieces for advanced students.

Blake, H (arr O'Sullivan and Gout): The Snowman
Faber £5.95.

Suite for trumpet and piano from the film of the Snowman.

Bolton, Cecil (arr): A Christmas Triptych
Studio Music Company £15.00.

3 pieces arranged for brass band.

Carr, Gordon: Trombone Quartet
Neuschel/Studio Music Company £12.50.

4 pieces for 4 trombones.

Dodgson, Stephen: Concerto for Bass Trombone and Orchestra
Neuschel/Studio Music Company £12.00.

Piano reduction version.

Gout, Alan (arr): Play Gershwin
Faber £5.95.

A selection of solos for trumpet and piano from the songs of George Gershwin.

Harris, Paul: Know Your Scales!
Faber £3.95.

The essential learning method for scales and arpeggios for trumpet, Grades 1, 2 & 3).

Harris, Paul: Know your Scales!
Faber £4.95.

The essential learning method for scales and arpeggios for trumpet, Grades 4 & 5.

Jacques, Michael: Cantilena and Rondo Scherzoso
Neuschel/Studio Music Company £5.00.

For trombone and piano.

Jewell, F (arr P Smalley): March: Battle Royal
Studio Music Company £6.50.

For low brass brass quartet of euphoniums and tubas from the BTQ Collection Series.

Lake, Leslie (arr): Twelve Studies
Neuschel/Studio Music Company £6.00.

For bass trombone, euphonium or tuba.

Lang, C S (arr L Lake): Tuba Tune
Cramer £5.50.

For brass quintet.

Leven, M (arr J Moss): Cruella de Vil
Hal Leonard (distributed by Studio Music Company) £15.00.

From Walt Disney's 101 Dalmations, arranged for brass band.

Menken, A (arr C Custer): Hercules Soundtrack Highlights
Hal Leonard (distributed by Studio Music Company) £20.00.

From the Walt Disney film, arranged for brass band.

Miller, John (arr): The Baroque Trombone
Faber £6.95.

12 repertoire pieces for trombone and keyboard.

Miller, John (arr): The Baroque Trumpet
Faber £6.95.

16 repertoire pieces for trumpet in D, (or standard, Bb, or Piccolo) and keyboard.

Morley, T (arr. M Howard): April is in my Mistress' Face
Studio Music Company £4.50.

For low brass brass quartet of euphoniums and tubas from the BTQ Collection Series.

Mower, Mike: Musical Postcards for Trumpet
Boosey & Hawkes £9.25.

10 pieces in different styles from around the world, including an accompaniment CD.

Perrin, Roger: Seven Easy Brass Trios
Studio Music Company £4.00.

Bass clef/C edition.

Perrin, Roger: Seven Easy Brass Trios
Studio Music Company £4.00.

Treble clef/Bb edition.

Perrin, Roger: The Jazztet Series Volume One
Studio Music Company £14.50.

4 pieces for any combination of six or more brass instruments or saxophones.

Perrin, Roger: The Jazztet Series Volume Two
Studio Music Company £14.50 .

4 pieces for any combination of six or more brass instruments or saxophones.

Perrin, Roger: The Jazztet Series Volume Three
Studio Music Company £14.50.

4 pieces for any combination of six or more brass instruments or saxophones.

Rimsky-Korsakov (arr Mead): Notturno
Studio Music Company £4.00.

Arranged for four euphoniums.

Smalley, Peter: A Cool Suite
Studio Music Company £16.50.

For low brass quartet of euphoniums and tubas from the BTQ Collection Series.

Tchaikovsky, P (arr P Sparke): Four Dances from the Nutcracker
Studio Music Company £12.50.

For brass band.

Ward and Palmer (arr G. Richards): And the Band Played On
Studio Music Company £15.00.

For brass band.

Whettam, Graham: A Little Suite
Meriden Music £9.30 (score and parts).

An easy suite for brass quintet based on Christmas melodies.

Wiggins, Christopher: The Bakers Dozen
Neuschel/Studio Music Company £6.00.

For trombone and piano.

Wills, Simon: Concerto for Trombone
Neuschel/Studio Music Company £12.00.

Piano reduction version.

Music for Guitar

Rock School - Bass Guitar Grade 4
Faber £6.95.

Graded solo exams in rock, jazz and pop.

Rock School - Electric Guitar Grade 4
Faber £6.95.

Graded solo exams in rock, jazz and pop.

Blake, Howard: Prelude, Sarabande & Gigue
Faber £4.95.

For solo guitar.

Music for Keyboard

Easy Classic Piano 1
Universal £5.95.

Easy arrangements for piano solo.

Easy Pop Piano 1
Universal £5.95.

Easy arrangements for piano solo.

The Boosey & Hawkes 20th Century Piano Collection
Boosey & Hawkes £8.25.

A varied collection of music for piano written since 1945.

The Faber Book of TV Themes
Faber £6.95.

16 themes from popular TV shows arranged for piano or keyboard.

Barratt, Carol: Topsy-Turvy Tunes
Boosey & Hawkes £5.25.

24 pieces for young pianists.

Bolton, Cecil: Children's Favourite Nursery Rhymes
Cramer £4.95.

A book for beginner piano or keyboard, also suitable for recorder with guitar accompaniment, with pages for colouring.

Cornick, Mike: Boogie Piano
Universal £3.95.

6 easy pieces for solo piano.

Cornick, Mike: Piano Ragtime
Universal £3.95.

6 easy pieces for solo piano.

Cornick, Mike: Piano Ragtime Duets
Universal £6.50.

6 easy pieces for piano duet.

Bach, J S: Jesu, Joy of Man's Desiring
Fentone £2.95.

Arranged for piano duet.

Delibes: Flower Duet from 'Lakme'
Fentone £2.25.

Arranged for piano solo.

Offenbach: Can-Can
Fentone £2.25.

For easy-play piano solo.

Rossini: March from 'William Tell'
Fentone £2.95.

Arranged for piano duet.

Saint-Saens, C: The Swan
Fentone £2.95.

From the Carnival of the Animals arranged for piano duet.

McCarthy, Nic (arr): Scarborough Fair
Cool Music/Fentone £2.95.

Arranged in a jazzy style for piano.

McCarthy, Nic (arr): Nobody Knows The Trouble I Seen
Cool Music/Fentone £2.95.

Arranged in a jazzy style for piano.

Sousa, J: The Washington Post
Fentone 2.25.

For easy-play piano solo.

Tchaikovsky, P: Romeo and Juliet Theme
Fentone £2.95.

Arranged for piano duet.

Davis, Carl: A Dance to the Music of Time
Faber £3.50.

Themes from the TV series.

Davis, Carl: Great Film & TV Themes
Faber £6.95.

10 themes arranged for piano or keyboard.

Hall, P and Wooding, K: Spooky Piano Time
Oxford University Press £4.95.

Pieces, poems and puzzles for young pianists from the Oxford Piano Method suitable for Grades 2-3.

Hall, Pauline: Piano Time - Opera
Oxford University Press £5.25.

32 simple arrangements of operatic masterpieces for young pianists from the Oxford Piano Method suitable for Grades 2-3.

Harris, Richard (arr): Jane Austen's World
Faber £7.95.

Evocative music from Pride & Prejudice, Sense & Sensibility, Emma and Persuasion.

Kember, John: The Jazz Piano Master
Faber £8.95.

Jazz techniques through pieces and studies.

Marsden Thomas, Anne: A Graded Anthology for Organ Book One - A Practical Guide to Playing the Organ
Cramer £14.95.

Marsden Thomas, Anne: A Graded Anthology for Organ Book Two
Cramer £7.95.

Carefully selected studies with notes on

performance, registration, technique and practice tips, appropriate to Grade 2 standard.

Marsden Thomas, Anne: A Graded Anthology for Organ Book Three
Cramer £7.95.

Carefully selected studies with notes on performance, registration, technique and practice tips, appropriate to Grade 3 standard.

Marsden Thomas, Anne: A Graded Anthology for Organ Book Four
Cramer £12.95.

Carefully selected studies with notes on performance, registration, technique and practice tips, appropriate to Grade 4 standard.

Marsden Thomas, Anne: A Graded Anthology for Organ Book Five
Cramer £12.95.

Carefully selected studies with notes on performance, registration, technique and practice tips, appropriate to Grades 5-6.

Norton, Christopher: Essential Guide to Jazz Styles
Boosey & Hawkes £10.25 (book only); £14.25 incl. VAT (book and disk).

For keyboard, including an interactive disk.

Norton, Christopher: Microjazz Collection 1
Boosey & Hawkes £6.99 (book); £7.99 incl VAT (disk)

For piano or keyboard.

Norton, Christopher: Microjazz Collection 2
Boosey & Hawkes £5.99 (book); £7.99 incl VAT (disk).

For piano or keyboard.

Norton, Christopher: Microjazz Collection 3
Boosey & Hawkes £5.99 (book); £7.99 incl VAT (disk).

For piano or keyboard.

Norton, Christopher: Microjazz for Absolute Beginners
Boosey & Hawkes £5.99 (book); £7.99 incl. VAT (disk).

For piano or keyboard.

Norton, Christopher: Microjazz for Beginners
Boosey & Hawkes £5.99 (book); £7.99 incl. VAT (disk).

For piano or keyboard.

Sculthorpe, Peter: Three Pieces for Piano
Faber £4.95.

Suitable for advanced pianists.

Thompson, John: First Folk Songs
Wise £3.50.

Fun repertoire for beginner pianists complementing the Easiest Piano Course series.

Thompson, John: First Nursery Rhymes
Wi.se £3.95.

Fun repertoire for beginner pianists complementing the Easiest Piano Course series.

Wedgwood, Pamela: Up-grade!
Faber £3.95

Light relief between grades for piano Grades 0-1.

Wedgwood, Pamela: Up-grade!
Faber £4.95

Light relief between grades for piano Grades 3-4.

Wedgwood, Pamela: Up-grade!
Faber £4.95.

Light relief between grades for piano Grades 4-5.

Woolrich, John: The Little Piano Book
Faber £3.95.

5 pieces for piano suitable for Grade 3 standard.

Music for Percussion

Rock School - Drums Grade 4
Faber £6.95.

Graded solo exams in rock, jazz and pop.

Glennie, E and Cameron, P: African Dances
Faber £15.00.

From the 'Beat It!' group percussion for beginners series suitable for Key Stage 2 and above including CD.

Glennie, Evelyn (arr): Marimba Encores
Faber £4.95.

6 well-known tunes arranged for marimba.

Landmesser, Michael: Snare Drum Colours
Universal £6.95.

For 2 snare drums.

Whettam, Graham: The Kitchen
Meriden Music £18.00 (score and parts).

A suite for junior percussion ensemble.

Music for Recorders

55 for Fun
Fentone £5.95

For solo recorder.

Folk Times Two
Fentone £6.50

Blow the Wind Southerly and Londonderry Air arranged for recorder ensemble.

The Renaissance Recorder
Boosey & Hawkes £6.25.

A selection of renaissance tunes for descant recorder with keyboard accompaniment selected by Steve Rosenberg.

Brunner, H (arr): Harry Lime and Take Five
Universal £7.95.

2 pieces for recorder quartet.

Brunner, H (arr): The Little Drummer Boy and Hallelujah!
Universal £7.50.

2 pieces for recorder quartet.

Fortin, V and Heidecker, M (arr): Time & Rhythm 5
Universal £5.95.

Easy pieces for descant recorder ensemble with piano and percussion parts.

Gershwin, G: Summertime
Fentone £3.50.

Arranged for recorder and piano.

Handel, G F: Marching with Hande
Fentone £6.50.

Pieces for recorder ensemble.

Pitts, John: Recorder Duets from the Beginning Book 1
Chester £3.50.

Easy duets for descant recorders to complement the teaching scheme.

Pitts, John: Recorder Duets from the Beginning Book 2
Chester £3.50.

Easy duets for descant recorders to complement the teaching scheme.

Pitts, John: Recorder Duets from the Beginning Book 3
Chester £3.50.

Easy duets for descant recorders to complement the teaching scheme).

Russell-Smith, G (arr): A Carol Concert
Universal £10.95.

Arrangements of well-known carols for recorder ensemble, voices and piano, suitable for junior and middle schools).

Whettam, Graham: 6 into 37
Meriden Music £1.95.

6 simple unison pieces for recorders which are expanded into 2, 3 and 4-part pieces for younger players, including a teacher's guide.

Music for Strings

Londonderry Air
Fentone £6.75.

Arranged for string quartet.

Teacher and I Play Cello Duets Volume 1
Fentone £6.75

For 2 cellos.

Britten, Benjamin: Reflection
Faber £4.95.

For viola and piano.

Bruckner, C and Bruckner, K (arr): Christmas Concert
Universal £5.95.

6 pieces arranged for 2 violins or 2 flutes and piano.

Cohen, M and Spearing, R: Superstart Violin Level 1 Accompaniments
Faber £4.95.

For piano and/or violin.

Cohen, M and Spearing, R: Superstart, Violin Level 2 Accompaniments
Faber £4.95.

For piano and/or violin.

Cohen, Mary: Superstart Violin Level 1
Faber £3.95.

Basic skills and pieces for beginners.

Cohen, Mary: Superstart, Violin Level 2
Faber £3.95.

Pieces to develop skills for well-established beginners.

Gershwin, G: Simply Strings Volume 5
Fentone 9.95.

For easy string ensemble.

Gliere, Reinhold: 12 Album Leaves op. 51
Boosey & Hawkes £11.25

For cello and piano

Harris, Paul: Improve your Sight Reading!
Faber £5.50

A workbook for examinations for violin Grade 6.

Harris, Paul: Improve your Sight Reading!
Faber £5.95.

A workbook for examinations for violin Grades 7-8.

Hartley, Keith: Double Bass Solo 1
Oxford University Press £8.95.

50 graded melodies from the orchestral repertoire for double bass.

Hartley, Keith: Double Bass Solo 2
Oxford University Press £8.95.

60 graded melodies from the orchestral repertoire for double bass.

Howard, Gerald: The Essential String Method - Cello, Book 1
Boosey & Hawkes £4.99.

A first tutor integrating musical awareness, creativity and technical development.

Howard, Gerald: The Essential String Method- Cello, Book 2
Boosey & Hawkes £4.99.

A tutor integrating musical awareness, creativity and technical development.

Howard, Gerald: The Essential String Method - Double Bass, Book 1
Boosey & Hawkes £4.99.

A first tutor integrating musical awareness, creativity and technical development.

Howard, Gerald: The Essential String Method - Double Bass, Book 2
Boosey & Hawkes £4.99.

A tutor integrating musical awareness, creativity and technical development.

Huws Jones, E and Velagic, M (arr): Sevdah
Boosey & Hawkes £10.95 (set); £5.75 (violin part only).

Traditional music from Bosnia for violin and piano.

Jenkins, Karl: String Quartet No 2
Boosey & Hawkes £15.50 (score and parts).

For advanced players.

Legg, P and Gout, A: Thumb Position for Beginners
Faber £5.95.

Easy pieces for cello duet and cello and piano.

Legg, P and Gout, A: Thumb Position Repertoire
Faber £5.95.

Intermediate pieces for cello and piano.

Lloyd Webber, Andrew: Cats
Faber £5.95.

6 tunes from the show arranged for cello and piano.

Mann, Sylvia: Dr Downing's Cello Technique Doctor
Dr Downing Music £2.95.

A pocket book covering aspects of technique and caring for your cello.

Matthews, Colin: Five Duos
Faber £9.95.

For cello and piano.

Matthews, Colin: String Quartet No 3
Faber £12.95.

For advanced players.

Mower, Mike: Musical Postcards for Violin
Boosey & Hawkes £9.25.

10 pieces in different styles from around the world, including an accompaniment CD.

Mozart, W (arr B Dobretsberger): Selected pieces from the Magic Flute
Universal £5.95.

For 2 violins or 2 flutes and piano).

59

Nelson, Sheila: The Essential String Method - Viola Book 1
Boosey & Hawkes £4.99.

A first tutor integrating musical awareness, creativity and technical development.

Nelson, Sheila: The Essential String Method - Viola Book 2
Boosey & Hawkes £4.99.

A tutor integrating musical awareness, creativity and technical development.

Nelson, Sheila: The Essential String Method - Violin Book 1
Boosey & Hawkes £4.99.

A first tutor integrating musical awareness, creativity and technical development.

Nelson, Sheila: The Essential String Method - Violin Book 2
Boosey & Hawkes £4.99.

A tutor integrating musical awareness, creativity and technical development.

Norton, Christopher: Diversions
Boosey & Hawkes £6.75.

For violin and piano.

Osborne, Tony (arr): Hits from Broadway
Faber £15.95.

Music from 4 Broadway shows arranged for intermediate string ensemble from the Stringsets series.

Osborne, Tony (arr): Hits from the West End
Faber £15.95.

Music from Oliver!, Phantom of the Opera and Jesus Christ Superstar arranged for intermediate string ensemble from the Stringsets series.

Radanovics, M (arr): Gospels and Spirituals
Universal £5.95.

7 pieces arranged for 2 violins or 2 flutes and piano.

Radanovics, Michael (arr): Scarborough Fair and Midnight Special
Universal £9.50.

Arranged for string ensemble.

Schwertberger, Gerald: Happy Hour Sandwich
Doblinger £9.90.

(4 pieces for cello and piano).

Sculthorpe, Peter: First Sonata for Strings
Faber £6.95

Sculthorpe, Peter: Third Sonata for Strings
Faber £6.95.

Vine, Carl: Inner World
Faber £9.95.

For cello and pre-recorded tape or CD, for advanced performers.

Wilson, Peter (arr): Palm Court Trios Book 1
Boosey & Hawkes £17.50.

Popular classical and light music for violin, cello and piano.

Music for Woodwind

Abracadabra Clarinet Piano Accompaniments
A & C Black £9.99.

A companion to Abracadabra Clarinet, containing accompaniments to all the pieces.

Clarinettist's Choice Grade 1
Fentone £7.50.

For Bb clarinet and piano.

Masterclass Wind Starters Set 1
Masterclass Music £9.50.

3 pieces arranged for flexible wind ensemble, suitable for Grade 2-3.

The Light Touch Book One
Stainer & Bell £6.95.

Graded pieces for alto saxophone and piano - easy to intermediate standard).

The Light Touch Book Two
Stainer & Bell £7.50.

Graded pieces for alto saxophone and piano - intermediate to advanced standard).

Anderson, Julian: The Bearded Lady
Faber £8.95.

For clarinet and piano.

Anderson, Julian: The Bearded Lady
Faber £8.95.

For oboe/cor anglais and piano.

Barratt, Carol: Bravo Bassoon!
Boosey & Hawkes £8.25.

More than 25 pieces for bassoon and piano.

Bernstein, L (arr Elliot): Leonard Bernstein for alto saxophone
Boosey & Hawkes £8.25.

A selection of pieces for advanced students, also available for tenor saxophone.

Bernstein, L (arr ELliot): Leonard Bernstein for bassoon
Boosey & Hawkes £8.25.

A selection of pieces for advanced students.

Bernstein, L (arr Elliot): Leonard Bernstein for clarinet
Boosey & Hawkes £8.25.

A selection of pieces for advanced students.

Bernstein, L (arr Elliot): Leonard Bernstein for flute
Boosey & Hawkes £8.25.

A selection of pieces for advanced students.

Bernstein, L (arr Elliot): Leonard Bernstein for oboe
Boosey & Hawkes £8.25.

A selection of pieces for advanced students.

Bruckner, C and Bruckner, K (arr): Christmas Concert
Universal £5.95.

6 pieces arranged for two violins or two flutes and piano.

Cowles, Colin (arr): A Punnet of Classics
Cool Music/Fentone £2.95.

For solo saxophone.

Cowles, Colin (arr): Country Folk
Cool. Music/Fentone £2.95.

For solo flute.

Cowles, Colin (arr): Fancy Folk
Cool Music/Fentone £2.95.

For solo saxophone.

Cowles, Colin: All Jazzed Up
Fentone £5.95.

14 jazz influenced pieces for saxophones.

Cowles, Colin: Ebb and Flow
Cool Musie/Fentone £2.95.

For solo bassoon.

Cowles, Colin: Out of Character
Coo1 Music/Fentone £2.95.

For solo bassoon.

Cowles, Colin: Somerset Scenes
Coo1 Music/Fentone £2.95.

5 contemporary folk-tunes for solo clarinet.

Cowles, Colin: Somerset Scenes
Coo1 Music/Fentone £2.95.

5 contemporary folk-tunes for solo flute.

Cowles, Colin: Split Levels
Fentone £5.95.

A set of jazz influenced duets for 2 clarinets.

Cowles, Colin: Suite Quintessential
Studio Music Company £10.00.

For 2 flutes and 3 clarinets).

Elliott, Katie: The Fun Factory Clarinet Book
Boosey & Hawkes £3.99.

Fun, facts and puzzles for clarinet players everywhere.

Elliott, Katie: The Fun Factory Flute Book
Boosey & Hawkes £3.99.

Fun, facts and puzzles for flute players everywhere.

Gordon, C and London, E: 12 Clarinet Duets.
Janus Music/Studio Music Company £3.95.

Gordon, Christopher (arr): Mozart in London
Janus Music/Studio Music Company £5.00

A suite in 4 movements selected from Mozart's London notebook for Bb clarinet and piano.

Gordon, Christopher: 8 Flute Duets
Janus Music/Studio Music Company £3.50.

Gordon, Christopher: 8 Saxophone Duets
Janus Music/Studio Music Company £3.50.

Gordon, Christopher: A Little Suite
Janus Music/Studio Music Company £5.00.

A set of pieces for alto saxophone and piano.

Gordon, Christopher: A Little Suite
Janus Music/Studio Music Company £5.00.

A set of pieces for Bb clarinet and piano.

Gordon, Christopher: A Little Suite
Janus Music/Studio Music Company 5.00.

A set of pieces for flute and piano.

Gordon, Christopher: Haydn at Eszterhaza
Janus Music/Studio Music Company £8.00.

For flute, clarinet and bassoon.

Gordon, Christopher: Haydn at Eszterhaza
Janus Music/Studio Music Company £8.00.

For soprano, alto and tenor saxophones.

Gout, Alan (arr): Play Gershwin
Faber £5.95.

A selection of solos for alto saxophone and piano from the songs of George Gershwin.

Gout, Alan (arr): Play Gershwin
Faber £5.95

A selection of solos for Bb clarinet and piano, from the songs of George Gershwin).

Gout, Alan (arr): Play Latin
Faber £5.95.

A selection of hits from Latin America for Bb clarinet and piano.

Gout, Alan (arr): Play Latin
Faber £5.95.

A selection of hits from Latin America for flute and piano.

Harris, Paul: Improve your Sight Reading!
Faber £5.50.

A workbook for examinations for clarinet Grade 6.

Harris, Paul: Improve your Sight Reading!
Faber £5.95.

A workbook for examinations for clarinet Grades 7-8.

Harris, Paul: Improve your Sight Reading!
Faber £5.50.

A workbook for examinations for flute Grade 6.

Harris, Paul: Improve your Sight Reading!
Faber £5.95.

A workbook for examinations for flute Grades 7-8.

Harrison, Howard (arr): Amazing Studies - Clarinet
Boosey & Hawkes £9.25.

Pieces in a variety of styles to improve your technique.

Harrison, Howard (arr): Amazing Studies - Flute
Boosey & Hawkes £9.25.

Pieces in a variety of styles to improve your technique.

Harrison, Howard (arr): Amazing Studies - Saxophone
Boosey & Hawkes £9.25.

Pieces in a variety of styles to improve your technique.

Harvey, Paul: Brass Monkey Blues
Cool Music/Fentone £2.95.

A piece for solo saxophone.

Harvey, Paul: Broken Reed Blues
Cool Music/Fentone £2.95.

For solo clarinet.

Harvey, Paul: Dixie Pixie
Cool Music/Fentone £2.95.

For solo clarinet.

Harvey, Paul: Fantasia in one movement
Boosey & Hawkes £6.25.

For 4 Bb clarinets.

Harvey, Paul: Flamenco Jazz
Cool Music/Fentone £2.95.

A Spanish-style rhapsody for solo saxophone.

Harvey, Paul: Irish Gig
Cool Music/Fentone £2.95.

For solo clarinet.

Harvey, Paul: Jazz from the Beginning
Fentone £5.95.

For solo saxophone.

Harvey, Paul: Rock n' Reel
Cool Music/Fentone £2.95.

For solo clarinet.

Harvey, Paul: Rocking Reeds
Studio Music Company £5.75.

15 rock and jazz trios for clarinets.

Harvey, Paul: Rocking Reeds
Studio Music Company £5.75.

15 rock and jazz trios for flute, oboe and bassoon.

Harvey, Paul: Rocking Reeds
Studio Music Company £5.75.

15 rock and jazz trios for saxophones.

Harvey, Paul: Saxophone Sight-reading
Studio Music Company £8.50.

Sight-reading practice for Grades 1-8 including jazz.

Harvey, Paul: Snowball on the Rocks
Cool Music/Fentone £2.95.

A chromatic piece for solo saxophone.

Harvey, Paul: Swinginx
Cool Music/Fentone £2.95.

'Debussy meets the swing era' for solo saxophone.

Harvey, Paul: The Ice Maiden Cometh
Cool Music/Fentone £2.95.

A piece in swing style for solo saxophone.

Harvey, Paul: The Puce Penguin
Cool Music/Fentone £2.95.

A jazzy piece for solo saxophone.

Kenny, Terry (arr): Haydn's Andante from Surprise Symphony and Mozart's Minuet from Don Giovanni
Universal £10.45.

Arranged for flexible wind ensemble.

Matthews, Colin: Duologue and Night Spell
Faber £8.95.

4 studies for oboe and piano.

Matthews, Colin: Five Concertinos
Faber £8.95.

For wind quintet.

Mower, Mike: Musical Postcards for Alto Saxophone
Boosey & Hawkes £9.25.

10 pieces in different styles from around the world, including an accompaniment CD.

Mower, Mike: Musical Postcards for Clarinet
Boosey & Hawkes £9.25.

10 pieces in different styles from around the world, including an accompaniment CD.

Mower, Mike: Musical Postcards for Flute
Boosey & Hawkes £9.25.

10 pieces in different styles from around the world, including an accompaniment CD.

Mozart, W (arr B Dobretsberger): Selected pieces from the Magic Flute
Universal £5.95.

For 2 violins or 2 flutes and piano).

Norton, Christopher: Sonatina
Boosey & Hawkes £6.25.

For flute and piano.

Pachelbel: Canon
Fentone £4.50.

Arranged for flute and piano.

Radanovics, M (arr): Gospels and Spirituals
Universal £5.95.

7 pieces arranged for 2 violins or 2 flutes and piano.

Rae, James: Introducing the Clarinet Book 1
Universal £5.95.

10 pieces in popular styles playable as solos or duets with or without piano accompaniment.

Rae, James: Introducing the Clarinet Plus Book 2
Universal £5.95.

10 pieces in popular styles for clarinet playable as solos or duets with or without piano accompaniment.

Rae, James: Introducing the Saxophone Book 1
Universal £5.95.

10 pieces in popular styles playable as solos or duets with or without piano accompaniment.

Rae, James: Introducing the Saxophone Book 2
Universal £5.95.

10 pieces in popular styles for Eb saxophone playable as solos or duets with or without piano accompaniment.

Rae, James: Jazz Trios
Universal £6.95.

5 pieces for clarinet, alto saxophone and piano.

Rae, James: Jazz Trios
Universal £6.95.

5 pieces for flute, clarinet and piano.

Rae, James: Jazz Trios
Universal £6.95.

5 pieces for 2 alto saxophones and piano.

Sculthorpe, Peter: Two Easy Pieces
Faber £3.95

For flute and piano.

Strauss, J (arr Kenny): Champagne Polka
Universal £10.95.

From Die Fledermaus, arranged for flexible wind ensemble.

Music for Mixed Ensembles

Christmas Concert
Universal £10.95.

Easy arrangements of Christmas carols for flexible children's ensemble.

Anderson, Julian: Khorovod
Faber £25.00.

For 15 players - advanced.

Bartok, Bela: Concerto for Orchestra
Boosey & Hawkes £14.95 (full score).

For advanced orchestra from the Masterworks Library.

Benjamin, George: Sudden Time
Faber £30.00.

For large orchestra - advanced.

Britten, Benjamin: Orchestral Anthology No. 1
Boosey & Hawkes £16.95 (full score).

Includes Young Person's Guide to the Orchestra, Soirees Musicales, Matinees Musicales and Courtly Dances from Gloriana for advanced orchestra from the Masterworks Library.

Daugherty, Michael: Mxyzptlk
Peermusic/Faber £15.95.

From the Metropolis Symphony for advanced orchestra.

Grieg, E (arr B Dobretsberger): Selected pieces from Peer Gynt
Universal £10.45.

An easy arrangement for children's ensemble.

Holst, Gustav: Elegy - in memoriam William Morris
Faber £6.95.

For orchestra - advanced.

Matthews, Colin: Second Oboe Quartet
Faber £7.95.

For oboe, violin, viola and cello.

Matthews, David: The Sleeping Lord
Faber £12.00.

For soprano, flute, clarinet, harp and string quartet.

Moussorgsky (arr Ravel): Pictures at an Exhibition
Boosey & Hawkes £14.95 (full score).

For advanced orchestra from the Masterworks Library.

Mozart, W (arr V Kainzbauer): Selected pieces from A Musical Sleigh-Ride
Universal £9.50.

An easy arrangement for children's ensemble.

Rae, James (arr): Joshua Fought the Battle of Jericho
Universal £8.50.

From the jazz ensemble series for flexible ensemble.

Saint-Saens, C (arr B Dobretsberger): Selected pieces from Carnival of the Animals
Universal £12.35

An easy arrangement for children's ensemble.

Sculthorpe, Peter: Memento Mori
Faber £6.95.

For orchestra - advanced.

Stravinsky: The Rite of Spring
Boosey & Hawkes £14.95 (full score).

For advanced orchestra from the Masterworks Library.

Woolrich, John: A Farewell
Faber £9.50 (score and parts).

For clarinet, viola and piano.

Elizabeth Smith is the Administrator of the International Centre for Research in Music Education at the University of Reading.

RESOURCES FOR TEACHERS

Resource Centres

The centres listed below hold an extensive amount of musical literature in the form of periodicals, books, sheet music, etc, for reference by music teachers and other bona fide enquirers. Some centres also initiate projects, run courses for teachers and act as regional music centres for research purposes.

Andertons Music Company
Education Department, 58-59 Woodbridge Rd, Guildford, Surrey GU1 4RF
Tel: 01483 456888 *Fax:* 01483 456722
Email: edu@andertons.co.uk
Website: www.andertons.co.uk

Kevin Pawsey, mgr; Ian Timpson, mus educ consultant.
Suppliers of equipment and training to mus education establishments and schools.

British Institute of Organ Studies
17 Wheeleys Rd, Edgbaston, Birmingham B15 2LD
Tel: 0121 440 5491 *also fax*

Peter Williams, chmn; Jim Berrow, sec.
Dedicated to the scholarly study and conservation of historic British orgs, their source materials and repertoire. Operates an advisory service and administers the British Organ Archive, the National Pipe Organs Register and the Historic Organs Certificate Scheme. Regular day and residential conferences and publications.

The British Library National Sound Archive
96 Euston Rd, London NW1 2DB
Tel: 0171 412 7440 *Fax:* 0171 412 7441

Crispin Jewitt, dir.
Largest reference collection of sound recordings in the UK open to the public, full reference library of associated literature. Information on commercial discs and location of recordings around the UK. Groups from schools, universities, colleges welcome to listen by prior arrangement. W/shops, talks and seminars also offered by arrangement.

Centre for Intercultural Music Arts
Department of Education Studies, Goldsmith's College, Lewisham Way, New Cross, London SE14 6NW

Robert Kwami.
Organises w/shops, courses, symposia, seminars and other artistic and education programmes.

Homerton College Resource Centre
Cambridge CB2 2PH
Tel: 01223 507111 *Fax:* 01223 507120

John Finney, dir and head of mus.
The library holds a wide range of materials for use by primary and secondary teachers on request from the librarian. Details of Ad Dip, Gest-funded INSET course, other courses and consultancy work available from the director.

In Harmony
CIHE, The Avenue, Southampton SO17 1BG
Tel: 01703 216207

Tim Cain, dir.
Regular in-service courses for teachers held (approx 2 per term) with other occasional courses. *Music in the Curriculum* magazine, for dissemination of new ideas and materials.

International Centre for Research in Music Education
University of Reading, Bulmershe Ct, Woodlands Av, Reading RG6 1HY
Tel: 0118 931 8821 *Fax:* 0118 935 2080

Anthony Kemp, dir.
Permanent resource centre with wide programme to assist teachers, lecturers, students and advisers. The centre holds up-to-date collections of British publications for primary and secondary school mus. Wide selection of short courses offered including an annual day conference, modular course for primary curriculum leaders in mus, a three w/end course for nursery teachers and NNEB assistants and a distance-learning course for mus teachers in private practice.

Jewish Music Information Centre
The Sternberg Centre for Judaism, 80 East End Rd, London N3 2SY
Tel: 0181 349 4731; 0181 346 2288 *Fax:* 0181 343 0901

Viv Bellos, mus consultant.
Library of Reform Liturgical mus. Regular

seminars and w/shops on all aspects of Jewish mus.

Leeds College of Music
3 Quarry Hill, Leeds LS2 7PD
Tel: 0113 222 3459 *Fax:* 0113 243 8798
Website: www.netlink.co.uk/users/zappa/clcm/clcm.html

Gwyneth Allatt, librarian; Jay Glasby, mgr, library and resources.
Fully automated library with range of multi-media resources, including video and CD-Rom. Large archive of jazz and popular mus, including extensive collection of periodicals, sheet mus, recordings and other archive material for researchers into 20th C jazz and popular mus.

London Jewish Music Centre
PO Box 2268, Hendon, London NW4 3UW
Tel: 0181 203 8046 *also fax;*
Email: rad.74@dial.pipex.com

Rachel Wetstein; Daniel Tunkel.
A comprehensive Jewish mus information service.

Midland Centre for Music in Schools
Faculty of Education, University of Central England in Birmingham, Westbourne Rd, Birmingham B15 3TN
Tel: 0121 331 6097/6129/6100 *Fax:* 0121 331 6147
Email: helen.coll@uce.ac.uk

Helen Coll, dir.
Extensive resources bank holding books, mus, etc.

NIAS Music Team
Spencer Centre, Lewis Rd, Northampton NN5 7BJ
Tel: 01604 750333 *Fax:* 01604 758075

Sharon Green, John Smith, curriculum advisers; David Bray, inspector for mus.
Resource library holds comprehensive collection of publications on mus education. This includes books and periodicals, published materials for schools (including cassettes, CDs and videos) and collections of songs, cantatas, rcdr mus, etc.

A catalogue is available and a reference and free loan service is in operation. C/room insts including steel drum and samba kits are also available for hire at a nominal charge.

North West Consortium for Curriculum Music
c/o The Performing Arts Centre, The Professional Development Centre, Hindley, Wigan, Lancs WN7 2RY
Tel: 01942 255227 *Fax:* 01942 255217

Colin Edwards, team leader; Pam Harrison, deputy team leader.
Group of practising teachers and advisers from a consortium of LEAs (Bury, Knowsley, Salford, Stockport, Trafford, Wigan, Wirral) who meet to share ideas about the delivery of the mus curriculum. It aims to improve the quality of mus teaching in the classroom and provide a forum for professional discussion. Publishes *Early Ears, Primarily Pitch,* and *Hear Here*.

Piano Teachers' Information Centre (EPTA UK)
c/o Thames Valley University Learning Resource Centre, St Mary's Rd, Ealing, London W5 5RF
Tel: 0181 231 2648 *Fax:* 0181 231 2631
Email: colin.steele@tvu.ac.uk
Website: www.tvu.ac.uk

Colin Steele, mus librarian.
A reference collection including mus scores, a/v aids and videotapes of performances and pno teaching.

University of East Anglia (UEA)
School of Education and Professional Development, Norwich NR4 7TJ
Tel: 01603 56161 ext 2621

Sylvia McGregor, resource centre librarian.
The School's Curriculum and Learning Resources Centre holds a variety of mus resources including books, sound cassettes, sound discs, video cassettes, slides, computer software, wall charts, multi-media packs, games, mus insts and printed mus.

Advice and Consultancy Services

Certain organisations, firms and individuals offer advice and consultation, and some will arrange demonstrations and advisory workshops on various aspects of music education. Organisations specifically concerned with music for people with disabilities will be found in the **Music and Disability** section.

Association of British Choral Directors
46 Albert St, Tring, Herts HP23 6AU
Tel: 01442 891633 *also fax*

Howard Layfield, chair; Marie-Louise Petit, gen sec. Exists to promote education, training and development of choral directors from all choral sectors, and to provide a forum for choral conductors in the UK.

Barry Weinberg Associates
28 Blenheim Gardens, Wembley, Middx HA9 7NP
Tel: 0181 904 7025; 0956 372323 *Fax:* 0181 900 1130

Barry Weinberg, dir.
Specialist consultants in Jewish mus and education. Seminars, courses, lecture-recitals, etc for schools, colleges, graduate and p/grad programmes. Mus advisory service to radio, TV and film directors for programmes and features on Jewish themes.

British Kodály Academy
13 Midmoor Rd, London SW19 4JD
Tel: 0181 946 6528 *Fax:* 0181 946 6561
Email: enquiries@britishkodalyac.demon.co.uk
Website: www.britishkodalyac.demon.co.uk

Celia Cviic, treasurer and courses sec; David Vinden, dir of courses; Jane Platt, chmn; Brenda Harris, sec. Teacher training in mus teaching and musicianship according to the Kodály concept, which is relevant to early childhood education, all levels of the NC and higher education.

Brown, Carla
14 Danforth Dr, Framlingham, Woodbridge, Suffolk IP13 9HH
Tel: 01728 621052 *also fax*

Freelance mus education admin, fundraising and project management.

The Choral Centre
The Old Forge, Sand Hutton, York YO4 1LB
Tel: 01904 468472 *Fax:* 01904 468679
Email: banksramsay@mcmail.com

David Goodwin, admin.
Complete service provided to those requiring choral mus; advice, lists, inspection copies, etc. Phone or write for appointment to visit the centre.

CTI Centre for Music
Lancaster University, Dept of Music, Lancaster LA1 4YW
Tel: 01524 593776/592614 *Fax:* 01524 593939
Email: ctimusic@lancaster.ac.uk
Website: www.lancs.ac.uk/users/music/research/cti.html

Roger Bray, dir; Lisa Whistlecroft, co-ord; Barbara Hargreaves, admin.
CTI Music is a national centre which encourages better use of computers to improve the quality of teaching and learning in higher education. It offers seminars, w/shops, visits and demonstrations; maintains a software library; publishes the journal *Musicus*, the newsletter *CTImusic News*, a software directory and maintains an on-line information service on the WWW.

Educamus Music Education Consultancy and Employment Agency
71 Margaret Rd, New Barnet, Herts EN4 9NT
Tel: 0181 440 6919 *also fax*

Maxwell Pryce.
Consultancy, school inspection and register of mus teachers.

HummingBird Music Education Consultants
Edgcumbe, Kingston St Mary, Taunton, Somerset TA2 8HH
Tel: 01823 451588 *Fax:* 01823 451314
Email: mstocks@dial.pipex.com

Michael Stocks, snr consultant.
Specialises in support for schools and individual teachers of pupils aged 5-14. Services include the school management of mus, documentation, curriculum planning, in-class support and matters related to OFSTED inspection. Courses are held throughout UK. Enquiries from non-mus trained primary teachers are particularly welcome.

International Piano Teachers Consultants (IPTEC)
29 Beaumont Rd, Chiswick, London W4 5AL
Tel: 0181 994 4288

Meriel Jefferson, hon sec.
Consultative organisation formed to help pno teachers in their work. Specialist subjects covered and international co-operation fostered.

Kelsey, Xenophon
Ashley House, Ure Bank, Ripon, N Yorks HG4 1JG
Tel: 01765 602856

Freelance mus education consultant specialising in inst tuition, chmbr and orch mus provision and in-service training.

Murray, Andy

69 Riley Rd, Brighton, E Sussex BN2 4AG
Tel: 01273 699768 Fax: 01273 271737
Email: andy.murray@dial.pipex.com

Advisory consultancy in all matters relating to mus information technology in education. INSET needs, MIDI and recording systems design and training, independent purchasing advice, departmental and feasibility reports, custom software, courseware resources, commercial authoring, etc. Andy Murray is mus offr for the National Council for Educational Technology.

Music Education Arts Management Ltd

18 The Rotyngs, Rottingdean, Brighton BN2 7DX
Tel: 01273 300894 Fax: 01273 308394
Email: musedarts@fastnet.co.uk

Roy Wales, dir; Christine Wales, admin.

Music Education Council

54 Elm Rd, Hale, Altrincham, Cheshire WA15 9QP
Tel: 0161 928 3085 Fax: 0161 929 9648
Email: ahassan@easynet.co.uk

Roger Durston, chmn; Brian Ley, vice-chmn; Anna Hassan, admin.
The council operates as a forum for the development of commonly agreed national policies for presentation to government and other bodies. It is pro-active, addressing issues of national importance in mus education. The council operates through debate and resolutions at full meetings of member bodies plus an executive committee and a number of task groups.

National Institute of Adult Continuing Education (NIACE)

21 de Montfort St, Leicester LE1 7GE
Tel: 0116 255 1451 Fax: 0116 285 4514

Lou Brown, snr information offr.
Promotes lifelong learning opportunities for adults and works to develop increased participation in education and training, particularly for those who do not have easy access because of barriers of class, gender, age, race, language and culture, learning difficulties, disabilities or insufficient financial resources. NIACE publishes Adults Learning (10 issues), Studies in the Education of Adults (2 issues) and Time to Learn (2 issues), a guide to residential learning holidays, as well as a range of publications and monographs linking the best current theory and practice.

NIAS

John Dryden House, 8-10 The Lakes, Northampton NN4 7DD
Tel: 01604 237083 Fax: 01604 236240

David Bray, mus inspector.
Complete advice service on all aspects of the mus curriculum. This includes a wide range of consultancy services and a substantial programme of INSET.

Psychology for Music Teaching, Learning and Performing

28 Glebe Pl, London SW3 5LD
Tel: 0171 352 1666 also fax

Lucinda Mackworth-Young.
Freelance lecturer and consultant in psychology for musicians, students and pupils seeking help on mus teaching, learning and performing related problems. Specialist help in relationships between teachers, pupils and parents; motivation, traditional and creative mus skills, inst suitability, communication and anxiety in performance.

Royal School of Church Music

Cleveland Lodge, Westhumble, Dorking RH5 6BW
Tel: 01306 877676 Fax: 01306 887260

Harry Bramma, dir.
RSCM regional directors visit all parts of the UK to advise on all aspects of church mus.

Sound Sense, The National Community Music Association

Riverside House, Rattlesden, Bury St Edmunds, Suffolk IP30 0SF
Tel: 01449 736287 Fax: 01449 737649
Email: 100256.30@compuserve.com
Website: ourworld.compuserve.com/homepages/soundsense

Kathryn Deane, dir; Gloria Hall, admin.
Sound Sense is the development agency for participatory creative mus-making in the UK. It acts as a membership and information network, offers advice and information to arts and educational organisations and gives support, advice and training to community musicians and groups. Information services include publications and a Lottery help scheme for members.

Stent, Keith and Myrna

13 Savona Close, Wimbledon, London SW19 4HT
Tel: 0181 947 1034 Fax: 0181 879 1058
Email: 106361.2353@compuserve.com

Consultants offering seminar or individual preparation for mus exams, and assessment and advice for those seeking specialist mus education.

Trinity Music Education Consultancy

Trinity College of Music, 11 Mandeville Pl, London W1M 6AQ
Tel: 0171 935 5773 Fax: 0171 487 5717

John Stephens, dir of mus educ.
The college offers a consultancy service related to the needs of all involved in mus education. All members of the service have experience as teachers, advisers and inspectors and respond to the identified needs of institutions and individuals, including teachers, students, head teachers and governors. Where appropriate, written advice and guidance, reports, reviews and assessments can be provided.

Music Information Technology

Nigel Morgan

UK schools are acknowledged to be the world leaders in IT in education according to a DES survey (Statistical Bulletin 3/95) which shows that 94 per cent of secondary schools and virtually all primary schools in England get hands-on experience of computers. The position in Further and Higher Education is set to improve still further with the Dearing Report (1997) recommending the integration of IT and Communications Technology into all areas of teaching and learning.

The hybrid of IT known as Music Information Technology is a vibrant feature of UK education. Software and hardware suppliers continue to report buoyant sales during 1997 with many schools and colleges re-equipping and developing their Music IT resources, and the home-user investing in multimedia computers with CD quality soundcards and wavetable synthesisers as standard.

It is encouraging to report that BECTA (formerly NCET), the Government agency responsible for supporting information technology in education, has finally provided the music education community with a well researched and imaginative guide to choosing and using music IT for and in the classroom. The result of more than two years of consultation and preparation, the Music IT pack was published in the autumn of 1997. This heralds the beginning of regular publications on Music IT which will continue in 1998 with a series of Teacher Support materials. These will concentrate on four strands: MIDI and Sequencing, CD-Rom, Electronic Keyboards, Recording and Processing. Arranged in a series of units, these are designed as a practical program of advice and instruction suitable for supervised INSET opportunities and supported self-study.

The new agency taking over responsibility for these exciting and long overdue developments is the British Educational Communications and Technology Agency (BECTA). Launched in early 1998 it is part of the support strategy for the Government's National Grid for Learning, and will include co-ordinating the content of the Virtual Teachers Centre (VTC). The VTC is to be reached via a website address and is based around five 'rooms', Reception, Library, Meeting Room, Classroom Resources and Professional Development. The current content is made up of web-based resource materials developed with public funds. For further information on the websites for BECTA and the VTC, look at the new World Wide Web section in the Yearbook which follows the listing of Suppliers.

One of the most imaginative initiatives being progressed by BECTA for 1998 is in the collaborations it is making with music software developers and distributors to formulate a common code of description and language for working with MIDI applications. Steinberg, E-Magic and Cakewalk are among the companies who are already producing Companion Guides to their software that follow BECTA's identification of more than a hundred progressive stages and processes common to all music software use. This means that whatever software a teacher and student may use at any time, there is a common approach to reference and support available.

In the commercial world, Japanese companies Roland and Yamaha continue to provide important contributions to the development of practice in the use of IT in the classroom. In the autumn of 1997 Roland held their 4th bi-annual IT and Music Education Conference and Yamaha, in collaboration with Coda, continued to develop their innovative Education Supplement YES, currently the only journal providing an integrated view of music education and technology. There have also been changes in the pattern of music software distribution. Opcode, the major US software house, is now being handled by SCV and the Arbiter Group has acquired Harman who have for some years marketed the Steinberg range of products in the UK. During 1997-8 the integration between MIDI sequencing and digital audio recording within a single software format has continued to dominate developments in the marketplace. Soundcard technology is reaching a new level of sophistication with products like the Pinnacle which incorporate Kurzweil synthesis and sampling and E-Magic's AudioWerk8, a sub £500 PCI card with 8 individual outputs suitable for Mac or PC. Furthermore, this year will see the first sub £100 simultaneous 'play and record' card from Turtle Beach whose UK distributors, Et Cetera, are now well established as the major company dedicated to PC hardware and software for music. They are now handling Coda Finale, Cakewalk, and the new Music Master from Australia, a sequencer designed specifically for education.

In the area of recording, Sony's Minidisk format is slowly establishing itself as the portable and dedicated medium for stereo digital recording. Cost of disks is still a prohibitive factor for general classroom use but as an editing format it excels in comparison to DAT. Philips have now brought out the first sub £500 stand-alone CD recorder putting the mastering of CDs at last under the price of a portable DAT machine. High speed CD-R drives and software are now a practical alternative as an add-on to any recent Mac or PC computer system. But is in the area of recording known as sampling that the most interesting innovations in equipment are being pursued. The requirements of DJs who wish to use samplers along with record decks and mixers has produced sampling units like Akai's S-20 which enable instant loops, edits and transformations to be made via drum machine-like button pads.

The Exempla collaboration between Acorn and Apple has yet to result in new Music IT products offering a proper progression through ages and stages. Acorn third-party software contributes some valuable curriculum-led music software suitable for Key Stage 1 and 2 and there is at long last a robust digital audio and sequencer from Oregon Developments suitable for later Key Stages. Apple are busy improving Quicktime to version 3.0 to bring their General MIDI synthesizer in software up to the Roland GS specification, but have still little to offer in software to the lower Key Stages except for a few 'classic' CD-Rom titles, composer Morton Subotnik's Making Music being one highly recommended by the NCET (now BECTA) CD-Rom evaluation exercise.

Meanwhile the PC, as a computer platform for music, continues to show the greatest proliferation of new software developments and hardware add-ons. The Intel MMX technology and Microsoft's Direct Sound introduced in late 1996 have been taken up by Roland, in their Virtual MT and VS developments. It now looks likely that Windows 98 will include a full specification GS synthesizer in software. Meanwhile, the buzz phrase for 1998 in music for the PC is likely to be Downloadable Sounds. This system will allow the production of very inexpensive soundcards that enable the user to create, manage and download new sounds (from the Internet and CD-Rom) keeping them in the computer's RAM rather than on a ROM chip.

Despite the continuing rundown of music service support for Music IT in most local authorities, many independent organisations and agencies, often linked to established dealers and music shops, offer advice, guidance and INSET training. A point of excellence here continues to be Cheshire Micro Unit.

Music Technology is now an established academic subject in its own right and is offered by many VI forms and FE Colleges. The London University Examination Board (now known as Edexcel) has revised both Music Technology A and AS Level examinations with a syllabus structure that includes composition, performance and studio skills. At Key Stage 4 the RSA Music Technology Diploma provides an alternative to GCSE Music for those wishing to pursue a vocational course with links to GNVQs.

Product Listing and Information

Information is given under six headings: *Computer Hardware and Software, MIDI Instruments, Multimedia, Special Needs, Suppliers, World Wide Web Sites* and a *Glossary* of terminology. *Computer Hardware and Software* lists items by computer type; hardware items here are predominantly MIDI interfaces and patching systems. *MIDI Instruments* covers a selection of MIDI devices deemed appropriate to education situations such as the classroom or teaching lab, but not the electroacoustic or recording studio. *Multimedia* is divided into hardware and software and will include soundcards, desktop amplifiers and speakers for hardware, CD-Roms and MIDIfile collections. *Special Needs* will include recognised software and hardware, including some control systems that relate to music performance and composition.

Much music technology in use in schools and colleges has not been designed specifically for education, but has been found by many to be appropriate at certain levels. Increasingly, software and hardware is developed for a broader educational purpose and targets the home rather than the school. The lists aim to include all current specifically educational items. Home user and professional user products are included where there is evidence of their adoption by educational users and availability from educational suppliers.

In 1996-7 the move towards IBM-PC compatible and Apple Macintosh computers in the music education community has continued, most particularly in secondary, further and higher education. However, with the success of the remarkable Sibelius scorewriting system Acorn have found a niche in many schools, colleges and universities committed to 'other' platforms. The Atari ST, once the staple of both the music industry and the secondary-and-above music classroom, is now no longer produced and finding technical support and spare parts can be a problem in some areas of the country.

In the primary school the Acorn Archimedes and RISC PCs, and Research Machine Pentium PCs running Windows and Windows '95 are fast becoming the norm. Both platforms support a range of music-related software suitable for Key Stage 1 - 3. Surprisingly, there are few PC software titles for Key Stages 1 and 2 and almost no CD-Rom music titles for Acorn machines.

Entries for Acorn-related products are now solely for the Archimedes and RISC OS compliant computers. Although BBC machines are still found in many primary schools, sales of software for BBCs are negligible. There is no BBC music software or hardware in Acorn's 1997 catalogue. A similar situation occurs with the PC-186 or Nimbus computer from Research Machines, with Nimbus software and hardware for music now deleted from their product list. All software associated with Research Machines can be found under the heading IBM-Compatible Computers.

Computer Hardware and Software

The list is structured as follows: popular makes of computers are listed in bold type, each with lists of specific hardware add-ons and software programs for that computer. Packages that include both hardware and software are listed under hardware. Each listed item has the name of the product in (italics), a brief description, a price code and the name of the supplier. The price codes give a broad indication of price as follows:

A	under £50	E	under £1000
B	under £100	F	under £2000
C	under £250	G	over £2000
D	under £500		

The addresses and telephone numbers of suppliers are given in the **Suppliers** section immediately following. Suppliers are not given for computers, since these are generally available from the major educational suppliers.

Acorn Archimedes

Hardware

AKA12 A3000 MIDI Interface/Use Port

Midi interface for A3000 range with user port. Price code B: Acorn Computers.

AKA16 A5000 MIDI Interface

MIDI interface for the A5000. Price code B: Acorn Computers.

Armadeus Sampling Board

Sampling hardware for use with Armadeus sampling software. Price code C: Clares Micro Supplies.

AudioPort

Stand-alone or podule fitted SP/DIF, DSP and MIDI unit with expandable option to connect with external audio CODEC units (2in/6out or 8in/8 out. Designed as part of ProSound and Studio Sound systems. Price Code: Oregan Developments.

ESP MIDI Synth Plus

The lowest priced GM synth available! Designed for the RiscPC with a 16-bit sound facility. A version for machines with 8-bit sound will be available late 1997. Price Code: A.

ESP Parallel Port MIDI Interface

One IN, one OUT and THRU. Enables MIDI facility to be moved easily from machine to machine. Price Code: B.

ESP MIDIMaxII

Low budget MIDI Interface and sampling and MIDI facilities. Price Code B: ESP

Oak Recorder II

Sound sampler. Can be used with Hi-Fi/CD and includes SoundLab software. Price code A: Solent Computer Products.

Risc PC Sound Upgrade Card

Provides sound card support for PC cards fitted to Risc machines. Price Code B: Acorn Computers.

Software

Most of the software listed below is compatible with all models of Archimedes computer. Check with the supplier if in any doubt.

Armadeus

A sound sampling program enabling sounds to be recorded into the computer and processed in a number of ways. Requires sampling hardware. Price code B: Clares Micro Supplies.

Compose World

Uses pictures as a simple form of notation. Each picture is associated with a musical phrase. Based on the original Compose program but with additional features. MIDI optional. Price code B: ESP.

Compose World Files

A collection of extra files for use with Compose World. Price code A: ESP.
Keyboard Player: computer-aided learning for keyboard skills. Price code B: Chalksoft.

MidiWorks

Professional-level 64 track MIDI sequencer. Piano roll style, event list and drum pattern editors, boolean processor, MTC/SMPTE sync. Price Code C: Oregan Developments.

Music Box

Award-winning software using internal Archimedes sounds designed for children at Key Stage 1. Price Code A: Topologika.

Music Studio 32

32 track sequencer with graphic and notation editors configurable for different ages and abilities. Ability to add lyrics and print to A4 /A5 or output to Draw files. Price code B: Longman Logotron.

Notate

A music composition program based around traditional notation, configurable for different levels of user. MIDI is optional. Price code B: Longman Logotron.

ProSound

Professional-quality hard-disk multitrack recording software for Risc PCs and for A5000/7000 machines with suitable soundcard. Price Code C: Oregan

Rhapsody 4

Major rewrite and enhancement of Rhapsody 3. Choice of 3 operating levels - all user configurable. Support for GM, Intelligent 'capture' mode, typeset quality hardcopy, improved control over page layout. Ideal of Key Stage 2 and 3. Price Code B: Clares Micro Supplies.

Serenade

16-track MIDI sequencer with graphical user interface using 'piano-roll' type display. Requires MIDI interface and instrument. Price code C: Clares Micro Systems.

Sibelius Junior

Entry-level scorewriting package with MIDI step and flexitime input and realtime output suitable for Key Stage 2. Price code B: Sibelius Software

Sibelius 6

High-quality scorewriting package with MIDI step and flexitime input and realtime output. Educational user version of Sibelius 7 with some limitations of features. Price code C: Sibelius Software

Sibelius 7 Student

Professional 'expert-system' scorewriting package with MIDI flexitime input and realtime output. Student version has limited number of staves available. Reads and writes MIDI files. Price code D: Sibelius Software

Sibelius 7

Professional 'expert-system' scorewriting package with MIDI flexitime input and realtime output. Now reads and writes MIDI files. Includes drum-kit notation and Guitar and lute tablatures. New Sketch Mode format emulates sequencer piano roll displays. Price code E: Sibelius Software

Optical Manuscript

Developed for Sibelius 6, 7 and 7S users to enable scanning of printed music into Sibelius. Needs Acorn scanner, RISC PC, A7000 recommended. Price Code C: Sibelius Software.

Sound FX Maker and Editor (SFXM)

Digital sound synthesis software. Price code B: Cambridge International Software Ltd.

Soundtrack Keyboard Trainer

MIDI-based interactive trainer aiding note recognition, finger technique and rhythm. Teachers book available. Price code B: Starland Distribution.

Soundtrack Pitch Trainer

Teachers music listening skills using keyboard and notation displays. With or without MIDI. Price code A: Starland Distribution

Soundtrack Rhythm Trainer

Teaches rhythm and melody skills using standard music notation. With or without MIDI. Price code A: Starland Distribution.

Soundtrack Theory Trainer

Teaches basic musical skills, keys, notes on treble and bass clefs, note lengths and more. With or without MIDI. Price code A: Starland Distribution.

StudioSound

Multitrack audio sequencer. Allows sample crossfades. Components include mixer, real-time DSP effects, full sample control and timing. Uses industry standard sample file formats. Price Code C: Oregan Developments.

Vistamusic II

Music composition and performance software. Has applications for disabled and the visually impaired: Price code A: Enabling for Music Project.

Apple Macintosh (all models)

Hardware

Anatek Pocket Mac

One IN, two OUT MIDI interface. Price code B: MCMXCIX

E-Magic Log 2 Mac

One IN, three OUT MIDI interface. Price code B. Sound Technology.

E-Magic Audiowerk8

PCI based digital audio recording card. 8 outputs, stereo analogue ins and digital i/o. Complete with VMR recorder. Price code D. Sound Technology.

JL Cooper Mac Nexus

One IN, three OUT MIDI interface. Price code B. Sound Technology.

MIDIman Macman

One IN, three OUT MIDI interface. Price code B: Key Audio Systems.

MIDIman Mac Syncman

Two IN, six OUT MIDI interface with comprehensive tape synchronization facilities. Price code C: Key Audio Systems.

MIDI Edge Mac

One IN, three OUT MIDI interface. Price code A: Et Cetera.

Mark Of The Unicorn MIDI Time Piece AV

Eight-by-eight MIDI patchbay with SMPTE synchronization. Wordclock and video sync. Price code E: MusicTrack

Mark Of The Unicorn Fastlane

Simple one IN, three OUT serial port expander. Price Code B: MusicTrack

Opcode MIDI Translator II

One IN, three OUT MIDI interface. Price code B: SCV.

Opcode MIDI Translator Pro

Two IN, six OUT, 32 channels, switchable thru MIDI interface. Price code B: SCV.

Opcode Studio 4

MIDI interface supports 128 channels, 8 independent MIDI INs and 10 OUTs. Studio 4 reads all formats of SMPTE and converts to MIDI Time Code. Price Code C: SCV.

Opcode Studio 5LX

MIDI interface for Macintosh combines the functions of an interface, synchronizer, patchbay and processor in one unit. Studio 5LX provides 15 independent MIDI INs and OUTs, 240 MIDI channels per unit, networking capabilities and memory for user patches. Price Code E: SCV.

Opcode Studio 64X

A cross-platform MIDI interface. This interface is designed to automatically detect Macintosh or PC. Features include 4 MIDI INs, 6 MIDI OUTs, 64 MIDI channels, full SMPTE synchronization and powerful MIDI patchbay features. Price Code C: SCV.

Studio 64XTC

A cross platform, MIDI Interface/Patchbay with advanced synchronization features including ADAT sync, simultaneous Wordclock and Superclock Out, Video Reference and Blackburst In. Supports all SMPTE formats Sony P2 video control option late 1998. Price Code D: SCV.

Steinberg MicroMac

Basic one IN, one OUT MIDI interface. Price Code B: Arbiter Pro Audio.

Software

Adventures in Musicland

A collection of aural training games based on Lewis Carroll's 'Alice In Wonderland'. Uses the computer's own sound facility. Price code B: Off Planet Media.

Autoscore

Enables voice or instrument conversion to MIDI input. Suitable for using with MIDI scorewriters and sequencers. Price code C: Et Cetera.

Band in a Box 7.0

Auto-accompaniment software suitable for teaching harmony or creating instant 'music minus one' for rehearsal purposes. The program generates accompaniments in various musical styles from typed-in chord names, and enables the user to create original styles. Now with notation display. Price code B: Arbiter Pro Audio

Cubase 3.5

A professional sequencing package with many advanced features, originally developed for the Atari ST and now an 'industry standard'. Price code D: Arbiter Pro Audio

Cubase Audio 3.0

Similar to Cubase but with facilities for multitrack digital audio. Needs SoundTools or similar soundcard. Price code E: Arbiter Pro Audio.

Cubase Score

As above but with very comprehensive notation and music printing facilities. Price code D: Arbiter Pro Audio

Cubase 3.5 VST

As above but with integrated tracks of digital audio. Designed for DSP facilities of PowerPCs and requires no additional hardware. Price code D: Arbiter Pro Audio

Cubasis

Cubase style entry-level sequencer. Score, Key and List Editors and limited print facility. Price code C: Arbiter Pro Audio

Cubase Lite

Entry-level sequencer with Micromac interface. Price Code C: Arbiter Pro Audio.

Digital Performer (Education) 2.3

Integrated digital audio/MIDI sequencer with real time 32-bit effects and automated mixing. Price code D: MusicTrack

Encore 4.0 Academic

A music publishing and composition package. Supports up to 64 staves. Incorporates QuickTime Roland software GM synth. Price code D: Arbiter Pro Audio.

Finale 97

A comprehensive music publishing and score-based composition program. Enables scores to be written, edited, played back and printed. Supports up to 128 staves of music. Price code D: Et Cetera

Finale Allegro 1.0

A comprehensive music publishing and score-based composition program. Enables scores to be written, edited, played back and printed. Supports up to 32 staves of music. Price code C: Et Cetera

FreeStyle 2.01

Trackless sequencing and songwriting software. Unique colour display and MIDI control system. Ideal for disabled or visually-impaired. PowerPC native. Sense tempo feature. Price code C: MusicTrack.

Gospel Pianist

50 plus gospel-style piano standards with print out. Price code A: Arbiter.

Hearmaster

Aural training system covering chords, scales, melody and rhythm. Levels of difficulty may be fine-tuned. Price code C: Sound Technology.

Jazz Pianist

As for Pianist software. Also includes notation and displays guitar chords with print feature. Price code A: Arbiter Pro Audio.

Jazz Guitarist

As for Jazz Pianist but with guitar fret board display. Price code A: Arbiter Pro Audio.

Logic 2.5

An advanced sequencing and notation package from E-Magic with unlimited number of tracks. Notation features almost identical to Atari Notator SL. Price code D: Sound Technology.

Logic Audio Silver

Upgrade from the Audio Discovery software. Offers 24 audio tracks with 3 band EQ and adaptive mixer. Price Code D: Sound Technology.

Logic Audio Module 2.0

Hard-disk recording and editing software module for Logic 2.0. Needs SoundTools card or similar. Price code D: Sound Technology.

Logic Audio Gold

Full hard-disk recording integrated with Logic sequencing and scorewriting system. For use with Audiowerk PCI recording card, Digidesign Audiomedia cards, AW8, DAE, Korg 1212 I/O, Yamaha CBX for a total of 48 tracks. Price code D: Sound Technology.

Logic Audio Platinum

Full hard-disk recording integrated with Logic sequencing and scorewriting system. For use with 24-bit Audio Format (ProTools III/24), Soundscape SSHDR-1 for a total of 96 tracks. Price code D: Sound Technology.

MAX

MIDI Programming language aimed at experimental composers and performers. Now at version 3.5 with 'timeline' scoring facility and ability to produce stand-alone 'patches' as mini-applications. Price Code D: SCV

MasterTracks Pro 6.01

Very comprehensive sequencer now with notation editor. Good sequencer partner for Encore scorewriter. Price code B: Arbiter Pro Audio.

Metro 3.5

A 64-track sequencer with advanced graphic editing facility that integrates with the Macromedia Deck II digital audio software. Price code C: Et Cetera

MicroLogic 2

Entry-level version of E-Magic's Logic. Only 16 channels available. Notation editing and print facility. With Quicktime instruments. Price code B: Sound Technology.

MicroLogic AV

Entry-level version of E-Magic's Logic. 16 audio tracks with realtime effects and integrated sample editor. Notation editing and print facility. With Quicktime instruments. Price code C: Sound Technology.

MicroLogic XL

Entry-level version of E-Magic's Logic. Only 16 channels available. With GM files and keyboard shortcut support. Notation editing and print facility. With Quicktime instruments. Price code C: Sound Technology.

Mosaic Academic 1.58

A desktop publishing notation package by Mark of the Unicorn. MIDI step time input, realtime output. Price code C: MusicTrack

MusicShop 2.0

A cut-down 16-track version of the Vision

sequencer with improved music notation display (one grand stave at a time). As used by Brian Eno! Price code C: SCV.

MusicTime 2.0

Beginners notation software. Six and 12 stave versions, easy to use. Incorporates QuickTime Roland software GM synth. Price code C: Arbiter Pro Audio

New Orleans Pianist

As Jazz Pianist with over 65 New Orleans & Blues piano pieces with notation. Price code A: Arbiter Pro Audio.

Overture

Opcode's scorewriting program. MIDIfile compatible. Nearly professional graphics facilities. Power PC Native. Price code D: SCV

Nightingale

Professional quality scorewriter with step and realtime input. Incorporates NoteScan sheet music to MIDI facility. Price Code D: Et Cetera.

Performer 6.02

An advanced sequencer with unlimited tracks. Now with colour display and notation editing and printing. Price code D: MusicTrack.

Pianist

Contains over 200 pieces of music, biographies of composers and trivia quiz. Allows tempo and transpose change. Price code A: Arbiter Pro Audio.

Piano Discovery

Interactive piano tuition software. Price Code A: Et Cetera .

Ragtime Pianist

As Jazz Pianist with over 100 ragtime piano pieces with notation. Price code A: Arbiter Pro Audio.

Score Reader

Translates printed music into MIDIfile format via a scanning device. Price code D: Yamaha.

Studio Vision Pro 3.5

Integrated MIDI sequencing and digital audio recording software. Features include Power Mac native code, full support for Digidesign TDM bussing, advanced DSP features, enhanced integration with Apple's QuickTime and support for all major audio file types. Price code E: SCV

Symbolic Composer 4.0

Music composition language based on Common Lisp with realtime MIDI playback. Power PC native. Price code D: Tonality Systems (UK).

UNISYN 1.5

Graphic system exclusive editor/librarian system supporting over 230 synthesisers and MIDI devices. Price Code C: MusicTrack.

Vision 3.5

A complete software system for recording, editing and playback of MIDI-based music and audio recording with Sound Manager. Reads and writes QuickTime audio and MIDI files. Multimedia features include new DSP processing capabilities. Vision is Power Mac native and OMS compatible.Includes basic notation editing and printing. Price code D: SCV.

Vivace

Provides MIDIfile based musical accompaniments that tracks a musician's live performance in real time. At present all brass, woodwind and voice are available. Comes complete with Finale software. Price Code C/D/E (dependent on system): Dawsons.

Xpose

Visual sampler from Steinberg. Use with Quicktime movies and assign frames and sequences to MIDI keys. Visual effects can be added. Data can be used with Cubase sequencers to synchronize sound and image. Price Code D: Arbiter Pro Audio.

Atari ST, Mega ST, STE and Falcon (all models)

Hardware

E-Magic Unitor 2

2 MIDI OUTs and a tape synchronization device for optional use with Logic or Notator /Creator SL. Price code D: Sound Technology.

Geerdes Starport

128 channel expander. Price code D: Newtronic.

Heavenly Music statement

Extra MIDI out from the modem port. Price Code A: Roland.

Microdeal Replay 16

16-bit sampler plus editing software. Price code D: Microdeal.

Steinberg PC3
One IN/Three OUT MIDI Interface. Price code C: Arbiter Pro Audio

Steinberg Midex+
An optional tape synchronization device for use with Cubase. Price code D: Arbiter Pro Audio.

Software

Band In A Box 5.0
Auto-accompaniment software suitable for teaching harmony or creating instant 'music minus one' for rehearsal purposes. The program generates five instrument accompaniments in various musical styles from typed-in chord names, and enables the user to create original styles. Price code B: Arbiter Pro Audio.

Breakthru 1.2
Entry level MIDI and sample sequencer. Price code C: Software Technology. Price code B: Software Technology.

Breakthru 2
64 track sequencer with original graphic note editing system based on traditional piano-roll display. Support for sample replay. Price code C: Software Technology.

Breakthru 2 Plus
As above but with 32 channel MIDI expansion cartridge Price code C: Software Technology.

Cubase Score 2.0
A professional sequencing and scorewriting package with many advanced features, noted for its graphic music arrangement features and now considered an 'industry standard'. Price code C: Arbiter Pro Audio.

Cubase Audio 1.6
As above with hard-disk recording specifically for the Falcon. Price code E: Arbiter Pro Audio.

Cubase Lite
A 16 track entry level MIDI sequencer based on the professional Cubase package. Price code B: Arbiter Pro Audio.

Dr Tiricc
Phrase and lyric generator with computer voice. Price Code A: Intrinsic Technology.

Fractal Music Composer
Generates six-part music from fractal images on the computer screen, and can produce music and fractal images simultaneously. Price code B: Fractal Music Ltd.

Gospel Pianist
50 plus gospel-style piano standards with print out. Price code A: Arbiter Pro Audio.

Jazz Pianist
As for Pianist software. Also includes notation and displays guitar chords with print feature. Price code A: Arbiter Pro Audio.

Jazz Guitarist
As for Jazz Pianist but with guitar fret board display. Price code A: Arbiter Pro Audio.

John the Composer
An algorithmic composition program for beginners. Price Code A: Newtronic.

Logic 2.5
Object-oriented sequencing and notation package. Almost Notator SL but with radical multi-window concept. Price code D: Sound Technology.

MIDIGrid
A composition and performance system based on movements of the computer's mouse. Adaptable for special needs education. Price code B: CDP.

MIDIGrid Professional
As above, but with more advanced features. Price code C: CDP.

New Orleans Pianist
As Jazz Pianist with over 65 New Orleans & Blues piano pieces with notation. Price code A: Arbiter Pro Audio.

Pianist
200 classical piano works on disk plus a quiz and composer biographies. Price Code A: Arbiter Pro Audio.

Proscore 2.0
Features chord track with auto recognition. Price code C: GFA.

Ragtime Pianist
As Jazz Pianist with over 100 ragtime piano pieces with notation. Price code A: Arbiter Pro Audio.

Session Partner Profix
Style generator and auto-accompaniment software plus sequencer. Price code C: Newtronic.

Sharpscore Professional
A high-quality scorewriting package with real and

steptime MIDI input. 64 stave with Postscript printing. Price code C: Take Control.

Sharpscore Lite

4 system version of the above. Price code A: Take Control .

Sharpscore Educational

2 system version of the above. Price code B: Take Control.

Soundtrack Keyboard Trainer

MIDI-based interactive trainer aiding note recognition, finger technique and rhythm. Teachers book available. Price code B: Starland Distribution.

Soundtrack Pitch Trainer

Teachers music listening skills using keyboard and notation displays. With or without MIDI. Price code A: Starland Distribution

Soundtrack Rhythm Trainer

Teaches rhythm and melody skills using standard music notation. With or without MIDI. Price code A: Starland Distribution.

Soundtrack Theory Trainer

Teaches basic musical skills, keys, notes on treble and bass clefs, note lengths and more. With or without MIDI. Price code A: Starland Distribution.

Symbolic Composer 2.0

Music composition language based on Lisp. Needs 4Mbytes of RAM and hard disk. Price code D: Tonality Systems (UK).

Techo Grooves

Groove composer designed to operate like an analogue synth. Works as Desk Accessory. Price code B: Intrinsic Technology.

Tentrax

An easy-to-use sequencer designed for use with the Roland CM range of sound modules. Price code A: Starland Distribution

Twiddly Bits

MIDI recordings of valuable 'twiddly bits' and rhythm patterns recorded by top musicians. Several volumes available. Price code A: Roland.

IBM-Compatible Computers (all models)

The majority of music software now runs under Microsoft's Windows 3.1 and Windows '95. Some DOS-only programs are still available and are often extremely good value on slower PCs. Hardware is restricted in this section to a selection of MIDI interfaces. Look at the Multimedia section for information on soundcards and MIDI daughterboards. Although most soundcards have integral MIDI interfaces many are not MPU-401 compatible and cannot be recommended for serious MIDI recording.

Hardware

E-Magic Log 2 PC

MPU401 style 1/3 size MIDI interface card with one IN and three OUTs. Price code B: Sound technology.

E-Magic Audiowerk8

PCI based digital audio recording card. 8 outputs, stereo analogue ins and digital i/o. Complete with VMR recorder. Price code D. Sound Technology.

Midiator MS101

A serial port interface compatible with Microsoft Windows. Price code C: Arbiter Pro Audio.

Midiator MS124

As MS101 but with four MIDI outputs. Price code C: Arbiter Pro Audio.

MOTU MIDI Express

MIDI interface and SMPTE synchronizer essential

for hard disk recording. 128 channels. Price code E: MusicTrack.

MidiMan MM-401

MPU-401 compatible MIDI interface card. Price code B: Key Audio Systems.

MidiMan Portman PCP

MIDI interface using serial port, intended for use with laptop and portable PCs running Microsoft Windows. Price code B: Key Audio Systems.

MIDI Edge

Two IN, 4 OUT expandable interface card. Price code C: Et Cetera.

MusicQuest 2port/SE

Two IN, two OUT MIDI interface with message filters and multi-client drivers. Price code D: Et Cetera.

MusicQuest PC MIDI card

MPU 401 MIDI interface card. Price code B: Et Cetera.

MusicQuest MIDI Engine Note/1

Parallel port MIDI interface for notebooks and laptops. One IN, One OUT. Price code B: Et Cetera.

Opcode 2Port/SE

A 2 IN x 2 OUT, 32-channel MIDI interface with SMPTE that connects to the parallel port of any PC compatible. MIDI buffering, data compression, message filtering and SMPTE implementation. Price Code C: SCV.

Opcode 8Port/SE

A professional MIDI interface for all PC compatible computers. This interface features 8 INs, 8 OUTs, 128 MIDI channels and full SMPTE support. Price Code D: SCV.

PC-MIDI Flyer

Two IN, two OUT MIDI interface providing 32 MIDI channels. Compatible with Windows '95. Price Code B: MusicTrack.

Steinberg PC MIDI 1

Basic one IN, one OUT MIDI interface. Price code B; Arbiter Pro Audio

Roland MPU-IMC

Special MIDI interface for MCA machines. i.e. IBM PS/2. Price code B: Roland.

Steinberg PC 1

One IN, one OUT MIDI interface. Price code B: Arbiter Pro Audio.

Steinberg PC 3

One IN, three OUT MIDI interface. Price code C: Arbiter Pro Audio.

Voyetra V22

Two IN, two OUT MIDI interface. 32 channels. V22M has MPU-401 compatibility. Price code B: Arbiter Pro Audio.

Voyetra VP-11

Two IN, two OUT MIDI interface for parallel port. 32 channels. Suitable for laptops Price code C: Arbiter Pro Audio.

Software

Arranger Plus

Creates E86/KN2000/i3 styles on a PC with a soundcard. Price code B: Newtronic.

Autoscore

Enables voice or instrument conversion to MIDI input. Suitable for using with MIDI scorewriters and sequencers. Price code C: Et Cetera.

Band In A Box 7.0

Auto-accompaniment software capable of producing five-instrument backing tracks from input chord lists. Suitable for creating 'music minus one' or teaching harmony. Includes music notation display. Price code B: Arbiter Pro Audio.

Beat Brothers' Music Kit

Colourful and fun program with on-screen keyboard and simple sequencing via tape-machine style transport controls. Suitable for Key Stages 1 and 2. Price code B: AVP.

Cakewalk Professional 6.01 (for Windows 95 and NT 4.0)

A 256 track sequencer with notation editing and advanced features. Good for low-level PCs 486DX running Windows 95. Price code C: Et Cetera

Cakewalk Pro Audio 6.01 (versions for Windows 95 and 3.1)

A 256 track sequencer with notation editing and advanced features plus integration with digital audio. Number of audio tracks depends on PC and soundcard configuration. Includes JAMMER Hit session and Virtual Jukebox. Price code D: Et Cetera

Cakewalk Home Studio 6.01

A 16 track entry-level sequencer with most of the features of the Pro version. Now includes JAMMER interactive MIDI band. Price code B: Et Cetera

Compose World Junior

Windows 3.1 and Windows 95 version of popular Acorn package. Uses pictures as a simple form of notation. Each picture is associated with a musical phrase. Based on the original Compose program but with additional features. Price Code B: Single User; C: Site Licence. ESP

Cubase 3.0

A Windows version of the acclaimed professional sequencer already well-established for Atari and Apple machines. Score editing only. Price code D: Arbiter Pro Audio.

Cubase Audio 3.0

Combines digital audio tracks with MIDI sequencing. Needs quality 'play and record' soundcard. Up to 32 audio tracks, parametric eq,

4 effects sends per channel. Score editing only. Price code D: Arbiter Pro Audio.

Cubase Score 3.5.2

A Windows version of the acclaimed professional sequencer already well-established for Atari and Apple machines. Score editing and printing Price code D: Arbiter Pro Audio.

Cubasis A/V 2.0

Entry-level version of Cubase Audio with WAV recording support. Includes notation editing and printing. Designed for GM synths and modules with mixer and program list. Price Code C: Arbiter Pro Audio.

The Composer's Pen

A music notation program with printout facilities. Price code B (Amstrad PCW version), Price code C (IBM-compatible version): Composit Software. Digital Orchestrator Plus: Windows sequencer with integrated digital audio. Unlimited tracks, companion CD and video tutorial. Effects processing. Price code: C. Arbiter Pro Audio.

DO-RE-MIX 2

Composing and style-based arranging package using simple icons to create a virtual band. Only available with Roland soundcards. Price code B: Roland

Drumatix

Windows drum pattern generator and groove designer. Price code B: Newtronic.

Dr.T's Sing-A-Long

Non-MIDI sound and graphics software aimed at Key Stage 1. Over 25 classic children's songs with music notation, lyrics and animated graphics. Price code A: Starland Distribution.

Encore 4.2

A music publishing and composition windows package. Used by many European Conservatoires as a 'student-friendly' package. Supports up to 64 staves. Price code D: Arbiter Pro Audio.

FreeStyle 2.01

Trackless sequencing and songwriting software. Unique colour display and MIDI control system. Ideal for disabled or visually-impaired. New Sense Tempo feature. Price code C: MusicTrack.

Finale 97

A comprehensive music publishing and score-based composition program. Enables scores to be written, edited, played back and printed. Supports up to 128 staves of music. Price code D: Et Cetera

Finale Allegro 1.0

A comprehensive music publishing and score-based composition program. Enables scores to be written, edited, played back and printed. Supports up to 32 staves of music. Price code C: Et Cetera

Gospel Pianist

50 plus gospel-style piano standards with print out. Price code A: Arbiter Pro Audio.
Guitar Basics: innovative tutorial software including songs, tuner and audio chords. Price code A: Et Cetera.

Jammer Pro 3.0

Windows auto-style virtual band generator. Price code B: Et Cetera.

Jazz Pianist

As for Pianist software. Also includes notation and displays guitar chords with print feature. Price code A: Arbiter Pro Audio.

Jazz Guitarist

As for Jazz Pianist but with guitar fret board display. Price code A: Arbiter Pro Audio.

Keyboard Basics

Innovative tutorial software suitable for most home keyboards. Price code A: Et Cetera.

Kid Keys

Musical games for young (four to eight year old) children. Price Code A: AVP.

Koan Pro

Ambient music generator endorsed by Brian Eno! Price code C: SSEYO

Logic Audio Silver

Upgrade from the Audio Discovery software. Offers 24 audio traks with 3 band EQ and adaptive mixer. Price Code D: Sound Technology.

Logic Audio Gold

Full hard-disk recording integrated with Logic sequencing and scorewriting system. For use with Audiowerk PCI recording card, Digidesign Audiomedia cards, AW8, DAE, Korg 1212 I/O, Yamaha CBX for a total of 48 tracks. Price code D: Sound Technology.

Logic Audio Platinum

Full hard-disk recording integrated with Logic sequencing and scorewriting system. For use with 24-bit Audio Format (ProTools III/24), Soundscape SSHDR-1 for a total of 96 tracks. Price code D: Sound Technology.

MicroLogic AV

Entry-level version of E-Magic's Logic. 16 audio tracks with realtime effects and integrated sample editor. Notation editing and print facility. With Quicktime instruments. Price code C: Sound Technology.

MicroLogic v2

Entry-level version of E-Magic's Logic. Only 16 channels available. Notation editing and print facility. Price code B: Sound Technology.

MicroLogic XL

Entry-level version of E-Magic's Logic. Only 16 channels available. Notation editing and print facility. Includes GM files and keyboard shortcuts. Price code C: Sound Technology.

MasterTracks Pro6.5.3

Very comprehensive Windows sequencer now with notation editor. Good sequencer partner for Encore scorewriter. Digital Audio version available. Price code C: Arbiter Pro Audio.

MIDI Connections

Budget sequencer/scorewriter and auto-accompaniment style generator. Price code C: Starland Distribution.

MIDI Orchestrator Plus

Notation-based sequencer, 10 stave maximum. Price code C: Arbiter Pro Audio.

Music Ace

Very limited composing and music skills instruction software. Suitable for Key Stage 2. Price code A: AVP.

Musicator A/S Windows

32 stave notation / sequencer. Supports GM/GS instruments with integral sound editor. Integrated hard-disk recording with any sound card. Price code D: Arbiter Pro Audio.

Music Collage

Advanced graphical music arrangement and composing software, 2000+ musical patterns, 200+ musical styles. Price code A: Research Machines.

Music Master

Sequencing and publishing software for Windows (3.11, NT or 95). Designed in Australia expressly for music education. In Professional and Performa (less editing functions) versions with plug ins for video and timecode display. Price Code C & D: Et Cetera.

MusicTime PC

16 stave beginners notation software based on

Encore design. Six and 12 stave versions, easy to use. Price code B, C : Arbiter Pro Audio.

Musicware Piano 1 & 2

Interactive keyboard instruction software. 8 units and 200 lessons. Includes pitch training and music theory. Price code B: Et Cetera.

Personal Composer 1.3c

Windows sequencer with near professional music notation and printing features. Personal Composer I and II available with 18 and 16 stave options. Price code B, B C: Et Cetera.

Pianist

200 classical piano works on disk plus a quiz and composer biographies. Price Code A: Arbiter Pro Audio.

Power Chords

Sequencer and auto-style and accompaniment generator. Price code C: Digital Muse.

Recorder

Teaches the basic of music reading and writing through an on-screen tutor for the descant recorder. Shows which fingers to use as tunes are played from notation displays. Price code A: AVP.

Ragtime Pianist

As Jazz Pianist with over 100 ragtime piano pieces with notation. Price code A: Arbiter Pro Audio.

Rhapsody

Simplified and more accessible version of Passport's Encore software. Price Code C: Arbiter Pro Audio.

RM Music Explorer

Innovative Key Stage 2 and 3 composing and music exploring activity system with graphic and standard notation. Price code C: Research Machines.

Rhythm Maker

Drum-machine style software designed for Key Stage 2 and 3. Versions for Windows 3.1 or 95. Price Code: A single user; B site licence. ESP

Quickscore Elite 5.1 & Level II

Scorewriting package with limited, but effective, sequencing and editing facilities. Price Code B & C: Et Cetera.

Session Partner

Windows sequencer and style generator. Price code D: Newtronic.

Sound Forge XP 4.0

Express audio for multimedia and the Internet

Lessons for Life!

FROM ONE OF THE WORLD'S LEADING MUSIC EDUCATION RESOURCES

W hat you learn in school influences the choices you make later in life. Cubase is now the official software for music education and training in many countries. In recent public examinations and and educational testing. Steinberg has graduated with honours, beating the toughest competitors

The Complete Curriculum
Whatever the level of education, there's a Cubase program to suit all student and teacher requirements. From basic composing, producing examination scores and interactive study material, to the recording and editing of live performances, you can do everything in a single program

MIDI Recording & Editing...
Record musical ideas in real time or use step input. Cubase's graphic tools, cut, copy and paste functions allow students to build arrangements easily and to study musical form in an intuitive and visual way.

Scoring...
Notation and Score Printing is an integral part of the entire Cubase family. Cubasis and Cubase VST offer standard notation, text input and score printing. Cubase Score"and audio have a full range of notation styles to suit the most demanding composer! Layout, text and print options add a further dimension. Using one basic template, study material or scores for regular combinations of instruments and voices can easily be produced each week!

Audio...
A PC with a sound card, or a Power Macintosh is all you need for recording student performances, or for combining live vocals and instruments with MIDI tracks. Audio is an integrated part of all Cubase programs:record and edit your work in exactly the same way as MIDI using the standard Cubase tools

Educational Discount & MultiPacs...
Discount is available for schools and colleges. If you have several computers, Cubasis, Cubase Score and Cubase VST are available in 5 & 10-program MultiPacs

Phone or fax for your FREE demo CD ROM, and a copy of Steinberg's International Education Newsletter

Steinberg

Check out the latest product information on the Internet:http://www.steinberg.net

Arbiter Pro Audio, Wilberforce Road, London NW9 6AX Tel: 0181 207 5050 Fax: 0181 207 4572

File format support includes Microsoft WAV and AVI, RealMedia, Advanced Streaming Format, and Java AU. Dozens of audio effects and processing tools available. Price Code C: SCV.

Soundtrack Keyboard Trainer

Windows MIDI-based interactive trainer aiding note recognition, finger technique and rhythm. DOS, Junior version and Teachers book available. Price code A, B: Starland Distribution.

Super Jam!

8 part realtime auto-accompaniment software. Price code B: Et Cetera.

Twiddly Bits

MIDI recordings of valuable 'twiddly bits' and rhythm patterns recorded by top musicians. Several volumes available. Price code A: Roland.

Vision Windows 2.5

PC version of Opcode Macintosh sequencer. Does not include notation editor. Price Code D: SCV.

Voyetra Sequencer Plus

Well-established DOS-based sequencer with support for all major MIDI interfaces and sound cards. In Junior (64 track), Classic (500 track) and Gold (3000 track) options. Price code A, B, C: Arbiter Pro Audio.

Xpose

Visual sampler from Steinberg. Use with Quicktime movies and assign frames and sequences to MIDI keys. Visual effects can be added. Data can be used with Cubase sequencers to synchronize sound and image. Price Code D: Arbiter Pro Audio.

Multimedia

The listing below represents a selection from some two hundred and fifty CD-ROMs currently available. In addition to subject-related CD-ROMs there are extensive collections of CDs and CD-ROMs available that contain collections of ambient sounds, sound effects, vintage synthesisers and exotic instruments which are an invaluable addition to using a sampler or sampling soundcard. At present two companies respectively have the largest catalogues of subject-related and sampled sound CDs and CD-ROMs:

Education Interactive

Jordan House, Old Milton Green, New Milton, Hants, BH25 6QJ *Tel*: 01425 621218.

East-West (UK)

Suite 1 A, 25 Meeting House Lane, Brighton, East Sussex BN1 1 HB. *Tel:* 01273 736773

Multimedia - CD-ROMs for IBM-PCs and Archimedes RISC PCs

Playing CD-ROMs written for IBM-PCs on Archimedes RISC PCs is dependent on having an Aleph One PC card or similar and suitable soundcard emulation or connections to a PC soundcard.

A Question of Music

Interactive music quiz. Includes 5000 multi-choice spanning pop and classical music. Price code A: Music Sales.

Atticca Guide to Classical Music

4 hours of music from 200 classical pieces plus information on 350 classical works. Includes glossary of musical terms. Price code A: AVP.

Beethoven's 5th

Features each movement, orchestral instruments and life of the composer. Price code A: Research Machines.

Chart Toppers

3 volume set each containing around 25 songs arranged for GM, GS and Soundblaster AWE 32 formats. Price Code A: Music Sales.

Childrens Songs of the World

15 songs, lyrics and illustrations. Suitable for Key stage 1 and 2. Price code A: Education Interactive.

Composer's Toolkit

400 instruments sampled including a 6MB Yamaha Bay Grand, Fairlight stacks, most acoustic instruments, drum kits. Price code B: Et Cetera.

Corel CD Powerpak

Multimedia software utilities for CD-ROM. Price code B: Et Cetera.
Creative Essentials: series of 30 sound sample collections from Time and Space. Each disk features between 200 and 400 samples in 3 formats, audio, .WAV and .AIFF. Price Code A (each): Dawsons.

Encyclopaedia of Sound I & II

Collection of 500 sound files in 8 and 16-bit .WAV format. Basic sound effects to royalty free musical excerpts. Price code A: Et Cetera.

First Class Music

6 CD set of structured music activities conforming to Scottish 5 to 14 guidelines and English National Curriculum Key Stages 1 to 3. Price code D: Education Interactive.

Grooves

90 music tracks designed to be used and useful in all forms of Multimedia presentations. Price code A: Research Machines.

Hard Day's Night

See and hear The Beatles 90 minute movie, complete and uncut. With full script and essays about the film. Price code A: Et Cetera.

History of Blues

Follows the development of blues from field hollers and chants of American Slaves to 'rhythm and blues' and 'rock and roll'. Includes examples of Blind Lemon Jefferson, B.B. King. Price Code B: AVP

History of Jazz

Tracing the jazz sound from different cities in the USA from 1900s to present day. Includes music by Louis Armstrong, Duke Ellington, Benny Goodman. Price Code B: AVP.

History of Music Part 1 & 2

An interactive exploration covering most musical styles from the renaissance to the present day. Part 1 - Origins to Classical, Part 2 Romanticism into the 1990s. Lab Pack (5) available. Price code B (each): AVP.

Hutchinson Encyclopedia of Music

CD-ROM edition of the New Everyman Dictionary of Music. Price code B: AVP.

Learn to Play Guitar

Beginner to intermediate rock, heavy metal, R&B and country styles. Price code B: Et Cetera.

Let's Play Keyboard

In three volumes, Starter, Progress and Master.

Includes book and MIDIfiles on CD-ROM. Price Code A: Music Sales.

Lives of Great Composers

Acorn and PC with site licence. Composers featured are: Bach, Mozart, Haydn, Beethoven, Chopin, Brahms, Berlioz, Tchaikovsky, Verdi. Price Code B: AVP

Maestro Series 1

Contains clips from films, animations and adverts plus over half an hour's specially composed music. Developed out of the Royal Liverpool Philharmonic's Music and the Moving Image 1996 Schools Concerts. Key Stage 2 and 3. Price Code A: AVP.

Microsoft Multimedia Beethoven

The Ninth Symphony. Learn about Beethoven's world and follow the score whilst listening to the music recorded by the Vienna Philharmonic. Price code A: Research Machines.

Microsoft Multimedia Mozart

An exploration of Mozart's life and music featuring The Dissonance Quartet. Price code A: Research Machines.

Microsoft Multimedia Schubert

The Trout Quintet illustrated in sound and vision. Price Code A: Research Machines.

Microsoft Multimedia Stravinsky

Explores The Rite of Spring with text, score and images. Price code A: Research Machines.

Music Maker

Innovative drum and keyboard one key play along interactive disk introducing music notation. Version available with piano keyboard overlay for computer keyboard. Price Code A: Music Sales.

Swan Lake

Using the Tchaikovsky ballet as a starting point this CD-ROM provides a backdrop to learning basic music skills including playing the recorder. Key Stage 2/3. Price code A: AVP.

Tchaikovsky's 1812 Overture

An in-depth study of the overture, presentation of orchestral instruments and the life of the composer. Price code A: Research Machines.

Tekknotron

Techno track creator and arranger. Includes sequencer. All controller for QWERTY keyboard. No external MIDI instrument required. Price Code A: Music Sales.

85

The Great Green Mouse Disaster
For Key Stage 1 and 2. Disguised as a game this is an entertaining but instructive music activity disk from MacMillan. Price Code A: Education Interactive.

The Leading Edge
Drum loops, analogue synth patches, natural and synthesized effects. Price code B: Et Cetera.

The Orchestra Guided by Simon Rattle
Featuring the CBSO, a guided tour around the instruments and sections of the orchestra. Price Code A: Education Interactive.

Ultimate Computer Songbook
Interactive disk requiring external MIDI keyboard or controller. 3 titles: The Beatles, Classic Pop 1 & 2. 8 songs on each disk. Price Code A: Music Sales.

World Beat
40 different music style shown on video, info on 150 styles, music notations, detail from the World Music Encyclopaedia, discography from the All Music Guide. Price Code B: Et Cetera.

Multimedia - CD-ROMs and MIDIfile collections for Macintosh

A Question of Music
Interactive music quiz. Includes 5000 multi-choice spanning pop and classical music. Price code A: Music Sales.

Beethoven
String Quartet No.14. Price code B: Holdens

Chart Toppers
3 volume set each containing around 25 songs arranged for GM, GS and Soundblaster AWE 32 formats. Price Code A: Music Sales.

Childrens Songs of the World
15 songs, lyrics and illustrations. Suitable for Key stage 1 and 2. Price code A: Education Interactive.

Dvorak's New World Symphony
Price code A: Holdens.

First Class Music
6 CD set of structured music activities conforming to Scottish 5 to 14 guidelines and English National Curriculum Key Stages 1 to 3. Price code D: Education Interactive.

History of Blues
Follows blues from the field holler and chants of American slaves to the birth of 'rock and roll'. Music examples from Blind Lemon Jefferson, Muddy Waters, B.B. King. Price Code B: AVP.

History of Blues
Follows the development of blues from field hollers and chants of American slaves to 'rhythm and blues' and 'rock and roll'. Includes examples of Blind Lemon Jefferson, B.B. King. Price Code B: AVP

History of Jazz
Tracing the jazz sound from different cities in the USA from 1900s to present day. Includes music by Louis Armstrong, Duke Ellington, Benny Goodman. Price Code B: AVP.

History of Jazz
Tracing the jazz sound from different cities in the USA from 1900s to present day. Includes music by Louis Armstrong, Duke Ellington, Benny Goodman. Price Code B: AVP.

History of Music Part 1 & 2
An interactive exploration covering most musical styles from the renaissance to the present day. Part 1 - Origins to Classical, Part 2 Romanticism into the 1990s. Lab Pack (5) available. Price code B (each): AVP.

Jazz Multimedia History
Price code B: Holdens.

Jump
David Bowie's interactive music experience. Price code A: Holdens.

Mozart
The Dissonance Quartet. Price code B: Holdens.

Mozart
The Magic Flute. Price code B. Holdens.

Richard Strauss
Three Tone Poems. Price code A: Holdens.

Schubert
The Trout Quintet. Price code A: Holdens.

Stravinsky
The Rite of Spring. Price code B: Holdens.

The Great Green Mouse Disaster
For Key Stage 1 and 2. Disguised as a game, this is an entertaining but instructive music activity disk from MacMillan. Price Code A: Education Interactive.

The Orchestra
The instruments revealed. Based on Britten's Young Person's Guide to the orchestra. Price code A: Holdens.

Ultimate Computer Songbook
Interactive disk requiring external MIDI keyboard

or controller. 3 titles: The Beatles, Classic Pop 1 & 2. 8 songs on each disk. Price Code A: Music Sales.

Voyager Beethoven
Symphony No 9. Price code B: Holdens.

Multimedia - Soundcards and MIDI daughterboards for IBM-PC and Archimedes RISC PCs.

Most soundcards are sold with a bundle of software, usually a control panel for playing MIDIfiles, CD-ROM tracks, and .WAV files, an entry-level MIDI sequencer and multimedia utilities such as text to voice software.

CardDplus
Professional soundcard with digital and analogue interfaces and full .WAV compatibility. Price Code E: Et Cetera.

Creative Labs Sound Blaster
11 voice FM synth, voice recording, built-in MIDI interface. Price code B: Creative Labs.

Creative Labs Sound Blaster Pro
20 voice FM synth, voice recording, built-in MIDI and CD-ROM interface, sampling up to 44.1 khz. Price code B: Creative Labs.

Creative Labs Sound Blaster 16
16-bit CD quality stereo recording, 20 voice FM synth, voice recording, built-in MIDI and CD-ROM interface, Price code C: Creative Labs.

Creative Labs Sound Blaster 16ASP
16-bit CD quality stereo recording, 20 voice FM synth, voice recording, built-in MIDI and CD-ROM interface, advanced signal processing. WaveBlaster upgrade option. Price code C: Creative Labs.

Creative Labs Sound Blaster AWE32
16-bit CD quality stereo recording, 20 voice FM synth, voice recording, built-in MIDI and 3 format CD-ROM interface, 32 voice GM wavetable synth. Price code C: Creative Labs.

Ensoniq Soundscape 2000
GM wavetable and sampling card. Price code C: Sound Technology.

Roland RAP-10
For GM/GS sound source plus sampling facility at CD quality plus reverb/chorus. Price code C: Roland.

Roland ATW-10
Rap-10 card with Roland Audio Tools. Price code D: Roland.

Roland SCD-10
Sound Canvas daughterboard (GM) includes Do-Re-Mix software. Price code C: Roland.

Roland SCC-1
Sound Canvas 16 part, 24 voice GM/GS soundcard. Price code D: Roland.

SAW Multitrack
Pro quality hard disk recording software, editing and mixing. Needs 16-bit stereo soundcard. Price Code E: Et Cetera.

SAW Utilities
Software 'effects' rack for SAW Multitrack. Needs 16-bit stereo soundcard. Price code C: Et Cetera.

Sound Galaxy NXII
8-bit mono recording and playback, built-in amp, OPL2 FM synth. Panasonic CD-ROM interface. Price code B: SDL.

Sound Galaxy NXPro 16
16-bit stereo, 44.1khz recording and playback, CD-ROM interface, OPL3 FM synth, opt WavePower upgrade. Price code C: SDL.

Steinberg X-DMC
16-bit card with GM wavetable synth. Includes MusicStation software. Price code D: Arbiter Pro Audio.

TBS 2000
16-bit card with 32 voice GM sound set. Good general purpose card for Windows '95. With Pentium PC is bottom of the range simultaneous play and record card. Price code C: Et Cetera.

TripleDAT 3
Digital audio sound card with digital in and out interface. Includes sophisticated hard disk recording and sound editing software for PC. Price code F: Et Cetera.

Turtle Beach Malibu
16-bit 32-voice wavetable Kurzweil synth, CD-ROM interface, simultaneous play and record, Soundblaster compatible. Price code C: Et Cetera.

Turtle Beach Fiji
16-bit wavetable synth and sampler, CD-ROM interface, 16-bit digital audio play and record, optional digital i/o, MPU-401 compatible interface. Price code D: Et Cetera.

Turtle Beach Pinnacle
Kurzweil Synth engine, user expandable sample set, 16-bit digital audio play and record, optional digital i/o. Midi interface. Price code D: Et Cetera.

Turtle Beach Pinnacle Project Studio
Kurzweil Sampler and Synth engine, user expandable sample set, 20-bit digital audio play and record, S/PDIF digital i/o. 48 MIDI channel output. Midi interface. Voyetra Digital Orchestrator software included. Price code E: Et Cetera.

Yamaha SW60XG ISA XG
GM/XG compatible soundcard. 32 note polyphony, DSP effects processing. Includes Cakewalk Express. Price code C: Et Cetera.

Yamaha DB50X
XG format daughterboard. 32-note polyphony, DSP, 4 MBytes of ROM wave memory. Price code C: Et Cetera.

Multimedia - Soundcards and MIDI daughterboards for Archimedes and RISC PCs

16 Bit Minnie Audio Card
For Risc PC only. Plays back digital samples, Acorn Replay sound support. Emulates Archimedes sound system. General MIDI synth and MPC support upgrade available. Price code B: ESP.

DMI 50-S and PowerWAVE 50
2 independent MIDI interfaces, user port and PowerWAVE Ensoniq GM synth, 16-bit sampler. For A3000, A300, A400, A500 & RISC PC) Price code D: ESP

DMI 50 /XG /Sand PowerWAVE 50
2 independent MIDI interfaces, user port and Yamaha XG synth, 16-bit sampler. For A3000, A300, A400, A500 & RISC PC). Price code D: ESP

Irlam 24i16 Multimedia Digitiser
Combines a realtime 24bit video digitiser with a 16-bit audio capture and playback system. Price Code D: Acorn Computers.

Multimedia - DeskTop Music Peripherals

The keyboards listed below are of the MIDI controller type. They do not have their own sounds on board and must be used in conjunction with a soundcard or external MIDI sound module.

Evolution MK161
MIDI keyboard, 61 full-size keys, built-in amplifier and speakers. Price code C: Arbiter Pro Audio.

Fatar CMS 61
5 octave MIDI velocity sensitive keyboard. Price code C: Keyboards in Action.

Fatar Studio 610
5 octave MIDI velocity sensitive keyboard. Price code C: Keyboards in Action.

Kawai MDK61 II
61 key MIDI velocity sensitive keyboard. Price code C: London Music Shop.

Kawai DataCat
37 key MIDI velocity sensitive keyboard. Price code B: London Music Shop.

Roland PC-200 Mk11
49 key MIDI velocity sensitive keyboard. Price code C: Roland.

Roland MA-20
15 watt monitor amp, dual inputs. Price code B (each): Roland.

Roland MA-7
2 X 7w stereo monitor amps (pair). Price code C: Roland.

Publishers to the performing arts

RHINEGOLD PUBLISHING

R·

British & International Music Yearbook
Britain's most comprehensive and accurate directory of the classical music industry
Published each November £23.95

British Performing Arts Yearbook
The guide to performing companies, venues, suppliers, services, festivals, education and support organisations
Published each January £23.95

Music Education Yearbook
A guide for parents, teachers, students and musicians
Published each June £14.00

OTHER PUBLICATONS

The Musician's Handbook
A compendium of advice for the music profession
£14.95 (hardback)

Healthy Practice for Musicians
An expertly written self-help guide covering the whole spectrum of a musician's physical and mental well-being
£16.95 (hardback)

Arts Marketing
The definitive guide to audience-building through effective marketing
£18.95 (hardback)

Analysis Matters
A students' revision guide to the Group 1 London Examinations' Advanced Level Musical History and Analysis Papers for 1998 and 1999
£10.00

Kein Angst Baby
A singer's guide to German operatic auditions in the 1990s
£9.95

The Art of Conducting
A guide to essential skills
£12.95

MAGAZINES

Classical Music
The magazine of the classical music profession
Fortnightly £2.95
Annual UK Subscription £56.00

Music Teacher
Respected and enjoyed by music teachers for more than 85 years
Monthly £2.95
Annual UK Subscription £34.00

The Singer
For amateur and professional singers of every persuasion – from cabaret to grand opera
Bi-monthly £2.40
Annual UK Subscription £14.40

Piano
The magazine for performers and enthusiasts of classical, jazz and blues piano
Bi-monthly £2.40
Annual UK Subscription £14.40

Early Music Today
Britain's brightest early music news magazine
Bi-monthly £2.40
Annual UK Subscription £14.40

Opera Now
The international magazine for opera professionals
Bi-monthly £4.95
Annual UK Subscription £29.70

Music Scholar
A guide to scholarships for young musicians
Published November '97 £3.00

Rhinegold Publishing Limited
241 Shaftesbury Avenue
London WC2H 8EH
Tel 0171 333 1721 Fax 0171 333 1769
E-mail 100546.1126@compuserve.com

Roland CS-30
Computer stereo micro audio monitor, dual input. Price code C: Roland.

Yamaha CBX-K1
37 note MIDI velocity sensitive keyboard. Price code B: Yamah a.

Yamaha CBX-K3
49 note MIDI velocity sensitive keyboard. Price code C: Yamah a.

Yamaha CBX-S3
Single powered monitor, 10 watts. Price code C: Yamaha.

Yamaha YST-M10
Multimedia speaker. Price code B: Yamaha.

Yamaha YST-M5
Multimedia speaker. Price code A: Yamaha.

Yamaha YST-MSW10
Sub woofer. Price code C: Yamaha.

Multimedia - MIDIfile Collections

The MIDIfile is a data file containing synthesizer performance information. It can be read by most sequencers and scorewriters, and played direct from the Multimedia Control Panel of Windows 3.1 on IBM-PCs and from System 7.5 and above via QuickTime on the Macintosh. There are now many hundreds of MIDIfile collections ranging from editions of the major classical repertoire through most popular songs composed over the last 30 years, to instrumental tutors, Associated Board keyboard accompaniments, and collections of ethnic rhythms and patterns. The following represent a selection of those distributed by educational IT specialists and are all in General MIDI format.

Chester's Easiest Piano GM Edition
Carol Barratt's piano course in three volumes. Two formats of MIDIfile available - GM and Roland's ISM. Price Code A (each): Music Sales.

Making the Grade
Series for Clarinet and Flute with piano. Easy popular pieces arranged by Jerry Lanning. Price Code A (each): Music Sales.

Music Sales MIDIfiles
Interactive music packs includes Abba, Beatles, Clapton, Collins, Genesis, Madonna, Sting. RockScore MIDI Editions series has book and MIDIfile disk and includes Beatles, Genesis, Sting, and U2. Price code A: Music Sales.

Oscar Classical MIDI Library
Large collection of standard classical repertoire. Bach to Vivaldi. Price code B: Oscar Music Productions.

Roland Standard MIDIfiles
25 collections for GM/GS instruments ranging from a standard jazz collection to themes from movies and musicals, Sci-fi themes, concepts in reggae. Price code A: Roland.

Roland Tune 1000
59 collections of popular songs including compilations, Michael Jackson, Paul McCartney, Elton John, Frank Sinatra. Price code (each) A: Roland.

Roland Twiddly Bits
7 collections including gate effects, licks and tricks, guitars and LA rhythms. Price code A: Roland.

Starfile Classical MIDIfiles
6 volumes and an appetizer. Includes Mozart (3 collections) Mendelssohn, Romantic Period, 1st Viennese School. Price code A (each): Starland Distribution.

MIDI Instruments

The instruments selected here are confined to stand-alone sound modules, samplers and keyboards that are most commonly used in educational computer workstations.

Akai S-20
Desktop design with easy button controls. Auto-loop facility. 16 part multitimbral. Price Code D: Dawsons.

Casio CTK 501

5 octave, 128 voices, 16 part GM MIDI keyboard. Full size keys. Price code B: Keyboards in Action.

Casio WK1200

73 full size keys, touch sensitive. 24 note polyphony. GM MIDI keyboard with 6 track on-board sequencer. Price Code C: Dawsons.

Kawai X65-D

Multimedia workstation, 28 note polyphony, 16 part multi-timbral. C/w speakers and integral IBM-PC and Mac interface. Price code E: London Music Shop.

Korg X5DR

32 part, 64 voice, GM MIDI keyboard synthesiser, digital effects, integral IBM-PC and Mac interface, Price code D: Dawsons.

Roland E38

5 octave keyboard. GM/GS compatible 64 styles plus card access for 64 more. C/w speakers. Price Code E: Roland.

Roland XP10

5 octave, 28 voice programmable multi-timbral GM/GS synthesiser MIDI keyboard. Includes arpeggiator and interface for PC/Mac. Price code D: Roland.

Roland SC 88

64 note, 32 part sound module with integral IBM-PC and Mac interface. Price code E: Roland. Roland SK-50: 61 key GM/GS multi-timbral MIDI keyboard, built in sounds c/w speakers. Price code E: Roland.

Yamaha MU10

Described as an external music card. Can be hooked up to any computer. Basic General MIDI synth with the XG format. 32 note polyphony, 16 part multitimbral. Price Code C: Et Cetera.

Yamaha MU50

64 note, 32 part sound module with integral IBM-PC and Mac interface. A/D convertor enables unit to be used for external effects. Price code C: Yamaha.

Yamaha PSR330

61 key, fully GM Compatible c/w speakers. Price code C: Yamaha.

Yamaha PSR530

61 key, fully GM Compatible, on-board editable auto-styles, 4 track sequencer, digital effects c/w speakers. Price code D: Yamaha.

Yamaha PSR630

61 key, fully GM Compatible, on-board editable auto-styles, 4 track sequencer, digital effects c/w speakers. In built computer interface, 16 track sequencer and disk drive. Price code D: Yamaha.

Yamaha SU10

Sub £300 stereo sampler. Ideal for beginners. Up to 60 secs sample time, can run from batteries. Price Code D: Yamaha.

Yamaha CS1X

16 part multi-timbral GM 61 note touch sensitive keyboard. Arpeggiator and PC/Mac interface. Price code D: Yamaha

Yamaha AN1X

Analogue 'physical modelling' synthesiser. Rotary controls. Price code E: Yamaha

Special Needs

The devices and software listed here have been designed with use by those with Special Educational Needs. However, many of the items are highly suited to those requiring alternative control systems using MIDI for theatre lighting, sound effects and dance performance.

MIDICreator

A controller that connects a sound source with one or more switches. 14 inputs available linked to 8 preset programs. Can be linked to MIDIGrid. Price code D: Dawsons.

MIDIGesture

A proportional ultrasound switch device that plays sound through MIDICreator by detecting body movement. Price code C: Dawsons.

MIDISensor

Similar to MIDIGesture. Able to detect slightest movement at 150mm. Price code A: Dawsons.

MIDIGrid

A composition and performance system based on movements of the computer's mouse. Adaptable for special needs education. Price code B: Dawsons.

MIDIGrid Professional

As above, but with more advanced features. Price code C: Dawsons.

91

FreeStyle 2.01

Trackless sequencing and songwriting software. Unique colour display and MIDI control system. Ideal for disabled or visually-impaired. PowerPC native. Sense tempo feature. Price code C: Musictrack.

Soundbeam Kit A

Light beam controller for triggering sounds in MIDI synthesisers and samplers. One beam. Price code F: The Soundbeam Project.

Soundbeam Kit B

Light beam controller for triggering sounds in MIDI synthesisers and samplers. Two beams. Price code F: The Soundbeam Project.

Soundbeam Slave Kit

To add an extra beam to existing kit. Price code E: The Soundbeam Project.

Soundbeam Switcher 8

Links Soundbeam to mains controllers for multisensory rooms. Price code D: The Soundbeam Project.

Soundbeam Soundbox

Vibroacoustic resonator. A small, 4 speaker vibro-tactile box. Originally designed for use with Soundbeam by children with hearing impairment, and suitable for Vibroacoustic

Therapy, its surface is low enough for quite small children to be able to crawl on to it - or sit or lie on it - without coming to any harm if they roll off. Wheel chair users can also experience on it the physical vibrations of music. Dimensions 1128 mm (L) x 912 mm (W) x 180 mm (H) Price code E: The Soundbeam Project.

Soundbeam Soundbed

Vibroacoustic resonator. A sturdy, wooden, 6 speaker vibro-tactile bed for adults. Originally designed for use with Soundbeam by those with hearing impairment, it is also suitable for Vibroacoustic Therapy. Dimensions 1980mm (L) x 965mm (W) x 477mm (H to bed surface) + 280mm (to top of guardrail). Price code F: The Soundbeam Project.

Soundbeam Soundchair

A comfortable, wooden, reclining chair, with adjustable back and detachable leg-rest extension. It has 3 pairs of speakers, driving 3 separate, boxed, resonant cavities attached to the back, seat and leg-rest of the chair. Price code F: The Soundbeam Project.

Vistamusic II

Music composition and performance software. Has applications for disabled and the visually impaired: Price code A: Enabling for Music Project

Suppliers

Where an item listed above is available from more than one supplier, the name of the manufacturer or distributor is given - in such cases it may not be possible to order direct from the listed company.

The Advisory Unit
Wheathampstead Education Centre, Butterfield Rd, Wheathampstead, Herts A14 8PY
Tel: 01582 830260

Acorn
Acorn House, Newmarket Rd, Cambridge CB5 8PB
Tel: 01223 725000 *Fax:* 01223 725100

Arbiter Pro Audio
Unit 2, Borehamwood Industrial Park, Rowley La, Borhamwood, Herts, WO6 5PZ
Tel: 0181 207 5050 *Fax:* 0181 207 4572

AVP Computing
School Hill Centre, Chepstow, Monmouthshire NP6 5PH
Tel: 01291 625439

BECTA (British Educational Communications and Technology Agency)
Science Pk, Millburn Hill Road Road, Coventry CV4 7JJ
Tel: 01203 416994 *Fax:* 01203 411418

Cambridge International Software Ltd
7 Free Church Passage, St Ives, Huntingdon, Cambs PE17 4AY
Tel: 04180 467945

Capedia
Harford Centre, Norwich NR4 6DG
Tel: 01603 259900 *Fax:*01603 259444
Email: capedia@paston.co.uk
Range of musical software packages including *Nightingale, Notescan* and *Symbolic Composer.*

Casio Electronics Ltd
Unit 6, 1000 N Circular Road, London NW2 7JD
Tel: 0181 450 9131 *Fax:* 0181 452 6323

CDP
University Gate, Park Row, Bristol BS1 5UB
Tel: 0117 903 1147
Email: tendrich@cix.compulink.co.uk *or*
archer@pact.srf.ac.uk

Chalksoft
PO Box 49, Spalding, Lincolnshire, PE11 1NZ
Tel: 01775 769518 *Fax:* 01775 762618

Clares Micro Supplies
98 Middlewich Rd, Rudheath, Northwich, Cheshire CW9 7DA
Tel: 01606 48511 *Fax:* 01606 48512
Email: sales@clares.demon.co.uk

Composit Software
10 Leasowe Green, Lightmoor, Telford, Shropshire TF4 3BR
Tel : 01952 595436

Creative Labs
PO Box 877, Bristol, Avon BS99 5LA
Tel: 01272 244395

Creative Sounds
PO Box 877, Bristol, Avon BS99 5LA
Tel: 01272 244395

Datamusic
57 Cricketfield Rd, Hackney, London E5 8NR
Tel: 0181 985 5268 also fax

Dawsons MusicLtd
65 Sankey St, Warrington WA1 1SU
Tel: 01925 632591 *Fax::* 01925 417812

The Digital Muse
82 Tachbrook Street, London SW1V 2NB
Tel: 0171-828 9462

Education Interactive
Jordan House, Old Milton Green, New Milton, Hants, BH25 6QJ
Tel: 01425 621218 *Fax:* 01425 621260

Enabling for Music Project
21 Moreton House, Church La, Wolstanton, Newcastle, Staffs ST5 0E1
Tel: 01782 710607 *Fax:* 01782 238205
Email: delgarno@btinternet.com

ESP
21 Beech La, West Hallam, Ilkeston, Derbys DE7 6GP
Tel: 0115 944 4140 *Fax:* 0115 944 4150
Email: sales@exsoftpr.demon.co.uk
Website: www.cybervillage.co.uk/acorn/esp/

Et Cetera
Valley House, 2 Bradwood Ct, St Crispinb Way, Haslingden, Lancs BB4 4PW
Tel: 01706 228039 *Fax:* 01706 222989

Fractal Music
PO Box 1938, Hornsey, London N8 7DZ
Tel: 0181 340 1871

Garland Computing
35 Dean Hill, Plymouth, Devon PL9 9AF
Tel: 01752 40128 7

Holdens Computer Services Ltd
Chapel Lane, Longton, Preston PR4 5EB
Tel: 01772 610100 *Fax:* 01772 610101

Intrinsic Technology
PO Box 907 , London SE27 9NZ
Tel: 0181 761 0178

Key Audio Systems
Unit D, Robjohn's Road, Chelmsford, Essex CM1 3AG
Tel: 01245 344001 *Fax:* 01245 344002
Email: info@key.audio.co.uk

Keyboard Technology Ltd *see* **Resource**

Keyboards Direct
11 Boringdon Mill, Lister Close, Plympton PL7 4BA
Tel: 01752 346200 *Fax:* 01752 347598
Email: kd@starland.co.uk
Website: www.keyboards-direct.com

Keyboards in Action
9 Boringdon Mill, Lister Close, Plympton PL7 4BA
Tel: 01752 347595 *Fax:* 01752 347598
Email: kia@starland.co.uk
Website: www.starland.co.uk/kia

Korg (UK)
9 Newmarket Ct, Kingston, Milton Keynes MK10 0AU
Tel: 01908 857100 *Fax:* 01908 857199

Koch Media Ltd
East St, Farnham, Surrey GU9 7XX
Tel: 01245 714340

LMS Music Supplies
154 Sidwell St, Exeter EX4 6RT
Tel: 01392 428108 *Fax:* 01392 412521
Email: lmsmusic@compuserve.com

London Music Shop *see* **LMS Music Supplies**

Longman Logotron
124 Cambridge Science Park, Milton Rd, Cambridge CB4 4ZS
Tel: 01223 425558 *Fax:* 01223 425349

MCMXCIX *see* **TSC or The Synthesizer Company**

Meridian Software
East House, East Road Industrial Estate, East Road,
London SW19 1AR
Tel: 0181 543 3500

Microdeal
The Old School, Greenfield, Bedford MK45 5DE
Tel: 01525 713671

Millenium Music Software Ltd
172 Derby Rd, Nottingham NG7 1LR
Tel: 0115 955 2200 *Fax:* 0115 952 0876
Email: 100124.1103@compuserve.com
Website: www.millenium-music.co.uk
Mus software for PC and Macintosh. Also
pro-audio.

Music Hot-house
15 Burlington Dr, Beltinge, Herne Bay, kent CT6 6PG
Tel: 01237 375261 also fax
MIDIfile collections for educational use.

Music Sales Ltd
Newmarket Rd, Bury St.Edmunds, Suffolk IP33 3YB
Tel: 01284 702600
Email: music@musicsales.co.uk
Website: www.musicsales.co.uk

Music Software Express
PO Box 222, Plymouth, PL1 1BG
Tel: 0752 339400 *Fax:* 01752 347598
Email: mse@starland.co.uk
Website: www.musicsales.co.uk

MusicTrack
19a High St, Shefford, Beds, SG17 5DD
Tel: 01462 812010 *Fax:* 01462 814010
Email: musictrack@compuserve.com

Newtronic
62b Manor Av, London SE14 1TE
Tel: 0181 691 1087 *Fax:* 0181 691 2284
Email: newtronic@dial.pipex.xom
Website: www.musicians-mct.co.uk/newtronic

Off Planet Media Music Software
172 Derby Rd, Nottingham NG7 1LR
Tel: 0115 953 1131

Oregan
36 Grovesnor Av, Streetly, Sutton Coalfield B74 3PE
Tel: 0121 353 6044 *Fax:* 0171 353 6472

Oscar Music Productions
91 Brick La, London E1 6QN
Tel: 0171 377 6294

Perfect Fourth Software
11 Hempstead La, Potten End, Berkhampstead, Herts
HP4 2QJ
Tel: 01442 866311

Research Machines plc
New Mill House, 183 Milton Close, Abingdon, Oxon OX14 4SE
Tel: 01235 826000 *Fax:* 01235 826999
Email: rmd@rmplc.co.uk

Resource
The Resource Centre, 51 High St, Kegworth, Derby DE71 2DA
Tel: 01509 672222 *Fax:* 01509 672267
Email: info@resourceskt.co.uk

Roland (UK) Ltd
Atlantic Close, Swansea Enterprise Park. Swansea, West
Glamorgan SA7 9FJ
Tel: 01792 702701; 0941 121300 (educ) *Fax:* 01792
799644
Email: 100315.2425@compuserve.com
Website: www.roland.co.uk

SCV
6-24 Southgate Rd, London N1 3JJ
Tel: 0171 923 1892

Sibelius Software Ltd
75 Burleigh St, Cambridge CB1 1DJ
Tel: 01223 302765 *Fax:* 01223 351947
Email: info@sibeliussoftware.com
Website: www.sibelius-software.co.uk

Software Partners
Oaktree House, Station Rd, Claverdon, Warks CV35 8PE
Tel: 01926 842998 *Fax:* 01926 842384
Email: capella@softpart.demon.co.uk
Distribution includes capella mus notation
software, tonica harmony teaching and analysis
software and capella-scan and midiscan mus
scanning software.

Software Technology Ltd
23 Lyme Grove, Romiley, Stockport SK6 4DH
Tel: 0161 355 1980 *Fax:* 0161 355 1981
Email: sales@software-technology.com
Website: www.software-technology.com

Sound Technology
Letchworth Point, Letchworth, Herts SG6 1ND
Tel: 01462 480000 *Fax:* 01462 480800
Website: www.soundtech.co.uk

The Soundbeam Project
463 Earlham Rd, Norwich NR4 7HL
Tel: 01603 507786 *Fax:* 01603 507877
Email: tim@soundbeam.prestel.co.uk

SSEYO Ltd
Weir Bank, Monkey Island La, Berks SL6 2ED
Tel: 01628 629828 *Fax:* 01628 629829

Starland Distribution *see* Keyboards Direct *and* Keyboards in Action
Keyboards Direct is the consumer m/order division of Starland and Keyboards in Action is the educational division.

The Soundbeam Project
463 Earlham Road. Norwich NR4 7HL
Tel: 01603 507786

Studiocare Professional Audio
51-55 Highfield St, Liverpool L3 6AA
Tel: 0151 236 7800 *Fax:* 0151 284 0300
Email: sales@studiocare.demon.co.uk
Website: www.studiocare.co.uk
Audio equipment and associated hardware and software.

Take Control
Institute of Research and Development, University of Birmingham Research Pk, Vincent Dr, Birmingham B15 2SQ
Tel : 0121-415 4155 *Fax:* 0121 415 4156
Email: take-control@compuserve.com

Tobin Music Systems
The Old Malthouse, Knight St, Sawbridgeworth, Herts CM21 9AX
Tel: 01279 726625 *Fax:* 01279 722318
Basic Music Composition for BBC 3.5" and 5" disks.

Tonality Systems
18 Park Av, Thornes, Wakefield, W Yorks WF2 8DS
Tel: 01924 383017

Topologika Software
Waterside House, Falmouth Rd, Penryn, Cornwall TR10 8BE
Tel: 01326 377771 *Fax:* 01326 376755
Email: sales@topolgka.demon.co.uk
Website: www.topolgka.demon.co.uk

TSC or The Synthesizer Company
The CW Building, 1, Amalgamated Dr, West Cross Centre, Great West Rd, Brentford, Middx TW8 9EZ
Tel: 0181 400 9400 *Fax:* 0181 400 1240

Yamaha-Kemble Music (UK) Ltd
Sherbourne Dr, Tilbrook, Milton Keynes MK7 8BL
Tel: 09108 366700

World Wide Web Sites

Increasingly manufacturers, developers and distributors are making use of the World Wide Web to provide an information point for their customers and prospective users. For the teacher and lecturer this should prove an ideal way to find out the latest information on product specification, price, and availability. Regrettably, in researching this new section for the Yearbook it was found that few of the forty plus sites visited were being regularly updated. The small selection below include dedicated product and information sites as well as locations featuring MIDIfile and sample libraries, Internet radio, and shareware music software.

Cheshire Micro Unit
www.u-net.com/cmu/home.htm
Part of University College Chester, the Micro Unit are the longest established training provider for teachers in Music Technology for education.

Clares Micro Supplies
www.stcoll.ac.uk/uk/clares/
Developers and distributors of the Rhapsody software for Acorn Computers.

MusiciansNet
www.musicansnet.co.uk
The gateway to Future Music's web pages giving an overview of each month's magazine features.

Oregan Developments
www.oregan.demon.uk
Developers and distributors of ProSound and MIDIworks software for Acorn Computers.

Research Machines

rmplc.net/rmd/mustech/index..html
Full details of RM's Music Technology catalogue are available here.

Roland

roland.co.uk
Comprehensive website including complete product listing, spec sheets on individual equipment, information of workshops and roadshows.

SCV

www.scvlondon.co.uk
Distributors for Opcode, Sound Forge and other US and European software companies.

Sibelius OPUS Users Group

www.argonet.co.uk/opus
Dedicated and independent support site for all those working with the Sibelius range of music scorewriting products. Includes access to OPUS score library.

Steinberg

www.steinberg-us.com Information for the Cubase user.

Software Technology

www.software-technology.com
Web site devoted to searching for and supplying music software worldwide.

The National Grid for Learning

www.ngfl.gov.uk
Launched in 1998 in prototype format with teachers in 1000 schools and with specially commissioned focus groups. Ultimately the Grid will provide for learners in schools, FE, HE, libraries and lifelong learning.

The Virtual Teachers Centre

vtc.ngfl.gov.uk
During 1998 the prototype for this Centre will be developed by BECTA, its Structure and content based on the vision set out in the Government's consultation document 'Connecting the Learning Society'. Music and IT Resources are found under 'Classroom Resources'. Contains resources for Primary, Secondary and also CD-ROM reviews for KS1-4.

The Soundbeam Project

www.soundbeam.co.uk Latest information on products, courses and developments for the handicapped and those with visual and hearing impairment.

0171 Internet Radio

www.0171.com One of the best live radio sites in the UK. Needs Realtime audio player.

Sonic Arts Network

www.demon.co.uk/sonicart/
A national association of composers, performers, teachers and others interested in the creative uses of technology in the composition and performance of music. It has an active education division, director Paul Wright.

Standard MIDI files on the INTERNET

www.cs.ruu.nl/pub/MIDI/MIRRORS/SMF/search/Classic.html
A large collection of links to web sites carrying libraries of Standard MIDI files. Many of these sites do not provide descriptions of individual files beyond an eight character file name.

Sounds for Samplers or Soundcards

www.users.dircon.co.uk/-helicopt/
Banks of analogue synthesiser sounds and drum loops created by the Helicopter Collective. Use of the Shockwave software is recommended to audition items on this site in real time.

Downloadable Shareware

Sweet Sixteen

home1.swipnet.se/~w-11396/
Atari sequencer.

Anthem V107

www.loop.com/~hharris/
Macintosh sequencer.

Virtual Drummer

www.igs.net/~jonnichols/
Macintosh-based TR-707 style virtual drum machine

The Hit Factory:

www.mygale.org/01/newman/hit-factory/
Multi-module Macintosh software includes sampler, synthesiser (using Apple game-based sound technology), mixer, sequencer and effects.

Jazz 3.0

rokke.grm.hia.no/per/jazz.html
PC sequencer with novel features unusual from a shareware product. Versions available for Windows 3.1, 95 and Linus (the shareware Unix operating system).

Glossary

CD-ROM - a CD format and device for accessing information in text, audio, video and graphics. An essential prerequisite of Multimedia.

daughterboard - an add-on board to a soundcard, usually a GM synthesizer.

digital i/o - a feature found on some soundcards and samplers that enable digital audio recordings to be transfered in digital format (i.e. without loss of quality) to and from a DAT machine, CD or Minidisk player for storage or editing.

Dongle - a small device intended to prevent the use of unauthorised copies of an associated item of commercial software, through needing to be plugged in to the computer for the software to operate.

drum machine - an instrument for producing full drum rhythm parts, offering a range of percussion sounds and the means to enter a score part, usually with the option to repeat and re-order small sections.

GM or General MIDI - an agreed standard specification for multi-timbral instruments. Sequencer music created using one GM instrument will play back correctly on any other GM instrument.

hardware - the physical equipment components of a computer system as distinct from the software (programs and other information).

internal sound device - the computer's inbuilt sound generator. Though of limited sound quality, range and number of voices (typically 3), it offers a valuable and very low-cost introduction to sound creation and composition systems.

Joystick - a hand-held device allowing the control of a computer through continuous hand movements.

Microsoft Windows '95 - An operating system developed for IBM PCs by the Microsoft Corporation. It does away with the need to type instructions from the computer's keyboard by providing pull-down menus, icons, and movable, sizable windows on the screen. All of these may be controlled with the mouse alone.

MIDI - The Musical Instrument Digital Interface. A series of codes which have been agreed upon by musical instrument manufacturers. MIDI works like a language, enabling different devices to `talk' to each other.

Modular - modular design in software is that which enables a program to be configured for specific uses by adding or removing sections (software modules).

Monitor - the television-like screen that displays the picture produced by the computer. Monitors used in education usually have colour capability, and are available in a variety of sizes. The word monitor is also sometimes used to describe a loudspeaker used in a recording studio environment.

Multi-timbral - adjective applied to any MIDI device which is capable of playing more than one type of sound simultaneously.

Sampling - the recording of a short sound, `musical' or not, for replay as a musical instrument sound, either on a `hit', at different pitches under keyboard control, or with even further transformation. `Samplers' are used to give control over any sound, or accurately to reconstruct the sound of an acoustic instrument such as a piano.

Scorewriter - software package which enables the creation of musical scores on the computer screen which may then be printed.

Sensor - a device that can detect the position and movement of part or whole of the users body without being in contact with it, and, for example, translate this into musical sound.

Sequencer - a software or hardware device which enables music to be recorded, edited and replayed. A sequencer does not record actual sounds, but remembers information about notes played, how hard keys are pressed, and so on. Once inside the computer, this information may be processed in a number of ways, just as words may be processed in a word-processor; mistakes may be corrected and improvements made. The sequencer then relays this edited information to a keyboard or sound module for playback.

Software - the programs and other information components of a computer system, as opposed to the hardware .

software synthesis - describes a means of having a synthesiser resident inside the operating software of a computer. Macintosh computers have Quicktime Musical Instruments and Cybersynth. Roland launched their VSC-550W and VS-MT systems in 1997 to utilise the latest Pentium MMX technology. Microsoft's forthcoming operating system Windows 98 is likely to include a built in GS synthesiser in software.

soundcard - device installed inside a computer to support multimedia. Usually contains digital audio recording and playback facilities, a MIDI interface, and a GM MIDI synthesiser. Those supporting games formats have an OS2/3 FM synthesizer.

sound module - a device which can produce sounds in response to MIDI signals from a connected instrument or computer, but which does not itself incorporate a keyboard.

Voice - the fundamental note-playing element in a musical instrument, especially an electronic one. A synthesiser with eight voices can play chords of up to eight notes. The meaning derives from 'musical voice', a single line of notes and rests but, confusingly, it is sometimes used to mean an instrumental sound.

World Music

Since the development of the National Curriculum, the Music syllabus has broadened its content considerably. One of the major growth areas has been that of World Music or Non-Western Music. The following section has been devised this year to help to provide information to music teachers and students who are searching for contacts, activities and resources in the field of World Music and is divided into categories as follows: Organisations and Resource Centres, Performers of World Music, Book and Periodical Publishers, Music Publishers, Retailers and Suppliers, Courses and Training in Higher Education, Summer Schools and Short Courses.

Organisations and Resource Centres

Alice Schulmann Frank Collection *see* **The Horniman Museum** *in* **Museums and Other Collections**

Art Asia
Unit 7, Radcliffe Ct, Radcliffe Rd, Southampton SO17 0PH
Tel: 01703 226212 *also fax*

Helen Askins, admin; Vinod Desai, co-ord. Promotes arts of the Indian sub-continent in the Southern region. Hosts high-quality classical and popular concerts, drama and dance productions. Activities include mus and dance w/shops, demonstrations and performances for schools and colleges, information and advice service and programme of classes in Asian mus and dance.

Asian Music Circuit
Unit F (ground floor), West Point, 33-34 Warple Way, Acton, London W3 0RG
Tel: 0181 742 9911 *Fax:* 0181 749 3948

Kuldeep Jaf, sec; Penny King, mus co-ord. Promotes mus from the Indian sub-continent, SE Asia and the Far East, through concerts, w/shops and demonstrations.

British Forum for Ethnomusicology
Faculty of Music, University of Edinburgh, Alison House, 12 Nicolson Sq, Edinburgh EH8 9DF
Tel: 0131 650 8248 *Fax:* 0131 650 2425
Email: m.trewin@music.ed.ac.uk
Website: www.soas.ac.uk/centres/music/rw4bfe.html

A M Trewin, membership sec. UK National Committee of the International Council for Traditional Music. Publishes journal, newsletter; regular conferences, events, concerts, etc.

Centre for Intercultural Music Arts
Department of Education, Goldsmiths College, Lewisham Way, London SE14

Robert Kwami.

China People Promotions
28 Tonmead Rd, Northampton NN3 8HX
Tel: 01604 412922 *also fax*
Email: ljiang@globalnet.co.uk

Li Jiang, dir; Ket Y-Chiu, admin. Organises Chinese mus, dance, operatic face painting, etc and w/shops for schools, colleges and universities.

Drum Call
84 Bank Side St, Leeds LS8 5AD
Tel: 0113 248 6746

Promotes W African drumming through festivals and w/shops in the UK and France. Summer courses available and free quarterly magazine with listings.

Hampshire Intercultural Resources Centre
Warren Crescent, Southampton SO16 6AY
Tel: 01703 702721

Hilary Bates, intercultural resources offr. Centre provided for all Hampshire schools by Hampshire Inspection and Advisory Service. Offers range of intercultural teaching resources, including LEA-produced materials, books, teaching packs and mus insts. All resources available for loan to support intercultural aspects of the NC and have been chosen specifically to portray positive images of different cultures. Services offered will help schools to meet Framework for Inspection of Schools requirements. Venue for INSET courses.

International Shakuhachi Society
Lorien, Wadhurst, Sussex TN5 6PN
Tel: 01892 782045

Dan E Mayers, president; Clive Bell, sec and treasurer. Provides information on teachers, methods and recordings to devotees of Shakuhachi worldwide. Also provides Shakuhachi insts and bamboo blanks.

International Society for Music Education
International Centre for Research in Music Education,

University of Reading, Bulmershe Ct, Reading RG6 1HY
Tel: 0118 931 8846 *also fax; Fax:* 0118 935 2080
Email: e.smith@reading.ac.uk
Website: www.isme.org

Publishes *International Journal of Music Education* with articles on various aspects of research in world musics in mus education.

The Kodály Centre of London
64 Montpelier Rise, Wembley, Middx HA9 8RQ
Tel: 0181 904 8923 *also fax*
Email: dvinden@tcm.ac.uk

David Vinden, dir.
Musicianship classes in the Kodály method, teaching techniques and methodology for class teachers, inst teachers and singers. 3 levels of training carry Trinity College of Music acreditation. Publications include: Harmonic Foundations, the Modes, rhythm flip cards and flash cards.

Live Music Now!
4 Lower Belgrave St, London SW1W 0LJ
Tel: 0171 730 2205 *Fax:* 0171 730 3641

Virginia Renshaw, dir; Katherine Potter, asst dir.
Founded in 1977 by Yehudi Menuhin, Live Music Now seeks to enable young musicians of the highest calibre to perform for audiences with disabilities and other special needs. In addition to classical Western mus, there is a significant amount of world mus performed, representing the mus of India, China, Korea and folk mus from S America, Africa, Scotland and Ireland.

Music for Change
24 Hospital La, Canterbury, Kent CT1 2PE
Tel: 01227 459 243
Email: music.forchange@virgin.net

Tom Andrews, co-ord.

Charity working with mus from around the world. Organises w/shops in schools geared to fulfilling NC requirements in various subjects including Japanese Taiko drumming, African perc and Indian tabla playing. Also assists in projects overseas, collecting insts for community projects and encouraging local mus practice in Africa, Asia, Latin America and the Caribbean. Publishes free termly information bulletin for schools and community groups in Kent.

School of Scottish Studies
University of Edinburgh, 27 George Sq, Edinburgh EH8 9LD
Tel: 0131 650 3060/4159 *Fax:* 0131 650 4163
Email: scottish.studies@ed.ac.uk
Website: www.pearl.arts.ed.ac.uk

Francesca Hardcastle, librarian; Rhona Talbot, archive asst; Mark Trewin, lecturer in ethnomus. John Levy collection of ethnomusicological recordings (mostly South and East Asian); Peter Cooke collection of African mus and other smaller collections. Archive materials used in support of research and teaching at u/grad and p/grad levels.

The Traditions Library *see* Libraries and Museums

UK-Japan Music Society
27 Heron Close, Great Glen, Leicester LE8 9DZ
Tel: 0116 259 3891 *also fax*

Yorkshire Youth and Music
Dean Clough, Halifax HX3 5AX
Tel: 01422 383130 *Fax:* 01422 321823

Gillian Hall, dir.
Promotes concerts and w/shops for young people; Western and world. World mus concerts aimed at age 4 and above usually take place between Sep and Mar. Performers also lead w/shops in schools to precede concerts.

Performers of World Music

The groups and individuals listed below all work particularly in the area of World Music. Others who may also do some work in this field can be found in the **Performers in Education** section.

Aklowa
Aklowa Centre, Takeley House, Brewer's End, Takeley, Bishop's Stortford, Herts CM22 6QK
Tel: 01279 871062

David Laryea, dir.
Music, art and dance of Africa.

Badejo Arts
Harmood Community Centre, 1 Forge Pl, Ferdinand St, London NW1 8DQ

Tel: 0171 482 4292 *also fax*
Email: badejoarts@badejo.demon.co.uk

Peter Badejo, artistic dir.
Traditional and contemporary African mus and dance. Also annual summer school.

Caliche
Midlands Arts Centre, Cannon Hill Pk, Birmingham B12 9QH
Tel: 0121 446 5440 *Fax:* 0121 446 4372

Carlos Munoz, dir.
W/shops and concerts for schools introducing

mus of the South American Andes with insts such as the gui, mandolin, Andean pipes and other wind, str and perc insts.

The Carnival Collective
Flat 2, 5 Montpelier Rd, Brighton BN1 3JF
Tel: 01273 726793; 01273 419347 *also fax*

Pat Power.
Brazilian-based street mus, mainly samba-style; school w/shops and demonstrations in Brazilian perc. Also carnival arts education.

Cheneour, Paul
87a Queens Rd, E Grinstead, W Sussex RH19 1BG
Tel: 01342 300949 *Fax:* 01342 410846
Email: egsales@egnet.co.uk
Website: www.egnet.co.uk/clients/music/rgm.html

Composer and player of fl, alto fl, bs fl, picc, Arab, Indian, Chinese and Japanese bamboo fl. East-West fusion of musical styles. Also plays as part of flute duo 'Zhar' (fl and tabla). Recordings available and education work.

Chitraleka and Company
GFF, 40 Clarendon Sq, Leamington Spa CV32 5QZ
Tel: 01926 339640; 01827 52076 *Fax:* 01926 330747
Email: gvs@spa-arts.demon.co.uk

Chitraleka Bolar, artistic dir; Gwen Van Spijk, mgr.

Devi, Nilima
Centre for Indian Classical Dance, 48-50 Churchill St, Leicester LE2 1FH
Tel: 0116 255 2862 *Fax:* 0116 285 4472

Nilima Devi, artistic dir.
Live mus, solo and group performances, educational work including lecture demonstrations and w/shops in Indian classical dance. Diploma in Kathak dance available.

Eastwood-Kilvington Duo
40 Thornton Rd, Girton, Cambridge CB3 0NW
Tel: 01223 276763 *Fax:* 01223 277980

Lorraine Eastwood, Chris Kilvington.
Gui duo offering educational concerts including *Music From Around the World.*

Ebony Steelband
Ebony Steelband Trust, Acklam Playcentre, 6 Acklam Rd, London W10 5QZ
Tel: 0181 960 6424 *Fax:* 0181 964 4624

Concert performances and recordings ranging from the Albert Hall to small community nurseries and day-centres. Also appear regularly on TV, radio and at festivals and carnivals. Players range from 12-35 yrs and number between 30 and 100. The jnr band *Ebonique* has c30 players aged 8 and above.

Edwards, Glyn
15 Rosser St, Pontypool, Torfaen NP4 6EA
Tel: 01495 750156

Hands on w/shop for all age ranges using over 70 insts from a private collection.

Kokuma Dance Theatre Company
418-419 The Custard Factory, Gibb St, Digbeth, Birmingham B9 4AA
Tel: 0121 608 7744 *Fax:* 0121 608 7755

Anita Clarke, educ asst.
Education and outreach programme designed to reproduce African and Caribbean dance and music through w/shops, lecture demonstrations, INSET and long-term residencies. Teaching combines mus and dance and incorporates NC keystage targets.

Lockett, Mark
101 Summerfield Cres, Edgbaston, Birmingham B16 0EN
Tel: 0121 454 5922 *also fax*
Email: marklockett@ormuzd.demon.co.uk

Mark Lockett.
Gamelan and Brazilian perc in schools.

Metalworks Gamelan
13 Salegate La, Temple Cowley, Oxford OX4 2HQ
Tel: 01865 770272 *also fax*
Email: jsherbourne@bigfoot.com
Website: www.jags.co.uk/metalworks

Janet Sherbourne, w/shop leader.
Participatory w/shops in mus of Java and Bali, creative composition, mixed media and inst-making projects. Past activities have included work for education authorities, festivals, Classic FM and special needs. Also 8-piece gamelan ens available for concerts and demos. INSET for teachers.

Morley, Stephen
GFF, 11 Lansdowne St, Hove BN3 1FS
Tel: 01273 749561

Teacher of tabla. Also tabla and perc w/shops in primary and secondary schools in the Brighton area.

Peregrine
Grange Rd, St Michaels, Tenterden, Kent TN30 6TJ
Tel: 01580 764258 *also fax*

Priti Paintal, mus dir.
Asian, African and Western mus group. Education performances, festivals and tours.

Perkins, John
The Convent, Old Exeter Rd, Chudleigh, Newton Abbot, Devon TQ13 0DR
Tel: 01626 853387 *Fax:* 01626 854077

Player of the sitar and surbahar (bass sitar) acc on tabla (drums). Past activities have included

TV appearances, w/shops, recitals, recordings and concert and festival appearances.

Samba Wamba
10 The Promenade, Victoria Park, Nottingham NG3 1HB
Tel: 0115 958 2701; 0115 979 0085

Chris Lewis-Jones; Mat Anderson.
Carnival Arts-in-education company who offer w/shops, carnival art, performances, residencies, collaborations and festivals. Education work in schools and the community.

Sherbourne, Janet
13 Salegate La, Temple Cowley, Oxford
Tel: 01865 770272 *also fax*
Email: jsherbourne@bigfoot.com
Website: www.jags.co.uk/metalworks

Performer and composer specialising in gamelan projects (primary, secondary and in-service). Traditional Balinese/Javanese mus and composing for gamelan.

Steele, Jan
Salegate La, Temple Cowley, Oxford OX4 2HQ
Tel: 01865 770272

Composer of Indian light mus and involved with Metalworks Gamelan *see above.*

Traditional Arts Projects (TAPS)
South Hill Park Arts Centre, Bracknell, Berks RG12 7PA
Tel: 01344 302008 *Fax:* 01344 411427
Email: taps@dmac.co.uk

Lucy Wheeler, project admin.
Traditional Arts Development Agency from Southern Arts region, existing to promote and encourage traditional creative skills such as composition, arrangement, improvisation, choreography, songwriting, drama-writing and story-telling as well as to develop the traditional arts as a vehicle for community arts work and education. Projects include: The World Band (interactive concerts and hands-on w/shops for all stages of education); Millan (concerts and m/class w/shops); and Roots Progress (performances and w/shops using structured collective improvisation).

Underwood, Ruth
2 St John's Grove, London N19 5RW
Tel: 0171 272 8500

Schools w/shops for nursery, infant, primary and special schools including *Music Around the World,* musical storytelling, mus and history and composition. Also includes fl and gui concert with Martin Vishnick. Mus of different styles from around the world for children aged 3-11, including those with learning difficulties. Aims to meet NC attainment targets and makes cross-curricular links with all NC subjects.

Book and Periodical Publishers

Ashgate Publishing Ltd
Gower House, Croft Rd, Aldershot, Hants GU11 3HR
Tel: 01252 331551

Publish *World Music in Education* and *Composing the Music of Africa,* ed by Malcolm Floyd. Catalogue available. Orders should be addressed to Bookpoint Ltd, 39 Milton Pk, Abingdon, Oxon OX14 4TD *Tel:* 01235 400400 *Email:* orders@bookpoint.co.uk; enquiries@bookpoint.co.uk.

Cambridge University Press
Edinburgh Building, Shaftesbury Rd, Cambridge CB2 2RU
Tel: 01223 312393

Various titles.

Evans Brothers Ltd
2a Portman Mansions, Chiltern St, London W1M 1LE
Tel: 0171 935 7160 *Fax:* 0171 487 5034

S Pawley, mgr dir; B Jones, international publishing dir; J Hole, UK sales mgr.
The World of Music, available with a CD which has 38 world and classical mus extracts. £12.99 (book only); £24.99 (book and CD).

Folk Roots
Southern Rag Ltd, PO Box 337, London N4 1TW
Tel: 0181 340 9651 *Fax:* 0181 348 5626
Email: froots@froots.demon.co.uk
Website: www.froots.demon.co.uk/

Ian Anderson, ed; Beverly Hill, sales; Gina Jennings, advertising.
Folk Roots magazine. Monthly, £29.60 pa; £59.20 for 2-yr subscription (UK).

Heinemann Educational
Halley Ct, Jordan Hill, Oxford OX2 8EJ
Tel: 01865 311366 *Fax:* 01865 310043

Sue Walton, mus publisher.
Produce series of books with recordings in conjunction with WOMAD, exploring the mus of India, Indonesia and West Africa. All curriculum materials include some world mus examples, eg *Lively Music, Music Matters 14-16* and *New Music Matters 11-14.*

Oxford University Press
Walton St, Oxford OX2 6DP
Tel: 01865 556767 *Fax:* 01865 556646

Oxford Topics in Music series including The Steel Band, Jamaican Music and Indian Music; Teacher Resource Material including European Festivals pack with CD; Education/Trade: Saxon Way West, Corby, Northants NN118 9ES *Tel:* 01536 741519 *Fax:* 01536 746337.

Showcase Publications Ltd
38c The Broadway, London N8 9SU
Tel: 0181 348 2332 *Fax:* 0181 340 3750
Email: www.showcase-music.com

Kay Chestnutt, ed; Tony Tillmanns, sales and mkt.

Showcase International Music Book, published annually in January (£35). Also available on CD-Rom, published annually in March (£49.95).

Sussex Publications Ltd
Microworld House, 23 North Wharf Rd, London W2 1LA
Tel: 0171 262 2178; 0800 174147 *Fax:* 0171 262 1708
Email: microworld@ndirect.co.uk

Audiotapes including *Islands in the Sun, The Story of Reggae and Calypso, Instruments Around the World* and mus listening courses; Performing Arts in China series; videotapes: Music from the East; slide sets including *The Indian World of Arts and Architecture.* Address from summer 1998: Microworld House, 2-6 Foscote Mews, London W9 2HH.

Music Publishers

A & C Black Publishers Ltd
35 Bedford Row, London WC1R 4JH
Tel: 0171 242 0946 *Fax:* 0171 831 8478
Email: publicity@acblack.co.uk

Charlotte Burrows, press mgr.
Books and CDS: Mango Spice, Singing Sack, Listening to Music.

EG Music Ltd
63a Kings Rd, London SW3 4NT
Tel: 0171 730 2162 *Fax:* 0171 730 1330

Chris Kettle, dir; Sam Alder, chmn.

Faber Music Ltd
Sales & Marketing Dept, 3 Queen Sq, London WC1N 3AU
Tel: 0171 833 7931 *Fax:* 0171 278 3817
Email: sales@fabermusic.co.uk
Website: www.fabermusic.co.uk

Folksong Series covering the British Isles and Europe, America, The Caribbean, the Far East, India and Africa for KS1-3. Both English and original texts wherever possible. The majority of the books available with accompanying cassette, rendering them an ideal resource for the non-specialist teacher. Also *Beat It! - African Dances* by Evelyn Glennie and Paul Cameron, an ideal resource for both general and more specialised mus teachers working with beginner perc groups. Contains 16 contrasting w/shops based on 4 African dances. Ideal for Yr 4 and above. Pack provides CD of performances, printed melody lines for the pieces, pno parts with chord symbols for gui, 16 w/shops, assessment guidelines, illustrations and guidance on inst technique and general background. Related w/shop presented by Evelyn Glennie and Paul

Cameron is to be featured in the *Mad About Music* show at the London Arena on 20 Jun 1998. Complimentary tickets available to teachers from Faber Music.

Jewish Music Distribution
The London Jewish Music Centre, Box 2268, Hendon, London NW4 3UW
Tel: 0181 203 8046 *also fax*

Rachel Wetstein, dir; Daniel Tunkel, dir.
Distributors and suppliers of Jewish mus compilations and recordings from around the world.

Musicland Ltd
Beauchamp House, Churcham, Glos GL2 8AA
Tel: 01452 750253 *Fax:* 01452 750585

Educational mus for children.

Saydisc Records
Chipping Manor, Wotton-under-Edge, Glos GL12 7AD
Tel: 01453 845036 *Fax:* 01453 521056

Percussion Around the World resource pack for KS2-3, comprising CD or cassette and wallchart and teacher's notes, various world mus resources.

Schott & Co Ltd
48 Great Marlborough St, London W1V 2BN
Tel: 0171 437 1246 *Fax:* 0800 525567

Wendy Lampa, educ mus ed; J Webb, head of mkt and sales.
Publishes *World Sound Matters,* ed Jonathan Stocks, which is an anthology of mus from around the world and consists of 2 CDs of traditional mus recordings from 35 different countries and explanatory texts.

Retailers and Suppliers

Adaptatrap Percussion
26 Trafalgar St, Brighton BN1 4ED
Tel: 01273 672722

Les Sherwood, proprietor.
World mus insts especially perc; also w/wind and didgeridoos, etc. Clearing house for local tutors and performers of world mus. Educational discount available. M/order by arrangement.

Forwoods
35-37 Palace St, Canterbury, Kent CT1 2DZ
Tel: 0800 072 0354; 01227 464741 *Fax:* 01227 762836

Specialist supplier to independent schools with wide range of books and resources on world mus and other areas. Catalogue available.

Knock on Wood World Music
Unit 131, Glasshouses Mill, Pateley Bridge, Harrogate HG3 5QH
Tel: 01423 712712
Email: kow@globalnet.co.uk
Website: www.netlink.co.uk/users/nettle/kow

Andy Wilson.
Schools and education m/order service for mus insts, books and recordings from around the world, including Smithsonian/folkways video anthologies, World Music Press, etc. Shop available at Arch X Granary Wharf, Leeds LS1 4BR *Tel:* 0113 242 9146; 0113 245 9878 *also fax.*

Music Education Supplies
101 Banstead Rd South, Sutton, Surrey SM2 5LH
Tel: 0181 770 3866 *Fax:* 0181 770 3554

Ray Mason.

M/order perc from around the world, including Africa, India, Chile and Mexico.

Ray Man Eastern Musical Instruments
29 Monmouth St, Covent Garden, London WC2H 9DD
Tel: 0171 240 1776 *Fax:* 0171 240 9689

Large assortment of ethnic insts from all around the world. Catalogue and m/order available.

Recorder and Woodwind Centre
5 Dorset St, London W1N 3FE
Tel: 0171 935 3339

Jane Vickers, rcdr sales specialist.
Sells various ethnic wind insts including low whistles, tin whistles, bamboo fl and didgeridoos.

Soar Valley Music
15 Prince William Rd, Loughborough, Leics LE11 0GU
Tel: 01509 269629 *Fax:* 01509 269206

David Ledsam; Martin Tabraham.
Folk inst (w/wind and perc) wholesaler, also Latin and African perc. Products include African perc (Djembe, doum-doum, bougarabou, talking drum, caxixi, shekere); Middle East perc (dumbek, darrabuka, Azerbadjani def frame drum, sagat finger cymbals, bendir drums); Latin American/Samba band (cuica, repenique, surdo, ganza, tamborim, pandeiro); Celtic insts (low and high whistles, bodhrans, fl, highland and Irish bagpipes, hps); also didgeridoos and ocarinas.

Courses and Training in Higher Education

Badejo Arts
Harmood Community Centre, 1 Forge Pl, Ferdinand St, London NW1 8DQ
Tel: 0171 482 4292 *also fax*
Email: badejoarts@badejo.demon.co.uk

Peter Badejo, artistic dir.
Annual summer school in African People's Dance and Music: Bami Jo.

Bharatiya Vidya Bhavan
School of Indian Music, Dance, Yoga and Languages, Old Church Building, 4a Castletown Rd, London W14 9HQ
Tel: 0171 381 3086

H V S Shastry, academic dir.
Classical Indian mus and dance; group and individual tuition from beginners to advanced;

3-yr diploma and 2-yr post-diploma courses in Bengali mus, Karnatic vocal, Hindustani vocal, harmonium, keyboard and veena, sitar and vn or mridangam and tabla. Tutors may also teach p/grad classes on above topics. Also non-diploma tuition available.

Birmingham Conservatoire
Faculty of the University of Central England in Birmingham, Paradise Pl, Birmingham B3 3HG

Mark Lockett, head of world mus.
U/grad: BMus (Hons) Raga Samgeet (4 yrs), a new specialist degree course on the classical mus of N India, Pakistan and Bangladesh, including aural, historical and theoretical courses and study at Delhi University during 3rd yr. Interim academic

awards (Cert HE, Dip HE and BMus) available for those who do not wish to complete 4 yrs, (first intake Oct 1998). 26 wk course as part of 1st yr BMus (Hons) course, covering Africa, S Europe, Southeast Asia, N and S America; practical (optional) courses in gamelan, W African mus, N Indian classical and Brazilian mus for BMus and MA students. P/grad: MA in Ethnomusicology (1 f/t, 2 p/t); P/grad Diploma in Ethnomusicology (1 f/t, 2 p/t); MPhil and PhD research degrees. Other: Junior recital certificate in Raga Samgeet at the Birmingham Conservatoire Junior School.

Cambridge University
University Music School, West Rd, Cambridge CB3 9DP

Ruth Davis, lecturer in ethnomusicology.
U/grad: Several options within the BA Music (Hons) course, including Music in Middle Eastern societies (1 term), Westernisation and world mus (1 term), Andalusian nubat in Tunisia (2 terms), and for 1998-9, a term's Introduction to ethnomusicology. P/grad: MPhil in Musicology (ethnomusicology option). 1 yr. Normally requires first or second class BA Hons in Music for entry; PhD in Music (ethnomusicology).

City University
Dept of Music, Northampton Sq, London EC1V 0HB

Steve Stanton, acting head of dept.
U/grad: BMus and BSc Hons degree in mus (3 yrs) where students may specialise in ethnomusicology; modules include African mus, Arabic mus, African-American mus studies, European folk mus, Indonesian mus, Jewish mus, improvisation and cognition, intercultural jazz studies, mus traditions of the Far East, S Asian mus studies and mus in oral cultures. P/grad: MA in Ethnomusicology (1 f/t, 2 p/t). Practical facilities and tuition available in central Javanese gamelan, Sundanese gamelan, African drumming and N Indian classical mus.

Dartington College of Arts
Music Dept, Totnes, Devon TQ9 6EJ
Tel: 01803 862224 *Fax:* 01803 863569
Website: www.dartington.ac.uk

Trevor Wiggins, dir of mus; Kevin Thompson, principal.
World mus forms part of the BA Hons mus degree programme. Specialises in a wide range of contemporary musics and offers practical and theoretical electives in world mus. Almost any inst available as a main study and a number of ens including Balinese gamelan, W African drumming, Samba and Choral Singing. Opportunity to spend part of final year abroad.

Durham University
Dept of Music, The Music School, Palace Green, Durham DH1 3RL

Robert Provine, professor of mus.
U/grad: Music of the World (1), survey course; Ethnomusicology (1), discipline of ethnomusicology; Music in Culture and Society (1), selected studies; Music in China (1), survey of Chinese mus; various world mus components in gen u/grad course. P/grad: Taught MA and PhD research courses in ethnomusicology, including courses in discipline of ethnomusicology, area studies, set texts, etc.

King Alfred's University College Winchester
Sparkford Rd, Winchester, Hants SO22 4NR
Tel: 01962 841515 *Fax:* 01962 842280
Email: malcolmf@virgo.wkac.ac.uk

Malcolm Floyd, head of mus; June Boyce-Tillman, reader.
Modules on mus of E Africa and S E Asia. Certificate in Advanced Educational Studies in world musics in education. Short practical courses for teachers and pupils in E African and Thai mus.

Kingston University
School of Music, Kingston Hill, Kingston upon Thames, Surrey KT2 7LB
Tel: 0181 547 7149 *also fax*

Gloria Toplis, course dir.
World mus features in all of the courses and is a major area of research at Kingston. Part-time BA (Hons) Music for instrumental/vocal teachers with world mus component. Wide staff expertise in world mus and mus education.

Leeds College of Music
3 Quarry Hill, Leeds LS2 7PD
Tel: 0113 222 3400/3424/3416 *Fax:* 0113 243 8798
Website: www.netlink.co.uk/users/zappa/clcm/clcm.html

Dharambir Singh, Indian mus course co-ord; Roger Ladds, head of p/t courses.
2-yr foundation course in Indian mus; p/t courses, including afro-caribbean steelband samba w/shop (Brazil and Cuba), Indian insts and vocals, aural and theory, Punjabi folk dance, Indian film mus, folk fiddle and folk mus, jazz orch. Also courses in musicianship and w/shops for teachers taught by professional Indian, jazz and samba musicians.

London University: Goldsmith's College
New Cross, London SE14 6NW
Tel: 0171 919 7640 *Fax:* 0171 919 7644
Email: j.baily@gold.ac.uk

John Baily, reader in ethnomusicology.
U/grad: Ethnomusicology, world mus survey (1). P/grad: MMus in ethnomusicology (1 f/t, 2 p/t), foundation for doctoral research. 5 taught courses

in history, theory of ethnomusicology, special area, current issues and transcription and analysis. Also fieldwork in London. Other: wkly p/grad research seminar in ethnomusicology, Thu 11-1pm.

Morley College
61 Westminster Bridge Rd, London SE1 7HT

Helen Simpson, course leader.
Comprehensive 2 yr (or 1 yr 'fast track') mus Access course aimed at preparing students for u/grad mus studies. World mus taught both as theoretical and practical subject.

Roehampton Institute
Dept of Music, Southlands College, Roehampton La, London SW15
Tel: 0181 392 3432 *Fax:* 0181 392 3435
Email: music@roehampton.ac.uk
Website: www.roehampton.ac.uk/academic/arts+hum/music.html

Damian Day, mus programme convenor.
Courses in Javanese gamelan, mus of sub-Saharan Africa and Caribbean mus. Also modules in fieldwork.

School of Oriental and African Studies
University of London, Thornhaugh St, London WC1H 0XG
Tel: 0171 637 2388 *Fax:* 0171 436 3844
Email: kh@soas.ac.uk
Website: www.ulcc.ac.uk/

Keith Howard, mus studies centre chmn.

Southampton University
Dept of Music, Highfield, Southampton SO17 1BJ

U/grad: Music in a Multicultural World, looking at cross-cultural reception and fusions (non-western musics, non-western art and popular mus). P/grad: An individually negotiated topic, decided by the student and supervisor is one unit available on the modular MA course.

University College of North Wales (Bangor)
Dept of Music, College Rd, Bangor, Gwynedd LL57 2DG
Tel: 01248 382182 *Fax:* 01248 370297

Wyn Thomas, lecturer.
U/grad: Ethnomusicology/Organology (1), introductory course in first yr of degree; Ethnomusicology: Methodology, Music in Ireland and Scotland, Music in Wales, Women in Music or Harps and Harpists (each 1 semester) during 2nd and 3rd yr of course. P/grad: MA courses offered in Ethnomusicology, Music in Celtic Cultures and Music in Wales (each 1 yr), 2:1 Hons degree required for entry; MPhil and PhD research courses available (2-3 yrs), 2:1 Hons degree required for entry.

York University
Dept of Music, York University, York YO1 5DD

Neil Sorrell, snr lecturer in mus.
U/grad: Indian Music, Gamelan mus and Introduction to World Music 'Survey Course' as 4-wk modules with 2 months writing-up time; occasionally courses offered in Japanese and Thai musics. P/grad: MA in Ethnomusicology (1 f/t, 2 p/t), BA normally required for entry; MPhil, DPhil offered in any area of World Music (3-4), MA normally required for entry.

Summer Schools and Short Courses

Dartington College of Arts
Music Dept, Totnes, Devon TQ9 6EJ
Tel: 01803 862224/865988 *Fax:* 01803 863569
Website: www.dartington.ac.uk

Trevor Wiggins, dir of mus; Kevin Thompson, principal.
International summer school offers world mus as part of a 6-wk summer festival on the campus.

Drum Call
84 Bank Side St, Leeds LS8 5AD
Tel: 0113 248 6746

Drum convention in W Yorks, 30 Apr-4 May 1998.

For further details on Drum Call *see* **Organisations and Resource Centres** above.

Royal Festival Hall Gamelan Programme
SBC, Royal Festival Hall, London SE1 8XX
Tel: 0171 921 0848 *Fax:* 0171 401 9756

Robert Welch.
Regular evening classes and short courses for beginners, children and more advanced players. W/shops with teachers' packs also available.

Educational Recordings

The following list of educational learning aids includes recordings of set works for ABRSM exams on cassette and complete packages for use in the classroom.

Academy Rehearsal Tapes
PO Box 2288, Glastonbury BA6 9XJ
Tel: 0181 943 5329 *also fax*

B Snook, educ adviser.
Cassettes featuring accompaniment of exam pieces; also other titles for fl.

Beckmann
Meadow Ct, West St, Ramsey, Isle of Man IM8 1AE
Tel: 01624 816585 *Fax:* 01624 816589

Fiona Helleur, mkt mgr.
Specialist videos in entertainment, sport and leisure. M/order cat available.

Cramer Music
23 Garrick St, London WC2E 9AX
Tel: 0171 240 1612 *Fax:* 0171 240 2639

P J Maxwell, mgr dir.
Music Connections practical mus for primary teachers. *Listening In* a course in listening skills according to GCSE exam criteria. Schools musicals: *Trolls* by Peter Skellern, *A Christmas Soldier* by Stephen Chadwick.

Folktracks Traditions Centre (Library and Archive)
16 Brunswick Sq, Gloucester GL1 1UG
Tel: 01452 415110

P Kennedy, dir.
Audio-cassettes of authentic traditional mus and customs from Britain, Ireland and other countries.

Illman, Michael
47 Barton Rd, Woodbridge, Suffolk IP12 1JH
Tel: 01394 384347

Self-help aural tests: ABRSM gr 1-8; Trinity College of Music gr Initial-8; Diploma enquiries welcome. Specialises in accompaniment tapes. £8 per title (including postage).

Jewish Music Heritage Recordings
PO Box 232, Harrow, Middx HA1 2NN
Tel: 0181 909 2445 *Fax:* 0181 909 1030

Geraldine Auerbach, mgr dir.
Production of significant Jewish sacred and secular mus recordings including tapes for GCSE religious studies.

Karaoke Classics Ltd
PO Box 2288, Glastonbury BA6 9YJ
Tel: 0181 943 5329 *also fax*

B Snook, educ adviser.
Mus books with recorded accompaniment packages and exam rehearsal tapes for fl, ob, cl, bsn, vn and vc.

Kodály Institute of Britain
133 Queen's Gate School, London SW7 5LE
Tel: 0171 823 7371 *Fax:* 0171 584 7691

Mary Skone-Roberts, admin.
Video cassettes of musicianship training at primary and secondary level according to Kodály principles, including *Early Childhood Music Education* and *The Kodály Concept*. 5 musicianship training cassettes at elementary, intermediate and advanced levels; cassette *Music to Sing and Play* vocal and inst mus for jnr and snr schools.

Lees, Christine (Cassettes)
Pear Trees, Baughton La, Lower Strensham, Worcs WR8 9LL
Tel: 01386 750545

Cassettes contain explanation of exercises, examples and answers: ABRSM aural (1-8); dictation (1-15), from basic pitch/rhythm to 2-part and harmony; diploma aurals (1-3). Keyboard Musicianship Tutor Books 1 and 2, each containing 20 planned lessons.

Music Concepts
4 Warberry Rd, Wood Green, London N22 4TQ
Tel: 0181 888 9199 *also fax*

Aural in Practice (book and cassette).

Music Minus One
Forsyth Bros Ltd, 126 Deansgate, Manchester M3 2GR
Tel: 0161 834 3281 *Fax:* 0161 834 0630
Email: forsythmus@aol.com

Ian Taylor, Jean Colter.
Participational recordings for pno, rcdr and all orch insts.

MW Music
PO Box 78, Feltham, Middx TW13 7QW
Tel: 0181 890 2015 *also fax*

Sarah Lyle.
Pocket recordings to aid exam preparation covering performances, accompaniments recorded at various speeds, plus scales and aural.

Pocket Songs

Forsyth Bros Ltd, 126 Deansgate, Manchester M3 2GR
Tel: 0161 834 3281 *Fax:* 0161 834 0630
Email: forsythmus@aol.com

Jean Colter, Ian Taylor.
Sing along tapes; country and western, shows, standards, pop.

Saydisc Records

Chipping Manor, Wotton-under-Edge, Glos GL12 7AD
Tel: 01453 845036 *Fax:* 01453 521056

Listen To This! resource packs, comprising a CD or cassette and book. Packs for KS1-3. *Percussion Around the World* resource pack for KS2-3 comprising CD or cassette, wallchart and teachers' notes. World mus and key periods of British history.

Sound Wise Cassettes

Music Exchange (Manchester) Ltd, Claverton Rd, Wythenshawe, Manchester M23 9ZA
Tel: 0161 946 1234 *Fax:* 0161 946 1195
Email: mail@music-exchange.co.uk
Website: www.music-exchange.co.uk

John O'Brien, education dept.
Aural test cassettes (ABRSM gr 1-8 plus diploma), pno (gr 1-8) and vn mus (gr 1-7).

Sussex Publications Ltd

Microworld House, 23 North Wharf Rd, London W2 1LA
Tel: 0171 262 2178 *Fax:* 0171 262 1708
Email: microworld@ndirect.co.uk
Website: www.ndirect.co.uk/~microworld

Audiotapes: Music Listening Courses series. History of Music series. Performing Arts in China series. Videotapes: Music from the East (India, China, Far East, etc). Address from summer 1998 is: Microworld House, 2-6 Foscote Mews, London W9 2HH *Tel:* 0171 266 2202 *Fax:* 0171 266 2314.

Treasury of the Spoken Word

Drake Educational Associates, St Fagans Rd, Fairwater, Cardiff CF5 3AE
Tel: 01222 560333 *Fax:* 01222 554909

R G Drake, UK sales and mkt mgr.
Audio-cassette series, biographies of the great composers (illustrated with mus) plus other mus titles and four tape/slide programmes in the Welsh National Opera series.

Youngsong Music

53 Thornleigh Rd, Bristol BS7 8PQ
Tel: 0117 924 3960

Chris Adams, publisher.
Primary/middle and secondary/middle musicals: score, script and cassette kits for schools.

Performers in Education

This section is divided as follows: large organisations with active policies of educational projects; smaller groups and ensembles who make a feature of educational work; and solo performers who work on the same basis.

Performers have only been included where educational performances are an important part of their work, and special programmes have been devised for use with children. Groups and individuals who simply give the occasional school concert in a season are not included. Education programmes for people with special needs will be found in the **Music and Disability** section.

Many performers work in a wide range of community settings as well as in educational establishments. An asterisk denotes membership of *Sound Sense*, the representative and consultative body for community music work. It acts as an information exchange and gives advice and training to musicians and community groups. Further information can be obtained from Gloria Hall, administrator, Sound Sense, Riverside House, Rattlesden, Bury St Edmunds, Suffolk IP30 0SF *Tel:* 01449 736287 *Fax:* 01449 737649 *Email:* 100256.30@compuserve.com.

The *PRS Composers in Education Scheme* was established to encourage composition in the classroom (infants to secondary) as well as in community based projects. All kinds of music are considered, but projects must involve PRS composer members. Further information can be obtained from the Manager, Donations and Awards, Performing Right Society, 29-33 Berners St, London W1P 4AA *Tel:* 0171 306 4741.

Organisations

Academy of St Martin in the Fields
Raine House, Raine St, London E1 9RG
Tel: 0171 702 1377 *Fax:* 0171 481 0228

Elise Akseralian, educ co-ord.
The ASMF offers a wide range of projects as part of its commitment to work in schools and the community. Projects spanning from one day to several months are available to people of all ages and abilities. All schemes offer pre-project w/shops for players, teachers and leaders plus the opportunity to work with composers. Some projects also aim to develop ideas across other performing arts.

Arts Council of England
14 Great Peter St, London SW1P 3NQ
Tel: 0171 333 0100

The Arts Council of England is a non-political body which distributes public money at arm's length from government to a wide range of arts organisations and projects. It aims to develop and improve the knowledge, understanding and practice of the arts; increase the accessibility of the arts to the public; advise and co-operate with departments of government, local authorities and other bodies. The Arts Council also identifies and presents the best interests of the arts to government and others. It provides advice to arts organisations in every area of

arts management and conducts regular appraisals of the organisations it funds. It co-ordinates policies on such issues as education and disability, and advises on marketing techniques and press relations. Organisations funded through the Music Department are expected to demonstrate their educational commitment (most now employ education officers, working all year round on a wide range of projects). Nationally-significant educational research and training initiatives are supported from time to time.

BBC Philharmonic *
BBC New Broadcasting House, PO Box 27, Oxford Rd, Manchester M60 1SJ
Tel: 0161 244 4014 *Fax:* 0161 244 4010
Email: mmaris@bbc.co.uk

Martin Maris, educ and community co-ord.
The BBC Philharmonic through its education and community outreach work aims to provide its entire community with an exciting, highly active, accessible resource.
Through its work in schools, colleges, universities, specialised learning centres, prisons, hospitals, rural communities, multi-cultural centres, etc, the BBC Philharmonic aims to support and supplement

the work of teachers, lecturers, carers, nurses and prison officers. Orch members offer w/shops, m/classes, specialised instruction, improvisation sessions, composition-based projects.
Visits to studios, pre-recordings, live relays and outside broadcasts are all possible by prior arrangement. The orch offers approx 30 work experience places per season for mature mus students. Applications by letter and CV.

Bournemouth Sinfonietta and Bournemouth Symphony Orchestra
2 Seldown La, Poole, Dorset BH15 1UF
Tel: 01202 670611

Andrew Burn, educ and community dir; Andrew Baker, mus animateur.
Education is central to Bournemouth Orchestras' work. It covers a wide range of educational activities which centre upon the philosophy of practical involvement, whether it be composition, performing or directed listening tasks. As well as working with a school age range of 3-18, there is also an adult education programme.
Projects can range from day placements of players to seven week long residencies involving the entire orch, supplemented by structured preparatory work.

Britten Sinfonia *
6-8 Hills Rd, Cambridge CB2 1JP
Tel: 01223 300795 *Fax:* 01223 302092

Glyn Evans, educ consultant; Rachel Leach, educ offr.
Britten Sinfonia offers programmes of outreach and education for a wide variety of groups. Creative mus w/shops allow players, associated composers and animateurs the opportunity to work with schools, special schools, youth groups, disability groups and others throughout the year. Also offers extensive family events and concerts, pre-concert talks and coaching.

CBSO-City of Birmingham Symphony Orchestra *
Paradise Pl, Birmingham B3 3RP
Tel: 0121 236 1555

Ann Tennant, educ mgr; Josie Muirhead, educ offr.
The CBSO runs education projects in mainstream schools and special schools. The inspiration for many of these projects is a visit to a concert performance in Symphony Hall. A YES card (Young Persons Entertainments Scheme) from Birmingham Arts Marketing (£5) entitles holders to a 50% discount for all seats in the grand tier of the Symphony Hall.

Community Music East Ltd *
70 King St, Norwich NR3 3HY
Tel: 01603 628367 *Fax:* 01603 767863

CME runs both open and targeted community-based w/shops that are mixed ability and may be style or inst based. CME also works with specific groups including children and adults with physical and sensory disabilities and learning difficulties, the mentally ill, pre-school children, youth, young offenders and young people at risk, prisoners and the unemployed. CME works extensively in schools and has developed effective integration projects involving disabled and non-disabled students. CME runs nationwide training courses for community musicians, youth workers, teachers, community artists, care staff and other professionals in community music techniques.

Contemporary Music Network
Touring Dept, The Arts Council of England, 14 Great Peter St, London SW1P 3NQ
Tel: 0171 973 6504 *Fax:* 0171 973 6590
Email: beverley.crew.ace@artsfb.org.uk

Beverley Crew, admin.
This national touring scheme for high quality contemporary mus projects is run by the Arts Council of England. Some of the tours have associated educational activity.

English National Opera *
The Baylis Programme, The ENO Works, 40 Pitfield St, London N1 6EU
Tel: 0171 739 5808 *Fax:* 0171 729 8929

Steve Moffitt, head of the Baylis Programme; Alice King-Farlow, admin; Kate Cockburn, projects offr.
The Baylis Programme at ENO exists to introduce people of all ages, from all sections of the community, to the enjoyment of opera and to deepen their understanding and appreciation of this art form.
The aim is to stimulate creativity through participation. It runs 2 youth opera groups, Live Wires (age 8-12) and Live Culture (age 12-16), The Works (age 16-25), The Knack (a training course for young singers aged 18+), as well as schools w/shops and residencies, family days and opera-related projects for groups of all ages.

English Sinfonia
1 Wedgwood Ct, Stevenage SG1 4QR
Tel: 01438 350990 *Fax:* 01438 350930
Website: www.stevenage.gov.uk/englishsinfonia

David Bedford, composer in association; Janet Wright, educ offr; Pippa Vaughan, projects and mkt mgr.
Various school projects take place throughout the year involving children composing and performing with the orch.
Additional residencies include youth and adult

w/shops plus free adult educational recitals aimed at those who are not normally able to attend live performances on a regular basis.

English Touring Opera
W121 Westminster Business Sq, Durham St, London SE11 5JH
Tel: 0171 820 1131/1141 (minicom and voice) *Fax:* 0171 735 7008

Paul Reeve, educ mgr; Nicholas Skilbeck, artistic consultant.
ETO offers a wide variety of projects aiming to make opera accessible to as broad a section of the community as possible.
Schools w/shops encourage pupils to explore musical and dramatic themes. INSET training is an integral part of the project. ETO also runs an extensive programme of work for people with disabilities see **Music and Disability**.
There is also an opera summer school for adults and pre-performance talks for the audience at most venues.

Glyndebourne Education, Glyndebourne Touring Opera
Glyndebourne, Lewes, E Sussex BN8 5UU
Tel: 01273 812321 *Fax:* 01273 812783

Katie Tearle, head of educ and community projects; Phillipa Reive, project mgr; Tessa Chisholm, educ co-ord.
Glyndebourne Education organises activities across the community in schools, art centres, adult education centres, prisons and with special needs groups. Projects have been created with primary, secondary, special needs schools and adults. School w/shops include subsidised tickets for performances.
Pre-performance talks and adult w/shops presented during Glyndebourne Festival and on tour. Large-scale community projects in Hastings (1990), Ashford (1993), Peterborough (1995) and Glyndebourne (Feb 1997).

Guildford Philharmonic Orchestra
Millmead House, Millmead, Guildford, Surrey GU2 5BB
Tel: 01483 444666

Clare Lister, mus development officer; Nicola Goold, gen mgr.
School concerts in the Guildford area are a regular feature. All students/children under 18 can come to any concert for only £3. Concerts in association with Surrey Youth Music and Performing Arts. Education projects run with schools in the borough, culminating in a concert.

Hallé Orchestra *
The Bridgewater Hall, Manchester M2 3WS
Tel: 0161 237 7000 *Fax:* 0161 237 7029

Richard Wigley, educ dir.
The orch is seeking to add to its long established programme of family concerts by fostering the full range of the players' interests in a wide variety of outreach projects, with the aim of meeting a broader set of needs in the community than the conventional concert can address.
There are no restrictions on participant groups and w/shop projects are designed around the needs of both the participants and the members of the orchestra. The emphasis of all projects is on participation and creative work and, whenever possible, a project is backed by follow-up work.

London Mozart Players
92 Chatsworth Rd, Croydon CR0 1HB
Tel: 0181 686 1996 *Fax:* 0181 686 2187

Margaret Archibald, educ and community mgr.
The orch has an extensive education and community programme catering for all ages, ranging from pre-school to the elderly and including the disabled and special needs.
The programme includes story-telling with mus for the under fives, inst demonstrations and informal concerts adapted for all ages, creative mus-making, dance and creative writing w/shops, m/classes, chmbr mus coaching, as well as collaborative mus and dance projects for mixed audiences of children and older people.
Children's concerts and a scratch rehearsal for amateurs and students are organised annually in the Fairfield Concert Hall and musicians from the orch present weekly evening classes for adults.

The London Philharmonic
35 Doughty St, London WC1N 2AA
Tel: 0171 546 1600 *Fax:* 0171 546 1601

Maria Smith, educ and youth orch admin.
The London Philharmonic Education Department aims to provide a link between the orch and the community extending beyond the limits of traditional concert-going. Its education programme involves players in youth projects, primary, secondary and special schools.
The Education Department is committed to generating creative environments in response to the specific needs of each group. Projects are devised to address the requirements of the NC in mus (and in cross-curricular work where appropriate).

London Sinfonietta
Clove Building, 4 Maguire St, Butlers Wharf, London SE1 2NQ
Tel: 0171 378 8123 *Fax:* 0171 378 0937

Victoria Dawes, educ offr; Fraser Trainer, educ projects co-ord.
The Sinfonietta, an associate of the Royal Festival Hall, has a well-established education programme and has strong links with LEAs, mus colleges, universities, prisons, adult education

and special needs groups.

Projects involve composers and performers working in schools, colleges, prisons, etc, as part of audience development programmes designed to introduce contemporary mus to as wide a public as possible. In particular, the orch has developed composition projects with schools (many to co-ordinate with GCSE and NC requirements) based on the mus of 20th C composers such as Birtwistle, Turnage, Berio, Reich and Adès.

Projects often begin with practical w/shops for teachers, followed by several visits to the schools, culminating in the pupils performing alongside the London Sinfonietta. Projects can also involve dance, world mus, opera and mus theatre.

The Sinfonietta has also established a programme of training and creative projects with composers and professional musicians abroad, most notably to date in Finland, Norway and Japan.

London Symphony Orchestra *
Discovery Department, Barbican Centre, Barbican, London EC2Y 8DS
Tel: 0171 588 1116 *Fax:* 0171 374 0127
Email: discovery@lso.co.uk
Website: www.lso.co.uk

Karen Irwin, head of educ.
The LSO's education programme, *Discovery*, offers a wide range of projects, concerts and w/shops which open up accessibility to live classical mus and orch repertoire and enable people to work creatively with composers and members of the orch.

Activities include daytime concerts and creative projects for KS2-3 pupils, INSET for specialist and non-specialist teachers, new commissions, days in the Barbican Centre for primary schools, w/shops for nursery and pre-school children, pre-concert events for adult education groups, w/shops and access to open rehearsals for mus students.

The LSO has also produced a c/room mus resource, devised by Richard McNicol, entitled *Music Explorer*. This includes a 90-minute video featuring 12 pieces of mus, a listening guide and a composition project book and is available from the Discovery Department *Tel:* 0171 588 1116.

Lontano
Room 12, 2nd Floor, Toynbee Studios, 28 Commercial St, London E1 6LS
Tel: 0171 247 2950 *Fax:* 0171 247 2956

Lontano has a thriving educational programme which is planned in conjunction with the ensemble's performance work in London and throughout the UK. The ensemble has recently held large-scale schools projects in the London

borough of Islington. Also work in tertiary education with London University and the ensemble is in residence at the King's College mus dept. Lontano is also involved in INSET work and is able to undertake smaller scale w/shops and study days.

Milton Keynes City Orchestra
Acorn House, 369 Midsummer Boulevard, Milton Keynes MK9 3HP
Tel: 01908 692777 *Fax:* 01908 230099

Rod Birtles, gen mgr.
MKCO provides w/shops for schools, both secondary (focusing on GCSE repertoire and composition techniques) and primary (min age 8+); additionally the orch has commissioned a number of works for young performers and professional ensembles. Annual subscription season includes exploratory concerts with comprehensive musical and narrated introduction to a single work, and Sunday afternoon family concerts.

New London Orchestra
4 Lower Belgrave St, London SW1W 0LJ
Tel: 0171 823 5523 *Fax:* 0171 823 6373

Emma Chesters, gen mgr.
The NLO is committed to developing awareness and enjoyment of classical mus for children and adults from all areas of life through participation in a variety of w/shops and projects.

Primary, secondary and special needs school visits offering one-off or a series of hands-on w/shops. Also recitals and demonstrations in hospitals, hospices and sheltered accommodation as well as pre-concert talks before London concerts. Education w/shops and projects tailored to meet the needs of each individual school or organisation.

Northern Sinfonia *
The Sinfonia Centre, 41 Jesmond Vale, Newcastle-upon-Tyne NE2 1PG
Tel: 0191 240 1812 *Fax:* 0191 240 2668

Fiona Lockwood, educ admin.
The Open Sinfonia, Northern Sinfonia's education and outreach programme, provides an opportunity for the public to enjoy and participate in mus. Schools, colleges and groups of people with special needs have been the focus of the programme to date. This work is now extending to provide training for care staff and nursery nurses. Work in schools links with GCSE and NC requirements.

The programme is developing in the areas of higher education and INSET. The successful *Village Halls Tours* offer access to people living in rural areas. Open rehearsals are available to institutions and individuals by prior arrangement. The Young Sinfonia, a youth orch attached to the Sinfonia performs throughout the Northern Arts region.

Opera Factory
9 The Leathermarket, Weston St, London SE1 3ER
Tel: 0171 378 1029 *Fax:* 0171 378 0185

Sandy Balley, Claire Shovelton.
A performing opera company which aims to put the performer at the centre of its work. The extensive education and community programme aims to hand over the resources of the company to as many different groups of people as possible, bringing creative mus theatre projects into schools, prisons, adult education centres, etc. Full-scale operas have been created from scratch and performed in professional venues with groups of young unemployed people, or amateur musicians. W/shop programmes have been specially devised for adults with learning difficulties. Work may or may not be linked to the company repertoire.

Opera Integra
1 Sundew Av, London W12 0RT
Tel: 0181 746 2380

Brian Galloway, mus dir.
Self-funded w/shop.

Opera North *
Grand Theatre, 46 New Briggate, Leeds LS1 6NU
Tel: 0113 243 9999; 0113 244 4874 *Fax:* 0113 244 0418

The educational policy of the company aims at reaching as wide a public as possible through diverse residencies and w/shops for different age ranges and abilities. Much of the work is based on Opera North's current repertory; all of it is creative and has a strong related arts bias.
We do not regard 'education' as synonymous with 'school'. Larger-scale projects are also undertaken in schools or communities throughout northern England and further afield.

Opex 2000 - Opera in Education
87 Sumatra Rd, London NW6 1PT
Tel: 0171 433 1058 *Fax:* 0171 813 5486

C Humphreys, dir.
Specialised educational opera programmes for schools. W/shops linked to the NC and opera concerts for children.

Orchestra of St John's Smith Square
The Clove Building, Maguire St, London SE1 2NQ
Tel: 0171 378 1358 *Fax:* 0171 403 5620

Lucy Heslop, educ and audience development.
Education department offering long and short term projects; multimedia, cross-arts, contemporary mus or classical styles. Composition w/shops, inst

m/classes, orch coaching and performance opportunities nationwide.

The Philharmonia Orchestra *
76 Great Portland St, London W1N 5AL
Tel: 0171 580 9961 *Fax:* 0171 436 5517
Email: philharmonia@philharmonia.co.uk

Judith Robinson, educ mgr.
Works with people of all ages and abilities through a wide range of activities led by Philharmonia musicians and composers. Aims to help participants to compose, perform and increase understanding of mus.
Projects for groups from across the community are designed on an individual basis with an emphasis on participation and creativity. Also 'Music of Today' series presenting contemporary mus in the early evenings. Special ticket offers to schools at Royal Festival Hall.

Royal Festival Hall Music Education *
South Bank Centre, Royal Festival Hall, London SE1 8XX
Tel: 0171 921 0953 *Fax:* 0171 401 9756

Gillian Moore, head of educ.
Various educational projects covering a wide range of mus that corresponds to the current Royal Festival Hall programme. These projects include w/shops, lectures, performance-orientated events, summer school, teachers' courses, information packs, composers' days, special needs and regular gamelan classes and w/shops.

Royal Liverpool Philharmonic Society
Community Education Dept, Philharmonic Hall, Hope St, Liverpool L1 9BP
Tel: 0151 709 2895 *Fax:* 0151 709 0918

Jenny Isaacs, community educ offr; Christine Spriggs, community liaison offr.
The Society creates opportunities for people to participate in, enjoy and understand the arts. This involves creative projects, schools' concerts, 'Sounds Alive' events, community, gospel and youth choirs, artistic collaborations, training and skill building projects, activity-based rehearsal visits. 1998 will see the launch of a major new 3-yr initiative working with young people aged 18-25. This will be a dynamic music-led arts project culminating in 2001.

Royal Opera House
Education Department, Covent Garden, London WC2E 9DD
Tel: 0171 240 1200 *Fax:* 0171 212 9441

Darryl Jaffray, head of educ (ballet); Pauline Tambling, head of educ (opera).
The education department of the ROH encompasses both opera and ballet. The comprehensive programme of activities includes schools matinee performances, supported by

introductory teachers' study days and free teaching packs.

There is a programme of introductory lecture-demonstrations, a variety of courses for students and teachers, and a range of printed material including a free newsletter for teachers. In addition, large-scale creative projects in schools are organised.

Royal Philharmonic Orchestra
16 Clerkenwell Green, London EC1R 0DP
Tel: 0171 608 2381 *Fax:* 0171 608 1226

Judith Webster, head of educ.
The RPO organises a nationwide range of education projects including *Orchestra Now!* projects with youth orchs, creative mus w/shops, m/classes and community concerts.
Projects are organised in collaboration with participants and are tailor-made to suit their requirements wherever possible. Special ticket offers are made to schools in greater London, and group discounts and travel subsidies are offered for concerts in London.

Royal Scottish National Orchestra
73 Claremont St, Glasgow G3 7JB
Tel: 0141 226 3868 *Fax:* 0141 221 4317

Lyn Underwood, acting educ admin.
The RSNO education programme is committed to developing an extensive range of educational activities throughout Scotland involving primary, secondary and special schools, universities and mus colleges.
Activities include w/shops in creative mus-making and perc skills, teacher in-service support, m/classes and cross-arts projects. They welcome the opportunity to discuss specific project requirements from educationalists who have an interest in working with professional musicians.

Sadler's Wells
Community and Education Dept, White Lion Centre, White Lion St, London N1 9PW
Tel: 0171 278 1615 *Fax:* 0171 713 6215

Sheryl Aitcheson, community and educ mgr.
Arranges talks, w/shops, m/classes and outreach programmes with educational, schools and community groups. Co-ordinates the Lilian Bayh's Youth Dance Company, the Over 60s Club and the Over 60s Performance Group.

Scottish Chamber Orchestra *
4 Royal Terrace, Edinburgh EH7 5AB
Tel: 0131 557 6802 *Fax:* 0131 557 6933

Stephen Page, development dir; Fiona Vacher, educ development offr.
The orchestra has a development department committed to running an extensive programme of work in the community and in conjunction with the formal education sector in addition to universities and mus colleges. Projects have taken place in Eire, England, Germany, Japan and Scotland.
Its programme is varied and it welcomes approaches from educationalists, artists and possible collaborating organisations to discuss and plan future events, especially when there is the opportunity to link with other art forms.

Scottish Opera for All
39 Elmbank Cres, Glasgow G2 4PT
Tel: 0141 248 4567
Email: 101776.3172@compuserve.com
Website: www.arts.gla.ac.uk/tfts/scotop/scotop.html

Jane Davidson, project dir.
Company includes specialists in mus, dance, drama, visual arts. W/shops for children of all ages and adults on a wide variety of themes and topics.

Sinfonia 21
Office Unit 2, Free Trade Wharf, 350 The Highway, London E1 9HU
Tel: 0171 780 9434 *Fax:* 0171 780 9379

Tabby Bowers-Broadbent, educ mgr.
This highly-regarded orch has an established education and community programme. They offer a wide range of innovative projects to all members of the community from schools to senior citizens.
Current areas of work include secondary and primary schools, youth centres, festivals, hospitals, hospices and day-centre concerts, Voiceworks children's choir, INSET and support for teachers.

Society for the Promotion of New Music (SPNM)
Francis House, Francis St, London SW1P 1DE
Tel: 0171 828 9696 *Fax:* 0171 931 9928
Email: spnm@spnm.org.uk

Sarah Gibbon, educ offr; Katy Bignold, educ offr.
SPNM is a unique organisation dedicated to performing new works by composers right at the beginning of their careers. Education work includes courses for A-level pupils and teachers, education forums, training initiatives for composers, projects, w/shops and schemes.

Sound Sense - The National Community Music Association
Riverside House, Rattlesden, Bury St Edmunds, Suffolk IP30 0SF
Tel: 01449 736287 *Fax:* 01449 737649
Email: 100256.30@compuserve.com
Website: ourworld.compuserve.com/homepages/soundsense

Kathryn Deane, dir; Gloria Hall, admin.
Sound Sense was formed in recognition of the growing role of community mus and is concerned

with participatory mus-making.
The organisation acts as a membership and information exchange network and offers support, advice and training to community musicians and groups. Its membership is wide-ranging, including mus educators at all levels: therapists; students; individuals working in schools, prisons, hospitals and community centres; outreach programmes of festivals, orchs and opera companies; mus and recording studio co-operatives.

Wigmore Hall
36 Wigmore St, London W1H 0BP
Tel: 0171 486 1907 *Fax:* 0171 224 3800

Ruth Goldstein, educ offr.
A broad range of educational opportunities on offer to all members of the community based round the Wigmore Hall concert programme.
Events include lectures, INSET days, composers' w/shops and competitions, m/classes, schools' projects, summer schemes and family days, various ticket offer schemes, open rehearsal and educational concerts.

Yorkshire Youth and Music *
Dean Clough, Halifax HX3 5AX
Tel: 01422 383130 *Fax:* 01422 321823

Gillian Hall, dir; Sylvia Garvin, admin; Christina Butler, development offr.
Presents opportunities for young people to become involved in music related activities. Public events such as *Family Funday Concerts* aimed at age 3 and over, plus a range of w/shops in schools and youth centres for age 10-21.

Young Persons Concert Foundation
95 Wellington Rd, Enfield, Middx EN1 2PW
Tel: 0181 360 7390; 01923 859388 *Fax:* 0181 364 0185
Website: www.webcasting.com/stamps/found.htm

William Starling, artistic dir; Sally Needleman, special projects co-ord.
The foundation presents orch concerts and smaller, sectional (str, w/wind, br or perc) w/shops using young professional players as a series for schools, with items linked by narrator/presenter (often a well-known personality). Aim is to introduce children to live orch mus of all types. Concerts free to schools, where sponsorship is available.

Ensembles

Duos with no name other than the surnames of the performers are shown in square brackets.

A 1 Brass Ensemble
26 Wattleton Rd, Beaconsfield, Bucks HP9 1JD
Tel: 01494 674692 *Fax:* 01494 676428

Educational lecture and recital which includes the history of br, together with a demonstration of ancient and modern insts and mus.

Academia Wind Ensemble
c/o 61 Queen's Dr, London N4 2BG
Tel: 0181 802 5984 *Fax:* 0181 809 7436
Email: ann@paulrodriguezmus.demon.co.uk

W/wind based ens who works closely with students in both performance and w/shop situations. Also performs regularly in concerts and festivals throughout the UK and abroad.

Act of Creation
21 Reading Rd, Woodley, Reading, Berks RG5 3DA
Tel: 0118 969 6035
Email: n.j.c.bannan@reading.ac.uk

Nicholas Bannan.
Act of Creation is a multi-media creative team giving w/shops in mus, dance, video and sound sculpture. It has carried out residencies leading to large-scale musical performances, incorporating Rolf Gehlhaar's innovative musical tool *Soundspace,* at the Worfield and Henley Festivals.

Act of Creation is a flexible team which can comprise composers, singers, instrumentalists, dancers, choreographers, lighting and sound technicians and fireworks, and is available for school and community projects.

Act One Sing Too
7 Allington Ct, Allington St, London SW1E 5ED
Tel: 0171 828 1335

Children are encouraged to participate in these concert w/shops which, while being entertaining, also incorporate the educational concepts of the NC at KS1 and 2. Eileen Diamond performs her own songs, rounds and musical stories, accompanied by Stephen Clark on the pno, and the children readily join in with catchy choruses, actions and perc insts. Stephen also plays and demonstrates how the trb works in an entertaining and informative way. Duration to suit individual requirements. Additionally, a whole mus day can be arranged with a morning w/shop followed by a 'World Tour of Song'. Any size audience accommodated and schools may combine.

Actiontrack Performance Co
The David Hall, South Petherton, Somerset TA13 5AA
Tel: 01460 240472 *also fax;* 0385 564092

Actiontrack is a charitable association that works alongside educational organisations and institutions to make mus theatre performances from scratch. This entails groups performing their own material built alongside the company, often involving them in song and lyric writing, improvisation, theatrical techniques as well as the final performance.

Aguado Guitar Duo
c/o 24 Beaumont Pk Rd, Beaumont Pk, Huddersfield, W Yorks HD4 5JS
Tel: 01484 540255

Peter Batchelar.
3 programmes (age range 6-12, 12-16 and GCSE students) introducing gui techniques, history, stories covering gui mus of different centuries and countries. Duration 45-60 mins including question time. Other insts include lute and mandolin.

Alberni String Quartet
35 Musley La, Ware, Herts SG12 7EW
Tel: 01920 469839

Quartet regularly gives m/classes and w/shops for all ages and standards. School concerts are very informal and aimed primarily at age 7-11, using excerpts from entire quartet repertory and folk songs; children given opportunity of playing insts themselves. Duration 45 mins.
Composition projects for school children and string players also available. W/end courses for string players held throughout the year in Chichester, Hitchin, Ilminster, Shrewsbury and Wales, with a summer school held at Madingley Hall, Cambridge.

Albion Brass Consort
c/o Karen Durant Management, 298 Nelson Rd, Whitton, Twickenham, Middx TW2 7BW
Tel: 0181 893 3172 *Fax:* 0181 893 8090

Peter Rudeforth, admin.
Br quintet offering a range of educational programmes tailored to individual requirements of young people aged 18 and under. Special package for primary schools. Recitals from 30-60 mins. Wide ranging repertoire from the renaissance to improvised jazz. An entertaining display on insts from the hosepipe to piccolo tpt, natural hn and contrabass tb. Audience participation encouraged. Ens m/classes available.

Albion Ensemble
c/o Stephanie Williams Artists, 12 Central Chambers, Wood St, Stratford Upon Avon CV37 6JQ
Tel: 01789 266272 *Fax:* 01789 266467

Gareth Newman.
Wind quintet offering 4 different programmes for different age ranges between 5 and 15. All programmes 45-60 mins, examine aspects of listening to and making mus on an informal basis with participation. Up to 3 programmes can be presented in a school day. Mus includes standard wind quintet works plus popular arrangements and commissions.

Alibas
Halfpenny Cottage, 18 Greenfield Rd, Pulloxhill, Beds, MK45 5EZ
Tel: 01525 714398 *also fax*
Email: 100704.1557@compuserve.com
Website: www.demon.co.uk/creative-computing/bmn/

Alexandra Bass, fl; Liam Abramson, vc; Nigel Clayton, pno; Aliné Brewer, hp.

[Arnold]
Albertine, Horsham Rd, Handcross, Haywards Heath, W Sussex RH17 6DE
Tel: 01444 400643

Timothy and Helen Arnold give demonstration recitals on pno and/or hp. Children encouraged to 'help' the performers to play, and guided in playing themselves.

Arundo Clarinet Quartet
20 Spencer Gate, St Albans, Herts AL1 4AD
Tel: 01727 839516 *Fax:* 01727 762407

Angela Crispe, admin; Jill Sadler, Joanna Estall, Janet Spotswood, Angela Crispe. Educational seminars, w/shops and concerts in schools (ages 7-12 and 13-18). Also concerts in special schools. Extensive repertoire, varied and accessible (Bach, Mozart, Gershwin, Beatles).

austraLYSIS
23 Westfield Terrace, Longford, Gloucester GL2 9BA
Tel: 01452 22379; 00 612 523 2732 *Fax:* 00 612 527 2139

Roger Dean, dir.
Ensemble, usually of 3-6 players, specialising in the performance of contemporary compositions, improvised mus and jazz. Lysis can offer a comprehensive range of lecture recitals and w/shops on all aspects of 20th C Western mus, tailored to suit needs of institution concerned. Large-scale educational programmes can be arranged; a detailed synopsis of educational ventures is available on request.

[Barritt, Edwards]
1 Pendley Bridge Cottages, Tring Station, Tring, Herts HP23 5QU
Tel: 01442 822732 *also fax*
Email: barritt101765.465@compuserve.uk b

Paul Barritt, Catherine Edwards. Vn and pno duo offering demonstration and recitals for secondary age range. Solo and duo qualities of vn are examined, and balance of sounds. Also discussion on composers and virtuoso players.

119

Bass Metal
55 Heather Rd, Grove Pk, London SE12 0UG
Tel: 0181 857 4152

Leslie Lake.
Unique br quartet comprising 3 trbs and tb (including members of ENO orchestra). Programmes range from Bach to The Beatles, interspersed with inst demos. Age 7+. Duration 30-60 mins as required.

Beaufort Ensemble
32 St Michaels Rd, Sandhurst, Berks GU47 8HE
Tel: 01252 873313 *Fax:* 01252 871517
Email: camarts@dial.pipex.com

An introduction to wind insts and their repertoire. Tailor-made concerts to suit individual schools, ages 7-18. Duration from 30-90 mins. Audience participation encouraged.

[Benson, Philips]
Gothic Cottage, 22 Orchard St, Canterbury, Kent
Tel: 01227 767282

Gerald Benson, Jean Philips. Duo of storyteller and pianist presenting concert series in schools, festivals, music centres and other venues, for children aged 5-10 and parents. Involves both listening and participation for children. Tchaikovsky and modern works, some specially commissioned works by such as Leonard Salzedo, Jim Parker and Alan Ridout.

The Bold Balladiers
23 King Edward's Rd, Ruislip, Middx HA4 7AQ
Tel: 01895 635737

Michael Goldthorpe, artistic dir.
A flexible group of singers and insts featured on BBC radio specialising in Victorian and Edwardian popular repertoire. One-off or on-going projects with lottery funding range from KS2 to VI form level with emphasis on active participation by all pupils. Nationwide coverage.

[Brand, Brown]
Redwings, Linden Chase, Uckfield, E Sussex TN22 1EE
Tel: 01825 760046 *also fax*

Linda Brand, rcdrs and baroque ob, Helena Brown, hpd. School lecture-recitals for all ages. Programmes consist of demonstrations and information about the historical insts, the mus and composers along with relevant musical examples.

Caliche
Midlands Arts Centre, Cannon Hill Park, Birmingham B12 9QH
Tel: 0121 446 5440 *Fax:* 0121 446 4372
Email: caliche@munoz.demon.co.uk

Carlos Muñoz, dir.
Introduces the mus of the South American Andes. Familiar insts such as the gui and the mandolin are joined by the Andean pipes and other wind, string

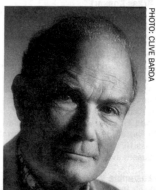

and perc insts. Performing projects based on the Amazon rainforest. W/shops and concerts suitable for all age groups with an emphasis on participation.

Carnival Band
c/o The Marketing Dept, Boosey & Hawkes MP Ltd, The Hyde, Edgware Rd, London NW9 6JN
Tel: 0181 205 3861 *Fax:* 0181 200 3737

Andy Watts, band leader.
Up to five professional musicians giving w/shops and performances to schoolchildren using different insts and styles to encourage improvisation and composition. Special emphasis on world mus and early mus w/shops.

[Carter, Thorby]
c/o Hazard Chase, Richmond House, 16-20 Regent St, Cambridge CB2 1DB
Tel: 01223 312400 *Fax:* 01223 460827
Email: hazard.chase@dial.pipex.com

Ally Smale, artist mgr.
Pamela Thorby, rcdrs; Bill Carter, lute, gui, theorbo. Pamela has a career as a soloist has experience of working with everything from 300 primary school children to mus college students.

City Waites
19 Patshull Rd, London NW5 2JX
Tel: 0171 485 3957 *Fax:* 0171 267 2957

Lucie Skeaping, admin.
Early mus from Middle Ages to Tudors and Stuarts played and sung with over 20 period insts. Participation; hands-on; mus of streets, theatre, tavern, court and countryside. Lively and accessible presentation style. Many school visits, BBC Schools and performances for National Theatre Education. For age 12 and over.

Compose Yourself!
21 Reading Rd, Woodley, Reading, Berks RG5 3DA
Tel: 0118 969 6035
Email: n.j.c.bannan@reading.ac.uk

Nicholas Bannan, organiser.
Partnership devoted to offering opportunities for student composers to work together and hear their works adequately performed and recorded; of particular value to those preparing for GCSE. Day-courses and residential w/shops on offer to students of all ages from primary to adult (including teachers). Studio and live electronics offered. Improvisation and performance w/shops on vocal techniques, computer mus and mus theatre courses also available.

Concerts for Schools
Finchingfield House, The Green, Finchingfield, Essex CM7 4JS
Tel: 01371 810289 *also fax*

Brian Patient, mgr; Lorraine Patient, artistic dir.
School-based educational concerts of excerpts from Gilbert and Sullivan operas performed by professional opera singers together with pupils. Also w/shops.

Courtlye Musick
38 Downs Park Av, Eling, Southampton, Hants
Tel: 01703 860327

Anita Felton.
Informal concerts for schools performed in period costume, using a large number of medieval and renaissance insts which introduce and demonstrate the history and social use of the insts and mus. Includes a question and answer session and the opportunity to learn some 16th C dance. Programmes to suit all age groups. Duration 45-60 mins.

Dragonsfire
9 Hillside Rd, Ashtead, Surrey KT21 1RZ
Tel: 01372 277703 *Fax:* 01372 278406

Nigel Perona-Wright, dir.
Vocal and multi-inst quartet offer specially tailored children's programmes using over 50 medieval, folk, ethnic and orch insts, in period costume when relevant.

Duo Basiliensis
58 Redhill Drive, Brighton BN1 5FL
Tel: 01273 552548 *also fax*

Marianne Mezger and Paul Simmonds offer informal concerts, demonstrations and lecture recitals on the rcdr family and hpd/clvd, illustrating historical events and colourful personages in the musical past. Language medium English or German.

Eastwood-Kilvington Duo
40 Thornton Rd, Girton, Cambridge CB3 0NW
Tel: 01223 276763 *Fax:* 01223 277980

Lorraine Eastwood and Chris Kilvington. Gui duo offering 1 hr education concert for children of all ages. Programmes entitled *Music From Around The World* and *Music of 5 Centuries* include performance, participation, gui history and technique.

Ebony Quartet
Redwings, Linden Chase, Uckfield, E Sussex TN22 1EE
Tel: 01825 760046 *also fax*

Philip Turbett, admin.
Four musicians playing combinations of cl, sax, fl, bsn with experience of school and community work from the *Live Music Now!* scheme.
They offer lecture recitals suitable for age 8-18, introducing w/wind insts with pieces ranging from

Thomas Morley to Benny Goodman including commissions from leading British composers.

Edinburgh Quartet
119 Craigleith Rd, Edinburgh EH4 2EH
Tel: 0131 332 8691 *Fax:* 0131 332 5084

Kenneth R Main, admin.
Str quartet offering schools concerts for children aged 5-18, striking a balance between entertainment and education.
Programmes individually tailored to schools and children concerned, with preference for performing to the whole school at once. Mus drawn from full quartet repertory, plus arrangements.

Endellion String Quartet
c/o Hazard Chase, Richmond House, 16-20 Regent St, Cambridge CB2 1DB
Tel: 01223 312400 *Fax:* 01223 460827
Email: hazard.chase@dial.pipex.com

Rachel Brasier, artist mgr.
Andrew Watkinson, Ralph de Souza, vn; Garfield Jackson, va; David Waterman, vc. Quartet offers informal concerts, m/classes, demonstrations and w/shops for all ages. Duration 45-60 mins.

Endymion Ensemble
55 Murchison Rd, London E10 6NA
Tel: 0181 556 2820 *also fax*

Carol Butler, admin.
Endymion offer a wide range of education and community work. Projects include composition, performance, m/classes and tutoring aimed at young people (including GCSE and pre-GCSE work) and amateurs.
The ensemble is well-known for educational residencies involving school and community w/shops, demonstration concerts, evening performances, etc. Repertoire extends from 18th C to the present day.

English Brass Ensemble
19 Exeter House, Putney Heath, London, SW15 3SU
Tel: 0181 788 9613 *Fax:* 0181 780 1768

Paul Archibald, dir.
W/shops and m/classes for children aged 18 and under (adult education programmes also offered) with comprehensive repertoire from renaissance to present day, and emphasis on contemporary repertoire and techniques. Members of ens provide tuition in all aspects of br chmbr mus performing from trio to large symphonic groups and br bands.

English Piano Trio
Victoria House, The Green, Sarratt, Rickmansworth, Herts WD3 6AY
Tel: 01923 265066 *also fax*

Timothy Ravenscroft, pno; Jane Faulkner, vn; Justin Pearson, vc. The English Piano Trio gives informal concerts for ages 5 to late teens. Repertoire ranges from Haydn to present day. Mus is interspersed with talking about different styles of writing for pno trio. Audience participation is encouraged and the emphasis is on learning and having fun.

Ensemble 32
32 Alexandra Rd, Norwich, Norfolk NR2 3EB
Tel: 01603 618575 *also fax*

Nigel Cliffe, artistic dir.
Vocal and pno ensemble offering programmes of mus and poetry. Programmes include *Now, what is love?* and *Christmas Collection, Introductions to Lieder and 20th C British Song*, and *Schubert: Such a Melodic Gift* which traces his development as a song writer.

Eos
Broomhill Trust, David Salomons Estate, Broomhill Rd, Southborough, Tunbridge Wells, Kent TN3 0TG

Charles Hazlewood, mus dir; Philip Dukes, leader; Mark Dornford-May, producer.
Flexible from between 6 to 40 young players, dedicated to making classical mus more accessible to a wider audience, especially young people.
Visual media often used, including lighting, sculpture, projection and costume design together with mus (often newly commissioned) of the highest quality.

Gamelan Sekar Petak
Music Dept, University of York, York YO1 5DD
Tel: 01904 432438 *Fax:* 01904 432450
Email: nfis1@york.ac.uk

Neil Sorrell, dir.
Concerts using a Javanese gamelan playing both traditional Javanese mus and modern Western works. W/shops and discussions aim to promote a wider understanding and appreciation of classical Javanese mus and insts.

Gemini
137 Upland Rd, East Dulwich, London SE22 0DF
Tel: 0181 693 4694 *Fax:* 0181 693 4426

Ian Mitchell, dir.
Flexible sized ensemble (usually up to 4 in w/shop) aiming to increase awareness of the possibilities and fun of working with mus, and to break down audience/performer barriers. W/shops with children, students of any age and background (primary, GCSE, A-level, university), and all involved in education. Experienced in leading courses for teachers. Content includes exploring aspects of mus through games, exercises, discussion and other art forms with creation leading to performance, frequently in Gemini concerts. Single w/shops available, longer term residencies ideal.

Gould Piano Trio
c/o Hazard Chase, Richmond House, 16-20 Regent St,
Cambridge CB2 1DB
Tel: 01223 312400 *Fax:* 01223 460827
Email: hazard.chase@dial.pipex.com

Ally Smale, artist mgr.
Following the success of their education projects
built around a new commission by British
composer Judith Bingham, the Gould Trio offer
m/classes or w/shops linked to recitals for
school and university/college students.

Grand Union Orchestra
14 Clerkenwell Green, London EC1R 0DP
Tel: 0171 251 2100 *Fax:* 0171 250 3009

Catherine Mummery, admin.
25 musicians from all over the world, reflecting the
diversity of cultures, musical practice, inst and vocal
expertise now resident in the UK. W/shops are
offered in which a great deal of singing and perc
work takes place. The skills of listening, responding
and playing by ear are encouraged.
The group devises projects suitable for a wide range
of ages and abilities, and for a diversity of school and
community sessions, one-off courses, longer courses
and residencies, or large scale community projects
leading to performance. Education pack and
teachers' notes available for participants on request.

Jigsaw
40 Beaconsfield Rd, London N15 4SJ
Tel: 0181 802 3575

Jill Sadler, cl, sax; Catherine Riley, pno. Specialising
in educational concerts for schools, w/shops and
inst demos. Catering for children of all ages and
offering plenty of opportunity for child participation.

The Lancing Trio
Albertine, Horsham Rd, Handcross, Haywards Heath, W
Sussex RH17 6DE
Tel: 01444 400643

Str insts and pno; introducing trios to children.

Leeds Wind Trio
27 Airedale Mt, Rodley, Leeds LS13 1JD
Tel: 0113 255 3005

Julia Breakspear.
Trio formed to perform mainly in schools and
other educational establishments. Group works
extensively for Leeds Education Authority, but is
available for bookings elsewhere.

The Lobster Quadrille
6 Arbour Sq, London E1 0SH
Tel: 0171 791 0330 *also fax*

Adey Grummet; Graham Coatman.
Offer a wide range of w/shops and creative
education projects tailored to the needs of almost

any kind of group. The company works in
combined media with special reference to
contemporary repertoire in mus and
mus-theatre.

Locke Brass Consort of London
55 Heather Rd, Grove Park, London SE12 0UG
Tel: 0181 857 4152
Email: llake@fundraising.co.uk
Website: www.fundraising.co.uk/other/lockebrass/index.html

Leslie Lake, mus dir.
Br ens offering combinations from 3-30 players;
usual number for informal lecture recitals is 5.
Musical items (16th C to popular modern tunes)
interspersed with inst demonstrations. Age
preferably 7+; duration 30-60 mins, depending on
age and requirements.

London Brass Virtuosi
74 Erskine Hill, Hampstead Garden Suburb, London
NW11 6HG
Tel: 0181 209 0452 *Fax:* 0181 458 5621

David Honeyball, dir.
Leading br players and teachers provide LEAs,
universities and colleges with courses which may
include schools concerts, m/classes, conducting
and inst m/classes. Emphasis on practical
involvement of children in schools concerts, with
highest standards of teaching for most standards of
br players.
M/classes also held for FE and advanced players,
plus in-service courses for teachers; director holds
conducting m/classes for teachers and students.
Number of tutors involved normally ranges from
3-11 depending on length and complexity of course
or residency; courses often linked to performances
by London Brass Virtuosi through mus festivals and
local arts centres.

London Chamber Ensemble
41 Queen's Gardens, London W2 3AA
Tel: 0171 402 0014 *Fax:* 0171 402 3134

Madeleine Mitchell, artistic dir, vn.
A flexible group of chmbr mus players with
extensive experience of educational work.
Concerts, w/shops, m/classes and coaching are
offered to schools and older students. Residencies
are possible.
A wide variety of projects are available including
the practical involvement of pupils, programmes
linked to attending concerts, exploring
contemporary mus, mus theatre, informal open
rehearsals and discussions on GCSE linked work, in
addition to programmes including most of the
varied standard repertoire for chmbr ens from 3-12
players (including voice).

London Gabrieli Brass Ensemble
22 Athenaeum Rd, London N20 9AE
Tel: 0181 445 3016 *also fax*

C M Larkin.
Br quintet offering programmes for young people explaining how both br insts and mus work and using examples from Bach to The Beatles, Gabrieli to Garfunkel. Adaptable for different age groups and languages, the programmes demonstrate early and modern insts. Also m/classes for more advanced students.

Lords Brass
Addiscombe, 10 Empress Av, Aldersbrook, Wanstead, London E12 5ES
Tel: 0181 518 8629 *also fax;* 0956 275554

Phillip Lawrence, admin.
10 piece and quintet br ens. Lectures, demonstrations, recitals and educational programmes offered. Insts include piccolo tpt, tpt, flugel, french hn, trb, bass trb, tb and perc. Demonstration tape available.

Los Angeles Guitar Quartet
c/o Hazard Chase, Richmond House, 16-20 Regent St, Cambridge CB2 1DB
Tel: 01223 312400 *Fax:* 01223 460827
Email: hazard.chase@dial.pipex.com

Juliet Allan, artist mgr.
Andrew York, John Dearman, Bill Kanengiser, Scott Tennant. Special schools concerts lasting c 40 mins, demonstrating styles and techniques, with a strong interactive element.

The Magic Cimbalom
20 Cornflower La, Shirley Oaks, Croydon, Surrey CR0 8XJ
Tel: 0181 656 9212 *also fax*
Email: kevin.murphy1@virgin.net

Kevin Murphy.
Educational performances from world mus to contemporary mus; vocal and inst improvisation and composition w/shops; projects which combine mus with theatre, film and dance; a junk band w/shop, Music from Scratch; a range of source materials for teachers. Promotes education events from w/shops to performances which aim to encourage children and adults of all abilities to develop their own creativity through mus and the arts. *See also* The Portable Museum of Exotic Instruments.

A Man, A Woman and a Double Bass
c/o Seaview Music, 28 Mawson Rd, Cambridge CB1 2EA
Tel: 01223 772690 *Fax:* 01223 772828
Email: silvius@dial.pipex.com

Alison Page, artist mgr (Seaview Music).
Versatile, entertaining duo presenting Lowri Blake (voice and vc) and Peter Buckoke (db), with wide experience of performing in schools and colleges. Programmes adjusted to suit age-group (5-teens) using combination of voice, vc and db with variety of classical, cabaret and contemporary mus.

Marini Quartet
46 Station Rd, Shepley, Huddersfield HD8 8DS
Tel: 01484 602401

Simon Mansfield, sec.
This trb quartet offers 3 education projects: *Stone Age to Space Age* a concert tracing the history of mus from man's first sounds to contemporary mus (age 5-14); *Blow by Blow*, a series of w/shops concentrating on the elements of the GCSE exam; and *Everything you wanted to know about the Trombone* a recital and w/shop for br players of any age and standard.

Metalworks Gamelan
13 Salegate La, Temple Cowley, Oxford OX4 2HQ
Tel: 01865 770272 *also fax*
Email: luke@jags.co.uk
Website: www.jags.co.uk/metalworks

Janet Sherbourne, w/shop leader.
Participatory w/shops in music of Java and Bali, creative composition, mixed media and inst-making projects.
15 students per session with 2 w/shop leaders and all insts provided. 8-piece gamelan ens available for concerts and demos. Also INSET for teachers.

Mexicolore
28 Warriner Gardens, London SW11 4EB
Tel: 0171 622 9577 *Fax:* 0171 498 3643

Ian Mursell; Graciela Sanchez.
W/shops and/or performances to introduce children to Mexico today and the world of the Aztecs through mus, dance, drama, artefacts, a special collection of Aztec insts and a/v materials. For all visits a wide range of traditional Mexican insts (wind, str and perc) are used, performed by the team and by children themselves.

The Musical Mystery Tour!
19 Patshull Rd, London NW5 2JX
Tel: 0171 485 3957 *Fax:* 0171 267 2957

Lucie and Roddy Skeaping, dirs.
The history of mus for children aged 5-12, mainly Tudors, over 20 period insts. Lots of participation, stories, slapstick, jokes and songs. A zany journey back in time: caveman 'music', minstrels, join Henry VIII's band, be a dragon and fight a knight on horseback, a 'bum fiddle' and find out why the vn was put in the washing machine! Krumhorns, rebecs, dressing up - over 300 w/shops throughout the UK and Middle East.

Off Stage Brass

15 Cherington Gate, Pinkneys Green, Maidenhead, Berks SL6 6RU
Tel: 01628 781094 *Fax:* 01628 672884

Lecture recitals on the history of br insts for all age groups. M/classes, group tuition, educational projects and evening concerts.

Olivers

c/o Fairhaven, 5 Tunwells La, Great Shelford, Cambridge CB2 5LJ
Tel: 01223 847330 *also fax*
Email: 106417.1721@compuserve.com

Selene Mills, admin.
Mus and history programmes: medieval, renaissance and baroque including musical Tudors, Shakespeare; concert w/shops. Robert and Andrea Oliver play viols, virginal, rebec, psaltery, early fl and obs, rcdrs and voice. Concert 50 mins, w/shop 90 mins. Pupils play own insts and sing pieces from same period. Listening, appraising, participation. Programmes to suit primary and secondary levels.

Orsino Ensemble

Lady Pl, Sutton Courtenay, Abingdon, Oxon OX14 4AW
Tel: 01235 847635
Email: cs@storrs.demon.co.uk

Charlotte Storrs, mgr.
The Orsino Ensemble provides a 'Magic Carpet' concert which tells the story of Jack and his magic carpet ride to far-away lands, in poems and mus. Lively str quartet mus from European classical tradition and narration by a professional actor. The w/shop introduces listening and appraising skills in accordance with NC guidelines for KS1-2. Discussions, demonstrations and audience participation.

Paragon Ensemble Scotland

20 Renfrew St, Glasgow G2 3BW
Tel: 0141 332 9903 *Fax:* 0141 332 9904
Email: paragon.ensemble@glasgow.almac.co.uk

David Davies, artistic dir; Ninian Perry, community educ dir; Alex Rutherford, admin.
A flexible ens undertaking invention and performance w/shops for primary, secondary, community and special needs groups.
Projects are designed to suit the abilities and resources of each group, and participants range from those with no mus experience or expertise to pupils studying Standard and Higher grades and mus students. W/shops are led by instrumentalists from the ensemble, composers, voice specialists, dancers, actors, writers and visual artists depending on the nature of the project. Projects range from half-day w/shops to ten-week residencies.

OFFSTAGE BRASS

Available for: Lecture recitals covering the history of brass instruments. Masterclasses on all brass instruments. Group tuition. All age groups. Inclusive educational project and evening concert option available.

contact: Tim Hawes
Tel: 01628 781094
Fax: 01628 672884

Parlour Quartet

63 Hemstal Rd, London NW6 2AD
Tel: 0171 624 2225 *Fax:* 0171 624 7731

Robert Carpenter Turner.
Victorian and Edwardian songs and ballads performed in period costume. Schools concerts for ages 6-12.

Phoenix

13 Poplar Close, Oversley Green, Alcester, Warwicks B49 6PL
Tel: 01789 762343 *also fax*

Audrey Douglas.
Fl and hp duo. Concerts and w/shops for children, including *Sounds of the Sea, Sounds of Europe, The Seasons, Birds and Beasts, Round and Round the Garden.* NC topics, eg water, the elements, plus KS1-2 and special schools.

The Portable Museum of Exotic Instruments

20 Cornflower La, Shirley Oaks, Croydon, Surrey CR0 8XJ
Tel: 0181 656 9212 *also fax*
Email: kevin.murphy1@virgin.net

Kevin Murphy.
A remarkable collection of ethnic insts from all over the world is brought to life in an exploration of the musical traditions of five continents.
School performances, lecture recitals, w/shops and a starting point for larger projects in which people can participate in improvisation, composition and performance. *See also* The Magic Cimbalom.

Roundelay

Waye House, Alston Cross, Ashburton, Devon TQ13 7ET
Tel: 01364 652114 *also fax*
Email: roundelay@compuserve.com
Website: www.classical_artists.com/roundelay

Roxana Gundry, Oliver Brookes.
Lecture-recitals employing a wide variety of medieval and renaissance insts. Roundelay offers programmes relevant to GCSE classes, and also a 45-min programme for primary schoolchildren.

[Ruhemann, Hand]

Flat 4, 8 Ainger Rd, London NW3 3AR
Tel: 0171 722 6858

Ileana Ruhemann, Richard Hand. Fl and gui duo. Wide range of mus, classical, folk and jazz. Programmes designed for different age groups. Extensive experience with children through the *Live Music Now!* Scheme (1986-8).

Saxology

110 Wantz Rd, Maldon, Essex CM9 5DE
Tel: 01621 852844 *Fax:* 01245 450192

Fiona Dermit.
Sax quartet available for concerts, demonstration recitals and educational w/shops.

Schidlof String Quartet

85 Asfordby Rd, Melton Mowbray, Leics LE13 0HN
Tel: 01664 60491 *also fax*

Keith Stubbs, educ co-ord.
Education programme presented by Russell Keable to schools and colleges in all phases, from presentation concerts to extended projects with group compositions and performance participation. Quartet in residence at De Montfort University, Associate Quartet to Norfolk and Norwich Festival and currently providing the National Education Programme for the London String Quartet Foundation.

Schubert Ensemble of London

32 Wolverton Gardens, London W6 7DY
Tel: 0181 563 0618 *Fax:* 0181 741 5233

Ann Senior, admin.
Vn, va, vc, db, pno, presenting wide variety of mus. Programmes introducing chmbr mus to young people can be adapted for any age group. Each inst is demonstrated and audience participation invited. Can offer mini m/classes and discussion with audience.

[Simpson, Mason]

22 Derwent Water Rd, London W3 6DE
Tel: 0181 992 8973

Introduction to the Maske a special programme of English mus, including dance, mime and a variety of insts (lutes, rcdrs, voice, early plucked insts).

Spice of Life Klezmer Ensemble

c/o Barry Weinberg Associates, 28 Blenheim Gardens, Wembley, Middx HA9 7NP
Tel: 0181 904 7025; 0956 372323 *Fax:* 0181 900 1130

Barry Weinberg, dir of mus.
Lecture recitals drawing on a wide variety of sources ranging from the Jewish folk mus of 19th C Eastern Europe to the songs of present-day Israel. Also programmes of Yiddish mus and songs complementary to Holocaust studies.

Three Down One Across

105 Priory Park Rd, London NW6 7UY
Tel: 0171 372 7311 *Fax:* 0181 537 9665
Email: sarafreedman@johnsonarts.demon.co.uk

Sara Freedman, mus dir.
Fl, ob, cl, bsn, and doubling insts. An energetic and experienced w/wind quartet specialising in w/shops and educational concerts for children aged 3-16 yrs (GCSE) and school mus clubs.
They have worked in education establishments for 4 yrs, providing a variety of w/shops including inst programmes, dance programmes, GCSE composition w/shops, history programmes based on forms in the periods, chmbr mus w/shops and journeys around the world using a mixture of

different styles of mus. Large repertoire of mus ranging from Bach to the 20th C, including narrated mus and songs. Strong emphasis on participation.

Programmes can be tailored to suit individual requirements and to tie in to the NC.

Three Reeds
The Old Meeting House, St James, Shaftesbury, Dorset SP7 8HF
Tel: 01747 854999

Jennifer Porcas.

Recitals covering a wide range of mus using ob, ob d'am, eh, bs ob and bsn. Also demonstrations and w/shops.

Tinderbox
93 Stradella Rd, London SE24 9HL
Tel: 0171 274 5314

David Moses.

Concerts, demonstrations and w/shops in schools, mus associations and libraries, etc, teaching through mus, story-telling, and audience participation. 2 players with wide range of familiar and unfamiliar insts (gui, lute, bass viol, bouzouki, banjo, sitar, db, rcdr, hpd, cl, sax, shawm, African and non-European traditional insts, pno, synthesizer, etc). Programmes for age ranges 3-7, 7-11 (5-11 in special circumstances), 9-13. Duration 50-60 mins.

Wessex Brass Quintet
Flat 1m, Springwater Rd, Bournemouth, Dorset BH11 8EZ
Tel: 01202 594278; 01962 877774

Br quintet or individuals offering wide range of programmes for age 18 and under. Special primary school package incorporating NC. Recitals 30-60 mins. Repertoire from renaissance to improvised jazz. Student participation encouraged. Ens m/classes also available.

Yorkshire Classic Brass
32 Heaton Grove, Bradford, W Yorks BD9 4DZ
Tel: 01274 487078 *also fax*

C Houlding, admin.

Br sextet with perc. Specially devised schools programme with participation by children.

Zephyr Winds
24 Gladston Rd, Neston, S Wirral, Cheshire L64 9PJ
Tel: 0151 336 4078

Chris Swann, admin.

Wind quintet of co-principals from Royal Liverpool Philharmonic and Hallé Orchestras (expanding to octet and including pno when required) with considerable experience of schools concerts, coaching and w/shop sessions. Concerts given to youth clubs, hospitals and centres for unemployed as part of local Liverpool scheme.

Individuals

Entries marked by a cross (+) indicate individuals who undertake PRS Composer in Education work.

Agnew, Elaine +
17 Deerpark Rd, Kilwaughter, Larne, Co Antrim BT40 2PW
Tel: 01574 277566
Website: www.kopco.demon.co.uk

Composer, education and community projects.

Alldis, Dominic
122 Dawes Rd, London SW6 7EG
Tel: 0171 381 2963 *Fax:* 0171 386 0337
Email: dominicalldis@canzona.cityscape.co.uk
Website: www.gold.net/dominicalldis

Jazz pianist and vocalist gives one-day w/shops on jazz, improvisation, jazz pno and singing, including a solo performance, or as a duo with bassist. Author of *A Classical Approach to Jazz Piano*, teaches jazz at the RAM and musicianship at the jnr department of the RCM.

Alvarez, Javier +
23 Barrington Rd, London N8 8QT
Tel: 0181 348 4973 *also fax;*
Email: musqja@herts.ac.uk

Composer.

Archibald, Margaret
17 Hayesford Park Dr, Bromley, Kent BR2 9DA
Tel: 0181 464 1645; 01306 880669

Lecture-demonstration *The Clarinet Family* gives a light-hearted introduction to 12 cls and 1 sax from 1730 to the present day. Adaptable for all ages from infant schools to homes for the elderly. The demonstration in schools can form part of a day of w/shops and m/classes.

Astle, Philip
Little Lodge Farm, Cloot Drove, Crowland, Peterborough PE6 0JH
Tel: 01733 210704

Nonsuch is a full-day participatory Tudor w/shop for one class (year 4-6) using drama, art, authentic mus and dance to recreate the story of Nonsuch, Henry VIII's lavish palace, now sadly demolished. Day ends with 40 min concert of Tudor mus performed for the whole school. *Tudor Music and Dance Workshop* is a half-day w/shop comprising a 1 hr demonstration of Tudor mus and insts for the whole school plus 2 or 3 short dance sessions for those year 4-6 classes actually studying the Tudors. *Tudor Concert* is 1 hr version of the above. *Medieval Music Workshop* is 1 hr demonstration with audience participation of medieval mus and insts which can be tailored to any age group.

Baillie, Alexander
39 Kingsmead Rd, London SW2 3HY
Tel: 0181 674 7221 *Fax:* 0181 674 8948

Cellist available for educational work including m/classes, teaching, coaching, working with youth orchs. Seminars on psychodynamics of study, practice, career development, etc.

Baker, Susan
Beckington Abbey, Beckington, Nr Bath BA3 6TD
Tel: 01373 830695 *also fax*

Programme entitled *Violins, Fiddles and Follies* played on a working museum of 20 rare and eccentric insts dating from 1650-1920 with their history and mus brought to life.

Bannan, Nicholas
21 Reading Rd, Woodley, Reading, Berks RG5 3DA
Tel: 0118 969 6035
Email: n.j.c.bannan@reading.ac.uk

A lecturer in mus education at Reading University, where he is researching the role of creativity in vocal development.
He has developed the Harmony Signing Method, an extension of Curwen and Kodály which permits young composers and arrangers to develop vocal pieces through interaction with their peers; and the Acoustic Mirror, a digital device for developing vocal confidence and imagination.
Available to schools, community groups and choral societies for w/shops on the creative use of the voice. Also for composition projects leading to public performance.

Barbour, Freeland +
6 The Steils, Edinburgh EH10 5XD
Tel: 0131 447 0991 *also fax*; 0831 779920

Composer.

Barley, Matthew
47 Waldemar Av, London SW6 5LN
Tel: 0171 731 1487 *Fax:* 0171 384 1490

Cello soloist with wide ranging experience of working with schoolchildren, students, amateurs and professional musicians in the UK and abroad. Provides composition and improvisation w/shops for the over 10s, always leading to performance. Special emphasis on performance and listening skills.

Bedford, David +
39 Shakespeare Rd, London NW7 4BA
Tel: 0181 959 3165

Composer whose education work centres around involving all children in a mus performance, not just those who can read mus, play or sing.
Set of pieces published by UE for use with an entire secondary class, children's operas with a large number of parts for non-musicians, w/shops and guided lectures which can be geared towards attending a performance of one of his works.
Object of w/shops is for all children to contribute to and participate in the creation of a composition. Specialises in GCSE groups.

Bennett OBE, William
50 Lansdowne Gardens, London SW8 2EF
Tel: 0171 498 9807 *Fax:* 0171 498 1155

Flautist available for m/classes. Held the posts of professor at Freiburg University in Germany and the Royal Academy.

Blake, Lowri
Warwick House, 34 Warwick Rd, Coulsdon, Surrey CR5 2EE
Tel: 0181 660 7877 *Fax:* 0181 763 0492
Email: silvius@dial.pipex.com

Solo cellist offering programmes with or without pno/hp accompaniment; also performs as singer and cellist in the duo *A Man, A Woman and a Double Bass* with Peter Buckoke. 3 programmes for primary, middle and snr schoolchildren aimed at making classical mus accessible to all ages by using the widest possible selection of mus.

Bruce, Stuart +
5 Brook Dr, Kinoulton, Nottingham NG12 3RA
Tel: 01949 81682 *also fax*

Composer.

Bryce, Iris and Owen
58 Pond Bank, Blisworth, Northants NN7 3EL
Tel: 01604 858192

Lectures on appreciation of jazz and practical tuition in jazz musicianship.

Bullard, Alan +
11 Christ Church Ct, Colchester CO3 3AU
Tel: 01206 562607

Composer of educational works for voices and insts; w/shops and lectures in schools and colleges.

Burn, Chris +
Garden Flat, 33 Grosvenor Rd, Wanstead, London E11 2EW
Tel: 0181 989 9640 *also fax*

Composer.

Burnett, Richard
Finchcocks, Goudhurst, Kent TN17 1HH
Tel: 01580 211702 *Fax:* 01580 211007

Pianist with remarkable collection of historic keyboard insts, largely in full playing condition. Operates a special scheme of school visits with courses, m/classes and concerts in which children take part.

Campbell, David
83 Woodwarde Rd, London SE22 8UL
Tel: 0181 693 5696 *also fax*

Clarinettist offering w/shops and m/classes possibly in conjunction with Boosey & Hawkes Musical Instruments (contact Jan Osmond *Tel:* 0181 952 7711).
Also gives demonstrations of 'Vivace' accompaniment system (contact Derek Baker at Dawsons *Tel:* 01925 632591).

Casey, Graham
Cornubia, 16 Edenfield, Orton Longueville, Peterborough PE2 7HY
Tel: 01733 235888
Email: gpcasey@compuserve.com

Clarinettist working as part of the Jupiter Ensemble. Educational w/shops. Also organises schemes encouraging young people to attend concerts and recitals.

Cashian, Philip +
Flat 2, 4 Granville Pk, London SE13 7EA
Tel: 0181 318 6998 *also fax*

Composer.

Coatman, Graham
4 Sunnybank, Shipley, W Yorks BD18 3RP
Tel: 01274 599379 *also fax*

Composer and mus director with many commissioned works for young people, especially in mus-theatre.
Extensive experience in leading and devising projects. Specialist in composition w/shops, collaborative creative projects (dance, drama, art), choral work, orch training days, INSET, etc.
Recent projects with ENO Baylis Programme, Orchestra of St John's Smith Square, BBC Philharmonic, Sinfonia 21, Leicester Haymarket/ Glen Parva Young Offenders Centre, Welsh National Opera, festival residencies, etc.

Coombes, Douglas +
c/o Lindsay Music, 23 Hitchin St, Biggleswade, Beds SG18 8AX
Tel: 01767 316521 *Fax:* 01767 317221

Composer with many commissioned works for young people offers miscellaneous programmes for children aged 5-12 with vocal, rhythmic and inst participation, in songs, puzzles and musical stories. Practical w/shops on creative mus-making, INSET courses for teachers around the UK and in Europe.

Cooney, John +
86 Bromfelde Rd, London SW4 6PR
Tel: 0171 498 2643 *also fax*

Composer, education. Composer in Residence with Academy of St Martin in the Fields.

Davies, Hugh
25 Albert Rd, London N4 3RR
Tel: 0171 272 5508

Composer and performer. Children's w/shops (KS2-3) building and playing simple bamboo insts. Minimum 3 hours; requires basic carpentry tools and appropriate workspace. Individual musical experience not necessary.
Longer projects continue with children inventing their own insts using a wider range of materials, and end with collective composition. Also lecture demonstrations.

Diamond, Eileen +
7 Allington Ct, Allington St, London SW1E 5ED
Tel: 0171 828 1335

Concert w/shops for nursery and infant children plus programmes for children with special needs. Varied programmes including musical stories arranged for age 3-5 and 5-7 using gui, pno, and taped accompaniment.
Strong emphasis on audience participation with actions, catchy choruses and perc insts. Teachers' w/shops and demos arranged. Video and cassettes available.

ó Dubhlaoidh, P
Hibernian Violins, 24 Players Av, Malvern Link, Worcs WR14 1DU
Tel: 01684 562947

School visits to talk about inst making and restoration, acoustics, care and maintenance of insts and directing mus-making activities.

Eastley, Max
Flat B, 551 Finchley Rd, London NW3 7BJ
Tel: 0171 794 3502 *also fax*

Composer, performer and visual artist. W/shops at KS2-3 making simple sculptures that make sound. Minimum 3 hrs. W/shop or art room required. Outdoor installations possible with extended time.

Evans, Patricia
41 Moorend Rd, Yardley Gobion, Towcester, Northants
Tel: 01908 542269

Pianist, lecture-recitalist and composer. W/shops and m/classes for all ages and abilities. Special

study of Russian mus. Also lecture recitals on spinet.

Fanshawe, David
PO Box 574, Marlborough, Wilts SN8 2SP
Tel: 01672 520211 *also fax*

Composer and explorer offers *One World-One Music* multi-media presentations suitable for all age groups. Focuses upon his life's work, preserving traditional mus from Arabia, Africa and the Pacific and featuring award-winning documentary films and compositions, including *African Sanctus*.

Frank, Marius
18 Lansdown View, Bath BA2 1BG
Tel: 01225 460459

Three educational projects are offered: *The Sounds of Music* a study of the physics of mus and how insts work, suitable for GCSE, A-level and degree students; *Rhythm City* a w/shop aimed at improving and developing the art of the jazz rhythm section, aimed at bassists, drummers, gui and keyboard players; *Rhythms from Around the World* a practical w/shop-based project that introduces the rich diversity of beats and patterns found in World Music. Suitable for ages 7-18+.

Geddes, John Maxwell +
21 Cleveden Rd, Glasgow G12 0PQ
Tel: 0141 357 2941

Composer in education.

Godman, Robert +
5 Nursery Dr, Sandy, Beds SG19 1DL
Tel: 01767 692161 *Fax:* 01462 850009

Composer, projects for all age ranges with emphasis on electro-acoustic technology. Also w/shops for teachers based on cross-arts projects for KS2.

Gregory, Julian
9 Rock Bank, Whaley Bridge, High Peak SK23 7LE
Tel: 01663 733331

BBC Philharmonic violinist sharing classic, jazz, folk, bluegrass and freeform mus with primary children. Inspires creative improvisation and spontaneous participation from all abilities. Traditional classical inst and hi-tech electronic vns.

Hardy, John +
Ael Y Garth, 3 Iron Bridge Rd, Tongwynlais, Cardiff CF4 7NJ
Tel: 01222 810653/5 *Fax:* 01222 810653

Composer, Channel 4 educational mus programmes, community opera project involving people of Fishguard and WNO (1997). Composes mus jointly with children in w/shop series.

Hope, Harvey
41 Arkwright Rd, Sanderstead, Surrey CR2 0LP
Tel: 0181 657 5840

Programme of gui mus, *Baroque to Rock*, which traces the history of the gui using a dozen rare insts dating from 17th to 20th C. Demos of each style include baroque, classical, flamenco, Latin-American, blues, etc. Suitable for all age groups.

Howells, David
67 Belsize La, Hampstead, London NW3 5AX
Tel: 0171 794 2077 *Fax:* 0171 916 0222

Pno recitals for ages 5-14, best given to whole school or large sections. Large repertoire, regular appearances at mus festivals and theatres, often with children's programmes. For younger audiences there are stories told from the pno (*The Snowman, Peter and the Wolf, Babar,* etc).
All performances are designed to encourage listening skills and aural awareness; specific programmes for KS1-3.

Ingman, Nick +
10 The Gardens, East Dulwich, London SE22 9QD
Tel: 0181 693 5608 *Fax:* 0181 693 9576
Email: 100712.153@compuserve.com

Composer.

Jackson, Andy +
13 West Rd, Bishop Auckland, Durham DL14 7PP
Tel: 01388 607060

Composer, community musicals and operas, orch works, gui recitals (with guitarra portuguesa).

Jarvis, Robert +
Ground floor flat, 169 Old Dover Rd, Canterbury, Kent CT1 3EP
Tel: 01227 472180 *also fax*

Trombonist, composer and animateur. Organises and oversees mus composition projects often involving other professional musicians and artists from different disciplines. Project length varies from couple of days to longer periods as composer in residence. Primary or secondary.

Kefala-Kerr, John * +
7 Swindon Terrace, Newcastle upon Tyne NE6 5RB
Tel: 0191 276 5347
Email: jkk@kopco.demon.co.uk
Website: www.kopco.demon.co.uk

Composer and artistic dir of the Karaoke Opera Company.

131

Kelsey, Xenophon
Ashley House, Ure Bank, Ripon, N Yorks HG4 1JG
Tel: 01765 602856

Experienced conductor and chmbr mus coach, specialising in work with young musicians. Director of Vacation Chamber Orchestras. Conducting, coaching, ens and individual m/classes, inst tuition, in-service sessions for teachers, etc.

King, Steve * +
c/o 4 Ferniebank Brae, Bridge of Allan FK9 4PJ
Tel: 01786 834449

Musician, composer and mus educationalist. In-service sessions and training for teachers and care staff. Creates and co-ordinates projects for children and adults, particularly those with disabilities or special needs.

Lockett, Mark +
101 Summerfield Cres, Edgbaston, Birmingham B16 0EN
Tel: 0121 454 5922 *also fax;*
Email: marklockett@ormuzd.demon.co.uk

Composer, gamelan, world mus and percussion.

McCullough, Andy
36 Bolton Cres, Windsor, Berks SL4 3JQ
Tel: 01753 861541

Two programmes based on the cl and its history and repertory, *The Clarinet Connection* and *Do you like my tone?* Mus includes pieces from Mozart to Poulenc, jazz and rock.

McNicol, Richard
Overdale, 145 Park Rd, Buxton, Derbys SK17 6SW
Tel: 01298 79598 *also fax*

Mus animateur to the London Symphony Orchestra and founder of Apollo Trust (founded to involve children of all backgrounds and abilities in live mus-making). Undertakes in-service training for teachers. Author of *Sound Inventions* (OUP) and *Music Explorer* (LSO).

Mitchell, Madeleine
41 Queen's Gardens, London W2 3AA
Tel: 0171 402 0014 *Fax:* 0171 402 3134
Website: www.classical-artists.com/madeleinemitchell

Violinist and professor at the Royal College of Music experienced in giving concerts and m/classes with or without pno for schools and older students. Inst demonstrations and illustrated talks.
Also str coaching m/classes and w/shops including mus with pictoral themes and an introduction to contemporary mus as well as standard repertoire. Lecture recitals for older students can include discussion on the life of a performer, collaborating with composers, etc.

Mitchell-Davidson, Paul +
25 Bannerman Av, Prestwich, Manchester M25 1DZ
Tel: 0161 798 9604 *also fax*

Composer, arranger and musician.

Morris, Keith +
5 Bentinck Rd, Newcastle upon Tyne NE4 6UT
Tel: 0191 273 5326

Composer, education and community projects.

Mosby, Paul
4 Creighton Av, London N10 1NU
Tel: 0181 444 9830

Oboist (The Oboe Man) offering formal and informal concerts, demonstrations and w/shops for all ages. Variety of insts, ethnic, baroque and 20th C, demonstrated with or without pianist. Children participate. Duration 45 mins (infants), 1 hr (primary and secondary).

Moses, David +
93 Stradella Rd, London SE24 9HL
Tel: 0171 274 5314

Multi-instrumentalist, singer, story-teller, author and composer of children's songs, teaching and resource material, children's radio and TV appearances. In-service course for teachers, concerts and w/shops for children. Songs, stories, insts from many countries, medieval to 20th C. 70+ str, wind and perc insts. Entertaining and informative, emphasis on audience participation. Programmes for age range 3-7, 7-11, 5-11. Duration 50-60 mins.

Patterson, Paul
31 Cromwell Av, London N6 5HN
Tel: 0181 348 3711 *Fax:* 0181 340 6489
Email: p.patterson@ram.ac.uk

Composer offering w/shops for teachers, school students and youth orchs involving a general introduction to practical contemporary mus-making (ability to play an inst not essential). C/room sessions (from half day to full week) cover new notation, 'group' composing from the children, helping to introduce the concept of new mus, either with the use of tapes and a synthesizer or with his own contemporary mus group. Other composers' works also studied, particularly A-level set works from contemporary repertory. Classes in Sibelius 7 mus notation system.

Peacock, Bob +
52 Reeth Rd, Linthorpe, Middlesbrough, Cleveland TS5 5JX
Tel: 01642 815943

Composer, specialises in teaching improvisation skills, aural perception and mus, transcription, jazz pianist.

132

Peggie, Andrew *
4 Colchester Av, London E12 5LE
Tel: 0181 514 2219 *Fax:* 0181 514 2219

Composer and musical director with extensive experience of organising and running musical and mus theatre projects with young people and adults, covering everything from song-writing to staging. Specialises in large scale projects (100+ participants).
Recent premieres include *Fabulous Fauna* (CBSO players and amateurs), *Of Bricks and Bones* (WNO community opera commission), *The Journey* (200 singers and players, Birmingham Town Hall) and *Making Musical Theatre* (performing arts students at Bretton Hall College).

Pratt, Stephen +
9 Wellington Av, Liverpool L15 0EH
Tel: 0151 733 9334 *Fax:* 0151 291 3170
Email: pratts@livhope.ac.uk

Composer, conductor.

Rachlin MBE, Ann
2 Queensmead, St John's Wood Pk, London NW8 6RE
Tel: 0171 722 9828 *Fax:* 0171 722 7981
Email: annrachlin@cis.compuserve.com

Presents *Fun with Music* a range of concert programmes for children aged 3-11. She has produced 20 cassettes and CDs and written 10 books on composers' childhoods published by Gollancz. Weekly classes, schools concerts and festival appearances.

Riley, Colin +
77 Godstone Rd, St Margarets, Twickenham TW1 1JY
Tel: 0181 891 0143

Composer in association with Bournemouth Orchestras 1995-1997. Freelance work in schools and colleges.

Rose, Michael
2 Neartown, Olney, Bucks MK46 4AN
Tel: 01234 713057 *also fax*

Conductor, composer, teacher and lecturer. Music published by Associated Board, OUP, Novello. Available for freelance conducting and educational work. Expert in youth mus, in-service teacher training, mus composed especially for young instrumentalists, choirs, etc.

Sherbourne, Janet
13 Salegate La, Temple Cowley, Oxford
Tel: 01865 770272 *also fax*
Email: jsherbourne@bigfoot.com
Website: www.jags.co.uk/metalworks

Performer and composer specialising in gamelan projects (primary, secondary and in-service).

Traditional Balinese/Javanese mus and composing for gamelan. Twice PRS Composer in Education.

Steedman, Heather
2 Thirlmere Gardens, Wembley, Middx HA9 8RE
Tel: 0181 904 9049 *also fax*

Recital and demonstration *Spotlight on Percussion* covering tuned perc, Latin-American insts, the drum kit, orch perc techniques and sound effects. Suitable for ages 5-18. Show includes pianist and drummer. Duration c 1 hr, with audience participation.

Steele-Perkins, Crispian
Random House, Sutton Abinger, Surrey RH5 6RN
Tel: 01306 730018 *Fax:* 01306 730013

Clinics, w/shops and lecture recitals illustrating tpt and wide variety of unusual historic brass insts with pno or org. Suitable for older students, either coached individually or in m/classes and tutorials.

Stuart, Amanda +
ZigZag Music Productions, Croeso, Church La, Hilton, Huntingdon, Cambs PE18 9NH
Tel: 01480 830073 *also fax*

Composer.

Treherne, John
10 Evesham Av, Whitley Bay, N Tyneside NE26 1QR
Tel: 0191 252 5144

Specialist programmes for primary or secondary schools. *Keyboards, Strings and Things* lecture recital for primary-age children with emphasis on audience participation, employing 20 different bowed, struck or plucked insts including hpd. Strong multi-ethnic and historical element, and focus on the science of sound. Duration 45-60 mins.

Underwood, Ruth
2 St John's Grove, London N19 5RW
Tel: 0171 272 8500

Flautist and mus teacher presents four w/shops in one school day: *Musical Storytelling, Music and History, Music Around the World* and *Composition* with composer Martin Vishnick, followed by a fl and gui concert. Mus of different styles from around the world for children aged 3-11, including those with learning difficulties. Aims to meet NC attainment targets and makes cross-curricular links with all NC subjects. Participation through songs, perc, movement and improvisation. Follow-on w/sheets and mus materials for non-mus specialist teachers.

LUCIE and RODDY SKEAPING'S

MUSICAL MYSTERY TOUR!

An introduction to the history of music from earliest beginnings to Medieval and Tudor times.
For primary school pupils aged 5 - 12

"AMUSING, LIVELY AND INFORMATIVE"
Times Educational Supplement

Songs of Tudors, Kings and Queens and Crusaders; lutes, rebecs, recorders, viols; songs and costumes, a life-size hobby-horse and the smallest violin ever! Using humour, drama, participation and over 20 period instruments, this lively workshop/show performs constantly in schools, arts centres and festivals in the UK and abroad.

Contact: Lucie Skeaping, 19 Patshull Road, London NW5 2JX
Tel 0171 485 3957   Fax 0171 267 2957

White, Barbara
Aldersyde, 72 Church La, Acklam, Middlesbrough, Cleveland TS5 7EB
Tel: 01642 826822

Pianist with wide experience of all types of schools: primary, secondary, VI form colleges, and special needs. Primary school programmes planned around themes or stories to stimulate the imagination, with opportunities for questions and participation. Secondary school programmes designed to make history of mus come alive through presentation of different styles. Duration of programme to suit age range, usually 30-60 mins.

Wiegold, Peter
82 Lordship Pk, London N16 5UA
Tel: 0181 802 9646 *also fax*
Email: p.wiegold@rhbnc.ac.uk

Performer and composer with wide experience of running practical mus and mus-theatre w/shops in schools and all kinds of educational establishments for orchs, ens and individuals, either working alone, with other professionals or using local resources. Led many training programmes in w/shop techniques for orchs, ens, etc. Lecturer in composition at Royal Holloway, University of London.

Wilson, Jeffery * +
5 Church Green, Boreham Village, Essex CM3 3EH
Tel: 01245 450192

Composer with an enthusiasm for community-based projects. Recent work includes projects with the National Youth Festival of Dance, the Gulbenkian Foundation in Lisbon and the London Festival Orchestra. Currently composer in association with the Chamber Academy Ensemble. Author of *Progressive Guide to Melodic Jazz Improvisation.*

York, John
c/o St Paul's Girls' School, Brook Green, Hammersmith, London W6 7BS
Tel: 0181 318 1824 *Fax:* 0181 244 7473

Pianist (professor at GSM, head of pno at St Paul's Girls' School) with experience of working with Youth & Music on overseas tours. Offers programmes for age 8-13 plus special programmes for GCSE and A-level courses. Also offers programmes of avant-garde and minimalist mus for pno duet with his partner, known as *York 2 Piano Duo.*

Zukerman, George
c/o Robert Gilder and Company, Enterprise House, 59-65 Upper Ground, London SE1 9PQ
Tel: 0171 928 9008 *Fax:* 0171 928 9755

Bassoonist offering graded series of schools programmes (age 6-11, 10-15, 14 and over) plus wind band w/shops, etc. Programmes for lowest age-group can be done without pno, but other groups require keyboard accompaniment for widely varied repertoire. Musical content encompasses a 'trip around the world'. Discussions are geared to specific age groups, but at all levels cover the history, development and mechanism of the bsn, and provide an introduction to the essential characteristics of the inst. Children handle the inst, try to play, and are involved in questions and discussions throughout. Sessions for older children include slides and ens work.

Youth Concession Schemes

Organisations offering concessions on ticket prices to young people are listed below. *Youth & Music* is listed first.

Youth & Music
28 Charing Cross Rd, London WC2H 0DB
Tel: 0171 379 6722 *Fax:* 0171 497 0345
Email: stagepass@dial.pipex.com

Monica Ferguson, exec dir.
Stage Pass for those under 30: up to 60% off tickets for concerts, opera, dance, ballet, musicals and theatre in Bath, Birmingham, Blackpool, Bradford, Bristol, Cardiff, Cheltenham, Coventry, Darlington, Durham, Edinburgh, Glasgow, Hull, Leeds, Leicester, Liverpool, London, Manchester, Newcastle upon Tyne, Northampton, Nottingham, Oxford, Perth, Sheffield, Stratford, Sunderland and Warwick. Annual Stage Pass membership £15 in the South East, £10.50 elsewhere. Annual school membership costs £68 in the South East and £46 elsewhere.

Bournemouth Orchestras
2 Seldown La, Poole, Dorset BH15 1UF
Tel: 01202 670611 *Fax:* 01202 687235

Millicent Jones, mkt mgr; Anthony Woodcock, mgr dir.
Students and under 18s admitted at half price. School parties over 20 are negotiable, with party leaders admitted free. Other schemes available.

Brighton and Hove Philharmonic Society
50 Grand Parade, Brighton BN2 2QA
Tel: 01273 622900 *Fax:* 01273 697887

Price reductions on most tickets for students, Youth & Music and school parties; 50% reduction on season tickets for students.

CBSO - City of Birmingham Symphony Orchestra
Paradise Pl, Birmingham B3 3RP
Tel: 0121 236 1555 *Fax:* 0121 236 4231
Email: information@cbso.co.uk
Website: www.cbso.co.uk

Ann Tennant, educ mgr; Andrew Biss, mkt mgr.
The YES card (Young Persons Entertainment Scheme) entitles holder to 50% discount for all CBSO concerts in Symphony Hall. £5 pa for age 21 and under, or those in f/t education. A Young Subscriber (age 21 and under, or those in f/t education) can get an additional 50% discount on regular subscription discounts (ranging from 15-30%). Applications for YES card through Birmingham Arts Marketing *Tel:* 0121 622 1234.

Children's Classic Concerts
Children's Music Foundation in Scotland, 537 Sauchiehall St, Glasgow G3 7PQ
Tel: 0141 248 1611 *Fax:* 0141 248 1989
Email: 106321.1441@compuserve.com

Louise Naftalin, mgr; Lizanne McKerrell, mgr.
Organises classical concert series for children.

Enjoy Opera
ENO, London Coliseum, St Martin's La, London WC2N 4ES
Tel: 0171 836 0111 *Fax:* 0171 497 9052

Catherine Lester, asst mkt offr; Barbara Bentley, group and sales promotions mgr.
Low-price ticket scheme for schools. Tickets are available at £5 per seat for operas in the current season; two selected dates per opera are offered; one of these dates is a sign language interpreted/audio introduced performance. The scheme is suitable for students aged 13-18.

Ernest Read Music Association (ERMA)
9 Cotsford Av, New Malden, Surrey KT3 5EU
Tel: 0181 942 0318

Noel Long, dir.
Concert series for children at RFH, schools, parties and season discounts. Ernest Read Symphony Orchestra; free membership for all players, also summer course discounts and special terms for students and under 25s.

Guildford Philharmonic Orchestra
Millmead House, Millmead, Guildford, Surrey GU2 5BB
Tel: 01483 444666 *Fax:* 01483 444732

Nicola Goold, gen mgr.
Price reductions of 50% on most tickets for students, Youth & Music and schoolchildren. All students/children under 18 can come to any concert for only £3.

Hallé Concerts Society
The Bridgewater Hall, Manchester M2 3WS
Tel: 0161 907 9000 *Fax:* 0161 907 9001

Concessions for school parties; concessions for those aged under 26, family concerts.

Junior Associates of The Friends of Covent Garden
Royal Opera House, Covent Garden, London WC2E 9DD
Tel: 0171 212 9412 *Fax:* 0171 212 9468

Those aged under 26 may join at the reduced fee of £17. This entitles the Junior Associate to all the benefits of full membership plus ten £5 vouchers per membership year. These vouchers can be used towards the cost of performance tickets. Junior Associates are also eligible for 'Saturday Special' reduced price tickets for certain performances.

London Mozart Players
92 Chatsworth Rd, Croydon CR0 1HB
Tel: 0181 686 1996 *Fax:* 0181 686 2187

Alice Walton, mkt mgr.
Tickets for children under 16 and those in f/t educ for any seating area at Fairfield Croydon, the Barbican and South Bank centres (subject to availability).

London Symphony Orchestra
Barbican Centre, Barbican, London EC2Y 8DS
Tel: 0171 588 1116 *Fax:* 0171 374 0127
Email: discovery@lso.co.uk
Website: www.lso.co.uk

Kate Mapp, educ and access asst.
Special benefits for schools and colleges include ticket discounts, pre-concert talks, *Meet the Orchestra* interval receptions and access to rehearsals. Benefits for other groups of 10 or more include discounts, receptions, talks and coffee/programme vouchers. There are also special family and school concerts. To join the LSO's free schools' and groups' mailing lists.*Tel:* 0171 588 0205 (24 hr line).

Northern Sinfonia
The Sinfonia Centre, 41 Jesmond Vale, Newcastle upon Tyne NE2 1PG
Tel: 0191 240 1812 *Fax:* 0191 240 2668

Fiona Lockwood, educ admin.
Children's concerts; Stage Pass concessions and student discounts; family tickets, rehearsal attendance by arrangement (for mus students). Education and outreach programme offers school group bookings at £1 per ticket for selected concerts.

The Philharmonia Orchestra
76 Great Portland St, London W1N 6HA
Tel: 0171 580 9961 *Fax:* 0171 436 5517
Email: info@philharmonia.co.uk
Website: www.philharmonia.co.uk

Jill Pridmore, sales and mkt mgr; Judith Robinson, educ mgr; Jane Leigh, group/schools sales.
The Philharmonia Orchestra offers school parties of 10 or more a discount of 50% on box office prices (subject to availability) for the orchestra's concerts at the Royal Festival Hall. Attendance at rehearsals may also be possible. To book tickets, or to be added to the free schools' mailing list *Tel:* 0171 580 5756.

Royal Liverpool Philharmonic Society
Philharmonic Hall, Hope St, Liverpool L1 9BP
Tel: 0151 709 2895; 0151 709 3789 (box office) *Fax:* 0151 709 0918

Student reductions for most concerts; Sat morning children's concerts, reductions for party booking. Young Friends of the Phil (RLPS Friends Society).

The Royal Opera House
Covent Garden, London WC2E 9DD
Tel: 0171 304 4000

Under 18s half-price matinee card, low-price standby tickets (subject to availability) for students and members of Youth & Music Stage Pass scheme.

Royal Philharmonic Orchestra
16 Clerkenwell Green, London EC1R 0DP
Tel: 0171 608 2381 *Fax:* 0171 608 1226

Stage Pass/Youth & Music discounts (age 14-29) *Tel:* 0171 379 6722. Group concessions (10 people or more), special offers for schools and colleges, free schools' mailing list.

Royal Scottish National Orchestra
73 Claremont St, Glasgow G3 7JB
Tel: 0141 226 3868 *Fax:* 0141 221 4317

Aberdeen, Dundee, Edinburgh and Glasgow; children £4 in advance, student and Young-Scot standby £4.50 on the day of the performance.

Sadler's Wells
The Peacock Theatre, Kingsway, London WC2A 2HT
Tel: 0171 278 6563; 0171 314 8800 (box office) *Fax:* 0171 314 9004

Discounts in advance, and standby tickets available 1 hr before show, subject to availability (students, under 18s, snr citizens and registered disabled only).

Scottish Chamber Orchestra
4 Royal Terrace, Edinburgh EH7 5AB
Tel: 0131 557 6800 *Fax:* 0131 557 6933

For main season concerts in Glasgow, the Glasgow Ticket Scheme enables students, Young-Scot card holders and schoolchildren to purchase any available ticket for £3.50 from one week prior. Students, Young-Scot card holders and schoolchildren are also eligible for £3.50 standby tickets for concerts in Edinburgh and £4 in Aberdeen and St Andrews. Bookable in advance, any available ticket for £6.50.

137

Wavendon Allmusic Plan Ltd
The Stables, Wavendon, Milton Keynes MK17 8LT
Tel: 01908 583928 *Fax:* 01908 281024
Jacky Scott, general mgr.
Discounted tickets for all events available to students and under 18s; also student standby tickets available on night at £4.

Young Persons Concert Foundation
95 Wellington Rd, Enfield, Middx EN1 2PW
Tel: 0181 360 7390; 01923 859388 *Fax:* 0181 364 0185
Website: www.webcasting.com/stamps/found.htm
William A J Starling, artistic dir; Sally Needleman, special projects co-ord.
Schemes to present all types of concert (from individual str, w/wind, br and perc sections to full orch) free to children in their own schools.

YOUTH PERFORMANCE

Organisations for Young Performers

The organisations below exist to promote excellence in performance for school age instrumentalists and singers.

Association of British Choral Directors (ABCD)
46 Albert St, Tring, Herts HP23 6AU
Tel: 01422 891633 *also fax*

Howard Layfield, chair; Marie-Louise Petit, gen sec. The national organisation and forum for choir leaders, teachers, students and choral conductors promotes the interests of all who work with young singers to lay a foundation for a life-long interest in choral singing. Courses, conventions, advice and discussion groups. International study and performing tours.

Boosey & Hawkes Youth Orchestra Award
Promotion Dept, Boosey & Hawkes, 295 Regent St, London W1R 8JH
Tel: 0171 291 7229 *Fax:* 0171 637 3490
Email: composers@boosey.com

Lloyd Moore.
A major award worth £1000 open to all participating orchs in the Edinburgh and Glasgow Festival of British Youth Orchestras held during the Edinburgh Festival. The prize is aimed at encouraging youth orchs to programme works by many of this century's greatest composers. Applicants must be members of NAYO and perform one work from the Boosey & Hawkes selected list. Designed to provide funds towards a recording, a concert in a major venue or to help towards a foreign or UK tour.

British Choral Institute
18 The Rotyngs, Rottingdean, Brighton BN2 7DX
Tel: 01273 300894 *Fax:* 01273 308394
Email: britchorinst@fastnet.co.uk

Roy Wales, dir; Christine Wales, admin.
A national organisation established as an advisory, promotional, educational and training body for choral singers, conductors, choral administrators and organisers from all sectors of the choral community with a special emphasis on developing international choral projects.

British Federation of Young Choirs (BFYC)
Devonshire House, Devonshire Sq, Loughborough, Leics LE11 3DW
Tel: 01509 211664 *Fax:* 01509 260630
Email: bfyc@foobar.co.uk

Susan Lansdale, chief exec; Andrew Fairbairn, hon sec.
Choral events for young people and training courses for teachers, conductors and singers. 450 members (180 choirs and 270 individuals). Choral animateurs in Scotland, Northern Ireland, East Anglia, London, West and East Midlands.

British Reserve Insurance Youth Orchestra Awards
NAYO, Ainslie House, 11 St Colme St, Edinburgh EH3 6AG
Tel: 0131 539 1087 *Fax:* 0131 539 1069
Email: admin@nayo.org.uk
Website: www.nayo.org.uk

Carol Main, dir.
5 awards of £500 each will be made to youth orchs within NAYO's membership towards a project to enhance the orchestras' activities. Deadline for applications Apr. Previous winners may reapply after an interval of one year.

Music for Youth
102 Point Pleasant, London SW18 1PP
Tel: 0181 870 9624 *Fax:* 0181 870 9935
Website: www.pjbpubs.co.uk/mfy

Larry Westland CBE, exec dir.
Platform for young musicians.

National Association of Choirs
21 Charmouth Rd, Lower Weston, Bath BA1 3LJ
Tel: 01225 426713

John Robbins, gen sec.

National Association of Youth Orchestras
Ainslie House, 11 St Colme St, Edinburgh EH3 6AG
Tel: 0131 539 1087 *Fax:* 0131 539 1069
Email: admin@nayo.org.uk
Website: www.nayo.org.uk

Carol Main, dir.
Has members from independent and LEA run orchs. Organises the Festival of British Youth Orchestras in Edinburgh and Glasgow along with

139

Boosey & Hawkes Youth Orchestra award, Anglo-German Youth Music Week, British Reserve Insurance Youth Orchestra Awards and the British Reserve Insurance Conducting Prize. NAYO also organises various Silver Baton award schemes in association with business sponsors, eg Salvesen Baton for young conductors. NAYO publishes a newsletter *Full Orchestra* three times pa. Also the Marion Semple Weir library of chmbr mus, free hire to members.

Sing for Pleasure
25 Fryerning La, Ingatestone, Essex CM4 0DD
Tel: 01277 353691 *also fax*
Email: choral@sfp.cix.co.uk
Website: www.sfp.cix.co.uk

Lynda Parker, dir.
Wide variety of day and residential courses for young singers and conductors. Singing day for children and INSET courses for teachers. Choir repertoire is available from above address.

Festivals for Young Performers

Aberdeen International Youth Festival
3 Nutborn House, Clifton Rd, London SW19 4QT
Tel: 0181 946 2995 *Fax:* 0181 944 6507

Nicola Wallis, festival dir.
5-15 Aug 1998. Youth orchs, choirs, jazz and rock groups, dance and theatre groups from all over the world. Mainly amateur, but some professional input.

The Festival of British Youth Orchestras in Edinburgh and Glasgow
NAYO, Ainslie House, 11 St Colme St, Edinburgh EH3 6AG
Tel: 0131 539 1087 *Fax:* 0131 539 1069
Email: admin@nayo.org.uk
Website: www.nayo.org.uk

Carol Main, dir.
15 Aug-5 Sep 1998; 14 Aug-4 Sep 1999. RSAMD box office *Tel:* 0141 332 5057; Central Hall box office *Tel:* 0131 229 7937 (during Festival period only).

Harrogate International Youth Music Festival
Perform Europe (Incoming), Deepdene Lodge, Deepdene Av, Dorking, Surrey RH5 4AZ
Tel: 01306 744360 *Fax:* 01306 744361
Email: smb.peurope@kuoni.co.uk

Sharon Brewster, festivals mgr.
10-17 Apr 1998. Celebrating its 26th year in 1998, the festival features varied and exciting performances from local and international choirs, bands, orchs and dance groups.

Music for Youth's National Festivals
102 Point Pleasant, London SW18 1PP
Tel: 0181 870 9624 *Fax:* 0181 870 9935

Larry Westland CBE, exec dir.
Up to 20,000 young musicians will perform at Symphony Hall, Birmingham, the Bridgewater Hall, Manchester and the Royal Festival Hall, London.

Schools' Prom
Music for Youth, 4 Blade Mews, London SW15 2NN
Tel: 0181 870 9624 *Fax:* 0181 870 9935
Website: www.pjbpubs.co.uk/mfy

Larry Westland CBE, exec dir.

West Sussex International Youth Music Festival
Perform Europe (Incoming), Deepdene Lodge, Deepdene Av, Dorking, Surrey RH5 4AZ
Tel: 01306 744360 *Fax:* 01306 744361
Email: mjl.peurope@kuoni.co.uk

Maria Llinares, festival mgr.
8-14 Apr 1998. Celebrating its 7th year in 1998. Non-competitive festival taking place in various venues throughout West Sussex and on the South coast, including Arundel Cathedral and Worthing Assembly Hall. Attracts both local and international bands, orchs, choirs and dance groups.

Competitions for Young Performers

Listed below are competitions open to young musicians. A more comprehensive list of competitions for a wider age range can be found in the *British Music Yearbook*.

Admira Young Guitarist of the Year Competition
c/o Bath International Guitar Festival, PO Box 3697, London NW3 2HQ
Tel: 0171 831 0345 *Fax:* 0171 831 0346

Aug 1998, applications by 15 Jun 1998. For age 20 and under. Application fee £30. First prize £1000.

Association of English Singers and Speakers Prize
13 Shaftesbury Av, Bedford MK40 3SA
Tel: 01234 355787 *also fax*

Open to students under the age of 30 at all UK institutions of higher education where singing and speech are taught and who are nominated by their institution. Aims to encourage singing and speaking of English. Candidates are required to introduce and sing a recital in English of up to 20 mins duration. Applications by early Mar for first round at end Mar. First prize: £1000; accompanist prize: £100.

BBC Young Musicians
BBC Music and Arts, EG30 East Tower, Television Centre, Wood La, London W12 7RJ
Tel: 0181 895 6143/4 *Fax:* 0181 895 6146
Email: young.musicians@bbc.co.uk

Jul 1999-Mar 2000. Str, w/wind, br, perc, keyboard. Open to UK citizens aged 19 and under (performers), aged 24 and under (composers). Stage one auditions for the next competition held in Jul 1999, entries by 1 Apr 1999. £2000 prize for each concerto finalist, plus Lloyds Bank Travel Award for the winner.

British Reserve Insurance Conducting Prize/Seminar
National Association of Youth Orchestras, Ainslie House, 11 St Colme St, Edinburgh EH3 6AG
Tel: 0131 539 1087 *Fax:* 0131 539 1069
Email: admin@nayo.org.uk
Website: www.nayo.org.uk

Biennial, next 1999. Age range 18-26. First prize £500.

Bromsgrove Festival Young Musicians' Platform
c/o 10 Evertons Close, Droitwich Spa, Worcs WR9 8AE
Tel: 01527 575441 *Fax:* 01527 575366
Email: lgharris@compuserve.com

May, applications by Feb. For young performers of any nationality aged 17-25 (any inst or voice) of gr 8 distinction standard. First prize £750, second prize £350, third prize £200. Application fee £15.

Caerphilly Young Musician of the Year Competition
Caerphilly County Borough Council, Council Offices, Caerphilly Rd, Ystrad Mynach, Hengoed CF82 7EP
Tel: 01443 815588 *Fax:* 01443 816998

Str, w/wind, br, singing, pno and perc. Open to those attending a Caerphilly County Borough Council secondary school or college. Maximum age of 19 at competition in Mar. First prize: £100 and 8 class prizes of £35 each. Prizewinners' schools receive matching cash prizes.

Eastbourne Symphony Orchestra Young Musician Awards
7 Prideaux Rd, Eastbourne, ESussex BN21 2NW
Tel: 01323 724763

Concerto competition for young soloists of any nationality. Jnr section (under 18) held Jan; snr section (under 23) held Feb-Mar, applications by Dec. First prize in snr competition £300 and an opportunity to play a concerto with the orchestra; jnr competition first prize £150. Application fee £10 (jnr), £20 (snr).

Essex Young Musician of the Year
Ongar Music Club, Corbetts House, Norwood End, Fyfield, Chipping Ongar, Essex CM5 0RW
Tel: 01277 899337 *also fax*

27-28 Jun 1998, applications by 31 May. Total prize money £1725. Winner receives £500, plus recitals for Ongar Music Club and others, and an invitation to appear at a leading London venue. Age limit 25, with two prizes for those aged 18 and under. Open to instrumentalists (except organists) and singers who were born, live or attend school or college in the Essex postal area. Application fee £25.

Gregynog Composers' Award of Wales
Festival Office, Gregynog, Newtown, Powys SY16 3PW
Tel: 01686 621493 *Fax:* 01686 650656

Entries by 4 Apr 1998. Open to all nationalities, no age limits. Special award available for composers aged 22 and under. Application fee £5. First prize £1000, 2 week residency at Gregynog and performance at 1998 Gregynog Festival. Application fee £5. Composition criteria to be confirmed.

The magazine for performers and enthusiasts of classical, jazz and blues piano

- Explore new styles with our in-depth features on the jazz and blues traditions

- Keep on top of new developments in keyboard technology - both acoustic and electric

- Gain an insight into the lives of today's great artists

- Find the best new music and editions available with the help of our growing review section

- Discover creative tips for teaching and learn about music therapy

Published bi-monthly, only available on subscription

Annual subscription prices
to UK addresses £14.40; airmail Europe £18.00 outside Europe £21.00

To subscribe please send a cheque in pounds Sterling, made payable to *Rhinegold Publishing Ltd*, to:
Rhinegold Publishing Ltd (PIANO SUBS), FREEPOST, Gravesend, Kent DA12 2BR

**CREDIT CARD SUBSCRIPTIONS
Tel: 01474 334500 (office hours)
Fax: 01474 325557**

For a FREE SAMPLE COPY please telephone
0171 333 1720

SHELL LSO MUSIC SCHOLARSHIP

£6,000

One of the most prestigious annual awards for young instrumentalists, the **Shell LSO Music Scholarship** features a different group of instruments each year working in a four-year cycle. Forthcoming Scholarships are:

**1999 Brass
2000 Timpani + Percussion**

Regional auditions and workshops are held early in the year, and the National Final takes place at the Barbican in London in the summer.

The Scholarship is open to candidates from all parts of the UK, aged between 15 and 22. The award of £6,000 is provided for the musical development of the winner. Further cash prizes are awarded to the winners of the Silver and Bronze medals and the Gerald McDonald Award.

*Detailed information and application forms are available in the previous October for any Scholarship year from: The Administrator, Shell LSO Music Scholarship, London Symphony Orchestra, Barbican Centre, London EC2Y 8DS.
Tel – 0171 588 1116*

International Early Music Network Young Artists' Competition

The Early Music Network, Sutton House, 2-4 Homerton High St, London E9 6JQ
Tel: 0181 533 2921 *Fax:* 0181 533 2922

Biennial. Next Jul 1999, applications by early Jan 1999. Open to vocal and inst ens (min 3 persons) aged 17-30 (aged 17-35 for singers) who specialise in repertoire from the Middle Ages to the 19th C and use the playing techniques and stylistic conventions of early mus. Part of the York Early Music Festival.

International Young Instrumentalist of the Year Competition

Eisteddfod Office, Llangollen, Denbighshire LL20 8NG
Tel: 01978 860236 *Fax:* 01978 869047
Email: lime@celtic.co.uk
Website: www.llangollen.org.uk

11 Jul 1998, applications by 15 Apr. Amateur insts aged 25 and under. Competition is part of Llangollen International Eisteddfod in Jul. Application fee £2 for UK competitors, no fee for overseas competitors. First prize £200 and trophy.

International Young Singer of the Year Competition

Eisteddfod Office, Llangollen, Denbighshire LL20 8NG
Tel: 01978 860236 *Fax:* 01978 869047
Email: lime@celtic.co.uk
Website: www.llangollen.org.uk

11 Jul 1998, applications by 15 Apr. Competition for amateur singers aged 16-32 as part of Llangollen International Eisteddfod in Jul. Application fee £2 for UK competitors, no fee for overseas competitors. First prize £200 and trophy.

Julius Isserlis Scholarship

Royal Philharmonic Society, 10 Stratford Pl, London W1N 9AE
Tel: 0171 491 8110 *Fax:* 0171 493 7463

Scholarship worth £20,000 over two years to fund study abroad. Awarded biennially by competition in selected performing categories to students aged 15-25 of any nationality permanently resident in the UK. Spring 1999: fl and ob. Entry fee £20.

Lloyds Bank Young Composers Workshop

BBC Young Musicians, Room EG 30, East Tower Television Centre, Wood La, London W12 7RJ
Tel: 0181 895 6143/4 *Fax:* 0181 895 6974
Email: young.musicians@bbc.co.uk

Open to UK citizens aged 16-24. Applications by 1 Apr 1999 to be returned with one example of recent composition not exceeding 15 minutes in duration.

Musicale Young Instrumentalist Competition

Musicale plc, 20 Salisbury Av, Harpenden, Herts AL5 2QG
Tel: 01582 460978 *Fax:* 01582 767343

Biennial, next 2000. Young instrumentalists aged 11-16. Cash prize plus concerto performance with the National Children's Chamber Orchestra of Great Britain at a major concert venue.

National Concert Band Festival

BASBWE, 7 Dingle Close, Tytherington, Macclesfield SK10 2UT
Tel: 01625 430807 *also fax*

Symphonic wind band categories: beginners (aged 14 and under), school, youth (aged 19 and under), community, open. 3 big band categories: school, youth, open. Regionals Nov-Dec, finals held April 1998 at the RNCM, Manchester.

National Mozart Competition

66 Talbot St, Southport, Merseyside PR8 1LU
Tel: 01704 530903

Annual. Nov, applications by Oct. For singers of any nationality aged under 28 (female), or under 30 (male). Preliminary rounds Oct in London, Manchester, Cardiff, Glasgow and Dublin. Application fee £25. Prize money of £2500 plus engagements. Also Verdi/Wagner prize of £250 for best performance by a male singer of a Verdi or Wagner aria.

National Youth Brass Band Championships of Great Britain

c/o Boosey & Hawkes plc, Deansbrook Rd, Edgware, Middx HA8 9BB
Tel: 0181 952 6747 *Fax:* 0181 951 1314
Email: amsizer@boosey.com
Website: www.boosey.com

Feb at University of Salford, applications by Nov. Jnr (aged 16 and under), intermediate, advanced and open (aged 19 and under) classes. First prize and trophy in each class. Application fee: £40.

Norfolk Young Musician Competition

Music at Saint George's, Wahnfried, 4 Church Close, Buxton, Norwich NR10 5ER
Tel: 01603 279742

Nov, entries by 30 Sep. For gr 8+ singers and instrumentalists aged 21 and under who either work, receive tuition or are resident in Norfolk. Three cash prizes plus sponsorship for a public concert later the same year as well as one in the Norfolk and Norwich Festival the following year.

Royal Philharmonic Society Composition Prize
10 Stratford Pl, London W1N 9AE
Tel: 0171 491 8110 *Fax:* 0171 493 7463

Annual award in Dec. Closing date as announced. Open to registered students past or present of any conservatoire or university within the UK, aged 28 and under on closing date. Application fee £20.

Sainsbury's Choir of the Year Competition
c/o Kallaway Ltd, 2 Portland Rd, Holland Pk, London W11 4LA
Tel: 0171 221 7883 *Fax:* 0171 229 4595
Email: kate@kallaway.co.uk

Biennial. Next Nov 1998, entries by 9 Jan 1998. Open to amateur choirs of 20-100 members. No age limit.
Three categories: youth choirs; single voice choirs; mixed voice choirs. Auditions Mar-May, finals held in Nov and televised on BBC2. First prize in each category of £2000; overall winner receives a further £1000 plus £1000 to commission a new piece of choral mus.

Shell LSO Music Scholarship
c/o The Scholarship Administrator, London Symphony Orchestra, Barbican Centre, Barbican, London EC2Y 8DS
Tel: 0171 272 4032 *Fax:* 0171 263 1831
Email: shell@lso.co.uk
Website: www.lso.co.uk

Information available Oct, entries by mid-Dec. Orch instrumentalists aged 14-22. Insts vary; 1999 br. £6000 annual scholarship. Auditions, w/shops and m/classes with LSO principals.

Texaco Young Musician of Wales
1 Westferry Circus, Canary Wharf, London E14 4HA
Tel: 0171 719 3000; 0181 549 7660 *Fax:* 0171 719 5175

Biennial event organised in partnership with Côr Meibion De Cymru (South Wales Male Choir). Preliminary rounds and regional finals held autumn 1998, final Mar 1999.
Open to instrumentalists age 14-19 who have lived or studied in Wales for a minimum of 3 years. The final is broadcast on television and the winner receives the Texaco Young Musician of Wales trophy and a prize of £1000. Second

prize £750; third prize £500; 3 runners up prizes £250 each. Application fee of £10 refunded on attendance at preliminary rounds.
For application forms contact June McCullough *Tel:* 0181 549 7660. Completed forms to be returned by 31 Jul 1998.

Tunbridge Wells International Young Concert Artists Competition
TWIYCA, Competition Office, MCL Group 77, Mount Ephraim, Tunbridge Wells, Kent TN4 8BS
Tel: 01892 510088 *Fax:* 01892 538547

Biennial. Next 2-4 Jul 1998, entries by 23 Feb 1998. Aged under 24 on date of final.
3 sections: pno, str, wind. Total prize money available £10,500 plus London recital. Application fee £45.

Yehudi Menuhin International Competition for Young Violinists
8 St Georges Terrace, London NW1 8XJ
Tel: 0171 911 0901 *Fax:* 0171 911 0903

Apr, applications by Oct. 2 sections: under 16 (jnr), under 22 (snr). Application fee: 450FF. First prizes 20,000FF (jnr) and 30,000FF (snr) plus performance at gala concert conducted by Yehudi Menuhin for the winner of each section.

Young Artists Platform
Tillett Trust, Courtyard House, Neopardy, Crediton, Devon EX17 5EP

Entry forms available in Oct, applications by Nov, auditions in Jan-Feb. Open to musicians residing or studying f/t in the British Isles. Age limits: inst soloists 20-25, singers 23-28, ens of up to 6 players all members must be within same age limits. Application fee £10, returned at audition. No cash prizes, successful candidates given concerts including Fairfield, Croydon, plus a demo tape, publicity photos and a publicity brochure.

Youth Choirs

The Youth Choirs below are listed under national, regional and local headings, depending on the method and scope of the audition procedure and from where the majority of the performers are drawn. A list of **Youth Opera and Music Theatre** companies appears at the end of the section. Unless otherwise indicated, the choirs consist of SSATB voices. Additional Youth Choirs run by the local authorities can be found in the **Local Music Education** section. School, music college and university choirs are not listed, unless membership of the choir is open to external applicants. An asterisk (*) indicates membership of the **British Federation of Young Choirs (BYFC)**, Devonshire House, Devonshire Sq, Loughborough, Leics LE11 3DW *Tel:* 01509 211664 *Fax:* 01509 260630 *Email:* bfyc@foobar.co.uk.

National

British Methodist Youth Choir
35 Westwood Rd, Sutton Coldfield, W Midlands B73 6UP
Tel: 0121 605 8766 *also fax*
Email: gjones@mcmail.com

Gilbert Jones, admin; Ashley Thompson, cond.
Entry requirements: Some experience of choral singing and mus reading plus recommendation from a present/recent choir dir. *Details:* SATB choir. Members from all over the country meet at three different venues pa in Jan, Apr and Sep-Oct for w/end of intensive rehearsal, leading to a concert and church services. Members need not be Methodist but must be willing to take part in church services. Some help with travel costs available.
Age range: 17-27. *Members:* 25-30.

Laudibus - The National Youth Chamber Choir
c/o Chameleon Arts Management, 32 St Michael's Rd, Sandhurst, Berks GU47 8HE
Tel: 01252 873313 *Fax:* 01252 871517
Email: camarts@dial.pipex.com

Mike Brewer, mus dir; Pete Csemiczky, promotions mgr.
Entry requirements: By audition, previous membership of the National Youth Choir necessary. *Details:* 1997 concerts held in Oxford and Cumbria.
Age range: 17-26. *Members:* 25.

National Youth Choirs of Great Britain *
PO Box 67, Holmfirth, Huddersfield, W Yorks HD7 1GQ
Tel: 01484 687023 *Fax:* 01484 681635

Carl Browning, exec dir; Michael Brewer OBE, mus dir; Danny Curtis, choir admin.
Entry requirements: Auditions held at regional centres annually in autumn and spring. *Details:* Courses at Christmas/New Year and in the summer. Fees: £240-300 (course); £20 (audition). SATB voices.
Age range: 12-18; 16-22. *Members:* 250.

National Youth Choir of Scotland and Chamber Choir *
18 Polmont Pk, Falkirk FK2 0XT
Tel: 01324 711749 *Fax:* 01324 713746
Email: nycos@ednet.co.uk

Robert Tait, admin; Christopher Bell, artistic dir and cond.
Entry requirements: By audition. *Details:* Summer course at Glenalmond College with concerts in Aberdeen, Perth, Edinburgh and Glasgow. Other w/ends for chmbr choir activities. SATB voices.
Age range: 16-24. *Members:* 100.

National Youth Choir of Wales
Welsh Amateur Music Federation, 9 Museum Pl, Cardiff CF1 3NX
Tel: 01222 394711 *Fax:* 01222 221447

Keith Griffin, dir; Bryn Terfel, president; Ralph Allwood, cond.
Entry requirements: Annual audition and re-audition. *Details:* Short courses and 8-day course. SATB voices.
Age range: 16-21. *Members:* 75.

The Rodolfus Choir
The Shepherd's Cottage, Gt Shelford, Cambridge CB2 5JX
Tel: 01223 845685 *Fax:* 01223 841980
Email: rallwood@netcomuk.co.uk

Ralph Allwood, cond; Lydia Smallwood, admin.
Entry requirements: Singers selected from those on Eton Choral Courses. *Details:* Few days of intensive rehearsals before concerts or recordings.
Age range: 17-25. *Members:* 50-60.

Regional and Local

Alicia Bardsley Singers
22 Greek St, Stockport SK3 8AB
Tel: 0161 429 7413 *also fax*

K Mullen, admin; Alicia Bardsley, cond.
Entry requirements: Audition. *Details:* Weekly rehearsals.
Mixed choir divided into jnr and snr sections.
Age range: Up to 14 (performance), 15+ (snr).
Members: 25 in each group.

Berkshire Boys' Choir
Berkshire Young Musicians Trust, Stoneham Ct, 100
Cockney Hill, Reading RG30 4EZ
Tel: 0118 901 2350 *Fax:* 0118 901 2351

Gillian Dibden, cond.
Entry requirements: Prepared solo song/hymn and
simple aural tests. Auditions in Jun for entry in
Sep, or mid-year by arrangement. *Details:*
Rehearsals Sat afternoon 4 times per term.
Toured Rheinland in 1997. SSA voices.
Age range: 9-13. *Members:* 60.

Berkshire Girls' Choir
Berkshire Young Musicians Trust, Stoneham Ct, 100
Cockney Hill, Reading RG30 4EZ
Tel: 0118 901 2350 *Fax:* 0118 901 2351

Gillian Dibden, dir.
Entry requirements: Auditions in Jun for entry in
Sep: prepared solo song or hymn and simple
aural tests. *Details:* Rehearsals Sat afternoon 4
times per term.
Age range: 9-14. *Members:* 50.

Berkshire Youth Choir
Berkshire Young Musicians Trust, 25 Whiteknights Rd,
Reading, Berks RG6 7BY
Tel: 0118 966 5015

Gillian Dibden, choral dir.
Entry requirements: Prepared solo song, aural and
sight-singing. Auditions in Jun for entry in Sep, or
by arrangement if vacancies occur. *Details:* Two
w/end courses per term. Winners of 1996
Sainsbury's Choir of the Year title. Outstanding
Award at National Choral Competition 1996.
Toured Czech Republic in 1997.
Age range: 14-18. *Members:* 80.

Boden Show Choir
6-12 Windmill Hill, Enfield, Middx EN2 6SA
Tel: 0181 367 2692 *Fax:* 0181 367 1836

Adam Boden, choir dir; Robert Hyman, choirmaster.
Entry requirements: Private auditions, simple
scales and pitch test. *Details:* Choir meets weekly
Tue evenings. Sings all kinds of mus from sacred
to rock'n'roll, but specialises in show mus.
Age range: 10-20. *Members:* 80.

The Bradford Choristers
8 Moorcroft, Eldwick, Nr Bingley, Yorkshire BD16 3DR
Tel: 01274 774758

Ann Foster, sec; Richard Darke, mus dir.
Entry requirements: By audition, mainly through
schools, although individual contact welcome.
Details: Boys' and gentlemens' choir, mainly
English church mus recitals. SATB voices.
Age range: 8-11. *Members:* 20-30.

Bridgwater Young People's Choir *
11 Morgans Rise, Bishops Hull, Taunton, Somerset TA1 5HW
Tel: 01823 252658 *also fax*

Andrew Maddocks, cond; Ann Fisher, sec.
Details: 2 choirs. SSA. Entry by audition to assess
voice potential and by informal interview.
Age range: 7-18. *Members:* 80.

Caerphilly Children's Choir
Plasyfelin Junior School, Churchill Pk, Caerphilly CF83 3FT
Tel: 01222 852523

Nigel Jones, mus dir.
Entry requirements: Ability to sing in tune. *Details:*
Weekly rehearsals. Local concerts. Unison and 2-part.
Age range: 8-12. *Members:* 50.

Calne Girls' Choir
18 Wyvern Av, Calne, Wilts SN11 8NZ
Tel: 01249 817470 *also fax*

Geoffrey Field, dir.
Entry requirements: Informal audition. No
previous choral experience necessary. *Details:*
Choir meets Wed 7.30-8.45pm. Members taken
from Calne, Chippenham, Devizes, Trowbridge
and surrounding areas.
Age range: 11-18. *Members:* 36.

Cambridgeshire Boys' Choir
35 Acorn Av, Bar Hill, Cambridge CB3 8DT
Tel: 01954 780307 *also fax; Fax:* 0385 597837
Email: cambridgeshire.boys.choir@dial.pipex.com
Website: dialspace.dial.pipex.com/cambridgeshire.boys.choir/

Nicholas Bergstrom-Allen, dir.
Entry requirements: Selection by audition. *Details:*
SSAA. Main choir rehearses twice weekly at King's
College School, plus a weekly rehearsal for the opera
group and an individual lesson for each boy in voice
production, solo singing and mus theory.
Professionally trained and fully prepared soloists or
ensembles for productions of all kinds worldwide.
Frequent concerts with wide-ranging repertoire.
Regular international touring, many TV appearances,
also provides singers for Royal Opera House.
Age range: 8-14. *Members:* 24 full members plus 6
probationers.

147

Cantamus *
c/o Camerata, 4 Margaret Rd, Birmingham B17 0EU
Tel: 0121 426 6208 also fax

Sheila Haslam, sec; Pamela Cook MBE, dir.
Entry requirements: By audition; solo piece and aural tests. Details: Female choir, SSAA; individual vocal tuition.
Age range: 12-22. Members: 35-50.

Cantate Youth Choir *
106 Potter St, Harlow, Essex CM17 9AW
Tel: 01279 304746
Email: cantate-choir@compuserve.com

Michael Kibblewhite, mus dir; Dawn Helder, gen mgr; Jan Eke, mkt mgr.
Entry requirements: Basic musicianship and commitment. Details: Rehearsals held in Bishop's Stortford, Hertfordshire. Wide repertoire including major SATB works. Concerts in East England and Central London. Foreign tours. Boy trebles welcome.
Age range: 10-21. Members: 100 +.

Cantores Novae *
269 Dobcroft Rd, Sheffield S11 9LG
Tel: 0114 235 0993 Fax: 0114 235 1883

Vivien Pike, cond.
Entry requirements: Auditions: good vocal technique, good sight-reading and aural. Details: SSAA choir consisting of students at college and university and advanced singers.
Age range: 14-40. Members: 55.

Capital Arts Children's Choirs
225 Shurland Av, East Barnet, Herts EN4 8DG
Tel: 0181 449 2342 also fax

Kathleen Shanks, mus dir; Pamela Horsepool, sec.
Entry requirements: Entry by audition. Details: The choir performs as a whole group, jnr choir (6-13) and snr choir (14-18). Participants in the National Festival of Music for Youth. Concerts at the Royal Festival Hall and Barbican. Broadcasts on BBC Radio 2, Classic FM and TV. Performances in Europe, USA and Canada. SSA voices.
Age range: 6-18. Members: 50.

Capital Arts Show Choir
225 Shurland Av, East Barnet, Herts EN4 8DG
Tel: 0181 449 2342

Kathleen Shanks, mus dir; Pamela Horsepool, sec.
Entry requirements: Entry by audition. Details: Performances, radio and TV broadcasts in Europe, USA and Canada. Royal Variety Performance, Dominion Theatre; London Palladium. SATB voices.
Age range: 7-18. Members: 50.

Cardiff County and Vale of Glamorgan Youth Choir *
The Friary Centre, The Friary, Cardiff CF1 4AA
Tel: 01222 640950/1 Fax: 01222 227471

Kelvin Thomas, mus dir; Stuart Burrows, president.
Entry requirements: Annual auditions. Details: Weekly rehearsals, courses, tours, recordings, concerts, festivals and competitions.
Age range: 15-21. Members: 90-100.

Central Berkshire Girls' Choir
Central Berkshire Music Centre, 25 Whiteknights Rd, Reading, Berks RG6 7BY
Tel: 0118 966 6914 Fax: 0118 935 3419

Michael Wood, dir and cond; Mrs E Bartley, admin.
Entry requirements: Audition. Details: Weekly rehearsals during term, 2 hrs. Toured USA in 1996.
Age range: 14-18. Members: 55.

Chamber Choir of The Arts Educational School
Tring Pk, Tring, Herts HP23 5LX
Tel: 01442 824255 Fax: 01442 891069

Vaughan Meakins, cond. Details: Twice weekly rehearsals. Female choir, formed from snr members of the school which combines an education with a vocational training in the arts of the theatre; dance, drama and music. SSAA. Past tours include Italy, France and USA. CDs with RPO and Tring International label.
Age range: 15-18. Members: 30-45.

Chelmer Youth Choir
34 Longmead Av, Gt Baddow, Chelmsford CM2 7EG
Tel: 01245 471649 also fax

Eric Withams, cond.
Entry requirements: No auditions. Details: Mixed voices.
Age range: 13-18. Members: 34.

Chelmsford Star Children's Choir
34 Longmead Av, Gt Baddow, Chelmsford CM2 7EG
Tel: 01245 471649 also fax

Eric Withams, cond.
Entry requirements: Auditions required. Details: Weekly rehearsals. Open to children from schools in the Chelmsford area. Upper voices.
Age range: 8-13. Members: 50.

Cheshire Youth Chamber Choir
Hadfield House, County Hall, Chester CH1 1SQ
Tel: 01244 602319 Fax: 01244 603813

Beverley Stanton, admin; Mervyn Williams, dir.
Entry requirements: Audition. Details: Formed in 1995. Engagements include Chester Festival, Eaton Hall and an appearance before the President of the European parliament. Toured Japan in 1997. Tour to South Africa planned.
Age range: 18-21. Members: 30.

Cheshire Youth Choir
Hadfield House, County Hall, Chester CH1 1SQ
Tel: 01244 602319 *Fax:* 01244 603813

Beverley Stanton, admin; Mervyn Williams, Martin Cooke, dirs.
Entry requirements: Audition required. *Details:* Monthly rehearsals plus singing courses. Appeared on BBC. Concert tours to Denmark and USA. Toured Austria in 1997.
Age range: 13-18 *Members:* 60.

Children's Voices of Enfield
20 Brycedale Cres, Southgate, London N14 7EY
Tel: 0181 882 0630 *also fax*

June Keyte, dir.
Entry requirements: Audition. *Details:* For musical children who have a real desire to perform in concerts and record for Educational Publications Worldwide as well as TV in the UK.
Age range: 8-18. *Members:* 50.

City of Birmingham Symphony Youth Chorus
Paradise Pl, Birmingham B3 3RP
Tel: 0121 236 1555/2461 *Fax:* 0121 236 4231
Email: information@cbso.co.uk

Simon Halsey, chorus dir; David Francis, chorus mgr; Hilary Parfitt, vocal coach; Shirley Court, cond jnr chorus; Adrian Partington, cond snr chorus.
Entry requirements: By audition in summer term.
Age range: 9-12 (jnr chorus), 12-18 (snr chorus).
Members: Snr 60; jnr 90.

City of Sheffield Young Choirs *
269 Dobcroft Rd, Sheffield S11 9LG
Tel: 0114 235 0993 *Fax:* 0114 235 1883

Vivien Pike, cond.
Entry requirements: Jnr choir: ability to sing in tune. Intermediate choir: audition, moderate sight-reading and aural test. Girls' choir: audition, vocal technique and sight-reading of a reasonable standard. *Details:* Weekly rehearsals. Jnr choir: mixed choir, SS trebles. Intermediate choir: mixed choir, SSA. Girls' choir: SSAA voices; peripatetic singing tuition.
Age range: Jnr 8-12; intermediate 10-16; girls 12-19.
Members: 55 (jnr), 50 (intermediate), 48 (girls' choir).

Durham County Youth Choir *
Darlington Music Centre, Borough Rd, Darlington DL1 1SG

John Allen, admin; Matthew Grehan-Bradley, cond.
Entry requirements: Auditions: solo of own choice and first verse of *I Vow to Thee My Country*; test for vocal range. *Details:* Weekly rehearsals and two weekend courses pa. Individual vocal tuition. County charge for non-LEA members. SATB voices.
Age range: 14-25. *Members:* 60.

Ealing Youth Choir *
169 Murray Rd, Ealing, London W5 4DD
Tel: 0181 560 4532 *also fax*

John Compton, chmn; Paul Ayres, cond.
Entry requirements: None. *Details:* Rehearsals Tue eves. European tours.
Age range: 12-21. *Members:* 25.

Farnham Youth Choirs *
21 Firgrove Hill, Farnham, Surrey GU9 8LH
Tel: 01252 723406 *also fax*

David Victor-Smith MBE, dir.
Entry requirements: Competitive entry to youth choirs *Details:* Weekly rehearsals, SSA (includes boys with unchanged voices); members usually from 15 mile radius of Farnham. National and international award winners. Regular foreign tours and recordings.
Age range: 7-9 (children's choir); 9-13 (jnr youth); 11-16 (youth, SSA); 15-25 (youth chmbr choir, 'Canzonetta', SATB). *Members:* Training choir 25; jnr youth choir 50; youth choir 50; youth chmbr choir 20+.

Fife Youth Choir
Auchterderran Centre, Woodend Rd, Cardenden KY5 0NE
Tel: 01592 414785 *Fax:* 01592 414641
Email: gwilson@itasdarc.demon.co.uk

Graeme Wilson, adviser in mus, Fife Council.
Entry requirements: Open to Fife pupils. *Details:* SATB.
Age range: 15-18. *Members:* 50.

Finchley Children's Music Group *
69 Etchingham Park Rd, Finchley, London N3 2ED
Tel: 0181 343 3847 *also fax*

Joan Lane, hon sec; Nicholas Wilks, mus dir.
Entry requirements: No audition for jnr group. Snr group by audition of song, scales and sight-reading. *Details:* Weekly rehearsals, single day half-term w/shops, residential summer school. Jnr group: unbroken voices, SSA. Snr group: SSA and SATB choirs.
Age range: 5-7 (infant), 7-10 (jnr), 10-18 (snr). *Members:* Infant group 50, jnr group 140, snr group 110.

Glasgow Youth Choir
30 Haggswood Av, Pollokshields, Glasgow G41 4RH
Tel: 0141 427 9921

Agnes F Hoey MBE, founder and cond.
Entry requirements: Jnr entry: ear test; snr entry: voice test. *Details:* Weekly rehearsals. Divided into mixed jnr (120) and snr girls/ladies (50). Now supported by Glasgow Caledonian University. Snr girls concert tour to Prague Jul 1998. SSA voices.
Age range: 6-23. *Members:* c 200.

Guildford Chorale
c/o Royal Grammar School, High St, Guildford, Surrey GU1 3BB
Tel: 01483 880600 *Fax:* 01483 306127

Andrew Wilson, cond and admin.

149

Entry requirements: Simple voice test. *Details:* 3 concerts pa, variety of styles. Weekly rehearsals Tue 4.30pm. *Age range:* 14-19. *Members:* 25-30.

Hampshire County Youth Choir
Hampshire Music Service, Gordon Rd, Winchester, Hants SO23 7DD
Tel: 01962 861502 *Fax:* 01962 863690

Keith Clark, mus dir and cond.
Entry requirements: By simple audition. *Details:* Weekly rehearsals, Friday eves. SATB voices. *Age range:* 14-19. *Members:* 50.

Hartlepool Youth Choir *
9 Granville Av, Hartlepool TS26 8ND
Tel: 01429 261124

Christopher J Simmons, mus dir; Daniel Raine, mgr.
Entry requirements: Pitch test. *Details:* Twice weekly rehearsals. Non-sectarian organisation. Europa Cantat, NAC, EFJC member. Also Hartlepool Training Choir, age 9-11 yrs; rehearsals Mon eves 6-7 pm. *Age range:* 11-25. *Members:* 35-40.

High Wycombe Music Centre Youth Choir
Sands Middle School, Mill End Rd, High Wycombe, Bucks HP12 4BA
Tel: 01494 445947 *Fax:* 01494 442773

Clem Virgo, cond; Eric Parsons, acc.
Entry requirements: Singers join on trial basis. *Details:* Rehearsals weekly Sat mornings. SATB choir, mostly unaccompanied but also major choral works. Open to all young people with good level of musicianship and committed to choral singing. Participants in National Festival of Music for Youth and Sainsbury's Choir of the Year Competition. Regular concerts in South Buckinghamshire and further afield. *Age range:* 13-19. *Members:* 60.

Hywel Girls' Choir and Hywel Boy Singers
6 Harries Av, Llanelli, Carmarthenshire SA15 3LF
Tel: 01554 772979 *also fax*
Email: hywel-williams@msn.com

John Hywel Williams MBE, dir of mus; Lady Mary Mansel Lewis OBE, president; Stuart Burrows, vice-president. *Details:* Tour to Poland, Denmark and Germany, tour of North of England. *Age range:* 8-16. *Members:* 80+.

Ipswich Girls' Choir
County Music Service, Northgate Arts Centre, Sidegate La West, Ipswich, Suffolk IP4 3DF
Tel: 01473 281866 *Fax:* 01473 286068

David Bramhall, cond. *Details:* SSA. Weekly rehearsals. *Age range:* 10-16. *Members:* 35.

Jersey Boys' Choir
Professional Development Centre, c/o PO Box 142,

Jersey, Channel Islands, JE4 8QJ
Tel: 01534 509491 *Fax:* 01534 509300

Malcolm Whittell, dir.
Entry requirements: By audition. *Details:* Vocal tuition. Also at same address Jersey Junior Girls' Choir, age 7-11, Mrs S de Gruchy, dir; Jersey Intermediate Girls' Choir, age 11-14, Mrs G Marquer, dir; Jersey Senior Girls' Choir, age 14-18, Mrs E du Feu, dir. *Age range:* 8-13. *Members:* 25.

Jewish Heritage Youth Choir
PO Box 232, Harrow, Middx HA1 2NN
Tel: 0181 909 2445 *Fax:* 0181 909 1030
Email: singing@jmht.org

Geraldine Auerbach, dir, Jewish Music Heritage Trust.
Entry requirements: Love of singing.
Age range: 8-14. *Members:* Performs Jewish repertoire for functions and concerts. Open to Jews and non-Jews.

Kent Youth Chamber Choir
Kent Music Centre, The Masters House, College Rd, Maidstone ME15 6YQ
Tel: 01622 688914 *Fax:* 01622 661318
Email: kmsho@cix.compulink.co.uk

Andrew Larner, dir of mus. *Details:* Two short courses pa. Consists of a group of snr members of the Kent Youth Choir; aims to sing more demanding, often unaccompanied mus. SATB voices. Also Kent Youth Barbershop, 4-8 members.
Age range: 18-25. *Members:* 15-20.

Kent Youth Choir
Kent Music Centre, The Masters House, College Rd, Maidstone ME15 6YQ
Tel: 01622 691212 *Fax:* 01622 661318
Email: kmsho@cix.compulink.co.uk

Andrew Larner, dir of mus.
Entry requirements: Audition required, good voice, high standard of general musicianship. *Details:* Three 4-day courses pa. SATB voices. *Age range:* 15-21. *Members:* 60.

Kent Youth Singers
Kent Music Centre, The Masters House, College Rd, Maidstone ME15 6YQ
Tel: 01622 688914 *Fax:* 01622 661318
Email: kmsho@cix.compulink.co.uk

Andrew Larner, dir of mus.
Entry requirements: Singers must show keen interest and have a voice which shows potential. *Details:* Training choir for the Kent Youth Choir. Three 4-day courses pa. SATB voices. *Age range:* 14-18. *Members:* 60.

The Manchester Boys' Choir
Zion Arts Centre, Stretford Rd, Manchester M15 5ZA
Tel: 0161 226 4411 *Fax:* 0161 226 1010

Adrian P Jessett, founder dir.
Entry requirements: No audition. *Details:* Choir in residence at The Bridgewater Hall with series of concerts each season. Radio and TV; engagement nationally and abroad. Works in association with Opera North and the Hallé Concerts Society. SSA voices.
Age range: 10-15. *Members:* 24.

Manchester Boys' Chorus
M E C Music Service, Medlock School, Wadeson Rd, Manchester M13 9UR
Tel: 0161 273 3630

Adrian P Jessett, founder dir.
Entry requirements: Chorus open entry, training chorus for boys with voice in transitional stage. *Details:* Weekly rehearsals. Regular engagements, usually for charitable organisations.
Age range: 15-22. *Members:* 24.

Manchester Grammar School Choir
The Manchester Grammar School, Old Hall La, Manchester M13 0XT
Tel: 0161 224 7201 *Fax:* 0161 257 2446

Andrew Dean, cond. *Details:* Five 30 min rehearsals each week. Boys voices. Foreign tour every two years. Regular performances with Hallé and BBC Philharmonic Orchestras.
Age range: 11-18. *Members:* 50.

Manx Youth Choir *
Music Centre, Lord St, Douglas, Isle of Man IM1 1LE
Tel: 01624 686555 *Fax:* 01624 686557

Entry requirements: Recommendation by own school choir director necessary if still at school. *Details:* Residential courses, new members accepted each year.
Age range: 13-21. *Members:* c 90.

Maureen Hunter Singers
14 Vine Close, Cottingham, E Yorks HU16 5RF
Tel: 01482 843344 *also fax*

J Graham Hunter, mgr.
Entry requirements: Selection by musical director, following audition. *Details:* Annual Christmas and spring concerts plus various charity concerts throughout year. Several tours made to USA and Canada, next in 1999.
Age range: Two groups, 8-13 and 14-adult (all female). *Members:* 30 and 65.

Methodist Association Youth Club Singers
2 Chester House, Pages La, London N10 1PR
Tel: 0181 444 9845

Craig McLeish, dir.
Entry requirements: Application form and audition

cassette of two pieces: 1 classical, 1 popular. *Details:* Performances in 1997 included Royal Albert Hall and Croydon Fairfield Hall, and tour of Northern and Republic of Ireland. SATB voices.
Age range: 14-26. *Members:* 120+.

New London Children's Choir *
41 Aberdare Gardens, London NW6 3AL
Tel: 0171 625 4641 *Fax:* 0171 625 4876

Ronald Corp, cond.
Entry requirements: No auditions for training choir. Audition required for snr, SSA and SATB choir. *Details:* Weekly rehearsals.
Age range: 8+ (training choir), 10-17 (snr choir, unbroken voices), 16-21 (SATB), 16-21 (New London Barbers, barbershop).
Members: Training choir 120, snr choir 120, SATB choir 60.

Northants County Youth Choirs
c/o Music Services, 125-129 Kettering Rd, Northampton NN1 4AZ
Tel: 01604 37117 *Fax:* 01604 603070

Peter Dunkley, head of mus service.
Entry requirements: Annual auditions held, but new members are admitted at any time during the year. *Details:* Four youth choirs. SATB, SSA, Boy Trebles.
Age range: 7-21. *Members:* 150.

Nottingham Choral Trust Youth Choir *
18 Hobart Dr, Stapleford, Notts NG9 8PX
Tel: 0115 939 0511

Angela Kay, cond; Susan Hatherly, sec.
Entry requirements: No auditions.
Age range: 6-18. *Members:* 300+.

Oldham Boys' Choir
Oldham Metropolitan Borough Music Centre, The Lyceum Building, Union St, Oldham OL1 1QG
Tel: 0161 627 2332 *Fax:* 0161 620 0259

Eileen Bentley, cond.
Entry requirements: Auditions, children selected from local schools. Sing a song they know, simple aural tests. *Details:* Weekly rehearsals. Some w/end w/shops throughout year. Participation in concerts and festivals.
Age range: 7-13/14. *Members:* 45.

Oldham Girls' Choirs *
Oldham Metropolitan Borough Music Centre, The Lyceum Building, Union St, Oldham OL1 1QG
Tel: 0161 627 2332 *Fax:* 0161 620 0259

Eileen Bentley, cond snr choir; Jacqui Hamlett, cond jnr choir.
Entry requirements: Auditions for all choirs. children selected from local schools. Sing a song they know, aural tests.
Details: Weekly rehearsals. Some w/end w/shops throughout years. Participation in concerts and

British Youth *Opera*

President *Valerie Masterson CBE*

British Youth Opera is this country's premier company for new and emerging operatic talent.

An annual Summer Season of two fully-staged productions takes place at major London and regional venues. Singers are aged 18 to 30 and many former members are now principals with leading opera companies in the UK and abroad.

"An unbelievably high standard"
Sunday Times

South Bank University, 103 Borough Rd London SE1 0AA
Tel **0171 815 6090**   Fax **0171 815 6094**
e-mail byopera@mailbox.co.uk

The essential magazine for professionals and amateurs who take their singing seriously.

Published bi-monthly.
Annual UK subscription £14.40
(overseas rates on application).

For a free sample copy please telephone **0171 333 1720**.

the **Singer**

THE NATIONAL YOUTH MUSIC THEATRE

"Britain's finest youth company"
The Scotsman

• Performances at major UK venues & festivals; national & international tours

• Varied repertoire including new commissions, musicals, opera, music theatre

• Open auditions throughout the UK for cast & orchestral performers

• Certificated, open access music theatre courses available at local, regional and national centres

• Work experience opportunities in stage management, wardrobe and arts administration

NATIONAL YOUTH MUSIC THEATRE
—— Supported by ——
ANDREW LLOYD WEBBER

NYMT
5th Floor
Palace Theatre
Shaftesbury Avenue
London W1V 8AY
Tel: 0171-734 7478
Fax: 0171-734 7515
Internet: www.nymt.org.uk

GUILDFORD CATHEDRAL CHOIR

The Dean and Chapter offer an

Organ Scholarship and **Choral Scholarships for Altos/Tenors/Basses**
in conjunction with the University of Surrey and **Choristerships**
(Boys aged 7 – 9) in conjunction with Lanesborough Preparatory School (day-school).

*For further information, please contact the Organist's Secretary, Guildford Cathedral, Stag Hill, Guildford GU2 5UP.
Telephone: 01483 565287*

festivals. SSA/SSAA.
Age range: 8-13 (jnr), 13-19 (snr). *Members:* Jnr 60, snr 55.

Oxford Girls' Choirs
The Old Manse, Leafield, Witney, Oxon OX8 5NN
Tel: 01993 878200 *Fax:* 01993 878375

Mary Taylor, admin.
Entry requirements: By audition. *Details:* SSAA.
Age range: 5-8, 8-11, 12-18. *Members:* Training choir 20, snr choir 30.

Royal Scottish National Orchestra Junior Chorus
Royal Scottish National Orchestra, 73 Claremont St, Glasgow G3 7HA
Tel: 0141 226 3868 *Fax:* 0141 221 4317
Email: rsno@glasgow.almac.co.uk
Website: www.scot-art.org/rsno

Christopher Bell, chorus master; Jill Mitchell, chorus mgr.
Entry requirements: By audition. *Details:* Weekly rehearsals for concerts with RSNO. Performances at the Edinburgh Festival.
Age range: 5-18.
Members: Jnr chorus 120, training chorus 80.

St Catherine's Chamber Choir
St Catherine's School, Bramley, Guildford, Surrey
Tel: 01483 893363 *Fax:* 01483 893003

Robert Gillman, cond and admin.
Entry requirements: Auditions. *Details:* Twice weekly rehearsals. Tours of Venice, Florence and Prague. SSAA.
Age range: 15-18. *Members:* 32.

Southend Boys' Choir
PO Box 6, Civic Centre, Southend on Sea, Essex
Tel: 01702 215436 *Fax:* 01702 215110

Roger Humphrey, cond.
Entry requirements: Auditions (ear and pitch tests).
Details: Weekly rehearsals. SSA. Frequent performances in London and abroad with major orchestras and conductors, plus recordings and broadcasts.
Age range: 8+. *Members:* 60.

Southend Girls' Choir
PO Box 6, Civic Centre, Southend on Sea, Essex
Tel: 01702 215436 *Fax:* 01702 215110

Roger Humphrey, cond.
Entry requirements: Auditions. *Details:* Weekly rehearsals and local performances. Toured Seychelles 1997. Performances in London, broadcasts and tour to Australia 1998.
Age range: 8-18. *Members:* 100.

Stockport Youth Choirs and The Maia Singers
23 Buttermere Rd, Gatley, Cheadle, Cheshire SK8 4RH
Tel: 0161 428 5456

John Pomphrey, dir; Lynda Whitney, admin.
Entry requirements: By audition. *Details:* Weekly rehearsals. 4 choirs: 2 girls' choirs (SSA); boys' choir (SA); young adult (SSATB).
Age range: 7-16+. *Members:* c 150.

Suffolk Jubilee Choir
County Music Service, Northgate Arts Centre, Sidegate La West, Ipswich, Suffolk IP4 3DF
Tel: 01473 281866 *Fax:* 01473 286068

David Bramhall, cond.
Entry requirements: Annual auditions. *Details:* SSA, including boy trebles and altos. Rehearsals, residential course and foreign tours in school holidays.
Age range: 12-20. *Members:* 45.

Vivace Girls' Choir *
c/o 7 Park La, Charvil, Reading, Berks RG10 9TR
Tel: 0118 934 0589

Miss S Newman, mus dir.
Entry requirements: Informal auditions. *Details:* Vocal tuition. Participates in festivals, concerts and competitions. SSA voices. Toured Holland in 1996. Member of BFYS. Proposed tour to France in 1999.
Age range: 9-16. *Members:* 50.

The Voice Squad
Fish and Bell Management, PO Box 175, Bury St Edmunds, Suffolk IP32 7DY
Tel: 01284 756204
Email: fishbell@aol.com

Birgitta Kenyon, dir.
Entry requirements: Trial session. *Details:* Specialises in mus theatre and jazz. Sat morning rehearsals, regular festivals and concerts, annual production at Theatre Royal.
Age range: 8-18. *Members:* 25+.

West Sussex Girls' Choir
Crawley Area Music Centre, c/o Hazelwick School, Mill La, Three Bridges, Crawley, W Sussex RH10 1SX
Tel: 01293 537197

Janet McCleery, cond.
Entry requirements: Auditions. *Details:* Weekly rehearsals. SSA voices.
Age range: 8-18. *Members:* 40.

Worcester Festival Junior Chorus
40 The Hill Av, Worcester WR5 2AW
Tel: 01905 351292 *also fax*

Christopher Hand, cond.
Age range: Aged 9 and above. *Members:* 40.

Youth Opera and Music Theatre

British Youth Opera
South Bank University, 103 Borough Rd, London SE1 0AA
Tel: 0171 815 6090 *Fax:* 0171 815 6094

Timothy Dean, mus dir; Denis Coe, exec chmn; Mikel Toms, admin dir.
Entry requirements: Applicants must be either studying in, or from the UK. Auditions from Nov in London and other centres. *Details:* Summer season mid-Jul to mid-Sep. Two operas performed in London and at least one other venue. Rehearsals are 3-hr sessions, during summer season a full-time commitment is required.
Age range: 22-30 (singers), 18-30 (insts and repetiteurs). *Members:* 100.

Hillside Opera
57 Gordon Av, Portswood, Southampton SO14 6WH
Tel: 01703 551088 *also fax*

Jill Meager, artistic dir; Kaarina Manzur, business mgr.
Entry requirements: Audition. *Details:* Opera company training singers preparing for a professional career.
Age range: 16+. *Members:* 50.

Live Culture and Live Wires Youth Opera Groups
Baylis Programme, English National Opera, The ENO Works, 40 Pitfield St, London N1 6EU
Tel: 0171 739 5808 *Fax:* 0171 729 8928

Johanne Davies, artistic dir, Live Culture; Tim Yealland, artistic dir, Live Wires.
Entry requirements: Informal w/shop auditions are held annually, children are not required to read mus or play an inst. *Details:* Both opera groups meet weekly (Sat) at the ENO Works from Sep to Jun. They are not purely singing-based but look at all aspects of opera including design, direction, composition and performing operas the groups have written.
Age range: Live Culture 12-16, Live Wires 8-12.
Members: c 30 in each group.

Music Box Children's Opera Group
Garden Flat, 29 West Park, Clifton, Bristol BS8 2LX
Tel: 0117 974 4666 *also fax*

Mark Lawrence, mus dir; Deborah Cranston, drama dir; Sue Hannam, membership sec.
Entry requirements: Annual auditions in Jul.
Details: A performing children's opera group (weekly rehearsals). Alternate concert/opera production termly. Performances have included *The Chime Rhyme* Mark Lawrence; *Noye's Fludde* Britten; *The Little Sweep* Britten; *The Green Children* Nicola le Fanu; *Brundibar* Hans Krasa.
Age range: 8-13. *Members:* c 50.

National Youth Music Theatre
5th Floor, Palace Theatre, Shaftesbury Av, London W1V 8AY
Tel: 0171 734 7478 *Fax:* 0171 734 7515
Website: www.nymt.org.uk

Jeremy James Taylor, artistic dir; Felicity Bunt, gen mgr; Vivienne Hughes, auditions admin.
Entry requirements: Auditions Oct-Dec for singers, actors, dancers and instrumentalists for the major mus theatre productions. *Details:* 4 major productions pa with residential and non-residential courses. Also open access mus theatre w/shops and regional satellite projects.
Age range: 11-19.

Youth Orchestras and Bands

This section is divided into lists of orchestras, wind bands and brass bands. Each list is subdivided under international, national, regional and local headings. This subdivision is based upon the method and scope of the audition procedure, and from where the majority of players are drawn.

An asterisk indicates membership of the **National Association of Youth Orchestras**, Ainslie House, 11 St Colme St, Edinburgh EH3 6AG *Tel:* 0131 539 1087 *Fax:* 0131 539 1069 *Email:* admin@nayo.org.uk, which draws its membership from amongst both independent and LEA-run orchestras. A full list of County Orchestras and Bands will be found in the **Local Music Education** section. School, music college and university groups are not listed, unless membership of the group is open to external applicants.

Youth Orchestras - International

European Union Baroque Orchestra
Hordley, Wootton, Woodstock OX20 1EP
Tel: 01993 812111 *Fax:* 01993 812911
Email: info@eubo.org.uk

Roy Goodman, mus dir; Paul James, gen admin; Emma Wilkinson, manager
Age range: Under 30 at time of audition. *Entry requirements:* Orchestral/audition courses, 14-20 Apr 1998 in France. *Additional info:* The EUBO brings together Europe's most talented young performers on authentic baroque instruments, providing a vital link between conservatoire study and a professional career. The orchestra is selected annually from EU nationals under the age of 30, during or following their conservatoire training. The EUBO offers 3-4 months' performing experience with leading baroque specialists including Roy Goodman, Ton Koopman, Andrew Manze, Monica Huggett and Paul Goodwin. Courses and concert tours take place throughout Europe; 1998 also includes tours to the Middle East.

European Union Youth Orchestra
65 Sloane Street, London SW1X 9SH
Tel: 0171 235 7671 *Fax:* 0171 235 7370

Bernard Haitink, mus dir; Joy Bryer, gen secretary.
Age range: 14-23. *Entry requirements:* Gr 8 min. *Additional info:* Prof Lutz Köhler, dir of studies. All member countries of the European Union.

Youth Orchestras - National

Britten-Pears Orchestra and Baroque Orchestra
Britten-Pears School for Advanced Musical Studies, High St, Aldeburgh, Suffolk IP15 5AX
Tel: 01728 452935 *Fax:* 01728 452715
Email: bps.admin@aldeburghfestivals.org

Elizabeth Webb, school director
Age range: 18+. *Additional info:* National orchs for advanced students and young professionals. Auditions are held annually. The orch meets 8 times pa for short courses in Snape, Suffolk and participates in the Aldeburgh Festival. Membership is restricted to UK residents.

Camerata Scotland *
NYOS, 13 Somerset Pl, Glasgow G3 7JT
Tel: 0141 332 8311 *Fax:* 0141 332 3915
Email: nyos@cqm.co.uk

Richard Chester, director
Age range: 18-28. *Entry requirements:* Member or recent past member of NYOS. By invitation. *Additional info:* Chmbr orch of the NYOS. UK and international tours.

ESO Youth Orchestra
Rockliffe House, 40 Church St, Malvern, Worcs WR14 2AZ
Tel: 01684 560696 *Fax:* 01684 560656
Email: info@eso.co.uk
Website: www.eso.co.uk

Marie Oldland, orch manager
Age range: 21 and under. *Entry requirements:* Minimum gr 8. *Additional info:* Annual course last week in Aug. Entry by audition in Mar, applications by end of Feb. Fee: £175.

Guildhall School of Music and Drama, Junior
Guildhall Symphony Orchestra
Junior School, Guildhall School of Music and Drama,
Silk St, Barbican, London EC2Y 8DT
Tel: 0171 382 7160 *Fax:* 0171 382 7212
Email: twait@gsmd.ac.uk
Website: www.gsmd.ac.uk

Derek Rodgers, head; Frederick Applewhite, cond.

Jewish Youth Orchestra of Great Britain
5 Bradby House, Carlton Hill, London NW8 9XE
Tel: 0171 624 1756

Sidney Fixman, dir of mus.
Age range: 13-18. *Entry requirements:* Gr 5+.

London Philharmonic Youth Orchestra
35 Doughty St, London WC1N 2AA
Tel: 0171 546 1600 *Fax:* 0171 546 1601

Maria Smith, educ and Youth Orch admin.
Age range: 18-26. *Entry requirements:* Auditions held in summer and when vacancies arise. Audition requirements: concerto (1st movt) and orch excerpts. *Additional info:* Performance at QEH and other UK venues.

London Schools Symphony Orchestra
Centre for Young Musicians, Morley College, 61 Westminster Bridge Rd, London SE1 7HT
Tel: 0171 928 3844 *Fax:* 0171 928 3454

Oliver Butterworth, head of performance, CYM.
Age range: 14-18. *Entry requirements:* By audition. *Additional info:* Courses take place in school holidays. Regular concerts at the Barbican, Kenwood Bowl and other venues; has toured Spain, France, Italy, Germany, Japan, Scandinavia and the USA.

Methodist Association of Youth Clubs Orchestra
2 Chester House, Pages La, London N10 1PR
Tel: 0181 444 9845 *Fax:* 0181 365 2471

Craig McLeish, director
Age range: 14-26. *Entry requirements:* Min gr 8. Send for application form. *Additional info:* Toured Ireland in 1997.

National Children's Chamber Orchestra of Great Britain
The Bourne, 20 Salisbury Av, Harpenden, Herts AL5 2QG
Tel: 01582 760014 *Fax:* 01582 767343

Gillian Johnston, David Johnston, mus dirs; Caroline Marriott, admin.
Age range: 10-16. *Entry requirements:* Str players gr 7+. Auditions in autumn term. *Additional info:* Residential course at Easter with concerts at major venues around the country, such as QEH (London), RNCM (Manchester) and The Maltings, (Snape). The orch plays without a cond and each programme includes an overture, classical symphony and a work from the 20th C. Chmbr repertoire also studied for a mid-week public chmbr concert.

National Children's Orchestra *
157 Craddocks Av, Ashtead, Surrey KT21 1NU
Tel: 01372 276857 *Fax:* 01372 271407

Vivienne Price MBE, dir of mus; Elisabeth Humphreys, admin.
Age range: 7-13. *Entry requirements:* Annual audition held Oct, open to all. *Additional info:* Concerts for age under 14 orch: 12 Apr (Chesterfield), 29 Aug (Huddersfield), 30 Aug (Northampton), 20 Dec (QEH), 4 Jan 1999 (Bridgewater Hall); age under 13 orch: 11 Apr (Buxton), 15 Aug (York), 20 Dec (QEH); age under 12 orch: 7 Aug (Pontefract); training and intro orch: 31 Jul (Pontefract).

National Children's Orchestra of Scotland *
NYOS, 13 Somerset Pl, Glasgow G3 7JT
Tel: 0141 332 8311 *Fax:* 0141 332 3915
Email: nyos@cqm.co.uk

Richard Chester, director
Age range: 8-14. *Entry requirements:* Annual auditions and resident in Scotland. *Additional info:* Residential courses in Scotland, providing tuition from professional musicians in addition to ens and orch experience, including public performances.

National Youth Jazz Orchestra of Great Britain
11 Victor Rd, Harrow, Middx HA2 6PT
Tel: 0181 863 2717 *Fax:* 0181 863 8685
Email: bill.ashton@virgin.net
Website: www.classical-artists.com/nyjo

Bill Ashton, dir of mus.
Age range: 11-25. *Entry requirements:* No formal auditions. Min gr 8. Players should attend rehearsals. Lesser standard acceptable for NYJO2. *Additional info:* Weekly rehearsals. NYJO has nearly 40 albums by British composers and gives 100 concerts pa. Does not enter competitions. Voted Best Big Band in 1995 British Jazz Awards, (Critics Choice 1995).

National Youth Jazz Orchestra of Scotland *
NYOS, 13 Somerset Pl, Glasgow G3 7JT
Tel: 0141 332 8311 *Fax:* 0141 332 3915
Email: nyos@cqm.co.uk

Richard Chester, director
Age range: 12-21. *Entry requirements:* Resident in Scotland. *Additional info:* Residential summer course with tuition from experienced tutors and public performances.

157

National Youth Music Theatre Orchestra
Fifth Floor, Palace Theatre, Shaftesbury Av, London W1V 8AY
Tel: 0171 734 7478 *Fax:* 0171 734 7515
Website: www.nymt.org.uk

Jeremy James Taylor, artistic dir; Felicity Bunt, gen mgr; Vivienne Hughes, auditions admin.
Age range: 11+. *Entry requirements:* Min gr 7 for auditions in Oct-Dec. *Additional info:* 4 major productions pa with extensive touring in the UK and abroad. Recruitment for open access regional activities at any time.

National Youth Orchestra of Great Britain *
32 Old School House, Britannia Rd, Bristol BS15 8DB
Tel: 0117 960 0477 *Fax:* 0117 950 0376
Email: nyo@btinternet.com
Website: www.btinternet.com/~nyo

Jill White, dir of mus; Michael de Grey, chief exec.
Age range: 10-19. *Entry requirements:* Annual auditions in autumn, applications by Jul. Min gr 8 (distinction) standard, applicants need not have taken exams. *Additional info:* NYO brings together talented musicians 3 times pa (Dec-Jan, Mar-Apr, Jul-Aug) for residential courses followed by concerts in major halls.

National Youth Orchestra of Scotland *
13 Somerset Pl, Glasgow G3 7JT
Tel: 0141 332 8311 *Fax:* 0141 332 3915
Email: nyos@cqm.co.uk

Richard Chester, director
Age range: 12-21. *Entry requirements:* Annual auditions. Resident in Scotland. *Additional info:* Winter and summer residential courses providing tuition from professional musicians and rehearsals with internationally renowned conductors and soloists prior to concert tours. Easter residential training course.

National Youth Orchestra of Wales *
Welsh Joint Education Committee, 245 Western Av, Cardiff CF5 2YX
Tel: 01222 265247 *Fax:* 01222 575894

Beryl Jones, admin; Pauline Crossley, expressive arts offr.
Age range: Up to 21. *Entry requirements:* By audition, gr 8 min. Members must be nominated by local authority. *Additional info:* Wales region. Annual summer course followed by concert tour.

National Youth String Orchestra and String Training Orchestra of Scotland
Scottish Amateur Music Association, 18 Craigton Cres, Alva, Clackmannanshire FK12 5DS
Tel: 01259 760249

Margaret Simpson, hon sec; Mark Duncan, dir of mus.
Age range: 12-21 (str orch), 8-16 (str training orch). *Entry requirements:* By audition, gr 7 (str orch), gr 3-7 (str training orch). *Additional info:* Courses for each orch held at St Andrews College, Bearsden, Glasgow, 10-15 Aug 1998.

Pro Corda (The National School For Young Chamber Music Players)
Leiston Abbey House, Theberton Rd, Leiston, Suffolk IP16 4TB
Tel: 01728 831354 *Fax:* 01728 832500

Pamela Spofforth MBE, president and dir emeritus; Mererid Crump, admin.
Age range: 8-18. *Entry requirements:* Auditions by appointment. *Additional info:* An orch formed from the ens at each of the jnr, intermediate and snr levels rehearse major works from the repertoire daily during the bi-annual 8-10 day residential courses. Concerts given annually in London and provincial venues.

Royal College of Music Junior Dept Symphony Orchestra
Junior Dept, Royal College of Music, Prince Consort Rd, London SW7 2BS
Tel: 0171 591 4334 *Fax:* 0171 589 7740
Email: phewitt@rcm.ac.uk
Website: www.rcm.ac.uk

Peter Hewitt, jnr dept dir; Neil Thomson, cond.
Age range: 14-18. *Entry requirements:* Annual auditions from members of Junior Dept. External applications by 1 Mar (details in prospectus). *Additional info:* 1 of 5 orchs at RCMJD. 3 concerts pa at RCM; also at St John's Smith Square, etc. Weekly rehearsals.

Royal Scottish Academy of Music and Drama Junior Academy Orchestra *
Junior Academy, Royal Scottish Academy of Music and Drama, 100 Renfrew St, Glasgow G2 3DB
Tel: 0141 332 4101 *Fax:* 0141 353 0372

Anne Strachan, head of jnr academy.
Age range: 10-17. *Entry requirements:* By audition. *Additional info:* Weekly rehearsals.

Young Musicians' Symphony Orchestra
11 Gunnersbury Av, London W5 3NJ
Tel: 0181 993 3135; 0181 440 6927 *Fax:* 0181 993 2635
Email: ymso@dircon.co.uk

James Blair, mus dir; Theresa Bampton-Clare, development director
Age range: 18-25. *Entry requirements:* Annual auditions held in spring term. *Additional info:* For advanced orchestral mus students at mus colleges nationally and in Ireland. Exceptionally talented non-mus students are very occasionally accepted. Also Schools Scheme: cut-price seats for school children and interval receptions with members of the orch aiming to make classical mus more accessible to children.

Youth Orchestras - Regional and Local

Bedfordshire County Youth Orchestras *
Emerald Court, Pilgrim Centre, 20 Brickhill Dr,
Bedford MK41 7PZ
Tel: 01234 213439 *Fax:* 01234 363516

John Shayler, Nick Quinn, joint acting mus service mgrs.
Age range: Youth orch 12-21; 2nd orch 11-19; 3rd orch 10-17; 4th orch 9-13; 5th orch 8-11. *Entry requirements:* Youth orch gr 8; 2nd orch gr 6-7; 3rd orch gr 5; 4th orch (strs only) gr 3-4; 5th orch (strs only) gr 2. Auditions for places in top 3 orchs. Resident or in f/t education in Bedfordshire. *Additional info:* Intensive courses during main school holidays. Youth orch foreign tours to Hungary, Czech Republic, Russia and Cyprus. 2nd orch plays at the Edinburgh Festival of British Youth Orchestras.

Brentwood Cathedral Youth Orchestra
Cathedral Office, Brentwood Cathedral, Ingrave Rd,
Brentwood CM15 8AT
Tel: 01277 261310 *Fax:* 01277 214060

Angela Harris, admin; Andrew Wright, cond.
Age range: 10-19. *Entry requirements:* Min gr 4.
Additional info: Rehearsals on Sun afternoons.

Brighton Youth Orchestra *
Brighton Youth Orchestra Trust, University of Brighton,
Falmer, Brighton BN1 9PH
Tel: 01273 643450 *Fax:* 01273 643534
Email: byo@bton.ac.uk
Website: www.brighton.ac.uk/byo/

Andrew Sherwood, dir of mus and cond; Natasha Atthill, admin.
Age range: 6-24. *Entry requirements:* By audition. 1st orch min gr 6-7 up to 21 yrs; 2nd orch gr 3+ and age 11-18; jnr youth orch, str gr 1+, age 6-12; fun str for elementary vns; advanced str ens. *Additional info:* Also folk orch and jazz big band. Annual tours, comp w/shops, chmbr mus, scholarship scheme and annual training course.

Bromley Youth Chamber Orchestra *
Bromley Youth Music Trust, Southborough La, Bromley,
Kent BR2 8AA
Tel: 0181 467 1566 *Fax:* 0181 468 7595

Nicholas Woodall.
Age range: 11-18. *Entry requirements:* Audition. Min gr 7. *Additional info:* Weekly rehearsals. Extensive schedule and tour to Canada Jul 1998. Biennial recording of CD. Performances in major London venues. Outstanding Performance Award in 1996 National Festival of Music for Youth.

Bromley Youth Symphony Orchestra *
Bromley Youth Music Centre, Southborough La, Bromley
BR2 8AA
Tel: 0181 467 1566 *Fax:* 0181 468 7595

Peter M Mawson, principal.
Age range: 8-18. *Entry requirements:* Annual audition in spring term. *Additional info:* Weekly rehearsals and short courses throughout year. Tour to the Hague in 1996.

Cambridgeshire County Youth Orchestra *
CIMA, The Old School, Papworth Everard, Cambs CB3 8RH
Tel: 01480 831695 *Fax:* 01480 831696

Peter Britton, director
Age range: Up to 21. *Entry requirements:* Gr 7 for str; gr 8 for w/wind and br. *Additional info:* 1998 performances in Cambridgeshire and Youth Orch Festival in Edinburgh and Glasgow. Winner of 1996 Boosey & Hawkes Youth Orchestra Award.

Cardiff County and Vale of Glamorgan Youth Orchestra
The Friary Centre, The Friary, Cardiff CF1 4AA
Tel: 01222 640950/1 *Fax:* 01222 227471

Eric Phillips, mus dir; Stuart Burrows, president.
Age range: 14-21. *Entry requirements:* Annual auditions. *Additional info:* Weekly rehearsals, courses, tours, recordings, concerts, festivals and competitions.

Cheshire Youth Orchestra
Cheshire School of Music, Woodford Lodge Professional Centre, Woodford Lane West, Winsford, Cheshire CW7 4EH
Tel: 01606 557328 *Fax:* 01606 862113

Valerie Hayward, Marilyn Shearns, orch dirs; Timothy Redmond, principal cond.
Age range: 12-21. *Additional info:* Toured USA, Germany and Denmark. 1997 tour to Prague. Regular performances with professional soloists.

City of Coventry Youth Orchestra *
Performing Arts Service Office, Leasowes Av, Coventry CV3 6BH
Tel: 01203 692348 *Fax:* 01203 692717

Brian Chappell, dir.

City of Hull Youth Symphony Orchestra *
The Albemarle Music Centre, Ferensway, Hull HU2 8LZ
Tel: 01482 223941 *Fax:* 01482 320565

Chris Maynard, cond.
Age range: 13-21. *Entry requirements:* By audition. *Additional info:* Biennial foreign tour. 1998 tour to Barcelona.

City of Sheffield Youth Orchestra *
The Cottage, Park Head, Birds Edge, Huddersfield
HD8 8XW
Tel: 01484 606114 *also fax*
Email: csyo@nayo.org.uk
Website: www.moffatt.demon.co.uk/csyo/

Edward Woodhead, dir; Christopher Gayford, cond.
Age range: 13-21. *Entry requirements:* By audition.
Gr 6+. *Additional info:* 3 courses (residential and non-residential) each year during the academic vacations. Tours have included Germany, Prague, Switzerland, Norway, Poland and Spain.

Colchester Youth Chamber Orchestra *
Weltevreden, Mount Pleasant, Hundon, Nr Sudbury,
Suffolk CO10 8DW
Tel: 01440 786337

George Reynolds, dir of mus; Edna Robson, hon secretary.
Age range: 7-18. *Entry requirements:* Audition gr 5 and above. *Additional info:* North East Essex and Suffolk borders. Residential course held during Oct half-term.

Cornwall Youth Orchestra *
c/o The Music Service, Dalvenie, County Hall, Truro TR1 3BA

John A Harries, head of mus service.

Derbyshire City & County Youth Orchestra
Music Activities, Derby City Education Service, Middleton
House, 27 St Mary's Gate, Derby DE1 3NN
Tel: 01332 716886 *Fax:* 01332 716920

Philip King, adviser; Peter Stark, guest cond.

Dorset Youth Orchestras *
Dorset Music Services, c/o Carter Community School,
Blandford Close, Hamworthy, Poole BH15 4BQ
Tel: 01202 678233 *Fax:* 01202 679381

David Norton, David Kenyon, dirs.
Age range: 6-18. *Entry requirements:* Auditions held in Sep. *Additional info:* Concert tours to Europe. Also Dorset Youth Choir and Dorset Youth gui ens.

Dudley Schools Symphony Orchestra *
Dudley Music Centre, Lawnwood Rd, Wordsley,
Stourbridge DY8 5PQ
Tel: 01384 813865 *Fax:* 01384 813866
Email: keith.horsfall@nayo.org.uk
Website: dudley-gatesay.co.uk

Gerald Johnson, head of service; Keith Horsfall, deputy head of service; Clive Kempton, mus inspector.
Age range: 12-18. *Entry requirements:* Auditions.
Gr 6 for str, gr 7-8 for w/wind and br. *Additional info:* Fortnightly rehearsals, annual summer mus school. Regular concerts and international tours

including Australia and Singapore during summer 1998. Based at Dudley Music Centre which also organises 6 str orchs, 7 wind bands, 7 br bands and 7 choirs.

Dundee Schools Symphony Orchestra *
Dundee City Council, Gardyne Rd, Dundee DD5 1NY
Tel: 01382 462857 *Fax:* 01382 462862
Email: advisers@educational-development-service.dundeecity.
sch.uk

Charles Maynes, director
Entry requirements: Competitive audition. *Additional info:* Participation in 1998 Edinburgh Festival of Youth Orchestras. 1998 tour to Germany.

Edinburgh Youth Orchestra *
92 St Alban's Rd, Edinburgh EH9 2PG
Tel: 0131 667 4648 *Fax:* 0131 662 9169
Email: eyo@ednet.co.uk
Website: www.ednet.co.uk/~eyo

Marjory Dougal, admin; Christopher Adey, cond.
Age range: Up to 21. *Entry requirements:* Gr 6+.
Resident in Scotland. *Additional info:* Course at Easter and occasional summer courses. Tour to Italy Jul 1999.

Enfield Young Symphony Orchestra
Enfield Arts Support Service, Aylward School, Windmill
Rd, Edmonton, London N18 1NB
Tel: 0181 807 8881 *Fax:* 0181 807 8213

Debbie Goldman, orch mgr; John Forster, cond.
Age range: 11-20. *Entry requirements:* Entry by audition, standard gr 6+. *Additional info:* 1997 tour to Spain. Previous tours to Paris and Edinburgh. Rehearsals run on professional model - 4-day intensive course in school holidays followed by concert.

Ernest Read Symphony Orchestra *
9 Cotsford Av, New Malden, Surrey KT3 5EU
Tel: 0181 942 0318

Noel Long, dir; Peter Stark, principal cond.
Age range: 17+. *Entry requirements:* Members accepted on audition or trial. Outstanding ability in performance and sight-reading required.
Additional info: 9-10 concerts given Oct-May, the majority of which are in Royal Festival Hall.

Fife Youth Jazz Orchestra *
Beath High School, Cowdenbeath, Fife
Tel: 01383 512114 *Fax:* 01383 610589

Richard Michael, cond; Jim O'Malley, Carlo Madden, Denis Boyd, asst conds.
Age range: 10-22. *Entry requirements:* None.
Additional info: Weekly rehearsals. Winners of BBC Big Band Competition Junior Section and Daily Telegraph Young Jazz Competition 1994. Concerts in Fife and throughout Scotland.

Fife Youth Orchestra *
Auchterderran Centre, Woodend Rd, Cardenden KY5 0NE
Tel: 01592 414785 Fax: 01592 414641
Email: gwilson@itasdarc.demon.co.uk

Graeme Wilson, adviser in mus, Fife Council.
Age range: 12-18

Goldsmiths' Youth Orchestras *
Dept of Professional and Community Education,
Goldsmiths College, University of London, Lewisham
Way, London SE14 6NW
Tel: 0171 919 7171 Fax: 0171 919 7223

Elinor Corp, cond.
Age range: Jnr orch, 9-13; snr orch, 12-20. Entry
requirements: Gr 6+ (str), gr 7+ (wind, br). Solo piece
(own choice), orch sight-reading, viva voce. Jnr orch
no audition and all welcome. Additional info: Mainly
boroughs of Lewisham, Greenwich and Southwark.
Performed at the National Association of Youth
Orchestras Festival, in Edinburgh and Glasgow.
Tours to France, Portugal, Scotland, Cornwall; mus
w/shops, m/classes.

Grimsby, Cleethorpes and District Youth Orchestra *
1 Maple Grove, New Waltham, Grimsby DN36 4PU
Tel: 01472 824463

Leo Solomon, chmn; Mrs S Parr, secretary.
Age range: Up to 25. Entry requirements: Training
wind band, str group and orch gr 1; jnr wind
band gr 3; jnr str group and orch gr 2;
intermediate symphony orch: strs gr 4, wind gr 5;
snr wind band gr 5; str orch gr 6; snr symphony
orch: strs gr 6, wind gr 5; snr swing band gr 4-5,
jnr swing band gr 2-4.

Hackney Youth Orchestras *
1 Frobisher House, Dolphin Sq, London SW1V 3LL
Tel: 01582 494794
Email: hyot@fjopp.demon.co.uk

Nicholas Ridout, director
Age range: 6-21. Additional info: Weekly
rehearsals, Saturday school and holiday courses.

Hemsted Forest Youth Orchestra
Music Dept, Benenden School, Cranbrook, Kent TN17 4AA
Tel: 01580 242030 Fax: 01580 240280

Patricia M Gane, dir of mus and cond.
Age range: 12-19+. Entry requirements: Termly
auditions by appointment. Additional info: Based
at the school, this orch also welcomes young
players from the surrounding areas. Regular
performances are given in a range of venues.

Hull Junior Philharmonic Orchestra *
11 Lynwood Av, Anlaby, Hull HU10 7DP
Tel: 01482 651128

J B Harston, secretary.

Age range: Up to 19. Entry requirements: Gr 5 for concert
orch; gr 1 for training orch. Additional info: Sat morning
rehearsals for training orch, Fri evening rehearsals for
concert orch. Tour planned in 1999. Recent tours to
Prague and Northern France.

Jordan Junior Strings
17 Meadow Cottages, Little Kingshill, Great Missenden,
Bucks HP16 0DX
Tel: 01494 862861

Elaine Jordan, director
Age range: 4-14. Additional info: 60 young str
players mostly trained in Suzuki method. 8 South
Bank concerts, several TV appearances and
demonstration at Kodály Music Institute in
Hungary.

Lydian Orchestra *
1 Molyneux Park Gardens, Tunbridge Wells, Kent TN4 8DL
Tel: 01892 530548

Victor Clements, chmn.
Age range: 15-25. Entry requirements: Min gr 7 (str),
gr 8 (wind) with merit or distinction. Additional
info: 3 courses each year.

Malden Young Strings *
242a Tolworth Rise South, Tolworth, Surrey KT5 9NB
Tel: 0181 330 7876

George Steven, director
Age range: Up to 18. Additional info: Summer
tours and concerts. Pre-instrumental classes for
young children.

Merseyside Youth Orchestra *
Philharmonic Hall, Hope St, Liverpool L1 9BP
Tel: 0151 709 2895 Fax: 0151 709 0918

L Clark Rundell, mus dir; Andrew Bentley, dir of
community education.
Age range: 13-23. Entry requirements: Min gr 6, 2
short contrasting pieces, all scales, prepared
sight-reading. Additional info: Short courses and
occasionally Sunday rehearsals.

Midland Youth Orchestra *
23 Hazelton Rd, Marlbrook, Bromsgrove, Worcs B61 0JG
Tel: 01527 876928
Website: ourworld.compuserve.com/homepages/anthony_
bradbury/myo.htm

Stephen Williams, mus dir and chmn; Anthony
Bradbury, associate cond; Caroline Jephcott,
hon secretary.
Age range: 12-25. Entry requirements: Gr 6 for
strs, gr 8 for w/wind, br and perc. Auditions Sat
pm, Aston University, Birmingham B4.
Additional info: Weekly rehearsals, annual
weekend residential course. Recently
celebrated 40th Anniversary with a concert at
the Symphony Hall, Birmingham. Host

orchestra of the 1996 Aberdeen International Youth Festival. 1998 concerts at Symphony Hall, Birmingham (18 Jul) and at Adrian Boult Hall (7 Nov).

Milton Keynes Youth Orchestra

Milton Keynes Music Service, Stantonbury Campus, Stantonbury, Milton Keynes MK14 6BN
Tel: 01908 224250 *Fax:* 01908 224201

Age range: 11+. *Entry requirements:* Gr 6+.

Newcastle Youth Chamber Orchestra *

58 Lansdowne Gardens, Jesmond, Newcastle upon Tyne NE2 1HH
Tel: 0191 281 1034

Layton Ring, dir of mus; Stephen McWeeney, manager
Age range: Up to 21. *Entry requirements:* Gr 6-8 depending on age and inst. *Additional info:* 6 rehearsals per term for 1 or more concerts in professional venues.

North Lincolnshire Schools Orchestras *

North Lincolnshire Music Support Service, c/o John Leggott College, West Common La, Scunthorpe DN17 1DS
Tel: 01724 297157 *Fax:* 01724 863907

S Fareham, head of service; E Hardy, deputy head of service; S Russell, co-ord.
Age range: 10-19. *Entry requirements:* Auditions. *Additional info:* Divided into 7 groups of increasing standards beginning with gr 2.

North Norfolk Youth Orchestra *

11 Cromwell Close, Cromer, Norfolk NR27 0DE
Tel: 01263 511433/512129 *Fax:* 01263 515378
Email: cromerhig.norfolk.ss@connect.bt.com

Richard Baker, dir of mus; Keith Paterson, treasurer; Valerie Crowe, Alan Morris, assoc cond.
Age range: 10+. *Entry requirements:* Gr 5 (str), gr 7-8 (w/wind, br). *Additional info:* Weekly rehearsals. Concerts in UK and Europe. Annual partnership with the International Youth Orchestra Stade-Elbe.

Northamptonshire County Youth Orchestra

Northamptonshire County Music Service, 125-129 Kettering Rd, Northampton NN1 4AZ
Tel: 01604 37117 *Fax:* 01604 603070

Peter Dunkley, cond and head of mus service.
Age range: School age. *Entry requirements:* Annual auditions, gr 6-8+. *Additional info:* Regular concerts, festivals, tours and competitions.

Nottingham Youth Orchestra *

1 Arlington Dr, Mapperley Park, Nottingham NG3 5EN
Tel: 0115 960 6723
Email: djfwoodhouse@enterprise.net
Website: www.innots.co.uk/jackw/nyo/derek.html

Alwyn Foster, chmn; Colin Tuck, sec; Derek Williams, cond; Chris Castleden, admin.
Age range: 12-21 in full-time education. *Entry requirements:* Auditions, Jun. Gr 6 for str, gr 7-8 for all others. *Additional info:* Weekly rehearsals. Tour to Cyprus in 1997.

Perth Youth Orchestra

20 Spoutwells Rd, Scone PH2 6RW
Tel: 01738 551162

Hazel Mackinnon, secretary.
Additional info: Tour to Spain, Jul 1998.

Reading Youth Orchestra

69 Bulmershe Rd, Reading RG1 5RP
Tel: 0118 926 1506/1828 *Fax:* 0118 926 3070

Rupert D'Cruze, director
Age range: 13-19. *Entry requirements:* By audition. *Additional info:* 1997 exchange visit with Dusseldorf Youth Orchestra.

Rehearsal Orchestra

4 Lucerne Ct, Abbey Pk, Beckenham, Kent BR3 1RB
Tel: 0181 663 1927 *Fax:* 0181 658 6261
Website: www.rehearsal_orchestra.org

Bridget Whyte, admin; Harry Legge OBE, artistic director
Age range: 16+. *Entry requirements:* Min gr 8, with good sight-reading. *Additional info:* Advanced orch training for students and young professionals, experience of working with orch for inst and vocal soloists, in-service training for more mature musicians, w/end courses held in London and elsewhere during year. Residential summer course held annually at the Edinburgh Festival.

Ripon Youth String Ensemble

Ashley House, Ure Bank, Ripon, N Yorks HG4 1JG
Tel: 01765 602856

Xenophon Kelsey, mus director
Age range: 10-18. *Entry requirements:* Gr 5+. *Additional info:* First prize winners, European Festival of Music for Youth, Belgium 1997. Promote courses, w/shops, rehearsals and concerts.

Solihull Youth Orchestras *

Education Dept, Council House, Solihull B91 3QU
Tel: 0121 704 6619 *Fax:* 0121 704 8065

Joyce Rothschild, mus inspector; Tony Veal, head of mus service; Richard Hart, mgr of youth orch.

Age range: Up to 21. Entry requirements: Annual auditions. Additional info: Courses held twice pa.

South East Surrey Area Youth Orchestra *
South East Surrey Music Centre, Furzefield Primary School, Delabole Rd, Merstham, Surrey RH1 3PA
Tel: 01737 643310 Fax: 01737 645463

Christopher Pratt, cond.
Age range: Up to 21. Entry requirements: Gr 4. Additional info: Weekly rehearsals during school term. Sat 10am-12 noon.

Southampton Youth Orchestra
Southampton Music Service, 5th Floor Frobisher House, Nelson Gate, Southampton SO15 1GX
Tel: 01703 833635 Fax: 01703 833324

Keith Smith, mus dir and cond.
Age range: 13-19. Entry requirements: Gr 7+. Additional info: Weekly rehearsals. Toured in Hungary 1996, Italy in 1997. Tour to France 1998.

Stoneleigh Youth Orchestra *
52 Manor Rd, Teddington, Middx TW11 8AB
Tel: 0181 943 2661

Christine Blake, admin.
Age range: 12-21. Entry requirements: Auditions in Sep; applications accepted throughout the year. Gr 6 or equivalent. Additional info: Weekly rehearsals held at Tolworth Girls' School, Surbiton (Sun 5-8pm). Regular concerts throughout year. Summer tour to Poland in July 1998.

Strathclyde Youth Jazz Orchestra
Dept of Applied Arts, University of Strathclyde, Jordanhill Campus, 76 Southbrae Dr, Glasgow G13 1PP
Tel: 0141 950 3476 Fax: 0141 950 3314

Bobby Wishart, mus dir and admin.
Age range: 14-25. Entry requirements: Training group gr 4-5; orch gr 6-7. Additional info: Bi-weekly rehearsals. Invitation to play in USA. Possible tours of Switzerland and South Africa. Educational activities include jazz w/shops for schools and in-service courses for staff. Regular recitals and concerts throughout year.

Suffolk Youth Orchestra
County Music Service, Northgate Arts Centre, Sidegate La West, Ipswich, Suffolk IP30 9HG
Tel: 01473 281866 Fax: 01473 286068

Philip Shaw, cond.
Age range: 12-21. Entry requirements: Annual auditions in Oct. Also Suffolk Youth Sinfonia, membership by invitation. Additional info: Rehearsal courses in school holidays, foreign tours.

Sussex Youth Chamber Orchestra *
168 Downs Rd, Hastings, East Sussex TN34 2DZ
Tel: 01424 440929; 0973 734572

Warwick Potter, mus dir; Derek Norcross, patron.
Age range: 15+. Entry requirements: Min gr 8.

Thames Vale Youth Orchestra
Lane House, Eynsham Rd, Farmoor, Oxford
Tel: 01865 862877

Mrs J Cumming, sec; M Stinton, dir of mus.
Age range: 13-18. Entry requirements: Min gr 6 on all insts. Additional info: Weekly rehearsals.

Ulster Youth Orchestra *
Chamber of Commerce House, 22 Gt Victoria St, Belfast BT2 7LX
Tel: 01232 278287 Fax: 01232 333845

Helen Henson, gen manager
Age range: 12-21. Entry requirements: Auditions in Dec and Jan. Gr 7-8 or equivalent. Additional info: Annual summer residential course and concerts. Joint concert project with Ulster Orchestra, Apr 1998. Concert tour of Ireland in Aug 1998.

Vacation Chamber Orchestras
Ashley House, Ure Bank, Ripon, N Yorks HG4 1JG
Tel: 01765 602856

Xenophon Kelsey, mus director
Age range: 16-22. Entry requirements: Gr 8+. Additional info: Residential courses each vacation for advanced players. Frequent concerts in Yorkshire Dales, North York Moors, Northern Pennines, etc.

Wakefield Youth Symphony Orchestra *
County Hall, Wakefield

Geraldine Gaunt, mus adviser/inspector.
Age range: 11-18. Entry requirements: Min gr 5.

Warrington and District Youth Orchestra
338 London Rd, Appleton, Warrington, Cheshire WA4 5PW
Tel: 01925 265456

Mrs J Bingham, chmn.
Age range: Up to 21. Entry requirements: By audition and subject to vacancies. Additional info: Weekly rehearsals, foreign exchange and annual residential courses.

Warwickshire County Youth Orchestra *
Education Office, 22 Northgate St, Warwick CV34 4SR
Tel: 01926 412803 also fax

Ray Hutchinson, head of youth mus.
Age range: 13-21. Entry requirements: W/wind and br, gr 8; strs, gr 6.

West Norfolk Jubilee Youth Orchestra *
The Dairies, Stoney Rd, Roydon, King's Lynn, Norfolk

S Corbett, sec; Joan Hooke, head of orch; Robin Norman, head of band.
Age range: 12-21. *Entry requirements:* Min gr 5.

West of England Schools' Symphony Orchestra
Education School Services, PO Box 25 Riverside, Keynsham, Bristol BS31 1DN
Tel: 01225 395119 *Fax:* 01225 395120

J L Fowles, orch co-ord.

Weston super Mare Youth Orchestra
367 Locking Rd, Weston super Mare BS22 8NH
Tel: 01934 622519 *Fax:* 01934 641649

Dennis Cole, cond; Mrs S Philpott, admin.
Age range: 10-21.

Wirral Schools' Orchestras *
Education Centre, Acre Lane, Bromborough, Wirral L62 7BZ
Tel: 0151 343 1783 *Fax:* 0151 343 9352

Philip Chapman, director

Age range: 13-18. *Entry requirements:* By audition, gr5/6 +. *Additional info:* Tour of Germany 1996; proposed tour to Austria, summer 1998.

York Area Schools Symphony Orchestra *
Whitecross Lodge, 150 Haxby Rd, York YO3 7JN
Tel: 01904 673436 *Fax:* 01904 673439

Alison Goffin, head of mus centre; Gill Cooper, mgr of performing arts service.
Age range: 11-19. *Entry requirements:* Gr 5 or by audition. *Additional info:* Weekly rehearsals during school term, on Sat mornings.

Young Sinfonia *
The Sinfonia Centre, 41 Jesmond Vale, Newcastle upon Tyne NE2 1PG
Tel: 0191 240 1812 *Fax:* 0191 240 2668

Emma Welton, admin; Ilan Volkov, cond.
Age range: 19 and under. *Entry requirements:* Min gr 8 or equivalent. Associate membership gr 6-8. *Additional info:* The youth orch of Northern Sinfonia. Open to young players from the Northern Arts Region.

Wind Bands - National

National Children's Wind Orchestra of Great Britain
The Bourne, 20 Salisbury Av, Harpenden, Herts AL5 2QG
Tel: 01582 760014 *Fax:* 01582 767343

Gillian Johnston, David Johnston, mus dirs; Caroline Marriott, admin.
Age range: 10-15. *Entry requirements:* Gr 5-8. *Additional info:* For w/wind, br and perc players aged 10-16 at gr 5 and above. Course members divided into chmbr wind ens and 2 further symphonic wind orchs. Entry by audition during the autumn term for a residential course at Easter and concerts at major venues around the country later in the year. Study includes standard repertoire, new commissions and chmbr mus.

National Youth Concert Band of Great Britain
54 St Nicholas Rd, Plumstead, London SE18 1HH
Tel: 0181 854 6492

Mrs Z Bowness Smith, course dir; Mrs I Sharman, hon treasurer; Miss S Cox, hon secretary.
Age range: 13-23. *Entry requirements:* Entry by audition. Open to wind, perc and db players, min gr 7. *Additional info:* 3 mus courses pa including

lectures on harmony, orchestration, conducting, etc. Planned concert tour to Australia.

National Youth Wind Ensemble and Wind Band of Scotland
Scottish Amateur Music Association, 18 Craigton Cres, Alva, Clackmannanshire FK12 5DS
Tel: 01259 760249

Margaret Simpson, hon sec; Brian Duguid, dir of mus.
Age range: 12-21. *Entry requirements:* Gr 7 (wind ens), gr 5-6 (wind band). *Additional info:* Summer course 3-8 Aug 1998 at University of St Andrews.

National Youth Wind Orchestra of Great Britain *
32 Park Lawn, Church Rd, Farnham Royal, Bucks SL2 3AP
Tel: 01753 642223 *also fax*

Kit Shepherd, exec director
Age range: 15-21. *Entry requirements:* Aug-Oct auditions for entry the following year. Min gr 8. *Additional info:* Residential courses Easter, summer and autumn w/ends, focus courses and outreach days. 8 public concerts pa. M/classes, chmbr mus, w/shops for ens, sax, br, fls, etc. European tour summer 1998.

Wind Bands - Regional and Local

Ashford Youth Wind Orchestra
c/o Kent Music School, Gower House, 32 Maidstone Rd,
Ashford, Kent TN24 8UB
Tel: 01233 646269

Tony Spencer, director
Age range: 18 and under. *Entry requirements:* Min
gr 4. *Additional info:* Rehearsals Tue evening
during school term.

Bedfordshire County Bands *
Emerald Court, Pilgrim Centre, 20 Brickhill Drive,
Bedford MK41 7PZ
Tel: 01234 213439 *Fax:* 01234 363516

John Shayler, Nick Quinn, joint acting mus
service mgrs.
Age range: Concert band 14-21; 2nd band 12-19;
3rd band 10-16. *Entry requirements:* Concert band
gr 7-8; 2nd band gr 5-6; 3rd band gr 3-4. Resident
in Bedfordshire. *Additional info:* Short intensive
courses during school holidays. Biennial tours
for concert and 2nd bands.

Birmingham Schools Wind Orchestra
Music Centre, Martineau Education Centre, Balden Rd,
Harborne, Birmingham B32 2EH
Tel: 0121 428 1175 *Fax:* 0121 428 3755

John Wesley-Barker, cond and admin.
Age range: 12-18. *Entry requirements:*
Performance of two contrasting pieces. Gr 6+.
Additional info: Weekly rehearsals, residential
courses and frequent concerts in Birmingham,
London and abroad. Enters B&H National
Concert Band Festival and National Festival of
Music for Youth.

Bodmin Community College Band
Lostwithiel Rd, Bodmin, Cornwall PL31 1DD
Tel: 01208 72114 *Fax:* 01208 78680

Adrian Evans, dir of mus.
Age range: 11-18. *Entry requirements:* Gr 3+.
Additional info: Weekly rehearsals Wed 6.30-9pm.
Finalists for the B&H National Concert Band Festival
for the 9th successive year. 1996 tour to Brittany;
1998 tour to USA.

Bromley Youth Concert Band *
Bromley Youth Music Centre, Southborough La, Bromley BR2 8AA
Tel: 0181 467 1566 *Fax:* 0181 468 7595

Peter Mawson, cond.
Age range: 13-18. *Entry requirements:* Auditions gr
6+. *Additional info:* Weekly rehearsals. Annual
concert tours abroad. 1st prize at Valencia Music
Festival 1996. 1st prize at World Music Concours,
Kerkrade 1997.

Cardiff County and Vale of Glamorgan Youth Wind Band
The Friary Centre, The Friary, Cardiff CF1 4AA
Tel: 01222 640950/1 *Fax:* 01222 227471

Peter Knight, mus director
Age range: 14-21. *Entry requirements:* Annual
auditions. *Additional info:* Weekly rehearsals,
courses, tours, recordings, concerts and
festivals.

City of Leeds Youth Concert Band
83 Wakefield Rd, Gildersome, Leeds LS27 7HA
Tel: 0113 252 8100

Aubrey Beswick, director
Age range: Up to 18. *Entry requirements:* Min gr 6.
Additional info: Rehearses Sat morning during
term-time. Biennial foreign tours plus full concert
programme throughout the year. Appearances at
Royal Festival Hall, Royal Armouries, Leeds and
on TV. Concert tour of Switzerland planned for
summer 1998.

Derbyshire City & County Youth Wind Band
Music Activities, Derby City Education Service, Middleton
House, 27 St Mary's Gate, Derby DE1 3NN
Tel: 01332 716886 *Fax:* 01332 716920

Philip King, adviser; Murray Slater, cond.
Age range: 12-21. *Entry requirements:* Entry by
audition. Min gr 6.

Enfield Youth Wind Band
Enfield Arts Support Service, Windmill Rd, Edmonton,
London N18 1NB
Tel: 0181 807 8881 *Fax:* 0181 807 8213

Ruth Summers, activities co-ord.
Age range: 11-18. *Entry requirements:* Gr 5+.

Fife Youth Concert Band *
Auchterderran Centre, Woodend Rd, Cardenden KY5 0NE
Tel: 01592 414785 *Fax:* 01592 414641
Email: gwilson@itasdarc.demon.co.uk

Graeme Wilson, adviser in mus, Fife Council.
Age range: 12-18.

Harrogate and Skipton Area Schools Concert Band
3 Royd Pl, Cononley, Keighley, W Yorks BD20 8JT
Tel: 01535 636823

Bernard G Tierney, dir of mus.
Age range: 13-18. *Entry requirements:* Gr 5+ min.
Additional info: Weekly rehearsals. Youth Music
1998 and Concerto for Euphonium with soloist Bob
Childs in Jul 1998.

165

High Wycombe Music Centre Concert Band
Sands Middle School, Mill End Rd, High Wycombe, Bucks
Tel: 01494 445947 *Fax:* 01494 442773

John Davie, cond.
Age range: 14-19. *Entry requirements:* Gr 7.
Additional info: 13 past performances at the
National Festival of Music for Youth with 1997
Outstanding Performance Award. Performed at
Schools Prom 1997. Several tours of Germany
and most recently Sweden. Prague visit in Jul
1998.

Highbury Area Band
19 Brunswick Gardens, Bedhampton, Havant, Hants
PO9 3HZ
Tel: 01705 462614 *Fax:* 01705 595799

B H Strugnell, chmn; J Clelford, manager
Age range: 11-21+. *Entry requirements:* Min gr 4 or
by audition. *Additional info:* Weekly rehearsals.

Isle of Wight Youth Concert Band
9 Elm Close, Ryde, Isle of Wight PO33 1ED
Tel: 01983 565675

Martyn Stroud, dir of mus.
Age range: 14-22. *Entry requirements:* Auditions, min
gr 5. *Additional info:* Approx 25 concerts pa plus
tours. Competitions and audio recordings. Plays at
royal receptions on the island and has appeared in
two BBC Songs of Praise.

Kent Youth Wind Orchestra *
Kent Music Centre, College Rd, Maidstone, Kent
ME15 6YQ
Tel: 01622 691212 *Fax:* 01622 661318

Alan Hutt, dir of mus; Phillip Hyde, manager
Age range: 13-19. *Entry requirements:* Min gr 7+.
Additional info: CD of works for band by living
British composers. Short courses summer and
Easter. Smaller chmbr ens are formed from main
band.

Mancunian Winds
Zion Arts Centre, Stretford Rd, Manchester M15 5ZA
Tel: 0161 226 4411/22 *Fax:* 0161 226 1010
Email: musicservice@manchester.gov.uk

Allan Jones, head of mus service.
Entry requirements: Application and audition.
Additional info: Performances at major concert
venues including RNCM and Bridgewater Hall.

Milton Keynes Music Centre Youth Band
Milton Keynes Music Centre, Stantonbury Campus,
Stantonbury, Milton Keynes MK14 6BN
Tel: 01908 224250 *Fax:* 01908 225271

Nancy Duncan, sec; James Howson, cond.
Age range: 11-18. *Entry requirements:* Gr 4.

North Tyneside Concert Band
School Services, Stephenson House, Stephenson St,
North Shields NE30 1QA
Tel: 0191 200 5025 *Fax:* 0191 200 6091
Email: nteaiv@rmplc.co.uk

R Harrison, cond.
Age range: 13+. *Entry requirements:* Gr 5.
Additional info: Weekly rehearsals during school
term. 1997 tour to Spain. 1998 tour to Germany.

Northallerton Area Wind Orchestra
Northallerton Music Centre Office, c/o Bedale High
School, Fitzalan Rd, Bedale, N Yorks DL8 2EQ
Tel: 01677 422070

Trevor Wilson, director
Age range: 14-18. *Entry requirements:* Gr 5 or
above. *Additional info:* Termly concerts plus
entry in National Festival of Music for Youth.

Northamptonshire County Youth Concert Band
Northamptonshire County Music Service, 125-129
Kettering Rd, Northampton NN1 4AZ
Tel: 01604 37117 *Fax:* 01604 603070

Adele Sellers-Peck, cond; Peter Dunkley, head of
mus service.
Age range: School age. *Entry requirements:*
Annual auditions, gr 6-8+. *Additional info:*
Regular concerts, festivals, tours and
competitions.

Shrewsbury Concert Band
9 Greyfriars Rd, Longden Coleham, Shrewsbury SY3 7EN
Tel: 01743 367482 *Fax:* 01743 340412

Mike Dutton, chmn; Shelley Holloway, secretary.
Age range: 16 and above. *Entry requirements:* Gr 4
and above. *Additional info:* Rehearses Thu
7.30-10pm.

Solihull Youth Wind Band *
Lyndon Music Centre, Daylesford Rd, Solihull, W
Midlands B92 8EJ
Tel: 0121 743 2483 *Fax:* 0121 743 5682

Tony Veal, head of mus service; Clive Allsopp,
inst teacher.
Age range: 15-18. *Entry requirements:* Min gr 6.
Additional info: Weekly rehearsals during school
term. Biennial tours, charity concerts and
competitors in the B&H Concert Band Festival.

South East Surrey Area Wind Band *
South East Surrey Music Centre, Furzefield Primary
School, Delabole Rd, Merstham, Surrey RH1 3PA
Tel: 01737 643310 *Fax:* 01737 645463
Email: 101630.7149@compuserve.com

Hugh Craig, cond.
Age range: Up to 21. *Entry requirements:* Gr 5.

Additional info: Weekly rehearsals during school term.

Suffolk Youth Wind Band
County Music Service, Northgate Arts Centre, Sidegate La West, Ipswich, Suffolk IP30 9HG
Tel: 01473 281866 *Fax:* 01473 286068

Suzanne Dexter-Mills, cond.
Age range: 12-21. *Entry requirements:* Annual auditions in Oct. *Additional info:* Rehearsal courses in school holidays, foreign tours.

Surrey County Youth Wind Orchestra *
South East Surrey Music Centre, Furzefield Primary School, Delabole Rd, Merstham, Surrey RH1 3PA
Tel: 01737 643310 *Fax:* 01737 645463
Email: 101630.7149@compuserve.com

Hugh Craig, cond.
Age range: Up to 21. *Entry requirements:* Min gr 6. *Additional info:* Weekly rehearsals at George Abbot School, Guildford, during school term.

Swale Youth Wind Orchestra
Swale Music Centre, Highsted School, Highsted Rd, Sittingbourne, Kent ME10 4PT
Tel: 01795 420586

Alan Parris, head of Swale mus centre.
Age range: 7-18. *Entry requirements:* Gr 6+. *Additional info:* Weekly rehearsals during school term.

Tutbury Junior Band
62 Station Rd, Rolleston on Dove, Burton upon Trent DE13 9AA
Tel: 01283 814703

Malcolm Heywood, cond; Barbara Harvey, secretary.
Age range: 8+. *Additional info:* Rehearses Wed 6.30pm. Takes adult beginners.

Warwickshire County Youth Wind Band *
22 Northgate St, Warwick CV34 4SR
Tel: 01926 412803 *also fax*

Jim Norden, director
Age range: 14-21. *Entry requirements:* Gr 7-8 on most insts, gr 6 on minority insts. *Additional info:* Monthly rehearsals and 4-day residential summer course.

West Kent Youth Wind Band
Kent Music School, The Master's House, College Rd, Maidstone, ME15 6YQ
Tel: 01622 765072

Alun Cook, faculty head of w/wind.
Age range: 13-18. *Entry requirements:* Gr 6+. *Additional info:* Weekly rehearsals during school term.

West Wiltshire Concert Band *
113 Gloucester Rd, Trowbridge, Wiltshire BA14 0AE
Tel: 01225 753175 *also fax*

V S Blay, mus director
Age range: 11-19. *Entry requirements:* Min gr 5. *Additional info:* Weekly rehearsals during school term. Regular concerts and tours abroad including Lake Garda in Jul 1998.

West of England Schools' Symphonic Wind Band
Education School Services, PO Box 25 Riverside, Keynsham, Bristol BS31 1DN
Tel: 01225 395119 *Fax:* 01225 395120

J L Fowles, orch co-ord.
Age range: 13-19. *Entry requirements:* Annual auditions. Min gr 6. *Additional info:* Rehearsals take place each school holiday. Min of 4 annual concerts throughout the UK. Frequent tours abroad.

Wirral Schools' Concert Band *
Education Office, Hamilton Building, Conway St, Birkenhead L41 4FD
Tel: 0151 666 4324 *Fax:* 0151 666 4207

David Straughan, school mus inspector.
Age range: 11-18. *Entry requirements:* Auditions in Jul. *Additional info:* Residential courses alternate with concert tours abroad. Regular recordings made.

York Area Schools Concert Band *
City of York Council, Educational Services, PO Box 404, 10-12 George Hudson St, York YO1 1ZG
Tel: 01904 553917 *also fax*

Alison Goffin, head of mus centre.
Age range: 11-19. *Entry requirements:* Gr 5+. *Additional info:* Weekly rehearsals during school term on Sat mornings.

167

Brass Bands - National

National Youth Brass Band of Great Britain
21 The Coppice, Impington, Cambridge CB4 4PP
Tel: 01223 234090 *also fax;* 0410 505689
Email: nybbgb@bandstand.demon.co.uk

Philip Biggs, admin.
Age range: 12-18. *Entry requirements:* Successful audition. *Additional info:* Two residential courses annually Easter and summer.

National Youth Brass Band of Scotland
Scottish Amateur Music Association, 18 Craigton Cres, Alva, Clackmannanshire FK12 5DS
Tel: 01259 760249

Margaret Simpson, hon sec; Neil Cross, dir of mus.
Age range: 14-21. *Entry requirements:* Gr 6 or equivalent. Entry by audition. Gr 3 for the reserve section. *Additional info:* Tuition provided by experienced br tutors, course 27 Jul-2 Aug 1998.

National Youth Brass Band of Wales
c/o Welsh Amateur Music Federation, 9 Museum Pl, Cardiff CF1 3NX
Tel: 01222 394711 *Fax:* 01222 221447

Keith Griffin, admin; Edward Gregson, president; James Watson, mus adviser. *Age range:* 12-21. *Entry requirements:* Min gr 8. Annual audition and re-audition. *Additional info:* Summer course and concerts.

Brass Bands - Regional and Local

Beaumaris and District Youth Band
East Lodge, Henllys La, Beaumaris, Gwynedd L58 8HU
Tel: 01248 811538

R Kingman.
Age range: Up to 19.

Cardiff County and Vale of Glamorgan Youth Brass Band
The Friary Centre, The Friary, Cardiff CF1 4AA
Tel: 01222 640950/1 *Fax:* 01222 227471

Keith Griffin, mus director
Age range: 14-21. *Entry requirements:* Annual auditions. *Additional info:* Weekly rehearsals, courses, tours, recordings, concerts, festivals and competitions.

Cheshire Youth Brass Band
Cheshire School of Music, The Professional Centre, Woodford Lodge, Woodford Lane West, Winsford, Cheshire CW7 4EH
Tel: 01606 557328 *Fax:* 01606 862113

Sandy Blair; David Lancashire, conds.
Age range: 12-21. *Entry requirements:* Min gr 5. *Additional info:* 60 members. Toured USA, Germany, Denmark and Portugal. Performing with Cheshire Dance w/shop Jul 1998 (Crewe).

Dobcross Youth Band
42 Sandy La, Dobcross, Oldham, Lancs OL3 5AG
Tel: 01457 870895

Jenny Wood, secretary.
Age range: 7-18. *Additional info:* 1996 and 1997 National Youth Junior Champions of Great Britain. Applications from new members welcome.

East Riding Youth Brass Band
South Cattleholmes, Wansford, Driffield, E Riding of Yorks YO25 8NW
Tel: 01377 254293

Age range: 9-18. *Entry requirements:* Jnr band gr 1; intermediate gr 3; youth band gr 5.

Greater Gwent Youth Brass Band
Gwent Music Support Service, Melfort Rd, Newport, South Wales NP9 3FP
Tel: 01633 223196 *Fax:* 01633 252051

Alun F Williams.
Age range: 11-21. *Entry requirements:* By audition, gr 5+.

Greenhall Youth Band
2 Mortonhall Park Gardens, Edinburgh EH17 8SL
Tel: 0131 664 5125

J Robertson.

Guildhall School of Music and Drama Brass Band
Junior School, Silk St, Guildhall School of Music and Drama, Barbican, London EC2Y 8DT
Tel: 0171 382 7160 /Fax: 0171 382 7212
Email: twait@gsmd.ac.uk
Website: www.gsmd.ac.uk

Derek Rodgers, head; John Miller, cond.

Hampshire County Youth Band *
Hampshire Music Centre, Gordon Rd, Winchester, Hants SO23 7DD
Tel: 01962 861502 *Fax:* 01962 863690
Email: edmsmclr@hants.gov.uk

Leighton Rich, cond.
Age range: 10-19, supported by a training band and jnr band. *Entry requirements:* Jnr band (gr 4); training band (gr 5); county band (gr 7); all grades are guidelines and exams need not have been taken. Annual auditions. *Additional info:* 1997 Youth Brass Band Champions. Annually commissions a new work for the band; 1997 commission was premiered at the Royal Festival Hall, London. Concert Jul 1998 in Basingstoke with Sithobelumtheto School Choir from South Africa including traditional Zulu dance.

Hathern Youth Band
10 St Peters Av, Hathern, Loughborough, Leics LE12 5JL
Tel: 01509 842813

Mrs M Spencer, secretary.
Age range: 10-18.

North Ayrshire Youth Band
5 Daltoil Ct, Ralston, Paisley PA1 3AH
Tel: 0141 882 4242

R McNeil; H Brennan.
Age range: 8-22. *Entry requirements:* By audition. *Additional info:* Rehearsals twice weekly. Regular concerts and contests.

Northamptonshire County Youth Brass Band
Northamptonshire County Music Service, 125-129 Kettering Rd, Northampton NN1 4AZ
Tel: 01604 37117 *Fax:* 01604 603070

Rachel Coles, cond; Peter Dunkley, head of mus service.
Age range: School age. *Entry requirements:* Annual auditions, gr 6-8+. *Additional info:* Regular concerts, festivals, tours and competitions.

Oldham Music Centre Youth Band
Oldham Music Centre, Lyceum Building, Union St, Oldham, Lancs OL1 1QG
Tel: 0161 627 2332 *Fax:* 0161 620 0259

M Evans. *Age range:* 12-21.
Entry requirements: Gr 5.

Poynton Youth Brass Band
21 Hollymount Gardens, Offerton, Stockport, Cheshire SK2 7NE
Tel: 0161 487 1989

F Cox.
Age range: 8-19.

Ratby Co-operative Junior Band
12 Oxford Rd, Desford, Leics LE9 9JN
Tel: 01455 823883

Mrs L Plant.

Rotherham Schools Youth Brass Band *
Parkhurst Teachers Centre, Doncaster Rd, Rotherham, S Yorks S65 2BL
Tel: 01709 828191 *Fax:* 01709 379601

Jeremy Wade, cond.
Age range: 12-18. *Entry requirements:* Gr 5. *Additional info:* Weekly rehearsals. 1997 tour to Budapest. National Youth Brass Band Championships competition 1998; National Youth Entertainments Competition.

St Helens Youth Brass Band, Training Band and Beginners Band
20 Birchwood Dr, Lower Peover, Knutsford, Cheshire WA16 9QJ
Tel: 01565 722590

Miss L Nicholson, cond.
Age range: Training band 8-16; youth band 11-19; beginners band, 19 and under. *Entry requirements:* Youth band gr 3. Training band gr 1. Beginners band - none. *Additional info:* Rehearsals Sat during school term.

Spennymoor Youth Band
12 Co-operative Terrace, Coxhoe, Co Durham DH6 4DQ
Tel: 0191 377 0454

Mrs E M Jackson.
Age range: 10-19. *Entry requirements:* Basic knowledge of mus and the ability to play a br inst. *Additional info:* Weekly rehearsals at Spennymoor Town Hall in preparation for various mus activities (national and local contests, concerts, garden parties, etc). Also jnr and beginners bands.

Stantonbury Brass Band
Milton Keynes Music Service, Stantonbury Campus, Stantonbury, Milton Keynes MK14 6BN
Tel: 01908 224250 *Fax:* 01908 224201

Age range: 13+. *Entry requirements:* Gr 6+.

Stockport Schools' Senior and Intermediate Bands
6 Oakland Av, Dialstone La, Stockport SK2 6AX
Tel: 0161 285 0869 *also fax*

Gill Scourfield, admin.
Age range: Up to 18. *Entry requirements:* By audition. Intermediate, gr 4; snr, gr 6. *Additional info:* 1997 tour to France. Snr band 1997 Action Research Entertainment Champions of Great Britain, 1997 Boosey & Hawkes Advanced Youth Band Champions of Great Britain.

Wakefield Metropolitan Band and Schools Band
Band Room 1-2, Manygates Adult Education Centre,
Manygates La, Wakefield
Tel: 01924 257643

R Busby, manager
Age range: 7-19. *Entry requirements:* Informal.
Additional info: National Brass Band
Championships Youth (Intermediate) section.
Rehearsals held in evenings throughout the year.

Wirral Schools' Brass Band *
Professional Development Centre, Acre La,
Bromborough, Wirral L62 7BZ
Tel: 0151 343 1783

A Milnes, head of br teaching.
Age range: 14-18. *Entry requirements:* By audition,
gr 5+. *Additional info:* Touring Spain Easter 1998.

Band Pres Cenedlaethol Ieuenctid Cymru
National Youth Brass Band of Wales
President: Edward Gregson
Music Director: James Watson
Annual Summer course and concerts
(1998 from 17–24 July at Lampeter)
Auditions and re-auditions each year
Minimum grade VIII – age 12 to 21 years

Côr Cenedlaethol Ieuenctid Cymru
National Youth Choir of Wales
President: Bryn Terfel
Conductor: Ralph Allwood
Accompanist: Janice Ball
Annual Summer Course and concerts
(1998 from 11–20 July at Lampeter)
Auditions and re-auditions each year
Good sight singing essential – age 16 to 21 years

Further information from the Director, Keith Griffin,
9 Museum Place, Cardiff CF1 3NX
Tel: 01222 394711 Fax: 01222 221447

The National Youth Brass Band of Wales and
the National Youth Choir of Wales were founded, and are
funded and administered by the
Welsh Amateur Music Federation
Ffederasiwn Cerddoriaeth Amatur Cymru

EXAMINATIONS

GCSE Examination Boards

Names and addresses of the various boards are given below together with details of their music syllabuses. Syllabuses refer to the 1999 examining period, and details should be taken only as a guide to the standard required, not used as a basis for examination work.

Since the last edition, significant developments have taken place in the structure of some of the exam boards. OCR has been launched by UCLES and the RSA Examinations Board and will incorporate the existing Midlands Examining Group (MEG). The Assessment and Qualifications Alliance (AQA) has been established by the Associated Examining Board (AEB), City & Guilds and the Northern Examinations and Assessment Board (NEAB). In this edition, the boards are identified as before, with reference to their new governing bodies. In the immediate future, the syllabuses will continue to be maintained by the individual boards. For further details, please contact the examination board concerned. The Scottish Examination Board has been re-named the Scottish Qualifications Authority.

It cannot be overstated that syllabuses printed below do not represent the full text as published by the individual examining boards. Teachers wishing to enter students for examinations must first obtain copies of the syllabus and regulations for the correct year from the relevant board and refer to the full text as printed therein. Syllabuses are reproduced here by kind permission, for the purpose of comparing different requirements of each board, since all schools are free to select the board of their choice.

Edexcel Foundation London Examinations
formerly **University of London Examinations and Assessment Council**
32 Russell Sq, London WC1B 5DN
Tel: 0171 393 4444 *Fax:* 0171 393 4445

A full and short course are offered for examination (first full course exam 1998, first short course exam 1997). **Full Course.** The full course comprises the following three core papers, equally weighted at 30%. Paper 1 (Performing); Paper 2 (Composing); Paper 3 (Listening and Appraising). Paper 4 (10%) is chosen from five options: performance on 2nd inst; improvisation; a commissioned composition; set work; mus technology.
Paper 1 Performing: All candidates must offer solo and ensemble performing. The standard of the performance and the level of difficulty of the music will be assessed. Work will normally be marked by the teacher-examiner, but tape recordings must be made for the purposes of moderation and standardisation. Candidates may choose the mus played and perform one piece (or solo part) to demonstrate technical control, expression and appropriate interpretation in solo performing. Ensemble will be assessed on a log

of participation in ensemble work together with a tape recording of the candidate playing or singing an individual part, or a recording (preferably video) of the candidate rehearsing and directing an ensemble. The log must include details of a number of performances (in the c/room, school mus groups, or outside school) involving other players, at least three of which have been observed by the teacher.
Paper 2 Composing: Candidates must submit 2 pieces lasting at least 3 mins in total. Each submission should comprise information on the given or chosen brief, a notated score or a commentary, and a tape recording, all of which are teacher-assessed but available for moderation as required. All types and styles of composition acceptable including those involving the use of electronic insts, although the use of technology will not be separately assessed. Compositions must be written in response to a given or chosen brief.
Paper 3 Listening and Appraising: Candidates are expected to respond to mus from a wide variety of styles and traditions. Questions are based on recorded extracts of mus from western traditions, popular culture including jazz, pop, folk, etc and non-western sources with particular emphasis on

171

Indian, Gamelan and African mus and Latin American and Caribbean styles. Candidates will be expected to identify characteristics, relate style to context, make comparisons and give reasoned opinions on a piece.

Paper 4 Options (all submitted for external marking): (a) Performing on a second inst, where in addition to the core performing requirements, candidates must discuss their performance, covering aspects of interpretation, technical features, mus elements, style in relation to period of composition, etc; (b) Improvisation, where candidates may have 10 mins to prepare one improvisation selected from a list of stimuli including mus motifs, rhythm patterns and chord sequences; (c) Commissioned Composition, similar to core composing, but offering a choice of three commissions (which vary from year to year). To be completed within a 4-week period; (d) Study of Set Works, where candidates choose one work from a choice of three, all based on a written score which, unmarked, may be used for reference during the exam. An understanding and appreciation of phrase structure, cadence, instrumentation, texture, harmony and compositional technique is required. Works for 1998 will be Haydn, *Concerto for Trumpet in Eb*, 1st and 2nd mvts; Berlioz *Overture: Le Carnaval Romain*; Sting, five songs from Sting Rock Score, *An Englishman in New York, Fragile, They Dance Alone, Secret Marriage, Straight to my Heart* (all from the album *Nothing but the Sun*); (e) Music Technology, where candidates will be required to produce a sequenced performance of a single movement or section of a movement of their own choice lasting between 2 and 5 mins, including the simultaneous use of different timbres. Candidates are allowed four weeks to sequence their performance, and must submit their recording with a score or tape of their original source and an explanatory log.

Short Course. The short course is designed to require around half the teaching time demanded by the full course, but operates to the same standards and procedures despite the reduction in range and quantity of work to be completed. All candidates take Paper 3 (Listening and Appraising) which is the same as the full course except that the study of non-Western mus is not required and fewer questions will be asked, and then choose between Paper 1 (Performing and Creative Skills) and Paper 2 (Composing and Realisation).

Paper 1 Performing and Creative Skills: Comprises solo performing (as in full course), a viva (as in the full course second instrument option) and a choice between improvisation (as in full course improvisation option) or mus technology for which candidates produce a sequenced performance of a piece lasting 2-5 mins, including the simultaneous use of different timbres.

Paper 2 Composing and Realisation: Comprises composing (1 or 2 pieces, other details as in full course), a viva and a choice of either performing, rehearsing and directing performance, or preparing a sequenced performance (mus technology) of own composition.

Midland Examining Group (MEG) *part of* OCR
Head Office, Syndicate Buildings, 1 Hills Rd, Cambridge CB1 2EU
Tel: 01223 553311 *Fax:* 01223 460278
Email: helpdesk@ucles.org.uk
Website: www.ucles.org.uk

The syllabus meets the requirements of the School Curriculum and Assessment Authority for GCSE syllabuses and Subject Criteria for Music. It contains six components within a flexible assessment structure, based on Listening, Performing and Composing. The six components are: *Component 1* Listening question paper 30%; *Component 2* Further Listening Question Paper 10%; *Component 3* Performing 30%; *Component 4* Unprepared Performing 10%; *Component 5* Composing 30%; *Component 6* Composing using a given stimulus 10%. All candidates take the listening question paper (component 1), one Terminal Task (components 2, 4 or 6) and two coursework components (components 3 and 5).

Listening: Candidates must identify and compare distinctive musical characteristics from a variety of styles and traditions and relate them to the context in which the mus was created. They will also make critical judgements about mus, expressing and justifying their views using appropriate musical vocabulary.

Performing: Candidates will be required to demonstrate technical control, expression and appropriate interpretation by performing a solo part or piece and demonstrate a sense of ensemble either by performing an individual part or by rehearsing and directing a group.

Composing: Candidates will be required to demonstrate the ability to create and develop ideas by composing music and use musical elements and resources appropriately by producing completed compositions within a given or chosen brief.

Question Paper Requirements: For component 1, up to 12 listening questions will be set on extracts of music, using any of the following methods: multiple choice, short answer questions, structured questions, free response questions that require more than a sentence. *Terminal Task Requirements:* For component 2 (further listening) questions will be set on extracts of mus. There will be up to three questions with no choice. Question types will be as for component 1. Component 4 (unprepared performing) will assess the candidate's ability to perform short pieces of previously unseen music. Component 6 (composing using a given stimulus) will assess the candidate's ability to create and develop ideas from a simple stimulus. *Coursework Requirements:* in components 3 and 5 (performing and composing), credit can be obtained by demonstrating the ability to perform on a second instrument or compose in an additional genre.

Northern Examinations and Assessment Board (NEAB) *part of the* Assessment and Qualifications Alliance (AQA)
Devas St, Manchester M15 6EX
Tel: 0161 953 1180 *Fax:* 0161 273 7572
Website: www.aqa.org.uk

The **Music** syllabus covers the three elements of listening and appraising, performing and composing; there are no set works, although there are four areas for the assessment of understanding of continuity and change outlined in the subject content.

Listening and Appraising: A recorded test of aural perception will be supplied by the Board, consisting of a question/answer book and an accompanying cassette. Candidates will be expected to have a knowledge of staff notation sufficient for them to follow a simple score and answer questions relating to clefs, key/time signatures, note/rest values, terms, signs and ornaments, cadences, abbreviations and structural features. They will also need a knowledge of styles and forms and an awareness of the styles and conventions of particular times. Identification and/or comparison of the distinctive features of mus and the ability to comment on the evolution of mus over time will be required.

Performing: Candidates must offer 2 from solo performance (1 piece, to be chosen by the candidate) and ensemble performance (1 piece for an ensemble of at least 2 players, with no doubling of the candidate's part) or rehearsing and directing (candidates must direct a performance of 1 piece previously rehearsed, and submit a written and taped record of rehearsal progress). Whatever permutations of activity are selected an equal balance of solo and ensemble assessment must be achieved.

Composing: Candidates must submit a folio and/or annotated tape of original compositions and/or arrangements composed in conjunction with a given or chosen brief. The total playing time should not normally exceed 5 mins.

Northern Ireland Council for Curriculum Examinations and Assessment (NICCEA) *formerly* Northern Ireland Schools Examination and Assessment Council
Clarendon Dock, 29 Clarendon Rd, Belfast BT1 3BG
Tel: 01232 261200 *Fax:* 01232 261234
Email: ccea@nics.gov.uk

The exam assesses the 3 main activities of listening, performing and composing.

Listening (2 hrs): Assessment will be carried out via 2 written papers, each with accompanying cassette. Candidates will be required to respond to the general mood and character of various pieces of music, some with and some without a score. They will need to be able to recognise and identify points of detail in musical extracts, have sufficient knowledge of staff notation to follow a simple score, and to recognise and identify different styles of music of the past and present. Candidates must also undertake an aural study of set works drawn from the classified periods of musical history.

Performing: Candidates must offer prepared performance (candidate's choice of 2 from individual performance, ensemble performance, rehearsing/directing an ensemble).

Composing: This will be a coursework activity assessed by the teacher and moderated by the Council. Candidates will be expected to have composed a number of pieces over the period of the course, in styles/notations of their own choosing. The total playing time of the final submission should be approximately 5 mins.

Scottish Qualifications Authority *formerly the* Scottish Examinations Board
Ironmills Rd, Dalkeith, Midlothian EH22 1LE
Tel: 0131 663 6601 *Fax:* 0131 654 2664

Standard Grade Syllabus. Candidates are assessed as follows in the four elements of solo performing, group performing, inventing and listening.

Solo Performing: this is externally assessed by visiting examiner. Candidates are required to play a programme of not less than 4 mins and not longer than 10 mins consisting of 2 or 3 pieces contrasted in style.

Group Performing: this is internally assessed and the standard of assessment externally moderated by a Moderator. The instrument played should be of a different category from that of the solo instrument.

Inventing: this is also internally assessed and externally moderated. The activities which form the inventing element are composing, arranging and improvising.

Listening: 3 question papers (one for each level) are offered. The Foundation and General papers

173

each last 45 mins; the Credit paper lasts 1 hr. There is a 10 min break in the middle of each exam. All candidates are required to listen to excerpts of music and to display in their answers to questions a knowledge and understanding of musical concepts, music of the 20th C, and the indigenous music of Scotland. Further details are available in *Arrangements in Standard Grade Music,* available on request from the Board.

Southern Examining Group (SEG)
Central Administration Office, Stag Hill House, Guildford GU2 5XJ
Tel: 01483 506506 *Fax:* 01483 300152

The exam comprises three elements: performing, composing and listening, each tested in a separate paper.
Performing: Candidates will be assessed on prepared performing. Each candidate must offer solo performing, and either ensemble performing or rehearsing and directing an ensemble.
Composing: Each candidate presents a composing coursework file of between 2 and 4 pieces, or 1 substantial composition lasting 4-5 minutes in performance. The file must include an annotated tape and/or scores for each piece together with a statement of intention and an analysis of the outcome.
Listening: A written paper based on recorded excerpts of mus. Up to 10 compulsory questions which require use of a range of skills, knowledge and understanding of music. Candidates must identify and compare distinctive characteristics of music from a wide variety of styles; relate the music to its social, historical and cultural context; make critical judgements about music, expressing and justifying views using a musical vocabulary. Candidates should be familiar with a wide range of music including the classical tradition of Western European music (from renaissance to present day), folk music, popular music and music in African, Asian, South American and West Indian traditions.

Welsh Joint Education Committee (WJEC)
245 Western Av, Cardiff CF5 2YX
Tel: 01222 265000 *Fax:* 01222 575994

The exam covers the three elements of appraising, performing and composing.
Appraising: All questions based on music which will be heard in the exam. Candidates will be tested on: pitch, chord progression, rhythm, metre, major/minor key signatures up to 4 sharps/flats; phrases, cadences, contrast and development, simple musical forms; musical devices (eg imitation, ostinato, sequence; recognition of changes in tempo, rhythm and key); instrumentation; commonly used musical terms; developments in music from 1550 to the present day (including jazz, rock, pop, and music from some cultures other than those of Western Europe); recognition and comprehension of musical extracts from works set for detailed study: Weber, *Overture to Oberon*; and general study: English Madrigals (Morley, *Now is the Month of Maying,* Byrd, *Though Amaryllis Dance,* Gibbons, *The Silver Swan;* Vivaldi, *Four Seasons (Autumn);* Smetana, *Vltava;* Schoenberg, *Pierrot Lunaire* (first 7 songs); Alain Boublil and Claude-Michel Schoenberg, *Les Misérables* (I Dreamed a Dream, On My Own, Do You Hear the People Sing?); Grace Williams, *Fantasia on Welsh Nursery Tunes.*
Performing: Candidates will be required to sing or play a solo part or piece and either sing or play in an ensemble or rehearse and direct an ensemble. Candidates will be expected, in all divisions, to display elements of musicianship as follows: clarity/accuracy of rhythm/pitch; the use of appropriate tempi; effective use of dynamics; fluency of performance; sensitive balance of phrasing; stylistic awareness; technical control of the instrument. Singing or playing individually (5 mins of music selected from work prepared during the course); singing or playing in an ensemble (there must be no doubling of the candidate's part in the ensemble which must be 2 or more players, and the candidate must display awareness of, and empathy with, the other part(s)); rehearsing and directing an ensemble (10 mins of music selected from work done during the course, which candidates must be prepared to discuss with the examiner).
Composing: A selection of work done during the course should be presented with a playing time of 2-4 mins. Scores presented in graphic notation or recordings must be accompanied by explanatory notes or commentaries (written or taped). Free composition, pastiche and arranging will be accepted, in any genre and for any instrumental/vocal combination.

A-level and Higher Examination Boards

Since the last edition, significant changes have taken place in the structure of the exam boards. OCR has been launched by UCLES and the RSA Examinations Board and will incorporate the current OCEAC exams which include syllabuses offered by the Cambridge (UCLES), Oxford (UODLE) and Oxford and Cambridge (OCSEB) boards. The Assessment and Qualifications Alliance (AQA) has been established by the Associated Examining Board (AEB), City & Guilds and the Northern Examinations and Assessment Board (NEAB). In this edition the boards are identified as before, with reference to their new governing bodies. In the immediate future, the syllabuses will continue to be maintained by the individual boards. The Scottish Examination Board has been re-named the Scottish Qualifications Authority.

From the 1995 examination period, the common-core test of aural perception ceased to exist. The Northern Examinations and Assessment Board are administering an aural test which will be used by the Northern Ireland Council for the Curriculum Examinations and Assessment and the University of Oxford Delegacy of Local Examinations. The Edexcel Foundation London Examinations are administering an aural test which will be used by the Oxford and Cambridge Schools Examination Board. The Welsh Joint Education Committee and the University of Cambridge Local Examinations Syndicate have their own aural examinations, and the Scottish Examination Board conducts its own tests in practical musicianship.

Syllabuses refer to the 1999 examining period, and details should be taken only as a guide to the standard required, not used as a basis for examination work. **It cannot be overstated that syllabuses printed below do not represent the full text as published by the individual examining boards. Teachers wishing to enter students for examinations must first obtain copies of the syllabus and regulations for the correct year from the relevant board and refer to the full text as printed therein.** Syllabuses are reproduced here by kind permission, for the purpose of comparing the different requirements of each board.

Edexcel Foundation London Examinations
formerly **University of London Examinations and Assessment Council**
32 Russell Sq, London WC1B 5DN
Tel: 0171 393 4444 *Fax:* 0171 393 4445

A-level Syllabuses. The various A-level syllabuses are formed from different combinations of papers as follows: Music Syllabus A (9502) papers 1, 2 or 10, 4, 6; and one of 3, 5, 8, 10, 12A, 12B or 6 (second inst or voice); Music Syllabus B (9506) papers 1, 2 or 10, 4, 7; Theoretical Music (9508) papers 1, 2, 4, 3 or 10, 5 or 8; Practical Music (9509) papers 1, 9, 6, 7; Music Technology (9510) papers 11, 10, 6, 12.
Paper 1 Aural Perception (20%): Part I (45 mins). *Section A Dictation:* short diatonic melody, at least half of which will be given; short treble or bass melody which may be accompanied; 2-part

(short sections from one or both parts of a 2-part piece not exceeding 8 bars). *Section B Aural discrimination:* chords, keys and cadences (2-stave skeleton score provided); intonation (up to 5 errors in the solo part to be identified from a short passage for solo orchestral instrument and accompaniment); pitch and rhythm discrimination (up to 8 errors of pitch or rhythm to be identified in passage for up to 3 instruments). **Part II** (45 mins). *Aural and Stylistic Analysis:* A test to assess (by means of recorded extracts) a candidate's awareness of a variety of musical techniques and styles/forms of music from 1550 to the present day. Recorded extracts will not be drawn exclusively from Western high art music.
Paper 2 Musical Techniques I (20%): Compulsory harmonisation of a chorale melody in the style of Bach, and either Handelian

175

two-part counterpoint or the completion of a classical string quartet. **Paper 3 Musical Techniques II** (20%): Any two of late 16th C counterpoint; the completion of a piano part of an early romantic German song; the completion of a short piece by Bartók or one of his contemporaries.

Paper 4 Musical History and Analysis I (20%): A study of the broad sweep of music history, from the late 16th C to the 20th C, through the contextual analysis of 30 set works and extracts.

Paper 5 Musical History and Analysis II (20%): Musical history studied through analysis of 20 set works and extracts of one of five genres from sacred vocal, secular vocal, orchestral, chamber or keyboard music.

Paper 6 Performance (Minor) (20%): Prepared and unprepared performance assessed by visiting examiner plus coursework performing.

Paper 7 Performance (Major) (40%): As paper 6, but all work at a more advanced level.

Paper 8 Dissertation (20%): Coursework assessed by examination. Candidates may offer a dissertation on a chosen aspect of music.

Paper 9 Repertoire (20%): A written paper covering repertoire, performance practice and organology. Candidates are required to answer four essay questions, two from section A and two from section B.

Paper 10 Composition and Arrangement (20%): Available as an alternative to Paper 2. Coursework assessed by an external examiner. One or two compositions must be submitted together with an arrangement of one of three pieces of music which will be set by the Council.

Paper 11 Principles of Music Technology (20%): A written paper requiring short answers on the musical use and potential of technology in synthesis, sampling and sequencing; multi-track recording.

Paper 12 Studio Music (40%): Coursework assessed by an external examiner. Section A consists of the preparation of sequences of performances of two pieces of ensemble music, one in a popular idiom and the other selected from art music in the period from c 1550 to the present day. The stimuli for the sequencing will be set by the Council. Section B consists of the production of multi-track recordings and edited stereo master-tapes of two pieces of ensemble music of the candidate's choice.

Advanced Supplementary Syllabuses. The various Advanced Supplementary syllabuses are formed from different combinations of papers as follows: Music (8515) papers 1 (part II only), 6, and one of 2, 4, 10, 12A or 12B; Theoretical Music (8518) papers 1 (part II only), 2 or 10, 4; Practical Music (8520) papers 1 (part II only), 6, and one of 9 or 6 (second inst or voice); Music Technology (8522) papers 11A or 11B, 6, 12A or 12B. The percentage weighting of the papers varies in the Advanced Supplementary syllabuses.

Northern Examinations and Assessment Board (NEAB) *part of the* Assessment and Qualifications Alliance (AQA)

Devas St, Manchester M15 6EX
Tel: 0161 953 1180 *Fax:* 0161 273 7572
Website: www.aqa.org.uk

Syllabus available from NEAB Publications Dept, 12 Harter St, Manchester M1 6HL. In 1999 one Advanced syllabus and one Advanced Supplementary syllabus are provided, sharing common components with different weightings.

Music (Advanced). A common core, consisting of two components, will be taken by all candidates. In addition, three optional components will be selected from a list of six to complete the total of five components required to gain an award.

Common Core: *Listening (20%)* a Test of Aural Perception set by the NEAB which follows the format established in 1994 for the former Inter-Board Test of Aural Perception. *History and Analysis (20%)* an end of course examination in which candidates may choose to answer either three questions on different, specified historical topics or two on different, specified historical topics and one on a specified set work. In each year of examination there will be a choice of eight historical topics and four set works.

Options: Three from: *Composition (20%)* a coursework folio of original music lasting no more than 15 mins which must be the unaided work of the candidate. Folios will be externally assessed by NEAB examiners against the criteria outlined in the syllabus. *Harmony and Counterpoint (20%)* an end of course examination in which candidates must answer two questions, one on four-part harmony in either the style of a Bach Chorale or that of the classical string quartet, and one on two-part counterpoint, employing either appropriate techniques from the 17th to 20th C or specifically 20th C techniques. *Practical Musicianship (20%)* a test of ensemble playing and a demonstration of skills applied to previously unseen music. The ensemble performances should last for 5-8 mins and should normally involve three or more performers. Ensembles consisting of two performers should contain parts forming an equal partnership. Three tests of practical musicianship from the following list should also be selected: harmonisation of a melody; improvisation on a given stimulus; incorporation of a melody with keyboard accompaniment; realisation of a figured bass; sight-reading; sight-singing; transposition. The ensemble and tests may be performed on any instruments/voices (as appropriate) subject to the restrictions noted below. *Project and Report (20%)* a written report, initially assessed internally and then subject to external moderation on a project chosen by the student in consultation with the teacher. The report will be of 2000-3000 words and will include data gathering and research which then leads to an evaluative conclusion related to the topic selected. Project titles need not normally be approved by the NEAB but should enable students to experience music first-hand and to focus on an area which is sufficiently defined to allow for in-depth study. *Recital A (20%)* a recital of 15-20 mins on one instrument/voice, the music being selected by the student (see restrictions noted below). *Recital B (20%)* a recital of 12-15 mins on one instrument/voice and the performance of a previously unseen quick-study piece on the same instrument/voice following a 15 min preparation period (see restrictions noted below). Students may only offer two of the three practical and performing options of *Practical Musicianship, Recital A* and *Recital B*. Candidates selecting *Recital A* and *Recital B* must offer them on instruments from different families, defined as follows: brass, guitars, harp, keyboard, percussion, strings, voices, woodwind. Candidates selecting one of the *Recitals* and *Practical Musicianship* may offer them on the same instrument/voice if desired.

Music (Advanced Supplementary). A common core, consisting of a listening test, will be taken by all candidates. In addition, two optional components will be selected from a list of six to complete the total of three components required to gain an award. **Common Core:** *Listening (20%)* Part 2 of the Test of Aural Perception set by the NEAB which follows the format established in 1994 for the former Inter-Board Test of Aural Perception.
Options: Two from the following, the specification of which is identical to that contained above for Music (Advanced): *Composition, Harmony and Counterpoint, History and Analysis, Practical Musicianship, Recital A, Recital B* each weighted at 40%. Only one of the three practical and performing components may be selected at AS-level. Please note *Project and Report* is not available at AS-level.

Northern Ireland Council for the Curriculum Examinations and Assessment (NICCEA) *formerly* Northern Ireland Schools Examinations and Assessment Council

Clarendon Dock, 29 Clarendon Rd, Belfast BT1 3BG
Tel: 01232 261200 *Fax:* 01232 261234
Email: ccea@nics.gov.uk

The exam consists of 2 written papers, an aural paper, a practical exam and a commissioned composition.

Paper 1: Consists of 2 sections. Candidates must answer one question from each section. Section A will contain a question on each of the following: 4-part harmony; 2-part counterpoint. Section B will contain a question on each of the following: string quartet; orchestration.
Paper 2: Candidates are required to study two set topics from a choice of four and two set works from a choice of four. Two essay-type questions will be set on each of the topics and on each of the set works. 4 questions are to be answered; one on each of the two chosen topics and one on each of the two chosen set works.
Aural: This is the test administered by the NEAB *see above*.
Practical Exam: Candidates should perform a short programme lasting about 10 mins and a sight-reading test or improvisation.
Commissioned Composition: Candidates must choose 1 of 3 assignments and submit these for assessment by 31 Mar.
Music (Advanced Supplementary). Candidates will be required to take Paper 2 of the A-level syllabus outlined above. In addition they must take an Aural Perception test (Part 2 of the NEAB test).

OCEAC: University of Cambridge Local Examinations Syndicate (UCLES) *part of* OCR

Syndicate Buildings, 1 Hills Rd, Cambridge CB1 2EU
Tel: 01223 553311 *Fax:* 01223 460278

One Advanced syllabus and three Advanced Supplementary syllabuses are available (in June only). For the Advanced examination, there are 6 components: candidates must take Performing 1, Composing Folio 1 and Historical Topics, and choose one from either Performing 2, Composing Folio 2 or Project. For the Advanced Supplementary examination, candidates may select one from four options. This is not available to candidates taking Music at Advanced Level in the same session. In order to stress the fundamental importance of listening, the assessment of aural perception is fully integrated into all parts of the examination.
Advanced Level. Performing 1: *Section A* Recital: candidates will be required to perform a recital programme of approximately 15 mins duration, including at least one work by a 20th C composer. Singers will be expected to perform at least one work in a language other than English. Sight-reading tests will be given and candidates will also be required to do an individual improvisation in any style. *Section B* Coursework: candidates must be assessed in two disciplines, one chosen from each of the following lists: list 1 (a) performing as a member of an ensemble, (b) accompanying and/or playing from figured bass;

list 2 (a) conducting and rehearsing, (b) improvising in a group, (c) any two from harmonising melodies, transposing, score reading, sight-singing (not available to candidates who offer a vocal recital).
Composing Folio 1: Coursework folios must contain exercises in stylistic imitation in any two from a list of four compositional types and three compositions or creative arrangements.
Historical Topics: (3 hrs) Three topics will be set as a focus for historical study. In any year, study of one of two of these topics will be compulsory. For each topic, one prescribed work (or a group of shorter pieces) will be set; the edition cited in the syllabus must be used. Candidates will also be expected to explore the general repertoire of music associated with the topics. *Section A* a piece of music drawn from the repertoire of topic 2 or topic 3 will be recorded on cassette tape. A skeleton score of the music will be provided. Candidates will be required to answer up to ten questions about one of these pieces of music which may involve writing down sections of melody, harmonic progressions, rhythmical figures, articulation omitted from the skeleton score, commentary on matters of texture, instrumentation, phrase structure, form or style. Candidates will be expected to relate this piece of music to the wider repertoire of the topic. There is no restriction on the number of times a candidate may play the recording. *Section B* two questions will be set on each of the prescribed works and candidates will be expected to answer one of these. *Section C* three questions of a general nature will be set on each topic and candidates will be required to answer one of these. Topics and prescribed works for 1999 are as follows: Music in the Age of Humanism (c1550-c1640), prescribed work is Monteverdi, *Vespers* of 1610; Opera in the Classical and Early Romantic Periods (c1760-c1835), prescribed work is Beethoven, *Fidelio*; Music in France (c1890-1930), prescribed work is Stravinsky, *The Rite of Spring*.
Performing 2: The instrument used for this paper should be clearly distinct in technique and/or repertoire from the instrument offered for **Performing 1.** Sight-reading tests will be given.
Composing Folio 2: Courses of study related to this paper should aim to develop candidates' discrimination and imagination in creative work, and to give them the scope to use a wider range of techniques and styles than those offered in the syllabus for **Composing Folio 1.** Candidates are required to submit a folio containing representative examples of the work they have done throughout the course.
Project: Candidates who select this paper are required to submit some work of their own choice which does not duplicate work assessed in any other part of the examination.
Advanced Supplementary. Candidates are

required to take one of the following options:
Option A. *Performing:* As for Advanced Level Performing 1. *Composing Folio:* As for Advanced Level Composing Folio 1 except folios should contain exercises in stylistic imitation under one of the stated headings, together with either two compositions or one composition and one arrangement; or exercises in stylistic imitation under two of the stated headings, together with one composition. *Historical Topics:* As for Advanced Level except in the examination, candidates will be permitted to answer all three sections from the compulsory topic. **Option B.** *Performing:* As for Advanced Level Performing 1 except (a) candidates will be required to perform a recital of 10 mins duration, (b) they will be required to take the test(s) of either sight-reading, sight-singing or improvising, (c) they must be assessed in one coursework discipline only. *Project:* As for Advanced Level. *Composing Folio:* As described under Option A.
Option BB: As for Option B, except candidates offer Historical Topics instead of the Composing Folio.
Option C. *Performing:* As for Advanced Level Performing 1. *Project:* As for Advanced Level.

OCEAC: Oxford and Cambridge Schools Examination Board (O&C) *part of* OCR
Purbeck House, Purbeck Rd, Cambridge CB2 2PU
Tel: 01223 411211 *Fax:* 01223 211501

The board offers an Advanced (9640) and Advanced Supplementary (8486) Syllabus.
Advanced Course. Paper 1 Aural Perception: This is the test administered by the Edexcel Foundation London Examinations *see above.*
Paper 2 Composition: Candidates choose 2 from the following options. *Option 1* (1 hr) a chorale, or passage from a chorale, will be set, which candidates will be required to harmonise in four parts, in the style of J S Bach. The melody will be given throughout, along with at least one passage in complete four-part harmony. *Option 2* (2 hrs) opening of a short movement in each of the following styles will be set: a late renaissance 2-part texture, a baroque 3-part texture, a minuet from a classical string quartet, a short character piece for piano in romantic style. Candidates will be required to choose one of the passages and to compose, from this opening, a complete movement (or part of a movement) in the style of the given passage. In the case of the baroque 3-part, candidates will be required to add figuring to their bass part. *Option 3* comprises commissioned composition and arrangement. This allows candidates to develop skills through their own composition in any style they choose, to a general prescription set by the Board: composition using a specified form or technique; composition to a specified theme and length; setting text to music; instrumentation.

Option 4 (coursework) compose two original compositions for contrasting media or one substantial composition of 10-20 mins duration.

Paper 3 Music History and Analysis: *Section A* three topics will be set: Romantic Lieder (1814-1897); The Classical Symphony (1750-1825); The 20th C Musical. *Section B* three themes will be set and candidates must study one of these themes: 20th C Organ Music (1900-1990); the Solo Concerto in 18th and 19th C; Italian and English Madrigals (1530-1630).

Paper 4 Performance: *Section A* Practical Examination: candidates may offer for this component a pass at grade 6 in either instrumental performance or singing. Alternatively a public recital may be offered, details agreed with the board by 1 Nov. *Section B* Performing Options: candidates should select one of the three options offered: Ensemble Performance - to perform, rehearse or conduct an instrumental or vocal ensemble on a regular basis throughout the course; Musicianship Skills - course in improvising, sight-singing and instrumental transposition; Second Study - candidates may offer a second study on a different instrument to that offered in the practical examination. The instrument offered for a second study must be distinct in technique and repertoire from that offered in the first study.

Paper 5 Music Technology: Externally assessed coursework may be offered by A-level candidates in place of one of the options in Paper 2. Consists of four components of which the candidate must choose three. AS-level candidates may offer Paper 5 instead of Paper 3.

Advanced Supplementary Course. Candidates should take Paper 1 Aural Perception part II, or Paper 4 Performance (Section A Practical Examinations), plus Paper 2 Composition (any two options from 1 hr examination, 2 hr examination, directed coursework, free composition), plus Paper 3 Music History and Analysis (Section A, 1 topic only), or Paper 5 Music Technology.

Scottish Qualifications Authority
Ironmills Rd, Dalkeith, Midlothian EH22 1LE
Tel: 0131 663 6601 *Fax:* 0131 654 2664

Higher Grade Syllabus *formerly* Revised Higher Grade. Candidates are assessed in the 3 elements of performing, inventing and listening. Core and extension areas are identified for each element. Candidates will select one element for extension study. Candidates selecting extension in either listening or inventing will be assessed at both core and extension. Candidates undertaking performing (extension) will be assessed at extension only in that element. With the exception of inventing (core), all assessment is external.

Performing will be assessed by visiting examiner.
Performing: Core - solo or group performance lasting 6-10 mins. Extension - (i) solo performance lasting 12-15 mins (ii) either solo or group performance on a second instrument lasting 6-10 mins, or test of practical musicianship in extemporisation or practical harmony.
Inventing: Core - folio of inventions, with performance time of 3-8 mins. Extension - either one substantial invention or a written paper lasting 2 hrs 30 mins.
Listening: Core - a written paper lasting 1 hr 30 mins. Extension - a written paper lasting 45 mins and a written submission on an Investigative Study.
Further Endorsements: Each of the extensions may be attempted as an endorsement by candidates in the same year as the presentation or in a year subsequent to the award. The endorsement will be awarded only to those candidates who gain an award at Higher Grade of band C or above.
Certificate of Sixth Year Studies. This examination is offered in the sixth year of study in the Scottish secondary school and is open to those candidates with a SCE Higher Grade pass (or equivalent qualification) in music. The course offers a choice of specialised study in performing, inventing and listening. Three models of course design are offered, each containing compulsory components (including coursework) and a negotiated component. The following summarises the assessment arrangements. Each candidate will be examined in the following elements:
Compulsory Component: performing recital, inventing folio or listening dissertation. All of these are externally assessed and make up 45% of the total marks.
Coursework: (a) Work related to specialised study. This consists of a teacher's report, candidate's coursework reports and oral interview. Internally assessed and contributing 20% of total marks. (b) Analytical commentary. This is a study and comparison of at least two works from (a) above. Externally assessed and worth 15% of total marks.
Negotiated Component: Candidates will select one of three options; performing, composing and/or arranging, or tests of practical musicianship. Externally assessed worth 20% of total marks. External assessment will be done by a visiting examiner who will assess the recital together with, where appropriate, any short performances and tests of practical musicianship. Coursework (a) will be assessed by the teacher. In order to check the internal assessment of coursework (a) in each of the 3 models, the visiting examiner will interview each candidate for approximately 10 mins.

University of Oxford Delegacy of Local Examinations part of OCR

Ewert Pl, Summertown, Oxford OX2 7BZ
Tel: 01865 54291

Four papers are set: aural, composing, historical appreciation of music, and performing.

Paper 1 Aural: This is the test administered by the NEAB *see above*.

Paper 2 Composing: 3 compositions in varying styles are to be submitted, 2 of them related to commissions (to be announced in the 1st term of the academic year in which the final exam will be taken) chosen from a list of given topics (eg variation form); the third composition to relate to 1 of 5 prescriptions (eg a movement for percussion ensemble), the fifth of which is completely free.

Paper 3 Historical Appreciation of Music: 2 study periods are to be chosen out of 6 that cover together the period 1550 to the present day. In addition, 1 topic area is to be studied from each of the chosen study periods. Example: Study Period D (1828-1900); Topic Area Italian Opera in the 19th C (Verdi, *Aïda* and Wolf, *Mörike Lieder)*; the Concerto in the 19th C (Mendelssohn, *Violin Concerto* and Brahms, *Second Piano Concerto*). Clean copies of scores mentioned in the Topic Areas will be allowed to be taken into the examination room.

Paper 4 Performing: A performance is to consist of a brief recital, sight-reading, any one from a prescribed list (eg keyboard harmony). Performances will be assessed by the teacher, with moderation by Oxford.

Welsh Joint Education Committee (WJEC)

245 Western Av, Cardiff CF5 2YX
Tel: 01222 265000 *Fax:* 01222 575994

Two papers are set (A1 and A2) plus aural tests and a practical exam.

Paper A1 Composing (2 hrs 30 mins): A paper in harmony and counterpoint covering string quartet writing of the Viennese school, chorale harmonisation in the style of J S Bach, completion of a baroque trio sonata, and 2-part counterpoint in baroque style and the completion of a folio of compositions.

Paper A2 (2 hrs): Set works placed in their historical, stylistic and cultural perspective. 2 set works from 2 of the following 5 periods: renaissance, baroque, classical, romantic, modern. Either Weelkes and Wilbye, *The Oxford Book of English Madrigals* or Sweelinck, *Works for Organ or Clavier* (fantasias only) or Byrd, *Mass for 4 Voices* or Dowland *50 Songs* (songs 1-12); either Purcell, *Dido and Aeneas* or Handel, *Eight Great Suites Book II* or J S Bach, *Cantata Wachet Auf No 140* or Corelli *Concerto Grosso no 9, op 6 in F*; either Beethoven, *Piano Concerto No 4 in G* or Schubert, *Quintet in C Major Op 163* or Mozart, *Requiem* or Haydn *Symphony no 101*; either Cesar Franck, *Symphony in D Minor* or Chopin, *Preludes* or Brahms, *Violin Concerto in D* or Strauss *Till Eulenspiegel*; either Shostakovich, *Symphony No 5* or Messiaen, *Quatuor pour la fin du temps* or Grace Williams, *The Dancers* or *Songs from Wales* (Volume I) or Hoddinott *Dives and Lazarus*. A folio of original work arising from the set works and associated topics is also required.

Aural Tests: Set and administered by the Welsh Joint Education Committee.

Performing: Present piece(s) not exceeding 10 mins (basic); present a recital of music not exceeding 20 mins on one instrument or voice (additional). All candidates will be required to sing at sight, and offer either 2 (basic) or 3 (additional) of the following: melodic improvisation or improvisation of a counter melody in the Cywydd Metre; keyboard harmony or score reading; practical performance on a second instrument; sight-reading; ensemble work (not exceeding 5 mins) of two or more players. Candidates who do not choose to do the additional performance are required to offer additional work in either the composing component or the set works component.

Advanced Supplementary. All candidates are required to take Part II of the aural test (30%), and one of the following three components (70%): composing with additional folio; set works with additional folio; performing with additional performance. These are identical to the components as detailed in the A-level music syllabus.

External Examining Institutions

Principal Examining Institutions

Associated Board of the Royal Schools of Music
14 Bedford Sq, London WC1B 3JG
Tel: 0171 636 5400 *Fax:* 0171 436 4520
Email: chiefexec@abrsm.ac.uk
Website: www.abrsm.ac.uk

Richard Morris, chief exec.
Preparatory test, theory and practical graded exams, Advanced certificate, LRSM (composition, mus in the school curriculum, teaching, performance, direction, pno accompaniment); performance assessment scheme for adults; professional development courses for inst and singing teachers.

Guildhall School of Music and Drama
Examinations Service, Dept of Initial Studies, Silk St, Barbican, London EC2Y 8DT
Tel: 0171 382 7167 *Fax:* 0171 382 7212
Email: exams@gsmd.ac.uk
Website: www.gsmd.ac.uk

Eric Hollis, dir.
Syllabuses of graded exams, recital certificate, Teachers' Diploma and Performers' Diploma in pno, vn, vc, singing, fl, cl (classical and jazz), ob, bsn, sax (classical and jazz), rcdr, orch br and br band insts, contemporary, popular pno, elec org, gui (classical and plectrum), orch perc and drum kit.

London College of Music Examinations
Thames Valley University, St Mary's Rd, London W5 5RF
Tel: 0181 231 2364 *Fax:* 0181 231 2433
Email: lcm.exams@tvu.ac.uk

Gillian Patch, exams mgr; Keith Beniston, chief examiner in mus.
All insts, singing, sacred mus, mus theatre, duets and ens. Kindergarten, steps, leisure play, grs 1-8, certificate in advanced performance, ALCM, ALCM(TD), LLCM, LLCM(TD), FLCM (performance). Theoretical diplomas: AMusLCM, LMusLCM, FLCM (thesis, composition).

Trinity College London
16 Park Cres, London W1N 4AP
Tel: 0171 323 2328 *Fax:* 0171 323 5201
Email: info@trinitycollege.co.uk
Website: www.trinitycollege.co.uk

John Davey, chief exec; Nicholas King, chief examiner (mus); Mark Stringer, dir of exams (mus/speech).
Graded exams in all insts from initial to grs 1-8. First Concert Certificate (Brass), Performers Certificate, ATCL, AMusTCL, LTCL (teachers and performers), LMusTCL, ATCL and LTCL (mus education), Certificate in Music Education, FTCL, F(MusEd)TCL.

Other Examining Institutions

Birmingham Conservatoire
University of Central England in Birmingham, Paradise Pl, Birmingham B3 3HG
Tel: 0121 331 5912/5901 *Fax:* 0121 331 5906
Email: conservatoire@uce.ac.uk

Alastair Pearce, vice-principal.
ADBC, LDBC, FBC. Teachers', performers' and fellowship diplomas.

Faculty of Church Music
27 Sutton Pk, Blunsdon, Swindon SN2 4BB

Rev Mark Gretason, hon gen sec.
Examinations for the grade of Associate, Licentiate and Fellow open to church musicians of any denomination.

Guild of Church Musicians
St Katharine Cree, 86 Leadenhall St, London EC3A 3DH
Tel: 01883 743168 *Fax:* 01883 741854

John Ewington OBE, gen sec; Michael Nicholas, exams sec.
Membership is open to church musicians of all Christian denominations. The Guild administers the exams for the Archbishops' Award in Church Music; Archbishops' Certificate in Music (ACertCM); Fellowship of the Guild of Church Musicians (FGCM).

Independent Contemporary Music Awards (ICMA)
PO Box 134, Witney, Oxon OX8 7FS
Tel: 07000 780728; 0374 599698 (24 hours)

Margaret Woolway, registrar.
Diploma and grade exams in all traditional insts, plus elec org, elec keyboard, mus technology, composition, conducting, church mus, accordion, gui, rock gui, kit drumming, contemporary vocals and musicianship. Examinations are held throughout the year at venues chosen by applicants. Approved by the Secretary for State

for Education and Employment under Section 400 of the Education Reform Act 1996.

National College of Brass
242 Grimsby Rd, Cleethorpes, NE Lincs DN35 7EY
Tel: 01472 691623

Andrew White, chmn; J Hall, dir of exams. Grs 1-8 practical for br; also theory. Diploma in performing, theory and conducting.

National College of Music
4 Duffield Rd, Chelmsford, Essex CM2 9RY
Tel: 01245 354596

Eric Hayward, gen sec.
Grs 1-8; bronze, silver and gold medal exams; associate diploma (ANCM), licentiate diploma (LNCM), fellowship diploma (FNCM). All syllabuses approved by the Secretary of State for examinations in schools.

Phillips College
122 Horton Rd, Manchester M14 7GD
Tel: 0171 314 3057

Lee P Longden, dir; Nicholas Groves, academic dean; Ian Roche, admin dean.
The examination division of the Cambridge Society of Musicians, offering certificate, diploma and advanced diploma in band musicianship,

bandmastership, popular mus studies (rock, jazz and pop stylings), mus educ for c/room teachers, choir training, arranging and musicology.

Rock School/Trinity Graded Examinations for Guitar, Bass and Drums
Rock School Ltd, Broomfield Rd, Richmond, Surrey TW9 3HS
Tel: 0181 332 6303 *Fax:* 0181 332 6297

Norton York, chmn; Kathy Wells, programmes mgr. Grs 1-6 and 8 available in electric gui, bass gui and drums for solo players. Mus theory diploma exam (AMusTCL) available for rock guis, bass players and drummers. Performance diploma (ATCL) and Teaching Diploma (LTCL) available.

Royal College of Music
Prince Consort Rd, London SW7 2BS
Tel: 0171 589 3643

R Holloway, asst registrar (exams).
ARCM (performers).

Royal College of Organists
7 St Andrew St, London EC4A 3LQ
Tel: 0171 936 3606 *Fax:* 0171 353 8244

Alan Dear, snr exec.
Membership is open to any interested person; corporate membership is also available to groups. Those wishing to take any diploma must

first apply for membership. ARCO, FRCO; the Choir-training Diploma (Dip CHM) and Organ Teaching Diploma (Dip TCR) may be added to either of these. The Preliminary Certificate may be taken by members or jnr members.

Royal School of Church Music
Cleveland Lodge, Westhumble, Dorking, Surrey RH5 6BW
Tel: 01306 877676 *Fax:* 01306 887260

Geoff Weaver, dir of studies.
Foundation Certificate in Church Music Studies, a modular course for church musicians; Organist Training Scheme, focusing on service accompaniment;

St Nicholas and St Cecilia Awards, qualifications for advanced singers.

Victoria College of Music
9 Staple Inn, London WC1V 7QH
Tel: 0171 405 6483 *also fax*
Email: exams@vcm.telme.com

Jeffery Tillett, dir of exams; Sir Malcolm Arnold CBE, hon president; Martin Ellerby, principal.
AVCM, LVCM (teachers and performers), FVCM, AMusVCM, LMusVCM, grs 1-8, jnr bronze, silver and gold medals. All insts including elec keyboard.

SCHOOLS

Specialist Music Schools

Most of the schools listed below were recognised in the Gulbenkian Report *Training Musicians* as being specially devoted to the training of musically gifted children. Pimlico School is a comprehensive school under Westminster City Council offering a special music curriculum. Where ages are specified, the figure after the decimal point should be read as months.

Chetham's School of Music
Long Millgate Manchester M3 1SB
Tel: 0161 834 9644 *Fax:* 0161 839 3609

Canon Peter F Hullah, head; Stephen Threlfall, dir of mus.
Awards: All UK pupils eligible for means-tested DFEE fee remission scheme up to full fees; day choristerships at Manchester Cathedral also available under separate scheme, voice-trials by appointment age 7+. *Musical activities:* Individual tuition, many ens and comprehensive musical training, orch and choral work, tours, regular internal and external concert participation, m/classes by distinguished visiting musicians. Variety of musical styles and genres taught and encouraged. *Additional info:* Co-ed day and boarding school for gifted young musicians. Specialist tuition (1st and 2nd study) in all orch insts including perc, composition, gui, and voice. Entry assessed on musical potential and decided by mus audition only. Entrants may be accepted at any age. Assessment auditions and advice available throughout year; main auditions held Jan/Mar. Candidates should show outstanding mus potential and instinctive mus perception, instrumental progress, sustained inner motivation to make mus, expressive personality and authentic creative impulses in performing. Overseas candidates can apply on video and audio cassette.
Pupils: 280. *Age range:* 8-18. *Fees:* £4122 (day), £5325 (boarding), £824 (choristers).

The City of Edinburgh Music School
Broughton High School Carrington Rd Edinburgh EH4 1EG
Tel: 0131 332 7805 *Fax:* 0131 343 3296
Email: admin@broughtonhigh.edin.sch.uk

Tudor Morris, dir of mus.
Awards: All pupils funded by their LEA as agreed by all Scottish local authorities. *Musical activities:* Full range of orch, band and choral mus, strong emphasis on chmbr mus and composition (including electronic). *Additional info:* LA scheme offering specialist training to musically gifted children of all ages within framework of education at established LA primary and secondary schools (Flora Stevenson Primary School, Comely Bank, Edinburgh EH4 1BG and secondary school as above). Individual time-tabling allows musicians to spend at least a quarter of school day on specialist study integrated into broad general curriculum. Study includes tuition on all insts and voice, ens work, composition, exams to higher, advanced and diploma level; also extra curricular mus activities organised. Specialist mus staff and facilities including electronic mus studio. Selection by audition (final auditions held end of spring term); application not restricted to those resident in the City of Edinburgh region, but pupils from outside the authority must apply to own LA for financial support. Day school with boarding arrangements available for those living outside daily travelling distance.
Pupils: 40-50. *Age range:* Entry at all ages of primary and secondary school.

Music School of Douglas Academy
Mains Estate Milngavie Glasgow G62 7HL
Tel: 0141 956 2281 *Fax:* 0141 956 1533

Gordon Wilson, head teacher; Ronald McIntosh, course dir (mus). *Additional info:* Fees met by LEA grant; entrance procedure by 1st round auditions (Feb), then final round (Mar) held at residential school over a 2 day period. Auditions may be held at any time of the year. The Academy Music School provides and organises specialist tuition on any inst or voice for pupils showing exceptional talent at audition. Open to students of any nationality; day and boarding. Full range of subjects covered by the mus curriculum, with ample opportunity for practical music-making.
Pupils: 38. *Age range:* 11-18.

Pimlico School
Lupus St London SW1V 3AT
Tel: 0171 828 0881; 0171 821 1717 *Fax:* 0171 931 0549

Philip Barnard, head; David Murphy, dir of mus.
Awards: LA funded specialist intake of up to 15 young musicians pa. *Musical activities:* Orch, choral, ens work, internal and public performance, 5 major

concerts pa. *Additional info:* Westminster co-ed comprehensive school. Musicians fit specialist mus training into normal school curriculum (slightly extended hrs) with 2 hrs per week ens work substituted into time-table, as well as 1 hr per week on 1st study and 30 mins on 2nd study. Entry age normally 11 (or at any age according to vacancies) with facility for other pupils to transfer on to mus scheme at VI form level. The course is run by Westminster City Council but is open to any pupil in the Greater London Area.
Pupils: 1350; 75 (music). *Age range:* 11-18. *Fees:* None.

Purcell School
Aldenham Rd Bushey Herts WD2 3TS
Tel: 01923 331100 *Fax:* 01923 331166
Email: purcell.school@btinternet.com

John Bain, head; Jeffrey Sharkey, dir of mus.
Awards: The school offers aided places under the government's Music and Ballet Scheme. Other scholarships and bursaries available for overseas pupils. Sole criterion for entry is musical potential, assessed in preliminary and main auditions throughout the year. *Musical activities:* Individual tuition in str, pno, wind, br, perc, jazz, voice, composition, electronic mus. Ens include symphony and chmbr orchs, choir, pno class, contemporary ens and period ens. Many concerts in school and major London venues. Regular overseas tours. Weekly aural and Dalcroze eurythmics sessions. Regular m/classes and lecture recitals by visiting musicians. *Additional info:* Co-ed day and boarding school. Emphasis on integrated mus and academic curriculum to A-level. Spacious and accessible new premises in Bushey, 30 mins from the centre of London.
Pupils: 170. *Age range:* 7-18. *Fees:* £3020 (day), £5116 (boarding).

St Mary's Music School
Coates Hall 25 Grosvenor Cres Edinburgh EH12 5EL
Tel: 0131 538 7766 *Fax:* 0131 467 7289

Jennifer Rimer, head; John Grundy, dir of mus; Hazel Sheppard, admin.
Awards: Government aided places: 39 for instrumentalists (tuition and boarding fees), 6 for choristers, plus up to 18 choral scholarships *see also* **Choir Schools**. *Musical activities:* Individual tuition, choir, orch, chmbr ens, composition, m/classes by visiting musicians, concerts (including overseas), broadcasts, recordings. *Additional info:* Specialist co-ed day and boarding school. Pupils from UK and abroad. Entry at any stage, including VI and VII form. Majority of pupils are instrumentalists. Choristers at St Mary's Episcopal Cathedral are educated at the Music

SPECIALIST MUSIC SCHOOLS

School from P5-S2. Recruitment auditions each term. Advisory auditions can be arranged at any time. *Pupils:* 64. *Age range:* 9-19.

Wells Cathedral School
Wells Somerset BA5 2ST
Tel: 01749 672117 *Fax:* 01749 670724
Email: wellscs@rmplc.co.uk

John Baxter, head; Roger Durston, dir of mus.
Awards: Means tested DFEE specialist mus, school mus scholarship places available and scholarships for cathedral choristers *see also* **Choir Schools**. *Musical activities:* Considerable opportunities for public performances; m/classes with visiting artists, lectures, internal recitals, Cathedral choral and orch concerts, opera and concert trips to London, Bristol and Bath, annual South Bank concert, overseas tours. *Additional info:* Academically integrated specialist mus education for c 130 gifted musicians within co-ed boarding and day school. Intensive individual tuition in all orch insts, keyboard, gui and voice. Tuition includes 2 hrs per week on 1st inst plus chmbr mus, orch coaching and aural training. Broad academic curriculum maintained with individually structured mus and practice timetables. Entry according to mus potential at any age (normally aged 8-13 or VI form) with final auditions held Jan/Feb (preliminary auditions arranged throughout yr). Audition consists of 2 contrasting pieces on main inst and 1 piece on any 2nd inst, aural, sight-reading (2nd inst optional). *Pupils:* 794; 502 day, 292 boarding. *Age range:* 3-18.6. *Fees:* £977-2123 (day), £3045-3575 (boarding).

Yehudi Menuhin School
Cobham Rd Stoke d'Abernon Cobham Surrey KT11 3QQ
Tel: 01932 864739 *Fax:* 01932 864633

Nicolas Chisholm, head; Stephen Potts, dir of mus.
Awards: Means-tested DFEE funding guaranteed to all EC resident pupils; bursaries sometimes available for overseas students. *Musical activities:* Many concerts and public performing experience of widely varying kinds are part of school curriculum; also work with visiting professional musicians. *Additional info:* Small international co-ed boarding school. 2 hrs inst teaching per week (vn, va, vc, db, pno only studied); with emphasis on solo and chmbr mus, orch, accompaniment; broadly based mus training, including choral singing. Wide academic curriculum integrated, including GCSE, A-level and university entrance courses. Entry by audition only, based on mus potential. Auditions held throughout the yr, entry age normally 8-14. Candidates to perform on chosen inst, aural and sight-reading tests.
Pupils: 51. *Age range:* 8-18. *Fees:* Dependent on the financial means of parents.

SALISBURY CATHEDRAL CHOIR

VOICE TRIALS
1999

For boys and girls aged 7 - 9

Voice trials for both boy and girl choristers will be held in January and February 1999 for admission to **Salisbury Cathedral School** in September 1999.

Choristers all receive a full Preparatory School education at the Cathedral School.

For boy choristers, the Dean and Chapter provide scholarships which are worth half the full boarding fee. Details regarding scholarships and bursaries for girls are available on request.

Additional help may be available in cases of need.

For details apply to:
The Secretary (Dept. VTC),
Salisbury Cathedral School,
1 The Close, Salisbury, SP1 2EQ.
Tel: 01722 322652

Choir Schools

Schools providing choristers for cathedral, college and some parish church choirs are listed below. The list is in three parts: Anglican preparatory schools, Anglican independent and maintained secondary schools, and Roman Catholic schools. To avoid confusion, schools with similar names are also given a location in brackets. Boys (and in some cases girls) aged 7-10, with good singing voices and instrumental ability are auditioned. Where ages are specified, the figure after the decimal point should be read as months. Although the Government Assisted Places Scheme has been discontinued, some schools offer their own assisted places. Applicants are advised to enquire at the school of their choice for further information.

Most schools are members of the **Choir Schools Association**, The Minster School, Deangate, York YO1 2JA *Tel:* 01904 624900 *Fax:* 01904 632418, Mrs W A Jackson, administrator.

Preparatory Schools (age 7-13)

Abbey School
Church St, Tewkesbury, Glos GL20 5PD
Tel: 01684 294460 *Fax:* 01684 290797

J H Milton, head; Andrew Sackett, dir of mus. *Awards:* Choral scholarships worth up to 33% tuition fees. Age 7-10.6, voice trials Feb, or by appointment. *Musical Activities:* Orch, ens, choirs. *Pupils:* 21 choristers; 80 non-choristers. *Age range:* 2-13 (day), 7-13 (wkly boarding), 8-13 (choristers). *Fees:* £330-1904 (day), £2309-2649 (wkly boarding).

Bramdean School
Richmond Lodge, Exeter, Devon
Tel: 01392 273387 *Fax:* 01392 439330

Diane Stoneman, head; Glen Miller, master of choristers; Tony Connett, dir of mus. *Awards:* Choral scholarships awarded at age 7-9 to day boys and wkly boarders. *Musical Activities:* TV appearances, radio broadcasting, professional recording studio in school. *Additional info:* This school accepts both RC and Anglican pupils. *Pupils:* 198. *Age range:* 3-18. *Fees:* £1364 (day), £2225 (boarding).

Cathedral Choir School
Whitcliffe La, Ripon, N Yorks HG4 2LA
Tel: 01765 602134 *Fax:* 01765 608760

R H Moore, head; A J Bryden, dir of mus. *Awards:* 18 choral scholarships worth at least 50% boarding fees for boys. Girls cathedral choir has fees reduced by 20%. Age under 10, voice trials first Sat in Feb and at other times. *Musical Activities:* 2 orchs, wind ens, str quartet. *Additional info:* Day, boarding and wkly boarding. *Pupils:* 18 choristers; 107 non-choristers. *Age range:* 4.6-13.6 (day), 8-13.6 (boarding). *Fees:* £1200-1765 (day), £2230-2410 (boarding).

The Cathedral School (Llandaff)
Cardiff Rd, Llandaff, Cardiff CF5 2YH
Tel: 01222 563179 *Fax:* 01222 567752
Email: xrg85@dial.pipex.com

Lindsay Gray, head; Michael Hoeg, dir of mus. *Awards:* 20 choral scholarships for boys worth 66% fees. Age 7-10 at voice trial. 16 choral exhibitions for girls worth up to £1000 pa. Age 7-11 at voice trial. Voice trials for boys and girls held each term. *Musical Activities:* Orchs, chmbr orch, ens, choirs and chmbr choir. Professional concerts given and competitions entered. *Additional info:* Day and boarding. *Pupils:* 18 boy, 16 girl choristers; 353 non-choristers. *Age range:* 3-13. *Fees:* £1107 (pre-prep/yr 1), £1231 (pre-prep/yr 2), £1491 (day/yr 3), £1600 (day/yr 4), £1673 (day/yrs 5-8), £2675 (wkly boarding), £2727 (full boarding).

Cathedral School (Salisbury)
1 The Close, Salisbury, Wilts SP1 2EQ
Tel: 01722 322652 *Fax:* 01722 410910

Mrs C M Rolt, acting head; David Halls, dir of mus. *Awards:* 16 choral scholarships for boys worth 50% fees; 4 choral scholarships worth 40% fees; 1 mus scholarship. Age 7-10. Voice trials: Jan (boys), Feb (girls). Some scholarships and bursaries for girl choristers. *Musical Activities:* Orch, 2 school choirs, many inst ens. *Additional info:* The first all-girl cathedral choir was created in Sep 1991. £500,000 bursary and scholarship fund raised for girl choristers under presidency of Dame Kiri Te Kanawa. *Pupils:* 44 choristers and probationers; 174 non-choristers; 163 day; 55 boarding. *Age range:* 3-13. *Fees:* £2075 (day), £2875 (boarding).

193

The Chorister School
Durham DH1 3EL
Tel: 0191 384 2935

Stephen Drew, head; Mrs J Tasker, dir of mus. *Awards:* 23 choral scholarships of 50% boarding fees. Age 7-9 at May, Nov voice trial and by appointment. *Musical Activities:* Orch, ens, separate school choir.
Pupils: 180. *Age range:* 4-13. *Fees:* £1640 (day), £1285 (choristers with mus tuition), £2400 (boarding).

Christ Church Cathedral School
3 Brewer St, Oxford OX1 1QW
Tel: 01865 242561 *Fax:* 01865 202945

Allan Mottram, head; Simon Whalley, dir of mus. *Awards:* 18 cathedral choral scholarships, worth approx 60% boarding fees. Choristerships for Worcester College. Age 7, voice trials as advertised. *Musical Activities:* Choir concerts, recordings, tours; 2 choirs, orch, str orch.
Pupils: 145. *Age range:* 2.6-13; nursery 2.6-4, pre-prep 4-7. *Fees:* £350-803 (nursery), £1090 (pre-prep), £1827 (day/main school), £1118-2785 (boarding).

Exeter Cathedral School
The Chantry, Palace Gate, Exeter, Devon EX1 1HX
Tel: 01392 255298 *Fax:* 01392 491910

C I S Dickinson, head; S W Tanner, dir of mus. *Awards:* 24 choral scholarships for boys worth 50% boarding fees. Usually age under 9.6 at voice trial in Feb. 18 choral scholarships (up to 20% fees) for girls, voice trial in Feb. Mus scholarships also available for non-choristers. *Musical Activities:* School choir, jnr choir, orch, str ens, big band, barber shop ens, w/wind, br, guis. *Additional info:* Day and boarding.
Pupils: 22 boy choristers; 20 girl choristers; 135 non-choristers. *Age range:* 3-13. *Fees:* £845-1540 (day), £890-970 (boarding).

King's College School
West Rd, Cambridge CB3 9DN
Tel: 01223 365814 *Fax:* 01223 461388

A S R Corbett, head; Charmian Farmer, dir of mus. *Awards:* 22 choristerships worth 67% boarding fees. Age 6-7 at voice trials (various dates). King's College Chapel. *Musical Activities:* 2 orchs (c 150 children), 3 choirs, numerous chmbr mus groups, activities and concerts. *Additional info:* Day boys and girls. Dyslexia centre, 28 peripatetic mus teachers.
Pupils: 22 boarding choristers; 267 day and

boarding non-choristers. *Age range:* 4-13. *Fees:* £1504 (pre-prep), £1962 (day), £3040 (boarding), £979 (choristers).

King's School Junior School
Ely, Cambs CB7 4DB
Tel: 01353 660730 *Fax:* 01353 665281

M Anderson, head; N Porter-Thaw, head of mus. *Awards:* 20 choral scholarships worth 66% fees. Age 8-9.6 at entry. Bursaries of 33% fees are available to ex-choristers of Ely cathedral who remain at snr school. Mus scholarships at 11+. *Musical Activities:* Str ens, br ens, w/wind ens, wind band, orch, rcdr consort, gui group, perc ens, regular tours and jnr choirs. *Pupils:* 20 choristers; 300 non-choristers. *Age range:* 8-13. *Fees:* £1550-1845 (day), £2235-3100 (boarding).

Lanesborough School
Maori Rd, Guildford, Surrey GU1 2EL
Tel: 01483 880650 *Fax:* 01483 880651
Email: goodr@lanesboroughps.surrey.cabletel-schools.org.uk
Website: www.rgs-guildford.co.uk

S Deller, head; S Watts, dir of mus. *Awards:* 18 choral scholarships worth £1470 pa. *Musical Activities:* School choirs, orch, concerts and musical productions. *Additional info:* Junior department of the Royal Grammar School, Guildford. *Pupils:* 18 choristers; 310 non-choristers. *Age range:* 4-13. *Fees:* £640-1680.

Lichfield Cathedral School (St Chad's)
The Palace, Lichfield, Staffs WS13 7LH
Tel: 01543 306170 *also fax*

A F Walters, head; R W Dingle, dir of mus. *Awards:* 18 choral scholarships worth 50-60% fees. Age 7-9 at Jan voice trial, or at other times when candidates are ready. *Additional info:* Day and boarding. *Pupils:* 18 choristers; 3 probationers; 225 non-choristers. *Fees:* £1035 (pre-prep), £1610 (day/form 1-3), £1695 (day/form 3-6), £2170 (wkly boarding/form 1-3), £2255 (wkly boarding/form 3-6), £2385 (full boarding/form 1-3), £2470 (full boarding/form 3-6).

Lincoln Minster School
Eastgate, Lincoln LN2 1QG
Tel: 01522 523769 *Fax:* 01522 514778
Email: lms@legend.co.uk

Clive Rickart, head; Linda Hepburn-Booth, mus dir; Colin Walsh, master of the choristers. *Awards:* Choral scholarships of up to 50% fees for boys (22) and girls (22) aged 7-14. Voice trials late Jan or by arrangement. Also mus scholarships. *Musical Activities:* Chmbr choir, jnr choir, jnr and snr orchs, cl ens, fl ens, str group, rcdr group, mus and drama productions. *Additional info:* Educates boy and girl choristers. *Pupils:* 190 (prep); 210 (snr). *Age range:* 2-7 (pre-prep), 7-11 (prep), 11-18 (snr school). *Fees:* £1085 (day pre-prep/yrs 1-2), £1410 (day prep/yrs 3-6), £1585 (day snr/yrs 7-8), £2400-2775 (wkly boarding), £2585-3000 (boarding).

The Minster School
Deangate, York YO1 2JA
Tel: 01904 625217 *Fax:* 01904 632418

Richard Shephard, head; Jill Bowman, dir of mus. *Awards:* 50 choral scholarships worth 80% tuition fees. Annual voice trials for boys and girls aged under 9. *Musical Activities:* Orch, choir, chmbr ens. *Pupils:* 50 choristers; 150 non-choristers. *Age range:* 3-13. *Fees:* £895-1380 (day).

New College School
Savile Rd, Oxford OX1 3UA
Tel: 01865 243657

J Edmunds, head; R W Allen, dir of mus. *Awards:* Chorister places at greatly reduced fees. Age 7-9 at Feb voice trial. *Musical Activities:* Joint concerts with local groups, two choirs in school, orch groups, Sat creative arts morning. *Additional info:* Day for choristers. *Pupils:* 20 choristers; 115 non-choristers. *Age range:* 7-13. *Fees:* £1460-1595 (day).

The Pilgrims' School
3 The Close, Winchester, Hants SO23 9LT
Tel: 01962 854189 *Fax:* 01962 843610

B A Rees, head; Miss Hilary Brooks, dir of mus. *Awards:* 22 cathedral choir choral scholarships, 16 Winchester College quirister scholarships, all worth 50% boarding fees. Age 7.6-10; voice trials Nov. *Musical Activities:* 2 school orchs, school band. *Pupils:* 180. *Age range:* 8-13. *Fees:* £2065 (day), £2830 (boarding).

Polwhele House School
Truro, Cornwall TR4 9AE
Tel: 01872 273011 *also fax*

Richard White, head and dir of mus. *Awards:* 18 choral scholarships worth 75% tuition fees and free tuition in 1 inst plus 25% boarding fees. Age 7-9; voice trials Jan. Choristers for Truro Cathedral. *Musical Activities:* Rcdrs, chmbr groups, orch, musical productions, girls' choir and parents' choir. *Additional info:* Day and wkly boarding. Wkly boarding available for children aged 7-13. After school care and occasional boarding. *Pupils:* 18 choristers; 151 non-choristers. *Fees:* £197-984 (nursery), £1040-1138 (day/5-7), £1540 (day/7-11), £1678 (day/11-13), £1190 (wkly boarding/7-11), £1320 (wkly boarding/11-13).

The Prebendal School
53 West St, Chichester, W Sussex PO19 1RT
Tel: 01243 782026

Revd Canon G C Hall, head; Mark Wardell, dir of mus. *Awards:* 18 choral scholarships worth 50-100% fees. Age 7.6-9.6 at voice trials held whenever a vacancy occurs in the choir. *Musical Activities:* 3 orchs, 3 choirs, ens, 19 visiting inst staff. *Pupils:* 18 boarding choristers; 149 day, 22 boarding non-choristers. *Age range:* 3-13. *Fees:* £1840 (day), £2392 (boarding).

Queen Elizabeth Grammar Junior School
158 Northgate, Wakefield, W Yorks WF1 3QY
Tel: 01924 373821 *Fax:* 01924 366246

M M Bisset, head; David Turmeau, dir of mus. *Awards:* 12 choral places with 33% academic fee remission during time in choir (foundation awards available in snr school). *Pupils:* 237 day, including 12 choristers. *Age range:* 7-11. *Fees:* £1142-1207 (day).

St Edmund's Junior School
Canterbury, Kent CT2 8HU
Tel: 01227 454575 *Fax:* 01227 471083

R G Bacon, head; Ian Sutcliffe, dir of mus. *Awards:* 30 choral scholarships (Canterbury Cathedral Choristerships), normally 6 pa, worth 50% fees; other financial help may be available. Age under 9, Nov voice trials. *Musical Activities:* Orch, bands, choirs, chmbr ens and jazz group. *Additional info:* Day and boarding. *Pupils:* 30 choristers; 200 non-choristers. *Fees:* £2163 (day), £3090 (boarding).

St George's School
Windsor Castle, Berks SL4 1QF
Tel: 01753 865553 *Fax:* 01753 842093

Revd R P Marsh, head; J C Young, dir of mus. *Awards:* Up to 24 choral scholarship places worth £4665 pa. Age 6.9-9 at voice trials in Nov and Feb. Choir of Queen's Free Chapel of St George in Windsor Castle. *Musical Activities:* Orch, wind band, str orch, school choir (sings at Lower Chapel, Eton College), str ens; concerts and musicals. *Pupils:* 24 choristers; 132 non-choristers. 121 day; 35 boarding. *Age range:* 2.6-13. *Fees:* £450-650 (nursery), £1200-1375 (pre-prep), £2095-2315 (day), £3050 (wkly boarding), £3110 (boarding).

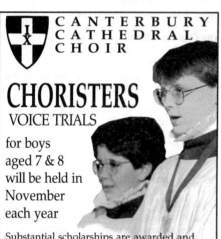

St John's College School
73 Grange Rd, Cambridge CB3 9AB
Tel: 01223 353532 *Fax:* 01223 315535
Email: enquiry@sjcs.demon.co.uk

K L Jones, head; E P Bryan, dir of mus. *Awards:* 20 choral scholarships worth 66% boarding fees. Age under 10 at Oct voice trial. St John's College Chapel. Also bursaries available at 11+. *Musical Activities:* 5 choirs, orch, full range of chmbr mus. *Additional info:* Co-ed day and boarding. *Pupils:* 440. *Age range:* 4-13. *Fees:* £1120-1857 (day), £2933 (boarding).

St Mary's Preparatory and Choir School
Chart La, Reigate, Surrey RH2 7RN
Tel: 01737 244880 *Fax:* 01737 221540

J A Hart, head; Marion Holmes, dir of mus; Jonathan Rennert, master of choristers. *Awards:* 14 choral scholarships worth 50% fees. Usually age 10 and under; St Mary's Church, Reigate. *Musical Activities:* Concerts and services in London and Surrey. Occasional recordings and radio broadcasts. *Pupils:* 14 choristers; 240 non-choristers. *Age range:* 3-13. *Fees:* £289-1440 (day).

St Paul's Cathedral School
2 New Change, London EC4M 9AD
Tel: 0171 248 5156 *Fax:* 0171 329 6568

Stephen A Sides, head; John Scott, Cathedral dir of mus. *Awards:* 40 places for boarding choristers. Age 6.9-9 at Feb, May or Oct voice trials. *Musical Activities:* Orchs, ens and chmbr groups; day boys' choir. All choristers learn 2 insts (included in fees). *Pupils:* 40 boarding choristers; 60 day non-choristers; 45 pre-prep boys and girls. *Age range:* 4-13. *Fees:* £1768 (day), £1066 (boarding choristers).

Westminster Abbey Choir School
Dean's Yard, London SW1P 3NY
Tel: 0171 222 6151 *Fax:* 0171 222 1548

Roger Overend, head; Martin Neary, organist, and master of choristers; Stephen Le Prevost, mus master. *Awards:* 38 places, all for boarding boy choristers. Voice trials 3 times pa. *Additional info:* Only school in country educating just boy choristers. *Pupils:* 38. *Fees:* £973 (boarding, including tuition on 2 insts).

Independent and Maintained Secondary Schools (age 7-18)

Bristol Cathedral School
College Sq, Bristol BS1 5TS
Tel: 0117 929 1872 *Fax:* 0117 930 4219
Email: webmaster@cathedral.demon.co.uk
Website: www.cathedral.demon.co.uk

K J Riley, head; Simon Holt, dir of mus. *Awards:* Up to 19 chorister places with means-tested financial support available, also £1400 pa non means-tested. Age 9-10, voice trials Feb. *Musical Activities:* 1st and 2nd orchs, str orch, concert band, str quartets, school choir, chmbr choir. *Pupils:* 470; 19 choristers. *Age range:* 10-18. *Fees:* £1454.

Chetham's School of Music *see* Specialist Music Schools

Hereford Cathedral School
Old Deanery, Cathedral Close, Hereford HR1 2NG
Tel: 01432 363522 (snr school) *Fax:* 01432 363525

H C Tomlinson, head of snr school; T R Lowe, head of prep school; J M Williams, dir of mus. *Awards:* 18 choral scholarships worth 50% of boarding and tuition fees for boarders, and 66% of tuition fees for day boys; may be supplemented by various trusts in case of need.

Age 8-10; voice trials Nov and sometimes May. Academic and mus scholarships may be awarded at 13 to ex-choristers. Potential Oxbridge choral scholars have opportunity to return to cathedral choir after voice has settled. *Musical Activities:* 2 orchs, chmbr choir, choral society, chmbr mus, 2 concert bands, regular productions of musicals. *Additional info:* Junior School at 29 Castle St, Hereford HR1 2NN *tel:* 01432 363511 *fax:* 01432 363515. *Pupils:* 18 choristers; 847 non-choristers (235 prep school, 630 snr school). *Age range:* 3-11 (jnr), 11-18 (snr). *Fees:* £1087 (day), £2007 (boarding).

King's School (Gloucester)
Pitt St, Gloucester GL1 2BG
Tel: 01452 521251 *Fax:* 01452 385275

Peter Lacey, head; Ian Fox, dir of mus. *Awards:* 24 choral scholarships worth 100% fees during time in choir; generous reduction in fees after leaving choir. Age under 9; Feb voice trials. *Musical Activities:* Orch, jnr orch, br ens, concert band, jnr br ens, wind group, str group, jnr str group, choral society, girls' choir, school choir, madrigal group, str quartet, wind octet and many other ens. *Additional info:* Day and boarding; choristers

are day boys.
Pupils: 500. *Age range:* 4-18. *Fees:* £900-2260 (day), £3445-3820 (boarding).

King's School (Peterborough)
Park Rd, Peterborough PE1 2UE
Tel: 01733 751541 *also fax*

G L Longman, head; N C Kerrison, dir of mus. *Awards:* VI form choral scholarships available to altos, tenors or basses. Students study for 3 A-levels. *Musical Activities:* 2 choirs, 2 orchs, jazz ens, br ens and concert band.
Pupils: 40 choristers; 820 non-choristers. *Age range:* 11-18. *Fees:* n/a. Day places only.

King's School (Rochester)
Satis House, Boley Hill, Rochester, Kent ME1 1TE
Tel: 01634 843913 *Fax:* 01634 832493

I R Walker, head; G R Williams, dir of mus. *Awards:* A number of choral scholarships worth 40% tuition fees. Age under 10, voice trials Nov and Feb. Up to 5 mus scholarships pa from 11+, 1 of up to 100% fees (means tested above 50%). Free inst tuition for holders of mus awards. *Musical Activities:* Orch, chmbr orch, quartet, wind band, choir, br group. *Additional info:* Co-ed; boarding from 8 yrs.
Pupils: 245 prep; 20 choristers; 327 snr. *Age range:* 8-13 prep. *Fees:* £1889-2169 (day/prep), £2530 (day/snr), £3354/3634 (boarding/prep).

King's School (Worcester)
College Green, Worcester WR1 2LH
Tel: 01905 23016 *Fax:* 01905 25511

J M Moore, head; D E Brookshaw, dir of mus. *Awards:* 22 choral scholarships worth over 50% fees. Age 7-9.6; voice trials Dec. *Musical Activities:* Concerts, broadcasts and choir tours.
Pupils: 1005 day; 22 boarding. *Age range:* 7-18. *Fees:* £1189-1846 (day), £3200 (boarding).

Lincoln Minster School *see* Preparatory Schools (age 7-13)

Magdalen College School
Cowley Pl, Oxford OX4 1DZ
Tel: 01865 242191 *Fax:* 01865 240379

P M Tinniswood, head; C J G Ives, organist; M N Pearce, dir of mus. *Awards:* 16 choral scholarships worth 50% tuition fees. Age under 10; voice trials Oct and Mar. *Musical Activities:* Jnr and snr orchs, choral society, madrigal choir, close harmony group, chmbr ens, jazz band.
Pupils: 16 choristers; 520 non-choristers. *Age range:* 9-18. *Fees:* £1798 (day).

Minster School
Nottingham Rd, Southwell, Notts NG25 0HG
Tel: 01636 814000/812911 (24 hr choir info)
Fax: 01636 814788

P J Blinston, head; Gill Baker, dir of mus. *Awards:* Voluntary aided C of E comprehensive day school. Financial assistance available to subsidise transport, meals and inst lessons. Voice trials and inst auditions Mar/May/Jun, age 8.6-10.6. *Musical Activities:* 4 choirs, 3 orchs, ens groups, 3 bands.
Pupils: 16 full choristers, 2 probationers, 12 jnrs; 1430 non-choristers. *Age range:* 8-19.

Norwich School
The Close, Norwich NR1 4DQ
Tel: 01603 623194 *Fax:* 01603 627036

C D Brown, head; Colin Dowdeswell, dir of mus. *Awards:* 20 choral bursaries for Cathedral choir worth 50% of fees. Age 8-10; voice trials Jan, Feb. *Musical Activities:* Choirs, orchs, bands, ens. *Additional info:* Mus scholarships (£300 to full fees) available age 11-13. Girls admitted in the VI form. VI form mus awards also available.
Pupils: 150 jnr; 630 snr; up to 20 choristers. *Age range:* 8-18. *Fees:* £1630-1696 (day).

St Edward's College
Sandfield Pk, Liverpool L12 1LF
Tel: 0151 281 1999 *Fax:* 0151 281 1909

John Waszek, head; John Moseley, dir of mus. *Musical Activities:* 3 orchs, 3 choirs, various ens; concerts given throughout yr.
Pupils: 860. *Age range:* 11-18. *Fees:* N/A, grant-maintained status.

St James' School
22 Bargate, Grimsby, S Humberside DN34 4SY
Tel: 01472 362093/4 *Fax:* 01472 351437

D J Berisford, head; Adrian King, dir of mus. *Awards:* 18 choral scholarships worth 50% fees (tenable up to age 16). Age 7-11; voice trials by appointment. *Musical Activities:* Snr and prep school orch, jazz ens, str ens, w/wind ens, snr school br ens; also lunchtime concerts, termly concerts and mus, art and drama festival.
Pupils: 241. *Age range:* 4-18. *Fees:* £800-1690 (day), £2040-2690 (wkly boarding), £2180-2830 (full boarding).

St Mary's Music School
Coates Hall, 25 Grosvenor Cres, Edinburgh EH12 5EL
Tel: 0131 538 7766 *Fax:* 0131 467 7289

Jennifer Rimer, head; John Grundy, dir of mus; T Byram-Wigfield, master of choristers. *Awards:* 24 chorister places (up to 18 with choral scholarships worth up to 75% academic fees); 6 government aided places). Boys and girls, 7-10. Entry by audition each term. Advisory auditions

can be arranged at any time. *Musical Activities:* Many outside engagements, broadcasts, recordings, tours. *Additional info:* Day and boarding. *See also* **Specialist Music Schools.**
Pupils: 25 choristers; 39 non-choristers. *Age range:* 9-19.

Wells Cathedral School
15 The Liberty, Wells, Somerset BA5 2ST
Tel: 01749 672117 *Fax:* 01749 670724
Email: wellscs@rmplc.co.uk

J S Baxter, head; Roger Durston, dir of mus.

Awards: 20 choral scholarships for boys worth 45% fees and 18 for girls worth 8% fees. Age under 10.6; voice trials Jan. Academic scholarships also available. *Musical Activities:* Tuition in all orch insts, keyboard, gui and voice. Chmbr mus, orch coaching and aural training. *Additional info:* Co-ed; day and boarding. *See also* **Specialist Music Schools.**
Pupils: 20 boy choristers; 18 girl choristers; 749 non-choristers. 487 day; 300 boarding; 150 studying inst. *Age range:* 3-18.6. *Fees:* £977-2123 (day), £3045-3575 (boarding).

Roman Catholic Choir Schools

Bramdean School *see* Preparatory Schools (age 7-13)

St Edward's Junior School
Sandfield Pk, Liverpool L12 1LF
Tel: 0151 281 2300 *Fax:* 0151 281 4900

Philip Sweeney, head; Brenda Bixter, dir of mus; Mervyn Cousins, dir of cathedral mus. *Awards:* 12 choral scholarships worth £250 pa. Age 3-11; voice trials Feb/Mar. Informal auditions throughout the year. *Musical Activities:* Orchs, choir, 3-4 concerts pa.
Pupils: 370. *Age range:* 3-11. *Fees:* £925 (nursery and reception), £975 (3-6 yrs).

St John's College
College Green, Newport Rd, Old St Mellons, Cardiff CF3 9YX
Tel: 01222 778936 *Fax:* 01222 360688

D J Neville, head; S J Maxson, dir of mus. *Awards:* From 10% fees upwards subject to performance at voice trial. *Musical Activities:* Mixed choir,

orch, br and wind ens, regular large-scale dramatic productions, many outside engagements, broadcasts, recordings, tours. Preparation for Oxford and Cambridge choral awards. *Age range:* 3-18. *Fees:* £850-1045.

Westminster Cathedral Choir School
Ambrosden Av, London SW1P 1QH
Tel: 0171 798 9081 *Fax:* 0171 798 9090

C Foulds, head; J O'Donnell, master of mus. *Awards:* Total of 30 choral scholarships offered (usually 6 pa), value approx 75% full fees with further remission available in cases of exceptional need. Age normally 8 (on entry); voice trials Feb, Jun, Nov or by arrangement for entry usually in Sep. *Musical Activities:* Chmbr mus, orchs and non-chorister choir. *Additional info:* Day and boarding.
Pupils: 30 choristers; 70 day. *Age range:* 8-13. *Fees:* £2225 (day), £1100-1225 (boarding).

Preparatory Schools Offering Music Scholarships

All of the preparatory schools listed below offer music scholarships. Additional preparatory schools with exceptionally active music departments will be found in the **Choir Schools** and **Independent Schools** sections. Children are normally taken from 7 or 8 years and move to an independent school at 13; some schools also have a pre-preparatory department for children as young as age 3. Where ages are specified, the figure after the decimal point should be read as months.

Ashford Junior School (Girls)
East Hill, Ashford, Kent TN24 8PB
Tel: 01233 625171 *Fax:* 01233 647185

Mrs P Metham, head; Miss J Hollis, dir of mus.
Awards: Mus scholarship, age 9 or under on 1 Sep in year of entry. 2 pupils gain mus scholarships to secondary schools. *Musical activities:* Choir, orch, rcdr group, perc group, theory class. Class vn lessons from age 5-7 for all pupils. Sat morning vn mus school from age 3.
Pupils: 165 day including pre-prep; 97 have lessons in school. *Age range:* 5-11. *Termly fees:* £1041-1647 (day), £3249 (boarding).

Badminton Junior School (Girls)
Westbury-on-Trym, Bristol BS9 3BA
Tel: 0117 905 5222 *Fax:* 0117 962 8963
Email: badminton.office@dial.pipex.com

Mrs A Lloyd, head; C Francis, dir of mus.
Awards: Mus scholarships available. Pupils can gain mus scholarships to secondary school. *Musical activities:* Orch and choir, wind and Suzuki groups.
Pupils: 67 (day); 10 (boarding); 72 (studying inst). *Age range:* 4-11. *Termly fees:* £1125-1550 (day), £2975 (boarding). *See also* **Independent Schools** Badminton School.

Bedgebury Junior School (Girls)
Bedgebury Park, Goudhurst, Kent TN17 2SH
Tel: 01580 211954

Mrs L J Griffin, head; Bryan Gipps, dir of mus.
Awards: Mus awards and bursaries at 7+. *Musical activities:* 2 choirs and orchs.
Pupils: 146 pupils (day, wkly and full boarding available). Majority of pupils study inst. *Age range:* Pre-prep 2.6-7.6; prep 7.6-11. *Termly fees:* £582-2483 (day), £2635-3998 (boarding). *See also* **Independent Schools** Bedgebury School.

Bishops Stortford Junior School (Co-ed)
Bishops Stortford College, Bishops Stortford, Herts CM23 2QZ
Tel: 01279 838607 *Fax:* 01279 306110

D J Defoe, head; Andrew Bruce, dir of mus.
Awards: 3 mus scholarships (choral and inst) value 20-50% fees available; age under 11, under 12. Min gr 3 required; scholarships tenable throughout prep and snr school career. *Musical activities:* Jnr school has own choir and orch; also mus productions, regular concerts and recitals. Musical integration with main college provides additional opportunities, especially to more advanced musicians.
Pupils: 410 day and boarding. *Age range:* 4-13. *Termly fees:* £1300-2230 (day), £2700-2940 (wkly boarding), £2700-2940 (boarding).

The Blue Coat School (Co-ed)
Somerset Rd, Edgbaston, Birmingham B17 0HR
Tel: 0121 454 1425 *Fax:* 0121 454 7757

B P Bissell, head; Christopher Johnson, dir of mus.
Awards: At least 2 mus scholarships available pa worth 45% of either day or boarding fees, covering ages 11+ to 13+. Continuation awards available at Bromsgrove School. *Musical activities:* School orch (with wkly sectional coaching from visiting specialists), wind band, 3 choirs, graded rcdr groups. 2 main concerts and 6 informal concerts annually. Keyboard lab, use of computers for composition, Kodály classes, full range of inst teaching and singing lessons available.
Pupils: 170 day; 70 boarding; 150 studying inst. *Age range:* 7-13+. *Termly fees:* £1715 (day), £2620 (boarding).

Bramdean School (Boys)
Richmond Lodge, Exeter, Devon
Tel: 01392 273387 *Fax:* 01392 439330

Diane Stoneman, head; Glen Miller, master of choristers; Tony Connett, dir of mus.
Awards: Choral scholarships awarded at age 7-9. Open to day boys and boarders depending on

Ashford
SCHOOL

<u>A World of Difference</u>

Ashford School's impressive record of achievement shows how traditional values and modern methods combine to provide every opportunity for bright girls to become successful women.

The broad curriculum, small class size and single sex environment encourage individual thinking and effective study, while personal expression through diverse leisure pursuits develops versatility and confidence. Over half of all our pupils study music, both instrumental and choral

Music Scholarships and Awards

Available to Year 4, Year 7, Year 8 and Year 9 students.

For further information, please contact
The Registrar
Ashford School, East Hill, Ashford
Kent. TN24 8PB
Telephone 01233 625171

Ashford School is a Charity, No 307848, which exists
for educational purposes

regional locality. *Musical activities:* TV appearances, radio broadcasts, professional recording studio in school.
Pupils: 198. *Age range:* 3-18. *Termly fees:* £1364 (day), £2225 (boarding).

Caterham Preparatory School (Co-ed)
Mottrams, Harestone Valley Rd, Caterham, Surrey CR3 6YB
Tel: 01883 342097 *Fax:* 01883 341230
Email: admoy@pncl.co.uk

A D Moy, head; N C Hickey, dir of mus. *Musical activities:* Orch, 2 choirs, rcdr group, wind and str ens. Further band and orch opportunities plus annual choral work with main school. Also mus productions and inst teaching (all insts). Group teaching to all.
Pupils: 50 studying inst. *Age range:* 3-11. *Termly fees:* £630-1850.

Catteral Hall (Co-ed)
Giggleswick, Settle, N Yorks BD24 0DG
Tel: 01729 822527 *Fax:* 01729 825505

M J Morris, head; N J Waugh, dir of mus.
Awards: 2 mus awards of up to 50% fees, plus 1 of up to 33% fees, all with free inst tuition in 2 insts; offered on grounds of mus ability. Age 12.6 or under on 1 Sep. At least 1 inst to be offered (2 preferable: 1 keyboard inst, 1 orch inst); singing an advantage. *Musical activities:* Catteral Hall is separate from main school, but has many integrated musical activities including chapel choir, orchs, bands. Jnr school has choir, orch groups, jnr concert band, plus annual concert, mus competitions and other productions including musicals. Mus society concerts twice a term, regular mus assemblies and arts festival in Lent term. Full range of inst tuition available.
Pupils: 58 day; 60 boarding; 85 studying inst. *Age range:* 7-13 (jnr school of Giggleswick School, to which pupils are normally expected to proceed).
Termly fees: £2160 (day/age 7-10), £2320 (day/age 11-13), £3230 (boarding/age 7-10), £3470 (boarding/age 11-13). *See also* **Independent Schools** Giggleswick school.

Clayesmore Preparatory School (Co-ed)
Iwerne Minster, Blandford, Dorset DT11 8PH
Tel: 01747 811707 *Fax:* 01747 811692
Email: hmcps@aol.com

M G Cooke, head; P F G Newson-Smith, dir of mus.
Awards: Mus awards to the value of 50% boarding fees, additional bursaries may be available in case of need and free inst tuition. *Musical activities:* Orch, chapel choir, str, w/wind, early mus and br groups; mus productions; organ recitals; outings by chapel choir to cathedrals and churches to sing evensong and give concerts; overseas tours by choir and concert band; visiting recitalists.

Pupils: 170 day; 79 boarding; 166 studying inst. *Age range:* 3-13. *Termly fees:* £2165 (day), £3035 (boarding).

Colet Court (Boys)
Lonsdale Rd, Barnes, London SW13 9JT
Tel: 0181 748 3461 *Fax:* 0181 563 7361

G J Thompson, head; Ian Hunter, dir of mus.
Awards: 1 mus scholarship offered annually, value according to parental means from 15% to full fees plus free inst tuition. Scholarships are awarded conditionally upon pupils' continuation to main school. Age 10-11 on 1 Sep; min gr 4 on main inst with 2nd inst preferred. 2 choral scholarships are also offered for boys entering Colet Court aged 7-8 and 10-11. *Musical activities:* Beginner's orch, 2 other orchs; 3 choirs (with outside concerts and recitals, annual choral w/end); also inst groups, jazz group, and annual jazz w/end. Full-scale mus production alternate yrs, also regular concerts, annual joint mus activity with snr school. Full range of inst tuition available.
Pupils: 430 day; 330 studying inst. *Age range:* 7-13. *Termly fees:* £2170 (day), £3181 (boarding). *See also* **Independent Schools** St Paul's School.

Colston Collegiate School (Co-ed)
Stapleton, Bristol BS16 1BA
Tel: 0117 965 5297

G N Phillips, head; Ian Holmes, dir of mus.
Awards: Unspecified number of awards at 11+. 6 pupils gain mus scholarships to secondary schools. *Musical activities:* Str orch, wind band, jazz groups, school and chapel choirs.
Pupils: 150 day (7-11); 150 day (11-13); 100 studying inst. *Age range:* 7-13. *Termly fees:* £1155-1334 (day).

Cranleigh Preparatory School (Boys)
Cranleigh, Surrey GU6 8QH
Tel: 01483 273666 *Fax:* 01483 277136

Malcolm Keppie, head; Chika Robertson, dir of mus.
Awards: No awards made on entrance. 1 pupil gaining mus scholarship to Cranleigh School pa including exhibitions. *Musical activities:* Chapel choir, second and jnr choirs, with in-school and outside activities (and recordings made), 'Big Sing Choir' open to all. Str and full orch; also wind band. Chmbr mus and ens for w/wind, br, perc, gui and str players, all with intensive specialist coaching. Vocal and inst tuition in all orch and keyboard insts available. Regular school concerts and annual mus competition. Theory and aural classes, regular informal concerts.
Pupils: 98 day; 80 boarding; 125 studying inst. *Age range:* 7-13. *Termly fees:* £2275 (day), £3060 (boarding).

Dean Close Junior School (Co-ed)
Lansdown Rd, Cheltenham, Glos GL51 6QS
Tel: 01242 512217/258000 ext 616 (mus dept)
Fax: 01242 258005

S W Baird, head; P E Auster, dir of mus.
Awards: Exhibitions up to value 50% fees available (choral or inst). Aged 10-11 on 1 Sep; auditions Mar. 6 mus scholarships pa to secondary schools. *Musical activities:* 2 orchs, str groups, wind band, jazz band, chapel choir, jnr choir, 2nd choir and smaller inst groups. 20 peripatetic staff offer tuition on any inst.
Pupils: 211 day; 88 boarding; 136 studying inst. *Age range:* 3-13+. *Termly fees:* £1000 (pre-prep reception/yr 1), £1060 (pre-prep/yr 2), £1440 (day/form 3), £1590 (day/form 4), £2730 (wkly boarding/age 7-8 only), £2210 (day), £3235 (boarding).

The Downs School (Co-ed)
Colwall, Malvern, Worcs WR13 6EY
Tel: 01684 540277 *Fax:* 01684 540094

Jenni Griggs, head; Michael Castle, dir of mus.
Awards: Mus scholarships available. 2 pupils pa gain mus scholarships to secondary schools. *Musical activities:* Large purpose-built mus school and concert hall. Teaching in all orch insts plus acoustic and elec guis, sax, perc/drum-kit. Orch, 2 choirs, str, w/wind, handbells and rock/jazz ens. School performs major works including world premiere of *Simpkin & Tailor of Gloucester*, published by Penguin Books.
Pupils: 45 in jnr school (age 4-7.6); 100 in main school (age 7.6-13); 88 day; 57 boarding. In main school every pupil studies at least 1 inst. *Age range:* 3-13. *Termly fees:* £442-1945 (day), £2645 (boarding).

Dunhurst School (Bedales Junior School) (Co-ed)
Petersfield, Hants GU32 2DP
Tel: 01730 300200 *Fax:* 01730 300600

Michael Lucas, acting head; Melanie Fuller, dir of mus.
Awards: Scholarships of up to 50% fees from age 8. *Musical activities:* Jnr and snr choirs, orch; w/wind, br, rcdr, str and perc chmbr groups. Festivals, competitions, performances internally and externally. Also mus, dance and drama productions. Mus lessons and practice are built into school time-table.
Pupils: 101 day; 52 boarding; 134 studying inst. All proceed to snr school. *Age range:* Dunhurst 8-13; Dunannie (pre-prep) 3-8. *Termly fees:* £2120-2260 (day), £3099-3232 (boarding). *See also* **Independent Schools** Bedales School.

Eagle House School (Boys)
Sandhurst, Berks GU47 8PH
Tel: 01344 772134 *Fax:* 01344 779039

S J Carder, head; A D Grafton, dir of mus.
Awards: 1 mus scholarship pa value up to 50% fees. Age 10-11; approx gr 3-4 on 1 inst, with 2nd inst/voice taken into consideration. Award continued at Wellington College given satisfactory progress. *Musical activities:* Chmbr orch, str orch, perc ens, concert band, 2 w/wind ens, br group and 2 choirs.
Pupils: 190 day; 36 boarding; 108 studying inst; 1-2 pupils gaining mus scholarships pa. *Age range:* 4-13. *Termly fees:* £2280 (day), £3250 (boarding).

Forest Preparatory School (Co-ed)
College Pl, Nr Snaresbrook, London E17 3PY
Tel: 0181 520 1744 *Fax:* 0181 520 3656

M Lovett, head; M Palmer, dir of mus.
Awards: Mus scholarships available at age 11+. *Musical activities:* Choir, band and c/room mus. This includes free tuition for 1 yr on a str, br pr w/wind inst. Jnr School has long tradition of concerts, musical plays etc, and also shares in main school's musical activities.
Pupils: 209: 2 class entry, boys and girls taught separately. *Age range:* 7-13 (boys), 7-11 (girls). *Termly fees:* £1400 (7+ yrs), £1583 (8-10 yrs). *See also* **Independent Schools** Forest School.

Hereford Cathedral Junior School (Co-ed)
28 Castle St, Hereford HR1 2NJ
Tel: 01432 363511

Rebecca Shepherd, dir of mus; T Lowe, head.
Awards: 2 mus scholarships pa offering up to 2 mus insts plus fees. *Musical activities:* Choir, orch, str group, theory classes, rcdr group, keyboard, musicals and shows. Also joint activities with Hereford Cathedral School choristers and snr school. Annual house mus competition.
Pupils: 260. Also boarding house for choristers. *Age range:* 4-11. *Termly fees:* £860-1260.

Hill House International Junior School (Co-ed)
17 Hans Pl, London SW1X 0EP
Tel: 0171 589 5925 *also fax*

Col H Stuart Townend, head; Richard Townend, dir of mus.
Awards: Total of 18 choral scholarships tenable throughout school career, with 4-6 awards usually available pa. Scholarships usually awarded internally to pupils aged 8-11 but may be awarded at other ages. Scholars must be proficient on at least 1 inst. Several mus scholarships to secondary schools pa. Over 30 pupils gaining mus scholarships to secondary schools in recent yrs. *Musical activities:* 2 orchs, 6 choirs, chmbr mus groups, str quartets, gui and w/wind ens, br and rcdr consorts, 21 f/t mus staff and full use of local resources. Many mus activities including tuition on full range of insts and voice. Termly mus tour in Britain or Europe, annual performance of major works and regular concerts. ABRSM inst exams are not taken. Provides choir for Holy Trinity, Sloane Square.
Pupils: 1100 day; 500+ studying inst. *Age range:* 4-13.6. *Termly fees: Annual fees:* £3400-5300 (day/according to age).

King's School (Rochester) (Boys)
Satis House, Boley Hill, Rochester, Kent ME1 1TE
Tel: 01634 843913 *Fax:* 01634 832493
Email: kingsroc@rmplc.co.uk
Website: www.rmplc.co.uk/eduweb/sites/kingsroc/index.html

I R Walker, head; G R Williams, dir of mus.
Awards: From 11+, up to 5 mus scholarships offered, including 1 up to 100% fees (means tested above 50%). Gr 5-6 in main inst at 13+ with second inst required. Free inst tuition. Exam Feb. A number of choral scholarships worth 40% tuition fees. Age under 10, voice trials Nov and Feb.
Pupils: 245; 20 choristers. *Age range:* 8-13. *Termly fees:* £1889-2169 (day), £3354-3634 (boarding). Boarding from 8 yrs.

Orwell Park School (Co-ed)
Nacton, Ipswich, Suffolk IP10 0ER
Tel: 01473 659225 *Fax:* 01473 659822
Email: headmaster@orwellpark.demon.co.uk
Website: www.ukschools.com/schools/orwell/

Andrew Auster, head; Andrew Cronin, dir of mus.
Awards: Mus scholarships available on entry for ages 7-11. *Musical activities:* Choirs, orch, str and w/wind ens, jazz group.
Pupils: 200; 141 studying inst. *Age range:* 3-13. *Termly fees:* £890-3360.

Port Regis
Motcombe Park, Shaftesbury, Dorset SP7 9QA
Tel: 01747 852566 *Fax:* 01747 854684
Email: office@portregis.com

P A E Dix, head; Stephen Binnington, dir of mus.
Awards: Mus scholarships worth up to £6000 pa. Auditions held throughout year. *Musical activities:* Orch, 3 choirs, ens include str, w/wind and br. All children follow structured course in c/room mus; particularly talented children follow special programme of study. Regular musicals, plays, concerts, also occasional recording opportunities. Wide range of individual inst tuition available.
Pupils: 300. *Age range:* 7-13 (also nursery and pre-prep). *Termly fees:* £2865 (day), £3840 (boarding).

St Edward's Junior School

Sandfield Pk, Liverpool L12 1LF
Tel: 0151 281 2300 *Fax:* 0151 281 4900

Philip Sweeney, head; Brenda Bixter, dir of mus. *Awards:* 12 mus scholarships value from £250 pa. *Musical activities:* Orchs, choir, 3-4 concerts pa. Choir school for Metropolitan Cathedral. *Pupils:* 370 day. *Age range:* 3-11. *Termly fees:* £925-975. *See also* **Choir Schools: Independent and Maintained Secondary Schools** St Edward's College.

Summer Fields (Boys)

Oxford OX2 7EN
Tel: 01865 554433 *Fax:* 01865 510133

Robin Badham-Thornhill, head; David Langdon, dir of mus.
Awards: 1-3 mus scholarships (inst and choral) awarded annually at age 8; scholarship exam end of Jan. *Musical activities:* 2 orchs, wind band, chapel choir, probationers' choir, jnr choir; str, w/wind, br, perc, rcdr, gui, jazz groups, concerts, mus competitions and mus society events. *Pupils:* 15 day; 240 boarding; 170 studying inst. *Age range:* 8-13. *Termly fees:* £2370 (day), £3540 (boarding).

Taverham Hall (Co-ed)

Norwich, Norfolk NR8 6HU
Tel: 01603 868206 *Fax:* 01603 861061

W D Lawton, head; Chris Bell, dir of mus.
Awards: 1 mus scholarship available, value up to 25% fees. Age under 10.6 on 1 Sep; gr 2 distinction (approx), with special consideration to orch players. 1 mus exhibition of free tuition in 2 insts also offered. Singing an advantage. 2-3 mus scholarships to secondary schools pa. *Musical activities:* Chapel choir, orch, concert band, also br, w/wind bands, small ens. Staged musicals, plus annual combined choral concert with neighbouring independent school. Wide range of mus taught, and mus actively encouraged as a performing art.
Pupils: 136 day; 42 boarding; 62+ studying inst. *Age range:* 3-7 (pre-prep), 8-13 (prep). *Termly fees:* £1035-2295 (day), £2990 (boarding).

Tettenhall College (Coed)

Tettenhall, Wolverhampton, W Midlands WV6 8QX
Tel: 01902 751119/741627 *Fax:* 01902 747283/741940

P C Bodkin, head; I F Wass, dir of mus.
Awards: Mus scholarships up to 66% fees and bursaries of free inst tuition at all ages. All mus insts and voice considered. *Musical activities:* Chmbr choir, 2 jnr choirs, wind band, orch ens. Tuition available in all insts. Annual mus competition. Regular concerts in school and outside.
Pupils: 343 day and boarding; 134 lower school; 209 upper school; 100 studying inst. *Age range:* Pre-prep 3.5-7, main school 7-13. *Termly fees:* £1611 (day), £2681 (boarding). *See also* **Independent Schools**.

Westminster Under School (Boys)

Adrian House, 27 Vincent Sq, London SW1P 2NN
Tel: 0171 821 5788 *Fax:* 0171 821 0458

Gerry Ashton, head; Jeremy Walker, dir of mus; Steven Wray, asst dir of mus.
Awards: Mus scholarships of up to 50% fees with free inst tuition are offered annually for boys at age 10 and 11 (external/internal candidates welcome) who show outstanding potential; gr 4 on main inst, 2nd inst/voice preferred. Several mus awards to secondary schools pa. Choristerships are offered in connection with St Margaret's Church, Westminster Abbey for boys from age 8. Mus bursary fund exists to provide assistance with tuition fees in cases of nees. *Musical activities:* Jnr and snr choirs, chmbr choir, jnr and snr orchs, advanced str orch, jazz/wind band, gui ens, early mus group, perc ens, etc. Regular concerts and outside activities, inter-house mus competition, biennial choir tour (Italy in 1997, South Africa in 1999). Parents, boys and old boys concerts and joint activities in St John's Smith Square with Westminster School. Full range of inst tuition available, free group tuition for beginners in yr 4.
Pupils: 270 day; 200+ studying inst. *Age range:* 8-13. *Termly fees:* £2300. *See also* **Independent Schools** Westminster School.

Ashford
SCHOOL
A World of Difference

Ashford School's impressive record of achievement shows how traditional values and modern methods combine to provide every opportunity for bright girls to become successful women.

The broad curriculum, small class size and single sex environment encourage individual thinking and effective study, while personal expression through diverse leisure pursuits develops versatility and confidence. Over half of all our pupils study music, both instrumental and choral

Music Scholarships and Awards

Available to Year 4, Year 7, Year 8 and Year 9 students.

For further information, please contact
The Registrar
Ashford School, East Hill, Ashford
Kent. TN24 8PB
Telephone 01233 625171

Ashford School is a Charity, No 307848, which exists
for educational purposes

Independent Schools Offering Music Scholarships

All the schools listed below offer music scholarships on the basis of musical ability. Most schools expect all children to sit a common entrance exam before a place is awarded. A cross (+) indicates that girls are accepted in the VI form of a boys' school. Schools with similar names are also given a location in brackets to avoid confusion. Although the Government's Assisted Places Scheme has been discontinued, some schools still offer some form of assisted places. Applicants are advised to enquire at the school of their choice for further information.

The majority of independent schools have signed the agreement of the *Headmasters Conference* (further details from 130 Regent Rd, Leicester LE1 7PG *Tel:* 0116 247 1167, David Prince, membership secretary) on a ceiling for entrance scholarships. The salient points are listed below:
(i) The ceiling of 50% of the advertised fees shall apply to entrance scholarships at 13 whether academic, art or music.
(ii) Any augmentation of an award above 50% shall be by means of a bursary. Such bursaries shall be awarded only after completion of a statement of parental income showing that the parents' means lie within the limits which the school would normally regard as making the applicant eligible for a bursary. The schools policy on the award of bursaries shall be contained in a short statement, available on request.

Abbots Bromley (School of S Mary and S Anne) (Girls)
Abbots Bromley, Staffs WS15 3BW
Tel: 01283 840232 *Fax:* 01283 840988
Email: 106342.440@compuserve.com

A J Grigg, head; Alison Evans, dir of mus.
Awards: 1 or more mus awards of up to 66% fees may be awarded for outstanding mus merit supported by academic ability shown in entrance exams. Age 10-14; gr 5 min on 1st inst, with 2nd inst. Mus awards only available exceptionally before age 10. Also awards available at VI form level. *Exam boards:* MEG (GCSE); Edexcel (A-level). *Exam candidates:* GCSE 10; A-level 6.
Musical activities: Snr and intermediate orchs; snr and jnr choirs, fl choir, rcdr group, pop group, choral society, mus productions. National and other competitions entered. Prep school for age 5-11, enjoying same mus facilities as main school. *Pupils:* 136 day; 144 boarding; 185 studying inst. *Termly fees:* £2595 (day/snr), £3885 (boarding/snr), £1625 (day/jnr), £3292 (boarding/jnr).

Abbotsholme School (Co-ed)
Rocester, Uttoxeter, Staffs ST14 5BS
Tel: 01889 590217 *Fax:* 01889 591001
Email: 100721.1173@compuserve.com

Timothy Moon, dir of mus.
Awards: At least one major mus scholarship (up to 50% fees) at age 11 and 13, plus minor awards and discretionary mus bursaries. Similar awards for VI form entrants. *Exam boards:* MEG, Oxford (GCSE and A-level). *Exam candidates:* GCSE 8; A-level 2.
Musical activities: Choral society, orch, wind bands, perc ens, str quartets and other smaller groups. Well-equipped recording studio. Arts society present series of concerts by world-class musicians.
Pupils: 78 day; 125 boarding; 103 studying inst. *Termly fees:* £2025-2785 (day), £4175-4337 (boarding).

Abingdon School (Boys)
Abingdon, Oxon OX14 1DE
Tel: 01235 521563 *Fax:* 01235 536449

M St John Parker, head; Michael Stinton, dir of mus.
Awards: Up to 3 means-tested scholarships (up to 50% fees) usually at age 13, and several exhibitions at age 11 or above. Gr 5 min on 1st inst with proficiency on 2nd inst. Small number of Foundation Places available. *Exam boards:* MEG (GCSE); UCLES (A-level). *Exam candidates:* GCSE 23; A-level 7.
Musical activities: Strong mus dept with choral society, chmbr choir, school choir, 3 orchs, snr wind, cl, sax, fl ens, 3 wind and br bands, big band, jazz ens, extensive str programme, chmbr mus.
Pupils: 780 day and boarding; 420 studying inst. *Termly fees:* £1982 (day), £3654 (boarding).

Ackworth School (Co-ed)

Ackworth, Pontefract, W Yorks WF7 7LT
Tel: 01977 611401 *Fax:* 01977 616225
Email: 100021.3420@compuserve.com
Website: www.ackworth.w-yorks.sch.uk

Martin Dickinson, head; Richard Ellis, dir of mus.
Awards: Several mus scholarships may be awarded, up to 50% of boarding or day fees; no age limit; awarded according to musical promise. *Exam boards:* NEAB (GCSE and A-level). *Exam candidates:* GCSE 9; A-level 2.
Musical activities: Snr and jnr choirs, snr and jnr orchs, jazz group, chmbr choir, chmbr mus groups, inter-house mus competitions, jazz and concert bands, br groups and numerous musical outings. Mus is housed in Music Centre opened 1994.
Pupils: 290 day; 110 boarding; 150 studying inst.
Termly fees: £1935 (day), £3400 (boarding).

Aldenham School (Boys)+

Elstree, Herts WD6 3AJ
Tel: 01923 858122 *Fax:* 01923 854410
Email: market@aldenhamschool.demon.co.uk

S R Borthwick, head; G J Barker, J Wyatt, dirs of mus.
Awards: Mus scholarships value up to 50% of fees. Special org scholarships available. *Exam boards:* Edexcel (GCSE and A-level). *Exam candidates:* GCSE 9; A-level 2.
Musical activities: School orch, regular concerts, concert visits, chapel choir, br ens, wind band, str quartet, mus technology.
Pupils: 250 day; 110 boarding; 90 studying inst.
Termly fees: £1821 (day/11+), £2865-3395 (day/13+), £4160 (boarding).

Alleyn's School (Co-ed)

Townley Rd, Dulwich, London SE22 8SU
Tel: 0181 693 3422 *Fax:* 0181 299 3671

C H R Niven, head; A T Kermode, dir of mus.
Awards: Mus scholarship value 50%. A number of exhibitions for free inst tuition will also be awarded. Age 11-13 entry; gr 5-6 min on principal inst, with 2nd inst normally expected; orch insts preferred. VI form bursaries available for mus. *Exam boards:* Edexcel (GCSE and A-level). *Exam candidates:* GCSE 20; A-level 6; AS-level 6.
Musical activities: 4 orchs, 2 wind bands, jazz band, br ens and over 30 chmbr groups. Snr, jnr and chmbr choirs. Numerous concerts, both formal and informal (1 at major venue).
Pupils: 930 day; 400 studying inst. *Termly fees:* £2085 (day).

Allhallows College (Co-ed)

Rousdon, Nr Lyme Regis, Dorset DT7 3RA
Tel: 01297 626110 *Fax:* 01297 626114

K R Moore, headmaster; Mrs M L Banting, dir of mus.
Awards: Mus scholarships and all-rounder awards. VI form scholarships also available. *Exam boards:* SEG, Edexcel. *Exam candidates:* 11.
Musical activities: Snr, jnr and special choirs. Str, wind, br, recorder, gui and chmbr ens. Orch and jazz w/shops.
Pupils: 160 day and boarding; 50 studying inst.
Termly fees: £1395-875 (day), £3125 (wkly boarding), £3550 (boarding).

Ampleforth College (Boys)

York YO6 4ER
Tel: 01439 788000 *Fax:* 01439 788330

Rev G F L Chamberlain, head; Ian Little, dir of mus.
Awards: Choral and inst scholarships at ages 13 (gr 5) and 16 (gr 8). 2 insts must be offered (can include voice). Potential will be considered alongside attainment. *Exam boards:* MEG (GCSE); Edexcel (A-level). *Exam candidates:* GCSE 3; A-level 3.
Musical activities: Schola Cantorum (international tours, recordings, broadcasts), symphony orch, wind and str orchs, chmbr ens; regular concert series.
Pupils: 508 day and boarding; 214 studying inst.
Termly fees: £2160 (day/snr school), £4185 (boarding).

Ardingly College (Co-ed)

Haywards Heath, W Sussex RH17 6SQ
Tel: 01444 892577 *Fax:* 01444 892266

J W Flecker, head; Robert Hammersley, dir of mus.
Awards: Up to 10 mus awards available (6 worth up to 50% fees), with free tuition in 2 insts (2 reserved for str players; 2 for ex-cathedral choristers; 2 open to players of any inst). 2 choral scholarships available pa up to value of 50%. Own jnr school at same address (7-13) with up to 4 mus awards (2 worth up to 50% and 2 may be choristerships). *Exam boards:* MEG (GCSE); London (A/AS-level); Edexcel (Practical A-level). *Exam candidates:* GCSE 8; A-level 4.
Musical activities: Orch, str orch, concert band, big band; br ens, cl ens, other chmbr mus; also chapel choir (has toured abroad, sings in cathedrals), chmbr choir and choral society. Jazz singers and jazz band.
Pupils: 460 day and boarding (snr school); 149 (jnr school); 45 (pre-prep); 200+ studying inst (snr school); 100+ studying inst (jnr school).
Termly fees: £1560-3310 (day), £2950-4270 (boarding).

Ashford School (Girls)

East Hill, Ashford, Kent TN24 8PB
Tel: 01233 625171 *Fax:* 01233 647185

Mrs J Burnett, head; J Fehr, dir of mus.
Awards: 1 scholarship at age 11 (gr 4-5) 50% of day fees, or more of less value. *Exam boards:* Edexcel (GCSE and A-level). *Exam candidates:* GCSE 10.
Musical activities: 2 orchs, str orch, band, 3 choirs, rcdr ens, 2 str quartets, chmbr mus. Musical production and oratorio each yr.
Pupils: 518 day and boarding; 250 studying inst. Ashford Junior School (age 3-11) at same address. *Termly fees:* £367-2334 (day), £3493-4056 (boarding).

Badminton School (Girls)

Westbury on Trym, Bristol BS9 3BA
Tel: 0117 905 5200 *Fax:* 0117 962 8963
Email: badminton.office@dial.pipex.com

Mrs J Scarrow, head; C Francis, dir of mus.
Awards: Mus scholarships available. *Exam boards:* MEG (GCSE); NEAB (A-level). *Exam candidates:* GCSE 6; A-level 4.
Musical activities: Mus school including Badminton Suzuki Group, 3 orchs, 4 choirs, numerous ens; also joint choral concerts with other schools; public concerts and tours abroad.
Pupils: 120 day; 230 boarding; 290 studying inst. *Termly fees:* £1050-1450 (day/jnr), £2200 (day/snr), £2850 (boarding/jnr), £3950 (boarding/snr).

Bancroft's School (Co-ed)

Woodford Green, Essex IG8 0RF
Tel: 0181 505 4821 *Fax:* 0181 559 0032
Email: staff@bancrofts.netkonect.co.uk

P R Scott, head; R M Bluff, dir of mus.
Awards: 2 mus scholarships offering part remission of fees may be awarded at age 11. *Exam boards:* Edexcel (GCSE and A-level). *Exam candidates:* GCSE 15; A-level 5.
Musical activities: 2 orchs, 4 choirs, inst ens, swing band, 2 wind bands.
Pupils: 975 day; 382 studying inst. *Termly fees:* £1613 (day/prep), £2128 (day/snr).

Barnard Castle School (Co-ed)

Barnard Castle, Co Durham DL12 8UN
Tel: 01833 690222 *Fax:* 01833 638985
Email: barnyscl@rmplc.co.uk
Website: www.bacaschl

M D Featherstone, head; Paul Harrison, dir of mus.
Awards: Inst, choral and org scholarships up to a value of 50% fees and free inst tuition are offered at 11+, 13+ and 16+. *Exam boards:* SEG (GCSE); Edexcel (A-level). *Exam candidates:* GCSE 14; A-level 4.

Musical activities: Chapel choir, chmbr choir, 2 orchs, choral society, concert band, wind, str and perc ens, jazz band. Annual singing competition, inst festival and staged mus production; major choral concert and numerous concerts and recitals. Annual overseas tours. Chapel choir sings regular cathedral evensongs.
Pupils: 357 day; 164 boarding; 180 studying inst.
Termly fees: £1870 (day), £3159 (boarding).

Bearwood College (Co-ed)

Wokingham, Berks RG41 5BG
Tel: 0118 978 6915 *Fax:* 0118 977 3186

R J Belcher, head; A R I Cummings, dir of mus.
Awards: Choral, org, pno and inst, value up to 50% fees; age approx 11-16+. *Exam boards:* MEG (GCSE); Edexcel (A-level). *Exam candidates:* GCSE 13; A-level 2.
Musical activities: Chapel choir, str ens, dance and dixie bands, jnr band, br ens; 2 concerts per term.
Pupils: 117 day; 105 boarding; 60 studying inst.
Termly fees: £1868-2075 (day), £3330-3700 (boarding).

Bedales School (Co-ed)

Church Rd, Steep, Petersfield, Hants GU32 2DG
Tel: 01730 300100 *Fax:* 01730 300500
Email: registr@bedales.org.uk

Alison Willcocks, head; Nicholas Gleed, dir of mus.
Awards: Offered at age 10+, 13+ and VI form (occasionally other ages). All insts considered equally; gr 8 required for VI form candidates, with potential and enthusiasm more important than formal qualifications at other levels. *Exam boards:* MEG (GCSE); Edexcel (A-level). *Exam candidates:* GCSE 12; A-level 4.
Musical activities: 3 orchs, 2 choirs, chmbr groups, ens, concert bands and regular performance opportunities. All musical styles encouraged.
Pupils: 420 boarding; 225 studying inst. Prep schools are Dunannie (pre-prep 3.6-8) and Dunhurst (8-13) at above address. *Termly fees:* £3617 (day), £4776 (boarding).

Bedford School (Boys)

De Parys Av, Bedford MK40 2TU
Tel: 01234 353436

I P Evans, head; Andrew Morris, dir of mus.
Awards: Major awards of max value 50% fees with free inst tuition; also several exhibitions of free tuition in 2 insts. Age 13+; gr 6 on 1st inst. *Exam boards:* MEG (GCSE); O&C (A-level). *Exam candidates:* GCSE 12; A-level 4.
Musical activities: 3 orchs, 3 bands, choral society, chapel choir; also str quartets, chmbr ens and mus club. Also a prep school, with 3

orchs, choirs, rcdr groups and inst tuition. *Pupils:* 1120 day and boarding; 500 studying inst. *Termly fees:* £2335 (day), £3715 (boarding).

Bedgebury School (Girls)
Bedgebury Pk, Goudhurst, Cranbrook, Kent TN17 2SH
Tel: 01580 211954 *Fax:* 01580 212252
Email: info@bedgebury.ndirect.co.uk
Website: www.bedgebury.ndirect.co.uk

Mrs L J Griffin, head; Bryan Gipps, dir of mus.
Awards: Mus scholarships and bursaries available at ages 7+, 11+, 13+, and 16+. *Exam boards:* SEG (GCSE); WJEC (A/AS-level). *Exam candidates:* GCSE 7; A-level 2.
Musical activities: 3 choirs, 2 orchs, wind band, regular concerts and recitals. Annual major choral and stage productions.
Pupils: 374 day and boarding; 250 studying inst and singing each week. *Termly fees:* £2483 (day), £3998 (boarding).

Bedstone College (Co-ed)
Bucknell, Shropshire SY7 0BG
Tel: 01547 530303 *Fax:* 01547 530740

Michael Symonds, head.
Awards: Choral scholarship worth up to 50% of fees and choral exhibitions worth up to 20% of fees at age 13+. Inst scholarship worth up to 50% fees and inst exhibitions worth up to 20% fees at age 14. *Exam boards:* MEG (GCSE); UCLES (A-level). *Exam candidates:* GCSE 2; A-level 1.
Musical activities: Chapel choir, choral society, orch, str group, regular concerts and musical productions.
Pupils: 23 day; 162 boarding; 60 studying inst. *Termly fees:* £1445 (day/prep), £2002 (day/snr), £2370 (boarding/prep), £3500 (boarding/snr).

Benenden School (Girls)
Cranbrook, Kent TN17 4AA
Tel: 01580 240592 *Fax:* 01580 240280
Email: schooloffice@benenden.kent.sch.uk

Mrs G duCharme, head; Patricia M Gane, dir of mus.
Awards: Annual mus scholarships, tenable throughout school career and VI form scholarships. *Exam boards:* SEG (GCSE); Edexcel (A-level). *Exam candidates:* GCSE 6; A/AS-level 1.
Musical activities: 3 choirs, orch, youth symphony orch, inst ens, big band, recording studio, orch and choral concerts, subscription concerts and specialist w/shops.
Pupils: 456 boarding; c 300 studying inst. *Termly fees:* £4735 (boarding).

Berkhamsted Collegiate School (Boys)+
Castle Campus, Castle St, Berkhamsted, Herts HP4 2BB
Tel: 01442 863236 *Fax:* 01442 877657

Christopher McDade, dir of mus.
Awards: Mus scholarships and exhibitions at 13+.
VI form mus scholarship (Beechwood Trust).
Exam boards: Edexcel (GCSE); NEAB (A and
A/S-level). *Exam candidates:* GCSE 11; A-Level 8.
Musical activities: Prep school: choir, orch, jnr br
ens, jnr str group. Senior school: sinfonietta, big
band, chmbr choir, br ens, early mus group, wind
band, str orch. Summer mus school and overseas
tour. *Termly fees:* £1353-1736 (day/prep),
£2178-2561 (day/jnr/snr), £2561 (day/VI Form),
£3657-3699 (boarding/jnr), £3937-4127
(boarding/snr), £4127 (boarding/VI Form).
Preparatory school (age 3-11) is fully
co-educational, as is the VI Form. The school is
single-sex from age 11-16 with girls being taught at
the campus below. The VI form is fully co-educational.

Berkhamsted Collegiate School (Girls)
Kings Campus, Kings Rd, Berkhamsted, Herts HP4 3BG
Tel: 01442 862168 *Fax:* 01442 876732

Christopher McDade, dir of mus.
Awards: For details of awards, musical activities
and fees, see Berkhamsted Collegiate School
(Boys) above. The teaching of girls aged 11-16 is
carried out at the Kings Campus. In the VI form,
the Boys' and Girls' colleges amalgamate and are
fully co-educational.

Bethany School (Co-ed)
Goudhurst, Cranbrook, Kent TN17 1LB
Tel: 01580 211273 *Fax:* 01580 211151

N D B Dorey, head; W Faram, dir of mus.
Awards: Scholarship value up to 40% fees and
tuition in 2 insts; scholarships value up to 10-20%
fees and tuition in 1-2 insts. *Exam boards:* SEG
(GCSE); UCLES (A-level). *Exam candidates:* 10.
Musical activities: Chapel choir, orch, choral
society, br ens, w/wind group, str group, rcdr
ens, jazz group and gui ens.
Pupils: 160 day; 126 boarding; 100 studying inst.
Termly fees: £2230 (day), £3486 (boarding).

Birkdale School (Boys)+
Oakholme Rd, Sheffield S10 2DH
Tel: 0114 266 8408 *Fax:* 0114 267 1947

Revd M D A Hepworth, head; Andrew Sanderson,
dir of mus.
Awards: 2 mus scholarships pa at 11+ and VI form
worth up to 25% of tuition fees. Additional
bursaries available on proof of need. *Exam
boards:* Edexcel. *Exam candidates:* GCSE 8; A-level 3.
Musical activities: Choir, 2 orchs, wind band, jazz
band, br group, early mus group, str group, str

quartets, rock bands, mus drama and major
concerts every term. Prep school: choir, chmbr
choir, wind band, str group, rcdr group.
Pupils: 830 day; 100+ studying inst. *Termly fees:*
£1127 (pre-prep), £1333 (prep), £1599 (snr).

Bishop's Stortford College (Co-ed)
Bishop's Stortford, Herts CM23 2PJ
Tel: 01279 838575 *Fax:* 01279 836570

J G Trotman, head.
Awards: 4 mus scholarships to a max value of
50% fees (possible additional bursaries) offered
at under 10, under 14 and in the VI form. *Exam
boards:* MEG (GCSE); UCLES (A-level). *Exam
candidates:* GCSE 8; A-level 4.
Musical activities: Orch, choral society, chapel
choir, chmbr choir, wind band, dance band.
Pupils: 220 day; 120 boarding. Prep school is
Bishop's Stortford College Junior School and
Pre-preparatory Department (age 4-6) *Tel:* 01279
838607 (same campus). *Termly fees:* £1300 (pre-prep),
£2230-2790 (day), £2840-3870 (boarding).

Bloxham School (Co-ed)+
Banbury, Oxon OX15 4PE
Tel: 01295 720222 *Fax:* 01295 721897

David K Exham, head; Christopher Fletcher-Campbell,
dir of mus.
Awards: Mus scholarships of up to 50% fees plus
free inst tuition. Bursaries also available. Age 11,
13 or 16 on 1 Sep. *Exam boards:* Edexcel (GCSE
and A-level). *Exam candidates:* GCSE 5; A-level 3.
Musical activities: Centrally located mus school,
orch, wind, br and str ens, swing band, choir,
annual choral event and/or musical, annual house
songs competition (whole school), concerts,
concert visits, mus society, mus computer.
Pupils: 350 mainly boarding; 100 studying inst.
Termly fees: £2330-3495 (day), £4460 (boarding).

Blundell's School (Co-ed)
Tiverton, Devon EX16 4DN
Tel: 01884 252543 *Fax:* 01884 243232
Email: blundadmin@aol.com

J Leigh, head; A H Barlow, dir of mus.
Awards: Value up to 50% fees plus free inst
tuition. *Exam boards:* SEG (GCSE); Edexcel
(A-level). *Exam candidates:* GCSE 12; A-level 6.
Musical activities: Choir, choral society, orchs,
mus club, military band, jazz band, jnr jazz band,
br ens, chmbr groups, jnr band, chmbr choir, jnr
choir and swing band. Regular tours abroad.
Pupils: 150 day; 312 boarding; 250 studying inst.
Termly fees: £1500-2595 (day), £2825-4250 (boarding).

Bootham School (Co-ed)
York YO3 7BU
Tel: 01904 623261 *Fax:* 01904 652106

Ian M Small, head; Alasdair Jamieson, dir of mus.
Awards: Entry scholarships of up to 50% fees. First term tuition free for new orch inst. Prizes awarded, some bursary help. *Exam boards:* SEG (GCSE); Edexcel (A-level). *Exam candidates:* GCSE 19; A-level 11.
Musical activities: Swing band, orch, str orch, wind band, 2 fl choirs, br and cl groups, 4 choirs, rock and jazz groups (some joint activities with The Mount sister school).
Pupils: 380; 109 boarding; 173 studying inst.
Termly fees: £2385 (day), £3665 (boarding).

Bradfield College (Boys) +
Reading, Berks RG7 6AU
Tel: 0118 974 4203 *Fax:* 0118 974 4195

P B Smith, head; M R Harding, dir of mus.
Awards: Up to 4 mus scholarships of between 20-50% full fees plus free tuition on up to 3 insts. Scholarships of free tuition on 2 insts. Candidates must be aged over 12 and under 14 on 1 Sep. *Exam boards:* Edexcel (GCSE); UCLES (A/AS-level). *Exam candidates:* GCSE 10; A-level 4.
Musical activities: Chapel choir, orch, concert and swing bands, str orch, chmbr mus, choral society, concert club, jazz bands, chmbr choir, lunchtime recitals, rock, jazz and country bands, str orch, VI form girls' choir, organ recitals and annual staged musicals. Major concerts termly; Easter holiday choir tour abroad. 3 orgs, new Steinway, computer mus studio, 1500 seat open-air theatre.
Pupils: 603 day and boarding; 302 studying inst.
Termly fees: £4075.

Brentwood School (Co-ed)
Ingrave Rd, Brentwood, Essex CM15 8AS
Tel: 01277 212271 *Fax:* 01277 262218

J A B Kelsall, head; David Pickthall, dir of mus.
Awards: A number of mus scholarships annually, value up to 50% fees plus free tuition in 2 insts. Age under 14 on 1 Sep. *Exam boards:* MEG (GCSE); Oxford (A-level). *Exam candidates:* GCSE 26; A-level 16.
Musical activities: Orchs, big band, chapel choir, choral society; br, gui, str ens; major concerts and recitals each term, house mus competition annually. Regular recordings.
Pupils: 1087 day; 68 boarding; 300 studying inst.
Termly fees: £2162 (day), £3760 (boarding).

Brighton College (Co-ed)
Eastern Rd, Brighton BN2 2AL
Tel: 01273 704202 *Fax:* 01273 704204
Email: admissions@brightoncollege.demon.co.uk

A F Seldon, head; C G Sandercock, dir of mus.
Awards: Several scholarships up to 50% fees which can be increased in the case of need by bursaries, plus free tuition in 2 insts available. William Stewart Scholarship could be as high as 50% fees and several other awards open for competition in Feb. Age under 14 on 1 Jun. Candidates should be proficient on 2 insts (or 1 inst and voice). Musical potential and lively interest will be given due recognition. VI form entry scholarships also offered. *Exam boards:* Edexcel (GCSE and A-level). *Exam candidates:* GCSE 9; A-level 2.
Musical activities: Choir, orch, choral society, concert band, br ens, chmbr mus groups, etc; mus lab with computers and synthesizer.
Pupils: 475; 140 studying inst. *Termly fees:* £2920 (day), £3975 (wkly boarding), £4525 (boarding).

Bristol Cathedral School (Boys) +
College Sq, Bristol BS1 5TS
Tel: 0117 929 1872 *Fax:* 0117 930 4219

K J Riley, head; S D Holt, dir of mus.
Awards: 5 mus scholarships value up to 50% fees awarded (2 at 11+, 1 at 13+, 2 at 16+); plus 2 awards of means-tested tuition in 2 insts (age 11+). 5 choral scholarships value up to £1400 for cathedral choristers, age 10+. *Exam boards:* MEG (GCSE); UCLES (A-level). *Exam candidates:* GCSE 21; A-level 10.
Musical activities: School choir, 1st and 2nd orchs, chmbr orch, wind, br groups and choral society.
Pupils: 470 day; 230 studying inst. *Termly fees:* £1347 (day).

Bristol Grammar School (Co-ed)
University Rd, Bristol BS8 1SR
Tel: 0117 973 6006 *Fax:* 0117 946 7485

C E Martin, head; J Gadsden, dir of mus.
Awards: Up to 6 mus scholarships with free tuition in 1 or more insts. Age 11, 13 or 16. *Exam boards:* NEAB (GCSE and A-level). *Exam candidates:* GCSE 10-12; A-level 2-3.
Musical activities: Choirs, orchs, bands, chmbr groups.
Pupils: 1042 day; 200 studying inst. *Termly fees:* £1431.

British School of Brussels (Co-ed)
Leuvensesteenweg 19, B-3080 Tervuren, Belgium
Tel: 00 32 2 766 0430 *Fax:* 00 32 2 767 8070

Jennifer Bray, principal; David Iliff, dir of mus.
Awards: Annual mus scholarships up to the value

of BF 59,000 pa. *Exam boards:* MEG (GCSE); UCLES, Edexcel (A-level).
Musical activities: Active mus dept; orchs and choirs perform regularly.
Pupils: 950 day; 400+ studying inst. Age range 3-18. *Termly fees: Annual fees:* BF 638,000; BF 677,000 (VI form).

Bromsgrove School (Co-ed)
Worcester Rd, Bromsgrove, Worcs B61 7DU
Tel: 01527 579679 *Fax:* 01527 576177

T M Taylor, head; A E Bird, dir of mus.
Awards: A number of awards, value up to 50% fees, with free tuition. May be supplemented in cases of need. Any inst or voice. Entry at 7+, 11+, 13+ and 16+. *Exam boards:* MEG (GCSE); Edexcel (A-level). *Exam candidates:* GCSE 10; A-level 3.
Musical activities: Orch, concert band, big band, jazz, rock and pop bands, chapel choir, close harmony group, choral society, biennial opera or musical, chmbr ens, keyboard lab, mus computers. Biennial tours (1996: Salzburg, Venice, Lucerne).
Pupils: 1130 day and boarding (in upper and lower schools); 400 studying inst. *Termly fees:* £1560-2240 (day), £2745-3575 (boarding).

Bryanston School (Co-ed)
Blandford, Dorset DT11 0PO
Tel: 01258 452411 *Fax:* 01258 484661
Email: headmaster@bryanston.co.uk
Website: www.brysch.demon.co.uk

T D Wheare, head; P A Lattimer, dir of mus.
Awards: 4 jnr mus scholarships, 2 snr mus scholarships, value up to 50% which may be supplemented with a means-tested bursary. Age under 14 on 1 Sept or VI form entry. *Exam boards:* MEG (GCSE); UCLES (A-level). *Exam candidates:* GCSE 16; A-level 7.
Musical activities: Orchs, choirs, bands; operettas, professional and amateur concerts.
Pupils: 86 day; 540 boarding. 600+ mus lessons taught weekly. *Termly fees:* £4765 (boarding).

Burgess Hill School (Girls)
Keymer Rd, Burgess Hill, W Sussex RH15 0EG
Tel: 01444 241050 *Fax:* 01444 870314
Email: staffnet@rmplc.co.uk

Rosemary Lewis, head; C R B Haslam, dir of mus.
Awards: Scholarships offered, value up to 50% fees. Age 7+, 8+, 11+, 12+, 13+ and 16+. Reasonable degree of inst proficiency required; 2 insts expected (preferably pno plus orch inst). *Exam boards:* SEG (GCSE); Edexcel (A-level); AS-levels also offered. *Exam candidates:* GCSE 10;

A-level 4.
Musical activities: 2 orchs, 2 choirs, rcdr groups, chmbr mus and jazz ens. Concerts and trips, concert visits organised, m/classes. Jnr school attached (age 5+) with orch, wind band, rcdr groups, choir.
Pupils: 600 day and boarding; 200 studying inst.
Termly fees: £930-1995 (day), £3375 (boarding).

Campbell College (Boys)
Belmont Rd, Belfast BT4 2ND
Tel: 01232 763076 *Fax:* 01232 761894

R J I Pollock, head; M McGuffin, dir of mus.
Awards: 1 scholarship of £200, 2 exhibitions of £100, all with free inst tuition. Age under 14 on 1 Jun, gr 5 min on at least 1 inst. *Exam boards:* NICCEA (GCSE and A-level). *Exam candidates:* GCSE 12; A-level 2; AS-level 2.
Musical activities: Choral singing, regular concerts.
Pupils: 690 day; 55 boarding; 45 studying inst.
Termly fees: Annual fees: £894-1044 (day), £5559 (boarding).

Canford School (Co-ed)
Canford Magna, Wimborne, Dorset BH21 3AD
Tel: 01202 841254 *Fax:* 01202 881009

J D Lever, head; D A Warwick, dir of mus.
Awards: Up to 4 scholarships of between 10-50% fees, each with free tuition in 2 insts. Age under 14 on 1 Sep; awarded on musical potential. Some VI form scholarships of up to 50%. Scholarships may be supplemented in cases of need. *Exam boards:* London (GCSE); Edexcel (A-level). *Exam candidates:* GCSE 8; A-level 5.
Musical activities: 1st orch, str orch, jnr strs, concert band, jazz band, wind and br ens. Also chapel choir, choral society and mus society with recitals and concert visits.
Pupils: 193 day; 369 boarding; 225 studying inst.
Termly fees: £3360 (day), £4475 (boarding).

Carmel College (Co-ed)
Mongewell Pk, Wallingford, Oxon OX10 8BT
Tel: 01491 837505 *Fax:* 01491 825305

Philip Skelker, head; Ian Jacobs, dir of mus.
Awards: Scholarships and exhibitions available. Age 10+ or VI form entry (boarding candidates must be Jewish). *Exam boards:* MEG (GCSE); Edexcel (A-level). *Exam candidates:* GCSE 10; A-level 2.
Musical activities: Ens, orch, choir, musical productions, light opera and concerts.
Pupils: 191 boarding; 9 day; 98 studying inst.
Termly fees: £2460 (day), £3000-4355 (boarding/UK), £4000-5880 (boarding/overseas).

Casterton School (Girls)
Kirkby Lonsdale, Carnforth, Lancs LA6 2SG
Tel: 01524 279200 *Fax:* 01524 279208

A F Thomas, head; D C Chapman, dir of mus.
Awards: Mus scholarships and bursaries offered up to value of fees in 2 insts plus some of academic fees subject to satisfying general entrance requirements. *Exam boards:* NEAB (GCSE and A-level). *Exam candidates:* GCSE 4-5; A-level 2-3.
Musical activities: Chmbr orch, snr orch and choir, madrigal group, training orch and jnr choir, choral society, wind band and other inst ens.
Pupils: 111 day; 238 boarding; 204 studying inst.
Termly fees: £1980-2280 (day), £2869-3585 (boarding).

Caterham School (Co-ed)
Harestone Valley, Caterham, Surrey CR3 6YA
Tel: 01883 343028 *Fax:* 01883 347795
Website: www.rmplc.co.uk/eduweb/sites/caterham/index.html

R A E Davey, head; Adrian Goss, dir of mus.
Awards: Scholarships with free tuition in 2 insts. Age under 14 on 1 Sep; additional VI form mus scholarship may also be considered. *Exam boards:* Edexcel (GCSE and A-level). *Exam candidates:* GCSE 12; A-level 5.
Musical activities: Orchs, choirs, barbershop group, concert bands, chmbr groups, jazz groups. Annual summer residential 1-wk mus course, residential chmbr w/end; also concert tours, and annual mus competition and singing prizes. Mus and dramatic productions performed.
Pupils: 550 day; 150 boarding; 290 studying inst.
Termly fees: £1932 (day), £3532-3732 (boarding).

Charterhouse (Boys) +
Godalming, Surrey GU7 2DX
Tel: 01483 291695/6 *Fax:* 01483 291637

Revd John Witheridge, head; Robin Wells, dir of mus.
Awards: At least 5 mus scholarships offered; value of scholarships and supplementary bursaries from £1500 to full fees. Age under 14 on 1 Jul; gr 6 (pno) or gr 5 other insts. For age 16 entry, at least 4 mus scholarships offered. *Exam boards:* MEG (GCSE); UCLES (A-level). *Exam candidates:* GCSE 8; A-level 6.
Musical activities: 2 orchs, str orch, concert band, chapel choir, chmbr choir, choral society, male voice group; wind, str, chmbr mus societies; various ens classes. A strong mus dept with composer in residence.
Pupils: 700 day and boarding. *Termly fees: Annual fees:* £3840 (day), £4647 (boarding).

Cheadle Hulme School (Co-ed)

Claremont Rd, Cheadle Hulme, Cheadle, Cheshire SK8 6EF
Tel: 0161 488 3330 *Fax:* 0161 488 3344

Donald Wilkinson, head; Michael Fletcher, dir of mus.
Awards: VI form mus bursaries; free str tuition for pupils aged 7-9 yrs. *Exam boards:* MEG, NEAB. *Exam candidates:* GCSE 10; A-level 4.
Musical activities: 3 orchs, 5 choirs, 2 wind bands, str groups, fl groups and additional ens. Regular snr choir exchange to Butzbach, Germany.
Pupils: 1150 day; 302 studying inst; 173 jnr dept (from 7+). *Termly fees:* £1091 (day/jnr), £1362 (day/snr).

Cheltenham College (Co-ed) +

Bath Rd, Cheltenham, Glos GL53 7LD
Tel: 01242 513540 *Fax:* 01242 265630
Email: college@cheltcoll.gloucs.sch.uk
Website: www.cheltcoll.gloucs.sch.uk

P A Chamberlain, head; G S Busbridge, dir of mus.
Awards: Various scholarships and exhibitions value up to 50% fees plus free inst tuition available. *Exam boards:* MEG (GCSE); Edexcel (A-level). *Exam candidates:* GCSE 14; A-level 4.
Musical activities: Chapel choir, madrigal group, choral society, orch, wind band, big band, str, orch, training orchs, numerous inst ens, jazz improvisation group and rock bands. Joint mus activities with Cheltenham Ladies' College.
Pupils: 543 day and boarding, 231 studying inst.
Termly fees: £3325 (day), £4400 (boarding).

The Cheltenham Ladies' College (Girls)

Bayshill Rd, Cheltenham, Glos GL50 3EP
Tel: 01242 520691 *Fax:* 01242 227882

Mrs V Tuck, head; A Lowen, dir of mus.
Awards: 2 major awards offered (1 jnr, 1 VI form) with additional awards according to merit, all carrying free inst tuition, in addition to the general fees concession. *Exam boards:* SEG (GCSE); Edexcel (A-level). *Exam candidates:* GCSE 12; A-level 4.
Musical activities: 2 orchs, 2 str orchs, 5 choirs (including madrigal choir), jnr wind band, 3 fl choirs, jazz band, rock groups, 15 chmbr groups.
Pupils: 215 day; 636 boarding; 500 studying inst.
Termly fees: £2765-3175 (day), £4515-4950 (boarding).

Chigwell School (Co-ed)

Chigwell, Essex IG7 6QF
Tel: 0181 501 5700/501 5745 (mus dept); 0181 501 5760
Fax: 0181 500 6232

D F Gibbs, head; David Thomas, acting dir of mus.
Awards: 3 scholarships, value usually up to 50% fees plus free tuition on 2 insts. Age 10-14; usually gr 5+ but awards are made mainly on mus

potential (inst ability, but voice may also be taken into account). 2 mus awards also made to VI form. *Exam boards:* MEG (GCSE); Edexcel (A-level). *Exam candidates:* GCSE 6; A-level 1.
Musical activities: 1st orch, wind band, jnr orch, chmbr orch (with tours abroad), br and wind groups, chapel choir, pop groups, swing band and choral society. Participation in chmbr mus competitions, Cathedral evensong visits, concerts by chapel choir.
Pupils: 709 day and boarding; 250 studying inst. Prep school is Chigwell Junior School at same address. *Termly fees:* £1496-2301 (day/according to age), £2220-3311 (wkly boarding), £2349-3498 (boarding).

Christ College (Co-ed)
Brecon, Powys LD3 8AG
Tel: 01874 623359; 01874 611603 (mus dept)
Fax: 01874 611478

D P Jones, head; M Dyer, acting dir of mus.
Awards: Up to 6 scholarships pa; max value 50% fees, with free tuition in 1 inst. Age under 12, under 14 or under 17 on 1 Jun. *Exam boards:* WJEC (GCSE); Edexcel (A-level). *Exam candidates:* GCSE 15; A-level 5.
Musical activities: Orch, jazz band, br band; br, wind and str groups; chapel choir, chmbr choir, choral society (all perform regular concerts).
Pupils: 360 boarding; 170 studying inst. *Termly fees:* £2430 (day), £3135 (boarding).

Christ's Hospital (Co-ed)
Horsham, W Sussex RH13 7LS
Tel: 01403 262833 *Fax:* 01403 276470

P C D Southern, head; Peter Allwood, dir of mus.
Awards: Entrance normally at age 11+, and mus ability offered as part of entrance exam. Financial assistance given to all successful candidates, value up to 100% fees as parental circumstances require. Mus tuition free to 40% of pupils, others assessed according to parental income. Free tuition awards given as a result of performance in entrance audition. *Exam boards:* MEG (GCSE); O&C (A-level). *Exam candidates:* GCSE 12; A-level 6; AS-level 1.
Musical activities: 5 choirs, 3 orchs, 3 bands, show band, many inst ens, regular performance opportunities, musicals, operas and other mus activities; also holiday tours and courses subsidised.
Pupils: 810 boarding; 470 studying inst. *Termly fees:* Fees assessed according to parental income.

City of London Freemen's School (Co-ed)
Ashtead Pk, Ashtead, Surrey KT21 1ET
Tel: 01372 277933 *Fax:* 01372 276165

D C Haywood, head; P M Dodds, dir of mus.

Awards: At least 2 mus awards of 50% and 33% fees (plus free inst tuition) at age 12-13 (not means tested). Many VI form scholarships possibly for mus. *Exam boards:* SEG (GCSE); UCLES (A-level); Edexcel (A-level mus technology). *Exam candidates:* GCSE 16; A-level 2.
Musical activities: 3 choirs, 2 orchs, wind band, jazz band; str, w/wind and br ens; chmbr mus, 2 orgs, recording and electronic mus studios, concert programme including operas, musicals. Occasional concerts in London. Tours to Europe and N America.
Pupils: 700 day; 50 boarding; 310 studying inst.
Termly fees: £2202 (day), £3387 (wkly boarding), 3498 (full boarding).

City of London School (Boys)
Queen Victoria St, London EC4V 3AL
Tel: 0171 489 0291 *Fax:* 0171 329 6887

W Duggan, head; M Smedley, dir of mus.
Awards: Up to 3 scholarships value up to 50% fees. Age 10-13, gr 5 min. Academic bursaries replacing former assisted places scheme. *Exam boards:* MEG, Edexcel. *Exam candidates:* GCSE 10; A-level 6.
Musical activities: School choirs, orchs, org.
Pupils: 870 day; 250+ studying inst. *Termly fees:* £2142 (day).

City of London School for Girls (Girls)
St Giles' Terrace, Barbican, London EC2Y 8BB
Tel: 0171 628 0841 *Fax:* 0171 638 3212

Y A Burne, head; Mrs M Donnelly, dir of mus.
Awards: 1 scholarship value £1800 pa (valid for pupil's school life) available in year 2000 plus 1 choral award value £400 made annually to snr school pupil; 1 annual VI form scholarship worth £300. A scholarship or exhibition at 11+ for mus excellence combined with good academic standards. Two Founder's Company awards, one for £250, one for £50 to musicians entering at VI form. *Exam boards:* MEG (GCSE); Edexcel (A-level). *Exam candidates:* GCSE 8-16; A-level 4-8.
Musical activities: Snr orch, jnr orch, prep dept orch, wind band, chmbr groups, str quartets, jnr choir, snr choir, madrigal group. Other activities include performance of lunchtime foyer concerts at Barbican Centre, performances in Bach Choir RFH concerts, at City of London Festival, City Livery Co church services and dinners, plus activities with City of London School for Boys and GSMD.
Pupils: 650 pupils; 350+ studying inst. *Termly fees:* £1962 (day).

Clayesmore School (Co-ed)
Iwerne Minster, Blandford, Dorset DT11 8LL
Tel: 01747 812122 *Fax:* 01747 811343

D J Beeby, head; D K Pigot, dir of mus.

Awards: Inst awards of 50%, 35%, 20% and 10% fees, all with free inst tuition (on 1st inst). Age under 14; usually gr 5 required in any orch inst. 2 choral awards also offered, value 5% fees; preference to ex-cathedral voices. *Exam boards:* SEG (GCSE); Oxford, Edexcel (A-level). *Exam candidates:* GCSE 14; A-level 6.
Musical activities: Chapel choir, school orch, concert band, barbershop singers, str orch, choral society, many small ens.
Pupils: 300 day and boarding; 100 studying inst. Prep school at same address *tel:* 01747 811707.
Termly fees: £2825 (day), £4035 (boarding).

Clifton College (Co-ed)
Clifton, Bristol BS8 3JH
Tel: 0117 973 9187 *Fax:* 0117 946 6826
Email: admissions@clifton-college.avon.sch.uk
Website: ds.dial.pipex.com/clifton-college

A H Monro, head; J C Heritage, dir of mus.
Awards: At least 1 major scholarship value 50% fees (index-linked) plus other awards of lesser value; age under 14 on 1 Jun. VI form scholarships value 50% fees. All awards include free inst tuition and may be supplemented; gr 5-8 required. *Exam boards:* MEG (GCSE); Edexcel (Practical A-level); O&C (A-level). *Exam*

candidates: GCSE 11; A-level 5.
Musical activities: Choral society, chapel choir, scholars' choir, folk choir, close harmony groups. Also 1st orch, training orch, str orchs; 2 wind bands, swing band, contemporary mus group, br and various other ens. Prep school attached with chapel choir, orch, str and wind ens, br ens; also rcdr groups and regular mus productions.
Pupils: 675 day and boarding; 300 studying inst.
Termly fees: £3035 (day), £4415 (boarding).

Clifton High School (Girls)
Bristol BS8 3JD
Tel: 0117 973 0201 *Fax:* 0117 923 8962
Email: clifton@rmplc.co.uk
Website: www.rmplc.co.uk/eduweb/sites/clifton/index.html

Mrs C Culligan, head; Jonathan Palmer, dir of mus.
Awards: 1 major mus scholarship, 2 inst scholarships to value of fees in 2 insts. Age under 13 in Feb. *Exam boards:* Edexcel (GCSE); NEAB (A-level). *Exam candidates:* GCSE 10; A-level 2.
Musical activities: 2 orchs, wind bands, chmbr groups, 4 choirs.
Pupils: 728 day; 290 studying inst. *Termly fees:* £425-1570 (day), £2345-2690 (family boarding).

Colfe's School (Boys)+
Horn Park La, London SE12 8AW
Tel: 0181 852 2283 *Fax:* 0181 297 1216

D J Richardson, head; P J Hopkins, dir of mus.
Awards: Various open scholarships, any of which may be awarded for musical promise supported by academic ability. Value up to 50% fees, or exhibitions value £900 pa. Age 11, 12, 13, 14 or VI form entry. *Exam boards:* SEG (GCSE); Edexcel (A-level). *Exam candidates:* GCSE 11; A-level 5.
Musical activities: 3 school orchs, br ens, wind ens, concert band, rcdr consort, chmbr mus groups, 4 school choirs, male voice group, house competitions, mus tours, musician in residence scheme.
Pupils: 990 day (including prep, nursery and pre-prep); 200+ studying inst. *Termly fees:* £1790 (day/snr).

Colston's Collegiate School (Co-ed)
Stapleton, Bristol BS16 1BJ
Tel: 0117 965 5207 *Fax:* 0117 958 5652

D G Crawford, head; I R Holmes, dir of mus.
Awards: Mus scholarships offering up to 50% fee remission, also minor awards for tuition fees on 2 insts or voice. *Exam boards:* MEG (GCSE); Edexcel (A/AS-level). *Exam candidates:* GCSE 7; A/AS-level 2.
Musical activities: Orch, choirs, choral society, br and wind bands, chmbr ens, rcdr group, pop groups.
Pupils: 570 day; 60 boarding; 140 studying inst. *Termly fees:* £1775-2010 (day), £3113-3706 (boarding).

Colston's Girls' School (Girls)
Cheltenham Rd, Bristol, Avon BS6 5RD
Tel: 0117 942 4328 *Fax:* 0117 942 6933
Email: cggadmin@aol.com

Judith Franklin, head; Alistair Mackenzie, dir of mus.
Awards: 2 exhibitions for free tuition on 2 insts, 2 VI form scholarships and discretionary awards. *Exam boards:* NEAB (GCSE); Oxford (A-level). *Exam candidates:* GCSE 8; A/AS-level 6.
Musical activities: 5 choirs, 3 orchs, 2 wind bands, rcdr groups, chmbr mus, CGS singers, 2 str groups, vc choir.
Pupils: 480 day; 140 studying inst. *Termly fees:* £1280.

Cranbrook School (Co-ed)
Waterloo Rd, Cranbrook, Kent TN17 3JD
Tel: 01580 712163/712554 *Fax:* 01580 715365
Email: registrar@cranbrook.kent.sch.uk
Website: www.cranbrook.kent.sch.uk

P A Close, head; Malcolm K Riley, dir of mus.
Awards: Mus scholarships available, with free tuition in 2 insts. Age 13, gr 5 expected. *Exam boards:* MEG (GCSE); UCLES (A-level). *Exam*

candidates: GCSE 4; A-level 2; AS-level 3. *Musical activities:* Orch, big band, jnr ens, 2 choirs, rock bands, str quartet, subscription concert series.
Pupils: 459 day; 275 boarding; 150 studying inst.
Termly fees: £1800 (boarding). No tuition fees.

Cranleigh School (Boys)+
Cranleigh, Surrey GU6 8QQ
Tel: 01483 273666 *Fax:* 01483 267398

Guy Waller, head.
Awards: Mus scholarships (major awards value 50% fees, 2 exhibitions value up to 25% fees) all with free inst tuition; age under 14 on 1 Sep, gr 4-8. VI form scholarships value 25% fees; ex-cathedral choristers particularly welcome. *Exam boards:* MEG (GCSE); Edexcel (A-level). *Exam candidates:* GCSE 15; A-level 4.
Musical activities: Orchs, bands, chapel choir, choral society, concert choir, chmbr choir; also other groups and ens.
Pupils: 106 day; 378 boarding; 150 studying inst.
Cranleigh Preparatory School is at the same address. *Termly fees:* £3380 (day), £4570 (boarding).

Culford School (Co-ed)
Bury St Edmunds, Suffolk IP28 6TX
Tel: 01284 728615 *Fax:* 01284 728631
Email: culford_edu@msn.com
Website: www.netlink.co.uk/users/culford

John Richardson, head; John Humphries, registrar; James Recknell, dir of mus.
Awards: Mus scholarships, HM Forces bursaries.
Exam boards: Edexcel (GCSE and A-level). *Exam candidates:* GCSE 4; A-level 3.
Musical activities: Orchs, groups, ens, choirs, mus productions.
Pupils: 390 day; 230 boarding; 200 studying inst.
Termly fees: £1929-2511 (day), £2290-3859 (boarding).

Dauntsey's School (Co-ed)
W Lavington, Nr Devizes, Wilts SN10 4HE
Tel: 01380 818441 *Fax:* 01380 813620

S B Roberts, head; C B Thompson, dir of mus.
Awards: Benson mus scholarship of 10% fees (with free tuition on 2 insts), Longsdon Exhibition (available as an academic or mus award) of 5% fees. Age under 14 on 1 Sep. Gr 5 min on 1st inst; 2nd inst or voice an advantage. 4 choral clerkships value £100 plus free singing lessons. *Exam boards:* MEG (GCSE); Edexcel (A/AS-level). *Exam candidates:* GCSE 18; A-level 2; AS-level 3.
Musical activities: Symphony orch, 4 str orchs, 2 wind bands, dance band, 3 fl choirs, 4 choirs, choral society, madrigal group, perc ens, 2 br groups.

Pupils: 369 day; 302 boarding; 350 studying inst. *Termly fees:* £2385 (day), £3874 (boarding).

Dean Close School (Co-ed)
Shelburne Rd, Cheltenham, Glos GL51 6HE
Tel: 01242 522640 *Fax:* 01242 258003

C J Bacon, head; R O Knight, dir of mus.
Awards: Mus awards of 50% (org), 50% and 25% fees (snr school), 25% fees (jnr school) with free inst tuition (total value up to £6000). Age 12.6-14 (snr) or 10-12 (jnr) on 1 Sep; gr 5 min on 1st inst, with 2nd inst or singing an advantage. *Exam boards:* SEG (GCSE); O&C (A-level). *Exam candidates:* GCSE 10; A-level 3.
Musical activities: Orch, chmbr orch, str group, wind band, br group, numerous ens, chapel choir, choral society, small choir, jazz band.
Pupils: 457 day and boarding; 132 studying inst. Prep school is Dean Close at same address.
Termly fees: £2210 (day/jnr), £3100 (day/snr), £3235 (boarding/jnr), £4450 (boarding/snr).

Denstone College (Co-ed)
Uttoxeter, Staffs ST14 5HN
Tel: 01889 590484 *Fax:* 01889 591295

D M Derbyshire, head; John York Skinner, dir of mus.
Awards: 3 inst, 5 choral scholarships and exhibitions (including VI form) value up to 50% fees (may be increased in cases of need). Special consideration given to choristers. *Exam boards:* Edexcel (GCSE); Edexcel, NEAB (A-level). *Exam candidates:* GCSE 14; A-level 5.
Musical activities: Schola Cantorum, choral society, opera group, orch, band, foreign choir tours.
Pupils: 300 day and boarding; 100 studying inst.
Termly fees: £1860-2694 (day), £3776 (boarding).

Douai School (Co-ed)
Upper Woolhampton, Reading, Berks RG7 5TH
Tel: 0118 971 5200 *Fax:* 0118 971 5241
Email: douai1@aol.com

Peter McLaughlin, head; David Bishop, head of mus.
Awards: 1 mus scholarship max value 1 term's school fees. Also minor awards of free inst tuition. *Exam boards:* SEG, Edexcel. *Exam candidates:* GCSE 6.
Musical activities: Choral society, snr orch, jnr orch, snr choir, jnr choir, concert band.
Pupils: 210 day and boarding; 75 studying inst.
Termly fees: £1920-2355 (day), £2930-3655 (boarding).

Dover College (Co-ed)
Dover, Kent CT17 9RH
Tel: 01304 205969 *Fax:* 01304 242208
Email: club@dcollege.demon.co.uk

H W Blackett, head; Roderick Spencer, dir of mus.

Awards: 1 or more mus awards value up to 50% including free tuition on all insts. Age under 14 on 1 Sep; gr 5 min on any inst. *Exam boards:* MEG (GCSE); O&C (A-level). *Exam candidates:* GCSE 5; A-level 3.
Musical activities: School orch, choral society, jnr and snr choirs which have performed nationally and internationally; br group, jazz group, male voice choir and annual house mus festival.
Pupils: 270 day and boarding; 70+ studying inst.
Termly fees: £1390-2260 (day), £2390-3260 (wkly boarding), £3195-3995 (full boarding).

Downe House (Girls)
Cold Ash, Hermitage Rd, Thatcham, Berks RG18 9JJ
Tel: 01635 200286

Miss S R Cameron, head; A Cain, dir of mus.
Awards: 1 mus scholarship value 50% fees plus free tuition in 2 insts; open exhibitions also available. Age under 13. VI form open mus scholarship value 50% fees plus free tuition in 2 insts. VI form mus exhibitions. *Exam boards:* MEG (GCSE). *Exam candidates:* GCSE 20; A-level 3.
Musical activities: 2 orchs, chmbr orch, rcdr consort, wind band, 4 choirs, choral society, chmbr groups, annual opera. Also choral and orch concerts with boys' schools; participation in festivals and national competitions; annual choral tour abroad. Also twice yearly competitions including chmbr mus, composition, solo inst and singing; visiting professional artists; m/classes.
Pupils: 30 day; 580 boarding; 450 studying inst.

Downside School (Boys)
Stratton on the Fosse, Bath, Somerset BA3 4RJ
Tel: 01761 235100 *Fax:* 01761 235105
Email: downside@rmplc.co.uk

Dom Antony Sutch, head; Chris Tambling, dir of mus.
Awards: 2-3 awards of up to 50% fees pa plus free inst tuition. Age under 14 on 1 May. Also choral exhibitions of up to 10% fees for members of Schola Cantorum. *Exam boards:* MEG (GCSE); NEAB (A-level). *Exam candidates:* GCSE 9; A-level 6.
Musical activities: Orch, Schola Cantorum, chmbr choir, jazz band, big band, choral society. Regular tours and concerts.
Pupils: 300 boarding; 185 studying inst. *Termly fees:* £1852/2060 (jnr/snr, day), £3256-4060 (jnr/snr, boarding).

Dulwich College (Boys) +
Dulwich Common, London SE21 7LD
Tel: 0181 693 3601; 0181 299 9256/8 *also fax*

G G Able, master; M Ashcroft, dir of mus.
Awards: 2 inst scholarships of up to 50% fees with free inst tuition. Age under 14 on 1 Sep; gr 5

225

(age 9-11), gr 6-7 (age 12-14) required. Orch insts preferred. Jnr dept takes boys from age 7 (eligible to compete for awards from within school). VI form scholarship also available. *Exam boards:* Edexcel (GCSE and A-level). *Exam candidates:* GCSE and A-level 25.
Musical activities: 3 orchs, 2 wind bands, 2 br groups, chmbr ens, big band. Twice yearly concerts in RFH and Fairfield Hall. Scheme for free loan of fine vns. Free tuition in vn and va to all from age 8.
Pupils: 1400 day and boarding; 500 studying inst.
Termly fees: £2090-2206 (day), £4234-4412 (boarding).

Dunottar School (Girls)
High Trees Rd, Reigate, Surrey RH2 7EL
Tel: 01737 761945 *Fax:* 01737 779450

Terry Lamont, dir of mus; Margaret Skinner, head.
Awards: 2 mus scholarships annually (to the value of 33% school fees plus free tuition on 1 inst), one for entry at year 7, one at year 10. Gr 3-4 at year 7, gr 5+ at year 10. *Exam boards:* Edexcel. *Exam candidates:* GCSE 7; A-level 4.
Musical activities: Jnr and snr str ens, jnr, intermediate and snr choirs, choral society, jnr and snr orchs, wind band.
Pupils: 430 (day), c 175 studying inst. *Termly fees:* £1090 (reception), £1780 (snr).

Durham School (Boys)+
Durham City, Co Durham DH1 4SZ
Tel: 0191 384 7977; 0191 386 6572 (mus school)
Fax: 0191 383 1025

N G Kern, head; Roger Muttitt, dir of mus.
Awards: A number of mus scholarships value 50% fees plus free inst tuition offered pa. Exams held 26 Feb; age under 14 on 1 Sep, gr 5 min (higher for pianists); 2 insts should be offered. Special consideration for str players and candidates with singing experience. Limited number of scholarships and exhibitions for 11+ and 16+ entrance, the latter for girls also. Org scholarship also available for 16+ candidates. *Exam boards:* MEG (GCSE); Edexcel (A-level). *Exam candidates:* GCSE 12; A-level 14.
Musical activities: Orch, str orch, band, chapel choir, cathedral visits, chmbr choir, choral society with local schools, chmbr ens, barbershop, jazz ens.
Pupils: 319 day and boarding; 138 studying inst.
Termly fees: £1791-2593 (day), £3372-3961 (boarding).

Eastbourne College (Co-ed)
Old Wish Rd, Eastbourne, E Sussex BN21 4JX
Tel: 01323 452320 *Fax:* 01323 452327

C M P Bush, head; Graham Jones, dir of mus.

Awards: Inst and choral awards of up to 50% fees available. Age under 14 on 1 Sep, gr 5 min. Special consideration given to cathedral choristers and str players. Scholarships also available to VI form girls and boys. Org scholarship offered. *Exam boards:* MEG (GCSE); Edexcel (A-level).
Musical activities: Choir, chmbr choir, choral society, orch and training orch, str orch, Eastbourne Symphony Orchestra affiliated to dept and open to best players, big band, swing band, chmbr groups. Pro concert series, electronic w/shop.
Pupils: 500 day and boarding; 200 studying inst.
Termly fees: Annual fees: £9000 (day), £12,690 (boarding).

Edgbaston High School for Girls (Girls)
Westbourne Rd, Birmingham B15 3TS
Tel: 0121 454 5831 *Fax:* 0121 454 2363

Miss E M Mullenger, head; Miss M Harper, dir of mus.
Awards: 2 mus scholarships; 1 at 16+ of up to full fees; 1 at 11+ of up to 50% fees. *Exam boards:* NEAB. *Exam candidates:* GCSE 15-17; A-level 5.
Musical activities: Choirs, wind band, 2 orchs; str, rcdr, br and fl groups.
Pupils: 964 day (age 2.9-18); 471 prep and pre-prep on site; 512 (snr school); 120 (VI form); 225 studying inst. *Termly fees:* £1540 (day).

The Edinburgh Academy (Boys)+
Henderson Row, Edinburgh EH3 5BL
Tel: 0131 556 4603

J V Light, rector; P N Coad, dir of mus.
Awards: Mus scholarships value up to 50% fees offered. Age under 14 on 1 Mar. VI form entry also. *Exam boards:* MEG (GCSE); O&C (A-level). *Exam candidates:* GCSE 11; A-level 5.
Musical activities: Choral society, chmbr choir, symphony orch, str orch, jnr orch, snr and jnr concert bands, dance band. Major choral works and opera performances, regular concerts, chmbr mus groups and keyboard studio.
Pupils: 312 prep school; 482 upper school; 300+ studying inst. *Termly fees:* £1830 (day), £2072 (boarding).

Elizabeth College (Boys)+
Guernsey, Channel Islands
Tel: 01481 726544 *Fax:* 01481 714839
Website: www.elizcoll.demon.co.uk/

J H F Doulton, head; P C Harris, dir of mus.
Awards: 1 inst scholarship of free tuition in 1 inst, 1 choral scholarship value £300 pa. *Exam boards:* MEG (GCSE); Edexcel (A-level). *Exam candidates:* GCSE 4; A-level 0.
Musical activities: College choir, orch, wind band, chmbr groups and keyboard studio work.

Pupils: 674 day; 26 boarding; 145 studying inst. *Termly fees:* £910 (day), £2310 (boarding).

Ellesmere College (Co-ed)
Ellesmere, Shropshire SY12 9AB
Tel: 01691 622321 *Fax:* 01691 623286

B J Wignall, head; Christopher Deakin, dir of mus. *Awards:* 2 scholarships of up to 50% fees plus free tuition in 2 insts; 1 'Schulze' org scholarship of up to 50% of fees plus free tuition; also 3 exhibitions of up to 25% fees. Age under 14 on 1 Sep or VI form entry; gr 5 min; 2 insts (or voice) should be demonstrated. Particular consideration to singers, organists and str players. Awards also available to girls and boys at VI form entry. *Exam boards:* NEAB (GCSE); UCLES (A-level); Edexcel (A-level mus technology). *Exam candidates:* GCSE 6; A-level 5; mus technology A-level 5.
Musical activities: Chapel choir, choral society, orch, str orch, jnr band, concert band, jazz band, many ens including fl group, sax group, cl group and perc group. At least 2 major choral works performed pa; also professional concert series.
Pupils: 366 day and boarding; 144 studying inst. *Termly fees:* £1704 (day/jnr), £2572 (day/snr), £3884 (boarding/snr).

Emanuel School (Co-ed)
Battersea Rise, London SW11 1HS
Tel: 0181 870 4171 *Fax:* 0181 877 1424

T Jones-Parry, head (to Aug 1998); Anne-Marie Sutcliffe, head (from Aug 1998); J S Holmes, dir of mus. *Awards:* Up to 2 mus scholarships of up to 50% fees at ages 10-11+, 13+ and 16+, together with free mus tuition on 2 insts. *Exam boards:* Edexcel (GCSE and A-level). *Exam candidates:* GCSE 8; A/AS-level 4.
Musical activities: Chapel choir, orch, chmbr and br groups. Major concert each term, annual musical, annual choir tour.
Pupils: 760 day; 100+ studying inst. *Termly fees:* £1770 (day).

Epsom College (Co-ed)
Epsom, Surrey KT17 4JQ
Tel: 01372 821234 *Fax:* 01372 821005

Anthony Beadles, head; Ian Holiday, dir of mus. *Awards:* Usually 25 open awards, any of which may be for mus. Age under 14 on 1 May (boys only) or on entry to VI form (girls and boys). Mus can be offered as part of all-rounder award. *Exam boards:* MEG (GCSE); Edexcel (A-level). *Exam candidates:* GCSE 10-14; A-level 4-6.
Musical activities: Several choirs, orch, concert band, choral society, madrigal group, large

modern mus school.
Pupils: 660 day and boarding; 275 studying inst.
Termly fees: £3275 (day), £4215 (wkly boarding), £4275 (boarding).

Eton College (Boys)
Windsor, Berks SL4 6DW
Tel: 01753 671000 *Fax:* 01753 671159

J E Lewis, head; R Allwood, dir of mus.
Awards: 8 scholarships offered; 4 to the value of 50% fees and 4 to the value of sixth of fees. Awards may be supplemented up to the value of full fees in cases of need. 6 exhibitions are also offered carrying remission of inst fees. Age under 14 on 1 Sep; gr 5-8 on 1st inst. Special consideration will be given to cathedral choristers who would still be able to sing treble in the College Chapel Choir. 4 VI form scholarships are offered pa to boys whose prior education has been in state schools. 1 of these may be awarded to a boy of outstanding musical ability. All awards include free inst tuition. *Exam boards:* MEG (GCSE); Edexcel (A-level). *Exam candidates:* GCSE 13; A-level 3.
Musical activities: 3 orchs, 2 bands, 2 swing bands, 3 choirs and many chmbr groups.
Pupils: 1283 boarding; 715 studying inst. *Termly fees:* £4649.

Exeter School (Co-ed)
Exeter, Devon EX2 4NS
Tel: 01392 273679 *Fax:* 01392 498144

N W Gamble, head; S D Foxall, dir of mus.
Awards: Top mus scholarship for outstanding ability may be awarded at 11, 12, 13 and 16. Other mus scholarships, one each at 11, 12, 13 and 16, are means-tested, value 10-50%. Other mus exhibitions are available. 2nd inst an advantage. (Governors' and Academic awards also available). *Exam boards:* Edexcel (GCSE and A-level). *Exam candidates:* GCSE 23; A-level 16.
Musical activities: 4 orchs, concert band, 2 jazz bands, choral society, 3 choirs, many ens. Most orchs, choirs, bands joint with St Margaret's School. Outstanding Performance Award at 1996 National Festival of Music for Youth.
Pupils: 700 day and boarding (11-18); 100 day prep (7-11); 300 studying inst. *Termly fees:* £1565 (day), £1345 (prep) £2965 (boarding).

Farlington School (Girls)
Strood Pk, Horsham, Sussex RH12 3PN
Tel: 01403 254967 *Fax:* 01403 272258

P M Mawer, head; Coralie Moult, dir of mus.
Awards: 1 or 2 inst awards, value up to 50% fees and free inst tuition, awarded annually; age 11-14. Mus scholarships, mus potential assessed at age 9-12. VI form scholarship available, up to value of

50% fees plus free tuition in 1 inst, for which mus skills may be taken into consideration. *Exam boards:* SEG (GCSE); London (A-level). *Exam candidates:* GCSE and A-level 18.
Musical activities: 2 snr and 2 jnr choirs, chmbr groups, wind ens, rcdr groups; also voice training and madrigal group.
Pupils: 370 day and boarding; 180 studying inst.
Termly fees: £950-2150 (day), £2755-3485 (boarding).

Felsted School (Co-ed)
Dunmow, Essex CM6 3JJ
Tel: 01371 820258/820497 (mus school)
Fax: 01371 821179

Stephen Roberts, head; Jasper Thorogood, dir of mus.
Awards: Scholarships value up to 50% fees offered, with free tuition in 2 insts, at age 11+, 13+ and VI form. Approx gr 5-6 on pno, org or orch inst with 2nd inst (voice preferred). *Exam boards:* MEG (GCSE); Edexcel (A-level). *Exam candidates:* GCSE 6-8; A-level 4.
Musical activities: Orch, str orch, chapel choir (cathedral visits), concert choir (with local schools), vocal ens, jazz and concert bands, chmbr mus, annual inst competitions, annual professional subscription concert series.
Pupils: 500 day and boarding; 250 studying inst.
Termly fees: £2895 (day), £3960 (boarding).

Fettes College (Co-ed)
Carrington Rd, Edinburgh EH4 1QX
Tel: 0131 332 2281 *Fax:* 0131 332 3081

Michael Spens, head; David Goodenough, dir of mus.
Awards: Major mus scholarships pa of up to 50% fees, which in cases of financial need can be supplemented by bursaries. Further exhibitions for candidates with marked potential. All carry free tuition on 2 insts. Age 10-14 and VI form entries. *Exam boards:* MEG (GCSE); SEB (Higher); Edexcel (A-level). *Exam candidates:* GCSE 13; A-level 3; Highers 5.
Musical activities: Choral society, numerous concerts and recitals, chapel choir, madrigal choir, musicals, 3 orchs, pipe and jazz bands, chmbr ens, computer studio for composition. Strong cultural links with Edinburgh. Foreign tours. Fully integrated jnr house (Inverleith House, age 10-13) with thriving mus.
Pupils: 485 mostly boarding; 230 studying inst.
Termly fees: £1930 (day/jnr), £3030 (day/snr), £3075 (boarding/jnr), £4485 (boarding/snr).

Forest Girls' School (Girls)
Snaresbrook, London E17 3PY
Tel: 0181 521 7477 *Fax:* 0181 520 7381

Mrs R Martin, head; M D Palmer, dir of mus.
Awards: Mus scholarships available at age 11, 13

and 16. *Exam boards:* MEG (GCSE); Edexcel (A-level). *Exam candidates:* GCSE 20; A-level 8.
Musical activities: Classroom mus, 3 choirs; girls join in main school activities (orchs, chapel choir, wind band, swing band, ens); also concert and stage productions.
Pupils: 375 day; 200 studying inst. *Termly fees:* £2046 (day).

Forest School (Boys)+
Snaresbrook, London E17 3PY
Tel: 0181 520 1744 *Fax:* 0181 520 3656

A G Boggis, warden; M D Palmer, dir of mus.
Awards: Mus scholarships of up to 100% fees plus free tuition on 1 inst. Age 11, 13 or 16 on 1 Sep. 2 insts (1 of gr 5 approx) or 1 inst plus voice should be offered. *Exam boards:* MEG (GCSE); Edexcel (A-level). *Exam candidates:* GCSE 20; A-level 8.
Musical activities: Orchs and choirs, musical plays, etc. Joins with girls' school on same site for musical activities.
Pupils: 475 day and boarding; 200 studying inst. Prep school is Forest Preparatory School. *Termly fees:* £1493 (day/8-10), £1930 (day/11), £3029 (boarding/11).

Framlingham College (Co-ed)
Framlingham, Suffolk IP13 9EY
Tel: 01728 723789 *Fax:* 01728 724546

G M Randall, head; R Rogers, dir of mus.
Awards: Up to 5 awards ranging from 10-50% fees, which may include free tuition for up to 2 insts. Age range under 14 on 1 Sep; gr 5 on 1st inst, with 2nd inst or singing. Also VI form awards (gr 7). *Exam boards:* NEAB (GCSE); London (A-level). *Exam candidates:* GCSE 5; A-level 1.
Musical activities: Chapel choir, choral society, barbershop group, symphony orch, rock and jazz groups, swing band, chmbr mus and wind band.
Pupils: 129 day; 318 boarding; 149 studying inst. *Termly fees:* £2285 (day), £3560 (boarding).

Frensham Heights (Co-ed)
Rowledge, Farnham, Surrey GU10 4EA
Tel: 01252 792134 *Fax:* 01252 794335

Peter M de Voil, head; Edwin Rolles, dir of mus.
Awards: Singing scholarships offered on grounds of mus promise, inst and choral scholarships also available. *Exam boards:* NEAB (GCSE and A-level). *Exam candidates:* GCSE 12; A-level and diploma 14.
Musical activities: 3 choirs and 2 orchs, jazz band, vocal and inst ens. Annual madrigal choir tour abroad.

Pupils: 173 day; 117 boarding; 150 studying inst. *Termly fees:* £2900 (day), £4375 (boarding).

George Watson's College (Co-ed)
Colinton Rd, Edinburgh EH10 5EG
Tel: 0131 447 7931 *Fax:* 0131 452 8594
Email: n.mitchell@watsons.edin.sch.uk

F E Gerstenberg, principal; Norman Mitchell, dir of mus.
Awards: 3 org scholarships; 1 inst scholarship of up to 50% academic fees, 1 inst bursary of up to 10% academic fees offered annually for entrants to form 1. Exams held in Feb. *Exam boards:* SEB, Edexcel. *Exam candidates:* 38 Standard, Higher grade and CSYS.
Musical activities: 4 orchs, 2 concert and jazz bands; wind, br, str and chmbr ens; College Chorus; chmbr, middle and jnr school choirs; opera society, several concerts and musicals pa.
Pupils: 2138 day; 23 boarding; 785 studying inst. Jnr and nursery school on campus. *Termly fees:* £1504 (day), £3062 (boarding).

Giggleswick School (Co-ed)
Giggleswick, Settle, N Yorks BD24 0DE
Tel: 01729 823545 *Fax:* 01729 824187

A P Millard, head; Tim Harvey, dir of mus.
Awards: Generous mus scholarships available, with free inst tuition. Age 10, 11, 13, 14 and VI form entry. *Exam boards:* NEAB (GCSE and A-level). *Exam candidates:* GCSE 4; A-level 2.
Musical activities: Orch, str orch, concert band, choral society, chapel choir, jazz choir, swing band, rock band and ens.
Pupils: 430 pupils; 200 studying inst. Prep school is Catteral Hall. *Termly fees:* £2454 (day), £3700 (boarding).

Glenalmond College (Co-ed)
Glenalmond, Perthshire PH1 3RY
Tel: 01738 880442 *Fax:* 01738 880410
Email: registrar@glencoll.demon.co.uk

Ian Templeton, warden; Robert Gower, dir of mus.
Awards: Up to 5, ranging from 10-50% fees. Applications possible at any stage; all insts welcome. *Exam boards:* MEG (GCSE); O&C (A-level); SEG (Highers). *Exam candidates:* GCSE 9; A-level 3; Higher 2.
Musical activities: Full orch, str orch, concert band, pipe band, wind quintets, br group plus various smaller ens. Large chapel choir and choral society, chmbr choir, concert society and opera club.
Pupils: 54 day; 302 boarding; 200 studying inst. *Termly fees:* £2930 (day), £4395 (boarding).

The Godolphin School (Girls)
Milford Hill, Salisbury, Wilts SP1 2RA
Tel: 01722 333059 *Fax:* 01722 411700

Jill Horsburgh, head; Eileen Sharp, dir of mus.
Awards: Mus scholarships available for entry at 11+, 12+ and 13+. *Exam boards:* Edexcel (GCSE and A-level). *Exam candidates:* GCSE 20; A-level 10.
Musical activities: 5 choirs, 4 orchs, 3 bands, foreign mus tours; participate in county and local festivals, and county and national youth groups.
Pupils: 192 boarding; 203 day; 300 studying inst. *Termly fees:* £2373 (day), £3962 (boarding).

Gordonstoun School (Co-ed)
Elgin, Morayshire IV30 2RF
Tel: 01343 830445/830264 (mus dept)
Email: jdthomas@rmplc.co.uk
Website: www.gordonstoun.org.uk

M C S-R Pyper, head; M J Appleford, dir of mus.
Awards: 2 or 3 jnr and snr awards pa, value up to 50% fees. Age 13+, 16+; gr 5-8 on 1 or more insts expected. *Exam boards:* Edexcel (GCSE); UCLES (A/AS-level). *Exam candidates:* GCSE 4-6; A-level 2-3.
Musical activities: Orch, str orch, chmbr ens, br and wind ens, choir, opera group. Weekly student concerts; also major overseas orch tours. Emphasis on opera and musicals. 14 professional recitals pa.
Pupils: 430 boarding; 200 studying inst. Prep school is Aberlour House, Aberlour, Banff. *Termly fees:* £4035 (boarding).

Gresham's School (Co-ed)
Holt, Norfolk NR25 6EA
Tel: 01263 713271

John Arkell, head; Mark Jones, dir of mus.
Awards: Several new scholarships in mus at 13+ and VI form level. *Exam boards:* Edexcel (GCSE); UCLES, Edexcel (A-level). *Exam candidates:* GCSE 9; A-level 3; AS-level 1.
Musical activities: Choirs, orchs, concert band, chmbr groups and frequent recitals.
Pupils: 186 day; 336 boarding; 280 studying inst. *Termly fees:* £4435 (boarding).

Guildford High School (Girls)
London Rd, Guildford, Surrey GU1 1SJ
Tel: 01483 561440 *Fax:* 01483 306516

Mrs S H Singer, head; Graham Thorp, dir of mus.
Awards: Scholarships at 11+ up to 25% fees, and at 16+ up to 33% fees. Exhibitions also available. Auditions Jan (11+) and Nov (16+). *Exam boards:* Edexcel (GCSE and A-level). *Exam candidates:* GCSE 15; A-level 4; AS-level 2.
Musical activities: Choirs, chmbr choir, first and second orch, chmbr groups, concert band, jazz band, fl choir, rcdr consort, cl ens, br group, sax

group. Regular concerts, mus drama productions, world mus projects, national competitions and foreign tours. Mus technology studio.
Pupils: 830 day; 375 studying inst. *Termly fees:* £1125 (age 4-7), £1530 (age 7-11), £1895 (age 11-18).

Haberdashers' Aske's School (Boys)
Butterfly La, Elstree, Borehamwood, Herts WD6 3AF
Tel: 0181 207 4323 *Fax:* 0181 236 0282

J W R Goulding, head; C Muhley, dir of mus.
Awards: Several scholarships may be awarded at age 11 and 13 for free tuition in 1 inst. All scholars are also eligible to apply for means-tested bursary support. Choral or inst ability may be offered.
Exam boards: MEG (GCSE); O&C (A-level). *Exam candidates:* GCSE 20; A-level 2.
Musical activities: 5 choirs, 4 orchs, 2 jazz bands, 3 br ens, 3 wind bands, 4 rcdr groups, chmbr groups.
Pupils: 1300 day; 550 studying inst. *Termly fees:* £1950 (prep school), £2126 (main school).

The Haberdashers' Aske's School for Girls (Girls)
Aldenham Rd, Elstree, Herts WD6 3BT
Tel: 0181 953 4261

Mrs P Penney, head; Alexander Mitchell, dir of mus.
Awards: Mus scholarship for entry at age 11.

Exam boards: Edexcel (GCSE and A-level). *Exam candidates:* GCSE 10; A-level 4.
Musical activities: 3 symphony orchs, chmbr orch, 3 wind bands, jazz band, choral society, 4 choirs and various ens.
Pupils: 1200 day; 600 studying inst. *Termly fees:* £1240-1470 (day).

Haileybury (Co-ed) +
Hertford, Herts SG13 7NU
Tel: 01992 463353 *Fax:* 01992 467603
Email: stuartw@haileybury.herts.sch.uk

S A Westley, master; Alexander Anderson, dir of mus.
Awards: Up to 5 mus awards, value up to 50% fees with additional bursary in case of financial need. All including free inst tuition. Age under 14 on 1 Jun, gr 6 min. 1 str award; also VI form main awards, including an org scholarship. *Exam boards:* Edexcel (GCSE and A-level). *Exam candidates:* GCSE 6; A-level 5.
Musical activities: Chapel choir, choral society, orch, str orch, br ens, chmbr mus, concert band. Overseas tours and concerts at St Martin in the Fields.
Pupils: 600 day and boarding; 200 studying inst. *Termly fees:* £3224 (day), £4446 (boarding).

Hampton School (Boys)

Hanworth Rd, Hampton, Middx TW12 3HD
Tel: 0181 979 5526 *Fax:* 0181 941 7368

B R Martin, head; Iain Donald, dir of mus.
Awards: Up to 2 scholarships value 35% fees at ages 11 and 13. Gr 5 on 1st inst required, with 2nd inst (may also be rcdr or voice). 1 choral scholarship (in conjunction with the Chapel Royal, Hampton Court Palace) value 35% fees at age 11. Also exhibitions of 15% fees may be awarded. *Exam boards:* MEG (GCSE); O&C (A-level). *Exam candidates:* GCSE 15; A-level 2.
Musical activities: Orch, chmbr orch, str orch, choir, jnr choir, choral society, wind bands, jazz band, chmbr mus, str quartets, gui ens, contemporary mus group. Extensive concert programme, tours, musical productions.
Pupils: 930 day; 300 studying inst. *Termly fees:* £1760.

Harrogate Ladies' College (Girls)

Harrogate, Yorks HG1 2QG
Tel: 01423 504543 *Fax:* 01423 568893
Email: enquire@hlc.org.uk
Website: www.rmplc.co.uk/eduweb/sites/g0hca

Margaret J Hustler, head; David Andrews, dir of mus.
Awards: Mus scholarships and awards available. *Exam boards:* NEAB (GCSE); UCLES (A-level). *Exam candidates:* GCSE 6; A-level 2.
Musical activities: Mus school; special interest in mus and choral work through chapel choir, jnr and snr choirs, orch and ens; also concerts and frequent concert and opera visits. Majority of girls learn insts. *Termly fees:* £2048-2108 (day), £2998-3085 (wkly boarding), £3075-3165 (boarding).

Harrow School (Boys)

Harrow on the Hill, Middx HA1 3HW
Tel: 0181 869 1231 *Fax:* 0181 423 3112
Email: harrow@rmplc.co.uk

N R Bomford, head; R H Walker, dir of mus.
Awards: Mus scholarships min value 50% fees offered, plus some of lesser value. Age under 14 on 1 Sep; gr 6 (distinction) on 1st inst, with 2nd inst or singing. *Exam boards:* Edexcel (GCSE); UCLES (A-level).
Musical activities: All mus interests catered for.
Pupils: 784 boarding; 350 studying inst. *Termly fees:* £4765 (boarding).

Hereford Cathedral School (Co-ed)

Old Deanery, Cathedral Close, Hereford HR1 2NG
Tel: 01432 363522 *Fax:* 01432 363525

H C Tomlinson, head; J M Williams, dir of mus.
Awards: Scholarships, up to 50% fees, and exhibitions available to gifted instrumentalists. Age 11, 13, and VI form entry. *Exam boards:* SEG (GCSE); Edexcel, Oxford (A-level). *Exam candidates:* GCSE 28; A-level 12.
Musical activities: 2 orchs, 2 concert wind bands, choral society, chmbr choir, jnr choirs, chmbr mus ens, jazz band. Many informal concerts plus regular musicals and concerts in Cathedral and elsewhere. Fully-equipped mus technology centre.
Pupils: 627 day and boarding (snr school); 245 (jnr school); 350 studying inst. *Termly fees:* £1585 (day), £2845 (boarding). *See also* **Choir Schools**.

Highgate School (Boys)

North Rd, London N6 4AY
Tel: 0181 340 1524 *Fax:* 0181 340 7674

R P Kennedy, head; John March, dir of mus.
Awards: At least 2 scholarships up to 50% fees, including free tuition. Age under 14 on 1 Sep; gr 6 min on 1st inst. *Exam boards:* MEG (GCSE); Edexcel (A/AS-level). *Exam candidates:* GCSE 12; A-level 1; AS-level 1.
Musical activities: 2 orchs, dance orch, concert band, choral society, chapel choir (including trebles from jnr school), chmbr groups, staged musicals, overseas tours, w/shops and m/classes. Many joint activities with Channing Girls' School.
Pupils: 610 day; 207 studying inst. *Termly fees:* £2625 (day).

Howells School (Girls)

Denbigh, N Wales LL16 3EN
Tel: 01745 813631 *Fax:* 01745 814443

Mary Steel, head; Geoff Coward, dir of mus.
Awards: Mus scholarships awarded every year for entry into lower school and VI Form. *Exam boards:* NEAB (GCSE); UCLES (A-level). *Exam candidates:* GCSE 13; A-level 8.
Musical activities: Concert wind band, snr chapel choir, jnr choir, str ens, also various chmbr ens; concerts performed, mus drama productions. Prep school with inst tuition.
Pupils: 200 day; 70 boarding; 160 studying inst. *Termly fees:* £2195 (day), £2995 (boarding).

Hurstpierpoint College (Co-ed)

Hassocks, W Sussex BN6 9JS
Tel: 01273 833636 *Fax:* 01273 835257

S D A Meek, head; R A Burton, dir of mus.
Awards: Jnr school awards value up to 50% fees offered; age under 10.6. Snr scholarships value up to 50% fees with free mus tuition, plus several exhibitions; cathedral choristers given special consideration; approx gr 5 on 1st inst with 2nd inst. *Exam boards:* MEG (GCSE); Edexcel (A-level). *Exam candidates:* GCSE 10; A-level 10.
Musical activities: Orch, choir, bands, jazz band and smaller groups. Annual performance of major choral work, biennial mus production.

Pupils: 116 day; 225 boarding (358 snr school, 163 jnr school). *Termly fees:* £3240 (day/snr), £4180 (boarding/snr). £2085 (day/jnr), £2810 (boarding/jnr).

Hutchesons' Grammar School (Co-ed)
21 Beaton Rd, Glasgow G41 4NW
Tel: 0141 423 2933 *Fax:* 0141 424 0251
Email: rector@hutchie.demon.co.uk

David Ward, head; Keith Hamilton, dir of mus.
Awards: VI form scholarships include mus. *Exam boards:* Edexcel, SEB (Standard Grade and Highers). *Exam candidates:* Standard Grade 9; Highers 9; A-level 3; SYS 3.
Musical activities: Choral society, 8 choirs, 2 orchs, 2 wind bands, 2 str ens, 2 gui ens, rcdr groups plus 3 music-dramatic productions pa.
Pupils: 1944 day (age 5-17); 360 studying inst.
Termly fees: £1166-1407 (day).

Ibstock Place (Co-ed)
Clarence La, Roehampton, London SW15 5PY
Tel: 0181 876 9991 *Fax:* 0181 878 4897

Franciska Bayliss, head; Chris Artley, dir of mus.
Awards: Mus scholarships and exhibitions for ages 11-16. *Exam boards:* Edexcel (GCSE). *Exam candidates:* GCSE 5.
Musical activities: School orch, snr choir, various

chmbr ens, jazz and rock bands.
Pupils: 210 day; 94 studying inst. *Termly fees:* £1925 (day).

Ipswich High School for Girls (Girls)
Woolverstone, Ipswich IP9 1AZ
Tel: 01473 780201 *Fax:* 01473 780985

Miss V C MacCuish, head; Peter Clayton, dir of mus.
Awards: Awards of 25% fees at 11+. *Exam boards:* Edexcel (GCSE); UCLES (A-level). *Exam candidates:* GCSE 12; A-level 4.
Musical activities: 2 orchs, wind band, str ens, jnr str group, elementary str group, 3 choirs. Annual concert at Snape, opera, regular school concerts, mus competition, church carol service.
Pupils: 670 day; 350 studying inst. *Termly fees:* £1384 (day).

Ipswich School (Co-ed)
Henley Rd, Ipswich, Suffolk IP1 3SG
Tel: 01473 408300 *Fax:* 01473 400058
Email: registrar@ipswich.suffolk.sch.uk
Website: www.ipswich.suffolk.sch.uk

I G Galbraith, head; A D Leach, dir of mus.
Awards: Up to 3 awards of substantial fee reduction for age under 12 on 1 Sep, under 14 on 1 Sep and mus is considered for the all-rounder scholarship available at 16. *Exam boards:* Edexcel

(GCSE and A-level). *Exam candidates:* GCSE 16; A-level 8.
Musical activities: 2 orchs, big band, chmbr orch, wind ens; also chapel choir, school choir. Recitals and concerts regularly organised. Prep dept with choir and orch, str and rcdr groups.
Pupils: 727; 200 studying inst. *Termly fees:* £1699 (day/jnr), £1866 (day/snr), £1018 (wkly boarding/jnr), £1244 (wkly boarding/snr), £1066 (boarding/jnr), £1336 (boarding/snr).

James Allen's Girls' School (Girls)
East Dulwich Grove, London SE22 8TE
Tel: 0181 693 1181 *Fax:* 0181 693 7842

Marion Gibbs, head; Rupert Bond, dir of mus.
Awards: Mus awards at any age as appropriate. *Exam boards:* MEG, UCLES. *Exam candidates:* GCSE 14; A-level 4; AS-level 2.
Musical activities: Highest traditions: Gustav Holst and Vaughan Williams taught here; 4 choirs, 3 orchs, chmbr mus, bands; visiting composer scheme, latest electronic equipment. Integrated inst programme at jnr and snr level, ad hoc rock bands, fl and cl ens, perc ens, etc; also mus tours and courses.
Pupils: 750 snr day; 250 prep; 330 studying inst. *Termly fees:* £2067-2130 (day).

The John Lyon School (Boys)
Middle Rd, Harrow, Middx HA2 0HN
Tel: 0181 422 2046 *Fax:* 0181 422 5008

T J Wright, head; Stuart Miles, dir of mus.
Awards: Mus scholarships at 11+ and 13+ worth up to 50% fees with free tuition on 2 insts. Age 11, gr 5 on 1st inst, with 2nd inst or singing. Special consideration given to str players. *Exam boards:* MEG (GCSE); UCLES (A/AS-level). *Exam candidates:* GCSE 9; A-level 4.
Musical activities: 2 orchs, choirs, band, jazz band, chmbr groups.
Pupils: 525 day; 100 studying inst. *Termly fees:* £2025.

Kelly College (Co-ed)
Tavistock, Devon PL19 0HZ
Tel: 01822 613005 *Fax:* 01822 612050
Email: kirwinc@aol.com
Website: ourworld.compuserve.com/homepages/kelly-college

M Turner, head; Andrew Wilson, dir of mus.
Awards: Mus scholarships offered value up to 50% fees with free tuition in 2 insts. Age under 14 with gr 5 on main inst or VI form entry with gr 7 on main inst, with 2nd inst or voice; choral experience an advantage. *Exam boards:* MEG (GCSE); O&C (A-level). *Exam candidates:* GCSE and A-level 15.
Musical activities: Chapel choir, chmbr choir, jnr choir, opera group, pop groups, wind band, orch,

chmbr mus ens, m/classes and choral soc concert society presenting professional concer
Pupils: 190 day; 160 boarding; 130 studying inst.
Termly fees: £1695-2565 (day), £4065 (boarding).

Kent College (Co-ed)
Canterbury, Kent CT2 9TD
Tel: 01227 763231 *Fax:* 01227 764777
Email: kcollege@rmplc.co.uk

E Halse, head; R Johnston, dir of mus.
Awards: Several bursaries available, value 33% and 50% fees plus free inst tuition. Age 11; occasional additional bursaries of same value awarded at age 13. *Exam boards:* MEG (GCSE); UCLES (A-level). *Exam candidates:* GCSE 15; A-level 4.
Musical activities: 3 orchs, choirs, band, chmbr groups, madrigal group; regular concerts; mus groups regularly tour UK and abroad.
Pupils: 500 day and boarding; 190 studying inst.
Termly fees: £21376 (day), £3806 (boarding).

Kent College Pembury (Girls)
Old Church Rd, Pembury, Tunbridge Wells TN2 4AX
Tel: 01892 822006 *Fax:* 01892 820221
Email: kentcoll@rmplc.co.uk

Barbara Crompton, head; Jenifer Horbury, dir of mus.
Awards: Discretionary scholarships available at 11+, 13+ and 16+ for joint academic and musical ability; free mus tuition awards at the same stages. 11+ gr 4; 13+ min gr 5. *Exam boards:* MEG (GCSE); Edexcel (A-level). *Exam candidates:* GCSE 5; A-level 1.
Musical activities: 2 choirs, orch, fl and cl choirs, snr and jnr chmbr groups. Fully staged musicals and joint events with other schools; many internal concerts.
Pupils: 162 day; 76 boarding; 136 studying inst.
Termly fees: £2400 (day), £3755 (wkly boarding), £4040 (boarding).

King Edward VI School (Co-ed)
Kellett Rd, Southampton SO15 7UQ
Tel: 01703 704561 *Fax:* 01703 705937
Email: registrar@kes.hants.sch.uk
Website: www.kes.hants.sch.uk

P B Hamilton, head; M C Hall, dir of mus.
Awards: 1 mus scholarship, age 11 (gr 5 on 1 inst); 2 scholarships, age 13 (gr 6 on 1 inst). VI form mus scholarships also available. Scholarships value £500 pa; 2nd inst/singing an advantage. *Exam boards:* SEG (GCSE); UCLES (A-level). *Exam candidates:* GCSE 11; A-level 3-4.
Musical activities: Choir (country-wide performances in churches and cathedrals, European summer tour), jnr and snr orchs; also inst ens, jazz band, other small vocal groups, wind band, fl choir.

...) studying inst. *Termly fees:*

...l (Birmingham) (Boys)
...ingham B15 2UA

Tel: 0121 472 1672; 0121 471 1640 (mus dep) *Fax:* 0121 415 4327
Email: registrar@kes.bham.sch.uk
Website: www.kes.bham.sch.uk

H R Wright, chief master; M J Monks, dir of mus.
Awards: 3 mus scholarships of up to 50% fees at
11+, 13+ and 16+. *Exam boards:* NEAB. *Exam
candidates:* GCSE 26; A/AS-level 13.
Musical activities: Symphony orch, concert orch,
jnr str orch, concert band, wind band, swing
band, snr and jnr br ens, choral society, chapel
choir, chmbr choir, chmbr mus.
Pupils: 891 day; 300 studying inst. *Termly fees:*
£1638.

King Edward's School (Godalming) (Co-ed)
Witley, Wormley, Godalming, Surrey GU8 5SG
Tel: 01428 683960 (mus dept)

R J Fox, head; S C Pedlar, dir of mus.
Awards: Available up to 50% fees; assisted
bursaries and place scheme may augment. *Exam
boards:* Edexcel, MEG. *Exam candidates:* GCSE
6-12; A-level 1-5.
Musical activities: Concert and swing bands, ens,

chapel choir, chmbr choir, various ens, operatic
society, choral society and elec mus studio,
Father Willis Organ.
Pupils: 500; 210 studying inst. *Termly fees:* £2180
(day), £3150 (boarding).

King Henry VIII School (Co-ed)
Warwick Rd, Coventry CV3 6AQ
Tel: 01203 673442 *Fax:* 01203 677102

T J Vardon, head; Richard Hollingdale, dir of mus.
Awards: Two VI form mus scholarships are
offered, one of 50% fees, one of 25% fees. A
bursary for free inst tuition is available for a
GCSE mus student. *Exam boards:* Edexcel (GCSE);
Edexcel (A/AS-level). *Exam candidates:* GCSE 5;
A/AS-level 1.
Musical activities: 4 choirs, 2 orchs, wind band,
various ens. Many concerts and trips, regular
musical productions. Additional groups in jnr
school.
Pupils: 810 day: 300 studying inst. *Termly fees:*
£1405 (day).

King William's College (Co-ed)
Castletown, Isle of Man IM9 1TP
Tel: 01624 822551 *Fax:* 01624 824287

P Kerr Fulton-Peebles, principal; A T Roberts, dir
of mus.

Awards: 2 mus scholarships value 10% fees awarded to pupils aged 11 and over, augmentable in case of need, with free inst tuition. 2nd inst an advantage. Org scholarship may be available and real ability as a singer is advantageous. *Exam boards:* MEG (GCSE); O&C, Edexcel (A-level). *Exam candidates:* GCSE 8; A-level 6.
Musical activities: Jnr and snr orchs, chapel choir, schola cantorum, choral society, jnr choir, barbershop, jazz band, military band, house mus festival, UK and international choir tours.
Pupils: 500 day and boarding; 200 studying inst. Prep school is Buchan Prep School. *Termly fees:* £1275-1960 (day/jnr), £2120-2915 (day/snr), £2770-3140 (boarding/jnr), £3300-4095 (boarding/snr).

King's College (Co-ed)
Taunton, Somerset TA1 3DX
Tel: 01823 272708 *Fax:* 01823 334236
Email: info@kingscol.demon.co.uk

R S Funnell, head; C K Holmes, dir of mus.
Awards: Awards of 50%, 33% and 15% fees offered, all with free inst tuition. Awards may be increased in cases of need. Age under 14 or VI form entry; gr 5-8 on main inst. Preference given to str players and singers, especially those with cathedral choir experience. *Exam boards:* MEG (GCSE); Edexcel (A-level). *Exam candidates:* GCSE 11; A-level 9.
Musical activities: Symphony orch, chmbr orch, chapel choir, chmbr choir, wind band, jazz band. Many performing opportunities, plus new mus school with digital recording studio.
Pupils: 114 day; 344 boarding; 166 studying inst. Associated prep school is King's Hall. *Termly fees:* £2863 (day), £4347 (boarding).

King's College School (Boys)
Wimbledon Common, London SW19 4TT
Tel: 0181 255 5300 *Fax:* 0181 255 5309

A C V Evans, head; M D Jenkins, dir of mus.
Awards: 1 or more mus scholarships value up to 50% fees plus VI form org scholarship. Age under 14 on 1 Sep; gr 6-8 on 1st inst with 2nd inst; orch insts preferred. *Exam boards:* MEG (GCSE); UCLES (A-level). *Exam candidates:* GCSE 15; A-level 5.
Musical activities: 3 orchs, 4 choirs, 3 wind bands, 2 barbershop groups, chmbr mus groups, jazz groups; annual mus festival; up to 30 concerts pa.
Pupils: 1190 day; 450 studying inst. *Termly fees:* £2450 (day).

King's School (Bruton) (Co-ed)
Bruton, Somerset BA10 0ED
Tel: 01749 813326 *Fax:* 01749 813426
Email: kingshm@kingsbruton.somerset.sch.uk

R I Smyth, head; J P S Chesney, dir of mus.
Awards: Mus scholarships value 10-50% fees may be awarded according to musicianship. Age under 14 on 1 Jun; VI form mus scholarships available. All awards carry free tuition in 2 insts. Special consideration to choristers. *Exam boards:* MEG (GCSE); Edexcel (A-level). *Exam candidates:* GCSE 6; A-level 4.
Musical activities: Orch, military band, concert band, dance band, chapel choir, regular choral concerts. Mus society (organises regular concert trips). Regular formal and informal concerts and musical productions.
Pupils: 361 day and boarding; 170 studying inst. Prep and pre-prep schools attached. *Termly fees:* £2785 (day), £3930 (boarding).

King's School (Canterbury) (Co-ed)
Canterbury, Kent CT1 2ES
Tel: 01227 595501/595556 *also fax* (mus dept)

Revd K H Wilkinson, head; Stefan Anderson, dir of mus.
Awards: Up to 10 mus scholarships pa to boys and girls plus one or more awards for VI form entrants (value not exceeding 50% fees, but assistance may be available depending on parental income). Free tuition on 2 insts. Age under 14 on 1 Sep. Gr 5 min (more if pno only offered). Some awards reserved for str players and choristers. *Exam boards:* MEG (GCSE); UCLES (A-level). *Exam candidates:* GCSE 10, A-level 5.
Musical activities: Activities include 'King's Week' (school's own mus festival); 3 orchs, band, 4 choirs, early mus group, 4 jazz ens, chmbr mus and informal concerts.
Pupils: 740 day and boarding; 434 studying inst. *Termly fees:* £3200 (day), £4650 (boarding).

King's School (Ely) (Co-ed)
Ely, Cambs CB7 4DB
Tel: 01353 660741/2 *Fax:* 01353 662187/667485

R H Youdale, head; G P L Griggs, dir of mus.
Awards: Mus scholarships, up to max value 50% fees, may be awarded on entrance, with free tuition in 2 insts. Age under 14 on 1 May; gr 5-7 on main inst expected. Bursaries for ex-Ely Cathedral choristers and 11+ and VI form awards also available, including org scholarship in conjunction with Ely Cathedral. *Exam boards:* Edexcel (GCSE and A-level). *Exam candidates:* GCSE 3; A-level 5.
Musical activities: Snr, jnr orchs; chapel choir, chmbr choir, barbershop, jazz band, concert band, br groups, w/wind groups and various chmbr ens. Termly informal and major concerts and biennial mus and opera productions. House mus competition and inst festival held annually.
Pupils: 714 day and boarding (age 7-18); 350 studying inst. *Termly fees:* £2837 (day), £4222 (boarding). *See also* **Choir Schools**.

King's School (Gloucester) (Co-ed)
Pitt St, Gloucester GL1 2BG
Tel: 01452 521251/2/3/4 *Fax:* 01452 385275

Peter Lacey, head; Ian Fox, dir of mus.
Awards: Several scholarships available to gifted instrumentalists at ages 11, 13 and 16. *Exam boards:* MEG (GCSE); UCLES (A-level). *Exam candidates:* GCSE 10; A-level 6.
Musical activities: 2 orchs, jnr ens, br group, concert band, str group; school choir, jnr choir, madrigal group; annual oratorio performance in Cathedral with local state schools, plus regular concerts.
Pupils: 500 day and boarding; 210 studying inst.
Termly fees: £900-2260 (day), £3445-3820 (boarding). *See also* **Choir Schools**.

The King's School in Macclesfield (Co-ed)
Macclesfield, Cheshire SK10 1DA
Tel: 01625 260000 *Fax:* 01625 260009

A G Silcock, head; Andrew K Green, dir of mus.
Awards: VI form mus scholarship and 1 org scholarship. *Exam boards:* NEAB. *Exam candidates:* GCSE 20; A-level 5.
Musical activities: Choir, chmbr choir, girls' choir, foundation choir, orch, str orch, chmbr orch, concert band, jazz group, barbershop group, vc ens, gui ens, fl group, opera and musical group, jnr school orch and choir. Regular termly concerts, charity concerts, annual carol service in local cathedrals.
Pupils: 1320 day; 330+ studying inst (and many more outside school). Associated prep school is King's School Macclesfield Junior School. *Termly fees:* Annual fees: £3450 (day/jnr), £4395 (day/snr).

King's School (Rochester) (Co-ed)
Rochester, Kent ME1 1TE
Tel: 01634 843913 *Fax:* 01634 832493
Email: kingsroc@rmplc.co.uk
Website: www.rmplc.co.uk/eduweb/sites/kingsroc/index.html
I R Walker, head; G R Williams, dir of mus.
Awards: Up to 5 scholarships offered including 1 major mus scholarship of up to 100% fees (above 50% means-tested). Age 11+. Gr 5-6 in main inst at 13+ with 2nd inst required. Org scholarship of up to 100% fees (above 50% means-tested), age 15+. gr 8 org. All scholarships include free tuition on all insts studied. Exam in Feb. *Exam boards:* MEG (GCSE); O&C (A-level). *Exam candidates:* GCSE 11; A-level 4.
Musical activities: Choir performs in Chapel and concerts, orch, chmbr orch, prep school orch. Also br group, prep br group and various wind groups. Prep school on same site shares mus

facilities, and cathedral choristers are drawn from school. *See also* **Choir Schools**.
Pupils: 511 day; 61 boarding; 200 studying inst.
Termly fees: £2169-2530 (day), £3634-4390 (boarding).

King's School (Worcester) (Co-ed)
College Green, Worcester, Worcs WR1 2LH
Tel: 01905 23016 *Fax:* 01905 25511

J M Moore, head; D E Brookshaw, dir of mus.
Awards: At 13+ 2 scholarships offered, value up to 50% fees with free tuition in 2 insts; also up to 2 exhibitions with free tuition in 1 inst. Age over 12, under 14 on 1 Sep; gr 5-6 min. Mus awards also available at 7-8+, 11+ and 16+. Choral scholarships also available. *See also* **Choir Schools**. *Exam boards:* MEG (GCSE); Oxford (A-level). *Exam candidates:* GCSE 14; A-level 5.
Musical activities: 3 orchs, 3 choirs, wind band. Major concert termly, and many choral and org playing opportunities; also chmbr concert series. Jnr school (shares mus teachers) for age 7-11, with choir and orch, and termly concerts.
Pupils: 1003 day; 22 boarding; 300 studying inst.
Termly fees: £1189-1846 (day), £3200 (boarding).

Kingston Grammar School (Co-ed)
70-72 London Rd, Kingston upon Thames, Surrey KT2 6PY
Tel: 0181 546 5875 *Fax:* 0181 974 5177; 0181 547 1499
Email: kgs@rmplc.co.uk

C D Baxter, head; J L Thomas, dir of mus.
Awards: 2 mus scholarships worth 50% fees at age 11+ and 13+, together with free tuition on one inst. Special consideration given to str players. Expected levels: gr 4-5 (11+), gr 5-6 (13+). *Exam boards:* SEG (GCSE); Edexcel (A-level). *Exam candidates:* GCSE 9; A-level 3.
Musical activities: Jnr choir, 1st and 2nd orch, concert band, chmbr choir, wind ens and chmbr groups. Choral society present an oratorio annually; regular musicals in conjunction with drama dept. Regular lunchtime recitals, 2 major concerts per term. Regular visits to sing at cathedrals and colleges, and tours in the UK and abroad.
Pupils: 600; 140 studying inst. *Termly fees:* £2060.

The Lady Eleanor Holles School (Girls)
Hanworth Rd, Hampton, Middx TW12 3HF
Tel: 0181 979 1601 *Fax:* 0181 941 8291

Miss E M Candy, headmistress; Phoebe Woollam, dir of mus.
Awards: Approx 4 scholarships of up to 25% fees with free tuition on 1 inst. Below age 12, gr 4, auditions held end of Jan. Also VI form scholarships. *Exam boards:* SEG (GCSE); Edexcel (A/AS-level).

Exam candidates: GCSE 24; A/AS-level 8.
Musical activities: 3 orchs, 3 choirs, 5 bands, chmbr mus ens.
Pupils: 715 day; 200 studying inst. *Termly fees:* £1635-1950.

Lancing College (Boys) +
Lancing, W Sussex BN15 0RW
Tel: 01273 452213 *Fax:* 01273 464720

P M Tinniswood, head; P E Lewis, D N Cox, dirs of mus.
Awards: 8 mus awards value up to 50% fees. All awards may be augmented according to parental circumstances; all with free tuition on 2 insts. *Exam boards:* MEG (GCSE); UCLES (A-level). *Exam candidates:* GCSE 10; A-level 10.
Musical activities: 3 orchs, 2 bands, chmbr groups, chapel choir, choral society.
Pupils: 94 day; 408 boarding; 200 studying inst.
Termly fees: £3340 (day), £4445 (boarding).

Langley School (Co-ed)
Langley Pk, Norwich NR14 6BJ
Tel: 01508 520210 *Fax:* 01508 528058
Email: langley.school@dial.pipex.com

J G Malcolm, head; John Shooter, dir of mus.
Awards: 2 mus scholarships (up to 25% fees). No age limit. Exams in Mar, entry by early Feb. Gr 8 for VI form, gr 5+ at age 13. Occasional bursaries. *Exam boards:* MEG (GCSE); London (A-Level). *Exam candidates:* GCSE 4; A-level 2.
Musical activities: Choral society, chmbr choir, orch/wind band, jnr choir, cl choir, str ens, vc ens, br group, gui group. Termly productions and concerts. Langley School Professional Recital Series presents concert each term.
Pupils: 170 day; 80 boarding; 120 studying inst.
Termly fees: £1670-2040 (day); £3030-3675 (weekly boarding); £3240-3930 (boarding).

Latymer Upper School (Boys) +
King St, Hammersmith, London W6 9LR
Tel: 0181 741 1851 *Fax:* 0181 748 5212

C Diggory, head; Tony Henwood, dir of mus.
Awards: 4 mus scholarships of up to 50% fees with free tuition on 1 inst are available for boys entering the school in Sep at 11+ and 13+; also for boys and girls at 16. Gr 4-5 on 1st inst (11+), gr 5-6 (13+), gr 8 (16+) and ability to offer 2nd inst or singing preferable. Scholarship auditions held Feb. *Exam boards:* MEG (GCSE); NEAB (A/AS-level). *Exam candidates:* GCSE 21; A-level 5.
Musical activities: Choral society, 3 choirs, joint orch with Godolphin and Latymer, 2 other orchs, 2 bands, jazz band and chmbr groups.
Pupils: 1090 day; 350 studying inst. *Termly fees:* £2060 (day).

Leeds Girls' High School (Girls)
Headingley La, Leeds, W Yorks LS6 1BN
Tel: 0113 274 4000 *Fax:* 0113 275 2217
Email: postmaster@lghs.demon.co.uk
Website: www.lghs.demon.co.uk/

Sue Fishburn, head; Margaret Smith, dir of mus.
Awards: 2 mus scholarships for entry at age 11.
Up to 2 org scholarships pa and William Pitt
Award (internal) for mus contribution to school.
Exam boards: NEAB. *Exam candidates:* GCSE 2;
A-level 4.
Musical activities: Snr and jnr choirs, concert
band (cl choir, fl ens), str groups, rcdr groups,
chmbr groups, 2 orchs.
Pupils: 600 day; 200 studying inst. Associated
prep school is Ford House. *Termly fees:* £1612
(day/snr).

Leicester Grammar School (Co-ed)
8 Peacock La, Leicester LE1 5PX
Tel: 0116 222 0400 *Fax:* 0116 291 0505

J B Sugden, head; David M T Whittle, dir of mus.
Awards: Scholarships available from 11+. Other
bursaries also available. *Exam boards:* Edexcel
(GCSE/A-level). *Exam candidates:* GCSE 17; A-level
2; AS-level 2.
Musical activities: First and training orchs, chmbr
choir, chmbr groups, dance band, jazz band, rcdr
group, br ens, jnr choir and ens, concerts, annual
house mus evening.
Pupils: 640 day; 350 studying inst. *Termly fees:*
£1550 (day).

Leighton Park School (Co-ed)
Reading, Berks RG2 7DH
Tel: 0118 987 2065 *Fax:* 0118 986 6959

John Dunston, head; Stuart Beer, dir of mus.
Awards: Up to 25% fees (can be supplemented up
to 75% fees) available at age 11 and 13 entry. Gr 5
distinction on 1st inst required, preferably with
keyboard as strong 2nd study. *Exam boards:* SEG
(GCSE); Edexcel (A-level). *Exam candidates:* GCSE
18; A-level 5.
Musical activities: Choral and orch societies, wind
band, br ens, 4 jazz bands, big band, chmbr
groups, continental tours, regular mus
productions, professional concerts, annual house
mus competition, electronic mus studio, blues
band, sax quartet, perc ens, str ens, opera
productions.
Pupils: 365 day and boarding; 200+ studying inst.
Termly fees: £3204 (day), £4236 (boarding).

The Leys School (Co-ed)
Cambridge, Cambs CB2 2AD
Tel: 01223 508900 *Fax:* 01223 505303

J C A Barrett, head; Peter Noyce, dir of mus.
Awards: Index-linked mus scholarships, value up
to 50% fees. Age under 14 on 31 Jul (for prep
school candidates). VI form awards for boys and
girls; good gr 5 or above but potential important.
Exam boards: Edexcel (GCSE); UCLES (A-level).
Exam candidates: GCSE 8; A-level 2.
Musical activities: Choirs, orchs, bands, swing
band and chmbr ens.
Pupils: 430 day and boarding; 180 studying inst.
Termly fees: From £2790 (day), £4260 (boarding).

Llandovery College (Co-ed)
Llandovery, Carmarthenshire SA20 0EE
Tel: 01550 720315 *Fax:* 01550 720168
Email: llan.coll@virgin.net
Website: freespace.virgin.net/llan.coll

Claude Evans, headmaster; Richard Whitehead,
dir of mus.
Awards: Mus scholarships (including free tuition)
offered annually for entry at 11, 13 or 16. *Exam
boards:* WJEC, MEG, Edexcel, UCLES. *Exam
candidates:* GCSE 5; A-level 1.
Musical activities: Choir, choral society, chmbr
ens, musicals.
Pupils: 83 day, 139 boarding; 50 studying inst.
Termly fees: £2317 (day), £3489 (boarding).

Lomond School (Co-ed)
10 Stafford St, Helensburgh, Dunbartonshire G84 9JX
Tel: 01436 672476 *Fax:* 01436 678320

A D Macdonald, head; Anne Lyon, head of mus.
Awards: Scholarships up to 50% fees and
substantial boarding bursary. *Exam boards:* SEB,
Edexcel (A-level). *Exam candidates:* Standard
Grade, Highers and A-level 12.
Musical activities: Choirs, jazz, traditional mus
group, clarsach, Scots fiddle, bagpipes, voice.
Pupils: 470 day and boarding; 84 studying inst.
Termly fees: £1590.

Lord Wandsworth College (Boys)+
Long Sutton, Hook, Hants RG29 1TB
Tel: 01256 862482 *Fax:* 01256 862563

I G Power, head; R W Goodrich, head of mus.
Awards: Value up to 50% fees awarded, and
exhibitions also offered at all ages. Entry
requirements dependent on age. *Exam boards:*
SEG (GCSE); Edexcel (A-level). *Exam candidates:*
GCSE 4; A-level 1.
Musical activities: Big band, orchs, choir, chmbr
choir, choral society, other ens and mus
societies, modern jazz, gui groups, musicals,
swing band
Pupils: 460 day and boarding; 200 studying inst.
Termly fees: £2650 (day/jnr), £2792 (day/snr),
£3404 (boarding/jnr), £3588 (boarding/snr).

Loretto School (Co-ed)
Musselburgh, Midlothian EH21 7RE
Tel: 0131 653 4455 *Fax:* 0131 653 4445

Keith J Budge, head; Timothy Goulter, dir of mus; Hamish Alldridge, admissions dir.
Awards: Annual major and minor mus scholarships offering up to 30% fees. No age limit; 13+ and VI form entries. Various bursaries which could augment scholarships. Major org scholarships tenable at any level. Also piping bursaries and 13+ chanter players. *Exam boards:* MEG (GCSE); Edexcel (A-level); SEB (Revised Highers).
Musical activities: Chmbr choir, orch, choral and chmbr groups, concert and jazz bands, whole school singing, wind and str ens, pipes and drums, recording studio. Strong cultural links with Edinburgh. 3-manual pipe org (1989, Kenneth Jones). Loretto Concert Society; piping competitions and tours.
Pupils: 20 day; 299 boarding; 200 studying inst. Prep school is Loretto Nippers. *Termly fees:* £2157 (day/jnr), £2860 (day/snr), £3235 (boarding/jnr), £4290 (boarding/snr).

Loughborough Grammar School (Boys)
Burton Walks, Loughborough, Leics LE11 2DU
Tel: 01509 233233 *Fax:* 01509 210486
Email: hmpa@loughboroughgs.demon.co.uk
Website: www.argonet.co.uk/education/barrow.lgs

P J Underwood, dir of mus.
Awards: Choral and inst scholarships at 11+, 13+ and 16+. *Exam boards:* UCLES (IGCSE); UCLES (A-level). *Exam candidates:* GCSE 7; A-level 5.
Musical activities: Choir, concert band, orch, big band, jnr concert band, swing band, ens.
Pupils: 960 day; 30 boarding; 350 studying inst. *Termly fees:* £1524 (day), £2817 (boarding).

Magdalen College School (Boys)
Oxford OX4 1DZ
Tel: 01865 242191 *Fax:* 01865 240379

P M Tinniswood, head; M N Pearce, dir of mus.
Awards: 1 or more inst scholarships value up to £2500 pa plus free tuition in 1 inst. Age under 14 on 1 Sep. Choral scholarships also available, age 9-10.6. *See also* **Choir Schools.** *Exam boards:* MEG (GCSE); O&C (A-level). *Exam candidates:* GCSE 10; A-level 4.
Musical activities: Jnr and snr orchs, choral society, madrigal choir, close harmony group, chmbr ens, jazz band.
Pupils: 537 day; 200 studying inst. *Termly fees:* £1798 (day).

Malvern College (Co-ed)
College Rd, Malvern, Worcs WR14 3DF
Tel: 01684 892333 *Fax:* 01684 572398

H C K Carson, head; Rory Boyle, dir of mus.
Awards: Mus scholarships of up to 50% fees offered, with free tuition on up to 2 insts. Age under 14 on 1 Jun; gr 5 min; 2nd inst an advantage. Scholarship auditions in Jan and Feb. Also exhibitions available. *Exam boards:* MEG (GCSE); Edexcel (A/AS-level). *Exam candidates:* GCSE 12; A-level 9.
Musical activities: Chmbr orch, symphony orch, symphonic wind band, jnr band, br group, jazz band. Also numerous wind and str chmbr ens, plus jazz groups. Chapel choir, chmbr choir, choral society.
Pupils: 572 day and boarding; 290 studying inst. *Termly fees:* £3235 (day), £4450 (boarding).

Malvern Girls' College (Girls)
15 Avenue Rd, Malvern, Worcs WR14 3BA
Tel: 01684 892288 *Fax:* 01684 566204
Email: mgc@atlas.co.uk

Philippa M C Leggate, head; P K Redfern, dir of mus.
Awards: At least 2 major mus scholarships offered. *Exam boards:* MEG (GCSE); NEAB (A-level). *Exam candidates:* GCSE 17; A-level 6.
Musical activities: Snr and jnr orchs, chmbr orch, snr and jnr choirs, wind band, br ens, choral society, chmbr groups, mus productions.
Pupils: 464 day and boarding; 300 studying inst. *Termly fees:* £2895 (day), £4340 (boarding).

Marlborough College (Co-ed)
Marlborough, Wilts SN8 1PA
Tel: 01672 892300 *Fax:* 01672 892307
Email: marlboroughcollege@cccp.net

E J H Gould, master; R W Nelson, dir of mus.
Awards: Up to 6 index-linked scholarships available value up to 50% fees (may be supplemented in case of need). Age under 14 on 1 Sep; gr 5 (merit or distinction) or above on 1st inst; 2 insts preferred. 3 main awards offered for VI form entry. *Exam boards:* Edexcel (GCSE and A-level). *Exam candidates:* GCSE 15; A-level 2.
Musical activities: 2 orchs, chmbr orch, chapel choir, jnr singers, special choir, 2 wind bands, rock society, jazz group, close harmony, jnr and snr musical productions, choral works, subscription concert series of 6 concerts pa.
Pupils: 770 boarding, 30 day; 542 studying inst. *Termly fees:* £3380 (day), £4700 (boarding).

Mary Erskine School (Girls)
Ravelston, Edinburgh EH4 3NT
Tel: 0131 337 2391 *Fax:* 0131 346 1137

P F J Tobin, principal; Helen Mitchell, head of mus.

243

Awards: Janie Beeston Scholarship for str players and other scholarships, max 40% fees for entry up to S3; several bursaries for inst tuition. Applications by mid-Jan. *Exam boards:* SEB (Standard Grade, Highers); O&C (A-level). *Exam candidates:* Standard Grade 15; Highers 12; A-level 2.
Musical activities: Strong mus dept twinned with Stewart's Melville College *see below;* 3 orchs, 3 bands, jazz band, many chmbr ens, choirs; regular concerts, 3 staged musicals pa. Mus dept serves co-ed jnr school.
Pupils: 694 day and boarding; 260 studying inst.
Termly fees: £1510 (day); £3020 (boarding).

The Maynard School (Girls)
Exeter EX1 1SJ
Tel: 01392 273417 *Fax:* 01392 496199
Website: www.znet.co.uk.maynard/welcome.htm

Miss F Murdin, head; N Horton, dir of mus.
Awards: 1 scholarship 50% fees (can be shared); 4 exhibitions of £275; 1 VI form scholarship 50% fees. *Exam boards:* Edexcel (GCSE and A-level). *Exam candidates:* GCSE 11; A-level 2; AS-level 1.
Musical activities: 3 orchs, 3 choirs, chmbr ens, jazz band, wind band.
Pupils: 520 (115 in VI form); c 200 studying inst.
Termly fees: £1260-1560.

Merchant Taylors' School (Boys)
Sandy Lodge, Northwood, Middx HA6 2HT
Tel: 01923 820644 *Fax:* 01923 835110

J R Gabitass, head; Richard Hobson, dir of mus.
Awards: 1 scholarship up to the value of 25% school fees plus free tuition; 2 exhibitions up to the value of 10%. Mus bursaries also awarded to cover costs of tuition of up to 2 insts per pupil. *Exam boards:* MEG (GCSE); O&C (A-level). *Exam candidates:* GCSE 10; A-level 2.
Musical activities: Snr and jnr orchs, chmbr orch, wind band and various chmbr groups. Choral society, chmbr choir; annual major choral work performed, also other orch and chmbr concerts and regular mus stage productions, many in collaboration with St Helen's School.
Pupils: 757 day and boarding; 200 studying inst.
Termly fees: £2880 (day/Christmas term), £2160 (day/Easter and summer), £4608 (boarding/Christmas), £3456 (boarding/Easter and summer).

Merchiston Castle School (Boys)
Colinton, Edinburgh EH13 0PU
Tel: 0131 441 1722/1567 *Fax:* 0131 441 6060

D M Spawforth, head; P K Rossiter, dir of mus.
Awards: Up to 2 mus scholarships available, plus inst bursaries. *Exam boards:* MEG (GCSE); Edexcel (A-level). *Exam candidates:* GCSE 3; A-level 1.

Musical activities: Chapel choir (with regular tours), choral society, close harmony group, orch, jazz band, pipe bands, mus club, chmbr groups, concert society (promoting professional concerts) and musicals.
Pupils: 390 day and boarding; 160 studying inst.
Termly fees: £1990-2830 (day), £3050-4255 (boarding).

Methodist College (Co-ed)
1 Malone Rd, Belfast BT9 6BY
Tel: 01232 205205 *Fax:* 01232 205230

T W Mulryne, head; J McKee, dir of mus.
Awards: 2 org/vocal scholarships. *Exam boards:* NICCEA. *Exam candidates:* GCSE 20; A-level 15.
Musical activities: 2 orchs, concert and swing band, chapel choir, chmbr, snr girls' and jnr choirs, snr chorus, traditional Irish group, rcdr groups, glockenspiel group, chmbr groups, pop groups; 2 fine pipe orgs.
Pupils: 2360 day and boarding (including 590 prep); 400 studying inst. Prep schools are Fullerton House and Downey House. *Termly fees:* £80-2069.

Mill Hill School (Co-ed)
Mill Hill Village, London NW7 1QS
Tel: 0181 959 1221 *Fax:* 0181 906 2614

W R Winfield, head; Richard Allain, dir of mus.
Awards: Up to 50% fees. Age under 14 on 1 Jun; 2nd inst/singing an advantage. *Exam boards:* MEG (GCSE); Edexcel (A-level). *Exam candidates:* GCSE 10; A-level 3.
Musical activities: Chmbr orch, orch, band, choir, ens. Mus subscription club presents 6 professional concerts pa.
Pupils: 550 day and boarding; 100+ studying inst.
Termly fees: £2735 (day), £4216 (boarding).

Millfield School (Co-ed)
Street, Somerset BA16 0YD
Tel: 01458 442291 *Fax:* 01458 447276
Email: admissions@millfield.somerset.sch.uk
Website: www.millfield.somerset.sch.uk/millfield

P M Johnson, head; S D Pinnock, dir of mus.
Awards: Mus scholarships awarded at head's discretion. Age 13+, 16+ in Sep; outstanding ability required on one inst. *Exam boards:* Edexcel (GCSE and A/AS-level). *Exam candidates:* GCSE 22; A-level 5.
Musical activities: Symphony orch, str orch, wind band, br band, chmbr choir, 'show' choir, choral society, madrigal group; wind, str, br and mixed chmbr ens; regular concerts.
Pupils: 1250 day and boarding; 250 studying inst.
Termly fees: £2940 (day), £4595 (boarding).

Milton Abbey School (Boys)
Nr Blandford, Dorset DT11 0BZ
Tel: 01258 880484 *Fax:* 01258 881194

Jonathan Hughes-D'Aeth, head; Y F S Day, dir of mus.
Awards: At least 3 scholarships of up to 50% fees with free tuition in 2 insts. Age under 14 on 1 Jun; gr 5 min on 1st inst with credit for 2nd inst. (Gr 5 theory preferable.) *Exam boards:* SEG (GCSE); NEAB (A-level). *Exam candidates:* GCSE 3; A-level 5.
Musical activities: Abbey choir, chmbr choir, plainsong choir, various inst ens. Mus school offers any number of options for mus experience, including all genres and very modern technology options. Abbey provides an inspirational setting for the greater focus of choral mus and there are additional joint mus ventures with nearby girls' schools. Involvement in mus encouraged at all levels.
Pupils: 190 boarding; 21 day; 50 studying inst.
Termly fees: £2855 (day), £4275 (boarding).

Moira House School (Girls)
Upper Carlisle Rd, Eastbourne, Sussex BN20 7TE
Tel: 01323 644144 *Fax:* 01323 649720
Email: head@moirahouse.e-sussex.sch.uk
Website: www.moirahouse.e-sussex.sch.uk/moirahouse

A Harris, head; J Pendry, dir of mus.
Awards: Mus scholarships to the value of 50% fees awarded annually to girls who demonstrate a high level of musicianship on at least 1 inst, preferably 2 insts (including voice). *Exam boards:* SEG; MEG (1n 1999). *Exam candidates:* GCSE 15; A-level 4.
Musical activities: 2 orchs, wind ens, rcdr ens, groups, 6 choirs.
Pupils: 364 day and boarding; 140 studying inst.
Termly fees: £1350-2600 (day), £2820-3670 (wkly boarding), £3090-4030 (boarding).

Monkton Combe School (Co-ed)
Monkton Combe, Nr Bath, Avon BA2 7HG
Tel: 01225 721102 *Fax:* 01225 721181

M J Cuthbertson, head; B J Newman, dir of mus.
Awards: Up to 2 awards of 10-50% fees (augmentable in case of need) with free tuition on up to 2 insts. Age under 14 on 1 Sep; 2nd inst advisable. Singing accepted as additional or alternative inst. *Exam boards:* Edexcel (GCSE and A-level). *Exam candidates:* GCSE 9; A-level 3.
Musical activities: Choir, orch, choral society, big band, wind group, str quartet and other ens. House mus festival, professional concert series.
Pupils: 70 day; 275 boarding; 150 studying inst.
Termly fees: £2280 (day/form 1-2), £2800 (day/form 3-6), £3350 (boarding/form 1-2), £4065 (boarding/form 3-6).

Monmouth School (Boys)
Monmouth, Gwent NP5 3XP
Tel: 01600 713143 *Fax:* 01600 772701

Tim H P Haynes, head; Jeffrey Gray, dir of mus.
Awards: Mus scholarships at 11+, 13+ and 16+ up to value of 50% fees with free inst tuition. Former choristers welcomed. *Exam boards:* WJEC (GCSE); Edexcel (A-level). *Exam candidates:* GCSE 9; A-level 5.
Musical activities: New mus school with extensive facilities. Choral society (Handel *Judas Maccabeus*, Bach *St Matthew*, etc), chmbr choir, choral society, barbershop groups, symphony orch, 2 str orchs, 3 wind bands, swing band, chmbr mus. 8 professional concerts pa including 3 by BBC NOW, performances in Cardiff and Bristol with WNO. 1996 choir tour to Ireland, 1998 choir tour to Slovakia.
Pupils: 578 day and boarding; 300 studying inst. Prep school of 85 day boys. *Termly fees:* £1829 (day), £3047 (boarding).

Moreton Hall (Girls)
Weston Rhyn, Oswestry, Shrops SY11 3EW
Tel: 01691 773671 *Fax:* 01691 778552

Jonathan Forster, principal; Richard Meyer, head of mus.
Awards: 3 mus scholarships available, plus free tuition on 2 insts. Age 11-13 (approx gr 5) or VI form entry (gr 8). Several additional bursaries of free tuition on 2 insts. *Exam boards:* MEG (GCSE); NEAB (A-level). *Exam candidates:* GCSE 14; AS-level 1.
Musical activities: School orch, str orch, concert band, snr and jnr choirs, rock groups, br ens, w/wind ens and other chmbr mus groups.
Pupils: 280 boarding; 150 studying inst. *Termly fees:* £2900 (day), £4200 (boarding).

The Mount School (Girls)
Dalton Terrace, York YO2 4DD
Tel: 01904 667500 *Fax:* 01904 667524
Email: www.digital-yorkshire.co.uk/mount/

Barbara Windle, head; Derek Chivers, dir of mus.
Awards: Several awards offered, value up to 25% fees; standards required are 11+ gr 4; 13+ gr 6; 16+ gr 8+. *Exam boards:* NEAB (GCSE and A-level). *Exam candidates:* GCSE 9; A-level 2.
Musical activities: Orch, str orch, wind band, various chmbr groups, choirs, lunchtime concerts, elec mus studio, rock w/shops, opera alternate years.
Pupils: 205 day; 141 boarding; 189 studying inst.
Termly fees: £2085 (day), £3390 (boarding).

New Hall School (Girls)
Chelmsford, Essex CM3 3HT
Tel: 01245 467588 *Fax:* 01245 464348

Sister Anne-Marie, head; A Fardell, dir of mus.
Awards: VI form mus scholarship. 11+ mus scholarships. *Exam boards:* Southern (GCSE); Oxford (A-level). *Exam candidates:* GCSE 6; A-level 2.
Musical activities: Liturgical, chmbr, school choirs; snr and str orchs; wind and jnr ens, jazz group and rock group. Professional concert series.
Pupils: 248 day; 180 boarding; 150 prep school; 280 studying inst. *Termly fees:* £2310 (day), £3540 (wkly boarding); £3610 (boarding).

Norwich High School for Girls GDST (Girls)
95 Newmarket Rd, Norwich NR2 2HU
Tel: 01603 453265 *Fax:* 01603 259891

Mrs V C Bidwell, head; Mrs H Weiland, dir of mus.
Awards: 1 mus scholarship each year on entry to the snr school at 11+. This scholarship represents remission of a percentage of the academic fees. *Exam boards:* MEG (GCSE); UCLES (A-level). *Exam candidates:* GCSE 17; A-level 7.
Musical activities: 3 orchs, wind band, br group, 4 choirs, chmbr choir. Choral concerts in Norwich Cathedral, plus many other concerts and activities.
Pupils: 900 day; 206 studying inst. *Termly fees:* £996-1384.

Notting Hill and Ealing High School (Girls)
2 Cleveland Rd, Ealing, London W13 8AX
Tel: 0181 997 5744 *Fax:* 0181 810 6891

Susan Whitfield, head; Andrew Phillips, dir of mus.
Awards: 1 mus scholarship to snr school. *Exam boards:* Edexcel (GCSE); UCLES (A-level). *Exam candidates:* GCSE 11; A-level 4.
Musical activities: Madrigal choirs, chmbr orchs, fl sextet, rcdr ens. Madrigal choir tours Europe, St Paul's Cathedral Service.
Pupils: 830 day; 400+ studying inst. *Termly fees:* £1640 (day).

Oakham School (Co-ed)
Chapel Close, Oakham, Rutland, Leics LE15 6DT
Tel: 01572 722487 *Fax:* 01572 755786
Email: registrar@oakham.rutland.sch.uk
Website: www.oakhamsch.demon.co.uk

A Little, head; D N Woodcock, dir of mus.
Awards: Value varies from a percentage of academic tuition fee to full boarding fee. Age 11, 13, 16 entry; good gr 5 min on main inst expected for age 13 entry. All insts and singing considered. Choral boarding places available for Cathedral and Choir school choristers of value 15% of full fees; these may be held in addition to other

scholarships. *Exam boards:* MEG (GCSE); UCLES (A-level). *Exam candidates:* GCSE 9-12; A-level 4-6.
Musical activities: 4 orchs, concert band, big band, school choir, choral society, jnr choir, many smaller inst ens and singing groups. Mus dramatic productions, and many concerts organised in school and outside, also abroad.
Pupils: 1009 day and boarding; 450 studying inst.
Termly fees: £2480 (day), £4260 (boarding).

The Oratory School (Boys)
Woodcote, Nr Reading RG8 0PJ
Tel: 01491 680207 *Fax:* 01491 680020

S W Barrow, head; M J Crump, dir of mus.
Awards: Choral and inst scholarships value up to 50% fees available, with free tuition on 2 insts. Age under 14 on 1 Sep; gr 5 min on 1st inst, with 2nd inst or singing. *Exam boards:* MEG (GCSE); Edexcel (A-level). *Exam candidates:* GCSE 12; A-level 5.
Musical activities: Orch, str orch, chmbr mus ens, choir, very active mus society.
Pupils: 400 day and boarding; 175 studying inst.
Termly fees: £3010 (day), £4305 (boarding).

Oswestry School (Co-ed)
Oswestry, Shropshire SY11 2TL
Tel: 01691 655711 *Fax:* 01691 671194
Email: osschoolhm@aol.com

P K Smith, head; S J Morris, dir of mus.
Awards: Several inst bursaries. *Exam boards:* MEG (GCSE); UCLES (A/AS-level). *Exam candidates:* GCSE 5; A-level 1; AS-level 1.
Musical activities: 3 choirs, orch, 2 str ens, various inst ens, 2 concert bands. Lunchtime and professional recital series.
Pupils: 156 studying inst. *Termly fees:* £1783 (day/jnr), £2075 (day/snr), £3182 (boarding/jnr), £3483 (boarding/snr).

Oundle School (Co-ed)
Oundle, Peterborough PE8 4EN
Tel: 01832 272227 *also fax*

D B McMurray, head; Andrew Cleary, dir of mus.
Awards: 6 major scholarships; value 50% fees (1 for str player), plus various mus exhibitions and choral awards. Age under 14 on 1 Sep. *Exam boards:* Edexcel (A/AS-level), MEG (GCSE). *Exam candidates:* GCSE 21; A-level 12.
Musical activities: Choral society, chapel choir, schola cantorum, mus society, 3 orchs, 2 jazz bands; str, wind, br and pno ens; contemporary mus ens, RocSoc, elec mus studios, Oundle Concerts (professional concert series).
Pupils: 1050 day and boarding; 426 studying inst.
Termly fees: £2220 (day), £4640 (boarding).

Pangbourne College (Co-ed)
Pangbourne, Reading, Berks RG8 8LA
Tel: 0118 984 2101 *Fax:* 0118 984 5443

A B E Hudson, head; R J Barsby, dir of mus.
Awards: Several of up to 50% fees with free inst tuition offered annually. Age 11, 13 or VI form entry; test early Feb. Main inst with 2nd inst/voice expected; str players/cathedral choristers particularly welcome. *Exam boards:* MEG (GCSE); Edexcel (A-level). *Exam candidates:* GCSE 18; A-level 8.
Musical activities: 2 orchs; military, concert and jazz bands; chmbr groups. Chapel choir, chmbr choir, choral society, concert club, arts society; cathedral visits, European choir and concert band tours.
Pupils: 380 pupils; 199 studying inst. *Termly fees:* £2110-2910 (day), £3020-4160 (boarding).

Park School, Yeovil (Co-ed)
The Park, Yeovil, Somerset BA20 1DH
Tel: 01935 23514 *Fax:* 01935 411257

P Bate, head; Jo Jones, head of mus.
Awards: Mus scholarships at 8+, 11+ and 13+ of up to 50% fees. *Exam boards:* MEG (GCSE and A-level). *Exam candidates:* 4.
Musical activities: 3 choirs, orch.
Pupils: 132 day; 18 boarding; 75 studying inst. *Termly fees:* £590-1660 (day), £2600-2900 (boarding).

Plymouth College (Co-ed)
Ford Park, Plymouth PL4 6RN
Tel: 01752 203300 ext 36 (mus dept) *Fax:* 01752 203246

A J Morsley, head; S J Oxley, dir of mus.
Awards: 1 open scholarship (for 13+ entry) of up to £1200 pa. 1 open scholarship (for VI form entry) of up to £1200 pa. *Exam boards:* NEAB (GCSE). *Exam candidates:* GCSE 4; A-level 5; Diploma 4.
Musical activities: Symphony orch, main and jnr choirs, Schola Cantorum, jnr strs, snr and jnr wind bands, jazz band, rock groups, str quartet, wind quintet, cl choir, fl choir, sax ens, gui ens, br ens.
Pupils: 605 day and boarding; 150 studying inst. *Termly fees:* £1712 (day), £3342 (boarding).

Pocklington School (Co-ed)
West Green, Pocklington, York YO4 2NJ
Tel: 01759 303125 *Fax:* 01759 306366
Email: pocklington.school@dial.pipex.com

J N D Gray, head; J P Bird, dir of mus.
Awards: Mus scholarships from £1000 pa and/or free inst tuition. Age under 14 on 1 Sep; gr 5 min on 1st inst with 2nd inst an advantage. *Exam boards:* MEG, NEAB (GCSE); Oxford, SEG (A-level). *Exam candidates:* GCSE 20; A-level 6-10.
Musical activities: Mus society, orchs and choirs,

chmbr choir, swing band, snr str orch, variety of chmbr ens, rock band.
Pupils: 600 day; 150 boarding; 200 studying inst. *Termly fees:* £1703 (day), £2968 (boarding).

Polam Hall (Girls)
Darlington, Co Durham DL1 5PA
Tel: 01325 463383 *Fax:* 01325 383539

Mrs H Hamilton, head; Mrs E Sleightholme, dir of mus.
Awards: Awards with free inst tuition available at age 11+, 13+, 16+. *Exam boards:* NEAB (GCSE); UCLES (A/AS-level). *Exam candidates:* GCSE 9; A/AS-level 3.
Musical activities: Jnr and snr choirs, jnr and snr orchs, wind band, str and wind ens, musical alternate years.
Pupils: Snr school (age 11-18) 342 day and boarding; 130 studying inst. Prep school (age 4-11) 128 pupils; 78 studying inst. *Termly fees:* £656-1010 (day/jnr), £1422 (day/snr), £2350 (boarding/jnr), £2908 (boarding/snr).

The Portsmouth Grammar School (Co-ed)
High St, Portsmouth, Hants PO1 2LN
Tel: 01705 819125 *Fax:* 01705 870184

T R Hands, head; D J Swinson, dir of mus.
Awards: VI form mus scholarships; free mus tuition for mus A-level pupils; 50% mus fees for mus A-level pupils; 3rd form mus scholarships. *Exam boards:* SEG, UCLES. *Exam candidates:* GCSE 15; A-level 2; AS-level 1.
Musical activities: Concert band, swing band, choral society, chmbr choir, close harmony group, barbershop group, chmbr orch, jnr orch and middle school choir.
Pupils: 830 day; 200 studying inst. Prep school is Portsmouth Grammar Lower School. *Termly fees:* £1680 (day).

The Princess Helena College (Girls)
Preston, Hitchin, Herts SG4 7RT
Tel: 01462 432100 *Fax:* 01462 431497
Email: head@phc.zynet.co.uk

A-M Hodgkiss, acting head; Cynthia Neaum, dir of mus.
Awards: Available at 11+, 12+, 13+ and VI form entry. Candidates should be gr 3+ on main inst at 11+ and 12+; gr 5+ at 13+ and VI form. *Exam boards:* MEG, NEAB. *Exam candidates:* GCSE 8; A-level 1.
Musical activities: Orchs, snr and jnr choirs, school choral society, chmbr choir, jazz ens, rcdr consort, handbell ens, fl ens, wind ens.
Pupils: 150 day and boarding; 85 studying inst. *Termly fees:* £2030-3645.

248

Prior Park College (Co-ed)
Bath, Avon BA2 5AH
Tel: 01225 835353 *Fax:* 01225 835753

Giles Mercer, head; Roland Robertson, dir of mus.
Awards: Jnr mus scholarships for entry at 11+, major mus scholarships for entry at 13+ and VI form scholarships. Generous reductions of fees available at all levels. *Exam boards:* MEG (GCSE); Edexcel, UCLES (A-level). *Exam candidates:* GCSE 10; A-level 2.
Musical activities: Choral society, 3 chapel choirs, chmbr choir, orch, concert band, str ens, jazz band, rock bands, chmbr groups; 2 musicals performed annually.
Pupils: 357 day; 148 boarding; 220 studying inst. *Termly fees:* £2030 (day/11+), £2120 (day/13+), £3833 (boarding).

Prior's Field School (Girls)
Godalming, Surrey GU7 2RH
Tel: 01483 810551 *Fax:* 01483 810180
Email: admin@priorsfield.demon.co.uk

Mrs J M McCallum, head; Miss C C Harrisson, dir of mus.
Awards: 1 mus scholarship at 25% or 2 at 15% and 10% respectively of the fees may be awarded annually at 11+ or 16+ entry. At 11+, gr 4-5 on 1st inst, at 16+, gr 8 expected. *Exam boards:* Edexcel, UCLES (GCSE and A-level). *Exam candidates:* GCSE 10; A-level 1.
Musical activities: Orch, chmbr orch, choir, jnr chmbr choir, snr chmbr choir, vocal ens.
Pupils: 227; 120 studying inst. *Termly fees:* £2430 (day), £3635 (boarding).

Queen Anne's School (Girls)
Caversham, Reading, Berks RG4 6DX
Tel: 0118 947 1582 *Fax:* 0118 946 1498

Mrs D Forbes, head; Miss F Brewitt-Taylor, dir of mus.
Awards: 1 mus scholarship of 50% fees. Additional bursaries including free tuition on 2 insts. *Exam boards:* MEG (GCSE); Edexcel (A-level). *Exam candidates:* GCSE 6; A-level 2.
Musical activities: School orch, chmbr mus, chapel, concert and jnr choirs, training orch, stage productions, joint activities with other schools and m/classes.
Pupils: 125 day; 180 boarding; 200 studying inst. *Termly fees:* £2720 (day), £4155 (boarding).

Queen Elizabeth's Grammar School (Boys)+
Blackburn, Lancs BB2 6DF
Tel: 01254 59911 *Fax:* 01254 692314

D S Hempsall, head; G R Hill, dir of mus.
Awards: Discretionary bursaries are awarded for free inst tuition. *Exam boards:* NEAB (GCSE and A-level). *Exam candidates:* GCSE 5; A-level 5.
Musical activities: Choral society, chmbr and jnr choirs, orch, wind and swing bands, ens.
Pupils: 1000 day; 200+ studying inst. *Termly fees:* £1463 (day).

Queen Elizabeth's Hospital School (Boys)
Berkeley Pl, Clifton, Bristol BS8 1JX
Tel: 0117 929 1856 *Fax:* 0117 929 3106

R Gliddon, head; Richard Jones, dir of mus.
Awards: 3 mus scholarships available; 2 at age 11+, 1 offering 50% fee remission plus free tuition in 2 insts, 1 offering free tuition in 2 insts; 1 at age 13+ offering 50% fee remission plus free tuition in 2 insts. *Exam boards:* UCLES, MEG (GCSE and A-level). *Exam candidates:* GCSE 10; A-level 3.
Musical activities: School orch, choir, chapel choir; wind, br and str ens; wind band, training band; occasional TV and radio work, joint concerts with neighbouring independent schools.
Pupils: 425 day; 80 boarding; 170+ studying inst. *Termly fees:* £1445 (day), £2633 (boarding).

Queen Ethelburga's College (Girls)
Thorpe Underwood Hall, Ouseburn, York YO5 9SZ
Tel: 01423 331480 *Fax:* 01423 331007
Email: remember@compuserve.com
Website: www.queenethelburgas.edu

Mrs E I E Taylor, principal; S Jandrell, dir of mus.
Awards: Discretionary mus scholarship, value £1500 pa. *Exam boards:* NEAB (GCSE); UCLES (A/AS-level). *Exam candidates:* GCSE 4; A-level 2.
Musical activities: Choirs, orch, str and wind ens, handbells, gui ens, recorder ens, early mus group, annual competitions and productions, visiting professional recitalists.
Pupils: 350 day and boarding; 90 studying inst. *Termly fees:* £1775-2295 (day), £3499-3999 (boarding).

Queen Margaret's School (Girls)
Escrick Pk, York YO4 6EU
Tel: 01904 728261 *Fax:* 01904 728150

G Chapman, head; S Nettleship, dir of mus.
Awards: Several mus scholarships available up to 33% fees at 11+, 12+, 13+ and 16+ entry. Approx gr 4-6, according to age. *Exam boards:* Edexcel (GCSE), NEAB (A-level). *Exam candidates:* 7.
Musical activities: 2 orchs, 2 bands, various ens, chapel choir, choral society, jnr choir, vocal groups, chmbr mus groups, rock bands, str orchs, regular collaborations with drama.
Pupils: 30 day; 336 boarding; 180 studying inst. *Termly fees:* £2390 (day), £3772 (boarding).

Queen Mary's School (Girls)
Baldersby Pk, Topcliffe, Thirsk, N Yorks YO7 3BZ
Tel: 01845 577425 *Fax:* 01845 577368

Margaret and Ian Angus, heads; N Carter, dir of mus.

Awards: 2 jnr mus scholarships of up to 33% fees; plus free inst tuition for 1 inst. Age 11, gr 3 min (1st inst), or age 12, gr 4 (1st inst), 2nd inst or voice an advantage. Also 1 snr scholarship value 33% fees plus free inst tuition for 2 insts, age 13, gr 5 min (1st inst), 2nd inst or voice expected. Awards may also be made to children age under 11, according to mus potential. *Exam boards:* SEG (GCSE). *Exam candidates:* GCSE 6.
Musical activities: Orch, str orch, various chmbr ens; chapel choir (sings in York Minster, Ripon Cathedral), 3 other choirs. School competes in local and national festivals; also affiliated to RSCM. Regular concerts by pupils and visiting professionals.
Pupils: 225 day and boarding; 175 studying inst. *Termly fees:* £670-1000 (pre-prep), £1495-1620 (day/prep), £1855 (day/snr), £2605-2755 (wkly boarding), £2655-2815 (boarding/prep), £2975 (boarding/snr).

Queen's College (London) (Girls)
43-49 Harley St, London W1N 2BT
Tel: 0171 580 1533/1115 *Fax:* 0171 436 7607
Email: pioneers@queens.dircon.co.uk

The Hon Lady Goodhart, head; Miss C Lax, dir of mus (admin); R Taylor, dir of mus (academic).
Awards: One 2-yr scholarship available at Lower VI. Some bursaries for free inst tuition at any age. *Exam boards:* Edexcel (GCSE and A-level). *Exam candidates:* GCSE 18; A-level 6.
Musical activities: 2 orchs, 3 choirs, rcdr ens, br ens, concerts (chmbr mus ens, etc), visiting lecture recitals, and outings to concerts.
Pupils: 386 day; 151 studying inst. *Termly fees:* £1940 (day).

Queen's College (Taunton) (Co-ed)
Taunton, Somerset TA1 4QS
Tel: 01823 272559 *Fax:* 01823 338430

C T Bradnock, head; S C Bell, dir of mus.
Awards: 8 mus awards of not more than 50% fees. Age over 10 and under 14 on 1 Sep; plus VI form entry. *Exam boards:* SEG (GCSE); Edexcel (A-level). *Exam candidates:* GCSE 12; A-level 3.
Musical activities: Orch, chmbr orch, chapel choir, band, madrigal group, chmbr mus, choral society, br ens.
Pupils: 700 day and boarding; 220 studying inst. *Termly fees:* £2202 (day), £3360 (boarding).

Queenswood School (Girls)
Shepherds Way, Brookmans Pk, Hatfield, Herts AL9 6NS
Tel: 01707 652262 *Fax:* 01707 649267
Email: registry@queenswood.herts.sch.uk

Clarissa Farr, principal; Neil Bell, dir of mus.
Awards: Mus scholarships offered, value up to 50% fees, for years 7, 8, 9 and VI form entry.

Winifred Turner Bequest, up to 66% fees also available biennially (next 1998). *Exam boards:* MEG (GCSE); Edexcel (A-level). *Exam candidates:* GCSE 9; A-level 4; AS-level 1.
Musical activities: 3 choirs including chmbr choir Queenswood Singers, orch, wind band, str ens and numerous chmbr groups. Annual singing competition and VI form mus competition; professional concert series; elec mus facilities; musician in residence.
Pupils: 81 day; 324 boarding; 200 studying inst or voice. *Termly fees:* £2358-2569 (day), £3823-4165 (boarding).

Radley College (Boys)
Abingdon, Oxon OX14 2HR
Tel: 01235 543000 *Fax:* 01235 543106

Richard Morgan, warden; John Madden, dir of mus.
Awards: 2 value 50% fees; 2 value 33% fees; and 1 value 25% fees are offered, plus several exhibitions. Age under 14 on 1 Sep. Gr 6-7 for scholarships, gr 5 for exhibitions (less may be accepted with evidence of keen, intelligent musicianship). All scholarships include free inst tuition. *Exam boards:* MEG (GCSE); Edexcel (A-level). *Exam candidates:* GCSE 13; A-level 4.
  Musical activities: Orch, chapel choir, choral society, chmbr choir; wind bands, dance bands; many ens and chmbr groups. Regular mus trips. Close partnership with the school of St Helen and Katherine, Abingdon and Our Ladys Convent Senior School.
Pupils: 623 boarding; 300 studying inst. *Termly fees:* £4550 (boarding).

Reading Blue Coat School (Boys) +
Holme Pk, Sonning, Reading RG4 6SU
Tel: 0118 944 1005 *Fax:* 0118 944 2690

S J McArthur, head; Jonathan Bowler, dir of mus.
Awards: Mus scholarships and bursaries up to 30% academic tuition fees and free tuition on 1 inst at 11, 13 and VI form entry. *Exam boards:* MEG (GCSE); Edexcel (A-level). *Exam candidates:* GCSE 15; A-level 6.
Musical activities: Choir, orch, concert band, jnr band, Stompers, swing band, jnr jazz, chmbr mus, rock and pop groups and annual musicals.
Pupils: 607 day and boarding; 200+ studying inst. *Termly fees:* £1838 (day), £3245 (wkly boarding), £3350 (boarding).

Red Maids' School (Girls)
Westbury-on-Trym, Bristol BS9 3AW
Tel: 0117 962 2641 *Fax:* 0117 962 1687

Stephen J M Browne, dir of mus.
Awards: 2 mus scholarships to cover the cost of lessons on 2 insts to be taken at the school. The major scholarship also includes a reduction in

tuition fees. *Exam boards:* MEG (GCSE); NEAB (A-level). *Exam candidates:* GCSE 10; A-level 3. *Musical activities:* 2 orchs, wind band, rcdr consort, chmbr orch, 4 choirs. *Pupils:* c 200. *Termly fees:* £1360 (day); £2720 (boarding); £114 (mus per inst).

Redland High School for Girls (Girls)
Redland Ct, Bristol BS6 7EF
Tel: 0117 924 5796 *Fax:* 0117 924 1127

Carol Lear, headmistress; Nigel Davies, dir of mus. *Awards:* 2 of value 50% fees and tuition on 2 insts, available at 11+, 13+, 16+. *Exam boards:* MEG (GCSE); Edexcel (A-level). *Exam candidates:* GCSE 14; A-level 4. *Musical activities:* 4 choirs, 3 orchs, swing band, wind band, 4 chmbr ens, regular concerts, local evensongs. *Pupils:* 484 day, 150 studying inst. *Termly fees:* £1477.

Reed's School (Boys)+
Cobham, Surrey KT11 2ES
Tel: 01932 863076 *Fax:* 01932 869046
Email: hm@reeds.surrey.sch.uk
Website: www.reeds.surrey.sch.uk

David Jarrett, head; Richard Coulson, dir of mus. *Awards:* At 11+, min gr 3 on 1st inst and a pleasing voice with some choral experience would be an advantage. At 13+ min gr 5 on 1st

inst, with 2nd inst/singing an advantage. Preference given to choristers. Max value of all awards 50% fees. *Exam boards:* SEG (GCSE); UCLES (A-level). *Exam candidates:* GCSE 10; A-level 2. *Musical activities:* Choral society, chapel choir, wind band, br ens, chmbr ens, male voice part-song group and jazz band. *Pupils:* 250 day; 150 boarding; 100+ studying inst. *Termly fees:* £2384 (day/jnr), £2845 (day/snr), £3179 (boarding/jnr), £3764 (boarding/snr).

Rendcomb College (Co-ed)
Cirencester, Glos GL7 7HA
Tel: 01285 831213 *Fax:* 01285 831331

J N Tolputt, head; David White, dir of mus. *Awards:* 1 major scholarship, value up to £4200 pa; 2 scholarships, value up to £2400 pa; 4 minor scholarships, value £600. Scholarships open to any pupil joining college at 11, 13 or 16. *Exam boards:* MEG (GCSE); Oxford (A-level); Edexcel (A-level performance); UCLES (A-level performing arts). *Exam candidates:* GCSE 11; A/AS-level 6. *Musical activities:* Purpose built mus dept; college and chapel choirs, dixieland jazz, br, wind and str ens. *Pupils:* 60 day; 182 boarding; 125 studying inst. *Termly fees:* £2250-2990 (day), £2940-3780 (boarding).

Repton School (Co-ed)
Repton, Derbys DE65 6FH
Tel: 01283 559200 *Fax:* 01283 559210

G E Jones, head; Richard Dacey, dir of mus.
Awards: Scholarships of 25-50% fees, plus exhibitions, bursaries and tuition awards at 13+ and 16+. Usually gr 5-8 on 1st inst, with 2nd inst/voice, but musical ability and potential are more important. *Exam boards:* NEAB (GCSE); Edexcel (A-level). *Exam candidates:* GCSE 9; A-level 5.
Musical activities: Orch, str orch, concert band, chapel choir, choral society, chmbr mus groups and br ens.
Pupils: 560 day and boarding; 170 learning inst.
Termly fees: £3040 (day), £4040 (boarding).

Roedean School (Girls)
Roedean Way, Brighton BN2 5RQ
Tel: 01273 603181 *Fax:* 01273 680791
Email: roedean@offiah.demon.co.uk

Patricia Metham, head; Veronica Fewkes, head of academic mus.
Awards: Mus scholarships value 50% fees. Age under 14 on 1 Sep or VI form entry. *Exam boards:* Edexcel (GCSE and A-level). *Exam candidates:* 8.
Musical activities: 3 school orchs, 4 choirs, str orch, wind band, chmbr mus and jazz band.
Pupils: 420 pupils; 300 studying inst. *Termly fees:* £2900 (day); £4775 (boarding).

Rossall School (Co-ed)
Fleetwood, Lancs FY7 8JW
Tel: 01253 774200 *Fax:* 01253 772052

R D W Rhodes, head; Stephen H Carleston, dir of mus.
Awards: Up to 6 mus scholarships offered, value 15-75% fees with free inst tuition. Age 11, 13, or 16; vocal ability an asset. *Exam boards:* MEG (GCSE); Edexcel (A-level). *Exam candidates:* GCSE 12; A-level 4.
Musical activities: Chapel choir, orch, concert band, jazz band, choral society, chmbr choir, professional concert series, plus other smaller groups.
Pupils: 350 boarding/day; 130 studying inst. *Termly fees:* £1620 (day), £2730-4030 (boarding).

Royal Grammar School (Worcester) (Boys)
Upper Tything, Worcester WR1 1HP
Tel: 01905 613391 *Fax:* 01905 726892
Email: rgsw2@aol.com

W A Jones, head; J E Smith, dir of mus.
Awards: Scholarship value 33% fees plus free inst tuition; also exhibitions with free inst tuition. Age 13+, gr 5. *Exam boards:* MEG (GCSE); Oxford (A-level). *Exam candidates:* GCSE 6; A-level 2.
Musical activities: Orch, band, big band, main choir (80+), madrigal group, early mus consort, baroque ens, prep choir, orch, etc. Many concerts, annual trip abroad.
Pupils: 922 day; 125 studying inst. *Termly fees:* £1296-1614.

Royal Grammar School, Guildford (Boys)
High St, Guildford, Surrey GU1 3BB
Tel: 01483 502424 *Fax:* 01483 306127
Email: staff@rgs.netkonect.co.uk
Website: www.rgs-guildford.co.uk

Tim Young, head; Peter White, dir of mus.
Awards: 8 mus scholarships offered (1 of 50% fees, 2 of 25% fees, 5 of 10% fees). Age under 14 on 1 Sep; gr 6 on 1st inst, gr 3 on 2nd inst; str ability an additional recommendation. *Exam boards:* MEG (GCSE); Edexcel (A-level). *Exam candidates:* GCSE 10; A-level 2; AS-level 2.
Musical activities: Guildford Sinfonia (main orch), chmbr orchs, big band, concert band, wind quintet, 2 str quartets; also br group, jazz group, chmbr choir and choral society. Termly professional lunchtime concerts.
Pupils: 850 day; 220 studying inst. Prep school is Lanesborough School *see* **Choir Schools**. *Termly fees:* £2085 (day).

The Royal High School, GDST (Girls)
Lansdown Rd, Bath BA1 5SZ
Tel: 01225 313877

Margaret Winfield, head.
Awards: Scholarships awarded (up to 50% fees). Minor awards of free tuition. Bursaries also available. Exam in Nov or Jan. Gr 4+ at age 11, gr 5+ at age 13 and gr 7+ at age 16. Other bursaries and scholarships also available. *Exam boards:* Midland (GCSE); London (A-Level).
Musical activities: 4 choirs, orch, wind ens, str ens. Termly performances. Competitions entered.
Pupils: 470 day; 150 boarding. *Termly fees:* £1962 (day); £3667 (boarding).

Royal Hospital School (Co-ed)
Ipswich IP9 2RX
Tel: 01473 326200 *Fax:* 01473 326213

Nicholas Ward, head; Peter Crompton, dir of mus.
Awards: Mus scholarships awarded each year worth up to 50% school fees. Also 10 exhibitions awarded each year. *Exam boards:* Edexcel, O&C.
Exam candidates: GCSE 10; A-level 3.
Musical activities: Chapel choir, choral society, chmbr choir, band, orch, ens. Regular musical productions, house singing competition, mus society.
Pupils: 660; 250 studying inst. *Termly fees:* £3016.

Royal Wolverhampton School (Co-ed)

Penn Rd, Wolverhampton, W Midlands WV3 0EG
Tel: 01902 341230 *Fax:* 01902 344496

Mrs B A Evans, head; Mrs C Fellows, dir of mus dept.
Awards: Mus scholarships offered to snr school pupils max of 25% day fees and tuition in 1 inst. Various other scholarships also available. *Exam boards:* MEG (GCSE); O&C (A-level). *Exam candidates:* GCSE 12; A-level 2.
Musical activities: Chapel choir, choral society, internal mus competitions, regular mus productions, pop group, ens groups, keyboard club.
Pupils: 600 day and boarding; 247 studying inst.
Termly fees: £860-1795 (day), £2870-3515 (boarding).

Rugby School (Co-ed)

Rugby, Warwicks CV22 5EH
Tel: 01788 543465 *Fax:* 01788 579745

Michael Mavor, head; Peter Crook, dir of mus.
Awards: Generous funding for mus scholarships (from bursaries of free inst tuition to major awards, may be supplemented in cases of need) for pupils entering at 13+ and the VI form. *Exam boards:* MEG, WJEC (GCSE); Edexcel, O&C, UCLES (A-level). *Exam candidates:* GCSE 10; A-level 4.

Musical activities: 1st orch, 2nd orch, str sinfonia, chmbr orch, concert wind band, swing and jazz bands, br ens, chapel choir, chmbr choir, chmbr ens. Musicals produced. Subscription concerts for visiting celebrities.
Pupils: 680 day and boarding; 300 studying inst.
Termly fees: £2275-2880 (day), £4090 (boarding).

Rydal Penrhos Co-educational Division (Co-ed)

Pwllycrochan Av, Colwyn Bay, N Wales LL29 7BT
Tel: 01492 530155 *Fax:* 01492 531872
Email: rydal@rmplc.co.uk

N W Thorne, head; Mrs M Ireland, dir of mus.
Awards: 1 or more scholarships value up to 33% fees with free tuition in 1 inst. Age over 11, under 16 on 1 Sep; potential and enthusiasm sought. Foundation awards have been introduced to replace the former assisted places scheme. *Exam boards:* Edexcel (GCSE and A-level). *Exam candidates:* GCSE 13.
Musical activities: Orch, band, 3 choirs, choral society. Rydal Penrhos Preparatory School has similar facilities.
Pupils: 221 day; 183 boarding; 150 studying inst.
Termly fees: £2226-2586 (day/snr), £3087-3620 (boarding/snr).

Rydal Penrhos Senior Girls' Division (Girls)

Colwyn Bay, N Wales LL28 4DA
Tel: 01492 530333 *Fax:* 01492 533198
Email: penrhos@rmplc.co.uk

C M J Allen, head; C Enston, dir of mus.
Awards: Up to 2 mus scholarships pa, value 50% fees plus inst tuition. Any age (11-VI form) eligible: proficiency in 2 insts required, with gr 4+ (age 11), gr 6+ (age 16) expected. Str players preferred. *Exam boards:* NEAB (GCSE); UCLES (A-level). *Exam candidates:* GCSE 5; A-level 2; AS-level 1-2.
Musical activities: Main school orch, training orch, str quartets, snr and jnr choirs; perc, w/wind, rcdr groups.
Pupils: 105 day; 118 boarding; 103 studying inst. *Termly fees:* £2179-2331 (day), £3040-3435 (boarding).

St Albans High School (Girls)

3 Townsend Av, St Albans, Herts AL1 3SJ
Tel: 01727 853800 *Fax:* 01727 845011

Mrs C Y Daly, head; Nigel Springthorpe, dir of mus.
Awards: 1 mus scholarship at 11+ entry plus occasional bursaries. *Exam boards:* Edexcel (GCSE); UCLES (A/AS-level). *Exam candidates:* GCSE 12; A/AS-level 4.
Musical activities: 3 orchs, 2 bands, 6 other ens, 5 choirs, choral society.
Pupils: 715 day; 325 studying inst. *Termly fees:* £1680 (day).

St Antony's-Leweston School (Girls)

Sherborne, Dorset DT9 6EN
Tel: 01963 210691 *Fax:* 01963 210786

Miss B King, head; Jane Stein, dir of mus.
Awards: Variable number of mus awards towards school fees, plus free inst tuition. Age 11-13 or VI form entry. *Exam boards:* MEG (GCSE); Oxford (A-level). *Exam candidates:* GCSE 6; A-level 2.
Musical activities: 4 orchs, 3 choirs, chmbr mus ens, annual choral performance and mus production activities in conjunction with other Sherborne schools.
Pupils: 245 day and boarding; 154 studying inst. *Termly fees:* £2546 (day), £3900 (boarding).

St Bede's (Co-ed)

The Dicker, Hailsham, Essex
Tel: 01323 843252 *Fax:* 01323 442628

Andrew Barclay, dir of mus.
Awards: Up to 6 awards. *Exam boards:* SEG (GCSE); Edexcel (A-level). *Exam candidates:* GCSE 18; A-level 5.
Musical activities: Choir, chmbr choir, orch, chmbr mus groups, str orch, wind band, jazz and

---

pop groups.
Pupils: 210 day; 290 boarding; 110 studying inst.
Termly fees: £2500 (day), £4150 (boarding).

St Bees School (Co-ed)
St Bees, Cumbria CA27 0DS
Tel: 01946 822263 *Fax:* 01946 823657
Email: 101602.300@compuserve.com

Mrs J D Pickering, head; H M Turpin, dir of mus.
Awards: Mus scholarships of up to 50% fees
available. Age under 12 or under 14 on 1 Sep, or
VI form entry. Under 12, gr 3 on 1st inst; under
14, gr 5; VI form, gr 7. 2nd inst desirable at all
ages; singing an advantage. *Exam boards:* MEG
(GCSE); UCLES (A-level). *Exam candidates:* GCSE
8; A-level 5.
Musical activities: Orch, ens, wind band, choral
society, choirs, madrigal group, jazz group,
electronic mus studio.
Pupils: 290 day and boarding; 90 studying inst.
Termly fees: £2162 (day/jnr), £2665 (day/snr),
£2834 (boarding/jnr), £3874 (boarding/snr).

St Catherine's School (Girls)
Bramley, Guildford, Surrey GU5 0DF
Tel: 01483 893363 *Fax:* 01483 893003

Mrs C M Oulton, head; R E Gillman, dir of mus.
Awards: 2 mus scholarships up to 30% fees (11+,

VI form), 4 str awards (age 10), 8 choral awards
(age 15-18), 8 various awards for less familiar
insts and for general excellence. *Exam boards:*
Edexcel (GCSE and A-level). *Exam candidates:*
GCSE 15; A-level 4; AS-level 1.
Musical activities: 6 choirs, orch, 2 concert bands,
chmbr ens.
Pupils: 556 day; 138 boarding; 320 studying inst.
Termly fees: £1105 (reception), £1340
(kindergarten), £1580 (transitional), £1825
(day/jnr), £2210 (day/middle snr), £3265
(boarding/jnr), £3630 (boarding/middle snr).

St David's College (Boys)
Gloddaeth Hall, Llandudno LL30 1RD
Tel: 01492 876702 *Fax:* 01492 870383
Email: sdc@llandudno.co.uk
Website: www.llandudno.co.uk/sdc

William Seymour, head; Mark Q Dunnington,
head of mus.
Awards: Inst scholarships of up to 25% fees with
free inst tuition at 11+ and 13+. *Exam boards:* WJEC
(GCSE and A-level). *Exam candidates:* GCSE 4-6.
Musical activities: Orch, choir, jazz band, regular
concerts.
Pupils: 75 day; 135 boarding; 52 studying inst.
Termly fees: £2164-2268 (day); £3327-3488
(boarding).

St Dunstan's College
Music Scholarship & Awards

A Music Scholarship of up to half fees with
free tuition in one instrument is offered to
girls and boys at 11+ who qualify
academically for entry into the school.
Two Music Awards covering tuition in one
instrument are also available.

Music Scholars are expected to play a full role
in the school's musical activities.

The Director of Music, Mr Norman Harper,
will be pleased to advise applicants on the
standards expected.

*For a Prospectus and information about
Open Days please contact the Registrar on*
0181 516 7234

St Dunstan's College, Stanstead Road, London SE6 4TY
HMC Co-educational Independent Day School for Ages 4–18
Registered charity number 312747

ST EDWARD'S SCHOOL OXFORD

Generous scholarships and exhibitions are
awarded annually for both 13+ and 16+ entry.

A music staff of 34 oversees both academic
studies to GCSE, Advanced, University
and Music College entrance levels and
instrumental studies on a wide range of
orchestral and non-orchestral instruments.
In addition there are two Orchestras, a large
programme of Chamber Music, a Jazz Band,
Big Band, Concert Band and three Choirs.
Many concerts are given each term.

The Director of Music,
Anthony Kerr-Dineen, welcomes enquiries
about all musical acitivities at St Edward's.

*The Ferguson Music School,
St Edward's, Oxford, OX2 7NN.
Telephone: (01865) 319217*

St Dunstan's College (Co-ed)
Stanstead Rd, Catford, London SE6 4TY
Tel: 0181 690 1274; 0181 516 7272 *Fax:* 0181 314 0242
Email: stduncol@mail.rmplc.co.uk

D I Davies, head; Norman Harper, dir of mus.
Awards: 1 mus scholarship of 33% of full fees plus
mus tuition; 2 exhibitions with free mus tuition at
age 11+. *Exam boards:* Edexcel (GCSE and
A-level). *Exam candidates:* GCSE 6; A-level 1;
AS-level 3.
Musical activities: 4 choirs, choral society, 2
orchs, 2 br ens, 2 jazz bands, perc group, 2 wind
groups, close harmony choir, chmbr ens, gui
group.
Pupils: 960 day; 186 studying inst. *Termly fees:*
£1920 (day).

St Edmund's College (Co-ed)
Old Hall Green, Ware, Herts SG11 1DS
Tel: 01920 821504 *Fax:* 01920 823011
Email: registrar@secware.demon.co.uk

Donald McEwen, head; N D Howard, head of mus.
Awards: Mus scholarships value up to 33% fees
available. *Exam boards:* MEG (GCSE); Edexcel
(A-level). *Exam candidates:* GCSE 5; A-level 1.
Musical activities: School orch, wind band, choral
activities, inst ens.
Pupils: 520 pupils; 140+ studying inst. *Termly fees:*
£1795-2160 (day), £2610-3196 (wkly boarding),
£2780-3440 (boarding).

St Edmund's School (Co-ed)
Canterbury CT2 8HU
Tel: 01227 454575 *Fax:* 01227 471083

A N Ridley, head; I P Sutcliffe, dir of mus.
Awards: Several scholarships and exhibitions
worth up to 50% fees according to merit
(candidates are considered at any stage between
the ages of 11 and 16). 1 scholarship worth 50%
boarding fees for Canterbury chorister, gr 5-6.
Separate org scholarship. *Exam boards:* SEG
(GCSE); Edexcel (A-level). *Exam candidates:* GCSE
16; A-level 3.
Musical activities: Strong mus tradition:
symphony orch, str orchs, choral society, chapel
choir, jnr choir, madrigal group, wind and jazz
bands, chmbr ens (special timetables for mus
scholars). Staff and facilities shared by jnr and
snr schools.
Pupils: 339 day; 159 boarding; 240 studying inst.
Termly fees: £2163 (day/jnr), £2863 (day/snr),
£3090 (boarding/jnr), £4420 (boarding/snr). *See
also* **Choir Schools.**

St Edward's College *see* **Choir Schools (Co-ed)**

St Edward's School (Co-ed) +
Woodstock Rd, Oxford OX2 7NN
Tel: 01865 319200 *Fax:* 01865 319206

D Christie, warden; Anthony Kerr-Dineen, dir of mus.
Awards: Awards up to 50% fees plus free tuition
(may be supplemented in cases of need). Age
under 14 on 1 Sep; proficiency in org, pno or an
orch inst with 2nd inst expected (voice may be
offered by itself or as 2nd inst). Special
consideration to str players. VI form mus
scholarship also available. *Exam boards:* SEG
(GCSE); Edexcel (A-level). *Exam candidates:* GCSE
and A-level 25.
Musical activities: School symphony orch, chmbr
orch, concert band plus smaller groups including
big bands and jazz bands. Chapel choir with
regular concerts, chmbr choir, choral society,
regular mus productions and opera. Mus society
with talks, trips, concerts, etc.
Pupils: 570 mostly boarding, some day; 375
studying inst. *Termly fees:* £3200 (day), £4475
(boarding).

St Elphin's School (Girls)
Darley Dale, Matlock, Derbys DE4 2HA
Tel: 01629 733263 *Fax:* 01629 733956

Mrs V Fisher, head; A Teague, dir of mus.
Awards: 2 mus bursaries of £1500 pa, plus free
inst tuition in 2 insts. *Exam boards:* Edexcel
(GCSE and A-level). *Exam candidates:* GCSE 13;
A-level 2.
Musical activities: Orch, 4 choirs, str, w/wind, br
groups.
Pupils: 156 day; 81 boarding; 104 studying inst.
Termly fees: £1980 (day/snr), £3399
(boarding/snr).

St Felix School (Girls)
Southwold, Suffolk IP18 6SD
Tel: 01502 722175 *Fax:* 01502 722641

Mrs S R Campion, head; V Scott, dir of mus.
Awards: Hess mus scholarship, min value 33%
fees; orch exhibitions (free inst tuition). *Exam
boards:* Edexcel (GCSE and A-level). *Exam
candidates:* GCSE 17; A-level 3.
Musical activities: Chmbr orch, inst ens, choral
society, chapel choir, barbershop groups, str
orchs and ens.
Pupils: 200 day and boarding; 100 studying inst.
Termly fees: £2400 (day), £3700 (boarding).

St John's School (Boys) +
Leatherhead, Surrey KT22 8SP
Tel: 01372 372021 *Fax:* 01372 386606

C H Tongue, head; P S Lutton, dir of mus (to Sep
1998); B Noithip, dir of mus (from Sep 1998).
Awards: 1 mus scholarship value 50% tuition fees

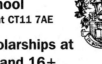

and 2 exhibitions value 25% tuition fees (13+); 1 mus scholarship value 50% tuition fees and 1 mus exhibition value 25% tuition fees (lower VI entry). Approx gr 5 on any inst with vocal excellence an advantage. *Exam boards:* MEG (GCSE); Edexcel (A-level). *Exam candidates:* GCSE 4; A-level 4.
Musical activities: Chapel, concert and madrigal choirs; school orch, wind band, jazz band.
Pupils: 430 day and boarding; 45 VI form girls; 150 studying inst. *Termly fees:* £2700 (day), £3900 (boarding).

St Lawrence College (Co-ed)
Ramsgate, Kent CT11 7AE
Tel: 01843 592680 *Fax:* 01843 851123
Email: slcthanet@aol.com

M Slater, head; E A Perkins, dir of mus.
Awards: Mus awards value 20% and 50% fees. Age under 14 on 1 Jun; gr 5 on any inst. Awards may be increased according to entrance exam performance (mus may also be offered as subject in exams for academic scholarships). *Exam boards:* MEG (GCSE); O&C (A-level). *Exam candidates:* GCSE 12; A-level 3.
Musical activities: Choir, jnr choir, orch, chmbr orch, stage band.
Pupils: 370 day and boarding; 120 studying inst. *Termly fees:* £2060-2800 (day), £3150-4200 (boarding).

St Leonards-Mayfield School (Girls)
Convent of the Holy Child, The Old Palace, Mayfield, E Sussex TN20 6PH
Tel: 01435 873652 *Fax:* 01435 872627

Jean Sinclair, headmistress; Kenneth Pont, dir of mus.
Awards: Scholarship at 11+ and 13+ for free tuition on 1 or 2 insts. 4 bursaries awarded annually by the Friends of Music in Mayfield. *Exam boards:* SEG (GCSE); Edexcel (A-level). *Exam candidates:* GCSE 11; A-level 2.
Musical activities: Chmbr orch, 5 choirs, opera and choral performances, opportunities to work with Malcolm Williamson, Paul Patterson, Francis Grier and Sir David Willcocks.
Pupils: 215 day; 275 boarding; 274 studying inst. *Termly fees:* £3933.

St Leonards School (Girls)
St Andrews, Fife KY16 9QU
Tel: 01334 472126/476345 (mus school) *Fax:* 01334 476152

Mrs M James, head; Marilyn Cleobury-Jones, dir of mus.
Awards: Mus scholarships max 33% of fees, awarded on entry (at any age). *Exam boards:* MEG (GCSE); UCLES (A-level). *Exam candidates:*

GCSE 13; A-level 3. *Musical activities:* 2 choirs, str and chmbr orch, various ens, concert wind band, jazz band, perc ens, Scots fiddle group, pipe band.
Pupils: 41 day; 234 boarding; 200 studying inst. *Termly fees:* £2075 (day), £3925 (boarding).

St Margaret's School (Girls)
Merry Hill Rd, Bushey, Herts WD2 1DT
Tel: 0181 950 1548 *Fax:* 0181 950 1677

M de Villiers, head; I Hope, dir of mus.
Awards: VI form mus scholarship offered, value up to £1600. Assisted places available at 5+, 8+, 11+ and 13+. *Exam boards:* MEG (GCSE); Edexcel (A-level). *Exam candidates:* GCSE 8-10; A-level 3.
Musical activities: Chapel choir, lower school choir, Oriana choir, school orch, ens. Concerts organised in collaboration with other schools.
Pupils: 488 day and boarding; 120 studying inst. Associated infant and prep school is Merry Hill House (age 4+). *Termly fees:* £1875 (day), £3070 (boarding).

St Margaret's School for Girls (Girls)
147 Magdalen Rd, Exeter EX2 4TS
Tel: 01392 73197 *Fax:* 01392 51402

Mrs M D'Albertanson, head; Miranda Ashe, dir of mus.
Awards: Mus scholarships and bursaries available. *Exam boards:* SEG (GCSE and A-level). *Exam candidates:* GCSE 10-13, A-level 2-11.
Musical activities: 4 orchs, 3 choirs, jazz band, wind band.
Pupils: 456 250 studying inst. *Termly fees:* £975 (kindergarten), £1248 (jnr), £1514 (snr).

St Mary's School (Ascot) (Girls)
St Mary's Rd, Ascot, Berks SL5 9JF
Tel: 01344 23721 *Fax:* 01344 873281

Sister Frances Orchard, head; Gareth Lloyd, dir of mus.
Awards: 1 scholarship each year (30% of fees). Free tuition on 2 insts. Also occasional bursaries. *Exam boards:* MEG (GCSE); O&C (A-Level). *Exam candidates:* GCSE 11; A-level 3.
Musical activities: Chmbr choir, chapel choir, jnr choir, orch, str orch, jnr orch, chmbr ens, pop groups, swing band. Fortnightly lunchtime concerts and 2-3 major concerts per term. Annual commercial CD recording, biennial production, triennial concert tour abroad, mus tech suite.
Pupils: 250 boarding; occasional day pupils, 224 studying inst. *Termly fees:* £2287 (day); £3811 (boarding).

259

St Mary's (Calne) (Girls)

Calne, Wilts SN11 0DF
Tel: 01249 857200 *Fax:* 01249 857207

Mrs C J Shaw, head; Keith Abrams, dir of mus. *Awards:* 1 mus scholarship of 33% fees plus several bursaries in the form of free inst tuition available to young musicians joining the school at age 11 or 12. A VI form scholarship of 33% fees is also available and may be awarded to an external or internal applicant. *Exam boards:* Edexcel (GCSE and A-level). *Exam candidates:* GCSE 13; A/AS-level 3.
Musical activities: Jnr, middle and snr choirs; chmbr choir, 2 orchs, wind band, jnr str orch, jazz band, many chmbr groups; choir and orch tours.
Pupils: 300 boarding and day; 260 studying inst.
Termly fees: £2545 (day), £4280 (boarding).

St Mary's School (Gerrards Cross) (Girls)

Gerrards Cross, Bucks SL9 8JQ
Tel: 01753 883370 *Fax:* 01753 890966

Rosemary Millward, dir of mus.
Awards: 1 award of 50% school fees awarded annually, age 12-16. *Exam boards:* SEG (GCSE); Edexcel (A-level). *Exam candidates:* GCSE and A-level 7.
Musical activities: Snr, middle school and jnr choirs; wind ens, rcdr group, madrigal and chapel choirs.
Pupils: 270 day; 75 studying inst. *Termly fees:* £1795 (day).

St Mary's School (Wantage) (Girls)

Wantage, Oxon OX12 8BZ
Tel: 01235 763571 *Fax:* 01235 760467
Email: stmarysw@rmplc.co.uk

Mrs S Bodinham, head; Ms F Eagar, dir of mus.
Awards: 2 mus scholarships offered at 13+, 1 at VI form, value 33% fees plus free inst tuition in 2 insts. Candidates should preferably offer 2 insts. Also mus exhibitions, value free tuition on 2 insts. *Exam boards:* SEG (GCSE); UCLES (A-level). *Exam candidates:* GCSE 8; A-level 2-3.
Musical activities: 2 orchs, ens, 2 choirs. Concerts organised, also visits and trips, including abroad. Some pupils play in national and regional youth orchs.
Pupils: 220 boarding; 150 studying inst. *Termly fees:* £2733 (day), £4100 (boarding).

St Mary's Westbrook (Co-ed)

Ravenlea Rd, Folkestone, Kent CT20 2JU
Tel: 01303 851222 *Fax:* 01303 249901

Christopher Fitzgerald, head; George Sharman, dir of mus.
Awards: Mus scholarships available. Additional bursaries available for inst tuition age 11 (approx gr 4-5). *Exam boards:* Oxford, SEG. *Exam candidates:* GCSE 4.

Musical activities: Snr and jnr orchs; snr and jnr chapel choirs.
Pupils: 250 day; 30 studying inst. *Termly fees:* £1155-2100 (day), £2253-2813 (boarding). The school is a newly created institution, formed through the merger of St Mary's College and Westbrook House.

St Paul's Girls' School (Girls)

Brook Green, Hammersmith, London W6 7BS
Tel: 0171 603 2288 *Fax:* 0171 602 9932

Janet Gough, high mistress; Derek Bourgeois, dir of mus.
Awards: Mus awards up to 100% fees according to parental means plus free tuition. Age 11 and 16.
Exam boards: Year 10-11 school directed course; O&C (A-level). *Exam candidates:* Year 11 school course 10; A-level 5.
Musical activities: School and chmbr orchs, joint orch with St Paul's Boys School, 2 wind bands, 4 choirs, opera group, early mus and jazz groups, str and wind groups.
Pupils: 644 day; 420 studying inst. *Termly fees:* £2331 (day).

St Paul's School (Boys)

Lonsdale Rd, London SW13 9JT
Tel: 0181 748 9162 *Fax:* 0181 748 9557
Email: pmt@stpauls.richmond.sch.uk

Stephen Baldock, high master; Mark Tatlow, dir of mus.
Awards: 2 means-tested mus scholarships value up to 100% fees available, with free tuition in 2 insts. Age under 14 on 1 Sep; min gr 6 on 1st inst with 2nd inst or voice. 1 or more VI form award available pa including biennial org scholarship (next 1998). Choral awards for treble voices available through Colet Court *see* **Preparatory Schools**. *Exam boards:* MEG (GCSE); UCLES (A-level). *Exam candidates:* GCSE 15+; A-level 5.
Musical activities: Several orchs including joint chmbr orch with St Paul's Girls' School; choral society, chapel choir, close harmony group; concert band and many wind, br and str groups. Chmbr mus tuition; jazz group plus tuition; keyboard tuition including hpd and synthesizer work. Alexander technique lessons available.
Pupils: 774 day and boarding; 350 studying inst.
Termly fees: £2995 (day), £4520 (boarding).

St Peter's School (Co-ed)

York YO3 6AB
Tel: 01904 623213 *Fax:* 01904 670407

A F Trotman, head; Andrew Wright, dir of mus.
Awards: Several mus bursaries offering part fees or free tuition in 1 or more insts. *Exam boards:* NEAB (GCSE); O&C (A-level). *Exam candidates:* GCSE 10; A-level 4.

Musical activities: Chmbr choir, school choir, choral society, 2 orchs, wind band, swing band, chmbr mus.
Pupils: 502 day and boarding; 180 studying inst.
Termly fees: £2082-2187 (day), £3577-3673 (boarding).

St Swithun's School (Girls)
Winchester, Hants SO21 1HA
Tel: 01962 861316 *Fax:* 01962 841874

H L Harvey, head; R Brett, dir of mus.
Awards: Mus exhibitions available at VI form, 12+ and 13+ providing free tuition in 1 or 2 insts throughout school career. *Exam boards:* MEG (GCSE); Edexcel (A-level). *Exam candidates:* GCSE 6; A-level 3.
Musical activities: 2 orchs, 3 choirs, fl and cl choirs, wind and concert bands, perc ens, 2 rcdr ens, br groups and jazz band.
Pupils: 237 day; 223 boarding; 337 studying inst.
Termly fees: £2430 (day), £4025 (boarding).

Seaford College (Co-ed)
Petworth, W Sussex GU28 0NB
Tel: 01798 867392 *Fax:* 01798 867606

R C Hannaford, head; Martin Essex, dir of mus.
Awards: Choral, vocal, inst scholarships awarded annually (Mar), value according to ability. Choral scholarship must be accompanied by academic

ability (academic scholarship or common entrance). *Exam boards:* Edexcel (A/AS-level).
Exam candidates: GCSE 4; A-level 3.
Musical activities: Chmbr groups, dance band, male voice choir, orchs, rock groups, swing band, opera and concert visits. Chapel choir; international tours, commercial recording schedule.
Pupils: 320 mostly boarding; 75 pupils studying inst. Also Junior House (11-13). *Termly fees:* £1980 (day/jnr), £2375 (day/snr), £2950 (boarding/jnr), £3610 (boarding/snr).

Sedbergh School (Boys)
Sedbergh, Cumbria LA10 5HG
Tel: 015396 20535 *Fax:* 015396 21301
Email: post@sedsch.demon.co.uk
Website: www.sedbergh.sch.uk

C H Hirst, headmaster; N D Wilby, dir of mus.
Awards: 6-8 mus scholarships and exhibitions available for inst/singers with potential, value up to 50% fees (augmentable with bursaries in certain cases) with free tuition in 2 insts. Age under 14 on 1 Jun or VI form entry. *Exam boards:* MEG (GCSE); Edexcel (A-level). *Exam candidates:* GCSE 10; A-level 3.
Musical activities: Orch, str orch, jazz groups, marching band, br band, vc quartet, plus various chmbr ens, chapel choir, chmbr choir, choral

society; musicals performed alternate yrs, including tours abroad; subscription concert series. *Pupils:* 350 boarding; 150 studying inst. *Termly fees:* £4050 (snr boarding).

Sevenoaks School (Co-ed)
High St, Sevenoaks, Kent TN13 1HU
Tel: 01732 455133 *Fax:* 01732 456143
Email: regist@admin.soaks.kent.sch.uk./
Website: www.soaks.kent.sch.uk

T R Cookson, head; Andrew Forbes, dir of mus. *Awards:* Around 10 scholarships and exhibitions awarded annually. *Exam boards:* Edexcel (GCSE and A-level); International Baccalaureate. *Exam candidates:* GCSE 10; A-level 4; IB 5. *Musical activities:* Choirs, orchs, bands, chmbr mus, summer festival. *Pupils:* 611 day; 337 boarding; 427 studying inst. *Termly fees:* £2454 (day/11-13+), £2733 (day/16+), £4029 (boarding/11-13+), £4308 (boarding/16+).

Sherborne School (Boys)
Sherborne, Dorset DT9 3AP
Tel: 01935 812030 (mus school) *Fax:* 01935 816628

P H Lapping, head; Paul Ellis, dir of mus. *Awards:* Up to 8 major scholarships awarded annually for age under 14 on 1 Sep. Bursaries are available to supplement these awards where necessary. Marion Packer scholarship of £600 pa for pianist. Free inst tuition for scholars. *Exam boards:* MEG (GCSE); Edexcel (A-level). *Exam candidates:* GCSE and A-level 15. *Musical activities:* 2 orchs plus chmbr orch, concert band, chapel choir, swing band, jazz bands; also wind, br, str ens. Various chmbr mus groups, choral society, subscription series, joint mus activities with Sherborne School for Girls and St Antony's-Leweston. Comprehensive collection of quality insts for boys' use. Separate mus school prospectus available. *Pupils:* 55 day; 500 boarding; 243 studying inst. *Termly fees:* £3190 (day), £4185 (boarding).

Sherborne School for Girls (Girls)
Sherborne, Dorset DT9 3QN
Tel: 01935 812245 *Fax:* 01935 814973

Miss J M Taylor, head; J Jenkins, dir of mus. *Awards:* Major mus scholarship at jnr and VI form levels up to 50% fees (plus free inst tuition in 2 insts). No age limit. Feb auditions. *Exam boards:* MEG (GCSE); Edexcel (A-level). *Exam candidates:* GCSE 10; A-level 4. *Musical activities:* Orchs, choirs, chmbr mus, opera, swing band, jazz and perc groups, br ens and rcdr consort. *Pupils:* 420 day and boarding; 350 studying inst. *Termly fees:* £2650 (day), £3850 (boarding).

Shrewsbury School (Boys)
Shrewsbury, Shrops SY3 7BB
Tel: 01743 344537/344135 (mus dept)
Fax: 01743 243107

F E Maidment, head; John Moore, dir of mus. *Awards:* At least 6 mus scholarships with free inst tuition, plus awards and exhibitions. Age under 14 on 1 Sep or VI form entry; potential rather than mere proficiency sought. *Exam boards:* MEG (GCSE); Edexcel (A-level). *Exam candidates:* GCSE 15; A-level 7. *Musical activities:* Orch, choral society, chapel choir, chmbr choir, concert choir, big band, concert band, traditional jazz band, flourishing rock bands, 5 str ens and other inst groups and ens. Chapel choir sings at cathedrals, churches; regular concerts, mus events, and annual competitions; also professional subscription concert series, weekly lunchtime series, visiting professional str quartet scheme and overseas tours organised each year. *Pupils:* 704 day and boarding; 280+ studying inst. *Termly fees:* £3200 (day), £4550 (boarding).

Sibford School (Co-ed)
Sibford Ferris, Banbury, Oxon OX15 5QL
Tel: 01295 781200 *Fax:* 01295 781204
Email: sibfordschool@dial.pipex.com
Website: dspace.dial.pipex.com/sibford.school/

Susan Freestone, head; Mark Paine. *Awards:* 2 scholarships (50% of day fees). Free tuition on 2 insts. Musicianship and inst potential of greater significance than achieved grades. Bursaries also available. *Exam boards:* MEG (GCSE); Edexcel (A-level). *Exam candidates:* GCSE 4; A-level 3. *Musical activities:* Str ens, br ens, wind ens, barber-shop group, orch, choral society. Termly performance opportunities. *Pupils:* 135 day; 162 boarding; 104 studying inst. *Termly fees:* £5580 pa (day, snr); £10,485 pa (boarding, snr).

Sidcot School (Co-ed)
Winscombe, N Somerset BS25 1PD
Tel: 01934 843102 *Fax:* 01934 844181
Email: sidcotad@aol.com

Angus Slesser, head; Timothy Bailey, dir of mus. *Awards:* 1 VI form scholarship value 75% fees (awarded by interview and audition). Also approx 4 mus bursaries of free tuition in 1-2 insts awarded annually, may be supplemented in cases of need by means-tested bursary of up to 30% boarding fees. Age 11+, 13+ (gr 3-4) or 16+ (gr 7-8). *Exam boards:* MEG (GCSE); UCLES (A-level). *Exam candidates:* GCSE 13; A-level 4. *Musical activities:* Orch, choirs, wind band, rock and jazz bands, chmbr mus playing; also regular

Shrewsbury School Music

SHREWSBURY SCHOOL

MUSIC SCHOLARSHIPS

Up to four or more Music Scholarships are awarded annually at 13+ after the competitive examination held in February. Scholarships are graded in value according to need and considerable flexibility is exercised in their award. Two further scholarships are available for sixth form entrants, one in particular for organists.

Music scholars play a full part in the lively musical life of the School and receive free tuition on any instrument or in singing.

There is a large Choral Society of over 200 voices, combining the Community and Student Choirs; a flourishing Chapel Choir; 3 School Orchestras; Big Band; Wind Band; Chamber Ensembles and Jazz Groups. In addition there is a Season of Concerts given by internationally acclaimed musicians, organised by the School and masterclasses and concerts by the School's professional visiting string quartet.

Scholars will very quickly be tackling advanced repertoire and an appropriate standard of instrumental playing and enthusiasm is therefore sought at audition. Cathedral choristers who would still be able to sing treble in the School Chapel Choir are particularly encouraged to apply.

For further particulars please apply to the Headmaster, The Schools, Shrewsbury SY3 7BA. The Director of Music, John Moore, will be pleased to answer enquiries or give advice at any stage. Please write or telephone Shrewsbury (01743) 344135.

concerts and visiting professional musicians.
Pupils: 406 day and boarding; 155 studying inst.
Termly fees: £1530 (day/jnr), £2050 (day/snr),
£3550 (boarding).

Silcoates School (Co-ed)
Wrenthorpe, Wakefield, W Yorks WF2 0PD
Tel: 01924 291614 *Fax:* 01924 368690

A P Spillane, head; G L Cox, dir of mus.
Awards: Mus awards available at head's
discretion. *Exam boards:* SEG (GCSE); Edexcel
(A-level). *Exam candidates:* GCSE 6; A-level 1.
Musical activities: Choirs, concerts, inst groups,
wind band.
Pupils: 600 day; 180 studying inst. *Termly fees:*
£1140 (day/7-8+), £1520 (day/9-10+), £1920
(day/11+).

Solihull School (Boys)+
Warwick Rd, Solihull, W Midlands B91 3DJ
Tel: 0121 705 4273 *Fax:* 0121 711 4439
Email: solsch@argonet.co.uk
Website: www.argonet.co.uk/users/solsch

P S J Derham, head; Stephen J Perrins, dir of mus.
Awards: 1 mus scholarship of 100% fees, 2 of 50%
fees offered; age over 11, under 14 on 1 Sep. Also
VI form award value 50% fees. *Exam boards:*
NEAB (GCSE and A-level). *Exam candidates:* GCSE
12; A-level 6.
Musical activities: 3 orchs, chapel choir, choral
society, opera group; str, wind and br ens; jazz
band and singers; girls' chmbr choir.
Pupils: 959 day; 300 studying inst. *Termly fees:*
£1580 (day).

Stamford High School (Girls)
St Martin's, Stamford, Lincs PE9 2LJ
Tel: 01780 484200

Patricia Clark, head; Paul White, dir of mus.
Awards: 2 mus scholarships of up to 50% school
fees plus free inst. Tuition in 1 or 2 insts at age
11+, 13+ or 16+. *Exam boards:* MEG (GCSE);
Oxford, Edexcel (A-level). *Exam candidates:* GCSE 6.
Musical activities: Orchs, choirs, chapel, bands,
ens, outings.
Pupils: 621 day; 97 boarding; 400 studying inst.
Termly fees: £1205-1508 (day), £2713-3016 (boarding).

Stamford School (Boys)
St Paul's St, Stamford, Lincs PE9 2BS
Tel: 01780 750300 *Fax:* 01780 750336

J Hale, head; Paul White, dir of mus; David Lovell
Brown, dir of chapel mus.
Awards: 2 mus scholarships of up to 50% fees
plus free inst tuition in 1 or 2 insts at age 11+, 13+
or 16+. *Exam boards:* MEG (GCSE); Oxford,
Edexcel (A-level). *Exam candidates:* GCSE 12;

A-level 6.
Musical activities: 3 orchs, 3 choirs, chapel choir,
3 bands, various ens.
Pupils: 720 day, 170 boarding, 300 studying inst.
Termly fees: £1508 (day), £3016 (boarding).

Stewart's Melville College (Boys)
Queensferry Rd, Edinburgh EH4 3EZ
Tel: 0131 332 7925 *Fax:* 0131 343 2432

P F J Tobin, principal; Roger Askew, dir of mus.
Awards: 1 scholarship, value up to 40% fees, for
entry at age 12-14, several bursaries for inst
tuition. *Exam boards:* SEB (Standard grade,
Highers); O&C (A-level). *Exam candidates:* 22.
Musical activities: Strong mus dept twinned with
girls' school *see* **The Mary Erskine School**. 3
orchs, 3 bands, 3 jazz bands, many chmbr ens,
choir. Regular concerts, 3 staged musicals pa.
Pupils: 800 day; 260 studying inst. Mus dept
serves co-ed jnr school on site. *Termly fees:*
£1533 (day), £2880 (boarding).

Stockport Grammar School (Co-ed)
Buxton Rd, Stockport, Cheshire SK2 7AF
Tel: 0161 456 9000 *Fax:* 0161 419 2407
Email: sgs@argonet.co.uk
Website: www.argonet.co.uk/users/sgs

I Mellor, head; Jackson Towers, dir of mus.
Awards: Mus bursaries (up to 4 pa) awarded to
entrants at age 11 with particular potential. *Exam
boards:* NEAB. *Exam candidates:* GCSE 30; A-level 6.
Musical activities: 2 orchs, str orch; jnr, boys,
girls and snr choirs; 3 wind bands, big band,
several jazz ens, chmbr groups, jnr school orch
and jnr school choir. Tours to the US,
appearances in professional concerts and TV, etc.
Pupils: 1275 day; 300 studying inst. Age range
4-18. *Termly fees:* £1095 (day/jnr), £1422
(day/snr).

Stonar School (Girls)
Cottles Pk, Atworth, Melksham, Wilts SN12 8NT
Tel: 01225 702309/702795 *Fax:* 01225 790830
Email: office@stonar.wilts.sch.uk

Caroline Homan, head; Nick Goodall, dir of mus.
Awards: 2 major awards worth approx £2000 pa; 2
minor awards at £1000 pa. Free tuition offered in
up to 2 insts. Gr 5/6+ at age 13. Also occasional
bursaries for talented musicians. *Exam boards:*
SEG (GCSE); Cambridge, London (A-Level). *Exam
candidates:* GCSE 3; A-level 2.
Musical activities: Choir, chmbr choir, orch, wind
band. Regular performances and productions.
Participation in competitions and festivals.
Pupils: 207 day; 221 boarding; 401 studying inst.
Termly fees: £839-1549 (jnr, day); £3132 (jnr,
boarding); £1895 (snr, day); £3420 (snr,
boarding).

265

Stonyhurst College (Co-ed) +
Stonyhurst, Lancs BB7 9PZ
Tel: 01254 826345 *Fax:* 01254 826013
Email: admissions@stonyhurst.ac.uk

A J F Aylward, head; R A Highcock, dir of mus.
Awards: Several mus scholarships and bursaries offered including org scholarship. Scholarships offered at 11+, 13+ and 16+. *Exam boards:* Edexcel (GCSE); OCEAC (A-level). *Exam candidates:* GCSE 7; A-level 4. *Musical activities:* All students study an orchestral inst free for at least 1 yr during school career. Orch, str orch, 2 wind bands, choir (wkly sung mass). Facilities include 4 orgs, Bösendorfer pno, large stock of orch insts and perc, keyboard studio, computer studio, perc studio.
Pupils: 386; 50% studying inst. *Termly fees:* £2600 (day), £4180 (boarding).

Stover School (Girls)
Newton Abbot, Devon TQ12 6QG
Tel: 01626 54505 *Fax:* 01626 335240

P E Bujak, head; Mrs S Farleigh, dir of mus.
Awards: Mus scholarships and exhibitions available at 11+, 12+, 13+ and VI form. *Exam boards:* SEG (GCSE); Oxford, Edexcel (A-level). *Exam candidates:* GCSE 6; A-level 2. *Musical activities:* Wide range of mus activities: choirs, bands, rcdr consort, sax ens, str group, chmbr orch.
Pupils: 182 day; 74 boarding; 52 studying inst. *Termly fees:* £1595 (day), £3100 (boarding).

Stowe School (Boys) +
Buckingham, Bucks MK18 5EH
Tel: 01280 813164 *Fax:* 01280 822769

Jeremy Nichols, head; John Cooper Green, dir of mus.
Awards: Several mus scholarships value up to 50% fees (may be increased in case of need) and bursaries of lower value. Age under 14 on 1 Sep; gr 5-6. Also occasional inst awards offered to outstanding VI form entrants. *Exam boards:* MEG, Edexcel. *Exam candidates:* GCSE 14; A-level 8; mus technology 4. *Musical activities:* 2 orchs, choirs, choral society, jazz band, professional concert series, electronic mus studio, 4 manual chapel org.
Pupils: 43 day; 514 boarding; 220 studying inst. *Termly fees:* £3310 (day), £4725 (boarding).

Strathallan School (Co-ed)
Forgandenny, Perth PH2 9EG
Tel: 01738 812546 *Fax:* 01738 812549

A W McPhail, head; D G Read, dir of mus.
Awards: Mus scholarships of up to 50% fees, or exhibitions each value 25% fees at all ages. Bursaries available on proof of financial need. *Exam boards:* NEAB (GCSE and A-level). *Exam candidates:* GCSE 10; A-level (Highers) 2. *Musical*

activities: 3 orchs, choirs, jazz band, wind band, folk band, baroque ens, pipe bands, chmbr and elec mus.
Pupils: 50 day; 430 boarding; 240 studying inst. *Termly fees:* £2220-2930 (day), £3200-4200 (boarding).

Sutton Valence School (Co-ed)
Sutton Valence, Maidstone, Kent ME17 3HL
Tel: 01622 842281/844092 (mus dept)
Fax: 01622 844093

N A Sampson, head; Adrian Leang, dir of mus.
Awards: Various choral and inst scholarships and exhibitions at ages 11, 13 and 16. *Exam boards:* Edexcel (GCSE and A-level). *Exam candidates:* GCSE 12; A-level 4. *Musical activities:* Chapel choir, choral society, secular choirs, orch; also inst ens, including big band, jazz band and rcdr consort, and mus society with 7 major winter concerts.
Pupils: 370 day and boarding; 200 studying inst or voice. *Termly fees:* £2495 (day), £3110 (boarding).

Talbot Heath (Girls)
Rothesay Rd, Bournemouth, Dorset BH4 9NJ
Tel: 01202 761881

Christine Dipple, head; A P Hill, Miss J Platt, mus dept.
Awards: Scholarships awarded at 11+, 12+ and 13+. Candidates must be at least gr 3, gr 4 and gr 5 respectively on their main inst. They will be expected to show a high degree of musical promise and documentary evidence of a candidate's musical standard will be required. *Exam boards:* MEG (GCSE); Cambridge (A-Level). *Exam candidates:* GCSE 4; A-level 6. *Musical activities:* 4 choirs, orch, str groups, fl choir, cl choir, rcdr groups, handbell groups, early mus group, various other ens. 2 main school concerts each year. Several recitals outside school. Close community involvement.
Pupils: 428 day; 27 boarding. *Termly fees:* £5790 pa (day); £9780 pa (wkly boarding); £10,050 pa (boarding).

Taunton School (Co-ed)
Taunton, Somerset TA2 6AD
Tel: 01823 349200/349224 *Fax:* 01823 349201

J P Whiteley, head; Philip Tyack, dir of mus.
Awards: Max 2 scholarships and assisted places at 13+ and VI form, of up to full remission of tuition fees with additional help from bursaries; orch insts preferred. *Exam boards:* SEG (GCSE); Oxford (A-level). *Exam candidates:* GCSE 4; A-level 3. *Musical activities:* Mus society, chapel choir, choral society, madrigal group, jazz band, str orch, wind orch, concert band, plus musical show productions and concerts.
Pupils: 450 day and boarding; 170 studying inst. *Termly fees:* £790-2520 (day), £1615-3935 (boarding).

267

SCHOOLS

TRINITY SCHOOL
CROYDON

NUMEROUS MUSIC AWARDS

For boys between 10 and 13, and Sixth Form entry, with exceptional musical promise on at least one instrument.

Music Scholarships
Up to half School fees (additional finance in case of need). Free tuition on two instruments at School or privately.

Music Tuition Scholarships
Free tuition on two instruments at School or privately.

Trinity Music is nationally known by boys' regular successes through instrumental competitions and public concerts. Trinity Boys Choir performs and records with professional London orchestras and opera companies in this country and abroad. Trinity Music has excellent facilities, extensive accommodation and a staff of thirty.

David Squibb, Director of Music, is pleased to see prospective candidates and parents by appointment.

Details from the Music Administrator, Trinity School, Shirley Park, Croydon CR9 7AT (0181 656 9541)

Trinity School is part of the Whitgift Foundation a registered charity which provides education for children

WARWICK SCHOOL

Junior School (7-11 years)   (200 boys)
Senior School (11-18 years) (800 boys)
DAY AND BOARDING PLACES

NEW MUSIC DEPARTMENT

MUSIC SCHOLARSHIPS
– to the value of 50% of the fees

ADDITIONAL ACADEMIC AWARDS
– at 11+, 12+, 13+ and Sixth Form

CHORAL SCHOLARSHIPS
– with St Mary's Church, Warwick

INSTRUMENTAL TUITION
– available to all boys entering at 11+

Further information from the Admissions Secretary or the Director of Music who is available by appointment to see prospective Music Scholars and their parents

Warwick School, Warwick, CV34 6PP
Telephone: (01926) 492484
Fax: (01926) 401259

Warwick School has charitable status and exists for the education of boys

TONBRIDGE SCHOOL

Up to **NINE Music Scholarships** of up to half fees, with free tuition in music, are offered in February 1999 to candidates of suitable calibre. Music may also be offered as an option in the school's Academic Scholarship Examination in May. The value of any Award may be increased, by any amount up to the full school fee, if assessment of the parents' means indicates a need. A number of Music Exhibitions, giving free instrumental tuition, can also be awarded.

Choral Exhibitions worth one-sixth fees are awarded without examination to choristers of Cathedral and Collegiate Choir Schools. Choristers can hold these awards and Music Scholarships simultaneously. The Chapel Choir maintains an exceptional Choral tradition: the magnificent rebuilt Chapel with a superb 4-manual organ by Marcussen opened in 1995.

Choral Scholarships worth approximately £1,320 per annum are awarded to the trebles of the Chapel Choir who attend either Hilden Grange or Yardley Court Preparatory Schools in Tonbridge.

Boys holding Music Awards are given extra time for practising within the curriculum. Special consideration will be given to string players although awards have also been made to other orchestral and keyboard players at every recent audition. Almost half the School receives music tuition from 6 full time and 31 visiting staff. Two orchestras, two bands, a large choral society and a variety of smaller ensembles provide a wide panorama of opportunity for high quality music making, both within and beyond the School. A major new Arts and Technology building opened in 1996, providing splendid additional facilities for Music.
The Director of Music, Hilary Davan Wetton, is always happy to meet with parents and their sons informally to give advice about preparation for the Scholarship Auditions.

Full details of all Scholarships are available from the Admissions Secretary, Tonbridge School, Kent, TN9 1JP. Telephone (01732) 365555.

Tonbridge School is a charitable foundation for the education of boys.
Registered Charity No. 307099

Teesside High School (Girls)
The Avenue, Eaglescliffe, Stockton on Tees TS16 9AT
Tel: 01642 782095 *Fax:* 01642 791207

Miss J F Hamilton, head; Miss S Lloyd-Jones, dir of mus.
Awards: Cover inst tuition and exam fees for up to 2 insts. *Exam boards:* NEAB (GCSE); Cambridge (A-Level). *Exam candidates:* GCSE 12; A-Level 1-2. *Musical activities:* Orch, str quartet, wind band, rcdr ens, fl ens, choir; regular concerts in school and local churches.
Pupils: 550 day; 375 studying inst. *Termly fees:* £1344-£1430.

Tettenhall College (Co-ed)
Wood Hall, Tettenhall, Wolverhampton, W Midlands WV6 8QX
Tel: 01902 751119/741627 *Fax:* 01902 747283/741940

P C Bodkin, head; I F Wass, dir of mus.
Awards: Mus scholarships up to 66% fees and bursaries of free inst tuition offered at all ages. All mus insts and voice considered. *Exam boards:* NEAB, Edexcel, UCLES. *Exam candidates:* GCSE 1; A-level 1.
Musical activities: Chmbr choir, 2 jnr choirs, concert band, orch ens. Regular concerts in school and outside; annual mus competitions. *Pupils:* 343 day and boarding; 100 studying inst. Prep school is Tettenhall College at the same address. *Termly fees:* £2013 (day), £3266 (boarding).

Tonbridge School (Boys)
Tonbridge, Kent TN9 1JP
Tel: 01732 365555 *Fax:* 01732 770853/363424
Email: tonbschl@demon.co.uk

J M Hammond, head; Hilary Davan Wetton, dir of mus.
Awards: Up to 9 mus scholarships value up to 50% fees with free inst tuition. Awards given for excellence in any inst. Age under 14 on 1 Sep. Choral scholarships value 17% fees also available to choristers of cathedral and other choir schools. Also VI form scholarships. *Exam boards:* MEG (GCSE); Edexcel (A-level). *Exam candidates:* GCSE 18; A-level 6.
Musical activities: 3 orchs, 2 concert bands, big band, chmbr mus ens, chapel choir, choral society. Additional practising arrangements made for scholars.
Pupils: 698 day and boarding; 350+ studying inst. *Termly fees:* £3204 (day), £4540 (boarding).

Trent College (Co-ed)
Long Eaton, Nottingham, Notts NG10 4AD
Tel: 0115 973 2737 *Fax:* 0115 946 3284

J S Lee, head; Patrick Burnham, dir of mus.
Awards: Mus scholarships and exhibitions awarded at 11+, 13+ and VI form up to 50% fees

remission and free inst tuition. *Exam boards:* MEG (GCSE); Edexcel (A-level). *Exam candidates:* GCSE 20; A-level 5; AS-level 5. *Musical activities:* Orch, specialist ens, bands, choirs.
Pupils: 434 day; 266 boarding; 450 studying inst. *Termly fees:* £2066-2230 (day), £3066-3633 (boarding)

Trinity School (Boys)
Shirley Pk, Croydon CR9 7AT
Tel: 0181 656 9541 *Fax:* 0181 655 0522
Website: www.trinity.croydon.sch.uk

B Lenon, head; David Squibb, dir of mus.
Awards: Numerous awards made to boys age 10-13 (1 Sep) on admission or subsequently, and at VI form. Choral experience considered. Up to 50% fees (augmented in cases of need). Free inst tuition, private or school. *Exam boards:* SEG (GCSE); Edexcel (A/AS-level). *Exam candidates:* GCSE 18; A-level 4; A-level mus technology 8.
Musical activities: Public performances (Fairfield, London halls, etc) with orchs, bands; str, w/wind and br groups. Trinity Boys Choir (with professional concert and opera engagements, radio and TV broadcasts, recordings in UK and abroad); Trinity Choristers (with annual residential Easter cathedral course).
Pupils: 900 day; 300 studying inst. *Termly fees:* *Annual fees:* £5961 (day).

Truro School (Co-ed)
Truro, Cornwall TR1 1TH
Tel: 01872 272763 ext 271 (mus school)
Fax: 01872 223431

G A G Dodd, head; D J Spedding, dir of mus.
Awards: Several, value up to 50% current fees. Any inst but preference given to orch players. *Exam boards:* Edexcel, O&C. *Exam candidates:* GCSE 16; A-level 10.
Musical activities: Full orchs, str orch, br band, wind orch, 3 choirs, chmbr ens, jazz band and ens.
Pupils: 799 day and boarding; 250 studying inst. *Termly fees:* £1604 (day), £2986 (boarding).

University College School (Boys)
Frognal, Hampstead, London NW3 6XH
Tel: 0171 435 2215 *Fax:* 0171 431 4385
Email: staff@ucs.u-net.com

K J Durham, head; Colin Myles, dir of mus.
Awards: 1 mus scholarship value 50% fees and/or exhibitions value of 25% fees, augmentable to 100% and 50% fees in cases of need. Age over 11 on 1 Sep; 2nd inst recommended; singing an advantage. *Exam boards:* MEG (GCSE); UCLES (A-level). *Exam candidates:* GCSE and A-level 20.
Musical activities: Chmbr and symphony orchs, concert band, school choir, choral society, various ens.
Pupils: 700 day. *Termly fees:* £2542 (day).

Uppingham School (Boys) +
Rutland, Leics LE15 9QE
Tel: 01572 822267 *Fax:* 01572 822792

Stephen Winkley, head; Neil Page, dir of mus.
Awards: Several mus scholarships value 50% fees
(may be supplemented to 100% fees in case of
need) plus several exhibitions. VI form
scholarships value 50% fees plus several
exhibitions. *Exam boards:* MEG (GCSE); UCLES
(A-level). *Exam candidates:* GCSE 20; A-level 10-12.
Musical activities: 1st orch, 2nd orch, chmbr
orch, concert choir, chapel choir, chmbr choirs.
Also 2 bands, big band, jazz bands. Series of
professional concerts; m/classes; consultants
scheme for mus specialists.
Pupils: 650 pupils; 400 studying inst. *Termly fees:*
£3000 (day), £4640 (boarding).

Walthamstow Hall (Girls)
Sevenoaks, Kent TN13 3UL
Tel: 01732 451334 *Fax:* 01732 740439

Mrs J S Lang, head; T J Daniell, dir of mus.
Awards: 1 open scholarship at age 11 and age 13; 1
internal scholarship at age 15. *Exam boards:* MEG
(GCSE); UCLES (A-level). *Exam candidates:* GCSE 7;
A-level 2. *Musical activities:* Jnr school: orch, choir,
rcdr ens. Snr school: 3 choirs, 2 orchs, wind band,
fl choir, chmbr ens, str quartet, wind quartet, rcdr

ens, musical dramas, visiting performers. Also
Ship Festival of Music and Drama, combined
concerts with Tonbridge School.
Pupils: 405 day; 40 boarding; 203 studying inst.
Termly fees: £1680 (day/jnr), £2390 (day/snr),
£3720 (boarding/jnr), £4430 (boarding/snr).

Warwick School (Boys)
Warwick CV34 6PP
Tel: 01926 492484 *Fax:* 01926 401259
Email: enquiries@warwick.warwks.sch.uk

P J Cheshire, head; Trevor G Barr, dir of mus.
Awards: 2 mus scholarships at 11+, 1 mus
scholarship at 13+, as well as additional
academic awards at 11+, 12+, 13+ and 16+ (all up
to 50% fees. Choral scholarships available at ages
7-10 in conjunction with St Mary's Warwick. *Exam
boards:* NEAB, Edexcel (GCSE and A-level). *Exam
candidates:* GCSE 6; A-level 2.
Musical activities: Choral society, chapel choir,
orch, swing band, str orch, jnr str orch, br group.
2 main concerts each year, numerous chmbr
concerts and year group concerts.
Pupils: Jnr school: 197. Snr school: 742 day; 58
boarding. *Termly fees:* £1515-1715 (day), £3219-3419
(wkly boarding), £3283-3473 (boarding).

Wellingborough School (Co-ed)

Irthlingborough Rd, Wellingborough, Northants NN8 2BX
Tel: 01933 222427 *Fax:* 01933 271986

F R Ullmann, head; P R Marshall, dir of mus.
Awards: Mus awards up to 50% fees plus choral awards; gr 5 on 1 orch inst; also VI form scholarships, gr 7 required. *Exam boards:* MEG (GCSE); Edexcel (A-level). *Exam candidates:* GCSE 7; A-level 5.
Musical activities: Chapel and concert choirs, orch, wind band, etc.
Pupils: 385 snr school; 255 jnr school; 125 pre-prep school; 300 studying inst. *Termly fees:* £1000 (pre-prep); £1820 (day/jnr), £1960 (day/snr), £3100 (wkly boarding/snr), £3450 (boarding/snr).

Wellington College (Boys) +

Crowthorne, Berks RG45 7PU
Tel: 01344 772639 *Fax:* 01344 771725

C J Driver, head; J D Holloway, dir of mus.
Awards: Major mus scholarships value up to 50% fees; several minor awards; all may be increased in case of need. Age under 14 on 1 Jun; also VI form scholarships of up to 50% fees; high standard on 1st inst with 2nd inst desirable. *Exam boards:* SEG (GCSE); Edexcel (A-level). *Exam candidates:* GCSE 12; A-level 8.
Musical activities: Choral society, 3 choirs, 2 orchs, 3 bands, 2 jazz orchs, chmbr mus, early mus groups, close harmony, specialist mus course.
Pupils: 132 day; 701 boarding; 358 studying inst. Prep school is Eagle House School *see* **Preparatory Schools**. *Termly fees:* £4450.

Wentworth College (Girls)

College Rd, Bournemouth, Dorset BH5 2DY
Tel: 01202 423266/422584 (mus dept)
Fax: 01202 418030

Miss S Coe, head; Mary Goodman, dir of mus.
Awards: Variable number of mus scholarships (up to 50% fees) plus bursaries for 11+ and 13+ entry, providing free mus tuition on up to 2 insts.
Exam boards: SEG (GCSE); UCLES (A-level). *Exam candidates:* GCSE 10; A-level 3.
Musical activities: Large orch, choir and numerous ens; participation in Bournemouth Festival encouraged; performances in continental Europe, frequent trips to concerts etc, locally and in London.
Pupils: 242 day and boarding; 75 studying inst.
Termly fees: £2038 (day), £3250 (boarding).

West Buckland School (Co-ed)

Barnstaple, Devon EX32 0SX
Tel: 01598 760281 *Fax:* 01598 760546

John Vick, head; Mark Richards, dir of mus.
Awards: Mus scholarships at 11+. *Exam boards:* SEG (GCSE); Edexcel (A-level). *Exam candidates:* GCSE 15-18; A-level 3-4. *Musical activities:* Choirs, orch, str orch, jazz orch, wind ens.
Pupils: 490 day; 125 boarding; 172 studying inst.
Termly fees: £1865 (day), £2865-3295 (boarding).

Westminster School (Boys) +

17 Dean's Yard, London SW1P 3PB
Tel: 0171 963 1003

David Summerscale, head; Guy Hopkins, dir of mus.
Awards: A number of mus awards value 50% fees tenable for 5 yrs including free inst tuition. Age under 14 on 1 Sep; gr 5-6 any inst. *Exam boards:* Edexcel (GCSE); UCLES (A-level). *Exam candidates:* GCSE 12; A/AS-level 7. *Musical activities:* Symphony orch, 2 choirs, opera, chmbr mus, musicals, jazz and wind bands, rock group. Contemporary mus society and choral society.
Pupils: 465 day; 200 boarding; 275 studying inst.
Termly fees: £3310 (day), £4800 (boarding).

Westonbirt School (Girls)

Tetbury, Glos GL8 8QG
Tel: 01666 880333 *Fax:* 01666 880364
Email: 101332.1005@compuserve.com

Mrs G Hylson-Smith, head; Malcolm Pike, dir of mus.
Awards: Annual means-tested mus awards value up to 50% fees. Age under 14 on 1 Sep. *Exam boards:* SEG (GCSE); Edexcel (A-level). *Exam candidates:* GCSE 4-10; A-level 2-4.
Musical activities: Orch, 4 choirs, various ens, electronic mus studio.
Pupils: 220 mainly boarding; 150 studying inst.
Termly fees: £2460 (day), £3780 (boarding).

Whitgift School (Boys)

Haling Pk, S Croydon CR2 6YT
Tel: 0181 688 9222 *Fax:* 0181 760 0682

C A Barnett, head; C G Tinker, dir of mus.
Awards: Several made pa on admission or subsequently to musically talented pupils for inst tuition, orch courses, etc; selection by audition.
Exam boards: MEG (GCSE); Edexcel (A-level). *Exam candidates:* GCSE 23; A-level 4.
Musical activities: School orch, jnr orch, wind band, jnr wind band, dance band, snr and jnr choirs, chmbr choir and chapel choir, choral society, various ens, advanced electronic mus, also international orch and choral exchanges.
Pupils: 1100 day; 250 studying inst. *Termly fees:* Annual fees: £6147 (day).

Winchester College (Boys)

Winchester, Hants SO23 9NA
Tel: 01962 621122 *Fax:* 01962 621123
Email: kmp@wincoll.ac.uk

J P Sabben-Clare, headmaster; Keith Pusey, master of mus.

Awards: Major mus awards (up to 50% fees) with free inst tuition offered; augmented to full boarding fees in cases of need. Age under 14 on 1 Sep; gr 6-8 on 1st inst with lesser ability on 2nd inst expected. Awards at 16+ also available. *Exam boards:* MEG (GCSE); Edexcel (A-level). *Exam candidates:* GCSE 17; A-level 9.
Musical activities: 3 orchs, 2 chapel choirs, choral society, early mus group, chmbr groups, regular opera productions, various ens; also jazz and swing bands. Professional subscription concert series.
Pupils: 25 day; 659 boarding; 400+ studying inst. *Termly fees:* £3636 (day), £4848 (boarding).

Wolverhampton Grammar School (Co-ed)
Compton Rd, Wolverhampton WV3 9RB
Tel: 01902 421326 *Fax:* 01902 421819

Bernard Trafford, head; Andrew Proverbs, dir of mus.
Awards: 1 mus exhibition (25% fees plus free mus tuition); also awards of free inst tuition for outstanding musicians of any age. *Exam boards:* MEG (GCSE); UCLES (A-level). *Exam candidates:* GCSE 26; A-level 7. *Musical activities:* 2 choirs, choral society, 2 orchs, 2 concert bands, big band, chmbr mus groups, tours abroad and occasional mus productions.
Pupils: 794 day; 200 studying inst. *Termly fees:* £1800 (day).

Woodbridge School (Co-ed)
Woodbridge, Suffolk IP12 4JH
Tel: 01394 385547 *Fax:* 01394 380944
Email: e-mail@woodbridge.suffolk.sch.uk

Stephen H Cole, head; John R Penny, dir of mus.
Awards: 2 mus scholarships of 25% fees plus free tuition in 2-3 insts; 1 bursary of free tuition in 2-3 insts. Age 11; usually gr 4-5. *Exam boards:* Edexcel (GCSE and A-level). *Exam candidates:* GCSE 7-11; A-level 2-3.
Musical activities: Chmbr orch (occasional tours), symphony orch, training orch, chmbr choir, jnr choir, choral society; also rcdr consort, medieval mus group; chmbr mus, band, br ens, str quartets, pop concerts, stage musicals.
Pupils: 550 day and boarding; 250 studying inst. Prep school is Abbey Junior School, Church St, Woodbridge *tel:* 01394 382675. *Termly fees:* £1986 (day), £3263 (boarding).

Woodhouse Grove School (Co-ed)
Apperley Bridge, Bradford BD10 0NR
Tel: 0113 250 2477 *Fax:* 0113 250 5290

D C Humphreys, head; Mrs J Johnston, dir of mus.
Awards: Mus scholarships and exhibitions with free inst tuition. Age 11, 13, or VI form entry; gr 5 on 1st inst with 2nd inst/voice expected. Other special awards also available to pupils over age limit, especially VI form entrants. *Exam boards:* NEAB (GCSE

and A-level). *Exam candidates:* GCSE 13; A-level 8.
Musical activities: 3 orchs, jnr choir, choral society, wind band, br and jazz groups, fl choir, str orch, cl groups, sax group.
Pupils: 565 day and boarding; 180 studying inst. *Termly fees:* £1945 (day), £3330 (boarding).

Worksop College (Co-ed)
Worksop, Notts S80 3AP
Tel: 01909 537127 *Fax:* 01909 537102

R A Collard, head; D R Evans, dir of mus.
Awards: Mus scholarships up to 50% fees pa including free inst tuition; augmentable in case of need. Age under 14 on 1 Sep. *Exam boards:* MEG (GCSE); NEAB (A-level). *Exam candidates:* GCSE 18; A-level 5. *Musical activities:* Chmbr orch, str quartets, ens, concert band, chapel choir, choral society.
Pupils: 350 day and boarding; 150 studying inst. *Termly fees:* £2660 (day), £3775 (boarding).

Worth School (Boys)
Paddockhurst Rd, Turners Hill, W Sussex RH10 4SD
Tel: 01342 710200 *Fax:* 01342 710201

Father Christopher Jamison, head; Michael Oakley, dir of mus.
Awards: Mus scholarships up to 50% fees and bursaries available. Special consideration will be given to str players and cathedral choristers. *Exam boards:* Edexcel (GCSE and A-level). *Exam candidates:* GCSE 6-10; A-level 2-4. *Musical activities:* Abbey choir, jnr choir, orchs, ens, choral society, wind band. New performing arts centre and mus school opening in 1998.
Pupils: 400 pupils. *Termly fees:* £2062 (day/jnr), £2865 (day/snr), £2972 (boarding/jnr), £4184 (boarding/snr).

Wrekin College (Co-ed)
Wellington, Telford, Shrops TF1 3BG
Tel: 01952 242305 *Fax:* 01952 240338

Peter Johnson, head; Francis Murton, dir of mus.
Awards: At least 2 mus awards, value 50%, 33% fees with free inst tuition. Age under 14 on 1 Sep; gr 5 on 1st inst an advantage. Age under 11 on 1 Sep; merit in gr 3. For VI form entry candidates should offer gr 6 on principal inst plus 2nd inst or voice. Several annual exhibitions also providing free inst tuition. Also special scholarship for the exceptionally gifted which includes free tuition at Birmingham Conservatoire Junior School. *Exam boards:* Edexcel (GCSE and A-level). *Exam candidates:* GCSE and A-level 6. *Musical activities:* Orch, choral society, chapel choir, concert band, jazz band, inst ens.
Pupils: 185 day; 125 boarding; 100 studying inst. *Termly fees:* £2100 (day/jnr), £2450 (day/snr), £4150 (boarding).

Wycliffe College (Co-ed)

Stonehouse, Glos GL10 2JQ
Tel: 01453 822432 *Fax:* 01453 827634
Email: senior@wycliffe.co.uk
Website: www.wycliffe.co.uk

D C M Prichard, head; C G Swain, dir of mus.
Awards: Several inst and vocal awards, values
5-50% full fees with free tuition on all insts. Age
under 14 on 14 Sep, gr 4 on 1st inst with 2nd inst
normally expected; or VI form entry. Extra
bursaries may be available for musicians. Orch
players preferred. *Exam boards:* Edexcel (GCSE
and A-level). *Exam candidates:* GCSE 10; A-level 8.
Musical activities: Chapel choir, choral society,
orch, chmbr choir, 2 bands, various chmbr
groups; professional concerts hosted.
Pupils: 127 day; 275 boarding; 150 studying inst.
Termly fees: £2990 (day), £4250 (boarding).

Wycombe Abbey School (Girls)

High Wycombe, Bucks HP11 1PE
Tel: 01494 520381 *Fax:* 01494 473836

Mrs J M Goodland, head; Judith Connett, dir of mus.
Awards: 1 mus scholarship available (awarded to
a girl with outstanding potential) value up to 50%
fees with free inst tuition. Age under 14; 1st study
inst required gr 5 with 2nd inst. Exhibitions may
be awarded. *Exam boards:* Edexcel (GCSE and
A-level). *Exam candidates:* GCSE 7; A-level 3.
Musical activities: 2 orchs; chapel choir, jnr
choir, choral society, chmbr, str and wind ens,
baroque and jazz groups, musical dramas.
Pupils: 25 day; 497 boarding; 368 studying inst.
Termly fees: £3375 (day), £4500 (boarding).

Yarm School (Boys) +

The Friarage, Yarm, Cleveland TS15 9EJ
Tel: 01642 786023 *Fax:* 01642 789216

R N Tate, head; Ben Wilson, dir of mus.
Awards: Mus scholarships offered value up to
33% fees. Awarded on grounds of mus promise,
usually on school entry. *Exam boards:* NEAB
(GCSE and A-level). *Exam candidates:* GCSE 8;
A-level 3. *Musical activities:* Snr school orch, wind
band, choir (SATB), chmbr group, ens etc. Jnr
school orch, wind band, choir and ens.
Pupils: 800 day; 210 studying inst. *Termly fees:*
£823-1712 (day).

G.A.M.P.A.
Gloucester Academy of Music and Performing Arts

JUNIOR DEPARTMENT

Senior Music
for 12-20 yr olds, minimum standard Gd. 7

Young String/Wind Project
for 9-14 yr olds, minimum standard Gd. 5

Music A-Level Courses

The Conservatoire for the South West

Tel/Fax: 01452 750585

Junior Department

Trinity College of Music
11-13 Mandeville Place
London W1M 6AQ
Telephone: 0171 935 5773
Facsimile: 0171 224 6278

Patron: HRH The Duke of Kent KG
Principal: Gavin Henderson

Trinity, with a long and innovative tradition of performance-based training prepares students for a professional career in music.

Trinity College's Junior Department offers gifted musicians aged 9-18 individual lessons and a range of group activities, choirs and orchestras through its thriving Saturday School.

The Department also holds **Open Days** throughout the year when visitors can see the Department at work – from the unique Creative Musicianship classes to instrumental ensembles, orchestras and choirs.

Particularly welcome to attend are parents and teachers considering their children's musical futures. A Junior Department Prospectus is available.

For details of Junior activities and a prospectus, please contact the *Junior Department* on extension 644.

TRINITY
college of music:

Junior Departments at the Conservatoires

In most cases partial or full local authority funding is available for specially talented children to attend their nearest conservatoire; travelling expenses may also be payable. See **Local Music Education** section for bursaries and additional lists of local Saturday Music Schools.

Birmingham Conservatoire

Junior School, Paradise Pl, Birmingham B3 3HG
Tel: 0121 331 5905 *Fax:* 0121 331 5906
Email: conservatoire@uce.ac.uk
Website: www.uce.ac.uk

Heather Slade-Lipkin, head of jnr school; Christine Lees, str co-ord; Luan Ford, w/wind and br co-ord; Jill Polyblank, pno co-ord; Andrea Calladine, vocal co-ord; John Leach, academic co-ord; snr conservatoire staff and CBSO players; Katherine Tomlinson, sec.
Course details: Specialist Sat morning tuition includes individual inst tuition on principal and 2nd inst. Supporting aural, theory and harmony tuition and A-level course (A-level exam centre). Chmbr mus for all pupils and symphony orch, wind orch, 2 choirs and Dalcroze Eurhythmics. Young strs from age 3. *Awards:* Means-tested bursaries. A few LEA awards available. *Entry requirements:* Competitive auditions; approx gr 5 at age 10 for main jnr school. Assessment tests only for young strs.
Pupils: 110. *Fees:* £475 (main jnr school); £110 (young strings).

Guildhall School of Music and Drama

Junior School, Barbican, London EC2Y 8DT
Tel: 0171 382 7160 *Fax:* 0171 382 7212
Email: twait@gsmd.ac.uk
Website: www.gsmd.ac.uk

Derek Rodgers, head of jnr school; Robert Pell, head of middle school; Valerie Kampmeier, head of lower school; Frederick Applewhite, head of orch studies; Detlef Hahn, head of strs; Robert Porter, head of w/wind and perc; John Miller, brass co-ord; Susan Tomes, head of keyboard studies; Mollie Petrie, head of singing; Faith Whiteley, head of prep course; Margaret Powell, head of chmbr mus; Heather Steedman, perc co-ord.
Course details: Specialist Sat training offered to young people aged 5-19 with exceptional musical ability. Inst tuition, musical awareness, GCSE and A-level tuition, plus many performance opportunities; activities include 6 orchs, chmbr mus, bands, choir, w/shops, m/classes. Prep course for young str players aged 5-8. *Awards:* Support available from many LEAs and charitable institutions. Some scholarships and bursaries available to others. *Entry requirements:* Entry by audition in Mar and Apr (for Sep entry); applications by end

of Feb. Approx expected standard gr 4-5 at age 10. Supplementary auditions throughout yr. *Pupils:* 270 music, 50 drama, 70 prep. *Fees:* £480 (basic), £280 (prep course).

London College of Music and Media at Thames Valley University

Junior Music School, St Mary's Rd, Ealing, London W5 5RF
Tel: 0181 231 2304/2677 *Fax:* 0181 231 2546

Peter Cook, dir; Peter Turton, head of strs; Christina Bailey, head of w/wind; Jean Reynolds, head of vocal studies; Jeremy Davis, head of keyboard; Martin Vishnick, head of composition; Philip Cunningham, head of GCSE/A-level; Russell Hepworth-Sawyer, head of mus technology.
Course details: Sat morning tuition includes individual inst instruction (snr course) and small group tuition (jnr courses). All courses include 'Discovering Music' and ens classes. New GCSE and A-level courses now available. Mus technology course covers the requirements of papers 11 and 12 of the London A/AS-level (MIDI, sequencing and recording). New for 1998, ens and mus theatre courses. Also performers w/shops, speech and drama classes, composition, orch and choir. *Awards:* Some students are LEA supported. Part-bursaries awarded by LCM to others in exceptional cases. *Entry requirements:* Entry on musical potential; auditions throughout yr.
Pupils: Approx 130. *Fees:* £55-95 (jnr courses), £185-205 (snr courses), specialist courses from £250.

Royal Academy of Music

Junior Academy, Marylebone Rd, London NW1 5HT
Tel: 0171 873 7380 *Fax:* 0171 873 7374

Jonathan Willcocks, dir.
Course details: A specialist mus provision for pupils aged 11-18 showing outstanding potential. Individual study on principal and optional 2nd inst, supporting aural and theory studies, chmbr mus for all pupils, symphony orch and supporting ens, choirs, many opportunities for solo performance. Full prospectus available. Also Primary Academy (age 8-11) and preliminary courses (from age 5). *Awards:* Some places are LEA supported; scholarships and means-tested bursaries available. *Entry requirements:* Open day in Feb, entries by 1 Mar. Audition in Mar-Apr for entry in Sep.
Pupils: 170 (Junior Academy), 110 (Primary

Academy and preliminary courses). *Fees:* £570 (Junior Academy), £315 (Primary Academy), £55+ (preliminary courses).

Royal College of Music
Junior Dept, Prince Consort Rd, London SW7 2BS
Tel: 0171 591 4334 *Fax:* 0171 589 7740
Email: jd@rcm.ac.uk
Website: www.rcm.ac.uk

Peter Hewitt, dir; Elisabeth Cook, asst dir; Andrea Robins, admin asst; John Mitchell, orch mgr and librarian.
Course details: Specialist training on Sats (am and pm) for students aged 8-18 who show outstanding talent and potential. First class individual tuition on principal and 2nd study insts (including voice and composition) with supporting musicianship, orch, choral and chmbr mus training of high calibre. Performance opportunities, w/shops, m/classes and lectures. Special Mini-Bass course for beginner db players (age 7-11). Preparation for mus college and university entrance. Full prospectus available.
Awards: Awards available from some LEAs; additional means-tested bursaries offered by RCM. *Entry requirements:* Entry by audition in Mar-Apr; applications by 1 Mar. Gr 5 distinction or equivalent on 1st inst usually expected of age 11 applicants. Usual age 9-13 (other ages considered). Wide catchment area.
Pupils: Approx 280. *Fees:* £680.

Royal Northern College of Music
The Junior School of Music, 124 Oxford Rd, Manchester M13 9RD
Tel: 0161 273 6283; 0161 907 5264 *Fax:* 0161 273 7611
Email: postmaster@fsi.rncm.ac.uk
Website: www.rncm.ac.uk/

Shirley Blakey, admin of jnr school; Karen Humphreys, acting admin, jnr school.
Course details: Independent concern offering specialist Sat tuition to pupils aged 7 and above. Tuition in principal study and subsidiary inst, with classes in aural training, theoretical work, ens playing, also orch training, perc classes. Graded system of concerts for performing experience. *Awards:* Wide catchment area; some pupils receive LEA support. Limited supply of bursaries available to others. *Entry requirements:* Auditions held in May for Sep entry; all pupils re-auditioned annually. Applications by 31 Jan.
Pupils: 70. *Fees:* £630.

Royal Scottish Academy of Music and Drama
Junior Academy of Music, 100 Renfrew St, Glasgow G2 3DB
Tel: 0141 332 4101 *Fax:* 0141 353 0372

Anne Strachan, head of dept; Sharon McGuire, sec.
Course details: Students aged 8-9 upwards. Specialist Sat tuition given on 1st inst with subsidiary inst tuition and opportunity to start 2nd inst study, plus class tuition in musicianship and theory. 2 orchs, chmbr orch, concert wind band, choir; also w/wind, br, chmbr mus ens, with opportunities for performing experience. Preparation during final yr for mus college application. *Awards:* Financial support offered by most Scottish Councils, with further scholarships offered by RSAMD in cases of exceptional ability or need. *Entry requirements:* Auditions during Feb and early Mar; applications by 31 Jan.
Pupils: 140.

Trinity College of Music
Junior Dept, Mandeville Pl, London W1M 6AQ
Tel: 0171 935 5773; 0171 487 9602/3 *Fax:* 0171 224 6278
Email: hjones@tcm.ac.uk

Harold Jones, head of jnr dept; Christopher Caine, snr asst and co-ord; Lettice Stuart, creative mus consultant; Janet Lasky, admin and concerts mgr; Ann Cherry, co-ord, w/wind and br; Gordon Pringle, co-ord, str; Philip Colman, co-ord, vocal and choral.
Course details: Pupils aged 9-18. Specialist tuition in principal study (and 2nd/3rd study where appropriate) with creative musicianship classes. Training also through symphony orch, chmbr orch, jnr str orchs, choirs, ens for fl, cl, sax, br, strs, rcdrs, perc; pno accompaniment; performing experience through concerts at the college, St John's Smith Square, the South Bank Halls and the Wigmore Hall. *Awards:* Junior exhibitions awarded by some LEAs; bursaries (on proof of need) and prizes also awarded (some preference for hn, bsn, va and db players). *Entry requirements:* Entry by audition, held during spring term. Approx standard expected is gr 4-5 at age 11, with strong musical potential. Proportionately higher standard expected of older entrants. Open days are held regularly.
Pupils: 170. *Fees:* £440 (40-min inst study, musicianship and ens activities); £159 per optional additional 30-min inst study.

Welsh College of Music and Drama
Junior Music and Access Studies Department, Castle Grounds, Cathays Pk, Cardiff CF1 3ER
Tel: 01222 394665 *also fax*
Email: jmas@wcmd.ac.uk
Website: www.wcmd.ac.uk

Edmond Fivet, principal; James Walker, head of jnr mus; Sally Craven, admin mgr, jnr mus.
Course details: Specialist pre-junior mus school (age 4-8) and junior mus dept (age 8-18) on Saturdays. Access courses offering individual tuition in performance and general musicianship. *Awards:* Limited number of bursaries available. *Entry requirements:* Entry by audition.
Pupils: 150. *Fees:* £110 (pre-junior), £425 (junior).

Local and Independent Music Schools

Most of the music schools listed below are independent. For additional local authority music schools refer to the **Local Music Education** section.

Academy of Contemporary Music
91 Haydon Pl, Guildford, Surrey GU1 4LR
Tel: 01483 456788 *Fax:* 01483 456070

Phil Brookes, dir; Bruce Dickinson, school mgr. *Courses:* F/t and p/t courses in contemporary mus for gui, bass, dr, vocals, mus production. *Entry requirements:* Audition. *Places:* 240.

Bela Bartók Centre for Musicianship
6 Frognal Ct, 158 Finchley Rd, London NW3 5HL
Tel: 0171 435 3685 *also fax*

Agnes Kory, dir.
Courses: Training courses for mus teachers and performers; also professional, amateur and children's classes including the Kodály system, history, analysis and performance skills. Adult classes credit-bearing for Trinity College of Music Certificate and Diploma for mus education. Both weekly classes and intensive holiday courses. *Status:* Registered charity.

Benslow Music Trust
Little Benslow Hills, off Benslow La, Hitchin, Herts SG4 9RB
Tel: 01462 459446 *Fax:* 01462 440171

Keith Stent, mus adviser.
Courses: The country's only adult residential mus centre, offering an annual programme of 100 mainly w/end (some week) courses, especially in chmbr mus (str, wind, pno and combined); also orchs, rcdr, pno, singing, early mus, jazz, big band, Alexander Technique, etc. All courses directed by experienced tutors including many international performers. *Status:* Private charity. *Fees:* W/end course: £111 (residential), £91 (non-residential). Some bursaries available. *Places:* Max 45 on some courses.

Berkley Music School
24 Brownside Rd, Cambuslang, Glasgow G72 8NL
Tel: 0141 641 0220

Helena McCracken, Eric McCracken, principals.
Courses: Classical, plectrum and folk gui tuition; also pno, keyboard and voice tuition. Beginners to advanced; individual or class tuition. 5 centres throughout Glasgow area.

Bharatiya Vidya Bhavan
School of Indian Music, Dance, Drama, Yoga and Languages, Old Church Building, 4a Castletown Rd, London W14 9HQ
Tel: 0171 381 3086

M N Nandakumara, exec dir.
Courses: Classical Indian mus and dance; group tuition; individual tuition; beginners to advanced; also 3 and 5-yr diploma course. *Entry requirements:* Beginners min age 7; diploma courses age 8+ with knowledge of subject. *Status:* Private school.
Fees: £55 per term for beginners, £135 per term for diploma courses. *Places:* 20 places on each course.

Blackburn School of Music
Eldon Pl, Preston New Rd, Blackburn
Tel: 01254 262888

Brian Morley, principal.
Courses: Pno, voice, str insts, w/wind insts, classical gui, all br insts; gr 1-8, diploma; theory (all grades). Also jnr mus courses and Music with Mum (babies and toddlers course). *Status:* Private. *Places:* 750.

Blackheath Conservatoire of Music and the Arts
19-21 Lee Rd, London SE3 9RQ
Tel: 0181 852 0234 *Fax:* 0181 297 0596

Marjorie Ayling, principal.
Courses: Tuition in most insts; beginners accepted, group tuition, gr 1-8; diploma; age 0-5/5-7 mus-making classes; Sat morning jnr choir, str and rcdr groups, special mus courses 7-16; theory classes; also tuition for GCSE, A-level. *Status:* Private school, registered charity.

Bolton Community Education Service
Clarence Street Centre, Clarence St, Bolton, Lancs BL1 2ET
Tel: 01204 525500 *Fax:* 01204 363962

Wilf Cox, snr area organiser; Tom Smith, curriculum team leader.
Courses: All courses p/t. Beginners accepted, group tuition, adult education and community classes in mus (practical and theory). Gr 1-4. Access courses (open college) into higher education. *Entry requirements:* No specific entry requirements. Students of all standards welcome. Also facilities for students with special educational needs. *Status:* Local government service.

Fees: 70p-£1.25 per hr and £1 per term registration fee with many free courses. Fee remission for students on benefits. *Places:* 90+.

Brighton Music Centre
Chesham House, 1 Chesham Pl, Brighton, Sussex BN2 1FB
Tel: 01273 606501

Linda Bhattachara, Vivienne Bott, co-dirs.
Courses: Tuition on all insts and voice (all ages, all levels beginners-diploma); adult mus-reading course. Advanced certificates and diplomas for Royal Schools of Music; ARSM, LRAM, ALCM, LLCM. Evening classes in diploma harmony and musicianship. *Entry requirements:* Gr 8 for all advanced courses. *Status:* Private school.
Fees: £20 per hr; £170 per 10-wk term; £200 per 10-wk term (advanced courses). *Places:* 10 in harmony group.

Britten-Pears School for Advanced Musical Studies
High St, Aldeburgh, Suffolk IP15 5AX
Tel: 01728 452935 *Fax:* 01728 452715
Email: bps.admin@aldeburghfestivals.org

Elizabeth Webb, dir; Ann Rawdon Smith, admin; Rachael Buxton, asst admin.
Courses: 10 day residential m/class advanced courses organised from Mar to Oct for instrumentalists and singers. Various courses available, with small number of places on each; entry by audition only (auditions Jan), usually advanced students and young professionals. Prospectus published Sep, and available on request. Also Britten-Pears Orchestra and Baroque Orchestra; national training orch meeting for short courses. *Status:* Private mus school.
Fees: Some bursaries available.

Cantica Voice Studio
55 Hayes Rd, Bromley, Kent BR2 9AE
Tel: 0181 460 6239 *Fax:* 0181 213 1857

Andrew Field, dir.
Courses: P/grad and professional voice training.

City of Belfast School of Music
99 Donegall Pass, Belfast BT7 1DR
Tel: 01232 322435 *Fax:* 01232 329201

R J Hewitt, principal tutor.
Courses: Sat morning centre with inst work including str, rcdr, choral work; many other w/shops, also various ens. Also evening and Sat tuition in all orch and band insts; pno, singing, gui, org, rcdr; aural and theory classes; plus group activities and ens, concerts, recitals and courses. Individual and group courses. *Entry requirements:* Audition and interview. *Status:*

Local authority establishment.
Fees: Under 18s £100 pa.

Clonter Opera Theatre
Swettenham Heath, Congleton, Cheshire CW12 2LR
Tel: 01260 244638 *Fax:* 01260 224742

Jeffery Lockett, artistic dir; Leonard Hancock, mus dir.
Courses: Annual inter-conservatoire opera competition. Prize of £1500. Also two residential Opera Studios pa in Apr and Jul each culminating in opera performances. Applications for auditions should arrive no later than 15 Sep for the following year. *Status:* Charitable trust.
Fees: No course fee is charged. Performance fees are paid and board and lodging are provided free of charge. *Places:* Variable.

Co-op Music School
11 Fore St, Ipswich IP4 1JW
Tel: 01473 218098 *also fax*

R Risebrow, member educ offr.
Courses: Tuition offered on most insts. Grade work encouraged. *Entry requirements:* Enrolment from waiting list prior to start of new term.
Fees: From £28.

College of Piping
16-24 Otago St, Glasgow G12 8JH
Tel: 0141 334 3587 *Fax:* 0141 337 3024

Dugald MacNeill, acting principal.
Courses: Piping tuition at all levels (tuition for Institute of Piping exams). 2 centres (Glasgow and Edinburgh), also international summer school. *Status:* Private college.
Fees: £10 per hr, £200 per week (f/t). *Places:* 20.

Derby Music Centre
c/o St Benedict School, Darley Abbey, Derby DE22 1JD
Tel: 01332 558007
Email: dmassos@aol.com

B Davies, admin.
Courses: Musical opportunities for children and young people aged 5-21. Rehearsal orchs and bands. Sat mornings in term time. Lessons available for beginners.
Fees: £27 per term; £45 family membership (any number of children). Bursaries available.

Dorset Rural Music School
The Music Centre, The Close, Blandford Forum, Dorset DT11 7HA
Tel: 01258 452511

Nigel Carver, dir.
Courses: Wide range of inst tuition available to children, teenagers and adults (day and evening); also various mus events organised. A retail sales

section stocks a healthy stock of publications, mus accs and insts. *Status:* Charitable trust.

Drumtech
The Powerhouse, 74 Stanley Gardens, Acton, London W3 7SZ
Tel: 0181 749 3131 *Fax:* 0181 740 8422

Francis Seriau, dir; Nick Bennett, gen mgr.
Courses: 2-yr diploma in higher education in association with Thames Valley University; 1-yr f/t course at 3 levels; 3-month f/t course at 3 levels; private lessons; 10-wk p/t courses; foundation courses; intermediate courses; reading and theory; advanced concepts and techniques; Funk Fusion courses; Latin courses. *Entry requirements:* Assessment lesson or audition for 2-yr diploma. *Status:* Private school. *Fees:* 1-yr course £3600. 3-month course £1200. Private lessons from £20 per hr. Foundation and intermediate courses £180. Reading and theory from £75. Advanced concepts and techniques and Funk Fusion courses £180. Latin course from £120. Discretionary grants may be obtained from LEAs for 1-yr course. 2-yr diploma fully grant funded. *Places:* No limitations.

The Elgar School of Music
16-20 Deansway, Worcester WR1 2ES
Tel: 01905 28613 *Fax:* 01905 723919

Donald Hunt, principal.
Courses: Tuition in all orch insts, pno, hpd, org, gui, rcdr, singing, aural training, mus theory; beginners accepted, gr 1-8, diploma; GCSE and A-level; ens playing, choral groups and special courses. Also jazz improvisation. *Status:* Private school.
Fees: From £18.50 to £200 per term. Bursaries from £50 to £200 pa. *Places:* 10-30 on courses (group tuition); up to 300 for individual tuition.

Ely School of Music
PO Box 1, Ely, Cambridge CB6 3DJ
Tel: 01353 663020 *also fax*

Courses: Tuition for beginners in keyboard, br insts and theory.

Essex Accordion, Organ and Guitar Centre
19 Colchester Rd, Southend-on-Sea, Essex SS2 6HW
Tel: 01702 340909

Jerry Mayes, principal.
Courses: Classical gui, gr 1-8; accordion, beginners to advanced (tuition for British College of Accordion exams, gr 1-8, teaching diploma); org, beginners to advanced; keyboard tuition for Trinity College of Music exams. *Status:* Private school.
Fees: £8 per 20-30 min private lesson. No funding available.

Flute Studio
Tamley Cottage, Hastingleigh, Nr Ashford, Kent TN25 5HW
Tel: 01233 750493 *also fax*
Email: 100610.2714@compuserve.com

Trevor Wye, principal.
Courses: F/t residential 7-month course for p/grad fl players. *Status:* Independent school.
Fees: £3000 pa. *Places:* 5 per course.

Gloucester Academy of Music and Performing Arts
The Management Suite, Merchants' Quay, The Docks, Gloucester GL1 2ER
Tel: 01452 750585 *also fax*

Caroline Lumsden, dir; Anne Ingram, admin.
Courses: The Junior Academy provides specialist tuition in mus and drama for ages 9-18. A-level mus (practical 1-yr); theoretical and academic (2 yrs).

Guitar Institute Guitar School
Basstech - Bass Guitar School, The Power House, 74 Stanley Gardens, Acton, London W3 7SZ
Tel: 0181 740 1031 *Fax:* 0181 749 0892

Alan Limbrick, dir; Paul Dhiman, gen mgr.
Courses: 2-yr Dip HE in Popular Music Performance. 1-yr and 3 month f/t courses, 10 wk p/t courses, private lessons 7 days per wk. *Entry requirements:* Applicants are advised to book an assessment lesson. 1 A-level pass and 5 GCSE passes for Dip HE course. *Status:* Private school and an accredited institution of Thames Valley University.
Fees: Limited number of Guitar Institute and major company scholarships available. Discretionary and mandatory LEA grants for some courses.

Harpenden Musicale
The Bourne, 20 Salisbury Av, Harpenden, Herts AL5 2QG
Tel: 01582 713333 *Fax:* 01582 767343

Gillian Johnston, David Johnston, dirs.
Courses: Individual tuition at all levels in all orch and band insts. Group mus activities include chmbr, str and symphony orchs; wind, concert and stage bands; rcdr groups; gui and folk gui groups. All ages and levels catered for. Annual nationwide summer courses also organised; other school activities include trips abroad, RFH concert, Barbican concert. Also the Musicale Primary Schools' inst teaching scheme offers inst teaching in primary schools out of school hours. *Status:* Private school.
Fees: £47-£120 per term. *Places:* No limit.

Hindhead Music Centre
Hindhead Rd, Hindhead, Surrey GU26 6BA
Tel: 01428 604941 *Fax:* 01428 607871

Ann Hughes-Chamberlain, principal.

Courses: Tuition in all orch insts, hp, pno, rcdrs, singing, composition, gui and keyboards (classical, folk, rock, blues, etc). Beginners to diploma. Mus appreciation classes age 3-7; adult mus appreciation talks. Ens, orchs, gui groups, rcdr ens, children's choir, chmbr mus. Summer specialist courses for pno, fls, cls, sax, children's summer mus courses. *Status:* Company limited by guarantee.
Fees: Around £28.50 per hour. *Places:* Individual tuition.

Horfield School of Music
22 Wellington Hill, Bristol BS7 8SR
Tel: 0117 975 6021

A G Stone, principal.
Courses: All wind and keyboard insts taught, plus general coaching. Beginners accepted, gr 1-8, diploma; also mus theory, arranging and popular singing. Group activities. *Status:* Private school.
Fees: £85 per term for ten 30 min sessions or five 1 hr sessions. *Places:* 10.

Huntingdonshire Regional College School of Music
California Rd, Huntingdon, Cambridge PE18 7BL
Tel: 01480 52346 *Fax:* 01480 450129
Email: college@huntcol.demon.co.uk

Roger J Tivey, dir, school of mus.
Courses: Extensive tuition gr 1-8 in pno and all orch insts including hpd, org, hp, perc, folk and elec gui and keyboard. Theory, practical study, tuition for teaching diplomas (gr 8+); A-level, HE foundation course, mus appreciation, singing studies. Activities include snr, jnr and prep concert bands; snr orch; str orchs; wind, br, fl, keyboard, gui ens; rock group; swing band; rcdr consorts; chmbr and children's choirs. Termly concerts, plus series of chmbr concerts. Open to all age groups, Sat am and pm, and weekdays. Main mus school, with further centres at St Neots and St Ives. Tutors also hired by county schools. *Status:* Private school and peripatetic service.
Fees: £60 (students); £70 (adults) per term. £20 for associate membership. *Places:* 1000.

Independent Academy of Music
66 Talbot St, Southport, Merseyside PR8 1LU
Tel: 01704 530903

Alexander Abercrombie, Barbara Dix, dirs.
Courses: P/t courses in singing, pno, str insts, w/wind, harmony and counterpoint; beginners to diploma and college entrance; ABRSM. Occasional m/classes (eg pno, pno accompaniment, opera); annual opera production. *Entry requirements:* Singing by audition. All others by interview. *Status:* Independent mus school.

Fees: Variable, staff set their own fees. *Places:* Variable.

International Cello Centre
Edrom House, Duns, Berwickshire TD11 3PX
Tel: 01890 818277

Christopher Cowan, Lucy Cowan, Donald Macdonald, dirs.
Courses: Historic country house with chmbr mus courses held in spring and summer. Private tuition available throughout the year. Centre aims to keep alive the mus and philosophy of Pablo Casals.
Fees: c £215 for chmbr mus courses. *Places:* 20.

John and Ingrid Gould Music School
5 Granshaw Close, Kings Norton, Birmingham B38 8RB
Tel: 0121 458 2781

John Gould, Ingrid Gould, principals.
Courses: Accordion, gr 1-8, diploma; pno, org, gui for beginners; also rcdr and theory. Individual tuition. *Status:* Private school.
Fees: £8-12 per 30 mins.

Kodály Centre of London
64 Montpelier Rise, Wembley, Middx HA9 8RQ
Tel: 0181 904 8923 *also fax*
Email: dvinden@tcm.ac.uk

David Vinden, Yuko Vinden, dirs.
Courses: Kodály musicianship and teacher training classes comprising solfège musicianship, c/room techniques and methodology, choral direction and folk-song analysis.
Fees: £130 per 10 wk term, £90 for students. *Places:* 15 per class.

Leo Baeck College
The Manor House, 80 East End Rd, London N3 2SY
Tel: 0181 349 4525 *Fax:* 0181 343 2558
Email: leo-baeck-college@mailbox.ulcc.ac.uk

Rabbi Dr Jonathan Magonet, principal; Rabbi Mark Solomon, dir of mus.
Courses: Training for student rabbis in the art of Cantillation and liturgical mus. *Status:* Private college.
Fees: £250 per course.

Lewisham Academy of Music
77 Watson's St, London SE8 4AU
Tel: 0181 691 0307

N Jacqueline Beckford, company sec; John Savage, mus worker.
Courses: Out of school mus project for children, young people and unemployed people, offering tuition in various insts and all musical styles, except classical, in well-equipped mus-making studios. Non-academic approach. All levels (beginners accepted and group tuition). Two

mus shows pa, chosen, written and performed by members of the Academy. Disabled access and facilities available in the recording studio. *Entry requirements:* Age limit 5-25. *Status:* Registered charity.
Fees: £3 per month for under 18s not working; £5 for unemployed and students; £12 if working. *Places:* 8-14 dependent on type of inst.

Liverpool Youth Music Committee
Roscommon Resource Centre, Roscommon St, Liverpool L5 3NE
Tel: 0151 207 4446 *also fax*

Martin Dempsey; Gerard Harrison, organisers.
Courses: Tuition in gui, perc, sax, fl; mus w/shops, mus theory, jnr band, jazz w/shop, drums and perc and bass gui. Tue-Thu evenings; basic keyboard and gui, Mon afternoon; singing w/shop, Fri morning; schools performance and w/shops by arrangement. *Entry requirements:* No formal qualifications necessary, just enthusiasm. *Status:* LEA supported mus centre.
Fees: 60p per session; £1. *Places:* 25-30 on each course.

London School of Singing and Dramatic Speech
18 Cranhurst Rd, London NW2 4LN
Tel: 0181 452 5502

Sarah Rose, principal.
Courses: Classical and modern popular singing: intensive vocal training at all levels, based on *The Singer and the Voice* by Arnold Rose. Rapid progress to highest standards of voice production for singing and dramatic speech, for leisure, professional work and diploma exams. Students taken at all levels. *Status:* Private school.
Fees: £100 per 4 lessons (individual). Group discount rates. Some scholarships available at the discretion of the principal. *Places:* Mainly individual tuition; group courses limited to 10 per group.

Manchester School of Music
6 Mount St, Manchester M2 5NS
Tel: 0161 834 4654

Sarah Duncan-Shorrock, principal.
Courses: Tuition in most insts, beginners, gr 1-8, diploma, professional training; also theory, singing, speech and drama. Private pop and rock vocal tuition. *Status:* Private school.
Fees: 10-wk course £109-118. No funding available. *Places:* Individual tuition but class tuition for theory.

The Mayer-Lismann Opera Centre
106 Gordon Rd, London W13 8PJ
Tel: 0181 991 0537

Jeanne Henny, artistic dir.

Courses: Operatic training centre for young singers, accompanists and conductors to study operatic scenes and roles in original language and to gain performance experience. Complete operas staged three times pa. *Entry requirements:* Entry by audition. *Status:* Private school. *Fees:* £500 per term (8 wks of 12 hrs per wk). *Places:* 15-20.

Medway School of Music
60-64 Canterbury St, Gillingham, Kent ME7 5UJ
Tel: 01634 855338 *also fax*

Peter Bailey; Debra Brennan, principals.
Courses: Inst tuition, group tuition, beginners, gr 1-8, diploma (all insts); mus theory gr 1-8; singing; children's mus club (2.5-5 yrs). *Status:* Private school.
Fees: £8.50 (adult), £8 (child) per 30 min lesson. *Places:* Mostly individual tuition. Max 5 in keyboard groups.

Midlands Arts Centre
Education and Outreach Dept, Cannon Hill Pk, Birmingham B12 9QH
Tel: 0121 440 4221 ext 266/7 *Fax:* 0121 446 4372

Gabrielle Oliver, educ and outreach programmer.
Courses: Adult courses in classical and folk gui, gr 5 theory, pno, voice w/shops, tabla, Indian vocal, Irish Bodhran, sax, br and steel pan. Children's courses include vn, pno, fl, rcdr, cl, gui and jnr orch. Also resident groups including Midland Youth Jazz Orchestra and Maestros Steel Orchestra. Various specialist study w/ends throughout the year including jazz (October). *Status:* Arts centre.

Millers School of Music
18 Pier Walk, Gorleston, Gt Yarmouth NR31 6DA
Tel: 01493 600481

Paul J Miller, Valerie Miller.
Courses: Pno, org, fl, rcdr; beginners, gr 1-8, diploma; also theory, GCSE, A-level, aural training, composition, pno accompaniment and coaching, diploma paperwork. *Status:* Private school.
Fees: c £18 per hour. *Places:* Individual lessons.

Mostly Music
28 Carlisle Close, Mobberley, Knutsford, Cheshire WA16 7HD
Tel: 01565 872650

Courses: Theory, diplomas, A-level, professional training. Church, early and choral mus.

Musicale Primary Schools' Instrumental Teaching Scheme
The Bourne, 20 Salisbury Av, Harpenden, Herts AL5 2QG
Tel: 01582 713333 *Fax:* 01582 767343

Liz Childs, dir.
Courses: W/wind and br teaching in primary

schools arranged directly between teachers and parents. Presently in Cambridgeshire, Bedfordshire and Hertfordshire.

Musicians Institute London Ltd
131 Wapping High St, London E1 9NQ
Tel: 0171 265 0284

Tony Muschamp, dir; Denise Roudette, president.
Courses: 1-yr f/t diploma course in gui, bass, drums or vocals, covering mus theory, band rehearsals, live performance and styles. World renowned visiting artists often hold m/classes.
Entry requirements: Entry by assessment. *Status:* Private school.
Fees: Some discretionary arts grants, grants and trust funds available. Also career development loans.

North East of Scotland Music School Ltd
21 Huntly St, Aberdeen
Tel: 01224 625554 *Fax:* 01224 626089
Website: www.mestonreid.com

Alan Young, admin.
Courses: Specialist inst and singing tuition organised from visiting professional teachers and musicians from all over the country to supplement local teaching facilities. Lessons available throughout the academic year. Pno, vn, vc, hn, ob, cl, db, bsn, singing, fl, rcdr, sax and tpt. Selection by audition and according to local tuition availability. Teaching takes place in Aberdeen, visits 9 times pa for 2-4 days. Serves particularly needs of N E Scotland. Mainly advanced tuition. *Entry requirements:* Audition. All ages accepted.
Fees: £14-21 per lesson.

Nottingham College of Music
2 Verney Dr, Stratford upon Avon, Warwicks CV37 0DX
Tel: 01789 294866

M S Sholl, principal.
Courses: Tuition mainly in keyboard insts; beginners, gr 1-8, diploma; mus theory correspondence courses; ABRSM, TCL and all diplomas. *Status:* Private school.
Fees: £10 per individual lesson. Correspondence courses approx £80 (UK), £100 (overseas) for 10 lessons. *Places:* All individual courses.

Open Academy of Music
35 Salisbury Rd, Harrow, Middlesex HA1 1NU
Tel: 0181 863 8275 *also fax*

Oliver Hunt, dir.
Courses: Keyboard-based distance learning. Aims to produce a fusion between jazz, rock, classical and early mus, including composition, improvisation and performance. Also both theoretical and practical preparation for grade

exams from gr 1 to Diploma level (all exam boards). *Status:* Private school.
Fees: £102-252.

Questors Young Musicians Club
Grange Junior School, Church Pl, Ealing, London W5
Tel: 0181 671 4579
Email: info@qymc.demon.co.uk
Website: www.qymc.demon.co.uk/

Fiona Johnson, mus dir.
Courses: Sat am mus school. Tuition offered on most orch insts, pno, rcdr, gui, perc and keyboard. Ens include w/wind, br, rcdr, jazz fl, str, jazz, vocal and orch. Introduction and taster courses available for children aged 4-7. Two concerts pa and an open day.
Fees: Fees start at £25 per 10-wk term. Assisted places scheme funded by the London Borough of Ealing.

Royal National College for the Blind
College Rd, Hereford HR1 1EB
Tel: 01432 265725 *Fax:* 01432 353478

Colin Housby-Smith, principal; Greg Barker, head of creative arts.
Courses: Offers FEFC and TEED funded training for blind and partially sighted people. Mus dept: practical and theoretical training in mus and musicianship. BTEC ND Music Technology specialising in sound recording. Pno tuning and repairs course (2-3 yrs). Beginners, gr 1-8; diploma; GCSE and A-level and studies in contemporary mus and mus technology. Also courses for sighted mus teachers of visually impaired people. Guest concerts and concert visits organised. Also BTEC First Diploma in Music Technology. *Entry requirements:* GCSE or equivalent in appropriate subjects. *Status:* Independent college. *Places:* 30+.

Royal School of Church Music
Cleveland Lodge, Westhumble, Dorking RH5 6BW
Tel: 01306 877676 *Fax:* 01306 887260

Harry Bramma, dir; Geoff Weaver, dir of studies.
Courses: Wide range of residential and non-residential courses at HQ and around the country; group lessons and beginners accepted; mus in religion studied in all aspects, all denominations. *Status:* Independent school.
Fees: Fees range from £6 per day for children to £465 for a 9-day choral course. *Places:* From 10 up to 250 on choral courses.

Saffron School/College of Music
121 Ashdon Rd, Saffron Walden, Essex CB10 2AJ
Tel: 01799 527098

Richard Godel, principal.
Courses: Individual lessons on wide range of

insts; beginners accepted, also group tuition, diploma. *Entry requirements:* By interview and consultation lesson. *Status:* Private school. *Fees:* £13 inst lessons (30 mins); £5 theory group. *Places:* 250.

Schools Music Service
PO Box 16, Liverpool L35 5HU
Tel: 0151 289 5365

Philippa Rosson, Kim Davies.
Courses: Inst teaching for schools. Qualified, reputable teachers for all insts. Help with rcdrs, bands, choirs and c/room mus. Advice on all aspects of KS. Mus tuition at mus centres in Liverpool, Frodsham and St Helens. Individual and group lessons, all ages, insts and abilities.

Spanish Guitar Centre (Bristol)
103 Coldharvour Rd, Westbury Rd, Bristol BS6 7SD
Tel: 0117 942 0479 *Fax:* 0117 914 6685
Email: bristol@spanish-guitar.co.uk
Website: www.spanish-guitar.co.uk/bristol/

Chris Gilbert, principal.
Courses: Tuition at all levels, beginners to advanced; mainly groups of 3-5 people. *Status:* Private school.
Fees: £80 per term.

Spanish Guitar Centre (London)
36 Cranbourn St, London WC2H 7AD
Tel: 0171 240 0754

Barry Mason, dir.
Courses: Classical and flamenco gui tuition offered to all levels, including exams gr 1-8.
Fees: £10 per lesson. *Places:* 40.

Spanish Guitar Centre (Nottingham)
44 Nottingham Rd, New Basford, Nottingham NG7 7AE
Tel: 0115 962 2709 *Fax:* 0115 962 5368

Ms C A Dickinson, principal.
Courses: Classical gui tuition, beginners, gr 1-8, diploma. *Entry requirements:* Individual assessment. *Status:* Private school.
Fees: £150 per term. *Places:* All individual lessons.

Spanish Guitar Centre (Penryn)
Goonhilland Barn, Burnthouse, St Gluvias, Penryn, Cornwall TR10 9AS
Tel: 01872 865802

Peter Budd, dir.
Courses: Classical and flamenco gui, beginners, gr 1-8, diploma; GCSE and A-level; also mus theory, arrangement of concerts, lectures, recitals, mus w/shops. *Status:* Private school.
Fees: £97 for 6-wk course of 1-hr per week. *Places:* Individual lessons and groups of 4-6.

Sycamore Piano School
10 Sycamore Close, Dukinfield, Cheshire SK16 5EN
Tel: 0161 338 2420 *also fax*

Mrs Caton-Greasley, Mrs L W Bunce, joint principals.
Courses: Specialist teaching of pno and theory, mobile and home-based teachers. Individual tuition 5-70 yr olds. Competitions, grades and diplomas available. *Status:* Private school.
Fees: £7.10 per half hour + 85p mobile. *Places:* Openings for 180 pupils. 30-50 vacancies.

Victoria College of Music
9 Staple Inn, London WC1V 7QH
Tel: 0171 405 6483 *also fax*
Email: exams@rcm.telme.com

Martin Ellerby, principal; Jeffery Tillett, exam dir; Sir Malcolm Arnold CBE, hon president.
Courses: Own board exams in mus, speech and drama held at local centres throughout the British Isles. Tuition by correspondence only. *Status:* Independent. *Places:* No limit.

West Hertfordshire Music School
Watford School of Music, Nascot Wood Rd, Watford WD1 3RS
Tel: 01923 225531 *Fax:* 01923 229089

Philip Ellis, principal.
Courses: Individual tuition in singing, all orch insts, pno, org, gui, perc; beginners accepted, group tuition, gr 1-8, diploma, theory; all ages; also A-level. Support received from local authority. Youth orch, chmbr, intermediate and jnr orchs, wind bands, br band, jazz big band, mus theatre, ens up to age 18. *Status:* County mus school.

Wiltshire Rural Music School
113 Gloucester Rd, Trowbridge, Wilts BA14 0AE
Tel: 01225 753175 *also fax*

Richard Young, hon dir.
Courses: School provides mus centre with w/end and evening activities. Sat pm chmbr mus playing and novice and elementary orch and chmbr mus, adult orch meetings, plus holiday courses for schoolchildren (including rcdr classes). Beginners accepted; group lessons in rcdr available. *Status:* Educational charity.
Fees: Variable depending on course. Closely linked to local authority, with partial funding. *Places:* No limit.

Yamaha Music Schools
c/o Yamaha-Kemble Music (UK) Ltd, Sherbourne Drive, Tilbrook, Milton Keynes MK7 8BL
Tel: 01908 366700

Nigel Burrows, mgr.
Courses: 100 UK schools for elec keyboard insts.

Publishers to the performing arts

RHINEGOLD PUBLISHING

YEARBOOKS

British & International Music Yearbook
Britain's most comprehensive and accurate directory of the classical music industry
Published each November £23.95

British Performing Arts Yearbook
The guide to performing companies, venues, suppliers, services, festivals, education and support organisations
Published each January £23.95

Music Education Yearbook
A guide for parents, teachers, students and musicians
Published each June £14.00

OTHER PUBLICATONS

The Musician's Handbook
A compendium of advice for the music profession
£14.95 (hardback)

Healthy Practice for Musicians
An expertly written self-help guide covering the whole spectrum of a musician's physical and mental well-being
£16.95 (hardback)

Arts Marketing
The definitive guide to audience-building through effective marketing
£18.95 (hardback)

Analysis Matters
A students' revision guide to the Group 1 London Examinations' Advanced Level Musical History and Analysis Papers for 1998 and 1999
£10.00

Kein Angst Baby
A singer's guide to German operatic auditions in the 1990s
£9.95

The Art of Conducting
A guide to essential skills
£12.95

MAGAZINES

Classical Music
The magazine of the classical music profession
Fortnightly £2.95
Annual UK Subscription £56.00

Music Teacher
Respected and enjoyed by music teachers for more than 85 years
Monthly £2.95
Annual UK Subscription £34.00

The Singer
For amateur and professional singers of every persuasion – from cabaret to grand opera
Bi-monthly £2.40
Annual UK Subscription £14.40

Piano
The magazine for performers and enthusiasts of classical, jazz and blues piano
Bi-monthly £2.40
Annual UK Subscription £14.40

Early Music Today
Britain's brightest early music news magazine
Bi-monthly £2.40
Annual UK Subscription £14.40

Opera Now
The international magazine for opera professionals
Bi-monthly £4.95
Annual UK Subscription £29.70

Music Scholar
A guide to scholarships for young musicians
Published November '97 £3.00

Rhinegold Publishing Limited
241 Shaftesbury Avenue
London WC2H 8EH
Tel 0171 333 1721 Fax 0171 333 1769
E-mail 100546.1126@compuserve.com

Further and Higher Education

Index to Further and Higher Education Establishments

Colleges, universities, etc, are listed below alphabetically, showing the sections in which they have an entry. Institutions starting their name with 'University of' or 'College of' are listed under the alphabetical component of the next part of the name, ie University of Central England in Birmingham is listed under C, and University College Scarborough under S. The following abbreviations are used in this index:

FE	**Colleges of Further Education**
HE	**Colleges of Higher Education**
Uni	**Universities**
Comparative	**Comparative Degree Tables**
Combined	**Combined Degrees**
Higher	**Higher Degrees**
Schols	**Scholarships at Universities and Music Colleges**
BEd	**BEd and BA(QTS) Courses**
PGCE	**Postgraduate Certificate of Education**
In-service	**In-Service Courses for Teachers**
Arts Admin	**Arts Administration Courses**
Inst Making	**Instrument Making and Repair Courses**
Rec & Tech	**Recording and Technology Courses**
Music Therapy	**Professional Training** under **Music and Disability**

Aberdeen College: FE

Aberystwyth, University College of Wales: Schols

Accrington and Rossendale College of FE: FE

Alchemea College of Audio Engineering: Rec & Tech

Alton College: FE

Anglia Polytechnic University, Cambridge: FE; Uni; Comparative; Combined; Higher; Arts Admin; Music Therapy; Jazz

Bangor, University of Wales: Uni; BEd; PGCE; Comparative; Higher; Schols; Rec & Tech

Barking College, Romford: FE

Barnsley College: HE

Bath Spa University College: Uni; Comparative; Combined; BEd; PGCE; Jazz; In-service

Birmingham Conservatoire: Conservatoires; Comparative; Higher

Birmingham University: Uni; Comparative; Combined; Higher; Schols

Bishop Grosseteste College, Lincoln: BEd; PGCE; Schols

Boston College: FE

Bournemouth and Poole College of FE, Poole: FE

Bournemouth University: Rec & Tech

Bretton Hall, University College, Wakefield: Uni; Comparative; Higher; BEd; PGCE; In-service

Brighton University: Uni; Combined

Bristol University: Uni; Comparative; Combined; Higher; Schols; Music Therapy; PGCE

Brockenhurst College: FE

Brunel University: Uni; Comparative; Combined; In-service; Jazz

Buckinghamshire College: Arts Admin

Bury College: FE

Cambridge University: Uni; Comparative; Higher; Schols

Cardiff, University of Wales: Uni; Comparative; Combined; Higher; Schols

Cardiff, University of Wales Institute (UWIC): BEd; PGCE

Central England in Birmingham, University of: Uni; BEd; PGCE

Chichester College of Arts, Science and Technology: FE; Jazz
The Chichester Institute of HE: HE; Comparative; Combined; Schols; BEd; Jazz
Christ Church College, Canterbury: HE; Comparative; Combined; Higher; BEd; PGCE; In-Service
City College, Manchester: Rec & Tech; Jazz
City of Liverpool Community College: FE; Jazz
City University, London: Uni; Higher; Comparative; Arts Admin; Rec & Tech; Music Therapy
Clarendon College of FE, Nottingham: FE
Cleveland Tertiary College: FE
Colchester Institute: FE; HE; Comparative; Higher; Music Therapy
Coleg y Drindod, Carmarthen see **Trinity College, Carmarthen**
Coventry University Performing Arts: FE; Uni; Jazz
Cricklade College, Andover: FE
Croydon College: FE

Dartington College of Arts: HE; Comparative; Combined; Jazz
De Montfort University: Comined; Arts Admin
Derby University: Uni; Comparative; Combined; Rec & Tech
Durham School of Education see **Durham University**
Durham University: Uni; Comparative; Combined; Higher; BEd; PGCE; Arts Admin

East Anglia University: Uni; Comparative; Higher; PGCE; Schols
Edge Hill University College: Uni; BEd; PGCE
Edinburgh University: Uni; Comparative; Higher; Schols; Rec & Tech
Essex University: Uni
Exeter College: FE
Exeter University: Uni; Comparative; Combined; Higher; PGCE

Fareham College: FE

Gateway School of Recording and Technology: Rec & Tech
Glasgow University: Uni; Comparative; Combined; Higher; Schols; Rec & Tech
Gloucestershire Initial Teacher Education Partnership: PGCE
Goldsmiths, University of London: Uni; Comparative; Higher; PGCE; In-service; Jazz; Music Therapy
Gorseinon College, Swansea: FE
Guildford School of Acting: FE
Guildhall School of Music and Drama, London: Conservatoires; Comparative; Higher; Schols; Music Therapy; Jazz

Gwent Tertiary College, Newport: FE
Gwent Tertiary College, Pontypool: FE

University of Hertfordshire: Uni; Comparative; Combined
Homerton College, Cambridge: BEd; PGCE
Huddersfield School of Education: BEd, PGCE
Huddersfield Technical College: FE
Huddersfield University: Uni; Comparative; Combined; Higher; Schols
Hull University: Uni; Comparative; Combined; Schols; Higher

Institute of Education, London University: Uni; Higher; PGCE; In-service

Joseph Chamberlain College, Birmingham: FE; Jazz

Keele University: Uni; Comparative; Combined; Higher; Schols; Rec & Tech
Kensington and Chelsea College: FE
Kidderminster College: FE; Rec & Tech; Jazz
King Alfred's College, Winchester: HE; Comparative; Higher; BEd; In-service
King's College, University of London: Uni; Comparative; Higher
Kingston University: Uni, Comparative; Higher; BEd; PGCE
Kingsway College, London: FE

La Sainte Union College of HE, Southampton: BEd; PGCE
Lancaster University: Uni; Comparative; Combined; Higher; Schols
Langside College, Glasgow: FE
Leeds College of Music: FE; Conservatoires; Comparative; Higher; Jazz; Inst Making
Leeds Metropolitan University: Uni; Combined; PGCE
Leeds University: Uni; Comparative; Combined; Higher; Schols; PGCE
Lewes Tertiary College: FE
Lewisham College of FE: FE
Liverpool Community College see **City of Liverpool Community College**
Liverpool Hope University College: Uni; Combined; BEd; PGCE; In-Service
Liverpool Institute of Performing Arts: HE
Liverpool University: Uni; Comparative; Combined; Higher
London College of Music [and Media] at Thames Valley University: Conservatoires; Comparative; Combined; Higher; Rec & Tech
London Guildhall University: Inst Making; Rec & Tech

Manchester College of Arts & Technology (MANCAT): FE

Manchester Metropolitan University: Uni; BEd; PGCE
Manchester University: Uni; Comparative; Higher; Schols
Media Production Facilities: Rec & Tech
Merton College, Morden: Inst Making
Middlesbrough College: FE
Middlesex University: Uni; PGCE; Combined; Jazz
Moray House Institute of Education, Edinburgh: BEd; PGCE
Moray House Institute, Edinburgh: Arts Admin

Napier University: Uni
National Opera Studio, London: Conservatoires; Higher
Neath College: FE
Nelson and Colne College of FE, Nelson: FE
Nene College, Northampton: HE; BEd; PGCE; Combined
New College, Durham: Jazz
Newark and Sherwood College: Inst Making; Rec & Tech
Newcastle College: FE; Rec & Tech; Jazz
Newcastle University: Uni; Comparative; Combined; Higher
Newport, University of Wales College: BA (QTS)
North Devon College, Barnstaple: FE
North East Surrey College of Technology, Ewell: FE
North East Worcestershire College, Bromsgrove: FE
North Hertfordshire College, Hitchin: FE; HE
North London University: Rec & Tech
North Riding College, Scarborough see University College, Scarborough
North Shropshire College, Oswestry: FE
North Warwickshire & Hinckley College: FE
North Warwickshire College of Technology and Arts, Nuneaton: FE
Northern College, Aberdeen: BEd; PGCE
Northumbria University: Uni; Arts Admin; Comparative
Norwich City College of FE and HE: FE
Nottingham Trent University: Uni; Comparative; Combined; PGCE
Nottingham University: Uni; Comparative; Higher; Schols

Oldham College of FE: FE
Open University, Milton Keynes: Uni; Comparative; Higher; PGCE
Oxford Brookes University: Uni; Combined; Comparative; BEd; Higher; PGCE
Oxford University: Uni; Comparative; Higher; Schols

Perth College of FE: FE; Rec & Tech
Peter Symonds' College, Winchester: FE

Peterborough Regional College: FE; Rec & Tech
Plymouth University: BEd; PGCE
Pontypool College see Gwent Tertiary College, Pontypool
Preston College: FE

Queen Mary's College, Basingstoke: FE; Jazz
Queen's University, Belfast: Uni; Comparative; Combined; Higher; Rec & Tech

Reading University: Uni; Comparative; Combined; Higher; BEd; PGCE; In-service
Redcar & Cleveland College: FE
Richmond upon Thames College, London: FE
Ripon and York St John, University College of: Uni; BEd; PGCE; In-Service
Roehampton Institute, London: HE; Comparative; Combined; Schols; BEd; PGCE; In-service; Arts Admin; Music Therapy
Rose Bruford College: Rec & Tech
Rotherham College of Arts and Technology: FE
Royal Academy of Music, London: Conservatoires; Comparative; Higher; Music Therapy; Jazz
Royal College of Music, London: Conservatoires; Comparative; Higher; Schols; Jazz
Royal Holloway, London University: Uni; Comparative; Combined; Higher; Schols
Royal National College for the Blind, Hereford: Inst Making; Rec & Tech; Music Therapy
Royal Northern College of Music, Manchester: Conservatoires; Comparative; Higher; Jazz; Schols
Royal Scottish Academy of Music and Drama, Glasgow: Conservatoires; BEd; Schols; Higher
Rugby College of FE: FE

SAE Technology College: Rec & Tech
St Andrew's College of Education, Glasgow: BEd
St Martin, University College of, Lancaster: Uni; Comparative; Combined; BEd; PGCE
Salford University: Uni; Comparative; Higher; Schols; Rec & Tech; Jazz
Scarborough, University College: Combined; BEd; PGCE
School of Oriental and African Studies, London University: Uni; Combined; Higher
Sheffield University: Uni; Comparative; Combined; Higher; Schols
South Cheshire College, Crewe: FE
South Derbyshire College, Ilkeston: Rec & Tech
South Devon College of Arts and Technology, Torquay: FE
South Downs College, Havant: FE
South East Derbyshire College, Heanor: FE; Jazz
South East Essex College, Southend: FE; Rec & Tech
Southampton University: Uni; Comparative; Combined; Higher
Southgate College, London: FE

Stevenson College of FE, Edinburgh: FE; Inst Making
Stockton-Billingham Technical College, Cleveland: FE
Stoke-on-Trent College: FE
Stranmillis College of Education, Belfast: BEd; PGCE
Stratford upon Avon College: FE
Strathclyde University: BEd; PGCE
Strode College, Street: FE
Sunderland University: Uni; Combined; BEd; PGCE
Surrey University, Guildford: Uni; Comparative; Higher; Schols; Rec & Tech
Sussex University, Brighton: Uni; Comparative; Higher; Schols
Sussex University, Institute of Education: PGCE
Swansea, University College of Wales: PGCE

Taunton's College, Southampton: FE
Thames Valley University, London: Uni
Trinity College, Carmarthen: BEd; PGCE
Trinity College of Music, London: Conservatoires; Comparative; Higher; Schols; In-service; Jazz
Ulster University, Jordanstown: Uni; Comparative; Higher; Schols; PGCE

Wakefield College: FE; Rec & Tech; Jazz
Warrington, University College: Arts Admin
Warwick University: BEd; Schols; Arts Admin
Welsh College of Music and Drama, Cardiff: Conservatoires; Comparative; Higher; Schols
West Cheshire College, Chester: FE
West Dean College, Chichester: Inst Making
West Herts College: FE
West Kent College, Tonbridge: FE
West London Institute of HE *see* **Brunel University College**
West Sussex Institute of HE, Chichester *see* **The Chichester Institute of HE**
Westminster University, Harrow: Uni; Comparative
Wigan and Leigh College: FE
Wirral Metropolitan College, Merseyside: FE
Wolverhampton University: Uni; Comparative; Combined; BEd
Worcester College of HE: PGCE; In-service

Yale College (Coleg Iâl), Wrexham: FE
Yeovil College: FE
York University: Uni; Comparative; Combined; Higher; Schols; Rec & Tech

Colleges of Further Education

An asterisk (*) indicates colleges offering specially designated foundation or pre-professional music courses. Certain Colleges of Higher Education offering this type of course are also included. Numbers in brackets denote the course's duration in years and are full-time unless stated otherwise. The following abbreviations are used throughout: BTEC ND (National Diploma), OND (Ordinary National Diploma), HND (Higher National Diploma), NC (National Certificate), HNC (Higher National Certificate).

Aberdeen College *
Balgownie Centre, Hutcheon Gardens, Aberdeen AB23 8HA
Tel: 01224 612581 *Fax:* 01224 612575

Dorothy Carnegie, course leader.
Courses: Foundation course in mus (1); mus diploma course (2); LLCM and LGSM diploma course (2). Grants may be awarded by the college. *Places:* c 20.

Accrington and Rossendale College of FE *
Division of Professional Services and Leisure, Rawtenstall Centre, Haslingden Rd, Rawtenstall, Lancs
Tel: 01254 354202/3

Paul Smith, head of division; Naomi Taylor, team leader performing arts.
Courses: BTEC First Diploma/Certificate Performing Arts (diploma 1 f/t, certificate 1 p/t); BTEC ND/Certificate Performing Arts (diploma 2 f/t, certificate 2 p/t); BTEC ND/Certificate Popular Music (diploma 2 f/t, certificate 2 p/t); HE Certificate/Diploma Band Studies (certificate 1, diploma 2); BA in Band Studies validated by Sheffield University (3).
Facilities: Practice rooms, studio rehearsal rooms, theatre studio, drama studio, dance studio, stagecraft room, keyboard lab, recording studio and sound engineering room. *Places:* 20 on each course.

Alton College
Old Odiham Rd, Alton, Hants GU34 2LX
Tel: 01420 88118 *Fax:* 01420 80012
Email: altoncollege@campus.bt.com

Martin Read, head of mus; Sylvia Harper, concerts co-ord.
Courses: A-level (London); ABRSM theory and practical. Tuition available on all insts. Wide-ranging chmbr, orch and choral experience offered including jazz band, big band, br band, choral society, chmbr choir, chmbr orch and wind band (all certificated by the Open College). Electronic mus w/shops, synthesizer and recording studio skills taught as part of A-level mus technology module. Adult evening classes.
Facilities: Recital room and concert hall with grand pnos; practice rooms. *Places:* 16 per group (2 groups pa).

Anglia Polytechnic University *
East Rd, Cambridge CB1 1PT
Tel: 01223 363271 *Fax:* 01223 352973

Richard Prior, head of mus.
Courses: P/t mus foundation course covering aural perception, theory, composition and performance.
Facilities: Students have access to university facilities including the library and mus ens. *Places:* 25.

Barking College
Dagenham Rd, Romford, Essex RM7 0XU
Tel: 01708 766841 ext 247 *Fax:* 01708 731067

Heather Carmel, head of mus.
Courses: BTEC ND Performing Arts (2). Mus options include language of mus, performance, composition, introduction to mus technology, recording techniques, singing. *Places:* 20.

Boston College
Sam Newsom Music Centre, South St, Boston, Lincs PE21 6HT
Tel: 01205 313227 *Fax:* 01205 311478

Courses: GCSE and A-level (f/t or p/t); preparation for diplomas; inst tuition; BTEC ND Popular Music; BTEC ND Applied Music.
Facilities: Recital hall (housing regular professional concerts), 2 lecture rooms, library, 7 practice rooms, 4 studios, rehearsal room, listening facility, coffee lounge, professional recording studio. Student accommodation available.

Bournemouth and Poole College of FE *
North Rd, Parkstone, Poole, Dorset BH14 0LS
Tel: 01202 465733/747600 *Fax:* 01202 205952

Mark Bellis, dir of mus.
Courses: Advanced studies in mus, including double A/AS-level mus (Edexcel), with mus technology options, inst tuition, orch and choral work, plus other GCSEs and A-levels (2); BTEC

ND Popular Music including mus technology, recording, composition, improvisation and performance (2); BTEC First Diploma in Performing Arts, intensive musical training for those not yet qualified for college diploma or BTEC Popular Music (1); p/t GCSE mus; p/t mus theory; p/t orchs, ens, jazz, etc.
Facilities: Large concert hall with technology suite, practice facilities, purpose-built popular mus studios. *Places:* Advanced studies 22; BTEC ND 44; BTEC First 25.

Brockenhurst College
Lyndhurst Rd, Brockenhurst, Hants
Tel: 01590 625555 *Fax:* 01590 625526

M C Newton, head of performing arts and media.
Courses: A/AS-level mus; A-levels in practical mus and performing arts. *Facilities:* Recital room, practice rooms, recording studio, mus technology studio.

Bury College
Peel Centre, Parliament St, Bury, Lancs BL9 0TE
Tel: 0161 280 8280 *Fax:* 0161 280 8228

Rob Nash, mus co-ord.
Courses: BTEC ND Popular Music; A/AS-level mus technology. Also inst w/shops, college orch, choir, pop/rock ens and other groups.
Facilities: 24-track recording studio and mus technology suite. Performances include a number of productions combining mus and performing arts courses.

Chichester College of Arts, Science and Technology *
Visual and Performing Arts, Dept of Music, Westgate Fields, Chichester, W Sussex PO19 1SB
Tel: 01243 786321 *Fax:* 01243 775783
Email: mdobson@inetgw.chichester.ac.uk
Website: www.chichester.ac.uk

Martin Seath, head of dept; Mike Dobson, head of school of mus.
Courses: Mus foundation course, complete preparation for HE covering A-level mus (single or double) plus other A-levels as appropriate (2); pre-professional mus course suitable for post A-level study covering performance, community mus, mus technology and composition (1); diploma in jazz studies, performing, recording and preparation for HE or work (1); BTEC ND Popular Music covers performance, mus technology and recording (2); mus foundation course (pre-degree) including GCSE mus theory, EFL and needs of overseas students supported (1); mus technology foundation course including A-level mus technology with other A-levels as appropriate (2); BTEC ND Music Technology;

BTEC First Diploma Performing Arts (Music) as ND but one year lower level popular mus course; BTEC ND Music in the Media; BTEC ND Instrumental Music Technology.
Facilities: Specialist mus block, computers, analogue and digital sound studio. Halls of residence. *Places:* Foundation mus 30; pre-professional 20; diploma in jazz 60; BTEC ND 120; mus technology foundation 16; BTEC ND Mus Tech 20; BTEC ND Mus in Media 20; BTEC ND Mus Inst Tech 15.

City of Liverpool Community College *formerly* Sandown College *
School of Performing Arts, Greenbank Centre, Mossley Av, Liverpool L18 1JB
Tel: 0151 733 5511 *Fax:* 0151 734 2525

Brian Wishaw, head of mus; Glyn Williams, HND.
Courses: BTEC HND Music (2); diploma in jazz and commercial mus (1); pre-professional course in mus (1); foundation course in commercial mus (1); BTEC ND Popular Music (2); introductory course in mus (1).
Facilities: Students from all courses are able to participate in mus-making activities within the school. Public concerts are an integral part of the work of the students. *Places:* 30-40 on each course.

Clarendon College *
Pelham Av, Mansfield Rd, Nottingham NG5 1AL
Tel: 0115 960 7201

A H Allcock, H Gelhaus, programme mgrs.
Courses: Mus with A-levels; mus diploma course; mus study programme; BTEC Popular Music; access courses in mus for both jazz and classical, BTEC First Diploma in mus; HNC Popular Music Production; GCSE Music.

Colchester Institute *
Faculty of Music and Art, School of Music, Sheepen Rd, Colchester, Essex CO3 3LL
Tel: 01206 718633 *also fax*
Email: colinst@rmplc.co.uk
Website: www.eduweb/sites/colinst

Bill Tamblyn, professor and head of school.
Courses: Foundation diploma in mus (2), foundation diploma in contemporary popular mus (2); BTEC ND in Music.
Facilities: Residential accommodation available on Clacton sites, but many students prefer to live in Colchester; excellent accommodation service. There are ramps and special WCs for disabled students. *Places:* 120.

Coventry University Performing Arts
Leasowes Av, Coventry CV3 6BH
Tel: 01203 418868 *Fax:* 01203 692374

Patricia Thompson, head of performing arts.
Courses: BTEC ND Music Techniques and Performance (2); BTEC ND Performing Arts (2); BA Hons in Music Composition and Professional Practice.
Facilities: 3 well-equipped electronic studios, recording studios, individual booths for private composition and computer-aided notation work, numerous practice rooms, library. Also 3 performance spaces: recital room, theatre and dance studio. *Places:* BTEC Music Techniques 20; BTEC Performing Arts 25; BA Hons 18.

Cricklade College *
Charlton Rd, Andover, Hants SP10 1EJ
Tel: 01264 363311 *Fax:* 01264 332088
Email: info@cricklade.ac.uk
Website: www.cricklade.ac.uk

Mark Ray, dir of mus; Mark Osborne, lecturer in mus; Janet Weston, lecturer in mus.
Courses: GCSE mus; pre-professional mus course including A-levels plus high level of performance tuition in 2-3 insts (1-2); A-level mus and mus technology; mus diploma; BTEC ND Popular Music; leisure courses; mus for special needs students.
Facilities: New purpose-built facilities opened Jan 1997 include recital room, mus technology studio, practice and rehearsal studios, teaching studios. College theatre capacity 270. *Places:* Pre-professional 10; other courses unlimited.

Croydon College
Fairfield, College Rd, Croydon CR9 1DX
Tel: 0181 686 5700 *Fax:* 0181 760 5880

John Parkes, programme mgr.
Courses: BTEC ND Performing Arts including mus, studio recording and mus technology (2); p/t courses in mus technology and studio recording.
Facilities: Performance hall, rehearsal and practice facilities, 16-track recording studio. *Places:* BTEC 35; 15 max on p/t courses.

Exeter College
Hele Rd, Exeter EX4 4JS
Tel: 01392 384154

Iorwerth Pugh, head of mus.
Courses: A-level (practical and theoretical) (2); other courses include adult education, jazz w/shop, 2 big bands, choral society and orch, gui w/shop, chmbr orch and student choir; BTEC ND Popular Music (2). Free inst and/or vocal tuition available to A-level and BTEC students on 1 inst.
Facilities: New mus suite consisting of 8 practice rooms, 2 lecture/rehearsal rooms, rehearsal hall

and sound studio and computer suite. Full digital facilities based around Apple Macintosh computers. *Places:* A-level, no limit (90 at present); BTEC ND 18.

Fareham College
Bishopsfield Rd, Fareham, Hants PO13 1NH
Tel: 01329 815000 *Fax:* 01329 822483

Shirley Taylor, head of performing arts.
Courses: GCSE and A/AS-levels in performing arts subjects; GNVQ in Performing Arts; inst tuition, recreational support programmes and evening classes.

Gorseinon College
Belgrave Rd, Swansea SA4 6RD
Tel: 01792 890723 *Fax:* 01792 898729
Email: p.ryan@gorseinon.ac.uk
Website: www.gorseinon.ac.uk

Penelope Ryan, principal; Leslie Ryan, mus; John Quirk, mus.
Courses: GCSE A/AS-level in mus, mus technology, performing arts, theatre studies and dance; BTEC ND Performing Arts; BTEC First Diploma Performing Arts with options in mus, drama, dance, arts admin and marketing; ABRSM and GSMD grade exams; coaching for mus diplomas and advanced certificate; theory exams; inst tuition on all orch insts and pno.
Facilities: Mus suite with keyboard studio, recording studio. Computers with Cubase Score (v3) and Sibelius 7 (Student), sampling, sequencing, notating and printing scores. Dance studio, theatre, rehearsal spaces, concert hall, library with mus scores, CDs and CD-Roms. *Places:* Up to 30 on each course.

Guildford School of Acting (GSA)
Millmead Terrace, Guildford, Surrey GU2 5AT
Tel: 01483 560701 *Fax:* 01483 535431

Gordon McDougall, principal.
Courses: BA Hons in Theatre (acting, musical theatre and production and design) (3); mus theatre course Diploma (3); Acting Course Diploma (acting and mus theatre option for graduates and mature students (1) (all NCDT accredited). Annual 10-day youth summer school in acting and singing for those aged 14-16, plus 3 courses for students aged 17 and above. *Places:* 220.

Gwent Tertiary College (Newport)
Crosskeys Centre, Newport, Gwent NP1 7ZA
Tel: 01495 333438 *Fax:* 01495 333386

David Price, dir of mus and head of performing arts.
Courses: A/AS-level covering theory, performance, mus technology and general musicianship; BTEC ND/First Diploma Performing

293

Arts based on pop and rock mus with drama and dance options.
Facilities: Recording studio, dance and drama studios, mus suite, electronic and acoustic equipment. *Places:* A-level 40; AS-level 15; BTEC ND 100; BTEC First Diploma 30.

Gwent Tertiary College (Pontypool) *formerly* Pontypool College *
Pontypool Campus, Blaendare Rd, Pontypool, Gwent NP4 5YE
Tel: 01495 762242

Mrs S Griffiths, head of mus.
Courses: GCSE and A-level (2); foundation mus course encompassing BTEC Media modules.
Facilities: Synthesizers, portable multi-track recording studio, ATARI 1040. *Places:* 15 per course.

Huddersfield Technical College *
New North Rd, Huddersfield HD1 5NN
Tel: 01484 536521 *Fax:* 01484 511885
Email: htcstaff@htcflex8.demon.co.uk

Mark Ellis, head of mus; Rick Cocker, tutor, mus tech and popular mus.
Courses: Preparatory mus course (2) incorporating GCSE, A-level and ABRSM, individual tuition, ens, composition, etc. Students are prepared for entry to university, mus colleges or HE colleges. BTEC ND Popular Music (2) incorporating performance techniques, history of pop, band skills; BTEC ND Performing Arts (2) with options in mus, dance, drama and stagecraft; BTEC ND Music Technology (2) incorporating sound recording, digital audio and MIDI systems, acoustics and synth techniques. BTEC First Diploma Popular Music (1) enables progression to Music Technology and Pop courses. Also ASET p/t courses in Sound Recording, Electronic Music, Modern Music Techniques. Also p/t courses in theory, voice, pno, gui.
Facilities: Concert hall, recording studios, PC-based mus IT suite, synth lab, MIDI studios, band rehearsal studios, pno lab, drama w/shop, etc. *Places:* 40.

Joseph Chamberlain College *
Balsall Heath Rd, Highgate, Birmingham B12 9DS
Tel: 0121 440 4288 ext 63

David Henson, dir of performing studies.
Courses: GCSE; A-level practical (Edexcel) (2); A-levels in mus and performing arts (Cambridge) including jazz musicianship; ABRSM gr 5-8; BEd (mus); access courses to Birmingham Conservatoire.
Facilities: Mus technology suite, recording studio, 2 tutorial rooms, 8 rehearsal studios, orch perc studio. Composer-in-residence. Links with Birmingham Contemporary Music Group and Birmingham Conservatoire. *Places:* 25.

Kensington and Chelsea College *
Faculty of Performing Arts, Sports, Health and Food, Hortensia Rd, London SW10 0QS
Tel: 0171 573 5233 *Fax:* 0171 351 0956

Tim Downs, lecturer in mus.
Courses: Mus foundation courses at three levels; A-level.

Kidderminster College
Dept of Community Studies, Hoo Rd, Kidderminster, Worcs DY10 1LX
Tel: 01562 820811

J Shepherd, lecturer in mus; J Bates, lecturer in mus and audio engineering.
Courses: A-level; BTEC Performance Studies; HND Theatre and Education; BTEC ND/First Diploma including rock performance and jazz modules, recording technology and pop business studies; BTEC Audio Engineering. Recreational classes, in-service courses and full range of inst and vocal tuition.
Facilities: Studio facilities. *Places:* 30 pa on each course.

Kingsway College *
Regents Park Centre, Longford St, London NW1 3HB
Tel: 0171 306 5700 *Fax:* 0171 306 5950

Malcolm Morrison, dir of perf arts; Philip Flood, head of mus.
Courses: London Young Musicians Course, incorporating A-level (2), further modules in composition, performance, jazz and popular mus, etc. Popular mus course incorporating BTEC ND (2) covering mus technology, live performance, mus business, composition and arrangement and studio recording.
Facilities: 16-track recording studio, 5 MIDI studios, extensive practice facilities, mus performance studio, theatre, well-equipped classrooms. Open learning centre with internet access and desktop publishing facilities. Lift access. Applications encouraged from candidates with disabilities. *Places:* LYMC/A-level courses 25; f/t BTEC 20.

Langside College
50 Prospecthill Rd, Glasgow G42 9LB
Tel: 0141 649 4991 *Fax:* 0141 632 5252

Anna Young, head of school, languages and communication.
Courses: A-level (1); SCE Higher Grade (1); evening class to prepare students for external mus college diplomas. *Places:* 20 on each course.

Leeds College of Music *
3 Quarry Hill, Leeds LS2 7PD

HAMPSHIRE SPECIALIST MUSIC COURSE

Peter Symonds' College
Winchester SO22 6RX
Hampshire LEA Co-educational
Sixth Form College (n.o.r. 1800)

13 places for outstanding young musicians between 16-18 are awarded after auditions held each year in February.

Students are provided with individual tuition in at least two studies (including piano) with eminent teachers, and have extensive opportunities for chamber music, orchestral and choral performances.

The academic curriculum consists of the London A level (double or single) combined with one or two other A levels or other appropriate AS or GCSE courses. A wide range of extra-curricular activities is offered.

Students are prepared for entrance to Music College and a range of Higher Education courses. Boarding facilities are available.

Further particulars are available from the College Office (tel: 01962 852 764, fax: 01962 849 372)

Tel: 0113 222 3400 *Fax:* 0113 243 8798
Website: www.netlink.co.uk/users/zappa/clcm/clcm.html

Peter Whitfield, head of FE programmes; Ian Smith, asst head of FE programmes.
Courses: BTEC ND Music Technology; BTEC ND Popular Music; BTEC ND Commercial Mus Production and Management; BTEC ND DJ Technology; BTEC ND Musical Instrument Technology; City and Guilds certificate in mus inst technology; BTEC HND Musical Instrument Technology (developed with Leeds Metropolitan University); foundation courses in preliminary, western mus, Indian mus and access course.
Facilities: No residential accommodation, but students are helped to find lodgings by the Welfare and Accommodation officer at the college and via Leeds Metropolitan University Lodgings Office. The college has a refectory and bar where mus is performed three lunchtimes a week. Students with disabilities are fully catered for in new purpose-built premises beside the West Yorkshire Playhouse.

Lewes Tertiary College *
East Sussex Academy of Music, Fisher St, Lewes

Roy Wales, dir.
Courses: E Sussex pre-professional mus course (2), organised in association with county mus centre; f/t foundation course including double mus A-levels with at least one other subject, tuition on at least 2 insts including pno, plus opportunities for performance; A-level mus technology.
Facilities: Mus annexe with recital hall, 15 teaching/practice rooms and electronic mus studio. *Places:* 25 students pa.

Lewisham College of FE *formerly* South East London College *
Lewisham Way, London SE4 1UT
Tel: 0181 692 0353 *Fax:* 0181 692 6258

D Moses, mus course tutor.
Courses: BTEC ND Popular Music (2); foundation course in popular mus (intermediate and advanced levels) (1); City and Guilds Sound Engineering (1); p/t LOCF accredited sound engineering courses; LOCF mus technology (1).
Facilities: Teaching and rehearsal rooms; studio, computer and keyboard suites. *Places:* Foundation intermediate 16; foundation advanced 16; BTEC ND 25; City and Guilds 16; LOCF mus technology 16; p/t LOCF sound engineering 16.

Manchester College of Arts and Technology (MANCAT)
Centre for Music and Performance Skills, 65-76 Lever St, Manchester M1 1FL
Tel: 0500 500 058 (free course enquiry line)
Fax: 0161 953 2259
Email: mail@mancat.ac.uk

Anne Bourner, head of mus and perf skills
Courses: Music Industry Level III (BTEC ND) and Level II (GMOCF); NVQ Level III Artform Development Worker. P/t courses include circus skills, Asian Band beginners, sound recording, mus technology.
Facilities: rehearsal rooms, performance area, recording studio, technical room/computer suite.

Middlesbrough College
Acklam Campus, Hall Drive, Acklam, Middlesbrough, Cleveland TS5 7DY
Tel: 01642 333398 *Fax:* 01642 333310

L Harrison, mus co-ord and lecturer; E Round, lecturer in mus.
Courses: GCSE; A/AS-level; mus for pleasure TROCN courses; theory classes; inst classes; composition classes; studio w/shop; ALCM diploma.
Facilities: Large suite of teaching and practice rooms, recording studio, performing arts theatre.

Neath College *
Dwr Y Felin Rd, Neath, W Glamorgan SA10 7RF
Tel: 01639 634271 ext 253 *Fax:* 01639 637453
Email: alan.good@neath.ac.uk

Alan Good, course co-ord.
Courses: A-level mus and theatre studies, mus technology; ALCM; LLCM; BTEC ND Performing Arts with options in popular mus, dance, theatre and stagecraft; BTEC HND Performing Arts (popular mus) in conjunction with the Welsh College of Music and Drama, Cardiff. Evening classes in recording technique and basic mus theory.
Facilities: Several multi-track digital recording studios, video studios and editing rooms, drama studio and mus practice rooms. *Places:* BTEC ND 40; HND 50; A-level mus technology 12; A-level mus 20; A-level theatre studies 20.

Nelson and Colne College of FE *
Scotland Rd, Nelson, Lancs BB9 7YT
Tel: 01282 440200 *Fax:* 01282 440274

Alison Birkinshaw, head of creative arts; Rosemary White, lecturer in mus.
Courses: Lancashire mus foundation course provides intensive training to prepare all musicians for a career in the mus industry; GCSE and A-level mus; Open College mus and courses

in recording technology including A-level in Music Technology.
Facilities: 3 fully-equipped recording studios (16-track and 8-track digital), 8 computer workstations running Cubase Score, 6 practice rooms, 3 Sibelius stations. *Places:* 26.

Newcastle College *
Faculty of Visual and Performing Arts, Maple Terrace, Newcastle upon Tyne NE4 7SA
Tel: 0191 200 4000 *Fax:* 0191 272 4020

Ian Spencer, head of faculty.
Courses: BTEC GNVQ Intermediate Performing Arts; foundation mus course; A-level mus; HND Jazz, Popular and Commercial Music; BTEC ND/HND Music Technology; BTEC HND Music Production; BTEC ND Popular Music; BMus (Hons) in Jazz, Popular and Commercial Music. *Places:* HND 50; ND 100; GNVQ 70; no limit on other courses.

North Devon College
Sticklepath, Barnstaple, Devon
Tel: 01271 388164 *Fax:* 01271 388121

Steve Edwards, head dept of arts and sciences.
Courses: A-level (2); BTEC ND Performing Arts. *Places:* 40.

North East Surrey College of Technology
Reigate Rd, Ewell, Surrey KT17 3DS
Tel: 0181 394 1731

P Batterham, head of humanities.
Courses: BTEC, A-level and HND in Performing Arts.

North East Worcestershire College *
Blackwood Rd, Bromsgrove, Worcs B60 1PQ
Tel: 01527 572813/572824 *Fax:* 01527 572900

Alastair Greig, head of mus studies.
Courses: New college mus foundation course; A-level (2); special intensive pre-professional course in A-level (1); mus diploma courses; in-service training; theory classes; professional recitals; composition w/shops. Free tuition in 2-3 insts and voice, keyboard harmony. Also evening classes for beginners and Access students.
Facilities: Large recital studio, 10 practice rooms, 2 concert halls (2 Steinway grands), 2-manual pipe organ.

North Hertfordshire College
Cambridge Rd, Hitchin, Herts SG4 0JD
Tel: 01462 424242 *Fax:* 01462 424380

Helen Corkill, mus lecturer.
Courses: BTEC ND Performing Arts with options in mus, dance, drama and stagecraft (2); BTEC ND Popular Music (from 1998); A/AS-levels in

Music, theoretical, practical and mus technology.
Facilities: Purpose-built mus centre including mus recital hall, teaching and practice facilities, new mus technology suite opened 1998. Centre for the arts includes 2 dance studios, theatre, teaching and rehearsal space. *Places:* BTEC ND Performing Arts 70; BTEC ND Popular Music 12; A-level 15.

North Shropshire College
College Rd, Oswestry, Shrops SY11 2SA
Tel: 01691 688000 *Fax:* 01691 688001

Odilon Marcenaro, head of mus.
Courses: A/AS-level mus and mus technology.
Facilities: Fostex 8 and 4-track recorders, Atari and Macintosh computers, Roland keyboards, Alesis effects units, Fostex 8-12-2 mixing desk, Audio Technica microphones.

North Warwickshire and Hinckley College
Performing Art & Media Centre, London Rd, Hinckley, Leics LE10 1HQ
Tel: 01203 243000 ext 3002 *Fax:* 01455 633930

Simon Edwards, head of popular mus; Ian Wynd, head of media production; Vince Brosnan, head of performance arts.
Courses: BTEC ND in popular mus (2 f/t); BTEC ND Media Production offers modules in sound recording; BTEC ND Performing Arts; GNVQ Media (intermediate and advanced offers modules in radio production; p/t inst tuition.
Facilities: 2 16-track digital studios including MIDI setup; 2 analogue radio studios; 5 VHS video edit suites; large performance studio; rehearsal areas.

North Warwickshire College of Technology and Arts *
Hinckley Rd, Nuneaton, Warwicks CV11 6BH
Tel: 01203 349321 *Fax:* 01203 329056

Judith Norden, head of f/t mus studies.
Courses: GCSE; A/AS-level mus technology; A/AS-level dance; BTEC Performing Arts; foundation mus course (2) including 2 A-levels.

Norwich City College of FE and HE
Ipswich Rd, Norwich NR2 2LJ
Tel: 01603 773162/3

David Morgan, head of dept.
Courses: A/AS-level mus (NEAB) with additional specialist inst tuition in most subjects including voice (2) f/t or p/t.
Facilities: Mus room with 4 mus technology workstations; practice rooms and drama/mus studio. *Places:* 25 pa.

Oldham College
Rochdale Rd, Oldham OL9 6AA
Tel: 0161 624 5214 ext 4243; 0161 785 4243 (direct)
Fax: 0161 627 3635

Nick Middleton, head of mus.
Courses: BTEC ND Popular Music; BTEC ND Asian Popular Music; Access course in mus (1). *Facilities:* Mus technology and recording studios; modern on-site theatre. *Places:* 25 pa, subject to audition and interview.

Perth College
Faculty of Arts, School of Music and Audio Engineering, Crieff Rd, Perth PH1 2NX
Tel: 01738 621171 *Fax:* 01738 440050

Pamela McLean, head of faculty of arts.
Courses: HNC Music Performance; HND Music Performance; Rock Music studies; The courses cover all aspects of performance, individual inst study, sound recording and the mus business.
Facilities: Two fully automated 24-track digital recording studios, 4 rehearsal studios, keyboard and sequencing lab, MIDI lab, TV broadcast facility; vocal, bass and gui studios. *Places:* NC 50; HNC 15-20; HND 15-20.

Peter Symonds' College *
Owens Rd, Winchester, Hants SO22 6RX
Tel: 01962 852764 *Fax:* 01962 849372

Anna Bennetts, head of mus incl Hampshire specialist mus course.
Courses: Hampshire specialist mus course, a f/t pre-professional foundation performers course incorporating double A-level plus 1/2 other academic courses, tuition in 2-3 insts (2); college course, single A/AS-levels (Edexcel); wide-ranging chmbr, orch and choral experience offered.
Facilities: Recital room with recording studio; practice rooms; Sibelius 7 and Atari C-Lab technology packages. Separate house for the specialist course. *Places:* Specialist course 12; A-level 25.

Peterborough Regional College *
Park Cres, Peterborough, Cambs PE1 4DZ
Tel: 01733 67366

Ian Burton, dir of mus.
Courses: Foundation course (A-Level); GCSE; BTEC ND Performing Arts; BTEC First Diploma in Performing Arts; BTEC ND Popular Music; modern studio recording techniques; inst tuition (ABRSM/Trinity College/Rock School); intensive mus studies. Also orch, choir, mus theatre group, substantial events programme; annual Festival of Visual and Performing Arts, etc.
Facilities: 8-track recording studio and portable studio facilities; suite of practice and teaching rooms; performing arts studio; 400 seat hall; live studio links with Cable TV. *Places:* Foundation course 12; modern studio recording techniques 15; BTEC 15 on each course.

Preston College *
Park School, Moor Park Av, Preston, Lancs PR1 6AP
Tel: 01772 254145

C H Pollington, head of mus; E Proctor, executive offr.
Courses: BTEC ND Music Technology; BTEC ND Popular Music; HNC Music Technology; BTEC First Diploma Performing Arts (Music); BA (Hons) Music and the Creative Arts (with University of Central Lancashire).
Facilities: Fully-equipped digital and 16-track analogue studios. Computer mus suites, PC, Mac, ST, hard disc recording, editing and sampling. *Places:* BTEC 20; HNC 12.

Queen Mary's College
Cliddesden Rd, Basingstoke, Hants RG21 3HF
Tel: 01256 20861

David Coggins, head of mus.
Courses: F/t and p/t courses include A-level in mus, practical mus, mus technology, performing arts; mus appreciation, improvisation (jazz and rock studies), mus theory, synthesizer and sequencing techniques, inst lessons.
Facilities: 2 teaching rooms, 4 practice rooms, synthesizer computer set-up, studio theatre adjacent to dept. *Places:* 40.

Redcar and Cleveland College
Corporation Rd, Redcar, Cleveland TS10 1EZ
Tel: 01642 473132 *Fax:* 01642 490856

S Colbert, head of mus.
Courses: GCSE (1); A-level (2); BTEC Performing Arts (2). *Facilities:* Purpose-built mus suite and recording studio. *Places:* 18 on each course.

Richmond upon Thames College
Egerton Rd, Twickenham, Middx TW2 7SJ
Tel: 0181 607 8223/4

Chris Mitchell, head of mus; Peter Garvey, Paul Jenkins, lecturers in mus.
Courses: GCSE, A-level mus; A-level Performing Arts; BTEC Performing Arts.
Facilities: Mus centre comprises 8 rehearsal rooms, seminar room and recording studio. *Places:* GCSE and A-level 20; BTEC 25-30.

Rotherham College of Arts and Technology
Eastwood La, Rotherham, S Yorks S65 1EG
Tel: 01709 360765

John Sleet, course tutor for popular mus.

Courses: BTEC ND Popular Music. *Facilities:* Studio theatre, mus room, practice rooms. *Places:* BTEC 18.

Rugby College of FE *
Rugby, Warwicks CV21 3QS
Tel: 01788 541666 *Fax:* 01788 538575

Linda Wainscot, curriculum mgr, performing arts.
Courses: Courses in most insts and singing; BTEC ND Performing Arts (2); BTEC First Diploma in Performing Arts; BTEC ND in Popular Music; flexible foundation courses in mus and dance (1); flexible diploma in mus. Active as LEA centre for out-of-school mus-making for children aged 6-18.
   Facilities: Mus centre, dance studio, drama studio. *Places:* No limit.

South Cheshire College
Dane Bank Av, Crewe, Cheshire CW2 8AB
Tel: 01270 654654 *Fax:* 01270 651515

J R Pyatt, head of mus dept.
Courses: A-level (2); BTEC ND (2) and First Diploma (1) Performing Arts. *Places:* 20 on each course.

South Devon College
Newton Rd, Torquay TQ2 5BY
Tel: 01803 386235/386381 *Fax:* 01803 386403
Website: www.torbay.gov.uk/sdc

Ian Bentley, principal.
Courses: BTEC First Diploma Performing Arts with mus options (1); A-level mus plus either 2 additional A-levels or 1 other A-level and 2 GCSEs; BTEC ND Performing Arts with mus options (2); HND Drama in the Community with mus options (2).
Facilities: Practice rooms, mus equipment, sound recording equipment. *Places:* BTEC First Diploma 25; A-level 16; BTEC ND 25.

South Downs College *
College Rd, Purbrook Way, Havant, Hants
Tel: 01705 257011

Peter Rhodes, head of mus.
Courses: A-level; pre-professional foundation mus course (1-2) including A-level plus high-level performance tuition in 2-3 insts (1); p/t AMusTCL diploma course for mature students; BTEC First Diploma Performing Arts; course in popular mus (1); BTEC ND Performing Arts (2); A-level in mus technology; A-level in contemporary and popular mus. *Facilities:* Theatre, 7 lecture rooms, practice facilities equipped with quality insts and recording studio. *Places:* No limit.

South East Derbyshire College
Cavendish Centre, Ilkeston, Derbys DE7 5AN
Tel: 0115 930 2942 *Fax:* 0115 944 7181

Steve McAlone, programme co-ord, mus and the performing arts.
Courses: BTEC ND Popular Music; BTEC First Diploma Performing Arts; BTEC ND Music Technology (subject to approval); A-levels theory, performance and technology; ABRSM exams; external diplomas, rock school, etc. Students attend on a f/t or p/t basis.
Facilities: Recording studio, TV and video studio, editing suite, theatre, practice and rehearsal rooms. *Places:* A-level 40; BTEC c 50; evening course 20+.

South East Essex College
Carnarvon Rd, Southend-on-Sea, Essex SS2 6LS
Tel: 01702 220400/220639 *Fax:* 01702 432320

Mark Vinall, head of media and performing arts.
Courses: Wide range of performing arts and mus courses including; A-level, BTEC, GNVQ and vocational courses; Access to HE mus diploma and mus theatre courses. College has won National Training Awards for its work with students with learning difficulties and disabilities.

Southgate College *
High St, Southgate, London N14 6BS
Tel: 0181 886 6521 *Fax:* 0181 982 5051

Neil Cloake, head of school of performance; Paul Goodey, co-ord jnr arts centre.
Courses: GCSE; A-level; foundation in mus (f/t or p/t). Opera, choral and orch societies, theory of mus.
Facilities: Practice rooms, concert hall, theatre, recital room, studio recording, Atari and Mac based workstations. *Places:* No limit.

Stevenson College of FE *
Carrickvale Centre, Stenhouse St West, Edinburgh EH11 3EP
Tel: 0131 535 4621 *Fax:* 0131 535 4622

A D Knight, snr lecturer; Morag Campbell, head of section.
Courses: SCE Higher; A-level; foundation in mus. *See also* **Instrument Making and Repair Courses**. *Facilities:* 4 c/rooms equipped with hi-fi, pnos and electronic keyboards; 16 soundproof booths for inst practice; Resource base with computers, MIDI, keyboards and listening stations. *Places:* Practical courses 15-20; SCE Higher 12-24; A-level 12.

Stockton-Billingham Technical College *
The Causeway, Billingham, Cleveland TS23 2DB
Tel: 01642 552101 *Fax:* 01642 551194

Anne Attwood, head of performing arts; Andrew McIntyre, GNVQ mus tutor.
Courses: GNVQ Performing Arts, including mus; range of leisure courses including jazz, rock and pop mus skills. *Facilities:* Keyboard suite, high-tech facilities: Atari C-Lab Notator, mus sequencers, etc. *Places:* GNVQ 25-30.

Stoke-on-Trent College *
Art, Design and Performing Arts, Burslem Campus, J Block, Moorland Rd, Burslem, Stoke-on-Trent ST6 1JJ
Tel: 01782 208208 *Fax:* 01782 603103

Richard Longden, programme mgr (mus).
Courses: BTEC HND Music (2); BTEC HND Popular Music (2); BTEC ND Popular Music and Recording; GCSE (1); A-level (1-2); p/t diploma courses 6-7 hrs per wk, for teachers, performers and accompanists (1); pre-GCSE course (1); joint diploma and A-level course (2); diploma in professional mus studies (2); pre-diploma in professional mus studies (1); college diploma in performing arts, or in mus, drama or dance (1-2); jazz diploma LGSM; BTEC Diploma Performing Arts.

Stratford upon Avon College
The Willows, Alcester Rd, Stratford upon Avon CV37 9QR
Tel: 01789 266245

Will Allen, head of mus.
Courses: GCSE mus (1); BTEC ND Performing Arts with mus options (2).

Strode College
Church Rd, Street, Somerset BA16 0AB
Tel: 01458 844400 *Fax:* 01458 844411

Tess Baber, section head; James Phippen, lecturer in charge of mus.
Courses: A-level (2); BTEC ND Performing Arts with mus options. *Facilities:* 400-seat theatre.

Taunton's College
Hill La, Southampton SO15 5RL
Tel: 01703 511811 *Fax:* 01703 511991

Jane Higgins, head of mus and performing arts.
Courses: A/AS-level. Entry to colleges and universities. Free inst tuition on 1 inst for A-level students. London 'double' A-level offered.
Facilities: Excellent new facilities. Wide-ranging chmbr, orch and choral experience offered.

Wakefield College *
School of Music, Thornes Park Centre, Horbury Rd, Wakefield WF2 8QZ
Tel: 01924 789874 *Fax:* 01924 789875

Tony Davis, dir of mus; Andy Cholerton, Kevin Dearden, lecturers.
Courses: A-level combinations including classical, popular or mus technology; p/t external diploma courses leading to LTCL, LRSM and LGSM (classical and jazz); BTEC ND Popular Music; Intermediate Diploma in Popular Music; BTEC ND Classical Music. *Facilities:* Keyboard lab; computer suite; 3 recording studios; rehearsal, practice and recital rooms; well-equipped theatre.

West Cheshire College
Handbridge Centre, Eaton Rd, Handbridge, Chester CH4 7ER
Tel: 01244 677677 *Fax:* 01244 680131

Rosalind Rice, head of mus.
Courses: Inst mus at Saturday mus school; group and individual tuition. A-level mus (1); BTEC Performing Arts with mus option. *Facilities:* Music practice rooms at Handbridge and Blacon sites. *Places:* A-level 14; BTEC Performing Arts 25.

West Herts College *
Watford Campus, Hempstead Rd, Watford, Herts WD1 3EZ
Tel: 01923 240311 Fax: 01923 247525

G Warner, mus lecturer
Courses: BTEC ND Performing Arts; HND/degree courses Performing Arts; BA Performance for the Arts, Entertainment and Media (3) in planning for Sep 1998; Foundaation course in contemporary mus (Access to Music) for age 16+ with mus inst experience.

West Kent College *
Brook St, Tonbridge, Kent
Tel: 01732 358101 *Fax:* 01732 771415

Nigel Scaife, head of mus.
Courses: Foundation course (2); p/t diploma (2); preliminary course (GCSE) (1); general and theoretical A-levels (2); practical A-level (1); mus technology A-level (2); BTEC ND Performing Arts (Music) (2); BTEC ND Music Technology; BTEC ND Popular Music; Access to music.
Facilities: Sound recording studio and computer mus suite, practice and rehearsal facilities, hall with sound and lighting system, TV studio and edit suite. *Places:* No limit.

Wigan and Leigh College
Leigh Campus, Railway Rd, Leigh, Lancs WN7 4AH
Tel: 01942 761726 *Fax:* 01942 761771

Mrs A J Boardman, centre mgr, performing arts.
Courses: BTEC ND Performing Arts specialising in

popular mus; BTEC HND Popular Music; GCSE and A-level mus. *Facilities:* Hi-tech suite, 24-track digital recording studio, 16-track analogue recording studio, rehearsal rooms, practice rooms. *Places:* HND 30.

Wirral Metropolitan College
Performing Arts and Media Studies, Borough Rd, Birkenhead, Wirral, Merseyside L42 9QD
Tel: 0151 551 7583 *Fax:* 0151 551 7401
Email: greg.williams@wmc.ac.uk

Greg Williams, head of school, arts and design. *Courses:* Creative arts course with A-Level (2); foundation certificate in mus with GCSE (1); BTEC Popular Music (2); BTEC Performing Arts with Music (2). Facilities: Mus suite, sound recording studio, practice and rehearsal rooms, dance studio, drama studio, video suite. *Places:* No limit.

Yale College (Coleg Iâl) *
Grove Park Rd, Wrexham, Clwyd LL12 7AA
Tel: 01978 311794 *Fax:* 01978 291569
Email: gmarshman@yale.ac.uk
Website: www.yale.ac.uk

Emlyn R Jones, principal; Sam Wyse, co-ord for performing arts.

Courses: A/AS-level mus courses including theoretical, practical and mus technology; BTEC ND Performing Arts (Popular Music); foundation diploma. *Facilities:* 2 mus studios, practice rooms, 16-track recording studio, concert venue. *Places:* BTEC 20; foundation diploma 20; A-level 20.

Yeovil College *
Hollands Campus, Mudford Rd, Yeovil, Somerset BA21 4DR
Tel: 01935 23921 ext 312 *Fax:* 01935 429962
Email: oayeovil@rmplc.co.uk
Website: www.rmplc.co.uk/eduweb/sites/oayeovil/index.html

Stephen Knight, head of mus. *Courses:* A-level in mus and performing arts; A-level mus technology; A-level theatre studies; BTEC Certificate in singing, mus technology; BTEC ND Performing Arts, including core units in mus, dance, drama and stagecraft with mus options. Rock w/shop, ens, chmbr orch, choir and production in professional theatre within general studies. Rock musicians welcome on BTEC ND/Certificate. *Facilities:* Include electro-acoustic mus studio. *Places:* 20 on each course.

Degree and Graduate Diploma Courses

There are three types of institution to be considered, all of which offer opportunitities to study music from many different angles for those who are not interested in becoming a classroom teacher. Details of teacher training degrees, now mainly BA (QTS), are not included here but in a separate section under **Teacher Training Courses.** Details of single subject degrees, combined subject degrees, and higher degrees (MMus, PhD, etc) are also listed in tabular form.

Colleges of Higher Education now offer many modules or options towards degree courses which include music. Although the music content of these courses varies from one institution to another, all those listed below include music as a major option. Courses such as these often provide a wider context for the study of music, with practical and critical work across the arts.

At the **Conservatoires**, music is studied principally under the guidance of internationally regarded musicians. Most of the colleges offer a degree and/or a degree equivalent course together with various internal diplomas, but these are chiefly geared towards the performance of music. Students intending to make a career on the concert platform are well advised to choose this type of institution, either for a three or four-year course or a one-year post-graduate course following a university degree. Academic courses at conservatoires require qualifications similar to those needed for university entrance, but exceptionally talented players may be accepted for performers courses with a minimum of formal qualifications.

The **Universities** offer the chance to study music in a wider educational context, where interaction with other disciplines is possible. Research is an important element in the work of all university departments, therefore specialist lines of musical thought are pursued by the full-time academic staff. Most university courses are now modular but incorporate the opportunity to make a detailed study in one area of a specific interest (which might be performance). The universities that were formerly polytechnics concentrate largely on imparting musical skills in a manner similar to that of the conservatoires, whilst at the same time offering the juxtaposition of courses in other subjects. These establishments have also initiated some highly individual modular degree courses.

All Colleges of Higher Education, Conservatoires and Universities offering degree or degree-level courses with a music content above 66% are listed below, divided alphabetically according to the type of institution. The content, entrance requirements and examination procedure of the degrees is also listed in tabular form for easy comparison *see* **Comparative Degree Tables.**

Colleges of Higher Education

Students should apply for admission to colleges of higher education through the **Universities and Colleges Admissions Service** (UCAS), Fulton House, Jessop Av, Glos GL50 3SH *Tel:* 01242 222444 where application materials may be obtained. Higher education establishments which have become University Colleges can now be found in the **Universities** section.

Barnsley College
Church St, Barnsley, S Yorkshire
Tel: 01226 730191
Email: music@barnsley.ac.uk

Courses: BA Hons in Band Studies; BA Hons in Popular Music Studies; BA Hons Creative Music Technology; BA Hons Popular Music Studies (extended 4 yr degree); HND Creative Music Technology; BTEC ND Popular Music.
Course details: All courses are modular in design with a strong practical content. Students develop a broad range of skills in the first yr of the course taking modules including musicianship, history, performance, mus technology, recording techniques, performance management and mus business. Some courses offer an international pathway with 8 weeks of study in Los Angeles.
Careers and counselling: All work is supervised by a personal tutor. The college has extensive facilities to support students through its Client Services team of specialist tutors.
Campus facilities: The mus centre is located at the Honeywell campus close to the town centre and has a refectory on site. A newly opened learning centre gives students access to word processing facilities and a quiet study area; also a specialist library on campus.
Music facilities: The college has a well-equipped mus centre including a suite of practice rooms, large rehearsal hall, two recording studios and multimedia suites. On site there is a mus technology suite with 24 workstations, a video studio and a newly opened multimedia centre. A wide range of insts for bands is available, including guis and amps, keyboards, drumkits and perc. Situated between Leeds, Sheffield, Manchester and Huddersfield where a wide variety of mus is accessible.

The Chichester Institute of HE
Music Dept, Bishop Otter Campus, College La, Chichester PO19 4PE
Tel: 01243 816000 *Fax:* 01243 816080

Arthur Robson, head of mus.
Courses: BA Hons Music (4). Mus may be studied as a single honours subject and as a single honours, major, joint or minor subject, with a selection from a wide range in the BA Modular Degree scheme. BA (QTS) (4). In addition, anyone with an Advanced Diploma is eligible, under certain conditions, to enter the BA course in the 2nd year. Mphil; PhD.
Careers and counselling: Careers service provided by college; professional counselling service.
Campus facilities: Accommodation offered to most 1st yr students. College dining rooms provide 2 meals daily; also self-catering facilities, coffee and snack bars. There is some provision for disabled students.
Music facilities: The facilities offered at the Bishop Otter Campus are particularly suited to such a course, with excellently equipped studios for w/shop presentations, and the nearby stimulus of the Chichester Festival Theatre and the annual Chichester Festival. Specific mus amenities include a suite of practice rooms, a recently established electronic studio, weekly performance options including choral singing and opportunities for opera and mus theatre. Instrumental and/or vocal tuition is available to all. There is also an org scholarship tenable jointly at the institute chapel and at Chichester Cathedral. Although the college has strong links with the traditions of the Anglican church, applications are welcomed from students of all religious persuasions or none.

Christ Church College
School of Music, North Holmes Rd, Canterbury, Kent CT1 1QU
Tel: 01227 767700 *Fax:* 01227 782244
Email: g.r.hancox@canterburk.ac.uk

Grenville Hancox, head of dept; Dalwyn Henshall, dir joint hons; Roderick Watkins, dir single hons; Derek Hyde, dir p/grad studies; Faith Whiteley, str consultant; David Campbell, head of w/wind; Benjamin Luxon, vocal studies consultant; Ronald Smith, pno consultant.
Courses: BA Joint Studies (Ordinary and Hons) (3) *see* **Combined Degrees**; BA (Single Hons); BSc Music and Maths; Access to mus, certificate in mus. P/grad: MA Piano Accompaniment; MA Composition; MA Performance; MA Electronic and Computer Composition; MPhil; PhD. T/T: BA QTS Hons (4); PGCE (mus).
Course details: The degree courses are modular in structure, enabling students to combine courses relevant to their own interests, strengths

and career intentions. Students earn credits for the modules successfully completed each year, and the degree is awarded on the basis of these credits in addition to final examinations at the end of each year. Both the BA and the BSc degrees are two-subject honours degrees: mus may be combined with art, education, geography, tourism, English, religious studies, sports science, IT, mathematics or radio, film and TV studies.

The BA single honours degree requires students to study mus and one elective from other disciplines in yr 1 (4 modules), and to study mus exclusively in yrs 2 and 3. A range of courses is offered including mus theatre studies, electronics (MIDI and electro-acoustic recording), advanced performance and composition. In yr 3 of BA and BSc Joint Hons students may opt for a concentration of mus modules, studying 3 in mus and one in their other subject.

Students receive tuition on 2 insts on a regular basis in yr 1. Mus modules for the BA and BSc degrees are grouped under the two headings of performance and critical studies, together with written and practical musicianship. Individual and vocal instrumental tuition forms a major element of the course, students receiving tuition in one study and able to arrange a second study. All elements of the course relate to each other, with mus studied also being performed, compositions and arrangements realised, and practical mus skills put into practice in a public setting.

A wide style of composition is encouraged by staff with expertise ranging from jazz to contemporary mus, baroque to gamelan. MA degree courses offer the opportunity to continue study in an area of specialisation developed at u/grad level.

Careers and counselling: All students allocated to a tutor; careers advice service also provided.

Campus facilities: Many students can be accommodated on campus in their 1st yr. Student canteen, student union bar, excellent practice facilities and a concert hall.

Music facilities: A weekly programme of concerts given by visiting professionals, students and staff in the St Gregory's Centre, a converted church owned by the college, is augmented by concerts in the cathedral and in Europe. Christ Church College is situated in the city of Canterbury just outside the precincts of the cathedral. The mus dept is housed in a fine Georgian house amidst the modern campus of the college. A comprehensive college library, departmental library and resource centre serves students and staff. 3 newly-equipped studios, Apple Mac/Finale, 24-hour access.

Colchester Institute

School of Music and Performance Arts, Sheepen Rd, Colchester, Essex CO3 3LL
Tel: 01206 718633/718000 *Fax:* 01206 718633
Website: www.rmplc.co.uk

Bill Tamblyn, prof and head of school; Mark Messenger, head of strs; Charles Hine, head of w/wind; Jennifer Lilleystone, head of vocal studies; Lesley Young, head of keyboard studies; Alan Bullard, head of composition.

Courses: BA Hons (3); Preliminary and Advanced certificate for overseas students; 8 joint degrees (3) with the University of Essex; BTEC ND in mus; Foundation Diploma in Music (1 or 2); Foundation Diploma in Contemporary Popular Music (2); P/grad: MA (Music) (1 f/t, 2 p/t); MPhil; PhD.

Course details: The BA Hons Music is for those who intend to devote most of their time to peripatetic, class or private teaching, performance, research or careers within the mus industry. The course offers a wide range of options in yrs 2 and 3 including business studies, Christian liturgical mus, composition, musicology, mus in education, mus for people with special needs, mus technology and performance. The Preliminary Certificate in Music (1) is for self-supporting students from outside the EEC who are seeking a career in mus. The Advanced Certificate in Music (1) has both practical and academic components and is designed as a refresher/Access course for overseas students. The MA in Music is a modular programme with a wide range of core and elective studies. The Foundation Diploma and BTEC ND in Music are 2-yr preparatory courses for conservatoire or university entry. Suitable students may enter this course in yr 2. The Foundation Diploma in Popular Music is a 2 yr preparatory course for HE in this subject. 1st and 2nd practical study lessons are available in all years of all courses. Specialisms in the courses have been devised with future careers in mind and include business studies for musicians, mus for people with special needs, and Christian liturgical mus, as well as performance, composition and dissertation options.

Careers and counselling: Colchester Institute has its own careers officer. Each student is allocated to a personal tutor who can advise on any aspect of work or welfare. The tutor can also direct a student to other specialist advisers for careers, welfare, residence, etc.

Campus facilities: Residential accommodation available on Clacton sites, but many students prefer to live in Colchester; excellent accommodation service. There are ramps and special WCs for disabled students.

Music facilities: The purpose-built mus school is

located at the main Colchester site near the centre of the town with easy access to the town's considerable attractions and cultural activities. Specialist accommodation for the mus department is located on the ground floor and top two floors of one of the large blocks at Sheepen Road and includes an auditorium (the Swinburne Hall), 4 mus technology studios, an early mus room and a series of small practice studios and teaching rooms. There is a keyboard laboratory which enables students to follow training schemes at their own speed, and the Stephens Library with eleven listening booths and a stock of over 45,000 scores, books, periodicals, records and tapes. There are many performing groups including a symphony orch and a full choir, a chmbr choir and ladies choir, br, wind and jazz bands, str orch, opera group, baroque and world mus groups. Public concerts, often with guest artists, are given frequently. The school of mus and performance arts offers the advantages of a medium-size conservatoire (over 300 students) combined with a university-style department and a course of study balanced between the practical and the academic. A further 3-storey building with drama studio is due for completion in 2000.

Dartington College of Arts
Music Dept, Totnes, Devon TQ9 6EJ
Tel: 01803 862224 *Fax:* 01803 863569
Website: www.dartington.ac.uk

Trevor Wiggins, dir of mus; Prof Kevin Thompson, principal.
Courses: BA Hons (3) see **Combined Degrees**.
Course details: The BA Hons is a modular course offering a number of outcomes: a specialist mus route leading to single honours; a specialist mus route with work extended into theatre, visual performance, performance writing or arts management leading to a combined honours award; a specialist route in theatre, visual performance, performance writing or arts management with mus leading to a combined honours award. The programme of study is highly innovative and stimulating. Within mus, the focus is on contemporary mus across a wide range of styles and genres, including western art mus, world mus and ethnomusicology, popular mus, jazz, folk, etc. Three compulsory subjects are taken by all students: practical, theory and mus in context. Practical work involves performance or composition in any style or on any inst, with opportunities for both solo and ens work and composers are encouraged to arrange performances of their work. Theoretical work

examines the nature of contemporary mus, locating it in time and place, aiming for a global view, not merely a European/American axis. Mus in context involves students working outside the immediate college environment and considering their response to a new location and the musical needs of people. Students often travel considerable distances, eg, New Zealand, India, Gambia, USA, as well as within Europe on the Erasmus/Socrates exchange programme. Experience of cross-disciplinary work is provided for all students with later opportunities to extend this both personally and through co-operation with students from other disciplines. The first year is basically a foundation year, providing a range of skills and experience. From the second year there is an increasing level of choice about the time spent on each of the compulsory strands of work and considerable flexibility about the style of mus studied and developed.
Careers and counselling: Personal tutors supervise students' work throughout course.
Campus facilities: On-site accommodation offered; also self-catering accommodation and local lodgings. Licensed dining room, bar, coffee bar. Campus is not level; wheelchair users may experience some difficulties.
Music facilities: A wide range of facilities is available to support the work of the college. The Service and Production unit provides lighting, PA, portable digital recording, video cameras and projectors. There are sound-proofed practice rooms as well as larger studios. The Performance Technology Centre provides extensive high quality digital recording, editing, sound processing and video facilities. Computers are available for student work together with email and internet access. Dartington is in a countryside location about a mile from Totnes. There is a full programme of over 200 mus, theatre and film events every year, together with college w/shops and visits by international artists. Student ens cover choral and chmbr mus, contemporary mus, jazz, rock, Balinese gamelan, African mus, Samba, mus theatre, etc. Students also have the opportunity to participate in the Dartington International Summer School in Jul-Aug.

King Alfred's College
Sparkford Rd, Winchester, Hants SO22 4NR
Tel: 01962 841515 *Fax:* 01962 842280
Email: malcolmf@virgo.wkac.ac.uk

June Boyce-Tillman, reader; Malcolm Floyd, head of dept; Ernest Piper; Jay Deeble; Francis Silkstone.
Courses: BA Performing Arts. P/grad: MPhil; PhD in Music Education, Gender in Music, Ethnomusicology and Music in Religion/Ritual.

Course details: Mus contributes significantly to this new interdisciplinary course.
Careers and counselling: Individual and group sessions are arranged.
Campus facilities: Theatre, chapel (with org), arts centre, dance studio.
Music facilities: Lecture rooms, practice rooms, mus technology facilities, recital room.

Liverpool Institute of Performing Arts
Mount St, Liverpool L1 9HF
Tel: 0151 330 3095 *Fax:* 0151 330 3131

Arthur Bernstein, head of mus; Jill Halstead, admissions tutor.
Courses: BA Hons Performing Arts (Music).
Music facilities: 5 recording studios, practice rooms, venues and theatres. Sponsorship from TDK, Gibson (USA), etc.

Nene College
Music Dept, Moulton Pk, Northampton NN2 7AL
Tel: 01604 735500 *Fax:* 01604 720636

J L Cranmer, course leader.
Courses: BA Hons Music (3); BA Combined Honours (3), BSc Combined Honours (3) *see* **Combined Degrees**; BA Hons Performance Studies (3).
Course details: The Music BA course offers the opportunity for study in the following areas: performance (including individual tuition), composition (acoustic and electro-acoustic), historical studies, popular mus and technology (including studio work), analysis, and Music: Society and Ideas. 1st yr students take courses in each area after which a flexible programme structure offers the opportunity to specialise. Final yr students also undertake a dissertation on a music-related subject of their choice. The programme is characterised by an emphasis on contemporary approaches to all areas of mus study. Combined Honours students (BA and BSc) select 2 of the areas of study from the single honours curriculum (according to qualifications and/or experience) and pursue these subjects for 2 or 3 yrs. Final yr students with mus as their major subject also undertake a dissertation on a music-related subject of their choice. BA Performance Studies includes work in mus, dance and drama. The mus element consists of a 1-yr foundation course followed in years 2 and 3 by intensive periods of study in specialised areas (eg popular mus studies, mus theatre etc). Students also engage in regular performance projects which focus on devised work and a theoretical course concerned with performance theory across all 3 disciplines. Final yr students undertake a dissertation on a performance -related subject of their choice. The Music dept is an expanding one and provides a friendly and

stimulating environment in which students can develop independence of thought, self-confidence and collaborative abilities to the full. As well as student lunchtime recitals there is a series of evening concerts.

Careers and counselling: A careers advice and personal counselling service is available to all students.

Campus facilities: Accommodation available in halls of residence (preference given to 1st yr students) and college houses located in town. There are full student union facilities. Disabled students are welcomed.

Music facilities: Suite of practice studios, purpose-built teaching rooms, sound studio, electro-acoustic/digital recording studio, Javanese gamelan, good quality grand pnos, hpd, theorbo, public concert series.

North Hertfordshire College

Hitchin Centre, Cambridge Rd, Hitchin, Herts SG4 0JD
Tel: 01462 424242 *Fax:* 01462 424580

Helen Corkill, lecturer in mus.
Courses: BA Hons Performing Arts with options in mus, dance and drama (3).
Music facilities: Purpose-built mus centre including mus recital hall, teaching and practice facilities; new mus technology suite opened 1998.

Roehampton Institute London

Dept of Music, Southlands College, Roehampton La, London SW15 5SL
Tel: 0181 392 3432 *Fax:* 0181 392 3435
Email: music@roehampton.ac.uk
Website: www.roehampton.ac.uk/academic/arts+hum/music/music.html

Damian Day, mus programme convener.
Courses: BMus; BA Joint Hons (3) *see* **Combined Degrees**. P/grad: MPhil/PhD by research; MA 20th C mus; Advanced Diploma/MA Music Education (1-4); MA Education Studies (with mus option) (1). T/T: BA(QTS) (4); PGCE (1). Other: MA/Diploma in Music Therapy (1) *see* **Music and Disability**; Diploma in the Teaching of Music.
Course details: U/grad courses offered in mus have a strong practical bias. Students on the BMus course pursue an integrated core course in harmony, history and general musicianship in yrs 1 and 2. Higher level study is focused on specialist pathways in harmonic language and composition, non-Western mus, solo performance, mus history and dissertation. Other courses are offered in conducting, mus therapy and studio-based work. The BA students follow a core course similar to the BMus in yrs 1 and 2, whilst students also take courses in another subject (art for community, business studies, business computing, dance, drama and theatre studies, education, English, English language, environmental studies, film and TV studies, French, geography, history, media studies, psychology, social policy, social admin, Spanish, sports studies, theology and religious studies).
Careers and counselling: Large careers advice unit with 4 f/t staff. A special counselling service is also available.
Campus facilities: 60% of students are resident and there are 4 canteens. Disabled students are accepted; provision depends on disability.
Music facilities: Southlands College has moved to new, purpose-built premises. Mus is housed in an air-conditioned, sound-proofed, fully networked block. The dept is well equipped, with 2 electronic keyboard laboratories for musicianship training, and additional electronic equipment for self-programmed aural training. For those interested in electronic mus there are 3 computer studios, together with good recording equipment. There are insts for early mus performance, a set of classical Indian insts, a West Africa *drum gahu* ens and Zimbabwean mbira. The institute has a strong team of instrumental teachers, all of whom are professionally engaged in the musical life of London. At present approximately 150 students are registered for courses in mus, of whom more than 100 are following degree courses. There are strong choral and orchestral activities. Recent choral performances have been given in Guildford Cathedral, St Martin in the Fields, St James's, Piccadilly and other London venues. In addition to the dept's musical activities, each of the 4 constituent colleges has its own domestic musical life. Each has good practising facilities; 2 have orgs.

312

Conservatoires

Applications for places at the following institutions should be made directly to the registrar of the establishment concerned who will forward the necessary forms.

Birmingham Conservatoire

Faculty of the University of Central England in Birmingham, Paradise Pl, Birmingham B3 3HG
Tel: 0121 331 5901/2 *Fax:* 0121 331 5906
Email: conservatoire@uce.ac.uk

Prof George Caird, principal; Prof Alastair Pearce, vice-principal; Prof Janet Hilton, head of w/wind; Prof Keith Darlington, head of vocal studies; Prof Malcolm Wilson, head of keyboard studies; Reginald Reid, head of br; Prof Andrew Downes, head of composition and creative studies; Prof Jacqueline Ross, head of inst studies; James Strebing, head of perc; Mark Racz, head u/grad studies; Peter Johnson, head p/grad studies.
Courses offered: BMus (3 or 4 Hons). P/grad: MA; various degree and diploma courses (1:2); MPhil, PhD. T/T: BEd (2).
Course details: The conservatoire offers degree, diploma and p/grad courses to about 550 students. This number is large enough to provide a wide range of musical activities but small enough to ensure a friendly and personal environment. The BMus (Hons) course is designed for students who wish to concentrate on performance or composition, developing expertise, theoretical and historical knowledge, creativity and versatility for the professional musician. Great emphasis is placed on practical work, including individual principal study tuition, orch and inst ens programme, opera, choral performance, jazz, world mus, contemporary and early mus. Harmony and aural are taught in w/shop sessions which also develop improvisation and compositional skills. An options unit allows students to explore both practical and academic interests in greater depth, including baroque performance, gamelan, jazz and community mus. Various p/grad programmes are available. The PGDip and MA provide advanced study in performance, composition, musicology and world mus, with further academic study in the MA. The DPS is designed for the near-professional performer and includes opportunities for public performance including opera. The MPhil and PhD research degrees can be taken in composition, performance-study (with or without recital), aspects of world mus, 18th C studies, various aspects of 20th C musicology, aesthetics and analysis.
Careers and counselling: A member of staff acts as adviser for matters of vocational and professional nature; personal counsellor available through normal university channels. A series of careers seminars is arranged each yr.
Campus facilities: Single study bedrooms available in Cambrian Hall; hall of residence accommodation on university's education campus. University accommodation officer can assist with private lodgings. Refectory open weekdays.
Music facilities: Birmingham Conservatoire has a unique place among British mus colleges in that, while enjoying the benefits of being a faculty of the University of Central England, it is essentially a practically orientated college recognised as one of the major national conservatoires. As a member of the European Association of Music Conservatoires, it expects a high, professional level of instrumental/vocal performance from its students, whose practical work is informed and supported by sound theoretical and historical knowledge and understanding. Each student's programme of work is supervised by a personal tutor from the full-time staff who, in a pastoral capacity, is also responsible for the student's general welfare. The present building is purpose-built, situated at the heart of the city's cultural and administrative amenities in excellent modern accommodation. The facilities include the Adrian Boult Hall and recital hall with a ground floor extension adding 35 practice rooms, recording studio and a lecture theatre. There is of course Symphony Hall (which is part of Birmingham's International Conference Centre), an active repertory theatre, a distinguished art gallery, a fine public library as well as the town hall, all of which stand within a spacious pedestrian area served by an efficient and convenient transport network. New Street station, two cathedrals and the main shopping centre are all within 10 minutes' walk of Paradise Circus. From its foundation the conservatoire has been closely identified with the cultural life of the city and its local interests and loyalties have been strengthened by long-standing ties with the CBSO, whose performing home, Symphony Hall, is adjacent to the site. Many of the orchestra's principal players are on the staff of the conservatoire. There are also well-established links with Birmingham University (Department of Music) and various faculties of the University of Central England, notably those of Art and Design, and Education and Teacher Training. Entry scholarships are available for u/grads and p/grads.

314

Guildhall School of Music & Drama
Silk St, Barbican, London EC2Y 8DT
Tel: 0171 628 2571 *Fax:* 0171 256 9438

Ian Horsbrugh, principal; Damian Cranmer, dir of mus; Bernard Lanskey, asst dir of mus; Andrew Schultz, head of mus studies; David Takeno, head of strs; Peter Gane, head of wind and perc; Iain Burnside, head of keyboard studies; Robin Bowman, head of vocal studies; Robert Saxton, head of composition; Yfrah Neaman, head of advanced studies; Clive Timms, head of opera studies; Scott Stroman, head of jazz.
Courses offered: BMus (4) (degree for performers with 3-yr diploma exit point). P/grad: P/grad Diploma in Musical Performance (1); Certificate of Advanced Study for performers (1); Concert Recital Diploma (1+). Others: MMus in Composition; Dip MTh in music therapy (GSMD-York) (1) (validated by the University of York); Advanced Certificate in Jazz and Studio Music (1); Diploma in Continuing Professional Development (GSMD) (modular, 1-2).
Course details: As well as the BMus course, there is a variety of advanced and post-diploma courses catering for the specialist needs of performing musicians: advanced instrumental studies, opera, conducting, composition, jazz and studio mus, early mus, vocal training, orchestral training, pno accompaniment, repetiteur training and mus therapy. All the courses are designed with the flexibility to meet the needs of individual students. For instance, students on the u/grad course with a particular aptitude for early mus or jazz may be involved in some of the activities of these specialist courses, and the opera course may offer opportunities to singers on the u/grad or post-diploma vocal training courses. Many of the 100 overseas students are attracted to the advanced instrumental studies course, designed for potential soloists.
Careers and counselling: Most problems are the responsibility of the welfare officer, but counsellors are also available to advise, as are officers of the Students' Union.
Campus facilities: Assistant manager (Sundial Court) assists with finding lodgings, and places are available in Sundial Court, the school's hall of residence which consists of 3, 4 and 5 bed flats for 178 students, situated 5 mins walk from the school. Sandwich, tea and coffee bar available Mon-Fri, and lunch available at Lauderdale Tower.
Music facilities: In addition to the practice facilities within the School, there is an annexe with 46 practice studios. As part of the Barbican Centre complex, the school has been able to develop close links with the London Symphony Orchestra and the Royal Shakespeare Company. The Guildhall Symphony Orchestra and other ens are also able to give public concerts in the Barbican Hall. The school's own theatre is superbly equipped for the production of opera (for which the GSMD has an international reputation), and the presence of the stage management course ensures a professional level of presentation. The annual musical takes advantage of having both actors and musicians under the same roof. The teaching staff includes many leading performers and the school's policy is to draw on established practitioners to work with orchs, ens, chmbr mus groups, song classes and opera productions. A Leverhulme Foundation grant has enabled the school to invite conductors like Christopher Seaman (the School's principal guest conductor), Sir Colin Davis and Mstislav Rostropovich to conduct the orchs.

Leeds College of Music
3 Quarry Hill, Leeds LS2 7PD
Tel: 0113 222 3400 *Fax:* 0113 243 8798
Website: www.netlink.co.uk/users/zappa/clcm/clcm.html

David Hoult, principal; Graham Hearn, p/grad certificate course leader; Jonathan Stockdale, head of HE programmes; Peter Whitfield, head of FE programmes; Philip Greenwood, head of technology programmes; Roger Ladds, head of p/t programmes; David Smith, head of performance studies; Anthony Langford, head of academic studies and quality assurance.
Courses offered: BA Hons in Jazz Studies (3); Bachelor of Performing Arts Hons (Music) (3); Graduate Diploma in Music (3); BTECs in Music Technology, Instrument Repair, Popular Music, Music and Media, Foundation Programme (including preliminary, Access, Indian and Western. P/grad: Certificate in Jazz, Contemporary and Popular Music (1).
Course details: Entry requirements for the HE courses are normally five subjects, including English, two of which should be at A-level or equivalent. There may be exceptions and exemptions for mature and overseas students. Gr 5 theory plus practical can be offered in lieu of A-level mus. Although gr 8 theory and practical are not course requirements, prospective students must demonstrate an equivalent standard at audition.
Careers and counselling: The College has a careers officer to supply advice and information. A student counsellor and welfare officer are available for personal counselling. Course managers and personal tutors will also give advice.
Campus facilities: There is no residential accommodation, but students are helped to find lodgings by the Welfare and Accommodation officer at the College and via Leeds Metropolitan University Lodgings Office. The college has a

refectory and coffee bar where mus is performed 3 lunchtimes a week. Students with disabilities are fully catered for in LCM's new purpose-built premises next to the West Yorkshire Playhouse.

Music facilities: Facilities at the college include an extensive library, 24-track recording studio, electronic music lab, computer composition studio, an aural lab, a large collection of musical insts (including Indian and Caribbean), and Britain's first archive for jazz and popular mus. In addition to theoretical 1st and 2nd studies, emphasis is placed on practical work through improvisation, big band, jazz orch and small ens. Individual enterprise is encouraged: students are given the opportunity to hear their compositions performed and there are many student ens. The college organises an annual concert season featuring visiting artists as well as staff and students. Recent artists include Django Bates, Julian Bream, John Dankworth, Ensemble Bash, Kathryn Stott and Ron Goodwin.

London College of Music and Media at Thames Valley University

St Mary's Rd, Ealing, London W5 5RF
Tel: 0181 231 2304 *Fax:* 0181 231 2546

Linda Merrick, head of mus; Donald Ellman, pathway leader, p/grad studies; Charles Ford, pathway leader, u/grad studies; Nigel Clarke, head of w/wind, br and perc; Pamela Bowden, head of vocal studies; Raphael Terroni, head of keyboard; Peter Sheppard, head of strs; Martin Ellerby, head of composition.

Courses offered: DipHE Popular Music Performance (2); DipHE Music Technology (2); BMus (Performance/Composition) (3). P/grad Performance: MMus in Composing Concert Mus, Composing for the Theatre, Composing for New Media, Composing for Film and TV. There are also programmes running in media and creative technology. MA/P/grad Dips also available. Prospectus available.

Course details: Degree programmes are structured around a modular scheme allowing students to choose from a broad range of vocational options. The BMus (Performance/ Comp) is designed to develop all-round musicianship with an emphasis on performance, composition and related skills. It is a programme in the conservatoire tradition and provides a wide variety of opportunities for performance throughout the duration of the course. Students will study core modules in performance and composition on their first inst, ens and orch playing and stylistic studies.

Careers and counselling: Careers adviser available at all times to students; also comprehensive

---

The musical time of your life

The Academy offers a unique four-year BMus (Performance) degree course as well as advanced postgraduate courses. The attractions of the Academy include:

Royal Academy of Music

Principal: Curtis Price

For a Prospectus please write to:
The Registrar
Royal Academy of Music
Marylebone Road
London NW1 5HT
tel: 0171 873 7372
fax: 0171 873 7374

- an outstanding teaching staff, many of whom are leading international performers
- the opportunity to reach the highest level of performance, from classical to commercial music
- a renowned orchestral training programme led by the Director of Music for the European Union Youth Orchestra
- a gateway to music-making in London and beyond
- help with self-promotion and marketing to prospective employers
- a lively and friendly environment which attracts the finest young performers from all over the world
- courses tailor-made to suit the individual
- excellent facilities for practice, private study, recording and research

counselling and welfare service provided by university counsellor. Careers advice includes regular lectures and w/shops from leading figures in the mus profession and a specialist mus careers advice team.

Campus facilities: There are no halls of residence but accommodation service assists in finding lodgings close to the college. Large refectory and a staff/student bar. Provisions for handicapped students. TVU job/temp agency on-site.

Music facilities: London College of Music and Media is an integral part of Thames Valley University. The college has a chmbr choir, a chmbr orch, a str ens, a symphonic wind ens, wind band and a big band as well as numerous smaller ens. There are fully-equipped recording studios, some with workstations. There is a whole block dedicated to mus technology (including Sibelius 7 and Vivace), a recital hall and purpose-built teaching rooms.

National Opera Studio
Morley College, 61 Westminster Bridge Rd, London SE1 7HT
Tel: 0171 928 6833; 0171 261 9267 *Fax:* 0171 928 1810

Richard Van Allan, dir; Roy Laughlin, head of mus; Isobel Flinn, head of studies; Hugh Lloyd, admin.

Courses offered: 1-yr course of advanced training for post-diploma level singers about to enter the profession.

Course details: The National Opera Studio caters for approximately 12 singers and 3 repetiteurs pa and works in close collaboration with the principal opera companies. There is an emphasis on the study and interpretation of specific roles and on the relevant ensembles and scenes. The artistic development of such study is supervised by the director of the studio, the distinguished British bass, Richard Van Allan. Visiting artists from both British and foreign opera houses also participate in the studio's work during the academic year. Advanced musical coaching is given by guest repetiteurs from the main opera companies. There is also tuition in stagecraft, movement, characterisation and language from visiting specialists. The National Opera Studio is operated by a company limited by guarantee with charitable status. Its funding comes mainly from the Arts Council of England, from awards and scholarships from charitable trusts, the major opera companies and from individual and corporate donations. The board of management includes the heads of Great Britain's 6 main opera companies with Brian McMaster CBE as chairman. The studio was founded in 1978 for the purpose of providing advanced opera training. The work of the studio takes place mainly on the premises of Morley College, London. At least one public presentation is offered each year at which the talents of all those participating in the course are displayed for the benefit of potential employers, the press, agents and opera-lovers in general.

Campus facilities: Students must arrange their own accommodation, but other facilities (refectory, etc) are shared under an arrangement with Morley College.

Royal Academy of Music
Marylebone Rd, London NW1 5HT
Tel: 0171 873 7373 *Fax:* 0171 873 7374

Curtis Price, principal; Jonathan Freeman-Attwood, vice-principal and dir of studies; John Wallace, head of br; David Strange, head of strs; Christopher Elton, head of keyboard studies; Melanie Daiken, head of composition; Mark Wildman, head of vocal studies; Sebastian Bell, head of w/wind; Laurence Cummings, head of historical performance.

Courses offered: BMus Hons (4) (London). P/grad: performers course; MMus (2) (London).

Course details: The BMus course seeks to develop the artistic and intellectual qualities necessary to succeed in the music profession. Its integral approach, with performance as the core, is awarded a BMus (London). The Royal Academy of Music is the oldest institution for advanced musical training in England, and aims to provide the highest possible professional training in all aspects of performance. This involves continuous study of technique and interpretation, both solo and ens, in chmbr, choral and orch mus and opera. Students are trained primarily by individual lessons, but with strong support from frequent classes and regular opportunities for public performance. Care is taken to discover and develop the innate talent of each student in relation to their ambition and the known demands of the profession. Students are expected not only to absorb established techniques, knowledge and attitudes, but to think for themselves in preparation for the professional musical world. Formal examination, while stringent, is kept to a minimum, with increasing emphasis on continuous assessment and the self-assessment inherent in any artistic activity. The aim is to produce an articulate performer equipped to become an advocate for his profession and to continue self-development as a necessary means of achieving a productive and rewarding career. There are 500 students, of whom 25-30% come from outside the UK, representing some 40 countries.

Careers and counselling: Course tutors advise on careers; comprehensive counselling service also available.

Campus facilities: Accommodation (chiefly 1st yr students) in London University hostels.

Subsidised catering and student union bar. Blind and deaf students accepted.

Music facilities: The specially designed premises in Marylebone Road contain 70 teaching and practice rooms, the Sir Jack Lyons Theatre, a concert room, a recital room, 3 electronic studios, and a recently refurbished library. The Duke's Hall is the main concert venue, seating 400. New practice rooms have been installed and substantial improvements have been made to the teaching, administrative and recreational accommodation.

Royal College of Music
Prince Consort Rd, London SW7 2BS
Tel: 0171 589 3643 *Fax:* 0171 589 7740
Website: www.rcm.ac.uk

Janet Ritterman, dir; Jeremy Cox, dean of p/grad studies; Graham Caldbeck, head of u/grad studies; Ruth Gerald, head of keyboard studies; Brian Hawkins, head of strs; Neil Mackie, head of vocal studies; Edwin Roxburgh, adviser for 20th C mus; Colin Bradbury, head of w/wind; Peter Passano, head of br.

Courses offered: BMus Hons (4). P/grad: PGDip in solo performance, orch training, concert singing, conducting, early mus, opera, repetiteur, chmbr mus, composition; MMus (RCM) in Performance Studies (1) (applied research or advanced performance); MMus (RCM) in Composition (1) (pure composition or composition for screen); DMus.

Course details: The college is first and foremost a conservatoire and is particularly concerned with those who aspire to be performers, whether instrumentalists, singers, orch players, conductors or composers. It also caters particularly for those intending to teach, and who, as an alternative to university courses, are seeking a course of musical training where greater emphasis is placed on the development of practical skills. At p/grad level, the practical emphasis is allied to scholarly study up to doctoral level. U/grad applicants should understand that classroom techniques are not generally covered in the curriculum. Lessons are provided in all the normal instruments and subjects and a limited number of students (other than those in their first u/grad year) may take orchestral conducting as part of their curriculum provided they show potential. Opportunities exist for composers to undertake practical work in electronic mus. Lessons in the Alexander technique may be provided for those suffering from muscular tension.

Careers and counselling: College has a f/t professional welfare officer; careers advice is also available from individual tutors.

Campus facilities: The college has one hall of residence, accommodating 180 students. Details

of other available accommodation can be obtained from the welfare officer. Student canteen, bar and shop. No special provision for disabled students, but applications considered sympathetically. College has experience of blind and partially-sighted students.

Music facilities: There are many ensemble activities within the college, including two symphony orchs, a chmbr orch, str ens, big band, wind ens, chmbr choir, chorus of about 200 voices, 20th C ens (undertaking rehearsal and performance of contemporary mus), composers group and baroque orch (covering medieval, renaissance and baroque mus). A considerable number of chmbr mus groups receive regular coaching from specially qualified members of the teaching staff. M/classes and lectures by eminent performers and teachers are arranged from time to time, including series of coaching sessions and performances by members of the Chilingirian String Quartet, London Brass Ensemble, His Majesty's Sagbutts and Cornetts and other ens. College facilities include two concert halls, an opera theatre, an electro-acoustic and recording studio, a museum specially designed for the display and preservation of the college's valuable collection of historic musical instruments, a large number of teaching studios and practice rooms and a new three-manual org. There is a spacious library with an extensive collection of books and mus for loan and for reference, a large reading room for quiet study and good listening facilities where a wide range of records and tapes can be consulted. The library also houses the college's large and valuable collection of early printed mus and manuscripts, to which students and visitors may seek access. The college also possesses an extensive collection of portraits and ephemera associated with the musical profession.

Royal Northern College of Music
124 Oxford Rd, Manchester M13 9RD
Tel: 0161 273 6283 *Fax:* 0161 273 7611

Edward Gregson, principal; Christopher Yates, vice-principal; Colin Beeson, dir of development; Charles Bodman Rae, dir of studies; Rodney Slatford, head of strs; Renna Kellaway, head of keyboard studies; Patrick McGuigan, head of vocal studies; Timothy Reynish, head of wind and perc; David Young, academic registrar.

Courses offered: MusB/BA (Music) (4) (joint course offered in conjunction with University of Manchester); BMus Hons (4); BA (Music) (4); PPRNCM (4) also available in chmbr mus (for established groups). P/grad: MusM (2); p/grad diploma (1 or 2); p/grad extension (1+).

Course details: The principal aim of the Royal Northern College of Music is to train musicians to the highest possible professional standard. To this end, all u/grad courses are studied over 4 yrs. All courses with practical principal study are suitable for intending performers and carry equal performance opportunities, the difference lying chiefly in the level and the amount of supporting academic study involved; the u/grad courses may equally well lead to a teaching career. A course with an academic principal study is also available. Each student belongs to one of six schools of study: academic, composition, keyboard, strings, wind and perc or vocal. The regular working contact between heads of schools and their students gives a feeling of personal identity and involvement within the college.

Careers and counselling: Careers advice and counselling available.

Campus facilities: Accommodation for 176 students in college hall of residence. Some help available to students looking for private lodgings. Full catering services available at the college and its hall of residence.

Music facilities: Each school of study organises m/classes, w/shops and coaching sessions throughout the year, given by distinguished artists and chmbr ens. All students take part in a monitored internal concert system. The college employs a concerts manager to arrange external engagements for selected students who are

encouraged to undertake professional work. As well as u/grad symphony and chmbr orchs, there are numerous chmbr groups in all practical disciplines, which reflects the high degree of emphasis given to chmbr music, including Italian song, Lieder and French song classes in the vocal dept. In addition to regular orchestral concerts, the college usually presents at least two full-scale opera productions each year; there is a well-equipped and professionally-staffed opera theatre, a purpose-built concert hall with a fine Hradetsky organ, and an extensive library with study, IT, listening and video facilities. All this activity reflects the emphasis which the college places on the acquisition of professional performance skills. The RNCM has much to offer prospective students. It has its own hall of residence, set in pleasant grounds, and offering practice facilities and first-class recreational facilities. The college itself is open every day from 7am to midnight, including vacations, and is housed in a modern building close to the city-centre bases of the Hallé and BBC Philharmonic Orchestras, and to the university, which all enjoy close links with the college. Additionally, the RNCM is an arts centre, serving the north-west, presenting performances by distinguished visiting companies, ensembles and soloists.

Royal Scottish Academy of Music and Drama
100 Renfrew St, Glasgow G2 3DB
Tel: 0141 332 4101 *Fax:* 0141 332 8901; 0141 353 0372
Email: registry@rsamd.ac.uk
Website: www.rsamd.ac.uk

Philip Ledger CBE, principal; Rita McAllister, vice-principal and dir of mus; Christopher Underwood, head of vocal studies; Philip Jenkins, head of keyboard studies; David Davies, head of orch studies and w/wind; Bryan Allen, head of br; Peter Inness, head of academic studies; Walter Blair, associate dir of mus; Timothy Dean, head of opera.

Courses offered: BA Hons (Musical Studies) (4); BA (Scottish Music) (3); BMus Hons (Performance) (4). T/T: BEd Hons (Music) (4). P/grad: MMus (1)

Course details: The Royal Scottish Academy of Music and Drama offers a wide range of courses to students of both mus and drama. The school of mus aims to provide an all-round musical education; its courses also prepare students for entry into the musical and teaching professions. The BEd mus course additionally provides the award of a class-teaching certificate. The aim in all courses is to broaden students' horizons while at the same time building on their talents and interests. While the acquisition of a sound instrumental or vocal technique is fundamental to the mus courses, the personal development of character, temperament, insight and sensitivity are an essential part of the academy's approach to musical training. This training aims to prepare individual students not only for their chosen profession but also to develop awareness of the role of the profession in society. Great emphasis is laid on public performance and communication and on personal discipline and commitment. Underlying all is the enjoyment of mus, and the fulfilment derived from communicating this enjoyment to others.

Careers and counselling: Managing career development is an essential element of every course. The academy counsellor also has responsibility for students with special needs.

Campus facilities: The registrar maintains a list of suitable accommodation. The academy buffet and café bar offers a full range of meals and snacks. Disabled students are accepted; provisions include special facilities, ramps, etc.

Music facilities: The Academy is situated next to the Theatre Royal, the home of Scottish Opera. The extensive building has provided the school of mus with a wide range of fully-equipped teaching facilities, practice and rehearsal rooms, including an org room, c/rooms and lecture theatre, recording studio and electronic mus w/shop. The Stevenson Hall seats 360 people, while the recital hall seats 100. In 1998 the new, purpose-built Alexander Gibson Opera School at the RSAMD is due to be opened. The Royal Scottish Academy of Music and Drama is able to offer to its students and to Scotland the unique combination of a long tradition of excellence in both mus and drama with a modern, fully-equipped building situated in one of the major cultural centres of Europe.

Trinity College of Music
11-13 Mandeville Pl, London W1M 6AQ
Tel: 0171 935 5773 *Fax:* 0171 224 6278
Email: info@tcm.ac.uk
Website: www.tcm.ac.uk

Gavin Henderson, principal; Derek Aviss, deputy principal; Roger Pope, warden; Philip Meaden, dir of studies; John Stephens, dir of mus educ; Simon Young, dir of performance; Christopher Ellicott, academic registrar; Philip Fowke, head of keyboard dept; Linda Hirst, head of vocal dept; Jeffrey Bryant, head of wind, br and perc dept; Elizabeth Turnbull, head of str dept.

Courses offered: BMus (TCM) (4) (validated by the University of Westminster). P/grad: MMus in Performance Studies (1) (validated by the University of Sussex); MA (Music Education) (1) (validated by the University of Westminster); P/grad Certificate performers course (1); P/grad Certificate accompanying course (1); diploma courses of special study (1).

Course details: The BMus (TCM) is a performance-based vocational degree with added career options. The MMus in Performance Studies is intended for specialist performance studies with complementary academic support. The MA in Music Education provides for the development of teaching and communication skills for composers, teachers and performing musicians. There is also a p/grad certificate course for advanced performers (a few p/t places are available). Special study diploma courses are based around individual inst or vocal tuition and are tailored to the needs of the individual.

Careers and counselling: Careers advice offered through heads of departments, individual tutors and warden's office. Counselling available through warden, welfare officer and medical services.

Campus facilities: No accommodation on site, but available at Henry Wood House; advice given to students looking for other hostel accommodation, rooms, flats, etc. Applications are considered on an equal basis from disabled students; facilities for those with mobility problems are available in some of the college buildings. The college is sympathetic to those affected by dyslexia.

Music facilities: Founded in 1872, Trinity College is an independent foundation receiving an annual

TRINITY
college of music:

get into music

Trinity, with a long and innovative tradition of performance-based training, prepares students for a professional career in music

For further information and a prospectus contact:
The Development Office, Trinity College of Music, 11-13 Mandeville Place, London W1M 6AQ
Telephone: 0171. 935 5773 Facsimile: 0171. 224 6278

Patron: HRH The Duke of Kent KG. Principal: Gavin Henderson

Registered Charity No. 309998

HEFCE grant. It currently offers tuition to approximately 500 students on u/grad and p/grad courses. Trinity has been at the forefront of many developments in mus education. It was the first college to devise a system of graded external examinations, and the first to inaugurate a junior exhibitioners' scheme, subsequently adopted by many other colleges. The college provides a complete training for the vocational needs of students as professional musicians. The BMus (TCM) provides performance and professional studies plus related vocational options in the final year. Communication and teaching skills also form an important part of the curriculum for all students.

Welsh College of Music and Drama
Castle Grounds, Cathays Pk, Cardiff CF1 3ER
Tel: 01222 342854/640054 *Fax:* 01222 344906
Email: music.admissions@wcmd.ac.uk
Website: www.wmcd.ac.uk

Edmond Fivet, principal; Malcolm Goldring, asst principal; Jeremy Ward, head of performance studies; Richard Adams, head of w/wind, br and perc studies; Roger Butler, head of mus technology; Peter Esswood, head of str studies & orch training; Richard McMahon, head of keyboard studies; Elizabeth Ritchie, head of vocal studies; James Walker, head of jnr mus and access studies; Lucy Robinson, BA/MA course leader; Timothy Raymond, LWCMD/AD course leader.
Courses offered: BA Hons Performing Arts (Mus) (3). Others: Performers Diploma course (3); Advanced Diploma course (1 or 2); MA Performing Arts (1 or 2); P/grad Diploma in Music Therapy (1).
Course details: All courses place heavy emphasis on performance, although there are more

non-practical components within the BA Hons course. Irrespective of the course undertaken, each student has equal opportunity of access to performance activities, and the needs of students are paramount. Individual tuition, supported by a wide range of ens experiences, is at the core of a student's studies, and there are considerable opportunities for students to explore individual interests, either through course options, or as a result of the varied recital and concert programme both inside and outside the college. At p/grad level, students are encouraged to participate in as much practical activity as possible, with emphasis on individual learning.
Careers and counselling: Provided by college and visiting staff. Advice also available from professional agencies, including college counsellors.
Campus facilities: Students have access to Student Union accommodation service and usually find suitable accommodation within 1 mile radius of college. Refectory with meals and snacks; student bar.
Music facilities: The WCMD premises are within the parkland setting of Cardiff Castle grounds, and within walking distance of the compact city centre. Facilities include lecture theatres, teaching studios, orchestral and recital spaces, the Bute Theatre (used for mus and drama), electronic, recording and TV studios. The practice rooms are available 6 days per week. College ens perform regularly in outside venues such as St David's Hall, Llandaff Cathedral, Birmingham Symphony Hall and the Fairfield Hall. The college has developed close links with BBC National Orchestra of Wales, Welsh National Opera, the Sherman Theatre and Chapter Arts Centre. Students are able to benefit from the rich artistic life of Cardiff and mus students benefit from the existence of acting, stage management and design courses in the same college.

ANGLIA BUSINESS SCHOOL

MA ARTS ADMINISTRATION
CAMBRIDGE

Designed in co-operation with Eastern Arts, the regional arts board, this course offers specialist business skills for arts management professionals and recent graduates with an interest in the arts. Areas studied include:

- **Marketing**
- **Human Resource Management**
- **Information Technology**
- **Finance**

A work placement with an arts organisation is an integral part of the programme. Available full-time (one year) or part-time (two years) from September 1998.

For further information contact:
Barbara Mornin, Anglia Business School
Anglia Polytechnic University
Cambridge CB1 1PT
Tel: (01223) 363271 ext 2366
Fax: (01223) 352900
E-mail: bmornin@bridge.anglia.ac.uk

Anglia Polytechnic University

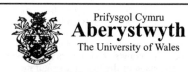

Prifysgol Cymru
Aberystwyth
The University of Wales

MUSIC FOR ALL!

At the University of Wales, Aberystwyth, we are committed to providing excellent opportunities for student musicians. Because we do not offer music degree courses, the scene is not dominated by music students - which means that everyone gets an equal chance to take part. A highly successful programme includes symphony and chamber orchestras, wind and brass bands, choirs and a huge number of superb concerts, Instrumental and vocal tuition is also available.

Orchestral players can apply for the valuable **MUSIC BURSARIES** awarded annually to new undergraduate and postgraduate students of any subject.

For a general prospectus and/or further details of Music at Aberystwyth (including 1st year courses and Music Bursaries) contact:

The Director of Music,
The Music Centre,
The University of Wales, Aberystwyth,
10 Laura Place,
ABERYSTWYTH,
Ceredigion, SY23 2AU
Tel: (01970) 622685 Fax: (01970) 622686

Prifysgol Cymru · University of Wales
BANGOR

DEPARTMENT OF MUSIC
YR ADRAN GERDD

A lively and forward looking Department offering a variety of well structured courses at undergraduate and postgraduate levels. The Department is housed in its own separate building with a range of library, teaching, practice-room and studio facilities.

UNDERGRADUATE
B.A. (Honours)
B.Mus (Honours)
3-year courses with options in:
    Composition
    Music History
    Performance
    Ethnomusicology
    Music Technology
    Studio Composition

For further details, please contact:-
The Academic Manager,
Department of Music,
University of Wales,
BANGOR, Gwynedd LL57 2DG

POSTGRADUATE
Master's and Diploma courses (1-year full-time, 2-year part-time) with options in Western music history, Ethnomusicology and Celtic music, Editorial studies, Music and the Christian Church, Composition, Electroacoustic Composition, Performance, Music for film, media and the arts, Sound recording and editing, and Research skills.

Research Degrees: MPhil and PhD
(1, 2 or 3 years full-time; part-time options) in Composition, Electroacoustic composition, Historical studies.

Studentships available

Tel - (01248) 382181   Fax - (01248) 370297   e-mail: muso20@bangor.ac.uk

324

Universities

Applications for admission to undergraduate courses at all of the following universities and University Colleges (except the Open University) are made through the *Universities and Colleges Admissions Service* (UCAS), Fulton House, Jessop Av, Cheltenham, Glos GL50 3SH *Tel:* 01242 222444. For a comparison between the content, entry requirements and examination procedures of music degree courses refer to the **Comparative Degree Tables**, **Combined Degree Tables** and **Higher Degree Tables**.

Anglia Polytechnic University

Music and Performing Arts Division, East Rd, Cambridge CB1 1PT
Tel: 01223 363271 *Fax:* 01223 352935

Richard Prior, head of dept (from Sep 1998); Robert Reeve, dir of extended curriculum; David Crilly, MA mus course leader; Richard Hoadley, BA mus field leader; Alan Rochford, admissions tutor; Nicholas Toller, international degree access course leader; Paul Jackson, dir of practical studies; Helen Odell-Miller, course leader, MA mus therapy.
Courses: BA (Single or Combined) Hons. Others: mus foundation course. International Degree Access Course. P/grad: MA Music Therapy; MA Music; Mphil; Phd.
Course details: At Anglia there is a strong commitment to the study and performance of the 'many musics' with jazz, electro-acoustic mus, ethnic mus, improvisation and composition standing alongside mus of the Western classical tradition. The course has a vocational emphasis and seeks to develop a wide variety of transferable skills (eg, the arts administration and enterprise modules) which will be invaluable to the graduate in both the musical profession and other occupations. Practical studies covers tuition on two insts (subject to required standards) and is provided by a large team of visiting specialists of national reputation. Students are encouraged to work towards a high standard in performance, and to value critical appraisal by staff and fellow students.
Careers and counselling: University careers service, field leaders, academic advisers and personal tutors.
Campus facilities: Accommodation on campus. Outside accommodation monitored by the university is available within a few minutes' walk. The university and the students' union run cafeterias. Applications from disabled, mature and overseas students are particularly encouraged. Open days are held periodically and individual visits can be arranged through the admissions tutor.
Music facilities: A wide range of ens activities offer a generous choice for students electing to take the practical studies modules. There is a comprehensive schedule of concerts and operas held on campus in Anglia's Mumford Theatre and in Cambridge. Anglia also runs a comprehensive community programme of concerts and w/shops in schools and art centres covering a wide radius, emphasising its role as a regional institution. Foreign concert tours are also a popular feature of vacation work, leading to close educational ties with many similar institutions worldwide. The Study Abroad programme offers formal academic exchanges usually for one semester in Year Two. In addition to its lecture, seminar and practice rooms, the Department of Music has outstanding electro-acoustic studios and a/v equipment. There is a well-stocked mus library and students can use Cambridge University Library for completion of dissertations. Generous provision is made for sporting, welfare and recreational facilities. Anglia seeks to promote critical mus awareness and personal development in an artistic and cultural environment.

Bangor, University of Wales

Dept of Music, College Rd, Bangor, Gwynedd LL57 2DG
Tel: 01248 382181 *Fax:* 01248 370297
Email: s.e.collick@bangor.ac.uk
Website: www.bangor.ac.uk/music/musichome.html

John M Harper, head of dept; Stephen Rees, admissions tutor; Bruce Wood, snr lecturer; David Evans, dir of studies.
Courses: BMus Hons (3) (80-120 credits in mus with up to 40 credits in other subjects in yr 1 only); BA Hons (3) (at least 60 credits in mus with up to 60 credits in other subjects in yr 1; option of 20 credits in another subject in yr 2). P/grad: MA (1) in editorial musicology, ethno-musicology, historical musicology, performance, and mus and media; MPhil; MMus (composition and/or electro-acoustic composition); PhD (2 or 3) by research or composition, Diplomas in musical performance, mus technology and sound recording.
Course details: The dept's activities cover five

325

principal areas of study: history, culture and society (including Western, world and celtic musics); applied mus studies; performance and practical skills; composition and contemporary studies (including acoustic and electro-acoustic composition); technology, media and popular culture. There are level one modules available in each of these five areas. The level one course allows the student to develop specific interests, skills, knowledge and understanding by choosing options from a wide range of courses in yrs 2 and 3. This allows the student to study specific areas in depth, or to maintain a broader balance, according to individual wishes and needs, and provides an opportunity to undertake special projects in one or more of these five areas. Students may undertake individual inst or vocal study and this may lead to a recital as a project in yrs 2 and 3. The dept has 7 f/t academic staff, 3 of whom teach in both English and Welsh, and a large number of visiting lecturers and teachers. Many modules may be studied in both languages and students may submit written coursework, assignments or projects in either English or Welsh. Formal written examinations are sat only in yr 1.

Careers and counselling: Careers advice is available during the course and after graduation. Students have personal tutors, year group tutors (and female advisers) within the department. The relationship between staff and students in the dept is close.

Campus facilities: Students are accommodated in halls of residence or flats. Student canteens are open for meals and light refreshments. Applications from disabled students are considered individually.

Music facilities: The department is large enough to maintain its own orch, choir, opera group and ens, but teaching has been organised to keep seminar and tutorial groups as small as possible. This enables students to take part in a rich variety of practical mus-making, but at the same time to receive individual attention. A wide range of studies in mus history and analysis is offered, with a broad approach in the early stages to give experience and confidence, practical guidance in study skills, and the opportunity to specialise. Performance and tuition is offered in all three years, and may lead to a recital as a special project. Mus technology and studio composition are areas of major development. There are four studios with some of the most advanced computer and digital facilities in the UK. There are applied courses such as recording, editing and mus processing, and creative options in studio composition. History, culture and society addresses mus in world, Western and Celtic

cultures. Modules take advantage of Bangor's geographical position for study of mus in Welsh culture, but a collection of over 300 world insts and a special library of recordings are available for wider studies. The department also houses the national archive devoted to traditional Welsh mus. Practical activities range from individual performance, chmbr mus, specialist ensembles, chmbr orch and choir, to a large symphony orch and choral society. The department has a number of outstanding resident and visiting performer-teachers. The concert series is one of the most extensive and varied of any British university and there are close links with the Welsh Arts Council and the BBC. In addition to the electronic studios, there are lecture, seminar, tutorial and practice rooms and an audio listening room. As well as a substantial collection of scores and black vinyl recordings, the mus library has over 3000 CDs. There are 2 concert halls and 2 rehearsal rooms together with a full complement of keyboard insts, harps and perc.

Bath Spa University College *formerly* Bath College of HE

Newton Pk, Bath BA2 9BN
Tel: 01225 873701 *Fax:* 01225 874438
Website: www.bathhe.ac.uk/am/som1.html

Alan Carter, dean of faculty of art and mus; Keith Bennett, course dir BA mus.

Courses: BA Hons (3); BA Hons Sound and Image (3) (mus in collaboration with BA Fine Arts); BA/BSc Combined Awards (3) (mus as major, joint or minor subject within the modular scheme); BA Creative Arts (3) *see* **Combined Degrees**. P/grad: MA in Contemprary Music and Culture. T/T: BA (QTS) (primary) with mus specialism; PGCE (1) for secondary specialist musicians (also general primary course offering mus as a foundation subject area).

Course details: The BA Hons is a modular degree offering a programme of foundation studies in yr 1, specialist (performance, composition, musicology) or generalist routes in yrs 2 and 3, a vocational studies programme in yr 2 which develops future career prospects through practically focused study (options in arts admin, mus education, mus technology, mus therapy, musical inst making), and a mus in the community module. The BA Hons Sound and Image route (yrs 2 and 3, entry via BA Hons) involves interdisciplinary study in mus and visual imagery. A new BA Hons Creative Music Technology route is being planned. The BA Creative Arts has a practical emphasis focusing on composition and performance individually and in w/shops and ens. The BA/BSc Combined Awards offers a choice of modules from BA Music or BA Creative Arts programmes; mus can

be studied with a wide range of other subjects within the modular scheme. There are about 200 students on all courses, 110 on the BA at present and 25 on the 1-yr PGCE secondary specialist course. There are 9 f/t and a large number of visiting specialist teachers.

Careers and counselling: The college has a professional counselling service and an active careers advisory service; students are assigned to a personal tutor upon entering college.

Campus facilities: Accommodation is provided in halls of residence and there are canteen facilities. There are on-site leisure and sports facilities. There is limited provision for disabled students (eg wheelchair users); places have been offered to partially-sighted applicants.

Music facilities: The mus dept at Bath is one of the largest and best resourced of its kind in the UK. There is a deep commitment to mus education at all levels, with extensive contact with schools throughout the region. Most of the mus staff are actively involved in performing or composing commitments outside the college; staff are highly qualified, with a good research and creative record.

The recently opened Michael Tippett Centre incorporates a 200-seat auditorium with wide rehearsal/performance space and a 16-track recording and electro-acoustic sound studio. The Centre is currently being extensively extended with the aid of lottery funding. There are 22 practice rooms, a mus technology room equipped with Macintosh based workstations, 3 lecture/seminar rooms and other large rooms for ens work and inst teaching. The courses are supported by an adventurous and varied season of professional concerts in the *Rainbow over Bath* concert series.

Birmingham University

Dept of Music, Barber Institute of Fine Arts, Edgbaston, Birmingham B15 2TT
Tel: 0121 414 5782 *also fax;*
Website: www.bham.ac.uk

Stephen Banfield, head of dept; John Whenham, dir of p/grad studies; Vic Hoyland, u/grad admissions tutor.

Courses: BMus Hons; BA Combined Hons (mus plus one other subject) *see* **Combined Degrees**. P/grad: MA (1); MPhil (1); MMus (1); MLitt (2); PhD including composition (2 or 3).

Course details: In Combined Hons, mus is 50% of degree, the other subject totalling 50%. Minor in another subject (33%) is often possible on entry with BMus (Hons).

Careers and counselling: University careers service provides general careers advice, and a student's personal tutor can advise on more specific musical questions as well as on personal matters.

Campus facilities: 1st year students are guaranteed places in university accommodation, thereafter in hall, flats or lodgings. Guild of Students runs full catering facilities in university. Disabled students would be welcomed, but might find geographical 'spread' of the dept a hindrance.

Music facilities: The presence of a first-class symphony orch in the city has influenced the dept's ethos which is based on mus as living sound. The dept is of a size (about 180 u/grads and 50 p/grads at any one time) to offer not only large-scale musical experiences but also the facilities, for composers, orchestrators, scholars of performance practice and conductors to hear their efforts come to life. It is this access to living mus that is pursued as a deliberate educational end in historical as well as creative studies. Collaboration with the dept of drama and theatre arts in the fields of opera and mus-theatre enables students to take options in drama and dance. The introduction to studio techniques in yr 1 is held in well-equipped electro-acoustic mus studios, which are available with specialist guidance for advanced composition. The dept also boasts large and small student orchs and choirs, a new suite of 16 practice rooms, and the support of the Barber Trust. The Barber Institute, home of the department, houses a comprehensive library of mus, books and recordings and a picture gallery of international importance. It is also a venue for the annual Birmingham Early Music Festival. Other concerts of international standard, professional opera, and mus-theatre are all on the student's doorstep.

Bretton Hall University College
West Bretton, Nr Wakefield, W Yorks WF4 4LG
Tel: 01924 830261 *Fax:* 01924 832006
Website: www.bretton.ac.uk

Courses: BA Hons in Contemporary Musics (3) (University of Leeds); BA Hons in Popular Music Studies (3) (University of Leeds); BA Hons in Music Performance Studies (3) (University of Leeds); BA Hons in Arts and Education (Music) (3) (University of Leeds). P/grad: MA Contemporary Performing Arts (1 f/t, 2.5 p/t) (University of Leeds); MA (Research); MPhil/ PhD (research). T/T: BA (QTS) (4) (primary) (University of Leeds); PGCE (1) (University of Leeds); MA (Music Education) (2.5 p/t) (University of Leeds).

Course details: There are about 200 music students in the dept following three major 3-yr u/grad courses. The BA Hons Contermporary Musics offers a broad technological basis, specialisation in composition, performance, mus in the community, electro-acoustic mus and mus

technology based on scholarship and discovery of creativity. The bias of the BA Hons in Popular Music is to provide vocationally-orientated training integrated with an academic course in a range of popular musics, reflecting and serving contemporary society. The MA in Contemporary Performing Arts is focused on the theory and practice of contemporary mus. The MA in Music Performance Studies is a performance specialist course combining theory and practice through its campus facilities. The PGCE provides for good graduates seeking teacher training for secondary work, with a peripatetic inst course option.

Careers and counselling: Careers advice from mus school and general college service. Personal counselling available from tutors.

Campus facilities: Bretton Hall is a spacious country campus of about 260 acres, surrounded by parklands and lakes, and incorporating the now nationally known 'Yorkshire Sculpture Park' and the Lawrence Batley Centre for the National Education Arts Archive. Accommodation available to all students, and there is a refectory. Special provision for disabled students. Nursery facilities on campus.

Music facilities: The mus dept possesses a large contemprary and world mus sound archive as well as an inst collection and is proud of the balance it maintains between practical and academic work, composition, computer and sound recording, jazz and world mus. The Cornelius Cardew Ensemble is the resident ens.

Brighton University
Grand Parade, Brighton BN2 2JY
Tel: 01273 600900

Billie Cowie, course leader (mus).

Courses: BA Hons Music with Visual Practice (3).

Course details: The BA Hons Music with Visual Practice is 50% mus and 50% visual art (there are parallel courses in dance with visual practice and theatre with visual practice). The emphasis of the course is on practical work focusing on electronic mus, composition and multi-media practices.

Careers and counselling: A full counselling and careers service is available to all students.

Campus facilities: The university has several halls of residence, and preference is given to 1st yr students. Canteen facilities on all university sites.

Bristol University
Dept of Music, Victoria Rooms, Queens Rd, Clifton, Bristol BS8 1SA
Tel: 0117 954 5028 *Fax:* 0117 954 5027
Email: m.e.peirson@bris.ac.uk
Website: www.bris.ac.uk/depts/music/

Wyndham Thomas, head of dept; T J Samson,

prof of mus; A Beaumont, reader in composition; W G Jenkins, snr lecturer in mus; J Irving, J Cross, lecturers in mus.

Courses: BA Hons (4); BA Joint Hons (3) *see* **Combined Degrees**. P/grad: MA in Composition for Film, Television and Theatre (1); MA in advanced mus studies (1 f/t, 2 p/t); MMus in Composition (2 f/t; 3 p/t); MLitt (2 f/t; 3 p/t or combination); PhD (3 f/t; 4 p/t); DMus.

Course details: Please contact the dept for further details.

Careers and counselling: Careers advice and personal counselling is available to all students.

Campus facilities: Accommodation may be provided for all 1st year students who wish to take advantage of it. Widespread eating facilities in students' union plus a university refectory. Disabled students are accepted, but there are no special facilities for them.

Music facilities: Accommodation for the mus dept now provided in the Victoria rooms includes a theatre/concert hall, a recital room, an electronic/recording studio as well as teaching and practice space. The new premises are only a few minutes' walk from all the principal university buildings, including the Great Hall (used for some larger concerts and org recitals), refectory, Senate House and Arts Library. The mus dept has its own score and record collection with video and listening facilities, together with a newly acquired chmbr org and hpd.

A multi-track MIDI studio is available to p/grad composers for electro-acoustic and other recorded forms of composition and is of special use to those on the Film, Television and Theatre Composition course. It is hoped that yr 3 composing options may be available in this area and there are foundation courses in mus technology and recording techniques in yr 1. Students are taught through a combination of lectures, classes, tutorials and seminars. Composition techniques are taught in classes, an exercise being set weekly. Each student is allocated a personal tutor. The dept is also visited by distinguished scholars, composers or performers (ens) who normally hold seminars on their special musical interests or coach student composers and performers.

Brunel University

Faculty of Arts, Dept of Performing Arts, Twickenham Campus, 300 St Margaret's Rd, Twickenham TW1 1PT
Tel: 0181 891 0121 *Fax:* 0181 891 8316
Email: arts-faculty@brunel.ac.uk
Website: www.brunel.ac.uk

Peter Rudnick, head of mus.
Courses: BA Single Hons (3); BA Joint Hons (mus studied conjointly with 1 other subject); p/t one-day Diploma course. P/grad: MPhil (by research) and PhD in composition, ethno-musicology, musicology, 20th C mus, improvisation and jazz studies, English renaissance mus, Persian classical mus.

Course details: The aim of both the Single and Joint BA Hons courses is to develop creative, performance, critical and analytical skills and a sense of the importance of the social and cultural context of mus. The bias of each course is performance, composition or critical musicology as determined by the student after compulsory studies in yr 1. The programme of modules is ideally suited to those seeking a career in mus or arts performance, production, business and admin, teaching or in preparation for further advanced study. P/grad work is by research (submission of thesis or portfolio of compositions only).

Careers and counselling: University careers service. F/t student counsellor available at all times.

Campus facilities: Students not living at home are accommodated either in halls of residence or in approved lodgings. Refectory and student lounge, plus bar/snack bars. There are no specific provisions for disabled students, but each application will be treated individually.

Music facilities: From September 1998 Single and Joint Honours mus degrees will be based in a new, purpose-built arts block on the Uxbridge campus in west London. The one-day diploma course will continue to run at the Twickenham campus.

Mus is studied as a modular degree programme and can be combined with American studies, drama, English, film and TV studies and history. The study of mus is rooted in practical work where performance and composition feature prominently. Students choose from a range of options including performance studies, composition, historical and analytical studies. Opportunities exist to collaborate with students of drama and dance within the dept of performing arts. Regular public concerts and recitals are given by students and staff. The range of musical activity includes orch, str ens, jazz, big band, chmbr choir, 20th C ens, Handel choir and a variety of other chmbr mus opportunities.

Cambridge University

University Music School, West Rd, Cambridge CB3 9DP
Tel: 01223 335176 *Fax:* 01223 335067

Alexander Goehr, prof of mus; Susan Rankin, chmn of faculty board; Dean Sutcliffe, sec of faculty board; Ian Cross, sec of degree committee; John Butt, Laura Davey, Ruth Davis, Martin Ennis, Iain Fenlon, Robin Holloway, Andrew Jones, Hugh Wood.

Courses: BA (3). P/grad: MusB; MPhil (1) in composition, musicology or ethnomusicology; MLitt; PhD.

Course details: Candidates should possess a good musical ear, a proficiency in working written musical exercises, a command of clear written English, a facility in playing and sight-reading at the keyboard, and an acquaintance with the standard musical repertory. It is also desirable that they should be reasonably familiar with one or more languages such as German, French, Italian, or Latin. Candidates should note that the Faculty of Music does not provide practical tuition on insts or voice; for information concerning financial provision made by the colleges, candidates should enquire at the college(s) of their choice. The course of study and instruction underlying the BA is designed to give a deeper appreciation of the art of mus and of its history than is obtainable from a predominantly vocational training at a conservatoire. It provides opportunities to study the art in its historical and cultural context, to examine and analyse the principles and techniques of musical composition, notation and interpretation from both stylistic and scholarly viewpoints, to pursue the study of ethnomus, musical acoustics and psycho-acoustics and to exercise the practice of composition itself. Perf nance has its place as one among several asp cts of the course which is meant for those with the inclination and aptitude for a range of academic studies of mus, rather than for those who are primarily or exclusively interested in performance. In these studies, a balance is sought between giving the student a grasp of basic intellectual skills that are necessary to any informed and intelligent appreciation of mus, stimulating and satisfying each student's individual interests, and introducing advanced musical studies which the student may not have met before. Although most u/grads who study mus enter some sector of the musical profession, the course can also be profitably undertaken by people who enter other occupations. Two or three subjects in the history of mus are offered each year; their subject-matter varies from year to year, as does that of the additional papers, in accordance with the interests of the lecturing staff responsible for teaching them. Keyboard skills are studied through the medium of small classes, each of four or five students, at which attendance is considered obligatory. The MusB examination consists of an inst or vocal recital of at least 40 minutes' mus, a dissertation of between 10,000 and 15,000 words and a single written paper on the background of the dissertation. The MusB is usually taken as a 4th year course by students who have already completed the Cambridge BA Degree.

Cardiff University *of* Wales

Adrian Thomas: *Professor of Music and Head of Department*
David Wyn Jones: *Undergraduate Admissions*
Stephen Walsh: *Postgraduate Admissions*

Cardiff is a city with a vibrant musical life (Welsh National Opera/BBC National Orchestra of Wales) in which the University Music Department plays a full part. The Department is a stimulating place to study and has a strong record of achievement in musicology, performance and composition. All its facilities are housed in one building, including an extensive library, concert hall, study and lecture facilities, computer lab (Macintosh/Sibelius), electronic studio and practice rooms.

Undergraduate Courses:
BMus Single Honours
(all or mostly music modules)
BA Single Honours
(with subsidiary modules)
BA Joint Honours
(with a range of other subjects)
BSc in Physics and Music
(one third in Music)

Postgraduate Courses:
Taught MA in Musicology
Taught MA in Performance Studies
Taught MMus in Composition
MPhil *(research)*, PhD *(research or composition/research)*

Further information is available from:
The Department of Music, Cardiff University of Wales, Corbett Road, Cardiff CF1 3EB
tel. (01222) 874816, fax. (01222) 874379

Undergraduate Email Enquiries:
music-ucasenq@cardiff.ac.uk

Music Web Site:
http://www.cf.ac.uk/uwcc/music/homepage.html

Careers and counselling: All u/grads are assigned to a tutor responsible for the student's well-being, and supervisors responsible for the student's work. There is also a university counselling service, with professional counsellors, and a careers service.

Campus facilities: Most colleges can accommodate all 1st year students and those from one other year. All colleges have dining halls, some also have cafeterias and bars. Suitably qualified disabled students would be accepted, and there is wheelchair access to the mus school; other provision depends on the individual colleges.

Cardiff, University of Wales
Dept of Music, Cardiff CF1 3EB
Tel: 01222 874816 *Fax:* 01222 874379

Adrian Thomas, professor and head of dept; Robin Stowell, professor; Stephen Walsh, reader; David Wyn Jones, Richard Elfyn Jones, snr lecturers; Derek Carew, Kenneth Gloag, David Humphreys, Caroline Rae, Timothy Taylor, lecturers; Stephen Price, tutor.

Courses: U/grad: BMus Hons (3); BA Hons (3); BA Joint Hons (3); BSc Physics and Music (3) *see* **Combined Degrees**. P/grad: Taught courses leading to MMus (in composition) and MA (in musicology, performance studies or Music, Culture and Politics (1); research opportunities leading to MPhil (2) and PhD (3).

Course details: Mus at Cardiff is studied at u/grad level through a combination of individual tuition, lectures and seminars where there is the opportunity to discuss issues in depth. Students taking the practical musicianship modules receive a weekly private lesson of 30 mins on their main inst or voice, and this provision doubles if the recital module is taken in yr 3. Yr 1 (BMus) has core instruction in analysis, study skills, harmony and counterpoint, with optional modules in comp, electro-acoustic mus, acoustics and historical topics. In Yr 1, BMus students take 10-12 modules in mus, while BA/BSc students take 4 in mus, but with free choice. In Yrs 2 and 3, all students select from groups covering compositional and electro-acoustic studies, written and practical musicianship, analytical and critical skills and historical studies. In Yr 2, BMus students take core modules in analysis. In Yr 3, all students are entitled to choose the dissertation option, while BMus students in addition have options in composition and recital. In Yrs 2 and 3, BMus students take a minimum of 10 mus modules (a full 12 in Yr 3), BA Hons 8 or more, BA Joint Hons 6, and BSc 4 modules. The BA Hons allows for up to 4 free-standing, non-mus modules to be taken in each of Yrs 2 and 3, while the BA Joint Hons

offers equal weighting in Yrs 2 and 3 with another subject (often a modern language, with an option of a year abroad after Yr 2). The BSc is run by the physics dept and is geared towards students with strengths in that field. The MMus involves the study of compositional techniques and idioms, contemporary orchestration, extended inst and vocal techniques, repertoire, the submission of a portfolio of original compositions as well as a practical test where students conduct rehearsals of one of their own works.

Taught MAs are examined by a range of continual assessment and examination depending on current staff research. MA in Musicology covers mus mainly from 1700, with options in historical, analytical and contextual studies plus a core course in research skills and a concluding project. MA in Performance Studies involves the study of methodology, performance practice, organology, techniques and repertoire of the student's main inst and recital presentation. MA in Music, Culture and Politics is an interdisciplinary course shared with staff from other depts at Cardiff, covering a range of aesthetic, theoretical and historical issues which range beyond the mus of our own time.

Careers and counselling: Careers advice offered by individual tutors in addition to the university careers service. Personal counselling is available whenever required.

Campus facilities: Accommodation is provided in extensive halls of residence and cafeterias are nearby. The students' union is 5 mins walk from the dept. Acceptance of disabled students depends largely on the nature of the disability; some provision is made, but there would still be some problems for those in wheelchairs.

Music facilities: The mus dept is housed in a purpose-built facility including both the mus library and concert hall as well as teaching rooms, IT facilities and practice rooms. There is a very active concert programme by both professional visitors and the dept's own ens. The student-run Music Society organises regular lunchtime concerts and membership of either the university choir or the symphony orch are regarded as obligatory at u/grad level. Other activities include m/classes and visiting lectures. The dept's principal objective is to enable each student to realise his/her artistic and intellectual potential by offering experience of mus through historical, analytical, theoretical and practical studies. It has a thriving student population, staff who are nationally and internationally known for their publications, performances and broadcasts, a concert schedule which serves both the university and the wider community, and facilities which are intended to enhance each student's progress.

University of Central England in Birmingham

For course details refer to Birmingham Conservatoire see **Conservatoires**.

City University

Dept of Music, Northampton Sq, London EC1V 0HB
Tel: 0171 477 8284 *Fax:* 0171 477 8576
Website: www.city.ac.uk/music

Denis Smalley, head of dept; Steve Stanton, BMus/BSc admissions tutor; Jim Grant, Dip/MIT dir; Annegret Fauser, MA dir; Simon Emmerson, research dir.

Courses: BMus/BSc Hons (3). P/grad: MA in Music (1 f/t; 2 p/t), with options in performance studies, composition, electro-acoustic mus, women and gender in music, women and gender in mus with performance, ethnomusicology and musicology; Dip/MSc in Music Information Technology (1 f/t; 2 p/t); MPhil (2 f/t; 5 p/t); PhD (3 f/t; 6 p/t); Master of Musical Arts/Doctor of Musical Arts in performance (3 f/t; 6 p/t).

Course details: The City University BMus/BSc Hons in Music is a unique combination of courses and options which are designed to help bridge the gaps between mus as art, mus as science and mus in performance. The course is concerned essentially with the study of the position and role of mus in society, rather than providing the more traditional historical survey of European Art mus. Ethnomusicology and Western musicology are juxtaposed to establish a global view of mus-making, and scientific and technological applications offer new perspectives of the world of sound today. Inst and vocal tuition is provided at conservatoire standard by the Guildhall School of Music and Drama with whom the dept has a valuable and wide-ranging collaborative relationship.

Careers and counselling: The university has an extensive careers office and each student has a personal tutor within the dept.

Campus facilities: 1st yr students from outside London are guaranteed places in hall. Some furnished flats are available for 2nd and 3rd yrs. There are 3 canteens and cafeterias open to all university members. Provision for disabled students would be made according to specific need.

Music facilities: There are strong vocational courses, such as mus therapy, sound recording and performance. Performance opportunities exist in the chamber choir, a chmbr orch, gamelan, Indian mus group and student ens (including jazz, folk and mus theatre groups). The City University Symphony Orchestra has given British premieres of Lutoslawski, Panufnik, Peter Sculthorpe and John Harbison at St John's Smith Square. The Anderson Collection of early insts includes an original Grancino cello, a fully restored 1799 Stodart grand pno, a hpd and two virginals. In addition to Javanese gamelans there is a substantial collection of South Asian and Far Eastern insts. The department also houses 3 Steinways, a Yamaha MIDI grand, and 8 practice rooms with upright pnos. Electro-acoustic and sound recording studios provide facilities for computer mus composition, classical and multi-track recording, and advanced research in computer mus applications. Audio and a/v editing facilities are available to all students along with portable systems for location recording and fieldwork projects. An extensive p/grad programme offers a wide spectrum of opportunity. In addition to the f/t staff, the dept has several visiting lecturers representing diverse musical specialisms, including a research fellow in mus therapy and a research assistant in Indian mus.

Coventry University

Performing Arts, Leasowes Av, Coventry CV3 6BH
Tel: 01203 418868 *Fax:* 01203 692374

Patricia Thompson, head of perf arts.
Courses: BA (Hons) Music Composition and Professional Practice.
Music facilities: 3 well-equipped elec studios, recording studios, individual booths for private composition and computer-aided notation work, numerous practice rooms, library. Also 3 performance spaces, recital room, theatre and dance studio.

Derby University

School of Art and Design, Western Rd, Mickleover, Derby DE3 5GX
Tel: 01332 622222 *Fax:* 01332 514323
Website: www.derby.ac.uk

Richard Hodges, head of mus.
Courses: BA/BSc Modular Hons (3 f/t; or p/t) *see* **Combined Degrees**; BA Hons Performing Arts; BA Hons in Popular Music with Music Technology (3 f/t).
Course details: BA Hons in Popular Music with Music Technology is taught by the School of Art and Design in collaboration with the Department of Engineering, and is characterised by the study of both practical and theoretical skills, with integrated performance, composition, critical theory and mus technology. Mus is available within a BA/BSc Hons degree combined subject modular scheme, which allows students to determine their own programme of study from a wide range of subject options. Mus can be taken at two levels: joint (50% mus) or minor (33% mus). Mus courses include both theoretical and practical elements and topics covered include mus technology, critical theory, contemporary mus and mus in popular culture. The BA Hons Performing Arts incorporates a mus pathway,

and involves the study of dance, theatre studies and writing.

Careers and counselling: Each student has a tutor, and academic counsellors and members of staff have special responsibility for grant matters, accommodation, careers and welfare. Also careers education and advisory services and confidential counselling services.

Campus facilities: Accommodation offered for all years in college annexes. Student Union bar on site. Ramps, wheelchair access and facilities for the disabled.

Music facilities: BA Hons mus students are taught on the Mickleover campus. Derby itself is an excellent centre for work and leisure, within easy reach of Birmingham, Chesterfield, Nottingham and Sheffield. Inst and vocal studies are taught on a continuous basis during the course, and students are encouraged to take external diplomas and examinations. The department of mus runs choirs and inst groups, and smaller students' ens are encouraged. There is a students' mus society which organises informal concerts within the university, and trips to concerts and performances outside Derby.

Durham University

Dept of Music, The Music School, Palace Green, Durham DH1 3RL
Tel: 0191 374 3221 *Fax:* 0191 374 3219

Jeremy Dibble, chmn of dept; Jonathan Stock, co-ord combined courses.
Courses: BA (3); BA Joint Hons in Arts (3 or 4); BA Hons Combined Studies in Arts (3) *see* **Combined Degrees**. P/grad: MA (1); MMus (2); PhD (3). T/T: BA (Hons) Ed (4).
Careers and counselling: The university has a large careers advisory service and every student has a college tutor.
Campus facilities: The university is fully residential, operating on the collegiate system. Disabled students are accepted, although no special provisions exist for them.
Music facilities: Musical life at Durham is both comprehensive and vigorous. Apart from the formal courses in the dept there are numerous opportunities for mus-making. Concerts of one kind or another take place several times a week, generally organised by the University Music Society, membership of which is open to all. There is also a series of professional concerts which emphasises 20th C works, and which is frequently associated with w/shops and critical lecture recitals. The dept is particularly strong in the fields of ethnomusicology, composition, electronics, analysis and British mus of the 19th and early 20th C. A-level mus is normally an essential qualification for entry to the dept, and keyboard skills (ABRSM gr 6) are also required.

University of East Anglia

School of Music, Norwich NR4 7TJ
Tel: 01603 592452 *Fax:* 01603 250454
Email: e.varge@uea.ac.uk
Website: www.uea.ac.uk/menu/acad_depts/mus/

Peter Aston, prof of mus; Ian Biddle, lecturer in mus; David Chadd, snr lecturer in mus; Sharon Choa, lecturer in mus; Simon Waters, lecturer in mus.
Courses: BA Hons (3). P/grad: MMus(1); MPhil (2); PhD (3). T/T: PGCE.
Course details: The mus degree course is a comprehensive one, providing a framework within which students are able to develop their individual talents and interests. Particular features of the course are the emphasis placed on practical musicianship and performance studies, the large element of choice within general subject areas, and the extensive facilities for sound recording and electro-acoustic mus. In yr 1, all students take courses in practical musicianship (covering aural perception, keyboard skills and conducting), composition, mus history and musical style and analysis. In yrs 2 and 3, students choose units from the three main areas of historical studies, technical studies and creative and performance studies, any one of which may count for 40% of the degree assessment. Whichever units are chosen, students are encouraged at all times to relate their historical, analytical and stylistic studies to a broad perspective of mus as a creative and performing art.
Careers and counselling: The university has a careers centre, and every student has a personal tutor. Professional counselling is available in the Dean of Students' Office.
Campus facilities: Most 1st year and a large proportion of second and final year students are accommodated in university residences. University accommodation service helps with finding external accommodation. Campus has restaurant, refectory, self-service buffet plus snack bars. Applications from disabled students are welcomed, and students are accepted subject to confirmation from the Dean of Students' Office that the necessary special arrangements can be made.
Music facilities: Teaching takes place in the University Music Centre in the form of seminars, lectures, tutorials and practical classes. The centre houses a concert room, 3 professionally-equipped sound recording and electro-acoustic mus studios, seminar and rehearsal rooms, staff offices and tutorial rooms, stores for insts, scores and records, and 8 sound-proofed practice rooms. As well as providing facilities for teaching, the mus centre is the natural focal point for a range of musical activities.

333

The concert room is used for chamber concerts and recitals by visiting professional musicians and for rehearsals of the university choir and orch, the students' chmbr choir and chmbr orch, various chmbr ens, mus-theatre and early mus groups. Students reading mus at UEA take a leading part not only in university activities such as these but, if they wish, in mus outside the university. The dept has close links with Norwich Cathedral, the Norfolk and Norwich Festival and the Aldeburgh Festival, which provides students with opportunities to participate in a wide range of mus-making in Norwich and the surrounding area.

Edge Hill University College
St Helens Rd, Ormskirk, Lancs L39 4QP
Tel: 01695 575171 *Fax:* 01695 579997

Courses: BA Hons in Music with Media (3) (through the integrated honours scheme).
Course details: The BA Hons in Music and Media is available as an integrated honours scheme and is designed to develop areas of expertise in both mus and media production. Current modules in the 1st yr include performance studies of first study inst or voice, general mus studies, composition and arrangement, an introduction to media and music technology, historical studies and communication studies. Yrs 2 and 3 include performance studies, composition, popular mus, musicology project, communication studies, technology, studying new media, cultural context of media practice, digital media production, photographic reproduction, radio production, discourse and communication, international media policy and professional context.

Edinburgh University
Faculty of Music, Alison House, Nicolson Sq, Edinburgh EH8 9DF
Tel: 0131 650 2423 *Fax:* 0131 650 2425
Email: music@ed.ac.uk
Website: www.music.ed.ac.uk

D R B Kimbell, head of dept and prof; N Osborne, prof; E J Harper, R J Monelle, readers; J P Kitchen, P W Nelson, T N O'Regan, T M Turnbull, snr lecturers; L Coates, E Sheinberg, lecturers; A M Trewin, ethnomusicology; G G O' Brien, organology.
Courses: BMus (3 or 4); BMus in Music Technology (3 or 4); MA (3 or 4). P/grad: DipMus/MMus (1); MPhil (2); PhD (3). An Honours MA in History of Art and History of Music is offered in conjunction with the Department of Fine Art.
Course details: The Scottish tradition of the 3-yr Ordinary and/or 4-yr Honours degree makes it possible for the Faculty of Music at Edinburgh to provide a curriculum of studies that offers thoroughness and breadth, and in its later stages

enables students to choose between a specialised or a wide-ranging group of subjects. For two years all students pursue a common course. From yr 3 onwards they select their own courses (subject to certain constraints) from a wide variety of options which are roughly grouped as compositional studies, historical studies, performance studies and scientific studies.

Students may also make a submission in the form of either compositions, dissertation, an edition, a portfolio of recordings, portfolio of orchestrations or a recital. A BMus in Music Technology is also available. This brings together scientific and artistic approaches to the academic discipline of mus and is run in collaboration with the Dept of Physics.

Careers and counselling: University careers advisory service. Personal counselling is offered by the directors of studies.
Campus facilities: Accommodation is provided in halls of residence. There are various student refectories in the university, plus a common room in the mus dept. Some special provisions are made for disabled students and, depending on the disability, they may be accepted.
Music facilities: The dept is fortunate in possessing the Russell Collection of early keyboard insts and the Collection of Historic Musical Instruments, two concert halls (the Reid and St Cecilia's), many practice studios, an electronic studio, and one of the finest mus libraries in the UK. Student groups take part in the faculty concert series and there is also a great deal of professional mus-making in Edinburgh from the Royal Scottish National Orchestra, the Scottish Chamber Orchestra, the Scottish Ensemble and Scottish Opera in the winter season, to the Edinburgh Festival events in the summer. The Festival Theatre, an important venue for opera and ballet, is adjacent to the dept.

Essex University
Wivenhoe Pk, Colchester, Essex CO4 3SQ
Tel: 01206 873333 *Fax:* 01206 873702

Christopher Holden, arts offr.
Courses: 8 joint mus degrees run conjointly with Colchester Institute. For details *see* **Colleges of Higher Education** Colchester Institute.

Exeter University
Music Dept, Knightley, Streatham Dr, Exeter EX4 4PD
Tel: 01392 263810 *Fax:* 01392 263815

Nicholas Sandon, prof of mus; Richard Langham-Smith, reader and head of dept; Philip R Grange, reader in composition; Timothy Jones, lecturer; Alan Street, lecturer and admissions tutor; Peter C Allsop, lecturer in mus; Paul

Morgan, p/t lecturer.

Courses: BA Hons (3); BMus (3) (course as for BA for yrs 1 and 2); BA Combined Honours (Arts Group) (3; 4 with modern lang combination) *see* **Combined Degrees**. P/grad: MMus in composition; MA in musicology; MPhil (1); PhD (history, musicology, composition) (3). P/grad courses may also be taken in Education Dept.

Course details: The u/grad course ranges over the literature of Western mus in a syllabus which co-ordinates theoretical and practical study. Students are encouraged and enabled to develop their particular abilities. Yr 1 concentrates upon achieving competence in the academic, technical and practical skills associated with mus. Students examine mus in its historical context, sample various analytical methods, practise composition, explore the language of late baroque and classical mus, receive individual tuition on their 1st inst and group coaching in ens performance, and take a non-mus subject. Yr 2 and Yr 3 students have increasing opportunities to develop their skills and interests. A wide range of mus history courses examine in detail individual repertoires and topics. Courses on mus analysis and techniques are closely focused on particular methods and repertories. Students may qualify to continue to take solo performance, while ens performance remains open to all. Other courses offer an introduction to specialist musical skills such as musical direction, mus therapy, mus education, editing, DTP, aesthetics, and mus psychology. Students may take a non-mus subject.

Teaching takes the form of lectures, seminars, individual tuition and supervision, and practical w/shops and rehearsals.

Careers and counselling: The university runs a careers advisory service. All students have a personal tutor from their own dept.

Campus facilities: Accommodation is always available in university halls and flats. There are several canteens. Disabled students are admitted if it is considered that they can satisfactorily complete the course, but no special provisions are made.

Music facilities: All students are encouraged to participate extensively in the extra-curricular musical activities of the university, which include a symphony orch and chmbr orch, several choirs, an early mus group, a madrigal society, etc. Students will hardly need encouragement to attend the concerts given almost every week in the Great Hall by professional orchs, ens and soloists.

Glasgow University

Dept of Music, 14 University Gardens, Glasgow G12 8QH
Tel: 0141 330 4093 *Fax:* 0141 330 3518
Email: marjorie@music.gla.ac.uk
Website: www.music.gla.ac.uk

Graham Hair, composition; Marjorie Rycroft, head of dept, baroque and classical mus; Warwick Edwards, medieval and renaissance mus; Eduardo Miranda, mus technology; Stephen Arnold, contemporary composition, computer mus; Stuart Campbell, Russian and Soviet mus.

Courses: BMus (3 or 4); MA (3 or 4) (mus taken p/t within general arts degree or as single or combined hons); BEng (4) (mus taken p/t within electronics and mus degree) *see* **Combined Degrees**. P/grad: MMus (1); MLitt (2); PhD (3).

Course details: The University of Glasgow caters for f/t (BMus) and f/t or p/t (MA/BEng) students in mus, MA students taking mus within a general arts degree and BEng students taking mus (with special emphasis on audio processing) within the programme of the Engineering faculty. All three degrees are available as Ordinary or Honours degrees. The emphasis for MA students is on mus as a cultural phenomenon with options in technical applications (composition, performance or electronics) if desired. BMus students have a ground course covering nearly every musical discipline, followed by specialisation in either history, performance or composition, with a choice of supporting studies. Students may thus offer their degrees in their strongest and preferred subjects. A 1-yr p/grad MMus (by research) degree is offered in musicology, composition, performance or computer mus.

Careers and counselling: Careers advice and personal counselling both available.

Campus facilities: Accommodation provided in halls of residence. Canteen facilities on campus. Disabled students accepted, but no special provision is made for them.

Music facilities: Mus students can benefit from the abundance of professional mus-making in Glasgow, with Scottish Opera, the Royal Scottish National Orchestra and the BBC Scottish Symphony Orchestra all resident in the city. Students may participate in the university's orch and choruses, and are encouraged to join in chmbr groups.

Goldsmiths College

Music Dept, University of London, New Cross, London SE14 6NW
Tel: 0171 919 7640 *Fax:* 0171 919 7644
Email: music@gold.ac.uk
Website: musicinfo.gold.ac.uk

Simon McVeigh, head of dept and head of p/grad studies; Roger Wibberley, deputy head of dept; Colin Lawson, chair of performance studies; John Baily, reader in ethnomusicology and p/grad admissions; Frank Dobbins, reader; Keith Potter, snr lecturer/international admissions; Anthony Aldridge, dir of elec mus studio; Craig Ayrey, lecturer; Peter Driver, lecturer and u/grad admissions; Marina Frolova-Walker, lecturer; Sadie Harrison, lecturer; Anthony Pryer, lecturer; Roger Redgate, lecturer; Benedict Sarnaker, head u/grad studies; Noelle Mann, head of Centre for Russian Studies. *Courses:* BMus (3; 4 p/t). P/grad: MMus in Ethnomusicology, Theory and Analysis, Historical Musicology, Composition, or Performance and Related Studies (1 f/t; 2 p/t); MPhil (2 f/t; 3 p/t); PhD (3 f/t; 4 p/t).

Course details: Throughout the BMus course, contemporary mus and historical studies are compulsory. In the final 2 yrs students are able to choose from a wide range of options. The course is modular. Inst and vocal tuition is available on this course.

Careers and counselling: Students have access to general college careers advisory service and a departmental careers advisor, and are allocated to personal tutors within dept.

Campus facilities: Accommodation provided for a large number of students in 11 halls of residence, mostly self-catering. Large refectory offers meals and snacks, plus student union coffee bar also serving snacks. Physically handicapped students would be accepted if suitably qualified; partial wheelchair access.

Music facilities: The character of the mus dept at Goldsmiths is influenced by its size, its academic and practical diversity, and its proximity to the musical centres of London. As one of the largest mus depts in the established university sector it has some 200 u/grads (f/t or p/t), 80 p/grads, 12 f/t members of staff and many p/t teachers. This enables it to present a wide choice of courses and performance activities; the latter are professionally directed, of a very high standard and take place at established public venues. Student compositions are recorded at concerts and w/shops given by professional as well as student ens. Central London naturally offers a great international focus both for its concerts and libraries. Goldsmiths itself, however, is a hive of activity in performance, composition and research into many historical periods and culture, and there are regular research seminars and one-day conferences.

The ethnomusicology section has a separate studio, while the newly-founded Centre for Russian Music houses the Prokofiev archive and other Russian sources. A well-equipped electronic mus studio, with a f/t studio mgr, contains a recording suite, individual studios for technology and composition students, and a computer room with a range of mus software

packages. The main college library has a large mus section, staffed by mus specialists and in addition the dept has its own library and CD collection. A purpose-built block of practice rooms has recently been opened.

University of Hertfordshire
College La, Hatfield, Herts AL10 9AB
Tel: 01707 284441 *Fax:* 01707 285098
Website: www.herts.ac.uk

Howard Burrell, prof of mus and head of dept; Martyn Parry, head of academic studies; John Palmer, head of research.
Courses: BSc (Hons) Electronic Music; BSc Hons Electronic Music with Mathematics; BSc Hons Combined Studies (elec mus major). MSc in Composition (f/t and p/t).
Course details: The university's approach to the teaching of mus has been specifically designed by a team of professional composers and performers to utilise fully the range of technology currently available. With a core focus on the computer, the courses aim to embrace the demand for a contemporary approach to mus and its vocational applications, whilst enabling the student to develop creative skills and abilities.
Campus facilities: Accommodation in halls available for 1st years. Accommodation Office will assist in finding accommodation in subsequent years. Student union offices, shop, and bar.
Music facilities: 2 mus studios equipped with individual workstations, typically PowerMac/Akai S3000/Yamaha DMP7/DAT Recorder. There is a choral society, big band, concert band and the university is home to Hatfield Philharmonic Orchestra, the leading amateur orch in the area. Hatfield campus is located only 30 mins from central London.

Huddersfield University
Dept of Music, Queensgate, Huddersfield HD1 3DH
Tel: 01484 472003 *Fax:* 01484 472656
Email: music@hud.ac.uk
Website: www.hud.ac.uk/schools/music+humanities/music

Peter Lawson, head of dept; Michael Holloway, admissions offr; John Bryan, performance leader; Margaret Lucy Wilkins, composition leader; Michael Clarke, electro-acoustic mus leader; Graham Cummings, musicology leader.
Courses: BMus Hons (3); BA Hons in Music with a Modern Language (3 or 4) *see* **Combined Degrees**; BA Hons in Music with Theatre Studies (3); BA Hons in Music with English (3); BA Hons Music Technology (3 or 4). P/grad: MA in Composition, Performance, Electro-Acoustic Composition, Contemporary Music Studies or Historical Musicology (1 f/t; 2 p/t); MPhil; PhD.

Course details: The BMus Hons offers a programme of study in which performance, composition, electro-acoustic mus and musicology are treated with equal importance. A range of options in all 3 yrs allows for increasing specialisation, either in one of the above disciplines, early mus, br band, org or church mus or contemporary mus. The BA Hons mus with a modern language (French, German or Spanish), English or theatre studies provides a balanced educational experience in two subjects. The combination of mus with non-music studies offers an integration of practical and academic elements in all disciplines. Mus technology combines electro-acoustic mus with modules in computing and electronic engineering. The MA in performance has a high practical profile, and aims to produce a more flexible, adaptable musician prepared for a variety of careers in the mus industry. The MA in composition provides an opportunity to consolidate composing experience and development of techniques largely unfettered by other intellectual demands. All u/grads take original composition as part of their course and 7 active composers are available on the staff. The MA in electro-acoustic composition adopts a similar approach and exploits the potential of the dept's 5 electro-acoustic studios. In the MA in contemporary mus studies, students study various analytical approaches and apply them to a group of case studies of their own choice, culminating in an extended dissertation on their main area of interest. The MA in historical musicology focuses on research methods and analytical skills linked to case studies and final dissertation on a modern topic.
Careers and counselling: Course tutors supervise each student's work. In addition all 1st year students are placed with a personal tutor. The university careers service and the dept's careers tutor provide continuous cover in this area.
Campus facilities: Most 1st yr students are offered accommodation in halls of residence on campus. Other accommodation (lodgings, rented rooms, etc) are within easy distance of the university. Student refectories. Suitably qualified disabled students are accepted.
Music facilities: As part of their academic programme students participate in a wide range of supplementary mus studies, and in orch, br band, choirs, chmbr mus, early mus, new mus ens, wind orch, str orch, big band, opera, etc. The student strength of the dept is approx 350, large enough to promote ens activities yet small enough to give a friendly close-working environment, within a university which provides welfare services and other facilities including sport. Housed in purpose-built accommodation, the dept provides extensive facilities for study.

These include 2 concert halls (St Paul's Hall, converted from a fine Georgian church on campus, contains a new 41-stop tracker-action org), extensive practice and teaching accommodation, mus library, electro-acoustic mus studios (well-equipped with analogue and digital facilities), perc studio and other mus and ancillary accommodation. The dept also has a wide range of insts many of which are available for student loan. Situated centrally in Huddersfield, department students are easily able to participate in the many musical events in the locality. Huddersfield Town Hall is the regular venue for concerts by major British and foreign orchs, while the city of Leeds (less than 30 miles away by road or rail) is the home of Opera North and Manchester boasts the Hallé and BBC Philharmonic Orchestras. The Huddersfield Contemporary Music Festival annually brings personal visits by such figures as Xenakis, Pierre Boulez and Ligeti. In this festival, the university dept of mus plays a major part, with concession prices for students, competitions for student composers, and regular appearances by department ens.

Hull University

Dept of Music, Hull University, Hull HU6 7RX
Tel: 01482 465998

Brian Newbould, prof of mus; Ian Denley, head of w/wind; Delia Fletcher, head of vocal studies; Ann Airton, head of keyboard studies; Richard Quick, head of strs.
Courses: BMus Single Hons (3); BA Special Hons (3); BA Joint Hons (3) *see* **Combined Degrees**. P/grad: MMus; MA; MPhil; PhD (minimum length for all courses 1 yr).
Course details: The mus courses aim to cultivate well-balanced musicians with some ability and knowledge in most traditional aspects of the subject but with specialist skills in particular areas of their choice including performance. Tuition in mus technology is available and there are 6 mus scholarships. Yr 1 is designed to give the student secure foundations for further musical study and to reveal the student's individual talents. These individual talents may then be developed in yrs 2 and 3 of the course through options which include composition, performance, a study of editing techniques of early mus, orchestration and analysis.
Careers and counselling: Hull offers an established programme of careers advice, with personal counselling where necessary.

Campus facilities: All 1st year students guaranteed a place in university accommodation. Applications from disabled students are considered.

Music facilities: Students belong to an active musical community in which choral, orch and chmbr mus are fostered, with inst tuition provided by the university. M/classes, coaching sessions and open rehearsals are given by visiting musicians, including regular visits by the Allegri String Quartet. Visiting lecturers contribute to the dept's courses from time to time, and numerous visiting artists give concerts. There are special facilities for learning to play early insts (string, wind or keyboard) and there is an established viol consort: tuition and insts provided. A Lammermuir pipe organ is one of three new orgs recently installed. A chapel choir is directed by the university org scholars, who are normally u/grads studying mus. The dept aims to provide an informal, friendly atmosphere for the pursuit of musical studies to a high level. Students enjoy a good social life, and are happy to be at hand on days when sixth-formers arrive for interview, to discuss any aspect of life in the university and its mus dept.

Keele University

Dept of Music, Keele University, Keele, Staffs ST5 5BG
Tel: 01782 583295 *also fax;*
Email: mua09@mus.keele.ac.uk
Website: www.keele.ac.uk/depts/mu/index.htm

David Nicholls, prof; Mike Vaughan, head of dept and snr lecturer; Katharine Preston, visiting prof of mus (Jan-Jul 1998); Jane Manning, hon prof; Raymond Fearn, Rajmil Fischman, Philip Jones, Barbara Kelly, Sohrab Uduman, Alastair Williams, lecturers.

Courses: BA (3 or 4); BSc (4); (both joint hons); BA Joint Hons (mus/electronic mus and humanities/social sciences) (3 or 4); BSc Joint Hons (mus/electronic mus and natural sciences) (3 or 4) *see* **Combined Degrees**. P/grad: MA in Modern Music; MA/MSc or P/grad Diploma in Digital Music Technology; MPhil; PhD (all p/grad courses p/t or f/t).

Course details: Mus and electronic mus can only be studied on a joint honours course, in combination with one other principal subject chosen from an unusually wide range. Some of these combinations are unique to Keele and have particular advantage for those hoping to pursue careers in school teaching, the recording industry, arts management and admin, in addition to those entering the mus profession. Four-year students may take the concurrent Certificate in Education course. Research interests include American, British, French, German and Italian mus, mus aesthetics and analysis and acoustic and electro-acoustic

composition. Inst lessons are provided for all 1st and 2nd yr students plus those offering a recital in their final-year programme. Recitalists are encouraged to present traditional repertoire together with more wide-ranging programmes including early and contemporary mus, folk and jazz. In the field of computer mus the dept offers p/grad courses in digital mus technology. The versatility of Keele mus graduates is well recognised by employers.

Careers and counselling: University has careers and counselling services; students are also helped by individual tutors.

Campus facilities: Accommodation is provided for most students, and there are several restaurants and cafes. The computer centre operates the main campus network to which over 1000 terminals and PCs are connected.

Music facilities: Most of the mus dept's teaching takes place in the Clock House, an early 19th C building on the edge of the campus, which contains practice rooms (also available at the Lindsay Studio Theatre and in some halls of residence), lecture rooms, offices, the electronic studios and the computer room. The Lindsay Studio Theatre, where some concerts are also held, is equipped with two concert grand pnos, a Goble Dulcken harpsichord and a chmbr org in the early 18th C tradition. A full-size Steinway concert grand pno, along with the main org, is housed in the University Chapel, where most large-scale concerts are held. The dept owns a full range of orch insts, including perc, plus viols, rcdrs and other early insts.

Plans are currently being drawn up for a new concert hall on campus. There are 4 electronic mus studio areas at Keele designed to meet the needs of both student and professional users. The Tim Souster Studio is a digital multitrack recording and composition studio. Studio 1 is dedicated to MIDI equipment in combination with digital audio. Studio 2 is designed primarily for the composition of electro-acoustic mus using traditional analogue techniques. The Garagem a purpose-built computer mus laboratory, houses sound synthesis and processing computer workstations which make use of software for sound synthesis, mixing, editing and spectral manipulation. The university library contains about 18,000 items of printed mus, 5500 mus books, 5000 sound recordings and a collection of periodicals, many of which have current subscriptions. Special listening facilities are available in the library's mus section. The mus dept's own library contains cassettes, video tapes, some books and periodicals, student dissertations plus single and multiple copies of scores.

There are many performance groups at Keele, some affiliated to Keele Philharmonic Society. In addition, students can join Keele Swing Band, Keele Jazz Orchestra, the Chapel Singers or the Chapel Choir. The Keele Concert Society presents an international series of subscription concerts on Monday evenings. Mus students are eligible for up to 75% reduction on tickets. Keele Music Forum exists to promote the dissemination of research within the dept. Lectures and seminars are given by visiting guest speakers, students and staff. In addition there are several m/classes and w/shops featuring the visiting professor, Jane Manning with student singers, ens and student and staff composers.

King's College, London

Dept of Music, Strand, London WC2R 2LS
Tel: 0171 873 2029 *Fax:* 0171 873 2326
Email: irene.auerbach@kcl.ac.uk
Website: www.kcl.ac.uk/kis/schools/hwms/music/

Laurence Dreyfus, head of dept; Michael Fend, mus history, dir of u/grad studies; Sir Harrison Birtwistle, professor composition; John Deathridge, professor of mus, mus history; Daniel Chua, mus analysis; Tim Crawford, applied computing and mus; Cliff Eisen, mus history; Robert Keeley, composition; Silvina Milstein, composition and mus analysis; David Trendell, gen musicianship, mus history; Irene Auerbach, departmental sec.

Courses: BMus (3). P/grad: MMus (in theory and analysis, composition or historical musicology) (1 f/t; 2 p/t); MPhil/PhD (min 2/3). Others: Certificate of Advanced Musical Studies.

Course details: The u/grad course concentrates the main commitment of the student's time into yr 1, leaving yrs 2 and 3 free for students to pursue various options: performance, composition, mus history and analysis. For p/grad students, the proximity of the British Library offers considerable advantages, which staff are quick to exploit. There is also the opportunity for BMus students to perform and conduct in lunchtime concerts, and there are frequent cheap or free concert and opera tickets offered. All u/grads, in addition, take the required instrumental or vocal lessons at the Royal Academy of Music, with which King's is associated.

Careers and counselling: Careers advice offered informally by members of department; also university and college careers advisers. Each student has a personal tutor to advise on academic and personal matters.

Campus facilities: Hall of residence places are offered to all 1st yr students not living at home. There is a canteen in the college close to the dept building. Disabled students would be

accepted, but unfortunately the building is unsuitable for most physical disabilities.

Music facilities: At King's College the aim is to develop hand, ear and mind in step with each other. The dept attracts many excellent performers and composers who are anxious to study with leading London teachers and to exploit the concert and operatic life of the capital. The important role of performance and composition in the dept notwithstanding, it is not forgotten that the university's main business is with musical thought, with the historical and theoretical approaches to the art, studied as part of the scholarly traditions of the humanities. The dept can call on a large number of visiting scholars to supplement its small staff, not to mention the wide-ranging facilities and resources of the associated Royal Academy of Music. Many internationally known musicologists, passing through London, are happy to give papers at the research Colloquia on Wednesdays, which u/grads are also encouraged to attend. The international perspective is very important, and valuable connections abroad are maintained through the various past teachers and research graduates of the dept who now hold chairs or senior positions in such places as Princeton, Chicago, Ferrara, Rome and Paris (CNRS).

Kingston University
School of Music, Kingston Hill Centre, Kingston on Thames, Surrey KT2 7LB
Tel: 0181 547 7149 *Fax:* 0181 547 7118
Website: www.kingston.ac.uk/~ed-s450/school_of_music/welcome.htm

Edward Ho, professor and head of school of mus; Roger Beeson, principal lecturer; Kevin Jones, reader; John Bate, principal lecturer; Carol Gartrell, principal lecturer; Gloria Toplis, snr lecturer; Michael Searby, snr lecturer; Maria Busen-Smith, snr lecturer.
Courses: BA Hons Music (3); BA Hons Music (post-diploma; p/t). P/grad: MPhil; PhD; MA (1 f/t, 2 p/t). T/T: M Teach (4); PGCE (1).
Course details: There are two different BA Hons Music syllabuses. Both provide a broad practical mus degree with increasing specialisation through the years and many opportunities to perform. Syllabus A includes inst studies whereas Syllabus B involves mus technology including sound recording, studio techniques and the use of computers.
Careers and counselling: Careers advice and personal counselling both available.
Campus facilities: Accommodation provided both on site and in approved lodgings. Eating facilities in student canteen. Applications from disabled students considered sympathetically and individual arrangements can be made although

there are no special provisions.
Music facilities: The mus centre at Kingston University offers an excellent environment for musical study. Resources include a digital pipe org, 2 hpds, more than 40 pnos, orch and c/room insts, 5 electronic mus studios, computer workstations and an inst repair w/shop. There is a specialist library with excellent listening facilities, containing a comprehensive collection of books, anthologies, CD-Roms of Music Index and RILM, periodicals, scores, sheet mus, CDs, gramophone records and tapes. The holding of scores features the complete works of no fewer than 30 major composers. A major development has been the collaboration with the Gateway School of Recording and Music Technology which runs 5 recording studios and teaches mus technology.
There are various performing groups including symphony orch, chmbr orch, chorus, chmbr choir, early mus group, new mus ens, wind band, baroque ens, world mus ens, string quartets, br ens big band, wind and mixed enss which give regular concerts within and outside the University. The resident ens, the Fibonacci Sequence, gives concerts, w/shops and m/classes. In addition, m/classes, w/shops and short courses given by eminent musicians are organised from time to time. Free visits to concert halls on the South Bank and opera houses in London are arranged for students.

Lancaster University
Music Dept, Bailrigg, Lancaster LA1 4YW
Tel: 01524 65201 *Fax:* 01524 63806

Anthony Pople, prof and head of dept.
Courses: BMus (3); BA Hons (3) single or joint *see* **Combined Degrees**. P/grad: MMus; MPhil; PhD (both research degrees; MPhil may include performance or composition).
Course details: The dept aims to allow the student a realistic choice of areas of specialisation within a framework strong in the basic features of musical knowledge. Consequently all students take a course integrating harmony, counterpoint and analysis, and courses in history and performance as these basic skills are appropriate not only for a future career within the mus profession, but also for those who may wish to use their degree as a basis for work in another field. The choice of specialisation is made carefully in consultation with the staff, with the result that students generally find it not too difficult to proceed to the next stage of their training, which in most cases is a p/grad course at a university (for composers and historians), or at a mus college (for performers), or a PGCE course (for inst or school teachers). Increasing numbers of students are finding that their degree

341

is an appropriate qualification for entry into immediate employment, in commercial or public service management, or in the computer industry.

Careers and counselling: The mus dept has one of the best records within the university for placing students at the end of their course. There is a college tutor system, a dept tutor system and a university counselling service.

Campus facilities: Accommodation is provided for all 1st yr students, 3rd yr students who require it, and for some 2nd yr students. There are several student canteens on the campus. Enquiries from disabled students are welcomed; the dept has had some experience of blind students.

Music facilities: The dept aims to co-ordinate practice with theory and history, and encourages students to draw on their historical and technical knowledge when performing, and vice versa. It is felt to be important not to regard the various parts of the course as compartments which have no relationship with each other. Inst tuition is provided free. Courses are offered in arts admin and conducting. The range of interests of the academic staff is broad and this is reflected in the courses of study. Members of staff are fully involved in practical activities (2 orchs, 2 choirs, wind band, big band and smaller groups), and

the university itself promotes a series of professional concerts in order that students may see and hear musicians at work. For the same reason there are 5 artists-in-residence (the Medici String Quartet and the pianist Andrew West) and 2 orchs (BBC Philharmonic and Manchester Camerata). The dept is a comfortable size (about 100 students and 6 staff) which prevents anonymity. This also means that advice may be readily sought and given. Weekly seminars are in small groups. The dept is, amongst other things, particularly interested in the application of microcomputers to certain aspects of teaching, and willing students are encouraged to help develop this work.

University of Leeds

Dept of Music, Leeds LS2 9JT
Tel: 0113 233 2583 *Fax:* 0113 233 2586
Email: c.l.noble@leeds.ac.uk
Website: www.leeds.ac.uk/music/music.html

Julian Rushton, prof of mus, p/grad admissions; Graham Barber, head of dept and dir of performance studies; David Cooper, dir of electronic studio; Richard Rastall, musicology; Philip Wilby, composition; Kate Daubney, film mus, u/grad admissions; Steven Sweeney-Turner, research fellow.

Courses: BMus (4); BA Hons (3); BA Joint Hons (3); BSc (3); Graduate Diploma in Music (2) (all except BMus and Grad Diploma available p/t). *See also* **Combined Degrees.** P/grad: Diploma in Music Studies (1); MMus; MA; MPhil; PhD; PhD in Composition. T/T: PGCE (1) secondary and primary.

Course details: The modular u/grad course starts from a broad base and incorporates progressive specialisation. It begins by sharpening traditional knowledge and skills in hearing, writing, and analysing mus, as well as practical work and musical history. All 1st yr students do some free composition and are introduced to the electronic studio; all students may take inst lessons. The main areas of specialisation in yrs 2 and 3 are composition, performance, musicology, criticism and mus technology. All students write a dissertation. There is a wide range of other historical courses related to the special interests of staff (eg 17th C English str mus, Mozart's Italian operas, film mus, the mus of Lutoslawski; other courses include projects in performance, harmony, analysis and orchestration. Assessment is spread across exams, take-away papers, dissertations, assessed essays and coursework. The 4-yr BMus for advanced performers includes a year abroad in a conservatoire environment on the continent or in the USA. We offer a modular p/grad taught course (MMus) which includes options in advanced analysis and criticism, composition, performance, musicology, technology and opera studies, as well as a core module in research training. Research degrees (including composition) may be undertaken over 1, 2 or 3 years.

Careers and counselling: Well-staffed, experienced careers office. Personal tutors offer additional guidance and counselling. Occasional seminars.

Campus facilities: The university has halls of residence and self-catering flats, with canteen facilities. Leeds is committed to making courses possible for disabled students.

Music facilities: All mus students at Leeds may take inst or singing lessons. As well as a performance course, the department organises w/shop sessions as part of the course and contributes to the concert series promoted by the university. The department benefits from excellent inst teaching and coaching from Leeds teachers and visitors such as the Allegri String Quartet, and from the very active musical life of the city of Leeds, especially Opera North.

Leeds Metropolitan University

Calverley St, Leeds LS1 3HE
Tel: 0113 283 5912 *Fax:* 0113 283 3110
Email: j.hardman@lmu.ac.uk
Website: www.lmu.ac.uk/ies

R Ward, P Greenwood, course leaders; P Conway, course mgr.

Courses: BEng Hons Electronics, Music and Media Technology (3; 4 sandwich; 4 p/t); *see* **Combined Degrees.** BSc Hons Electronics, Media and Communications (3; 4 sandwich; 4 p/t), BSc Hons Music Technology (3; 4 sandwich; 4 p/t).

Course details: The BEng Hons in Electronics, Music and Media Technology combines electronic engineering with the technological and creative aspects of radio, TV, mus and other media technologies. Central to this course is a student's creative ability to appraise sound systems and images as well as the ability to maintain engineering excellence. The BSc Hons in Electronics, Media and Communications is a specialism which caters for those students wishing to pursue a career in electronics, but who also have a real interest in applying electronics to mus, media and supporting audio/acoustic technology. Topics include mus skills and media technologies, studio recording, mus technology, integrated systems design, digital and analogue electronics, communication electronics and a major project. The BSc Hons Music Technology provides well trained technicians with a knowledge of technology and the ability to use it creatively within the mus industry. 5 main themes run through the course: technology, computing, recording, mus systems and mus. Graduates may expect to gain employment as recording engineers, sound technicians or studio designers.

Campus facilities: Kirkstall Brewery student residences accommodate over 1000 1st yr students.

Music facilities: Many mus-related modules taught at Leeds College of Music.

Liverpool University

Music Dept, PO Box 147, Liverpool L69 3BX
Tel: 0151 794 3096 *Fax:* 0151 794 3141
Email: music@liv.ac.uk
Website: www.liv.ac.uk/~music/

John Williamson, head of dept; Robert Orledge; David Horn, popular mus dir; Colin Iveson, head of vocal studies; James Wishart, head of composition and electronic studio; John Gough, head of keyboard studies; Tony Shorrocks, head of performance studies.

Courses: BA Hons (3); BA Hons Music/Popular Music; BA Combined Hons (3) *see* **Combined Degrees.** P/grad: MA Popular Music (1); MMus (1); MPhil (2); PhD (3) both by research and thesis. All p/grad courses can also be taken p/t.

Course details: The dept's aim is to secure the best possible balance between the academic and the 'practical' aspects of mus, while recognising the extent to which they are complementary.

Careers and counselling: Advice from dept's careers liaison officers, Michael Talbot and Philip

Tagg, plus much help from university's careers and appointments board. Each student has a personal tutor within the dept.
Campus facilities: Accommodation provided in university halls of residence. Several canteens on campus. Disabled students are accepted although the dept is not specifically adapted for the severely disabled.
Music facilities: The university maintains an excellent library of scores, theoretical and critical works, facsimiles, reference material, etc. Students are encouraged, as a major part of their training, to pursue independent research, presenting their findings in the form of written (and read and discussed) papers. Original composition is strongly encouraged, and student work is tested (and criticised) in live performance, in some instances by professional players from the Royal Liverpool Philharmonic Orchestra.
Performance plays a major role in student life. Many students are skilled instrumentalists who find an important outlet in regular orch and chmbr playing, and virtually all are involved to some extent in vocal mus, participating in large-scale choral works, in sacred and secular works from all periods for smaller groups, and in opera.
Professional performance of the highest calibre (orch, chmbr, opera, etc) is provided in the city of Liverpool and students have exceptional inexpensive opportunities to attend concerts and rehearsals.
To cater for the considerable measure of specialisation demanded by present-day students the course provides an unusually large range of options in all yrs: musicology, composition, performance, editing, orchestration, popular mus modules (various), and electronic studio techniques.
The individual research activities of various staff members greatly enrich the quality of their teaching, and the special expertise of graduate students working for higher degrees is fostered by maintaining good research facilities.

Liverpool Hope University College
Music Dept, Hope Pk, Liverpool L16 9JD
Tel: 0151 291 3457/3459 *Fax:* 0151 291 3170
Website: www.livhope.ac.uk

Stephen Pratt, head of mus; Mary Black, Robin Hartwell, Jonathan Powles, Ian Sharp.
Courses: BA Hons combined subjects (3). T/T: BEd Hons (4); PGCE (primary or secondary) (1).
Course details: The courses are accredited by the University of Liverpool.
Careers and counselling: College provides full careers advisory service.
Campus facilities: Accommodation available, with

canteen on campus. Disabled students are admitted. Liverpool Hope is based upon the halls of Christ's and Notre Dame and S Katharine's, and is situated on an attractive campus about 20 mins from the city centre.
Music facilities: The mus department is situated in a new purpose-built centre. It is well appointed with lecture and practice rooms, an electro-acoustic studio, listening and recording facilities, a recital room, a mus technology laboratory and a wide range of insts including 3 orgs and 2 hpds. There is a wide range of practical activity within the dept ranging from large scale choral performances, orch and band, through to opera and chmbr mus. The college runs a concert society, *Concordia*, which has become established as one of the most significant in the North West having brought many artists of international stature to the campus for both concerts and w/shops.

University of London Institute of Education
Dept of Music, 20 Bedford Way, London WC1H 0AL
Tel: 0171 612 6740 *Fax:* 0171 612 6741

Keith Swanwick, chair of dept.
Courses: Diploma/BEd. T/T: PGCE. P/grad: MA in Music Education; MPhil; PhD.
Course details: The BEd for serving teachers provides an opportunity for practitioners to extend their academic and practical knowledge and upgrade professional qualifications. The MA and Research degrees offer opportunities for extended studies in the field of mus educ.
Campus facilities: As a centre for the study of education there are excellent facilities for teaching, library and resources, art exhibitions, concerts and drama productions, in addition to the wider educational resources of the University of London. Accommodation is provided in university halls of residence. Canteen located in the students' union. Applications from disabled students are accepted and there is wheelchair access on several levels. Concert halls and theatres, galleries and museums are all within easy distance of the central location in Bloomsbury.
Music facilities: The mus faculty has a spectrum of research interests including mus aesthetics, psychology and sociology of mus, the musical development of children, mus and gender, assessment, evaluation and curriculum innovation. Teaching rooms, keyboard, electronics/rehearsal and recording room, research students rooms and practice areas. Reference and advanced study rooms provide places for informal meetings, group work and individual study. Resources include journals and other information on mus and mus education, sets of c/room material, choral and inst mus,

records and tapes, a collection of mus educ and a/v material and a range of mus insts.

Manchester Metropolitan University (Crewe and Alsager Faculty)
Hassall Rd, Alsager, Stoke-on-Trent ST7 2HL
Tel: 0161 247 2000 *Fax:* 0161 247 6377

Grahame Shrubsole, head of mus.
Courses: BA Hons in Creative Arts (3); BA Joint Hons (3) *see* **Combined Degrees**. DipHE (2) may be awarded on completion of yr 2 of all degree courses to successful students. Mus is studied as one of 2 or 3 subjects on each course.
Course details: The BA in Creative Arts offers 2-3 subjects grouped around a compulsory core which is designed to give focus and integrity to the course. This core subject, Live Arts, is studied throughout the course as a double unit, equal in weight to the other 2 arts being studied in the first 2 yrs and as a maj/min component in the final year. The other subjects available in this degree are visual arts, dance, drama and writing. In the Joint Honours there is no core subject. Mus students add units chosen from English, history, American studies, cultural studies, philosophy, geography, business studies, sport, writing and the other arts subjects of dance, drama and visual arts. There is a maj/min option on this route. The subject area emphasises creativity in the context of composition, scholarship and performance.
Careers and counselling: Careers guidance service, careers library; Dean of Undergraduate Studies, student counsellors, tutorial system (personal and subject) provides comprehensive support service.
Campus facilities: Campus accommodation available for substantial number of students; comprehensive catering facilities and bars. Disabled students accepted whenever possible, but special provision is not comprehensive. Well-equipped, self-contained mus block including electronic studios and practice, teaching, ens rooms, together with storage facilities for students' insts. Regular free bus service between campuses. Extensive lending and reference materials in library including CDs, performance materials, etc.
Music facilities: As a faculty of Manchester Metropolitan University, the mus dept is housed on the Alsager site from which access is easy to major cultural centres such as Manchester, Liverpool and Birmingham as well as nearby Stoke on Trent. There is a stimulating series of public arts events including recitals held during term-time on the Alsager campus. Regular concert trips are organised by the student mus society. Students are given the opportunity to be assessed on inst and vocal skills (1 or 2 insts),

either individually or in ens, to pursue musicological interests and to study techniques of composition, acoustic and electronic, with particular emphasis on the development of a personal style.
There is considerable student choice available within the programme, which is marked by continuous assessment. A broad view of musical development is taken with a particular emphasis placed on the diversity of 20th C mus. The student body encompasses many diverse musical interests and backgrounds, supporting a wide range of ens. There is a strong collaborative spirit between students from all degree routes and backgrounds such as popular and classical, electronic and acoustic. Additional and alternative units of study encompassing popular musics and devised work are available. Prospective students with unconventional qualifications and practical experience are encouraged to apply.

Manchester University
Dept of Music, Denmark Rd, Manchester M15 6HY
Tel: 0161 275 4987 *Fax:* 0161 275 4994

John Casken, prof of mus; Keith Elcombe, head of dept; David Fallows, prof/admissions offr; Julie Bray, lecturer; Barry Cooper, snr lecturer, p/grad admissions; David Fanning, snr lecturer; Crawford Howie, lecturer; Geoffrey Poole, snr lecturer.
Courses: MusB Hons (3). P/grad: MusM (1 f/t; 2 p/t); MPhil (1 f/t; 2 p/t); PhD (3 f/t; 6 p/t). Also special joint courses with RNCM for a small number of exceptionally gifted students, MusB (3) and GRNCM (1).
Course details: The dept, rated excellent for both its teaching and research, aims to provide a broad and interesting musical training and to create a lively musical environment. It aims to develop skills, encourage critical awareness and stimulate a creative imagination through a study of mus in its historical context, performance, analysis and composition. The objective is to equip students with an all-round competence which will serve them well both inside and outside the mus profession, and to allow them to specialise in the areas of musicology, performance and composition in their final year. A wide range of teaching methods is employed, from individual tutorials to seminars and lectures.
Careers and counselling: Large university careers and appointments service available. Also university counselling service plus personal tutors for students.
Campus facilities: All single 1st year undergraduates are guaranteed accommodation and the Accommodation Office helps with finding

flats, etc for other students. Large refectory including self-service and snack bars. Disabled students are accepted, and there is purpose-built accommodation but at present the mus dept is not well-equipped for disabled students.
Music facilities: Staff special interests embrace all periods of Western mus, with a particular strength in 20th C mus and composition, medieval and classical mus. The Lindsay String Quartet are p/t lecturers and in addition to regular concerts, they give seminars, teach and coach chmbr ens. The dept is comparatively large (approx 150 u/grads, 20 p/grads and 8 lecturers), and the mus dept's own building includes concert hall, practice rooms, electronic mus studio facilities and a small library. Students are often attracted by the vigour of Manchester's musical life with regular concert-giving provided by the Hallé and BBC Philharmonic Orchestras in the new Bridgewater Hall and at the BBC, by the orchs and ens of the RNCM, the Lindsay String Quartet and the university's own orchs, choirs and ens. In addition there are excellent visiting theatre and ballet companies. The library has extensive facilities: 30,000 scores, 6000 records, specialist periodicals and historical manuscripts.

Middlesex University
Trent Park, Bramley Rd, London N14 4YZ
Tel: 0181 362 5684 *also fax*

Michael Bridger, head of mus.
Courses: BA Hons Music (3); BA Hons Jazz (3); BA Hons Sonic Arts (3); BA Hons Performing Arts (3); Mus can be combined with a large range of other subjects as a major or minor study. T/T PGCE (1).
Course details: Practical w/shops form the main method of teaching. The BA Performing Arts brings together students specialising in mus, dance and drama and gives opportunities for interdisciplinary work. The BA Sonic Arts programme explores the newly developing world of electronic sound. Applications for all programmes are welcome from those who do not possess the normal entry requirements, but who do have good practical skills and experience.
Careers and counselling: Full university careers service available, also welfare officers and counsellors.
Campus facilities: Trent Park is an attractive country park within easy reach of central London. Accommodation in hall for some students; welfare officers can advise about alternatives. Refectory and bar facilities. Disabled students are accepted, but the

dance/drama element in the BA Performing Arts may be unsuitable in some cases.

Music facilities: Well-equipped, purpose-built mus block; a Learning Resources Centre with a large stock of sheet mus, scores and CDs.

Napier University

The Ian Tomlin School of Music, Craighouse Campus, Craighouse Rd, Edinburgh EH10 5LG
Tel: 0131 455 6200 *Fax:* 0131 455 6211
Email: p.sawyer@napier.ac.uk
Website: www.napier.ac.uk/depts/mushome.html

Philip Sawyer, head of School of Music; Anna Butterworth, snr lecturer; Nicholas Ashton, lecturer; Andrew Doig, lecturer; Frederick Frayling-Kelly, lecturer; Ian Macpherson, lecturer; Jim Doyle, technician.

Courses: BMus Hons (4); HND in Music Studies (2). Students who take the HND course may, subject to suitability, transfer to BMus1 after HND1 or into BMus2 after HND2.

Course details: HND students take compulsory core subjects in principal inst, voice or composition, prescribed scores and history, notation and stylistic harmony, aural perception and sight singing. They may choose options from subsidiary inst, voice or composition (subject to standard and availability), mus technology, keyboard skills, fretboard skills, composition and arranging, jazz improvisation, techniques of conducting and essay writing. Entry is by audition and interview, applicants should be of gr 7+ in the principal inst or voice. Composers should send a portfolio of their work prior to interview. BMus students take core subjects in principal study inst (voice or composition), history and stylistic studies and general mus skills (BMus1 only). In yrs 2 and 3, students may choose options from arranging and composition, mus technology, fretboard skills, keyboard skills, techniques of conducting, jazz improvisation and light mus performance styles. In yr 4 students choose modules to suit their career aspirations and special interests. Entry is by audition and interview and students should be of gr 8+ standard in their principal inst or voice.

Careers and counselling: The university careers service is available throughout the year. There is a student counselling service and a student-run welfare advice service.

Campus facilities: Napier University occupies 4 main campuses and a number of minor sites, mostly on the south and west sides of Edinburgh. There is a wide range of accommodation available throughout Edinburgh, some of is owned by the University, with one hall of residence at the Craiglockhart campus. Other facilities include a residential accommodation service, occupational health service, physical

education unit at Sighthill and Craiglockhart campuses, chaplaincy, access fund office, libraries and refectories on the four main campuses. Students benefit from the wide-ranging and lively cultural life of Edinburgh, with its fine concert halls, galleries, museums, theatres and libraries.

Music facilities: The Ian Tomlin School of Music is housed in a purpose-converted villa at the University's Craighouse campus in the Morningside area of Edinburgh. The villa is set high up on the campus with fine wiews over Edinburgh to the west, north and east. Facilities include recital room, recording control room, seminar, class and lecture rooms, teaching and practice studios, computing and mus technology facilities. The department of mus is the focal point for the university's chmbr orch, symphonic winds and jazz band.

Newcastle University

Dept of Music, Armstrong Building, Newcastle upon Tyne NE1 7RU
Tel: 0191 222 6736 *Fax:* 0191 222 5242

Eric Cross; Richard Middleton, head of dept; David Clarke; Agustín Fernández; Ian Biddle; Jennifer Burchell; Magnus Williamson.

Courses: BA Hons (3 f/t, 6 p/t); BA Hons in Combined Studies *see* **Combined Degrees**. P/grad: MA; MA or Diploma in Music Technology; MA in Music, Meaning and Culture; MA in Popular Music; MMus or Diploma in Performance or Composition (1 f/t, 2 p/t); MLitt; MPhil; PhD.

Course details: The BA Hons in Music modular degree programme aims to provide a thorough grounding in all the main areas of the subject. The recently introduced syllabus covers issues in mus history with particular emphasis on the links between mus and culture, analysis, mus technology, aesthetics and theory, various compositional techniques and performance. In yrs 2 and 3 students choose from a wide range of options (including such areas as mus and computing, conducting studies, orchestration, popular mus and detailed historical projects), and final year specialisations include composition, performance and musicology. Teaching is done mainly in small groups. Examinations involve a mixture of formal 3-hr papers, 1-wk 'take-away' papers and assessed course work. In addition to the single honours degree in mus, Newcastle offers a combined honours degree for which mus may be taken for 1, 2 or 3 yrs. In theory, mus can be combined with any subject, although in practice some combinations are excluded by timetable clashes. Students choose two or three subjects to study each year, with a total of not more than five subjects during the 3-yr course. All subjects are

studied in depth, as students attend the same courses as single honours u/grads. A new set of p/grad degree programmes has just been introduced, allowing a wide range of choice and specialising in areas such as composition, performance, mus technology, popular mus and mus, meaning and culture.
Careers and counselling: Career advice and personal counselling available to all students.
Campus facilities: Halls of residence are available, as are canteen facilities. Disabled students are accepted, but there is no special provision.
Music facilities: Academic courses are balanced by an atmosphere of practical mus-making, with a large university orch and choir and various smaller groups ranging from a chmbr orch and madrigal choir to a viol consort and new mus group. All students taking practical studies modules can receive free practical tuition throughout the course, often from members of the Northern Sinfonia. Newcastle is a lively university in a lively city, with the campus occupying a precinct close to the city centre. Newcastle has a great variety of accommodation, societies for every interest, some of the best outdoor facilities for sport in this country, and a flourishing concert series. The city has its own chmbr orch, the Northern Sinfonia, the Avison Baroque Ensemble, several theatres, which are visited frequently by Opera North, the Royal Ballet and other touring companies (including the Royal Shakespeare Company), and the city regularly plays host to visiting orchs from all parts of the world.

University of Northumbria at Newcastle
Dept of Visual and Performing Arts, Lipman Building, Sandyford Rd, Newcastle upon Tyne NE1 8ST
Tel: 0191 227 3920

John Kefala Kerr, head of mus and route leader.
Courses: BA Hons Music (3).
Course details: The mus degree route (in the university's unitised programme), provides vocational training in mus in the community. The route aims to increase popular access to the arts by training musicians in the uses of mus in the community. This includes producing performances which meet the needs of specific groups and audiences, and working with people to produce their own musical statements. The focus of the work is popular mus, and there are three progressive strands of activity: core theory, musical and contextual analysis and criticism, and practical work (improvisation, composition and arrangement, group performance, basic technical skills, voice, keyboards, perc, gui, recording, computers). A strong emphasis is placed on group work in all aspects. Students gain increasing control over their work, allowing specialisation in musical

forms and types of community. The route includes placements and professional residencies as an essential element of community-based arts development. In addition students take an elective unit each semester.
Careers and counselling: Careers advice available from university student services and from head of mus. All students allocated to a personal tutor who can deal with other problems.
Campus facilities: Some students are accommodated in halls of residence in single rooms and shared flats. Canteen housed in same building as BA course. Disabled students welcome to apply; there are lifts and special WCs.
Music facilities: Mus room, practice room, digital and analogue studios, theatre and small studio.

Nottingham Trent University
Dept of Visual and Performing Arts, Victoria Studios, Nottingham NG1 4BV
Tel: 0115 941 8418

Simon Lewis, head of dept; Piers H Nicholls, course leader; Jeremy Peyton Jones, subject leader mus.
Courses: BA Hons Contemporary Arts (3) *see* **Combined Degrees** (mus studied with either art, dance or performance).
Course details: The course encourages interdisciplinary work between visual art, dance, performance and mus. Mus is studied as one of two subjects in the BA Hons Creative Arts course. Emphasis is placed upon original and innovative practical work in each of its 4 main disciplines of which each student takes 2. In yrs 1 and 2 both subjects are studied, with one subject only in yr 3. The course demands motivation, concentration and commitment to achieve a high standard of expertise and a deep understanding of the arts. Composition (including studio and computer mus techniques), performance, presentation and musical direction, along with interdisciplinary projects and complementary critical studies are included.
Careers and counselling: University careers and counselling service available to students, also counselling from personal tutors.
Campus facilities: Most 1st year students and certain students in yrs 2 and 3 are offered accommodation. Eating facilities are available in a student canteen. There is no provision for accepting disabled students.
Music facilities: Nottingham Trent boasts a lively, stimulating arts environment in the heart of the city. There are generous opportunities to pursue individual interests and enthusiasms in a creative context with excellent facilities and technical support. Facilities include a fully equipped studio theatre (100 seats), recital room, 3 large rehearsal studios, 7 practice

rooms, 2 Yamaha grand pnos and several uprights. There are also 3 recording studios, 2 computer rooms, a range of orch and perc insts, stage amplifiers, etc. Mus and visual arts students also have access to film and video recording and editing facilities.

Nottingham University

Dept of Music, University Pk, Nottingham NG7 2RD
Tel: 0115 951 4755 *Fax:* 0115 951 4756
Website: www.nottingham.ac.uk/~amxal/musdept.htm

Robert Pascall, head of dept; John Morehen, conducting and musicology; Peter Wright, composition, medieval, renaissance, contemporary; Nick Sackman, composition and contemporary mus; Mervyn Cooke, Britten, jazz, composition, ethnomusicology; Philip Weller, 18th C opera, 19th and 20th C song; Nigel Simeone, 20th C French and Czech mus, conducting.
Courses: BA Hons (3). P/grad: MA; MPhil; PhD (musicology, composition); AMusM; AMusD (composition).
Course details: Nottingham's degree course is modular, wide ranging, and offers opportunities to specialise from an early stage. It is designed to allow the student with historical, philosophical or sociological interests, the scientifically-minded student, the composer or the performer to pursue a course of study slanted in one of these directions. The dept does not teach harmony and counterpoint as a separate discipline. Rather it is regarded as one method of investigating a given period, along with analyses and the adducing of historical evidence. By this means, any such technical work is always 'applied' rather than abstract; and the historical period can be examined in stylistic depth. Mus history is never studied as a dry account of past events; students learn about mus as a living art by re-creating it, and it is for this reason that they are encouraged to take part fully in university musical activities. There is a strong tradition of student composition in the dept, and composers have plentiful opportunities to have their works performed. The dept has 3 composers on its staff, and has strong interests in 20th C mus. The option of composition in the degree is for the serious composer with original talent: it is in no sense a mere extension of harmony and counterpoint. The dept has electronic studios including an advanced digital synthesis facility. Students can learn computer programming for purposes of mus analysis. Performance is not compulsorily examined in the degree. It is available as an option at Part I and/or Part II for the serious performer, who must give 2 recitals in public (total 50 mins for Part I, 60 mins for Part II) and take a written paper in performance practice and interpretation.

Departmental staff are keenly involved in research. Particular fields of research interest are: the renaissance and early baroque, the 19th C, contemporary mus, the mus of Brahms, the mus of Janácek and Czech mus, mus theory and analysis, bibliography, opera and computer applications.
Careers and counselling: Both careers advice and personal counselling are available.
Campus facilities: Ample accommodation in halls of residence for all students; also canteen facilities. Disabled students are accepted, and access to dept is good. There is special provision for the visually handicapped.
Music facilities: There is an early inst collection and a video archive of opera.

Open University

Walton Hall, Milton Keynes MK7 6AA
Tel: 01908 274066
Website: www.open.ac.uk/ou/academic/arts.html

Donald Burrows, professor and head of mus dept; Trevor Herbert, snr lecturer and staff tutor; J Barrie Jones, David Rowland, Robert Samuels, Fiona Richards, Martin Clayton, Patricia Howard, lecturers in mus; Kevin Dawe, staff tutor.
Courses: U/grad: BA. P/grad: BPhil; MPhil; DPhil. T/T: Various in-service and updating courses available in School of Education, and PGCE in mus. U/grad courses are also available to non-degree students.
Course details: The Open University offers part-time university education to home-based students. The university uses primarily distance teaching methods (print, a/v media), together with a certain amount of regionally organised face-to-face tuition, supplemented for some courses by a one-week summer school. The u/grad degree is modular. Apart from a very few restrictions, students can choose any combination of courses from any faculty, putting together 360 points on the CAT scheme (courses are 30 or 60 points, each course lasting for one year) for an ordinary degree, or 360 points (with at least 120 points at level 3), for an honours degree. Like other subjects, mus is taught as part of inter-disciplinary courses and through specialist courses. At present there are mus elements in the following interdisciplinary courses: A103 An Introduction to the Humanities; A205 Culture and Belief in Europe 1450-1600; A206 The Enlightenment. The following specialist mus courses are offered: A214 Understanding Music: Elements Techniques and Styles (basic harmony, orchestration, stylistic and formal analysis: second level, 60 points); A341 Beethoven (historical and social context plus analysis: third level, 30 points); AA302 From Composition To Performance: Musicians At Work

349

(historical and social context plus analysis: third level, 60 points). In all these, the package provided comprises teaching material (in print, broadcast and cassette forms, video for A214 and AA302, and CDs for AA302), scores and recordings. A103 and A214 have summer schools. While it is not yet possible to do a mus degree at the Open University, students can slant their studies significantly towards mus (up to about 50% of the total). A Diploma in Music is available, requiring A214 plus any 60 point specialist mus course. Advanced Standing is awarded for recognised diplomas from other institutions, and successful completion of some OU courses exempts candidates from theoretical components of some conservatoire diplomas. Facilities for f/t and p/t p/grad research are available.

The interests of the central staff are focused on Handel, romantic and nationalist mus, British br inst mus since 1500, history and performance practice of the pno, 19th and 20th C mus, cultural theory of mus, 17th and 18th C opera, Indian mus and theory of rhythm. All the specialist mus courses listed above are available to non-undergraduates, as one-off packages. In addition, PA 543 Introduction to Music, a short continuing education course, is available on a similar basis plus an Access module in the Living Art course, entitled 'Sounds'.

Careers and counselling: Students are allocated a tutor and have access to a counselling service. Arrangements are administered by the University's regional offices in Britain.

Campus facilities: The campus is non-residential, except for a small number of f/t research students.

Oxford Brookes University

Music Dept, School of Art, Publishing and Music, Music and Publishing, Gipsy La, Headington, Oxford OX3 0BP
Tel: 01865 484986 *Fax:* 01865 484952

Dai Griffiths, principal lecturer and head of mus; Christina Bashford, snr lecturer in musicology; Tim Howle, snr lecturer and studio mgr; Michael Young, snr lecturer in composition.

Courses: BA/BSC Combined Studies (Ordinary and Hons) (3) *see* **Combined Degrees**; BA Hons in Music. P/grad: MA in Electronic Media; MA in Music, History and Culture; MPhil/PhD in musicology and composition.

Course details: At u/grad level, mus may be taken either on its own as a single honours degree, or with one of more than 40 other subjects as part of a combined degree. Both are modular and require the completion of 24 modules during the degree programmes. The mus course has

pathways in musicology, composition (studio and acoustic), performance and popular mus. There is choice and flexibility within the course, enabling each student to construct an individual and coherent programme of study.

The 1st yr has compulsory modules in structure and tonality, mus history and acoustic composition. Single honours students must also take a module in mus technology and 2 modules from other subject areas. In the yrs 1 and 2 students choose from a wide range of modules, including opera and politics, mus in society, modernism, after modernism, understanding jazz, ens performance, solo performance, electronic mus, compositional styles and structures. A dissertation or extended composition is undertaken in the final year. The MA in Electronic Media allows p/grad students to study the composition of electronic mus alongside developments in digital technology in fine art and publishing, with core options on electronic text, digital, image-making, computer mus and time-based media. The MA in mus, history and culture is run in conjunction with the School of Humanities, offering p/grad students the opportunity of studying mus in its historical and cultural context and absorbing the approaches and methods of a range of humanities disciplines. The programme offers special studies in mus (Music in London Society, 1800-1850; Music, Nationalism and National Identity; the Aesthetics of Popular Song) alongside a wide range of subjects in English, history and history of art. Supervision is available in musicology and composition for the MPhil and PhD research degrees. It is also possible to undertake inter-disciplinary research, with joint supervision in mus and another discipline in the humanities.

Careers and counselling: Each student is assigned a personal tutor within the university whom they see regularly to discuss academic progress and general well-being. In addition, the mus dept runs a year-tutor system as part of the university's profiling process.

Campus facilities: The accommodation office helps students to find accommodation. Most 1st yr u/grads choose to be in a hall of residence or lodgings, whilst 2nd and 3rd yr students often share houses. The 12 halls of residence provide more than 2000 study bedrooms. Applications from people with special needs are welcome. The Student Centre on the Headington Hill campus houses the Students' Union, shops, catering outlets, bars, the chaplaincy and the advice centre. The university bookshop and sports centre are nearby and the city of Oxford is close enough for students to take advantage of the many museums, galleries, shops and concert halls.

Music facilities: The mus dept enjoys spacious and well-equipped accommodation in the Richard Hamilton building. There is a large lecture theatre, small lecture room, practice rooms, a recording studio and a mus technology room. The studio has traditional sound-recording technology as well as 'state of the art' computer hardware and software. It is possible to experiment with hard-disk recording, synthesis, sound manipulation and the synchronisation of audio to video in the mus technology room. There are also two IT studios with a range of word-processing, DTP and graphics softwares, email, internet and other networked facilities. The university library stocks books, journals, scores, CDs, LPs, tapes and CD-Roms. There are many musical activities taking place; choral and orch societies, musicals, jazz big band, str quartets, vocal groups and rock ensembles. The department owns a number of pnos, a hpd, a spinet, a double bass and a range of perc insts. Student lunchtime concerts take place on Thursdays during term-time.

Oxford University

Faculty of Music, St Aldate's, Oxford OX1 1DB
Tel: 01865 276125 *Fax:* 01865 276128
Email: office@music.ox.ac.uk

Reinhard Strohm, Heather prof of mus; Roger Parker, prof; Bojan Bujic, reader, fellow of Magdalen College; John Caldwell, reader; Stephen Darlington, organist at Christ Church; Peter Franklin, reader, fellow of St Catherine's College; Edward Higginbottom, organist at New College; Harry Johnstone, fellow of St Anne's College; Hélène La Rue, curator of the Bate Collection; Nicholas Marston, reader, fellow of St Peter's; Edward Olleson, fellow of Merton College; Owen Rees, fellow of Queen's College; Robert Sherlaw Johnson, tutorial fellow of Worcester College; Roger Parker, reader; Susan Wollenberg, fellow of Lady Margaret Hall.

Courses: BA Hons (3). P/grad: MPhil; MSt; MLitt; DPhil; BMus.

Course details: The BA course covers the whole span of Western mus and introduces the student to a variety of different kinds of study: historical, critical, analytical, technical, compositional and performance-related. Students may choose which studies they wish to explore from a wider spectrum including electro-acoustic mus, composition or solo performance. The degree is awarded on the results of the final examination taken at the end of three years. There are four compulsory papers: two papers on the general history of mus, one paper (or exercise) on the techniques of composition from the 16th C until the present day. Other papers are chosen from a wide range of subjects, including analysis, orchestration, composition, a dissertation or transcription and commentary, solo performance and performance practice, history of insts or specialisms in a particular period or topic. Topics available change from year to year. Lectures, classes and seminars are offered throughout the course. Much of the teaching is by tutorials which are on a one-to-one or two-to-one basis. This maintains independence of work and also allows a close working relationship between student and tutor.

Careers and counselling: Careers advice is offered both informally by tutors and formally by the university appointments committee. Personal counselling is also offered by tutors and if needed by the university's counselling service.

Campus facilities: Oxford is a collegiate university with all colleges making their own arrangements for accommodation, catering, etc. All 1st year students and most others are provided with rooms. Provision for disabled students also depends on the individual colleges.

Music facilities: Oxford is one of the best places to study Western Music on a broad and comprehensive basis. It has one of the largest teaching faculties for mus in the country, the internationally known Bate Collections of musical insts and excellent libraries of mus, books on mus and recordings. It offers the student a very rich life of practical mus whether as performer, listener or composer. The Faculty encourages and subsidises student performing groups of various kinds.

Queen's University

School of Music, Belfast BT7 1NN
Tel: 01232 335105 *Fax:* 01232 238484
Email: c.fegan@qub.ac.uk
Website: www.music.qub.ac.uk

Ian Woodfield, dir and u/grad admissions; Jan Smaczny, p/grad admissions.

Courses: BMus Single Hons (min 3), BA Joint Hons (min 3) *see* **Combined Degrees**. Also BA, Diploma, MA and PhD in Ethnomusicology available in the Dept of Social Anthropology. P/grad: MA (1 f/t; 2 p/t) in Renaissance, 20th C Mus, Performance Studies; MA/Diploma in Music Technology (1 f/t; 2 p/t); MPhil by Thesis; MPhil in Composition; PhD by Thesis or in Composition.

Course details: The BMus course at Queen's aims to cover a broad span of Western mus from several points of view: historical, technical and analytical. Special historical topics cover smaller areas in detail. Students are also able to specialise in performance, composition, electro-acoustics, various musicological skills

such as editing, and many other areas, some of which, such as ethnomusicology, are taught in co-operation with other depts.

Careers and counselling: Careers advice and counselling available if required.

Campus facilities: Accommodation provided in halls of residence and other houses; canteens on campus. Applications are welcome from disabled students. There is limited wheelchair access to the school of mus.

Music facilities: The school is strong in renaissance mus, composition, electro-acoustic mus, computer applications and 19th and 20th C mus. U/grads are encouraged to pursue their interest in the editing and study of 16th C and early 17th C mus, and 20th C mus is well served by the 20th C technique and style options in which a range of techniques of important composers is analysed, studied and imitated. Composition is an important specialism. There is also the provision of advanced electro-acoustic studios and a networked computer studies room. Although the school has in many respects a traditional academic approach to mus in a university, mus-making of all kinds is fostered.

The school runs a university choir, consort and a university symphony orch, whilst the students (through the Music Society) organise a chmbr choir, a chmbr orch and a series of lunchtime recitals. The university hosts many professional recitals and concerts, some under its own auspices, others under the auspices of outside bodies such as the Belfast Music Society. Noteworthy are the annual 'Early Music' and 'Sonorities' festivals. As part of the general revival of cultural life in Belfast, students have the opportunity also of hearing live professional concerts given by the Ulster Orchestra, which is now resident next to the university campus and whose members teach and perform within the dept.

Reading University
Dept of Music, 35 Upper Redlands Rd, Reading RG1 5JE
Tel: 0118 931 8411 *Fax:* 0118 931 8412

Jonathan Dunsby, head of dept.
Courses: BA Hons, Music (3); BA Combined Hons (3 or 4) *see* **Combined Degrees**. P/grad: MA (1 f/t; 2 p/t) (musicology, mus theory and analysis or organ historiography); MMus (1 f/t; 2 p/t) (composition, performance studies); MPhil; PhD (3).
Course details: Those wishing to study mus at Reading should have a lively approach to the subject, together with a keen interest and acquaintance with mus which goes well beyond the limits of the works prepared for the GCSE and A-level. Mus may be studied as a single subject or in combination with another subject. English Literature, French, German, History of Art or Italian may be combined with mus within the Faculty of Letters and Social Sciences. The

courses in combination with a foreign language are 4-yr courses with 1-yr spent abroad; the remainder are 3-yr courses. Teaching is by lecture, class and tutorial group. The aims of the BA (Hons) are to provide a strong foundation in musicianship and knowledge and critical understanding of the repertoire in yrs 1 and 2; thereafter to offer the opportunity for a deeper and more intense study of two specialist areas chosen from four options.
Careers and counselling: The university careers advice service is supplemented by advice and counselling from personal tutors.
Campus facilities: Accommodation is provided and there is a student canteen on the campus. Applications from disabled students are accepted, and each is assessed individually; wheelchair access to ground floor of mus dept only.
Music facilities: The dept's mus librarian guides students in their reading and directs them to useful material in musical scores, critical literature or recorded performances, all readily available in the university mus library which is housed in the dept building. It is the aim of the dept to stimulate and foster the musical interests of its students. Part of the work of a university mus dept is to provide different kinds of musical activity for the benefit of the rest of the university, and indeed the town, for listeners as well as performers. Students in the dept involve themselves in these activities as singers or players. The choral society and university orch, both including town membership, meet weekly during term and perform major works in their concerts. The university chmbr orch also gives concerts, particularly of mus which is outside the scope of the larger groups. The University Singers, a group run by students, tends to specialise in *a cappella* mus. The university opera society, another student organisation, has for a number of years put on a succession of enterprising productions, usually of 19th C opera. There are opportunities for chmbr mus and solo playing, and students participate in the lunchtime Campus Concerts in the Faculty of Letters. A regular series of guest recitals is presented in the dept's Recital Room.

University College of Ripon and York St John
The Ripon Campus, College Rd, Ripon HG4 2QX
Tel: 01765 602691 *Fax:* 01765 600516

Marilynne J R Davies, head of performance studies; Bonnie Martin, Daniel Lancaster, snr lecturers in mus; Josephine Peach, snr lecturer in mus p/t; Bruce Cole, lecturer in mus p/t.
Courses: BA Hons (3) in Communication Arts Studies in Media and Performance; BA (QTS) Hons (4).

Course details: Mus courses at Ripon and York St John are designed to further the student's understanding, knowledge and sensitivity to mus. The courses are taught through a series of projects which are practically based and include individual and group performance. There is the opportunity to take options in performance, composition and musicology. The BA requires an interest in mus and communication arts. The course is in modules and combines theory and practice in mus and the arts, particularly dance and drama.

Careers and counselling: College careers service; also careers education resources centre on both campuses. Qualified counsellors and counselling available for personal problems.

Campus facilities: All 1st yr students normally offered places in hall; remainder are assisted to find accommodation. Student union bar, coffee bar, plus cafeteria offering full meals. Applications are welcomed from disabled students who will be given every support to help them complete their course.

Music facilities: The College is a Church of England college affiliated to the University of Leeds. At Ripon, the college has close links with the cathedral. The resources available include a recently restored 2-manual Willis org, 2-manual hpds, electronic keyboards, computers and individual practice rooms equipped with pnos. Regular performances are given by students as soloists and as members of large and small ens, and compositions by students are also given their first public performance at either lunchtime or evening concerts. Campus libraries house a large and comprehensive collection of records, sheet mus, scores and journals and over 3000 books on mus. Concerts are given by visiting artists, and lunch-time programmes (open to the public) provide valuable opportunities for students to participate in making mus. Ripon Cathedral choral and org scholarships are open to male u/grads with an interest in singing and church mus. The college itself offers annually one choral and one org scholarship as well as orch scholarships. There are opportunities for u/grads to spend a term studying in Germany, France, the Netherlands, Sweden, Scandinavia, Austria or the USA at one of the universities with whom the college has close links.

Royal Holloway

University of London, Egham Hill, Egham, Surrey TW20 0EX
Tel: 01784 434455 *Fax:* 01784 439441
Email: uhwm013@sun.rhbnc.ac.uk
Website: www.rhbnc.ac.uk/music/index2.html

Tim Carter, prof of mus and head of dept; Erik

Study Opportunities in Music

- Largest Music Department with maximum 5* rating in 1996 Research Assessment Exercise
- Outstanding international research strengths in historical musicology, theory & analysis, performance studies, composition
- MPhil/PhD degree programmes in all subjects above; studentships & teaching assistantships available
- Innovative taught MMus in Advanced Musical Studies
- High-recruiting BMus and BA degrees, featuring specialist options chosen by students
- Excellent library facilities and performing opportunities
- Beautiful campus setting only 35 minutes from London's South Bank

Further info: The Administrator, Dept. of Music, Royal Holloway, University of London, Egham, Surrey TW20 0EX. Tel: 01784 443532. Fax: 01784 439441.

E-mail: uhwm010@rhbnc.ac.uk

Home page: http://www.sun.rhbnc.ac.uk/Music

Levi, Lionel Pike, John Rink, snr lecturers in mus; Geoffrey Chew, snr lecturer in mus; James Dack, lecturer in mus; Katharine Ellis, lecturer in mus and p/grad admissions tutor; Brian Dennis, lecturer in mus and u/grad admissions tutor; John Woolrich, Peter Wiegold, p/t lecturers in composition; David Charlton, Andrew Watney, readers in mus.

Courses: BMus (3); BA (3) *see* **Combined Degrees**. P/grad: MMus (1-yr f/t, 2-yr p/t); supervision of research for MPhil, PhD.

Course details: The London BMus degree as taught in the college was devised to give flexibility to the teaching of the dept and to offer a curriculum both broad and deep, aimed at students whose interest and experience of mus is wide ranging and whose approach is expected to be intelligent, enquiring and enthusiastic. In yr 1 all students take the same subjects, including musical techniques, analysis, history of mus, inst and/or vocal performance, and aural. In subsequent years students choose subjects of special interest to themselves from a range of options, the only principle of limitation being that specialisation must not be pursued at the expense of reasonable all-round achievement in technical, historical and performance areas. The approach, nevertheless, is not vocational. Some graduates may go on to become teachers, composers, performers, musicologists, but the primary aim is to open up horizons for all, whether or not the intention is to follow a career in mus. In fact, quite a high proportion of graduates do, but others are just as likely to get jobs in commerce, industry, the professions and public service.

Careers and counselling: Both provided by University of London Careers Advisory Service with other counselling and guidance from college counsellors and departmental tutors.

Campus facilities: Royal Holloway, though a college of London University, is predominantly residential, and 1st and 3rd year students may expect to be allotted a place in one of the halls of residence or in self-catering accommodation.

Music facilities: The annual intake for the BMus is approximately 50 students, but the dept has one of the highest number of applicants in the country. There are about 200 u/grad and p/grad students in the dept, with 11 f/t staff and numerous p/t tutors and visiting inst and vocal teachers. Together with the extensive mus library the dept is situated opposite the main college buildings, while nearby are 18 practice and mus teaching rooms. There is the opportunity for students to spend all or part of yr 2 in a European university under the Socrates/Tempus scheme. Inst and choral scholarships are awarded on a competitive basis

for talented musicians. Application forms available from the Registrar.

University College of St Martin
Lancaster LA1 3JD
Tel: 01524 63446 *Fax:* 01524 68943
Email: r.mcgregor@ucsm.ac.uk
Website: www.ucsm.ac.uk

Richard McGregor, head of perf arts; Gillian Cummins, Gerard Doyle, snr lecturers in mus; Kevin Hamel, lecturer in mus; Clive Walkely, lecturer (p/t).

Courses: BA Performing Arts (3) with mus as main specialism (performance plus drama and/or dance); BA Modular Studies (3) (mus available as minor or joint subject) *see* **Combined Degrees**. T/T: BA (QTS) (4) (mus studies over all 4 yrs); PGCE secondary (from Sep 1999).

Course details: For the BA Hons (modular studies), mus may be studied at minor or joint level with another subject. For the BA (QTS), mus is studied as a main subject within a degree combining subject study with education studies and block placements related to teaching in primary school. BA (QTS) students also take courses which prepare them for class mus teaching in primary schools. The main elements of the mus courses are the same for all students, involving performance (with weekly lessons throughout the course in the student's chosen inst or voice), composition and arranging, and study of selected topics of style and repertoire focusing on the 20th C, conducting and composition. Supporting courses are also taken in keyboard harmony, sight-singing (also rcdr, gui, and vocal ens for QTS). 4th-yr QTS students develop subject application in the classroom involving work with children in local schools, and are given the opportunity to develop skills in extended composition, major performance, conducting and/or dissertation. Courses with different emphases may be available at Lancaster and Ambleside campuses. The Performing Arts degree has a strong performance strand (eg aspects of perf practice, editions, presentation, etc) with supporting topic-based modules exploring mus and ritual and mus aesthetics. The degree allows for subsidiary study in drama or dance, with important core elements where issues such as gender, politics, semiotics, therapies etc are explored. There is a final year inter-arts project for all students.

Careers and counselling: Each student is assigned to a tutor with opportunities for regular meetings; programme of careers guidance in yr 3; confidential counselling service available.

Campus facilities: 1st-yr students are normally offered a room in one of seven halls of residence and assistance is given to other students by the

college accommodation officer. Student union bar/coffee bar and college refectory.

Music facilities: The mus courses provide opportunities for students to develop a range of practical skills, and to gain experience in performing, composing and arranging mus. They also examine many of the techniques and styles which are found in Western mus, with an emphasis on aspects of 20th C mus. All students sing in one or more of the three choirs and, as appropriate, play in the college orch, band or jazz group. The mus dept is purpose built and well-equipped with practice rooms, keyboard lab and listening facilities. Students have many opportunities to take part in mus making, and there are annual scholarships awarded to an organist, a chorister and an orch player. The college is used as a concert venue by schools and local societies, and also organises concerts given by well-known professional recitalists.

University of Salford
Faculty of Media and Music, Dept of Music, Adelphi, Peru St, Salford, Manchester M3 6EQ
Tel: 0161 295 5000 *Fax:* 0161 295 6106

Keith Wilson, dean of faculty; Derek Scott, head of dept and prof of mus; Mick Wilson, head of band musicianship; Robin Dewhurst, head of popular mus; David King, head of perf; Sheila Whiteley, associate dir of Institute for Social Research.
Courses: BA Hons Band Musicianship (3 or 4); BA Hons Popular Music and Recording (3); BSc Hons Music Acoustics and Recording (3). P/grad: MA in Composition Studies (popular mus, jazz, bands); MA in Performance (popular mus, jazz, bands); MPhil Popular Music; PhD.
Course details: The aim of the BA Hons Popular Music and Recording (3) is to provide an alternative to conventional mus courses. The course is related directly to the musical and vocational requirements of the jazz and popular mus student with particular emphasis on recording studio work. There are options in video production, computer studies, arts admin and the popular arts in society. The BA Hons Band Musicianship was the first course of its kind in Europe and offers specialisms in jazz, br and wind band with an option in conducting.
Careers and counselling: Careers officers in regular attendance; careers information available through library. College welfare officer, counsellor and chaplain available for consultation.
Campus facilities: The accommodation officer will help with various types of living premises in Manchester and Salford including university residences. Student union offices, shop, bar and recreation rooms. Refectories at both campuses.
Music facilities: The University of Salford is

strategically placed both geographically and culturally to offer students access to some of the finest mus-making and allied artistic endeavours in the country, including the Hallé, BBC Philharmonic and some of the most famous br bands. The mus dept is closely associated with the popular mus explosion in Manchester and works in connection with the International Media Centre at Adelphi. The mus division has 13 f/t staff, 36 visiting specialists and attracts distinguished professional performers, conductors and composers to work with students. University bands are involved in broadcasting and recording and undertake concert tours playing, for example, in Brazil and Ecuador. Visiting conductors have included the late Sir Charles Groves, Sir Malcolm Arnold, Sian Edwards and Elgar Howarth. Sir Harrison Birtwistle composed *Salford Toccata* for the br band and Arnold *Little Suite No 3*. All students have the chance to become acquainted with electro-acoustic mus and recording techniques. Students choose an associated study, arts admin, recording techniques or mus theatre. Centre facilities include a resource base, a library, four multi-track recording studios, electro-acoustic studios equipped with PPG system, practice rooms, plus facilities provided for drama and media students. Mus students co-operate with media, drama and dance students in all major productions providing original scores and bands for performers and tours. There are approximately 360 f/t students on the mus courses. The mus dept has an established popular mus research base. It is also creating a br band research archive.

School of Oriental and African Studies
University of London, Thornhaugh St, London WC1H 0XG
Tel: 0171 637 2388 *Fax:* 0171 436 3844

Keith Howard, mus studies centre chmn; David Hughes, Richard Widdess, snr lecturers, mus; Owen Wright, prof of Near and Middle Eastern mus; Lucy Durán, lecturer in African mus.
Courses: BA Music (3); BA Language and Music (3 or 4); BA combinations of mus with social anthropology, art, geography, development studies, religious studies, history (3) *see* **Combined Degrees**. P/grad: MMus in ethnomusicology and MA Area Studies (1 f/t; 2 or 3 p/t); MPhil (2); PhD (3).
Course details: All courses relate to the traditional musics of Asia and Africa and to the discipline of ethnomusicology. The single subject BA Music Studies incorporates study of Western mus at King's College London. Mus courses form constituent parts of broader degrees including other subjects (eg Asian or African languages,

357

history, etc). Courses include African mus, South Asian mus, East Asian mus, South East Asian mus, mus of the Middle East, ethnomusicology. Most subjects available at BA, MA (Area Studies), MMus in ethnomusicology, MPhil and PhD levels. A comprehensive range of performance options in non-western musics is offered.

Careers and counselling: Careers advice and counselling offered.

Campus facilities: University of London Accommodation Office assists with finding places and School of Oriental and African Studies has its own accommodation block. There is a canteen.

Music facilities: Practice suite, Javanese and Balinese gamelans, Thai mahori ens, African, Asian and Near and Middle Eastern instrument collections, teaching and research a/v collections.

Sheffield University

Dept of Music, Western Bank, Sheffield S10 2TN
Tel: 0114 222 0470 *Fax:* 0114 266 8053
Email: v.r.messenger@sheffield.ac.uk

Eric Clarke, head of dept; A F Bennett; A M Brown; J W Davidson; P H A W Hill; M J Hindmarsh; G Nicholson.

Courses: BMus Hons (single subject); BA Dual Hons *see* **Combined Degrees**. P/grad: MMus; MA in Music; MA Psychology of Music (all 1 f/t, 2 p/t); MPhil, PhD (2-3 f/t, 4-6 p/t). MPhil and PhD courses in performance practice and in original composition are also available.

Course details: BMus students concentrate on mus in its various aspects and take two non-mus modules in yr 1, within the Faculty of Arts. The aim is to produce graduates with wide musical sympathies, a good general knowledge of the subject and appropriate practical skills. The course has no particular bias: all students are expected to deal with mus in its historical, analytical, creative and practical aspects in yr 1, with considerable opportunities for specialisation in yrs 2 and 3. The BA Dual Honours course is appropriate for those with an equally strong interest in mus and another arts subject. Applicants who are called for interview are required to perform (BMus applicants only) and to discuss their musical knowledge and interests; aural tests may also be given. There is no written test in connection with the interview. The examination at the end of yr 1 must be passed, but it does not count towards the final degree class. The courses have a modular structure; modules taken in yrs 2 and 3 count equally towards the final degree.

Careers and counselling: University Careers and Advisory Service; departmental careers advisor; also personal tutors. Any member of staff may be approached informally for guidance on academic

or other matters.

Campus facilities: Accommodation is provided in university halls of residence and flats. There are full catering services in the main university and student common room facilities in the mus dept. Applications from disabled students are considered, but no special provision is made for them.

Music facilities: The mus dept of Sheffield University has an annual intake of about 40 students, a staff of 9 and a large number of visiting inst tutors. It occupies a Victorian building, Hadow House, adjacent to Tapton Hall of Residence and within half a mile of the main university. Most modules are taught by lectures or seminars, often backed up by individual tutorials. Individual tuition is given for dissertations, composition, and performance. Students are actively taught for only a small proportion of their time, perhaps 8-hrs per week, and need to plan their own programme of work around these 'student contact hours'. The dept's large library is well equipped for private study, with two reading rooms, a fine collection of complete editions and a substantial CD and record collection with a listening room. In addition to inst or vocal tuition, students take part regularly in ensemble activities, such as str and wind chmbr groups, early mus group, 20th C mus group, and chmbr choir. About 50 public concerts are sponsored by the dept every year. These include a subscription series given mainly by visiting professional artists, concerts by the university orch and chorus and other performers of the appropriate standard. The dept strongly encourages performing activity.

Southampton University

Dept of Music, Highfield, Southampton SO17 1BJ
Tel: 01703 593425 *Fax:* 01703 593197
Email: musicbox@soton.ac.uk
Website: www.soton.ac.uk/-musicbox/

Mark Everist, prof of mus and head of dept; William Drabkin, snr lecturer; Robynn Stilwell, lecturer in mus; Nicholas Cook, prof of mus; Anthony Pople, prof of mus; José Bowen, lecturer in mus; Julie Brown, lecturer in mus and u/grad co-ord; Laurie Stras, lecturer in performance studies; Jeanice Brooks, lecturer in mus and p/grad co-ord; Pete Thomas, head of jazz and popular mus studies; Paul Cox, head of str studies; Keith Davis, head of vocal studies; Deborah Meager, head of keyboard and perc studies; Robin Soldan, head of w/wind studies; Peter White, head of br studies.

Courses: BA Hons (3); BA Combined Hons (3) *see* **Combined Degrees**. P/grad: MA in musicology (includes historical, analytical and critical studies); MPhil; PhD (research).

Course details: The dept aims to strike a balance between practical and academic studies, and in the single honours mus degree, performance can account for up to a third of the degree. A foundation year which prepares students for advanced musical study is followed by two years in which the students pursue various combinations of subjects, e.g. performance, history of mus, studio work, composition, etc. Mus is defined in its broadest terms, and courses are offered on all aspects of western mus from the 12th to the 20th C, including jazz and popular mus. The flexible course structure is designed to allow students to tailor their study to a particular interest, while ensuring that basic skills necessary for any mus-related career are grasped. The MA course offers a taught curriculum that combines core courses that develop essential research skills alongside a programme of specialised topic work that leads to a dissertation. Applicants for research degrees (MPhil, PhD) are welcome in any area of staff expertise; students working in performance-related areas may offer recital work towards their degree. On graduation, students go on to further study in performance or research, into teaching or the professions.
Careers and counselling: Careers advice and personal counselling available to all students. A special one-day programme on careers for mus graduates is held annually.
Campus facilities: With 8 halls of residence, all 1st year students are offered places, and a high proportion of senior students. There are several canteens. A special hostel is provided on the campus for disabled students and there is easy access to all mus buildings.
Music facilities: The department takes full advantage of a purpose-built concert hall housing a fine collection of historical and modern keyboard insts (including an outstanding classical organ). Solo, ensemble, orch and choral performances given by students, together with an extensive series of professional concerts, ensures a diverse range of programmes from Bach and Boulez to jazz and non-Western mus. Visiting artists offer w/shops and m/classes, some of them (such as the Allegri Quartet) on a regular basis. There are also resident performers who work with students; in 1996-7 this was the versatile Double Image ensemble. Specialised tuition in the performance of early mus, jazz and popular mus is provided. Practice teaching and rehearsal facilities include 22 solo and 2 ensemble practice rooms, a rehearsal room with instrument store, a p/grad study room and 2 additional teaching rooms. The department houses a music-dedicated computer lab and a recently refurbished electronic studio and live room. The research of the department is internationally acknowledged in all fields of musical scholarship from the middle ages to the present.

University of Sunderland
School of Arts, Design and Communications, Clifton Hall, Burdon Rd, Sunderland SR2 7EE
Tel: 0191 515 2179 *Fax:* 0191 515 3375

Jim McAvoy, snr lecturer in mus.
Courses: BA Hons combined programme *see* **Combined Degrees**; BA Hons Creative Arts Studies; BA Arts and Design.
Course details: The BA may be taken as joint honours (an equal proportion of two subjects); major/minor (two subjects with a bias for one of them); combined (three subjects in equal proportion); and independent (modules studied from a range of subjects). Mus is available both in a minor mode and as one of three subjects in combination. In the BA Creative Arts Studies and BA Arts and Design mus may be taken as a major or minor area of study.
Careers and counselling: Confidential service offered by the Chaplaincy in health, finance, special needs and childcare.
Campus facilities: Sports centre, Bede Tower Theatre and Students Union.
Music facilities: Specialist mus studio, electronic studio, practice suite block and small theatre/concert hall. Choral singing, inst ens and university big band.

University of Surrey
Dept of Music, Guildford, Surrey GU2 5XH
Tel: 01483 300800/259317 *Fax:* 01483 259386

Thomas Messenger, head of dept, renaissance and baroque mus; Sebastian Forbes, prof and dir of mus, composition; Dave Fisher, dir of Tonmeister studies; Nicholas Conran, conducting, opera, jazz, Feldenkrais technique; Stephen Downes, 19th-20th C mus and aesthetics; Christopher Mark, analysis, 18th and 20th C mus; Francis Rumsey, digital audio technology; George Mowat-Brown, composition, 20th C mus; Tim Brookes, acoustics, psycho-acoustics, mus technology; Matthew Head, late baroque and classical, gender and sexuality.
Courses: BMus Hons Music (3); BMus Hons Music and Sound Recording (Tonmeister) (4). P/grad: MMus (1); MPhil; PhD.
Course details: The dept specialises in performance studies, composition, historical and analytical musicology, sound recording and audio engineering. These areas of expertise are reflected in both our u/grad degree courses. The BMus mus course concentrates on both academic and practical musical studies, and the Tonmeister course combines theoretical and

practical sound recording studies with selected musical subjects. One of the chief attractions of the BMus mus course is its flexibility: after exposure to core topics in yr 1 (history, analysis, etc), students choose subjects from a range of options in yrs 2 and 3 which cater for their individual interests and allow them to specialise in performance, composition, conducting and/or musicology. The University has recently restructured from Faculties to Schools. The Dept of Music is now part of the School of Performing Arts, which also contains the Dept of Dance Studies. The Music and Sound Recording (Tonmeister) course aims to provide students with a solid foundation in the principles and practice of mus and sound recording. A key strength is the course's integration of technical, practical and musical study. It is intended that students will acquire both a broad academic background and a portfolio of professional skills. The department's Professional Training Programme combines real-life work experience with a course of academic study.

Careers and counselling: Academic and personal tutorial schemes are well developed within the dept and in addition students may be referred to university professional counsellors. The university offers a full careers service to all students. Mus students are guaranteed accommodation for yr 1 and are eligible to apply for accommodation for their final year.

Campus facilities: There are 3 restaurants (including one for vegetarians) all close to the mus department. Disabled students are accepted, but should contact the university to discuss access and facilities.

Music facilities: The dept is housed in the purpose-built Performing Arts Technology Studios opened in 1988. The facilities include 2 recording studios with control rooms and 4 editing suites (comparable to the best commercial installations); studio 1 also contains a new Steinway concert grand pno and is used for many of our concerts. There are 10 practice rooms (all with pnos), a hpd, a portable Copeman-Hart org and perc equipment. A mobile recording van is available to take equipment to outside locations for concerts and recordings. A radiophonic workshop and computer workstations, including Sibelius 7, are available for student use. The size of the dept, some 160 u/grads and 20 p/grads, fosters a relaxed, friendly atmosphere and makes participation possible in a wide range of practical activities, eg weekly lunch-hour recitals, concerts of student compositions, recording sessions and performance/ composition w/shops. Students are further encouraged to organise other ens,

---

University of Surrey
Department of Music • Postgraduate Study

• The Department specialises in **historical** and **analytical musicology, composition, performance, conducting, sound recording, audio engineering** and **music technology**.

• **Two Music Department Research Scholarships** of £4,750 per annum are now available.

• The Department organises regular **Research Seminars, Postgraduate Study Days, Celebrity Concerts, Master Classes** in **Performance**, the biennial **Guildford International Music Festival**, and enjoys **close links** with **major arts organisations** and the **audio and recording industry**.

Courses offered:

• **MMus:** an innovative and flexible course with **new options** allowing specialisation in composition, performance, conducting, and studio production. Other options include aesthetics, analysis, renaissance studies, criticism and reviewing.

• **MPhil, PhD by Composition:** submission of a composition folio comprising compositions, recordings, analyses, programme notes and written projects.

• **MPhil, PhD:** original research leading to a substantial thesis.

Artists in Residence, **The Medici String Quartet**; Visiting Professor of Piano, **Nikolai Demidenko**.

Contact: Mrs P Johnson,
Postgraduate Secretary, Department of Music, University of Surrey, Guildford, GU2 5XH.
Tel: 01483 259317   Fax: 01483 259386   e-mail:P.B.Johnson@surrey.ac.uk

rock/pop groups, etc. The Medici String Quartet is the resident ens and Nikolai Demidenko is a Visiting Professor. The dept has professional links with external organisations such as South East Arts, Neve Electronics, the BBC, APRS, AES and West German Radio. It also enjoys close associations with distinguished performers. Most teach at the university, whilst others are chosen by students in consultation with the dept and are visited for tuition in London or nearby. In addition to departmental lectures and concerts we invite renowned lecturers and performers from outside the university to provide students with exposure to the performing profession and the worlds of research and composition, and the recording industry. Our graduates enjoy excellent employment prospects in a wide range of careers. These include orchestral and freelance performance, teaching, lecturing, research (both academic and technical), arts admin, journalism, marketing, television and radio engineering and production, and record production. We are also successful in preparing students for careers outside mus. The dept is considering the addition of an optional professional training period for BMus students in year 3.

Sussex University

Faculty of Music, Falmer, Brighton BN1 9QR
Tel: 01273 678019 *Fax:* 01273 678466

Martin Butler, chair of music, reader in mus; Jonathan Harvey, honorary prof of mus; Michael Finnissy, research fellow (mus); Donald Mitchell, visiting prof in mus; David Osmond-Smith, prof of mus; Julian Johnson, lecturer in mus; Robert Adlington, lecturer in mus.
Courses: BA Hons (3) in mus, 20th C mus studies or mus and media studies. P/grad: MA in 20th C mus analysis, musical aesthetics and ideology, topics in contemporary musical thought and culture or composition; MPhil (by thesis or composition); DPhil (by thesis or composition).
Course details: The aim of the BA course is to understand both the inner workings of mus and its place in the historical, cultural and intellectual development of society. Sussex offers unique degree programmes in 20th C mus studies and mus and media studies. Students with an interest in composition are particlarly welcome at Sussex. Students also take 'contextual' courses in their schools of studies - either English and American studies or cultural and community studies.
Careers and counselling: Careers advice and personal counselling available to all students.
Campus facilities: Accommodation provided for all 1st year students. There is a large refectory and a range of other eating places and all residential rooms on campus have access to kitchens. Disabled students are accepted.
Music facilities: The belief that close scrutiny of mus enhances its enjoyment and that to understand mus fully you need to study both its inner workings and its place in the historical, cultural and intellectual development of society, underlies the mus courses at Sussex. Students are able to study their selected main subject in the context of different Schools of Studies; in the case of mus these are the School of Cultural and Community Studies and the School of English and American Studies. This arrangement enables students to choose the course combination that suits them best, brings them into contact with tutors with varying backgrounds and specialisms, and gives them a chance to broaden their own perspectives. Sussex University's mus course has a strong creative element with maximum opportunity for composition. Students are given the opportunity to discover what it is like to work as a composer in present-day British society. The 20th C mus studies degree allows a rare specialisation in the mus of our time. The mus and media studies degree offers the opportunity to study classical and contemporary mus in conjunction with the technologies and social aspects of new media. Musical activities at Sussex are lively and varied. Professional concerts are held regularly in the Gardner Centre for the Arts. Student orchs, choirs, and ensembles include groups specialising in contemporary mus, medieval mus, rock, jazz, folk and mus theatre. Organ and choral scholarships are available for suitably qualified applicants. Facilities available to students include a Steinway grand pno, a two-manual Goble hpd, a Grant, Degans and Bradbeer org, two chmbr orgs, pnos, various other keyboard insts, a large collection of tuned and untuned perc, and an expanding electronic mus studio. Practice, listening and computing facilities are available. The mus faculty has a substantial library of scores, records, CDs and videos.

Thames Valley University

London College of Music and Media, St Mary's Rd, Ealing, London W5 5RF
Tel: 0181 579 5000 *Fax:* 0181 566 1353

Keith Bemiston, admissions and chief examiner; Helen Swann, acting dean; Linda Merrick, head of mus; Donald Ellman, principal lecturer academic studies; Charles Ford, Allan Moore, snr lecturers.
Courses: For course details refer to London College of Music *see* **Conservatoires**.
Course details: BMus; MA; Diploma of Higher Education in mus technology (popular mus).
Music facilities: Teaching suites, concert hall,

extensive recording facilities, 40 rooms available for rehearsal or practice.

Ulster University

Dept of Music, Shore Rd, Newtownabbey, Co Antrim BT37 0QB
Tel: 01232 366690 *Fax:* 01232 366870
Email: hm.bracefield@ulst.ac.uk
Website: www.ulst.ac.uk

Mrs H M Bracefield, head of mus.
Courses: BMus Hons (3). P/grad: MPhil/DPhil in musicology, composition or performance; Cert/Dip/MA (1 p/t; 1.5 p/t; 2.5 p/t) in 20th C Music. T/T: PGCE (1). Others: Foundation Certificate in Music (1 p/t).
Course details: A special feature of the mus courses has always been the integral part played by practical study of musical performance, enabling students to develop their executant skills alongside academic knowledge. The aims of the 3-yr BMus course are to provide a sound knowledge of Western mus from 1450 to the present day together with analytical, compositional and performance skills. Performance is an integral part of the course. There is the possibility of a greater choice of path of study in yr 3. Ulster offers special expertise in early mus, analysis, composition and modern mus. The dept received a rating of 'excellent' in the HEFCE Teaching Quality Assessment, and received funding for a project on peer assessment in mus.
Careers and counselling: Careers advice offered continuously in yrs 2 and 3; each student has an adviser of studies who is available for other guidance and counselling; professional advisers on campus.
Campus facilities: Accommodation usually available to 1st year and some 3rd year students in student residences. Several canteens are open to staff and students. Applications considered individually from disabled students and there are ramps, disabled toilet, secure parking and special furniture on premises.
Music facilities: The dept of mus is situated on the Jordanstown campus, 8 miles north of Belfast, in attractive grounds on the side of Belfast Lough. The dept occupies Dalriada House, a beautiful old house of architectural merit which has recently been well restored and decorated. The dept was established in 1972, and has been offering honours degree courses in mus since 1980. The present student body is about 100 strong, a number large enough for many different kinds of practical mus-making. Staff research interests cover a wide field, including transcription, editing and performance of early mus, 20th C techniques of composition and analysis (and the application of them to computing), American mus, contemporary

experimental mus, the evolution of 18th C and 19th C styles, and the development of mus for the handicapped. All members of the f/t and p/t staff are practising performers, an emphasis reflected in constant interaction between musical scholarship and performance and in regular visits by distinguished musicians to coach and address mus students. All students are expected to take part in the department's practical activities. The choir and orch give 2 or 3 major concerts each year, but there are many smaller ens activities as well, and students are encouraged to form groups themselves. Students may join the chmbr choir, wind, br and str groups, early mus groups, the Mushroom Group (experimental mus). Regular lunchtime recitals are given by students, staff and visiting performers, and the dept also promotes evening concerts by distinguished visiting artists. The dept's 25 rooms comprise a keyboard laboratory, a practice room suite, electronic and computing studios, the Heather Clarke Recital Room, and rooms suitable for lectures, seminars, tutorials and practice. There is a large stock of mus insts (keyboards, strs, w/wind, br and perc), electronic and computer equipment, miniature scores and sheet mus. A three-manual org has recently been installed in the Assembly Hall.

Westminster University

Commercial Music Dept, Watford Rd, Norwick Pk, Harrow HA1 3TP
Tel: 0171 911 5000 ext 4033 *Fax:* 0171 911 5934

Norton York, course leader; John Eacott, Keith Harris, Mykael Riley, Simon Pitt, Helen Reddington, course tutors.
Courses: BA Hons Commercial Music (3).
Course details: This course includes production, composition, and business studies. It is directly related to contemporary practice in all forms of commercial mus. It is aimed at people with a sound musical grounding or with a practical aspiration to work in the management of the mus industry.
Careers and counselling: On campus counselling service.
Campus facilities: The university's Harrow campus is a premier site for art and media education with high quality media facilities to support work in film, television, digital media and mus.
Music facilities: A complex of 9 recording studios is available for student projects, and an extensive library of pop mus literature and recordings. On-campus TV and film studios are available for performances and multi-media projects. In addition, the course benefits from the facilities of the HMV Music Business Research Project.

University of Wolverhampton

School of Education, Sport and Performance Studies,
Gorway Rd, Walsall WS1 3BD
Tel: 01902 323236 *Fax:* 01902 323177

John Pymm, principal lecturer and joint head of
mus; Kevin Stannard, snr lecturer and joint head
of mus; Shirley Thompson, baroque mus; Gay
Leese, head of w/wind; Robert Williams, head of
vocal studies; Hilary Middleton, head of
keyboard studies; Malcom Procter, head of
project work.
Courses: BA Hons (3); T/T: BEd (3).
Course details: The aim of the BA Hons is to
produce a skilled musician. The modular course
enables students to gain a wide range of
musicianship skills and experience but also
enables them to specialise in an area of
particular interest. Mus may be taken as a
specialist subject in a BA Hons degree or as part
of a joint honours BA of BSc Hons degree.
Popular Music may be taken as a major or joint
honours route in the degree, and may be
combined with mus.
Other subjects that may be combined with mus
include science, economics, politics, business
studies, computer studies, and the more usual
arts subjects. The mus modules are varied and
include performance, composition and
musicology. Composition forms part of many
modules and various styles are introduced from
very modern techniques to popular styles.
Other modules include jazz, non-European mus,
conducting and arranging, renaissance mus, mus
therapy, solo performance, computers, church
mus and editing early mus.
Careers and counselling: Each student is allocated
a personal tutor who can help and advise on the
choice of modules and careers. Student counselling
is available and advice on accommodation and
welfare subjects.
Campus facilities: Most 1st year students are
accommodated in halls of residence and priority
is given to students whose homes are at a
distance from the university. Accommodation is
in single study bedrooms with kitchens on each
floor; there are canteen facilities on all sites.
Disabled students are accepted although there is
no lift to the mus area.
Music facilities: The mus area is well equipped
with practice rooms and two electronic studios.
Concerts and rehearsals for the choir, swing
band, wind band, orchs and baroque consort are
held in the refurbished theatre.
The university has a large choir, an orch and a
band which meet weekly. There is a flourishing
Gilbert and Sullivan Society and the resident mus
group is the English Serenata who tour
nationally.

York University

Dept of Music, York University, York YO1 5DD
Tel: 01904 432446 *Fax:* 01904 432450
Email: music@york.ac.uk
Website: www.york.ac.uk/depts/music/welcome.htm

Prof Nicola Lefanu, head of mus and
composition; Prof David Blake, composition;
Bruce Cole, community mus composition;
Ambrose Field, computer mus composition; Tim
Howell, analysis; Nicky Losseff, medieval
polyphony, gender and mus, performance; Roger
Marsh, mus theatre composition; Tony Myatt,
computer mus composition; Neil Sorrell, world
mus and composition; Peter Seymour,
performance; Jonathan Wainwright, renaissance
and early baroque mus.
Courses: BA Hons (3); BA Hons (Mus with
Education) (3) *see* **Combined Degrees**; BA/BSc
(Music Technology) (3). P/grad: MA (1); MA/MSc in
Music Technology (modular); MA in community
mus (modular); MPhil (min 2); DPhil (min 3) by
Thesis or Composition or Thesis plus recital.
Course details: The principal aim of the first
degree course is to draw out and build upon
student interests, and to develop musical insight
in scholarship, performance and composition
rather than attempting historical coverage for its
own sake. The BA in Music Technology is based
on analysis, composition, performance, electronics,
software engineering and acoustics. It can be
taken as a BSc. This course provides essential
background for audio engineers alongside a
broad education in mus and an interdisciplinary
study for students in both science and mus. The
taught MA course offers pathways in analysis,
composition/electroacoustic/acousmatic composition,
contemporary studies, ethnomusicology,
historical studies, performances and includes
opportunity for small-scale research or
composition on an advanced recital programme.
The MA is also available in Music Technology;
this may be taken as an MSc; and both Masters
courses are available on a p/t basis. Applications
for research degree places (MPhil and DPhil)
are welcome from good honours graduates
interested in mus, ethnomusicology,
composition, medieval, baroque and renaissance
mus, and contemporary mus.
Careers and counselling: Careers advice and
personal counselling both available.
Campus facilities: York is a collegiate university,
with accommodation, canteens, etc, available
within each college. Mus dept well adapted for
disabled students (ramps, wheelchair lifts, etc)
and structure of course is well suited for
students to work at their own pace. Applications
from mature students also welcomed.
Music facilities: The dept is fundamentally
concerned with the study of mus through its

practice, in composition and performance, in the belief that musical scholarship should flow from first-hand acquaintance with musical sound and structure. The staff of composers, performers and musicologists have research interests covering many aspects of style and interpretation; chamber mus; historically informed performance of renaissance, baroque and other 'early' mus; Javanese, Thai, Japanese, African and Indian mus; jazz, improvised mus and electro-acoustic mus. The dept is also widely known for its work in mus education. The emphasis upon study through musical participation is greatly assisted by a number of established departmental ens: the university choir and orch, chmbr choir, chmbr orch, new mus ens, Javanese gamelan and jazz orch - to which are added from time to time many smaller groups, such as consorts of viols and renaissance wind insts, str quartets and other chmbr groups, br ens, etc. Analysis and discussion of musical procedures, writing about mus, and other aspects of traditional musical scholarship are also closely related to musical experience. Likewise with training in written musical skills (composition, aural, musical techniques). All these studies are encompassed within the cycle of 'projects' arranged in three categories (musicological and historical; interpretation and performance; harmony, counterpoint, analysis and composition). Final assessment is based upon the presentation of folios of work produced by students as a result of participation in the projects of their choice.

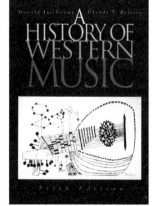

Comparative Degree Tables

Degree and Graduate Diplomas

The comparative degree tables on the following pages are a brief guide to available music courses and highlight some of the differences in course content and examination procedure.

The tabular information on the following pages is divided into two parts. The first part lists information concerning the bias of the course, the compulsory elements and the available options or modules.

In the first set of tables the compulsory elements of each course are listed under the respective year and the options available are listed separately. Many courses are now modular but for ease of comparison have been listed in 'years'. *No. pa* refers to the number of places per annum on a particular course. In the *Staff* column, the former figure denotes full-time staff and the latter figure refers to part-time staff members. If the relevant information could not be obtained, or was not available, the entries have been left blank.

The tables include all institutions offering degree or degree equivalent courses in music. For a fuller description of courses and facilities see the chapters on **Universities**, **Conservatoires** and **Colleges of Higher Education**.

While every effort has been made to ensure the information is accurate at the time of going to press, it is advisable to confirm specific points with the institution concerned.

The second set of tables, concerning selection procedures, level of practical tuition and types of assessment, appears on p 379.

Institution / Course	No. pa	Staff f/t, p/t	Bias of course	Year 1	Year 2	Year 3	Options and additional information
Anglia Polytechnic University BA Hons (Music)	65 +20 c/h	6/40	Practical and academic aspects incorporated within flexible vocational emphasis	Practical studies, musicianship, crit skills, aural, kybd, mus tech, comp & improvising	Enterprise in mus, advanced musicianship	Dissertation	**Yrs 2/3:** Modules offered include practical studies, 20th C mus, baroque and renaissance mus, classical & Romantic mus, analysis and aesthetics, anthropology of mus, arts admin, choral conducting, comp, creative process,rock & pop mus, ethnomusicology, jazz, mus teaching, mus technology, mus therapy, rehearsing & directing,recording techniques, opera w/shop, mus in India and modules in non-mus subjects
Bangor, University of Wales BA	37	7/+	Broad base, with wide opportunities for choice and specialisation	At least 60 credits (from 120) of modules offered in these areas: hist, culture & soc, applied mus studies, perf and practical skills, comp and contemporary studies, technology, media & popular culture	At least 100 credits (of total 120) in mus	All studies in mus	**Yrs 2/3:** 60 optional modules from choice of 12 study areas (Western mus history; mus & the Christian Church; mus & ideas; ethnomusicology; popular culture; mus in Wales; mus analysis and aesthetics; transcription and editing; comp; electro-acoustic comp; perf and perf practice) and applied studies (including orchestration and instrumentation; tonal studies); training studies (including cond; acc and kybd skills; mus processing and publishing; recordin g and editing); practical studies (including mus in the community and early mus)
Bangor, University of Wales BMus	37	7/+	As BA	As BA except at least 80 credits in mus from level one modules	All studies in mus	All studies in mus	**Yrs 2/3:** As BA
Bath Spa University College BA (Hons) (Music)	40	9/35	Foundation studies in yr 1, specialism or general programme in yrs 2-3 (modular); opportunity for career-orientated study and community involvement. New Creative Mus Technology route being planned	Perf, musicology, comp, musicianship (aural, kybd, stylistics, conducting; choir, mus technology, ens)	Musicianship (aural, stylistic composition, choir, jazz or conducting or pno accompaniment), vocational study	Interdisciplinary core module	**Yr 1:** 2nd inst, inter-related arts. **Yr 2:** Specialism in comp, perf, musicology or sound & image; vocational study choice from arts admin, mus educ, mus therapy, mus in the community; inter-related arts mus and theatre,phil of art, 20th C world lit, various musicology modules (including early mus, world mus, women in mus). **Yr 3:** as Yr 2 with additional optiorıs in electro-acoustic comp and stylistic writing

367

Institution Course	No. pa	Staff f/t, p/t	Bias of course	Year 1	Year 2	Year 3	Options and additional information
Birmingham Conservatoire BMus Hons	120	14/165	Aims to prepare students for entry into rapidly changing mus profession (orchs, ens, etc)	1st study; specialist activities (orchs, ens, etc); ICHA (improvisation, comp, harmony, aural) w/shops; mus history; analysis; world mus; optional studies; sound & recording	1st study; specialist activities; ICHA; mus history; analysis; style and perf; optional studies	As yr 2	Wide variety of options available in all yrs, eg baroque, renaissance, pop, jazz, world mus. **Yr 4:** 1st study, specialist activities, mjr project, style and perf, new mus, options
Birmingham University BMus (Hons)	37-39	9/1	Practical tuition, continuous assessment, progression from set yr 1 to flexible yr 3	Hist, techniques, comp, perf, ancillary subject	Hist, some perf		Available in yrs 2 and 3
Bretton Hall University College BA (Hons) Music	30	6/22	Focus on contemporary mus, with equal balance between practical musicianship, comp & academic disciplines	Perf, musicology, musicianship with Faculty Arts Project	As yr 1	Perf, musicology, dissertation with elective chosen from comp, perf or applied mus studies	Yrs ½: Dance, English film & photography or creative writing, fine art, drama. Yr 3: mus, English
Bretton Hall University College BA Hons (Popular Music)	30	4/10	Vocationally-based training in a range of popular musics	Comp and arrangement, tech skills, inst skills, practical projects	Same as yr 1 plus professional studies	Core theory, practical project, professional practice	Details as for BA (Music)
Bristol University BA (Music)	30	7/1	European mus tradition, development of historical, creative or practical fields	Comp, contemp culture, mus hist, analysis, kybd, perf, conducting, aural	Hist of mus	Hist of mus	
Brunel University BA (Music)	34	5.5/25	Perf, comp or critical musicology; chosen by student after yr 1 compulsory studies	Aural awareness in practice, intro to comp, mus in society, analytical and critical skills, intro to studio mus technology, ens for perf 1		Project (special exercise in comp, perf or musicology).	Yrs 2/3: Perf techniques, comp, renaissance, 19th and 20th C mus, popular mus, mus theatre, world mus, advanced perf, advanced studio mus, ethnomusicology, special topic, ens perf 2

Institution / Course	No. pa	Staff f/t, p/t	Bias of course	Year 1	Year 2	Year 3	Options and additional information
Cambridge University BA Hons	50-60	13	No bias - a wide range of comp, historical and musico-technical studies possible	Harmony, counterpoint, hist of mus 1, hist of mus 2, notation, analysis, set work, practical (aural and kybd)	Hist of mus 1, hist of mus 2, ethnomusicology, analysis, acoustics, practical (aural and kybd)	Fugal forms, set works	**Yr 2:** 1 from stylistic comp or portfolio of tonal comps. **Yr 3:** 1 additional paper (special subjects). Also 3 from notation of early mus 1 and 2, perf practice, test of perf, stylistic comp, portfolio of free comps, portfolio of tonal comps or an extra additional paper or dissertation
Cardiff, University of Wales BA Hons	c 10	12/48	Balance between analysis, hist, harmony, comp and practical musicianship	None	None	None	Free choice in all yrs
Cardiff, University of Wales BMus Hons	60	12/48	Very similar to BA				**Yrs 2/3:** Free selection of modules
The Chichester Institute of HE BA (Music)Single Hons, major or joint	24	3/20	Comp, improvisation, 20th C and 19th C mus theatre	20th C mus, perf, improvisation and comp	Style and genre, techniques of musical expression	Mus theatre and therapy, towards individual style	**Yr 2:** Classical style or jazz, studio techniques
Christ Church College BA Single Hons	25	5/41	Perf and comp	100% of time studying mus	Solely mus with a choice of 4 from 10 options	As yr 2	
Christ Church College BA Joint and Combined Hons	70	5/41	To develop a practical creative approach	Mus, arts and ideas, craft of mus, perf studies, Kodály, studio studies			**Yr 2:** Practical mus, studio, improvisation, theatre studio, comp. **Yr 3:** Special study, comp, advanced perf and theatre studies.
City University BMus/BSc Hons	34	8	Mus in Society, ethnomusicology, perf and perf arts, applied technology	Mus anthropology and non-literate sound worlds, north Indian classical mus, perf, Western mus, applied technology, electro-acoustic studio project, comp, acoustics		12,000 word dissertation on specialism of student's choice	12 modules taken from a wide range of cultural studies topics; applied studies, comp and perf
Colchester Institute BA Hons (Music)	90	16/60	Balance of practical and academic elements with major vocational options	1st inst, orch or choir, ens, mus hist, mus comp; modular course with core studies plus electives	1st practical study, orch or choir, major vocal study	Special hons studies	**Yrs 2/3:** Major options include perf, comp, arts admin, mus educ, mus therapy, dissertation, Christian liturgical mus. Other electives also available. Two Practical studies available in all 3 yrs

Institution / Course	No. pa	Staff f/t, p/t	Bias of course	Year 1	Year 2	Year 3	Options and additional information
Dartington College of Arts BA (Hons)	50+	5/32	Many styles of mus (especially 20th C); practical work with analysis/musicology in a socio-cultural framework	Interdisciplinary arts and subject specialism	Comp or perf	As yr 2	**Yr 1:** Perf writing, theatre, visual, perf opportunities; project-based work. **Yr 2:** Same as Yr 1 plus arts mgt, comp, 20th C art or popular mus. **Yr 3:** Same as Yr 2 plus off-campus work in the UK or Europe
Derby University BA/BSc Hons	25	3/12	Perf/practical bias				Mus studied as 50% or 33% of course. Wide range of options for other modules
Durham University BA (Music)	41	9		Western mus 1700-1830, musical techniques, analysis, composition	Western mus	Western mus, 1 choice from dissertation, comp, perf	**Yrs 2/3:** 8 from 20th C, electro-acoustics, mus techniques, orch, ethnomusicology, analysis, and special topics
East Anglia University BA Hons	25	5/1+	Perf, comp and student choice within subject areas	Hist, analysis, harmony and counterpoint, comp, aural, kybd, perf, conducting, bibliographical method & research techniques	Hist, technical studies, creative and perf studies (choice of areas)	Continuation of yr 2 studies plus dissertation	**Yrs 2/3:** 2 from perf, comp, conducting, hist, technical studies; a wide-ranging list, including extra-musical disciplines
Edinburgh University BMus (3/4)	30	9/3	Breadth of study with possibility of specialisation at later stages	Harmony and counterpoint, analysis, history, acoustics, ethnomusicology, kybd	Harmony and counterpoint, comp, orchestration, analysis, aesthetics, hist, kybd		**Yrs 3/4:** From the groups of technical and compositional, hist and musicology, perf and organological, scientific and theoretical studies
Edinburgh University MA (3/4)	30	9/3	Historical	Hist of music	Hist of music	2 courses from the BMus	**Yr 3:** Subjects from BMus options
Edinburgh University BMus in Music Technology	5	9/2	Scientific and artistic approach to mus with Dept of Physics	Counterpoint, harmony, analysis, acoustics, maths, electronics	Counterpoint, harmony, hist of mus, analysis and aesthetics, mus tech	Analysis and synthesis of sound, acoustics of musical insts, mus technology	
Exeter University BA (Hons)	30	6/2	Hist, analysis, comp	Mus in context, analysis, techniques, aural, comp, perf, kybd	Min of 2 historical courses		**Yr 3:** Topics in the history of mus, dissertation, recital. Also composition 1, composition 2, orchestration, special topic, additional analysis, editorial exercise, advanced kybd skills, conducting and musical direction
Exeter University BMus	5	6/2	Comp, hist and analysis in yrs 1/2	As BA	As BA	Comp, orchestration	**Yr 3:** As BA

Institution / Course	No. pa	Staff f/t, p/t	Bias of course	Year 1	Year 2	Year 3	Options and additional information
Glasgow University BMus	16+	6/4	Specialisation in comp, hist or perf	Integrated musicianship: harmony (written and practical), orchestration, analysis, aural, perf, hist, comp		Historiography and criticism	**Yr 2/3:** 9 from dissertation, comp, electronic comp, perf, counterpoint and harmony, 1 or 2 hist papers, 1 or 2 special papers, analysis, notation, perf practice
Glasgow University MA	30+	6/4		Integrated musicianship			Courses of 4 hrs pw leading to 2 papers chosen from hist (1 period), integrated musicianship, special paper, listening and repertory, mus and technology
Goldsmiths College, University of London BMus (3/4)	58/5	12/35	Broad and deep curriculum; students may specialise if they wish. Modular course: 12 modules over 3 yrs (f/t) or 4 yrs (p/t)	Language of tonal mus; practical mus; comp; intro to western mus	Contemporary and historical studies	Contemporary mus or historical studies	**Yr 2:** 2 from perf, analysis, comp, mus technology, ethnomusicology, jazz and popular mus, aesthetics and criticism, techniques. **Yr 3:** 3 from recital perf, advanced comp, mus technology, analysis, ethnomusicology, jazz and popular mus, aesthetics and criticism, research. **Yrs 2/3:** Interdisciplinary studies and approved studies in other areas are available as options
Guildhall School of Music & Drama BMus (Hons) (4)	90		Development of all-round musicianship in both practical and academic areas				Degree for the performing musician
University of Hertfordshire Bsc Hons (Elec Mus)	20	2/10	Practical.electro-acoustic comp	Foundation, studio practice, musicianship, electro-acoustic	Creative projects (30 points) plus choice of modules to the value of 90 points	Project or dissertation (30 points) plus choice of modules to the value of 90 points	Options in Yrs 2 & 3 include mixing and processing, sound editing on the computer, sound and image, orchestration, notation, styles and textures, perspectives of electronic mus, vocational visits
Huddersfield University BMus/BA Hons	110	11/58	Student selection in Part 2	Part 1: Musicology; 2 from perf, comp, electro-acoustic mus		Part 2: 1 element from part 1	Various electives in all years eg conducting, instrumentation, concert management, mus processing, mus in the community, intro to analysis, br band scoring/arranging
Hull University BMus	27	7/25	Balance of basic musicianship and development of individual talents	Harmony and counterpoint, historical studies, analysis, chmbr mus, aural, kybd, conducting, practical skills	Harmony and counterpoint, practical skills		**Yr 1:** free composition, set works, early mus to 1600; **Yrs 2/3:** 2 from perf, comp, musicology, orchestration, practical musicianship, analysis, set works, opera the symphonic tradition, church mus, tradition, 20th C mus, historical and critical perspectives. Tuition on early insts available

Institution Course	No. pa	Staff f/t, p/t	Bias of course	Year 1	Year 2	Year 3	Options and additional information
Keele University BA/BSc	50	8/25	Broad historic perspective, focus on 20th C, with opportunity for specialism; electronic mus combines with specialist modules	General introduction to listening/analytical strategies; inst/vocal tuition; selective study of aspects of 1700-1900 repertoire (mus students); introduction to theory and practice and studio techniques of electro-acoustic mus (ele mus students); specialist options	20th C and other mus hist modules (mus students); intro to computer mus and MIDI (elec mus students); inst and vocal tuition, specialist options	Readings in musicology and aesthetics module; specialist options. Electronic mus students have a compulsory special subject	Comp, recital, conducting, orchestration, mus theatre, repertoire based courses, analysis, folk and world musics, mus perf etc.
King's College, University of London BMus (3)	30	10/6	Flexible, allowing students to follow their own interests	General musicianship, hist, techniques, chmbr mus, choir, analysis, perf studies, introduction to 20th C mus	Hist, chmbr mus, choir, perf studies and options	Chmbr mus, choir and options	**Yrs 2/3:** Comp, analysis, hist, perf studies, techniques
Kingston University BA Hons (Music)	50	8/30+	Broad, practical degree with increasing specialisation	1st/2nd inst, harmony and counterpoint, comp, musicianship, hist, analysis, world mus, mus perf and communication	1st/2nd inst, comp, musicianship, hist, analysis	2 specialisms chosen from perf, comp, dissertation	**Yr 2:** Lang, aesthetics and criticism, mus and bus, ethnomus, tech, mus perf and communication. **Yr 3:** Hist, analysis, mus and business, mus educ and society, cond, ens, lang, repertoire and style, accompaniment
Kingston University BA Hons (Music and Technology)	20	8/3	Course taught jointly by School of Music and Gateway School of Recording and Music Technology	Mus and recording tech, comp, mus perf and communication, world mus, hist, analysis, harmony and counterpoint, musicianship	Mus and recording technology, comp, mus and business, hist, analysis, musicianship	Project, recording technology	**Yr 2:** Ethnomusicology, mus perf and communication, lang. **Yr 3:** Hist, analysis, mus and business, mus educ and society, cond, ens, lang, repertoire and style, comp, accompaniment
Lancaster University BMus	25	6/3+		Musicology, musical techniques, practical, hist and repertoire	Hist, musical techniques, practical, hist and repertoire	Special study, musical techniques, practical, hist and repertoire	Wide range of courses in all years
Lancaster University BA			Same as BMus - flexibility allows study of other subjects				
Leeds College of Music BA (Hons) Jazz Studies	30						

Institution / Course	No. pa	Staff f/t, p/t	Bias of course	Year 1	Year 2	Year 3	Options and additional information
Leeds College of Music BPA (Music)	30						
University of Leeds BA (Hons) (3)	29	7/20	Broad-based course with ample room for specialisation	Hist studies, theory, comp, mus tech, mus study skills	Harmony & analysis	Dissertation, analysis	**Yr 1:** Comp, perf, tech, aural. **Yr 2:** Comp, perf, hist studies, musicology, orch. **Yr 3:** Comp, perf, musicology, hist and criticism, hist studies, analysis, orch
University of Leeds B Mus (4)	12	7/20	Specialisation in perf including 1 yr abroad in a conservatoire	Theory, lang, aural, mus study skills, perf	Perf, chmbr mus, lang	Yr abroad in a conservatoire. Compulsory elements of Yr 4 include perf and Year Abroad log	**Yr 2:** Harmony, hist stud, comp, musicology, criticism, tech, orch. **Yr 3:** Dissertation, comp, musicology, hist and criticism, hist studies, analysis, orch, mus processing. **Yr 4:** Performance
Liverpool University BA (Music)	24	8/20	Hist, 20th C mus and analysis, with provision for studio work, editing, popular mus and comp	General hist, analysis, recital	Hist, analysis	Hist, analysis	**Yr 1:** 2 from style comp, comp, recital 2, aural. **Yr 2:** 3 or 4 from recital 1, recital 2, perf stud, style comp, comp, kybd skills, editing, studio techniques, orchestration, intro to popular mus, popular mus in the US, mus business skills, film and TV mus. **Yr 3:** 2 or 3 from recital, style comp, comp, editing, studio techniques, orchestration, dissertation, popular mus in the US, issues in stud of contemporary mus, anthropology of popular mus, film and TV mus
Liverpool University BA Hons Mus/Popular Mus	13	8/20	To show how classical and popular music inter-relate within a broad and multi-national cultural perspective.	Hist of mus, popular mus stud, popular musicology	Hist of mus, popular mus in the US, mus business skills	Hist of mus (modern or early period) with projects or analysis	**Yr 1:** 2 from analysis, style comp, comp, recital, aural. **Yr 2:** 2 or 3 from analysis, style comp, recital, perf stud, comp, kybd skills, editing, studio techniques, orchestration, film and TV mus, issues in stud of contemporary mus, anthropology of popular mus. **Yr 3:** 3 or 4 from dissertation, special projects and same options as yr 2. **This course can be taken by non-performers**
London College of Music and Media BMus (3)	60	5/90	Perf/comp/vocational modular course including 20th C studies	1st study (inst/vocal/comp), ens studies; core course (arranging, analysis), history	1st study (inst/vocal/comp), ens studies; core course (arranging, analysis) education w/shop	1st study (inst/vocal/comp), ens studies; core course (arranging, analysis), 20th C mus perf w/shop	**Yrs 2/3:** Options from perf practice, concert management, dissertation, mixed-media project

Institution / Course	No. pa	Staff f/t, p/t	Bias of course	Year 1	Year 2	Year 3	Options and additional information
Manchester University MusB Hons	60	7/1	All round competence	Style and context in western mus, musicianship, perf, classical analysis, harmony & counterpoint, principles of mus structure	Choice of core elements: harmony & counterpoint, analysis, hist, comp, instrumentation	1 or 2 from comp, dissertation, recital	**Yr 1**: hist topic, concerts and criticism, comp, mus notation. **Yr 2**: perf, mus notation, acoustics, studio techniques, arts management, gamelan, chmbr mus perf, mus bibliography, special topics, other dept. **Yr 3**: perf practice, comp (small folio), analysis, special subject, editing, aesthetics
Newcastle University BA Hons (Music)	26	6/3	General grounding with student choices shaping yrs 2/3	Mus hist, mus structure, mus technology, mus in contemporary culture, contemporary compositional teachniques	World musics, historical/cultural option	Musical aesthetics and theory	**Yr 2/3**: Various modules from topics such as conducting, orchestration, chant studies, fugue, editorial techniques, popular mus, detailed historical options, etc. **Yr 3**: 1 or 2 from comp, perf, dissertation, project
Northumbria University BA Hons Music	18	3/3		Composition, perf, core theory, improvisation, basic tech skills, electives	Enabling, devising, ens, basic tech skills, core theory, electives	Project, project support, core theory, electives	
Nottingham Trent University BA (Contemporary Arts)	80	8	Encourages creative work and critical awareness; interdisciplinary work between visual art, perf, mus and dance	Induction module, mus level 1 module	Mus level 2 modules	Mus level 3 modules	**Yr 1**: Visual art or performance. **Yr 3**: Options in art and design
Nottingham University BA (Music)	30	7/16	Wide-ranging; catering for generalists, historians, performers and composers	Perceptual (acoustics and aural), stylistic (historical and analytical), mus from 1900, creative (perf, comp, studio)		Colloquium (aesthetic, cultural and technical issues in mus)	**Yr 1**: lang and style, hist and critical approaches; 20th C mus, creative studies. **Yr 2**: Middle Ages, renaissance, baroque, classic, romantic, 20th C, analysis, computer studies, notation and transcription, perf, comp, sound tech. **Yr 3**: Seminar, dissertation, analysis, edition, notational studies, perf, comp
Open University BA	c750	9/60	Students can take mus courses within the modular system				
Oxford Brookes University BA (Hons) in Music	7	4/10	Broad base, with choice and specialisation within musicology, comp, perf, pop mus	4 compulsory modules: structure and tonality, gen history, comp, mus tech		Dissertation or comp project (2 module credits)	Modular course, 8 taken per yr. **Yr 1**: 4 modules of student's choice (2 from other subject areas). **Yrs 2/3**: 16 modules. Wide range of topics, jazz, early mus, opera and politics, ethnomusicology, modernism, advanced comp (studio/acoustic) and perf. Up to 2 modules from other subject areas possible

Institution / Course	No. pa	Staff f/t, p/t	Bias of course	Year 1	Year 2	Year 3	Options and additional information
Oxford University BA Hons (Music)	50+	13/10	All round competence	Hist, mus techniques, analysis, keyboard	Hist (800-1970), comp techniques, analysis and criticism	As yr 2	**Yr 3:** All courses lead towards final examinations, 4 from 30 in 2 lists (perf, advanced keyboard, opera studies, perf practice, org studies,comp portfolio, dissertation. edition with commentary, analysis, electro-acoustics, orchestration, inst studies, others
Queen's University BMus Hons	30	7/4	Historical/analytical basis, with option to major in perf, comp or electro-acoustics	Western mus from medieval to present day, aural, kybd, 1st (2nd) study, technique and style	Historical topics, analysis	Historical topics	**Yr 1:** Comp. ethnomusicology, electro-acoustics. **Yrs 2/3:** Electro-acoustics, comp, historical topics, analysis, aesthetics, mus in worship, musical insts, orchestral studies, notation and transcription, psychology of mus. **Yr 3:** Analysis, perf, pno accompaniment, dissertation, computer mus, comp
Reading University BA Hons (Music) (3)	25	5/18	General core training, specialised Yr 3 chosen from 4 options	History, strict comp, practical, set works/general musicianship	Hist, strict comp, free comp, analysis, practical	None	**Yr 1:** Mus syllabus 2/3 of courses; 1/3 chosen from arts subjects. **Yr 3:** Analysis, comp, hist, perf and special (non-mus) subject
Roehampton Institute London BMus	30	5/25	Broad base with opportunity to specialise in practical or academic work	1st study, history, harmony, analysis, 20th C mus, composition	1st study, history, harmony, analysis	1st study	**Yrs 2/3:** Modules in mus therapy, 20th C and early history, comp, studio techniques, non-Western mus, advanced harmony and counterpoint, ens perf.
Roehampton Institute London BA	20	5/25	As BMus but with combined honours subjects	As BMus	As BMus		
Royal Academy of Music BMus (Perf) (4)	80	7/103	Strongly practical with relevant academic and supporting studies	Perf or comp, history, mus techniques, analysis, aural, ens	As yr 1 except history	Perf or comp, ens. Performance practice and professional preparation, art of teaching	**All years:** 2nd study, and a wide range of practical and academic electives. **Yr 3:** Specialism according to need, aspiration and ability. **Yr 4:** As yr 3 except art of teaching. Course run in conjunction with University of London
Royal College of Music BMus Hons (4)	c100	12/185	Perf	Hist, practical studies, aural, stylistic studies	Hist, practical studies, aural, stylistic studies	Teaching & professional skills	**Yrs 3/4:** Wide range of options and practical studies
Royal Holloway, London University BMus	50	10/2	Broad base, allows specialisation in hist, analysis, perf or comp	4 compulsory course units (historical, practical, technical)	2 compulsory course units (historical, practical, technical/analytical)	Compulsory general paper	**Yrs 2/3:** 5 units from a list of specialist courses including perf, comp, historical and analytical options. Also some non-musical options, eg langs, computing

Institution / Course	No. pa	Staff f/t, p/t	Bias of course	Year 1	Year 2	Year 3	Options and additional information
Royal Northern College of Music BA (4)	100		Practical and academic course but intended for performers	1st study, kybd, aural, hist, theory, practical musicianship	1st study, hist, theory, practical musicianship	1st study, hist	**Yr 2:** Choice of hist period. **Yrs 3/4:** Choice of academic and practical
Royal Northern College of Music BMus Hons	100		Similar in content to BA. Greater concentration on academic areas in all 4 yrs; intended for practical musician	1st study, kybd, aural, hist, theory, practical musicianship	1st study, aural, hist, theory	1st study, hist, theory	**Yr 2:** Choice of specialist hist period, practical. **Yr 3/4:** Specialist hist topics; theory options and practical
Royal Northern College of Music MusB/GRNCM	8		Very high perf attainment and abilities in academic mus needed	1st study	1st study	1st study	Combination of GRNCM and MusB of Manchester University. Practical options are taken at RNCM, academic options at the University of Manchester. **Yr 4:** Practical only
University College of Saint Martin BA Perf Arts (University of Lancaster)	40-45	5/3	Perf and social context	Mus specialist modules	2 specialist mus units, subsidiary specialism plus core unit	2 specialist units, project, core unit	**Yr 1:** 1 module each in drama and dance
University of Salford BA Hons (Popular Music and Recording)	40	7/2	Bias towards popular mus perf: rock, jazz folk and commercial; emphasis on recording studio work or studio perf	Perf, improvisation, ens, comp, arranging, aural, transcription, pop mus, hist, analysis, mus technology, sound recording & production, mus synthesis, latin perc	As yr 1		**Yr 1:** Kybd proficiency. **Yr 3:** Mus technology (comp), studio production (recording), comp, perf, popular mus studies, arranging, session musicianship, mus direction
University of Salford BA Hons (Band Musicianship) (3)	100	16/45	Band mus, including br and wind bands, popular mus and jazz	Perf, bands, ens, comp, arranging, analytical and hist studies, mus synthesis, conducting	As yr 1 plus arranging		**Yr 3:** 2 major options from analysis, arranging, arts admin, comp, conducting, dissertation, perf, mus criticism, mus theatre and recording studies
University of Salford BA Hons (Band Musicianship) (4)	25		Academic and practical study of br, wind, jazz and popular band mus	Perf, bands, composition, aural and transcription, analysis and hist studies, conducting and kybd	Same as yr 1 plus mus theatre, arts admin, computer studies and recording studies		

Institution / Course	No. pa	Staff f/t, p/t	Bias of course	Year 1	Year 2	Year 3	Options and additional information
Sheffield University BMus (3)	35	8/1	Broad based course, opportunity for specialisation in yrs 2-3	Critical responses to mus, perf with composition, stylistic studies, topics in hist of mus			Technical options include mus technology, psychology of mus, editorial method, development of musical ability. **Yr 2:** 6 modules from a range including historical, stylistic and technical studies. **Yr 3:** Comp, dissertation or recital may be taken as a double module
Southampton University BA Hons	70	10/35	Balance of practical and academic study, subject to individual interests in yrs 2-3	Foundation for advanced mus studies: perf, comp, analysis, mus technology, musicianship, (keyboard, aural, conducting), critical and repertory studies, writing skills			**Yrs 2/3:** Wide range of options, including ens/solo perf, comp, mus computing and hist/critical topics. Extensive scope for project work. Modular course with core subjects in Yr 1
Surrey University BMus Hons	28	8/35	Firm musical foundation with opportunities for specialisation for students with both academic and practical mus interests	20th C repertoire, tonal analysis, instrumentation, perf, harmony and kybd skills, acoustics, style, hist of mus to 1900		General repertoire knowledge	**Yr 2:** 8 from tonal analysis, historical perf practice, classical studies, orchestration, contemporary mus studies, 18th C harmony and counterpoint, 19th C mus thought, opera after 1850, hist perf practice, 20th C analysis, comp, perf, research project. **Yr 3:** 6 from analysis, baroque fugue, baroque studies, jazz, romantic, 20th C British mus, mus of the 2nd Viennese School, mus in Eastern Europe 1830-1930, Revolting or Popular?, plus 1 or 2 from conducting, comp, dissertation, perf
Surrey University BMus Hons Tonmeister (Music and Sound Recording)	16	8/35	Solid foundation in the principles and practice of mus and sound recording; professional training programme combines work experience with academic study	Acoustics, electronics, maths, practical and lab sessions, recording techniques, harmony/kybd skills, style hist, instrumentation, pno, aural tonal analysis	Electro-acoustics, mus tech, microprocessor applications, audio laboratory, recording techniques	Industrial/professional training	**Yr 2:** 4 from: Classical studies, 18th C harmony and counterpoint, tonal analysis, opera after 1850, orchestration, hist perf practice, 19th C mus thought, analysis, contemporary mus stud (perf, comp, research project). **Yr 4:** Compulsory elements: electro-acoustics, technical project, portfolio of recordings. Options: analysis, baroque studies, jazz studies, romantic studies, renaissance historical studies, 20th C Brit mus (perf, comp, conducting) commercial mus studies
University of Sussex BA Hons (3)	20-25	4	Concentrating on the 20th C, or combining with media studies	Hist, analysis, harmony and counterpoint	As yr 1		**Yr 3:** Wide range of options. Perf optional in all yrs

Institution Course	No. pa	Staff f/t, p/t	Bias of course	Year 1	Year 2	Year 3	Options and additional information
Trinity College of Music BMus (TCM)	70-100	128	Perf, professional and vocational qualification	Individual studies, prof studies, musicianship, communication skills, contextual studies (techniques, analysis, history)	As yr 1 plus communication and teaching skills	Perf and prof studies	Study options available from level 1. Vocational options level 3
University of Ulster BMus (Hons)	25	6/18	Balance between practical and theoretical, with options to specialise. Perf integral to course	Analysis, technique, baroque/classical studies, musicianship, inst studies, introduction to musicology	Comp, electronic comp, analysis, harmony, inst studies, romantic and renaissance studies	20th C analysis, late 19th and 20th C studies, project, technical studies	**Yr 2:** 1 from American mus 1900-1939, notation. **Yr 3:** 2 from perf (advanced), popular mus in contemporary America, special topics
Welsh College of Music and Drama BA Hons Performing Arts (Music); Performers Diploma	30-40	15/110	Combined perf with academic supporting studies to provide integrated approach to whole musician	Perf, style, aural, kybd, history, analysis, short courses early music, electro-acoustic, drama, movement for singers	As yr 1	As yr 1	**Yr 2:** Wide range of options, eg br band, comp, br studies, cond, mus tech, kybd, mus therapy, contemporary mus, early mus, str studies, Welsh mus. **Yr 3:** 1 of dissertation, composition, mus technology, early mus
Westminster University BA Hons in Commercial Music	58	5	Commercial mus production and business, students specialise in one of these	Perf and style, law and the mus market, recording and technology, business and the mus market, mus and its audiences	Single production, mus production for theatre, live perf, film and tv, managing in the mus business, record release project, pop mus and culture	Thesis, major project in mus productions or mus business, contemporary mus criticism	Option level 1: commercial scorewriting and arranging I, leading entrepreneurial teams, digital mus technology; option level 2: commercial scorewriting and arranging II, repertoire and back catalogue project; option level 3: experimental mus production; work experience
Wolverhampton University BA Hons	40	4/15	To produce skilled practical musicians who have developed skills in comp and musicology	Core subjects plus options; modular course.			**Yr 1:** Gui, vocal, mus w/shop, 18th-19th C vocal/inst styles. **Yr 2:** Inst tuition, also non-European mus, early 20th C mus styles. **Yr 3:** Mus therapy, mus and drama, solo perf, conducting and arranging, renaissance mus, jazz, pop studies, pop comp and arranging
York University BA Hons, BA/BSc Hons (Mus Technology)	40	10	Perf, comp, analysis, ethnomusicology	Analysis, aural perception, performance	Projects	Projects	Recital, composition, perf practice. Also joint course with dept of electronics

Comparative Degree Tables

Details of the course bias, compulsory elements and available options can be found on p 366.

Selection procedures

A-level Music. The letter indicates the grade of A-level music required, and YES means the qualification is necessary, but may be at any grade.

Other A-levels. If other A-levels are required then the grades are specified here. A blank indicates that no other grades are required. For the total number of A-level passes required, this column should be read in conjunction with the previous column.

ABRSM Grades. If ABRSM grades are specified, then the grade will be indicated here. The second grade refers to a second instrument, and (K) indicates that the grade should be obtained on a second instrument.

Interview. A means always, S means sometimes and N means never.

Practical. YES or NO indicates the likelihood of a practical test at the interview.

Availability of Practical Tuition

Instrumental. If instrumental tuition is included within the course, then it is indicated by YES or the frequency of tuition. If left blank, then no provision is made for instrumental tuition in the course structure.

Orchestral/Chamber. If orchestral or chamber music tuition is part of the course, it is indicated by YES or the frequency of tuition.

Choral/Vocal. If choral or vocal tuition is part of the course, it is indicated by YES or the frequency of tuition.

Languages. This lists the availability of language tuition, the specific languages which may be studied and the frequency of tuition. This is frequently compulsory for singers.

Academic. Frequency of academic tuition is indicated.

Assessment

Non-Exam Assessment. Most courses now include varying amounts of continuous assessment and portfolio submissions.

While every effort has been made to ensure the information is accurate at the time of going to press, it is advisable to confirm specific points with the institution concerned.

Institution / Course	A-Level Music	Other A-Levels	ABRSM Grades	Interview	Practical	Instrumental	Orchestral/Chamber	Choral/Vocal	Languages	Academic	Non Exam Assessment
Anglia Polytechnic University BA Hons (Music)	C	CD (12 points)	VII (1st study)	S	S	1 hr pw	up to 7 hrs pw	up to 2 hrs pw	Fr, Sp, Ger, It	8 hrs pw	Assessed in perf, seminar presentation & portfolio
Bangor, University of Wales BA	B/C	CC	VIII/V	S	YES	30-60 mins per inst pw	up to 6 hrs pw	up to 9 hrs pw	Fr, Ger, It, Sp, Russ 2 hrs pw, Wel 6 hrs	8-10 hrs pw	100% is non-exam in yrs 2-3
Bangor, University of Wales BMus	B/C	CC	VIII/V	S	YES	30-60 mins each inst	up to 6 hrs pw	up to 9 hrs pw	Fr, Ger, It, Rus, Sp 2 hrs pw, Wel 6 hrs	8-10 pw	100% is non-exam in yrs 2-3
Bath Spa University College BA (Hons) (Music)	C	D	VIII or equiv	A	YES	45 mins-1 hr pw	2 hrs pw	2 hrs pw		8-15 hrs pw	Projects, folios, essays, negotiated contracts/profiles, dissertation, recitals, professional performance of compositions, continuous assessment
Birmingham Conservatoire BMus Hons	NO	E	VII+ all insts	A	YES	1 hr pw	5-10 hrs pw	Up to 5 hrs pw	It, Fr, Ger	Up to 10 hrs pw	Variable
Birmingham University BMus (Hons)	A	BB	VIII/VI (K)	S	S	1 hr pw	2 hrs pw	2 hrs pw	Available	12 hrs pw	50% in yr 1 increasing to 70% in yr 3
Bretton Hall University College BA (Hons) Music	B	CC	VIII	A	YES	Bursary	3 hrs pw	3 hrs pw	YES	8hrs pw	Coursework, portfolio, practical
Bretton Hall University College BA Hons (Popular Music)	NO	2		A	YES	Bursary			All European lang modules	9 hrs pw + group work	Continuous assessment with practical perf
Bristol University BA (Music)	B	CC	VIII/V(K)	S	NO	fortnightly (1 hr)	2 hrs pw	3.5 hrs pw	NO	10 hrs pw in yr 1	Most of the course is examined by assessed work.

Institution / Course	A-Level Music	Other A-Levels	ABRSM Grades	Interview	Practical	Instrumental	Orchestral/ Chamber	Choral/Vocal	Languages	Academic	Non Exam Assessment
Brunel University BA Hons (Music)	C	12 points	VIII prac & theory	A	A	30 mins pw (15 wks)	1.5 hrs pw	1.5-2.5 hrs pw (30 wks)	YES	30 wks	Continuous assessment, coursework, practical fieldwork c 70%
Cambridge University BA	A	AB		A	S	NO	NO	NO	voluntary, at univ lang centre	Daily	Portfolios, thesis
Cardiff, University of Wales BA Hons	B	B or CC	VII	A	YES	0.5 hr pw	3-4 hrs+ pw	2-4 hrs+ pw	Fr, Ger, It	10-14 hrs	Continuous assessment; variable, depending on courses selected
Cardiff, University of Wales BMus Hons	B	B or CC	VII/VI	A	YES	0.5-1 hr pw	3-4 hrs+ pw	or 2-4 hrs+ pw	Fr, Ger, It	10-14 hrs	Continuous assessment; variable, depending on courses selected
The Chichester Institute of HE BA (Music: major or joint)	NO		NO	S	YES	1 hr pw	Wkly	Wkly	NO	Major 9 hrs, joint 6 hrs pw	Coursework, take-away papers, practical
Christ Church College BA Single Hons	B	B	VIII	A	YES	1.25 hrs pw	Wkly	Wkly	YES	16 hrs pw	75%; portfolio of compositions, critical analysis and assessed essays
Christ Church College BA Joint and Combined Hons	C	CC+	VII	A	YES	0.5 + 1 hr group pw	2 hrs + pw	2 hrs + pw	Y	8 hrs pw	Continuous assessment: comp/harmony, orch; seminars, special study
City University BMus/BSc Hons		BBC/BCC	VIII/VII	A	YES	Wkly	NO	NO	YES		50% projects, essays, practical
Colchester Institute BA (Hons) (Music)	B	D	VIII	A	YES	1 hr pw (1) 0.5 hrs pw (2)	4 hrs pw	2 hrs pw	Opt 1.5 hrs pw	8 hrs pw	Coursework, assignments, concert giving, concert organisation, placements
Dartington College of Arts BA (Hons)	C	D	VIII	S	YES	Various up to 25 hrs pa	Various 25-50 hrs pa	Various 25-50 hrs pa	YES	22 hrs pw	Continuous assessment

Institution / Course	A-Level Music	Other A-Levels	A-Levels	ABRSM Grades	Interview	Practical	Instrumental	Orchestral / Chamber	Choral / Vocal	Languages	Academic	Non Exam Assessment
Derby University BA/BSc Hons	NO	2 (14 points)	S	VII for joint pathway	NO		0.5 hr pw	1.5 hrs pw	1 hr pw	N/A		Continuous assessment
Durham University BA (Music)	B	CC	S	VI(K)	YES	YES	YES	YES	YES	Fr, Ger, It, Lat, Sp, Russ	YES	Take-away papers, projects, practicals, compositions
East Anglia University BA Hons	B	CC	A	VII/VII/ VII(K)	YES	YES	Wkly - or less	Wkly +	Wkly +	YES by special arrangement	Daily	Periodic tests, coursework, portfolio, practical
Edinburgh University BMus (3/4)	B	BC/C; B (Highers)	A	VII(K)	YES		By individual arrangement	N/A	N/A	Yr 1: It, Ger 2 hrs pw	F/t academic course	**Yr 1/2:** written and practical exams. **Yrs 3/4:** examined by submissions and written/practical exams
Edinburgh University MA (Music) (3/4)		BC/C	S		NO					YES		Some continuous assessment
Edinburgh University BMus in Music Technology	B	B (mus) C (maths)	A	VII	YES		By arrangement	N/A	N/A	F/t		Some submissions in yrs 3 and 4
Exeter University BA (Hons)	B	CC	A	VIII/V	YES		12 pa	NO	NO	YES		Recital, continuous assessment in many subjects
Exeter University BMus	B	CC	A	VIII/V	YES		14 pa	NO	NO	YES		Recital, continuous assessment in many subjects
Glasgow University BMus	B/C	BC; BBB (Highers)	A	VII/V	YES			3 hrs pw	2 hrs pw	All langs	6+ hrs pw	All courses are continuously assessed
Glasgow University MA	NO	AB or BBC	N	NO	NO			3 hrs	2 hrs	All langs	3-4 hrs pw	All courses are continuously assessed

Institution / Course	A-Level Music	Other A-Levels Music	ABRSM Grades	Interview	Practical	Instrumental	Orchestral/ Chamber	Choral/Vocal	Languages	Academic	Non Exam Assessment
Goldsmiths, University of London BMus (3/4)	B	BC	VI;V (pref)	A	YES	40 mins (up to 19 annually)	3 hrs pw	2 or 4 hrs pw		Most langs available	4-6 hrs pw	Orch and choral perf are course requirements (non-assessed)
Guildhall School of Music & Drama BMus Hons (4)	YES	EE; 2 but equal accepted		A	YES	1-2 hrs pw	3-6 hrs pw	1-2 hrs pw	Singers 1.5 hrs pw: Fr, Ger, It, Eng	6-8 hrs pw	Various
University of Hertfordshire Bsc Hons (Elec Mus)	C	1	V (Theory)	A	NO						Coursework, in-class tests, practicals, projects
Huddersfield University BMus/BA Hons	B/C	E	VIII/IV	A	YES	1hr	4 hrs pw	2 hrs pw	Fr, Ger, It, Jap, Sp	5-7 hrs pw	Composition, electro-acoustic mus, musicology coursework
Hull University BMus	B	CC or CD	VIII/V	S	YES	Fortnightly 1 hr	Wkly	Wkly	YES		33% examination, 33% continuous assessment, 33% practical
Keele University BA/BSc	B/C	BB/CC	VII	S	S	0.5 hrs pw	Various	Various	YES	4 hrs pw+	Almost entirely continuous assessment
King's College, University of London BMus (3)	A	B	VIII/V/V(K)	S	YES	0.5-1 hr pw	2 hrs pw	1 hr+ pw	It, Fr, Ger, Jap, Sp	Approx 18 hrs pw	Continuous assessment
Kingston University BA Hons (Music)	C	D	VIII/III(K)	S	YES	1.5 hrs pw	2.5 hrs pw	2 hrs pw	Fr, Ger, It, Sp, Jap, Rus	12 hrs pw	Mainly by coursework in written subjects, exam in practical areas
Kingston University BA Hons (Music and Technology)	B	D	III(K)	S	YES		2.5 hrs pw	2 hrs pw	Fr, Ger, It, Sp, Jap, Rus	12 hrs pw	Mainly coursework and projects
Lancaster University BMus			VIII	A	YES	45 mins pw	2 hrs pw	2 hrs pw	NO	2 hrs pw	Coursework

Institution / Course	A-Level Music	Other A-Levels	ABRSM Grades	Interview	Practical	Instrumental	Orchestral/ Chamber	Choral/Vocal	Languages	Academic	Non Exam Assessment
Lancaster University BA	B	B/C	VIII	A	YES	45 mins pw	2 hrs pw	2 hrs	YES		Coursework
Leeds College of Music BA (Hons) Jazz Studies	NO	2	VIII	A	YES	20 hrs pa	NO	Available	Fr and others	900 hrs pa	Continuous assessment in coursework, project, practical according to module
Leeds College of Music BPA (Music)	NO	2	VIII	A	YES	20 hrs pa	Variable 25-50 hrs pa	Available	Fr and others	900 hrs pa	Continuous assessment in written and practical assignments according to module
University of Leeds BA (Hons) (3)	B	CC	VII/VIII	S	NO	30/50 mins pw	Variable, 4-6 hrs typical	Variable, 2-4 hrs typical	Most langs + Chinese, Jap	10-12 hrs pw	Dissertation, essays, projects, portfolios, recital, ens perf, viva voce
University of Leeds B Mus (4)	B	CC	VIII (dist)	A	YES	45-60 mins pw	Variable, 4-6 hrs typical	Variable, 2-4 hrs typical	Most Eur langs	10-12 hrs in Yr 1	Recital, chmbr mus, perf, dissertation, essays, projects, viva voce
Liverpool University BA (Music)	B	CC/BB	VI+	S	YES	30 mins pw per study	N/A	Singers only	Fr, Ger, It, Sp, Dutch 1-2 hrs pw	Yr 1: 10 hrs pw; Yrs 2 & 3: 9 hrs pw	Continuous assessment, portfolio, dissertation, 3-wk take-away paper
Liverpool University BA Hons Mus/Popular Mus	B	CC/BB	NO	S	NO	30 mins pw per study	N/A	Singers only	1-2 hrs pw; Dutch, Fr, Ger, It, Sp	9-10 hrs pw	Continuous assessment, portfolio, dissertation, take-away 3 wk paper
London College of Music and Media BMus (3)	ABC	BCDE	VIII	A	YES	1 hr pw (min 22 wks)	3 hrs pw (min 20 wks)	2 hrs pw (min 30 wks)	Ger, Fr, It	10+ hrs pw	Greater proportion of modules are non-exam
Manchester University MusB Hons	B	BB	VII/VI(K)	N		1 hr pw	3 hrs pw	3 hrs pw	YES	10 hrs pw	Harmony, counterpoint and comp portfolios, history essays, analysis projects, thesis, instrumentation, studio techniques, topics

Institution / Course	A-Level Music	Other A-Levels	ABRSM Grades	Interview	Practical	Instrumental	Orchestral / Chamber	Choral / Vocal	Languages	Academic	Non Exam Assessment
Newcastle University BA Hons (Music)	B	CC	VIII / S	YES	Wkly or fortnightly	Wkly	Wkly	Wkly	As subsidiaries		Coursework, take-away papers, practical (70%)
Northumbria University BA Hons Music	C	C	VIII / A	YES	1 hr per wk basic skills			Optional choir	As an elective	Approx 6 hrs per wk	Entirely continuous assessment except for some electives.
Nottingham Trent University BA (Contemporary Arts)	NO	3	VII / A	YES	N/A	2 hrs pw	2 hrs pw	1.5 hrs pw			No written examination. Folio, continuous assessment
Nottingham University BA (Music)	B	AC	S	NO	1 hr pw	2 hrs pw	2 hrs pw	2 hrs pw	Most European langs	10 hrs pw	Most modules include coursework
Open University BA	No formal entry requirements. Students undertake c 15 hrs pw independent study, plus a small amount of face-to-face tuition										50% of each course
Oxford Brookes University BA Hons Music	B	C	NO / S	NO	Yes	Yes	Yes	Yes	Modules in Fr, Ger and It	10-12 hrs per week	100% coursework assessment, eg essays, comps, group presentations, recitals, projects, dissertation
Oxford University BA Hons (Music)	A	EE+	A	YES	N/A	N/A	N/A	N/A	Almost all langs	12 hrs pw	Up to c30% in finals with certain options
Queen's University BMus Hons	C	BB or CCC	NO / A	YES		0.5-1 hrs pw	2.5 hrs pw	1hr pw; 2-3 hrs pw	All common Eur lang	15 hrs pw	Essays, projects, practicals, continuous assessment
Reading University BA Hons (Music) (3)	B	CC	VIII/V(K) / S	YES	0.5 hrs pw	2 hrs pw	2 hrs pw	2 hrs pw	Fr, Ger, It		**Yr 2:** hist 33% coursework, analysis 50% coursework; free comp; portolio; strict comp: 33% portfolio. **Yr 3:** each option, dissertation; comp and analysis, portfolio

Institution / Course	A-Level Music	Other Music A-Levels	ABRSM Grades	Grades	Interview	Practical	Instrumental	Orchestral/Chamber	Choral/Vocal	Languages	Academic	Non Exam Assessment
Roehampton Institute London BMus	C	1	VIII	S	YES	Wkly	2 hrs pw	2 hrs pw	2 hrs pw	Fr, Sp, It, Ger, Russ	3 days	Coursework, recitals, seminars, portfolio, take-away papers, thesis
Roehampton Institute London BA	C	1	VIII	S	YES	Wkly	2 hrs pw	2 hrs pw	2 hrs pw	Fr, Sp, It, Ger, Russ	2 days for mus, 2 for second subject.	Coursework, recitals, seminars, portfolio, take-away papers, thesis
Royal Academy of Music BMus (Perf) (4)	B	B/C	VIII dist	A	YES	1-1.5 hrs pw		6 hrs pw	singers: 2 hrs pw	Fr, Ger, It, Sp & others 1-2 hrs pw	Yrs 1-2: 6 hrs pw; Yrs 3-4: 3 hrs pw	Internal assessment
Royal College of Music BMus (Hons) (4)	E	E	VIII or Adv Cert	A	YES	1-1.5 hrs pw		6 hrs pw	2 hrs pw	Fr, It, Ger, Russ 1-2 hrs pw	Up to 6 hrs pw	None
Royal Holloway, London University BMus	B	BB	VIII; VI	A	YES	30-60 mins pw	N/A	N/A	N/A	Fr, Ger, It, Sp	10-12 hrs pw	Most courses are assessed on portfolio/recital work as well as written exams
Royal Northern College of Music BA (4)	NO	NO	None	A	YES	up to 2 hrs pw		up to 6 hrs pw	variable	EFL; vocal students - It, Fr, Ger, Russ, Czech	Approx 5 hrs pw	Continuous assessment in perf; also academic
Royal Northern College of Music BMus Hons	NO	2		A	YES	up to 2 hrs pw		up to 6 hrs pw	variable	EFL; vocal students - It, Fr, Ger, Russ, Czech	5 hrs pw	Continuous assessment in perf and academic studies

Institution / Course	A-Level Music	Other A-Levels	ABRSM Grades	Interview	Practical	Instrumental	Orchestral/Chamber	Choral/Vocal	Languages	Academic	Non Exam Assessment
Royal Northern College of Music MusB/GRNCM	YES	A-levels specified by Univ of Manchester		A	YES	up to 2 hrs pw	up to 6 hrs pw	variable	EFL; vocal students - It, Fr, Ger, Russ, Czech	As stipulated by Univ of Manchester	Continuous assessment, performance
University College of Saint Martin BA Perf Arts (University of Lancaster)	C	C	VII or equiv standard	A	YES	16-19 per yr	Wkly	Wkly	May be available	Yr 1: 100-120 hrs; Yr 2: 75-85 hrs	Approx 50% coursework
University of Salford BA Hons (Popular Music and Recording)	YES	2	VIII	A	YES	1 hr pw	5-7 hrs pw (ens tuition)	N/A	YES	7 hrs pw	Continuous assessment, coursework
University of Salford BA Hons (Band Musicianship) (3)	YES	2/3	VIII	S	YES	1 hr pw	3+ hrs pw	N/A	Available in college	10 hrs pw	Coursework continuously assessed
University of Salford BA Hons (Band Musicianship) (4)	YES	1	VIII	S	YES	45 mins pw	3 hrs+ pw		Available in college	6-8 hrs pw	Continuous assessment
Sheffield University BMus (3)	A/B	BC	VIII/V(K)	S	YES	1 hr pw	2-3 hrs pw	2+ hrs pw		8 hrs pw	Continuous assessment in yrs 2-3; ens class option; other courses also assessed
Southampton University BA Hons	B	BC	VIII/V(K)	A	YES	50 mins pw; 80 mins finalists	2 hrs pw	1 hr pw	3 hrs pw; most available	10 hrs pw	All yr 1 and some yr 2/3 courses
Surrey University BMus (Hons) (Music)	B	CC	VIII	A	YES	1-1.5 hrs pw	4 hrs pw	2 hrs+ more for specialists	Fr, Ger, It, Rus, Sp, 2 hrs pw	20-25 hrs pw	Continuous assessment, final yr specialisation
Surrey University BMus Hons Tonmeister (Music and Sound Recording)	B	BB	VII	A	YES	1-1.5 hrs pw	4 hrs pw	2 hrs pw	Fr, Ger, Sp, It, Russ, etc	25 hrs pw	Continuous assessment, final yr specialisations

Institution / Course	A-Level Music	Other A-Levels	A-Levels	ABRSM Grades	Interview	Practical	Orchestral/ Chamber	Choral/Vocal	Languages	Academic	Non Exam Assessment
University of Sussex BA Hons (3)	B	BC	VIII	S	YES	0.5 hrs pw	N/A	N/A	Most Eur langs	8 hrs pw	Dissertation, extended essay, portfolio of comp or orchestration
Trinity College of Music BMus (TCM)	YES	2	VIII	A	YES	1 hr pw	3-6 hrs pw + ens	Singers 1 ind; 2 choir	Singers; 3 hrs pw	4.5 hrs pw & dept studies	Continuous and annual assessment of all studies
University of Ulster BMus (Hons)	B/C	AB/BCC	VII/VIII	A	YES	1 hr pw	3 hrs pw (voluntary)	1 hr choir; 0.5 hrs vocal	NO	9-12 hrs pw	Continuous assessment, coursework, performance, peer assessment
Welsh College of Music and Drama BA Hons Performing Arts (Music); Performers Diploma	YES	2	VIII min	A	YES	1 hr pw minimum	6 hrs pw	3 hrs pw	It, Fr, Ger, Wel	An average of 10 hrs	Continuous assessment, projects, submitted work
Westminster University BA Hons in Commercial Music	C	CC	N/A	A	YES				Poly lang scheme offers most langs	4 days pw	Assessed by regular coursework and by presentations
Wolverhampton University BA Hons	C/D	D (12 point average)	VIII	S	YES	4 hrs per semester	1 hr pw	1.5 hrs pw	Lang modules available	12 hrs pw	All modules contain a variety of methods of assessment including coursework, written/practical examinations, presentations and audio tapes, although there are relatively few written examinations
York University BA Hons, BA/BSc Hons (Mus Technology)	A/B	BC	VIII	S	YES	Variable - 1hr/fortnight	Wkly	Wkly	By arrangement		Whole course continuous assessment

Combined Degrees

The following tables of combined degrees list the courses at **Universities** and **Colleges of Higher Education** in which music may be studied in combination with one or more subjects for at least a third of the course time.

Joint-subject degree courses tend to offer students the opportunity to study selected parts of each single-subject degree course, usually with some interdisciplinary study to link them. Students are likely to find themselves studying with single-subject students. and the work load may be greater.

Most combined subject courses are now modular and allow the student to tailor the course to his or her own interests. Music takes its place in an organised whole made up of a number of different areas studied in relation to one another.

Brief details are given under the headings: *Institution, Course title, Subject choice,* and *Additional information*. For additional information refer to the **Universities** and **Colleges of Higher Education** sections and to their prospectuses.

The following subject abbreviations have been used to indicate subject choice:

Acc	Accountancy, Accounting	Int	International
Am	American	IT	Information Technology
Anc	Ancient (eg Anc Hist)	Ital	Italian
Anthrop	Anthropology	Jap	Japanese
Arab	Arabic	Lang	Language(s)
Arch	Archaelogy	Lat	Latin
Bib Stud	Biblical Studies	Ling	Linguistics
Biochem	Biochemistry	Lit	Literature
Biol	Biology	Math	Mathematics
Bus Stud	Business Studies	Med Eng	Medieval English
Chem	Chemistry	Mgt	Management
Civ	Civilisation (Greek, Roman, etc)	MIT	Music Information Technology
Class	Classics/Classical	Mod	Modern
Comm	Communication	Phil	Philosophy
Comp	Computing/Computer	Phy	Physics
Contemp	Contemporary	Phys	Physical
Econ	Economics	Pol	Politics
Egy	Egyptian	Port	Portuguese
Elec	Electronic(s)	Psy	Psychology
Eng	English	Rel	Religious/Religions
Engi	Engineering	Russ	Russian
Env	Environment	Sci	Science
Ethnomus	Ethnomusicology	Scot	Scottish
Fin	Finance	Soc	Social
Fr	French	Soci	Sociology
Geog	Geography	Sp	Spanish
Geol	Geology	Stats	Statistics
Ger	German	Stud	Studies
Gk	Greek	Tech	Technology
Heb	Hebrew	Theo	Theology
Hisp	Hispanic	Turk	Turkish
Hist	History	Vis	Visual
Hum	Humanities	Wel	Welsh

Institution	Course	Subject	Additional Information
Anglia Polytechnic University	BA, BA Hons (3)	Art History, Audio Tech, Bus, Comm Stud, Econ, Eng, Eng Lang Stud, Euro Bus, Euro Phil and Lit, Fr, Geog, Ger, Graphic Art, Hist, Ital, Law, Math, Psy, Sp	2 subjects studied equally, or as major/minor
Bath Spa University College	BA Creative Arts	**Majors:** Art, Creative Stud in Eng, Textile Design Stud, Mus. **Elective modules:** Applicable Math, Bus Stud, Cult Stud, Dance, Design & Tech, Eng Stud, Env Biol, Food Studies, Geog, Global Futures, Health Stud, Hist, Int Educ, Irish Studies, Mass Comm, Remote Sensing and Geographic Info Systems, Soci, Stud in Visual Culture, Study of Rel, Psy	Majors in Creative Stud in Eng and in Mus may also be taken as elective modules. Availability of elective modules can depend upon timetable. Yr 1: mus with 2 or 3 subjects. Yrs 2/3: mus with 1 or 2 subjects. BA Creative Arts is a specialised award within the modular scheme
Bath Spa University College	BA/BSc Hons Combined Awards (3)	Eng Stud, Env Biol, Geog, Health Stud, Hist, Soci, Study of Rel. Joint or minor only: Applicable Math, International Educ, Psy	Elective modules in other subjects also available. Combined awards degrees are fully modular
Birmingham University	BA Hons Combined Subjects (3; 4 for combinations inc foreign lang)	Class Stud, Comp Stud, Dance, Drama, Eng, Fr, Ger, Gk (Anc & Mod), Hisp Stud, Hist, Hist of Art, Ital, Lat, Math, Media & Cultural Stud, Med Eng, PE, Phil, Russ, Theo	Yr 1: hist, techniques or comp, perf. Yrs 2-3: includes optional courses - students specialise as composers, scholars or performers or combine 2 of these tracks.
Brighton University	BA Hons Music with Visual Practice (3)	Vis Arts	50% mus, 50% vis arts
Bristol University	BA Hons Music and 1 foreign lang (4)	Fr, Ger, Ital	Can be done equally between the subjects or split 66%-33% either way
Brunel University	BA, BA Hons (3)	Am Stud, Drama, Eng, Film & TV Stud, Hist	2 subjects studied equally, or as major/minor
Cardiff, University of Wales	BA Joint Hons (3; 4 for combinations with foreign lang)	Cult crit, Econ, Educ, Eng, Fr, Ger, Hist, Ital, Phil, Pure Math, Rel Stud, Soc Phil, Soci, Wel	All Humanities Faculty students study 3 subjects in yr 1. (Math also available by arrangement.) In yrs 2-3 time divided equally between mus and 2nd subject
Cardiff, University of Wales	BSc Hons Music (3)	Phy	A minimum of 120 mus credits is taken. For students intending to go into mus recording, studio mgt or elec comp

Institution	Course	Subject	Additional Information
The Chichester Institute of HE	BA Hons (3)	Art, Dance, Educ Stud, Eng, Env Sci, Geog, Hist, Math, Media Stud, Related Arts, Rel Stud	Mus can be studied as a major subject (75%), joint (50%) or minor (25%) as well as a single hons subject.
Christ Church College	BA Hons/Ordinary (3)	Am Stud, Art, Bus Stud, Childhood Stud, Educ, Eng, Geog, Hist, Marketing, Math, MIT, Radio/Film/TV Stud, Rel Stud, Sci, Sports Sci, Tourism	2 subjects studied on modular basis allowing for specialisation in yr 3
Christ Church College	BSc Hons/Ordinary (3)	Math, IT	More than 50% of modules studied must be in Math
Dartington College of Arts	BA Hons (3)	Perf Writing, Theatre, Visual Perf, Arts Management (major or minor)	Major subject mus and a choice of c20 modules per semester linking with work in other arts disciplines and Arts Management
De Montfort University	BA Hons Performing Arts (3)	Dance, Theatre	Mus and mus technology as specialist subject studied, with theoretical stud in perf and practical perf w/shops. Experience of other arts and arts admin offered
Derby University	BA/BSc Hons (3)	Wide choice (modular)	Mus available as joint subject (50%) or minor (33%)
Durham University	BA Hons Joint (3 or 4)	Eng, Fr, Ger, Lat, Russ, Sp, Theo	2 subjects studied. If a modern lang is taken yr 3 is spent abroad
Durham University	BA Hons Combined Studies (3)	Chinese Hist, Eng, Fr, Ger, Gk, Gk and Roman Civ, Ital, Lat, Ling, Math, Phil, Russ, Russ Stud, Sp, Theo	3 subjects chosen in yr 1. 3 final courses studied in yrs 2 and 3 (normally subjects led to by yr 1 courses). Sci and Soc Sci may be available. Mus may not be studied with Phil or Sp in yrs 2 and 3
Exeter University	BA Combined Hons (3; 4 with modern lang)	Fr, Ger, Ital, Sp	
Glasgow University	MA Hons Music (4; 5 for combinations with foreign lang)	Arab, Arch, Celtic, Church Hist, Class Civ, Comp, Czech, Drama, Econ, Eng, Film & TV, Fr, Geog, Ger, Gk, Heb, Hist of Art, Hist Stud, Ital, Lat, Lit, Math, Phil, Phy, Polish, Pol, Pol Econ, Psy, Rel Stud, Russ, Scot Hist, Scot Lit, Soci, Social Policy, Theatre Stud, Theo	

Institution	Course	Subject	Additional Information
Glasgow University	BEng Electronics and Electrical Engineering with Music (4)	Elec, Electrical Engineering	Compulsory courses: audio process, advanced MIDI, electro-acoustic concert presentation. Mus is 35% of programme. Mus components focus on mus tech
University of Hertfordshire	BSc Combined Hons elec mus.	Astronomy, Bus, Chem, Comp, Econ, Elec, Env, Euro Stud, Human Biol, Ling Sci, Operational Research, Phil, Applied Phy, Applied Stats.	
Huddersfield University	BA Hons (3; 4 with lang or mus tech)	Fr, Ger, Mus Tech, Sp, Theatre Stud	Mus tech combines electro-acoustic mus with modules in comp and elec engi
Hull University	BA Joint Hons (3; 4 with lang)	Drama, Eng, Fr	
Keele University	BA Joint Hons (mus or elec mus & hum/soc sci) (3). BSc Joint Hons (mus or elec mus & natural sci) (3)	Am Stud, Applied Soc Stud, Biochem, Biol, Chem, Class Stud, Comp Sci, Criminology, Econ, Educ Stud, Eng, Finance, Fr, Geol, Ger, Human Resource Mgt, Int Hist, Int Pol, Math, Mkt, Medicinal & Biol Chem, Phil, Pol, Psy, Soci, Vis Arts or a double language combination	
Keele University	BA/BSc Joint Hons (4; 3)	Am Stud, Anc Hist, Applied Soc Stud, Astrophys, Biochem, Chem, Class Stud, Comp Sci, Criminology, Econ, Educ Stud, Elec, Eng, Env Mgmt, Finance, Fr, Geog, Geol, Ger, Human Resource Mgmt, Int Hist, Int Pol, Law, Math, Medicinal & Biol Chem, Phys, Pol, Psy, Russ, Russ Studies, Soci, Stats, Vis Arts, Double lang combination	Foundation year has modular structure with central core lecture course. Intensive transfer course in mus enables admission to 3-yr courses for those without necessary qualifications
Lancaster University	BA Joint Hons	Eng, Fr, Ger, Hist, Ital, Sp	
Leeds Metropolitan University	BEng Hons	Elec, Mus and Media Tech	

Institution	Course	Subject	Additional Information
University of Leeds	BA Hons (3; 4 with foreign lang); BSc Hons (all available p/t)	Eng, Fr, Ger, Hist, Hist of Art, Ital, Comp, Math, Phil, Rel Stud, Theo, Elec Engi	Liberal choice of courses can be made in combination within the modular degree structure
Liverpool Hope University College	BA (Combined Subjects) with Hons (3)	Am Stud, Art, Drama and Theatre Stud, Eng, Env Stud, Euro Stud, Fr, Human and Applied Biol, IT, Math, Soci, Sport, Recreation and PE, Theo	3 subjects studied in yr 1; 2 subjects in both yrs 2 and 3. Course fully modularised on basis of 360 credits
Liverpool University	BA Combined Hons (3)	Arch, Biol, Catalan, Class Civ, Comm Stud, Dutch, Econ, Egy, Eng, Fr, Geog, Geol, Ger, Gk, Heb, Hist, Lat, Ling, Math, Phil, Pol, Port, Psy, Russ, Sci, Sp	3 subjects chosen from a wide list of 36 subjects in yr 1, 2 of which are continued in yrs 2 and 3. (Geol may only be studied in yr 1)
Liverpool University	BA Combined Hons (Popular Music)	Biol, Comm Stud, Econ, Geog, Geol, Math, Pol, Psy, Sci	Can be taken as 1-yr or 3-yr part of Comb Hons and is open to non-performers
London College of Music and Media	BA 'major' in one of the following subjects with mus	Am Stud, Eng, Fr, Media Arts	6 modules per year. Yr 1: hum foundation plus 2 mus; Yrs 2 & 3: major modules (or 2 from each of 2 minors) plus 2 mus, pa
Middlesex University	BA Hons Performance Arts (3), BA/BSc Hons Combined Stud	Wide variety of subjects in Arts, Hum or Sci	Mus chosen as major subject, with basic skills in Dance and Drama
Nene College	BA/BSc Hons Combined Honours (3)	Wide range of subjects inc Arts, Bus Stud, Comp, Hum, Law, Math, PE, Sci, Soc Sci	3 or 4 subjects studied in total, with 1 subject read throughout 3 yrs. yr 1: subject 1 + 2 others, yr 2: subject 1 + 2 others, yr 3: subject 1 (66% time) + 1 other
Newcastle University	BA Hons Combined Studies (3)	Choice of over 30 subjects inc Comp Sci, Math, Soc Sci	2 or 3 subjects studied per yr (usually not more than 5 subjects in total to be studied). Entry does not have to be for specific combination of subjects
Nottingham Trent University	BA Hons Contemporary Arts (3)	Dance, Perf, Vis Art	Mus studied with one other subject. In yrs 1 and 2 both subjects are studied with only 1 in yr 3

Institution	Course	Subject	Additional Information
Oxford Brookes University	BA/BSc Hons/Ordinary (3 f/t or p/t or mixed mode)	Acc & Fin, Anthrop, Biol, Bus Admin and Mgt, Cartography, Comp Systems, Comp, Comp Math, Econ, Educ Stud, Elec, Eng Stud, Env Biol, Env Policy, Env Sci, Exercise & Health, Fine Art, Fr & Contemp Stud, Geog, Geol, Geotechnics, Ger & Contemp Stud, Ger Lang & Lit, Ger Stud, Hist, Hist of Art, Hospitality Mgt, Info Systems, Intelligent Systems, Law, Leisure Planning & Mgt, Mkt Mgt, Math, Planning Studies, Pol, Psy, Publishing, Soci, Software Engi, Stats, Telecommunications, Tourism, Transport Planning.	Modular course, in which 2 'fields' are combined, allowing for wide choice within the student's degree programme. Some flexibility in balancing of the 2 subjects. Final-yr students may opt to write an interdisciplinary dissertation, combining 2 areas of stud
Queen's University	BA Joint Hons (3; 4 with foreign lang); BA Combined Hons	Anc Hist, Arch, Bib Stud, Bus Admin, Byz Stud, Celtic, Class Stud, Comp Sci, Econ & Soc Hist, Eng, Ethnomus, Fr, Geog, Ger, Gk, Hist & Phil of Sci, Ital, Lat, Mod Hist, Phil, Political Sci, Psy, Russ, Scholastic Phil, Soc Anthrop, Soci, Sp, Women's Stud	All courses modular. BA Joint Hons 50% mus; BA Combined Hons mus in varying proportions
Reading University	BA Hons Music (3) + Art History or Eng; (4) + either Ger, Ital or Fr	Eng, Fr, Ger, Hist of Art, Ital	Strong foundation in musicianship; intense study of specialist area chosen from 4 options
Roehampton Institute London	BA Combined Hons (3; 4 in combination with Fr or Sp)	Art, Bus Stud, Bus Comp, Dance, Drama, Educ, Eng, Eng Lang, Env Stud, Film & TV, Fr, Geog, Hist, Math, Media Stud, Psy, Soc Admin, Soci, Sp, Sports Stud, Theo and Rel Stud	2 subjects studied equally in yr 1; opportunity in yrs 2 and 3 to place more emphasis on 1 subject
Royal Holloway	BA Hons Music Combined (Hons) (3) (4 in combination with Ger, Fr or Ital)	Drama/Theatre Stud, Econ, Fr, Ger, Gk, Ital, Jap, Lat, Maths, Mgt Stud, Phys, Pol Stud, Psy, Public Admin, Soci, Sp	Broad foundations but with opportunities to specialise at higher level in selected areas of perf, mus hist or comp
University College of St Martin	BA (Modular Studies) (University of Lancaster)	Variety of subjects available	BA Hons (Music) is taught in 1st year with BA QTS students and in year 2/3 with PA students. Available as minor or joint degree with another subject and includes main study inst or voice tuition

Institution	Course	Subject	Additional Information
University College, Scarborough: The North Riding College	BA Combined Hons, BSc Combined Hons	Mus may be studied with a variety of subjects in the arts and social sciences areas	Students may opt to study mus as a major, minor or third subject within a modular framework
School of Oriental and African Studies	BA Hons (3 or 4)	Art, Development Stud, Geog, Hist, Rel Stud, Soc Anthrop, Langs inc Jap, Mid East, S & SE Asia and others	Combinations with Arab, Jap, Turk, Persian, Korean, Chinese are 4 yrs (yr 1 mainly lang); otherwise flexibility in balance between subjects
Sheffield University	BA Dual Hons (3; 4 with foreign lang)	Bib Stud, Eng, Fr, Ger, Phil, Sp	Music and the other subject count equally in these courses
Southampton University	BA Combined Hons (3; 4 with foreign lang)	Eng, Fr, Ger	
Southampton University	BSc Combined Hons (3)	Acoustics, Math	
University of Sunderland	BA Joint Hons (3 f/t; 5 p/t)	Variety of subjects	
University of Wolverhampton	BA Hons (3)		May be taken as a single honours, joint honours, three subjects, or minor subject. A course in Music/Theatre Stud/Dance is available as a triple option
York University	BA Hons (mus with education) (3)		This course does not incorporate a teaching qualification

Higher Degrees

Students may read for a higher degree only after completing a first degree or degree equivalent. Applications should be addressed to the individual establishment. Courses carrying a recognised qualification (MMus, PhD, etc), fall into two main categories: taught, where a student's own work is supplemented by lectures and tutorials, culminating in an examination, and research, where students work largely at their own pace, with the minimum of supervision, and submit a thesis. Both are covered in the first list, **Academic Courses**, which excludes advanced degrees in music education (see **Teacher Training** section). Figures in brackets indicate the course length in years; (1:2) implies one year of full-time study or two years of part-time study. The second list, **Practical Courses,** covers courses for performers and composers run by the conservatoires.

Degrees for External Students

A BMus degree for external students is offered by the University of London. This is the only body which awards an honours degree as a single subject on an external basis. At the Open University, music may not be studied as a single subject. As a way of studying for a degree, external study is suitable for those who do not wish or are unable to be resident in a university.

The syllabus and examinations for the BMus degree of the University of London are rigorously controlled and external students are examined by the same standards as internal students. Some guidance is provided by the University of London for its external BMus students in the form of subject introductions. Registration for the BMus degree is available worldwide, but examinations are held only in London.

At London University, the MPhil and PhD are also offered externally at postgraduate level. These research degrees are open only to graduates of the University of London.

Prospectuses and application forms for the BMus or the MPhil/PhD may be obtained from the External Programme, Room 1, University of London, Senate House, Malet St, London WC1 7HU *Tel:* 0171 636 8000 ext 3150 *Fax:* 0171 636 5841 *Email:* enquiries@eisa.lon.ac.uk *Website:* www.lon.ac.uk/external.

Any graduate of the University of London may enter for the DMus. This higher doctorate is awarded only for published work of a high standard containing original contributions to the advancement of knowledge. Further details may be obtained from the Academic Registrar, Room 16, University of London, Senate House, Malet St, London WC1 7HU *Tel:* 0171 636 8000 ext 3018.

Academic Courses

Institution	Type of Study (Taught)	(Research)	Details
Anglia Polytechnic University	MA Mus Therapy, MA Mus (1:2)	MPhil, PhD (3)	
Bangor, University of Wales	*MA (1), MMus (1)	MPhil (1:2), PhD (2:3)	*Editorial Musicology, Ethnomusicology, Historical Musicology, Mus and the Media, Perf Comp and/or Electro-acoustic Comp
Birmingham Conservatoire	#MA (Music), #P/grad Diploma (Music) (1:2)	*MPhil, *PhD	*F/t or p/t. Most areas of hist and contemp mus may be covered. #Linked by common units but MA requires further theoretical study and seminar work. Available in Perf, Comp, Musicology, World Mus.
Birmingham University	*MA (1:2)	*MPhil (1), #MMus (1), MLitt (2), *PhD (2 or 3)	*Comp or Musicology #Comp only
Bretton Hall, University College	MA Music Education; MA Contemporary Performing Arts	MPhil; PhD; MA	
Bristol University	◆MA (1), *MA (1:2)	♣MMus/PhD (2:3), MLitt (2:3 or 1:2), PhD (3:4), DMus	*Advanced Musical Stud (Musicology or Comp) ◆Comp for Film, TV and Theatre ♣Comp
Cambridge University	*MPhil (1)	MLitt, PhD	*Musicology, Comp or Ethnomusicology
Cardiff, University of Wales	MMus (1), *MA (1)	PhD (3), MPhil (2)	*Musicology, Perf Stud or Mus, Culture and Pol
Christ Church College	*MA	MPhil, PhD	*Comp, Pno Accomp, Perf, Electronic & Computer Comp, Jazz
City University	MA (1:2), Diploma MIT (1:2)	MPhil (2:5), PhD (3:6), MSc MIT (1), MMA/DMA (3:6).	Perf Stud, Comp, Electro-acoustic Mus, Ethnomusicology, Musicology
Colchester Institute	*MA (1:2) Liturgical Mus, Comp, Perf, Mus Technology, Musicology.	MPhil, PhD	*Modular

Durham University	MA (1), MMus (2)	PhD (3), MA (1), MMus (2)	Research in hist and critical stud, analytic stud, ethnomusicology and elec studio tech and elec sound synthesis, comp
East Anglia University	*MMus (1 f/t, 2 p/t)	#MPhil (2 f/t, 4 p/t), #PhD (3 f/t, 6 p/t)	*Comp, Conducting, Eng Church Music, Mus Perf Stud, Musicology #Comp, Hist Musicology, Mus Theory and Analysis, Aesthetics and Phil
Edinburgh University	*DipMus/MMus (1)	#MPhil (2), #PhD (3)	All may be studied p/t *Specialised area, or general level #Comp or Research
University of Exeter	MPhil (1 min), MMus (1 min), MA (1 min)	PhD (3 min)	All may be studied p/t
Glasgow University		*MMus (1), MLitt (2), PhD (3)	*Musicology, Comp, Perf, Computer Mus
Goldsmiths College, University of London	*MMus (1:2)	MPhil (2:3), PhD (3:4)	*Ethnomusicology, Mus Theory and Analysis, Historical Musicology, Comp, Perf and Related Stud
Guildhall School of Music & Drama	*MMus (1)		*Comp
Huddersfield University	*MA (1:2)	MPhil (3), PhD (3:6)	*Perf, Comp, Electro-Acoustic Comp, Contemporary Mus Stud or hist musicology
Hull University	*MMus (1)	MPhil (2), PhD (3)	*Comp, Perf, Musicology or Analysis
Institute of Education	MA (Mus Ed) (1:2)	MPhil, PhD	Mus Educ, Aesthetics, Soci & Psy of Mus, Curriculum Development, Pop and World Mus.

Keele University	*P/grad Dip/MA/MSc in Digital Mus Tech Dip/MA in Modern Mus	◆PhD, ◆MPhil	*Final projects may consist of software project (MSc) or folio of electro-acoustic comp (MA) Final project in musicology/analysis, comp or perf ◆ Both may be either academic (Thesis) or Comp. All may be studied p/t
King Alfred's College		#MPhil (2), #PhD (3)	#Mus Educ, Gender in Mus, Ethnomusicology, Music and Rel/Ritual.
King's College	*MMus (1:2)	MPhil (min 2), PhD (min 3)	*Theory & Analysis, Comp, Historical Musicology
Kingston University	*MA in Mus (1:2)	MPhil, PhD	*2 from: Comp for Schools, Comp, Mus in Schools, Studio Comp, Perf Stud, Ethnomus, Mus Analysis, Mus Culture and Ideas; Research Project in yr 2 in wide range of subjects including perf and comp
Lancaster University	MMus (1)	*MPhil, PhD	F/t or p/t *May include Musicology, Perf or Comp
University of Leeds	MMus (1:2), Dip in Mus Stud (1)	MA (1:2), *MPhil (2:3), *PhD (3-6)	*Research or Comp
Liverpool University	*MMus (1), #MA (Popular Music) (1)	MPhil (2), PhD (3)	All may be studied p/t. *Available in any 2 of Dissertation, Analysis, Editing, Comp, Perf, Electronic Studio Techniques; #At associated Inst of Popular Mus
London College of Music and Media	*MA/P/g Dip(1:2), P/g Dip (1:2), ◆MA/P/g Dip (2 yrs p/t), MMus		*In Film and the Moving Image; Radio; ◆Cultural and Textual Studies and in Visual and Literary Studies
Manchester University	MusM (1:2)	*PhD (3:6), M Phil (1:2)	Also in Comp

Newcastle University	*MA (1:2), MMus (1:2)	MLitt, MPhil (1:2), ◆PhD (3:5)	*In Mus, Meaning and Culture, Popular Mus, Mus Tech; Perf, Comp; ◆including Comp
Nottingham University	MA (1)	*MPhil (2), *PhD (3), #AMusM (2), #AMusD (3)	*Comp or Musicology #Comp
Open University		BPhil, MPhil, DPhil	All usually studied p/t (though opportunity exists in Arts Faculty for limited numbers of f/t research students), length equivalent to 1/2/3 (respectively) f/t
Oxford Brookes University	MA in Electronic Media (1: 2); MA in Music, History of Culture (1: 2).	MPhil (min 18 mths: 30 mths); PhD (min 33 mths: 45 mths).	
Oxford University	*BMus (1), #MSt (1), #MPhil (2)	MLitt (2), DPhil (3)	*Comp, Oxford graduates only #Part taught, part thesis
Queen's University	*MA (1:2), #MA/Dip (1:2)	◆MPhil (2:4), ◆PhD (3:6)	*Renaissance, 20th C Mus, Perf Stud #Mus Tech ◆Research or Comp
Reading University	*MA (1), #MMus (1)	◆MPhil (3), ◆PhD (3)	*Musicology, Theory & Analysis, Org historiography; #Comp, Perf ◆May also be studied p/t
Royal Academy of Music	MMus (London) (2)		
Royal College of Music	MMus (RCM) (1)	DMus (2:4).	Perf stud or comp
Royal Holloway, University of London	*MMus (1:2)	MPhil, PhD	*Available in Theory & Analysis, Comp, Perf, Historical Musicology
Royal Northern College of Music	MusM (2) (University of Manchester)		Equal balance between practical and academic elements

University of Salford	MA (1)	*MA/MPhil Popular Music, #PhD	*Comp or Perf; also in Popular Mus, Jazz, Bands. Dissertation-based, min 3 months in Europe #Comp or research, especially in sociomusicology or mus tech
School of Oriental and African Studies	*MA (1:2), MMus (1:2/3)	MPhil (min 2), PhD (min 3)	*Area Stud, Ethnomusicology
Sheffield University	#MA	PhD (3:6), MPhil (2:4), *MMus (1:2)	*2 from Comp, Perf, Musicology, Folio #Psychology of Mus
Southampton University	MA (1)	MPhil (1), PhD (3)	
University of Surrey	*MMus (1:2)	MPhil, PhD (3:4)	*Compulsory core research unit taken with 1 from Mus, Orientalism and Eroticism, 20thC Brit Musi analytical and crit studior Applied Musicianship (1 major from Performance, Conducting, Compositionand 2 minor from Classical Studio Production, Crit and Reviewing, Comp, Conducting, Performance) followed by dissertation, recital or composition folio.
University of Sussex	*MA	MPhil, DPhil	*2 areas from Composition, Analysis, Aesthetics, Contemporary Mus Thought, Thesis or Composition
Trinity College of Music	MMus (TCM) (1) (validated by Univ of Sussex); MA (Mus Educ) (1) (validated by Univ of Westminster)		Performance and Comp with practical projects
University of Ulster	PG Cert/Dip/MA (1:1) in 20th C mus.	*MPhil (2:4), *DPhil (3:5)	*Musicology, Comp, Perf
York University	MA (1) f/t or p/t, *MA/MSc (f/t or p/t)	MPhil (min 2 yrs f/t) #DPhil (min 3 yrs f/t)	*Mus Technology #Thesis or Composition, or Thesis and recital

Practical Courses	Details
Birmingham Conservatoire	Diploma in Professional Studies (1 or 2) for performers and composers which integrates advanced study and professional work
Guildhall School of Music & Drama	Certificate of Advanced Study (1 yr p/grad perf course), P/grad Dip in Musical Perf (1 yr), Dip in Continuing Professional Development (modular 1-2 yrs for prof musicians), Concert Recital Diploma, Adv Cert in jazz and studio music
Leeds College of Music	1 yr f/t (or 2 yrs p/t) p/grad cert in jazz, contemporary and popular music, for perfs, comps, arrangers etc. Many specialisms offered. P/grad theatre mus scheme in conjunction with W Yorks Playhouse
London College of Music and Media	P/g Dip and MMus in Perf (1:2), MMus in Composing for concert mus, Film and TV, New media and theatre (all 1 yr f/t)
National Opera Studio	1 yr course for post-diploma level singers and repetiteurs
Royal Academy of Music	1 or 2 yr p/grad perf course (can be extended); opera
Royal College of Music	1 or 2 yr p/grad diploma for perf, comps and conds; also in early mus.
Royal Northern College of Music	1 or 2 yr p/grad diploma course for advanced students in all practical disciplines, and composers (in affiliation with the Univ of Manchester). Perf with supervised dissertation
Royal Scottish Academy of Music and Drama	1 yr (2 yrs p/t) course in perf, comp, conducting. 1 yr course in opera and advanced opera
Trinity College of Music	1 yr p/grad perf course; also special course for accompanists
Welsh College of Music and Drama	MA in Performance (1:2): p/grad advanced course for perf. Practical & vocational with integral academic studies. Advanced Diploma course (1:2)

Scholarships at Universities and Music Colleges

This section lists scholarships awarded by universities and music colleges which are tenable only at the awarding institutions. Refer to the relevant entries in **Universities** and **Conservatoires** for addresses and **Scholarships and Grants for Study and Research** for additional awards.

Aberystwyth, University of Wales

Music Bursaries. 4 or more awarded to orch instrumentalists; £400 pa; 3 yrs. Open to u/grads and p/grads in any discipline. Closing date 20 May.

Bangor, University of Wales

Choral Scholarships (3). Competitive u/grad or p/grad entrance awards; renewable throughout university career. Offered in conjunction with Bangor Cathedral; application forms from Registrar.

Drapers' Scholarships. £2000 towards p/grad fees.

Instrumental and Vocal Awards. For talented singers and players to finance additional individual tuition.

Organ Scholarships (2). Competitive p/grad or u/grad entrance awards; renewable throughout university career. Offered in conjunction with Bangor Cathedral; applications to Registrar by 30 Apr.

Birmingham University

Barber Postgraduate Scholarship in Music (1 or more). Award(s) for p/grad musical studies; total value £2000. Open to recommended Birmingham graduates.

Barber Undergraduate Scholarship in Music (1 or more). Award(s) made to best 2nd yr (occasionally 1st yr) mus students on basis of exam performance; for purchase of books, scores or recordings; total value £500.

Cunningham (G D) Postgraduate Scholarship in Music. P/grad study award; £200 pa; 1 yr. Open to recommended Birmingham graduates (for study towards a higher degree in mus at any approved centre) or other mus graduates (for study at Birmingham).

Goldsbrough (A) Prize. Award made to u/grad or p/grad student, preferably a performer showing excellence in baroque mus; £95.

Gregory (R) Prize. Award made to final year u/grad, preferably an organist, to assist towards a professional career; £50.

Hyperion Award and West Bequest. Amount and use at discretion of head of dept.

Bishop Grosseteste University College

Chapel Organ Scholarship.

Choral Scholarships (3). In conjunction with Lincoln Cathedral. Competitive entrance awards; open to f/t students; annual review.

Organ Scholarship (1). In conjunction with Lincoln Cathedral. Competitive entrance award; open to f/t students; annual review.

Bristol University

Choral Scholarships. Available at Bristol Cathedral.

Organ Scholarships. Award, tenable for 3 yrs at St Paul's Church, Clifton; awarded biennially. Award offered triennially at St Mary Redcliffe. Award offered triennially at Bristol Cathedral. Not restricted to members of the Church of England.

Cambridge University

Choral Exhibitions (approx 70). Competitive entrance awards (occasionally awarded to current u/grad student); £80 pa; 3 yrs.

Instrumental Awards (20-30). Competitive entrance awards (occasionally awarded to current u/grad student); £80 pa; 3 yrs.

Organ Scholarships (approx 30). Competitive entrance awards; £100 pa; 3 yrs.

Stewart (John) of Rannoch Scholarships in Sacred Music (9). Competitive u/grad awards; £300 pa; maximum 3 yrs.

Cardiff, University of Wales

A B Dally Prize. U/grad award: £200; to an outstanding student whose home is in Gwent.

Choral Scholarships. U/grad or p/grad award; in association with the Metropolitan Cathedral of St David, Cardiff. U/grad or p/grad award; £633; in association with Llandaff Cathedral.

David Evans Memorial Prizes. U/grad awards: total value £250; to meritorious students.

David Lloyd Scholarship. Two u/grad awards each of £175; one to a promising singer on first entry to the dept and one to an outstanding singer entering or finishing the final year of study.

Eleanor Amy Bowen Award. P/grad awards: £1000

403

awarded annually to an outstanding student pianist in the dept; preference may be given to a student who has registered for a taught p/grad MA scheme in performance studies.

Sir Geraint Evans Prize. U/grad award: £750; to an outstanding graduating singer who requires extra lessons.

John Morgan Lloyd Scholarship. U/grad award(s) to student(s) intending to make a career in the practice or teaching of mus.

Organ Scholarships. U/grad award: £750; in association with the Church of St Andrew and St Teilo. U/grad or p/grad award; in association with the Metropolitan Cathedral of St David, Cardiff.

Qualitex Prize. U/grad awards: £100; to a meritorious student.

Scholarships for String Players (3). U/grad award: £200; awarded to str players reading for a degree in mus.

Williams-Hughes Prize. U/grad award: £350; awarded to singers/pianists in alternate years for advanced study abroad.

The Chichester Institute of HE

Organ Scholarship. Award tenable jointly at the Institute Chapel and Chichester Cathedral.

East Anglia University

Choral Scholarships (max 6). Competitive u/grad or p/grad entrance awards; £1500 pa plus concert, broadcasting and recording fees; normally 3 yrs. Choir at Norwich Cathedral; applications to Cathedral Organist and UEA by 31 Oct.

Organ Scholarship. Competitive u/grad entrance award (p/grad entrants may compete); £1200 pa plus concert, broadcasting and recording fees; normally 3 yrs. Applications preferably by 31 Oct; normally offered trienially (next awards 1998, 2001). Organ at Norwich Cathedral.

Performance Scholarships (max 25; inst or vocal). Competitive u/grad award (BA Hons students taking performance option in 2nd, 3rd yrs of study eligible); up to £600 pa; 12 months (renewable further 12 months).

Edinburgh University

Faculty Entrance Scholarship. U/grad entrance scholarship awarded annually, non instrumental.

Helen Doig Bursary. Award intended for study or research relevant to Scottish mus; £600-800 pa; 1 yr, renewable to maximum of 3 yrs. Closing date 1 May.

Mackey Piano Scholarship. U/grad entrance scholarship offered periodically (every 3-4 yrs).

Smart Organ Scholarship. U/grad entrance scholarship offered periodically (every 3-4 years).

Sir Thomas Beecham Scholarship for Instrumentalists. U/grad entrance scholarship offered annually.

Glasgow University

Choral/Organ Scholarships. Awards offered to appropriate students after admission (choral), at admission (org).

General Bursaries (approx 40). Competitive u/grad entrance awards; £100-500 pa. Bursaries allocated on the basis of performance in Higher Grades and A-levels. Awards made Sep, no exam.

Guildhall School of Music & Drama

Postgraduate Scholarships. Awards to p/grads made at the discretion of the Principal may cover fees and/or maintenance allowance. Applications only from those offered places.

Eastern Europe. Two scholarship schemes for students from Eastern European countries intended mainly for str players.

Huddersfield University

John Myatt Scholarships. For bassoon.

Organ Scholarships.

Sellars Engineering Scholarships. For br band instrumentalists.

Yamaha Scholarships. For acoustic and electro-acoustic mus.

Hull University

Beverley Minster Choral Scholarships. Competitive entrance scholarships (two available annually), £300 pa; 3 yrs.

Marchant Music Scholarship. Competitive entrance scholarship, £300 pa; 3 yrs.

Organ Scholarship. Competitive entrance scholarship (two overlapping scholarships are offered); £500 pa; 3 yrs. Next award available 1999.

Ouseley Choral Scholarship. Competitive entrance scholarship, £200 pa; 3 yrs. Next award available 1998.

Sir Thomas Beecham Music Scholarship. Competitive entrance scholarship, £250 pa; 3 yrs.

Keele University

Bach Choir Scholarship. Accompanist £300 pa; 1 yr.

Chapel Music Scholarships. Choir conductor £300 pa; 1 yr. Organist £300 pa; 1 yr.

Montford Scholarship. Instrumentalist or vocalist; £300 pa; 1 yr.

Orchestral Leader Scholarship. £300 pa.

Lancaster University

Dalton (Eualie More) String Scholarship (vn, va or vc). Competitive u/grad award (student entering 1st yr or current u/grad student); £150 pa; up to 3 yrs. Automatic application through UCAS form.

Music Appeal Instrumental Scholarship (no inst restriction). Competitive u/grad award (student entering 1st yr or current u/grad student); £100 pa; up to 3 yrs. Automatic application through UCAS form.

University of Leeds

With the exception of the Edward Boyle Organ and Choral scholarships and the Snowden Opera Award, scholarships are awarded at the beginning of the second year of studies on the basis of progress, commitment and potential shown at level 1.
Boyle (Edward) Choral Bursaries. U/grad award; £250 pa; up to 3 yrs; by competition in term 1. Male singers only eligible (2nd and 3rd yr students may also compete). Applicants should indicate interest at interview. Award offered in association with Leeds Parish Church.
Boyle (Edward) Instrumental Scholarship. Any inst or voice £250 pa; up to 2 yrs.
Boyle (Edward) Organ Scholarship. U/grad award; £300 pa; 3 yrs; usually by interview in Jan before entering university. Available every 2-3 yrs. Applicants should indicate interest by letter to head of dept before Christmas. Award in association with Leeds Parish Church. *Brotherton (Charles) Trust Award.* U/grad award; p/grad discretionary.
Gaunt (Luther and Ernest) Instrumental Scholarships (strs or pno). U/grad award; £250 pa; up to 2 yrs.
Leigh (Blanche L) Instrumental Scholarship (strs or pno). U/grad award; £250 pa; 3 yrs.
Mills (Catherine). U/grad, p/grad £250 pa; inst/vocal. Annual.
Silversides (Alison Christine). U/grad award £250 pa; inst or vocal; 1 yr.
Snowden Award for Opera Studies. P/grad award; £250; 1 yr. Award made at discretion, on arrival, to student on MMus (Opera Studies) course.
Snowden Travel Bursaries. U/grad or p/grad, awarded annually to registered students on submission of a travel project.
Tebb (Robert) Instrumental Scholarship (any inst or voice). £250 pa; up to 2 yrs.
Toothill (Frank). U/grad award, £250 pa; inst or vocal; 1 yr.

Manchester University

Knowles (Margaret Ann) Music Scholarship. U/grad entrance award; £200 pa; 3 yrs. Award offered triennially to candidates who have been resident (or whose parents have been resident) in Cheshire, Staffs, Derbys, Notts, Lincs or further north for the last 3 yrs. May be extended for further yr for advanced study after graduation.
McMyn Scholarship (3). U/grad entrance award; £250 pa; 3 yrs. Awards for str players to study with Lindsay String Quartet.
Procter-Gregg Music Awards. U/grad or p/grad awards; up to £150 (total value of awards £750);

for travel or composition and performance study outside the university, or for composition and performance study within the university involving visits by eminent teachers or composers.

Nottingham University

Barber Organ Scholarship. Competitive award (current u/grad or p/grad mus student, or entrance award); £500 pa; 1 yr (renewable). Scholarship trials Oct.
U/grad Scholarships. 5 scholarships for voice or any inst (current u/grad mus student or entrance award); £500 pa; 1 yr (renewable). Scholarship trials Oct.

Oxford University

Awards may be made by individual colleges to u/grad students on the basis of academic attainment. Several colleges also offer senior scholarships and/or junior research fellowships in arts subjects. Most colleges offer support for inst or vocal lessons to qualified u/grad students. There are also mus dept subsidies available for p/grads to speak at conferences.
Choral Awards (about 20 pa). For all voices at many colleges.
Halstead and Osgood Travelling Scholarship. Awarded to p/grad students already in residence working towards a higher degree.
Instrumental Awards. Several colleges offer these to current u/grads.
Organ Awards (about 20 pa). Competitive entrance awards; average £200 pa; 3 yrs.
Conway Fund. For performance studies for current u/grad and p/grad students.

Roehampton Institute London

Director of Chapel Music. Awarded annually at Digby Stuart and Whitelands Colleges.
Organ Scholarships. £350 and capital fund for mus; awarded annually at Southlands College.

Royal College of Music

Foundation Scholarships (up to 40). Awards to u/grad, p/grad course entrants and current students; £300 pa; tenable throughout course. Some special awards, value up to full fees plus maintenance, may also be offered on merit (usually for p/grad study).

Royal Holloway and Bedford New College

Choral Scholarships (several). Competitive awards (priority to u/grad entrance candidates; others then considered); £200 pa; 1 yr (renewable). Exam held Jan.
Instrumental Scholarships and Exhibitions. 3-5 competitive awards (priority to u/grad entrance candidates; others then considered). £350 pa

(scholarships), £100 pa (exhibitions); 1 yr (renewable).

Organ Scholarships (several). Competitive awards (priority to u/grad entrance candidates; others then considered); £200 pa; 1 yr (renewable). Exam held Jan.

Royal Northern College of Music

Ida Carroll Research Fellowship. Candidates should have first degree and research experience; 1 offered every 2-3 years; awarded for research/composition, some teaching normally required; £8000.

Royal Scottish Academy of Music and Drama

Adams (Mary D) Scholarship for Singing. Entrance award (made on merit, on basis of entrance audition); £300 pa; 3 yrs.

Associated Board Scholarship. Entrance award (made on merit, on basis of entrance audition); £300 pa; 4 yrs. Candidates must have ABRSM gr 8 distinction (practical), gr 6, 7 or 8 (theory).

Boden (Ernest) Scholarship for Piano. Entrance award (made on merit, on basis of entrance audition); £200 pa; 3 yrs.

Fraser (Steven) Harp Scholarship. Entrance award (made on basis of entrance audition); £250 pa; 3 yrs.

Macfarlane Scholarship for Wind Instruments. Entrance award (made on merit, on basis of entrance audition); £250 pa; 3yrs.

MacLean (Elizabeth) Scholarship for Violin. Entrance award (made on merit, on basis of entrance audition); £250 pa; 3 yrs.

Miller (Peter Lindsay) Scholarship for Piano. Entrance award (made on merit, on basis of entrance audition); £500 pa; 1 yr.

Mooney (Peter) Scholarship for Singing. Entrance award (made on merit, on basis of entrance audition); £150 pa; 1 yr.

Stevenson Scholarships. Entrance awards (made on merit, on basis of entrance audition); £500 pa; 1 yr.

University of Salford

Elgar House Shield for Composition. Awarded annually following internal nomination and assessment.

Harry Mortimer Award for Performance. Competitive annual award for br players.

Sir Malcolm Arnold Prize for Performance. Competitive annual award for players of tr, cornet or flugel hn.

Riyadh Composition Prize. Awarded annually for best composition for wind band.

Roy Newsom Prize for Conducting. Competitive annual award for br band conducting.

Sheffield University

Beecham (Sir Thomas) Scholarship. Awarded annually to a 1st yr student; £250 pa; 3 yrs.

Coward (Sir Henry) Organ Scholarship. Competitive u/grad entrance award; £600 pa; 1 yr.

University of Surrey

Choral and Organ Scholarships. Offered in conjunction with Guildford Cathedral.

Prizes. Students can compete annually for prizes in composition, dissertation, performance, musicology and sound recording.

Sussex University

Choral Scholarships (3). All students (current u/grad, p/grad or new entrant) eligible; £100 pa; 1 yr (renewable).

Organ Scholarship. All students (current u/grad, p/grad and new entrants) eligible; £200 pa; 1 yr (renewable).

Trinity College of Music

U/grad and P/grad Scholarships. Offered on strength of normal entrance audition; tenable throughout course, subject to annual review.

Ulster University

Clarke (Heather) Scholarship. Award to final yr BMus student intending to further musical career; approx £400. Applications by 31 Mar.

University of Warwick

Choral, Instrumental, Keyboard and Organ. Open to all 1st yr u/grad candidates. Auditions held in Mar prior to Oct admission. Applications by 10 Feb; £300 and £30 lessons subsidy pa.

Welsh College of Music and Drama

Choral Scholarships. Awards for p/grad and u/grad study offered on basis of entrance auditions, in association with Llandaff Cathedral.

Entrance Scholarships. Occasionally available as a result of audition.

General Scholarships from the Sir Geraint Evans Scholarship Fund. Contribution to course fees for p/grad students.

Organ Scholarships. Awards for p/grad and u/grad study made on basis of entrance auditions in association with Llandaff Cathedral.

Other Awards. Occasional scholarships, £100-200 pa; offered through commercial sponsorships. Awards available from college trust funds in cases of financial difficulty; applications considered on merit.

York University

Vinson Award. U/grad or p/grad award (usually for entrance, sometimes to current student) offered at discretion of awarding body to candidate who is ineligible for conventional grant; approx £3000; 1 yr.

York Minster Choral Scholarship. Competitive awards (male entrance candidates and current students eligible); £868 pa; tenable throughout university career. Applications to Philip Moore, Church House, Ogleforth, York.

York Minster Organ Scholarship. Competitive u/grad or p/grad entrance award; £1254 pa; 1 yr (extendable to 3 yrs). Applications to Philip Moore, Church House, Ogleforth, York.

Nonhabel Scholarship. P/grad award. 1 yr renewable, approx £3000.

Scholarships and Grants

The Department for Education publishes leaflets on state scholarships. The Musicians Benevolent Fund publishes annually the *Handbook of Music Awards and Scholarships*; it is available each September from 16 Ogle St, London W1P 7JB *Tel:* 0171 636 4481.

The *Directory of Grant-Making Trusts* is published by CAF (Charities Aid Foundation) and is available from Biblios Publishers' Distribution Services Ltd, Star Rd, Partridge Green, W Sussex RH13 8LD *Tel:* 01403 71085. The *Grants Register* is published by Macmillan and is available from Macmillan Reference Ltd, 25 Eccleston Pl, London SW1W 9NF *Tel:* 0171 881 8027. Scholarships tenable at UK universities by UK and/or other commonwealth graduates are contained in *Awards for Postgraduate Study at Commonwealth Universities 1997-99* which is available from Publications Sales, Association of Commonwealth Universities, 36 Gordon Sq, London WC1H 0PF *Tel:* 0171 387 8572. This list excludes awards restricted to a single teaching institution or performing company, but a list of internal scholarships offered by universities and conservatoires can be found under Scholarships at Universities and Music Colleges.

This list *exludes* awards restricted to a single teaching institution or performing company, but a list of internal scholarships offered by universities and conservatoires can be found under **Scholarships at Universities and Music Colleges.**

A K Holland Award
c/o Rushworths Music of Liverpool Ltd, 42-46 Whitechapel, Liverpool L1 6EF
Tel: 0151 709 9071 *Fax:* 0151 709 9073

W D C Rushworth, sec.
Small awards for choral societies and solo singers living within a 60-mile radius of Liverpool.

Alfreda Hodgson Bursary/Raymond Fox Bursary
c/o NFMS, Francis House, Francis St, London SW1P 1DE
Tel: 0171 828 7320 *Fax:* 0171 828 5504

Kate Fearnley, award admin.
Award of £750 in alternate years for singers and instrumentalists respectively as part of the NFMS Award for Young Concert Artists. Applications are invited from European Community citizens aged 21-30 (singers) or 21-27 (instrumentalists) who are at the beginning of their professional careers in mus and normally resident in the UK. Application forms available early Jan. Annual auditions in spring.

Allcard Grants
The Worshipful Company of Musicians, Allcard Grants, 74-75 Watling St, London EC4M 9BJ
Tel: 0171 489 8888 *Fax:* 0171 489 1614

Singers, str players, pno accompanists and (in exceptional circumstances) wind players; for three p/grad scholarships of £3000 for an advanced course of performance study within the EU. Applications only through the heads of conservatoires or University music depts.

Nominations by 30 Apr, final selection by audition and interview in May/June.

Anna Instone Memorial Award
Capital Radio, 30 Leicester Sq, London WC2H 7LA

Kevin Appleby, admin.
Award of £5000 for a p/grad aged 26 and under studying at a London mus college. Candidates must be nominated by the principal; applications through nominators only by 1 Mar.

Sir Arthur Bliss Memorial Scholarship
The Secretariat, Royal College of Music, Prince Consort Rd, London SW7 2BS
Tel: 0171 589 3643 *Fax:* 0171 589 7740

1-yr p/grad scholarship, tenable at the RCM in alternate years (next award Sep 1999). Open competition for composers of any age (usually under 25) and of all nationalities after acceptance at RCM. Applications by 1 Oct. Application fee £40. Award of £1000.

Australian Music Foundation in London
c/o Richards Butler, Beaufort House, 15 St Botolph St, London EC3A 7EE
Tel: 0171 247 6555 *Fax:* 0171 247 5091
Email: jfe@richardsbutler.com

John F Emmott, hon sec.
Major award for Australian singers and instrumentalists of p/grad or equivalent standard for advanced course of study in Europe. Max age 30 on 31 Dec prior to application in Apr.

Awards for Advanced Study in Music
Arts Council of Wales, Music Dept, 9 Museum Pl,
Cardiff CF1 3NX
Tel: 01222 394711 *Fax:* 01222 221447

Lyn Davies, snr mus offr.
Awards have been made to musicians under 28,
born and educated in Wales; also open to those
now permanently resident in Wales and normally
having lived in Wales for 2 yrs. Applications by 1
Feb annually. Award of c£2000.

Benslow Musical Instrument Loan Scheme
Little Benslow Hills, off Benslow La, Hitchin, Herts SG4 9RB
Tel: 01462 420748 *Fax:* 01462 440171

Jenny Dann, sec; Sara Hewitt, mkt sec.
Applicants must be in f/t education.

Bob Harding Bursary
c/o 152 West St, Havant PO9 1LP
Tel: 01705 483228

Peter Craddock, mus dir.
Opportunity for young conductor to assist in and
observe rehearsals and concerts of the Havant
Symphony Orchestra throughout a season. Must
be under 30, on an advanced conducting course
and resident in UK. Travel and subsistence grant
up to £350. Selection by audition; open to
candidates nominated by London mus colleges.
Applications by Jun annually.

Boise Foundation Scholarship
c/o Royal Academy of Music, Marylebone Rd,
London NW1 5HT

Jean Shannon, hon sec.
Biennial award worth £5000 (next 1999) for
performers aged 30 and under who are resident
in the UK or Ireland. Applicants must be
nominated by heads of mus colleges, etc.
Application fee £10. Details available Nov 1998.
Auditions Apr 1999, applications by Mar.
Enquiries in writing only.

Catherine and Lady Grace James Foundation
9 Market St, Aberystwyth SY23 1DL
Tel: 01970 612806

Richard Morgan, exec sec.
For Welsh students requiring support for
approved courses, excluding private study.
Applications by 31 Jul annually.

Professor Charles Leggett Awards for Young Wind and Brass Players
c/o Musicians Benevolent Fund, 16 Ogle St, London W1P 8JB
Tel: 0171 636 4481 *Fax:* 0171 637 4307

Annual awards of £4000 for wind and br players
aged 18-24. In 1998 the awards will be for cl and

tb. Applications from Oct for auditions in Jan.
Application fee £10.

Craxton Memorial Trust
50 Hatherleigh Rd, Ruislip, Middx HA4 6AU

Jane Craxton, admin.
Biennial awards worth £250-700 for outstanding
young pianists and instrumentalists (excluding
org, perc and hpd) beginning their career. Max
age 26. Send sae for application form. Application
fee £5. Auditions Apr/May 1999, applications by
31 Jan 1999.

Donald Tovey Memorial Prize
Board of the Faculty of Music, University Offices,
Wellington Sq, Oxford OX1 2JD
Tel: 01865 270001 *Fax:* 01865 270708

J M J Maloney, sec, board of the faculty of mus.
Awarded irregularly for research in philosophy,
history or understanding of mus. May also be
awarded to assist publication of research already
completed. Awards normally for postdoctoral or
advanced work.

Emanuel Hurwitz Chamber Music Charitable Trust
44 Church Cres, London N3 1BJ

Miriam Keogh, founder and admin.
Bursaries for str players to further their studies
in chmbr mus (college/university fees will not be
paid). UK citizens only. Must apply in writing
with sae. Applications by 1 Jun.

Emily English Award
c/o Musicians Benevolent Fund, 16 Ogle St, London W1P 8JB
Tel: 0171 637 4481 *Fax:* 0171 637 4307

Award of £10,000 to assist young vn p/grad
students aged 24 and under. Applications open
Nov for auditions in Apr. Application fee £10.

English Speaking Union Music Scholarships
Cultural Affairs, The English-Speaking Union,
Dartmouth House, 37 Charles St, London W1X 8AB
Tel: 0171 493 3328 *Fax:* 0171 495 6108

Lucy Passmore.
The English-Speaking Union offers the following
mus scholarships to musicians of outstanding
ability to study at summer schools in the UK:
International Musicians Seminar (Cornwall);
Britten-Pears School for Advanced Musical Study
(Aldeburgh). Applications in Nov for placements
the following year.

Eric Thompson Trust
c/o The Royal Philharmonic Society, 10 Stratford Pl,
London W1N 9AE
Tel: 0171 491 8110 *Fax:* 0171 493 7463

Geraint Jones, chmn; Richard Fisher, clerk to the
trustees.

Modest cash awards given at the Trustees' discretion to help aspiring professional organists. No fixed age range, but younger applicants preferred. Applications in writing by 31 Dec annually.

ESTA Nannie Jamieson Nutshell Fund
6 Ember La, Esher, Surrey KT10 8ER
Tel: 0181 398 4691

Sylvia Palmer, hon sec.
European String Teachers Association, British Branch. Modest bursaries awarded annually for students and teachers of str insts (ESTA members) for help to attend w/shops, conferences and teaching courses. Applications by 1 May.

Francis Chagrin Fund
c/o SPNM, Francis House, Francis St, London SW1P 1DE
Tel: 0171 828 9696 *Fax:* 0171 931 9928
Email: spnm@spnm.org.uk

Peter Craik, admin.
Grants available towards cost of reproducing performance materials of unperformed works by British composers and composers resident in Britain of any age (pieces must have scheduled date for performance).

Gemini Fellowship
The Worshipful Company of Musicians, 74-75 Watling St, London EC4M 9BJ
Tel: 0171 489 8888 *Fax:* 0171 489 1614

S F N Waley, clerk.
2-yr fellowship awarded to composers who must write a major work during this time. The Company will arrange for a first performance of works meeting the required standard. Award £5000 annually.

Gillian Sinclair Music Trust
KPMG/Martin Musical Scholarship Fund, Lawn Cottage, 23a Brackley Rd, Beckenham, Kent BR3 1RB
Tel: 0181 658 9432

Martyn Jones, admin.
Offers annual sponsored recitals at the Wigmore Hall to Martin Musical Scholarship Fund recipients.

Grace Williams Memorial Award
Arts Council of Wales, 9 Museum Pl, Cardiff CF1 3NX
Tel: 01222 394711 *Fax:* 01222 221447

Lyn Davies, snr mus offr.
Awards for advanced study to musicians aged 14-30 born and educated in Wales. Annual closing date 1 Feb.

Graucob Music Awards
34 Chiltern Dr, Hale, Altrincham, Cheshire WA15 9PN
Tel: 0161 941 1522

Sharon Martin, admin.
10 annual awards of up to £750 each. Open to young musicians with gr 8+, aged 19 and under on 1 May and living in Greater Manchester, W Yorks, Lancs and Cheshire LEAs. Applications by 1 Mar.

Guilhermina Suggia Gift for the Cello
c/o Musicians Benevolent Fund, 16 Ogle St, London W1P 8JB
Tel: 0171 636 4481 *Fax:* 0171 637 4307

Biennial award of £2000 to assist exceptionally talented vc students aged 21 and under. Next award Apr 1998. Application fee £10.

H A Thew Fund
c/o Rushworths of Liverpool Ltd, Whitechapel, Liverpool L1 6EF
Tel: 0151 709 9071 *Fax:* 0151 709 9073

W D C Rushworth, sec.
Small awards made to mus students and organisations in Merseyside. Must be based within 60-mile radius of Liverpool.

H J C Stevens Organ Scholarship
St Bride's Church, Fleet St, London EC4Y 8AU
Tel: 0171 353 1301 *Fax:* 0171 583 4867

Canon John Oates, rector; Robert Jones, mus dir.
Award to 2nd or 3rd yr org student at London mus college or university; p/grad student applications also considered.

Harriet Cohen Memorial Music Awards Trust
Manches & Co, Aldwych House, 81 Aldwych, London WC2
Tel: 0171 404 4433 *Fax:* 0171 430 1133

John Rubinstein, admin trustee.
Discretionary annual awards to max £1500 made to British performers, composers, academics or singers of outstanding excellence and promise. Open to those aged 18-30. No individual applications will be considered; candidates will be nominated by main mus institutions upon invitation only and will be auditioned and interviewed.

Hattori Foundation For Young Musicians
72e Leopold Rd, London SW19 7JQ
Tel: 0181 944 5319 *Fax:* 0181 946 6970

Kim Gaynor, admin.
Awards up to £7000. Aims to assist exceptionally talented insts (aged 15-20 and 21-27) to pursue a solo career. Also awards to ens of average age under 27. Awards are not for tuition fees in f/t study courses. Open to UK residents and foreign nationals studying in the UK subject to certain conditions. Applications by 1 May 1998 for snrs and at any time for jnrs.

Sir Henry Richardson Award
c/o Musicians Benevolent Fund, 16 Ogle St, London W1P 8JB
Tel: 0171 636 4481 *Fax:* 0171 637 4307

Annual award of £6000 available alternately to accompanists and repetiteurs aged under 30 (repetiteurs in 1998). Applications from Jan for auditions in May. Application fee £10.

Hinrichsen Foundation
10-12 Baches St, London N1 6DN

Lesley Adamson, admin.
Awards only in the areas of contemporary composition and its performance and musicological research. Costs of degree and study courses, recordings and the purchase of insts and equipment excluded. Preference shown to UK applicants. Applications by 1 Jan, 1 Apr, 1 Jun, 1 Oct (subject to change).

Holst Foundation
43 Alderbrook Rd, London SW12 8AD
Tel: 0181 673 4215 *Fax:* 0171 228 2358

Funds available to applicants of any age, primarily for the performance of contemporary mus.

Ian Fleming Music Education Awards
c/o Musicians Benevolent Fund, 16 Ogle St, London W1P 8JB
Tel: 0171 636 4481 *Fax:* 0171 637 4307

Awards for mus education and help with inst purchase to outstanding young musicians beginning a career. Aged 26 and under (insts), 30 and under (singers). Applications from Nov-Mar for auditions in Apr. Application fee £10.

Ida Carroll Research Fellowship
Royal Northern College of Music, 124 Oxford Rd, Manchester M13 9RD
Tel: 0161 907 5200 *Fax:* 0161 273 7611
Email: info@rncm.ac.uk
Website: www.rncm.ac.uk

Colin Beeson, dir of development.
1-yr award worth £8000 for research at doctoral or post-doctoral level, tenable at the RNCM.

Sir James Caird's Travelling Scholarships Trust
Thorntons Solicitors, 50 Castle St, Dundee DD1 3RV
Tel: 01382 229111 *Fax:* 01382 202288

A F McDonald, admin and sec.
Grants and scholarships of up to £3500 available to Scottish p/grad students. Scholarships are tenable for 1 yr but may be renewed for up to 2 further yrs. Wiseman Prize (£600) for best performance and Joseph Bloch LRAM Prize (£200) for best str player. Auditions in Mar or Apr in London and Glasgow, applications by 31 Jan.

John Tunnell Trust
4 Royal Terrace, Edinburgh EH7 5AB
Tel: 0131 556 4043 *Fax:* 0131 556 3969

Jonathan Tunnell, chmn.
Awards in form of paid engagements in conjunction with Scottish mus societies to young professional inst chmbr ens (max 8 players). Preference given to British-based groups aged up to 27. Application forms supported by tapes. Applications by Jun 1998 for following season.

June Allison Award
KPMG/Martin Musical Scholarship Fund, Lawn Cottage, 23a Brackley Rd, Beckenham, Kent BR3 1RB
Tel: 0181 658 9432

Martyn Jones, admin.
Offered annually for outstanding w/wind performers. Award also includes recital in 'La Dolce Musica Series.' Applications by 1 Dec for award the following year; auditions in Jan. Send sae for application form.

KPMG/Martin Musical Scholarship Fund
Lawn Cottage, 23a Brackley Rd, Beckenham, Kent BR3 1RB
Tel: 0181 658 9432 *also fax*

Martyn Jones, admin.
Annual awards for instrumentalists aged 25 and under, mainly of p/grad standard, to finance tuition fees and maintenance. Preference to UK citizens. Applications by 1 Dec. Auditions Jan. Application fee £10.

L D F Casbolt Memorial Award
KPMG/Martin Musical Scholarship Fund, Lawn Cottage, 23a Brackley Rd, Beckenham, Kent BR3 1RB
Tel: 0181 658 9432

Martyn Jones, admin.
Offered annually for an outstanding violinist. Applications by 1 Dec for award the following year; auditions in Jan. Send sae for application form.

Loan Fund for Musical Instruments
16 Ogle St, London W1P 8JB
Tel: 0171 436 4816 *Fax:* 0171 637 4307

Marjorie Dickinson, sec.
Low-interest loans to talented young professional musicians towards the purchase of fine insts.

London Arts Board/NFMS Special Activities Fund
c/o NFMS, Francis House, Francis St, London SW1P 1DE
Tel: 0171 828 7320 *Fax:* 0171 828 5504
Email: postmaster@nfms.demon.co.uk

Robin Osterley, chief exec.
Funding of up to £30,000 available to choral societies, chmbr choirs, amateur orchs, concert promoters (including steel bands and non-western

411

mus) to help them commission professional composers, engage professional soloists and hire venues. Applications by Mar 1998.

Maisie Lewis Young Artists Fund
Musicians' Company Concerts, 6 Pembridge Cres, London W11 3DT
Tel: 0171 229 2610 *also fax*

Jan Lowy, admin.
Assists young artists of British residency aged 30 and under to gain experience on the concert platform. Application forms available from 1 May for completion by 31 July.

Manoug Parikian Award
c/o Musicians Benevolent Fund, 16 Ogle St, London W1P 8JB
Tel: 0171 636 4881 *Fax:* 0171 637 4307

Award of £3500 to assist young vn students aged 21 and under of any nationality. Applications from Nov-mid Feb for auditions in Apr. Application fee £10.

The Mario Lanza Educational Foundation
1 Kenton Gardens, Minster, Ramsgate, Kent CT12 4EN

Wendy Stilwell, sec.
Various awards for students who are engaged in a f/t course of classical singing at a college or conservatoire.

Mendelssohn Scholarship Foundation
c/o Royal Academy of Music, Marylebone Rd, London NW1 5HT

Jean Shannon, hon sec.
Award min £5000 for composers aged 30 and under, of any nationality but resident in the UK or Republic of Ireland. Application fee £10. Details available Nov 1999. Applications by Mar 2000. Enquiries in writing only.

Michael Tippett Musical Foundation
1 Dean Farrar St, London SW1H 0DY

Gwyn Rhydderch, sec.
Individual study or research costs are not funded. Leaflet available giving guidelines on performance and education project policy.

Miriam Licette Scholarship
c/o Musicians Benevolent Fund, 16 Ogle St, London W1P 8JB
Tel: 0171 636 4481 *Fax:* 0171 637 4307

Biennial award of £5000 to assist a female student (aged 18-30) of French Song. Next award Apr 1998. Application fee £10.

Muriel Taylor Scholarship
The Warehouse, 13 Theed St, London SE1 8ST
Tel: 0171 928 9251 *Fax:* 0171 928 9252

Kate Beresford, sec.
£2000 awarded annually to cellist aged 17-23 for advanced study. Send sae for further details. Application fee £15.

Music Sound Foundation
c/o 4 Tenterden St, Hanover Sq, London W1A 2AY
Tel: 0171 355 4848

Janie Orr, admin.
Charitable trust aiming to provide funds for the education of the public, and young people in particular, in all aspects of mus.

Myra Hess Trust
c/o Musicians Benevolent Fund, 16 Ogle St, London W1P 8JB
Tel: 0171 636 4481 *Fax:* 0171 637 4307

Limited number of awards towards fees, cost of inst or recital debut for outstanding young instrumentalists aged 18-30 beginning a performing career. Awards not open to org, hp, hpd, jazz gui, br, perc, and pno acc. Applications open from Sep-Apr for auditions in Jan-Jun. Application fee £10.

Peter Whittingham Trust
c/o Musicians Benevolent Fund, 16 Ogle St, London W1P 8JB
Tel: 0171 636 4481 *Fax:* 0171 637 4307

Annual award of £5000 open to individuals for projects in popular mus or jazz. Applications for course fees not accepted. Applications from Jul-Aug, interviews Nov.

Pocklington Apprenticeship Trust
Town Clerk and Chief Executive, RB of Kensington and Chelsea, Town Hall, Hornton St, London W8 7NX
Tel: 0171 361 2239 *Fax:* 0171 361 2764

Julia Carroll, admin offr.
Small educational awards for young people aged 21 and under in financial need, born and/or living in the Royal Borough for 10 yrs. Max grant awarded £300.

PRS/NFMS Awards for Enterprise
Francis House, Francis St, London SW1P 1DE
Tel: 0171 828 7320 *Fax:* 0171 828 5504
Email: postmaster@nfms.demon.co.uk

Robin Osterley, chief exec.
Awards made Jul for voluntary mus societies, choirs and orchs that show enterprise in concert programming. Application forms available in Jan. Applications by 31 Mar.

Sir Richard Stapley Educational Trust
PO Box 57, Tonbridge, Kent TN9 1ZT

Small grants worth £250-1000 for graduates aged over 24 on 1 Oct of the proposed academic year with a first or upper second degree studying for higher degrees at a university in the UK, or courses considered to be equivalent to a higher degree by the university or conservatoire, and who are not in receipt of local authority, research council, British Academy or other similar public bodies awards. Send sae for application form. Applications by 31 Mar, with two academic references in sealed envelopes.

Royal College of Organists
7 St Andrew St, Holborn, London EC4A 3LQ
Tel: 0171 936 3606 *Fax:* 0171 353 8244

Alan Dear, snr exec.
A number of trusts available to organists who are members of the College (non-members considered in exceptional circumstances). Applications by 30 Apr 1998.

RVW Trust
7th Floor, Manfield House, 1 Southampton St, London WC2 0LR
Tel: 0171 379 6547 *Fax:* 0171 240 6333

Bernard Benoliel, admin and sec.
Founder, Ralph Vaughan Williams. Corporate Trustee, Musicians' Benevolent Fund. Assists with the cost of first Master's Degrees in mus composition (non electro-acoustic) for British applicants or those of British residency. Does not consider applications towards cost of other degrees, summer courses or PhDs. Applications by mid-May.

Ryan Davies Memorial Awards
1 Squire Ct, The Marina, Swansea SA1 3XB
Tel: 01792 301500 *also fax*

Michael Evans, sec.
Awards worth £500-2000 to assist young Welsh performers aged 16-30 in mus and drama. Applications by 30 May.

Sascha Lasserson Memorial Trust
5 Cook Ct, 151A Rotherhithe St, London SE16 1QT

Ann Fischer, hon sec.
Grants for study purposes for violinists aged 18 and under, resident in UK.

Schools Music Association Founder's Fund
71 Margaret Rd, New Barnet, Herts EN4 9NT
Fax: 0181 440 6919

Maxwell Pryce, hon sec.
Small awards made to help with purchase costs of mus insts and summer schools available to British school pupils and students aged 18 and under in further and higher education.

Scottish Arts Council Travel and Training Bursaries
Performing Arts Dept (Music), 12 Manor Pl, Edinburgh EH3 7DD
Tel: 0131 226 6051 *Fax:* 0131 225 9833
Email: helen.jamieson.sac@artsfb.org.uk

Helen Jamieson, mus offr.
Bursaries of up to £1500 for instrumentalists, singers, composers and conductors to extend skills (f/t study excluded). Applicants of any age must be based in Scotland and have worked in the profession for 2 yrs. Applications by Feb. Full details and application forms from the mus offr.

Scottish International Education Trust
22 Manor Pl, Edinburgh EH3 7DS
Tel: 0131 225 1113 *also fax*

J F McClellan, dir.
Grants to promote individual Scottish talent or for projects contributing to the quality of life in Scotland. Applications in writing to above address.

Shell LSO Music Scholarship
London Symphony Orchestra, Barbican Centre, Barbican, London EC2Y 8DS
Tel: 0171 272 4032 *Fax:* 0171 263 1831
Email: shell@lso.co.uk
Website: www.lso.co.uk

Helen Smith, admin.
Annual competition with a first prize of £6000 for orch instrumentalists aged 14-22. Auditions, w/shops and m/classes with LSO principals. 1999 (br). Applications by Dec.

South East Music Schemes
19 Bourne Rd, London N8 9HJ
Tel: 0181 340 4116

Deborah Rees, admin dir.
Awards of up to £1000 for p/grad singers, instrumentalists and composers based in the SE Arts region, who may not receive mandatory awards towards further study in the UK or abroad. Age limit 30. Applications by 22 May 1998, send sae for application form from Mar 1998. Funded by South East Arts. Application fee £15.

Stephen Arlen Memorial Fund
London Coliseum, St Martin's La, London WC2N 4ES
Tel: 0171 836 0111 ext 355 *Fax:* 0171 240 7730

Teresa Howell, exec asst to dir of business and admin.
Annual award of £3000 (may be split) to a UK resident aged 18-30, following a career in opera, mus, dance or drama for a specific project. This is specifically not intended for the funding of

study or education of any kind. Next award autumn 1998, applications by end of Feb.

Sybil Tutton Awards
c/o Musicians Benevolent Fund, 16 Ogle St, London W1P 8JB
Tel: 0171 636 4481 *Fax:* 0171 637 4307

Awards to assist exceptionally talented opera students aged 18-30 with the cost of training on a recognised course. Applications from Nov-Apr for auditions in spring. Application fee £10.

Sydney Perry Foundation Award
KPMG/Martin Musical Scholarship Fund, Lawn Cottage, 23a Brackley Rd, Beckenham, Kent BR3 1RB
Tel: 0181 658 9432 *also fax*

Martyn Jones, admin.
Specifically for p/grad study. Two scholarships awarded annually. Applications by 1 Dec for award the following year; auditions in Jan. Send sae for application form.

Tait Memorial Trust
4/80 Elm Park Gardens, London SW10 9PD
Tel: 0171 351 0561 *Fax:* 0171 349 0531

Isla Baring, chmn.
Bi-annual, May-Jun and Nov-Dec. Awards to provide training and performance opportunities and generally to help further the careers of young professional Australian musicians in the UK. Age limit 30. Apply with CV, two references and project budget. Please send sae and tape if possible.

Thalben-Ball Memorial Awards
St Michael's Vestry, Cornhill, London EC3V 9DS
Tel: 01737 244604 *also fax;* 0171 626 8841

Jonathan Rennert, trustee and hon sec.
Annual funds ranging from £100-2000 for young organists and church musicians of any nationality studying in the UK. Age limit usually 26. Applications by 1 Apr annually. Also funds available for annual scholarship for Assistant Organist at St Michael's Church, Cornhill, City of London.

Sir Thomas Beecham Trust
15 North Pallant, Chichester, W Sussex PO19 1TQ
Tel: 01243 789855

Lady Beecham, trustee.
Scholarships, tenable for 3 yrs, established in partnership with certain universities. Available to 1st year students studying for a mus degree and nominated by the university.

Sir Thomas White's Educational Foundation
General Charities City of Coventry, Old Bablake, Hill St, Coventry CV1 4AN
Tel: 01203 222769 *also fax*

Mus scholarship, tenable in a higher education institution approved by Trustees. For students with local connections only. Advertised annually in local press.

Tillett Trust
Courtyard House, Neopardy, Crediton, Devon EX17 5EP

Katie Avey, admin.
Limited financial assistance to young professional musicians, usually aged under 30, of exceptional talent, to further their performing careers. British or residing f/t in British Isles. No application forms available but write giving full CV, references and details of budget for project. Funds not available for the purchase of insts, for normal u/grad or p/grad courses, or for funding commissions.

Trevor Snoad Award
KPMG/Martin Musical Scholarship Fund, Lawn Cottage, 23a Brackley Road, Beckenham, Kent BR3 1RB
Tel: 0181 658 9432 *also fax*

Martyn Jones, admin.
Open to outstanding va player aged 25 and under of p/grad standard. Preference given to UK citizens. Award of £500 pays for tuition fees and/or maintenance. Auditions held in London. Application forms available early summer. Applications by 1 Dec annually. Auditions Jan. Application fee £10, sent with sae.

W T Best Memorial Scholarship
Worshipful Company of Musicians, 74-75 Watling Street, London EC4M 9BJ
Tel: 0171 489 8888 *Fax:* 0171 489 1614

S F N Waley, clerk.
Provides financial assistance (£3000 a year) to an org scholar showing exceptional promise for a maximum of 3 yrs. Nominations from certain professors or principals of mus colleges. Applications through nominators only.

William Cox Memorial Fund for Young Singers
Badger Bungalow, 41 Findon Av, Witton Gilbert, Durham DH7 6RF

Antony Elton, hon admin.
Grants to help very talented advanced students of professional solo singing to purchase scores, etc. For age 19-29 inclusive. Trustees meet late Mar, mid Jun and late Sep/early Oct. Enquiries and applications by post only; those not sending sae will be ignored.

William Rushworth Memorial Trust

c/o Rushworths of Liverpool Ltd, 42-46 Whitechapel, Liverpool L1 6EF
Tel: 0151 709 9071 *Fax:* 0151 709 9073

W D C Rushworth, sec.
For instrumentalists. Small awards for societies and individuals within 60-mile radius of Liverpool.

Wingate Scholarships

38 Curzon St, London W1Y 8EY

Jane Reid, admin.
Awards of up to £10,000 pa made to people undertaking original work in almost any field and to outstanding musicians for advanced training. Open to citizens of the UK, Commonwealth, Ireland or Israel resident in British Isles during period of application, and to EU citizens who have been resident in the UK for at least 5 years. All applicants should be aged 24 and over. Shortlisted candidates auditioned/interviewed in London during May and results announced in Jun 1998.

Yamaha Music Foundation of Europe

Yamaha-Kemble Music (UK) Ltd, Sherbourne Dr, Tilbrook, Milton Keynes MK7 8BL
Tel: 01908 366700 *Fax:* 01908 368872

Karen Watts.
3 annual scholarships of £2000 each. Disciplines rotate.

Young Concert Artists Trust

23 Garrick St, London WC2E 9AX
Tel: 0171 379 8477 *Fax:* 0171 379 8467

Rosemary Pickering, chief exec.
Charity created in 1984 to identify and promote outstanding young soloists and chmbr musicians emerging into the profession. Known as YCAT, it is the only agency of its kind. Preliminary auditions in Feb and Mar with semi-finals in Apr and final auditions on 27 May. Applications by 23 Jan. Insts and singers normally resident in UK and under age 28 (insts) and 32 (singers) on 1 Jan 1998. No grants available. Categories vary from year to year.

Young Musicians' Recording Trust

26 Cleveland Sq, London W2 6DD
Tel: 0171 262 9066 *Fax:* 0171 262 3235

Mark Sutton, admin.
Student recording scheme open to final year inst and singing students. Nominations from heads of mus colleges only.

Rose BRUFORD COLLEGE
A University Sector College
Principal: Robert Ely

Opera Studies (BA) Hons
by distance learning

A full-length degree course, that studies opera as music theatre. A unique chance to broaden your knowledge of opera from the earliest forms to the opera of today. Modular structure, study at home, plus annual residential school.

Music Technology (BA) Hons

A 3 year full-time course designed for musicians who wish to work with the latest technology to bring together composition, performance and recording as a single activity.

Degrees validated by University of Manchester

For full details contact: The Admissions Office, Rose Bruford College, Lamorbey Park, Sidcup, Kent, DA15 9DF, UK
Tel: 0181 300 3024 Fax: 0181 308 0542
Email: Admiss@bruford.ac.uk

Choral Scholarship Trials

St Martin-in-the-Fields appoints eight student Choral Scholars each academic year 1998/9.

The annual scholarship is a challenging and high-profile position providing experience in Consort Singing and drawing on the rich repertory of Church Music.

There is good financial reward (£1,200) reflecting the required commitment.

Further details from: Paul Stubbings
Master of the Music, St Martin-in-the-Fields,
Trafalgar Square
LONDON WC2N 4JJ
Tel: 0171-930 1538

St Martin-in-the-Fields is a charitable foundation No. 261359

CLASSICAL
music

The magazine the music professionals read

Classical Music focuses on the people who make concerts happen – venue managers, agents, publicists, composers, festival directors, marketing and public relations people, and, of course, musicians. And every fortnight we bring you some of the best jobs around – playing jobs, management jobs, teaching jobs and marketing jobs with recruitment ads from all areas of the music industry.

SUBSCRIPTION PRICES:
United Kingdom £56 (26 issues) Airmail Europe £70 (26 issues); Airmail outside Europe £75 (N & S America, Africa, Middle East and Hong Kong); £84 (Australia, New Zealand, Japan and Far East) Surface mail worldwide £62

To subscribe please send your cheque (in pounds Sterling made payable to *Rhinegold Publishing Ltd*) to:
**Rhinegold Publishing Ltd (CM SUBS),
FREEPOST, Gravesend, Kent DA12 2BR**

**Fortnightly
£2.95**

**CREDIT CARD SUBSCRIPTIONS
Tel: 01474 334500 (office hours) Fax: 01474 325557**

FOR A FREE SAMPLE COPY Telephone 0171 333 1720 during office hours

Specialist Courses

Alexander Technique Training Courses

The **Society of Teachers of the Alexander Technique** can provide a list of members who teach in the UK. The Society can be contacted at 20 London House, 266 Fulham Rd, London SW10 9EL *Tel:* 0171 351 0828 or via the training centres listed below.

Alexander Centre for Training
142 Thorpedale Rd, London N4 3BS
Tel: 0171 281 7639 *Fax:* 0171 281 9400

D Gorman, dir.
Courses: 3-yr f/t training as an Alexander teacher. *Status:* Private school. *Entry requirements:* Interview and lessons. *Fees:* £1900 per term (including VAT). *Places:* 2-4 pa, entry in Jan, May and Sep.

Brighton Alexander Training Centre
57 Beaconsfield Villas, Brighton, E Sussex BN1 6HB
Tel: 01273 501612 *Fax:* 01273 552002
Email: nicholls@pavilion.co.uk

J Nicholls, dir; C Nicholls, co-dir.
Courses: Individual lessons; some evenings for small groups. Also 3-yr teacher training programme. *Status:* Private school. *Entry requirements:* Personal experience of Alexander Technique, education to at least A-level, plus interview. *Fees:* £1150 per term. Very occasional LEA discretionary awards. *Places:* 20.

Bristol Alexander Technique Training School Ass.
37 Bellevue Cres, Cliftonwood, Bristol BS8 4TF
Tel: 0117 987 2989 *also fax*

Ali Burrows, head of training; Linda Jordan, asst.
Courses: 3-yr teacher training course. Also short courses for personal interest and private lessons. School address: Long Ashton Guide Headquarters, Long Ashton, Bristol. *Status:* Non-profit making association. *Entry requirements:* Some experience in Alexander Technique. *Fees:* £1000 per term. *Places:* Max 15 students, intake in Sep.

Centre for the Alexander Technique
46 Stevenage Rd, London SW6 6HA
Tel: 0171 731 6348

P Ribeaux, Mrs E Ribeaux, dirs. *Status:* Private school. *Entry requirements:* Good general education, some work experience. *Fees:* £1200 per term. *Places:* 12.

Constructive Teaching Centre
18 Lansdowne Rd, London W11 3LL
Tel: 0171 727 7222

W H M Carrington, D M G Carrington, dirs.

Courses: 3-yr teacher training course in Alexander Technique. *Status:* Private college. *Entry requirements:* A thorough course of individual lessons. *Fees:* £1410 per term. Discretionary grants may be available from local authorities. *Places:* 40.

Essex Alexander School
65 Norfolk Rd, Ilford, Essex IG3 8LJ
Tel: 0181 220 1630

K Thompson, dir.
Courses: 3-yr course with three 10-wk terms pa. *Status:* Private school (STAT approved). *Entry requirements:* Interview with director. *Fees:* £950 per term. No funding available. *Places:* 15.

Hampstead Alexander Centre
4 Marty's Yard, Hampstead High St, London NW3 1QW
Tel: 0171 435 4940 *Fax:* 0171 794 2652

R J Simmons, dir.
Courses: 3-yr teacher training, p/grad training and individual lessons.
Entry requirements: Adequate prior instruction in the technique with interview. *Places:* 10-11 trainees in total.

Headington Alexander Training School
10 York Rd, Headington, Oxford OX3 8NW
Tel: 01865 765511 *Fax:* 01865 454112
Email: stephen.cooperalextech@btinternet.com

Stephen Cooper, dir.
Courses: 3 yr STAT-recognised teacher training course; p/grad training courses.
Entry requirements: Interview with director and familiarity with the technique. *Fees:* £1100 per term. *Places:* 12.

North London Alexander Technique Teachers Training Centre
10 Elmcroft Av, London NW11 0RR
Tel: 0181 455 3938

M Magidov, dir.
Courses: 3-yr course. *Status:* Private school. *Entry requirements:* Experience of Alexander Technique lessons. *Fees:* £1250 per term. No funding available. *Places:* Variable.

ALCHEMEA
College of Audio Engineering

CREATING THE NEXT GENERATION of AUDIO PROFESSIONALS

What does it take to be a good Audio Engineer?
How do you get a job in a recording studio?

The truth is that it is quite difficult, recording studios are inundated with applications from people hoping for a chance to work and learn to become recording engineers. The problem from a studio managers point of view is that it is very difficult for them to judge if the person is going to be a useful asset, or just someone who takes up lots of time asking silly questions and costing them valuable time and therefor money.

So though it is sometimes possible to gain employment with little or no studio experience, then work ones way up from tea making to assisting, to engineering, it is highly probable that this is going to be in one of the many small studios. This can be highly limiting. There will likely be just one style of music, one way of doing things, in short the exact opposite of the skill base that is going to be needed to be employable in the future. The job for life is a very out of date idea, this is true in most fields, in pro audio it is especially true. The rate of change in the tools & techniques that a sound engineer uses is quite phenomenal. What's needed is appropriate training, a broad knowledge base to enable one to understand not only how to use state of the art equipment but also have a good understanding of the underlying principles so as new technology appears you will be able to understand its potential.

ALCHEMEA College of Audio engineering was set up in 1992. It's a non profit making Co-operative that came about because the 4 founding members were sure they could provide better quality training than was available any where else. The aim of the ALCHEMEA Diploma Course is quite simply to provide the skills needed for the **next generation of recording engineers**, with a great emphasis on practical work using as far as possible state of the art, industry standard equipment. For example when the college started up it was felt imperative to have an brand new SSL Console, this very powerful and expensive mixer was at that time undeniably THE high end console used in most top recording studios but no educational facilities had one. It was obvious when it appeared that the Yamaha O2R was going to be of great importance. The implication of using an assignable digital desk with extensive automation facilities requires new areas of knowledge. Alchemea built a new 4th studio that also includes surround sound capability to meet this challenge. More recently we have identified the Euphonix CS3000 digitally controlled Analogue console as being the way forward in mixer development, so we got one even though it costs well over £100,000.

ALCHEMEA's training is successful, judged by the perception employers have that ALCHEMEA graduates are useful, eminently employable people, the high proportion of ex students employed & our 1993, NTA Award for training excellence. The skills learnt are relevant and enjoyable, placing one in an ideal position to benefit from emerging technology such as Multimedia & established industries such as Record production,TV, Radio & Live sound. The skills taught, particularly in the area of information technology based MIDI & Digital audio techniques, are relevant across the ever convergent Film/TV, Music & Multimedia worlds.

Contact Alchemea ,The Windsor Centre, Windsor St, London N1 8QH Tel 0171-359 4035 www.alchemea.demon.co.uk : Email Info@alchemea.demon.co.uk FAX 0171 359 4027

North of England Teaching Centre for the F M Alexander Technique
Flat 3, Park House, 39 Hanover Sq, Leeds LS3 1BQ
Tel: 0113 244 9713 *Fax:* 0113 246 7240

Margaret Rakusen, dir.
Courses: 3-yr teacher training courses. *Status:* Private school (STAT approved). *Entry requirements:* Mature character with a minimum of 30 Alexander Technique lessons. Probationary term. *Music facilities:* Based at the Yorkshire Dance Centre in central Leeds. *Fees:* £1200 per term. *Places:* 15.

Oxford Alexander Technique Teaching Centre
63 Chalfont Rd, Oxford OX2 6TJ
Tel: 01865 558477

Mrs Walker, dir.

Courses: Training course for teachers and private lessons.

Victoria Training School for the Alexander Technique
50a Belgrave Rd, London SW1
Tel: 0171 821 7916

Mrs S Kaminitz, dir.

West Sussex Centre for Alexander Technique
5 Coates Castle, Pulborough, W Sussex
Tel: 01798 865503

A and R Nott, dirs.
Courses: Training course (nine terms) for teachers of Alexander Technique. *Status:* Private school. *Entry requirements:* Full course (20-30) of lessons in the Alexander Technique. *Fees:* £1000 per term. *Places:* 10.

Arts Administration Courses

Anglia Polytechnic University
East Rd, Cambridge CB1 1PT
Tel: 01223 363271 *Fax:* 01223 352900

Barbara Mornin, course admin; Tony Smith, pathway leader.
Courses: MA in Arts Administration, includes work placement. *Status:* University. *Entry requirements:* Degree (min 2.2) or equivalent. *Fees:* £3500 f/t, £2900 p/t. *Places:* 25 f/t; 15 p/t.

Buckinghamshire University College
Wellesbourne Campus, Kingshill Rd, High Wycombe, Bucks HP13 5BB
Tel: 01494 522141 *Fax:* 01494 465432
Email: md@rncb.ac.uk
Website: www.rncb.ac.uk

John Beaven, course leader.
Courses: BA Hons Music Industry Management. *Status:* University College. *Entry requirements:* 2 A-levels or BTEC ND or GNVQ Advanced at appropriate level. *Music facilities:* Recording studio, venue for performance. *Places:* 70-100.

City University
Dept of Arts Policy and Management, Level 12, Frobisher Cres, Barbican, London EC2Y 8HB
Tel: 0171 477 8000 *Fax:* 0171 477 8887
Email: artspol@city.ac.uk
Website: www.city.ac.uk/artspol

Eric Moody, head of dept; Ursula Hedgley, admissions; Mary Dines, admin.
Courses: MA in Arts Management (p/t or f/t), MA in Museum/Gallery Management (p/t or f/t), MA in Arts Criticism (p/t or f/t); Diploma in Arts Administration (1); research degrees MPhil, PhD

(p/t or f/t).
Entry requirements: Degree or equivalent and work experience. For Arts Criticism, degree and interest in the arts.
Music facilities: Departmental resource centre, computer work stations. *Places:* 40 arts management; 30 museum/gallery management; 30 arts criticism; 30 diploma.

De Montfort University
Dept of Performing Arts, Scraptoft Campus, Scraptoft, Leicester LE7 9SU
Tel: 0116 255 1551 *Fax:* 0116 250 6199

Andrew Hugill, head of dept.
Courses: BA in Performing Arts (3) (arts admin, drama, mus, dance) with one subject chosen as major option; short in-service courses in arts admin (intensive 2-day residential courses on specialist topics for experienced arts administrators).

Durham University Business School
Mill Hill La, Durham DH1 3LB
Tel: 0191 374 2233 *Fax:* 0191 374 1230
Email: mba.ft@durham.ac.uk
Website: www.dur.ac.uk/dubs/

A M Nevin, C Cumming, MBA programme mgrs.
Courses: Master of Business Administration (MBA) including optional arts management specialisms (1). Course includes foundation management course, research, plus elective courses.
Entry requirements: Degree and 2 yrs work experience. *Fees:* £8750. *Places:* 100.

419

Moray House Institute
Chessel's Land, Heriot-Watt University, Edinburgh EH8 8AQ
Tel: 0131 558 6506 *Fax:* 0131 558 6505

Courses: MSc in Cultural Policy Management; MSc in Cultural Services Management.

University of Northumbria at Newcastle
Department of Historical and Critical Studies, Squires Building, Newcastle upon Tyne NE1 8ST
Tel: 0191 227 4933

Courses: P/grad diploma in arts management (1 f/t, 2p/t).

Roehampton Institute London
Roehampton La, London SW15 5PH
Tel: 0181 392 3269 *Fax:* 0181 392 3289
Email: hamdanic@roehampton.ac.uk

Peter Reynolds, head of drama and theatre studies; Robert Henry, programme convener, arts management.
Courses: Diploma (2 evenings per week) in arts management. The course combines financial management, arts funding, law, publicity and marketing, general administration, arts policy. *Status:* Institute of HE. *Entry requirements:* First degree or equivalent preferred but those experienced in arts admin will be considered. *Fees:* £816, registration £78. *Places:* 60.

University College, Warrington
Padgate Campus, Fearnhead La, Warrington WA2 0DB
Tel: 01925 494494 *Fax:* 01925 816077

David Grimshaw, snr lecturer.
Courses: BA Hons courses which include commercial mus production, radio production, TV production, performing arts, media and cultural studies and multimedia. Also Masters degrees in TV production and media and cultural studies.

Warwick University
Centre for the Study of Cultural Policy, School of Theatre Studies, Coventry CV4 7AL
Tel: 01203 523020 *Fax:* 01203 524446

Oliver Bennett, dir MA cultural policy.
Courses: MA European Cultural Policy and Arts Administration (1 f/t, 2 p/t). *Status:* University. *Entry requirements:* 2nd class hons degree or equivalent experience. *Music facilities:* Computers, language centre, excellent teaching facilities and the university has the largest arts centre in the UK outside London. *Fees:* £3080 f/t, £1540 p/t. Funding could be available. *Places:* 20.

Instrument Making and Repair Courses

Leeds College of Music
3 Quarry Hill, Leeds LS2 7PD
Tel: 0113 222 3400 *Fax:* 0113 243 8798
Website: www.netlink.co.uk/users/zappa/clcm/clcm.html

Philip Greenwood, head of technology programmes; Ted Lee, course leader.
Courses: BTEC ND, City and Guilds/LCM certificate in mus inst technology (w/wind, br, str, classical gui, electric gui, perc, pno repair and tuning, electronics) (2); general training for career in inst repair; BTEC HND in mus inst technology (various strands). *Status:* College of FE.
Entry requirements: Interview and aptitude tests, flexible qualifications for mature students.
Music facilities: Full range of machinery, equipment, teaching aids, w/shop and lecture rooms. *Fees:* LA discretionary awards available. *Places:* Max 48 pa.

London Guildhall University
Sir John Cass Dept of Design and Technology, 41 Commercial Rd, London E1 1LA
Tel: 0171 320 1842/1000 *Fax:* 0171 320 1830

Courses: BTEC ND Music Instrument Technology with specialist options in pno construction, tuning and maintenance; early keyboard inst construction; making of vns, early stringed insts, guis, wind insts and electronics for the music industry (2); BTEC HND Music Instrument Technology with specialist fields of study as above (2); p/t courses in making of vns, guis, early fretted insts; wind inst construction, maintenance and repair; pno tuning and repair; BSc Hons Music Technology with specialist project options as above (3). *Status:* University.
Entry requirements: ND, GCSE; HND and BSc, A-level or equivalent. *Music facilities:* Specialist w/shops for each inst family, fully-equipped electronic lab and electronic mus studio, acoustics lab, wood mills and finishing facilities, materials testing, computing cad-cam and specialist library.
Fees: LEA grants available. *Places:* ND 35; HND 55; BSc 40.

Merton College
London Rd, Morden, Surrey SM4 5QX
Tel: 0181 640 3001 ext 1812 *Fax:* 0181 640 0835

T Head, K Graves, tutors.
Courses: Course in mus inst repair leading to City and Guilds Advanced Craft Certificate (2). Yr 1 study areas include br inst repair and restoration, w/wind inst repair and restoration, orch str inst repair and restoration, gui making

and repairing, org design and building. Specialist hand and machine-tool training in woodwork and metalwork. Yr 2 students may specialise in 3 of the above subject areas. City and Guilds Higher Award in Mus Inst Repair (1) (in 2 specialist areas). Entry from 2-yr course or equivalent qualification and experience. P/t study to max 2 days per week available in any of the above areas. Evening courses also available, leading to a jointly awarded NCFE and Merton College certificate. *Status:* College of FE.

Entry requirements: Appropriate examination passes, work experience, and/or production of work pieces. Interview and practical assessment test for f/t courses only. *Music facilities:* Dedicated w/shops for most specialist areas, fully equipped with machine and hand tools. *Fees:* Free tuition for f/t courses. Some LEA grants available. *Places:* 20 pa (f/t); approx 8 p/t places per specialism.

Newark and Sherwood College
School of Violin, Woodwind and Piano Technology, Friary Rd, Newark on Trent, Notts NG24 1PB
Tel: 01636 680680 *Fax:* 01636 680681
Email: mhunt@newark.ac.uk

Malcolm Hunt, college mgr; Kerry Boylan, J Lord, G Else, R Summerfield, M Harrison, course tutors. *Courses:* Pno tuning and repair course (3); w/wind making and repair course (3); vn making and repair course (3); classical gui making course (2); vn foundation course (1); elec gui course. *Status:* College of FE.
Entry requirements: No formal entry requirements. Selection is by interview and practical tests. *Music facilities:* Full college facilities. *Fees:* No fees for EU students. *Places:* 16 places per course.

Royal National College for the Blind
Piano Tuning and Repairs, College Rd, Hereford HR1 1EB
Tel: 01432 265725 *Fax:* 01432 353478
Email: md@rncb.ac.uk
Website: www.rncb.ac.uk

Michael Wigmore, deputy head of creative arts. *Courses:* Pno tuning and repair course for the visually impaired (3). *Status:* College of FE.
Entry requirements: No formal qualifications

required. *Music facilities:* Very extensive. *Fees:* Details on application. *Places:* Flexible.

Stevenson College
Carrickvale Centre, Stenhouse St West, Edinburgh EH11 3EP
Tel: 0131 535 4621 *Fax:* 0131 535 4622

Andrew Knight, snr lecturer, mus inst technology; Ken Thomson, course mgr, orch inst technology; Morag Campbell, head of section. *Courses:* NC in pno servicing (1) leading to HND in stringed keyboard inst technology (2); NC in orch inst repair (1) leading to HND in wind inst technology (2) or HND in stringed inst technology (2). All courses also available p/t. *Status:* College of FE.
Entry requirements: NC course: 3 GCSEs or equivalent and 16+. HND: NC or equivalent educational and technical experience. *Music facilities:* Purpose-built w/shops equipped with range of tools, equipment and insts. 16 sound-proofed booths for pno tuning and inst practice. 2 c/rooms equipped with hi-fi, pnos and electronic keyboards. Resource base with keyboards, Apple Macs with MIDI, listening stations.
Fees: NC: £740 (£3095 overseas) plus £4 registration fee; HND: £1600 (£5580 overseas) plus £92.50 course assessment fee. SAAS or equivalent funding available. No external funding available for p/t students. *Places:* Pno servicing 12-14; orch inst repair 20-26; all HNDs 12-14.

West Dean College
West Dean, Chichester, W Sussex PO18 0QZ
Tel: 01243 811301 *Fax:* 01243 811343
Email: westdean@pavilion.co.uk
Website: www.pavilion.co.uk/westdean

Roger Rose; Martin Haycock, course tutors. *Courses:* 3-yr apprenticeship in mus inst making (renaissance and baroque bowed str insts, renaissance and baroque plucked insts). *Status:* Private educational trust.
Entry requirements: Practical test and interview with the tutors and principal. *Music facilities:* Excellent w/shops. *Fees:* £6960 (fees), £3540 (residential accommodation). Help in obtaining funding is available from the college at the discretion of the principal. *Places:* 8.

Professional Development Courses for Private Music Teachers

Associated Board of the Royal Schools of Music
14 Bedford Sq, London WC1B 3JG
Tel: 0171 467 8257 *also fax;*
Email: profdev@abrsm.ac.uk

Richard Crozier, professional development dir.
Courses: CT ABRSM: Professional Development Course for Instrumental and Singing Teachers (1 p/t). Includes some f/t study plus group study sessions, independent work and specialist mentoring of students. Students must complete 3 written assignments, 2 projects, plus a diary of teaching. Held at 12 regional centres in the UK.

Entry requirements: Applicants are not required to hold any formal qualification, but are expected to be teaching pupils on a regular basis. Age limits: min 21 (insts), min 25 (singers).

Bela Bartók Centre for Musicianship
6 Frognal Ct, 158 Finchley Rd, London NW3 5HL
Tel: 0171 435 3685 *also fax*

Agnes Kory.
Courses: Training courses to further the musical skills of mus teachers and performers. Professional and amateur classes focus on comprehensive mus education including the Kodaly system, history, analysis and performance skills. Courses are credit-bearing for the Trinity College of Music Certificate and Diploma for Music Education. *Status:* Registered charity.

British Suzuki Institute
39 High St, Wheathampstead, Herts AL4 9BB
Tel: 01582 832424 *Fax:* 01582 834488

Birte Kelly, gen sec.
Courses: P/t teacher training courses in vn, pno, vc and fl leading to the diploma of the European Suzuki Association. *Status:* Educational charity. *Entry requirements:* Diploma level preferred. Entry by audition and interview. *Places:* 40.

Goldsmiths
University of London, New Cross, London SE14 6NW
Tel: 0171 919 7229 *Fax:* 0171 919 7223

Jeremy Peyton-Jones, mus programme co-ord.

University of Reading
International Centre for Research in Music Education, Bulmershe Ct, Reading RG6 1HY
Tel: 0118 931 8843/8837 *Fax:* 0118 935 2080

Anthony Kemp, professor of mus educ.
Courses: P/grad Diploma/MA course in Music Teaching in Private Practice, developed by the University of Reading in collaboration with the Incorporated Society of Musicians (2-4). Designed specifically for those working in the field of private mus teaching, the course will involve long distance learning techniques of learning packs, regional seminars and local action research groups. *Entry requirements:* Recognised qualification and professional training on an inst or voice. *Fees:* Modules 1-3: £225 each; Module 4: £390.

Psychology for Musical Performance Courses

Psychology for Music Teaching, Learning and Performing
28 Glebe Pl, London SW3 5LD
Tel: 0171 352 1666 *also fax*

Lucinda Mackworth-Young.
Courses: Courses in the practical application of psychology, eurhythmics, psychotherapeutic principles, dance through the ages and other contingent disciplines for performers, teachers and students. Courses may be validated by Trinity College of Music as bearing credit to the ATCL and LTCL (Music Education) or Certificate in Music Education.

Recording and Technology Courses

Alchemea College of Audio Engineering
2-18 Britannia Row, The Angel, London N1 8QH
Tel: 0171 359 4035 *Fax:* 0171 359 4027
Email: info@alchemea.demon.co.uk
Website: www\alchemea.demon.co.uk

Courses: Foundation and Advanced Diploma Course in Audio Engineering; various courses in Audio Engineering and production. 16-wk f/t Foundation and Advanced courses. Practically orientated intensive, vocational courses commencing Jan, Mar, Jun and Sep. *Music Facilities:* 4 state-of-the-art studios, with Euphonix CS3000, Soundcraft, Trident, and yamaha 02R consoles. SSL also available. MIDI W/stations running Logic Audio, Cubase and Notator. Soundscape, Spectral and Cooledit Pro, Digital Audio w/stations. Film/TV post-production capacity in 2 studios.

Bangor, University of Wales
Dept of Music, College Rd, Bangor, Gwynedd LL57 2DG
Tel: 01248 382181 *Fax:* 01248 370297
Email: mus018@bangor.ac.uk
Website: www.bangor.ac.uk/music/musichome.html

John M Harper, head of dept; Jochen Eisentraut, Andy Lewis, course organisers.
Courses: University P/grad Diploma in Music Technology and Sound Recording Techniques. *Entry requirements:* A degree in a relevant descipline (not necessarily mus). *Music facilities:* 4 studios. *Fees:* Funding often obtained from the European Social Fund. *Places:* 12.

Bournemouth University
School of Media Arts and Communication, Poole House, Talbot Campus, Fern Barrow, Poole, Dorset BH12 5BB
Tel: 01202 524111/595469

Stephen Deutsch, course dir.
Courses: P/grad MA in Music Design for the Moving Image; P/grad MA in Sound Design for the Moving Image. *Status:* University. *Entry requirements:* BMus, BA Mus, or industrial experience; BA, BSc, NBus or industrial experience. *Music facilities:* Individual student workstations. Digital sound recording and editing. *Fees:* £3050 (for EU Citizens). *Places:* 8; 12.

City College Manchester
Arden Centre, Sale Rd, Northenden, Manchester M23 0DD
Tel: 0161 957 1721

David Gibson, principal.
Courses: BTEC HNC Music Technology (1 f/t; 2 p/t). Two strands to the course: one for skilled and experienced musicians; the other for people with a technological or scientific background.

BTEC HND Music Technology (2). *Entry requirements:* At least 4 GCSEs at grade C or above and A-levels or BTEC ND Performing Arts or Music Technology (at least merit), or relevant industrial experience. *Music facilities:* Facilities in two sites, including 2 16-track studios, MIDI and multimedia suite (using PC, Mac and Atari platforms) and keyboard lab, teaching and practice rooms. Abraham Moss Centre houses cutting rooms, professional 8 and 16-track digital and 24-track recording studios.

City University
Northampton Sq, London EC1V 0BH
Tel: 0171 477 8284 *Fax:* 0171 477 8576
Website: www.city.ac.uk/music

Anna Woodward, sec.
Courses: Diploma/MSc in Music Information Technology (1 f/t, 2 p/t). This course is primarily for recent graduates, mus professionals, teachers, etc and includes MIDI principles, mus-based software and the application of IT to mus-making. *Status:* University. *Entry requirements:* Degree or relevant professional experience. *Music facilities:* Mus computing lab (Apple Macs with tone modules and keyboards). The dept's facilities are connected to the university's Ethernet network.

University of Derby
Western Rd, Mickleover, Derby DE3 5GX
Tel: 01332 622222 ext 2066 *Fax:* 01332 514323
Website: www.derby.ac.uk

Richard Hodges, head of mus.
Courses: BA (Hons) in Popular Music with Music Technology (3 f/t). Modular programme taught by the School of Art and Design in collaboration with the School of Engineering, offering CertHE and DipHE at Levels 1 and 2 respectively and leading to honours degree on completion of Level 3. Integrates performance composition, critical theory and mus technology. *Status:* University. *Entry requirements:* For age 21 and under: min 2 A-levels and 5 passes (C+) in GCSE or equivalent (Highers, GNVQs, BTec, etc). For age 21 and above: no formal educational qualification necessary (Access course available for those with no recent experience or formal education). *Music facilities:* New 24-track digital recording studio at Green Lane campus. *Places:* 20.

Edinburgh University
Faculty of Music, Alison House, Nicholson Sq, Edinburgh EH8 9DF
Tel: 0131 650 2423 *Fax:* 0131 650 2425

Email: music@ed.ac.uk
Website: www.music.ed.ac.uk

Courses: BMus in Music Technology (3) brings together scientific and artistic approaches to the academic disciplines of mus. This course is run with the Dept of Physics. *Status:* University.

Entry requirements: 2 A-levels: music (B), maths (C). *Music facilities:* The facilities available for students comprise three separate studios and a recording room. The main studio contains professional quality 8-track recording facilities with digital (DAT) mastering. There are also 2-track and 4-track tape recorders. Synthesis is by a Yamaha TG77 FM tone generator and DX-7 keyboard. There are also Akai S1000 and Roland S-760 samplers, and MIDI control through applications running on a Mac LCIII computer. A separate recording room, linked to the main studio, offers a controlled recording environment, and a selection of microphones. The digital studio contains a Mac Quadra 700 running Digidesign Soundtools. There is also a lexicon 300 digital signal processor with digital connections and DAT mastering. Studio 3 houses a computer connected to the main campus network.

Work is underway on a special BMus Tech studio. *Places:* c 5.

Gateway School of Recording, Music Technology and Music Business Studies

Kingston Hill Centre, Kingston-upon-Thames, Surrey KT2 7LB
Tel: 0181 549 0014 *Fax:* 0181 547 7337

Dave Ward, dir; Sarah Tuakli, company mgr.
Courses: 2 yr f/t and 18 month p/t course in recording, mus technology and mus business studies; several short courses covering many diverse areas. Gateway also organises in-service training for teachers in mus technology and provides the recording technology modules of the Kingston University BA Hons in Music. *Status:* Private school. *Entry requirements:* For the f/t or p/t diploma: 2 A-levels or equivalent. *Music facilities:* Sited on the campus of Kingston University, the facilities include two 16-track and two 24-track teaching studios, two mus technology suites, and three pre-production sequencing suites. SSL training is given in association with other professional studios. There is also a 24-track recording studio, run commercially for orchestral and popular recording purposes. *Fees:* Variable. Funding available for the Kingston University Diploma. *Places:* Up to 10 on short courses; 56 on Diploma.

Glasgow University

Dept of Music, 14 University Gardens, Glasgow G12 8QH
Tel: 0141 330 4093 *Fax:* 0141 330 3518

Email: stephen@music.gla.ac.uk
Website: www.music.gla.ac.uk

Stephen Arnold, dir of computer mus studies; Eduardo Miranda, lecturer in mus technology.
Courses: BEng (Engineering with Music) (4); p/grad MMus degree in computer mus (1). *Status:* University. *Entry requirements:* BEng: 5 Highers (grade B), 3 A-levels (grades CCD). MMus: a good honours degree. *Music facilities:* 2 computer mus studios, audio lab and labs in electronics and electronic engineering. *Places:* BEng 30, MMus 8-10.

Keele University

Dept of Music, Keele, Staffs ST5 5BG
Tel: 01782 583295 *also fax*
Email: mua09@mus.keele.ac.uk
Website: www.keele.ac.uk/depts/mu/index.htm

Michael Vaughan, head of dept.
Courses: BA Joint Hons (electronic mus and humanities/social science subjects) (4;3), BSc Joint Hons (electronic mus and natural science). Recommended combinations of subjects with electronic mus are visual arts, maths, computer science or languages. *Status:* University. *Entry requirements:* 3-yr courses require fulfilment of the University's general entrance requirements including one of the following combinations: A-level mus and ABRSM gr 7; A-levels in practical mus and theoretical mus (London); gr 8 (theory), gr 8 (practical). 4-yr courses require students who do not have the qualifications listed above to take a transfer course in mus (gr 6 required). *Music facilities:* 4 electronic mus studio areas designed to meet the needs of both student and professional users. The Tim Souster studio is a digital multitrack recording and composition studio. Studio 1 is dedicated to MIDI equipment in combination with digital audio. Studio 2 is designed primarily for the composition of electro-acoustic mus using traditional analogue techniques. The Garage, a purpose-built computer mus laboratory, houses sound synthesis and processing computer workstations which make use of software for sound synthesis, mixing, editing and spectral manipulation. *Places:* 15.

Kidderminster College

Dept of Community Studies, Hoo Rd, Kidderminster, Worcs DY10 1LX
Tel: 01562 820811

J Shepherd, lecturer in mus; Jon Bates, lecturer in mus technology.
Courses: BTEC ND Sound Recording and Audio Technology. *Status:* College of FE. *Entry requirements:* 4 GCSE's. *Music facilities:* 2 digital studios; Cubase audio, logic audio 16-track ADAT and mixers; outboard FX. *Fees:* Available via LEA. *Places:* 14.

London College of Music at Thames Valley University

St Mary's Rd, London W5 5RF
Tel: 0181 231 2304 *Fax:* 0181 231 2546

Jolyon Forward, programme leader, lecturer (sound, multimedia); Lezli-An Barrett, lecturer (video).
Courses: Diploma in Higher Education in mus technology. *Status:* University. *Entry requirements:* For applicants under age 21, NVQ Level 3; one A-level or equivalent; success on a recognised Access programme. For applicants over age 21, NVQ Level 2; appropriate employment; other relevant experience. *Music facilities:* 10 sound studios, 3 with live rooms, 3 video studios, TV studio and multimedia studio. Extensive support for MIDI, sampling, synthesis, digital recording, hard disc recording and analogue formats. *Fees:* LEA mandatory awards. *Places:* 30.

London Guildhall University

Sir John Cass Dept of Design and Technology, 41 Commercial Rd, London E1 1LA
Tel: 0171 320 1842/1000 *Fax:* 0171 320 1830

Courses: BSc (Hons) Musical Instrument Technology, modular with emphasis on coursework and projects (3). BTEC HND Musical Instrument Technology (2). The courses specialise in the design, construction and servicing of electronic hardware systems and musical insts, and not performance and recording.
Status: University. *Entry requirements:* HND and BSc: A-level or equivalent. *Music facilities:* Fully-equipped electronic lab and electronic mus studio, acoustics lab and specialist library. *Fees:* LEA grants available. *Places:* HND 55; BSc 40.

Media Production Facilities

Bon Marche Building, Ferndale Rd, London SW9 8EJ
Tel: 0171 737 7152 *Fax:* 0171 738 5428

Paul Halpin, head of media training.
Courses: Diploma in Advanced Sound Recording and Production Techniques (1 f/t), comprising three 3-month certificate modules that may also be taken independently. Combines lectures with extensive hands-on session. Intakes in Jan and Sep; Semester Certificate (16 wks), offering analogue recording and mixing, digital/MIDI production and creative mus production techniques (starts May). *Status:* Private school. *Entry requirements:* Previous relevant practical experience and/or 2 GCSEs in maths and physics. *Music facilities:* 24-track studio with 32-channel automated Amek Mozart console with Superloc and Virtual Dynamics; digital suite with Mackie 24 Channel console, Tascam DA-88s, computer-based sequencing and hard disk

editing software; Various modules and synths, also a/v suites. *Fees:* £6350 plus VAT (diploma), £2750 plus VAT (certificate), registration fee £100. £3500 (semester) all inclusive, £295 plus VAT (1 wk), registration fee £35. Discretionary awards only from LEAs. *Places:* 15 (diploma, certificate), 8 (1 wk course).

Newark and Sherwood College

Chauntry Pk, Friary Rd, Newark on Trent, Notts NG24 1PB
Tel: 01636 680680 *Fax:* 01636 680681

Colin Boothman.
Courses: BTEC ND Musical Instrument Technology. *Status:* College of FE. *Entry requirements:* 4 GCSEs gr C or above, including maths and science. *Music facilities:* Electronics labs, recording facilities, w/shops, library. *Fees:* Discretionary awards. *Places:* c 30.

Newcastle College

Faculty of Visual and Performing Arts, Rye Hill Campus, Scotswood Rd, Newcastle upon Tyne NE4 7SA
Tel: 0191 200 4211 *Fax:* 0191 200 4729
Email: enquiries@ncl-coll.ac.uk
Website: www.ncl-coll.ac.uk

Ian Spencer, head of faculty; A Hooper, curriculum co-ord, mus.
Courses: BTEC ND and HND Music Technology; BTEC HND Music Production. *Status:* FE College. *Entry requirements:* HND Music Technology requires 2 A-levels or equivalent with considerable mus technology experience (sequencing, recording and synthesis). HND Music Production also requires playing and mus reading ability in addition. ND requires 4 GCSE passes and some mus technology experience. *Music facilities:* 8 recording studios, computer sequencing labs, keyboard labs. *Fees:* HND carries mandatory award status, ND carries discretionary award status. *Places:* 25 each HND, 50 ND mus technology.

University of North London

School of Communications Technology & Mathematical Sciences, 166-220 Holloway Rd, London N7 8BD
Tel: 0171 607 2789 *Fax:* 0171 753 7002

P C Prigmore, course admin.
Courses: University Certificate in Sound Recording Technology run in conjunction with Alchemea Studios (32 wks); p/t c/room at university and 70 hrs practical work at Alchemea (32 wks). University Certificate in Sound Studios & Recording (21 wks); p/t c/room and practical (MIDI and Cubase). *Status:* University. Both courses accredited by ASET. *Entry requirements:* Minimum of maths and science GCSE, prior experience or musical training. *Music facilities:* Practical studio facilities provided by Alchemea

Studios include latest recording studio equipment and a full range of MIDI and editing facilities. PC-based sequencing and hard-disk recording facilities available at the university, plus other recording facilities. *Fees:* No funding available. Discretionary awards from LEAs. Courses qualify for Career Development Loans (subject to status of applicant). *Places:* Sound Recording Technology, 48 (24 afternoon, 24 evening). Sound Studios & Recording, 48 (24 afternoon, 24 evening).

Perth College
Faculty of Arts, School of Music and Audio Engineering, Crieff Rd, Perth PH1 2NX
Tel: 01738 621171 ext 128 *Fax:* 01738 440050

Pamela McLean, head of faculty of arts.
Courses: NC Sound Engineering (1) is an integral part of the rock mus course; HNC and HND Audio Engineering. *Status:* College of FE. *Entry requirements:* By interview. *Music facilities:* Studio complex: 2 fully automated 24 track digital recording studios, suite of rehearsal rooms, MIDI studio and sequencing lab, video studios, vocal studio, inst workrooms, live performance areas. *Fees:* Local authority. *Places:* c 20 NC; 12-15 HNC; 12-15 HND.

Peterborough Regional College
Music Dept, Park Cres, Peterborough, Cambs PE1 4DZ
Tel: 01733 67366

Ian Burton, dir of mus.
Courses: Modern Studio Recording Techniques. *Status:* College of FE/HE. *Entry requirements:* Interview. *Music facilities:* 8-track recording studio and portable studio facility; suite of practice and teaching rooms; performing arts studio. *Places:* 15.

Queen's University
Music Dept, Belfast BT17 1NN
Tel: 01232 335105 *Fax:* 01232 238484
Email: c.fegan@qub.ac.uk
Website: www.qub.ac.uk

Michael Alcorn.
Courses: Diploma/MA in Music Technology (1 f/t or 2 p/t). *Status:* University. *Entry requirements:* Mus as major degree component, or other degree with evidence of musical competence; class 2:1 degree standard. *Music facilities:* Fully-equipped electronic studio, computer music facilities including NEXT suite, recording facilities, networked word processing stations. *Places:* 6.

Rose Bruford College
School of Production, Lamorbey Pk, Sidcup, Kent DA15 9DF
Tel: 0181 300 3024 *Fax:* 0181 308 0542
Email: admiss@bruford.ac.uk

Mark Constable, course tutor.

Courses: Music Technology BA (Hons), validated by University of Manchester. *Status:* University sector college. *Entry requirements:* 2 A-levels and gr 6 mus, or equivalent. *Music facilities:* Fully-equipped studio, recording and rehearsal rooms, MIDI laboratory. *Fees:* Government grant available.

Royal National College for the Blind
College Rd, Hereford HR1 1EB
Tel: 01432 265725

Martin Sayer, course tutor.
Courses: College certificate in music technology; BTEC First Diploma in Performing Arts and Mus Technology; BTEC ND Performing Arts and Sound Recording. *Music facilities:* MIDI teaching room, two 8-track recording studios, video editing suite, 16-track digital recording studio, radio studio, performance studio with sound and lighting facilities.

SAE Technology College *formerly* School of Audio Engineering
United House, North Rd, Islington, London N7 9DP
Tel: 0171 609 2653 *Fax:* 0171 609 6944
Website: www.sae.edu.au

Courses: Audio Engineering Diploma; Diploma in Multimedia; Studio Sound Certificate; DJ Certificate; BA degrees in Audio and Multimedia. Various short courses related to audio and multimedia. *Entry requirements:* Variable, according to course. *Music facilities:* Purpose-built 8-track and 24-track studios; numerous analogue and digital/computer workstations. *Fees:* Variable, according to course; grants available in certain circumstances. *Places:* 10-60 per course.

University of Salford
Dept of Music, Adelphi, Peru St, Salford, Manchester M3 6EQ
Tel: 0161 834 6633 *Fax:* 0161 834 3327

Derek B Scott, prof of mus and head of dept; Mark Grimshaw, head of mus technology and studio production.
Courses: BSc Mus Acoustics Recording (3). Specialist courses including recording techniques, composition, performance and popular mus repertoire studies. *Status:* University. *Entry requirements:* 3 GCSEs and 2 A-levels or 5 Scottish Certificates of Education and 2 Highers; relevant foundation course or BTEC. *Music facilities:* Two 24-track, one 40-track and one 48-track recording studios; popular mus and recording suite, specialist library, drum rooms, rehearsal rooms and 5 concert halls on campus. *Fees:* £1600 pa. Mandatory grant available. *Places:* 40 places on each course pa.

South Derbyshire College
Cavendish Centre, Music Dept, Cavendish Rd, Ilkeston, Derby DE7 5AN
Tel: 0115 930 2942 *Fax:* 0115 944 7181

Steve McAlone, programme co-ord, mus and perf arts.
Courses: A-level mus technology; BTEC ND Popular Music; p/t studio recording and mus technology courses. *Status:* College of FE. *Music facilities:* Recording studio, TV and video studio, editing suite. *Fees:* £70 pa. *Places:* 20 plus.

South East Essex College
Carnarvon Rd, Southend-on-Sea, Essex SS2 6LS
Tel: 01702 220400/220639 *Fax:* 01702 432230

Mark Vinall, head of media and perf arts.
Courses: BSc Hons Media Production and Technology (p/t and f/t); BSc Hons in Multimedia Technology (f/t); BTEC mus technology planned for 1998. *Status:* College of FE. *Music facilities:* New media centre enabling students to learn TV, radio, print, photography and IT at a high level.

Surrey University
Dept of Music, Guildford, Surrey GU2 5XH
Tel: 01483 300800/259317 *Fax:* 01483 259386

Dave Fisher, Tonmeister course dir.
Courses: BMus (Hons) (Tonmeister) specialises in the theory and practice of sound recording and mus. *Status:* University. *Entry requirements:* Maths, physics and mus A-levels. *Music facilities:* Purpose-built performing arts building incorporates 2 recording studios (1 with large live recording space, the other a multi-track studio), 4 editing suites and a MIDI programming suite with digital hard disk recording, analogue and digital transfer suite and computer workstations with Macintosh machines. *Places:* 16.

Wakefield College
School of Music, Thornes Park Centre, Horbury Rd,
Wakefield WF2 8QZ
Tel: 01924 789789

Tony Davis, dir of mus; Andy Cholerton, Kevin Dearden, lecturers.
Courses: A-level mus technology; BTEC ND Popular Music including mus technology and recording. *Status:* College of FE. *Entry requirements:* 4 GCSEs at gr C (including mus) plus ABRSM gr 3 theory. *Music facilities:* 3 recording studios, MIDI lab, keyboard lab, theatre, practice rooms, rehearsal rooms, recital room. *Fees:* Discretionary awards available from LEAs. *Places:* 24 pa.

University of York
Graduate Office, Dept of Music, Heslington, York YO1 5DD
Tel: 01904 432142 *Fax:* 01904 432450
Email: music@york.ac.uk
Website: www.york.ac.uk/depts/music/welcome.htm

Tony Myatt, course tutor.
Courses: BA/BSc Hons in Music Technology (3). This is taught jointly by the depts of mus and electronics. The BA in Music Technology is based on analysis, composition, performance, electronics, software engineering and acoustics. It can also be taken as a BEng. This course provides essential background for audio engineers, designers and composers, alongside a broad education in mus and an inter-disciplinary study for students in both science and mus. MA/MSc in Music Technology; Diploma in Music Technology. Taught courses include digital synthesis, MIDI, signal processing, electro-acoustic mus, composition, psycho-acoustics, software for composition and techniques of digital mus studio. *Status:* University. *Entry requirements:* BA/BSc: 3 A-levels (gr A-C) including mus and maths; gr 8 on 1st inst plus keyboard skills. MA/MSc: good 1st degree. *Music facilities:* 2 recording studios, 2 computer mus suites with 10 mus workstations and access to a further 14 high performance UNIX workstations. *Fees:* Funding available for MA/MSc SERC studentships. *Places:* BA/BEng 10; MA/MSc and Diploma 24.

Services Schools of Music

Royal Air Force Headquarters Music Services
RAF Uxbridge, Middx UB10 0RZ
Tel: 01895 237144 ext 6345/6286 *Fax:* 01895 810846

Flt Lt D J G Stubbs, dir of mus.
Courses: Initial 1-yr course leads to employment in a band. Training provided on a single course split into 5 modules designed to qualify musicians progressively through ranks from instrumentalist to bandmaster. Incorporates training for mus leadership and band management, inst teaching, conducting and orchestration. *Entry requirements:* Entry to RAF as musician (interview at a RAF Careers Information Office) followed by audition at Headquarters Music Services.

Royal Marines School of Music
HMS Nelson, Queen St, Portsmouth PO1 3HH
Tel: 01705 722351

Lt-Col R A Waterer, principal dir of mus.
Courses: Snr dept provides promotion courses for band sergeant, bandmaster and director of mus. Intensive broad curriculum includes harmony, counterpoint, aural training, musical history, arranging, orchestration, conducting leading to LRSM Diploma in Military Band Conducting. Jnr dept (Music Wing) offers 2 yrs 8 months, pupil inst course qualifying jnr musicians to join formed bands. Musical instruction includes individual professorial and uniformed instructor tuition, aural, choir and theory training, inst ens experience (marching, concert and dance bands; orchs, chmbr ens) plus a comprehensive syllabus of educational subjects, religion, ceremonial drill, physical training, sport and military training. Entry age 16+; proficiency on 1 or more insts advisable but not essential; selection on audition.

Royal Military School of Music
Kneller Hall, Twickenham, Middx TW2 7DU
Tel: 0181 898 5533 ext 8623 *Fax:* 0181 898 7906

Lt-Col S A Watts, principal dir of mus (army).
Courses: Mus training school for serving male/female members only who join Army as band musicians. After initial military training, members enter RMSM for 1 yr foundation course, depending on ability and learning capacity. Instruction and training available on all insts (primary and secondary), academic subjects, marching band and public concerts. Also career promotion courses of varying lengths available, including 3-yr f/t grad Bandmasters course (age 28-33), which provides conducting and practical/academic subjects to advanced level as well as human resource development and tuition on wind, br, perc, keyboard and str insts. Other diplomas and exams may be taken during courses. *Status:* Military training establishment. *Entry requirements:* Entry from age 16 by audition and interview (by arrangement through an Army Careers Office) for serving members who join the army as band musicians.

Colleges of Bagpipe Music

College of Piping
16-24 Otago St, Glasgow G12 8JH
Tel: 0141 334 3587 *Fax:* 0141 337 3024

Dugald MacNeill, acting principal.
Courses: Varied courses from beginner to advanced. Also evening courses. *Status:* Private school. *Music facilities:* Library (books and tapes), practice rooms available for weekly or extended courses only. *Fees:* £150 per week, £10 per 1-hr lesson. *Places:* 20.

Royal Scottish Band Association College
45 Washington St, Glasgow G3 8AZ
Tel: 0141 221 5414 *Fax:* 0141 221 1561

J Mitchell Hutcheson.
Courses: Annual summer school. 19-25 Jul 1998. Other classes at branch level throughout UK. Jan/Mar each yr.

Teacher Training Courses

In order to become a qualified classroom music teacher, students should follow either a three or four year course leading to a Bachelor of Education (BEd) degree or take a first degree (or degree equivalent) in music and follow this up with a one year Post-Graduate Certificate in Education (PGCE). The BEd course is currently being phased out and being replaced by the BA (QTS), a Bachelor of Arts degree with Qualified Teacher Status.

The BEd, BA (QTS) and PGCE courses are covered below. Students taking these courses specialise in the teaching of a particular age-range which is usually chosen at the beginning of the course. The majority of BEd, BA (QTS) and PGCE courses are now aimed at the primary and middle school age-ranges. Primary age-range courses aim to train graduates, whatever their subject, to be 'across the board' class teachers capable of teaching the whole primary curriculum including the arts. DfEE regulations stipulate that a certain number of hours must be allocated to the study of classroom music in all courses, together with varying opportunities to consolidate a student's musical training and, in some cases, to train them as 'curriculum leaders' in music.

Licensed teachers are appointed by LEAs; applicants must be over 26 and this qualification only leads to a qualified teacher status. The licensed teacher qualification is only recognised within the UK.

Teaching is now a degree entry profession in Scotland, with the main music teaching qualification being the music degree plus PGCE. Students may also train via a four-year BEd degree. Both routes lead to registration in respect of a teaching qualification (Secondary Education) Music but the dividing line between primary and secondary training in music is not as rigid as in England and Wales. It is possible for secondary courses to include an introduction to primary teaching (many teachers will teach both age ranges concurrently). Special regulations apply to non-Scottish graduates wishing to teach in Scottish secondary schools *see under* **Postgraduate Certificate of Education** below.

BEd and BA (QTS) Courses

Applications are usually made through the *Universities and Colleges Admissions Service* (UCAS), Fulton House, Jessop Av, Cheltenham, Glos GL50 3SH *Tel:* 01242 222444, and in a few instances directly to the college. In this section t/p is used to mean teaching practice. Applications for courses in Northern Ireland are dealt with by the individual colleges. Initial enquiries should be sent to the Department of Education for Northern Ireland, Rathgael House, Balloo Rd, Bangor, Co Down BT19 7PR *Tel:* 01247 279279.

Bath Spa University College
Newton Pk, Bath BA2 9BN
Tel: 01225 873701 *Fax:* 01225 874438

George Odam, subject leader mus educ; Jo Glover, snr lecturer in mus educ.
Courses offered: BA/BSc Hons (QTS) (4). Competence required on 1 inst to gr 7 plus A-level mus, or gr 8 plus GCSE mus. Non-traditional applicants encouraged. *Age range:* 3-11.
Music content: Subject study in yrs 1 and 2 includes inst and vocal performance, composition and mus technology and links with live concert series of a wide range of mus. The course provides a practical and balanced approach. It is taught in two strands; inst studies including individual inst lessons, ens and choral singing; and mus w/shop including improvisation, composition, European and world mus.
Educational studies: Modules available on curriculum studies in mus, mus curriculum specialism and school-based project in mus. *Music facilities:* Purpose-built auditorium, sound studio, mus technology workbase, primary mus professional studies base, 20 practice cubicles, 2 lecture/seminar rooms, keyboard practice facilities. Choir, orch and opera project provide opportunity for large-scale performance; there is also wide-ranging provision of student performing groups including jazz, big band, new mus ens and an annual concert series 'Rainbow over Bath'. *Places:* 20.

Bishop Grosseteste College
Newport, Lincoln
Tel: 01522 527347 *Fax:* 01522 530243
Email: bgc@hull.ac.uk

John Bannister, dir of mus.
Courses offered: BA (QTS) (4) (University of Hull). A-level mus preferred. Competence on 2 insts expected and assessed at interview, one at least to gr 7 standard. Cathedral org and choral scholarships available. Also BA (QTS) (3) for primary range which offers mus as an optional subject. *Age range:* 3-12, with specialism in 3-8 or 7-12.

Music content: 33% of course time. Practical approach covers individual tuition on 2 insts, group work, composition and arranging for the c/room plus history topics. Chance to specialise in yrs 3 and 4.
Educational studies: About 33% of course time; remaining 33% spent in c/room experience. *Music facilities:* Include electronic mus studio, mus library, practising facilities, recital room and theatre. *Places:* 20.

Bretton Hall College of HE
Music Dept (College of University of Leeds), Wakefield, W Yorks WF4 4LG
Tel: 01924 830261 *Fax:* 01924 830521

Graham Chambers, course leader; Valerie Tee, mus.
Courses offered: BA (QTS) (4) (University of Leeds). A-level mus (gr C+) or BTEC and gr 7 on 1st inst. Interview may involve performance. Also BA Hons Arts and Education with specialism in mus. *Age range:* Primary 5-11 with specialism in 7-12.
Music content: Course includes inst study, composition, musicianship, world mus, computer and recording work. Students are able to work with those on other mus degrees.
Educational studies: T/p included in each yr of course. *Music facilities:* Inst collection, computer-suites, recording studios. *Places:* 30.

Canterbury Christ Church College
North Holmes Rd, Canterbury, Kent CT1 1QU
Tel: 01227 767700 *Fax:* 01227 785761

Courses offered: BA (QTS) (3: optional yr 4).
Music content: Allows students to specialise in mus. Practical curriculum sessions, professional studies and substantial school experience. Specialist mus teaching from mus dept particularly focusing on application in the primary school.
Educational studies: 50% of course in yrs 1-3. 20 wks t/p plus observation and visits. Entire yr 4 spent in teacher education with mus specialism. *Places:* 30.

University of Central England in Birmingham

Faculty of Education, Westbourne Rd, Edgbaston B15 3TN
Tel: 0121 331 6098/6110 Fax: 0121 331 6147
Email: john.biddulph@uce.ac.uk
Website: www.uce.ac.uk

John Biddulph, pathway leader.
Courses offered: BEd Music (Secondary) (2). Qualifications or experience equivalent to 1 yr HE required in mus. Also GCSE in maths and English language, or equivalent through university test. Age range: 11-18 (including working experience with primary children).
Music content: Students study mus at the Birmingham Conservatoire and Faculty of Education. Mus education covers principles and methods of mus teaching. Practical w/shops, mus technology, world mus and performing, arranging and directing. No specific inst teaching option, but optional inst teaching on t/p and experience in w/shops.
Educational studies: General educational issues.
Music facilities: Centre for technology in mus education, open access computer and word-processing facilities, educ library, access to email and internet. Places: 17.

The Chichester Institute of HE formerly West Sussex Institute of HE

Music Dept, Bishop Otter Campus, College La, Chichester PO19 4PE
Tel: 01243 816000 Fax: 01243 816080

Michael Waite, head of mus.
Courses offered: BA (QTS) (4) (University of Southampton). A-level mus normally required (gr 8 in main inst may be accepted in lieu). Yrs 1-2 teaching as for BA Music major. QTS is optional route for yrs 3-4. Age range: 5-8, 8-13.
Music content: 50% of course time, with 1 hr 45 mins per wk inst study. Tuition also in history and form, practical musicianship (w/shops), electronic studio activities. Much extra-curricular mus-making and opportunities for performance along with BA students.
Educational studies: 50% of course, with yrs 1 and 2 mainly educational theory and mus major; yrs 3-4 are mainly practical professional training. 3 blocks of 5-wk t/p sessions plus 1-day attachments all through course. Music facilities: Practice rooms, recording studios, rehearsal studios, computer facilities, pipe org, synthesizers, hpd, pnos, etc. Places: 20.

University of Durham

School of Education, Leazes Rd, Durham DH1 1TS
Tel: 0191 374 2000 Fax: 0191 374 3506

Ruth Thomas, Stuart Button, lecturers, mus educ.
Courses offered: BA(Ed) Hons (3). Gr C in A-level mus normally required. Mus must be combined with a core subject of the NC (combinations of

more than 2 subjects are discouraged). Mus may also be studied along with art and drama on the Arts in Human Experience course, formal qualifications not essential. Age range: 5-8 or 7-11, chosen on application. Music facilities: Well-equipped mus rooms, full range of resources, full access to wide range of university mus activities.

Edge Hill University College

St Helens Rd, Ormskirk, Lancs L39 4QP
Tel: 01695 575171 Fax: 01695 584649
Email: biggint@staff.ehche.ac.uk
Website: www.ehche.ac.uk

Tony Biggin, head of mus; Avril Tisdall, snr lecturer.
Courses offered: BA (QTS) Hons Music and Education (4) (University of Lancaster). Grade 7 on inst and 2 A-levels at DD or GNVQ (merit), GNVQ (pass) and D at A-level, or BTEC with distinction and merit levels. Musicality and good standard of competence on main inst must be demonstrated at audition/interview. Age range: 3-8 or 7-12.
Music content: 50% of total course time. Mus elements covered include main inst, c/room inst (pno), rcdr, voice, language, repertoire and history, creative work, composition and arrangement (including use of computers and studio applications).
Educational studies: Parallel curriculum course throughout all 4 yrs. T/p of 3, 4, 5, 7 wks in yrs 1-4 respectively, plus additional observation and projects. Music facilities: Concert hall, theatre, recording studio; electronic music lab with Apple Mac, Roland, etc.

Homerton College

Hills Rd, Cambridge CB2 2PH
Tel: 01223 507111 Fax: 01223 507120

John Finney, head of mus; John Hopkins, dir of studies.
Courses offered: BEd Hons (4) (University of Cambridge). A-level mus expected, with gr 8 standard on main inst, plus gr 5 on pno (if not main inst). BA Hons (3) (University of Cambridge). 3 A-levels (gr A in mus and gr 8 on main inst, plus gr 5 on pno). Age range: 4-8 or 7-14.
Music content: BEd Hons: yrs 1 and 2 concentrate on main subject work in mus and its application to the c/room, including performance, improvisation, composition, stylistic studies, mus education, inter-arts, conducting, ethnomusicology, history of mus. BA Hons: content as BEd plus additional Tripos papers in yr 3.
Educational studies: Core and foundation subject study in yrs 3 and 4, plus professional and education studies (philosophy, sociology,

psychology of education) with extended school experiences through which to develop an understanding of the curriculum leadership role. *Music facilities:* Large library containing school-based printed materials and teachers' support books, recorded mus, western and non-western insts, concert hall, recital rooms and electronic mus studio. Also thriving college orchs, choirs, steel pans, etc. *Places:* BEd 18; BA 6.

University of Huddersfield School of Education and Professional Development
Holly Bank Rd, Lindley, Huddersfield HD3 3BP
Tel: 01484 478232 *Fax:* 01484 514784
Email: l.pearson@hud.ac.uk
Website: www.hud.ac.uk/

Lesley Pearson, snr lecturer.
Courses offered: BEd (Hons optional) (2) in secondary schools mus. GCSE gr C minimum in Music and English Language with HND or BTEC diploma and minimum of 2 years attendance on suitable course required for entry. *Age range:* 11-18.
Music content: 1st and 2nd study (2nd study composition unless already covered on a previous course). Keyboard skills, drum kit and gui. Covers principles and methods of mus teaching. Practical w/shops, mus technology, world mus and performing, arranging and directing. *Music facilities:* Students study at main Queensgate campus and at Holly Bank Faculty of Education. Mus technology suite available, IT facilities, access to email and internet, word processing and education library. *Places:* 9.

King Alfred's College
Sparkford Rd, Winchester, Hants SO22 4NR
Tel: 01962 841515 *Fax:* 01962 842280
Email: malcolmf@virgo.wkac.ac.uk

Malcolm Floyd, head of dept; Jay Deeble, applied studies co-ord; June Boyce-Tillman, Francis Silkstone, Ernest Piper.
Courses offered: BA (QTS). (4). Gr 7 in ABRSM exam (or equivalent) may be offered in place of 1 of 2 stipulated A-level passes. *Age range:* 4-7 or 7-11 chosen on entry (change of choice possible within yr 1).
Music content: 33%, spread evenly over whole course in context of general primary course (about 25% of this time spent on mus education related studies). Emphasis on practical skills (solo and ens work) including composing, critical studies and performing in a variety of world mus traditions, with practical experience of Caribbean steel pans, Thai and African mus with many visiting musicians.
Educational studies: 60% of course time. 30 wks school experience, plus at least 15 day visits spread over 4 yrs. *Music facilities:* Several practice rooms and mus technology facilities, recital room, chapel with org. *Places:* 25.

Kingston University
School of Music, Kingston Hill Centre, Kingston Hill, Kingston upon Thames, Surrey KT2 7LB
Tel: 0181 547 2000 *Fax:* 0181 547 7118
Website: www.kingston.ac.uk/~ed_5450/school.of_music/welcome.htm

Edward Ho, head of school of mus; Carol Gartrell, mus co-ord.
Courses offered: Master in Primary Teaching (Music) (4). A pass in A-level mus or performing arts plus gr 4+ standard on inst or voice normally required. Reasonable keyboard ability desirable. Those with gr 8 on an inst and gr 5 theory or GCSE mus also considered as well as those with experience of popular mus field. *Age range:* 3-8 or 7-11, chosen on application.
Music content: Yr 1: musicianship, composition, aural, practical skills and vocal work, mus teaching and learning in theory and practice (available for all 4 yrs); yr 2: world mus, composing and arranging for inst ens; yr 3: pop mus, contemporary composition and related issues; yr 4: ethnomusicology, composition for schools, mus project, dissertation.
Educational studies: About 33% of course, integrated with subject study and t/p plus regular weekly c/room contact. *Music facilities:* Gateway School of Music Technology. *Places:* 25.

Liverpool Hope University College *formerly* Liverpool Institute of HE
Hope Park, Liverpool L16 9JD
Tel: 0151 291 3457; 0151 291 3251 (admissions)
Fax: 0151 291 3170
Website: www.livhope.ac.uk

Stephen Pratt, head of mus dept; Mary Black, Ian Sharp, Robin Hartwell, Jonathan Powles.
Courses offered: BEd Hons (4) (University of Liverpool). A-level mus preferred plus inst or vocal competence to gr 6 or above. Consideration given to individual cases, especially those showing skill in composition. The department also runs an Access course for mature students. *Age range:* 3-8 or 7-11.
Music content: Nine modules, over 5 semesters. At level I includes inst or vocal performance, mus techniques, historical and analytical studies. Students select from a range of modules in analysis, composition, electro-acoustic studies, keyboard studies, history, performance, rehearsing and conducting, orchestration and style composition.
Educational studies: Mus students follow general and specialist courses in mus education (yrs 1-4). The remainder of the course (semesters 6,7 and 8) is divided between educational studies,

curriculum studies and school-based experience (160 days over 4 yrs).

Manchester Metropolitan University
Faculty of Community Studies, Didsbury School of Education, Wilmslow Rd, Manchester M20 8RR
Tel: 0161 247 2000 *Fax:* 0161 247 6392
Email: psjones@mmu.ac.uk
Website: www.mmu.ac.uk

Patrick Jones, mus co-ord; Peter Matson, Christine Robson, snr lecturers; Maurice Hope, snr lecturer, p/t.
Courses offered: BEd Hons (4). 1 inst or voice at gr 6 would normally be offered, but equivalent experience is acceptable. *Age range:* 3-11.
Music content: The course has a strong c/room and practical bias. Mus may be studied as one of a range of special subjects. Practical skills relevant to the c/room are offered including singing, gui and rcdr playing. Performance, arranging and composition are developed with a range of historical and contemporary mus perspectives. Tuition on one inst is offered.
Educational studies: Methodology studies integrated with special subject time. General subject studies offered in yrs 2 and 3. Education studies throughout yrs 1-4. *Music facilities:* A purpose-built mus suite containing two studios with excellent collections of c/room and world insts, practice rooms, listening lounge/library, electronic keyboards, mus technology studio. There is a good stock of orch insts, concert org, steel band and 12 pnos. *Places:* 25.

Moray House Institute of Education
Heriot Watt University, Holyrood Rd, Edinburgh EH8 8AQ
Tel: 0131 556 8455/6013/6007 *Fax:* 0131 557 3458

Neil W Houston, subject leader.
Courses offered: BEd Hons. *Age range:* 3-11.
Music content: The students follow a modular course through all 4 yrs with an additional elective course in yrs 3 and 4. Application of popular and ethnic mus within the primary c/room are considered. Composition and recording technology processes are offered in a yr 3 and 4 elective.
Educational studies: Course length 32 wks with a single day serial t/p visit and larger block allocations extending to 9 wks in yr 4. Vocational degree with remainder for college work focusing on professional studies. *Music facilities:* Mus w/shop spaces, mus technology centre, world mus facility and practice accommodation. *Places:* 100-200; 25-50 places available on elective courses.

Nene College
Moulton Pk, Northampton NN2 7AL
Tel: 01604 715000

M W Pettitt, BEd course leader.
Courses offered: BEd Hons (4) (University of Leicester). Proficient standard on at least 1 inst and an understanding of the rudiments of mus. *Age range:* 3-8 or 7-12.
Music content: All students study mus foundation course (14 hrs) in yr 1, with curriculum mus sessions (22 hrs) in yrs 2 and 3. Subject study of mus (250 hrs) occupies yrs 2-4, covering academic, creative and practical elements equally, with emphasis on application to teaching and much school-based work. Contemporary and traditional approaches to mus education covered. Group inst instruction and performance seminars.
Educational studies: About 50% of course time. T/p 22 wks equivalent throughout course. *Music facilities:* Keyboard lab, Javanese gamelan, practice rooms, performance studio and recording studio. *Places:* 36.

Northern College
School of Music, Dept of Aesthetic Education, Hilton Place, Aberdeen AB24 4FA
Tel: 01224 283500 *Fax:* 01224 283900

Prof Jonathan Stephens, dir of mus, head of aesthetic educ; Pam Robertson, deputy dir of mus.
Courses offered: BEd Hons Music (4), secondary specialist with primary input (yr 1) (Aberdeen Campus). BEd Hons Primary (4), general including mus, (Aberdeen Campus and Dundee Campus). Qualifications validated by the Open University. *Age range:* BEd Music: 5-12 (yr 1), 12-18 (yrs 2-4) (qualification is as a secondary mus specialist and as a visiting primary mus specialist). BEd Primary: 5-12.
Music content: The BEd Music course includes free composition, improvisation, stylistic techniques, arranging, transcribing, orchestrating, practical musicianship, solo and ens performance, keyboard versatility, social and historical studies, a range of electives including world mus, mus technology, mus therapy and special education, jazz, Scottish mus, integrated arts. Both courses are modular in structure.
Educational studies: BEd Music: placements in each yr of the course (yr 1, primary schools; yrs 2-4, secondary schools). BEd Primary: sessions in mus and the expressive arts in yrs 1-3, yr 4 option of expressive arts dissertation. *Music facilities:* World Music Centre (including Balinese gamelan, African drums, steel pans, samba/salsa insts), mus technology facility (including purpose-built electro-acoustic studio), keyboard lab, library and resource centre, theatre, mus

therapy special education centre (in process of development). *Places:* BEd Music 37; BEd Primary 98 (Aberdeen Campus), 70 (Dundee Campus).

Oxford Brookes University
School of Education, Wheatley Campus, Wheatley, Oxford OX33 1HX
Tel: 01865 741111 *Fax:* 01865 485838

Richard Bainbridge, admissions tutor.
Courses offered: BA (QTS). *Age range:* 3-7, 7-11.
Music content: General primary provision across the NC with the opportunity to take an additional mus module.

University of Plymouth
Rolle Faculty of Education, Douglas Av, Exmouth, Devon EX8 2AT
Tel: 01395 265344 *Fax:* 01395 255303

Philip Hull, head of dept.
Courses offered: BEd Hons (4) (University of Plymouth). *Age range:* 4-8 or 7-11.
Educational studies: 1-wk school experience in yrs 1 and 2; block practices in yrs 1, 2 and 4. *Music facilities:* Large mus suite, practice rooms, recital halls, MIDI-based recording studio and computer workstations. *Places:* 26.

University of Reading
Dept of Arts and Humanities in Education, Bulmershe Ct, Woodlands Av, Reading RG6 1HY
Tel: 0118 931 8839; 0118 987 5123 *Fax:* 0118 935 2080

Gwyn Parry-Jones, dir of mus studies and head of mus activities.
Courses offered: BA(Ed) Hons (4) QTS with optional specialism in inst and vocal teaching. The course structure allows for prolonged periods of exclusively mus study. Normal entry requirements with gr 8 practical sometimes accepted in lieu of 1 of 2 required A-levels. Otherwise minimum practical standard gr 7. *Age range:* 3-11.
Music content: More than 50% of course time. Candidates are now offered the option of a 4th yr specialism in inst and vocal teaching for those interested in becoming visiting teachers or specialists in performance tuition. This option combines appropriate school-based experience with a range of related studies. For all students main elements are inst or vocal performance (1 principal study included in the course), composition and arrangement including projects with children, mus technology, mus c/room skills, including ens direction, studies of mus history and style. The emphasis is on developing both the student's mus ability and an understanding of the place of mus in the primary school curriculum.
Educational studies: Nearly 50% of course time with frequent school visits and block practices.

Music facilities: Course takes place in excellent purpose-built facilities where there is a lively and stimulating mus environment. Well-established performing groups including chorus, orch, jazz orch, wind band and chmbr choir. *Places:* c 20.

University College of Ripon and York St John
College Rd, Ripon HG4 2QX
Tel: 01765 602691 *Fax:* 01765 600516
Email: m.davies@ucrysj.ac.uk

Marilynne J R Davies, head of performance studies.
Courses offered: BA (QTS) Hons (4) (University of Leeds). A-level mus plus gr 8 standard on main study normally required. Keyboard proficiency desirable. Course arranged on modular basis. *Age range:* Rising 5-11.
Music content: 35% of total course time.
Educational studies: 50% of total course time. 24 wks of school experience. *Music facilities:* Wide range of extra-curricular activities, well-equipped practice rooms, mus technology rooms, Clavinova studio, good concert facilities. Also pno studies, mus technology, course for children with special needs and opportunities to spend semester abroad. *Places:* 20.

Roehampton Institute London
Music Education, Southlands College, Roehampton La, London SW15 5SL
Tel: 0181 392 3424 *Fax:* 0181 392 3435
Email: music@roehampton.ac.uk
Website: www.roehampton.ac.uk/academic/arts+hum/music/music.html

Damian Day, BA (QTS) mus course co-ord; Colin Durrant, MA course leader.
Courses offered: BA (QTS) Hons (4). A-level mus (or equivalent) preferred, plus gr 8 on an inst or voice. Also new modular MA in mus education. *Age range:* 5-9 or 9-13, selected at interview.
Music content: 33% of yr 1 and variable in yrs 2-4 depending on student choice. Students pursue an integrated study of harmony, mus history and musicianship in yrs 1-2. In addition, inst lessons on main inst are offered, and on a 2nd inst for 1 yr. Options include electro-acoustic mus, composition, non-western mus (including steel pans, West African drumming, Zimbabwean mbira, Javanese gamelan and folk mus), conducting, mus therapy and mus history. The MA in mus education explores key issues of mus education from a philosophical standpoint and addresses specific practical issues to enable students to correlate theory and practice.
Educational studies: At intervals over all 4 yrs. *Music facilities:* 2 concert halls (one with Steinway grand), practice facilities, digital electronics studio, keyboard labs; Indian, West Indian and African insts for ens work. The college

has moved to new purpose-built premises. Mus will be housed in an air-conditioned, sound proofed, fully networked block. *Places:* 16.

Royal Scottish Academy of Music and Drama
100 Renfrew St, Glasgow G2 3DB
Tel: 0141 332 4101 *Fax:* 0141 353 0372
Email: registry@rsamd.ac.uk
Website: www.rsamd.ac.uk

Rita McAllister.
Courses offered: BEd Music Ord/Hons (4). Course offered jointly with St Andrew's College and University of Strathclyde Faculty of Education; students must apply to UCAS or direct to RSAMD and study at all 3 institutions. Pass in Higher grade English plus two others (mus desirable but not essential) required plus gr 7-8 on main inst; keyboard skills also essential. Entry by interview and entrance exam which includes performance. *Age range:* 11-18, with some coverage of primary age range in yr 1.
Music content: 50% time. Bias towards studies relevant to contemporary class teaching, with emphasis in all yrs on keyboard versatility, practical musicianship, compositional studies, 20th C studies; classes also in arranging and orchestration, electronic and recording techniques, techniques of singing and inst teaching, historical studies.
Educational studies: 50% time. Total of 30 wks of school experience spread over 4 yrs of course. *Places:* c 25.

St Andrew's College
Bearsden Campus, Bearsden, Glasgow G61 4QA
Tel: 0141 943 1424 *Fax:* 0141 943 0106

John Pitcathley, head of dept.
Courses offered: BEd Mus Ord/Hons (4) offered jointly with University of Strathclyde Faculty of Education and RSAMD *see* **Royal Scottish Academy of Music and Drama**.
Music content: Principal performance study and additional inst.
Educational studies: Concurrent degree course which offers an in-depth musical training underpinned by educational theory and supported by a number of school placements in both the primary and secondary sections. *Music facilities:* Practice rooms, recording, performing areas, mus IT. *Places:* c 30.

University College of St Martin
Lancaster LA1 3JD
Tel: 01524 384339 *Fax:* 01524 384593
Email: r.mcgregor@ucsm.ac.uk
Website: www.ucsm.ac.uk

Richard McGregor, head of performing arts; Gerard Doyle, snr lecturer in mus; Gillian Cummins, snr lecturer in mus; Kevin Hamel,

lecturer in mus.
Courses offered: BA (QTS) Hons (4) (University of Lancaster). A-level mus preferred if possible (gr 8 theory accepted in lieu), normally with gr 7 playing standard. *Age range:* 3-8 or 7-12, chosen at the end of yr 1.
Music content: 33% of course in yrs 1-3, 50% in yrs 2-4 (excluding time on t/p) including tuition on main inst or voice and other performance skills, composition, historical studies (focusing on 20th C), and related activities, eg choirs, orch, etc.
Educational studies: 50-66% of course time plus time spent on t/p. Latter organised in 3 block practices, 1 of which is a full term, plus regular school attachments. *Music facilities:* Purpose-built mus block with practice rooms, well-stocked library, listening facilities, keyboard lab, a variety of perc and other educational resource material. *Places:* 20-25.

University College Scarborough
Filey Rd, Scarborough YO11 3AZ
Tel: 01723 362392/503228 *Fax:* 01723 370815

Andrew Bates, mus courses leader; Caroline Wilkinson, course leader, QTS mus; Celia Wand, Howard Wilde, lecturers in mus.
Courses offered: BA (QTS) Hons (3). *Age range:* 3-11.
Music content: In addition to mus education, students take modules in mus history, composition, mus technology and performance.
Educational studies: 2 blocks of t/p during 3 yrs of course study. *Places:* 18.

Stranmillis College of Education
Stranmillis Rd, Belfast BT9 5DY
Tel: 01232 381271 *Fax:* 01232 664423
Email: h.grindle@stran-ni.ac.uk
Website: www.stran.ni.ac.uk

Harry Grindle, head of mus.
Courses offered: BEd Hons (4) (Queen's University). Usual requirement is gr C in A-level mus. *Age range:* KS1 and 2.
Music content: 33% of time spread equally over 4 yrs, covering history, keyboard and written musicianship, aural training, study of pno plus another (orch) inst or voice.
Educational studies: About 50% of course time, spread equally, plus t/p of 5-6 wks block practice in each year. *Places:* c10 per year.

University of Strathclyde
Faculty of Education, 76 Southbrae Dr, Glasgow G13 1PP
Tel: 0141 950 3000 *Fax:* 0141 950 3268

Courses offered: BA Hons in Applied Music (4). *Age range:* 11-18 (and primary).
Music content: The three specialist areas of study within this mus degree are business, community and education. All students follow core modules which include solo performance, keyboard

versatility, vocal techniques, ens work, creative skills, mus in its social, historical and cultural context, mus and computers, recording and media integration. The education specialism covers all the competences required of a secondary or primary teacher in Scotland. *Music facilities:* Purpose-built arts building houses state of the art mus labs and practice rooms. *Places:* Approx 30.

University of Sunderland
School of Education, Hammerton Hall, Gray Rd, Sunderland SR2 7JB
Tel: 0191 515 2395 *Fax:* 0191 515 2629
Email: katharine.gailard@sunderland.ac.uk
Website: www.sunderland.ac.uk

Judith Hills, snr lecturer in educ.
Courses offered: BA Hons Music Education Secondary (2), HND, mus diploma or equivalent experience required. *Age range:* Secondary.
Music content: Options include world mus, mus technology.
Educational studies: School-based year. *Places:* 15.

Trinity College (Coleg y Drindod)
Carmarthen SA31 3EP
Tel: 01267 676767 *Fax:* 01267 676766

Marion Thomas, head of mus.
Courses offered: BA (Ed) Hons (3) (University of Wales). A-level mus required or GCSE (or equivalent) plus performing standard of at least gr 5 ABRSM (or equivalent). College is affiliated to the Church in Wales. Most aspects of course available in Welsh. *Age range:* 4-12. Infant and juniors specialisation from yr 3.
Music content: 50% of course time, plus individual inst or vocal tuition.
Educational studies: Academic and professional training runs concurrently throughout the course.

University of Wales, Bangor
School of Education, Normal Site, Bangor LL57 2PX
Tel: 01248 370171 *Fax:* 01248 370461

Delyth H Rees, mus educ co-ord; Ann Hopcyn, lecturer in mus educ.
Courses offered: BEd Hons (3). A-level mus should be offered with inst or vocal competence of gr 5+. *Age range:* 3-8, 7-12; English and Welsh medium.
Music content: Mus units include composition, musicianship, history, world mus, mus technology. *Educational studies:* 24 weeks t/p over 3 yrs. *Music facilities:* Well-equipped mus rooms, wide variety of c/room, IT equipment and some world insts; resources library. *Places:* 15.

University of Wales Institute, Cardiff (UWIC)
Faculty of Education and Sport, Cyncoed Campus, Cyncoed Rd, Cardiff CF2 6XD

Tel: 01222 506554/506513 *Fax:* 01222 506589
Email: croese@uwic.ac.uk

Caryl Roese, dir of mus; Paul Thomas, PGCE (secondary); Julie Piacentini, course dir (2 yr secondary course).
Courses offered: BA (Ed) Hons (QTS) Primary (3) mus specialism in yrs 2 and 3; BA (Ed) Hons (QTS) Secondary Music Specialism (2); PGCE secondary (mus specialism). *Age range:* Primary and secondary.
Music content: Subject study and subject application. World mus, IT. *Music facilities:* IT, practice rooms. *Places:* Primary 15, secondary 15-18.

University of Wales College, Newport
Caerleon Campus, PO Box 101, Newport NP6 1YH
Tel: 01633 432432 *Fax:* 01633 432850
Website: www.newport.ac.uk

Jill Lawton, head of mus.
Courses offered: BA Primary. GCSE mus required, plus gr 5 on 1 inst. *Age range:* 4-11.
Music content: Emphasis is practical, composition (including use of technology) and performance (study of 1 inst). Strong primary school focus.
Educational studies: Links with schools are established in school-focused w/shops. 22 wks t/p in total. Infant or junior options selected in yr 2. *Music facilities:* Library, media resources centre, practice suite, recording studio and computer suite.

University of Warwick
Institute of Education, Coventry CV4 7AL
Tel: 01203 523523 ext 22303/23631
Email: p.v.ellis@warwick.ac.uk; r.c.green@warwick.ac.uk

P Ellis, R Green, course dirs.
Courses offered: BA (QTS) (4). *Age range:* Primary (lower and upper).
Music content: The course is designed to provide for the independent and personal development of students as musicians and teachers. The curriculum courses are designed to apply this subject knowledge in the c/room. Mus units are concerned with knowledge and skills in mus composing (including 20th C techniques), performing, history, development of mus (western and non-western), development of inst and vocal skills.
Educational studies: While training to teach the whole primary curriculum this course prepares students to become mus co-ordinators with a broad arts perspective in the primary school. Mus in education is explored together with a range of practical teaching activities to develop teaching and planning skills. Basic instruction is provided on the gui, in mus technology and class teaching methodology focused primarily but not exclusively on the NC. *Music facilities:* The

Institute of Education's mus centre comprises teaching rooms, electro-acoustic studios and other aspects of mus technology and a number of practice rooms. There is also the University Music Centre, housed in the Warwick Arts Centre, which runs a symph orch, large chorus, chmbr choir, wind orch, br society, big band, Gilbert and Sullivan Society, etc. Regular tours and concerts. Inst and vocal tuition available and mus scholarships awarded each year by competitive audition. *Places:* 15.

Wolverhampton University

School of Education, Walsall Campus, Gorway, Walsall, W Midlands WS1 3BD
Tel: 01922 720141 *Fax:* 01922 323177

John Pymm, principal lecturer and joint head of dept; Kevin Stannard, snr lecturer and joint head of dept; Shirley Thompson, baroque studies; Malcolm Procter, project co-ord.
Courses offered: BEd Hons (3). 2 A-levels (including mus). Students on Access or BTEC or without A-level mus may be accepted if they have a high level of performance skill (gr 7-8). Keyboard skills desirable but not essential. *Age range:* 4-11.
Music content: Modules in performance (especially ens), composition and arrangement, listening, analysis and appraisal of mus from contemporary art mus to popular and ethnic mus. Individual lessons on 1st inst, plus group lessons in voice, gui and keyboard. Students have the opportunity to work with multi-track and computer equipment.
Educational studies: Students take 1 subject at specialist level and 5 subjects at intermediate level (3 core subjects English, maths and science, plus 2 others from NC). School contact begins in yr 1 with visits and small group work, with longer periods of teaching practice in yrs 2 and 3. *Music facilities:* 4 main teaching rooms, 7 practice rooms, main theatre, lecture theatre, 2 recording studios, video editing and TV studio and multi-track/computer room. *Places:* 12.

Postgraduate Certificate of Education

Students with a degree may become qualified teachers by following a one-year Postgraduate Certificate of Education course (PGCE). Courses for both primary and secondary teachers are listed below. A one-year course, which has to prepare graduates for all aspects of teaching and includes a minimum of 12 weeks teaching practice, can offer very little in the way of music instruction which is not geared to classroom activities. Instrumental tuition is sometimes offered, but it is usually left to the individual student to arrange.

Graduates wishing to teach in Scottish secondary schools may apply for the one-year Teaching Qualification in Secondary Education (TQSE) course, but must first take the Scottish Teacher Education Institute entrance test in music. Fully-qualified teachers of music who have been trained outside Scotland do not have to retrain, but may also be required to take elements of the test in music if there is a mismatch in their qualifications.

Courses are divided according to recruitment. For courses in England and Wales, students should apply through the Graduate Teacher Training Registry (GTTR), Fulton House, Jessop Av, Cheltenham, Glos GL50 3SH *Tel:* 01242 223707 (for application enquiries) or 01242 544788 (general enquiries). Applications for courses in Northern Ireland are dealt with by the individual colleges and universities, and graduates should send initial enquiries to the Department of Education for Northern Ireland, Rathgael House, Balloo Rd, Bangor, Co Down BT19 2PR *Tel:* 01247 279279. Enquiries about courses in Scotland should be addressed to the Advisory Service on Entry to Teaching, c/o General Teaching Council for Scotland, Clerwood House, 96 Clermiston Rd, Edinburgh EH12 6UT *Tel:* 0131 3146000 *Website:* www.gtcs.co.uk. Applications should be made through TEACH, PO Box 165, Edinburgh EH8 8AT.

Bath Spa University College *formerly* Bath College of HE
Newton Park, Bath BA2 9BN
Tel: 01225 875875 *Fax:* 01225 875505

George Odam, subject leader, secondary mus educ; Joanna Glover, primary mus educ. *Age range:* 5-12, 11-18. *Course length:* 36 wks with 15 wks t/p. *Musical element:* Mus is a foundation subject in the primary course. Secondary course covers professional studies, practical projects, inst teaching and working with children under guidance of mus tutors. The course is two thirds school-based, continuously assessed and emphasises self-appraisal. *Music facilities:* Mus technology room, practice facility, world mus insts. *Places:* Primary 60; secondary 25.

Bishop Grosseteste College
Newport, Lincoln LN1 3DY
Tel: 01522 527347 *Fax:* 01522 530243

John Bannister, dir of mus; Peter Stopp, PGCE course tutor. *Age range:* 5-11. *Course length:* 38 wks with 19 wks t/p. *Musical element:* Mus covered in context of general PGCE primary course with opportunities for special mus options and extra-curricular mus

work. Cathedral org and choral scholarships available. The course is practical with small group w/shop focus. *Music facilities:* Extensive in specialist primary college. *Places:* 20.

Bretton Hall College of HE
W Bretton, Wakefield, W Yorks WF4 4LG
Tel: 01924 830261 *Fax:* 01924 830521

Philip Priest, secondary; Valerie Tee, primary. *Age range:* 7-12, 11-18. *Course length:* 38 wks with 19 wks t/p (primary), 36 wks (secondary) with part of every wk in school (equivalent 24 wks t/p). College to school balance, primary 50:50; secondary 66:33. *Musical element:* Course covers principles and methods of mus education, computer technology, composition and arranging for c/room, multi-cultural mus. Peripatetic inst teaching course can be taken as subsidiary option by secondary students, including 1 day per wk of school-based work. Other secondary students follow the mus management course which deals with the role of the mus specialist beyond classwork. *Music facilities:* World mus centre, mus technology facility (including purpose-built studio), keyboard lab, library and resource centre. *Places:* Primary 15; secondary 45.

University of Bristol

School of Education, PGCE Division, Helen Wodehouse Building, 35 Berkeley Sq, Bristol BS8 1JA
Tel: 0117 928 7002 *Fax:* 0117 929 9110

Paul Taylor, PGCE mus tutor.
Age range: 11-19. *Course length:* 1 yr. *Musical element:* Main subject course at secondary level. *Music facilities:* IT mus suite. *Places:* 11.

Cambridge University Faculty of Education

Homerton College, Faculty Registry, Hills Rd, Cambridge CB2 2PH
Tel: 01223 507111 *Fax:* 01223 507120

John Finney, course dir.
Age range: 4-9, 7-11, 11-18. *Course length:* 36 wks with 24 wks in school. *Musical element:* The primary (4-11) course provides a foundation course for all students (12 hrs) and a specialist course for those becoming curriculum leaders in mus (24 hrs). The secondary course (11-18) with a module in creative arts places emphasis on children's development as improvisers, composers, performers, listeners and appraisers/analysts. The issues addressed include interculturalism, vocal work, differentiation and assessment, special needs and mus technology. Regular school-based experience; 2 days per wk in term 1, 12 wks in term 2 and 5 wks following a special interest in term 3. *Music facilities:* Concert hall, studio and seminar rooms, practice facilities. Library containing school-based printed materials, teachers' support books, recorded mus, listening facilities and insts. *Places:* 25 secondary; 90 primary.

Canterbury Christ Church College

North Holmes Rd, Canterbury, Kent CT1 1QU
Tel: 01227 767700 *Fax:* 01227 785761

Chris Philpott, course tutor.
Age range: Secondary. *Course length:* 1 yr f/t. *Musical element:* 1 day per wk mus curriculum studies and w/shops, 2-5 days per wk with partnership schools. Practical curriculum sessions, professional studies, 18 wks school experience. *Places:* 20.

University of Central England in Birmingham

Faculty of Education, Westbourne Rd, Birmingham B15 3TN
Tel: 0121 331 6084/6110 *Fax:* 0121 331 6147
Email: janet.hoskyns@uce.ac.uk

Janet Hoskyns, course dir.
Age range: 11-18. *Course length:* 37 wks including 10 days home-based school experience and total school experience 24 wks. *Musical element:* The course is run jointly by schools and the faculty, and covers principles and methods of mus teaching; practical w/shops including general c/room technology relating to NC and examination syllabuses at KS4 and beyond. No specific visiting inst teacher option, but optional inst teaching experience on t/p and experience in w/shops. *Music facilities:* C/room mus facilities include a range of perc, keyboards, etc. Mus technology studio equipped with recording and mixing facilities, drum machines, sampling equipment, mus computers. Also practice rooms, library and mus resource centre for teachers, as well as facilities available in partner schools. *Places:* 28.

University of Durham

School of Education, Leazes Rd, Durham DH1 1TS
Tel: 0191 374 2000 *Fax:* 0191 374 3500

Ruth Thomas, Stuart Button, lecturers in mus educ.
Age range: 5-8, 7-11, 11-18. *Course length:* 38 wks with 22 wks t/p secondary, 22 wks t/p primary. *Musical element:* Mus as part of general primary curriculum, and as a specialist option for secondary teachers. *Music facilities:* Well-equipped mus rooms, practice rooms, full range of resources. Access to all university mus activities. *Places:* Primary 80; secondary 17.

Edge Hill University College

St Helens Rd, Ormskirk, Lancs L39 4QP
Tel: 01695 575171 *Fax:* 01695 584649
Email: biggint@staff.ehche.ac.uk
Website: www.ehche.ac.uk

Tony Biggin, head of mus; Avril Tisdall, snr lecturer.
Age range: 5-8, 7-12. *Course length:* 36 wks with 8 wks t/p. *Musical element:* In context of general primary PGCE course, 40 hrs (including art and drama). Extra-curricular opportunities in mus dept. *Music facilities:* Concert hall, theatre, recording studio; electronic mus lab with Apple Mac, Roland, etc. *Places:* Early years 50; juniors 50.

University of Exeter

School of Education, Heavitree Rd, Exeter EX1 2LU
Tel: 01392 264797 *Fax:* 01392 264736

Piers Spencer, subject chair; Sarah Hennessy, PGCE primary programme leader.
Age range: 7-12. *Course length:* 39 wks. *Musical element:* Mus is taken as a semi-specialism within a course for primary class teachers. The course is 90 hrs within the primary course. It comprises weekly practical seminars and w/shops which aim to give students a broad and balanced experience and training in all aspects of mus teaching and making in the primary school. There are opportunities for developing inst skills. *Music facilities:* Specialist lecture rooms; practice rooms, recording studios, a wide variety of c/room perc, resources library. *Places:* 18.

TEACHER TRAINING COURSES

Gloucestershire Initial Teacher Education Partnership
St Peter's High School, Stroud Rd, Tuffley, Glos GL4 0DE
Tel: 01452 520594 *Fax:* 01452 385135

Chris Arnold, course dir.
Age range: 11-18. *Course length:* 1 yr. *Musical element:* Course covers all the required standards. Trainee teachers are placed and trained in schools that offer very good practice and appropriate facilities in mus. *Music facilities:* Works in close partnership with Cheltenham and Gloucester College of HE. *Places:* 11.

Goldsmiths
University of London, Lewisham Way, New Cross, London SE14 6NW
Tel: 0171 919 7171 *Fax:* 0171 919 7313
Website: www.gold.ac.uk

Robert Kwami, main subject tutor.
Age range: 5-11 or 11-18 (also includes working experience with junior pupils). *Course length:* Primary: 36 wks with substantial t/p throughout year. Secondary: 36 wks with 24 wks t/p (block and serial practice). *Musical element:* Aims to develop understanding of current issues in mus education and their implications for c/room practice. Ideas and materials explored through collaborative work in schools, which forms a point of focus for seminars and w/shop sessions in college. Practical courses include non-western mus, mus technology, improvisation and inst skills. *Places:* Primary 76; secondary 20.

University of Huddersfield
School of Education, Holly Bank Rd, Lindley, Huddersfield HD3 3BP
Tel: 01484 478232 *Fax:* 01484 514784
Email: l.pearson@hud.ac.uk
Website: www.hud.ac.uk/

Lesley Pearson, course dir.
Age range: 11-18. *Course length:* 1 yr (36 weeks). *Musical element:* Focus on mus composition, preparation and evaluation of resources, world mus and mus technology. Professional issues are dealt with in schools and at the School of Education. *Music facilities:* Library, IT, email and internet access and mus technology facilities. *Places:* 20.

Institute of Education
University of London, 20 Bedford Way, London WC1H 0AL
Tel: 0171 612 6740 *Fax:* 0171 612 6741

Keith Swanwick, prof of mus educ; Pauline Adams, mus course leader.
Age range: 5-12, 11-18. *Course length:* 36 wks with at least 18 wks in school. *Musical element:* The secondary course covers principles and methods of mus teaching and offers further mus skills relevant to education. Beginner teachers are able to gain practical experience in a range of different mus styles and traditions, to use and develop IT skills and to examine their application in the c/room. There is scope for improvising, composing and performing in small groups or as individuals and in gaining experience in arranging for, conducting and directing school ens. Within the primary course, mus is a 6-hr foundation subject at KS1. A 9-day mus specialism option is offered at KS2 for those beginner teachers who have some mus expertise. The course allows for opportunities to assess current trends and issues in mus education and to examine ways of implementing a progressive mus curriculum within the primary school. *Music facilities:* Lecture rooms, recital halls, practice, reference and advanced research study rooms, IT, keyboard and recording facilities and a wide range of c/room perc. *Places:* 40.

Kingston University
School of Music, Kingston Hill Centre, Kingston Hill, Kingston-upon-Thames, Surrey KT2 7LB
Tel: 0181 549 1141 *Fax:* 0181 547 7118
Email: g.toplis@kigston.ac.uk

Edward Ho, head of school of mus; Maria Busen-Smith, course tutor PGCE.
Age range: 11-18. *Course length:* 36 wks with 18 wks block t/p and 2 days per wk of the remaining 18 wks spent in school. *Musical element:* In line with TTA requirements, the delivery of the course is shared between the university and partnership schools. The mus component focuses on the mus curriculum, composing, preparation and evaluation of resources, world mus and mus technology. Professional issues are dealt with in schools and in the university during sessions shared with students from other subject areas. *Music facilities:* Gateway School of Recording, Music Technology and Music Business Studies. Purpose-built mus education block with mus technology room, wide range of c/room and world mus insts and resources. *Places:* 19.

Leeds Metropolitan University
School of Teaching and Education Studies, Beckett Pk, Leeds LS6 3QS
Tel: 0113 283 2600

Paul Hurst, mus co-ord.
Age range: KS1 or KS2. *Course length:* 1 yr. *Musical element:* Mus unit of 12 hrs within context of general primary course. *Music facilities:* Roland keyboard lab. *Places:* 47.

University of Leeds
School of Education, Leeds LS2 9JT
Tel: 0113 243 1751 *Fax:* 0113 243 4545
Email: v.gammon@education.leeds.ac.uk./
Website: education.leeds.ac.uk/~edu/initial/main.html

Vic Gammon, lecturer in mus educ.
Age range: 5-12, 11-18. *Course length:* Secondary: 36 wks with at least 24 wks t/p or c/room experience. Primary: 38 wks with at least 18 wks t/p or c/room experience. *Musical element:* All aspects of secondary mus teacher's work covered, with significant emphasis on creative mus-making for the whole class. Primary PGCE has general creative arts unit for all teachers with option for mus specialists. *Music facilities:* Orch, choir, mus groups, mus technology, libraries and resource collection. *Places:* 75+ primary; 16 secondary.

Liverpool Hope University College *formerly*
Liverpool Institute of HE
Hope Park, Liverpool L16 9JD
Tel: 0151 291 3457/3217 (PGCE) *Fax:* 0151 291 3170
Website: www.livhope.ac.uk

Stephen Pratt, head of mus; Ian Sharp, snr lecturer; Mary Black, Jill Simms, lecturers.
Age range: 3-8, 7-11, 11-18. *Course length:* 36 wks (38 wks primary) including 120 days (98 days primary) school-based experience in partnership scheme with schools. *Musical element:* For all 3 age ranges, mus elements include creative activities, singing, rhythm, pitch, listening skills, notation, NC requirements. The course is practically orientated, considerable input from teachers in the field. *Music facilities:* New purpose-built facilities with lecture and practice rooms, electro-acoustic studio, listening and recording facilities, a mus technology lab and a wide range of insts including 3 orgs, 2 hpds. The dept is involved in a great deal of mus-making, ranging from choirs, orch and band to chmbr mus. *Places:* 18 secondary.

Manchester Metropolitan University
Faculty of Community Studies, Didsbury School of Education, Wilmslow Rd, Manchester M20 2RR
Tel: 0161 247 2000 *Fax:* 0161 247 6392
Website: www.mmu.ac.uk

Alan Dean, mus co-ord; Maurice Hope, snr lecturer.
Age range: Secondary. *Course length:* Secondary programme of school-based initial teacher training: 36 wks. 2 yr variant in conjunction with Royal Northern College of Music with special emphasis on str teaching, Kodaly and Dalcroze: 72 wks. *Musical element:* Basic c/room skills are learned and developed in a variety of schools

moving from a highly supported teaching role to more independent activity. During the course students develop a variety of inst and vocal skills, knowledge of mus technology and an awareness of children's creative potential, focusing on the elements of composing, performing, listening and appraising, also teaching for assessment. GCSE, A-level and other 16+ opportunities are covered. 2nd subjects offered include Instrumental Music and its Management, and in depth mus technology. *Music facilities:* A purpose-built mus suite containing two studios with excellent collections of c/room and world insts, practice rooms, listening lounge, library, electronic keyboard lab, mus technology studio. There is a good stock of orch insts, concert org, steel band and 12 pnos. Spacious hall available for concerts, conferences and whole-course teaching sessions. *Places:* 60.

Middlesex University
Trent Pk, Bramley Rd, London N14 4XS
Tel: 0181 362 5686 *Fax:* 0181 362 5684

Michael Bridger, head of school of mus.
Age range: 11-18. *Course length:* 36 wks with at least 120 days t/p. *Musical element:* In addition to the theory and practice of mus education and professional studies, w/shops are offered in mus technology, stylistic diversity (including popular and world mus) and mus in the whole curriculum. A unique element of the course is the provision for intending inst teachers to focus on their particular musical area.

Moray House Institute of Education
Heriot Watt University, Holyrood Rd, Edinburgh EH8 8AQ
Tel: 0131 556 6007

Neil W Houston, subject leader.
Age range: 5-18. *Musical element:* Preparation of student teachers for the mus c/room. 18 wks in college, 18 wks in school including one day per wk in primary school setting. *Music facilities:* Mus technology centre, world mus centre, wide performance base for choral, inst work.

Nene College
Moulton Pk, Northampton NN2 7AL
Tel: 01604 71500

Joanna Moxham, PGCE course tutor.
Age range: 3-8, 7-12. *Course length:* 40 wks, 33% of which is spent on t/p. *Musical element:* Mus covered only in context of general PGCE course. *Places:* 58.

Northern College

School of Music, Dept of Aesthetic Education, Hilton Place, Aberdeen AB24 4FA
Tel: 01224 283500 *Fax:* 01224 283900

Jonathan Stephens, dir of mus, head of aesthetic educ; Pam Robertson, acting deputy dir of mus. *Age range:* 5-12 (PGCE primary, general, available on the Dundee Campus only), 12-18 (PGCE secondary mus, specialist) with some input in the 5-12 range. PGCE secondary mus will not be offered in 1998-9, but may run on the Aberdeen Campus in 1999-2000. Qualifications are validated by the Open University. *Course length:* 36 wks including 18 wks school experience. *Musical element:* Secondary: all aspects of c/room mus are covered with a focus on listening and appraising, composing, performing and practical versatility. Course also includes primary methodology and prepares students to teach mus at all levels. Primary: all students have regular sessions in mus and the expressive arts, together with general preparation for teaching in the primary school. The mus course covers the main areas appropriate to work with pupils in the 5-12 age range. *Music facilities:* Aberdeen Campus: world mus centre (including Balinese gamelan, African drums, steel pans, samba/salsa insts), mus technology facility (including purpose-built electro-acoustic studio), keyboard lab, library and resource centre, theatre and mus therapy special education facility (new centre in process of development). *Places:* Primary 64 (Dundee Campus).

Nottingham Trent University

Faculty of Education, Clifton Hall, Clifton Village, Nottingham NG11 8NJ
Tel: 0115 941 8418 *Fax:* 0115 948 6747

Ian Gibbons, Deliah Pawluch, joint PGCE course leaders; John Scott, lecturer.
Age range: 5-11 (covering infant and jnr). *Course length:* 38 wks with approx 19 wks t/p. *Musical element:* Mus covered in the context of the general course for all students. *Places:* 50.

Open University

The School of education, Walton Hall, Milton Keynes MK7 6AA
Tel: 01908 274066

Gary Spruce.
Age range: 11-18. *Course length:* 18 months p/t PGCE in mus available at the School of Education. *Places:* 80.

Oxford Brookes University

PGCE Courses Admissions Registry, Headington, Oxford OX3 0BP
Tel: 01865 483025; 01865 485873

Sarah Maidlow, course dir.
Age range: 11+.

University of Plymouth

Rolle Faculty of Education, Douglas Av, Exmouth, Devon EX8 2AT
Tel: 01395 265344 *Fax:* 01395 255303

Philip Hull, head of dept.
Age range: Secondary. *Course length:* 36 wks with 24 wks based in school, in line with DFE guidelines. *Musical element:* An innovative course for intending secondary mus specialists, with subsidiary subject option. *Music facilities:* Large mus suite with MIDI-based electronics studio. *Places:* 16.

University of Reading

Dept of Arts and Humanities in Education, Bulmershe Ct, Woodlands Av, Reading RH6 1HY
Tel: 0118 931 8839 *Fax:* 0118 935 2080

Paul Wells, Gordon Cox, course dirs.
Age range: 5-12 (primary), 11-18 (secondary). *Course length:* Primary: approx 38 wks with 18 wks t/p. Secondary: 36 wks, 24 school-based, 12 university-based. *Musical element:* Primary: includes specialised mus and all curriculum areas in terms 1 and 2, arts project (drama, movement and art) in term 2. Secondary: includes study of the principles and methods of mus education with special reference to current developments and issues concerning c/room mus. Course aims to broaden students' experience of contemporary mus, composition, improvisation, pop, blues, jazz, ethnic, electronic and computer-generated mus, multi-cultural mus with particular emphasis on composition, microtechnology and the development of performance and communication skills in teaching via the innovative Community Music Project. Both courses are based on a close relationship between theory and practice. *Music facilities:* Purpose-built studio and practice rooms together with a comprehensive inst collection, resource centre and microtechnology studios. All courses work closely with local schools and students are encouraged to participate in the flourishing musical life of the campus which includes choirs, orchs, jazz band, contemporary mus group. *Places:* Early years 29; jnr 29; secondary 20.

University College of Ripon and York St John

York Campus, Lord Mayor's Walk, York YO3 7EX
Tel: 01904 616851

Marilynne J R Davies, head of perf studies; Carol Gaibett, PGCE mus; David Lancaster, snr lecturer in composition; Bruce Cole, mus technology.
Age range: 11+. *Course length:* 1 yr. *Music facilities:* Wide range of extra-curricular activities, well-equipped practice rooms, mus technology rooms, Clavinova studio and concert facilities.

Also pno studies, mus technology, course for children with special needs and opportunities to spend semester abroad. *Places:* 15.

Roehampton Institute London
Music Education, Southlands College, Roehampton La, London SW15
Tel: 0181 392 3000 *Fax:* 0181 392 3435
Email: c.durrant@roehampton.ac.uk

Colin Durrant, co-ord of mus educ.
Age range: 5-11, 11-18. *Course length:* 36 wks with 2 periods of block school experience (6 wks each) plus school-based course for remaining wks. *Musical element:* In the primary programme mus is taught as a NC foundation subject. The secondary programme includes subject extension in the area of management and methodology of inst teaching as well as the exploration of the nature of creative arts and mus technology. *Places:* 25.

University College of St Martin
Lancaster LA1 3JD
Tel: 01524 384339 *Fax:* 01524 384593
Email: r.mcgregor@ucsm.ac.uk
Website: www.ucsm.ac.uk

Richard McGregor, head of performing arts; Gerald Doyle, early years PGCE; Gillian Cummins, Kevin Hamel, upper primary PGCE.
Age range: 3-8, 7-12, 11-18. *Course length:* Primary: 36 wks with 13 wks t/p. Secondary (from 1999): autumn term is 34 days t/p school-based, 36 college-based; spring term block t/p; summer term is 23 days college-based, 27 school-based. *Musical element:* Primary course covers all subjects including mus. Secondary provides full specialist options including principles and methods of mus teaching, curriculum issues, mus technology and skills in performance management, direction and arranging for school groups as well as methods for promoting pupil's learning in mus. *Music facilities:* Purpose-built mus block with practice rooms; well-stocked library; keyboard lab, listening facilities, plus a variety of perc and other educational resources. All facilities currently being enhanced through Performing Arts Departmental provision. *Places:* Primary 70; secondary 20 (from 1999).

University College Scarborough
Filey Rd, Scarborough YO11 3AZ
Tel: 01723 362392 *Fax:* 01723 370815

Andrew Bates, lecturer in mus.
Age range: 3-11. *Course length:* 36 wks, about 25% of which is t/p (including block practices and 2 days per wk school attachments). *Musical element:* Mus covered as part of Creative and Expressive Arts course (1 of 6 general courses covering primary curriculum). *Places:* 8.

Stranmillis College of Education
Stranmillis Rd, Belfast BT9 5DY
Tel: 01232 381271 *Fax:* 01232 664423
Email: h.grindle@stran-ni.ac.uk
Website: www.stran.ni.ac.uk

Harry Grindle, head of mus.
Age range: 3-8, 5-13. *Course length:* 30 wks, including 15 wks t/p. *Musical element:* Pedagogical course, covering all aspects of school mus teaching. *Places:* 5.

University of Strathclyde
Faculty of Education, 76 Southbrae Dr, Glasgow G13 1PP
Tel: 0141 950 3000 *Fax:* 0141 950 3268
Email: c.g.byrne@strath.ac.uk
Website: www.strath.ac.uk/departments/appliedarts/

Charles Byrne, dir of mus in Teacher Educ programmes; Mark Sheridan, dir of research at the NJI; Iain Massey, lecturer in mus technology.
Age range: 11-18 (with a component on mus in the primary school). *Course length:* 36 wks including 22 wks t/p. *Musical element:* Course covers acquisition of c/room skills (lesson planning, c/room management, use of teaching aids, eg computers), plus elements of class mus teaching (performing: vocal and inst, listening, children's compositions, c/room ens work, exam preparation, projects). Also introductory modules on playing gui, bass gui, drum kit and multi-tracking and computer technology. *Music facilities:* Purpose-built arts building houses mus labs and practice rooms. *Places:* 10.

University of Sunderland
School of Education, Hammerton Hall, Gray Rd, Sunderland SR2 8JB
Tel: 0191 515 2395 *Fax:* 0191 515 2629
Email: katharine.gailard@sunderland.ac.uk
Website: www.sunderland.ac.uk

Elizabeth Holden, snr lecturer in educ.
Age range: Secondary. *Course length:* 1 yr, school-based. *Places:* 5.

University of Sussex Institute of Education
Initial Teacher Education, PGCE Admissions, Education Development Building, Falmer, Brighton BN1 9RG
Tel: 01273 678405 *Fax:* 01273 678411
Email: m.p.searls@sussex.ac.uk

Marian Metcalfe, Chris Hiscock, course tutors.
Age range: 11-18. *Course length:* 1 yr f/t, 19-21 months p/t. *Musical element:* The course is designed and taught by practising teachers in close partnership with mus depts in Sussex schools. Trainees gain considerable workshop-based practical experience in

developing the skills and knowledge relevant to teaching NC Music at KS3, and other courses at KS4 and KS5 including GCSE and A/AS levels. Trainees also take a hands-on course in mus technology, become familiar with aspects of world mus in an educational context, and develop competence in directing extra-curricular mus activities. *Music facilities:* Teaching equipment as required. All mus facilities are available in partnership schools where trainees spend most of their time. *Places:* 12. Numbers expected to be increased shortly.

Trinity College (Coleg y Drindod)
Carmarthen SA31 3EP
Tel: 01267 676767 *Fax:* 01267 676766

Marian Thomas, head of mus.
Age range: 5-12 (course taught in Welsh and English). *Course length:* 36 wks including 12 wks t/p plus 2 wks school experience. *Musical element:* Lectures, tutorials, simulated teaching sessions, concentrating on teaching techniques, c/room management. Class teaching only. *Music facilities:* Inst tuition and practice facilities available.

University of Ulster
Coleraine Campus, Cromore Rd, Coleraine, Co Londonderry BT52 1SA
Tel: 01265 44141 *Fax:* 01265 324923 ext4918
Email: b.burgess@ulst.ac.uk

Harry McMahon, head of school of educ; Barry Burgess, PGCE course tutor.
Age range: 8-13, 11-18. *Course length:* 36 wks including 24 wks in secondary and grammar schools, 4 wks school-based project and 1 wk in a primary school. *Musical element:* Importance attached to 1st study performance and development of keyboard skills. Choral and orch work with courses in conducting, arranging and mus teaching methods, ethnic mus, mus for people with special needs, mus technology (especially the use of keyboards and computers), issues arising from the Northern Ireland Curriculum and curriculum development through c/room based research. Students pursue courses in IT and micro-electronics in mus. *Music facilities:* Mus educ c/room, 2 Apple Mac labs, video conferencing facility, email centre for interaction with schools and students on teaching practice, staffed resources area, micro teaching suite, drama studio and educ library. *Places:* 16.

University of Wales Bangor
School of Education, Normal Site, Bangor LL57 2PX
Tel: 01248 370171 *Fax:* 01248 370461

Delyth H Rees, mus educ co-ord; Ann Hopcyn, lecturer in mus educ.
Age range: 3-8, 7-12, 11-18 (new course). English and Welsh medium. *Course length:* Primary: 38 wks with approx 18 wks t/p. Secondary: 36 wks with 24 wks school experience. *Musical element:* Primary: all aspects of primary teaching covered with mus unit within curricular studies; emphasis is on practical work. Secondary: principles and methods of mus educ, lesson planning, c/room organisation, assessment, NC requirements, GCSE and A-level mus. *Music facilities:* Well-equipped mus rooms, wide variety of c/room and IT mus equipment and some world insts. Resources library. *Places:* Primary 65; secondary 10.

University of Wales Institute, Cardiff (UWIC)
Faculty of Education and Sport, Cyncoed Campus, Cyncoed Rd, Cardiff CF2 6XD
Tel: 01222 506554/506513 *Fax:* 01222 506589
Email: croese@uwic.ac.uk

Paul Thomas, snr lecturer.
Age range: Secondary. *Course length:* 1 yr. *Musical element:* Subject study, subject application, world mus, IT components. *Music facilities:* IT facilities. Practice rooms. *Places:* 15-18.

Worcester College of HE
Henwick Grove, Worcester WR2 6AJ
Tel: 01905 738080

Jenny Hughes, head of mus.
Age range: Secondary. *Course length:* 1 yr. *Musical element:* Students should have an honours degree that is at least 66% mus. Students can be offered a wide range of school placements both in state and private sectors of education. *Music facilities:* The facilities include a suite of practice cubicles, teaching rooms, listening room and two small electronic studios. Two grand pnos, including a new Steinway, a hpd and a set of crumhorns are available for practice. There is a good collection of recorded mus from a range of cultures in addition to a stock of teaching material for use in school. The college computer centre and the mus dept work collaboratively to keep an up to date selection of mus software available on a range of computers likely to be found in schools. *Places:* 10.

In-Service Courses for Teachers

In-service training is widely available for music teachers. The following tables list full-time and extended part-time courses of study. Courses for music teachers vary from those leading to a recognised qualification (eg BEd/BA (QTS) degrees) to those which provide additional training in a particular area of teaching. Many short courses are also organised, often to meet more specific needs, which require little or no time off from teaching.

The local music adviser should be consulted for details of local in-service provision (INSET) arranged by the LEA both at LA music centres and at local schools (*see* **Local In-Service Courses for Classroom Teachers** at the end of this section).

Some areas are also served by a Teachers Centre (*see* **Resource Centres**). Most of these centres are active in investigating new teaching developments (particularly the Music Education Information and Research Centre at the University of Reading).

The DfEE publishes *HMI Short Courses for Teachers*, which contains details of their annual series of short, residential courses, some of which include music teaching. Many organisations arrange their own courses and summer schools, several of which offer training for teachers (eg Dalcroze Society, British Kodaly Society, British Suzuki Institute, Orff Society, and the Benslow Music Trust *see* **Summer Schools and Short Courses**). For in-service training in music therapy and the teaching of people with disabilities *see* **Music and Disability**.

In-Service Courses

To be eligible for secondment on salary to full-time courses of one year's duration, serving teachers (other than teachers in special education) must normally have had at least 5 years' teaching experience. Applicants for admission to the courses must satisfy the admission requirements of the institution offering the course.

All serving teachers are eligible to apply for admission to part-time courses, although the time allowed for study and financial assistance will depend upon the employer.

Details of BA(QTS) and PGCE courses and addresses will be found elsewhere in the **Teacher Training Courses** section.

Higher Degrees

The following list contains details of the few structured higher degree courses organised for serving teachers, usually requiring previous teaching experience. These courses normally take 1 year of study on a full-time basis, and 2-4 years part-time.

Bath Spa University College
Newton Park, Bath BA2 9BN

Jo Glover, snr lecturer in mus educ.
MA in professional studies in education. Up to 5 yrs p/t.

Bretton Hall, University College
West Bretton, Nr Wakefield, W Yorks
Tel: 01924 830261 *Fax:* 01924 830521

Valerie Tee, programme co-ord.
MA/MEd in Music Education. 27 months p/t. Mus modules available in theory and practice of mus

education, world musics as a teaching resource, popular mus in education, performance and composition at student's own level, dissertation.

Institute of Education
Institute of Education, 20 Bedford Way, London WC1H 0AL

Lucy Green, course co-ord.
MA in Music Education. 1 yr f/t or 2-4 yrs p/t. Taught course with dissertation or report. Applicants must be qualified teachers (either BEd or mus degree plus t/t), or graduates with a musical background. tudents will develop a sophisticated knowledge of thinking, research and practice, apply critical faculties to their own musical and educational research and practice and carry out a piece of small-scale empirical or theoretical research.

Reading University
Faculty of Arts and Humanities in Education, Bulmershe Ct, Reading RG6 1HY
Tel: 0118 931 8821 *Fax:* 0118 935 2080

Gordon Cox, course dir.
MA in Music Education. 1 yr f/t, 2-4 yrs p/t. Modular course designed to extend the understanding of the theoretical basis of educational practice, provision and curriculum development in mus. For graduates with teaching

experience. Course comprises 6 modules followed by dissertation. Individual modules can be taken separately.

Roehampton Institute
Music Education Dept, Froebel Institute College, Roehampton La, London SW15 5PJ
Tel: 0181 392 3382 *Fax:* 0181 392 3664
Email: cedarr@roehampton.ac.uk

Colin Durrant, programme convener.
MA Choral Education (Roehampton Institute). 1 yr f/t, up to 4 yrs p/t. Modular course mainly for mus teachers in primary and secondary schools and also for others such as conductors, church musicians etc. Designed to enhance professional knowledge, skills and competence in the choral area within an educational context.

Trinity College of Music
Music Education Dept, 11-13 Mandeville Pl, London W1M 6AQ
Tel: 0171 935 5773; 0171 224 1626 *Fax:* 0171 487 5717

John Stephens, course dir.
MA (Music Education). 1 yr f/t, 2-3 yrs p/t. For teachers and professional musicians to develop practical skills relevant to their professional work. The course is based on a series of assessed projects undertaken within the context of the students' normal professional activity or by specialist placements.

BEd Degree Courses in Music For Serving Teachers

These are 1 year full-time or 2-3 year part-time courses for teachers with initial training and 2-3 years' teaching experience. Normal matriculation requirements are expected.

Christ Church College
School of Music, North Holmes Rd, Canterbury, Kent CT1 1QU

BA(Ed) (University of Kent). 1 yr f/t, 3 yrs p/t. Initial teacher training with 3 yrs teaching experience required.

Institute of Education
20 Bedford Way, London WC1H 0AL

Charles Plummeridge, snr lecturer in mus educ.
BEd Hons. 3 yrs p/t. 50% of Part II may be devoted to mus education. The course covers the nature of musical experience, resources and

mus teaching strategies, curriculum design and development, and the organisation, management and evaluation of mus education in schools. Initial t/t plus 1 yr teaching experience required.

Liverpool Hope University College
Hope Park, Liverpool L16 9JD
Tel: 0151 737 3457

Stephen Pratt, head of mus.
BEd (Hons) (University of Liverpool). Mus, education studies, curriculum studies and t/p (300+ hrs).

One Year Full-Time Courses

Full-time courses are available at the **Institute of Education**, 20 Bedford Way, London WC1H 0AL. Charles Plummeridge, snr lecturer in mus education. These courses offer further training in music teaching and are arranged to meet more specialised needs than other courses. The 1 year course may also be studied part-time over 2 years and is an individually tailored course in which students select their own area of study (eg music education or work with a particular age group). The course involved lectures, seminar attendance, visits and research. Certificates are then awarded on the basis of a report to be submitted after study has ended. The 1 term course is offered during a particular term and is organised to provide supplementary training to meet particular needs. It involves supervision of a project along with attendance at relevant seminars.

Extended Part-Time Courses
(with occasional full-time study)

These courses, of at least 60 hours study, are studied on a part-time basis over an extended period of time so that teaching may continue with the minimum of disruption to pupils and classes. Courses fall into two categories :

i) those suitable for music specialists (eg primary curriculum leaders, secondary teachers) and class teachers with some music teaching experience, providing supplementary training to investigate and develop skills in a particular area of music teaching.
ii)those suitable for non-specialists and teachers with little or no musical skill who are called upon to teach class music. These courses aim to cover the rudiments of elementary music teaching, and to develop the application of existing musical skills to classroom music teaching.

(i) Music specialists/class teachers with some music teaching experience

Brunel University
Dept of Creative//Performing Arts, Gordon House, 300 St Margaret's Rd, Twickenham TW1 1PT
Fax: 0181 891 0487

Shiela McQuattie, course leader.
Music Diploma Course (for study of mus college diplomas). 1 yr p/t, Weds. Course for those wishing to take performers or teachers diplomas from a conservatoire or ABRSM theory exams.

Goldsmiths, University of London
Professional and Community Education, Lewisham Way, London SE14 6NW
Tel: 0171 919 7229 *Fax:* 0171 919 7223
Email: cen01cce@gold.ac.uk

Jeremy Peyton Jones, mus programme co-ord.
Certificate in Music Teaching to Adults. 1 yr p/t. Course for competent musicians and mus teachers wishing to specialise in adult teaching, continuing, further and higher education.
Course develops musicianship for teachers (composing, improvising, aural perception, singing skills) and puts teaching principles into action through teaching practice and placement in college.

Goldsmiths, University of London
Professional and Community Education, Lewisham Way, London SE14 6NW
Tel: 0171 919 7229 *Fax:* 0171 919 7223
Email: cen01cce@gold.ac.uk

Jeremy Peyton Jones, mus programme co-ord.
Certificate in Music Workshop Skills. 2 yrs p/t. Course for competent musicians wanting to run w/shops, group tuition, and community-based mus making.
The course combines practical and theoretical aspects of mus w/shop leading and self management through experience in placements in a community setting.

Institute of Education
20 Bedford Way, London WC1H 0AL

Charles Plummeridge, snr lecturer in mus educ.
Associateship. 2 yrs p/t. *See* **One-Year Full-Time Courses.**

King Alfred's College of HE

Winchester SO22 4NR
Tel: 01962 841515 *Fax:* 01962 842280
Email: malcolmf@virgo.wkac.ac.uk

Malcolm Floyd, course co-ord.
Three Certificates in Advanced Educational Studies. 10 days p/t with school-based assignments.
The Expressive Arts in Education, Child Development in Music and the NC, An Intercultural View of the Music Curriculum. Can be taken as a pathway to a Diploma in Advanced Educational Studies.
Applicants need qualified teacher status. Validated as double credits for the LTCL (Mus Ed). Also various shorter courses.

Reading University

International Centre for Research in Music Education, Bulmershe Court, Reading RG6 1HY
Tel: 0118 931 8821 *Fax:* 0118 935 2080
Email: e.smith@reading.ac.uk

Laurel Pegg, course dir.
Music Curriculum Co-ordination and Consultancy in the Primary School. 4120 hrs made up of school-based work and p/t attendance. For all teachers who are, or who aspire to be, primary mus co-ordinators developing a collaborative role with staff.

Roehampton Institute, London

Music Education Dept, Froebel Institute College, Roehampton La, London SW15
Tel: 0181 392 3382 *Fax:* 0181 392 3664
Email: cedarr@roehampton.ac.uk

Susan Young.
Diploma in Teaching of Music (Roehampton Institute). 2 yrs (5.30-7.30pm Thu).
Course mainly for primary school teachers with responsibility for organisation of mus in their schools. Modular course dealing with aspects of mus in the NC (composition, singing, technology, performing arts and inter-cultural approaches).

Trinity College of Music

Music Education Dept, 11-13 Mandeville Pl, London W1M 6AQ
Tel: 0171 935 5773 *Fax:* 0171 487 5717

John Stephens, dir of mus educ.
ATCL (Music Education) and LTCL (Music Education) for teachers. Course organised on a module basis within 3 yrs p/t.
Mus teaching course for those seeking to extend their musical skills. Modules appropriate for teachers in primary, secondary and special schools as well as in the private sector.
Courses include two summer schools at the college.

Trinity College of Music

Music Education Dept, 11-13 Mandeville Pl, London W1M 6AQ
Tel: 0171 935 5773 *Fax:* 0171 487 5717

John Stephens, dir of mus educ.
Special Course in Music. Up to 3 terms p/t. Aims to develop mus and teaching skills. Tuition in practical subjects is arranged within a programme of mus studies. Entrance audition.

Worcester College of HE

Henwick Grove, Worcester WR2 6AJ

College Certificate in Primary Music (Oxford Modular Scheme). 2 modules stretching across 2 terms. Course members attend practical sessions at college, and plan a mus policy for the whole of the primary age range.

(ii) Non-specialists/class teachers with little or no music teaching skills

Bath Spa University College

Newton Park, Bath BA2 9BN

R Ritchie, in-service admin; Jo Glover, snr lecturer in mus educ.
Certificate of Advanced Professional Studies: Music in the Primary School. 1 yr p/t. For generalist teachers in primary schools who require more mus training.

Reading University

International Centre for Research in Music Education, Bulmershe Ct, Reading RG6 1HY
Tel: 0118 931 8821 *Fax:* 0118 935 2080
Email: e.smith@reading.ac.uk

Laurel Pegg, course dir.
Music and Creative Development in the Nursery. 3 w/ends over 3 terms or arranged in other formats around the country. Mus and creative development presented within an holistic framework of all the desirable outcome learning areas. The course is for all teachers and assistants within nursery settings. No mus experience is necessary.

University College of Ripon and York St John

Lord Mayors Walk, York YO3 7EX

Certificate in Music Education 'Make Music Matter'. 1 yr p/t (1 evening per wk plus occasional w/end attendance). 4 modules of 30 hrs each. Course to enable class teachers to acquire skills, expertise, knowledge, confidence and curriculum insight in order to teach mus effectively to 5-11 yr olds. Includes mus for children with special needs. Each module is free standing and can be taken as part of the Advanced Diploma in Applied Educational Studies.

Local In-Service Courses for Classroom Teachers

In-service, INSET and twilight courses run by Local Education Authorities and local music centres are listed below by region: London, Rest of England, Scotland, Wales, Northern Ireland

London

Camden Borough Council
Education Development Centre, The Crowndale Centre, 218-220 Eversholt St, London NW1 1BD
Tel: 0171 911 1677 *Fax:* 0171 911 1536

Peter West, mus co-ord; Gina Edwards, admin.
A range of primary and secondary courses for teachers. Areas include practical approaches to c/room mus, planning, assessment, listening, devising policy, planning schemes of work, induction for newly qualified teachers, mus technology, composing and performing, working with visiting artists.

Ealing Education Centre
Westlea Rd, off Boston Manor Rd, London W7 2AD
Tel: 0181 579 5151

Tony Shield, gen inspector for mus.
Courses frequently held for mus teachers.

Enfield B C Education Dept
PO Box 56, Civic Centre, Silver St, Enfield, Middx EN1 3XQ
Tel: 0181 967 9250

Stephen Block, gen adviser, mus and perf arts.
INSET courses for primary and secondary class teachers, mus with technology; inst tutors. Performing arts courses and other cross-curricular collaborations.

Greenwich Professional Development Centre
Eltham Green Complex, 5th Floor, 1a Middle Park Av, Eltham, London SE9 5HH
Tel: 0181 850 5043 *Fax:* 0181 850 8937

Christopher Harrison, inspector for mus.
Full programme of courses and meetings for teachers at all KS.

Hackney Professional Development Centre
Albion Dr, London E8 4LI
Tel: 0171 241 5522

INSET courses published in termly brochure.

Haringey Music Centre
PDC, Downhills Park Rd, London N17 6AR
Tel: 0181 829 5033 *Fax:* 0181 365 8253

Leonora Davies, inspector for mus and mus services.
Half-day in-service courses for inst staff each term. General mus curriculum courses for c/room teachers throughout the year.

London Borough of Harrow
PO Box 222, Civic Centre, Harrow HA1 2UZ
Tel: 0181 424 1645 *Fax:* 0181 427 0810

Kevin Sadler, schools mus and arts service mgr.
C/room, inst and vocal in-service training courses for borough schools and mus service staff.

Islington Education Dept
Laycock St, London N1 1TH
Tel: 0171 457 5540 *Fax:* 0171 457 5829

Full in-service training programme for teachers.

Royal Borough of Kensington and Chelsea
Isaac Newton Centre, Professional Development, 108a Lancaster Rd, London W11 1QS
Tel: 0171 221 4031 *Fax:* 0171 243 1570

Mus courses for primary and nursery class teachers, inst tutors and for teachers in all phases.

Kingston Music Service
37 Fullers Way North, Surbiton KT6 7LQ
Tel: 0181 391 9248 *Fax:* 0181 391 5185

Joan Child, head of mus service.
Programme of in-service training for primary, secondary, special and inst teachers.

Lambeth Education Dept
234-244 Stockwell Rd, Briston, London SW9 9SP
Tel: 0171 926 2559

In-service training is available through consultancies with a community mus resource centre 'Musicworks'.

Lewisham Education QAD Team
Lewisham Professional Development Centre, Kilmorie Rd, London SE23 2SP
Tel: 0181 291 5005 *Fax:* 0181 291 6259

Christopher Harrison, gen adviser (mus).
Courses on all aspects of the mus curriculum are organised at the professional development centre and school-based support is arranged on request. A range of publications is available.

Merton Music Foundation
MMF Office, Chaucer Building, Canterbury Rd, Morden, Surrey SM4 6PX
Tel: 0181 640 5446; 0181 687 1846

John Mander, dir.

Regular INSET courses for inst and class mus teachers. Day, half-day and twilight courses.

Redbridge Music Service
John Savage Centre, Fencepiece Rd, Hainault, Ilford, Essex IG6 2LJ
Tel: 0181 501 3944 *Fax:* 0181 500 3893

Eric Forder, mus service dir.
INSET for primary, secondary and special school teachers as advertised in the Redbridge LEA INSET booklet.

Southwark Education Resource Centre
Cator St, London SE15 6AA
Tel: 0171 525 2808 *Fax:* 0171 525 2849

Tom Deveson, mus advisory teacher.
Termly courses on mus in the NC; mus for class teachers and planning for mus in schools; cross-curricular courses combining mus with other subjects; courses on mus policy, schemes and units of work. All courses can be run for individual schools/institutions by negotiation.

Wandsworth Borough Council Education Dept
Curriculum and Professional Development Service, Professional Centre, Franciscan Rd, London SW17 8HE
Tel: 0181 682 3759 *Fax:* 0181 682 4016
Email: rcrockes@profcent.edex.co.uk
Website: www.shared.insnet.net/profcent

Roger Crocker, development offr, mus.
Package 1: nursery, early years, KS1. Package 2: primary and KS2. Starting points for the generalist teacher; using ethnic insts from Asia and Africa; nursery and early years mus provision; mus technology in the classroom; in-school mus support; developing mus from KS2 to KS3. Twilight w/shop each half term.

Rest of England

Barnsley Performing Arts Development Service
Grove St, Barnsley
Tel: 01226 291525

Lesley Hepworth, head of service.
Courses for teachers covering all aspects of mus and performing arts in education.

Bedfordshire Education Dept
Emerald Court, Pilgrim Centre, 20 Brickhill Dr, Bedford MK41 7PZ
Tel: 01234 213439 *Fax:* 01234 363516

Ian Smith, county mus offr.
Portfolio of in-service courses available for specialist and non-specialist c/room teachers on a wide range of topics including current aspects of mus education. Half-day or day courses.

Birmingham Music Education
Birmingham Advisory and Support Service - Music Team, Martineau Education Centre, Balden Rd, Birmingham B32 2EH
Tel: 0121 428 1177 ext 334 *Fax:* 0121 428 1180

Susan Scarsbrook, teacher adviser co-ord.
In-service courses for all phases (validated by Trinity College of Music) and w/shops provided throughout the city.

Cornwall Education Advisory Service
Pondhu House, Penwinnick Rd, St Austell PL25 5DP
Tel: 01872 327516 *Fax:* 01726 77041

Derek Kitt, county adviser (mus).
2-day residential courses; twilight courses for cluster groups and individual schools; training days for clusters and individual schools; cross-curricular courses; joint departmental and instrumental service staff courses.

County Durham Music Support Service
Darlington Music Centre, Borough Rd, Co Durham DL1 1SG
Tel: 01325 380757 *Fax:* 01325 352473

J Allen, head of service.
In-service courses for teachers; vocal course, basic curriculum for non-specialist course, jazz and improvisation course and curriculum support to schools.

Coventry Performing Arts Service
Leasowes Av, Coventry CV3 6BH
Tel: 01203 692348 *Fax:* 01203 692717

Owen Dutton, head of service.
Regular INSET opportunities with a different focus, eg world arts, technology, singing, dance and drama.

Derby Music Activities
Derby City Education Service, Middleton House, 27 St Mary's Gate, Derby DE1 3NN
Tel: 01332 716886 *Fax:* 01332 716920

Philip King, adviser.
Various in-service courses for all phases.

Devon Curriculum Advice
Expressive Arts Base, Salisbury Rd, Plymouth PL4 8QZ
Tel: 01752 223581 *Fax:* 01752 253537
Email: jforster@www.devon-cc.gov.uk

John Forster, adviser for mus.
Programme of courses supporting school teachers in raising the quality of mus teaching and learning at all KS. Brochure available on request.

Doncaster
William Appleby Music Centre, Danum Rd,
Doncaster DN4 5HE
Tel: 01302 323556 *Fax:* 01302 323605

Peter Bear, dir of mus services.
In-service courses for teachers on various aspects of mus teaching.

Dorset Professional Development Services
County Hall, Dorchester, Dorset DT1 1XJ
Tel: 01305 224203 *also fax*

Kevin Rogers, mus adviser.
A wide range of courses offered through Professional Development Services.

Essex Advisory and Inspection Service
INSET Unit, County Hall, A Block, Chelmsford, Essex CM1 1LD
Tel: 01245 436007 *Fax:* 01245 344652

Jo Brockis, mus adviser.
Wide range of accredited courses and w/shops for teachers within the annual and termly programme, covering pre-KS1 to post-16.

Gateshead Dryden PDC
Evistones Rd, Low Fell, Gateshead, Tyne-and-Wear NE9 5UR
Tel: 0191 482 4133

J C Treherne, head of mus service.
Music in the NC. Courses at KS1, KS2 and KS3 levels. Day, half-day and twilight.

Hampshire Music Service
Hampshire Music Centre, Gordon Rd, Winchester SO23 7DD
Tel: 01962 861502 *Fax:* 01962 863690
Email: edmsmcrh@hants.gov.uk

Richard Howlett, head of mus service.
Extensive range of in-service courses for primary (KS1-2) and secondary (KS3-4) teachers; special schools.

Havering Inspection and Advisory Service (HIAS)
Broxhill Centre, Broxhill Rd, Harold Hill RM4 1XN
Tel: 01708 773813

John Morris, adviser for mus.
INSET courses available for both inst and c/room teachers.

Isle of Man Music Centre
Government Buildings, Lord St, Douglas, Isle of Man IM1 1LE
Tel: 01624 686555 *Fax:* 01624 686557

Bernard Osborne, John Cain, Stuart Loaring, INSET.
Various INSET packages arranged throughout the year for primary, secondary and peripatetic mus teachers.

Isle of Wight Music Service
Directorate of Education, County Hall, Newport,
Isle of Wight PO30 1UD
Tel: 01983 823435 *Fax:* 01983 826099

Neil Courtney, head of inst mus.
In-service courses for specialist and non-specialist mus teachers held regularly.

Kent Curriculum Services Agency
South Borough Buildings, Loose Rd, Maidstone,
Kent ME15 6TL
Tel: 01622 672202 *Fax:* 01622 691412

Derek Blease, county lead consultant for mus.
Support for the NC mus implementation. Cross-county INSET courses, demonstration lessons, w/shops and curriculum support projects.

Kirklees Music School
The Oastler Centre, 2nd Floor, Co-operative Buildings, 103 New St, Huddersfield HD1 2UA
Tel: 01484 426426 *Fax:* 01484 480490

David Williams, principal.
Provides curriculum support and INSET to specialist and non-specialist teachers for Kirklees Local Education Authority.

Knowsley Training and Conference Centre
219 Knowsley La, Huyton, Merseyside L36 8HW
Tel: 0151 443 5615/6 *Fax:* 0151 480 4411

Stephen Titchmarsh, head of perf arts service.
NC courses in mus and inst skills courses for teachers.

Leeds City Council Dept of Education
Music Support Service, The West Park Centre, Spen La,
Leeds LS16 5BE
Tel: 0113 230 4074 *Fax:* 0113 230 4073

C P Brackley Jones, head of mus support service.
A variety of in-service courses are offered for inst teachers and teachers in primary, secondary and special schools.

Leicestershire Arts in Education
Leicestershire Education Dept, Knighton Fields, Herrick Rd,
Leicester LE11 2HD
Tel: 0116 270 0850 *Fax:* 0116 270 4928

Anice Paterson, arts development consultant.
In-service courses for teachers both in school and centrally organised, including courses accredited by Leicester University and Trinity College of Music.

Lincolnshire Education and Cultural Services Directorate
County Offices, Newland, Lincoln LN1 1YQ
Tel: 01522 552222 *Fax:* 01522 553257

Joy Stopher, educ and mus adviser.
In-service courses provided by the Curriculum and Monitoring Branch.

Liverpool Education Offices
14 Sir Thomas St, Liverpool L1 6BJ
Tel: 0151 225 2707 *Fax:* 0151 225 2718

Aelwyn Pugh, inspector for curriculum (with mus).
Range of in-service courses for teachers at all levels and at special schools.

Manchester Music Service
Zion Arts Centre, Stretford Rd, Manchester M15 5ZA
Tel: 0161 226 4441/22 *Fax:* 0161 226 1010

Allan Jones, gen adviser (mus).
Full in-service training programme for mus teachers.

Newcastle upon Tyne Advisory Service
Education Dept, Civic Centre, Newcastle upon Tyne NE1 8PU
Tel: 0191 232 8520 *Fax:* 0191 211 4983

Steve Halsey, gen adviser (mus).
Regular programme of in-service courses for teachers.

NIAS
John Dryden House, 8-10 The Lakes, Northampton NN4 7DD
Tel: 01604 237083 *Fax:* 01604 236240

David Bray, mus inspector.
30+ courses per year on all aspects of the mus curriculum, devised to reflect national and local priorities.

Norfolk Centre for Arts in Education
Bull Close Rd, Norwich, Norfolk NR3 1NG
Tel: 01603 618914 *Fax:* 01603 764419

David Sheppard, mgr arts in educ services.
Frequent INSET courses organised. Courses at all key stages to support c/room mus.

Northumberland County Council
Education Development Centre, Hepscott Pk, Morpeth, Northumberland NE61 6NF
Tel: 01670 533518 *Fax:* 01670 533591

Alison Rushby, snr adviser.
Range of curriculum and management in-service courses.

Oxfordshire Music Service
Oxford School, Glanville Rd, Oxford OX4 2AU
Tel: 01865 779959 *Fax:* 01865 712438

Richard Hallam, dir of mus, inspector.

In-service training for special school teachers, general primary, specialist primary, specialist secondary teachers and instrumental teachers.

Rotherham Education Dept
Norfolk House, Walker Pl, Rotherham S65 1AS
Tel: 01709 382121/822576 ext 3698 *Fax:* 01709 839771

Geoffrey Thomas, adviser for mus and perf arts.
INSET book published annually including day, half-day, twilight and evening courses. Topics include NC mus, mus and IT, ethnic mus, preparing for examinations. Inst repair.

Sefton Education Dept
Town Hall, Bootle, Merseyside L20 7AE
Tel: 0151 934 3343

Jacqui Emery, acting mus adviser.
In-service courses for teachers.

Shropshire Music Service
Longmeadow, Bayston Hill, Shrewsbury SY3 0NU
Tel: 01743 874145 *Fax:* 01743 872666

Keith Havercroft, county mus adviser.
Large annual programme of courses and w/shops for mus teachers KS1-4 and post-16.

Solihull Education Dept
PO Box 20, Council House, Solihull, W Midlands B91 3QU
Tel: 0121 704 6619 *Fax:* 0121 704 8065

Joyce Rothschild, inspector for schools (mus).
Regular in-service courses for teachers.

Staffordshire - QLS
Kingston Centre, Fairway, Stafford ST16 3TW
Tel: 01785 277900/1

Nigel M Taylor, county inspector for mus and perf arts.
Wide variety of mus and performing arts courses for teachers in primary, special, middle and secondary schools. Programme published on a termly basis.

Stockport Music Centre
Dialstone Centre, Lisburne La, Stockport SK2 7LL
Tel: 0161 474 2233 *Fax:* 0161 474 2218

Colin Edwards, advisory teacher.
Wide range of INSET courses for specialist and non-specialist primary teachers including residential w/end courses for secondary teachers.

Suffolk County Music Service
Northgate Arts Centre, Sidegate La West, Ipswich, Suffolk IP4 3DF
Tel: 01473 281866 *Fax:* 01473 286068

Residential and and non-residential in-service courses for specialist and non-specialist mus teachers.

Sunderland INSET Agency
Broadway Education Development Centre, Springwell Rd, Sunderland SR4 8NW
Tel: 0191 553 5600 *Fax:* 0191 553 5633

Stephen Auster, mus adviser.
Primary, secondary and special mus in-service courses; also mus/IT centre.

Surrey Curriculum and Management Consultancy
The Runnymede Centre, Chertsey Rd, Addlestone, Surrey KT15 2EP
Tel: 01932 569663 *Fax:* 01932 570249

Keith Clark, county consultant for the arts.
Extensive in-service training programme.

Sussex (East)
PO Box 4, County Hall, St Anne's Cres, Lewes, E Sussex BN7 1SG
Tel: 01273 481208 *Fax:* 01273 481902

Karen Brock, county mus adviser. 1 and 2-day courses with follow up work alongside teachers in the classroom. Full, varied programme of in-service courses for primary, secondary and special school teachers. Based on own materials at KS1 and KS2 as well as courses which explore cross-curricular themes, IT, world mus across all key stages. Courses are also run in partnership with outside agencies such as Glyndebourne.

Sussex (West) Education Dept
Western Area Professional Centre, Stockbridge Rd, Chichester, W Sussex PO19 2EF
Tel: 01243 532970 *Fax:* 01243 531080

David Williams, gen adviser (mus).
Regular in-service courses for teachers are provided.

Tees Valley Music Service
The Oakland Centre, Fakenham Av, Middlesbrough TS5 4QQ
Tel: 01642 819903 *Fax:* 01642 852104

David Kendall, head of service.
In-service courses for all KS and curriculum enrichment programme.

Wakefield Music Service
Manygates Education Centre, Manygates La, Sandal, Wakefield WF2 7DQ
Tel: 01924 303306

Val Jennings, head of inst service.
A whole range of INSET training courses in mus.

Warwickshire County Music Service
22 Northgate St, Warwick CV34 4SR
Tel: 01926 412803 *Fax:* 01926 412746

Inspection, curriculum and in-service support, frequent in-service courses and conferences.

Wigan Music Advisory and Support Service
The Performing Arts Centre, The Professional Development Centre, Park Rd, Hindley, Wigan WN2 3RY
Tel: 01942 255227/254280 *Fax:* 01942 255217

Wide range of in-service courses for Wigan teachers.

Wolverhampton - Jennie Lee Professional Centre
Lichfield Rd, Wednesfield, Wolverhampton WV11 3HT
Tel: 01902 555957 *Fax:* 01902 555966

Denise Hopkins, advisory teacher for mus.
Regular in-service training for teachers.

Scotland

Argyll and Bute Council
Education Dept, Argyll House, Alexandra Parade, Dunoon, Argyll PA23 8AJ
Tel: 01369 704000

Ronald M Gould, head of support service.
In-service courses for class and inst teachers relating to 5-14, standard grade and highers.

Dumfries and Galloway
Dept for Education, 30 Edinburgh Rd, Dumfries DG1 1NW
Tel: 01387 260435 *Fax:* 01387 260453
Email: colin.brett@dumgal.gov.uk

C Brett, educ offr.
Regional staff development days. Primary mus courses. Various activities relating to secondary yrs 1 and 2. Comprehensive in-service programme for inst instructors.

Dundee City Council
Educational Development Service, Gardyne Rd, Dundee
Tel: 01382 462857 *Fax:* 01382 462862
Email: advisers@educational-development-servicedundee city.sch.uk

Charles Maynes, co-ord, expressive arts.
Continuous staff development programme.

East Ayrshire Music
Curriculum Management, Kilmarnock Academy, Elmbar Drive, Kilmarnock KA1 3BS
Tel: 01563 525509 *Fax:* 01563 542683
Email: kilmnkacad@aol.com

Alexander Ferguson, chmn curriculum management group (mus).
Teacher support for 5-14, standard grade and highers.

City of Glasgow Department of Education

Glasgow City Council, Charing Cross Complex, House 1, 20 India St, Glasgow G2 4PF
Tel: 0141 287 8182 *Fax:* 0141 287 8212
Email: rmackie@essglasgow.org.uk

Ronnie Mackie, adviser in creative & aesthetic subjects.
In-service courses for 5-14 expressive arts, standard grade mus, revised higher mus and higher still mus.

Highland Education Centre

Castle St, Dingwall, Ross-shire IV15 9HU
Tel: 01349 863441 *Fax:* 01349 865637

H C Richardson, regional mus adviser.
Regular INSET courses such as computing in mus and special needs.

Lothian Advisory Service

Westwood House, 498 Gorgie Rd, Edinburgh EH11 3AF
Tel: 0131 469 3043 *Fax:* 0131 469 3311

Andrew Kerr, mus adviser.
Extensive in-service provision for school mus and inst staff.

Wales

Carmarthenshire

Griffith Jones Centre, St Clears, Carmarthenshire SA33 4BT
Tel: 01994 231223 *Fax:* 01994 231255
Email: ewjonescarm@satproj.org.uk

Emyr Wynne Jones, mus adviser.
In-service for primary, secondary teachers and curriculum leaders. Also in-service for peripatetic staff. Half-day, day and twilight. Also, school-based consultancies.

Northern Ireland

North-Eastern Education and Library Board

Music Service, County Hall, 182 Galgorm Rd, Ballymena, Co Antrim BT42 1HN
Tel: 01266 662565/6/7 *Fax:* 01266 46071

Eric Boyd, head of mus services.
In-service courses for teachers; centre-based training for all post-primary mus teachers; centre-based training for non-specialist primary teachers; school-based in-service to primary schools. Half days twice a year, plus stand alone days as required.

Southern Education and Library Board

3 Charlemont Pl, The Mall, Armagh BT61 9AX
Tel: 01861 523811

Margaret Yeomans, creative and expressive studies adviser.
Various in-service policy and practice courses for specialist and non-specialist primary teachers; courses for post-primary mus teachers; c/room based in-service to primary schools.

Western Education and Library Board

Music Service, 1 Spillars Place, Omagh, Co Tyrone BT78 1HL
Tel: 01662 244821 ext 145 *Fax:* 01662 246716

Dónal Doherty, mus adviser.
INSET courses related to NIC for secondary and primary teachers.

INTERNATIONAL STUDY
Scholarships for Study Abroad

Organisations

The general advice is to contact the Embassy or High Commission in Britain of the country in which you wish to study. The organisations listed below can offer advice in certain countries.

Association of Commonwealth Universities
Publication Sales, John Foster House, 36 Gordon Sq,
London WC1H 0PF
Tel: 0171 387 8572 *Fax:* 0171 387 2655
Email: info@acu.ac.uk
Website: www.acu.ac.uk

Sue Kirkland, mgr ed directory publishing.
Students and staff wishing to study in a country other than their own, primarily, but not exclusively, within the Commonwealth, should refer to the following publications available from the above address: Awards for First Degree Study at Commonwealth Universities; Awards for Postgraduate Study at Commonwealth Universities; Awards for University Teachers and Research Workers; Awards for University Administrators and Librarians.

British Council
Overseas Appointments Services, Bridgewater House, 58 Whitworth St, Manchester M1 6BB
Tel: 0161 957 7383 *Fax:* 0161 957 7397

Mark Hepworth, applications offr.
The British Council itself does not offer scholarships to attend courses outside the UK. The funds administered by the British Council are channelled through schemes which enable overseas students to study in Britain. It does, however, administer a certain number of scholarships which are offered by the Chinese government.

Czech Ministry of Culture
Foreign Relations Dept, Valdstejnska 10, CZ-118 11
Praha 1, Czech Republic
Tel: 00 420 2 513 2628 *Fax:* 00 420 2 245 10346

Renata Romanova.
Czech artists, agents or representatives may seek support directly from the Ministry of Culture of the Czech Republic. The Ministry of Culture liaises with the Embassy's Cultural Dept, seeking their advice.

Embassy of Brazil
32 Green St, London W1Y 4AT
Tel: 0171 499 0877 *Fax:* 0171 493 5105
Email: ademar@infolondres.org.uk
Website: www.demon.uk/itamaraty

Ademar Seabra da Cruz Junior, head of cultural section.
All requests for support should be addressed to the head of the Cultural Section at the Brazilian Embassy which has a budget for support towards Brazilian cultural activity in the UK. The type and level of support is determined by each application. Proposals should be presented in writing or by fax and interviews will be arranged where appropriate. The cultural section of the Embassy can advise on sponsorship opportunities. It is essential that such requests be presented at least six months before the intended date of the recital or concert.

Embassy of Mexico
Cultural Section, 42 Hertford St, London W1Y 7TF
Tel: 0171 499 8586 *Fax:* 0171 495 4035

Juan Manuel Santin, minister for cultural affairs.
As part of a cooperative program between the Mexican and British governments, the Mexican government, through the Ministry of Foreign Affairs, offers student scholarships for British nationals on 3 programs: the Bilateral covers a wide range of academic disciplines together with specific projects involving various Mexican educational institutions; the Multilateral program invites applications for p/grad studies and collaborative academic research projects; the Special Program is specifically for research about Mexico. Application deadlines vary according to the academic timetable of the institution involved. Students must establish individual contact with the appropriate university or institution and obtain written confirmation of their acceptance on their chosen course of study. More information about higher education establishments in Mexico can be obtained

through a visit to the ANUIES (National Association of Universities and Institutes of Higher Education) website at www.anuies.mx

Embassy of Peru
52 Sloane St, London SW1X 9SP
Tel: 0171 235 2545 ext 20 Fax: 0171 235 4463

Juan Manuel Tirado, first sec.
The Peruvian Embassy does not have a budget to support the UK presentation of arts from Peru but can offer limited support, such as publicity in the Embassy's press releases, to selected projects. It cannot offer financial assistance direct to the promoter. However, it can offer selective advice on sponsorship opportunities. The Instituto Nacional de Cultura (INC) at Jiron Ancash 390, Lima 1, Peru, and the Ministry of Foreign affairs can also advise on potential sources of private funding and sponsorship opportunities.

Embassy of Venezuela
Cultural Centre, 58 Grafton Way, London W1P 5LB
Tel: 0171 388 5788

Gloria Carnevali, cultural attaché.
UK promoters seeking advice or support for projects should contact the Cultural Centre which can liaise with the relevant Ministry in Venezuela. The Cultural Centre has a small budget to supplement some of the costs of projects involving the presentation of the Venezuelan arts in the UK. In order to qualify for a grant the project must be supported by an institution or an official body.

German Academic Exchange Service
34 Belgrave Sq, London SW1X 8QB
Tel: 0171 235 1736 Fax: 0171 235 9602

Offers scholarships to p/grad students based at UK institutions of higher education to study in Germany. Next application deadline for mus one-yr grants, end Nov 1998 for study commencing Oct 1999.

The Italian Institute
The Bursary Dept, 39 Belgrave Sq, London SW1X 8NX
Tel: 0171 235 1461 Fax: 0171 235 4618
Email: italcultur@martex.co.uk

Provides information on advanced training and scholarships in Italy (including study at some opera centres attached to principal opera houses).

Japan Information and Cultural Centre
The Embassy of Japan, 101-104 Piccadilly, London W1V 9FN
Tel: 0171 465 6500 Fax: 0171 491 9347
Email: jicc@jicc.demon.co.uk
Website: www.embjapan.org.uk

Jane Anthony, educ offr.
The Embassy deals directly with the Japanese Ministry of Education (Monbusho) scholarship which is annual and open to all UK passport holders aged under 35 who have a first degree in any discipline.
Scholarships are held for 18 months to 2 yrs, tenable from Apr or Oct. Participants spend the first 6 months on an intensive Japanese course, then pursue their specialist subject. Living expenses, a return air ticket and university fees are covered by the Japanese Government. Application forms available from Mar for scholarships taken up the following year. A maximum of 20 scholarships offered annually.

Open Society Institute
888 Seventh Av, New York, NY 10106
Tel: 00 1 212 757 2323 Fax: 00 1 212 974 0367
Email: osnews@soros.org

Michael Vachon, dir of public affairs.
The network of Soros foundations supports Central and Eastern European projects and people. Where non-indigenous organisations and people receive grants, Central and Eastern European projects and individuals must be direct beneficiaries.

The Polish Embassy
34 Portland Pl, London W1N 4HQ
Tel: 0171 636 6032 Fax: 0171 637 2190
Email: pci-lond@pcidir.demon.co.uk

Provides details of study in Poland and administers the Polish Government Postgraduate Scholarship scheme. This scheme enables exchanges to take place in the fields of sciences, humanities and arts, lasting from 3-9 months. The scholarship provides exemption from tuition fees, free medical care and book grants, but does not cover travel costs between the UK and Poland. Candidates must be British citizens aged under 35, and should hold at least a BA, BSc or equivalent degree.
Application forms must be submitted by the end of Dec for the following year. Five Polish government scholarships are available annually for 4-week 'Polonicum' Polish language courses held at the University of Warsaw, Jagiellonian University in Cracow and the Marie Curie-Sklodowska University in Lublin during the summer. Short visits to Poland are also available for individuals under age 50 wishing to visit Poland for professional academic purposes. Visits normally last 2-3 weeks and proposals should be submitted not later than 12 weeks prior to the proposed arrival date. Funding covers internal travel, accommodation and daily subsistence costs, but does not cover travel to and from Poland.

Scholarships

American Foundation Harriet Hale Woolley Scholarships
15 Boulevard Jourdan, F-75690 Paris Cedex 14, France
Tel: 00 33 1 5380 6888 *Fax:* 00 33 1 5380 6899
Email: fondusa@iway. fr

Scholarships of $8500 awarded each year to artists for the study of art and mus in Paris. Must be a single American graduate aged 21-29, with evidence of artistic or musical accomplishment, and enrolled at an institute of higher learning in Paris. Applications by 31 Jan annually.

Anna Instone Memorial Award
Capital Radio, 30 Leicester Sq, London WC2H 7LA

Kevin Appleby, admin.
Award of £5000 for a p/grad student at a London mus college who must be nominated by the principal. Applications through nominators only by 1 Mar. Award may be used for study abroad.

Arts Council of Wales Awards for Advanced Study in Music
Music Dept, 9 Museum Pl, Cardiff CF1 3NX
Tel: 01222 394711 *Fax:* 01222 221447

Lyn Davies, snr mus offr.
Awards made to musicians aged 28 and under, born and educated in Wales. Also open to those now permanently resident in Wales and normally having lived in Wales for 2 yrs. May be used for study in UK or abroad. Applications by 1 Feb annually.

Australian Music Foundation
Beaufort House, 15 St Botolph St, London EC3A 7EE
Tel: 0171 247 6555 *Fax:* 0171 247 5091
Email: jfe@richardsbutler.com

John F Emmott, hon sec.
Major award for Australian singers and insts of p/grad or equivalent standard for advance course of study in Europe. Max age 30 on 31 Dec prior to application in Apr.

Countess of Munster Musical Trust
Wormley Hill, Godalming, Surrey GU8 5SG
Tel: 01428 685427 *Fax:* 01428 685064

Gillian Ure, sec.
Tuition and maintenance grants for UK and Commonwealth mus students, tenable at home and abroad. Age range: 18-25 for insts, 18-27 for female singers, 18-28 for male singers. Auditions Apr-Jun. Applications by 31 Jan.

Emanuel Hurwitz Chamber Music Charitable Trust
44 Church Cres, London N3 1BJ

Miriam Keogh, founder and admin.
Bursaries for str players to further their studies in chmbr mus at home or abroad (college/university fees will not be paid). Applications will only be accepted in writing with sae. Applications by 1 Jun. UK citizens only.

English Speaking Union Scholarships
The English Speaking Union, Dartmouth House, 37 Charles St, London W1X 8AB, UK
Tel: 0171 493 332 *Fax:* 0171 495 6108

Phil Ward, cultural affairs.
The ESU offers the following mus scholarships, varying from 3 to 9 weeks, to musicians of outstanding ability to study at summer schools in North America, Canada and Europe: Aspen Music School, Steans Institute (Ravinia Festival), Tanglewood Music Center, Dallas Symphony/Conservatory Music in the Mountains (Colorado), Yale University School of Music (Norfolk Chamber Music Festival), Banff Centre for the Arts, Académie Internationale de Musique Maurice Ravel (France) and International Kodály Seminar (Hungary). Applications in Nov for placements the following year.

Fulbright Awards
US-UK Fulbright Commission, Fulbright House, 62 Doughty St, London WC1N 2LS
Tel: 0171 404 6880 *Fax:* 0171 404 6834
Website: www.fulbright.co.uk

Lisa Davey, programme dir.
For 1st year of p/grad academic study and research in the US, covering round-trip travel and maintenance allowance. Any discipline, must have or expect a 2:1 degree, possess UK citizenship and be able to demonstrate leadership qualities; deadline for submission of application forms is Nov. These awards cover 9 months of academic year only. A number of awards are also available for research and lecturing for a minimum stay of 3 months in the US; £1750 (inclusive of round trip travel). Application forms should be submitted in the spring. Send large (A4) sae (for 100g) to British Programme Administrator for application form, stating clearly the award for which details are required. Further information and application forms can be obtained by visiting the Commission's website.

Harriet Cohen Memorial Music Awards Trust

Manches & Co, Aldwych House, 81 Aldwych, London WC2
Tel: 0171 404 4433 *Fax:* 0171 430 1133

John Rubinstein, admin trustee.
Annual awards to young British National professional musicians which may be used for study or performances abroad. Max age 30. Trust invites nominations from main mus institutions in rotation. No individual applications considered. Candidates will be auditioned and interviewed.

Ian Fleming Music Education Awards

c/o Musicians Benevolent Fund, 16 Ogle St, London W1P 7LG
Tel: 0171 636 4481 *Fax:* 0171 637 4307

Awards for mus education and help with inst purchase to outstanding young musicians beginning a career. May be used for study abroad. Max age 25 (insts), 29 (singers). Application fee £10. Applications from Nov, auditions Apr.

Julius Isserlis Scholarship

Royal Philharmonic Society, 10 Stratford Pl, London W1N 9AE
Tel: 0171 491 8110 *Fax:* 0171 493 7463

Richard Fisher, gen admin.
Awarded biennially by competition to students aged 15-25, of any nationality, permanently resident in the UK, in selected performing categories (spring 1999, fl and oboe) for study abroad. Value £20,000 over 2 yrs. Entry fee £20.

KPMG/Martin Musical Scholarship Fund

Lawn Cottage, 23a Brackley Rd, Beckenham, Kent BR3 1RB
Tel: 0181 658 9432 *also fax*

Martyn Jones, admin.
Annual awards for instrumentalists aged 25 and under to study in UK or abroad. Fund aims to assist exceptional talent with specialist and advanced study and to help bridge the gap between study and fully professional status. Not open to organists, singers, conductors, composers or academic students. Includes tuition fees and subsistence grants. Application fee £10. Selection of candidates is by audition. Auditions held in Jan. Applications by 1 Dec. Awards payable from 1 Apr. Send sae.

Nadia and Lili Boulanger International Foundation

3, pl Lili Boulanger, F-75009 Paris, France
Tel: 00 33 1 47 07 05 93

Alexandra Laederich, sec.
Scholarships are awarded to musicians of all nationalities and to scholars who propose research into the history or theory of mus who have shown ability for musical achievement and creativity. Open to those aged 20-35.

Nannie Jamieson Nutshell Fund

6 Ember La, Esher, Surrey KT10 8ER
Tel: 0181 398 4691

Sylvia Palmer, admin.
European String Teachers Association, British Branch. Modest bursaries awarded annually for students and teachers of str insts (ESTA members) for help to attend w/shops, conferences and teaching courses. May be used abroad. Applications by 1 May.

Richard Tauber Prize

Anglo-Austrian Music Society, 46 Queen Anne's Gate, London SW1H 9AU
Tel: 0171 222 0366 *Fax:* 0171 233 0293

Tony Fessler, gen sec.
Travel bursary and public recital in London open to British or Austrian singers. Next prize awarded in spring 1998.

Scottish Arts Council Travel and Training Bursaries

Performing Arts Dept (Music), 12 Manor Pl, Edinburgh EH3 7DD
Tel: 0131 226 6051 *Fax:* 0131 225 9833
Email: sac@artsfb.org.uk

Helen Jamieson, mus offr.
Bursaries to professional instrumentalists, singers, composers and conductors to extend expertise through study in UK or abroad. Bursaries cannot be made in connection with f/t study or training. Applicants must be Scottish based and have worked in the profession for 2 yrs. Applications by Feb 1998. Awards unlikely to exceed £1500.

South East Music Schemes

19 Bourne Rd, London N8 9HJ
Tel: 0181 340 4116

Deborah Rees, admin dir.
Awards for p/grad singers, instrumentalists and composers who live (or have lived) in the South East Arts region and who may not receive mandatory awards towards further study in the UK or abroad. Age limit 30. Applications available from Mar 1998 with sae, closing date 22 May 1998. Funded by South East Arts. Application fee (non-refundable) £15.

Sybil Tutton Awards

c/o Musicians Benevolent Fund, 16 Ogle St, London W1P 8JB
Tel: 0171 636 4481 *Fax:* 0171 637 4307

Awards to assist exceptionally talented opera students aged 18-30 on recognised operatic study courses; intended primarily for maintenance.

May be used for study abroad. Applications from Nov for auditions in Apr. Application fee £10.

Trevor Snoad Award

Martin Musical Scholarship Fund, Lawn Cottage, 23a Brackley Rd, Beckenham, Kent BR3 1RB
Tel: 0181 658 9432 *also fax*

Martyn Jones, admin.
An award granted to an outstanding va player aged 25 and under of p/grad standard. Preference to UK citizens. To finance tuition fees and/or maintenance. May be used for study abroad.

Winston Churchill Memorial Trust

15 Queen's Gate Terrace, London SW7 5PR
Tel: 0171 584 9315 *Fax:* 0171 581 0410

Miss R Conner, mgr.
Travelling fellowships in arts subjects, not necessarily mus. Applications Sep-Oct.

Yamaha Music Foundation of Europe

Yamaha-Kemble Music (UK) Ltd, Sherbourne Dr, Tillbrook, Milton Keynes MK7 8BL
Tel: 01908 366700 *Fax:* 01908 368872

K Watts.
3 scholarships of £2000 each; disciplines rotate annually.

International Courses

The following list details postgraduate courses available at overseas educational institutions. Applicants are advised to contact the institution concerned well before the start of the course to check availability of places for overseas students.

The Department for Education and Employment publishes a guide to opportunities for higher education in Europe entitled *The European Choice,* which contains many useful addresses for students wishing to study in Europe. It is available from DFEE Publications, PO Box 5050, Sudbury, Suffolk CO10 62Q *Tel:* 0845 602260.

Australia

Australian National University
Institute of the Arts, Australian Centre for the Arts and Technology, GPO Box 804, Canberra ACT 0200, Australia
Tel: +612 6249 5640 *Fax:* +612 6247 0229
Email: julie.fraser@anu.edu.au
Website: online.anu.edu.au/ita/acat/acathome.html

Julie Fraser, exec offr.
Courses: PhD; MA in Electronic Arts (by coursework, MA in Electronic Arts (by research); Graduate Diploma in electronic arts (including computer animation, computer music and multimedia options).

Elder Conservatorium of Music
Faculty of Performing Arts, University of Adelaide, South Australia 5005, Australia
Tel: +61 8 8303 5786 *Fax:* +61 8 8303 4423

Patrick Brislan, associate dean (international students).
Courses: Undergraduate: BMus in performance, composition, music education, musicology and ethnomusicology, jazz.
Postgraduate: BMus (Hons) in performance, musicology, music theory; Graduate Diploma in performance, music education, theory, ethnomusicology, jazz; MMus in performance, theory.

University of Melbourne
Faculty of Music, Parkville, Victoria 3052, Australia
Tel: +61 3 9344 5256 *Fax:* +61 3 9344 5346

Warren Bebbington, dean.
Courses: MMus in musicology, performance, composition, music education, music therapy; Master of Arts in musicology; Graduate Diploma in music therapy, guided imagery and music, electroacoustic, film and TV and instrumental composition; PhD in musicology, music therapy; DMus in advanced instrumental teaching, music research, composition.

University of New South Wales
Faculty of Arts and Social Sciences, School of Music and Music Education, Sydney, New South Wales 2052, Australia
Tel: +61 2 385 4871 *Fax:* +61 2 313 7326

Jill Stubington, head of school.
Courses: Research degrees: MMus (Hons), MMusEd (Hons), PhD. Taught degrees: MMus, MMusEd, BMus/BEd (double degree).

University of Newcastle
Faculty and Conservatorium of Music, Auckland St, Newcastle, New South Wales 2300, Australia
Tel: +61 49 294133 *Fax:* +61 49 265450

Robert Constable, dean of faculty.
Courses: BMus, BMus (Hons), DipMus, MMus, MA (Music), PhD in performance, composition, church mus.

Queensland Conservatorium of Music, Griffith University
PO Box 28, Brisbane Albert St, Queensland 4002, Australia
Tel: +61 7 875 6333 *Fax:* +61 7 875 6282

Heather Crombie, mgr, overseas office.
Courses: MMus in performance research, performance, contemporary musicology, music theory, aural and keyboard musicianship, composition; Graduate Diploma in instrumental or vocal performance, opera, opera repetiteur, composition, conducting, musicology. Undergraduate courses are also available.

University of Queensland
Faculty of Music, St Lucia, Queensland 4072, Australia
Tel: +61 7 365 4949 *Fax:* +61 7 365 4488

Malcolm Gillies, faculty dean.
Courses: MMus in composition, performance, music therapy, musicology, music education; MA in musicology; PhD in composition, musicology, music education; DMus in advanced musicological research, composition; Diploma in music therapy; Diploma in music studies (aural

studies and choral conducting); MMusSt in aural studies and choral conducting; Graduate Certificate in mus studies (aural studies and choral cond).

University of Sydney

Department of Music, Sydney, New South Wales 2006, Australia

Tel: +61 2 9351 2923 *Fax:* +61 2 9351 7340
Email: chris.miles@music.sydu.edu.au

A Marett, postgraduate course convenor.
Courses: PhD in musicology, ethnomusicology and composition; MPhil; MA; MMus in performance, composition, musicology and ethnomusicology; diploma in musical composition.

Sydney Conservatorium of Music

University of Sydney, Macquarie St, Sydney, New South Wales 2000, Australia

Tel: +61 2 230 1222 *Fax:* +61 2 252 1243
Email: mkoskelainen@greenway.usyd.edu.au
Website: www.usyd.edu.au/su/conmusic/

Mia Koskelainen, international student liaison offr.
Courses: Graduate Diploma in performance, accompaniment, repetiteur, opera; Master of Music in music education, performance, conducting, composition, musicology; Master of Performance.

Tasmanian Conservatorium of Music

GPO 252C, Hobart, Tasmania 7001, Australia
Tel: +61 02 21 7314 *Fax:* +61 02 21 7318

S de Haan, head of dept.
Courses: Associate Diploma of Music; Graduate Diploma of Music in performance; MMus in performance, composition, music education, research; PhD.

University of Western Australia

School of Music, Nedlands, Western Australia 6907, Australia

Tel: +61 9 380 2056 *Fax:* +61 9 380 1076
Email: dsymons@cyllene.uwa.edu.au

David Symons, senior lecturer.
Courses: MusM in composition, performance; MMusEd in music education; MA in musicology; PhD in musicology, music education; MusD in composition; DLitt in music research; Grad DipMusEd and Grad CertMusEd in music education.

Austria

Bruckner Konservatorium of Upper Austria

Wildbergstr 18, A-4040 Linz, Austria
Tel: +43 732 731 3060 *Fax:* +43 732 731 30630

Reinhart von Gutzeit, dir.
Courses: Performance, music education, conducting, music theory and history, opera, dance and jazz.

Franz Schubert Conservatorium of Music and the Performing Arts

Mariahilfer Strasse 51/II, A-1060 Wien, Austria
Tel: +43 1 587 4787 *Fax:* +43 1 587 7819

Evelyn Brandstetter, vice-dir.
Courses: State-recognised mus school and conservatoire founded in 1867. Diploma or teachers certificate; performance, theory, composition, jazz; all instruments and voice, chamber music, orchestra, also sound studio.

Tiroler Landeskonservatorium

Paul-Hofhaimer-Gasse 6, A-6020 Innsbruck, Austria
Tel: +43 512 583447 *Fax:* +43 512 58 344716

Michael Mayr, dir.

Courses: Performance, church music direction, opera, repetiteur training, theory, music history.

University of Music and Drama in Graz

Palais Meran, Leonhardstr 15, A-8010 Graz, Austria
Tel: +43 316 389 1207/1210 *Fax:* +43 389 1710
Email: petra.ernst@mhsg.ac.at
Website: www.mhsg.ac.at

Petra Ernst-Kühr, head of international programmes.
Courses: Students with a Master's degree or equivalent may take courses in a particular artistic field for a limited period of time.
No degree can be awarded. Also 3-yr diploma for advanced students in the fields of pno chamber music, pno vocal accompaniment, church music, lied and oratorio, music drama performance.

University of Music and Performing Arts, Vienna

Lothringerstrasse 18, A-1030 Wien, Austria
Tel: +43 1 58 806 *Fax:* +43 1 58 806110

Erwin Ortner, rector and prof.
Courses: Opportunities for postgraduate study as a guest student for two years.

Belarus

Belorussian Academy of Music
Internasionalaya 30, 220030 Minsk, Belarus
Tel: +7 0172 274942/271103 *Fax:* +7 0172
270013/209125

Vadim Yakonyuk.

Courses: Postgraduate courses in theory, history
of music, performance, music education.

Belgium

Royal Conservatory of Music, Liege
14 Rue Forgeur, B-4000 Liege, Belgium
Tel: +32 41 22 0306 *Fax:* +32 41 22 0384

Bernard Dekaise, dir.
Courses: Performance, contemporary music.

Royal Flemish Conservatory
Hogeschool Antwerpen, Department of Dramatic Art,
Music and Dance, Desguinlei 25, B-2018 Antwerp, Belgium

Tel: +32 3 244 1800 *Fax:* +32 3 238 9017
Email: secr@deptd.hogant.be

H Marien, head of dept.
Courses: Masters degrees (2 + 3 yrs) covering all
insts and voice; theory of mus, composition,
conducting (choir, orch, windbands); jazz and
popular mus. Diploma of Specialisation (1 or 2
yr) in inst, voice, conducting or composition.

Brazil

University of Brasilia Foundation
Department of Music, Institute of Arts, Campus
Universitario, Asa Norte, 70910 Brasilia, Brazil
Tel: +55 61 348 2335/2337 *Fax:* +55 61 272 1053

Beatriz Magalhaes-Castro, prof of fl.
Courses: Postgraduate courses in fl, bsn,
composition, choral conducting and music
education.

Federal University of Rio Grande Do Sul
Rua Prof Annes Dias, 112-15o andar, 90020-090 Porto
Alegre RS, Brazil
Tel: +55 512 26 87 72 *also fax*

Maria Elizabeth Lucas, chair.
Courses: Graduate programme in mus (MA/PhD in
Music Education); conference courses on topics
related to music education.

Bulgaria

State Academy of Music
94 Evlogi Georgiev Boulevard, Sofia 1505, Bulgaria
Tel: +35 9 2 470181/442715 *Fax:* +35 9 2 441454/463677

Nikolaj Nikolov, vice rector.
Courses: PhD and Master of Arts (2). Training in
all orchestral instruments including pno and

classic gui, singing, musical pedagogy,
composition, conducting (choral and
opera-symphonic), musicology and sound
engineering. Fees: US $6000 pa. Also,
departments of variety and jazz (voice and jazz
insts) and ballet (studies include ballet
pedagogy, theory and staging).

Canada

University of Alberta
Faculty of Arts, Department of Music, 3-82 Fine Arts
Building, Edmonton, Alberta T6G 2C9, Canada
Tel: +1 403 492 3263 *Fax:* +1 403 492 9246

Fordyce Pier, chair.
Courses: MA in music; MMus in composition,
performance, choral conducting; MEd in music
education; DMus in performance (pno or org);
PhD in music.

The Banff Centre for the Arts
Office of the Registrar, Box 1020, Station 28, Banff,
Alberta, T0L 0C0, Canada
Tel: +1 403 762 6180 *Fax:* +1 403 762 6345
Email: arts_info@banffcentre.ab.ca
Website: www.banffcentre.ab.ca/registrar/index/html

Karen Harper, mus registrar.
Courses: Offers professional and aspiring
musicians and audio engineers m/classes,
residencies, audio work/study, performance

and recording opportunities in a dynamic, international, multi-disciplinary arts environment in the Canadian Rockies.

Brandon University
School of Music, Brandon, Manitoba R7A 6A9, Canada
Tel: +1 204 727 9633 *Fax:* +1 204 728 6839
Email: music@brandonu.ca
Website: www.brandonu.ca/departments/music/

T Patrick Carrabré, acting dean, school of mus.
Courses: MMus in music education, performance and literature.

University of British Columbia
School of Music, 6361 Memorial Rd, Vancouver, British Columbia V6T 1Z2, Canada
Tel: +1 604 822 3113 *Fax:* +1 604 822 4884

Jesse Read, dir.
Courses: MA in musicology, ethnomusicology, theory; MMus in composition, performance; DMA in composition, performance; PhD in musicology, historical studies and theoretical studies.

University of Calgary
Department of Music, 2500 University Drive North West, Calgary, Alberta T2N 1N4, Canada
Tel: +1 403 220 5379 *Fax:* +1 403 284 0973
Email: 19202@ucdasnml.admin.ucalgary.ca
Website: www.ffa.ucalgary.ca/ffa/music

Malcolm V Edwards, head.
Courses: MA in musicology; MMus in composition, performance, music education. Graduate diplomas in Kodály concept of music education and wind ensemble conducting; PhD in musicology, composition and music education.

Université Laval
Faculté de Musique, Quebec, Province of Quebec G1K 7P4, Canada
Tel: +1 418 656 7061 *Fax:* +1 418 656 7365
Email: raymond.ringuette@mus.ulaval.ca
Website: www.ulaval.ca/mus/accueil.html

Raymond Ringuette, dean.
Courses: MMus in musicology, music education, instrumental teaching, composition, performance; DMus in music education, musicology.

McGill University
Faculty of Music, Strathcona Music Building, 555 Sherbrooke St West, Montreal, Quebec H3A 1E3, Canada
Tel: +1 514 398 4546 *Fax:* +1 514 398 8061
Email: johanne@music.mcgill.ca

Veronica Slobodian, admissions offr.
Courses: MA in computer application, theory, musicology, music education, MMus in performance, composition, sound recording; PhD in musicology, theory, music education; DMus in

composition; Licentiate in Music in advanced performance; Artist Diploma in performance.

University of Montreal
Faculty of Music, CP6128 Sta Centre-Ville, Montreal, Province of Quebec H3C 3J7, Canada
Tel: +1 514 343 7998 *Fax:* +1 514 343 5727

Marie-Thérèse Lefebvre, vice-dean graduate studies.
Courses: MMus in composition, performance; Doctor of Music in composition, performance; MA (musicology or ethnomusicology); Doctor of Philosophy in Music (musicology or ethnomusicology).

University of Ottawa
Faculty of Arts, Department of Music, Perez Hall, 50 University, Ottawa, Ontario K1N 6N5, Canada
Tel: +1 613 564 2481 *Fax:* +1 613 564 5643

Jocelyne Guilbault, dir of graduate studies.
Courses: BMus, MMus, BA(Hons), BA.

University of Regina
Faculty of Fine Arts, Department of Music, Regina, Saskatchewan S4S 0A2, Canada
Tel: +1 306 585 5532 *Fax:* +1 306 585 5549

Kathryn Laurin, head of mus dept.
Courses: BMus, BA, BMusEd, MMus in performance, composition, conducting.

Royal Conservatory of Music
273 Bloor St West, Toronto, Ontario M5S 1W2, Canada
Tel: +1 416 408 2824 *Fax:* +1 416 408 3096

Shannon Paterson, programme mgr.
Courses: Performance Diploma, 4-yr BA equiv in performance; Artist-Teacher Diploma, 3-yr pedagogy and performance course; Artist Diploma, 2-yr p/grad level diploma in advanced performance available in solo and orch streams; Resident ARCT (Hons) Diploma, 4-yr u/grad level diploma in performance and pedagogy.

University of Toronto
Faculty of Music, Edward Johnson Building, Toronto, Ontario M5S 1A1, Canada
Tel: +1 416 978 3750 *Fax:* +1 416 978 5771
Website: www.utoronto.ca/music

Courses: MA in musicology; MusM in composition, music education, performance; PhD in musicology/theory; Mus Doc in composition; Diploma in operatic performance.

Vancouver Academy of Music
S K Lee College, 1270 Chestnut St, Vancouver BC V6J 4R9, Canada
Tel: +1 604 734 2301 *Fax:* +1 604 731 1920
Website: www.sloth.com/uam/

Jerold C Gerbrecht, mus dir.

Courses: Artist Diploma involving private study, ensemble participation and 2 full solo recitals over 2-3 yrs.
Professional Studies programme for post-degree students with emphasis on private lessons, practice, ensemble participation and preparation for professional auditions.

University of Victoria
School of Music, PO Box 1700, Victoria, British Columbia V8W 2Y2, Canada
Tel: +1 604 721 7902 *Fax:* +1 604 721 6597
Email: pc0689@uvvm.uvic.ca

Harald Krebs, graduate adviser.
Courses: MA in musicology, musicology with performance; MMus in composition, performance; PhD in musicology.

Victoria Conservatory of Music
839 Academy Close, Victoria BC V8X 3Y1, Canada
Tel: +1 250 386 5311 *Fax:* +1 250 386 6602

Denis Donnelly, dir.
Courses: Diploma in Music (2), conservatory-style performance and pedagogy programme, majors in pno, pno accompaniment, vn, vc, gui, voice and fl; Certificate Programme in Music and English (1), combining ESL with mus studies in most inst areas.

University of Western Ontario
Faculty of Music, Talbot College, Ontario N6A 3K7, Canada
Tel: +1 519 661 2043 *Fax:* +1 519 661 3531
Email: clements@julian.uwo.ca

Peter Clements, associate dean.
Courses: Undergraduate: BMus (Hon) in music education, theory and composition, music history, performance; BMusA in general music; BA (Music), BA (Hons Music). Postgraduate: MMus in music education, composition, literature and performance, theory; MA in musicology; PhD in systematic musicology; Artist Diploma in performance.

York University
Faculty of Fine Arts, Department of Music, 225 Winters College, North York, Ontario M3J 1P3, Canada
Tel: +1 416 736 5186 *Fax:* +1 416 736 5321
Email: ccraft@yorku.ca

Robert Witmer, chair, dept of music.
Courses: MA and PhD in musicology and ethnomusicology. Emphasis on interdisciplinary research in North American music; (religious, jazz, folk, urban popular, world, concert) and cultural issues in the Americas.

China

Shanghai Conservatory of Music
20 Fen Yang Rd, Shanghai 200031, People's Republic of China
Tel: +86 21 6433 0536 *Fax:* +86 21 6433 0866

Xianping Zhang, dir, international exchange centre.
Courses: Performance, composition, theory, musicology, conducting.

Croatia

Music Academy of Zagreb University
Gunduliceva 6, 41000 Zagreb, Croatia
Tel: +385 1 420276/7 *Fax:* +385 1 422856

Pavel Rojko, vice-dean.
Courses: MA in performance, conducting, voice, all insts (except cembalo, harp and tuba); MA in musicology; MA in music education.

Czech Republic

Conservatory of Prague
Na Rejdisti 1, Stare Mesto, CZ-11000 Praha, Czech Republic
Tel: +42 2 231 9102 *Fax:* +42 2 232 6406
Email: conserv@prgcons.cz

Milan Jíra, deputy dir.
Courses: Performance, composition, conducting. Free information brochure available.

Janácek Academy of Music and Dramatic Arts
Faculty of Music, Komenského nám 6, CZ-66215 Brno, Czech Republic
Tel: +42 542 321307 *Fax:* +42 542 213286

Marie Kánová, foreign relations dept.
Courses: Composition, conducting, singing and opera directing, keyboard insts, wind, percussion and strings. Applications, including tape and repertoire list, by 5 Mar. Tuition fees US$4000 pa.

Denmark

Carl Nielsen Academy of Music, Odense
Islandsgade 2, DK-5000 Odense C, Denmark
Tel: +45 66 110663 Fax: +45 66 177763
Website: www.dfm.dk/

Bertel Krarup, rector.
Courses: Undergraduate and graduate courses in classical music, folk music, jazz and rock.

Copenhagen University
Department of Music, Klerkegade 2, DK-1308
Copenhagen K, Denmark
Tel: +45 35 323739 Fax: +45 35 323738

Jens Westergaard Madsen, head of dept.
Courses: PhD in musicology.

The Opera Academy
The Royal Theatre, PO Box 2185, DK-1017 Copenhagen K, Denmark
Tel: +45 33 696790/1 Fax: +45 33 696792
Email: admin@kgl-teater.dk
Website: www.kgl-teater.dk

Friedrich Gürtler, principal.
Courses: An education department of the Royal Theatre and the Royal Danish Academy of Music.

The Academy offers a three-year postgraduate study of opera and other forms of music drama.

Royal Academy of Music, Aarhus
26 Fuglesangs Allé, DK-8210 Aarhus V, Denmark
Tel: +45 89 483388 Fax: +45 89 483322

Courses: Graduate programmes in solo performance, repetiteur, accompaniment, composition.

Royal Danish Academy of Music
Niels Brocks Gade 1, DK-1574 Copenhagen V, Denmark
Tel: +45 3369 2269 Fax: +45 3369 2279
Email: dkdm.kum.dk

Steen Pade, principal.
Courses: Graduate programmes in solo performance, repetiteur, accompaniment, composition, music theory, conducting, music drama (opera).

West Jutland Conservatory of Music
Islandsgade 50, DK-6700 Esbjerg, Denmark
Tel: +45 75 126100 Fax: +45 75 180659

Axel Momme, dir.

Finland

Abo Akademi University
Department of Musicology, Biskopsgatan 17, FIN-20500, Abo 50, Finland
Tel: +358 2 215 4338 Fax: +358 2 251 8528
Email: pirkko.moisala@abo.fi
Website: www.abo.fi/tak/hf/musik

Pirkko Moisala, professor.
Courses: Courses at all levels are open to foreign students who have been accepted at Abo Akademi University. Contact Abo Akademi, International Office, Domkyrkotorget 3, FIN-20500, Abo, Finland for further information before applying.

The Music Conservatory of Central Finland
Pitkäkatu 18-22, FIN-40700 Jyväskylä, Finland
Tel: +358 14 618131 Fax: +358 14 211803
Website: www.music.jypoly.fi

Courses: Diploma in Music Pedagogy (4). 160 credit units offering two alternatives for specialism (music college teacher programme; music playschool teacher programme); Musician

degree programme (4), 160 credit units; Music pedagogue postgraduate studies.

The Sibelius Academy
PO Box 86, FIN-00251 Helsinki, Finland
Tel: +358 9 40 5441 Fax: +358 9 40 54600
Website: www.siba.fi/

Kristiina Saalonen, international relations co-ord.
Courses: BMus; MMus; Licentiate of Music (artistic or research option); DMus (artistic or research option). Degree programmes in performance, jazz music, folk music, church music, music education, opera, orchestral and choral conducting, composition, music theory and arts management.

Turku University
Department of Musicology, 20014 Turku, Finland
Tel: +358 2 333 5277 Fax: +358 2 333 6677

Pirkko Moisala, professor.
Courses: PhD in musicology and ethnomusicology.

France

Conservatoire National de Région, Amiens
3 Rue Desprez, F-80000 Amiens, France
Tel: +33 3 22 91 57 83 *Fax:* +33 3 22 91 94 23

Alain Voirpy, dir.
Courses: Performance, electro-acoustic music, dance, theatre, jazz.

Conservatoire National de Région, Angers
26 Avenue Montaigne, F-49100 Angers, France
Tel: +33 2 41 24 14 50 *Fax:* +33 2 41 88 66 59

J R Lowry, dir.
Courses: Opportunity for a year's study in France; it is possible to combine musical and linguistic studies with the local universities, suitable for foreign study years as part of a degree.

Conservatoire National de Région, Besançon
Place de la Revolution, F-25000 Besançon, France
Tel: +33 3 81 81 11 44 *Fax:* +33 3 81 83 09 15

Pierre Migard, dir.

Conservatoire National de Région, Bordeaux
22 Quai Saint-Croix, F-33800 Bordeaux, France
Tel: +33 5 56 92 96 96 *Fax:* +33 5 56 92 22 30

Michel Fusté-Lambezat, dir.
Courses: Courses for vn, va, vc, sax.

Conservatoire National de Région, Boulogne-Billancourt
22 Rue de la Belle-Feuille, F-92100 Boulogne-Billancourt, France
Tel: +33 1 55 18 45 85 *Fax:* +33 1 55 18 45 86

Marina Herzog, public relations.
Courses: Courses accessible only by competition. Performance, early music, composition, analysis, chamber music.

Conservatoire National de Région, Caen
1 Rue de Carel Cedex, F-14027 Caen, France
Tel: +33 2 31 86 42 00 *Fax:* +33 2 31 86 18 92

Conservatoire National de Région, Clermont-Ferrand
3 Rue Maréchal Joffre, F-63000 Clermont-Ferrand, France
Tel: +33 4 73 91 43 64 *Fax:* +33 4 73 91 78 20

Jean-Claude Amiot, dir.

Conservatoire National de Région, Douai
87 Rue de la Fonderie, F-59500 Douai, France
Tel: +33 3 27 88 79 74 *Fax:* +33 3 27 97 62 04

Pierre Vigneron, dir.

Conservatoire National de Région, Grenoble
6 Chemin de Gordes, F-38100 Grenoble, France
Tel: +33 4 76 46 48 44

Bernard Commandeur, dir.
Courses: Places available for European Union students. Admission by written application and audition.

Conservatoire National de Région, La Courneuve
40 Avenue Gabriel-Péri, F-93120 La Courneuve, France
Tel: +33 1 48 37 49 15

Michel Rotterdam, dir.
Courses: All insts and voice; jazz (strings and piano).

Conservatoire National de Région, Lille
Place du Concert, F-59800 Lille, France
Tel: +33 3 20 74 57 50 *Fax:* +33 3 20 42 13 76

Philippe Lefebvre, dir.
Courses: All insts, voice; jazz. Auditions in Jun, Sep-Oct.

Conservatoire National de Région, Lyon
4 Montee de Fourviere, F-69321 Lyon, France
Tel: +33 4 78 25 91 39 *Fax:* +33 4 72 38 77 08

René Clement, dir.
Courses: Music and dance.

Conservatoire National de Région, Nancy
3 Rue Michel Ney, F-54000 Nancy, France
Tel: +33 3 83 35 27 95 *Fax:* +33 3 83 36 47 85

Jean-Marie Quenon, dir.

Conservatoire National de Région, Poitiers
5 Rue Franklin, F-86000 Poitiers, France
Tel: +33 5 49 01 83 67 *Fax:* +33 5 49 60 76 28

Eric Sprogis, dir.
Courses: Diploma of Musical Studies; Diploma of Dance Studies.

Conservatoire National de Région, Saint-Maur-des-Fosses
25 Rue Krüger, F-94100 Saint-Maur-des-Fosses, France
Tel: +33 1 48 83 14 67 *Fax:* +33 1 48 83 05 29

C Verrom, admin mgr.

Conservatoire National de Région, Strasbourg
2 Avenue de la Marseillaise, F-67000 Strasbourg, France
Tel: +33 3 88 15 08 88 *Fax:* +33 3 88 15 08 99

M C Ségard, dir.
Courses: All courses available to foreign students.

Conservatoire National de Région, Tours
2 Ter, Rue du Petit Pré, F-37000 Tours, France
Tel: +33 2 47 05 57 64 *Fax:* +33 2 47 05 91 14

Jean Dekyndt, acting dir.
Courses: Early music, performance, chamber music.

Conservatoire National Supérieur de Musique de Lyon
3 Quai Chauveau, CP 120, F-69009 Lyon, France
Tel: +33 4 72 19 26 26 *Fax:* +33 4 72 19 26 00

Gilbert Amy, dir.
Courses: Diplôme National d'Etudes Supérieures for most orch insts, voice, composition, electro-acoustic music. Principal studies are complemented by music theory and analysis, chamber music, choral, orch, ethnomusicology, music history and pedagogy.

Conservatoire National Supérieur de Musique et de Danse, Paris
Cité de la Musique, 209 Avenue Jean-Jaurès, F-75019 Paris, France
Tel: +33 1 40 40 45 45 *Fax:* +33 1 40 40 45 00
Email: cnsmdp@worldnet.fr

Gretchen Amussen, international relations.
Courses: 1-2 yr advanced course for solo instrumentalists (str, wind, keyboard, voice) or chamber music ensemble.

Ecole Normale de Musique de Paris Alfred Cortot
114 Bis Boulevard Malesherbes, F-75017 Paris, France
Tel: +33 1 47 63 85 72 *Fax:* +33 1 47 54 02 73

M Pierre-Petit, Henri Heugel, dir gen.
Courses: Postgraduate diplomas in solo performance, chamber performance, singing, conducting, composition. Also higher diploma of teaching, higher diploma of performance and higher diploma of concert performance (piano, instrument or voice). Complete undergraduate and postgraduate study programmes also offered including all insts, voice, music theory, orch conducting, composition and film music.

Germany

Berlin College of Music
Fasanenstr 1, Postfach 12 6720, D-10595 Berlin, Germany
Tel: +49 30 3185 2320 *Fax:* +49 30 3185 2687

Martin Rennert, dean of faculty.
Courses: Performance, music education, musicology, early music, composition and opera studies.

Bundesakademie für Musikalische Jugendbildung
Postfach 11 58, D-78635 Trossingen, Germany
Tel: +49 74 25 94 930 *Fax:* +49 74 25 94 9321
Email: bak.trossingen@t-online.de
Website: home.t-online.de/home/bak.trossingen

Reinhard Froese, dir.
Courses: Theory, musicology, pedagogy, performance, music education.

College of Music and Theatre Hannover
Emmichplatz 1, D-30175 Hannover, Germany
Tel: +49 511 31001 *Fax:* +49 511 310 0200

Peter Becker, president.
Courses: Performance, choral and orchestral conducting, musicology, music education, studio music teaching, psychology of music, philosophy of music, composition, form, church music, electronic music, early music, new music, jazz and pop, jazz arranging, eurhythmics, speech training, opera, stage management, music and theatre history, theatre law, drama, dance, fencing, history of dance, journalism, media management.

College of Music Detmold
Münster Institute, Ludgeriplatz 1, D-48151 Münster, Germany
Tel: +49 251 482330 *Fax:* +49 251 4823330

Reinbert Evers, dean.
Courses: Performance (all insts, also traverso, gamba, voice), music education, eurhythmics.

College of Music, Köln
Department Wuppertal, Friedrich-Ebert-Str 141, D-42117 Wuppertal, Germany
Tel: +49 202 37 1500 *Fax:* +49 202 37 15040

Prof Zarius, dean.
Courses: String and wind insts, pno, perc, gui, mandoline, accordion, singing. Also theory, form, mus history, mus pedagogy, new mus, speech training.

Frankfurt am Main College of Music and Performing Arts
Eschersheimer Landstr 29-39, D-60322 Frankfurt am Main, Germany
Tel: +49 69 154 0070 *Fax:* +49 69 154 007108

Hamburg College of Music
Hochschule für Musik und Theater, Harvestehuder Weg 12, D-20148 Hamburg, Germany
Tel: +49 40 441950 *Fax:* +49 40 44 195666

Hermann Rauhe, president.
Courses: Music theory, instrumental music, performing arts, music education, studio

teaching, music therapy, church music, opera, drama, stage management.

Hanns Eisler Music College
Charlottenstr 55, D-10117 Berlin, Germany
Tel: +49 30 20309 2411 *Fax:* +49 30 20309 2408

Christoph Poppen, rector and professor.
Courses: Inst, vocal and conducting classes. Jazz.

Hochschule für Musik Detmold
Neustadt 22, D-32756 Detmold, Germany
Tel: +49 5231 9755 *Fax:* +49 5231 975972

Edmundo Lasharas.
Courses: Performance, choral and orchestral conducting, music education, church music, sound engineering, studio teaching, opera, eurhythmics, musicology, composition, theory, music history and analysis, speech training.

Leopold Mozart Conservatorium of Augsburg, Music Academy
Maximilianstr 59, D-86150 Augsburg, Germany
Tel: +49 821 324 2891 *Fax:* +49 821 324 2892

Christian Pyhrr, dir.
Courses: Composition, voice (opera, concert, choir), all orchestral instruments, piano, organ, guitar, recorder, musical education, wind ensemble, conducting, music and computer, choral and orchestral conducting.

Lübeck College of Music
Grosse Petersgrube 17-29, D-23552 Lübeck, Germany
Tel: +49 451 15050 *Fax:* +49 451 1505300

Inge-Susann Römhild.
Courses: Performance, choral and orchestral conducting, composition, theory, form and analysis, arranging, music history and repertoire, musicology, functional keyboard, opera, church music, music literature, acoustics, speech training, early music, new music, music education, studio teaching, philosophy of education, eurhythmics, drama, history of theatre.

Meistersinger Conservatorium of Nurenberg
Am Katharinekloster 6, D-8500 Nürnberg, Germany
Tel: +49 911 231 2373

Burkhard Rempe.
Courses: Choral and orchestral conducting, composition, music theatre, music education, church music.

Munich College of Music
München 2, Arcisstr 12, D-80333 München, Germany
Tel: +49 89 289 27 403 *Fax:* +49 89 289 27 409

Robert M Helmschrott, president.
Courses: Choral and orchestral conducting, composition, instrumental courses.

Peter Cornelius Conservatorium of Mainz
Klarastr 4, D-55116 Mainz, Germany
Tel: +49 6131 122624 *Fax:* +49 6131 122947

Wolfgang Schmidt-Köngernheim, dir.
Courses: Performance, choral and orchestral conducting, theory, form and analysis, music history, organology, acoustics, music education, studio teaching, functional piano, opera, eurhythmics, early music, speech training, solfège.

Robert Schumann College of Music
Fischerstrasse 110, D-40476 Düsseldorf, Germany
Tel: +49 211 49180 *Fax:* +49 211 491 1618

Herbert Gallhoff.
Courses: Performance courses.

Ruhr State College of Music
Folkwang College of Music, Theatre and Dance, Essen-Werden, Abtei, D-4300 Essen, Germany
Tel: +49 201 49030 *Fax:* +49 201 490 3288

Courses: Performance, conducting, composition, musicology, form, music education, eurhythmics, music theatre.

State College of Music and Drama, Heidelberg-Mannheim
N7, 18, D-68161 Mannheim, Germany
Tel: +49 621 292 3577/3500 *Fax:* +49 621 292 2072
Email: info@muho-mannheim.de

Rudolf Meister, rector.
Courses: Performance, conducting, music education, opera, composition, theory, musicology, dance, jazz.

State College of Music Detmold (Dortmund)
Dortmund Institute, Dortmund, Emil-Figge-Str 44, D-44227 Dortmund, Germany
Tel: +49 231 755 4872 *Fax:* +49 231 755 4998

Richard Braun, deacon.
Courses: Performance, music history, form and analysis, theory, music education, music literature, church music, organology, speech training, contemporary music, jazz.

State College of Music, Karlsruhe
Postfach 6040, D-76040 Karlsruhe, Germany
Tel: +49 721 662950 *Fax:* +49 721 662966
Website: www.karlsruhe.de/kultur/musikhockschule

Fany Solter, rector.
Courses: Performance, conducting, composition, form, musicology, new music, music education, opera, Catholic church music, music editing for broadcasting.

State College of Music, Köln
Institute Aachen, Theaterstr 2-4, D-52062 Aachen,
Germany
Tel: +49 241 455415 *Fax:* +49 241 455221

Prof Herbert Nobis, deacon.
Courses: Performance, choral conducting,
composition, theory, jazz harmony, music
history and analysis, solfège, opera, speech
training, eurhythmics, music education.

State College of Music, Saarbrücken
Saarbrücken 3, Bismarckstrasse 1, D-66111

Saarbrücken, Germany
Tel: +49 681 967 3115 *Fax:* +49 681 967 3130

Thomas Krümer, professor.
Courses: School music, church music interpretive
arts, orchestral and ensemble music, music
education.

Wurzberg Academy of Music
Hofstr 13, D-8700 Würzburg, Germany
Tel: +49 931 37493 *Fax:* +49 931 37719

Courses: Performance, choral and orchestral
conducting, all instruments, opera and concert
singing, music education, Catholic church music,
form, musicology, early music, Orff method, jazz,
electronic music, eurhythmics.

Hong Kong

Chinese University of Hong Kong
Department of Music, Chung Chi College, Shatin, New
Territories, Hong Kong
Tel: +852 0 2609 6510 *Fax:* +852 0 2603 5273

Wing-Wah Chan, chmn of mus dept.
Courses: MPhil in musicology, ethnomusicology
and theory; MMus in composition; PhD in

musicology, ethnomusicology and theory; DMus
in composition.

University of Hong Kong
Department of Music, Pokfulam Road, Hong Kong
Tel: +852 2 859 2893 *Fax:* +852 2 858 4933

Allan Marett, prof of mus.
Courses: MPhil and DPhil in musicology,
ethnomusicology, research, composition,
analysis, performance practice.

Hungary

Liszt Ferenc Academy of Music
Liszt Ferenc tér 8, H-1061 Budapest, Hungary
Tel: +36 1 321 4406 *Fax:* +36 1 321 4097

Courses: Diploma (5 yrs) and postgraduate

courses in all insts, singing and opera, chamber
music, composition, musicology, choral
conducting.

Indonesia

Sekolah Tinggi Seni Indonesia (STSI)Surakarta
Jl Ki Hajar Dewantara 19, Kentingan, Jebres, Surakarta
57126, Indonesia

Tel: +62 271 47658 *Fax:* +62 271 46175
Email: stsisolo@idola.net.id

Rahayu Supanggah, dir.
Courses: Courses in traditional Gamelan music
and song (1 and 2 years).

Israel

The Jerusalem Rubin Academy of Music
Campus Givat-Ram, Jerusalem 91904, Israel
Tel: +972 2 675 9913 *Fax:* +972 2 652 7713

Rina Gordon, academic adviser.
Courses: BMus, BEdMus, Artist Diploma, MMus, MA.

Rimon School of Jazz and Contemporary Music
46 Shmuel Hanagid St, Morasha, Ramat Hasharon

47295, Israel
Tel: +972 3 540 1012; +972 3 540 8882
Fax: +972 3 549 6163

Courses: Performance, composition, arrangement
and production, mus theory and general mus
skills. Electives include song writing, mus for
theatre, computerised mus and studio
production, private lessons, ensembles, analysis.

Tel-Aviv University
Faculty of Visual and Performing Arts, Samuel Rubin
Israel Academy of Music, Ramat-Aviv 69978,
Tel-Aviv, Israel
Tel: +972 3 640 8415/8 *Fax:* +972 3 640 9174
Tova Zur, students' sec.
Courses: Artist Diploma; MA; MMus.

Italy

Institute of String Instrument Making (Stradivari School)
Palazzo dell'Arte, Piazza Marconi n 5, I-26100 Cremona, Italy
Tel: +39 372 27129 *also fax*
Email: stradivari@graffiti.it
Torrisi Francesco, dir of teaching.
Courses: Diploma in violin making.

Istituzione Teatro Lirico Sperimentale di Spoleto 'A Belli'
Piazza Giovanni Bovio 1, I-06049 Spoleto (PG), Italy
Tel: +39 743 221645/220440 *Fax:* +39 743 222930
Email: teatrolirico@mail.caribusiness.it
Website: www.caribusiness.it/lirico
Claudio Lepore, admin.
Courses: Professional 45-day training course for orch players. The institute pays for board and lodging. Str players should be aged 27 and under, wind instrumentalists 25 and under.

State Conservatoire of Music Giovanni Battista Martini
Piazza Rossini 2, I-40126 Bologna, Italy
Tel: +39 51 221483/233975 *Fax:* +39 51 223168
Email: consmus@iperbole.bologna.it
Website: www.comune.bologna.it/iperbole/conservatorio

Japan

Elisabeth University of Music
4-15 Nobori-cho, Naka-ku, Hiroshima-shi, Hiroshima 730, Japan
Tel: +81 82 221 0918 *Fax:* +81 82 221 0947
Courses: Masters Degree in music theory, sacred music, vocal music and instrumental music, combined with elective courses. Doctoral programme in theoretical studies (musicology, composition, conducting, sacred music or music education), vocal music or instrumental music.

Kunitachi College of Music
5-5-1 Kashiwa-cho, Tachikawa-shi, Tokyo 190, Japan
Tel: +81 425 36 0321
Courses: MMus in composition, instrumental music, vocal music, musicology, music education.

Kurashiki Sakuyo University
3515 Nagao Tamashima, Kurashiki-shi, Okayama 710-02, Japan
Tel: +81 86 523 0888 *Fax:* +81 86 523 0811
Courses: A variety of courses available. Japanese fluency is required and placements are made upon the basis of written examinations and interview.

Kyoto City University of Arts
Faculty of Music, 13-6 Kutsukake-cho, Ooe, Nishikyo-ku, Kyoto-shi, Kyoto 610-1197, Japan
Tel: +81 75 332 0701 *Fax:* +81 75 332 0709
Website: www.kuca.ac.jp/indexj.html
Courses: Graduate courses in composition and musicology, instrumental music and vocal music.

Musashino Academia Musicae
1-13-1 Hazawa, Nerim-ku, Tokyo 176, Japan
Tel: +81 3 3992 1121 *Fax:* +81 3 3991 7599
Uichi Nakamura, dir of academic affairs dept.
Courses: MMus in composition, instrumental music, vocal music, musicology, music education.

Toho Gakuen School of Music
1-41-1 Wakaba-cho, Chofu-shi, Tokyo 182, Japan
Tel: +81 3 3307 4101 *Fax:* +81 3 3307 4354
Nobuyoshi Iinuma, acting president.
Courses: Many part-time foreign students study at the school.

Tokyo College of Music
3-4-5 Minami-Ikebukoro, Toshima-ku, Tokyo 171, Japan
Tel: +81 3 3982 3186 *Fax:* +81 3 2986 2883
Courses: Master of Arts in inst, vocal music, composition, conducting, music education; Performance Diploma course in vocal music, instrument, composition, conducting; auditors course in instruments, vocal music, composition, conducting, music education.

Tokyo University of Fine Arts
Faculty of Music, 12-8 Ueno Koen, Taito-ku, Tokyo 110, Japan
Tel: +81 3 5685 7500 *Fax:* +81 3 5685 7760

Courses: MMus in composition, conducting, preformance, Japanese music performance, musicology; Dphil.

Ueno Gakuen University
Faculty of Music, 4-24-12 Higashi Ueno, Taito-ku, Tokyo 110, Japan
Tel: +81 3 3842 1021 *Fax:* +81 3 3843 7548

Akiko Yamawaki, head of international dept
Courses: 1-yr graduate programme specialising in musicology, instrumental music or vocal music.

Latvia

Jazeps Vitols Latvian Academy of Music
Kr Barons St 1, LV-1708 Riga, Latvia
Tel: + 371 222 8684; +371 722 8684 *Fax:* +371 782 0271
Email: mailja@imuza.lv
Website: www.lmuza.lv

Maija Sipola, international relations manager
Courses: MA in composition, piano, strings, music education, vocal art, choir conducting, symphonic conducting, music theory.

Lithuania

Lithuanian Academy of Music
Pr Gedimino 42, 2600 Vilnius, Lithuania
Tel: +370 2 224967/612691 *Fax:* +370 2 220093
Email: muzakd@mafd.vno.osf.it

Laima Bakiene, head of international relations dept.

Courses: Performance (piano, strings, winds, chamber music, voice, opera), ethnomusicology, musicology and composition.

Luxemburg

Conservatoire de Musique
Rue d'Audun 50, Esch-sur-Alzette, Luxemburg
Tel: +352 54 97 25 *Fax:* +352 54 97 31

Netherlands

Brabants Conservatorium
Zwysenplein 1, Postbus 90907, NL-5000 GJ Tilburg, Netherlands
Tel: +31 13 539 4999 *Fax:* +31 13 535 8118
Email: conservatorium@fontys.nl
Website: www.fontys.nl/bc/welcome.html

Marcel Pinkse, faculty dean
Courses: Early vocal music (1250-1750), all modern isnts with clavichord and organ. Musical theatre courses include singing, dancing and acting.

College of Enschede Conservatory
Van Essengaarde 10, NL-7511 PN Enschede, Netherlands
Tel: +31 53 871730 *Fax:* +31 53 301689

C W A Fictoor, dir.
Courses: Performance, composition, theory, choral and orchestral conducting, church music, electronic music, opera, music education, music therapy, jazz, dance.

Conservatorium Hogeschool Enschede *formerly* **Twents Conservatorium**
PO Box 70 000, 7500 KB Enschede, Netherlands
Tel: +31 53 487 1730 *Fax:* +31 53 430 1689
Website: www.hen.nl

Frank Deiman, public relations.

THE POOL OF NORDIC OPERA ACADEMIES

Opera Academy under
The Royal Danish Academy of Music &
The Royal Theatre
* 3-year music-dramatic course

OA – DKDM   Niels Brocksgade 1,
                     DK-1574 Copenhagen V,
                     Tel: 45 33 69 22 69
                     Fax: 45 33.14 09 11

OA-DKT   Post Box 2185,
                     DK-1017 Copenhagen K,
                     Tel: 45 33 69 69 33
                     Fax:45 33 69 67 92

**Sibelius Academy
Department of Opera**

5.5-year Master degree & 4-year Bachelor degree

Sibelius Academy Department of Opera
                     PO Box 86
                     SF-00251 Helsinki
                     Tel: 358 94 05 45 48
                     Fax: 358 94 05 45 96

Norwegian Academy of Opera

* 3-year opera and music-dramatic course

Norwegian Academy of Opera
                     Tjuvholmen inng.B,
                     N-0250 Oslo
                     Tel: 47 22 99 57 60
                     Fax: 47 22 99 57 70

**School of Theatre and Opera,
University of Göteborg**

* 3½-year opera studies course
* 3½-year acting studies course
* 3-year musical-theatre studies course

School of Theatre and Opera
                     P.O. Box 210,
                     S-405 30 Göteborg
                     Tel: 46 31 773 41 03
                     Fax: 46 31 773 41 18

**Stockholm University College
of Opera**

* 3½-year and 1½-year opera training course for
advanced singers
* 2 year course for repetitors
* courses and seminars for opera directors

Stockholm University College of Opera
                     Strandvägen 82,
                     S-115 27 Stockholm
                     Tel: 46 8 545 81060
                     Fax: 46 8 545 81061

Conservatorium van Amsterdam
Postbus 78022, NL-1070 LP Amsterdam, Netherlands
Tel: +31 20 527 7550 *Fax:* +31 20 676 1506
Email: postmaster@sca.ahk.nl

Ton Hartsuiker, dir
Courses: Postgraduate courses in music: chamber music, performance diploma, song accompaniment.

Groningen Conservatory
Veermarkstraat 76, NL-9724 GA Groningen, Netherlands
Tel: +31 50 3660666 *Fax:* +31 50 3131591
Email: c.a.smilde@pl.hanze.nl
Website: www.hanze.nl

Rineke Smilde, dir, classical mus
Courses: Certificates in forte-piano, organ, brass, band conducting, accordion, piano.

Hilversum Conservatorium
Snelliuslaan 10, NL-1222 TE Hilversum, Netherlands
Tel: +31 35 646 0949 *Fax:* +31 35 642 2246

Martin Kamminga, dean
Courses: MMus in jazz performance (2) in co-operation with the University of Miami, Florida.

Hogeschool Maastricht
Conservatorium Maastricht, Bonnefantenstraat 15, NL-6211 KL Maastricht, Netherlands
Tel: +31 43 346 6680 *Fax:* +31 43 346 6689
Email: p.e.vanderpol@muz.hsmaastricht.nl

H J G M Custers, general dir; J Stulen, artistic dir
Courses: Courses in classical music and jazz.

Netherlands Institute for Church Music
Mariaplaats 28, 3512 CA Ultrecht, Netherlands
Tel: +31 30 231 4044 *Fax:* +31 30 231 4004

K Koetsveld, dir.
Courses: Courses include choir conducting, organ improvisation, gregorian chant, liturgy, hymnology.

Rotterdam College of Music and Dance
Pieter de Hoochweg 222, NL-3024 BJ Rotterdam, Netherlands
Tel: +31 10 477 3750 *Fax:* +31 10 476 8163
Email: rc@hmtr.nl
Website: www.hmtr.nl

Ms M Hendriks, international dept.
Courses: BA and advanced courses in classical music, jazz and popular music, world music, school music, modern dance.

Royal Conservatory of Music and Dance
Juliana van Stolberglaan 1, NL-2595 CA Den Haag, Netherlands
Tel: +31 70 381 4251 *Fax:* +31 70 385 3941
Website: www.koncon.nl

Frans De Ruiter, principal.
Courses: Certificate of Advanced Studies in performance (including early music and opera), conducting, theory, composition, jazz. Sonology course.

Utrecht School of the Arts
Faculty of Music, Mariaplaats 28, NL-3511 LL Utrecht, Netherlands
Tel: +31 30 231 4044 *Fax:* +31 30 231 4004

Courses: Chamber music course.

New Zealand

University of Auckland
Faculty of Music, Private Bag, Auckland, New Zealand
Tel: +64 9 373 7599 ext 7408 *Fax:* +64 9 373 7446
Email: m.staff@auckland.ac.nz
Website: www.mus.auckland.ac.nz/

Michelle Staff, school admin.
Courses: MA in music research; MMus in performance, composition, musicology; PhD in musicological research; DMus in composition; AdvDipMus in performance; Dip Performing Arts (opera).

University of Canterbury
School of Music, Private Bag 4800, Christchurch, New Zealand
Tel: +64 3 364 2183 *Fax:* +64 3 364 2728

Email: s.wallis@music.canterbury.ac.nz
Website: www.canterbury.ac.nz/music/musichome.htm

Roger M Buckton, head of dept; Susan J Wallis, sec.
Courses: Mus B (Hons) in composition, performance, musicology, music education; BA (Hons) in musicology, music education;
MA in musicology or music eduation; MMus in composition, performance; PhD in music education or musicology.

University of Otago
Department of Music, PO Box 56, Dunedin, New Zealand
Tel: +64 34 79 8885 *Fax:* +64 34 79 8885
Email: music@otago.ac.nz
Website: www.otago.ac.nz/music/home_page.html

Patrick Little, course adviser.
Courses: MA in musicology; MMus in performance,

composition; PhD in musicology, ethnomusicology; Postgraduate diploma in composition, performance, musicology, ethnomusicology.

Victoria University of Wellington
School of Music, PO Box 600, Wellington, New Zealand
Tel: +64 04 471 5369 *Fax:* +64 04 495 5157

Marianne Taylor, sec.
Courses: MA in music history and literature; MMus in music history and literature, composition, performance, ethnomusicology; PhD; DMus in composition; Graduate Diploma in Arts.

Norway

The Agder College Conservatory of Music
Kongensgt 54, N-4610 Kristiansand, Norway
Tel: +47 38 14 19 00 *Fax:* +47 38 14 19 01
Email: konservatoriet@hia.no
Website: www.krs.hia.no/kunstfag/konsen/

Knut Tonsberg, dir of studies.
Courses: One semester, two semester and two year courses in all insts, accompaniment, piano duo.

Barratt Due Institute of Music
Lyder Sagens Gate 2, N-0358 Oslo, Norway
Tel: +47 2 465878 *Fax:* +47 2 566377

Hans Olav Gressli, leader of education.

Conservatory of Music
School of Arts Education, Stavanger College, Bjergsted, N-4007 Stavanger, Norway
Tel: +47 51 834000 *Fax:* +47 51 834050
Email: postmottak@his.no
Website: www.his.no

Per Dahl, dean.
Courses: Performance, music education, music production.

The Grieg Academy, University of Bergen
Lars Hillesgate 3, N-5015 Bergen, Norway

Tel: +47 55 586950 *Fax:* +47 55 586960
Website: www.hf.uib.no/i/griaka/griaka.html

Kari Johnsen, dir.
Courses: Performance.

Norwegian State Academy of Music
Postboks 5190 Majorstua, N-0302 Oslo, Norway
Tel: +47 22 464055 *Fax:* +47 22 467074
Email: mh@mnh.no
Website: www.nmh.no

Courses: Solo performance, chamber music, accompaniment, conducting, music education, composition.

Trømso College, Music Conservatory
Krognessveien 33, N-9005 Tromso, Norway
Tel: +47 77 660304 *Fax:* +47 77 618899
Email: kunst@hitos.no

Courses: P/grad studies: Advanced Performance Studies in inst, accompaniment or vocal performance.

Poland

Academia Muzyczna im Karol Szymanowski Katowice
Ul Zacisze 3, PL-40 025 Katowice, Poland
Tel: +48 32 255 4017/33/49 *Fax:* +48 32 256 4485

Leon Markiewicz, head of dept of mus education.
Courses: Master of Arts, Doctor of Musicology.

Academy of Music, Kraków
Ul Starowislna 3, PL-31 089 Kraków, Poland
Tel: +48 12 22 0455 *Fax:* +48 12 22 2343
Email: zbmaleck@cyf-kr.edu.pl
Website: www.cyf-kr.edu.pl/asc/krakow/am/index.html

Teresa Malecka, rector for student affairs.
Courses: MA; Certificate of Music. P/grad studies

in composition, conducting, music theory and instrumental performance available to suitably qualified applicants.

Academy of Music, Lodz
Ul Gdanska 32, PL-90 716 Lodz, Poland
Tel: +48 42 336740 *Fax:* +48 42 399960
Email: rektorat@sp.amuz.lodz.pl
Website: www.amuz.lodz.pl

Bogdan Dowlasz, rector.
Courses: Master of Arts in composition, theory of music, music education, eurhythmics, instrumental and vocal/acting performance. Advanced foreign students may study subjects of their choice for 1 or 2 semesters.

Frederic Chopin Academy of Music, Warsaw
Ul Okolnik 2, PL-00 368 Warszawa, Poland
Tel: +48 22 827 7241 ext 223 *Fax:* +48 22 827 8308

Joanna Zawadzka, admissions officer.
Courses: Composition, conducting (opera, symphonic, wind, choir), music theory, keyboard studies (piano, organ, harpsichord), all instrumens, voice, music education, sound recording, music pedagogy.

Stanislaw Moniuszko State Academy of Music
Lagiewniki 3, PL-80847 Gdansk, Poland
Tel: +48 58 31 7715 *Fax:* +48 58 31 4365

Andrzej Zawilski, postgraduate courses exec.

Republic of Ireland

National University of Ireland
University College, Belfield, Department of Music, Belfield, Dublin 4, Republic of Ireland
Tel: +353 1 269 3244 *Fax:* +353 1 269 4409

H M White, prof of mus.
Courses: MA (1) in musicology; PhD; Dmus.

National University of Ireland
University College, Cork, Music Department, Western Rd, Cork City, Republic of Ireland
Tel: +353 21 902440 *Fax:* +353 21 271595
Email: music@ucc.ie
Website: www.ucc.ie/ucc/depts/music

David Harold Cox, prof.
Courses: MA; MPhil; MMus in Performance; PhD.

National University of Ireland Maynooth
Department of Music, Maynooth, Co Kildare, Republic of Ireland
Tel: +353 1 708 3733 *Fax:* +353 1 628 9432
Email: ggillen@vax1.may.ie; ggillen@ailm.may.ie

G T Gillen, professor of music.

Courses: MA in interpretation and performance, composition, musicology; PhD.

Royal Irish Academy of Music
36 Westland Row, Dublin 2, Republic of Ireland
Tel: +353 1 676 4412

John O'Conor, dir.
Courses: Certificate in Conducting. Associate Diploma in Music Performance and Teaching. MMus in Performance. Diploma in Music, Speech and Drama.

Trinity College
University of Dublin, School of Music, 5 Trinity College, Dublin 2, Republic of Ireland
Tel: +353 1 608 1120 *Fax:* +353 1 670 9509

Martin Adams, head of dept.
Courses: MLitt in musicological research and composition; PhD in musicology.

Romania

Academia De Muzica Gheorghe Dima
Str I C Bratianu 25, 3400 Cluj-Napoca, Romania
Tel: +40 64 191242/196938/193879 *Fax:* +40 64 193879
Email: katonai@amgd.edu.soroscj.ro

Iosif Katona, mus sec/PR.
Courses: Postgraduate courses in a wide variety of subjects including theory, stylistics, musical form, musical history and pedagogy. Doctorates in ethnomusicology, history of music, music aesthetics and music folklore (4 yrs f/t; 6 yrs p/t). Also opera and singing m/classes 19 Jun-3 Jul 1998 and the annual Bach Academy held in the second half of Nov 1998.

Academy of Music
Str Stirbei Voda 33, 79551 Bucharest, Romania
Tel: +401 614 6341 *Fax:* +401 615 8396

Tereza Lazar, sec.
Courses: Performance (instruments and voice), conducting, composition, musicology, music education.

Russia

St Petersburg N A Rimsky-Korsakov State Conservatory
Teatralnaya Pl 3, 190000 St Petersburg, Russia
Tel: +7 812 312 2129; +7 812 314 9693
Fax: +7 812 311 8288

Alexander Pataman, dean of foreign students.

Courses: Opera and symphony conducting, choral conducting, composition, instrumental, vocal performance, musicology, history of music, choreography, folk insts.

Slovak Republic

Academy of Music and Dramatic Arts, Bratislava
Faculty of Music and Dance, Zochova 1, 81301 Bratislava, Slovak Republic
Tel: +42 75 312070 Fax: +42 75 317081

Peter Krbat'a, dean.

Courses: PhD in performance, composition, conducting, music history, theory, opera, opera direction, music education.

South Africa

University of Cape Town
SA College of Music, Private Bag, Rondebosch 7700, South Africa
Tel: +27 21 650 2626 Fax: +27 21 650 2627
Email: musprw@bremner.uct.ac.za
Website: www.uct.ac.za

James May, dir (SACM).
Courses: MMus in practical, dissertation, composition; MPhil; PhD; DMus; Graduate Diploma in performance, opera; BMus and Performers diploma in solo performance, accompaniment, jazz studies, orchestral studies.

University of the Free State
Department of Music, PO Box 339, Bloemfontein 9300, South Africa
Tel: +27 51 401 2810 Fax: +27 51 448 4402
Email: lampregp@rd.uovs.ac.za

G P Lamprecht, head of dept.
Courses: BA Hons; BMus Hons; MMus in performance or by dissertation; PhD.

University of Natal
Department of Music, Durban 4014, South Africa
Tel: +27 31 260 3351 Fax: +27 31 260 1048
Email: ballanti@mtb.und.ac.za
Website: www.und.ac.za

Christopher Ballantine, prof of music.
Courses: MMus or MA in music education, music technology, ethnomusicology, musicology; MMus in composition, performance, jazz studies; PhD in ethnomusicology, musicology, music education; DMus in composition.

University of Port Elizabeth
Department of Music, PO Box 1600, Port Elizabeth 6000, South Africa
Tel: +27 41 504 2250 Fax: +27 41 504 2574

Albert Troskie, head, dept of music.
Courses: MMus in academic studies, composition, performance; DMus; DPhil; Soloist's Diploma in Music.

University of Pretoria
Department of Music, Brooklyn, Pretoria 0181, South Africa
Tel: +27 12 420 2316 Fax: +27 12 420 2248
Email: heyden@libarts.up.ac.za
Website: www.up.ac.za/academic/music/music.html

H Temmingh, head of dept.
Courses: MMus in performance, musicology, composition, methods of pno teaching, music education; DMus in composition, musicological research.

Rhodes University
Department of Music, PO Box 94, Grahamstown 6140, South Africa
Tel: +27 46 603 8489 Fax: +27 46 603 8492
Email: mutr@warthog.ru.ac.za
Website: www.music.ru.ac.za

T E K Radloff, snr lecturer.
Courses: MMus in composition, by thesis or by performance; DPhil in composition, by thesis or treatise; DMus in composition or music research.

University of South Africa (UNISA)
Department of Musicology, PO Box 392, Pretoria 0001,
South Africa
Tel: +27 12 429 6419 *Fax:* +27 12 429 3400
Email: reiddj@alpha.unisa.ac.za

D J Reid, head.
Courses: MA in musicology; MMus; DMus; DLitt; Dphil.

University of Stellenbosch
Private Bag X1, Matieland 7602, South Africa
Tel: +27 21 808 2336 *Fax:* +27 21 808 4336

R E Ottermann, professor.
Courses: MMus by performance, composition or
research; DMus; Dphil.

University of the Witwatersrand
School of Music, PO Box Wits 2050, Johannesburg,
South Africa
Tel: +27 11 716 2700 *Fax:* +27 11 716 8030
Email: 180carl@muse.arts.wits.ac.za

Carl van Wyk, head of school of mus.
Courses: PhD; MMus; Dmus.

Spain

Real Conservatorio Superior de Musica de Madrid
c/Doctor Mata, No 2, E-28012 Madrid, Spain
Tel: +34 1 539 2901 *Fax:* +34 1 527 5822

D Miguel de Barco Gallego, dir.

Sweden

University of Lund
Department of Musicology, Biskopsgatam 5, S-22362
Lund, Sweden
Tel: +46 46 222 8649 *Fax:* +46 46 222 4215
Email: musvet@musvet.lu.se

Greger Andersson, professor.
Courses: 4 yrs of full-time studies; PhD in
musicology.

Malmö Academy of Music
Box 8203, SE-20041 Malmö, Sweden
Tel: +46 40 325468 *Fax:* +46 40 325470
Email: margaretha.bergkvist@mhm.lu.se

Margaretha Bergkvist-Persson, vice-dir of
performance and composition.
Courses: Tuition on main instrument, chamber
music and orchestra, m/classes and
interpretation seminars; advanced course in
interpretation for foreign students, details as
above (60 ECTS credits); interpretation of
baroque music I and II, tuition in interpretation
and chamber music from the baroque period
(p/t, 15 ECTS credits).

Royal University College of Music
PO Box 27711, S-115 91 Stockholm, Sweden
Tel: +46 8 161800 *Fax:* +46 8 664 1424
Website: www.kmh.se

Sven Hamberg, co-ordinator of international
relations.
Courses: Advanced courses and diploma studies
in instruments, singing, conducting, theory and
composition.

School of Music and Musicology, Göteborg University
PO Box 5439, SE-402 29 Göteborg, Sweden
Tel: +46 31 773 4023 *Fax:* +46 31 773 4030
Email: christiane.bergreth.aune@musik.gu.se

Christiane Bergroth-Aune, international secretary.
Courses: For information on p/grad courses,
contact Mona Lisa Sandow *tel:* +46 31 773 4062 *fax:*
+46 31 773 4030.

Switzerland

Conservatoire of Music and Theatre, Berne
Kramgasse 36, CH-3011 Bern, Switzerland
Tel: +41 31 311 6221 *Fax:* +41 31 312 2053
Courses: Advanced course in performance.

Conservatorium of Lucerne
Dreilindenstrasse 93, CH-6006 Luzern, Switzerland
Tel: +41 41 429 0808 *Fax:* +41 41 429 0809
Thüring Bräm.
Courses: Soloist Diploma; master courses.

Conservatorium of Music, Lausanne
2 Rue de la Grotte, CH-1003 Lausanne, Switzerland
Tel: +41 21 321 35 35 *Fax:* +41 21 321 35 36
Jean-Jacques Rapin, dir.
Courses: Performance, accompaniment, orchestration, composition, theory, solfège.

Conservatoire de Neuchâtel
Clos-Brochet 30-32, CH-2007 Neuchâtel 7, Switzerland
Tel: +41 32 725 20 53 *Fax:* +41 38 725 70 24
François-Xavier Delacoste, dir.

Courses: Performers Diploma; diplomas in inst and vocal training and in musical theory with solfa and composition options; advanced certificates in instrumental and vocal performance, chamber music and accompaniment.

Geneva Conservatorium of Music
CP 5155, CH-1211 Genève 11, Switzerland
Tel: +41 22 319 60 60 *Fax:* +41 22 319 60 60
Website: musnov1.unige.ch/
Philippe Dinkel, dir.
Courses: Advanced courses in performance, accompaniment, chamber music, conducting and musical culture.

Music Academy of Basel
Musikhochschule and Schola Cantorum Basiliensis,
Leonhardsstr 6, Postfach, CH 4003 Basel, Switzerland
Tel: +41 61 264 5757 *Fax:* +41 61 264 5713
Website: www.unibas.ch/mab/
Courses: Advanced courses in performance, chamber music, composition, conducting, theory, music history, electronic music, opera, music education.

Ukraine

Ukranian National Tchaikovsky Academy of Music
Ul Gorodetsky 1-3/11, 252001 Kiev, Ukraine
Tel: +7 44 229 07 92 *Fax:* +7 44 229 35 30
Oleg Tymoshenko, Rector.
Courses: The Academy trains students to be scientists and teachers in the theory and history of music and music pedagogy. Postgraduate courses are also available in performance for instrumentalists (including folk instruments) and vocalists, and in choral and opera conducting and composition. Special subjects include the psychology of creative work and the performance and perception of music, aesthetics, and musical interpretation. Candidates for doctoral degrees are also accepted.

USA

Boston Conservatory
Music Division, 8 The Fenway, Boston, MA 02215, USA
Tel: +1 617 536 6340 *Fax:* +1 617 536 3176
Email: admissions@bostonconservatory.edu
Website: www.bostonconservatory.edu/
James O'Dell, chair, mus division.
Courses: MM in choral conducting, composition, music education, opera and music theatre, performance, vocal pedagogy; Artist Diploma in performance, opera.

Boston University
School for the Arts, School of Music, 855 Commonwealth Av,
Boston, MA 02215, USA
Tel: +1 617 353 3341 *Fax:* +1 617 353 7455
Phyllis Hoffman, dir, mus division.
Courses: MA in musicology, composition, music history, music theory, music education; MM in performance, collaborative pno, composition, theory, history and literature of music, conducting, music education; MusAD (Doctor of Musical Arts) in performance, historical performance, composition, music education; PhD in musicology, music history and theory; opera certificate; artist diploma certificate.

University of California, Berkeley
Department of Music, Berkeley, CA 94720, USA
Tel: +1 510 642 2678

Bruce Alexander, student affairs offr.
Courses: MA in composition, ethnomusicology, history and literature of music; PhD in historical musicology, composition, ethnomusicology.

University of Cincinnati
College-Conservatory of Music, PO Box 210003, Cincinnati, OH 45221-0003, USA
Tel: +1 513 556 3737 *Fax:* +1 513 556 0202

Robert J Werner, dean.
Courses: MA in arts administration; MFA (Master of Fine Arts) drama and music in theatre performance, directing and theatre design and production; MM in pno accompaniment, composition, conducting, music education, music history, performance, theory; DMA in composition; conducting, performance; DME music education; PhD in musicology and music theory; Artist Diploma in performance and opera directing.

Cleveland Institute of Music
11021 East Boulevard, Cleveland, OH 44106, USA
Tel: +1 216 795 3107 *Fax:* +1 216 791 1530
Email: cimadmission@po.cwru.edu
Website: www.cwru.edu/cim/cimhome.html

E William Fay, dir of admissions.
Courses: MM in performance, composition, Suzuki pedagogy, accompaniment, orchestral conducting; DMA in composition, performance.

University of Colorado at Boulder
College of Music, Campus Box 301, Boulder, CO 80309-0301, USA
Tel: +1 303 492 6352 *Fax:* +1 303 492 5619
Email: sherd@colorado.edu
Website: www.colorado.edu/music/

Daniel Sher, dean.
Courses: MMus in composition, conducting, music literature, performance, pedagogy; MMusEd in music education; DMA in literature and performance of choral music, composition, instrumental conducting and literature, performance, pedagogy; PhD in music (musicology, music education).

Cornell University
Department of Music, Lincoln Hall, Ithaca, NY 14853-4101, USA
Tel: +1 607 255 4097 *Fax:* +1 607 254 2877
Email: grad_music@cornell.edu
Website: www.arts.cornell.edu/music/

Rebecca Harris-Warrick, dir of graduate studies.
Courses: DMA in historical performance and in composition; PhD in musicology.

Curtis Institute of Music
1726 Locust St, Philadelphia, PA 19103, USA
Tel: +1 215 893 5252 *Fax:* +1 215 893 9065

Gary Graffman, dir.
Courses: MM in opera; Diploma; Bachelor of Music.

Eastman School of Music
University of Rochester, 26 Gibbs Street, Rochester, NY 14604, USA
Tel: +1 716 274 1000 *Fax:* +1 716 263 2807

Robert Freeman, dir.
Courses: MA in music education, musicology, theory, pedagogy; MM in composition, choral conducting, jazz and contemporary studies, music education, performance and literature; DMA in composition, conducting, music education, performance and literature; PhD in composition, musicology, music education, theory.

Esther Boyer College of Music
Temple University, 13th and Norris St, Philadelphia, PA 19122, USA
Tel: +1 215 204 8301 *Fax:* +1 215 204 4957
Website: www.temple.edu/music

Jeffrey Cornelius, dean.
Courses: MM in choral conducting, composition, music education, music history, performance, piano accompaniment and chamber music, piano accompaniment and opera coaching, piano pedagogy, string pedagogy, music theory; Master of Music Therapy; DMA in composition, performance; PhD in music education; Diploma in performance.

University of Florida
College of Fine Arts, Department of Music, Box 117900 MUB130, Gainesville, FL 32611-7900, USA
Tel: +1 352 392 0223 *Fax:* +1 352 392 0461
Email: music@nervm.nerdc.ufl.edu
Website: www.arts.ufl.edu/music/

Linda Black, dir of mus admissions.
Courses: MM in composition, conducting, music history and literature, pedagogy, performance, sacred music, theory, music education; PhD in music education.

The Hartt School
University of Hartford, 200 Bloomfield Av, West Hartford, CT 06117, USA
Tel: +1 203 243 4454 *Fax:* +1 203 768 4441
Email: maslin@uhavax.hartford.edu

James Jacobs, dir of admissions.
Courses: MM in performance, conducting, composition, liturgical music, music history, opera, theory, piano pedagogy, music education;

DMA in performance, composition, conducting, music educucation; PhD in music education; Graduate Professional Diploma and Artist Diploma in performance, conducting, composition, opera.

Harvard University
Department of Music, Music Building, Cambridge, MA 02138, USA
Tel: +1 617 495 2791 *Fax:* +1 617 496 8081

Kay K Shelemay, prof and chair.
Courses: PhD in composition, musicology, ethnomusicology, theory.

University of Houston
College of Humanities and Fine Arts, Moores School of Music, 4800 Calhoun, Houston, TX 77204-4201, USA
Tel: +1 713 743 3009

David Tomatz, dir of Moores school of mus.
Courses: MM in composition, theory, performance, music literature, music education, performance pedagogy; DMA in composition, conducting, music education, performance.

Indiana University - Bloomington
School of Music, Music Building, Bloomington, IN 47405, USA
Tel: +1 812 855 1582 *Fax:* +1 812 855 4936

Charles H Webb, dean.
Courses: MA in musicology, performing arts administration; MM in performance, composition, conducting, early music performance, jazz studies, theory, electronic and computer music, organ and church music, music education; DMus in composition, conducting, opera, music literature and performance, music literature and pedagogy, early music, organ and church music; PhD in musicology, music education, theory; Performer Diploma; Artist Diploma; opportunity for one or two semesters as non-degree visiting student.

Institute for Policy Studies of the Johns Hopkins University (Peabody Conservatory)
3400 N Charles St, Baltimore MD 21218-2696, USA
Tel: +1 410 516 7827 *Fax:* +1 410 516 4717

Eileen T Cline, dean emerita, Peabody Conservatory of Music.
Courses: The Arts and Development of Public Policy.

Juilliard School
60 Lincoln Center Plaza, New York, NY 10023, USA
Tel: +1 212 799 5000 *Fax:* +1 212 724 0263
Website: www.juilliard.edu

Mary Gray, dir of admissions.
Courses: BM in music performance; BFA in dance and drama; MM in performance; DMA in composition, performance; Certificate; Advanced Certificate; Young Artists programmes in opera, directing; professional studies in performance.

University of Kansas
School of Fine Arts, Department of Music and Dance, Lawrence, KS 66045, USA
Tel: +1 913 864 3436 *Fax:* +1 913 864 5387

Stephen C Anderson, chairman.
Courses: MM in church music, composition, conducting, musicology, performance, accompaniment, theory, music education, music therapy; DMA in composition, conducting, performance, church music; PhD in music education, musicology, theory.

University of Kentucky
School of Music, Lexington, KY 40506-0022, USA
Tel: +1 606 257 4900 *Fax:* +1 606 323 1050

W Harry Clarke, dir.
Courses: MM in performance, composition, music education; MA in theory and musicology; DMA in composition, performance; PhD in music education, musicology, theory.

Longy School of Music
One Follen St, Cambridge, MA 02138, USA
Tel: +1 617 876 0956 ext 144 *Fax:* +1 617 876 9326

Kurt Piemonte, admissions offr.
Courses: Opera Performance Diploma; Performance Diploma, all insts, voice and composition; Master of Music, all insts, voice, opera, early music, composition, Dalcroze, eurhythmics, jazz and American music; Artist Diploma, all insts, voice, chamber music.

Manhattan School of Music
120 Claremont Av, New York, NY 10027-4698, USA
Tel: +1 212 749 2802 *Fax:* +1 212 749 5471

Richard E Adams, dean of faculty and performance.
Courses: MM in composition, accompaniment, jazz and commercial music, performance, orchestral performance; DMA in composition; performance, accompaniment.

Mannes College of Music
150 West 85th St, New York, NY 10024, USA
Tel: +1 212 580 0210 *Fax:* +1 212 580 5281

Lisa C Wright, dir of admissions.
Courses: MM in performance, historical performance, conducting, composition, theory; Professional Studies Certificate in performance, composition, theory and conducting.

University of Maryland

Division of Arts and Humanities, School of Music, College Pk, MD 20742, USA
Tel: +1 301 405 5560 *Fax:* +1 301 314 9504

William Montgomery, dir of graduate studies in mus.
Courses: MM in composition, theory, performance, conducting, music history and literature, music education; PhD in musicology, music education, theory; DMA in composition, performance.

The University of Memphis

College of Communication and Fine Arts, Department of Music, Memphis, TN 38152, USA
Tel: +1 901 678 3532

John Baur, prof, graduate mus.
Courses: MM in composition, jazz studies, music history, Orff Schulwerk, performance, sacred music, Suzuki pedagogy, music education; DMA in composition, music education, performance, sacred music; PhD in musicology.

University of Miami

School of Music, PO Box 248165, Coral Gables, FL 33124, USA
Tel: +1 305 284 2241 *Fax:* +1 305 284 6475
Email: whipp@umiamiym.ir.miami.edu
Website: www.music.miami.edu

William Hipp, dean; David Boyle, associate dean for graduate studies.
Courses: MM in accompanying and chamber music, composition, conducting, jazz pedagogy, jazz performance (instrumental, vocal), keyboard performance and pedagogy, media writing and production, music business and entertainment industries, music education, music therapy, musicology, performance (pno, vocal, instrumental), studio jazz writing, theory; MS in music engineering technology, DMA in accompanying and chamber music, composition, conducting, jazz performance (instrumental vocal), jazz composition, keyboard performance and pedagogy, performance (pno, vocal, instrumental); PhD in music education; Advanced Diploma in Performance (orch insts, pno, voice, and jazz).

University of Michigan - Ann Arbor

School of Music, 1100 Baits Drive, Ann Arbor, MI 48109-2085, USA
Tel: +1 313 764 0590 *Fax:* +1 313 763 5097

Karen Frye.
Courses: MA in composition, ethnomusicology, musicology; MFA (Master of Fine Arts) in dance, musical theatre; MM in arts administration, composition, church music, conducting, early keyboard instruments, music education, performance, theory; DMA in composition, conducting, performance; PhD in ethnomusicology, musicology, music education, theory, theatre.

University of Minnesota - Twin Cities

School of Music, 100b Ferguson Hall, 2106 Fourth St South, Minneapolis, MN 55455, USA
Tel: +1 612 624 0071 *Fax:* +1 612 626 2200
Email: mus-adm@maroon.tc.umn.edu

David Grayson, dir of graduate studies.
Courses: MA in musicology, ethnomusicology, music education and therapy, theory, composition; MM in accompanying and coaching, choral conducting, orchestral conducting, wind ensemble and band conducting, pno pedagogy, church music, performance; DMA in performance, accompanying and coaching, orchestral conducting; PhD in theory and composition, music education and therapy, musicology, ethnomusicology.

University of Missouri - Columbia

Department of Music, 140 Fine Arts Building, Columbia, MO 65211, USA
Tel: +1 314 882 0933 *Fax:* +1 314 884 7444

Dan Willett, dir of graduate studies in mus.
Courses: MA in music education, music history; MM in conducting, composition, performance, pno accompaniment and pedagogy, theory; MEd in music education; PhD in music education.

University of Missouri - Kansas City

Centre for the Performing Arts, Conservatory of Music, 4949 Cherry, Kansas City, MO 64110-2229, USA
Tel: +1 816 235 2731 *Fax:* +1 816 235 5265
Email: cadmissions@cctr.umkc.edu
Website: cctr.umkc.edu/www/w3/dept/conservatory/index.html

Terry Applebaum, dean.
Courses: MA; MM in composition, conducting, music history and literature, performance, theory; Masters in music education; DMA in composition, conducting, performance; PhD in music education.

University of North Carolina at Greensboro

School of Music, Greensboro, NC 27412, USA
Tel: +1 910 334 5789 *Fax:* +1 910 334 5497
Website: www.uncg.edu/mus

Arthur Tollefson, dean.
Courses: MM in accompaniment, composition, conducting, music education, performance, theory, vocal pedagogy; DMA in conducting, performance; PhD in music education.

481

North Carolina School of the Arts

School of Music, 200 Waughtown St, PO Box 12189, Winston-Salem, NC 27117, USA
Tel: +1 919 770 3255 *Fax:* +1 910 770 3248

Sheeler Lawson, asst to the dean.
Courses: MM in performance, pedagogy, film composition.

Northwestern University

School of Music, 711 Elgin Rd, Evanston, IL 60208, USA
Tel: +1 847 491 3141 *Fax:* +1 847 491 5260
Email: musiclife@nwu.edu
Website: nuinfo.nwu.edu/musicschool

Heather Landes, dir of mus admission and financial aid.
Courses: MM in church music, composition, conducting, musicology, music education, performance, technology, theory, library and information science, jazz pedagogy; DMus in church music, composition, performance, conducting, collaborative arts; PhD in musicology, music education, theory, technology; Graduate Certificate in performance.

Oberlin College

Conservatory of Music, 77 West College St, Oberlin, OH 44074-1588, USA
Tel: +1 216 775 8200 *Fax:* +1 216 775 8942

Karen Wolff, dean.
Courses: MM in conducting, historical performance, opera theatre; Master of Music Education; Master of Music in teaching; Performance and Artist Diplomas.

University of Oklahoma

College of Fine Arts, School of Music, 560 Parrington Oval, Norman, OK 73019, USA
Tel: +1 405 325 2081 *Fax:* +1 405 325 7574

Allan Ross, dir.
Courses: MM in composition, music history, performance, choral conducting, instrumental conducting, theory; DMA in choral conducting, instrumental conducting, composition, performance; PhD in music education.

University of Oregon

School of Music, Eugene, OR 97403, USA
Tel: +1 503 686 5661 *Fax:* +1 503 346 0723

Anne Dhu McLucas, dean.
Courses: MA in music education, music history, music theory; MM in choral conducting, composition, music education, performance and music literature, piano pedagogy, conducting; MM in jazz studies; DMA in composition, music education, performance; PhD in music education, composition, music history, music theory.

Princeton University

Department of Music, Princeton, NJ 08544, USA
Tel: +1 609 258 4241 *Fax:* +1 609 258 6793
Email: imcelroy@princeton.edu
Website: www.music.princeton.edu/

Paul Lansky, professor and chair.
Courses: MFA (Master of Fine Arts) in composition, musicology, theory; PhD in composition, musicology, theory.

Rutgers the State University of New Jersey

Department of Music, Marryott Music Building, Douglass Campus, 100 Clifton Av, New Brunswick, NJ 08901-1568, USA
Tel: +1 732 932 9302 *Fax:* +1 732 932 1517
Email: mgsa.rutgers.edu/music

William Berz, chair.
Courses: MA in history, theory, composition; MAT in teaching; MM in performance, jazz; DMA in performance; PhD in musicology, theory, composition; AD in performance.

San Francisco Conservatory of Music

1201 Ortega Street, San Francisco, CA 94122, USA
Tel: +1 415 564 8086 *Fax:* +1 415 759 3499
Email: colleenk@sirius.com
Website: www.sfcm.edu

Colleen Katzowitz, dir of student services.
Courses: MM in performance, composition, conducting, chamber music, keyboard accompaniment; Postgraduate Diploma in vocal performance.

Shepherd School of Music

Rice University, PO Box 1892, Houston, TX 77251 1892, USA
Tel: +1 713 527 4854 *Fax:* +1 713 285 5317
Email: musi@rice.edu

Gary Smith, asst dean.
Courses: MMus in performance, composition, conducting, musicology, theory; DMA in composition, performance (strings, fl, cl, pno, org only).

University of South Carolina

School of Music, Columbia, SC 29208, USA
Tel: +1 803 777 4280 *Fax:* +1 803 777 6508
Email: gradmusic@mozart.sc.edu.usa
Website: www.music.sc.edu/

William Bates, dir of graduate studies.
Courses: Certificate of Graduate Study in Music Performance; MM in music history, performance, composition, conducting, jazz studies, piano pedagogy, music theory; Master of music education; DMA in composition, conducting, performance, piano pedagogy; PhD in music education.

University of Southern California
School of Music, University Park, Los Angeles, CA 90089-0851, USA
Tel: +1 213 740 6935 *Fax:* +1 213 740 3217
Email: uscmusic@mizar.usc.edu

Larry Livingston, dean.
Courses: MA in music history and literature, early music performance, music theory; MM in choral music, church music, composition, conducting, music education, performance, jazz studies; DMA in choral music, church music, composition, music education, performance; PhD in musicology, theory.

Southern Methodist University
Meadows School of the Arts, Division of Music, PO Box 750356, Dallas, TX 75275-0356, USA
Tel: +1 214 768 2643 *Fax:* +1 214 768 4669
Email: jnobles@mail.smu.edu
Website: www.smu.edu/~meadows/

Martin Sweidel, chair, division of music.
Courses: MM in composition, conducting, music history, music education, performance, pno pedagogy, theory, music therapy, sacred music; Artist Certificate in performance.

Stanford University
Department of Music, Stanford, CA 94305, USA
Tel: +1 650 725 3101 *Fax:* +1 650 725 2686
Email: asultan@leland.stanford.edu
Website: www-leland.stanford.edu/group/music

Annie Sultan, student services officer.
Courses: MA in composition, music history, music science and technology, performance practice; DMA in composition; PhD in musicology, computer-based theory and acoustics.

University of Tennessee at Knoxville
Colleges of Arts and Sciences, Dept of Music, Knoxville, TN 37996-2600, USA
Tel: +1 423 974 3331 *Fax:* +1 423 974 1941
Email: mmoore7@utk.edu
Website: orpheus.la.utk.edu

Marvelene C Moore, chair, music education.
Courses: MM in performance, conducting, pno pedagogy, composition, theory, accompaniment, sacred music, jazz studies, music education, musicology.

University of Texas at Austin
School of Music, 25th and East Campus Dr, Austin, TX 78712, USA
Tel: +1 512 471 7764 *Fax:* +1 512 471 2333
Email: utmusic@www.utexas.edu
Website: www.utexas.edu/cofa/music/

Ronald Crutcher, dir.
Courses: MM in composition, musicology, ethnomusicology, music education, music literature and pedagogy, performance, theory; DMA in composition, music education, performance; PhD in musicology, ethnomusicology, music education, theory.

Texas Christian University
College of Fine Arts and Communication, Department of Music, PO Box 297500, Fort Worth, TX 76129, USA
Tel: +1 817 921 7602 *Fax:* +1 817 921 7344
Email: mthomas@gamma.is.tcu.edu

Kenneth R Raessler, chairman.
Courses: MA; MFA (Master of Fine Arts); MM in musicology, performance, theory and composition, music education; Artist Diploma in piano; Graduate Diploma in piano.

University of Utah
Department of Music, 204 David Gardner Hall, Salt Lake City, UT 84112, USA
Tel: +1 801 585 6972 *Fax:* +1 801 581 5683
Email: rebecca.richmond@m.cc.utah.edu
Website: www.music.utah.edu/

Rebecca Richmond, graduate sec.
Courses: MA in musicology; MM in conducting, music education, music history, performance, theory, composition; PhD in composition, music education.

University of Washington
College of Arts and Sciences, School of Music Box 353450, Seattle, WA 98195-3450, USA
Tel: +1 206 543 1201 *Fax:* +1 206 685 9499
Email: rmccabe@u.washington.edu
Website: weber.u.washington.edu/~musicweb

Robin McCabe, dir.
Courses: MA in ethnomusicology, music history, music education, theory; MM in composition, conducting, opera production, performance; DMA in composition, conducting, opera production, performance; PhD in ethnomusicology, music history, theory, music education.

Wichita State University
College of Fine Arts, School of Music, 185 Fairmount, Wichita, KS 67208, USA
Tel: +1 316 689 3500 *Fax:* +1 316 689 3951

Harold A Popp, chair.
Courses: MM in history and literature, performance, pno pedagogy, theory and composition, conducting; MME in music education.

Yale University

Graduate School of Music, Stoeckel Hall, 96 Wall St, New Haven, CT 06520, USA
Tel: +1 203 432 4155 *Fax:* +1 203 432 7448
Website: www.yale.edu/schmus/

Judith B Long, dir of admissions and student affairs.

Courses: MM, MMA and DMA in composition, voice, orch and choral conducting, inst performance; Certificate in Performance; Artist Diploma. The graduate school of performance (Yale School of Music) does not offer degrees in theory or mus history. Candidates seeking PhD degrees should apply to the Yale University Graduate School of Arts and Sciences which has a department of music.

Conferences, Recreational and Part-Time Courses

Conferences

Listed below are major conferences in the UK and abroad which may be of interest to those working in the field of music education. The information given is that which was available at the time of going to press; for further details, enquiries should be addressed to the organisation concerned. It should be noted that some conferences operate on a membership-only basis.

For residential and short courses *see* **Summer Schools and Short Courses.**

Association of British Choral Directors
46 Albert St, Tring, Herts HP23 6AU
Tel: 01442 891633

Marie-Louise Petit, gen sec.
Annual 3-day convention. Wide range of events for choral conductors and trainers, including a concert. 28-30 Aug 1998 in Exeter.

Association of British Orchestras
Francis House, Francis St, London SW1P 1DE
Tel: 0171 828 6913 *Fax:* 0171 931 9959
Email: abo@orchestranet.co.uk
Website: www.orchestranet.co.uk

Alex Knight, Libby Macnamara.
Annual Conference. 22-24 January 1999 in Belfast.

Association of Teachers of Singing
The Sideways House, 146 Greenstead Rd, Colchester, Essex CO1 2SN
Tel: 01206 867462 *also fax*

Norman Tattersall, conference dir, sec, treasurer.
3-day conference 6-9 Aug 1998 in Cheltenham Spa; 1-day conference autumn 1998 at the RAM; 3-day conference 15-18 Jul 1999 in Bournemouth; 1-day conference spring and autumn 1999 at the RAM.

Association of Woodwind Teachers
36 Durler Av, Kempston, Bedford MK42 7DG
Tel: 01234 301236 *Fax:* 0181 907 8428

Caroline Barlow.
Conference w/end. 25-27 Sep 1998 in Little Benslow Mills, Hitchin.

British Association of Symphonic Bands and Wind Ensembles
7 Dingle Close, Tytherington, Macclesfield SK10 2UT
Tel: 01625 430807 *also fax*
Email: 113074.3547@compuserve.com

Liz Winter, admin.
Annual conference. 3-6 Apr 1998, RNCM Manchester.

British Federation of Young Choirs
Devonshire House, Devonshire Sq, Loughborough, Leics LE11 3DW
Tel: 01509 211664 *Fax:* 01509 260630

Annette Mitchell, admin.
Adolescent Voice Conference. 11-13 Sep 1998 at Loughborough University. Will include mus theatre, vocal health, conducting technique, singing in the c/room.

British Institute of Organ Studies
Llanedren, Hayscastle, Haverfordwest, Pembs SA62 5HT
Tel: 01348 840545

Annual residential conference. 17-20 Aug 1998 at Bath College of HE. Includes visits to local orgs, papers on local org builders and related topics. Also 1-day conferences throughout the year at different venues.

British Society for Music Therapy
25 Rosslyn Av, E Barnet, Herts EN4 8DH
Tel: 0181 368 8879 *also fax;*
Email: denize@bsmt.demon.co.uk

Denize Christophers, admin.
Annual Conference. Nov.

British Suzuki Institute
39 High St, Wheathampstead, Herts AL4 8PB
Tel: 01582 832424 *Fax:* 01582 834488

B Kelly.
Suzuki teachers' conference. 5-6 Sep at Bath College.

Clarinet and Saxophone Society of Great Britain
167 Ellerton Rd, Surbiton, Surrey KT6 7UB
Tel: 0181 390 8307

S D Moss.
Easter Teachers' Seminar.

Contemporary Music-Making for Amateurs (COMA)
4 Lamb St, Spitalfields, London E1 4EA
Tel: 0171 247 7736 *Fax:* 0171 247 7732
Email: coma@compuserve.com

Frances Pace.
Key to Change, re-call conference. Oct 1999 at the South Bank Centre. Pre-conference working groups, including *Teaching Pathways to Contemporary Music*, through 1998-9.

Dartington Violin Conference
Dartington Hall, Totnes, Devon TQ9 6EL
Tel: 01803 866688

Helen Chaloner.
British Violin-Making Association conference. Speakers on violin-making, its history and related subjects. 19-21 Sep 1998 at Dartington Hall, Devon.

European Music Educators Association (EMEA)
CMR 411, Box 2032, APO AE 09112, USA
Email: gary.bogle@asam.baynet.de

Gary Bogle, president elect.
Conferences held in Mar and Sep.

European Piano Teachers Association UK Ltd
3 Alexandra Rd, Richmond, Surrey TW9 2BT
Tel: 0181 332 7291

Peter A Gitsham.
International conference including m/classes, recitals, demonstrations, discussions, w/shops and individual consultations. 25-29 Aug 1998 at the College of Ripon and York St John in York.

Federation of Music Services
Wheatley House, 12 Lucas Rd, High Wycombe, Bucks HP13 6QE
Tel: 01444 439572

Richard Hickman.
Annual conference. May.

The Headmasters' and Headmistresses' Conference
Hanbury Cottage, Cocking Midhurst, W Sussex GU29 0HF
Tel: 01730 815635 *Fax:* 01730 815225

5-8 Oct 1998 on Jersey. Only heads of HMC schools and guests are eligible to attend.

Incorporated Society of Musicians
10 Stratford Place, London W1N 9AE
Tel: 0171 629 4413 *Fax:* 0171 408 1538
Email: membership@ism.org
Website: www.ism.org

Annual Conference 6-9 April 1999, Chichester. Music in Education seminar held Feb/Mar and Private Teachers seminar held Sep each yr.

International Music Council of UNESCO
Oster Farimagsgade 45A, DK-2100 Copenhagen, Denmark
Tel: 00 45 3268 6742 *Fax:* 00 45 3268 6766
Email: janole45@inet.uni2.dk
Website: inet.uni2.dk/home/jt/imc/

Jan Ole Traasdahl, congress co-ord.
Music Education in a Multicultural Society congress for mus educators, musicians and all involved with mus and multiculturalism in education. Held in Aarhus, Denmark, 2-5 Jul 1998.

International Society for Music Education
International Centre for Research in Music, University of Reading, Bulmershe Ct, Reading RG6 1HY
Tel: 0118 931 8846 *also fax*
Email: e.smith@reading.ac.uk
Website: www.isme.org

Elizabeth Smith, admin.
23rd World Conference to be held 19-25 Jul 1998 in Pretoria, South Africa. ISME conferences are held in a different country every two years. The conference in 2000 will be in Edmonton, Canada.

International Society for the Study of Tension in Performance
28 Emperor's Gate, London SW7 4HS
Tel: 0171 373 7307 *Fax:* 0171 373 5440

Carola Grindea, admin.
Health and the Performing Arts conference.

XXVI International Viola Congress
3 Victoria Circus, Glasgow G12 9LB
Tel: 0141 334 4867
Email: durrant@dial.pipex.com

John White, host chmn; James Durrant, consultant.
Congress held by the International Viola Society 16-19 Jul 1998 at the RSAMD, Glasgow. Includes daily w/shops, m/classes, discussions, talks and concerts.

Jazz and the Media Conference
Leeds College of Music, 3 Quarry Hill, Leeds LS2 7PD
Tel: 0113 222 3454 *Fax:* 0113 222 3455

Emma Hall, conference admin.
Held by the Association of British Jazz Musicians. Apr, at Leeds College of Music.

Manchester Metropolitan University International Music Symposium
Royal Northern College of Music, 124 Oxford Rd, Manchester M13 9RD
Tel: 0161 907 5289 *Fax:* 0161 273 7611

Allan Taylor, events mgr.
Held at RNCM, 6-8 Sep 1998.

Music Masters' and Mistresses' Association (MMA)
Three Ways, Chicks La, Kilndown, Cranbrook, Kent TN17 2AS
Tel: 01892 890537

Annual conference for members only plus invited guests, Bryanston School 2-4 May 1998.

National Association of Choirs
21 Charmouth Rd, Lower Weston, Bath BA1 3LJ
Tel: 01225 426713

Annual conference.

National Association of Music Educators
52 Hall Orchard La, Frisby-on-the-Wreake, Melton Mowbray, Leics LE14 2NH
Tel: 01664 434379 *Fax:* 01664 434137
Email: musiceducation@name.org.uk

Jane Easton, prof offr.

Annual national conference. 27-29 Jun at Bretton Hall in Wakefield.

National Early Music Association
Holly Bush House, 18 High St, Caythorpe, Grantham, Lincs NG32 3BS
Tel: 01400 273795
Website: www.brainlink.com/~starmus/unison/nema/nema.html

Elspeth Fraser-Darling.
Monophony to Polyphony.

National Jazz Education Conference
Leeds College of Music, 3 Quarry Hill, Leeds LS2 7PD
Tel: 0113 222 3454 *Fax:* 0113 222 3455

Emma Hall, conference admin.
Apr, at Leeds College of Music.

National Operatic and Dramatic Association National Conference
Noda House, 1 Crestfield St, London WC1H 8AN
Tel: 0171 837 5655 *Fax:* 0171 833 0609

Alexandra Gibbons.
2-4 Oct 1998 in Kenilworth. 11 other conferences held throughout the UK.

National Union of Teachers
Hamilton House, Mabledon Pl, London WC1H 9BD
Tel: 0171 388 6191

Karen Cresswell, admin.
Annual conference in Blackpool.

Pianoforte Tuners' Association Annual Convention
10 Reculver Rd, Herne Bay, Kent CT6 6LD
Tel: 01227 368808 *also fax*
Website: www.pianotuner.org.uk

Valerie Addis, Lewis Flisher.
May.

Schools Music Association Annual Conference
71 Margaret Rd, New Barnet, Herts EN4 9NT
Tel: 0181 440 6919

Maxwell Pryce, hon sec, chief exec.
23-25 Oct in the Midlands. INSET course for school mus teachers, lecturers, inspectors, mus trade.

Sound Sense: Wales Event
Riverside House, Rattlesden, Bury St Edmunds, Suffolk IP30 0SF
Tel: 01449 736287 *Fax:* 01449 737649
Email: 100256.30@compuserve.com
Website: ourworld.compuserve.com/homepage/soundsense

Gloria Hall, admin.
Jun 1998 in Wales.

Conference Organisers

The following conference organisers are those who have organised major arts conferences in the past or who devote a significant proportion of time to arts clients.

C P H Exhibition Consultants
87 Bridge St, Pinner, Middx HA5 3HZ
Tel: 0181 866 6230 *Fax:* 0181 866 5489

Colin Holdsworth.

First Conferences Ltd
85 Clerkenwell Rd, London EC1R 5AR
Tel: 0171 404 0404 *Fax:* 0171 404 7733
Email: clara@firstconf.com
Website: www.firstconf.com

Clara Attridge, Guy Grant.
Run leading-edge international events in a range of industries.

Metaphor Conferences and Exhibitions
21 Kirklees Close, Farsley, Pudsey, LS28 5TF
Tel: 0113 255 0752 *Fax:* 0113 257 5755

Michael Phillips.
Organises *Resource*, Information Technology for Teachers. Nov 1998.

PMW International Ltd
Dresden House, 51 High St, Evesham, Worcs WR11 4DA
Tel: 01386 422408 *Fax:* 01386 422465

Peter Weston, dir.
Work primarily in the field of association conference and exhibition management.

Summer Schools and Short Courses

Alexander Technique for Pianists

50 Weston Way, Weston Favell, Northampton NN3 3BN
Tel: 01604 401862 *also fax*

John Naylor, admin.
Courses on the application of Alexander Technique to pno study and performance. Individual and group tuition in both pno and Alexander Technique.

Alston Hall College

Alston La, Longridge, Preston, Lancs PR3 3BP
Tel: 01772 784661 *Fax:* 01772 785835

Graham Wilkinson, principal.
1998: Courses include chmbr mus for str, wind and pno 6-8 Apr; chmbr mus for str quintets 21-23 Nov; also day courses. Fees: from £75 (residential), £14 (day). For those aged 18 and over.

The Amadeus Chorus and Orchestra Summer School

41 Cahir St, London E14 3QR
Tel: 0171 537 2329 *Fax:* 01453 843557

Philip Mackenzie, dir.
For players aged 18-30 min gr 8 (higher for wind, br and perc). Also places for 4 conductors (u/grads). Repertoire includes Copland, Fanfare for the Common Man; King, concert overture; Bernstein, symphonic dances from West Side Story; Shostakovich, symphony no 10. Fees: £75 (half-price bursaries are available). 12-19 Jul 1998 in Gloucestershire.

Amadeus Summer Course

100 Harvist Rd, London NW6 6HL
Tel: 0181 960 4780 *Fax:* 0181 964 5510

Robin Anderton, admin.
For p/grad and young professional str quartets. 1-2 weeks concentrated study of the quartet repertoire, with members of the Amadeus Quartet. 26 Jul-8 Aug 1998 at the RAM, applications by May (some scholarships available).

The Andover Harp Course

44 Church Cres, London N3 1BJ
Tel: 0181 349 4067 *also fax*

Miriam Keogh, admin.
Classes in technique, repertoire and ens groups; aspects of orch hp playing, plus care and maintenance of the hp. Held at Farleigh School, Red Rice, Andover in Aug. Residents aged 14-25, non-residents aged 12-14. Fees: £225.

Anglo-German Youth Music Week

NAYO, 2 Gilberyn Dr, Worle, Weston-super-Mare, Somerset BS22 0TR
Tel: 07050 622403; 0802 437919 *Fax:* 01934 512380
Email: malcolm.goodman@nayo.org.uk
Website: www.nayo.org.uk

Malcolm Goodman, NAYO course admin.
1-10 Aug 1998 in Oberwesel-am-Rhein, Germany. Annual residential mus week, alternately in Germany and the UK. Wide range of orch and chmbr mus with students from other European countries. Full symphony orch also forming 2 chmbr orchs. For age 15-25 of gr 7-8+ standard on first inst. Fees: £240.

Association for Cultural Exchange - Study Tours

Babraham, Cambridge CB2 4AP
Tel: 01223 835055 *Fax:* 01223 837394

Hugh Barnes.
Programme of study tours, residential courses in UK and worldwide, including visits to Haydn Festival in Eisenstadt, Music in Bavaria, Schubert at Feldkirch, Tanglewood in New England, Three Choirs Festival. Average age 40-75. Fees: £600-1000.

Ayton Castle Summer School

Music-Makers, 17 North Gardner St, Glasgow G11 5BU
Tel: 0141 339 2708 *Fax:* 0141 337 6923

Gusztáv Fenyö, artistic dir.
7-19 Jul 1998. Applications by 1 May. Courses for strs, pno and chmbr mus. Combines with 2-week festival (Summer Music at Ayton Castle) of evening chmbr mus concerts. For age 14-30. Fees: £200-295 (residential); £100 (non-residential).

Baroque Week

13 Brackley Rd, Monton, Eccles, Manchester M30 9LG
Tel: 0161 281 2502
Email: baroquew@silverfe.demon.co.uk
Website: www.newn.cam.ac.uk/prlw/winchester/baroque.html

Peter Collier.
Baroque mus-making at King Alfred's College, Winchester. Open to players of baroque insts, historically aware players of modern insts and singers. Fees: £335 (residential); £230 (non-residential); reduction of £35 for participants under 25.

Bath International Guitar Festival '98

25th July - 8th August

Summer Schools
for classical, flamenco, jazz, rock and blues guitar.

Competitions

Admira Young Classical Guitarist of the Year

Takamine Young Acoustic Guitarist of the Year

Contact: Emmanuelle Ginn
Bath International Guitar Festival,
Bath Spa University College,
Newton Park, Bath BA2 9BN
Tel: +44 (0) 1225 875522
Fax: +44 (0) 1225 874444
E-mail: e.ginn@bathspa.ac.uk

Courses 1999

BEAUCHAMP HOUSE
INTERNATIONAL MUSIC COURSES

Junior String Course	Mar. 30- Apr.1
Choir Weekend	July 16 - 17
JESTA International Chamber Course	July 25 - 31
Adult Early Music Course	July 25 - 31
International Singing, Dance and Drama	Aug. 1 - 7
Junior Orchestra	Aug. 8 - 14
Intermediate Orchestra	Aug. 15 - 21
Senior Orchestra	Aug. 22 - 28
Grade 5 Theory	Aug.2 - Sept.4
Big Band	Aug.2 - Sept.4

Churcham Gloucester GL2 8AA. music@beauchamp.demon.co.uk
Tel +44 (0)1452 750382   Fax +44 (0)1452 750585

Cambridge Early Music Summer Schools

Short courses in early music for Baroque instrumentalists and accomplished singers, with...

The Hilliard Ensemble
The Parley of Instruments

The Parley of Instruments, director Peter Holman (26 July-2 August 1998): 'The Purcell Tradition' - English music from Purcell to Handel, for a maximum of 16 singers with Baroque strings, woodwind and continuo, at A=415. Cantatas, odes, orchestral and chamber music for every imaginable combination of solo and consorted voices and instruments.

The Hilliard Ensemble with guest tutors Linda Hirst and Richard Wistreich, and Composer-in-Residence Paul Robinson (2-9 August 1998): vocal ensembles (individual groups and individual applicants) studying your choice of contemporary and early music. At least two opportunities for each ensemble to perform in public, including a specially composed premiere by Paul Robinson.

Come and enjoy an intensive and rewarding week at Trinity Hall, one of Cambridge's most charming colleges. Expert technical and stylistic tuition for professional and amateur singers and players by world-famous specialists; wide musical repertoire, good food, student and professional concert series, friendly and inspiring atmosphere.

Free brochure from Selene Mills, CEMSS, Trinity Hall, Cambridge CB2 1TJ.
Telephone/fax: 01223 847330.   E-mail: cemss@btinternet.com

Bass-Fest 1998

Studio Ten, Farnham Maltings, Farnham, Surrey GU9 7QR
Tel: 01252 319610 *also fax*
Email: bibf@classical-artists.com
Website: www.classical-artists.com/bibf

David Heyes.
25-30 Aug 1998 at Leighton Park School, Berks.
Db w/shops with international tutors.

Bath International Guitar Festival

PO Box 3697, London NW3 2HQ
Tel: 0171 831 0345 *Fax:* 0171 831 0346

Philip Castang, mgr.
First 3 weeks of Aug at Prior Park College, Bath. Top performers and teachers in all styles of gui, from classical to rock. Applications by 15 Jun 1998. All levels and ages welcomed for m/classes, lectures, seminars and study modules. Full concert series, two major competitions for snr (Albert Augustine Memorial International Guitar Competition) and jnr (Admira Young Guitarist of the Year Competition) performers. Private and shared accommodation available, as well as some scholarships.

Beauchamp House Holiday Music Courses

Churcham, Gloucester GL2 8AA
Tel: 01452 750382 *Fax:* 01452 750585

Alan and Caroline Lumsden, dirs; Margaret Nelson, admin.
3-day and 1-week w/shops for children throughout school holidays including orch courses (jnr, intermediate, snr and international chmbr), big band, international singing, dance and drama week, choir w/end, gr 5 theory. Beginners up to gr 8+, aged 8 and above. Also early mus week for adults. Residential fees from £58-240 pw.

Beechwood Easter Guitar Course

Elizabeth's Cottage, The Green, Leigh, Tonbridge, Kent TN11 8QW
Tel: 01732 832459

Raymond Love.
4-day residential course for classical gui; solo and ens playing. Emphasis on ens playing and concerts. Age 16 and above. Fees: £140-150.

Bela Bartók Centre for Musicianship

6 Frognal Ct, 158 Finchley Rd, London NW3 5HL
Tel: 0171 435 3685 *also fax*

Agnes Kory, dir.
Professional, amateur and children's classes focus on comprehensive mus education including the Kodály system, history, analysis and performance skills. Regular classes and occasional intensive holiday courses.

Benslow Harp Course

33 Sandbrook Rd, London N16 0SH
Tel: 0171 254 0419

Charlotte Seale; Imogen Barford.
26-30 Jul 1998 in Hitchin. Intensive residential course open to students and young professionals. Non-competitive environment and small classes. Recitals, m/classes, w/shops with guest artists, private practice rooms. Early application advised as numbers strictly limited.

Benslow Music Trust

Little Benslow Hills, off Benslow La, Hitchin, Herts SG4 9RB
Tel: 01462 459446 *Fax:* 01462 440171

Keith Stent, mus adviser.
Residential w/end and holiday courses for amateur musicians, students and teachers. Annual programme of over 100 different courses includes many for chmbr mus (strs, wind, pno and combinations), orchs of different standards, rcdrs, solo singing and insts, early mus, Alexander Technique, etc. Summer programme includes weeks and w/ends for Tudor mus, viol, str quartet, hp, big band, banjo, wind band, w/wind and orch.

Bochmann String Courses

BMCC, The Barns, Village Farm, Ford, Cheltenham, Glos GL54 5RU
Tel: 01386 584539 *also fax*

Gina Bochmann, admin; Michael Bochmann, dir.
Numerous courses throughout the year for students, p/grads and young professionals aged 18 and over. For str ens and solo vn with or without pno. Dates arranged according to mutual convenience.

Border Marches Early Music Forum

3 Upper Linney, Ludlow, Shropshire SY8 1EF
Tel: 01584 876175

Jenny Sayer, sec; Alison James, newsheet distribution.
Day w/shops held on Sundays in Leominster, Herefordshire, approximately 6 times pa, vocal and inst from medieval to baroque. Day w/shops in 1998: Ockeghem, 10 May (tutor, Edward Wickham); Spanish Composers from the New World, 21 Jun (tutor, Peter Syms). Also w/end residential w/shop on Florentine Intermedii at Trefeca, nr Brecon 25-27 Sep (tutors, Philip and Margaret Thorby); for details *Tel:* 01874 625346.

Brass Band Summer School

c/o The Old Barn, 10 Vicarage Rd, Bradwell Village, Milton Keynes MK7 8BL
Tel: 01908 321505

c/o Gordon Higginbottom.

Aug 9-16 1998 at Oxford Brookes University. All ages welcome.

Brien Stait String Course
31 Kidmore End Rd, Emmer Green, Reading, Berks RG4 8SN
Tel: 0118 947 2547

Mar and May at Reading University.

The British Kodály Academy
c/o 13 Midmoor Rd, London SW19 4JD
Tel: 0181 946 6528 Fax: 0181 946 6561
Email: enquiries@britishkodalyac.demon.co.uk
Website: www.britishkodalyac.demon.co.uk

Celia Cviic, treasurer and courses sec; John Wood, chmn.
Adult diploma courses, certificate in Kodály mus education, w/end courses, w/shops and INSET throughout the UK. Summer school in Cheltenham, Aug 1998 studying the Kodály approach to musicianship, c/room techniques and choral conducting. Special course for singers. Tutors from Hungary and the UK. All courses credit bearing for Trinity LTCL and Cert-Ed. Summer school 2-9 Aug 1998.

British Suzuki Institute
39 High St, Wheathampstead, Herts AL4 8BB
Tel: 01582 832424 Fax: 01582 834488

Birte Kelly, gen sec.

Suzuki teacher training in vn, pno, vc and fl. P/t courses lead to Diploma of European Suzuki Association. Regular p/t courses open to observers. 1998 courses: vn, pno (vc, fl), 16-18 May; vn, pno, vc, fl, 19-21 Jun; vn, 18-24 Jul; vn, pno (vc, fl), 16-18 Oct; vn, pno, vc, 20-22 Nov. 1999 courses: vn, pno, vc, fl, introductory LTCL, 8-10 Jan; vn, pno, 5-7 Feb; vn, pno, vc, 27 Mar - 1 Apr; vn, pno, vc, fl, 14-16 May.

British Youth Opera
South Bank University, 103 Borough Rd, London SE1 0AA
Tel: 0171 815 6090 Fax: 0171 815 6094

Timothy Dean, mus dir; Denis Coe, exec chmn; Mikel Toms, admin dir.
Singers from 22-30, insts and repetiteurs from 18-30. Auditions from Nov, summer season mid Jul-mid Sep; also year round programme. Performances in London and other locations.

Britten-Pears School for Advanced Musical Studies
High St, Aldeburgh, Suffolk IP15 5AX
Tel: 01728 452935 Fax: 01728 452715
Email: bps.admin@aldeburghfestivals.org

Elizabeth Webb, dir; Ann Rawdon Smith, admin; Rachael Buxton, asst admin.
10-day residential m/class advanced courses and

British Kodály Academy

**Musical Literacy through singing,
the voice as the main instrument.**

Courses for music & instrumental teachers; non-specialist primary teachers; early years and Special Needs teachers; singers and musicians, both amateur and professional.

International Summer School & Singers Course
2–9 August 1998

Cheltenham Ladies' College
Classroom Methodology, Solfège
Musicianship at all levels and Choral Training with leading Kodály experts from Hungary and Great Britain.

Part-Time Musicianship Courses at three levels
starting September 1998

Weekend Course Spring 1999

With Music in Mind

BKA c/o 13 Midmoor Rd London SW19 4JD
Tel 0181 946 6528 Fax 0181 946 6561
e-mail enquiries@britishkodalyac.demon.co.uk
(http://www.britishkodalyac.demon.co.uk)

Reg.Charity No. 326552

Symposium for Young String Quartets

(Promoted by The London String Quartet Foundation)

Founder The Lord Menuhin OM KBE

Girton College, Cambridge

26 - 29 March 1999

Under the Direction of Yfrah Neaman OBE

Ideal for Quartets in Schools and Junior Departments of Music Colleges

Please apply for further details from :
Dennis Sayer, Administrator,
62 High Street, Fareham, Hampshire PO16 7BG
Tel : (01329) 283603 Fax : (01329) 281969
Closing date for applications - 1 December 1998

opera courses organised from Apr-Sep for insts and singers. Various courses available with small number of places on each; entry by audition only (Jan), usually advanced students and young professionals. Courses for singers include A Midsummer Night's Dream, French Song, Russian Song, oratorio; inst courses include str quartets, br and str ens, contemporary performance and composition, vn and vc m/classes. Prospectus published Oct, and available on request. Also Britten-Pears Orchestra; advanced national training orch and Britten-Pears Baroque Orchestra meeting for short courses. Applications by mid Dec.

Bryanston Summer School
London Suzuki Group, 96 Farm La, London SW6 1QH
Tel: 0171 386 8006 *also fax*
Email: lsg@pullinger.prestel.co.uk

Aug 23-30 1998. Individual and group lessons for Suzuki vn, va, vc and pno students. Four levels of orch, chmbr mus, choirs, Dalcroze, Kodály and theory. Residential. Age range 5-16. Fees: £225-310, parents £285. Non-residential and observer rates available.

Bude Jazz Summer School
South West Jazz, c/o Exeter and Devon Arts Centre, Gandy St, Exeter EX4 3LS
Tel: 01392 218368 *Fax:* 01392 420442

Kevin Buckland, regional development offr. An intensive but fun week of courses for musicians aged 30 and under who have already acquired a reasonable level of musical ability with their chosen inst or voice, either as sight readers or by ear. W/shops developing understanding, interpretation and improvisation; m/classes; public performances. Courses suitable for various levels of experience in jazz skills, including beginners. 23-29 Aug 1998, applications by 1 Aug. Fees: £280 (residential), £200 (non-residential).

Burton Manor
Burton, S Wirral, Cheshire L64 5SJ
Tel: 0151 336 5172 *Fax:* 0151 336 6586

Janet Hooper, course admin. Various courses. 1998: Music's Marriage with Dance and Drama (tutor - John Hursey), 26-28 Jun; Women Composers - the Lost Traditions Found (tutor - Rosemary Evans), 11 Jul; The Life and Works of Leos Janacek (tutor - Graham Melville-Mason), 11-13 Sep; 100 Years of Music (tutor - Colin Tarn), 18-20 Dec. Fees: £25 (day), £98 (w/end residential).

Cambridge Early Music Summer Schools
Trinity Hall, Cambridge CB2 1TJ
Tel: 01223 847330 *also fax*
Email: cemss@btinternet.com

Website: www.btinternet.com/~nick.webb/cemsshomepage.htm

Selene Mills, admin. Hilliard Summer Festival 2-9 Aug 1998. For ens singers age 16 and above. Course emphasis is on performance, focusing on early and contemporary vocal ens mus. Fees: £540 (residential) or £440 (non-residential). The Purcell Tradition (The Parley of Instruments) 26 Jul-2 Aug 1998. Odes, anthems, theatre mus, orch works, and vocal and inst chmbr mus focusing on English mus up to Handel. Fees: £495 (residential) or £395 (non-residential).

Cambridge School of Music
1 Sleford Close, Balsham, Cambridge CB1 6DP
Tel: 01223 893972 *Fax:* 01223 893099

Mrs Barker, course dir. Residential orch course 26 Jul-1 Aug 1998, applications by 15 Jul. Age 7 to adult (gr 1-5). Fees: £235.

Cambridge Symposium for Young String Quartets
62 High St, Fareham, Hants PO16 7BG
Tel: 01329 283603 *Fax:* 01705 281969

Dennis Sayer, admin. Suitable for str quartets in schools and jnr depts of mus colleges. Combined age of quartet 76. Held at Girton College, Cambridge. Next 26-29 Mar 1999, applications by 1 Dec 1998. Fees: £100 per quartet, £30 per teacher.

University of Cambridge
Board of Continuing Education, Madingley Hall, Madingley, Cambridge CB3 8AQ
Tel: 01954 210636 *Fax:* 01954 210677

Sue Hoskins, courses registrar. W/end appreciation courses and coaching for str players aged 18 and above. Fees: £120 (w/end), £390 (week).

Canford Summer School of Music
5 Bushey Close, Old Barn La, Kenley, Surrey CR8 5AU
Tel: 0181 660 4766 *Fax:* 0181 668 5273

Malcolm Binney, mus dir. 26 Jul-16 Aug 1998, applications by mid-Jul: orch, wind band and choral conducting, chmbr mus for w/wind, composition, jazz, m/class for pno, pno accompaniment and voice, wind orch, choirs, br band, opera, orchs, str orch, perc, mus and dyslexia and mus teaching techniques. Age 16 and above.

Centre For Young Musicians
Morley College, 61 Westminster Bridge Rd, London SE1 7HT
Tel: 0171 928 3844

Fiona Johnson. School holiday courses in venues around

London. 1997 courses include: London Schools Concert Band, 28 Jul-1 Aug; London Schools Symphonic Band, 28 Jul-2 Aug; London Schools Concert Orchestra, 28 Jul-2 Aug; str ens, Jnr w/wind, jnr strs, jnr rcdrs, jnr guis, jnr perc, rcdr ens, jnr musicianship, jnr br, 28-31 Jul.

Chamber Music Holidays and Festivals
57 Chatsworth Rd, Bournemouth BH8 8SL
Tel: 01202 528328 *Fax:* 01202 524081

Vivienne Pittendrigh.
Bournemouth, Vienna, Corfu, Prague, Florence, Ireland and Budapest. Holidays for chmbr mus players and listeners. Scheduled playing, m/classes, concerts and various festival activities in historically and scenically interesting places.

Charterhouse Summer School of Music
Music Office, Charterhouse, Godalming, Surrey GU7 2DX
Tel: 01483 291696

Robin Wells, dir of mus.
Symphony, str and chmbr orchs, chmbr mus, gui, accompaniment, solo and choral singing, org. Age 18 and above. 25 Jul - 1 Aug 1998, applications by 1 Apr. Fees: £180-340.

Cheltenham Woodwind/Horns Chamber-Music Course
c/o Lindsey Music, 42 St Mary's Pk, Louth, Lincs LN11 0EF
Tel: 01507 605244

Jeff Brown, events organiser.

Choral Workshop
6 Clive Rd, Balsall Common, Coventry CV7 7DW
Tel: 01676 532436

Jill Pacey, admin.
Choral w/end for age 16 and above with professional artists and orch for singers. Rossini, Petite Messe Solennelle at the Warwick Arts Centre. Some bursaries available. 10-11 Oct 1998.

The City Lit
Music Dept, Keeley House, Keeley St, London WC2B 4BA
Tel: 0171 430 0546 *Fax:* 0171 831 8508

Moira Hayward, head of mus section; Della Rhodes, jazz co-ord.
Adult education courses from elementary to advanced level in inst, vocal, choral, operatic, musicianship, composition, chmbr mus, ens, jazz, pop, world mus, mus appreciation and mus technology. Enrolment Jul-Sep for year courses. Also runs a series of short summer courses in Jul, details available on request.

Clarinetwise
Pengribyn, Cilrehydn, Llanfyrnach, Pembs SA35 0AA
Tel: 01239 698602

Jacqueline Browne, events organiser; Michael

Collins, president.
Regular cl w/shops, courses and m/classes. Quarterly journal available. 1 day teachers, jnr and w/wind courses during summer term 1998. Workshop 98, 29 Nov 1998 in Nottingham, includes playing sessions, classical, jazz, w/shops, demos, talks, m/classes, recitals. All ages and standards welcome.

Clonter Opera Farm
Swettenham Heath, Congleton, Cheshire CW12 2LR
Tel: 01260 224638 *Fax:* 01260 224742

Jeffery Lockett, artistic dir; Leonard Hancock, mus dir.
Two residential opera studios culminating in public performances for singers aged 20-35. Jul 1998 (Bizet, Carmen or Mozart, Marriage of Figaro), applications by end Sep for the following year. Performance fees and travel costs paid; free board and lodging.

Coleg Harlech
Harlech, Gwynedd LL46 2PU
Tel: 01766 780363 *Fax:* 01766 780169
Email: ifans@harlech.ac.uk

M Ifans.
Orch mus summer school for ages 16 and above. 8-15 Aug 1998, applications by 31 May. Fees: £250 (concessions for students).

Colla Voce Enterprises
Ridgeside, Eastfield Rd, Redhill, Surrey RH1 4DY
Tel: 01737 763292 *also fax*
Email: scook@netcomuk.co.uk

Sue Cook, business dir.
Two summer schools held at Leighton Park, Reading and directed by Alison Pearce accompanied by a team of international tutors. Inspiration, Responsibility, Creativity: a highly specialised course in 2 parts for managers and singers wishing to develop personal presentation and mkt skills. Includes concerts, m/classes and individual tuition. 27-31 Jul 1998. Summer school for singers and accompanists: a week of tuition for musicians at all levels, focusing on essential skills needed for performance including voice, drama, interpretation and posture. 3-8 Aug 1998.

Colourstrings/Colourkeys Course for Teachers
The Szilvay Foundation, 4 Ullswater Close, Kingston Vale, London SW15 3RF
Tel: 0181 547 3073 *also fax*

Pat Wislocki, Deborah Harris, dirs.
Annual residential/day courses including mus kindergarten and primary school mus (4-7), pre-instrumental mus, vn, vc, mini-bass, pno and gui teaching methods. Kodály-based, using relative sol-fa to train the inner ear prior to

learning an inst and continuing this approach in inst tuition. Musicianship and Dalcroze Eurhythmics classes included. All 5-day courses are credit bearing for the LTCL (MusEd) and Cert (MusEd). 8-13 Aug 1998; mus kindergarten Associate Teacher (Certificate) introductory training course and follow-up courses Apr and May.

The 4th Conspiracy of Flutes
41 Devon Av, Twickenham TW2 6PN
Tel: 0181 241 7572 *also fax*

Julie Wright.
A booster course for adult flautists of all levels held 28-31 Aug at Bloxham School, near Oxford. Hosted by Atarah Ben-Tovim MBE and directed by Julie Wright. Further courses for both students and teachers available Jul in Hindhead and Oct at Château Pitray in Dordogne.

Contemporary Music Making for Amateurs (COMA)
13 Wellington Way, Bow, London E3 4NE
Tel: 0181 980 1527 *also fax*
Email: coma@compuserve.com

Chris Shurety, dir; Frances Pace, admin.
Residential summer school, 25 Jul-1 Aug at Bretton Hall, Yorkshire. W/shops for age 18 and above in composition, improvisation, contemporary inst, vocal and electro-acoustic techniques, ens and orchs, concerts of commissioned and students' works, recording and computer facilities, creative mus project. Tutors include Michael Finnissy, Deirdre Gribbin, Joanna MacGregor and Jane Manning. Fees: £380 (£240 concessions).

Countrywide Holidays Association
Grove House, Wilmslow Rd, Didsbury, Manchester M20 2HU
Tel: 0161 448 7112; 0161 446 2226 (reservations)
Fax: 0161 448 7113
Email: 101573.1452@compuserve.com

Patricia Percival, reservations mgr.
Various coures, Jul-Aug.

Creative Dance Artists Trust
15b Lauriston Rd, London SW19 4TJ
Tel: 0181 946 3444 *Fax:* 0181 879 0642

Gale Law, admin.
International course for professional choreographers and composers. Fosters creative collaboration between essential elements of dance, mus and movement. Participants are selected by committee. No age restriction, but evidence of talent in a professional context required. 2 weeks in Jul 1998, applications by Mar.

Curwen Institute
56 Creffield Rd, Colchester, Essex CO3 3HY
Tel: 01206 572411

Yvonne Lawton, sec.
New Curwen Method. Recommended for class mus teachers. Specially arranged local courses on application.

Dalcroze Society
41a Woodmansterne Rd, Coulsdon, Surrey CR5 2DJ
Tel: 0181 645 0714 *also fax*

Mrs P Piqué, sec.
Summer course of mus education through movement for all ages. Rhythmics, improvisation, ear training and therapy for all age groups. 27-31 Jul 1998 at Christ Church College, Canterbury.

Dartington International Summer School
Dartington Hall, Totnes, Devon TQ9 6DE
Tel: 01803 865988/867068 *Fax:* 01803 868108

Gavin Henderson, artistic dir; Justine Peberdy, admin.
18 Jul-29 Aug 1998. Summer course for those of any age, with opportunity for advanced tuition and m/classes, informal mus-making, plus concerts, talks, etc. Composer in residence; mus-theatre, masque and opera. Fees: £160-660 per week.

Dillington House
Ilminster, Somerset TA19 9DT
Tel: 01460 52427/55866 *Fax:* 01460 52433

W/end courses throughout the year. Various courses plus day schools and concerts every month.

Dolmetsch Summer School
Heartsease, Grayswood Rd, Haslemere, Surrey GU27 2BS
Tel: 01428 643235/651473 *Fax:* 01428 654920/651473
Email: brian@be-blood.demon.co.uk
Website: www.be-blood.demon.co.uk

Dr Blood, course sec.
Bishop Otter College, Chichester, W Sussex. Rcdr; also optional classes for viols, chmbr orch, c/room techniques, choir, rcdr orch, conducting and composition. For any age group. 9-15 Aug 1998, applications by 1 Jun. Fees: £400 (residential); £200 (non-residential).

Double Bass Summer Holiday Course *see* Oxford Cello School

Double Bass Summer School
7 St Clair Dr, Worcester Pk, Surrey KT4 8UG
Tel: 0181 330 3188 *also fax*
Email: peter.emery@kcl.ac.uk

P W Emery, hon sec.

Separate courses for beginners, intermediate and advanced db players aged 8-25. Ens playing, m/classes, technique classes and chmbr mus. Aug, applications by 1 Aug. Fees: £150.

Early Music Wales
Welsh College of Music and Drama, Castle Grounds, Cathays Park, Cardiff CF1 3ER
Tel: 01222 342854 *Fax:* 01222 237639
Email: w-d@baynet.co.uk

Andrew Wilson-Dickson, Lucy Robinson, dirs. Courses for age 17 and above. Places for singers, lutenists, baroque guis, keyboard players, vns, fls, rcdr and str players who are keen to specialise in renaissance and baroque mus. Period insts essential. 19-26 Jul 1998, applications by end Jun. Fees: c £300.

The Earnley Concourse
Earnley, Chichester, W Sussex PO20 7JL
Tel: 01243 670392 *Fax:* 01243 670832
Email: earnley@interalpha.co.uk

W/end and week-long study courses for age 16 and above, featuring mus history, chmbr and jazz w/shops. Ages 16 and over. Fees: c £150+ (w/end); c £380+ (week).

East Anglia Summer Music School
c/o Opera da Camera, 7 Meadow Rd, New Costessey, Norwich NR5 0NF
Tel: 01603 744584 *Fax:* 01603 507720

Jeffrey Davies, organiser and dir. Residential and w/end classes for adults at the University of East Anglia, covering concert repertoire, opera and technique. M/classes, opera w/shops and w/shops for singers. 21-30 Aug 1998, applications by mid-Jul. Fees: £110 (residential), £60 (non-residential).

Edinburgh University Centre for Continuing Education
11 Buccleuch Pl, Edinburgh EH8 9LW
Tel: 0131 650 4400 *Fax:* 0131 667 6097
Email: cce@ed.ac.uk
Website: www.ed.ac.uk/~cce/summer

Bridget Stevens, admin dir. Music at the Edinburgh Festival, 29 Aug-4 Sep 1998; piano w/shop, 10-28 Aug 1998. Also weekly classes in mus theory and appreciation. For age 18 and above. Fees: 9 weekly classes c £35, summer courses £140-250 per wk. Applications taken until one month before start date.

DARTINGTON INTERNATIONAL SUMMER SCHOOL

17 July – 28 August 1999
50ᵗʰ ANNIVERSARY SEASON

Six glorious weeks of concerts, courses, masterclasses, workshops, exhibitions and lectures – open to people of all ages and abilities and set in the beautiful Dartington Hall Estate.

A faculty of internationally renowned artists direct the following projects:

Chamber Music, Choral Singing, Composition, Music Theatre, Conducting, Jazz, Improvisation, Wind Band, Repertoire Orchestra, African Drumming, Balinese Gamelan, Indian Singing, Flamenco, Tango, Salsa, Early Opera Performance, Opera Masterclasses, The Rock Shop, Vocal and Instrumental Masterclasses, and much, much more...

'The Quality of teaching on offer is not far short of celestial' Norman Lebrecht, Daily Telegraph

For a free copy of the 1998/99 Summer School brochure please contact:
Jenny Pink, Dartington International Summer School, Dartington Hall, Totnes, Devon TQ9 6DE Tel: 01803 867068 Fax: 01803 868108 e-mail: brochure@dissorg.u-net.com

Dartington International Summer School is a department of The Dartington Hall Trust, a registered charity for education and the arts.

Edrom House Summer Schools
Edrom House, Duns, Berwickshire TD11 3PX
Tel: 0189 081 8277; 0181 340 0897 *Fax:* 0181 341 5292

Christopher Cowan, Lucy Cowan, Penelope Lynex.
Chmbr mus, vn and vc courses, for age 11 upwards. Apr, Jul, Aug and Sep. Chmbr mus course 1-9 Aug 1998. Fees: £170-215.

Elizabeth College (Guernsey) Summer Orchestral Course
Shalom, Les Marettes Villas, St Martin's, Guernsey
Tel: 01481 38980

Miles Attwell, admin; Richard Dickins, principal cond.
Gr 5+. Age 9-19. All orch and wind insts; 3 orchs, 3 bands. 17-22 Aug 1998, applications by 1 Jul. Fees: £130 including accommodation.

Emanuel Hurwitz Chamber Music Course
44 Church Cres, London N3 1BJ
Tel: 0181 349 4067 *also fax*

Miriam Keogh, admin.
Held at Farleigh School, Red Rice, Andover, Hants. Aug. M/classes, str orch, ens coaching. Age 15-27, gr 8+. Serious students only, not for amateurs. Aug. Fees: £260. Bursaries available.

Emscote Lawn Music School
Emscote Rd, Warwick
Tel: 01926 428135

Paul Russell.
Orch course for young musicians aged 8-14.

Eton Choral Courses
The Shepherd's Cottage, Gt Shelford, Cambridge CB2 5JX
Tel: 01223 845685 *Fax:* 01223 841980
Email: rallwood@netcomuk.co.uk

Ralph Allwood, dir; Lydia Smallwood, admin.
3 courses at Eton College 4-30 Jul 1998; 2-10 Aug, applications by Apr. Age 16-20. Fees: £325.

European Federation of Young Choirs
9 Fairmount Dr, Loughborough, Leics LE11 3JR
Tel: 01509 263954 *Fax:* 01509 232310

Mrs S E Rastall, sec.
Loughborough Singing Week for age 16 and above. Next 1999.

European Piano Teachers' Association UK (EPTA)
1 Wildgoose Dr, Horsham RH12 1TU
Tel: 01403 267761 *also fax*

Frances Bryan, admin; Kendall Taylor CBE, president; Frank Martin, chmn.
EPTA has 34 regional centres throughout UK which organise regular seminars, w/shops, m/classes, pupils' and teachers' concerts. Annual pno pedagogy courses. Annual residential summer conference end Aug with m/classes, pno teaching, recitals, lectures. Open to non-members. Ages 18 and above. EPTA UK International Conference 25-29 Aug 1998 in York with lectures, demonstrations and m/classes. Pedagogy course Jan-May.

European String Teachers' Association (ESTA)
247 Hay Green La, Bournville, Birmingham B30 1SH
Tel: 0121 475 3345 *also fax*

Olive Goodborn, admin.
Summer school 16-21 Aug 1998 at the Purcell School, Herts, with Jaäp Schroder, Anna Shuttleworth, Simon Fisher and Jenny Ward-Clarke. For str teachers.

European Youth Summer Music
Festivals House, 198 Park La, Macclesfield, Cheshire SK11 6UD
Tel: 01625 428297 *Fax:* 01625 503229
Email: festivals@compuserve.com
Website: ourworld.compuserve.com/homepages/festivals/eysm.htm

Liz Whitehead, course organiser.
A summer orch course for young musicians aged 11-21 at Haileybury College, Herts. 25 Jul-2 Aug 1998, applications by 1 Jul. Fees c £265.

Fantasia Music School
5 Aspen Way, Middleton on Sea, W Sussex PO22 6PW
Tel: 01243 586068

Mrs M Sutton, admin.
3 summer courses held at Dorset House School, nr Arundel for young musicians aged 8-18. Residential and day; Aug. Fees: £120-155 (day), £230-255 (boarding).

Fawley Court Music Courses
37 Calluna Ct, Heathside Rd, Woking, Surrey GU22 7HU
Tel: 01483 769490 *also fax*

Pippa Dice, admin; Michael Procter.
W/end courses near Henley on Thames for singers with good sight-reading abilities.

Fife Summer Jazz Course
Arts in Fife, The Tower Block, ASDARC, Woodend Rd, Cardenden KY5 0NE
Tel: 01592 414714 *Fax:* 01592 414727

Anne Chalk, publicity and development offr.
Jazz Course directed by Richard Michael. For all ages. Jul 1998, applications by 12 Jun.

Flutewise Residential Courses
9 Beaconsfield Rd, Portslade, E Sussex BN41 1XA
Tel: 01273 702367 *Fax:* 01273 888864
Email: flutewise@i-gadgets.com

Liz Goodwin, Christine Mead, admin.
Courses for fl players of all ages and standards.

CANOLFAN Y CELFYDDYDAU ABERYSTWYTH ARTS CENTRE

MUSICFEST

Aberystwyth International Music Festival & Summer School

Last two weeks of July.

Week long courses for strings, woodwind, piano, horn, saxophone, trombone, jazz, Improvisation, choral, percussion and composition.

Chamber Music from top artists and ensembles.

Information and Application forms from:

Louise Amery,
M.F.I.S.S.,
Aberystwyth Arts Centre,
Penglais,
Aberystwyth SY23 3DE
or phone 01970 622889
email: lla@aber.ac.uk

GUILDHALL SUMMER SCHOOL LONDON

Scott Stroman, Director

For all singers and instrumentalists, at any level of experience, The Guildhall Summer School, offers the following courses:

JAZZ, ROCK AND STUDIO MUSIC
One week – Sunday 19 - Friday 24 July
Bands, ensembles, vocal groups, classes, instrumental/vocal tuition available, workshops and concerts for musicians from beginner to professsional level.
Two weeks – Monday 13 - Friday 24 July
A more intensive course for intermediate and advanced students.

THE SINGERS WEEK
Monday 13 - Friday 17 July
An exciting course in group singing in many styles – Gospel, Latin, African and Jazz with leaders from around the world. Additional sessions in rhythm, theory and reading.

INTRODUCTION TO JAZZ WEEKEND
Sat/Sun 18 - 19 July
Designed for students with little or no jazz experience, it covers all the basics.

JAZZ EDUCATION FOR TEACHERS
Sat/Sun 18 - 19 July
Focuses on teaching methods for GCSE, A Level, primary children and adults.

INTRODUCTION TO RECORDING ENGINEERING
Monday 13 - Friday 17 July
Monday 20 - Friday 24 July
Two weekly courses in recording techniques, live sound and production.

MUSIC TECHNOLOGY
Sat/Sun 11 - 12 July
Sat/Sun 18 - 19 July
Two one-day workshops on computers, MIDI, sequencing, notation and applications, for musicians and teachers.

Further details from:
Heather Swain, Manager
Guildhall Summer School
c/o Guildhall School of Music and Drama
Barbican, London EC2Y 8DT
Telephone 01702 714733 (evenings and weekends)

Group accommodation, discounts and bursaries available.

May and Oct 1998 at Corsica Hall, Seaford, E Sussex.

Gathering of the Clans
c/o The Villa, Tollerson, York YO6 2EQ
Tel: 01347 838273

Courses and m/classes for cellists aged 14 and above. Various venues around the country.

Glamorgan Summer School
Welsh Jazz Society Ltd, 26 The Balcony, Castle Arcade, Cardiff
Tel: 01222 340591 *Fax:* 01222 665160
Email: jazzwale@compuserve.com

Brian Hennessey, dir.
A jazz education summer course held at University of Glamorgan, Treforrest.

Glasgow University
Dept of Adult and Continuing Education, 57-61 Oakfield Av, Glasgow G12 8LW
Tel: 0141 339 8855 ext 4394 *Fax:* 0141 307 8025

J G Macdonald, deputy dir.
Joint study days with Scottish Opera. Mus appreciation and theory, 8, 10 and 20 week courses from Oct. For age 18 and above. Fees: from £40 for 10 week courses.

Gloucestershire Choral Weekend
Cotswold House, Naunton, Cheltenham, Glos GL54 3AA
Tel: 01451 850796

Geoffrey Mitchell, mus dir; Cedric Virgin, organiser.
Study of classical and contemporary choral works for mixed voices at Wycliffe College in Gloucestershire. No age limit. Apr and Mar. Fees: c £89.95 (residential), c £57.95 (non-residential). Easter course 1999 in Gloucestershire.

Gloucestershire Summer Orchestral Course
Colwell Centre for Arts in Education, Derby Rd, Gloucester GL1 4AD
Tel: 01452 330300 *Fax:* 01452 330311

Brenda Whitwell, office mgr.
Residential orch summer course for insts aged 9-18. Caters for all grades, but min gr 1 required for entry. 26 Jul-1 Aug 1998, applications by 26 Jun.

Goldsmiths
University of London, Continuing and Community Education, Lewisham Way, London SE14 6NW
Tel: 0171 919 7200/7229 *Fax:* 0171 919 7223
Email: cen01cce@gold.ac.uk

Louise Gibbs, programme co-ord; Jeremy Peyton Jones, mus programme co-ord.
Courses for musicians and teachers, of 10 weeks duration: Afro-Latin perc; African drumming; jazz improvisation for singers; principles and

practices of teaching. Also Afro-Latin perc w/shop, 9-10 May 1998; jazz improvisation for singers, 20-21 Jun 1998; jazz pno w/end w/shop, 27-28 Jun 1998; listening, composing, performing, 28-31 Jul 1998.

Guildhall Summer School
Guildhall School of Music and Drama, Silk St, Barbican, London EC2Y 8DT
Tel: 01702 714733 (eves)

Heather Swain, mgr.
2 week jazz, rock, studio and world mus summer school 11-24 Jul 1998 for age 12 and above. Fees: £70 (intro to jazz w/end), £80 (mus technology w/end), £200 (jazz, rock and studio 1 week), £350 (jazz, rock and studio 2 weeks), £160 (singers week).

H F Holidays Ltd
Imperial House, Edgware Rd, London NW9 5AL
Tel: 0181 905 9558; 0181 905 9388 (24 hr brochure line)
Fax: 0181 205 0506

Laura Livingston, admin.
Wide variety of mus-making and appreciation holidays with expert tuition throughout the year. Courses include Elgar in the Dales, Composers of Gloucestershire, Monteverdi to Mozart, Barber-shop singing, Choral Music in England, Singing for Beginners, Gilbert and Sullivan.

Harrogate Woodwind/Horns Chamber-Music Course
c/o Lindsey Music, 42 St Mary's Pk, Louth, Lincs LN11 0EF
Tel: 01507 605244

Jeff Brown, events organiser.
8-15 Aug 1998.

Hawkwood Short Courses
Hawkwood Residential College, Painswick Old Rd, Stroud, Glos GL6 7QW
Tel: 01453 759034 *Fax:* 01453 764607

W/end courses for str, chmbr mus, mus appreciation. Summer orch week (wind and str). Various w/end and mid-week courses throughout year. Hawkwood chmbr orch for str, w/wind and br players of moderate ability. Baroque chmbr mus w/end, open to all str, keyboard and w/wind players and singers.

Haworth Chamber Music Weekend
14 Dunstarn Dr, Leeds LS16 8EH
Tel: 0113 267 5821 *also fax*

Elizabeth Altman.
Apr 1999, applications by mid Mar. Residential w/end course of m/classes and coaching for students and adults in strs, w/wind and pno. Arrangements for repertory carefully designed and course includes a walk, talk and participants'

concert. Also B&B accommodation in character village cottages, meals and rehearsal in historic buildings. Wealth of activity for non-playing partners. Bursaries offered. Groups and individuals welcome. Fees: £140. Further information also available from Haworth Tourist Information Centre *Tel:* 01535 642329.

Headington Summer School
1/1 Corrennie Dr, Edinburgh EH10 6EQ
Tel: 0131 447 1557

Heather Thomson, sec; E King, treasurer.
M/classes for solo singers and accompanists and ens singing. Peter Gellhorn, David Coleman, Paul Hamburger and Jean Alhster. 18-26 Jul 1998 at Headington School, Oxford.

Hereford International Summer School
Flat 1, 54 Lullingstone La, Hither Green, London SE13 6UH
Tel: 0181 695 1685

David Battersby, admin.
Courses for choral singers, choral conducting, solo singers, pno performance, young pianists, pno teachers and pno accompaniment. For age 13 and above. Aug. Fees: £350.

Higham Hall College
Bassenthwaite Lake, Cockermouth, Cumbria CA13 9SH
Tel: 017687 76276 *Fax:* 017687 76013
Email: higham.hall@dial.pipex.com
Website: www.higham-hall.org.uk

A Galbraith, dir.
Jazz ens, Aug. Also various courses throughout yr for age 18 and above. Fees: from £105.

Hindhead Music Centre
Hindhead Rd, Hindhead, Surrey GU26 6BA
Tel: 01428 604941 *Fax:* 01428 607871

Ann Hughes-Chamberlain, dir.
Summer mus m/class courses with international artists. Jul-Aug.

Holiday Music in the Cotswolds
34 Stanton Rd, London SW20 8RJ
Tel: 0181 947 5538

Muriel Levin, dir.
'Piano Plus' day courses in converted barn for pianists and ens (str, w/wind, vocal) for age 15 and above. Recitals, w/shops. Apr, Jul, Sep, Oct 1998. Fees: £150.

Ideas for Cellists
c/o Penelope Lynex, 20 Hillway, London N6 6QA
Tel: 0181 340 0897 *Fax:* 0181 341 5292

Penelope Lynex, vc; Mary Pells, baroque vc.
23-26 Jul 1998, applications by 2 Jun. Tutors' recitals, lessons, classes, vc ens, sight-reading. For age 12 and above (gr 6+). Fees £125

(residential), £95 (non-residential), pianists £15 reduction off either rate.

Incorporated Association of Organists Festival and Summer School
11 Stonehill Dr, Bromyard, Herefordshire HR7 4XB
Tel: 01885 483155 *Fax:* 01885 488609

Richard Popple MBE, sec; Margaret Phillips, president.
Annual summer school held in Oxford for a week in Aug including concerts, recitals, lectures and m/classes. Open to all who study or enjoy org mus. Applications by May. Fees: c £350. Bursaries available for f/t students.

Incorporated Society of Musicians (ISM)
10 Stratford Pl, London W1N 9AE
Tel: 0171 629 4413 *Fax:* 0171 408 1538
Email: membership@ism.org
Website: www.ism.org

Neil Hoyle, chief exec.
Conferences of special interest to school and private teachers, performers and composers. Also w/shops, seminars, lecture recitals at various regional centres. Open to non-members. Annual conference 6-9 Apr 1999, Chichester.

The Inner Voice
The White House, Aston Hill, Aston Rowant, Watlington, Oxon OX9 5SG
Tel: 01844 351561 *Fax:* 01844 354891
Email: elisabeth@innervoice.demon.co.uk

Elisabeth Wingfield; Ali Gordon-Creed.
Courses designed to help performers free themselves of problems associated with nerves, lack of self-confidence and the inner critic. Training enables performers to use their potential more effectively and reduce the negative effecrs of stress. Also, psychology for musical performance courses in England and Italy for teachers, students and professional singers and musicians.

The 9th International Brass Band Summer School
Sedbergh School, Sedbergh, Cumbria LA10 5HG
Tel: 01539 622230 (day); 01539 620001 (eve)
Fax: 01539 621301

Alan Lewis, course dir; Geoffrey Brand, mus dir.
Annual summer school at Sedbergh School, open to br and perc players of all abilities and ages. Wide repertoire of band and ens mus, optional theory classes and inst tutorials. 19-26 Jul 1998. Fees: £247-295.

International Musicians Seminar
IMS, Prussia Cove, 32 Grafton Sq, London SW4 0DB
Tel: 0171 720 9020 *Fax:* 0171 720 9033

Rosanna Yeatman, sec.

M/classes in Cornwall given by eminent musicians (Steven Isserlis, Ralph Kirshbaum, Andras Schiff), for str players, pianists and chmbr ens aged 16-30. sFees: c £675 per 10-day course.

International Piano Teachers Consultants (IPTEC)
29 Beaumont Rd, Chiswick, London W4 5AL
Tel: 0181 994 4288

Meriel Jefferson, hon sec.
1-day courses, consultations available in specialist subjects. Seminar for pno teachers, Brockenhurst, Hants, 25 Jul 1998.

International Society for Study of Tension in Performance (ISSTIP)
School of Music, Kingston University, c/o 28 Emperor's Gate, London SW7 4HS
Tel: 0171 373 7307 *Fax:* 0171 244 0904

Carola Grindea, chm; Pamela Bowden, co-dir London Performing Arts Clinic.
Annual 1-day w/shops and seminars open to non-members. Special courses on prevention of physical injuries and pyschological problems. For age 18 and above. Performing Arts Clinic 1st and 3rd Weds at London College of Music.

Islington Arts Factory
2 Parkhurst Rd, London N7 0SF
Tel: 0171 607 0561 *Fax:* 0171 700 7229
Website: www.artec.co.uk/artec/iafnet

Dominic Chennell, publicity offr.
Community arts centre offering courses and w/shops for adults and children. Vocal classes, drumming. Waged/concession rate. Fees from £20 per 3-month term.

Jackdaws Educational Trust
Bridge House, Great Elm, Nr Frome, Somerset BA11 3NY
Tel: 01373 812383 *Fax:* 01373 812083

Maureen Lehane Wishart, mus dir.
Residential w/end mus courses offered every w/end, Mar-Aug 1998, catering for students, proficient amateurs, mus teachers and professional musicians. Young people of a required standard are encouraged and appropriate concessions in course fees are made. Fees: residential w/ends £95 plus B&B at £15 per person per night; for age under 14, £50 plus B&B; for age under 22, £70 plus B&B.

Jazz Academy
Regent's College, Regent's Pk, London NW1 4NS
Tel: 0171 487 7495; 01908 648945 *also fax*

Michael Garrick, dir; Arthur Lockwood, admin.
Jazz skills, Easter 1998; Summer Jazz, mid Aug 1998; Piano People, 28-30 Dec 1998. Courses held at Royal Academy of Music, London. Fees on application. For any age.

Kato Havas One-Day Workshop for Strings
72 Victoria Rd, Oxford OX2 7QE
Tel: 01865 514094 *also fax*

Release of Tension and Stage Fright in Performance, held at St Edmund Hall, Oxford. 25 Jul 1998. Fees: £10 (Khana members); £30 (non-members).

Keele Summer Schools
Centre for Continuing and Professional Education, Keele University, Keele, Staffs ST5 5BG
Tel: 01782 583436 *Fax:* 01782 583248
Email: ada02@cc.keele.ac.uk

Helen McGarry, course sec.
Chamber Music Summer School, for amateurs, students and teachers aged 18 and above, 22-29 Aug 1998. Applications by 26 Jun.

Kenneth van Barthold Intensive Piano Workshop
Arvenis, Stour La, Stour Row, Shaftesbury, Dorset SP7 0QJ
Tel: 01747 838 318 *also fax*

Kenneth van Barthold.
2 tutors for 12 students, 12 practice rooms, recording facilities, final public recitals on Steinway concert grand. Presented in association with the University of Edinburgh Music Faculty and Centre for Continuing Education. 10-28 Aug 1998.

The Knack
Baylis Programme at English National Opera, ENO Works, 40 Pitfield St, London N1 6EU
Tel: 0171 739 5808

Mary King, course dir; Steve Moffitt, head of the Baylis Programme.
For singers aged 18-40 developing skills in mus and singing, text and drama, movement and dance. Taught in evening sessions Oct-Jun, auditions in May. No previous formal qualifications needed. Fees: £500 per term.

Knuston Hall
Irchester, Wellingborough, Northants NN29 7EU
Tel: 01933 312104 *Fax:* 01933 357596

John Herrick, principal.
Various w/end and week adult residential courses throughout year. For age 16 and above. Fees: £89.50.

The Kodály Institute of Britain
133 Queen's Gate, London SW7 5LE
Tel: 0171 823 7371 *Fax:* 0171 584 7691

Mary Skone-Roberts, admin.
International summer school 1-8 Aug 1998 in London. Courses for kindergarten, primary, secondary and tertiary educators, singers and

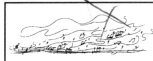

pno teachers. Musicianship training for all. M/classes and recitals.
1-yr p/t courses in musicianship according to the Kodály Principles at 3 levels: elementary, intermediate, advanced, begin late Sep, credit bearing for Trinity College LTCL (Music Ed) Cert and Dip. W/end courses in early childhood, primary and secondary mus education, London and Edinburgh, 1998.

Lacock Summer School
Cantax House, Lacock, Chippenham, Wilts SN15 2JZ
Tel: 01249 730468 *also fax*

Andrew van der Beek.
19-24 Jul, 26-31 Jul 1998. For singers and players of renaissance and baroque insts. All ages. Fees: £230, £140 (age 25 and under).

Lake District Summer Music
Stricklandgate House, 92 Stricklandgate, Kendal, Cumbria LA9 4PU
Tel: 01539 733411 *Fax:* 01539 724441
Email: ldsmdetails@hotmail.com

Andrew Lucas, admin.
Residential snr summer school 1-12 Aug 1998: chmbr mus and solo inst coaching and m/classes with top international artists for str players, ens and pianists at conservatoire and young professional level. Children's w/shop/Young String Venture 2-7 Aug 1998: non-residential courses for young str players aged 6-18. Technique, ens, orch, eurhythmics (mus and movement) under specialist tutors.

Lambent Books
4 Coombe Gardens, New Malden, Surrey KT3 4AA
Tel: 0181 715 2560 *also fax*
Email: lambent@well.com

Joseph O'Connor.
Courses and individual consultations for performers and teachers on performance anxiety, communication skills and psychology of learning.

Lancaster Rehearsal Orchestra
Dept of Music, University of Lancaster, Lancaster LA1 4YW
Tel: 01524 593777/593013 *Fax:* 01524 847298
Email: d.mccaldin@lancaster.ac.uk

Denis McCaldin, cond; Ronald Adelson, sec.
1-day symphony orch courses 3 times pa. Mahler, 8 Nov 1998; Stravinsky, 7 Feb 1999; Bruckner, 25 Apr 1999. Entry by audition, age 16 and above. Applications by one month before event. Fees: £5 per event.

Latour International Festival of Music and the Arts (France)
c/o Mananan Festival Office, Erin Arts Centre, Port Erin,

Isle of Man IM9 6LD
Tel: 01624 835858 *Fax:* 01624 836658

John Bethell, dir.
Vocal and opera study courses with Jeffrey Lawton for professionals and amateurs aged 19-35. Opportunity to appear in opera performance. 26-30 Jul 1998, applications by 1 May.

Lauderdale House Society
22 Gresley Rd, London N19 3JZ
Tel: 0171 272 5664 *also fax*

Murray Gordon, mus chmn.
M/classes for pno, voice, vc, vn, fl. Concerts, gui society, Singers Guild, Suzuki, etc.

Learn at Leisure (Continuing Education)
University of Nottingham, Cherry Tree Buildings, Nottingham NG7 2RD
Tel: 0115 951 6526 *Fax:* 0115 951 6556
Email: ce.residential@nottingham.ac.uk

David Bodger, residential courses dir.
Educational courses for adults. Welsh National Opera *Tosca* and *La traviata,* 19-21 Jun (Llandudno); Haydn at Esterhaza, 3-5 Jul (Oxford); introduction to chmbr mus, 4-6 Sep (Knuston Hall); intro to contemporary mus, 18-20 Sep (Nottingham); Glyndebourne w/end, 16-18 Oct.

Leeds College of Music
3 Quarry Hill, Leeds LS2 7PD
Tel: 0113 222 3400 *also fax*

Aug bank holiday week. Annual residential jazz summer school for all standards, grouped by experience. Maximum number around 60.

Lights, Music, Action
Fish & Bell Management, PO Box 175, Bury St Edmunds, Suffolk IP32 7DY
Tel: 01284 756204
Email: fishbelluk@aol.com

Annual residential summer school 21-28 Aug 1998. Auditions by arrangement. Held in Suffolk. Ages 9-18. Jazz musicians (gr 4+); drama, dance and music theatre (all standards, grouped by experience); backstagers training (make-up, scenery, costume). Large scale final production.

Lionel Tertis International Viola Workshop
Erin Arts Centre, Victoria Sq, Port Erin, Isle of Man IM9 6LD
Tel: 01624 835858 *Fax:* 01624 836658
Website: www.enterprise.net/arts/tertis.htm

John Bethell, dir.
Study courses and m/classes for professional and amateur va players of all ages. Next 2000, applications by 31 Mar 2000. Fees £90 plus £15 registration.

505

Llandaff Summer Music Course

50 Parc-y-Coed, Creigiau, Cardiff CF4 8LY
Tel: 01222 892388 *also fax*

Jenny Vale, admin; Christopher Vale, course dir.
Aug. Orch course for age 10-17.

MAC (Midlands Arts Centre)

Cannon Hill Pk, Birmingham B12 9QH
Tel: 0121 440 4221 ext 266/7 *Fax:* 0121 446 4372

Gabrielle Oliver, educ programmer.
Specialist mus w/end courses for all ages including jazz and early mus. Mus courses for adults and children (Western and Asian insts and styles) during term-time and holidays.

Manchester University

Centre for the Development of Continuing Education (CDCE), Humanities Building, Oxford Rd
Tel: 0161 275 3290 *Fax:* 0161 275 3300

Glyn Davies, mus tutor.
Learning for pleasure - a term's course on variety of mus topics; Certificate programme (humanities), weekly meeting over 2 years (modular) on jazz and popular mus. Residential w/end courses at Chancellors: choral, orchestral and mus appreciation.

Marlborough College Summer School

Marlborough, Wilts SN8 1PA
Tel: 01672 892388 *Fax:* 01672 892476

Alex Scott, sec.
12 Jul-1 Aug 1998. Weekly courses for residents and non-residents of all ages: singing, pno for beginners and improvers, gui, choral w/shop, conducting and directing mus w/shop, gamelan, unlock your voice and jazz improvisation. Plus over 160 different courses for all the family. Fees: from £84 (5 half days); accommodation from £100.

Mayer-Lismann Opera Centre

106 Gordon Rd, London W13 8PJ
Tel: 0181 998 7854 *Fax:* 0181 991 2105

Jeanne Henny, dir.
Opportunity for young singers, accompanists and conductors to gain practical experience of the operatic and concert repertoire. Four operas are staged every year.

Mid-Pennine Arts

Yorke St, Burnley BB11 1HD
Tel: 01282 421986 *Fax:* 01282 429513

Nick Hunt, dir.
Arts Development Agency for Burnley, Hyndburn, Pendle, Rossendale, Todmorden. Various mus in education projects.

Missenden Abbey

Gt Missenden, Bucks HP16 0BD
Tel: 01494 890295/6 *Fax:* 01494 863697
Email: enquiries@missendenabbey.ac.uk
Website: www.aredu.demon.co.uk/missendenabbey

Rosa Maria Welsh, educ co-ord.
W/end courses all year round including mus appreciation, singing and jazz. Age 16 and above. Fees: £159.20 (residential); £69.20 (non-residential). Summer school 2-29 Aug 1998. Fees: £499 (residential); £154.20 (non-residential).

Morland Choristers' Camp

Garden Flat, Morland, Penrith, Cumbria CA10 3AZ
Tel: 01931 714654

Revd Canon Gervase W Markham, camp chief.
A residential course approved by the Royal School of Church Music for age 9-18 who are members of church choirs or school choirs. Church mus, secular mus and outdoor activities. 26 Jul-2 Aug 1998. Fees: £170.

Morley College

61 Westminster Bridge Rd, London SE1 7HT
Tel: 0171 928 8501 ext 238 *Fax:* 0171 928 4074

Robert Hanson, dir of mus.
Large range of adult education courses, including ens, solo performance, singing, electronic mus, history and theory; all levels from beginners to advanced. Special theme days held regularly.

Mostly Music

28 Carlisle Close, Mobberley, Knutsford, Cheshire WA16 7HD
Tel: 01565 87265

Roger Wilkes.
Courses and events throughout the year, in Greater Manchester and NW England: choral, rcdr, early mus, study courses, church mus, private and correspondence tuition. Singing holidays at home and abroad (spring, summer).

Music at Madingley

Board of Continuing Education, University of Cambridge, Madingley Hall, Madingley, Cambs CB3 8AQ
Tel: 01954 210636 *Fax:* 01954 210677
Email: laf@cam.ac.uk

Linda Fisher, programmes mgr.
Various w/end and week-long residential practical courses for ages 18 and above. Alberni m/class 24-31 Jul 1998. Fees: £390 (residential). £278 (non-residential). 2-9 Apr 1999. Fees: £399 (residential), £285 (non-residential).

Music Summer School

Wedgwood Memorial College, Barlaston, Stoke-on-Trent
ST12 9DG
Tel: 01782 372105 *Fax:* 01782 372393

D Tatton.
Short courses throughout the year. 1998 courses: circle dance, 19-21 Jun; jazz on a summer w/end, 3-5 Jul; mus tutorial w/ends from Sep 1998 - Mar 1999.

Music Theatre Summer School

Cumbria College of Art and Design, Brampton Rd, Carlisle
CA3 9AY
Tel: 01228 25333 *Fax:* 01228 514491
Email: cum@cumbriacollart.ac.uk
Website: www.cumbriacollart.ac.uk

Judith Todd, mkt.
Aug. One week summer school for students, practitioners and teachers of composition, inst, singing, dance, acting and design. Fees: £250-275 (non-residential), £400-439 (residential).

Musicale Holidays

The Bourne, 20 Salisbury Av, Harpenden, Herts AL5 2QG
Tel: 01582 460978 (24 hrs) *Fax:* 01582 767343

David Johnston, Gillian Johnston, dirs.
Residential course at Harpenden for high standard orch and symphonic wind orch players, plus other non-residential courses held at venues throughout UK during 27 Jul-15 Aug 1998. Caters for insts aged 5-18 of all standards and non-insts aged 5-9 in the form of a mus activity course. Applications welcome until opening date of course.

Musicfest International Summer School

Aberystwyth Arts Centre, Penglais, Aberystwyth, Ceredigion SY23 3DE
Tel: 01970 622882 *Fax:* 01970 622883
Email: lla@aber.ac.uk
Website: www.aber.ac.uk/~arcwww/index.htm

Louise Amery, mkt mgr.
Runs in conjunction with Musicfest, Aberystwyth International Music Festival. Provides the opportunity for children over 14, mus students, professional and amateur adults to work on chmbr mus and solo repertoire and to play in orchs with a team of British chmbr musicians of international standing. 18-31 Jul 1998, applications by Jul.

Musicosophia United Kingdom

PO Box 3030, Littlehampton, W Sussex BN16 2QT
Tel: 01903 786745 *also fax*

Catherine Brophy, dir; A Haizel, sec.
Organises courses for listeners as part of an international movement of music lovers. Music Meditation, 26-28 Jun 1998 in London; The

Listener's Bruckner, 27-28 Jul; Shakespeare and Mendelssohn, 14 Nov; The Listener's Beethoven, 20-22 Nov at Benslow Music Trust; Bach, Feb 1999; Mozart, Mar; Beethoven Apr; Schubert, May. Other short courses available. Fees £25-125 (concessions available). Applications by one month before course begins.

National Chamber Music Course

3 Grand Av, London N10 3AY
Tel: 0181 883 2275 *Fax:* 0181 372 6465

Caroline Stone, admin; Elisabeth Waterhouse, dir. 2-8 Aug 1998, applications by end Mar. Held at Temple Dinsley, Herts. Chmbr mus course for str players aged 10-18. (2 chmbr ens, inst classes, orch and choir). Fees: £310.

The National Children's Chamber Orchestra of Great Britain

The Bourne, 20 Salisbury Av, Harpenden, Herts AL5 2QG
Tel: 01582 760014 *Fax:* 01582 767343

Gillian and David Johnston, dirs; Caroline Marriott, admin.
For str players aged 10-16 at gr 7 and above. The players will play in quartets and in a chmbr orch combining with wind players from the National Children's Wind Orchestra of Great Britain. Entry is by audition during the autumn term for a residential course at Easter - concerts at major venues around the country later in the year. Also training str orch for promising younger players.

National Children's Music Camps

61 Crown Rd, Sutton, Surrey SM1 1RT
Tel: 0181 715 4048 *also fax*
Email: ncm@edcrown.demon.co.uk

Avril Dankworth, founder-president; David Edwards, campers' admin.
Annual mus camps for age 8-17 in the grounds of the Old Rectory, Wavendon, Bucks. Teenage camps 26 Jul-1 Aug and 2-8 Aug 1998, jnr camps 9-15 Aug and 16-22 Aug 1998, applications by Feb. Fees: £183 (teenage), £168 (jnr).

National Children's Orchestra

157 Craddocks Av, Ashtead, Surrey KT21 1NU
Tel: 01372 276857 *Fax:* 01372 271407

Vivienne Price MBE, admin; Elisabeth Humphreys, admin.
Easter and summer holidays. Auditions in autumn. 5 orchs divided into age groups: under 14, under 13, under 12, under 11 (2 orchs). 1998: under 14 orch, 4-12 Apr, 22-30 Aug; under 13 orch, 3-11 Apr, 7-15 Aug; under 12 orch, 31 Jul-7 Aug; training and introductory orchs, 24-31 Jul; w/wind, br, perc course, 31 Jul-7 Aug.

PRO CORDA

THE NATIONAL SCHOOL FOR
YOUNG CHAMBER MUSIC PLAYERS

CHAMBER MUSIC COURSES FOR YOUNG STRING
PLAYERS AND PIANISTS AGED 8-18 AT PREPARATORY,
PRIMARY, JUNIOR, INTERMEDIATE AND SENIOR LEVELS

DIRECTOR OF MUSIC – ROBERT MAX

MEMBERS OF THE FACULTY INCLUDE CHAMBER MUSIC
PLAYERS AND TEACHERS OF THE HIGHEST CALIBRE

**THE RESIDENTIAL COURSES ARE DESIGNED TO
PROVIDE EXCELLENT OPPORTUNITIES FOR A
PROGRESSIVE TRAINING IN THE CHAMBER MUSIC
REPERTOIRE DURING THE SCHOOL HOLIDAYS**

AUDITIONS WILL BE HELD DURING THE SPRING IN
LONDON AND THE PROVINCES.

FURTHER DETAILS FROM:
**THE ADMINISTRATOR,
PRO CORDA, LEISTON ABBEY,
LEISTON, SUFFOLK IP16 4TB.
Tel: 01728 831354   Fax: 01728 832500**

Pro Corda: registered charity no: 312772

The National Children's Wind Orchestra of Great Britain
The Bourne, 20 Salisbury Av, Harpenden, Herts AL5 2QG
Tel: 01582 760014 *Fax:* 01582 767343

Gillian and David Johnston, dirs; Caroline Marriott, admin.
For w/wind, br and perc players aged 10-15 at gr 5 and above. 2 orchs are formed. Entry by audition during the autumn term for a residential course at Easter and concerts at major venues around the country later in the year. Study includes standard repertoire, new commissions and chmbr mus.

National Isis Strings Academy
7 Scot Grove, Pinner, Middx HA5 4RT
Tel: 0181 428 7174
Email: vrnisa@queenswood.herts.sch.uk

Viviane Ronchetti, mus dir.
Patron, Sir Neville Marriner CBE. High-quality chmbr orch training for str players gr 7+ and aged 13-19. 5-day residential course at Queenswood School, Hatfield, 26 Jul-1 Aug. Fees: £35 (w/ends), £140 (5-day residential).

National Junior Music Club of Great Britain
23 Hitchin St, Biggleswade, Beds SG18 8AX
Tel: 01767 316521 *Fax:* 01767 317221

Douglas Coombes, dir; Carole Lindsay-Douglas, organiser.
1-day courses in mus games for primary teachers at various venues nationwide. Subject for all courses is 'Themes and schemes in music with vocal composing'. 1998 dates: 5,8,12 and 19 May, 26 Sep. Fees: £50.

National Operatic and Dramatic Association (NODA)
NODA House, 1 Crestfield St, London WC1H 8AU
Tel: 0171 837 5655 *Fax:* 0171 833 0609

Mark Thorburn, chief executive.
Residential week-long theatre training course for age 18 and above. University of Warwick in Coventry, 8-15 Aug 1998.

National Scout and Guide Symphony Orchestra Course
c/o Youth Activities Section, Guide Association, 17-19 Buckingham Palace Rd, London SW1W 0PT
Tel: 0171 834 6242 *Fax:* 0171 828 8317

Karen Rogers, youth activities asst; exec asst.
3-9 Aug 1998 in Durham. Applicants must be aged 13-26, members of the Scout or Guide Associations and proficient in at least 1 orch inst. Fees: c £250.

National Youth Choir of Scotland
18 Polmont Pk, Polmont By Falkirk FK2 0XT
Tel: 01324 711749 *also fax*
Email: nycos@ednet.co.uk

Robert W Tait, admin; Christopher Bell, artistic dir and cond.
Residential courses in Jul, Oct and Apr for mixed voices aged 16-24, born, resident or studying in Scotland. Auditions annually in Mar. Also chmbr choir by invitation and training choir (age 14-17). *Fee:* £250-300 (summer course).

National Youth Choirs of Great Britain
PO Box 67, Holmfirth, Huddersfield, W Yorks HD7 1GQ
Tel: 01484 687023 *Fax:* 01484 681635

Carl Browning, exec dir; Michael Brewer OBE, mus dir; Danny Curtis, choir admin.
Residential courses for members of the National Youth Choirs. Auditions held annually in Jun, Jul, Oct and Nov for age ranges 12-19 (training choir) and 16-22 (main choir). Courses at New Year, Easter and summer. Fees: £240-300 (course), £20 (audition).

National Youth Jazz Orchestra of Scotland
13 Somerset Pl, Glasgow G3 7JT
Tel: 0141 332 8311 *Fax:* 0141 332 3915
Email: nyos@cqm.co.uk

Richard Chester, dir.
Residential summer course with tuition from experienced tutors and public performances. Ages 12-21. Applicants must be resident in Scotland.

National Youth Music Theatre
5th Floor, The Palace Theatre, Shaftesbury Av, London W1V 8AY
Tel: 0171 734 7478 *Fax:* 0171 734 7515
Email: bird@clearsite.com
Website: www.clearsite.com/nymt/

Jeremy James Taylor, artistic dir; Felicity Bunt, gen mgr.
Application throughout year for open access mus theatre w/shops and regional satellite projects. Auditions Oct-Dec for singer/actor/dancers and insts for 4 major mus theatre productions pa. Courses are residential and non-residential, usually during school holidays and w/ends.

National Youth Orchestra of Great Britain
32 Old School House, Britannia Rd, Bristol BS15 8DB
Tel: 0117 960 0477 *Fax:* 0117 960 0376
Email: nyo@btinternet.com
Website: www.btinternet.com/~nyo

Michael de Grey, chief exec; Jill White, dir of mus.
Residential courses 3 times pa. In 1999 the NYO will perform in major venues throughout the UK and abroad, including Barbican Hall, London; Symphony Hall, Birmingham; and The

Bridgewater Hall, Manchester. Auditions annually for players aged 10-19 (gr 8 dist standard, applicants need not have taken exams). Applications for 1999 orch by 31 Jul 1998. Fees: £225. Bursaries available.

National Youth Orchestra of Scotland
13 Somerset Pl, Glasgow G3 7JT
Tel: 0141 332 8311 *Fax:* 0141 332 3915
Email: nyos@cqm.co.uk

Richard Chester, dir.
Winter and summer residential courses providing tuition from professional musicians and rehearsals with internationally renowned conductors and soloists prior to concert tours. Easter residential training course. Ages 12-21. Summer residential courses in Jun-Jul followed by public performances. Annual auditions held in Jan-Feb for courses at Easter, in Jul-Aug and Dec-Jan; application deadline Nov. Applicants must be resident in Scotland.

National Youth Wind Orchestra of Great Britain
2 High Green, Woodham Village, Aycliffe, Co Durham DL5 4RZ
Tel: 01753 642223 *also fax*

Kit Shepherd, exec dir.
Autumn auditions for residential courses held 15-31 Aug 1998 and at Easter. Chmbr mus m/classes, ens courses and w/shops. Age 15-21 at gr 8+.

Nelly Ben-Or Piano Courses Incorporating the Alexander Technique
23 Rofant Rd, Northwood, Middlesex HA6 3BD
Tel: 01923 822268 *also fax*

Roger Clynes, course sec.
11-15 Jul 1998, early Jan 1999. Courses at the Guildhall School of Music and Drama, London, for pianists, teachers and advanced students. Individual sessions at the keyboard and in the Alexander Technique. The courses incorporate the principles of the Alexander Technique in details of pno playing and creative study of mus for performance.

Nonsuch Summer School
101 St Stephens Rd, Canterbury CT2 7JT
Tel: 01227 462871

Sian Jones, admin.
29 Jul-9 Aug 1998 at Hockerill School, Bishops Stortford. W European court dances of 12th-19th C. Fully residential. Age 16 and above. Fees: £90-450.

North East Early Music Forum (NEEMF)
43 Beckett's Park Cres, Leeds LS6 3PH
Tel: 0113 278 6886 *Fax:* 0113 230 7818
Email: bmb6jlj@bmb.leeds.ac.uk

Jillian Johnson, hon sec.
Day w/shops throughout year in performance and interpretation of early mus for age 16 and above. Residential w/end at the University of Leeds for singers and insts. Lully: Isis with Jeffrey Skidmore, 11-13 Sep.

North Wales Summer School of Music
Capcoch, Tal-y-bont, Bangor, Gwynedd LL57 3UU
Tel: 01248 351186 (after 7pm)

Pat Morrell, course admin.
Vocal m/class, 10-12 Jul 1998; choral course, 3-5 Jul 1998; wind group, 10-12 Jul 1998. For age 16 and above.

Northern Junior Philharmonic Orchestra Course
Moorcroft, South Rd, Prudhoe, Northumberland NE42 5LB
Tel: 01661 832605 *Fax:* 01661 833526

Peter Swan, organising sec.
Orch course for instrumentalists aged 12-23 of gr 8 standard. Sir Michael Tippett Award (£500) available for the most promising musician(s) on the course. Programme: Edward Rushton, new work; Berg, Lulu Suite; Mahler, Symphony no 10. 22 Jul-4 Aug 1997, auditions Apr, applications by Feb. Fees: £260.

Northern Recorder Course
41 Grosvenor Rd, Sale, Cheshire M33 6WL
Tel: 0161 973 2050

D A Bamforth.
Held at University College, Chester, 7-14 Apr 1999. St Matthews Hall, Stretford, 24 Oct 1998 and 23 Oct 1999. Any age.

Northern Sax Course (Harrogate)
c/o Lindsey Music, 42 St Mary's Pk, Louth, Lincs LN11 0EF
Tel: 01507 605244

Jeff Brown, events organiser.
14-17 Apr 1998.

Northumbrian Recorder and Viol School (NORVIS)
5 Birchgrove Av, Gilesgate Moor, Durham DH1 1DE
Tel: 0191 386 4782
Email: marlene.austin@durham.ac.uk

Marlene Austin, admin.
Held at College of St Hild and St Bede, Durham, 1-8 Aug 1998. Course for any age covers all aspects of early mus: rcdrs, viols, baroque strs, renaissance insts, plucked insts, keyboard, singing and dancing.

Nottingham University School of Continuing Education
Cherry Tree Buildings, University Pk, Nottingham NG7 2RD
Tel: 0115 951 3715 *Fax:* 0115 951 3711
Email: philip.olleson@nottingham.ac.uk

Philip Olleson, lecturer in mus.

Day and eve courses in mus appreciation and history. 2 choirs. Holiday courses and mus courses from Feb-Nov.

The Old Rectory Music Courses
Fittleworth, Pulborough, W Sussex RH20 1HU
Tel: 01798 865306 *also fax*
Email: oldrectory@mistral.co.uk
Website: www3.mistral.co.uk/oldrectory/index.html

Tony and Sue Dawkins, principals.
Wide range of week, w/end and mid-week courses in singing, hpd, mus appreciation, w/wind, handbells, strs, rcdr and va da gamba. 1998: singers summer school, 29 May-5 Jun; Three Great Symphonies, 10-12 Jul; close harmony and barber-shop singing, 24-26 Jul; Ivor and Noel singing w/shop, 4-11 Sep; mus appreciation, 11-13 Sep; singing for the tone deaf, 23-25 Oct; rcdr playing, 30 Oct-1 Nov; singing w/shop, 23-27 Nov; mus appreciation, 4-6 Dec.

The Opera School Wales
Rhydyberry Cottages, Merthyr Cynog, Brecon, Powys LD3 9SA
Tel: 01874 690339; 01874 690254 *also fax*

Bridgett Gill, dir.
Intensive 3-week spring course (Mar-Apr) for young professional singers combining stage and vocal training, make-up and stage-fighting instruction, culminating in several fully-staged performances with orch ens, touring theatres in Wales and London. Auditions Nov. Fees: £320-380.

Orff Society (UK)
7 Rothesay Av, Richmond, Surrey TW10 5EB
Tel: 0181 876 1944 *also fax*
Website: www.catan.demon.co.uk/orff/

Margaret Murray, hon sec.
Introductory course, Apr 1998; Accent on Rhythm, 6-7 Jun 1998; Hands on Music, 25-31 Jul at University of Warwick. Creative mus courses mainly for teachers in primary and middle schools.

Oundle International Festival and Summer School for Young Organists
The Old Crown, Glapthorn, Oundle, Peterborough PE8 5BJ
Tel: 01832 272026 *also fax*

James Parsons, dir; Patricia Ryan, admin.
Summer School for up to 50 organists based in Oundle, Northants. Age range 14-23. Four courses offered, with valuable recital awards and week of festival events, professional concerts, exhibitions, etc. 12-19 Jul 1998, applications by 1 Apr. Fees: c £365.

Oxenfoord International
25 Frogston Rd West, Edinburgh EH10 7AB
Tel: 0131 445 7491 *Fax:* 0131 445 7492
Email: joan@buzbee.demon.co.uk
Website: www.napier.ac.uk/depts/music/courses.html

Joan Busby, course dir; Denise Borland, admin.
Opera, mus theatre, early mus, French song, Lieder, vocal technique, etc for solo singers and accompanists aged 17 and above. St Leonards School, St Andrews, Fife. 16-26 Aug 1998.

Oxford Baroque Chamber Music Week
13 Brackley Rd, Monton Green, Eccles, Manchester M30 9LG
Tel: 0161 281 2502 *Fax:* 01223 461143
Email: baroquew@silverfen.demon.co.uk
Website: www.newn.cam.ac.uk/prlw/winchester/baroque.html

Peter Collier.
9-16 Aug 1998 at Headington School, Oxford. Course for wind, str and keyboard players of baroque or modern insts at old or modern pitch. A secure technique and good sight-reading is required.

Oxford Cello School
67 Oxford Rd, Abingdon, Oxon OX14 2AA
Tel: 01235 530572 *Fax:* 01235 555952
Email: ocs@infotrade.co.uk

Marianne Gottfeldt, dir.
Residential and non-residential summer schools for vc and db in Jul and Aug. Technique m/classes, individual lessons, scales, video analysis, improvisation, ens, vc and db orch and choir. Gr 6-8 aural training and theory for the younger student. Solo performance with orch for performance students. Possibility of taking AEB exams during course. Also, performance course for post gr 8 students, adult improvers course and AEB Advanced Certificate. Visiting professor Maud Tortelier.

Oxford Chamber Music Courses
80 St Bernard's Rd, Oxford OX2 6EJ
Tel: 01865 553892

Tom Patterson.
Three-day meeting, 22-25 Aug. Fees: £155 (residential), £120 (non-residential), reduction for students in f/t education (£35). For any age group.

Oxford Flute Summer School
32a Gregories Rd, Beaconsfield HP9 1HQ
Tel: 01494 681566 *Fax:* 01865 514409
Email: ofss@compuserve.com

Clive Conway, Janet Way, dirs; Katie Bycroft, admin.
Annual course for fl players of all standards age

16 and over, held at The Queen's College, Oxford. Concerts, classes, ens and individual tuition for ages 16 and above. 10-16 Aug 1998. Three options offered: general course for players of all ages and standards; performance course, daily individual lesson and public performance; audition course for students aged 16-18 auditioning for mus colleges and universities. Fees: £210 (general), £310 (performance and audition).

Oxford Summer Sessions

d'Overbroeck's College, Beechlawn House, Park Town, Oxford OX2 6SN
Tel: 01865 310000 *Fax:* 01865 552296
Email: doverb@rmplc.co.uk

Sami Cohen, dir.
Aug 1998. Non-residential mus summer school organised by d'Overbroeck's College, Oxford, for str players of gr 5+ standard. Strings in solo, chmbr mus and orch forces are brought to concert pitch by principals of Oxford's New Chamber Orchestra under the direction of Andrew Zreczycki, culminating in a public concert at the Holywell Music Room. Ages 11-21. Auditions.

Oxford University Department for Continuing Education

1 Wellington Sq, Oxford OX1 2JA
Tel: 01865 270360 *Fax:* 01865 270309

Anna Sandham, co-ord; Jonathan Darnborough, associate tutor in mus.
Wide ranging programme of weekly courses and day schools in Oxford and surrounding area. Fees: from £24. Also runs a number of residential summer schools for adults 18 Jul-22 Aug 1998. Fees from £260.

Pendrell Hall College

Codsall Wood, Wolverhampton, Staffs WV8 1QP
Tel: 01902 434112 *Fax:* 01902 434113

David Evans, principal; Linda Reeve, admin offr.
Mus study w/ends for ages 18-80. Includes exploring chmbr mus, 27-29 Jul 1998.

Pipers' Guild

121 Hallam Way, West Hallam, Derbys DE7 6LP
Tel: 0115 930 8323
Email: margent@rmplc.co.uk
Website: www.quantine.co.uk/~piper/pgpage/htm

Stephanie Payne, sec; Mary Argent, chmn; Betty Roe, president.
Summer school, 6-11 Aug 1998 at Royal School for the Deaf in Derby.

Practical Psychology for Instrumental Music Teachers

Music, Mind and Movement, 28 Glebe Pl, London SW3 5LD
Tel: 0171 352 1666 *also fax*

Lucinda Mackworth-Young, dir.
Jul 1998, applications by 31 May. Practical psychology for inst mus teaching and performing, including teacher-pupil-parent relationships, emotions and motivation, teaching styles and learning strategies, practice, communication and anxiety in performance. Also Eurhythmics, Dance through the Ages and Improvisation. The course bears credit towards the ATCL and LTCL (mus educ) or Certificate of Music Education of Trinity College, London. Also shorter courses.

Pro Corda Trust (National School for Young Chamber Music Players)

Leiston Abbey House, Theberton Rd, Leiston, Suffolk IP16 4TB
Tel: 01728 831354 *Fax:* 01728 832500

Pamela Spofforth MBE, founder; Robert Max, dir of mus; T Boulton, M Parrington, course dirs; Mererid Crump, admin.
Residential courses during school holidays for young str players and pianists aged 8-18 attending twice yearly at preparatory, primary, jnr, intermediate and snr levels. Specialist ens tuition under the direction of distinguished musicians. Entry by audition. Application forms from Administrator at above address. 1998 courses: Preparatory, 23-30 May; primary, 31 Jul-8 Aug Jul and 25-31 Oct; jnr, 31 Jul-8 Aug; intermediate, 10-18 Aug; snr, 20-29 Aug.

Randazzo Opera

24 Bladon Ct, Barrow Rd, London SW16 5NE
Tel: 0181 677 8821; 0181 309 1309

Arlene Randazzo, admin and stage dir; Janet Haney, mus dir.
On-going w/shops with performances in Jun and Jul throughout London. All ages. Auditions.

Rathbone-Dickson Chamber Music Course

31 Chepstow Pl, London W2 4TT
Tel: 0171 229 0219 *also fax*

Joyce Rathbone, David Waterman, dirs.
2-10 Aug 1998. Held at Westonbirt School, Tetbury, Glos. Pno and str players aged 16-26.

Recorder Summer School

113 Birchwood Rd, Marton, Middlesbrough TS7 8DE
Tel: 01642 310628

Miss S Foxall, sec.
Classes and ens for rcdr players aged 16 and above (age 15 accepted if accompanied by an adult on the course). All grades including beginners. Renaissance groups, baroque chmbr

mus, concert and mus w/shops. Aug 1998 at Bretton Hall, Wakefield.

The Rehearsal Orchestra
4 Lucerne Ct, Abbey Pk, Beckenham, Kent BR3 1RB
Tel: 0181 663 1927 *Fax:* 0181 658 6261
Email: bwhyte@rehearsal-orchestra.org
Website: www.rehearsal-orchestra.org

Harry Legge OBE, artistic dir; Bridget Whyte, admin.
Advanced orch training for students and young professionals, teachers and experienced players. Wide range of orch repertoire studied, including new mus. 1 and 2-day sessions throughout the year, plus residential week in Edinburgh during the festival. Min gr 8, age 16+ with good sight-reading. Student and non-student rates given on application.

Royal College of Organists
7 St Andrew St, Holborn, London EC4A 3LQ
Tel: 0171 936 3606 *Fax:* 0171 353 8244

Study trip to Stockholm for organists 4-8 Sep 1998. Residential course for organists 2-4 Jan 1999 in Cambridge (provisional).

Royal School of Church Music
Cleveland Lodge, Westhumble, Dorking RH5 6BW
Tel: 01306 877676 *Fax:* 01306 887260

Geoffrey Weaver, dir of studies.
1-day and longer residential courses for singers and insts aged 10-25 at many locations around the country. Training events for choristers of all ages during Easter, applications by 1 Mar and summer holidays, applications by 1 Jun. Fees: £120-190.

Royal School of Church Music Harwich Summer Courses
Cherry Trees, 23 Stanley Rd, Wivenhoe, Essex CO7 9EN
Tel: 01206 824036

Graham Wadley, admin.
Boys' course 26-28 Jun 1998; girls' course 18-20 Sep 1998; students' course 31 Oct - 1 Nov 1998.

Royal Scottish Pipe Band Association
45 Washington St, Glasgow G3 8AZ
Tel: 0141 221 5414 *Fax:* 0141 221 1561

J Mitchell Hutcheson, exec offr.
Organises education classes run by 12 branches. Annual summer school, last week of Jul. All ages.

St Andrews International Flute Summer School
151 West Princes St, Glasgow G4 9BZ
Tel: 0141 333 0828 *also fax*

Ruth Morley, dir.
Annual course for fl players to study with Peter Lloyd, including m/classes, chmbr mus, daily student concerts, daily warm-up class, acting and performance skills, tone development. May be attended by performers, participants or observers. 12-18 Jul 1998 at St Leonard's School, St Andrews.

Sarum College Courses
Sarum College, 19 The Close, Salisbury, Wiltshire SP1 2EE
Tel: 01722 424800 *Fax:* 01722 338508

Robert Fielding.
Residential courses held in Salisbury. Summer course for young composers, 22-25 Jul 1998 has places for 10 students who will receive free tuition. Summer chmbr mus course for str and accompanists, 21-25 Jul 1998 is aimed at gifted pupils aged 12-19 of AB gr 7-8 or above; participants prepare work for concerts in Salisbury Cathedral, The Medieval Hall and Sarum College Chapel.

Schools Music Association of Great Britain
71 Margaret Rd, New Barnet, Herts EN4 9NT
Tel: 0181 440 6919 *also fax*

Maxwell Pryce, hon sec and chief exec.
Annual residential course and conference on mus in schools, 23-25 Oct 1998. Courses for mus teachers at regional centres throughout year.

Scottish Amateur Music Association
18 Craigton Cres, Alva, Clackmannanshire FK12 5DS
Tel: 01259 760249

Margaret Simpson, hon sec.
Summer courses include traditional fiddle school, National Youth Wind Ensemble of Scotland, 3-8 Aug 1998; National Youth Brass Band of Scotland 27 Jul-2 Aug 1998; National Youth String Orchestra of Scotland (and Training School), 10-15 Aug 1998 at St Andrew's College, Bearsden; National Recorder School of Scotland, Craigie Campus, University of Paisley, 11-13 Sep 1998.

Sheffield University Division of Adult Continuing Education
196-198 West St, Sheffield S1 4ET
Tel: 0114 282 5400

Adam White, mus co-ord.
Courses in mus theory, pop mus, women in mus, mus appreciation, improvisation, composition, Sep-May, applications by Sep. Particularly suited to those over age 17 who wish to study mus without the need to give up work. Modules are accredited and validated by the University of Sheffield. Fees: £30-120 per 20 credit modules (24 wks), or £360 pa (concessions also available).

513

The Shell Expro Music School
3 Nutborn House, Clifton Rd, London SW19 4QT
Tel: 0181 946 2995 *Fax:* 0181 944 6507

Nicola Wallis, festival dir.
Part of Aberdeen International Youth Festival.
Provides advanced level tuition and w/shops for
individual insts, chmbr ens and singers. Ages
16-23 for inst course, 18-30 for singers. 3-15 Aug
1998, applications by end May.

Sing for Pleasure
25 Fryerning La, Ingatestone, Essex CM4 0DD
Tel: 01277 353691 *also fax*
Email: choral@sfp.cix.co.uk
Website: www.sfp.cix.co.uk

Lynda Parker, dir.
Residential and day courses for children,
teachers, singers and choral conductors of all
ages, throughout the country. 1998: Superweek
singing holidays for ages 10-14, 11-20 Aug and
21-30 Aug; youth singing week for ages 14-18,
15-22 Aug; summer school for singers,
conductors and teachers, 22-30 Aug; primary
teachers, 15-22 Aug; course for primary teachers
leading to accreditation with Trinity College of
Music, 24-25 Oct. International festivals through
the 'A Coeur Joie' movement. Publishes
repertoire suitable for schools and choral groups.

Southampton University
Dept of Adult Education, Southampton SO9 5NH
Tel: 01703 592833

Ann Hayter, mkt co-ord.
Mus courses for the general public in
Southampton and throughout Hampshire, Dorset
and W Sussex. Opera study days,
interdisciplinary courses, jazz w/shop, beginners
courses. There is an accredited mus pathway
within the Certificate of Higher Education:
Humanities. Courses available through the
academic year.

Southend Summer School for the Performing Arts
PO Box 63, Southend-on-Sea, Essex SS21 6FE
Tel: 01702 588700/541595/586790 *also fax*

Roger Humphrey, dir; Rosemary Pennington,
co-dir.
Intensive week-long summer school for ages 8-16,
17-21 Aug 1998. Mus, drama, dance, arts and
crafts. Mus with specialist tutors includes strs,
w/wind groups, perc, composition, keyboard. All
activities culminate in a final public performance
and demonstration. Fees: £40.

Spode Music Week
66 Cornish House, Green Dragon La, Brentford, Middx TW8 0DF
Tel: 0181 568 1072

Email: ims@moose.co.uk
Website: www.moose.co.uk/userfiles/sjd/spode.html

Ian Saxton, bursar.
Choir, orch, children's orch, lectures, recitals.
Informal mus making encouraged and families
welcomed; children under 14 must be
accompanied by an adult. Creche facilities and
bursaries available. 20-27 Aug 1998, applications
by 7 Aug. Fees: £260 (adults); £175, aged 12-15;
aged 11 and under free.

Stratford-upon-Avon Flute Festival
PO Box 7, Stratford upon Avon CV37 9GB
Tel: 01789 269247 *Fax:* 01789 269843

Elena Durán, dir; Michael Emmerson, chmn.
Annual m/classes for flautists of all levels at King
Edward VI School, Stratford upon Avon.
Emphasis on performance; special sessions for
young flautists. 17 Jul-1 Aug 1998, applications by
1 Jul. Fees: £450 (including accommodation).

Stringwise
3 Dresden Rd, London N19 3BE
Tel: 0171 561 0864; 0171 382 7167

Chris Poon, Cecily Mendelssohn.
A team of specialists, led by Sheila Nelson,
offering professional development courses for all
str teachers with emphasis on musicianship and
freedom of movement in playing. 'Music Matters'
residential course at GSMD, 2-5 Sep 1998.
Accommodation available. 4-day courses in
London for young str players aged 6-13, Apr and
Jul.

Summer Flute Academy
Oak Cottage, Elmsted, nr Ashford, Kent TN25 5JT
Tel: 01233 750543 *also fax*

Ann Nichols, sec; Trevor Wye, Clifford Benson,
m/class teachers.
18-25 Jul 1998. Annual week held at Wye College,
Kent for age 16 and above. Fl and pno duo
repertoire. Fees: £340 (B&B), £440 (full board),
£195 (course only).

Summer School for Piano Teachers
Ian Tomlin School of Music, Napier University,
Craighouse Campus, Queens Craig, Edinburgh EH10 5LG
Tel: 0131 455 6200 *Fax:* 0131 455 6211
Email: a.butterworth@napier.ac.uk

Anna Butterworth, dir.
Lectures, m/classes and survey of ABRSM pno
syllabus 1998-9. 3-7 Aug 1998. Chief guest
speaker: Ruth Gerald.

Gain a Professional Music Teaching Qualification

Trinity College of Music has a long tradition in the training of music teachers alongside performers and in providing continuing support for those in the music profession.

The Music Education Department arranges a programme of courses designed to enhance the professional development of those engaged in music education. Many of the courses carry accreditation on a modular basis for teachers who are registered.

Trinity, with a long and innovative tradition of performance-basedtraining, prepares students for a professional career in music.

Qualifications

- **Certificate in Music Education** is an initial qualification for class teachers and others who are at the early stages of development.
- **LTCL (Music Education)** a diploma for teachers, instrumental tutors and private teachers.
- **FMusEd (TCL)** for advanced levels of study.
- **MA (Music Education)** a one year full time or two/three year part-time study. (Subject to validation by the University of Westminster).

Courses

Courses in the termly programme are relevant for teachers working in primary, secondary or special schools, in youth and adult education, as an advisory, classroom or instrumental tutor or as a private teacher.

Consultancy

The Consultancy team with a wide range of experience in music education, responds to identified needs of institutions and individuals. It offers advice in professional and career development, resourcing and delivering the curriculum and the specialist needs of pupils and students.

If you would like to receive further information about the qualifications, a programme of courses for teachers or details of the consultancy, please complete and return the coupon below.

- -

To: **Elaine Hardy, the Music Education Department**
Trinity College of Music, 11-13 Mandeville Place, London W1M 6AQ
Telephone 0171 935 5773, Facsimile 0171 487 5717

EYB98

Name _____

Address _____

_____

_____ Post Code _____

- ☐ Qualifications in Music Education
- ☐ MA (Music Education)
- ☐ Programme of Courses for Teachers
- ☐ TCM Music Education Consultancy

Sussex University

Centre for Continuing Education, Education Development Buildings, Falmer, Brighton, E Sussex BN1 9RG
Tel: 01273 678527/678040/678025 *Fax:* 01273 678848

F Gray, dir.
P/t certificate in mus; day schools and weekly classes for adults throughout the year.

Talbot Lampson Choral School

18 Amersham Ct, Craneswater Pk, Southsea, Hampshire PO4 0NX
Tel: 01962 867682 *also fax*

Rupert D'Cruze, course dir; Kathleen Edwards, hon sec.
Course for conductors, accompanists and choral singers at University of Greenwich, Avery Hill Campus, Eltham, London. Ages 14 and over. 20-23 Aug 1998, applications by 27 May. Brochure available from 31 Jan. Fees: £220 (residential).

Temple Dinsley Summer School

86 Cromwell Av, London N6 5HQ
Tel: 0181 340 8362 *Fax:* 0181 341 7616

Elisabeth Waterhouse, dir.
Suzuki camp in Herts for children aged 4-11 playing vn, vc or pno. Inst lessons, group lessons and related activities. 9-12 Aug 1998, applications by 1 Jul.

Trinity College of Music

Music Education Dept, 11-13 Mandeville Pl, London W1M 6AQ
Tel: 0171 935 5773; 0171 224 1626 *Fax:* 0171 487 5717

John Stephens, dir of mus educ.
Vacation course for teachers. Week one: 20-24 Jul 1998, provides opportunities for study appropriate for teachers in special schools and private inst teachers. Week two: 27-31 Jul 1998, specialist summer school for mus teachers in primary and secondary schools. Applications by Jun 1998. Fees: £150 (non-residential).

Urchfont Manor

Devizes, Wilts SN10 4RG
Tel: 01380 840495 *Fax:* 01380 840005

Patricia Howell, dir.
Courses for adults.

Wansfell College

Theydon Bois, Epping, Essex CM16 7LF
Tel: 01992 813027 *Fax:* 01992 814761
Website: www.aredu.demon.co.uk/wansfellcollege

Marilyn Taylor, principal.
W/end and midweek courses throughout year in all subjects including mus, mus appreciation, history and performance. Age 18 and above. Fees: from £87.

Wavendon Allmusic Plan

Wavendon Courses, The Stables, Wavendon, Milton Keynes MK17 8LT
Tel: 01908 582522/583928 *Fax:* 01908 281024

John Dankworth, Dame Cleo Laine, presidents; Jacky Scott, gen mgr; Chris Loney, admin offr.
W/shops, m/classes and courses running all year for all types of mus and all ages. Mus summer camps and courses for those aged 8-16. Adult summer jazz course 23-29 Aug at Silsoe College, Bedford, £325 (full board), £225 (course only). Beginners and advanced improvisation courses throughout year.

Wessex Youth Band Courses

7 High Bank, Thurlstone, Sheffield S36 9QH
Tel: 01226 765579 *also fax*

John Grinnell, Margaret Grinnell, organisers.
Courses held at Sturminster Newton, Dorset, for br and wind band players aged 7-21. Snr (gr 4+ and max age 21) and jnr (pre gr 3-4 standard). 27 Jul-2 Aug 1998. Fees: £32.

West Dean College

West Dean, Chichester, Sussex PO18 0QZ
Tel: 01243 811301 *Fax:* 01243 811343
Email: westdean@pavilion.co.uk
Website: www.pavilion.co.uk/westdean

Rosemary Marley, mus course organiser.
1998 courses include: Summer School in Early Music Performance, 15-21 Aug; Classical Guitar Festival of Great Britain, 22-28 Aug; New Vocal Repertory w/end for singers and composers 9-12 Jul; Chilingirian str quartet course, 18-24 Jul; fl m/classes with Susan Milan (gr 5+), 12-17 Jul; The Faust Legend in Music (lectures), 18-20 Sep; Beethoven, Schubert and the Early Romantics (lectures), 9-11 Oct; Opera and Recital, m/classes for advanced singers and pianists, dates tbc; viol consort mus, dates tbc. Age 16 and above. Further information on application which should be 6 weeks before start of course.

William Bennett Flute Summer School

50 Lansdowne Gardens, London SW8 2EF
Tel: 0171 498 9807 *Fax:* 0171 498 1155

Michie Bennett, sec.
Course I, 11-19 Jul 1998; course II, 22-30 Jul 1998. Fees: £295 (performer), £275 (participant), £235 (auditor), plus £140 residential fee.

Winchester Summer Music Course

37 St David's Rd, Clifton Campville, nr Tamworth, Staffs B79 0BA
Tel: 01827 373586 *Fax:* 01827 373437

James Maddocks, dir; Joan Maddocks, sec.
1-8 Aug 1998, applications by 4 Jul.

Workers' Music Association Summer School
17a Newton Rd, London NW2 6PS
Tel: 0181 450 4958

Jacqui Selby, hon organiser.
Participatory courses held at Wortley Hall, Yorks, for amateur musicians of any age and standard. Br band, orch, chmbr mus, folk, jazz, wind band, conducting, composition, harmony, rudiments, sight reading, choral, solo and ens singing. 1-8 Aug 1998, applications by Feb. Fees: £275 (residential), £195 (day student), £115 (external student).

Wycombe Music Summer School
c/o New London Music Society, 83a Vincent Gardens, Dollis Hill, London NW2 7RH
Tel: 0181 452 8739

Philip Meaden, dir; Cynthia Gomme, admin; Peggy Lewis, sec.
Symphony and intermediate orchs, choir, late learner ens, br and w/wind courses, all held at Wycombe Abbey School, Bucks, 1-8 Aug 1998. For age 16 and above. Applications by 31 May. Fees: £156-300.

Youth Music Centre Summer School
58 Cyprus Av, Finchley, London N3 1SR
Tel: 0181 343 1940 *Fax:* 0181 343 1595

Jane Barnett, sec.
26 Jul-2 Aug 1998, applications by end of May. Held at Farleigh School, Andover, Hants. For str and wind players aged 9-16, orch and chmbr mus. Principal teacher Emanuel Hurwitz CBE. Fees: £225.

Youthful Promise
278 Gillott Rd, Edgbaston, Birmingham B16 0RU
Tel: 0121 454 3087

Sara Clethero, artistic dir; Rob Mrozek, hon chair.
Trains individual student singers of all ages to as near professional standards as possible. Provides dramatic and vocal training in a group setting. W/end w/shops and classes in movement, singing technique, Alexander Technique and staging operatic productions, choral work and m/classes. Fees: £40 (w/end). Also summer school for adult choral and solo singers at Ashfold School in Buckinghamshire, 27 Jul-4 Aug 1998. Fees: £295.

University Adult and Continuing Education Departments

All the universities below offer music courses. For additional short courses refer to **Summer Schools and Short Courses** and the courses provided by the **Local and Independent Music Schools.**

Aberystwyth, University of Wales
Dept of Continuing Education, 10-11 Laura Pl, Aberystwyth, Ceredigion SY23 2AU
Tel: 01970 622685

Lyn Davies, mus lecturer; David Russel Hulme, collegiate dir of mus.
Variety of courses, no formal qualifications or previous experience required. Also inst and choral activities.

Bangor, University of Wales
Dept of Continuing Education, Bangor, Gwynedd LL57 2DG
Tel: 01248 383761 *Fax:* 01248 382044
Email: emsoob@bangor.ac.uk

Mrs D Murphy, course admin.
Courses include afternoon and evening courses for adults, 1 or 2 w/end chmbr mus courses pa, 1-day orch class every month from Oct to Apr.

Birkbeck College
Centre for Extra-Mural Studies, London University, 26 Russell Sq, London WC1B 5DQ
Tel: 0171 631 6660 *Fax:* 0171 631 6686
Email: j.oulton@cems.bbk.ac.uk

M W R Symes, mus offr.
Courses in history and appreciation of mus for adult students. *See also* **Goldsmiths.**

Birmingham University
School of Continuing Studies, Edgbaston, Birmingham B15 2TT
Tel: 0121 414 5613 *Fax:* 0121 414 5619

Paul Naylor-Gray, academic adviser, mus.
2 yr p/t Certificate programmes (Cert HE) in music, primary mus education, mus technology, popular mus studies, jazz. Free-floating accredited modules include introduction to mus, mus theory gr 5-8, keyboard skills, aural skills and harmony and counterpoint.

Bristol University
Dept for Continuing Education, 8-10 Berkeley Sq, Queens Rd, Clifton, Bristol BS8 1HH
Tel: 0117 928 7135; 0117 925 4975 *also fax*

John Pickard, lecturer and mus course organiser.
Courses range from basic appreciation courses through to a p/t degree course, mus certificates and p/grad 2-yr p/t diploma in mus therapy for qualified mus students.

University of Cambridge
Board of Continuing Education, Madingley Hall, Madingley, Cambridge CB3 8AQ
Tel: 01954 210636 *Fax:* 01954 210677
Email: laf@cam.ac.uk

Linda Fisher, programmes mgr.
Some w/end mus interest courses.

Cardiff, University of Wales
Dept for Continuing Education and Professional Development, 38-39 Park Pl, Cardiff CF1 3BB
Tel: 01222 874000 ext 5397 *Fax:* 01222 668935
Email: coepd@cf.ac.uk

Royston Havard, mus lecturer.
Extensive programme of daytime and evening classes in Southeast Wales. Day and residential schools (mainly w/end) on a variety of musical subjects, plus interpretation of song, choral mus and jazz w/shops. Some multi-disciplinary courses.

Edinburgh University
Centre for Continuing Education, 11 Buccleuch Pl, Edinburgh EH8 9LW
Tel: 0131 650 4400 *Fax:* 0131 667 6097
Email: cce@ed.ac.uk
Website: www.ed.ac.uk/~cce

J Miller, mus offr.
Term-time courses (weekly, day and evening) at various levels in mus theory and appreciation. Also summer schools, Music at the Edinburgh Festival (29 Aug-4 Sep 1998) and Piano Workshop (10-28 Aug 1998).

Exeter University
Dept of Continuing/Adult Education, Cotley, Streatham Rise, Exeter EX4 4PE
Tel: 01392 411905 *Fax:* 01392 436082

Different mus courses held each yr.

Glasgow University
Dept of Adult/Continuing Education, 57-61 Oakfield Av, Glasgow G12 8LW
Tel: 0141 339 8855 ext 4394 *Fax:* 0141 307 8025

J G MacDonald, deputy dir.
Course for credit (SCOTCAT) in theory of mus; short courses in mus appreciation, joint study days with Scottish Opera.

Goldsmiths, University of London
Professional and Community Education, London
University, Lewisham Way, London SE14 6NW
Tel: 0171 919 7229/7200 *Fax:* 0171 919 7223
Email: cen01cce@gold.ac.uk

Jeremy Peyton-Jones, mus programme co-ord.
A wide variety of mus courses are available,
covering both classical and popular mus styles,
aimed at levels from absolute beginners to
pre-degree and diploma preparation. There are
certificate courses in mus studies, popular mus
and jazz, mus teaching to adults, mus w/shop
skills; short courses for teachers including
specialist refresher and in-service (INSET) courses.

Hull University
Faculty of Arts, c/o Centre for Lifelong Learning, Hull, N
Humberside HU6 7SZ
Tel: 01482 466143; 01724 732477 *also fax*

G G Saunders, lecturer, co-ord for continuing edu.
Leisure study courses for adults; p/t degrees and
p/grad studies.

Keele University
Centre for Part-time and Continuing Education, Keele,
Staffs ST5 5BG
Tel: 01782 625116

Raymond Fearn, lecturer in mus.
Summer schools in early mus, chmbr mus and
bell-ringing.

University of Kent at Canterbury
School of Continuing Education, Keynes College,
Canterbury, Kent CT2 7NP
Tel: 01227 823507 *Fax:* 01227 458745

Mus appreciation courses (1-day courses held on
Sats).

King Edward VI College
The Mansion, Fore St, Totnes, Devon
Tel: 01803 862020

Larry Rudling, dir of studies; Susan Greenhalgh,
asst dir of studies.
Access to the arts in HE, options in mus, theatre
and visual arts, 1 year course, 2 days per week.

Kingston University
School of Music, Kingston Hill, Kingston upon Thames,
Surrey KT2 7LB
Tel: 0181 547 7149 *also fax*
Email: g.toplis@kingston.ac.uk
Website: www.kingston.ac.uk/university.htm

Gloria Toplis, course dir.
BA (post-diploma). P/t 'top-up' course leading to
Hons degree in mus. Applicants need mus college
diploma and some instrumental or vocal
teaching experience.

Leeds College of Music
3 Quarry Hill, Leeds LS2 7PD
Tel: 0113 222 3400 *Fax:* 0113 243 8798

Roger Ladds, mgr of p/t courses.
Large range of adult education courses, including
annual adult residential jazz summer school for
all standards in Aug.

Leeds University
School of Continuing Education, Leeds LS2 9JT
Tel: 0113 233 3222 *Fax:* 0113 233 3246
Email: d.char@leeds.ac.uk

Ms D Char, admin offr.
Various daytime, w/end and evening courses
available in Leeds, Middlesbrough and many
centres around Yorkshire.

Liverpool University
Centre for Continuing Education, 19 Abercromby Sq, PO
Box 147, Liverpool L69 3BX
Tel: 0151 794 6900 *Fax:* 0151 794 2512

David Horn, academic organiser for mus.

London College of Music and Media
Thames Valley University, Faculty of Extra-Mural Studies,
St Mary's Rd, London W5 5RF
Tel: 0181 231 2304/2677 *Fax:* 0181 231 2546

Peter Cook, dir.
Individual tuition in all insts, speech and drama.
Classes in theory (basic and advanced),
composition, basic keyboard skills, pno, gui, mus
technology, singing, w/wind consort and jazz
w/shop. Courses for ALCM, LLCM and LLCM(TD)
diplomas. Also evening courses in GCSE and
A-level. Special summer courses in Jun-Jul.

Manchester University
Centre for Development of Continuing Education,
Manchester M13 9PL
Tel: 0161 275 3290

Glyn Davies, p/t programme organiser and tutor.
A range of day and evening courses in the history
and appreciation of mus; residential w/ends,
some choral.

Nottingham University
School of Continuing Education, Cherry Tree Buildings,
University Pk, Nottingham NG7 2RD
Tel: 0115 951 3715/6526 *Fax:* 0115 951 3711

Philip Olleson, lecturer in mus.
Day-time and evening courses on mus history
and appreciation, keyboard skills and rudiments
of mus. Also w/end and longer mus courses held
from Feb to Nov.

Oxford University
Dept for Continuing Education, 1 Wellington Sq,
Oxford OX1 2JA
Tel: 01865 270360 *Fax:* 01865 270309

J Leatherby, course admin.
Day, evening, w/end and holiday mus courses.

Reading University
International Centre for Research in Music Education,
Bulmershe Ct, Reading RG6 1HY
Tel: 0118 931 8821 *Fax:* 0118 935 2080

Elizabeth Smith, admin.
A selection of courses and conferences designed
to meet the needs of primary and secondary
school teachers with a responsibility for mus.

Rose Bruford College
School of Distance Learning, Lamorbey Pk, Sidcup,
Kent DA15 9DF
Tel: 0181 300 3024 *Fax:* 0181 308 0542
Email: admiss@bruford.ac.uk

Anthony Hozier, head of school.
BA (Hons) Opera Studies validated by the
University of Manchester. A full-length degree by
distance learning, studying opera as well as mus

theatre. Modular structure, annual residential
school. Course runs in collaboration with Royal
Opera House, ENO, Opera North, Welsh National
Opera and Glyndebourne.

Sheffield University
Division of Adult Continuing Education, 196-198 West St,
Sheffield S1 4ET
Tel: 0114 222 7000 *Fax:* 0114 222 7001

Adam White, mus co-ord.
The division offers a wide range of mus courses
covering not only the traditional mus
appreciation of classical mus and opera, but also
jazz and non-Western mus. Evening and daytime
classes available in Sheffield. There are mus
modules offered in the university p/t degree
course, and a certificate in mus studies.

University of Southampton New College
The Avenue, Southampton SO17 1BJ
Tel: 01703 592329 *Fax:* 01703 594060

Sarah Champion, course co-ord.
Level 1 mus courses, practical and theoretical,
for 1st yr level p/t students as part of Humanities
Certificate degree course.

Workers Educational Association

National Office WEA
Temple House, 17 Victoria Park Sq, London E2 9PB
Tel: 0181 983 1515 *Fax:* 0181 983 4840
Email: wea-uk@mcr1.poptel.org.uk

Robert Lochrie, gen sec.
Workers' Educational Association (WEA) is an independent body made up of its students, individual subscribers and affiliated organisations, employing professional staff in a nationwide network of courses and classes for adults. The list below shows only the 14 district offices, but WEA branches can be found in most towns. Courses are often run in consultation with local authority adult education departments and university continuing education departments, but remain independent of both.

District Offices of the WEA

Cheshire, Merseyside and West Lancashire WEA
7-8 Bluecoat Chambers, School La, Liverpool L1 3BX
Tel: 0151 709 8023 *Fax:* 0151 708 0046
Email: office@cmwl.wea.org.uk

Greg Coyne, district sec.
Cheshire (part), Cumbria (part), Lancashire (part), Merseyside (Knowsley, Liverpool, St Helens, Sefton and Wirral).

East Midlands WEA
16 Shakespeare St, Nottingham NG1 4GF
Tel: 0115 947 5162 *Fax:* 0115 924 3513

Russell Gent, district sec.
Derbys (part), Leics, Lincs (part), Notts (part).

Eastern WEA
Botolph House, 17 Botolph La, Cambridge CB2 3RE
Tel: 01223 350978 *Fax:* 01223 300911

Carolyn Daines, district sec.
Beds, Cambs, Essex (most), Herts (most), Norfolk, Northants, Suffolk.

London District WEA
4 Luke St, London EC2A 4NT
Tel: 0171 387 8966 *Fax:* 0171 383 5668

Philippa Langton, district sec; Fred Osborne, subject offr, mus.
Essex (part), Herts (part), London, Middx, Surrey. WEA local branches organise a wide range of musical appreciation courses.

North Western WEA
4th Floor, Crawford House, University Precinct Centre, Oxford Rd, Manchester M13 9GH
Tel: 0161 273 7652 *Fax:* 0161 274 4948

Ian Harford, district sec.
Cheshire, Derbys, Greater Manchester area, Lancs (part). Mus appreciation, rcdr playing, harmony singing and learn to sing courses.

Northern Ireland WEA
1 Fitzwilliam St, Belfast BT9 6AW
Tel: 01232 329718 *Fax:* 01232 230306
Email: wea@wea-ni.thegap.com

Paul Nolan, dir.
Adult education.

Northern WEA
51 Grainger St, Newcastle upon Tyne NE1 5JE
Tel: 0191 232 3957 *Fax:* 0191 230 3696
Email: wea-n@mcr1.poptel.org.uk

Lesley Gillespie, district sec.
Teesside, Cumbria, Durham, Northumberland, Tyne and Wear.

Scottish Association
Riddle's Ct, 322 Lawnmarket, Edinburgh EH1 3PG
Tel: 0131 226 3456 *Fax:* 0131 220 0306

Joyce Connon, Scottish sec.
Highland, Aberdeenshire, Moray, Aberdeen City, Fife, Clackmannanshire, Falkirk, Stirlingshire, City of Edinburgh, W Lothian, Midlothian, E Lothian, Glasgow, S Lanarkshire, N Lanarkshire, E Renfrewshire, Renfrewshire, Inverclyde, Argyll & Bute, E Ayrshire, N Ayrshire, S Ayrshire, E Dunbartonshire, W Dunbartonshire.

South Eastern WEA
4 Castle Hill, Rochester, Kent ME1 1QQ
Tel: 01634 842140 *Fax:* 01634 815643

Vernon Hull, district sec.
Kent, Sussex, London Boroughs of Bexley and Bromley. Music appreciation and history courses available in most areas.

South Western WEA
Martin's Gate Annexe, Bretonside, Plymouth PL4 0AT
Tel: 01752 664989 *Fax:* 01752 254195

Liz Weightman, district sec.
Cornwall, Devon.

Thames and Solent WEA
6 Brewer St, Oxford OX1 1QN
Tel: 01865 246270 *Fax:* 01865 204282
Email: office@t&s.wea.org.uk

Sarah Grylls, district sec.

Berks, Bucks, Hants, Isle of Wight, Oxon. A range of mus appreciation evening and daytime classes available.

Wales North WEA
33 College Rd, Bangor, Gwynedd LL57 2AP
Tel: 01248 353254 *Fax:* 01248 371181
Email: weanw@nwales.wea.org.uk

Annie Williams, dir.
Several mus appreciation courses in all areas.

Wales South WEA
10 Coopers Yard, Curran Rd, Cardiff CF1 5DF
Tel: 01222 235277 *Fax:* 01222 233986
Email: yprice@swales.wea.org.uk

Graham Price, gen sec.
Provides a wide range of adult education through 21 branches and in collaboration with partners in the voluntary and state sectors

West Mercia WEA
78-80 Sherlock St, Birmingham B5 6LT
Tel: 0121 666 6101 *Fax:* 0121 622 2526

Richard Copley, district sec.

Cheshire (part), Herefords, Shrops, Staffords, Warwicks, Worcs.

Western WEA
40 Morse Rd, Redfield, Bristol BS5 9LB
Tel: 0117 935 1764 *Fax:* 0117 941 1757
Email: jsmith@west.wea.org.uk

Joan Smith, district sec.
Bath and NE Somerset, Bournemouth, Greater Bristol, Dorset, Glos, S Glos, Poole, Somerset, N Somerset, Swindon, Wilts.

Yorkshire North WEA
6 Woodhouse Sq, Leeds LS3 1AD
Tel: 0113 245 3304 *Fax:* 0113 245 0883
Email: office@yn.wea.org.uk

Sam Herman, district sec.
Lincs (part), Yorkshire, (except the part included in Yorkshire South District).

Yorkshire South WEA
Chantry Buildings, 6-20 Corporation St, Rotherham S60 1NG
Tel: 01709 837001 *Fax:* 01709 372121
Email: ted.hartley@legend.co.uk

Edward Hartley, district sec.
N E Derbys, N Lincs, N Notts, S Yorks.

Jazz in Education

This section covers jazz in education regionally, including activities within the formal education sector together with community activities.

National Organisations and Competitions

European Jazz Competition
c/o Jazzwise, 2b Gleneagle Mews, London SW16 6AE
Tel: 0181 769 7725 *Fax:* 0181 677 7128

Charles Alexander, vice-president.
Annual jazz competition, entries by 30 Jun.

Jazz Services
Room 518, Africa House, 64 Kingsway, London WC2B 6BD
Tel: 0171 405 0737/47/57 *Fax:* 0171 405 0828
Email: jazz@dial.pipex.com
Website: ds.dial.pipex.com/town/square/ad663/

Chris Hodgkins, dir; Celia Wood, information offr.
Promotes the growth and development of jazz within the UK and provides services in touring, information, education and communication.

National Youth Jazz Association
11 Victor Rd, Harrow, Middx HA2 6PT
Tel: 0181 863 2717 *Fax:* 0181 863 8685

Email: bill.ashton@virgin.net
Website: www.classical-artists.com/nyjo

Bill Ashton, chmn.
NYJA organises two Sat rehearsals each week in London and w/shops and clinics by the National Youth Jazz Orchestra.

National Youth Jazz Orchestra of Great Britain
11 Victor Rd, Harrow, Middx HA2 6PT
Tel: 0181 863 2717 *Fax:* 0181 863 8685
Email: bill.ashton@virgin.net
Website: www.classical-artists.com/nyjo

Bill Ashton, dir of mus.
NYJO has made 30 albums by British composers and aims to give 100 concerts pa. No formal auditions, but please telephone before coming the first time. Age 11-25. First British jazz ens to have its mus studied for the GCSE syllabus and voted Best Big Band in the 1995 British Jazz Awards. No courses, but rehearsals are held every Sat unless the orch is on tour.

Jazz in Further Education

Pre-Diploma Foundation Courses

Brunel University
Faculty of Arts, Gordon House, 300 St Margaret's Rd, Twickenham, Middx TW7 5DU
Tel: 0181 891 0121 *Fax:* 0181 891 8270

Charles Beale, course leader.
Foundation course, A-level in mus technology and OCN accredited mus diploma with professional and access to HE routes (2). The course has a strong tradition in pop and rock, jazz and improvised mus. Course content includes song writing, composition and jazz w/shops. Work centred around the 8-track and 16-track studios and sequencing workstations. Emphasis on creativity, self-motivation and skills for professional and academic success in HE or the mus business. Transfer to degree possible. Min age 16; mature students welcome. Inst and

vocal skills (at least gr 6) and some theory knowledge. Consideration will also be given to those of good mus potential who are without these qualifications. Entry by audition.

Chichester College of Arts, Science and Technology
Dept of Visual and Performing Arts, Westgate Fields, Chichester, W Sussex PO19 1SB
Tel: 01243 786321 ext 2384/3 *Fax:* 01243 775783
Email: kendona@inetgw.chichester w
Website: www.chichester.ac.uk

Martin Seath, head of dept; Mike Dobson, head of school; Adrian Kendon, course dir.
Access Diploma in Jazz Studies, level 1, level 2 and level 3, provides training for careers in professional mus and access to HE.

City College
Arden Centre, Sale Rd, Northenden, Manchester M23 0DD
Tel: 0161 957 1775/1780 (admissions)
Fax: 0161 945 3854
Email: dfreedman@manchester-city-coll.ac.uk or
dennis@g3vsh.demon.co.uk
Website: www.manchestercitycoll./
Stuart Riley, course leader; Dennis Freedman, course co-ord.
BTEC HNC and HND Jazz Studies. Includes inst tuition, ens playing, harmony, improvisation, composing and arranging, keyboard skills, professional and business studies, mus technology, sound recording, history and repertoire.

City of Liverpool Community College
Greenbank Centre, Mossley Av, Liverpool
Tel: 0151 733 5511
Brian Wilshaw, head of mus.
Foundation course in Commercial Music (1). Diploma in Jazz and Commercial Music (1) follows on from the foundation course or an equivalent level of attainment. This advanced course concentrates on developing both theoretical and practical skills covering jazz and commercial mus styles. *Entry requirements:* Audition; good performance ability with a thorough knowledge of relevant theory.

Joseph Chamberlain College
Balsall Heath Rd, Highgate, Birmingham B12 9DS
Tel: 0121 440 4288 ext 63 *Fax:* 0121 440 0798
David Henson, dir of perf studies.
A-levels in mus and performing arts, including jazz musicianship.

Kidderminster College
Dept of Community Studies, Hoo Rd, Kidderminster, Worcs DY10 1LX
Tel: 01562 820811
J Shepherd, lecturer in mus; Andy Edwards, p/t lecturer in mus.
BTEC ND/First Diploma including rock performance and jazz modules.

New College Durham
Dept of Humanities, Framwellgate Moor Centre, Durham DH1 5ES
Tel: 0191 386 2421 *Fax:* 0191 386 0303
D A Blazey, head of mus.
BTEC ND in Popular Music (2) covering inst tuition, arranging and composition, aural skills, recording technology, MIDI. Opportunities for ens playing and public performance. *Entry requirements:* By interview and audition. Min 4 GCSE passes at gr C or above, or equivalent for mature students.

Queen Mary's College
Cliddesden Rd, Basingstoke, Hants RG21 3HF
Tel: 01256 20861 *Fax:* 01256 26097
David Coggins, head of mus.
Jazz and rock studies, including improvisation.

South East Derbyshire College
Cavendish Centre, Cavendish Rd, Ilkeston, Derbys DE7 5AN
Tel: 0115 930 2942 *Fax:* 0115 944 7181
Steve McAlone, programme co-ord, mus and perf arts.
BTEC ND Popular Music or various A-level mus qualifications including mus performance, composition and arranging, recording techniques, mus technology, improvisation, study of the mus business.

Wakefield College
Faculty of Performance, Media and Arts, Thornes Park Centre, Horbury Rd, Wakefield WF2 0DU
Tel: 01924 789809 *Fax:* 01924 789821
Website: www.wakcoll.ac.uk
Tony Davis, dir of mus; Andy Cholerton, lecturer; Kevin Dearden, lecturer.
BTEC ND Popular Music (2); Intermediate Diploma in Music; ABRSM exams; GCSE and A-level mus and A-level mus technology (2). Inst tuition, recording techniques, keyboard harmony, arranging, improvisation, ens work. Performance experience is considered a vital element of the course. LGSM Diploma (1 p/t) in advanced jazz techniques including performance, harmony, arranging, history and aural. The School of Music has over 20 tutored mus ens including 3 jazz ens.

Jazz in Higher Education

Diploma and Graduate Courses

Anglia Polytechnic University
Division of Music, East Rd, Cambridge CB1 1PT
Tel: 01223 63271 *Fax:* 01223 352973
Email: s.v.rands@anglia.ac.uk

Kevin Flanagan, module leader; Chris Ingham, module lecturer.
Modular course (3 f/t) provides a distinctive combination of practical and theoretical study, of which jazz is an important part. Students may take up to 2 insts as individual studies. In yr 1, students may take a composition and improvising module involving composition, jazz improvisation and free improvisation, in any style. In yrs 2 and 3, students may specialise further, through the three jazz modules. Group activities include the jazz orch and smaller bands which perform in a variety of styles in venues across the country. Normally 2 A-levels (including mus), plus gr 7 on 1st study inst and gr 5 keyboard standard. Applications from mature students are encouraged.

Bath Spa University College
Newton Pk, Newton St Loe, Nr Bath
Tel: 01225 873701 *Fax:* 01225 874438
Website: www.bathhe.ac.uk/am/som1.html

K M Bennett, course dir.
BA Hons in Music: jazz figuring and improvisation is obligatory for keyboard players in the general musicianship course. Jazz Improvisation II, a follow-on course to the above, is an option in the general musicianship course in yr 2. *Entry requirements:* Usually 2 A-levels (including mus at gr C) and gr 8 on 1st inst. 40 places pa on course. Wide range of facilities including concert hall, studio teaching and practice rooms.

Brunel University College
Performing Arts Section, Twickenham Campus, 300 St Margaret's Rd, Twickenham, Middx TW7 5DU
Tel: 0181 891 0121 *Fax:* 0181 891 0487

Peter Rudnick, head of mus.
BA Joint Hons mus degree (4-5 p/t) combining mus with one other subject at degree level. The course has a modular structure which offers a number of options including opportunities for jazz performance and composition. In addition, students undertake an individual project (extended essay, composition or community-based project) on a subject of their own choice, and those who wish to concentrate on

jazz-related subjects are encouraged to do so. There is also an individual performance option, and the opportunity to participate in small jazz ens and big band work. Refer to college for details of required formal qualifications. Audition and interview is usually an important part of the selection process.

The Chichester Institute of HE
College La, Chichester, W Sussex PO19 4PE
Tel: 01243 816000 *Fax:* 01243 816080
Website: www.chihe.ac.uk

Rod Paton, mus section.
Solo and group improvisation is at the core of all practical and creative mus courses, and students who offer jazz and other contemporary musical genres are welcomed. Within the degree programmes, modules are on offer in modern jazz, jazz improvisation, ens work, improvisation with dance and mus therapy, and individual tuition is available in jazz pno, gui, sax, drums, etc. Degree programmes: BA (Hons) Music as a single subject now available; BA (Hons) Music as major subject, with a wide choice of arts and humanities subjects; BA (Hons) Music joint with Art, Dance or Related Arts; BA (Hons) Music as minor subject, with English, Geography, History, or Religious Studies; BA (Hons) with QTS, mus as specialist subject for teaching in lower and upper primary.

Coventry University Performing Arts
Leasowes Av, Coventry CV3 6BH
Tel: 01203 418868 *Fax:* 01203 692374

Christopher Best, course tutor.
3-yr BA for composers offers students an opportunity to develop composition, arrangement, improvisation and technology skills together with competence and knowledge of the mus business.

Dartington College of Arts
Totnes, Devon TQ9 6EJ
Tel: 01803 861620/1 *Fax:* 01803 863569
Email: registry@dartington.ac.uk
Website: www.dartington.ac.uk

Trevor Wiggins, dir of mus.
BA Hons modular degree. Elective modules are available in other arts subjects. Candidates are asked to indicate if they are interested in combining their study with Arts Management modules leading to BA Hons Arts Management

527

with Music or BA Hons Music with Arts Management. There is the option to focus on popular mus and jazz. The jazz element consists of performance, composition, analytic and contextual study of jazz in the 20th C. Jazz element within BA Hons course involves tuition in jazz performance, modules dealing with jazz and popular mus history and style, plus the opportunity for individual research. A weekly improvisation w/shop session is led by Lewis Riley. 50+ places on course. Resources include Performance Technology Centre.

Goldsmiths, University of London
Professional and Community Education, New Cross, London SE14 6NW
Tel: 0171 919 7229/7200 *Fax:* 0171 919 7223

Jeremy Peyton Jones, mus programme co-ord. Certificate in Jazz and Popular Music Studies (1 p/t). Equivalent to 120 credit points of u/grad study at level one, the course aims to prepare students for a profession in mus or further study in FE and HE, although it can bring equal benefit to those primarily interested in their own mus development with no career aspirations. Also short courses in jazz pno, harmony and arranging for jazz and contemporary styles, jazz improvisation for singers, modern jazz w/shop, contemporary jazz pno, musicianship for improvisation, blues pno.

Leeds College of Music
3 Quarry Hill, Leeds LS2 7PD
Tel: 0113 222 3400
Website: www.netlink.co.uk/users/zappa/clcm/clcm.html

Peter Whitfield, head of foundation courses. Access (1 yr) and Western Music (2 yrs) courses including performance, aural, theory and analysis, repertoire studies, stylistic harmony and IT.

Middlesex University
Department of Music, Trent Park Campus, Bramley Rd Oakwood, London N14 4YZ
Tel: 0181 362 5000 *Fax:* 0181 362 5684

Stuart Hall, acting head of jazz programme. BA Hons Jazz (3). Emphasis on composing, performing and listening and on the practical w/shop as the main teaching mode. Students are expected to participate in ensemble activities. Applications welcome from those with good practical and performing skills but without the normal entry requirements.

Newcastle College
Faculty of Visual and Performing Arts, Maple Terrace, Newcastle upon Tyne NE4 7SA
Tel: 0191 200 4000 *Fax:* 0191 272 4020

James Birkett, programme leader. BMus (Hons) in Jazz, Popular and Commercial Music. 3-yr f/t programme covering practical, theoretical and organisational skills in all aspects of jazz, popular and commercial mus. Entry by audition and interview. Appropriate qualifications for degree-level study required.

University of Salford
Faculty of Media and Music, Adelphi, Peru St, Salford, Greater Manchester M3 6EQ
Tel: 0161 295 5000 *Fax:* 0161 295 6106

Derek B Scott, dir of mus. BA (Hons) in Band Musicianship (3/4); BA (Hons) in Popular Music and Recording; BSc Music, Acoustics and Recording. Band Musicianship encompasses jazz and rock ens, as well as wind and br bands. All 3 courses include jazz as a major element of their syllabus. The centre arranges a comprehensive series of concerts and w/shops. Visiting artists include: Bobby Shew, Martin Taylor, the Arguelles Brothers, Stan Sulzman, Norman Winstone, Iain Bellamym, Roy Williams, Don Lusher and Allan Vezutti. Regular jazz concerts at Band on the Wall (Manchester), Viewpoint (Salford), Barbican Centre (London).

Undergraduate Courses at the Conservatoires

Guildhall School of Music & Drama
Silk St, Barbican, London EC2Y 8DT
Tel: 0171 628 2571 *Fax:* 0171 256 9438
Website: www.gsmd.ac.uk

Scott Stroman, head of jazz and studio mus; Dorothy Cooper, admin.
BMus (4). At u/grad level the jazz stream is offered as a 4-yr option for students wishing to emphasise jazz performance within a broad programme of study. The course content is similar to the main BMus course, with practical skills being developed in both jazz and classical fields. Students' individual tuition is undertaken by specialists in both areas and they perform in both classical and jazz ens. Applicants should be proficient both as classical performers and as jazz improvisors.

Leeds College of Music
3 Quarry Hill, Leeds LS2 7PD
Tel: 0113 222 3400 *Fax:* 0113 243 8798
Website: www.netlink.co.uk/users/zappa/clcm/clcm.html

Jonty Stockdale, head of HE mus; Trevor Vincent, course co-ord, BA Hons; David Fligg, course co-ord, BPA Hons.
The BA Hons in Jazz Studies (3) (validated by the University of Leeds) embraces a wide range of activities practised in the field of jazz and contemporary mus. The Bachelor of Performing Arts Hons (Music) includes practical and theoretical aspects of jazz studies as part of a wider programme of study. Min age 18; min gr 8 principal inst; min of normally 2 A-levels in different subjects plus 3 GCSE passes including English Language.

Royal Academy of Music
York Gate, Marylebone Rd, London NW1 5HT
Tel: 0171 873 7338 *Fax:* 0171 873 7374
Email: jazz@ram.ac.uk

Graham Collier, artistic dir of jazz studies.
Principal study jazz for any inst and composition available as part of the 4-yr, f/t performer's course leading to a BMus. There are w/shops, seminars and m/classes with the regular faculty and visiting artists. The jazz course includes performing regularly with the big band and various other small groups. Jazz is also offered as an option for classical mus students. There may also be limited places available for p/grad study.

Royal College of Music
Prince Consort Rd, London SW7 2BS
Tel: 0171 589 3643 *Fax:* 0171 589 7740

Jazz activities are offered on an occasional basis within the context of w/shops, m/classes and big band rehearsals with visiting jazz musicians.

Royal Northern College of Music
124 Oxford Rd, Manchester M13 9RD
Tel: 0161 273 6283

Clark Rundell; Mike Hall; Steve Berry.
The college has 2 big bands and several smaller jazz ens, and regular improvisation classes.

Trinity College of Music
11-13 Mandeville Pl, London W1M 6AQ
Tel: 0171 935 5773 *Fax:* 0171 224 6278
Email: info@tcm.ac.uk
Website: www.tcm.ac.uk

Bobby Lamb, big band; Michael Garrick, pno; Herbie Flowers, double bs, improvisation; David Cliff, gui; Simon Woolf, bs gui.
Jazz provision exists within each department, including vocal studies, and the big band is drawn from throughout the college.

Postgraduate Courses at the Conservatoires

Guildhall School of Music & Drama
Silk St, Barbican, London EC2Y 8DT
Tel: 0171 628 2571 *Fax:* 0171 256 9438
Website: www.gsmd.ac.uk

Scott Stroman, head of jazz and studio mus; Dorothy Cooper, admin.
Advanced Course in Jazz and Studio Music (1) is intended for advanced players seeking to extend their experience in the styles of jazz and jazz influenced mus. Applicants should have achieved diploma standard on their principal inst(s) and have advanced knowledge of jazz harmony and performance practice. The course is planned around a performance programme involving a big band, small bands and singers' group, which allows students to apply skills in improvisation, composition and arranging that are developed in classwork. There are many lectures, w/shops and m/classes with visiting jazz musicians of national and international status. Applicants should normally have completed a mus course at mus college, university or college of HE. However equivalent experience and high performance ability could qualify for eligibility.

Leeds College of Music
3 Quarry Hill, Leeds LS2 7PD
Tel: 0113 222 3400 *Fax:* 0113 243 8798
Website: www.netlink.co.uk/users/zappa/clcm/clcm.html

Graham Hearn, p/grad course leader.
P/grad certificate in Jazz, Contemporary and Popular Music (1) for those with a good first degree or graduate diploma. The course can be tailored to each student with specialisations in performing, directing, arranging and song writing.

Solo Jazz Performers in Education

Beale, Charles
21 Westmorland Close, St Margarets, Twickenham, Middx TW1 1RR
Tel: 0181 892 6142 *also fax*
Email: charlieb@dircon.co.uk

Currently project mgr of the new ABRSM jazz pno and other syllabuses; freelance career includes p/t lecturer (Brunel, Thames Valley University), session work, research student (London University), jazz w/shops and gigs with own band.

Bryce, Owen
58 Pond Bank, Blisworth, Northants NN7 3EL
Tel: 01604 858192

Owen Bryce has been running courses for adults in jazz playing and appreciation for many years. These are organised in conjunction with mus organisations and many county councils, taking the form of residential w/ends or week-long summer schools and 1-day courses in basic improvisation. He also gives illustrated lectures on the history of jazz and is the author of *Let's Play Jazz*. Major courses are run in Feb, Mar, Apr, July, Aug, Oct and Nov. Members of the Owen Bryce Band are Owen Bryce, tpt; Jan Bryce, trb; Laurie Bielby, cl, alto/bar sax; Reg Jones, gui; Norris Gaselee, bs; Bill Bates, drums. The band plays a repertoire of jazz classics in a bright Dixieland style backed by a solid rhythm section. Also leads the Owen Bryce Quartet.

Carr, Ian
34 Brailsford Rd, London SW2 2TE
Tel: 0181 671 7195

Tpt player, composer and author Ian Carr combines his playing career with educational activities. He directs weekly jazz w/shops on the Weekend Arts Course (WAC) at Interchange in London and undertakes all kinds of educational projects. He was musical director of the Hull Jazz Summer School for several years in succession and is an associate professor at the GSMD. He is particularly keen to encourage the performance of contemporary mus and is the author of several books on jazz and a regular broadcaster on Radio 3.

Clyne, Jeff
10 Temple Gardens, Temple Fortune, London NW11 0LL
Tel: 0181 455 2893

Double bass and jazz studies at the GSM and the RAM. Course director of Wavendon Jazz Courses.

Collier, Graham
38 Shell Rd, London SE13 7TW
Tel: 0181 692 6250 *Fax:* 0181 692 5213
Email: graham@jazzword.demon.co.uk
Website: www.jazz.continuum.com

Graham Collier is the artistic director of Royal Academy's degree course in jazz. He also presents lectures and w/shops under the title *The Jazz Ensemble*. The w/shops are practical demonstrations of the ideas and techniques that he has developed in working with jazz ens of any size and any instrumentation. The methods used allow freedom with control for all the musicians and permit improvisation on many co-existing levels. The w/shops, which can use a conventional big band or a more ad-hoc grouping, are ideally held over a concentrated period of time leading to a performance.

Fairweather, Digby
see Jazz College under **Jazz Groups in Education**

Haslam, George
3 Thesiger Rd, Abingdon, Oxon OX14 2DX
Tel: 01235 529012 *also fax*

Saxophonist, presents jazz, blues, improvisation and sax w/shops in schools, universities, arts centres, etc. Runs *Learning the Blues* and *Improvisation Now*. Venues have included Oxford University Faculty of Music, Oxford Playhouse and schools and arts centres across England as well as Argentina, Hong Kong, Ukraine and USA. His work has been sponsored by the Musicians' Union, British Council and Southern Arts.

Ingham, Richard
31 Agbrigg Rd, Sandal Magna, Wakefield, Yorks WF1 5AB
Tel: 01924 257826 *Fax:* 01924 219272

Solo recitalist and member of the Northern Saxophone Quartet. He gives regular jazz w/shops and lectures and is a former chmn of the Clarinet and Saxophone Society of Great Britain. He is visiting professor of jazz at St Andrews University and lecturer in sax at Leeds College of Music.

Michael, Richard
6 Dronachy Rd, Kirkaldy, Fife, Scotland KYY 5QL
Tel: 01592 263087

F/t educator based in Scotland. Head of mus at a comprehensive school in Fife, where he has developed a method of introducing jazz improvisation in c/room work with pupils of all levels of mus ability. The approach is based on instant arrangements and scat singing and elements of the method are described in the following handbooks, each containing an audio cassette: *Jazz Beginnings* (Quickstep Music); *Creative Jazz Education* with Scott Stroman (Stainer & Bell). He is also musical director of Fife Youth Jazz Orchestra, organises the annual Arts in Fife Jazz Summer School, and directs the annual jazz course and big band of the National Youth Orchestra of Scotland. He operates a jazz consultancy service for mus teachers, and gives occasional w/shops, courses and lectures in other parts of the country. He is a member of the working party for the forthcoming jazz pno syllabus of the ABRSM and a national trainer for the new Higher Still exam in Scotland.

Purcell, Simon
15 Essex Rd, Forest Gate, London E7 0HL
Tel: 0181 257 0708

Currently prof of jazz improvisation and pno at GSM. Also involved with in-service training for teachers and tutors at Wavendon, Guildhall and Glamorgan Summer Schools and is the author of *Teaching Jazz - a Practical Guide.*

Stroman, Scott
91 Wilberforce Rd, London N4 2SP
Tel: 0171 354 5539

Trombonist, composer and singer. Head of jazz and studio mus at the GSMD, co-leader of Wellins-Stroman quintet and mus dir of the London Jazz Orchestra. UK co-ordinator of the International Association of Schools of Jazz. Also orch and choral conductor.

Tomkins, Trevor
14 Bellamy St, London SW12 8BU
Tel: 0181 675 1455

Teaches at the RAM, the GSM, the London College of Music and Goldsmiths. He is a co-director of the Wavendon course with Jeff Clyne and has given w/shops all over the country for local authorities.

Vas, Olaf
30 Sanderstead Ct, Sanderstead Av, Surrey CR2 9AG
Tel: 0181 657 3744

Clarinettist, saxophonist and flautist who has worked in radio, TV and film with large and small groups. He now teaches on several jazz courses including the Wavendon course and works frequently with Eddie Harvey.

Watson, Andy
64 Hill View Rd, Chelmsford, Essex CM1 7RX
Tel: 01245 258262 *also fax*

Guitarist who works as a p/t lecturer in jazz, rock and contemporary mus at Harlow College and combines this with work as a freelance educator and session guitarist. He has also directed many w/shops in schools (both independently and for the Arts Council Jazz in Education Scheme).

Weldon, Nick
24 Ryland Rd, London NW5 3EA
Tel: 0171 284 0226 *also fax*
Email: nick@weldon.demon.co.uk

Performer and composer. Teaches jazz pno at Royal Academy and privately. Runs beginners improvisation course at the Wavendon All Music Plan and teaches on the Wavendon Summer Course.

Jazz Groups in Education

Compose Yourself!
21 Reading Rd, Woodley, Reading, Berks RG5 3DA
Tel: 0118 969 6035
Email: n.j.c.bannan@reading.ac.uk

Nicholas Bannan.
Compose Yourself! has a core of 3 musicians and composers whose educ w/shops aim to encourage creativity through improvisation and composition in many styles, including jazz. Extra personnel are added to provide expertise in specific areas, such as jazz impro. W/shops are designed to meet the requirements of GCSE, and include sessions in group improvisation, rehearsal and performance of pupils' compositions, introduction to compositional techniques, courses covering specific areas of mus interest. The approach can be adapted to

meet the needs of all ages of pupil, and has been used for in-service training work. The group is based in Berkshire and has worked for several LEAs in the South, as well as giving w/shops at the RNCM.

Grand Union
14 Clerkenwell Green, London EC1R 0DP
Tel: 0171 251 2100 *Fax:* 0171 250 3009

Catherine Mummery, admin.
The Grand Union consists of some 2 dozen musicians from a variety of parts of the world, embracing a wide range of cultures, mus practice and inst and vocal expertise. About half of these musicians are engaged on a regular basis in an enormously varied programme of w/shop

531

projects. Although their educ work is based on a much broader mus reference than jazz, the key element of improvisation is fundamental to their work. In their w/shops, the group does not specify mus techniques or performance skills, but attempts to help people create their own original mus, regardless of inst expertise. A great deal of singing and perc work takes place, and the skills of listening, responding and playing by ear are encouraged. The group devises projects suitable for a wide range of ages and abilities, and for a diversity of school and community contexts. They can be single sessions, longer courses or residencies, or large-scale community projects leading to performance.

Jazz Attack
c/o Jazz Action, 1 Portrush Close, Darlington, Co Durham DL1 3HU
Tel: 01325 480454 *also fax*

Offers jazz and rock performance techniques with improvisation for both beginners and experienced players as an essential foundation for contemporary mus studies in schools and colleges today. Ideal for GCSE students, can provide 1-day w/shop, series of 1-day w/shops for LEAs.

Jazz College
c/o Inglemead, Waddington Rd, Clitheroe, Lancs
Tel: 01200 424839

Lesley Eastman, admin; Digby Fairweather, dir, tpt. Jazz College takes jazz w/shops into all sections of the educ system. W/shops and courses are designed to suit individual needs, and the number of musicians in the teaching team can be varied accordingly, from 1-6 players. The organisation works mainly in schools, both primary and secondary, but also undertakes projects in arts and community centres, colleges of FE and residential courses.

Michael Garrick's Travelling Jazz Faculty
12 Castle St, Berkhamsted, Herts HP4 2BQ
Tel: 01442 864989 *Fax:* 01442 384493

Travelling Jazz Faculty is led by pianist and composer Michael Garrick. It consists of a pool of professional musicians, their number varying according to the needs of each particular project. Specialises in jnr involvement recitals with his trio, though he caters for all ages, standards and groups, including choirs, strs, big bands and orchs, plus teachers' courses. As well as using standard jazz repertoire, he has pieces specifically designed to combine jnrs, snrs and adult learners with professional jazz musicians, and his projects are conceived to foster cross-curriculum work. Michael Garrick is director of Jazz Academy which offers vacation courses at the Royal Academy of Music, London.

Regional Jazz Organisations

Greater London

Jazz Services Information
Room 518, Africa House, 64 Kingsway, London WC2B 6BD
Tel: 0171 405 0737/47/57 *Fax:* 0171 405 0828
Email: jazz@dial.pipex.com
Website: ds.dial.pipex.com/town/square/ad663/
Chris Hodgkins, dir; Celia Wood, information offr.

Classes, Workshops and Short Courses

The City Lit
Music Dept, Keeley House, Keeley St, London WC2B 4BA
Tel: 0171 430 0546 *Fax:* 0171 831 8508

Moira Hayward, head of mus section; Della Rhodes, jazz co-ord.
Adult educ courses from elementary to advanced level in jazz and popular mus. Ear training, harmony, improvisation and ens playing.

Community Music
Unit G1, Clink St, Winchester Wharf, London SE1
Tel: 0171 234 0900

Evening courses on voice, sax, mus technology, also summer courses and teacher-training in w/shop skills. Mixed ability; previous experience helpful but not essential.

Goldsmiths
University of London, Continuing Education, New Cross, London SE14 6NW
Tel: 0171 919 7200 *Fax:* 0171 919 7223

Jazz Improvisation for Singers, 20-21 Jun 1998. Jazz Piano Weekend Workshop, 27-28 Jun 1998. Various jazz classes and courses throughout the year.

Islington Arts Factory
Islington Arts Factory, 2 Parkhurst Rd, London N7
Tel: 0171 607 0561 *Fax:* 0171 700 7229
Website: www.artec.org.uk/artec/iacnet

Community arts centre currently offering mus w/shops for adults in singing throughout the year for all levels of ability; mus w/shops for age 12-16 in kit drumming; 2 studios for hire, equipped with drumkit, pno, PA, microphones, backline.

The Saturday Jazz School
Richmond Adult and Community College, Parkshot, Richmond, Surrey TW9 2RE
Tel: 0181 940 0170 *Fax:* 0181 332 6560

Mark Mulley, mus course team leader. Opportunities for students to develop their jazz playing technique on a wide range of insts. Tuition by a team of performers and educationalists including Eddie Harvey, Charles Alexander, Terry Seabrook, Dave Jones, Tony Woods, Fred Lucas, Fergus O'Kelly, Mark Mulley and Dave Wickins. The course is not designed for complete beginners, students are advised to discuss their needs with the course tutor. All terms culminate in a concert, plus many other opportunities for students to perform in concerts and jam sessions.

Summer Schools

Guildhall Summer School (Jazz, Rock, Studio Music)
Guildhall School of Music and Drama, Silk St, Barbican, London EC2Y 8DT
Tel: 01702 714733 (eves)

Heather Swain, mgr.
2 wk summer school for ages 12 and above. 11-24 Jul 1998. W/end course Jazz Education for teachers 18-19 Jul 1998.

Jazz Academy Vacation Courses
12 Castle St, Berkhamsted, Herts HP4 2BQ
Tel: 01442 864989 *Fax:* 01442 384493

Michael Garrick, course dir.
Annual summer jazz course, mid-Aug. Annual jazz pno course, 28-30 Dec.

Jazz Rock Studio Music Summer School
Guildhall School of Music and Drama, Silk St, Barbican,

London
Tel: 01702 714733

Heather Swain, mgr.
Courses (for 1-2 wks and w/ends 11-24 Jul 1998) at the GSMD include Guildhall's own jazz faculty joined by professional musicians, to work on inst tuition, harmony and improvisation, large and small ens work, an introduction to jazz and improvisation for those with little or no experience. Also recording engineers course, jazz for mus educators (teachers' w/end course), mus technology w/ends and a singers world mus course.

Jazzwise Summer School
2b Gleneagle Mews, London SW16 6AE
Tel: 0181 769 7725 *Fax:* 0181 677 7128

Charles Alexander; Jamey Aebersold, course dir. Intensive improvisation jazz w/shop held in Jul at Richmond Adult and Community College.

Jazz in Central England

Jazz Central was disbanded in April 1993. Independent jazz activities are listed below.

Classes, Workshops and Short Courses

Campion School
Adult Education Dept, Bugbrooke, Northants
Tel: 01604 863948

Owen Bryce, tutor.
A practical course on Tue evenings 7.15-9.15pm, Jan-Mar and Sep-Dec.

Launde Abbey Jazz Course
c/o 58 Pond Bank, Blisworth, Northants NN7 3EL
Tel: 01604 858192

Iris Bryce, course dir; Owen Bryce, Bill Bates, tutors.
2-day practical w/end course every Nov at Launde Abbey, Leicestershire.

MAC (Midlands Arts Centre)

Cannon Hill Pk, Birmingham B12 9QH
Tel: 0121 440 4221 *Fax:* 0121 446 4372
Email: mac.birmingham@btinternet.com

Dorothy Wilson, programme dir; Alan James, perf programmer; Gabrielle Oliver, educ programmer. Term-long jazz pno courses are held at the centre, plus an annual jazz project w/end, catering for all levels of ability and experience. Monthly open jamming sessions are led by 'Tomorrow's Warriors'. The centre is also the rehearsal base of the Midlands Youth Jazz Orchestras, Jamma's Caribbean Jazz Band and Maestros Steel Orchestra.

Mill Arts Centre

Spiceball Pk, Banbury, Oxon OX16 8QE
Tel: 01295 252050/279002 *Fax:* 01295 279003

Deborah Clark, arts development worker.
Jazz jam session for all age groups and youth jazz w/shop for age 12-18 on Tue evenings.

Morley Jazz Course

c/o 58 Pond Bank, Blisworth, Northants
Tel: 01604 858192

Iris Bryce, course dir; Owen Bryce, Bill Bates, tutors.
Annual 2-day jazz course takes place Feb-Mar at Morley Retreat and Conference House, Derby. Concentrates on big band and dixieland jazz.

Musicians Unlimited Management (UK)

Dorothy Cooper and Associates, 4 Medland, Woughton Pk, Milton Keynes MK6 3BH
Tel: 01908 670306 *Fax:* 01908 674909
Email: dcooper@mum-uk.demon.co.uk

Provides a service to education authorities including Marion Montgomery performance m/classes, INSET days, touring jazz w/shops (introducing jazz history, improvisation, harmony and rhythm into the c/room), schools concerts, project work with all types of mus including Latin-American and Japanese. Tailor made for each school/college and NC based. Residential and non-residential courses.

Summer Schools

Knuston Hall

Irchester, Wellingborough, Northants NN29 7EU
Tel: 01933 312104 *Fax:* 01933 57596

Owen Bryce, tutor in charge.
W/end and week's practical course with Owen Bryce and Alan Jeanes. 15-22 Aug 1997.

Wavendon Courses

The Stables, Wavendon, Milton Keynes, Bucks MK17 8LT
Tel: 01908 582522/670306 *Fax:* 01908 281024/674909

Jacky Scott, gen mgr.
A comprehensive education programme including 2-day courses: Contemporary jazz, Latin American, Beginners improvisation, Rhythm section. Also 7-day summer jazz course.

Jazz in the East of England

Eastern Jazz was disbanded in 1991. Independent jazz activities are listed below.

Classes, Workshops and Short Courses

Anglia Polytechnic University

East Rd, Cambridge CB1 1PT
Tel: 01223 63271 *Fax:* 01223 352935

Kevin Flanagan, module leader for jazz; Chris Ingham, lecturer.
Jazz is an important constituent of the BA Hons Music degree and great emphasis is placed upon it in the mus life of the college. There is a jazz orch, small ens and evening classes are held in jazz improvisation and jazz orch. Concert and w/shop activities are open to the public, and some are run in conjunction with outside organisations.

Benslow Music Trust

Little Benslow Hills, off Benslow La, Hitchin, Herts SG4 9RB
Tel: 01462 459446 *Fax:* 01462 440171

Keith Stent, mus adviser.
This is a residential centre for mus courses which features jazz. Hosts an annual course in jazz playing and appreciation with Owen Bryce for musicians of average ability wishing to improve their ens playing and their improvisation techniques. Up to 40 on each course. Mainly w/end courses including Big Band Summer School with Paul Eshelby.

534

Cambridgeshire Instrumental Music Agency (CIMA)
The Old School, Ermine St North, Papworth Everard, Cambs CB3 8RH
Tel: 01480 831695 *Fax:* 01480 831696

Peter Britton.
Information about jazz in the Cambridgeshire area.

Cambridge Modern Jazz Club
18 Perowne St, Cambridge
Tel: 01223 362550

Joan Morrell.
Offers w/shops to schools and colleges by jazz musicians visiting Cambridge on the Jazz Club programme.

Colchester Arts Centre
Church St, Colchester, Essex
Tel: 01206 577301 *Fax:* 01206 764334

Anthony Roberts.
The Arts Centre has presented jazz improvisation w/shops, usually in series of 6 sessions, according to the availability of funding. The arts centre also stages occasional one-off workshops featuring top jazz players. Recently staged a 1-day gui w/shop with Jim Mullen and Dave Cliff, Jean Toussaint, Billy Jenkins, Paul Getting.

Harlow College
Harlow CM20 1CT

Martin Banks, head of perf arts dept.
This is a tertiary college which has occasional special jazz w/shops. Essex Open College Federation Certificate in Jazz Studies (p/t evening course).

Jazz Course
58 Pond Bank, Blisworth, Northants NN7 3EL
Tel: 01604 858192

Owen Bryce, Iris Bryce, tutors.
Practical jazz course with jam session each evening at Theobalds Park, Bulls Cross Ride, Cheshunt, Herts EN7 5HW, 25-27 Apr 1997.

Jazz East
18 Perowne St, Cambridge CB1 2AY
Tel: 01223 362550

Joan Morrell, jazz animateur.
In Apr 1998 Jazz Essex became Jazz East after a succesful lottery bid bringing together jazz services in Cambridgeshire and Essex. Runs 3-day w/shops in Leigh-on-Sea at Easter and Oct, open to all standards, styles and ages. Organises m/classes, placing jazz tutors in schools and colleges as set out in the NC for mus and covering composition and improvisation. Organises a jazz summer school at Writtle College, Chelmsford in Aug for Chelmsford Borough Council. Jazz musicians' co-operatives and w/shop groups meet weekly in Southend, Colchester and Chelmsford.

Wingfield Arts
The Old College, Wingfield, Eye, Suffolk IP21 5RA
Tel: 01379 384505 *Fax:* 01379 384034

Tracy Wingfield, sec.
Wingfield Arts and Music is an annual programme of arts events, and includes some jazz performances with major artists. There is also a scheme to hold occasional jazz w/shops with such artists, both for the general public and for schools.

Jazz Education Projects (South of England)

Jazz Education Projects
10 Wiston Av, Chichester, W Sussex PO19 4RJ
Tel: 01243 533752

Adrian Kendon, admin.
The organisation does jazz improvisation work in primary, secondary and tertiary education sectors. The programme is in 3 phases taking pupils from basic improvisation skills through to the development of more advanced skills in composition and improvisation. JEP publishes jazz improvisation materials for use by teachers in the c/room, covering the requirements for the NC, and the GCSE and A-level mus syllabuses. Also community projects.

Classes, Workshops and Short Courses

Denman College
Marcham, Nr Abingdon, Oxon OX13 6NW
Tel: 01865 391991

Carl Attwood.
Regular courses in jazz appreciation.

Queen Mary's College
Cliddesden Rd, Basingstoke, Hants RG21 3HF
Tel: 01256 20861 *Fax:* 01256 26097

David Coggins, head of mus; Andrew Dickens, lecturer.

1-yr courses in jazz/rock improvisation. Adult education evening classes in jazz improvisation.

Summer Schools

Earnley Concourse
Chichester, Sussex PO20 7JL
Tel: 01243 670392 *Fax:* 01243 670832
Email: earnley@interalpha.co.uk

Annual spring course for elementary musicians. Also annual jazz summer school which includes

practical and appreciation groups and visits to local jazz club.

South West Jazz

South West Jazz
c/o Exeter and Devon Arts Centre, Gandy St, Exeter, Devon EX4 3LS
Tel: 01392 218368 *Fax:* 01392 420442

Kevin Buckland, regional development offr; Rosie Jarvis, admin.
Regional development agency for jazz and associated musics in Avon, Cornwall, Devon, Gloucestershire, Somerset and W Dorset. Publishers of *The Jazz Education Pack*. Facilitates jazz in education projects and provides information, advice and database services.

Contributes editorial and information to *Jazz UK* magazine. Regular newsletters to promoters, professional and amateur musicians. Project management for festivals and events. Manages Bude Jazz Summer School for young musicians. Introduction to improvisation, ens and section w/shops, and m/classes. Also two-day course on improvisation teaching for teachers and musicians with Eddie Harvey. Development of education projects throughout the region.

Classes, Workshops and Short Courses

Bath Jazz Workshop
The Small School, Larkhall, Bath
Tel: 01373 452812

Ralf Dorrell.
Meets weekly during term-time to teach the basics of jazz and enable students to participate in a local jazz group. Workshop members often form their own bands.

Bodmin Community College Jazz Orchestra
Lostwithiel Rd, Bodmin, Cornwall PL31 1DD
Tel: 01208 72114 *Fax:* 01208 78680

Adrian Evans, dir of mus.
Gr 5+. Rehearsals Fri 4-6 pm. 5 consecutive Gold Awards at the B & H National Concert Band Festival.

Clyst Vale Community College
Station Rd, Broadclyst, Exeter EX5 3AJ
Tel: 01392 466643 *also fax*
Email: cvcomed@cvcomed.devon-cc.gov.uk

John Glanfield.
Weekly big band w/shops for insts of all ages, with the opportunity for up to 6 concert performances pa.

Exeter and Devon Arts Centre
Gandy St, Exeter
Tel: 01392 219741 *Fax:* 01392 499929

Andy Morley, arts mgr.
Occasional jazz w/shops with visiting tutors and vocal w/shops (including jazz styles) on a similar basis. Regular programme of jazz events. Continues in various venues while Arts Centre rebuild is underway.

Exeter College
Hele Rd, Exeter EX4 4JS
Tel: 01392 384154

Iorwerth Pugh, head of mus.
Jazz w/shop. 2 big bands, jazz improvisation and composition relating to BTEC ND in popular mus.

Gloucestershire Youth Jazz Orchestra
c/o Colwell Arts Centre, Derby Rd, Glos GL1 4AD
Tel: 01452 330300 *Fax:* 01452 330311

Tony Sheppard, mus dir.
Gloucester Education Authority has funded the development of jazz ens at their mus centres and have funded w/shops with leading jazz musicians for Gloucestershire Youth Jazz Orchestra.

536

Guildhall Arts Centre
23 Eastgate St, Glos
Tel: 01452 505086 *Fax:* 01452 384734
Email: pat@guildart.demon.co.uk

Pat Roberts.
Regular Mon evening improvisation w/shops led by Pete Rosser for any musician who has an interest in jazz.

King Edward VI College
The Mansion, Fore St, Totnes
Tel: 01803 862591

Mick Green.

There is a Tue evening jazz w/shop open to those with at least a basic inst facility and sight-reading ability. Activities include playing, jazz interpretation and different styles of improvisation.

Prema Arts Centre
South St, Uley, Nr Dursley, Glos GL11 5SS
Tel: 01453 860703 *Fax:* 01453 860123

Gordon Scott, dir and admin.
The centre presents occasional jazz w/shops with visiting musicians.

Summer Schools

Bude Jazz Summer School
South West Jazz, c/o Exeter and Devon Arts Centre, Gandy St, Exeter EX4 3LS
Tel: 01392 218368 *Fax:* 01392 420442

Kevin Buckland, regional development offr; Stan Barker, course dir.
An intensive but fun week of courses for young musicians who have already acquired a

reasonable level of musical ability with their chosen inst, either as sight readers or by ear. W/shops developing understanding, interpretation and improvisation; m/classes, public performances. Courses suitable for various levels of experience in jazz skills, including beginners. 24-30 Aug 1997, applications by 20 Jul. Residential course includes Bude Jazz Festival pass. *Fee:* £280 (residential), £200 (non-residential).

Jazz North West

Jazz North West
2a Church St, Malpas, Cheshire SY14 8NZ
Tel: 01948 861050 *Fax:* 01948 861066

Sefton Music Support Service
Central Music Centre, Redgate, Formby, Liverpool L37 4EW
Tel: 01704 872773 *also fax*

Geoffrey Reed, head of mus support service; Glenn Waite, dir of youth jazz orch and jazz in educ co-ord.
Sefton Music Support Service has two jazz groups as part of its extension activities: Sefton Youth Jazz Orchestra and Sefton Youth Jazz Workshop. Both rehearse weekly and perform regularly. Jazz is incorporated in a rolling presentation to primary schools given by mus support staff called *Music Alive*. Sefton *Jazz in Education Week* takes place annually in the spring term. It includes jazz college w/shops in schools and a concert bringing together the work of schools and authority groups. This work has grown out of a project in 1985 which used funding from the Jazz in Education pilot scheme to develop ground work in two schools. Although jazz w/shops were assisted in the mid-eighties, they are now entirely self-funding.

Wigan Education Department
Gateway House, Standishgate, Wigan, Lancs WN1 2NB
Tel: 01942 255227 *Fax:* 01942 25521/243974
Website: www.wiganmbc.gov.uk/pub/leis/jazz/festwyjo.htm

Ian Darrington, jazz and live mus.
The Education Dept of Metropolitan Wigan has made a major commitment to jazz education since 1978. This investment and continued support has produced the award winning and internationally renowned Wigan Youth Jazz Orchestra, the Wigan International Jazz Festival (an 8-day annual event) the Wigan Schools Swing Band, and the Wigan Jazz Club. Regular w/shops on jazz improvisation and related subjects are held in the schools throughout the Wigan Borough, additionally a large and varied programme of 'live' jazz is available to all the pupils in Wigan schools.
The Wigan Education Department owns its own record label, *Gateway Records*, on which the Wigan Youth Jazz Orchestra record and document their work. To date this has produced a single, 9 albums, and a 40 min documentary video.

Classes, Workshops and Short Courses

Burnley Mechanics Arts and Entertainment Centre
Manchester Rd, Burnley, Lancs BB11 1JA
Tel: 01282 430005; 01282 430055 *Fax:* 01282 457428
Website: www.newsquest.co.uk/lit/burnley/mechanics

Anthony Preston.
As well as running occasional jazz w/shops, this centre hosts an annual 1-wk jazz course for those who wish to improve their jazz playing. Beginners, intermediate and advanced stages are tutored by Jazz College. Also evening big band sessions. Course is usually held in last week in Jul. First jazz festival 27-31 Jul 1998. Also Stage Door Jazz Club promotes monthly performances by leading jazz artists.

City College Manchester
Arden Centre, Sale Rd, Northenden, Manchester M23 0DD
Tel: 0161 957 1500 *Fax:* 0161 945 3854
Email: admissions@manchester-city-coll.ac.uk
Website: www.manchester-city-coll.ac.uk

Dennis Freedman.
Four jazz courses all starting in Sep: Jazz Musicianship and Theory 1 (Tue 5.30-7.30pm) aims to provide the student with sound basic mus literacy and then to apply it to jazz playing and writing. Main course components are elements of notation, melody and harmony, jazz repertoire and improvisation. Jazz Musicianship and Theory 2 (Thu 5.30-7.30pm) provides a more advanced treatment than course 1, dealing with more complex rhythms, more difficult sight-reading, more chromaticism and modulation. The use of modes, diminished, whole tone, altered and pentatonic scales in improvisation is considered and an introduction to arranging techniques is given. Jazz Improvisation (Tue 7.30-9.30pm) is an entirely practical course which helps students to develop improvisation. Jazz Group Workshop (Thu 7.30-9.30pm) is a weekly w/shop based around a big band in order to allow players of all abilities to experience jazz and ens playing. Gigs given regularly in area.

City of Liverpool Community College
School of Performing Arts, Green Bank Centre, Mossley Av, Liverpool L18 1JB
Tel: 0151 733 5511 *Fax:* 0151 734 2525

Brian Wilshaw, head of mus.
Several of the f/t mus courses at this college offer a significant element of jazz and improvisation. The college also has regular visits from touring jazz groups, and related w/shop activity is often open to instrumentalists from the community.

Inner City Music
Musicroots, c/o Band On The Wall, 25 Swan St, Manchester M4 5JQ
Tel: 0161 834 1786 *Fax:* 0161 834 2559

The educational services of Inner City Music operates within an innovative scheme entitled *Musicroots*. A f/t education officer will be appointed in 1998 and a programme of w/shops, classes and other activities will be launched in Oct.

Liverpool Youth Music Centre
Roscommon Resource Centre, Roscommon St, Liverpool L5 3NE
Tel: 0151 207 4446 *also fax*

Gerard Harrison, asst organiser; Martin Dempsey, organiser.
Liverpool Community Education Dept fund a series of jazz-related weekly w/shops at this centre, including basic sax tuition, jazz improvisation techniques, jazz/rock gui tuition, perc, general musicianship. The classes are held eves during term-time, and are open to players of all ages and levels of experience. Fees: 60p per session. Also tuition in gui, perc, sax, fl. Fees: £1 per 2 hr session. LEA supported mus centre. No formal qualifications required, just enthusiasm.

Wigan International Jazz Festival
c/o Wigan Education Dept, Gateway House, Standishgate, Wigan, Lancs WN1 1XL
Tel: 01942 255227 *Fax:* 01942 255217

Ian Darrington, teacher adviser in mus.
There are a number of open w/shops organised within the annual Wigan International Jazz Festival in Jul. The International Jazz Festival administered by Wigan Education Authority features local, national and international artists in an 8-day annual event.

Wigan Youth Jazz Orchestra
c/o Wigan Education Dept, Gateway House, Standishgate, Wigan, Lancs WN1 1XL
Tel: 01942 255227; 01942 243974 *also fax;*
Fax: 01942 255217
Website: www.wiganmbc.gov.uk/pub/leis/jazz/festwyjo.htm

Ian Darrington, mus dir.
This award-winning orch is supported and administered by Wigan Education Dept. The orch has an extensive repertoire, has toured Britain, Canada, Czechoslovakia, France, Hong Kong, Hungary,

Southern Ireland, USA, Israel and the Faroe Islands, and has worked with many of the world's greatest jazz musicians. Since 1985 they have made 9 albums and a 40 min documentary video. The 1998 tour will include Singapore, Kuala Lumpur, Perth and Sydney. New album due for release Jun 1998. Rehearsals take place at the Cafe at the Pier on Mon evenings. New members are always welcome on sax, tpt, trb, bs, pno, drums and gui.

Summer Schools

Manchester Jazz Summer School
City College, Arden Centre, Sale Rd, Northenden, Manchester M23 0DD
Tel: 0161 957 1775 (admissions) *Fax:* 0161 945 3854
Email: dfreedman@manchester-city-coll.ac.uk or dennis@g3vsh.demon.co
Website: www.manchester-city-coll

Dennis Freedman, course leader.
Specialist inst tuition, guided group playing, rhythm section w/shops, lectures and demonstrations on jazz theory and composition, improvisation w/shops at all levels, talks on great jazz figures.

Jazz Action (North East of England)

Jazz Action
1 Portrush Close, Darlington, Co Durham DL1 3HU
Tel: 01325 480454 *also fax*

Adrian Tilbrook, jazz development offr.

Jazz Action runs a creative w/shop scheme which gives young bands the opportunity to rehearse and perform with established jazz artists. Jazz Action intends to continue this policy of school w/shops. *See* **Jazz Attack** below.

Classes, Workshops and Short Courses

Jazz Attack
c/o Jazz Action, 1 Portrush Close, Darlington, Co Durham DL1 3HU
Tel: 01325 480454 *also fax*

Adrian Tilbrook, jazz development offr.
Jazz Attack provides jazz and rock performance technique courses as an essential foundation for contemporary mus studies in schools and colleges. The package is ideal for GCSE students.

Sheffield Jazz Workshop *formerly* Hurlfield Jazz Workshop
19 Carterknowle Rd, Sheffield S7 2DW
Tel: 0114 258 6290

Graham Jones, admin.
W/shops for insts held on Sat mornings 10.00am-12.30pm at the Bannerdale Centre, Bannerdale Rd, near Abbeydale Rd, Sheffield.

Sheffield University Division of Adult Continuing Education
196-198 West St, Sheffield S1 4ET
Tel: 0114 222 7000 *Fax:* 0114 222 7001

Adam White, mus co-ord.
Wide range of mus courses including jazz.

Summer Schools

Higham Hall Courses
Highham Hall, Bassenthwaite Lake, Cockermouth, Cumbria CA13 9SH
Tel: 017687 76276 *Fax:* 017687 76013
Email: higham.hall@dial.pipex.com
Website: www.higham-hall.org.uk

Freda Shaw, bookings sec; Len Phillips, course dir.

Course on small group playing and improvisation, residential and non-residential, aimed at players with some experience. Also many mus appreciation courses.

Workers' Music Association Summer School
17a Newton Rd, London NW2 6PS
Tel: 0181 450 4958

Jacqui Selby, hon organiser.
Participatory jazz courses at Wortley Hall, nr
Sheffield, Yorks for amateur musicians of all ages

and standards. 1-8 Aug 1998. Fees: residential
£275; day student £195; external student £115.

Welsh Jazz Society

Welsh Jazz Society Ltd (Cardiff)
26 The Balcony, Castle Arcade, Cardiff, South Glamorgan
CF1 2BY
Tel: 01222 340591 *Fax:* 01222 665160

Brian Hennessey, dir.
A registered educ charity dedicated to the work
of mus educ through programmes of w/shops
and performance throughout Wales.

Welsh Jazz Society Ltd (Mold)
c/o Theatr Clwyd, Mold CH7 1YA
Tel: 01352 756331 *Fax:* 01352 758323

Allan Cumberland, jazz development offr.
Runs weekly jazz w/shops on Sats at Theatr
Gwynedd, Bangor, Gwynedd, N Wales *tel:* 01248
351707.

Summer Schools

Glamorgan Summer School Jazz Course
c/o Welsh Jazz Society, 26 The Balcony, Castle Arcade,
Cardiff CF1 2BY
Tel: 01222 340591 *Fax:* 01222 665160

Dave Wickins, tutor, organiser.
Jul-Aug, University of Glamorgan, Treforest,

Pontypridd. Administered by Welsh Jazz Society
on behalf of the University of Glamorgan. Tutors
include Simon Purcell, Jean Toussaint, Dave Cliff,
Geoff Simkins, Julian Arguelles, Stan Sulzmann
and Steve Watts.

Jazz in Scotland

Scottish Jazz Network was disbanded in 1992. Although there are no formal jazz music courses
in Scotland, it is possible to acquire the knowledge and skills involved through playing in a jazz
orchestra or attending a recreational course.

Classes, Workshops and Short Courses

Fife Youth Jazz Orchestra
6 Dronachy Rd, Kirkcaldy, Fife KYY 5QL
Tel: 01592 263087

Richard Michael, dir of mus.
This is available to young Scottish musicians
aged 25 and under. All aspects of jazz are taught
including harmony, improvisation and big band
charts. There are 3 editions of FYJO, a
contemporary big band of 20 insts, an
intermediate band of 25 insts (normal big band
plus strs and w/wind), and FYJO 3, a group for
age 12 and under.

Fife Council Arts
Tower Block, Auchterderran Centre, Woodend Rd,
Cardenden, Fife KY5 0NE
Tel: 01592 414714 *Fax:* 01592 414727

Anne Chalk, support services offr; Andrew Neil,
arts policy co-ord.
Fife Youth Jazz Orchestra meets every Thu at
Balwearie High School.

The Grampian Jazz School
c/o Assembly Direct, 89 Giles St, Edinburgh EH6 6BZ
Tel: 0131 553 4000 *Fax:* 0131 554 0454

Assembly Direct run courses in Aberdeen
throughout the year. Some of the leading jazz
musicians in Scotland, led by Tom Bancroft teach
their skills to musicians of all ages and all
capabilities. The school teaches jazz

improvisation and harmony through a series of inst and ens classes.

Jazz in Schools
c/o Assembly Direct, 89 Giles St, Edinburgh EH6 6BZ
Tel: 0131 553 4000 *Fax:* 0131 554 0454

Assembly Direct have a Jazz in Schools scheme which runs a variety of jazz mus w/shops. Run by leading Scottish musicians, each w/shop is designed in collaboration with the school and can cover various aspects of the NC guidelines for mus.

Jazz Music Teacher In-Service Days
c/o Assembly Direct, 89 Giles St, Edinburgh EH6 6BZ
Tel: 0131 553 4000 *Fax:* 0131 554 0454

Assembly Direct run in-service days for mus teachers in Scotland to teach them jazz improvisation and harmony. The teaching is directly tied to the requirements laid out in the NC guidelines for expressive arts. A post-course school visit by the in-service tutor is available for jazz mus tuition to work in collaboration with the teacher.

Strathclyde Arts Centre Jazz Workshop and Jazz Band
c/o Strathclyde Arts Centre, 12 Washington St, Glasgow G3 8AZ
Tel: 0141 221 4526 *Fax:* 0141 204 3368

John Gourlay, Eliot Murray, tutors.
A weekly w/shop funded by Glasgow City Council for age 14 and above to learn standard melodies and improvisation. Also Strathclyde Arts Centre Jazz Band, a performance group playing modern standards and original work.

Summer Schools

Fife Summer Jazz Course
Fife Council Arts, Tower Block, Auchterderran Centre, Woodend Rd, Cardenden, Fife KY5 0NE
Tel: 01592 414714 *Fax:* 01592 414727

Richard Michael, mus dir.

Jul, at Fife College Halls of Residence, The Priory, Kirkcaldy.

Jazz in Northern Ireland

International Jazz Summer School
c/o The Music Dept, University of Ulster, Shore Rd, Newtownabbey, Co Antrim BT37 0QB
Tel: 01232 366690 *Fax:* 01232 366870
Email: hm.bracefield@ulst.ac.uk

Hilary Bracefield, Brian Carson, joint admins;

Hugh Fraser, course leader.
The course is residential for up to 50 players wishing to develop their jazz knowledge and skills. Last week in Aug, applications by May. Organised in association with the Arts Council of Northern Ireland and the Arts Council/An Chomhairle Ealaion.

SUPPLIERS AND SERVICES

Retailers

The following is a brief list of major retailers of sheet music, books, and instruments. Retailers in Greater London are listed first, followed by those in the rest of Great Britain. A more comprehensive list, arranged by geographical location, can be found in the *British Music Yearbook*.

Greater London

All Flutes Plus
5 Dorset St, London W1H 3FE
Tel: 0171 935 3339 *Fax:* 0171 224 2053
Email: afp@allflutesplus.co.uk

Fl specialists; w/wind, mus, rcdrs, repairs, rentals.

Barbican Music Shop
Cromwell Tower, Silk St, Barbican, London EC2Y 8DD
Tel: 0171 588 9242 *Fax:* 0171 628 1080

Books, mus, insts, CDs, accs.

Bill Lewington Ltd
144 Shaftesbury Av, London WC2H 8HN
Tel: 0171 240 0584 *Fax:* 0171 240 2919
Email: sales@bill-lewington.com
Website: www.bill-lewington.com

Books, insts, mus. Also wholesalers.

Blackburn Stringed Instruments
75 Harrington Gardens, London SW7 4JZ
Tel: 0171 373 2474 *Fax:* 0171 373 5141

Vns, vas, vcs; also restoration and evaluation. Bows, buying and selling of str insts.

Boosey & Hawkes Music Shop
295 Regent St, London W1R 8JH
Tel: 0171 291 7255 *Fax:* 0171 436 2850

Books, mus, accs; m/order (cat), credit cards.

Britten's Music Ltd
136 George La, South Woodford, London E18 1AY
Tel: 0181 530 6432

K Moorcraft, mgr.
Mus, insts, accs.

Chappell of Bond Street
50 New Bond St, London W1Y 9HA
Tel: 0171 491 2777 *Fax:* 0171 491 0133

Insts, mus, pnos, keyboards, books, school mus.

Chas E Foote Ltd
10 Golden Sq, London W1R 3AF
Tel: 0171 437 1811 *Fax:* 0171 734 3095
Email: footesdrums@msn.com

W/wind, br, str and perc.

Chimes Music Shop
44 Marylebone High St, London W1M 3AD
Tel: 0171 935 1587; 0171 486 1303 *Fax:* 0171 935 0457
Email: musicman@marcus.fnet.co.uk

Ling Sam, mgr.
Books, insts, mus, CDs, sheet mus (comprises majority of stock), bargain books. Also m/order.

Dillons The Bookstore
82 Gower St, London WC1E 6EQ
Tel: 0171 636 1577 *Fax:* 0171 580 7680
Email: enquiries@gower.dillons.org.uk

Angela Stone.
Books, mus, CDs, video and all related expertise.

The Dulwich Music Shop
2 Croxted Rd, Dulwich, London SE21 8SW
Tel: 0181 766 0202 *Fax:* 0181 766 8689

Sheet mus, books, CDs, gifts, inst sales and repairs.

ENO Shop
MDC Classic Music, 31 St Martin's La, London WC2N 4ER
Tel: 0171 240 0270
Email: classic@mdcmusic.co.uk
Website: www.mdcmusic.co.uk

James Skeggs, mgr.
Books on opera, dance and ballet. CDs, videos and gifts.

Hampstead Pianos
133 Abbey Rd, London NW6 4SL
Tel: 0171 624 8895 *Fax:* 0181 245 4653

Tom Walter, mgr.
Acoustic pnos, restoration, tuning, removals and unique pno designs.

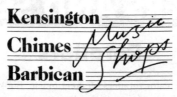

SHEET MUSIC • BOOKS • INSTRUMENTS & ACCESSORIES

An abundance of printed music and books
from worldwide publishers.

◆

Instrument hire, repairs and accessories.

◆

Gifts with a musical theme.

◆

Musically-qualified staff with substantial
experience in the trade.

◆

Prompt mail order service.

◆

Discounts for libraries, schools, professionals,
teachers and students.

◆

Free delivery service twice weekly to schools and
libraries in Central London.

Kensington Music Shop	**Chimes Music Shop**	**Barbican Music Shop**
9 Harrington Road	44 Marylebone High Street	Cromwell Tower
South Kensington	London W1M 3AD	Barbican
London SW7 3ES	Tel: 0171-935 1587	London EC2Y 8DD.
Tel: 0171-589 9054	Fax: 0171-935 0457	Tel: 0171-588 9242
Fax: 0171-225 2662		Fax: 0171-628 1080

Opening hours for all shops: 9-5.30, Sat 9-4

Harpsichord Workshop
130 Westbourne Terrace Mews, London W2 6QG
Tel: 0171 723 9650 *also fax*

Mark Ransom, mgr.
Tuning, repair and renovation, short and long-term hire, insts for sale and an agent for well-known makers.

Impact Percussion
120-122 Bermondsey St, London SE1 3TX
Tel: 0171 403 5900 *Fax:* 0171 403 5910
Email: impactperc@msn.com

Paul Hagen, proprietor.
Orch and latin perc and kits; also repairs and hire.

Islington Music
6 Shillingford St, off Cross St, London N1 2DP
Tel: 0171 354 3195 *also fax*

Sheet mus, tapes, accs, gifts, insts sales and hire, m/order.

Ivor Mairants Musicentre
56 Rathbone Pl, London W1P 1AB
Tel: 0171 636 1481 *Fax:* 0171 580 6272

Phil Lusher, mgr.
Fretted insts, guis, accs, m/order, repairs.

J P Guivier & Co Ltd
99 Mortimer St, London W1N 7TA
Tel: 0171 580 2560; 0171 636 6499 *Fax:* 0171 436 1461

Richard White, Robin Hamilton, dirs.
Dealers and restorers of insts and bows of the vn family. Also cases, accs and valuations.

J Reid Pianos
184 St Annes Rd, Tottenham, London N15 5RP
Tel: 0181 800 6907 *Fax:* 0181 809 0767

Pnos, repairs, restoration, educational discounts, retail and wholesale supplier.

Kensington Music Shop
9 Harrington Rd, London SW7 3ES
Tel: 0171 589 9054 *Fax:* 0171 225 2662

Mus, books, insts, accs.

Knightsbridge Pianos
88 Old Brompton Rd, London SW7 3LQ
Tel: 0171 584 2581

New and reconditioned uprights and grands for rental or purchase.

Markson Pianos
36-38 Artillery Pl, Woolwich, London SE18 4AB
Tel: 0181 854 4517 *Fax:* 0181 317 1076
Email: 106372.2523@compuserve.com

Pno sales, hire, restoration, tuning, maintenance, transport, concert hire, educational discounts.

The <u>only</u> showroom dedicated solely to hornplayers. Instruments for sale by **Paxman, Alexander, Engelbert Schmid, Yamaha, Holton** and others. Plus accessories, sheet music and an unrivalled on-site repair facility.

Paxman Musical Instruments Limited
Unit B4, Linton House, 164-180 Union Street, London SE1 0LH
Showroom: 0171-620 2077 Fax: 0171-620 1688

546

Markson Pianos Ltd
8 Chester Ct, Albany St, London NW1 4BU
Tel: 0171 935 8682 *Fax:* 0171 224 0957
Email: 106372.2523@compuserve.com

Pno sales, hire, tuning and repairs, restoration, transport; acoustic and electronic. 24-hr concert hire service.

Music Sales Ltd
Music Book Centre, 8-9 Frith St, London W1V 5TZ
Tel: 0171 434 0066 *Fax:* 0171 439 2848
Email: music@musicsales.co.uk
Website: www.musicsales.co.uk

Books, mus, karaoke, interactive MIDI mus software.

Paxman Musical Instruments Ltd
Unit B4, Linton House, 164-180 Union St, London SE1 0LH
Tel: 0171 620 2077 *Fax:* 0171 620 1688
Email: paxmanhorn@compuserve.com

Hns, mus, repairs.

Peters Music Shop
c/o Boosey & Hawkes, 295 Regent St, London W1R 8JH
Tel: 0171 291 7244

Stocks mus in Peters Edition and agencies.

Phelps Pianos
49 Fortess Rd, London NW5 1AD
Tel: 0171 485 2042 *Fax:* 0171 284 1404

Selection of new, nearly new, second-hand and reconditioned pnos for sale or hire. Tuning and repairs, restoration, free advice.

Phil Parker
106a Crawford St, London W1H 1AL
Tel: 0171 486 8206 *Fax:* 0171 935 6686

Br insts, accs, repairs and mus.

Ray Man
29 Monmouth St, Covent Garden, London WC2H 9DD
Tel: 0171 240 1776 *Fax:* 0171 240 9689

Eastern mus insts, recordings, tuition, hire.

Robert Morley & Co Ltd
34 Engate St, London SE13 7HA
Tel: 0181 318 5838 *Fax:* 0181 297 0720
Website: www.yell.co.uk/sites/morley

Julia Morley.
Spinets, virginals, clvds, hpds, pnos; stools, cabinets, mus stands; sale and rental, tuning, repairs. (Cat).

Schott/Universal Edition
48 Gt Marlborough St, London W1V 2BN
Tel: 0171 437 1246 *Fax:* 0171 437 0263
Email: 101627.166@compuserve.com
Website: www.schott-music.com

Classical mus.

Southgate Music Shop
110 Chase Side, London N14 5PH
Tel: 0181 886 9901 *Fax:* 0181 886 3426

Sarah Drake, mgr.
Sheet mus, insts for sale and hire, keyboards, accs and repairs; also second-hand insts.

Spanish Guitar Centre
36 Cranbourn St, London WC2H 7AD
Tel: 0171 240 0754

Classical and flamenco guis, accs, mus, CDs, tuition.

Steinway & Sons
44 Marylebone La, London W1M 6EN
Tel: 0171 487 3391 *Fax:* 0171 935 0466

G Oakley, mgr dir.
New and refurbished pnos, tuning, rebuilds and repairs, concert hire.

T W Howarth & Co Ltd
31 Chiltern St, London W1M 1HG
Tel: 0171 935 2407 *Fax:* 0171 224 2564
Email: sales@howarth.demon.co.uk
Website: www.howarth.demon.co.uk

W/wind, sheet mus, w/wind repairs, inst hire, m/order, w/wind accs.

Top Wind
2 Lower Marsh, London SE1 7RJ
Tel: 0171 401 8787 *Fax:* 0171 401 8788
Email: topwind@topwind.com
Website: www.topwind.com

Fl specialists. Also repairs and suppliers to schools and colleges. Full range of student and professional insts, sheet mus, rentals, books, accs and expert advice.

W & G Foyle Ltd
Music Dept, 113-119 Charing Cross Rd, London WC2H 0EB

Books, sheet mus, recordings.

Walthamstow Music
116 Hoe St, Walthamstow, London E17 4QR
Tel: 0181 520 2163 *Fax:* 0181 509 3005

Br, w/wind, str, keyboard and hi-tech insts. Sheet mus, repairs, hire.

Whone, Adam
86 Mill Hill Rd, London W3 8JJ
Tel: 0181 992 0619 *Fax:* 0181 992 8891

Vn restorers, makers and experts. Also vas, vcs and bows.

Rest of Great Britain

Abbey Music
48 Grosvenor Rd, Tunbridge Wells, Kent TN1 2AS
Tel: 01892 511611; 0800 526150 *Fax:* 01892 511115

School perc and c/room insts.

Allegro Music
82 Suffolk St, Queensway, Birmingham B1 1TA
Tel: 0121 643 7553 *Fax:* 0121 633 4773
Email: sales@allegro.co.uk

Books, mus, m/order.

Andy Lee Woodwind
195 Osborne Rd, Jesmond, Newcastle upon Tyne
Tel: 0191 281 3585 *also fax*

W/wind repairs, second-hand refurbished stocks of all w/wind insts specialising in sax.

Balaam's Music
103 Risbygate St, Bury St Edmunds, Suffolk IP33 3AA
Tel: 01284 766933 *Fax:* 01284 701605
Email: music@balaam.dungeon.com.uk

Mus, insts, books, repairs, insurance.

Band Box (Wolverhampton) Ltd
5 Worcester St, Wolverhampton WV2 4LD
Tel: 01902 421420

Books, mus, insts, repairs.

Bandsound
26 Mitre Copse, Eastleigh, Hants SO50 8QE
Tel: 01703 600444 *also fax*

Mus education products.

Blackwell's Music Library Services
Hythe Bridge St, Oxford OX1 2ET
Tel: 01865 792792 *Fax:* 01865 261395
Email: lbdmus@blackwell.co.uk

M/order suppliers to mus libraries, colleges and orchs; books, printed mus, recordings.

The Brighton Violin Shop Ltd
131-133 Edward St, Brighton BN2 2JL
Tel: 01273 673200

Str insts, accs, mus, repairs.

Bristol Music Shop
30 College Green, Bristol BS1 5TB
Tel: 0117 929 0390

Orch insts, mus, restorations, MIDI song files, accs.

Bristol Musical
88 Horfield Rd, Bristol BS2 8EQ
Tel: 0117 929 2758 *also fax*

New and used electric guis, basses; accs, equipment, PA systems.

The Bristol Violin Shop
12 Upper Maudlin St, Bristol BS2 8DJ
Tel: 0117 925 9990 *also fax*

Makers and repairers of bowed str insts; insts bought and sold; accs and specialist str mus; m/order.

Britannia Music Shop and Britannia Reeds
156 Hatfield Rd, St Albans, Herts AL1 4JD
Tel: 01727 846055 *Fax:* 01727 811164

W/wind specialist, also br and str. Insts, mus, accs.

Bruce Millers
363 Union St, Aberdeen AB9 1EN
Tel: 01224 592211 *Fax:* 01224 580085

Insts, keyboards, pnos, mus, recordings, books, tuning, repairs, hi-fi, accs, TV videos.

C Milsom & Son Ltd
Northgate, Bath BA1 5AS
Tel: 01225 465975

Books, insts, mus, recordings.

Cambridge Music Shop
1a All Saints' Passage, Cambridge CB2 3LT
Tel: 01223 351786 *Fax:* 01223 464178

Mus, books, facsimiles, insts, m/order.

Chappell of Bond Street
21 Silbury Arcade, The Shopping Centre, Central Milton Keynes MK9 3AG
Tel: 01908 663366 *Fax:* 01908 606414

Insts, keyboards, studio PA, mus, CDs, tuning, repairs, hire, pnos.

Clevedon Music Shop
19 Alexandra Rd, Clevedon, BS21 7QH
Tel: 01275 342090 *also fax;* 01275 791181

Insts, mus, books, accs, repairs, CDs.

Counterpoint Music Shop
38 Grantham St, Lincoln LN2 1LW
Tel: 01522 560065

Sheet mus, books, CDs, cassettes, educational specialist, m/order.

Countrywide Piano Centre Ltd
194 Penn Rd, Hazlemere, High Wycombe, Bucks HP15 7NU
Tel: 01494 813388 *Fax:* 01494 813994

Pnos (new and second-hand), repairs, tuning, restorations. School, churches, educ discount.

Courtney and Walker Ltd
82-86 Elm Grove, Southsea, Hants PO5 1LN
Tel: 01705 822036 *Fax:* 01705 780799

Education specialists, insts, hire, mus.

Cremona House Violin Shop
Cremona House, 7 Perry Rd (Park Row), Bristol BS1 5BQ
Tel: 0117 926 4617

Crowthers of Canterbury
10 Longport, Canterbury, Kent CT1 1PE
Tel: 01227 763965 *also fax*

Lorée obs, w/wind insts, accs, mus, rentals, repairs.

David Newton Violins at Potters Music Shop (Croydon) Ltd
12-16 High St, Merstham, Surrey RH1 3EA
Tel: 01737 645065 *Fax:* 01737 645808

Str insts, repairs, bow-makers; and Music In Print Ltd *Tel:* 01737 645334. Sheet mus, w/wind, br insts, guis. Also hire of most insts.

David Snelling Violins
9 Station St, Kibworth, Beauchamp, Leicester LE8 0LN
Tel: 0116 279 3212 *Fax:* 0116 279 6260

Sales of vns, vas and vcs. Valuations, insurance, repairs.

Dennis Todd Music
86 Front St, Bedlington, Northumberland NE22 5AE
Tel: 01670 822085 *Fax:* 01670 820592

Br, w/wind, perc, electronic keyboards, guis, sheet mus, educational mus, rental plan, repairs.

Derek Hossle Woodwind
26 Andrew St, Mossley, Lancs OL5 0DN
Tel: 01457 835656

W/wind, repairs, restoration.

Derek Roberts Violins
185 Leam Terrace, Leamington Spa, Warwicks CV31 1DW
Tel: 01926 428313 *also fax*

Orch strs, cases, bows, accs; also maker and restorer.

Duck Son & Pinker Ltd
9-12 Bridge St, Pulteney Bridge, Bath BA2 4AU
Tel: 01225 465975

Books, insts, mus, recordings, hi-fi.

554

Emma Newton Electric Violins at Potters Music Shop (Croydon) Ltd
12-16 High St, Merstham, Surrey RH1 3EA
Tel: 01737 645065 *Fax:* 01737 645808

Electric vns and vas.

Forsyth Brothers Ltd
126 Deansgate, Manchester M3 2GR
Tel: 0161 834 3281 *Fax:* 0161 834 0630
Email: forsythmus@aol.com

Mus, books, orch insts, guis, keyboards, digital pnos, grand and upright pnos (new and second hand) etc. Tuning, repair, hire. CDs, cassettes, videos, talking books, m/order.

Forwoods Music
35-37 Palace St, Canterbury, Kent CT1 2DZ
Tel: 01227 464741 *Fax:* 01227 762836
Email: forwoods.music@btinternet.com

Insts, mus, books; also m/order.

Frank Fidler
Rosehill Instruments, The Old Dairy, The Square, Ruardean, Glos GL17 9TJ
Tel: 01594 544053

Br, w/wind sales and repairs, accs.

Freeman & Neale's Music Shop
40-42 Lawford Rd, Rugby, Warwicks CV21 2DY
Tel: 01788 577064 *also fax*

Insts, mus.

Galleon Music
Aldeburgh Foundation, High St, Aldeburgh, Suffolk IP15 5AX
Tel: 01728 453298 *Fax:* 01728 452715

CDs, cassettes, scores, m/order. Britten specialist.

Goodmusic
PO Box 100, Tewkesbury, Glos GL20 7YQ
Tel: 01684 773883 *Fax:* 01684 773884

Mail order only. Mus, books.

The Guitar Makers
87 Gales Dr, Three Bridges, Crawley, W Sussex RH10 1QA
Tel: 01293 543055

Custom-made guis, accs, amps, repairs, Gibsons, Fenders Aria etc.

H Wright Greaves Ltd
11 Goose Green, Altrincham, Cheshire WA14 1DW
Tel: 0161 929 6949 *Fax:* 0161 926 8280

Mus, books, accs, gifts, m/order.

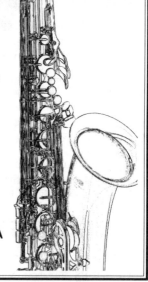
556

Herga Music
2a-4 High St, Wealdstone, Harrow HA3 7AA
Tel: 0181 861 1590 *Fax:* 0181 861 5501

Sheet mus, br, w/wind, str insts, guis, pnos, keyboards, educational products, mus books, gifts, repairs, hire, m/order.

Howorth Wrightson Ltd
Unit 2, Cricket St, Denton, Manchester M34 3DR
Tel: 0161 335 0220 *Fax:* 0161 320 3928

Manufacturers of own design of mus stands.

J & L Dawkes
652 Bath Rd, Taplow SL6 0NZ
Tel: 01462 604404

W/wind and br insts and service.

James Dace & Son Ltd
33 Moulsham St, Chelmsford, Essex CM2 0HX
Tel: 01245 352133 *Fax:* 01245 262841

Insts, mus, accs, CDs.

John Barnes
3 East Castle Rd, Edinburgh EH10 5AP
Tel: 0131 229 8018

W/shop drawings and information for builders of early keyboard insts, clvd kits (portable 18th C design), hpd and spinet kits. Covered strings for clvds and square pnos.

John Packer Ltd
1 Portland St, Taunton, Somerset TA1 1UY
Tel: 01823 282386 *Fax:* 01823 337653

Suppliers and repairers of wind and br insts. Educational contractor.

Just Flutes/Jonathan Myall (Musical)
36 Chipstead Valley Rd, Coulsdon, Surrey CR5 2RA
Tel: 0181 668 4444 *Fax:* 0181 668 7262
Email: justflutes@i-gadgets.com
Website: www.i-gadgets.com/justflutes/

Mus, books, insts, recordings, cassettes, accs; also m/order and repairs.

Kempster & Son (The Music Shop)
98 Commercial Rd, Swindon, Wilts SN1 5PL
Tel: 01793 535523 *Fax:* 01793 526375

Group and PA gear, multi-track recording and educational insts.

KGB Musical Instruments
61 Derby Rd, Birkenhead, Merseyside L42 7HA
Tel: 0151 647 3268

Guis, gui parts, strs and accs.

Knock on Wood
Arch X Granary Wharf, Leeds LS1 4BR
Tel: 0113 242 9146; 0113 245 9878 *also fax*

Schools/educational mail order: Unit 131, Glasshouses Mill, Harrogate, Pateley Bridge HG3 5QH *Tel:* 01423 712712 *also fax*. Multicultural supplies of insts, recordings, books and teaching resources.

Lindsay Music
23 Hitchin St, Biggleswade, Beds SG18 8AX
Tel: 01767 316521 *Fax:* 01767 317221

Books, mus and accs (strs, reeds, etc), mus gifts.

Machinehead Music
2 Bush House, Bush Fair, Harlow, Essex CM18 6NS
Tel: 01279 421744/453092

Group insts, guis, accs.

McQueens Musical Instruments
902 Chester Rd, Gorse Hill, Stretford, Manchester M32 0PA
Tel: 0161 865 9886 *also fax*

General musical inst retail shop.

Mail Order Music
Newmarket Rd, Bury St Edmunds, Suffolk IP33 3YB
Tel: 01284 703097/725725 *Fax:* 01284 702592
Email: mailorder@musicsales.co.uk
Website: www.musicsales.co.uk

Sheet mus: c/room, solo, ens, choral, musical shows, new media. Catalogues include Chester Music, Novello, Golden Apple, Shawnee Press, G Schirmer, UME and Youngsongs.

Marcus Musical Instruments Ltd
125 Royal Av, Belfast BT1 1FF
Tel: 01232 322871 *Fax:* 01232 439955
Email: musicman@marcus.dnet.co.uk

Full range of all types of mus inst.

Modern Music (Basingstoke) Ltd
3-4 Chelsea House, Town Centre, Basingstoke, Hants RG21 7JR
Tel: 01256 464663 *Fax:* 01256 818113

Insts, mus, pnos, orgs, hi-tech.

Mostly Music
28 Carlisle Close, Noberley, Knutsford, Cheshire WA16 7HD
Tel: 01565 872650

M/order of books, mus, recordings, tapes, CDs.

Music Cellar
12 Fox St, Preston, Lancs
Tel: 01772 251407 *Fax:* 01772 251412

Orch insts, pnos, clavinovas, keyboards, mus.

Music Direct
33 Tydfil Pl, Roath Pk, Cardiff CF2 5HP
Tel: 01222 496080 *Fax:* 01222 457760

Printed mus and books; specialist catalogues on request. UK and export.

Music Education Supplies
101 Banstead Rd South, Sutton, Surrey SM2 5LH
Tel: 0181 770 3866 *Fax:* 0181 770 3554

Agents of Sonor school perc and suppliers of Suzuki handchimes and perc, Nordoff-Robbins reed hns, Aulos rcdrs, books, insts, etc.

Music Exchange (Manchester) Ltd
12 St Peter's Sq, Manchester M2 3DF
Tel: 0161 236 1766

Books, mus, insts and accs.

Music for Brass Ltd
Unit 1, Warneford Av, Dewsbury Rd, Ossett, W Yorks WF5 9NJ
Tel: 01924 261154 *Fax:* 01924 280310

Own titles (br and wind band).

The Music House
27 Greenhill St, Stratford-upon-Avon, Warwicks CV37 6LE
Tel: 01789 268515 *also fax*

Mus, insts, accs.

The Music Shop
27 Church St, Inverness IV1 1DY
Tel: 01463 233374 *Fax:* 01463 713983

Books, insts including bagpipes and bodhrans, sheet mus, accs; educational discounts.

Music Store Group Ltd
4 Eastgate Sq, Chichester, W Sussex PO19 1ED
Tel: 01243 780536 *Fax:* 01243 783499

Insts, mus.

Music Warehouse
10 Northgate St, Aberystwyth, Ceredigion SY23 2JS
Tel: 01970 612349

Books, insts, mus, recordings.

Musicale plc
20 Salisbury Av, Harpenden, Herts AL5 2QG
Tel: 01582 769712 *Fax:* 01582 767343

Books, nationwide inst purchase scheme, mus, accs, m/order, repairs. Commission for teachers and mus depts.

Musicparts (UK)
426 Worsley Rd, Winton, Eccles, Manchester M30 8HQ
Tel: 07071 223698 *Fax:* 01942 889452

Custom making of br insts, customizing of

w/wind and br insts. Sales of new and secondhand br and w/wind insts.

Musisca Ltd
20 Wellington La, Montpelier, Bristol BS6 5PY
Tel: 0117 924 0934 *also fax*

Mus stands, pno stools and lighting, cond stands, desk stands.

Myatt (John) Woodwind and Brass
57 Nightingale Rd, Hitchin, Herts SG5 1RQ
Tel: 01462 420057 *Fax:* 01462 435464

Full repair w/wind and br workshop.

Newingtons Music Centre
Grove Hill Rd, Tunbridge Wells, Kent TN1 1RZ
Tel: 01892 526659 *Fax:* 01892 540611

Insts, keyboards, pnos, mus, cassettes, CDs, videos, books, accs, restoration and repair, m/order.

Oundle Music Shop
13 West St, Oundle, Peterborough PE8 4EJ
Tel: 01832 273669

Insts, mus, also repairs, education specialists and m/order service.

Oxford University Press Bookshop
116-117 High St, Oxford OX1 4BZ
Tel: 01865 242913 *Fax:* 01865 241701
Email: bookshop@oup.co.uk

Books, sheet mus.

Peter W Salisbury Ltd
24 Duke St, Henley-on-Thames, Oxon RG9 1UP
Tel: 01491 413019 *Fax:* 01491 411361

Pnos.

Presto Music
130 Station Rd, Knowle, Solihull B93 0EP
Tel: 01564 773100

Insts, mus, CDs, m/order.

Roadshow
64 Upper Craigs, Stirling FK8 2DS
Tel: 01786 471323 *also fax*

PA, guis, amps, drums, lighting; also sales, tuition, hire and repairs.

Rosehill Instruments Ltd
64 London End, Beaconsfield, Bucks HP9 2JD
Tel: 01494 671717 *Fax:* 01494 676428

Insts, mus, electronic pnos.

Salop Music Centre
St Michaels St, Shrewsbury, Shropshire SY1 2DE
Tel: 01743 365561/364111

Sheet mus, br, w/wind, keyboards, orch str, educational perc, gui specialists, hi tech, PA, folk, schools discount.

Seaford Music
24 Pevensey Rd, Eastbourne, E Sussex BN21 3HP
Tel: 01323 732553 *Fax:* 01323 417455
Email: mail@gic.co.uk
Website: www.gic.co.uk/sm

Mus, educational books, inst accs, classical CDs, cassettes.

Sheehan's Music Services
50 London Rd, Leicester LE2 0QD
Tel: 0116 255 7492 *Fax:* 0116 285 5932
Email: mel@sheehans.com

W/wind, br, electroacoustic and classical gui, folk insts, books and accs, repairs.

Stentor Music Co Ltd
Albert Rd North, Reigate, Surrey RH2 9EZ
Tel: 01737 240226 *Fax:* 01737 242748
Email: stentor@stentor-music.com

Wholesale specialist str inst supplier; also br, w/wind and guis.

Swales Music Centre Ltd
2-6 High St, Haverfordwest, Pembrokeshire
Tel: 01437 762059 *Fax:* 01437 760872

Mus, books, cassettes, CDs, insts, accs.

Telford Musical Instruments Ltd
7 Bell St, Wellington, Telford, Shropshire TF1 1LS
Tel: 01952 255310 *Fax:* 01952 223138

Insts, mus.

TR Music
233-236 Stafford St, Walsall, W Midlands WS2 8DF
Tel: 01922 613101

Guis, PA, amps, electric repairs, str insts, cl, fl, drums, mus books, accs, recording equipment, lighting, pyrotechnics.

Trevada Music
9 Chapel St, Camborne, Cornwall TR14 8EF
Tel: 01209 714353 *Fax:* 01209 718708
Email: trevada@netcomuk.co.uk
Website: www.trevadamusic.co.uk

Also at: 18 Wind St, Ammanford SA18 3DN *Tel:* 01269 596607. Pnos, keyboards, br, w/wind, perc, str, sheet mus, repairs, rental scheme.

Venables Pianos
1 Monmouth Ct, Ringwood, Hants BH24 IHE
Tel: 01425 476644 *Fax:* 01425 476645

New and second-hand pnos, uprights, specialising in grands; clavinovas, electronic keyboards.

Windband
9 Greyfriars Rd, Shrewsbury, Shropshire SY3 7EN
Tel: 01743 367482 *also fax;*

Fax: 01743 340412
Email: windband@cableinet.co.uk

W/wind and br specialist, folk and early insts, mus and accs m/order, rental purchase, inst hire schemes, repairs.

The Woodwind Exchange
38 Manningham La, Bradford BD1 3EA
Tel: 01274 721831

Publishers to the performing arts

RHINEGOLD PUBLISHING

YEARBOOKS

British & International Music Yearbook
Britain's most comprehensive and accurate directory of the classical music industry
Published each November £23.95

British Performing Arts Yearbook
The guide to performing companies, venues, suppliers, services, festivals, education and support organisations
Published each January £23.95

Music Education Yearbook
A guide for parents, teachers, students and musicians
Published each June £16.50

OTHER PUBLICATONS

The Musician's Handbook
A compendium of advice for the music profession
£14.95 (hardback)

Healthy Practice for Musicians
An expertly written self-help guide covering the whole spectrum of a musician's physical and mental well-being
£16.95 (hardback)

Arts Marketing
The definitive guide to audience-building through effective marketing
£18.95 (hardback)

Analysis Matters
A students' revision guide to the Group 1 London Examinations' Advanced Level Musical History and Analysis Papers for 1998 and 1999
£10.00

Kein Angst Baby
A singer's guide to German operatic auditions in the 1990s
£9.95

The Art of Conducting
A guide to essential skills
£12.95

MAGAZINES

Classical Music
The magazine of the classical music profession
Fortnightly £2.95
Annual UK Subscription £56.00

Music Teacher
Respected and enjoyed by music teachers for more than 85 years
Monthly £2.95
Annual UK Subscription £34.00

The Singer
For amateur and professional singers of every persuasion – from cabaret to grand opera
Bi-monthly £2.40
Annual UK Subscription £14.40

Piano
The magazine for performers and enthusiasts of classical, jazz and blues piano
Bi-monthly £2.40
Annual UK Subscription £14.40

Early Music Today
Britain's brightest early music news magazine
Bi-monthly £2.40
Annual UK Subscription £14.40

Opera Now
The international magazine for opera professionals
Bi-monthly £4.95
Annual UK Subscription £29.70

Music Scholar
A guide to scholarships for young musicians
Published each November £3.00

Rhinegold Publishing Limited
241 Shaftesbury Avenue
London WC2H 8EH
Tel 0171 333 1721 Fax 0171 333 1769
E-mail book.sales@rhinegold.co.uk

R·

Mail Order Suppliers

The following companies offer a mail-order system for their own products and the products of other companies. Most **Music Publishers** (see relevant section) will also supply music by post. Some retailers without an established mail-order service will also supply by post on request.

Aarabee Centre
Bhavan's Bookshop, Institute of Indian Art & Culture, 4a Castletown Rd, London W14 9HQ
Tel: 0171 381 3086; 0171 610 1575 *Fax:* 0171 381 8758

Mrs Amara, mgr.
Books on classical Indian mus, dance, yoga, Indian philosophy and religion. Mus insts and teaching accs.

Balaam's Music
103 Risbygate St, Bury St Edmunds, Suffolk IP33 3AA
Tel: 01284 766933 *Fax:* 01284 701605
Email: music@balaam.dungeon.com.uk

Mus insts, books, CDs, accs; worldwide (cat).

Banks and Son (Music) Ltd
18 Lendal, York YO1 2AU

Tel: 01904 658836 *Fax:* 01904 629547
Email: banksmusic@dial.pipex.com
Website: www.banksmusic.co.uk

Printed mus, mus text books, CDs, mus insts and accs, software.

Bill Lewington Ltd
144 Shaftesbury Av, London WC2H 8HN
Tel: 0171 240 0584 *Fax:* 0171 240 2919
Email: sales@bill-lewington.com
Website: www.bill-lewington.com

Samantha Pett.
Main agents for Earlham and other leading makers supplying mus insts suitable for schools and colleges (cat). Also Olds, Grassi, Iwao, Munamatsu and Hall Crystal Flutes. All brands stocked.

Black Cat Music
Bankside House, Vale Rd, Tonbridge, Kent TN9 1SJ
Tel: 01732 367123 *Fax:* 01732 367755

Sharon Street, sales exec.
Equipment and furniture for mus teaching: mus stands, chairs, staging, acoustic treatments (cat).

Boosey and Hawkes Music Shop
295 Regent St, London W1R 8JH
Tel: 0171 291 7255 *Fax:* 0171 436 2850
Website: www.boosey.com

B&H, Peters Edition, ABRSM and other major publishers (cat).

The Bristol Violin Shop
12 Upper Maudlin St, Bristol BS2 8DJ
Tel: 0117 925 9990 *also fax*

Rachel Whitworth, shop mgr.
Makers and repairers of str insts, accs; also special str mus (cat).

Britten's Music Ltd
3 Claremont Rd, W Byfleet, Surrey KT14 6DY
Tel: 01932 354898 *Fax:* 01932 350606

Dot Freeman, mgr.
Mus, books, accs.

Chimes Music Shop
44 Marylebone High St, London W1M 3AD
Tel: 0171 935 1587; 0171 486 1303 *Fax:* 0171 935 0457

Sam Fong, manageress.
Books, insts, mus, cassettes, CDs, vn strs and accs.

Cornelius Edition
29 Lansdown Pl, Lewes, Sussex BN7 2JU
Tel: 01273 473278 *also fax*

Insts, w/wind, br, guis, keyboard; printed mus specialists.

Counterpoint
Newton House, 38 Grantham St, Lincoln LN2 1LW
Tel: 01522 560065

Eileen Lee, proprietor.
Sheet mus, books, CDs, cassettes, educ specialist (cat).

Courtney and Walker Ltd
82-86 Elm Grove, Southsea, Hants PO5 1LN
Tel: 01705 822036 *Fax:* 01705 780799

Education specialists, computerised sheet mus dept. Complete range of insts (classical and rock).

Cremona House Violin Shop
Cremona House, 7 Perry Rd (Park Row), Bristol BS1 5BQ
Tel: 0117 926 4617

Dolmetsch Musical Instruments
Unit 1b, The Unicorn Trading Estate, Weydown Rd,
Haslemere, Surrey GU27 1DN
Tel: 01428 643235 *Fax:* 01428 654920/651473
Email: brian@be-blood.demon.co.uk
Website: www.be-blood.demon.co.uk/under.htm
Brian Blood, mgr dir.
Major suppliers of full range of rcdrs used in
schools and colleges throughout country (cat).

Farnsworth Musical Supplies Ltd
126 Nottingham Rd, Sherwood Rise, Nottingham NG7 7AH
Tel: 0115 960 8955

Byron Newton, company sec.
Insts, mus, accs.

Forsyth Bros Ltd
126 Deansgate, Manchester M3 2GR
Tel: 0161 834 3281 *Fax:* 0161 834 0630
Email: forsythmus@aol.com

Audrey Wilson, Ian Taylor.
Mus, insts, books, recordings, accs supplied.
Educ cats KS1 and 2, KS3 and beyond.

Forwoods Music
35-37 Palace St, Canterbury, Kent CT1 2DZ
Tel: 01227 464741 *Fax:* 01227 762836
Email: forwoods.music@btinternet.com

James Pertwee, Stephen Yarrow, sheet mus;
Keith Wilson, insts.
Sheet mus, books, insts, accs (cat).

Goodmusic
PO Box 100, Tewkesbury, Glos GL20 7YQ
Tel: 01684 773883 *also fax*

David Good, Elizabeth Good.
Mus and books (cat) by m/order only.

H Wright Greaves Ltd
11 Goose Green, Altrincham, Cheshire WA14 1DW
Tel: 0161 929 6949 *Fax:* 0161 926 8280

M W Greaves, mgr; R W Greaves, asst mgr.
Mus, books, accs, gifts.

Hamilton Caswell Violins
9-11 Perry Rd, Park Row, Bristol BS1 5BG
Tel: 0117 929 4642

H Caswell, proprietor; Amelie Caswell, mail-order
mgr.
Strs, bows, cases and accs (cat).

Henley Music
PO Box 2171, Reading RG4 9YS
Tel: 0118 972 4845

Linda Sargeant, proprietor.
Sheet mus, accs.

Hobgoblin Music
17 The Parade, Northgate, Crawley, W Sussex RH10 2DT
Tel: 01293 515858 *Fax:* 01293 851620
Email: post@hobgoblin.co.uk
Website: www.hobgoblin.com

Specialist supplier of insts: folk, ethnic and
education (cat).

Holywell Music Ltd
58 Hopton St, London SE1 9JH
Tel: 0171 928 8451 *Fax:* 0171 928 8284

Suppliers of hps, hp strings and sheet mus for hp
only.

Hope Education
Orb Mill, Huddersfield Rd, Oldham OL4 2ST
Tel: 0161 633 6611 *Fax:* 0161 633 3431

C Proctor, sales dir.
Wide variety of perc, w/wind, keyboard including
Sonor Orff and Yamaha. Plus mus, books, stands,
trollies, cassettes and audio equipment.

Jazzwise
2b Gleneagle Mews, Ambleside Av, London SW16 6AE
Tel: 0181 769 7725 *Fax:* 0181 677 7128

Charles Alexander.
Specialist supplier of jazz repertoire and
instructional material to schools, colleges and
bands.

John Myatt Woodwind & Brass
57 Nightingale Rd, Hitchin, Herts SG5 1RQ
Tel: 01462 420057 *Fax:* 01462 435464
Email: shop@myatt.co.uk
Website: www.myatt.co.uk

Peter Myatt, mgr dir; Clive Reeves, sales mgr.
W/wind and br inst specialists; full repair
w/shop, sheet mus, CDs and all insts (cat).

June Emerson Wind Music
Ampleforth, N Yorks
Tel: 01439 788324 *Fax:* 01439 788715

Tracy Battensby, mgr.
Specialist supplier and publisher of mus for wind
insts and mus from Albania. Catalogues include:
Great Big Flute catalogue; Music for Reed
instruments: ob, cl, saxophone, bsn; Music for
Wind Ensembles; Music for Brass Instruments.

Kensington Music Shop
9 Harrington Rd, London SW7 3ES
Tel: 0171 589 9054 Fax: 0171 225 2662

Mus, books, insts, accs (cat).

Knock on Wood
Unit 131, Glasshouses Mill, Harrogate HG3 5QH
Tel: 01423 712712 also fax
Email: kow@globalnet.co.uk
Website: www.netlink.co.uk/users/nettle/kow

Andy Wilson, partner.
Insts, books, recordings and posters for multicultural mus (cat).

Lindsay Music
23 Hitchin St, Biggleswade, Beds SG18 8AX
Tel: 01767 316521 Fax: 01767 317221

Printed mus specialists: educ, choral, inst, orch. Importer of titles published by World Music Press (USA); supplies UK and abroad (cat).

LMS Music Supplies
154 Sidwell St, Exeter EX4 6RT
Tel: 01392 428108 Fax: 01392 412521
Email: lmsmusic@compuserve.com

David Sharp, Edwina Sharp.
Mus, books, insts, keyboards, educ (cat).

Lovely Music
17 Westgate, Tadcaster, N Yorks LS24 9JB
Tel: 01937 832946 Fax: 01937 835696

Ray Lovely, dir; Lynda Robertson, mgr.
Specialist mus suppliers to schools, colleges, orchs, bands, choirs (various cats).

Mail Order Music
Newmarket Rd, Bury St Edmunds, Suffolk IP33 3YB
Tel: 01284 703097 Fax: 01284 702592
Email: mailorder@musicsales.co.uk
Website: www.musicsales.co.uk

C/room, solo, ens, choral, musical shows. Distributors for Chester Music, Novello, Golden Apple, Shawnee Press, G Schirmer, UME and Youngsongs (cats). See **Music Publishers** Music Sales Ltd, Chester Music and Novello.

Music Direct
33 Tydfil Pl, Roath Pk, Cardiff CF2 5HP
Tel: 01222 496080 Fax: 01222 457760

Bob Welch, mgr.
Mus (all educ categories) and books (specialist cats).

Music Exchange (Manchester) Ltd
12 St Peters Sq, Manchester M2 3DF
Tel: 0161 236 1766

Mrs J Lawless, mgr.
Sheet mus and mus books; also guis, br, w/wind and strs.

Music Supplies Ltd
33 Warwick St, Worthing, W Sussex BN11 3DQ
Tel: 01903 208692; 01903 203437 Fax: 01903 239004

Insts, keyboards, mus, educ supplies.

Musicale plc
The Bourne, 20 Salisbury Av, Harpenden, Herts AL5 2QG
Tel: 01582 769712 Fax: 01582 767343

All printed mus, insts, accs; nationwide and abroad.

Musisca Ltd
20 Wellington La, Montpelier, Bristol BS6 5PY
Tel: 0117 924 0934 also fax

D M Oboussier, dir.
Mus stands, lights, pno stools, cond stands, desk stands, cortols (cat).

N E S Arnold Ltd
Ludlow Hill Rd, West Bridgford, Nottingham NG2 6HD
Tel: 0115 971 7700 Fax: 0500 410420
Email: info@nesarnold
Website: www.nesarnold.co.uk

D J Lansom, divisional dir.
Insts: wind, str, br, tuned perc (glockenspiels, metallophones, xylophones, chimes, chimebars), beaters, untuned perc (African, Asian, Latin American), tambourines, drums, cymbals, guis, electronic keyboards, rcdrs, whistles, panflutes. Publications, mus paper, accs (cat).

Newingtons Music Centre
Grove Hill Rd, Tunbridge Wells, Kent TN1 1RZ
Tel: 01892 526659 Fax: 01892 540611

Helen Macnab.
Classical and educ mus, pnos, insts, keyboards, cassettes, CDs, books, accs, digital pnos, videos (string cat).

Normans Ltd
5 Lady Margaret Ct, Colchester Av, Cardiff CF3 7AW
Tel: 01222 486486 Fax: 01222 486047

W/wind, br insts, perc and tutor books.

Novello & Co Ltd
The Music Sales Group, Newmarket Rd, Bury St
Edmunds, Suffolk IP33 3YB
Tel: 01284 702600 *Fax:* 01284 768301
Email: music@musicsales.co.uk
Website: www.musicsales.co.uk

Harriet Gedge, sales mgr; Deborah Watson, mkt mgr.
Choral (including school cantatas), inst, wind and str ens, c/room mus at KS1-4, Science Press Books. Music Sales Education and Music Shows for Schools catalogues.

Out of the Ark Music
The School House, 15 Esher Green, Esher, Surrey KT10 8AA
Tel: 01372 463274 *Fax:* 01372 463351

M Johnson, partner; G Powell, sales mgr.
Songbook and cassette packages, resources for nursery, reception and KS1-3 musical plays and songbooks. Cat available with free sample cassettes.

Paxman Musical Instruments Ltd
Linton House, 164-180 Union St, London SE1 0LH
Tel: 0171 620 2077 *Fax:* 0171 620 1688
Email: paxmanhorn@compuserve.com

Makers and suppliers of French hns (including Studenti range); retailers of hns and repairs.

Rapid Music Ltd
Freepost GI 2353, 23 Old Malt Way, Woking, Surrey GU21 4QD
Tel: 01483 763603 *Fax:* 01483 720522
Email: mbarnett@macline.co.uk

Michael Barnett; Carol White, dirs.
Mus by m/order (cat).

Recorder & Woodwind Centre
5 Dorset St, London W1H 3FE
Tel: 0171 935 8252 *Fax:* 0171 224 2053
Email: afp@allflutesplus.co.uk

Jane Vickers, rcdr specialist.
Specialist suppliers of rcdrs, ranging from educ to professional insts (cat).

Robert Morley & Co Ltd
34 Engate St, Lewisham, London SE13 7HA
Tel: 0181 318 5838 *Fax:* 0181 297 0720
Website: www.yell.co.uk/sites/morley

Julia Morley.
Pnos and early keyboard insts (cat).

Schott Universal Edition
48 Great Marlborough St, London W1V 2BN
Tel: 0171 437 1246 *Fax:* 0171 437 0263
Email: 101627.166@compuserve.com
Website: www.schott-music.com

Classical sheet mus; publishers of classical and contemporary mus (cat).

Soar Valley Music
15 Prince William Rd, Loughborough, Leics LE11 5GU
Tel: 01509 269629 *Fax:* 01509 269206

David Ledsam, Martin Tabraham.
Folk and world sheet mus, celtic and latin insts, perc. UK agents Raul, Gope and Kambala perc (cat).

Sounds Write
56 Baswich Crest, Stafford ST17 0HJ
Tel: 01785 250405 *Fax:* 01785 663576

Keith Baskett, mgr of mkt and sales.
Theory work books for young beginners to gr 3 following the ABRSM syllabus. Material offers a structured and fun approach through its child-centred method of teaching. Applicable to any inst and does not require keyboard skills. Free brochure available.

Spanish Guitar Centre
44 Nottingham Rd, New Basford, Nottingham NG7 7AE
Tel: 0115 962 2709 *Fax:* 0115 962 5368
Email: 101772.613@compuserve.com

A Liepins, mus dir.
Specialists in classical guis, printed mus and accs (cat).

Stamford Music Shop
4 Cattlemarket Rd, Peterborough
Tel: 01733 345385 *also fax; Fax:* 01733 559158

Sheet mus, insts.

Stamford Music Shop
11 St Mary's Hill, Stamford, Lincs PE9 2DP
Tel: 01780 751275 *Fax:* 01780 752245

Sheet mus, CDs, cassettes, insts.

Swales Music Centre Ltd
2-6 High St, Haverfordwest, Pembrokeshire
Tel: 01437 762059/763261 *Fax:* 01437 760872

Pat Swales Barker, Freda Swales Shewry, dirs.
Large selection of sheet mus, books on mus, records, cassettes, CDs, insts and accs (choral cat).

Sycamore Learning Aids
22 Sycamore Close, Dukinfield, Cheshire SK16 5EN
Tel: 0161 338 2647 *also fax*

Christine Caton-Greasey, Lesley Bunce, partners.
Award and assessment systems, gifts, novelties,

medals, rossettes, Music Teacher Business Journal, progress certificates, theory products (cat).

Tapp (Music) Ltd
Time and Tune, 14-16 Otley St, Skipton, N Yorks BD23 1DZ
Tel: 01756 797513 *Fax:* 01756 701215

Sheet mus supply service for pno teachers (pno mus and other titles), insts, accs, CDs (cat £2.50).

Underground Sounds Ltd
108-110 St James' Rd, Tunbridge Wells, Kent TN1 2HH
Tel: 01892 533778 *Fax:* 01892 515026

Retailers of br, w/wind, guis, keyboards, drums, perc, mus books for inst and c/room use.

Whitwams Ltd
70 High St, Winchester, Hants SO23 9DE
Tel: 01962 865253 *Fax:* 01962 842064

LEA, school suppliers of printed mus, books, perc, pnos, guis, keyboard insts, educ recordings, CDs and cassettes, audio accessories.

William Elkin Music Services
Station Rd Industrial Estate, Salhouse, Norwich, Norfolk NR13 6NS
Tel: 01603 721302 *Fax:* 01603 721801

Peter Todd, retail mgr.
Sheet mus, books, mus gifts (cat).

Wind Mail Associates
The South Wing, Lullingstone Castle, Eynsford, Kent DA4 0JA
Tel: 01322 862455 *Fax:* 01322 866154

Trevor Edwards, mgr dir.
Publishers of the Wind Band Catalogue and the Jazz and Stage Band Catalogue.

Yamaha Software Direct
Yamaha-Kemble Music (UK) Ltd, Sherbourne Dr, Tilbrook, Milton Keynes, MK7 8BL
Tel: 01908 366700 *Fax:* 01908 368872

Yamaha disks, cartridges, accs, owner's guide videos, CDs, books.

Instrument Manufacturers

The following manufacturers, distributors and wholesalers are able to supply a wide range of instruments designed and produced specifically for educational use. Following this is the **Brand Name Directory** which lists educational instruments together with their source of distribution.

Acorn (Percussion) Ltd
Unit 33, Abbey Business Centre, Ingate Pl, London SW8 3NS
Tel: 0171 720 2243 (24 hrs) *Fax:* 0171 627 8883

Richard Benson, dir; Marguerite Vetter, dir of sales.
Manufacturer and supplier of multi-cultural and general schools perc insts. All age groups and abilities catered for. Tuned perc also available.

Andrew Wooderson Early Keyboard Instruments
5 Bourne Rd, Bexley, Kent DA5 1LG
Tel: 01322 525558 *also fax;* 01322 558326 (w/shops)

Hpds, spinets, virginals, f-pnos and clvds built to order. Also second-hand insts, hire, repair and maintenance.

Barnes and Mullins Ltd
155 Grays Inn Rd, London WC1X 8UF
Tel: 0171 278 4631/3 *Fax:* 0171 837 2184

Bill Lewington Ltd
144 Shaftesbury Av, London WC2H 8HN
Tel: 0171 240 0584 *Fax:* 0171 240 2919
Email: sales@bill-lewington.com
Website: www.bill-lewington.com

M Seymour, sales mgr.

Boosey & Hawkes Musical Instruments Ltd
Deansbrook Rd, Edgware, Middx HA8 9BB
Tel: 0181 952 7711 *Fax:* 0181 951 3556

Bösendorfer Pianos
142 Edgware Rd, Marble Arch, London W2 2DZ
Tel: 0171 724 3510 *Fax:* 0171 224 8692

Clive Morley Harps
Goodfellows, Filkins, Nr Lechlade, Glos GL7 3JG
Tel: 01367 860493 *Fax:* 01367 860659
Email: morley@harps.demon.co.uk
Website: www.demon.co.uk:80/harps/index.html

Cremona House Violin Shop
Cremona House, 7 Perry Rd, (Park Row), Bristol BS1 5BQ
Tel: 0117 926 4617

Richard Bristow.

Derek Roberts Violins
185 Leam Terrace, Leamington Spa, Warwicks CV31 1DW
Tel: 01926 428313 *also fax*

Vns, vas, vcs.

Dolmetsch Musical Instruments
Unit 1b, The Unicorn Trading Estate, Weydown Rd, Haslemere, Surrey GU27 1DN
Tel: 01428 643235 *Fax:* 01428 654920
Email: brian@be-blood.demon.co.uk
Website: www.be-blood.demon.co.uk/index.htm

Brian Blood, mgr dir.
Rcdrs, early keyboard and str insts, repairs and restoration of mus insts.

Forsyth Bros Ltd
126 Deansgate, Manchester M3 2GR
Tel: 0161 834 3281 *Fax:* 0161 834 0630
Email: forsythmus@aol.com

Hibernian Violins
24 Players Av, Malvern Link, Worcs WR14 1DU
Tel: 01684 562947

Padraig ó Dubhlaoidh, proprietor.
Str insts. Also restoration.

John Hornby Skewes & Co Ltd
Salem House, Parkinson Approach, Garforth, Leeds LS25 2HR
Tel: 0113 286 5381 *Fax:* 0113 286 8515

Robert Deakin, sales office mgr; Helen Byres, educ co-ord.
Also many accs from straps to amp equipment and inst cleaners.

Kemble & Co Ltd
Mount Av, Bletchley, Milton Keynes MK1 1JE
Tel: 01908 371771 *Fax:* 01908 270448
Website: www.airtime.co.uk/forte/kemble.htm

Brian Kemble, joint mgr dir.

Korg UK Ltd
9 Newmarket Ct, Kingston, Milton Keynes MK10 0AU
Tel: 01908 857100 *Fax:* 01908 857199

Distributor.

INSTRUMENT MANUFACTURERS

Musisca Ltd
Piccadilly Mill, Lower St, Stroud, Glos GL5 2HT
Tel: 01453 751911 *also fax*
Marc Oboussier, dir.

Percussion Plus
The Mill, Great Bowden Rd, Market Harborough, Leics
LE16 7DE
Tel: 01858 433124 *Fax:* 01858 462218

The Piano Warehouse
30a Highgate Rd, London NW5 1NS
Tel: 0171 267 9229 *Fax:* 0171 284 0083
Email: sales@piano.workshop.co.uk

Pilgrim Harps
Stansted House, Tilburstow Hill Rd, S Godstone, Surrey
RH9 8NA
Tel: 01342 893242 *Fax:* 01342 892646
Pedal and lever hps and accs.

Premier Percussion Ltd
Blaby Rd, Wigston, Leicestershire LE18 4DF
Tel: 0116 277 3121 *Fax:* 0116 277 6627

Robert Morley & Co Ltd
34 Engate St, Lewisham, London SE13 7HA
Tel: 0181 318 5838 *Fax:* 0181 297 0720
Website: www.yell.co.uk/sites/morley
Julia Morley.
Pnos, hpds, spinets, virginals, clvds, celestes (cat).

Rosetti Ltd
4 Tamdown Way, Springwood Industrial Estate, Braintree,
Essex CM7 2QL
Tel: 01376 550033 *Fax:* 01376 550042
Distributors.

Stentor Music Co Ltd
Albert Rd North, Reigate, Surrey RH2 9EZ
Tel: 01737 240226 *Fax:* 01737 242748
Email: stentor@webmusic.demon.co.uk

T W Howarth & Co Ltd
31-35 Chiltern St, London W1M 1HG
Tel: 0171 935 2407 *Fax:* 0171 224 2564
Email: sales@howarth.demon.co.uk
Website: www.howarth.demon.co.uk
W/wind insts: student and professional makes of obs d'amore and eh, professional cl and bsn.

Tucker, Anne and Ian
4 High St, Mistley, Essex CO11 1HA
Tel: 01206 393670/393884 *also fax*
Email: ian.tucker@virgin.net
Makers of hpds, spinets and clavichords; restoration, tuning and maintenance.

Vincent Bach International Ltd
Unit 71, Capitol Park Industrial Estate, Capitol Way,
Edgware Rd, London NW9 0EW
Tel: 0181 905 9505 *Fax:* 0181 905 9149

Whelpdale, Maxwell & Codd Ltd
154 Clapham Pk Rd, London SW4 7DE
Tel: 0171 978 2444 *Fax:* 0171 978 2347
K Beckingham, group sales mgr.
Pnos.

Woolley, Dennis
Tubhole Barn, Dent, Sedbergh, W Yorks LA10 5RE
Tel: 015396 25361
Hpd, f-pno.

Yamaha-Kemble Music (UK) Ltd
Sherbourne Dr, Tilbrook, Milton Keynes MK7 8BL
Tel: 01908 366700 *Fax:* 01908 368872

Brand Name Directory

The list features the brand names of orchestral instruments and string bows, but not replacement strings, tuners or electronic amplification.

Acme *Whistles and bird calls* see John Hornby Skewes & Co Ltd.

Acorn *Perc* see Acorn (Percussion) Ltd.

Adamas *Gui* see John Hornby Skewes & Co Ltd.

Adler *Rcdr* see John Hornby Skewes & Co Ltd.

Adler See Vincent Bach International Ltd.

Alfred Knoll *Bows* see Stentor Music Co Ltd.

Almansa *Gui* see John Hornby Skewes & Co Ltd.

Amati *Br, w/wind* see Rosetti Ltd.

AMR *Hand-made tpt, cornet, tb* see Bill Lewington Ltd.

Andreas Zeller *Vn, va, vc, db* see Stentor Music Co Ltd.

Angel *Perc* see John Hornby Skewes & Co Ltd.

Antoni *Vn, vc, va* see John Hornby Skewes & Co Ltd.

Antonio Lorca *Gui (student classical)* see Stentor Music Co Ltd.

Aoyama *Hp* see Clive Morley Harps.

Applause *Gui* see John Hornby Skewes & Co Ltd.

Aranjuez *Gui, str* see Stentor Music Co Ltd.

Asturias *Gui* see Stentor Music Co Ltd.

B & H 400 Series *Br, w/wind, str* see Boosey & Hawkes Musical Instruments Ltd.

Bach 300 *Br* see Vincent Bach International Ltd.

Beltone *Tpt, cornet* see Stentor Music Co Ltd.

Bentley *Pno* see Whelpdale, Maxwell & Codd Ltd.

Besson Brass Instruments *Br* see Boosey & Hawkes Musical Instruments Ltd.

The Blues *Harmonica* see John Hornby Skewes & Co Ltd.

Blüthner *Pno* see Whelpdale, Maxwell & Codd Ltd.

BM *Perc, flageolet* see Barnes & Mullins Ltd.

Bösendorfer *Pno* see Bösendorfer Pianos.

Broadwood *Pno* see Whelpdale, Maxwell & Codd Ltd.

Buffet Crampon *Cl, fl, ob, harmony insts* see Boosey & Hawkes Musical Instruments Ltd.

Camber *Cymbals* see John Hornby Skewes & Co Ltd.

Cecilia *Hp* see Clive Morley Harps.

Celebrity *Gui* see John Hornby Skewes & Co Ltd.

Century *Sax, fl, tpt, cl* see John Hornby Skewes & Co Ltd.

Chappell *Pno* see Kemble and Co Ltd.

Corelli *Vn, va, vc, db, str* see Stentor Music Co Ltd.

Cortol *Alto, tenor curtal* see Musisca Ltd.

Diamond *Perc* see Acorn (Percussion) Ltd.

Dogal *Vn, va, vc, db, str* see Stentor Music Co Ltd.

Dolmetsch *Rcdr, hpd, spinet, clvd, viol, hp, lute, rebec* see Dolmetsch Musical Instruments.

Dvorak *Vn family, gui* see Rosetti Ltd.

Earlham *Rcdr, sax, br, w/wind* see Bill Lewington Ltd.

Elkhart *Br, w/wind* see Vincent Bach International Ltd.

Elysian Harps *Hp* see Clive Morley Harps.

Elysian Pianos *Upright, grand pno* see Robert Morley & Co Ltd.

Encore *Gui and str* see John Hornby Skewes & Co Ltd.

Epiphone *Gui* see Rosetti Ltd.

Fairfield *Db* see Stentor Music Co Ltd.

Falcon *Gui* see John Hornby Skewes & Co Ltd.

Feddog *Whistles and tutors* see John Hornby Skewes & Co Ltd.

Gehr Steinberg *Pno* see Whelpdale, Maxwell & Codd Ltd.

Generation *Flageolet* see John Hornby Skewes & Co Ltd.

Gibson *Gui* see Rosetti Ltd.

Golden Spiral *Str* see Stentor Music Co Ltd.

Grassi *Sax, fl* see Bill Lewington Ltd.

Grotrian Steinweg *Upright, grand pno* see Robert Morley & Co Ltd.

Hall *Crystal fl and piccs* see Bill Lewington Ltd.

Hero *Harmonica, accordion* see John Hornby Skewes & Co Ltd.

Hibernian *Vn* see Hibernian Violins.

Hofner *Str* see Boosey & Hawkes Musical Instruments Ltd.

Hokada (Trio) *Gui (student models)* see Stentor Music Co Ltd.

Hopkinson *Pno* see Whelpdale, Maxwell & Codd Ltd.

Howarth *Ob, cl, bsn* see T W Howarth & Co Ltd.

Iwao *Fl* see Bill Lewington Ltd.

JHS Hornby *Rcdr* see John Hornby Skewes & Co Ltd.

Jo-Ral *Mutes* see Bill Lewington Ltd.

John Morley *Hpd, clvd, virginal, spinet, celeste* see Robert Morley & Co Ltd.

Joseph Bernard *Vn, va* see Stentor Music Co Ltd.

Jupiter *Br, w/wind* see Korg UK Ltd.

Keilwerth Sax See Boosey & Hawkes Musical Instruments Ltd.

Kemble *Pno* see Kemble and Co Ltd.

Knight *Pno* see Whelpdale, Maxwell & Codd Ltd.

Korg *Synthesizers, digital pnos* see Korg UK Ltd.

Kun *Vn, va* see Stentor Music Co Ltd.

Lark *Vn, cornet, tpt, fl, cl* see John Hornby Skewes & Co Ltd.

Latin Percussion *Perc* see Rosetti Ltd.

LP *Perc* see Acorn (Percussion) Ltd.

Manuel Contreras *Gui* see Stentor Music Co Ltd.

Manuel Rodriguez *Gui* see John Hornby Skewes & Co Ltd.

Mapex *Drums* see Korg UK Ltd.

Marshall & Rose *Pno* see Whelpdale, Maxwell & Codd Ltd.

Meinl *Perc* see Acorn (Percussion) Ltd.

Metro *School perc* see Barnes & Mullins.

Mistral *Fl, sax, cl* see Stentor Music Co Ltd.

Monington & Weston *Upright, grand pno* see Robert Morley & Co Ltd.

Monnig *Br, w/wind* see Vincent Bach International Ltd.

Moreno *Gui* see Stentor Music Co Ltd.

Morley *Hp* see Clive Morley Harps.

Muramatsu *Fl* see Bill Lewington Ltd.

Olds *Tpt, cornet, flugel hn, tb, hn, picc, fl, cl* see Bill Lewington Ltd.

Ozark *Gui, fretted insts* see Stentor Music Co Ltd.

P & H *Bows* see Stentor Music Co Ltd.

Paesold *Str* see Boosey & Hawkes Musical Instruments Ltd.

Palma *Gui* see John Hornby Skewes & Co Ltd.

Parker *Gui* see Korg UK Ltd.

Percussion Plus *Perc* see Percussion Plus.

Performance Percussion *Perc* see John Hornby Skewes & Co Ltd.

Pilgrim *Hp* see Pilgrim Harps.

Pirastro *Str* see Stentor Music Co Ltd.

Premier *Perc* see Premier Percussion.

Prince *Gui* see Rosetti Ltd.

Pro Arte *Vn, str* see Stentor Music Co Ltd.

Rahma *Rcdr* see Stentor Music Co Ltd.

Regal Tip *Perc* see John Hornby Skewes & Co Ltd.

Remo *Perc* see Acorn (Percussion) Ltd.

Rhythm Tech *Perc* see John Hornby Skewes & Co Ltd.

Ricardo Sanchis *Gui* see Stentor Music Co Ltd.

Richard Lipp & Sohn *Pno* see Whelpdale, Maxwell & Codd Ltd.

Rickenbacker *Gui* see Rosetti Ltd.

Rico *W/wind* see Barnes & Mullins.

Rogers *Pno* see Whelpdale, Maxwell & Codd Ltd.

Rosetti *W/wind, str orch* see Rosetti Ltd.

Rudolf Fiedler *Vn, va, vc, db* see Stentor Music Co Ltd.

Savarez *Gui, str* see Stentor Music Co Ltd.

Schimmel *Pno* see Forsyth Bros Ltd.

Schreiber *Bn* see Boosey & Hawkes Musical Instruments Ltd.

Selmer Paris I *Br, w/wind* see Vincent Bach International Ltd.

Selmer USA I *W/wind* see Vincent Bach International Ltd.

Shimro *Vn* see Stentor Music Co Ltd.

Signet *Br, w/wind* see Vincent Bach International Ltd.

Skylark *Vn, va, bows* see John Hornby Skewes & Co Ltd.

Sound *Perc* see Acorn (Percussion) Ltd.

Steinmeyer *Pno* see Piano Warehouse.

Stentor *Vn, va, vc* see Stentor Music Co Ltd.

Sterling *Br* see Stentor Music Co Ltd.

Takamine *Gui* see Korg UK Ltd.

Vandoren *W/wind and accs* see Rosetti Ltd.

Vantage *Gui* see Korg UK Ltd.

Vintage *Gui, concertinas and melodeons* see John Hornby Skewes & Co Ltd.

Weber *Pno* see Piano Warehouse.

Welmar *Pno* see Whelpdale, Maxwell & Codd Ltd.

Wolf *Vn, va* see Stentor Music Co Ltd.

Yamaha *Keyboard, pno, hi-tech synthesizer, br, w/wind, gui, drums* see Yamaha-Kemble Music (UK) Ltd.

Yanagisawa *Sax* see Barnes & Mullins.

Young Chang *Pno* see Piano Warehouse.

Zildjian *Cymbals* see Yamaha-Kemble Music (UK) Ltd.

Instrument Repairers

This section includes instrument repair workshops and retailers with on-site repair facilities. Some **Retailers** (see relevant section) act as outlets for repair workshops.

Aldershot Music Ltd
45 Station Rd, Aldershot, Hants GU11 1BD
Tel: 01252 343085 *Fax:* 01252 325560

John Malley, snr br repairer.
Br.

All Flutes Plus
5 Dorset St, London W1H 3FE
Tel: 0171 935 3339 *Fax:* 0171 224 2053
Email: afp@allflutesplus.co.uk

Danny Paul, w/shop mgr.
Specialist fl repairers.

Allen Organs
Trada Business Campus, Stocking La, Hughenden Valley, High Wycombe, Bucks HP14 4ND
Tel: 01494 563833 *Fax:* 01494 563546

Paul Arkwright, UK service mgr.
Repair of Allen orgs only.

Andrew Wooderson Early Keyboard Instruments
5 Bourne Rd, Bexley, Kent DA5 1LG
Tel: 01322 558326; 01322 525558 *also fax*

Tuning, maintenance, repair and restoration of early keyboard insts. Also concert hire, new insts built to order.

Ashton Instrument Repairs Ltd
13 Mewmarket Rd, Ashton-under-Lyne, Lancs OL7 9LL
Tel: 0161 330 7176

Br band insts.

Band Supplies
7 Hunslet Rd, Leeds LS10 1JQ
Tel: 0113 245 3097 *Fax:* 0113 234 1602

W/wind, br. Also sales.

Band Supplies (Scotland)
5 Old Dumbarton Rd, Glasgow G3 8QY
Tel: 0141 339 9400 *Fax:* 0141 334 8157

Ronnie Tennant, mgr; Raymond Tennant, rep; Andy Burnley, repairer.
W/wind, br, perc, strs.

Bill Lewington
144 Shaftesbury Av, London WC2H 8HN
Tel: 0171 240 0584 *Fax:* 0171 240 2919
Email: sales@bill-lewington.com
Website: www.bill-lewington.com

Samantha Pett.
Br, w/wind; discounts for schools.

Blackburn Stringed Instruments
75 Harrington Gardens, London SW7 4JZ
Tel: 0171 373 2474 *Fax:* 0171 373 5141

Repairs, restorations, valuations for vns, vas, vcs and bows.

The Bridge Fiddler
Riverside House, Chapel Milton, Chapel-en-le-Frith, High Peak SK23 0QQ
Tel: 01298 813813

John Goodborn.
Str inst and bow repairer, restorer and dealer, including db.

Bristol Music Shop
30 College Green, Bristol BS1 5TB
Tel: 0117 929 0390

Br and w/wind repairs and restoration.

Cambridge Music Shop
1a All Saints Passage, Cambridge CB2 3LT
Tel: 01223 351786 *Fax:* 01223 464178

Str, w/wind, bows.

Cambridge Pianola Company
The Limes, Landbeach, Cambridge CB4 4DR
Tel: 01223 861348 *Fax:* 01223 441276

F T Poole, proprietor.
Pno and pianola restoration, sales and rentals.

Cambridge Reed Organs
18 Hill Close, Newmarket, Suffolk CB8 0NR
Tel: 01638 660531 *also fax*

Bruce Dracott, proprietor.
Harmonium restoration, repair, tuning and hire. Also celeste hire.

Cavalier Music
145 Barncroft Way, Havant, Hampshire PO9 3AF
Tel: 01705 475923

B L Boughton.
Br and w/wind repairs.

Chandler Guitars
300-302 Sandycombe Rd, Kew, Richmond, Surrey TW9 3NG
Tel: 0181 940 5874 *Fax:* 0181 332 6255

Charlie Chandler, w/shop mgr.
3 f/t repairers. Fretted insts (including refinishing), gui amplifiers and FX.

Clevedon Music Shop
19 Alexandra Rd, Clevedon, Somerset BS21 7QH
Tel: 01275 342090 *also fax;* 01275 791181

Keyboards, small perc, insts.

Clive Morley Harps Ltd
Goodfellows, Filkins, Nr Lechlade, Glos GL7 3JG
Tel: 01367 860493 *Fax:* 01367 860659
Email: morley@harps.demon.co.uk
Website: www.demon.co.uk:80/harps/index.html

Hp restoration.

Coad, Lucy
Workshop 3, Greenway Farm, Bath Rd, Wick, Nr Bristol BS15 1RL
Tel: 0117 937 4949 *also fax*

Square pno conservation and repairs.

Countrywide Piano Centre Ltd
194 Penn Rd, Hazlemere, High Wycombe, Bucks HP15 7NU
Tel: 01494 813388 *Fax:* 01494 813994

Pno restoration, tuning; school, churches, educ discount.

Courtney & Walker Ltd
82-86 Elm Grove, Southsea, Hants
Tel: 01705 822036 *Fax:* 01705 780799

Pno, strs, fretted strs, w/wind, br.

Cremona House Violin Shop
Cremona House, 7 Perry Rd, (Park Row), Bristol BS1 5BQ
Tel: 0117 926 4617

Richard Bristow.
Vn repairs.

David Newton Violins at Potters Music
12-16 High St, Merstham, Surrey RH1 3EA
Tel: 01737 645065 *Fax:* 01737 645808

Emma Newton, mgr.
Strs, bows; also sales, vns and accs.

David Snelling Violins
9 Station St, Kibworth Beauchamp, Leicester LE8 0LN
Tel: 0116 279 3212 *Fax:* 0116 279 6260

Vn, va and vc repairs and sales.

Davies, Peter
The Woodwind Workshop, 2nd Floor, Byram Arcade, Westgate, Huddersfield HD1 1ND
Tel: 01484 533053 *also fax*

Glenn Groves, cl repairer; Stephen Crow, sax repairer.
Repair and restoration of ob family of insts, plus repair all other w/wind.

de Vere White, Graham
57 Nightingale Rd, Hitchin, Herts SG5 1RQ
Tel: 01462 421402 *Fax:* 01462 812473
Email: tracey@gdeverewtrepairs.demon.co.uk

W/wind, br.

Derek Hossle Woodwind Repairs
26 Andrew St, Mossley, Ashton-under-Lyne OL5 0DN
Tel: 01457 835656

W/wind, br.

Derek Roberts Violins
185 Leam Terrace, Leamington Spa, Warwicks CV31 1DW
Tel: 01926 428313

Maker and restorer of vns, vas, vcs.

The Dulwich Music Shop
2 Croxted Rd, Dulwich, London SE21 8SW
Tel: 0181 766 0202 *Fax:* 0181 766 8689

Inst repairs.

Dunkley, Clive
25 Foxenden Rd, Guildford, Surrey GU1 4DL
Tel: 01483 37685

Repair, tuning and maintenance of hpds, virginals and clvds.

Forsyth Bros Ltd
126 Deansgate, Manchester M3 2GR
Tel: 0161 834 3281 *Fax:* 0161 834 0630
Email: forsythmus@aol.com

Pno tuning and restoration, w/wind, br, strs.

Frank Fidler
Supplies and Repairs, The Old Dairy, The Square, Ruardean, Glos GL17 9TJ
Tel: 01594 544053

W/wind, br, perc; educ discount.

Frederick Phelps Ltd
67 Fortess Rd, London NW5 1AG
Tel: 0171 482 0316 *Fax:* 0171 813 4589

Rachel Douglas, dir; Andreas Hudelmayer, head of w/shop.
Vn family insts and accs: sales, restorations and valuations.

Frith, Stephen C
22 Ewhurst Close, West Green, Crawley, Sussex RH11 7EZ
Tel: 01293 543055

Gui maker and repairer.

G Morris & Sons
41 Palmerston Rd, Buckhurst Hill, Essex IG9 5PA
Tel: 0181 502 9988

Pno tuning, maintenance, repair and restoration.

George Veness Workshop
Stanhope Studio, Donald Way, Winchelsea, E Sussex TN36 4NH
Tel: 01797 225878

Hpd and clvd sales and repairs.

Gibson Music
5 St John Maddermarket, Norwich, Norfolk NR2 1DN
Tel: 01603 663262 *also fax*

All orch insts.

Glissando Music Repairs
2 Arthur Cottages, Frimley Rd, Ash Vale, Aldershot GU12 5PD
Tel: 01252 518098 *also fax*
Email: glissmus@aol.com

Specialises in services and repairs of w/wind, br and str insts for schools and colleges.

Gordon Stevenson Violins
6 Barclay Terrace, Bruntsfield, Edinburgh EH10 4HP
Tel: 0131 229 2051 *Fax:* 0131 229 9298

Dealer and restorer in fine vns and str insts.

Graham Webb Music
6-8 Bridge St, Leighton Buzzard, Beds LU7 7AL
Tel: 01525 376622 *Fax:* 01525 850628

Elec keyboard, org, pnos, w/wind, br and some guis.

Hampstead Piano Services
131 Abbey Rd, London NW6 4SL
Tel: 0171 624 8895 *Fax:* 0181 245 4652

Tom Walter, mgr.
Pno sales and repairs, new and second-hand, valuers and consultants.

Hansford, Neil
12 Upper Maudlin St, Bristol BS2 8DJ
Tel: 0117 925 9990 *also fax*

Viols; Eng, Fr, Ger, Ital baroque vcs.

The Harpsichord Workshop
130 Westbourne Terrace Mews, London W2 6QG
Tel: 0171 723 9650 *also fax*

Mark Ransom.
Tuning, repair, renovation and hire.

Hibernian Violins
24 Players Av, Malvern Link, Worcs WR14 1DU
Tel: 01684 562947

Padraig ó Dubhlaoidh, proprietor.
Str maker and restorer.

Hickies Ltd
153 Friar St, Reading, Berks RG1 1HG
Tel: 0118 957 5771 *Fax:* 0118 957 5775

Pno restorations; w/wind and br repairs; discount to schools.

Impact Percussion
120-122 Bermondsey St, London SE1 3TX
Tel: 0171 403 5900 *Fax:* 0171 403 5910
Email: impactperc@msn.com

Paul Hagen, proprietor; Steve Newton, engineer.
All perc. Discounts for schools on new parts or insts. Quick turn-around.

Ivor Mairants Musicentre
56 Rathbone Pl, London W1P 1AB
Tel: 0171 636 1481 *Fax:* 0171 580 6272

Phil Lusher, mgr.
Gui, fretted str insts. Electric gui repairs.

J & A Beare Ltd
7 Broadwick St, London W1V 1FJ
Tel: 0171 437 1449 *Fax:* 0171 439 4520

Restoration of fine strs; dealer and valuations.

J & L Dawkes
652 Bath Rd, Taplow SL6 0NZ
Tel: 01628 604404

W/wind and br insts.

J P Guivier & Co Ltd
99 Mortimer St, London W1N 7TA
Tel: 0171 580 2560; 0171 636 6499 *Fax:* 0171 436 1461

Richard White, Robin Hamilton, dirs.
Str repairs, also dealer in vn, va, vc, together with bows, cases, strs and other accs.

J Reid Pianos
184 St Ann's Rd, Tottenham, London N15 5RP
Tel: 0181 800 6907 *Fax:* 0181 809 0767

Pno repair and restoration; educ discount and retail.

Klef Music Ltd
118 Magdalen St, Norwich, Norfolk NR3 1JD
Tel: 01603 612396

Gui.

Len Stiles Musical Instruments
268 Lewisham High St, London SE13 6JX
Tel: 0181 690 7771 *also fax;* 0181 690 2958

Keyboards, pnos, synths, hi-tech, br, w/wind, vns, guis, amps. Also repairs.

Longstaff & Jones
6 Vicar St, Oakengates, Telford, Shropshire TF2 6BJ
Tel: 01952 613788 *also fax*

Restoration and maintenance of pipe orgs, tuning contractors.

Louandy's Music Shop
93 Albert Rd, Colne, Lancashire BB8 0BS
Tel: 01282 868045

Amps, elec gui, PA, plus all related accs.

Lyons Musicale Ltd
The Bourne, 20 Salisbury Av, Harpenden, Herts AL5 2QG
Tel: 01582 460978 *Fax:* 01582 767343

David Johnston, mgr dir.
Lyons C clarinet.

McQueens Musical Instruments
Sunset Business Centre, Manchester Rd, Kearsley, Bolton BL4 8RT
Tel: 01204 794600 *also fax*

Repairers of br and w/wind. Manufacturers of bugles, cavalry tpts. Contractors to MOD.

Maestros_including_ **Mainly Music**
19 Market St, Tavistock, Devon PL19 0DE
Tel: 01822 614074

Str, w/wind, br; educ discounts, sales of sheet mus; m/order.

Markson Pianos
36-38 Artillery Pl, Woolwich, London SE18 4AB
Tel: 0181 854 4517 *Fax:* 0181 317 1076

Repairs. Also sales, hire, restoration, tuning, transport, educ discounts.

Markson Pianos Ltd
8 Chester Ct, Albany St, London NW1 4BU
Tel: 0171 935 8682 *Fax:* 0171 224 0957
Email: marksonpianos@compuserve.com

Repairs. Also sales, hire (including short-term hire for concerts), restoration, tuning, maintenance, transport; educ discounts.

Martin Restall Violins
6 Stonemasons Ct, Parchment St, Winchester, Hants
Tel: 01962 841514

Musical Instruments Repairs and Sales
Hereward Rise, Halesowen, W Midlands B62 8AN
Tel: 0121 550 9707 *Fax:* 0121 501 3873
Email: mir@cableinet.co.uk

W/wind, br, gui, str, perc, keyboards, mus, new and secondhand.

Musical Instruments Repairs and Sales
57 Martley Rd, St Johns, Worcester WR2 6HH
Tel: 01905 420241 *also fax*

W/wind, br, gui, strs. Also sales.

Musicparts (UK)
PO Box 25, Tyldesley, Manchester M29 7GJ
Tel: 07071 223698 *Fax:* 01942 889452

Peter Pollard, master craftsman; Christopher Hirst, repair technician; Anne Langer, repair technician; Stewart Harrison, repair technician. Repairers and restorers of br and w/wind insts. Custom making of br insts. Customising of w/wind and br insts. M/order service for accs, etc. Courses in inst repair.

Myatt (John) Woodwind and Brass
57 Nightingale Rd, Hitchin, Herts SG5 1RQ
Tel: 01462 420057 *Fax:* 01462 435464

Full repair w/wind and br w/shop.

Odell, Nick
The Music Workshop, PO Box 45, Upwell, Wisbech, Cambs PE14 9AZ
Tel: 01945 772423 *also fax*

Repairer of str insts: vn family; guis, early and folk.

Oundle Music Shop
13 West St, Oundle, Peterborough PE8 4EJ
Tel: 01832 273669

Str, w/wind, br, all general repairs including educ perc.

Paxman Musical Instruments Ltd
Linton House, 164-180 Union St, London SE1 0LH
Tel: 0171 620 1990 *Fax:* 0171 620 1688
Email: 106156.2732@compuserve.com;
paxmanhorn@compuserve.com

David Botwe, w/shop mgr.
Br.

Perfect Pitch
72 The Broadway, Chesham, Bucks HP5 1EG
Tel: 01494 774826 *Fax:* 01494 778353

Str, w/wind.

Phelps Pianos
49 Fortess Rd, London NW5 1AD
Tel: 0171 485 2042 *Fax:* 0171 284 1404

Pno; repairs, restoration, sales, hire, tuning, educ discounts.

Phil Parker Ltd
106a Crawford St, London W1H 1AL
Tel: 0171 486 8206 *Fax:* 0171 935 6686

Br.

Ranger, Jonathan (Pianos)
5 Summerfield Rd, London W5 1ND
Tel: 0181 997 1793 *also fax*

Jonathan Ranger, dir.
Repairer, restorer and tuner of historic and modern pnos, hpds, square pnos, f-pnos, spinets, clvds, virginals. Preparation and tuning for concerts, etc. Information service.

Ransom, Mark
130 Westbourne Terrace Mews, London W2 6QG
Tel: 0171 723 9650 *also fax*

Tuning, maintenance, hire, transport of hpds.

Reg Thorp Woodwind Repair
13 Pinewood Way, Midhurst, W Sussex GU29 9LN
Tel: 01730 814782

Reg Thorp, proprietor.
W/wind repair and renovation, and making early cls.

Richmond Music Shop
16 Red Lion St, Richmond, Surrey TW9 1RW
Tel: 0181 332 6220/6477 *Fax:* 0181 332 0552
Email: richmondmusic@compuserve.com

Barnaby Marder, dir.

Robert Morley & Co Ltd
34 Engate St, London SE13 7HA
Tel: 0181 318 5838 *Fax:* 0181 297 0720
Website: www.yell.co.uk/sites/morley

Julia Morley.

Repair and restoration of pnos, f-pnos, hpds, spinets, clvds, virginals, celestes.

San Domenico Stringed Instruments
175 Kings Rd, Cardiff CF1 9DF
Tel: 01222 235881 *Fax:* 01222 344510

H Morgan, dir.
Fine vns, vcs, bows and student insts. Restoration, bow rehairing, insurance, valuation and appraisals.

Sheehan's Music Services
50 London Rd, Leicester LE2 0QD
Tel: 0116 255 7492 *Fax:* 0116 285 5932
Email: noel@sheehans.com

W/wind, br, fretted str, baroque insts.

Spanish Guitar Centre
36 Cranbourn St, London WC2H 7AD
Tel: 0171 240 0754 *also fax*

Largest stock of classical guis in Europe.

Springwood Music Workshops
Water St, Huddersfield, W Yorks HD1 4BB
Tel: 01484 530053 *Fax:* 01484 305303
Email: john.sw@ukonline.co.uk
Website: www.musiclink.co.uk/smw/

R A Sinclair Willis, admin.
Repair and restoration of str family of insts, f-pno, reed orgs, harmoniums, mechanical mus insts, pipe orgs.

Stevens, Mike
272 Louth Rd, Scartho, Grimsby, N E Lincs DN33 2LF
Tel: 01472 824138

Mike Stevens, repairer.
Str, w/wind and br repairs. Also school perc. Adaptions for disabled players. Parts made.

Swans Music Ltd
3 Plymouth Court Business Centre, 166 Plymouth Grove, Manchester M13 0AF
Tel: 0161 273 3232 *Fax:* 0161 274 4111

David Swan, w/shop mgr and company sec; Bill Swan, mgr dir.
Pno repair, restoration and tuning; keyboard, org; educ discount. Also sell and hire pnos, insts and accs.

Teagues
34 Orchard St, Newport, Isle of Wight PO30 1AU
Tel: 01983 523460 *Fax:* 01983 525171

Mus, orgs, pnos (elec and acoustic), keyboards, br, w/wind, str, guis, perc, accs, full tuning and repair facility.

Temple, Alex
Platt Lodge, 61 Barton Rd, Worsley, Manchester M28 2GX
Tel: 0161 794 3717
Email: alextemple@compuserve.com

Hpd, clvd; tuning, repairs and hire.

Thwaites
33 Chalk Hill, Oxhey, Watford, Herts WD1 4BL
Tel: 01923 232412 *also fax*

Str w/shop; vn, vc, db.

Top Wind
2 Lower Marsh, London SE1 7RJ
Tel: 0171 401 8787; 0171 928 8181 (repairs)
Fax: 0171 401 8788
Email: jon@topwind.com
Website: www.topwind.com

Specialist fl repairs.

Trainor, Brian
15 Stanmore Cres, Lanark ML11 7DF
Tel: 01555 664024

W/wind, br and str inst repairs.

Tucker, Anne and Ian
4 High St, Mistley, Essex CO11 1HA
Tel: 01206 393670/393884 *also fax*
Email: ian.tucker@virgin.net

Hpds, spinets, clvds and early pnos.

Walthamstow Music
116 Hoe St, Walthamstow, London E17 4QR
Tel: 0181 520 2163/5448 *Fax:* 0181 509 3005

Full repair service on all w/wind, br and str insts. Bow repair service for both professional and amateur players.

Ward, Alan
St Andrews, 27 Plomer Hill, Downley, High Wycombe, Bucks HP13 5JG
Tel: 01494 523371

Str restorer and repairer. Also maker, vn, va, vc, modern and baroque.

Whitham, J S
Faraway, Llandegla, Denbighshire LL11 3BG
Tel: 01978 790238 *also fax*
Email: jswhit@ptfoods.demon.co.uk

Repairs to all orch insts, also mobile service.

Wilks Music Stores Ltd
32-33 St Helens Rd, Swansea SA1 4AY
Tel: 01792 655953 *also fax*

Str, w/wind, br, restoration.

Wood, Wind & Reed
Russell St, Cambridge CB2 1HU
Tel: 01223 500442 *Fax:* 01223 362682

Daniel Bangham, proprietor; Brian Dent, head of repairs.
W/wind inst repair specialists, w/wind and br sales, also sheet mus and accs.

Woodward, Nicholas
The Bristol Violin Shop, 12 Upper Maudlin St, Bristol BS2 8DJ
Tel: 0117 925 9990 *also fax*

Maker of modern and baroque str insts.

Woolley, Dennis
Tubhole Barn, Dent, Sedbergh, W Yorks LA10 5RE
Tel: 015396 25361

F-pno, hpd.

The Associated Board of the Royal Schools of Music (Publishing) Limited

The Associated Board of the Royal Schools of Music is the leading international music examining body with over 500,000 candidates every year in more than 80 countries.

ABRSM (Publishing) Limited is renowned for:

- an extensive keyboard catalogue
- a wide-ranging catalogue of instrumental albums
- authoritative performing editions of classical works

Recent publications that have received critical acclaim include:

THE WELL-TEMPERED CLAVIER PART I J. S. Bach
Edited by DR RICHARD JONES
'Best Standard Publication' award, Music Retailers Association 1994

SPECTRUM *20 contemporary works for solo piano*
Compiled by THALIA MYERS
Music Industries Association's 'Standard Publication Award for Excellence' in 1996

BAROQUE FLUTE PIECES
Edited by DR RICHARD JONES
Winner, Newly-Published Music Competition 1997, National Flute Association, USA

ABRSM (Publishing) Limited

14 Bedford Square London WC1B 3JG United Kingdom
Telephone +44 171 636 5400 *Fax* +44 171 436 4520
E-mail publishing@abrsm.ac.uk
Website www.abrsmpublishing.co.uk

Music Publishers

This section lists publishers of educational printed music. Publishers of reference and educational books about music will be found in the **Book Publishers** section. If a catalogue is available, (cat) appears after the relevant entry. A more comprehensive list of music publishers is maintained in the *British Music Yearbook*.

A & C Black Publishers Ltd
Music Dept, 35 Bedford Row, London WC1R 4JH
Tel: 0171 242 0946 *Fax:* 0171 831 7489
Email: 100726.1035@compuserve.com

Sheena Roberts.
Primary and secondary songbooks, c/room mus, inst tutors and repertoire.

Alfred A Kalmus Ltd/Universal Edition (London) Ltd
38 Eldon Way, Paddock Wood, Kent TN12 6BE
Tel: 01892 833422/3 *Fax:* 01892 836038

A P Knowles, sales promotion.
Solo, ens, wind band, school orch, choir (cat); school mus, orch, vocal, books.

Alfred Lengnick & Co Ltd
c/o William Elkin Music Services, Station Rd Industrial Estate, Salhouse, Norwich, Norfolk NR13 6NS
Tel: 01603 721302 *Fax:* 01603 721801

Solo, ens, wind band, str orch, school orch, choir (cat).

Alfred Publishing Co (UK) Ltd
7 Amber Business Village, Tamworth, Staffs B77 4RP
Tel: 01827 311553 *Fax:* 01827 313011
Email: 100565.1116@compuserve.com

Pno methods and collections, classical and educ mus for all insts, gui, band, orch and choral, computer software (cat).

Andrews of Harrogate (Music Typography)
100 Duchy Rd, Harrogate HG1 2HA
Tel: 01423 504373 *also fax*
Email: music.man@zetnet.co.uk
Website: www.users.zetnet.co.uk/dandrews

David Andrews, proprietor.
Mus processing from ms to print.

Antico Edition
PO Box 1, Moretonhampstead, Newton Abbot, Devon TQ13 8UA
Fax: 01647 252085

Nick Sandon, gen ed.
Medieval and renaissance, sacred and secular mus.

Associated Board of the Royal Schools of Music (Publishing) Ltd
14 Bedford Sq, London WC1B 3JG
Tel: 0171 636 5400 *Fax:* 0171 436 4520
Email: publishing@abrsm.pub.uk

Julian Hodgson, mgr dir; C G P Morris, mkt mgr.
Extensive keyboard and inst catalogues, mus for examinations, theory of mus textbooks.

AV Music
51 Cannon La, Pinner, Middx HA5 1HN
Tel: 0181 866 3401 *Fax:* 0181 866 5929

Alec Gould, proprietor.
W/wind, br, wind band.

Banks Music Publications
The Old Forge, Sand Hutton, York YO4 1LB
Tel: 01904 468472 *Fax:* 01904 468679
Email: banksramsay@mcmail.com

Rosemary Goodwin, mgr.
Solo, ens, choir.

Bärenreiter Ltd
Burnt Mill, Elizabeth Way, Harlow, Essex CM20 2HX
Tel: 01279 417134; 01279 454823 (24 hrs)
Fax: 01279 429401

Solo, ens, str, wind, pno, org, orch, choir.

Bartholomew Music Publications
105 Bartholomew Rd, Kentish Town, London NW5 2AR
Tel: 0171 267 0437 *also fax*

Specialists in db mus.

Basil Ramsey Publisher of Music Ltd
604 Rayleigh Rd, Eastwood, Leigh-on-Sea, Essex SS9 5HU
Tel: 01702 524305 *also fax*

B Ramsey.
Solo, ens, wind band, str orch, school orch, choir (cat). All enquiries to Banks Music Publications.

BBC Educational Publishing
Room 3404, White City, London W12 7TS
Tel: 0181 752 5337 *Fax:* 0181 752 5340

Sally Lovell, publicity co-ord.
Solo, ens, wind band, str orch, school orch, choir, hymns and songs.

Bearsongs
PO Box 944, Birmingham B16 8UT
Tel: 0121 454 7020 *Fax:* 0121 454 9996

Jim Simpson, mgr dir; Clare Jepson-Homer, prof mgr.
Mainly jazz and blues (cat).

The Beauchamp Press
Beauchamp House, Churcham, Glos GL2 8AA
Tel: 01452 750253 *Fax:* 01452 750585

Alan Lumsden, dir.
Renaissance and baroque choral and inst mus.

Boosey & Hawkes Music Publishers Ltd
295 Regent St, London W1R 8JH
Tel: 0181 205 3861 *Fax:* 0181 200 3737

Catalogues available for c/room, str teachers, pno teachers, keyboard, strs, w/wind, br and perc, band and orch, vocal, choral, books and scores, SMF software, Microjazz, Essential String Method, Choral Music Experience, Bote & Bock, Editio Musica Budapest, Ricordi, Zen-On, Fazer, Guildhall School of Music.

Bosworth & Co Ltd
14-18 Heddon St, London W1R 8DP
Tel: 0171 734 4961 *Fax:* 0171 734 0475
Email: post@bosworthbn.demon.co.uk
Website: www.demon.co.uk/bosworth

Howard Friend, dir.
Solo, ens, wind band, school orch, choir (cat), rcdrs, str, orch, accordion band, pno, org, keyboard, theory, gui.

Brass Wind Publications
4 St Mary's Rd, Manton, Oakham, Rutland
Tel: 01572 737409 *also fax*

D N Triggel, D Triggel, partners.
Solo, ens, wind band (cat), c/room ens.

Breitkopf & Härtel
Walkmühlstraße 52, D-65195 Wiesbaden, Germany
Tel: +49 6128 966350 *also fax*
Email: sales@breitkopf.com

Publish editions of set works for ABRSM and Trinity College, including the new wind and br syllabus for Trinity 1999-2002. Backlist contains numerous methods for various insts in bilingual editions. Also education-oriented new pno edition, *Hello Mr Gillock, Hello Carl Czerny!*

The *Faber Young Voices* series is devised specifically to address the needs of young choirs. The series aims to span the fullest possible range of repertoire - both traditional and popular new material from folksongs and calypsos to show songs and Christmas favourites.

For further details of the series and to receive a copy of our FREE Upper Voice Choral Sampler CD, please contact our Sales and Marketing Department at the address below.

Sales and Marketing, Faber Music Ltd,
3 Queen Square, London WC1N 3AU
Tel: 0171-833 7931/278 7436
Fax: 0171-278 3817
E-mail: sales@fabermusic.co.uk
Website: http://www.fabermusic.co.uk

FABER MUSIC

Broadbent & Dunn Ltd
12 Tudor Ct, London E17 8ET
Tel: 0181 521 4275 *Fax:* 0181 520 8994

Marjorie Dunn, dir; William Dunn, sales mgr.
Mus for str, br, w/wind, and pno.

Cambridge University Press
Edinburgh Building, Shaftesbury Rd, Cambridge CB2 2RU
Tel: 01223 312393 *Fax:* 01223 315052
Email: information@cup.cam.ac.uk
Website: www.cup.cam.ac.uk/

Susan Taylor, commissioning ed.
Primary and secondary educ mus books.

Camden Music
19a North Villas, Camden Sq, London NW1 9BJ
Tel: 0171 267 8778 *also fax*
Email: 100770.3421@compuserve.com
Website: www.printed-music.com/camden

Andrew Skirrow, proprietor.
Orch, wind, br, vocal, urtext editions, educ mus.

Campion Press - Music Publishers
Sandon, Buntingford, Herts SG9 0QW
Tel: 01763 247287 *Fax:* 01763 249984

Cascade Music Publishing
30 College Green, Bristol BS1 5TB
Tel: 01454 323608 *also fax*
Email: cascademusic@hotmail.com

J E Fairhead, proprietor.
Classical and jazz-based pieces for w/wind and br solo and ens. Agent for Modern Music Jazz Catalogue and Attic Music.

Cathedral Music
Maudlin House, Westhampnett, Chichester, W Sussex PD18 0PB
Tel: 01243 776325 *Fax:* 01243 539604
Email: cathedralmusic@compuserve.com or 106771.64@compuserve.com

Richard Barnes, dir.
Org and choral specialist.

Chester Music
The Music Sales Group, Newmarket Rd, Bury St Edmunds, Suffolk IP33 3YB
Tel: 01284 702600 *Fax:* 01284 768301
Email: music@musicsales.co.uk
Website: www.musicsales.co.uk

Harriet Gedge, sales mgr; Deborah Watson, mkt mgr.
Contemporary mus, c/room mus, inst solo and ens, str orch, school orch, wind band, br ens, vocal, choral, scores and books.

Chiltern Music
Maudlin House, Westhampnett, Chichester, W Sussex PD18 0PB
Tel: 01243 776325 *Fax:* 01243 539604
Email: 106771.64@compuserve.com

R Barnes, dir.
Orch, inst, pno and secular choral.

Cinque Port Music Publishers
Bank House, Queen St, Deal, Kent CT14 6ET
Tel: 01304 362181 *also fax*

Stephen I Misson, Pamela M Misson, partners.
Military and br band mus. Specialists in Royal Marines band recordings.

Colne Edition
11 Christ Church Ct, Ireton Rd, Colchester, Essex CO3 3AU
Tel: 01206 562607

A Bullard, dir.
Solo, ens, br band, wind band, school orch, choir (including mus of Alan Bullard).

Comus Edition
Leach Cottage, Heirs House La, Colne, Lancs BB8 9TA
Tel: 01282 864985 *Fax:* 01282 860770
Email: wmd@comusic.demon.co.uk
Website: www.comusic.demon.co.uk

Michael Dennison, mgr.
Ens, br, w/wind mus.

Concord Partnership
5 Bushey Close, Old Barn La, Kenley, Surrey CR8 5AU
Tel: 0181 660 4766 *Fax:* 0181 668 5273

Concord Music Hire Library, EF Kalmus and Masters Music Windband, GIA Publication Inc, James Watson Unlimited Music, Maecenas Contemporary Composers, Maecenas Europe, Maecenas Music Ltd, Trigram and Wimbledon Music Inc.

Cornelius Edition
29 Lansdown Pl, Lewes, Sussex BN7 2JU
Tel: 01273 473278 *also fax*

Marcus Martin, dir.
Solo, ens, str orch, school orch (cat).

Cramer Music
23 Garrick St, London WC2E 9AX
Tel: 0171 240 1612 *Fax:* 0171 240 2639

P J Maxwell, mgr dir.
Solo, ens, c/room ens, mus courses, school orch, vocal mus (cat).

Cwmni Cyhoeddi Gwynn Cyf
Y Gerlan, Heol y Dwr, Penygroes, Caernarfon, Gwynedd
LL54 6LR
Tel: 01286 881797

Wendy Jones, admin.
Vocal and choral mus (cat).

Da Capo Music
26 Stanway Rd, Whitefield, Manchester M45 8EG
Tel: 0161 766 5950

Colin Bayliss, mgr dir.
British contemporary mus (approx grades with
each work).

Dolce Edition
15 Rock St, Brighton BN2 1NF
Tel: 01273 692974 *Fax:* 01273 622792

Specialists in rcdr mus.

Duettino Publications
16 Batchworth Heath, Rickmansworth WD3 1QB
Tel: 01923 825625

G R Gruner, dir.
Duet mus only.

Eaton Music Ltd
8 West Eaton Pl, London SW1X 8LS
Tel: 0171 235 9046 *Fax:* 0171 235 7193
Email: eatonmus@aol.com

Terry Oates, owner and dir; Mandy Oates, dir.
Film and TV mus, Hooked on Classics, popular
songs.

Ebony Edition
Redwings, Linden Chase, Uckfield, E Sussex TN22 1EE
Tel: 01825 760046 *also fax*

Philip Turbett.
Wind mus, specialist in cl and sax mus.

Elderslie Music
44 Batley Rd, Alverthorpe, Wakefield, W Yorks WF2 0AD
Tel: 01924 219794 *also fax*

Kevin S Bolton.
Specialist gui mus.

Emerson Edition Ltd
Windmill Farm, Ampleforth, Yorks
Tel: 01439 788324 *Fax:* 01439 788715

June Emerson, mgr dir.
Specialist publisher of mus for wind insts, solo,
ens, wind band, mus from Albania.

Eschenbach Editions
28 Dalrymple Cres, Edinburgh EH9 2NX
Tel: 0131 667 3633 *also fax*

J Douglas, dir.
Solo, ens, str orch, school orch, choir, rcdrs.

European Music Archive
33a Chestnut La, Amersham, Bucks HP6 6EN
Tel: 01494 722602

Martin Teale, dir.
17th-18th C mus for solo, ens.

Faber Music Ltd
3 Queen Sq, London WC1N 3AU
Tel: 0171 833 7931 *Fax:* 0171 278 3817
Email: sales@fabermusic.co.uk
Website: www.fabermusic.co.uk

Solo, str orch, school orch, choir, school mus, ens. Orders: Sales and Publicity Dept, Faber Music Ltd, 3 Queen Sq, London WC1N 3AU, tel no as above.

Fentone Music Ltd
Fleming Rd, Earlstrees, Corby, Northants NN17 4SN
Tel: 01536 260981 *Fax:* 01536 401075
Email: fentone.music@btinternet.com
Website: www.btinternet.com/~fentone.music/

Iain Fenton, dir.
Solo, str orch, school orch, rcdr series, gui, org, cl, fl, full orch, pno, ob, str, vocal, books.

Forsyth Brothers Ltd
126 Deansgate, Manchester M3 2GR
Tel: 0161 834 3281 *Fax:* 0161 834 0630
Email: forsythmus@aol.com

Jean Colter, Ian Taylor.
Theory, harmony, rcdr and pno mus.

Fraser-Enoch Publications
64 Tremaine Rd, London SE20 7TZ
Tel: 0181 659 7110 *Fax:* 0181 659 7716

Steve Kennett, partner admin.
Educational pno mus: solo, duets and trios (grs 1-8). Mss to Fraser-Enoch, 64 Tremaine Rd, London SE20 7TZ.

Friendly Music
PO Box 53, Cranbrook, Kent TN17 3ZX
Tel: 01580 713281

Jonathan Rutland, proprietor.
Cl quartets and wind quintets. Also beginner books for bsn, cl and sax.

Fulcrum Music Publications
10 Trafalgar St, Cheltenham GL50 1UH
Tel: 01242 226101 *also fax*

P T Lane.
Solo, ens, br band, school orch, choir (cat).

G Henle Verlag
Forstenrieder Allee 122, D-81476 Munich, PO Box 710466, D-81454 Munich, Germany
Tel: 00 49 89 75982 0 *Fax:* 00 49 89 759 82 40
Email: info@henle.de
Website: www.henle.de

Martin Bente, president CEO; Michael Ingendaay, sales mgr.
Urtext editions of the classics, study editions, orch works, complete editions, facsimiles, catalogues of mus, musicological books.

G Schirmer Ltd
The Music Sales Group, Newmarket Rd, Bury St Edmunds, Suffolk IP33 3YB
Tel: 01284 702600 *Fax:* 01284 768301
Email: music@musicsales.co.uk;
Website: www.musicsales.co.uk

Harriet Gedge, sales mgr; Deborah Watson, mkt mgr.
Classical and contemporary: inst, solo, chmbr, w/wind ens, str ens, br ens, concert bands and choral.

Gee Music Group Ltd
7 Fleetsbridge Business Centre, Upton Rd, Poole, Dorset BH17 7AF
Tel: 01202 686368 *Fax:* 01202 686363

David Gee, mgr dir; Len de Silva, sales mgr.
Incorporating Music Forte Ltd, Music Gifts Co (Poole) Ltd, Musigraphic Publishers Ltd. Orch, school orch, inst, pno tutor, chmbr, wind and br mus, musical gifts. Catalogues represented: Kalmus Orch, Masters Music, Music Gifts Co, Musigraphic, Southern Music of Texas, Wynn Music, Peanuts Piano Course.

Gemini Publications
58 Abinger Rd, London W4 1EX
Tel: 0181 994 8639 *also fax*

Cecilia McDowall
Schools musicals, choral music, vocal music and str arr. for schools

Golden Apple Productions
The Music Sales Group, Newmarket Rd, Bury St Edmunds, Suffolk IP33 3YB
Tel: 01284 702600 *Fax:* 01284 768301
Email: music@musicsales.co.uk
Website: www.musicsales.co.uk

Deborah Watson, mkt mgr; Harriet Gedge, sales mgr.

Musical plays, nativities and shows, inst, songbooks with actions, learning and topic work. NC KS1-3, pre-school and special needs.

Hallamshire Music
Bank End, N Somercotes, Nr Louth, Lincs LN11 7LN
Tel: 01507 358141 *Fax:* 01507 358034

D C Ashmore, dir.
Solo, ens, br band, wind band, school band.

Hampton Music Publishers
Hampton House, 84 Clare St, Northampton NN1 3JE
Tel: 01604 230939 *Fax:* 01604 621195

Harlequin Music
69 Eversden Rd, Harlton, Cambridge CB3 7ET
Tel: 01223 263795 *also fax*

Val Bell, dir.
Br and wind mus; solo, ens, wind and br band, perc.

HarperCollins Religious
77-85 Fulham Palace Rd, Hammersmith, London W6 8JB
Tel: 0181 741 7070 *Fax:* 0181 307 4064
Email: kathy.dyke@harpercollins.co.uk

Kathy Dyke, ed.
Christian mus, hymn books.

Hunt Edition and Pan Educational Music
c/o Spartan Press, Old Brewery House, Redbrook, Monmouth NP5 4LU
Tel: 01600 712482 *Fax:* 01600 712483
Email: spartanpress@compuserve.com

Simon Hunt, dir.
Educational mus for recreation and learning.

International Music Publications Ltd
Southend Rd, Woodford Green, Essex IG8 8HN
Tel: 0181 498 7200 *Fax:* 0181 551 1595

Richard Clarke, educ publishing assistant.
Br, w/wind and str, pno, perc, rcdr, solo, tutors, musical plays, songbooks, mus curriculum material.

Jewish Music Distribution
The London Jewish Music Centre, Box 2268, Hendon, London NW4 3UW
Tel: 0181 203 8046 *also fax*
Email: rad.74@dial.pipex.com

Rachel Wetstein, Daniel Tunkel, dirs.
Distributors and suppliers of Jewish mus compilations and recordings from around the world.

Joad Press
4 Meredyth Rd, London SW13 0DY
Tel: 0181 876 8634

Solo, ens, wind band, str orch, school orch, choir.

John Trotter Books and Manor House Books
Sternberg Centre, 80 East End Rd, London N3 2SY
Tel: 0181 349 9484 *Fax:* 0181 346 7430
Email: mhb@jt96.demon.co.uk

John Trotter.
Suppliers of Jewish mus compilations, CDs and books on Jewish musicology, including cassettes.

Josef Weinberger Ltd
12-14 Mortimer St, London W1N 7RD
Tel: 0171 580 2827 *Fax:* 0171 436 9616

Wensy Herring, Sean Gray, promotion.
Mus theatre, orch, str and wind orch, choral, ens and solo (cats available).

Jubilate Hymns Ltd
Southwick House, 4 Thorne Park Rd, Chelston, Torquay TQ2 6RX
Tel: 01803 607754 *Fax:* 01803 605682
Email: jubilatemw@aol.com

M Williams, financial and copyright mgr; David Peacock, editorial sec.
Church mus books, carol books, prayer books for choir and school assembly (cat).

Kevin Mayhew Publishers
Rattlesden, Bury St Edmunds, Suffolk IP30 0SZ
Tel: 01449 737978 *Fax:* 01449 737834
Email: kevinmayhewltd@msn.com

Mike Craig, customer services.
Full range of org, choral and inst mus. Carefully edited and clearly set out including musicals, rcdr, str, w/wind, br, keyboard and vocal mus.

Lindsay Music
23 Hitchin St, Biggleswade, Beds SG18 8AX
Tel: 01767 316521 *Fax:* 01767 317221

C Lindsay-Douglas, dir.
Ens, school orch, choir, c/room mus (cat); including works by Douglas Coombes (jnr, secondary), Vera Gray (infant), 'Albert House Press', musical novelties. Also UK supplier of World Music Press cat.

Lomond Music
32 Bankton Pk, Kingskettle, Fife KY15 7PY
Tel: 01337 830974 *Fax:* 01337 830653
Email: bruce.fraser@zetnet.co.uk

Bruce Fraser.
Br band, wind band mus; educ, ens mus (br, w/wind, strs, choral).

London Pro Musica Edition
15 Rock St, Brighton BN2 1NF
Tel: 01273 692974 *Fax:* 01273 622792

Solo, ens (cat).

Lovely Music
17 Westgate, Tadcaster, N Yorks LS24 9JB
Tel: 01937 832946 *Fax:* 01937 835696

Ray Lovely, dir; Lynda Robertson, mgr.
Mostly Music and Mayflower Publications, Jan Holdstock titles.

Lynwood Music
2 Church St, W Hagley, W Midlands DY9 0NA
Tel: 01562 886625 *Fax:* 0121 331 5906

Rosemary Cooper, mgr dir; Paula Lechantoux, sec; Anna Downes, promotions rep.
Works for children by contemporary British and European composers.

Maecenas Europe
5 Bushey Close, Old Barn La, Kenley, Surrey CR8 5AU
Tel: 0181 660 3914 *Fax:* 0181 668 5273

Keyboard, inst, pop, classical, choral, band, orch, textbooks.

Maecenas Music Limited
5 Bushey Close, Old Barn La, Kenley, Surrey CR8 5AU
Tel: 0181 660 4766 *Fax:* 0181 668 5273

Ens, wind band, br band; contemporary inst, choral and vocal mus (cat). Hire library.

Margaret Carpenter Publications
Out of the Ark Music, The School House, 15 Esher Green, Esher, Surrey KT10 8AA
Tel: 01372 463274 *Fax:* 01372 463351

M Johnson, G Powell.
Musical plays for primary schools.

Masterclass Music
12 Kelso Pl, Dundee DD2 1SL
Tel: 01382 667251 *Fax:* 01382 640775

Nigel Don, arranger.
Mus for mixed ens; secondary school (cat).

Meriden Music
Silverwood House, Woolaston, Nr Lydney, Glos GL15 6PJ
Tel: 01594 529026 *Fax:* 01594 529027

Graham Whettam, Janet Whettam.
Publishes works of Graham Whettam.

Middle Eight Music
23 Garrick St, London WC2E 9AX
Tel: 0171 240 1612 *Fax:* 0171 240 2639

P J Maxwell, mgr dir.
Solo, ens, c/room ens, mus courses, school orch (cat).

MSM Music Publishers (Inc Leonard, Gould & Bolttler)
406 Roding La South, Off Woodford Av, Woodford Green, Essex IG8 8EY
Tel: 0181 551 1282 *Fax:* 0181 550 8377

M L Wright, mgr dir.
Solo, ens, choir (cat).

Music Exchange (Manchester) Ltd
Tayborn Publishing, Claverton Rd, Wythenshawe, Manchester M23 9ZA
Tel: 0161 946 1234 *Fax:* 0161 946 1195
Email: mail@music-exchange.co.uk
Website: www.music-exchange.co.uk

John O'Brien, educ dept.

Music Sales Ltd
Distribution Centre, Newmarket Rd, Bury St Edmunds, Suffolk IP33 3YB
Tel: 01284 702600 *Fax:* 01284 768301
Email: music@musicsales.co.uk;
Website: www.musicsales.co.uk

Deborah Watson, mkt mgr; Harriet Gedge, sales mgr.
C/room, solo, ens, choral and musical shows. Catalogues including Chester Music, Golden Apple, Novello, Omnibus Press, G Schirmer, Science Press Books, Shawnee Press, UME, Youngsongs.

Musicland
Beauchamp House, Churcham, Glos GL2 8AA
Tel: 01452 750253 *Fax:* 01452 750585

Alan Lumsden, dir.
Educ mus for children.

Musisca Publishing
34 Strand, Topsham, Exeter EX3 0AY
Tel: 01392 877737 *also fax;* 0117 924 0934
Email: musisca@printed-music.com
Website: www.printed-music.com/musisca/index.htm

Philippe Oboussier, ed.
Solo, duo (vc), str quartet, ens.

Muskett Music
The Old Mill, Duntish, Dorchester, Dorset DT2 7DR
Tel: 01300 345412 *also fax*
Email: hurdyplay@aoc.com

M Muskett, dir.
Early mus; hurdy gurdy method.

New Wind Music Co
11 Park Chase, Wembley Pk, Middx HA9 8EQ
Tel: 0181 902 2073

G Lewin, dir.
Wind mus; solo, ens (cat).

Novello Publishing Ltd
The Music Sales Group, Newmarket Rd, Bury St Edmunds, Suffolk IP33 3YB
Tel: 01284 702600 *Fax:* 01284 768301
Email: music@musicsales.co.uk
Website: www.musicsales.co.uk

Harriet Gedge, sales mgr; Deborah Watson, mkt mgr.
Choral including school cantatas, inst, wind and str ens, c/room mus at KS1-4, Science Press books.

Oecumuse
52a Broad St, Ely CB7 4AH
Tel: 01353 663252 *Fax:* 01353 663371

Barry Brunton, dir.
Choir, org.

Out of the Ark Music
The School House, 15 Esher Green, Esher, Surrey KT10 8AA
Tel: 01372 463274 *Fax:* 01372 463351

M Johnson, partner; G Powell, sales mgr.
Songbook and cassette packages. Resources for KS1-3. Nursery and Reception including Christmas musicals.

Oxenford Imprint
c/o Cathedral Music (agent), Maudlin House, Westhampnett, Chichester, W Sussex PO18 0PB
Tel: 01243 776325 *Fax:* 01243 539604
Email: cathedralmusic@compuserve.com or 106771.64@compuserve.com

Richard Barnes, dir.
Choir.

Oxford University Press (Mus Dept)
Great Clarendon St, Oxford OX2 6DP
Tel: 01865 556767 *Fax:* 01865 267749
Email: music.enquiry@oup.co.uk
Website: www.oup.co.uk/music

J D Elloway, mgr of mus dept; C J Wood, mus educ ed; M R L Clare, sales and mkt mgr.
Orders: Saxon Way West, Corby, Northants NN18 9ES *tel:* 01536 454590 *fax:* 01536 746337. Choral, orch, educ, tutors, opera, insts, chmbr, church mus, etc.

Pan Educational Music and Hunt Edition
40 Portland Rd, London W11 4LG
Tel: 0171 727 5965

Simon Hunt, dir.
Specialists in wind mus.

Penguin Books Ltd
27 Wright's La, London W8 5TZ
Tel: 0171 938 2200

Solo, ens.

Peters Edition Ltd
10-12 Baches St, London N1 6DN
Tel: 0171 553 4000 (sales); 0171 553 4020 (hire)
Fax: 0171 490 4921
Email: info@edition-peters.com
Website: www.edition-peters.com

Classical.

Phoenix Music
Bryn Golau, Saron, Denbighshire LL16 4TH
Tel: 01745 550317 *Fax:* 01745 550560
Email: phoenixmus@aol.com
Website: www.printed-music.com/phoenix

Wind band, jazz band, c/room ens, inst ens.

Piccolo Press
10 Clifton Terrace, Winchester, Hampshire SO22 5BJ
Tel: 0171 724 3250; 01962 864755 *also fax*

Clifford Bevan, dir.
Publishers of mus for unusual ens and insts;
Music Students Practice Diaries; books on organology, etc.

Piper Publications
Dochroyle Farm, Barrhill by Girvan, Ayrshire KA26 0QG
Tel: 01465 821377
Email: piperpub@dircon.co.uk
Website: www.users.dircon.co.uk/~piperpub

P Spence, dir.
Solo, wind band, ens, str orch, school orch, choir, musical plays (cat); youth and amateur orch, tutors (vn, va, fl), mus and history combined projects (Footprints), KS1. Mus for steelpan, Panaphon, Piper New Classics. Complete Hook fl mus.

Power Music Co Ltd
Arrensdorff Edition, 1 Station Rd, Harecroft, Wilsden, Bradford, W Yorks BD15 0BS
Tel: 01535 272905 *also fax*

J Power, dir.
Solo, inst ens, wind band, school orch, jazz series, str series, br series, sax series, fl and cl quartets.

Primavera
110 Wyatt Park Rd, London SW2 3TP
Tel: 0181 674 1711

Solo, str orch, school orch, choir, wind duets, ABRSM listed pieces (cat).

Redcliffe Edition
68 Barrowgate Rd, London W4 4QU
Tel: 0181 995 1223 *also fax*

F J Routh, dir.
Choral mus.

Ricordi & Co (London) Ltd
Kiln House, 210 New Kings Rd, London SW6 4NZ
Tel: 0171 371 7501 *Fax:* 0171 371 7270
Email: ricordie@bmg.co.uk

Angelo Curtolo, mgr.

Roberton Publications
The Windmill, Wendover, Aylesbury, Bucks HP22 6JJ
Tel: 01296 623107

Kenneth Roberton, mgr partner.
Solo, ens, str orch, school orch, choir, pno.

Royal School of Church Music
Cleveland Lodge, Westhumble, Dorking RH5 6BW
Tel: 01306 877676 *Fax:* 01306 887260

H W Bramma, dir.
Choral, vocal, org, hymns and anthems, services, etc. Also mus for churches without choirs (cat).

St Annes Music Ltd
Kennedy House, 31 Stamford St, Altrincham, Cheshire WA14 1ES
Tel: 0161 941 5151 *Fax:* 0161 928 9491

Solo, ens, wind band, str orch, school orch, choir (cat).

Samuel French Ltd
52 Fitzroy St, London W1P 6JR
Tel: 0171 387 9373 *Fax:* 0171 387 2161

Paul Taylor, dir.
Musicals, musical plays for schools.

Sceptre Publishers
97 Elton Rd, Stibbington, Peterborough, Cambs PE8 6JX
Tel: 01780 782093 *Fax:* 01780 783159

Solo electronic org (cat) and a monthly newspaper *Organ and Keyboard Cavalcade*.

Schauer & May Ltd
Simrock House, 220 The Vale, London NW11 8HZ
Tel: 0181 731 6665 *Fax:* 0181 731 6667

Irene Retford, dir.
Solo, ens, str orch, choir, wind band.

Schott & Co Ltd
48 Great Marlborough St, London W1V 2BN
Tel: 0171 437 1246 *Fax:* 0171 439 1697

W Lampa, educ mus ed; J Webb, head of mkt and sales.
Marketing and Sales Dept: Brunswick Rd, Ashford, Kent TN23 1DX *tel:* 01233 628987 *fax:*

01233 610232. Solo, ens, wind band, str orch, school orch, choir; also rcdr, perc insts, Orff-Schulwerk, Eulenburg Miniature Scores, primary and secondary resource materials.

Shaftesbury Edition

16 Mitcham Rd, Dymchurch, Romney Marsh, Kent TN29 0TH
Tel: 01303 874449

Peter Aviss, dir.
Mus for solo, str orch, youth orch, choir, rcdr consort by Peter Aviss.

Shawnee Press

The Music Sales Group, Newmarket Rd, Bury St Edmunds, Suffolk IP33 3YB
Tel: 01284 702600 *Fax:* 01284 768301
Email: music@musicsales.co.uk
Website: www.musicsales.co.uk

Harriet Gedge, sales mgr; Deborah Watson, mkt mgr. Choral, inst, musical plays from primary to secondary.

Snell & Sons

68 West Cross La, West Cross, Swansea SA3 5LU
Tel: 01792 405727

Shirley Davies, proprietor.
Welsh mus specialists.

Sounds Write

56 Baswich Crest, Stafford ST17 0HJ
Tel: 01785 250405 *Fax:* 01785 663576

Keith Baskett, mgr of mkt and sales.
Offers a lively set of theory work books written for young beginners to gr 3. *Music Fun* follows the ABRSM Theory of Music syllabus and gives a structured and fun approach through its child-centred method of teaching. It is applicable to any inst and does not require keyboard skills. Free brochure available.

Spartan Press Music Publishers Ltd

Old Brewery House, Redbrook, Monmouth NP5 4LU
Tel: 01600 712482 *Fax:* 01600 712483
Email: spartanpress@compuserve.com

Mark Goddard, mgr dir; Marcus Creighton-Sims, sales co-ord.
Solo, flexible ens, pno, w/wind, br, str, vocal.

Sphemusations

12 Northfield Rd, Onehouse, Stowmarket, Suffolk IP14 3HF
Tel: 01449 613388

J Butt, dir.
Solo, school orch, choir, orch scores, chmbr mus; mus for 'music and movement' classes; keyboard, hp and voice (cat).

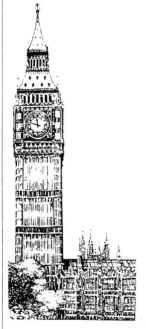

Stainer & Bell Ltd
PO Box 110, Victoria House, 23 Gruneisen Rd, Finchley,
London N3 1DZ
Tel: 0181 343 3303 *Fax:* 0181 343 3024
Email: post@stainer.co.uk
Website: www.stainer.co.uk

C Wakefield, joint mgr dir.
Solo, ens, wind band, str orch, school orch, choir.

Stanley Thornes (Publishers) Ltd
Ellenborough House, Wellington St, Cheltenham, Glos GL50 1YW
Tel: 01242 276280 *Fax:* 01242 221914
Email: cservice@thornes.co.uk
Website: www.thornes.co.uk

Moira Wood, mkt controller; Mary Maggs, list development mgr.
Sounds of Music, a complete streamlined primary mus scheme; Silver Burdett mus; Blueprints, photocopiable teacher resources; Music File, annual subscription service for secondary school teachers.

Stanza Music
11 Victor Rd, Harrow, Middx HA2 6PT
Tel: 0181 863 2717 *Fax:* 0181 863 8685
Email: bill.ashton@virgin.net
Website: www.classical-artists.com/nyjd

Bill Ashton, dir.
Inst and small jazz ens, large big band (cat). Now published in USA by Stanza USA.

Studio Music Co
77-79 Dudden Hill La, London NW10 1BD
Tel: 0181 830 0110 (sales/enquiries) *Fax:* 0181 451 6470

Paul Williams, sales mgr.
Solo, ens, c/room ens, wind band, big band, br band, str orch, choir, musical plays (cat).

Thames Publishing
14 Barlby Rd, London W10 6AR
Tel: 0181 969 3579 *Fax:* 0181 969 1465

John Bishop, publishing mgr.
Solo, ens, choir, str orch. No mss without preliminary letter.

Tinderbox Music
93 Stradella Rd, London SE24 9HL
Tel: 0171 274 5314

David Moses, dir.
Resource material for non-specialist and specialist teachers; primary, song books, rcdr and other inst mus for beginner and intermediate levels.

Tobin Music/Helicon Press
The Old Malthouse, Knight St, Sawbridgeworth, Herts CM21 9AX
Tel: 01279 726625

The Tobin Music System. Pre-school, primary

and secondary mus course for the c/room. Also rcdr, pno and classical gui tutors.

Tyne Music
38 West Moreland Rd, Newcastle upon Tyne NE1 4EN
Tel: 0191 232 2479 *also fax*

D A Westgate, dir.
Br band tuition books, choir, musicals, modern musicals, modern song books.

United Music Publishers Ltd
42 Rivington St, London EC2A 3BN
Tel: 0171 729 4700 *Fax:* 0171 739 6549
Email: ump@compuserve.com
Website: ourworld.compuserve.com/homepages/ump

Solo, ens, str orch, school orch, choral, scores, mus hire library. UK distributors of all major French editions (cats). Retail showroom and m/order service.

University of York Music Press Ltd
Department of Music, University of York, Heslington, York YO1 5DD
Tel: 01904 432434 *Fax:* 01904 432450

Jackie Glanville, admin; David Blake, dir; William Colleran, dir of promotions.
Company representing 16 composers. Cat available on request which includes the complete Olivan list of Elisabeth Lutyens.

Universal Edition (London) Ltd *see* Alfred A Kalmus

Useful Music
c/o Spartan Press, Old Brewery House, Redbrook, Monmouth
Tel: 01600 712 482 *Fax:* 01600 712 483

G Lyons, owner.
educ w/win mus.

Virgo Music Publishers
Virgo House, 47 Cole Bank Rd, Hall Green, Birmingham B28 8EZ
Tel: 0121 778 5569 *also fax*
Website: www.printed-music.com/virgo

K Shifrin, dir.
Classical; easy jazz-based mus for br, w/wind and flexible school insts, from 1 player to full band.

Ward Lock Educational Co Ltd
1 Christopher Rd, E Grinstead, W Sussex RH19 3BT
Tel: 01342 318980 *Fax:* 01342 410980

Penny Kitchenham, gen mgr.
Primary education books, favourite/traditional songs and rhymes (cat).

Warner-Chappell Music Ltd
Griffin House, 161 Hammersmith Rd, London W6 8BS
Tel: 0181 563 5867 *Fax:* 0181 563 5801

Mark Mumford, educ publishing mgr.
Popular, classical, education mus.

William Elkin Music Services
Station Road Industrial Estate, Salhouse, Norwich NR13 6NY
Tel: 01603 721302

Richard Elkin, dir.
Distributors for: AIM Music Gifts, Alfred Coppenrath, Allans of Australia, Ashley Dealers Service, Aureole, Bold Strummer, Braydeston Press, Carl Gehrmans, Chappell (Choral), Chas Colin, Coppelia, CPP/Belwin, Creative Concepts, J Curwen, Duettino Publications, Edition Delrieu, Edwin Ashdown, Ensemble, Fountain Publications, Freeman Easy, Grafton Classics, Hal Leonard (Choral), Hammond Publications, Hinshaw Music Inc, Hoffnung cards, Fr Hofmeister, Joad Press, Joel Rothman, Josef Weinberger, Joseph Patelson, Kahn & Averill, Karamar, Kendor Music, Kirklees Stickers, Lawson Gould, A Lengnick, Lorenz Music Corp, Margaux, Mayfair Music, Melodie Editions, Meredith, Music 70, Norton, Paraclete Press, Peer Southern, Pickboy Music Accessories, Plymouth Music Co, PP Music, Russian Music Publishers,

Sam Fox, Seresta Music, Shapiro Bernstein & Co, Sikorski, Souvenir Press, Spratt Music Publishing, Staff Music Publishing, Sunrise Publishing, Suvini Zerboni, Tecla, Tetra/Continuo, Thames Publishing, Toccata Press, TRO, Unicorn Music Co.

Wright & Round Ltd
The Cornet Office, PO Box 157, Gloucester GL1 1LW
Tel: 01452 523438 *Fax:* 01452 385631

Rachel Jones, mgr.
Br band, solo, ens, (cat).

Yorke Edition
31 Thornhill Sq, London N1 1BQ
Tel: 0171 607 0849 *Fax:* 0171 700 4577
Email: yvonne@yorkedition.co.uk
Website: www.yorkedition.co.uk

R Slatford, dir.
Solo (db only) (cat).

Youngsong Music
The Music Sales Group, Newmarket Rd, Bury St Edmunds, Suffolk IP33 3YB
Tel: 01284 702600 *Fax:* 01284 768301
Email: music@musicsales.co.uk
Website: www.musicsales.co.uk

Deborah Watson, mkt mgr; Harriet Gedge, sales mgr.
Musical shows for schools and youth theatre groups.

Book Publishers

This section lists publishers of reference and educational books about music. Publishers of printed music will be found in the **Music Publishers** section.

A & C Black Publishers Ltd
Music Dept, 35 Bedford Row, London WC1R 4JH
Tel: 0171 242 0946 *Fax:* 0171 831 7489
Email: 100726.1035@compuserve.com

Sheena Roberts, commissioning ed; Jane Sebba, Ana Sanderson, snr eds.
Primary, secondary, songbooks, c/room mus, inst tutors and repertoire.

Amadeus Press
10 Market St, Swavesey, Cambridge CB4 5QG
Tel: 01954 232959 *Fax:* 01954 206040
Email: timberpressuk@btinternet.com

Sue Smith, mkt exec (UK).
Specialist books on classical mus and musicians. Biographies of major figures such as Jussi Björling, Rosa Ponselle, Beethoven, Boulez and others.

Ashgate Publishing Ltd
Gower House, Croft Rd, Aldershot, Hampshire GU11 3HR
Tel: 01252 331551 *Fax:* 01252 344405
Email: ashgate@cityscape.co.uk

Titles include *Composing the Music of Africa* and works on Schubert, Delius and Finissy.

Blackwell Publishers
108 Cowley Rd, Oxford OX4 1JF
Tel: 01865 791100 *Fax:* 01865 791347
Email: lberrett@blackwellpublishers.co.uk
Website: www.blackwellpublishers.co.uk

Lorna Berrett, mkt.
Publishers of Music Analysis Journal and various mus reference titles including Blackwell History of Music in Britain, Early Twentieth Century Music, Music Before 1600 and Blackwell Guide to Recorded Jazz.

Boosey & Hawkes Music Publishers Ltd
The Hyde, Edgware, London NW9 6JN
Tel: 0181 205 3861 *Fax:* 0181 200 3737

Catalogues available: mus for schools, str

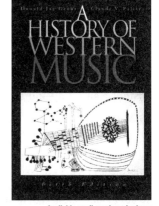

teachers, pno teachers, br and w/wind teachers, mus for children's choirs, vocal, choral, str, w/wind, br, perc, band and orch, w/shops; also Bote & Bock, Editio Musica Budapest, Fazer, Guildhall and Ricordi.

Cambridge University Press

Edinburgh Building, Shaftesbury Rd, Cambridge CB2 2RU
Tel: 01223 312393 Fax: 01223 315052
Email: information@cup.cam.ac.uk
Website: www.cup.cam.ac.uk

Penny Souster, snr commissioning ed; Victoria Cooper, commissioning ed; Susan Taylor, ed.
Primary and secondary educ mus books; gen mus books; books for scholars and students on the history of mus, mus performance, theory and analysis, popular mus and opera. Books series include Cambridge Companions to Music, Cambridge Music Handbooks, Musical Lives, Music in the Twentieth Century, Cambridge Studies in Opera and Cambridge Opera Handbooks.

Cassell plc

Wellington House, 125 Strand, London WC2R 0BB
Tel: 0171 420 5555 Fax: 0171 240 7261

Philip Sturrock, mgr dir.
Primary.

Evans Brothers Ltd

2a Portman Mansions, Chiltern St, London W1M 1LE
Tel: 0171 935 7160 Fax: 0171 487 5034

S Pawley, mgr dir; B Jones, international publishing dir; J Hole, UK sales mgr.
World of Music (book and CD), Tell us about Mozart and Tell us about Chopin.

Faber & Faber Ltd

3 Queen Sq, London WC1N 3AU
Tel: 0171 465 0045 Fax: 0171 465 0034

Belinda Matthews, mus ed.
Gen mus books, including Composers Remembered series, biographies and letters, history, criticism, theory, reference and popular mus titles.

Gresham Books Ltd

The Gresham Press, PO Box 61, Henley-on-Thames, Oxon RG9 3LQ
Tel: 0118 940 3789 also fax
Email: greshambks@aol.com

Mary Green, mgr dir; Lewis Green, liaison offr; Liz O'Brian, copyright mgr.
Hymn books (standard and special), hymn books for schools; prayer books (special), orch and choir portfolios.

Grove's Dictionaries of Music
25 Eccleston Pl, London SW1W 9NF
Tel: 0171 881 8029/8030 *Fax:* 0171 881 8109
Email: grove@macmillan.co.uk

Julia Bullock, Sehaam Cyrani, Catherine Jones, mkt execs.
The New Grove Dictionary of Music and Musicians (20 vols, hardback and paperback editions), The New Grove Dictionary of Opera (4 vols, hardback), The New Grove Dictionary of Jazz (2 vols, hardback), The New Grove Dictionary of Musical Instruments (3 vols, hardback), The New Grove Dictionary of American Music (4 vols, hardback), The Grove Concise Dictionary of Music.

Guinness Publishing
338 Euston Rd, London NW1 3BP
Tel: 0171 891 4567 *Fax:* 0171 891 4501
Email: guinness_publishing@guinness.com

Ian Castello-Cortes, Michael Feldman, publishing dirs; David Roberts, Helen Weller, projects mgrs.
The Guinness Book of British Hit Singles; The Guinness Book of British Hit Albums; Guinness Rockopedia (autumn 1998); Guinness Classical 1000; Guinness Guide to Classical Music.

Heinemann Educational
Halley Ct, Jordan Hill, Oxford OX2 8EJ
Tel: 01865 314130 *Fax:* 01865 314140

Sue Walton, mus publisher.
Primary and secondary.

Hodder & Stoughton
338 Euston Rd, London NW1 3BH
Tel: 0171 873 6000 *Fax:* 0171 873 6024

Philip Walters, mgr dir; Jan Mitchener, mkt mgr.
Primary, Bookshelf series, Teach Yourself series, book and cassette packs for teachers.

Holt, Rinehart & Winston Ltd
Harcourt Brace and Company Ltd, 22-24 Oval Rd, London NW1 7DX
Tel: 0171 424 4200 *Fax:* 0171 482 2293
Email: college@hbuk.co.uk

Madelene Hyde, college mkt mgr.
Small list covering mus theory and methods of teaching mus.

Holt-Saunders Ltd *see* Holt, Rinehart & Winston Ltd

Indiana University Press
c/o Open University Press, Celtic Ct, 22 Ballmoor, Buckingham MK18 1XW
Tel: 01280 823388 *Fax:* 01280 823233
Email: enquiries@openup.co.uk
Website: www.indiana.edu/~iupress/

Academic books for students, academics and

professionals. Specialisms include publications of The Early Music Institute, American mus history, 17th and 18th C mus, Russian and 20th C mus, voice and song, and practical reference volumes for musicians. Distributed by Open University Press.

Jessica Kingsley Publishers
116 Pentonville Rd, London N1 9JB
Tel: 0171 833 2307 *Fax:* 0171 837 2917
Email: post@jkp.com
Website: www.jkp.com

Books focusing on mus therapy, mus for children with special needs and mus and health.

Keyrandom Ltd
PO Box 2013, Bath BA1 5JU
Tel: 01225 480964 *also fax*

Graham Couch, dir.
The Virtual School of Music (CD-Rom).

Little, Brown and Company (UK) Ltd
Brettenham House, Lancaster Pl, London WC2E 7EN
Tel: 0171 911 8000 *Fax:* 0171 911 8100

Philippa Harrison, chief exec and publisher; David Young, mgr dir; Alan Samson, Barbara Boote, editorial dirs.
Selected titles of interest to musicians, including reference guides and numerous popular mus titles.

Melrose Press Ltd
Trade Dept, 3 Regal La, Soham, Ely, Cambs CB7 5BA
Tel: 01353 721091 *Fax:* 01353 721839

Nicholas S Law, mgr dir; Jean Pearson, chief exec; Sean Tyler, ed.
International Who's Who in Music and Musicians' Directory Vol 1 (classical), International Who's Who in Music Vol 2 (Popular Music).

Open University Press
Celtic Ct, 22 Ballmoor, Buckingham, Bucks MK18 1XW
Tel: 01280 823388 *Fax:* 01280 823233
Email: enquiries@openup.co.uk
Website: www.bookshop.co.uk/openup/

Academic books for students, academics and professionals. Popular Music in Britain series focuses on the history of popular mus culture.

Oxford University Press
Great Clarendon St, Oxford OX2 6DP
Tel: 01865 556767 *Fax:* 01865 556646
Email: phillipb@oup.co.uk
Website: www.oup.co.uk

Bruce Phillips, commissioning ed, mus.
Academic, general, reference, college, paperbacks and Master Musicians series. Education/Trade:

Saxon Way West, Corby, Northants NN18 9ES *Tel:* 01536 741519 *Fax:* 01536 746337. Choral, orch, educ, courses, tutors, insts, church mus, etc.

Pendragon Press
Crag House, Witherslack, Grange-over-Sands, Cumbria LA11 6RW
Tel: 015395 52286 *Fax:* 015395 52013
Email: musicbks@rdooley.demon.co.uk
Website: www.rdooley.demon.co.uk

Rosemary Dooley, UK distributor.
Aesthetics, dance and mus, Liszt, French opera, analysis, Czech mus, performance guides, thematic catalogues, mus history.

Penguin Books Ltd
Bath Rd, Harmondsworth, Middx UB7 0DA
Tel: 0181 899 4000 *Fax:* 0181 899 4099

Clare Fletcher, mkt dir; Helen Drake, mkt mgr.
Reference books on mus, including Penguin Guide to Compact Discs, Penguin Guide to Compact Discs Yearbook, Penguin Opera Guide, Penguin Price Guide for Record and CD Collectors.

Phaidon Press
Regents Wharf, All Saints St, London N1 9PA
Tel: 0171 843 1234 *Fax:* 0171 843 1111

20th C composer series of biographies and other titles, including a new translation and commentary of Der Ring des Niebelungen by Rudolph Sabor.

Random House UK
20 Vauxhall Bridge Rd, London SW1V 2SA
Tel: 0171 840 8400 *Fax:* 0171 828 6681

Encyclopedia, opera, history.

Rhinegold Publishing Ltd
241 Shaftesbury Av, London WC2H 8EH
Tel: 0171 333 1721 *Fax:* 0171 333 1769
Email: info@rhinegold.co.uk

Tony Gamble, mgr dir; Keith Diggle, mkt dir; Sarah Williams, publishing mgr; Richard Thomas, mkt mgr.
Rhinegold Publishing Ltd publishes magazines and reference books for the arts, specialising in the mus industry.
The company began with the magazine Classical Music and has expanded to include Music Teacher, Piano, Early Music Today, The Singer, and Opera Now.
Works of reference include the British and International Music Yearbook, Music Education Yearbook and British Performing Arts Yearbook. Other books include The Musician's Handbook, Arts Marketing, Healthy Practice for Musicians and Analysis Matters.

Robert Hale Ltd
Clerkenwell House, Clerkenwell Green, London EC1R 0HT

Tel: 0171 251 2661 *Fax:* 0171 490 4958
Website: www.bookweb.co.uk

Martin Kendall, mkt dir; Emma Norledge, promotions mgr.
Various books including reference, Christmas carols, classical mus guides, violin-making, etc.

Robson Books Ltd
5-6 Clipstone St, London W1P 8LE
Tel: 0171 323 1223; 0171 637 5937 *Fax:* 0171 636 0798

Secondary (and above). Books include the Contemporary Composers series, biographies of Placido Domingo, Luciano Pavarotti, Toscanini and Bernard Haitink, and Opera Lover's Guide to Europe.

Royal Musical Association
Crag House, Witherslack, Grange-over-Sands, Cumbria LA11 6RW
Tel: 01539 552286 *Fax:* 01539 552013
Email: musicbks@rdooley.demon.co.uk
Website: www.rdooley.demon.co.uk

Rosemary Dooley, RMA distributor.
RMA monographs series. 7 titles to date.

Schofield & Sims Ltd
Dogley Mill, Fenay Bridge, Huddersfield HD8 0NQ
Tel: 01484 607080 *Fax:* 01484 606815
Email: 100641.252@compuserve.com

Jack Brierley, sales dir.
Primary and secondary.

Shelwing Ltd
4 Pleydell Gardens, Folkestone, Kent CT20 2DN
Tel: 01303 850501 *Fax:* 01303 850162

Eileen Marshall, publicity mgr; Iris Farrar, book sales.
Sole agents for Scarecrow, McFarland cats.
Secondary and above.

Showcase Publications Ltd
38c The Broadway, London N8 9SU
Tel: 0181 348 2332 *Fax:* 0181 340 3750
Email: showcase-music.com

Kay Chestnutt, ed; Tony Tillmanns, sales and mkt.
Showcase International Music Book (formerly Kemps International Music Book).

Sounds Write
56 Baswich Crest, Stafford ST17 0HJ
Tel: 01785 250405 *Fax:* 01785 663576

Keith Baskett, mgr of mkt and sales.
Theory work books for young beginners to gr 3 following the ABRSM syllabus. Material offers a structured and fun approach through its child-centred method of teaching which is applicable to any inst and does not require keyboard skills. Free brochure available.

Stanley Thornes (Publishers) Ltd
Ellenborough House, Wellington St, Cheltenham, Glos GL50 1YD
Tel: 01242 267280 *Fax:* 01242 221914
Email: cservice@thornes.co.uk
Website: www.thornes.co.uk

Moira Wood, mkt controller; Mary Maggs, list development mgr.
Sounds of Music: NC mus scheme for nursery and primary teachers.
Silver Burdett Music: mus scheme for teachers of 4 to 14 year olds. Blueprints Music: curriculum resource books for primary teachers. Music File: annual subscription service for secondary school teachers.

Victor Gollancz
Wellington House, 125 Strand, London WC2R 0BB
Tel: 0171 420 5555 *Fax:* 0171 240 7261

Secondary.

Warner Books
Brettenham House, Lancaster Pl, London WC2 7EW

Various reference publications and popular mus titles.

Wise Publications
8-9 Frith St, London W1V 5TZ
Tel: 0171 434 0066 *Fax:* 0171 439 2848
Email: music@musicsales.co.uk
Website: www.musicsales.co.uk

Mus personalities (pop and classical), mus technology, mus careers, theory, pop mus, jazz.

Woodwind Plus
42 St Mary's Pk, Louth, Lincs LN11 0EF
Tel: 01507 605244

Mus for w/wind ens, w/wind, pno. Tutorial publications.

WW Norton & Company Ltd
10 Coptic St, London WC1A 1PU
Tel: 0171 323 1579 *Fax:* 0171 436 4553

Alan Cameron, mgr dir; Victoria Keown-Boyd, mkt mgr.
Norton Introduction to Music History, Norton History of Music, Marsalis on Music, musicology titles, Norton Critical Scores series and Grout: History of Western Music.

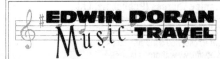

Tour and Travel Companies

ABC Executive Travel
Tower Bridge Piazza, Butlers Wharf, London SE1 2LH
Tel: 0171 357 8322 *Fax:* 0171 357 8323
Email: info@abc-extra.co.uk
Website: www.abc-extra.co.uk

Andreas Schwalbe, gen mgr.
Complete tour management for individuals, orchs and choirs, including travel arrangements, aircraft charter, ground handling, accommodation, transfers, passport and visa service.

ACFEA Tour Consultants
12-15 Hanger Green, London W5 3EL
Tel: 0181 991 2200 *Fax:* 0181 998 7965
Email: information@specialised-travel.co.uk
Website: www.specialised-travel.co.uk

Matthew Grocutt, operations mgr.
Organise concert tours in UK, Europe, the Baltic States, S Africa, USA, Australia and Japan for youth and adult choirs, bands and orchs.

Aircraft Chartering Services Ltd
7 High St, Ewell, Epsom, Surrey KT17 1SG
Tel: 0181 394 2795 *Fax:* 0181 393 6154
Email: aircraftch@aol.com

Mark Hugo, mgr dir; Philip Mathews, Andrew Richley, touring mgrs.
The charter of aircraft for the touring orch.

The Albatross Travel Group
Albatross House, 31 Rochester Rd, Aylesford, Kent ME20 7TT
Tel: 01622 790700/790800 *Fax:* 01622 790701

Bethan Jones, sales mgr.
Travel consultants to the entertainment industry.

Club Europe Concert Tours
Fairway House, 53 Dartmouth Rd, London SE23 3HN
Tel: 0181 699 7788 *Fax:* 0181 699 7770
Email: music@club-europe.co.uk

Alison Moore, concert tours mgr; David Drummond, mus dir.
International concert tours for adult, youth and school groups.

Congress Travel
13 Newtown, Bradford on Avon, Wilts BA15 1NE
Tel: 01225 867865 *Fax:* 01225 867505
Email: artsman@btinternet.com

Anthony Goodchild, UK representative.
Performing tours, exchanges, festivals worldwide. Specialises in USA and Canada.

Edwin Doran Music Travel
54 King St, Twickenham, Middx TW1 3SH
Tel: 0181 288 2921/3 *Fax:* 0181 288 2959

Edwin Doran, dir; Philippa Newnham, sales mgr.
Mus and drama tours to and from UK for schools and youth groups. Specialist concert tour operations for choirs, orchs and bands.

Edwin Doran Music Travel
Gardale House, Gatley Rd, Gatley, Cheadle, Cheshire SK8 4AU
Tel: 0161 491 6969 *Fax:* 0161 428 9754

Edwin Doran, dir.
Specialist in mus and educational tours.

Euro-Academy Ltd
77a George St, Croydon, Surrey CR0 1LD
Tel: 0181 686 2363 *Fax:* 0181 681 8850

Mrs M B Malone.
Mus tours to Germany, Holland and Austria for schools, youth orchs and choirs, br bands, folk groups, etc.

Gower Music International
2 High St, Studley, Warwicks B80 7HJ
Tel: 01527 854822 *Fax:* 01527 857236
Email: gower@gowstrav.demon.co.uk
Website: www.gowertours.com/gowermusic/

Peter Cook, gen mgr; Julian Edwards, mus tours mgr.
Specialist tour operator arranging performance tours and festivals abroad for choirs, bands and orchs.

HF Holidays
Imperial House, Edgware Rd, London NW9 5AL
Tel: 0181 905 9558 (reservations); 0181 905 9388 (brochure line) *Fax:* 0181 205 0506

Laura Livingston.
Wide range of mus holidays including orch and choral weeks, opera w/shops and mus appreciation and festivals.

Hotelink (UK) Ltd
Silver House, Church La, Lower Fyfield, Marlborough, Wilts SN8 1PY
Tel: 01672 861111 *Fax:* 01672 861100
Email: 106513.724@compuserve.com

Jean R Grant, John Silver, dirs.
Specialists in negotiating best quality hotel accommodation at lowest rates for orchs and other groups on tour in the UK or abroad.

605

606

Interchange
Interchange House, 27 Stafford Rd, Croydon, Surrey CR0 4NG
Tel: 0181 681 3612 *Fax:* 0181 760 0031

Gordon Burnett, mgr dir.
Specialists in group tours worldwide catering to individual group requests.

International Arts and Music
PO Box 1, St Albans, Herts AL1 4ED
Tel: 01727 841115 *Fax:* 01727 851676

Stuart Harding, mgr dir.
Central booking point for theatre (opera, music and art), travel and accommodation UK and worldwide.

Legato Music Tours
8 Meadow La, Alvechurch, Birmingham B48 7LH
Tel: 0121 445 4938

Christine Read, Nigel Morley, dirs.
Specialist mus tours throughout Europe for schools, youth groups, choirs, bands and orchs.

Maestro Travel & Touring Company
6th Floor, 32 Hanover St, Liverpool L1 4AA
Tel: 0151 707 1234 *Fax:* 0151 707 1747
Email: maestro@compuserve.com
Website: www.maestrotravel.com

Ken Grundy; Nigel Foo.
International travel arrangements for the classical mus business from individual artists to ens and full scale orch touring.

Martin Randall Travel Ltd
10 Barley Mow Passage, Chiswick, London W4 4PA
Tel: 0181 742 3355 *Fax:* 0181 742 7766

Martin Randall, dir.
Operators of special lecture tours to European festivals and opera houses.

Music and Travel Ltd
124 Village Way, Beckenham, Kent BR3 3PA
Tel: 0181 663 3037 *Fax:* 0181 663 3012
Email: info@music-and-travel.co.uk
Website: www.music-and-travel.co.uk/

David Horsburgh, dir.
Travel and tour arrangements specialising in Europe and N America. Tailor-made tours, festivals and exchanges.

Musica Europa
7a Farm Rd, Maidenhead, Berks SL6 5HX
Tel: 01628 776795 *Fax:* 01628 32112

Ben Gunner, dir.
Organises concert tours, w/shops, courses, exchanges and visits to the European festivals for both performers and listeners.

Nst Music Tours
Chiltern House, 181 Bristol Av, Blackpool, Lancs FY2 0FA
Tel: 01253 352525 *Fax:* 01253 356955
Email: nst@nstgroup.co.uk

Sarah Foden, mus tours mgr.
Tailor-made performance tours for bands, choirs and orchs throughout Europe. Arrangements for travel and accommodation only are also available.

Onyx International Travel Services Ltd
26 Woodford Close, Caversham, Reading, Berks RG4 7HN
Tel: 0118 947 2830 *Fax:* 0118 946 3104

Specialists in orch and choir travel including flight, hotel bookings worldwide, air charter and tailor-made tours.

Perform Europe
Deepdene Lodge, Deepdene Av, Dorking, Surrey RH5 4AZ
Tel: 01306 744360 *Fax:* 01306 744361
Email: peurope@kuoni.co.uk

Maria Llinares, Sharon Brewster, operations.
Specialists in performing arts tours for amateur groups in the UK and Ireland. Agents for the Bournemouth Music Makers Festival. Organisers of the Harrogate and W Sussex International Youth Music Festivals.

Progressive Tours Ltd
12 Porchester Pl, London W2 2BS
Tel: 0171 262 1676 *Fax:* 0171 724 6941
Email: 101533.513@compuserve.com

L R Temple, mgr.
Specialists in travel to former USSR, most European countries, Cuba and South Africa for choirs, orchs, cultural groups, etc. Exchange enquiries welcome.

Rayburn Tours Ltd
Rayburn House, Parcel Terrace, Derby DE1 1LZ
Tel: 01332 347828 *Fax:* 01332 371298

Catherine Astle, Sarah Middleton, Anne Johns, mus tours orgs; Daniel Carriett, mus tours mgr.
Tailor-made concert tours for all types of amateur youth and adult bands, choirs, orchs and ens.

St Albans Travel Service
4a Spencer St, St Albans, Herts AL3 5EQ
Tel: 01727 842276 *Fax:* 01727 847418

Catherine Neal, mgr.
UK and international travel service, hotel bookings, many discounts.

School Rail
PO Box 1, St Albans, Herts AL1 4ED
Tel: 01727 834475 *Fax:* 01727 851676

Pat Kearley, mgr.
Educational tours, reduced rail travel, overnight accommodation, ticket bookings, lecture and tour arrangements. Theatre and mus events. Worldwide tours for choirs, orch, etc.

Specialised Travel Ltd
12-15 Hanger Green, Park Royal, London W5 3EL
Tel: 0181 998 1761 *Fax:* 0181 998 7965
Email: information@specialised-travel.co.uk
Website: www.specialised-travel.co.uk

Richard Savage, chmn.
ABTA, IATA and CAA bonded travel consultants to the mus industry since 1955. Competitive quotes for travel to any part of the world. Concert tours organised to E and W Europe, USA and Canada, Japan and South Africa.

Travel for the Arts
117 Regent's Park Rd, London NW1 8UR
Tel: 0171 483 4466 *Fax:* 0171 586 0639

Clare Temple, mgr.
Operates a programme of visits to opera houses and summer festivals for opera, ballet and mus lovers.

Upbeat Tours
29 High St, Llandovery, Carms SA20 0PU
Tel: 01550 720978 *also fax*

Meryl Goodwin, Hugh Thomas, dirs.
Specialists in concert tours of Brittany for choirs, orchs and chmbr musicians.

Wyvern Schooltours Ltd
28 Westbourne Gardens, Trowbridge, Wilts BA14 9AW
Tel: 01225 766346 *Fax:* 01225 777936

Ashley Scarlett, operations dir.
Tailor-made tours to Western Europe for orch, inst and choral groups.

Young Travellers Ltd
Dept Music and Leisure, Travel House, 34 Station Rd, London SE20 7BQ
Tel: 0181 778 6850 *Fax:* 0181 778 9754
Email: musicleisure@young-travellers.co.uk

S Williamson, dir; A McIntyre, programme consultant.
Transportation by coach of orchs and choirs in the UK and abroad including accommodation arrangements if required.

Financial Services

The following companies offer specialist accountancy and insurance services to individuals and organisations in the music profession.

Accountancy Services

Bruton Charles Chartered Accountants
60 Valley Rd, Henley on Thames RG9 1RR
Tel: 01491 411322 *Fax:* 01491 410951
Email: 101565.2202@compuserve.com

Jonathan Lawrence-Archer.
Tax and accounts, VAT returns and personal financial planning.

Bruton Charles Chartered Accountants
Ashland House, 20 Moxon St, Marylebone High St,
London W1M 3JE
Tel: 0171 935 7872 *Fax:* 0171 486 7639

Tax and accounts, VAT returns and personal financial planning.

Chantrey Vellacott
Russell Sq House, 10-12 Russell Sq, London WC1B 5LF
Tel: 0171 436 3666 *Fax:* 0171 436 8884

Eric Longley, Chris Jones.
Auditing and accounting services; personal financial planning and taxation.

Chantrey Vellacott
Derngate Mews, Derngate, Northampton NN1 1UE
Tel: 01604 639257 *Fax:* 01604 6231460
Website: www.chantry-vellacott.co.uk

Elliot Harris.
Auditing and accounting services; personal financial planning and taxation.

David Smith & Co
41 Welbeck St, London W1M 8HH
Tel: 0171 224 1004 *Fax:* 0171 486 8705

D C Smith, practitioner; R Shah, qualified snr. Accounts preparation and taxation advice to self-employed musicians and teachers. Clients need not be local.

Guy Rippon Organisation
24 Pepper St, London SE1 0EB
Tel: 0171 928 9777 *Fax:* 0171 928 9222

Guy Rippon, snr partner.
Chartered certified accoutants. Comprehensive accountancy services to the mus industry. Also registered auditors.

John Seeley & Co
1 Upper Saint Mary's Rd, Bearwood, Warley, W Midlands B67 5JR
Tel: 0121 429 1504 *Fax:* 0121 429 3121

John Seeley, principal.
Full range of accountancy and taxation services for the mus industry. Free financial guide for musicians available on request.

Lloyd Piggott Chartered Accountants
Blackfriars House, Parsonage, Manchester M3 2JA
Tel: 0161 833 0346 *Fax:* 0161 832 0045

Colin Lomas, snr partner; Gary Dodds, Christopher Swallow.
Accountancy and taxation services for musicians throughout the UK.

Martin Greene Ravden
55 Loudoun Rd, St John's Wood, London NW8 0DL
Tel: 0171 625 4545 *Fax:* 0171 625 5265
Email: mgr@mgr.co.uk

Lionel Martin, David Ravden, Steve Daniel, Ed Grossman, Harish Shah, partners.
Business management, tour accounting and admin, VAT, royalty examinations, litigation support and other financial services.

Nyman Libson Paul Chartered Accountants
Regina House, 124 Finchley Rd, London NW3 5JS
Tel: 0171 794 5611 *Fax:* 0171 431 1109

Specialist knowledge of the entertainment and mus industry.

Pearson & Co (Chartered Accoutants)
Faircross House, 116 The Parade, High St, Watford,
Herts WD1 2AX
Tel: 01923 238140 *Fax:* 01923 210991

Richard Pearson, partner.
Accountancy, audits, taxation and financial
management services.

Pryor, Begent, Fry & Co
The Great Barn Studio, Cippenham La, Slough SL1 5AU
Tel: 01753 554613 *Fax:* 01753 553520

Accountants.

Trevor Ford & Co
151 Mount View Rd, London N4 4JT
Tel: 0181 341 6408 *Fax:* 0181 340 0021

Client list full at present.

Willott Kingston Smith and Associates
Quadrant House, Air St Entrance, 80-82 Regent St,
London W1R 5PA

Steve Waring, Geraint Howells.
Financial management, contract reviews,
litigation support, international tax, personal
financial planning, audit and accounting, taxation
and VAT.

Insurance Services

Berkeley Alexander (Insurance Advisory Services)
28 High St, Lewes, E Sussex BN7 2SB
Tel: 01273 477784 *Fax:* 01273 478994

E York.

Brass Band Insurance
312 High St, Harlington, Hayes, Middx UB3 5BT
Tel: 0181 759 0825 *Fax:* 0181 564 9063

Mr and Mrs J Beeston.

British Reserve Insurance Co Ltd
Musical Instrument Dept, Cornhill House, 6 Vale Av,
Tunbridge Wells, Kent TN1 1EH
Tel: 01892 515244 *Fax:* 01892 511080

Hibernian Violins
24 Players Av, Malvern Link, Worcs WR14 1DU
Tel: 01684 562947

Padraig O Dublaoidh.
Advice on insuring str insts and bows.

HSBC Gibbs (HCA) Ltd
Bishops Court, 27-33 Artillery La, London E1 7LP
Tel: 01883 741854 *also fax*

John Ewington.

Jack Hayward Harps
Harp Strings Insurance, 5 Sun Gardens, Burghfield
Common, Reading RG7 3JB
Tel: 0118 983 3922 *Fax:* 0118 983 3868

Jack Hayward, proprietor.

Lowndes Lambert International Ltd
Crowley Colosso Division, Friary Court, Crutched Friars,
London EC3N 2NP
Tel: 0171 560 3000 *Fax:* 0171 560 3655

Musicover: Golden Valley Insurance
The Olde Shoppe, Ewyas Harold, Herefordshire HR2 0ES
Tel: 01981 240536/241062 *Fax:* 01981 240451
Email: goldenvalleyins@mcmail.com

Sharon O'Gorman.

NW Brown Music Division
Richmond House, 16-20 Regent St, Cambridge CB2 1DB
Tel: 01223 357131 *Fax:* 01223 353705
Email: music@nwbrown.co.uk

Mark Boon.

PJ Jenkins & Co
Bristan House, Colham Mill Rd, W Drayton, Middx UB7 7AE
Tel: 01895 431448 *Fax:* 01895 434055

Roger Lark & Sedgwick
Wigham House, Wakering Rd, Barking, Essex IG11 8PB
Tel: 0181 557 2300 *Fax:* 0181 594 7083

Associations

This list contains educational organisations and musical associations with some relevance to education. A fuller list of musical associations can be found in the *British Music Yearbook*.

Adult Residential Colleges Association (ARCA)
Headlands, Church La, Washbrook, Ipswich, Suffolk IP8 3HF
Tel: 01473 730737
Website: www.aredu.demon.co.uk

Short courses averaging 2 to 7 days. Many member colleges include mus in the range of subjects covered.

Arts Foundation
The Countess of Huntingdon's Chapel, The Vineyards, Bath BA1 5NA
Tel: 01225 315775 *Fax:* 01225 317597
Email: pru.skene.ace@artsfb.org.uk

Prudence Skene, dir.
A private, charitable organisation established to foster innovation and patronage in the arts by awarding Fellowships to individual artists. No open applications accepted; nominations only.

Associated Board of the Royal Schools of Music
14 Bedford Sq, London WC1B 3JG
Tel: 0171 636 5400 *Fax:* 0171 436 4520
Email: abrsm@abrsm.ac.uk
Website: www.abrsm.ac.uk

Richard Morris, chief exec; Suzannah Power, head of mkt.
The Associated Board offers a graded system of mus exams from preparatory level to professional diploma. Exams are offered in 35 insts, singing, choral singing, practical musicianship and theory. Over half a million candidates are examined each year worldwide. A Professional Development Course is available for inst and singing teachers, leading to the qualification of CT ABRSM. Examinations in jazz will be available in the UK from 1999.

Association for the Advancement of Teacher Education in Music *see* National Association of Music Educators

Association of British Choral Directors (ABCD)
46 Albert St, Tring, Herts HP23 6AU
Tel: 01442 891633 *also fax*

Marie-Louise Petit, gen sec; Howard Layfield, chair.
The association and forum for choral conductors.

Promotes education, training and development for choral conductors and teachers in all sectors of activity.

Association of British Jazz Musicians
Jazz Services, Africa House, 64-78 Kingsway, London WC2B 6BD
Tel: 0171 405 0737 *Fax:* 0171 405 0828
Email: jazz@dial.pipex.com

Chris Hodgkins.
Represents the interests of jazz musicians in the UK who are members of the Musicians' Union.

Association of British Orchestras
Francis House, Francis St, London SW1P 1DE
Tel: 0171 828 6913 *Fax:* 0171 931 9959
Email: abo@orchestranet.co.uk
Website: www.orchestranet.co.uk

Libby MacNamara, dir.
Representation of the collective interests of professional UK orchs: conferences, seminars, negotiation, training and general advocacy. Incorporating Opera and Music Theatre Forum.

Association of Educational Advisers in Scotland
Cunninghame House, Irvine, KA12 8EE
Tel: 01294 324450 *Fax:* 01294 324444

Alistair Horne, president; Jan Ward, sec.

Association of English Singers and Speakers
13 Shaftesbury Av, Bedford MK40 3SA
Tel: 01234 355787 *also fax*

Jacob de Vries, chmn.
Aims to encourage the communication of English words in speech and song with clarity, understanding and imagination.

Association of Heads of Independent Schools
Wispers School, Haslemere, Surrey GU27 1AD
Tel: 01428 643646 *Fax:* 01428 641120

L H Beltran, chmn.
Member schools, accredited by ISJC, tend to be small all-ability schools, both boarding, weekly boarding and day.

Association of Irish Choirs
4 Drinan St, Cork, Republic of Ireland
Tel: 00 353 21 312296 *Fax:* 00 353 21 962457

Barbara Heas, admin.
Established in 1980 to promote choral mus and singing. Organises annual summer school and other courses; publishes choral mus; administers the Irish Youth Choir; issues newsletter In-Choir.

Association of Professional Music Therapists
38 Pierce La, Fulbourn, Cambs CB1 5DL
Tel: 01223 880377 *Fax:* 01223 881679

Diana Asbridge, admin.
Deals with the needs of professional mus therapists in relation to standards of practice, employment career structure, training, etc.

Association of Teachers and Lecturers (ATL)
7 Northumberland St, London WC2N 5DA
Tel: 0171 930 6441 *Fax:* 0171 930 1359
Email: info@atl.org.uk
Website: www.atl.org.uk

Peter Smith, gen sec.
Provides over 150,000 members (4,877 mus teachers) with full trade union services. Also curriculum development.

Association of Teachers of Singing
146 Greenstead Rd, Colchester, Essex CO1 2SN
Tel: 01206 867462 *also fax*

Coral Gould, membership sec; Norman Tattersall, conference dir; Colin J Schooling, sec and treasurer. For qualified teachers of singing; holds annual conference in different venues and spring and winter conference in London.

Association of University Teachers
United House, 9 Pembridge Rd, London W11 3JY
Tel: 0171 221 4370 *Fax:* 0171 727 6547
Email: hq@aut.org.uk

David Triesman, gen sec.

Association of University Teachers (Scotland and Northumbria)
6 Castle St, Edinburgh EH2 3AT
Tel: 0131 226 6694 *Fax:* 0131 226 2066
Email: scotland&ne@aut.org.uk
Website: www.aut.org.uk/auts.html

David Bleiman, asst gen sec; Tony Axon, research offr.
Professional association for academic and related staff in universities.

The Association of Woodwind Teachers

Honorary President: June Emerson
Vice President: Bernard Parris
Patrons: Susan Milan, Gordon Lewin, William Waterhouse,
Celia Nicklin, Colin Bradbury
Chairman: Angela Fussell

Professional masterclasses, information exchange, woodwind repair workshops, newsletters, meetings, lists of repairers and reed makers

A friendly forum for all your ideas and problems

for more information contact:

**Norman Blow
26 Gouge Avenue, Northfleet, Gravesend
Kent DA11 8DP** ☎ **01474 322881**

BRITISH ASSOCIATION
~ OF ~
SYMPHONIC BANDS
~ AND ~
WIND ENSEMBLES

BASBWE is **the** Association for anyone with an interest in Wind Music – players, conductors, composers, teachers and publishers - promoting interest nationwide in wind bands and wind ensembles. BASBWE is particularly committed to the performance of original music and the commissioning of new works for wind bands at all levels – School, Community and Professional.

BASBWE's Annual Conference gives the ideal opportunity for wind enthusiasts to meet and discuss the development of wind music, hear new music and attend workshops and lectures by leading clinicians from this country and abroad. Also, **BASBWE** has taken over the management of the **National Concert Band Festival**, sponsored by **Boosey & Hawkes Plc.**

For more information please contact:
Liz Winter, 7 Dingle Close, Tytherington,
Macclesfield SK10 2UT
Tel/Fax: 01625 430 807

Association of Woodwind Teachers
90 Becmead Av, Kenton, Middx HA3 8HB
Tel: 0181 907 8428 *also fax;* 0410 520539

Angela Fussell, chmn; Caroline Barlow, sec.
The aims of the association are to promote and encourage high standards of w/wind teaching and to give support and practical help to w/wind teachers both specialist and general. Also encourages professional development through exchange of information and mutual support.

Association of Workers for Children with Emotional and Behavioural Difficulties
18 Thornton Ct, Girton, Cambridge CB3 0Ns
Tel: 01223 277096 *also fax*

Sue Panter, gen sec.
Serves all disciplines involved with children with emotional and behavioural difficulties.

Bagpipe Society
25 Baden Rd, Evington, Leicester LE5 5PA
Tel: 0116 273 4453

Tim Garland, publicity offr.
For all types of folk, early and art bagpipes. Regular newsletters, journals, diary of bagpipe events and other publications.

BBC Education
White City, Wood La, London W12 7TS
Tel: 0181 746 1111 *Fax:* 0181 752 4398
Email: edinfo@bbc.co.uk
Website: www.bbc.co.uk/education

Supplies information concerning forthcoming schools radio and TV broadcasts as well as supporting publications, time-tables, etc.

Beecham (Sir Thomas) Trust
15 North Pallant, Chichester, W Sussex PO19 1TQ
Tel: 01243 789855

Shirley, Lady Beecham, trustee; A M Mackarel Davies, trustee; Christopher R Hopper MVO, chmn.
The provision of scholarships and awards at certain universities and musical institutions throughout the UK.

Benslow Association
Little Benslow Hills, off Benslow La, Hitchin, Herts SG4 9RB
Tel: 01462 459446 *Fax:* 01462 440171

Chris Blackman, chmn.
The Friends of Benslow Music Trust.

Benslow Music Trust
Little Benslow Hills, off Benslow La, Hitchin, Herts SG4 9RB
Tel: 01462 459446 *Fax:* 01462 440171

Keith Stent, mus adviser.
National centre for residential mus courses and meeting place for amateur musicians of all standards. Over 100 short courses each year.

Berkshire Young Musicians Trust
Stoneham Ct, 100 Cockney Hill, Reading, Berks RG30 4EZ
Tel: 0118 901 2350 *Fax:* 0118 901 2351

David Marcou, principal.
Provides a wide range of musical opportunities in schools, mus centres and at county level.

British and International Double Bass Forum
Studio Ten, Farnham Maltings, Farnham, Surrey GU9 7QR
Tel: 01252 319610
Email: bibf@classical-artists.com
Website: www.classical-artists.com/bibf

David Heyes, admin.
Promotes the db in all aspects of performance and educ. International membership. Quarterly newsletter.

British Arts Festivals Association
3rd Floor, Whitechapel Library, 77 Whitechapel High St, London E1 7QX
Tel: 0171 247 4667 *Fax:* 0171 247 5010
Email: bafa@netcomuk.co.uk
Website: www.artsfestivals.co.uk

Gwyn Rhydderch, co-ord.
Association of more than 50 leading professional arts festivals for promotion of festivals to audiences at home and abroad and as a forum for exchange of expertise. Includes Festivals Education Group for festival personnel organising education and community programmes. Free annual arts festivals brochure.

British Association for Early Childhood Education
111 City View House, 463 Bethnal Green Rd, London E2 9QY
Tel: 0171 739 7594 *Fax:* 0171 613 5330

Mrs B Boon, snr admin offr; Mrs J Rabin, project mgr.
BAECE is concerned with all aspects of learning for children aged 0-9. Organises national conferences, seminars and meetings; also publishes a newsletter.

British Association of Symphonic Bands and Wind Ensembles (BASBWE)
7 Dingle Close, Tytherington, Macclesfield SK10 2UT
Tel: 01625 430807
Email: basbwe@interbs.demon.co.uk
Website: www.interbs.demon.co.uk/basbwe

Liz Winter, sec; John Myatt, chmn; Charles Hine, chmn elect; Sir Simon Rattle, president.
Promotes interest nationwide in wind bands and wind ens. Quarterly journal *Winds*.

British Choral Institute
18 The Rotyngs, Rottingdean, Brighton BN2 7DX
Tel: 01273 300894 *Fax:* 01273 308394
Email: britchorinst@fastnet.co.uk

Roy Wales, dir; Christine Wales, admin.
Advisory, promotional, education and training body for choral singers, conductors, choral administrators and organisers, with a special emphasis on developing international choral projects.

British Double Reed Society
9 Hamlyn Gardens, Church Rd, London SE19 2NX
Tel: 0181 653 3625
Email: john.wingfield@bdrs.demon.co.uk

Sarah Francis, chmn; David Moore, hon sec.
Registered charity established to further the interests of all involved with the ob and bsn.

British Federation of Brass Bands
17 Kiln Way, Badgers Dene, Grays, Essex RM17 5JE
Tel: 01375 375831

Norman Jones, gen sec; Peter Parkes, pres.
The national body representing the interests of br bands throughout the UK.

British Federation of Festivals
Festivals House, 198 Park La, Macclesfield, Cheshire SK11 6UD
Tel: 01625 428297 *Fax:* 01625 503229
Email: festivals@compuserve.com
Website: ourworld.compuserve.com/homepages/festivals

Elizabeth Whitehead, chief exec.
Headquarters of the amateur mus, speech and dance festival movement.

British Federation of Young Choirs
Devonshire House, Devonshire Sq, Leics LE11 3DW
Tel: 01509 211664 *Fax:* 01509 260630
Email: bfyc@foobar.co.uk

Susan Lansdale, dir; Andrew Fairbairn, hon sec.
Offers events, courses, training and encouragement to people of all ages involved with choral singing. Choral animateurs employed in Scotland, Northern Ireland, the South East, Midlands, East Anglia and London.

British Flute Society
61 Queen's Dr, London N4 2BG
Tel: 0181 802 5984 *Fax:* 0181 809 7436

Ann Cherry, sec; Nick Wallbridge, membership sec.
Promotes fl playing from beginner to professional standard. Events held throughout the country. Quarterly journal *Pan.*

British Horn Society
50 Kings Hall Rd, Beckenham, Kent BR3 1LS
Tel: 0181 289 8864

Email: 100530.2575@compuserve.com
Website: www.foresight.co.uk/horn/

Shirley Hopkins, chmn.
Promotes the hn and its mus. Student, amateur and professional membership. Organises festivals, w/shops and publishes *The Horn* magazine.

British Institute of Organ Studies
c/o 17 Wheeleys Rd, Edgbaston, Birmingham B15 2LD
Tel: 0121 440 5491 *also fax*

Jim Berrow, sec; Peter Williams, chmn.
Dedicated to the scholarly study and conservation of historic British orgs, their source materials and repertoire. Operates an advisory service and administers the British Organ Archive, the National Pipe Organs Register and the Historic Organs Certificate Scheme. Regular day and residential conferences and publications.

British Kodály Academy
13 Midmoor Rd, London SW19 4JD
Tel: 0181 946 6528 *Fax:* 0181 946 6561
Email: enquiries@britishkodalyac.demon.co.uk
Website: www.britishkodalyac.demon.co.uk

Celia Cviic, treasurer and courses sec; Jane Platt, chmn.
Offers teacher training according to the Kodály concept in mus education through w/shops and INSET courses throughout the UK. Also w/end courses, diploma courses and an annual summer school.

British Music Information Centre
10 Stratford Pl, London W1N 9AE
Tel: 0171 499 8567 *Fax:* 0171 499 4795
Email: bmic@bmic.co.uk
Website: www.bmic.co.uk

Matthew Greenall, dir; Simon Woolf, information mgr.
Reference library of 20th C British classical mus. Free admission; open Mon-Fri noon-5pm. Concerts, usually Tue and Thu 7.30pm.

British Music Society
30 Chester Rd, Watford, Herts WD1 7DQ
Tel: 01923 230111

David Burkett, hon sec.
Concentrates particularly on promoting an interest in neglected British composers through learned publications, professionally produced recordings and live concerts.

British Society for Music Therapy
25 Rosslyn Av, E Barnet, Herts EN4 8DH
Tel: 0181 368 8879 *also fax*

Denize Christophers, admin.
Promotes the use of mus therapy in the treatment, education and rehabilitation of

619

children and adults suffering from emotional, physical or mental handicap. Holds meetings and conferences, publishes papers and a journal for members. Membership is open to all interested in mus therapy.

British Suzuki Institute
39 High St, Wheathampstead, Herts AL4 8BB
Tel: 01582 832424 *Fax:* 01582 834488

Birte Kelly, gen sec.
Suzuki teacher training in vn, pno, vc and fl. P/t courses lead to Diploma of European Suzuki Association.

British Trombone Society
PO Box 817, London SE21 7BY
Tel: 0181 658 0405 *also fax;* 01763 848208

John Edney, membership sec; Christopher Greening, ed.
Open to all ages and abilities interested in the trb.

Calouste Gulbenkian Foundation
98 Portland Pl, London W1N 4ET
Tel: 0171 636 5313 *Fax:* 0171 637 3421

Ben Whitaker, dir.
Grant-giving foundation which also publishes books within the three policy areas of social welfare, arts and education.

Cambridge Society of Musicians
122 Horton Rd, Manchester M14 7GD
Tel: 0171 314 3057
Email: csm@music-services.demon.co.uk

Lee P Longden, dir; Ian Roche, admin dean; Nicholas Groves, academic dean.
A learned society which elects experienced musicians to membership, and formally qualified musicians to the higher grades of Associateship and Fellowship. The Society's College, Phillips College, offers certificate and diploma exams.

Careers and Occupational Information Centre
PO Box 298a, Thames Ditton, Surrey KT7 0ZS
Tel: 0181 957 5030 *Fax:* 0181 957 5019

Publishes a wide range of careers and occupational books.

Careers Research and Advisory Centre (CRAC Ltd)
Sheraton House, Castle Pk, Cambridge CB3 0AX
Tel: 01223 460277 *Fax:* 01223 311708
Email: enquiries@crac.org.uk
Website: www.crac.org.uk/crac

Alison Manners, snr admin, business relations; Donald McGregor, dir.
CRAC is an independent development agency and registered educational charity founded in 1964. It provides information, informs policy, anticipates developments and identifies practical solutions in the careers and guidance field.

Cathedral Music, Friends of
Aeron House, Llangeitho, Tregaron, Dyfed SY25 6SU

Michael Cooke, hon sec; Alan Thurlow, chmn.
To assist cathedrals financially in maintaining their mus and to increase public awareness of the unique heritage of cathedral mus.

Cello Club
12 Pierrepoint Rd, London W3 9JH
Tel: 0181 248 9067
Email: celloclub@wbruce.demon.co.uk

William Bruce, dir; Christopher Bunting, president.
A non-profit making national club for young cellists. Members receive three magazines and three newsletters each year on everything to do with the vc world, the opportunity to participate in special vc events and discounts on vc supplies.

Chance for Children Trust
Freepost (SE 6892), London SE25 4TJ
Tel: 0181 997 5831

Helen Ranger.
Mus w/shops for children and young people who have been through a period of trauma.

Children's Music Foundation In Scotland
537 Sauchiehall St, Glasgow G3 7PQ
Tel: 0141 248 1611 *Fax:* 0141 248 1989
Email: childclasscon@compuserve.com
Website: www.childclassic.co.uk

Louise Naftalin, Lizanne McKerrell, mgrs.
Organises the 'Children's Classic Concerts' series, and encourages an appreciation of classical mus in children through concerts and educational w/shops.

Choir Schools' Association
The Minster School, Deangate, York YO1 2JA
Tel: 01904 624900 *Fax:* 01904 632418

Mrs W A Jackson, admin.
Membership includes over 40 schools which educate boy and girl choristers for cathedrals, churches and collegiate chapels. Also administers a Bursary Trust Fund, which aims to ensure that no chorister is denied a place at choir school on financial grounds.

Christian Copyright Licensing (Europe) Ltd
PO Box 1339, Eastbourne, E Sussex BN21 4YF
Tel: 01323 417711 *Fax:* 01323 417722
Email: info@ccli.co.uk
Website: www.ccli.com

Chris Williams, sales.

Issues and administrates the Church Copyright Licence on behalf of over 2500 copyright owners. The licence allows reproduction and recording of the words of copyright worship songs and hymns to churches, schools and Christian organisations for non-commercial use.

Church Music Society
8 The Chandlers, The Calls, Leeds LS2 7EZ
Tel: 0113 234 1146 *also fax*

Simon Lindley, hon sec.
Leading publisher of all kinds of church mus in association with OUP mus dept. Annual lecture and other events.

Clarinet and Saxophone Society of Great Britain
167 Ellerton Rd, Tolworth, Surbiton, Surrey KT6 7UB
Tel: 0181 390 8307

Susan Moss, membership sec.
Advice and consultancy service; library, discount insurance, quarterly journal (including *Young Reeders* supplement), annual conference, teachers' course, regional events.

Clarinet Heritage Society
47 Hambalt Rd, London SW4 9EQ
Tel: 0181 675 3877

Stephen Bennett, hon sec.
Publishes and records new and rare cl mus and promotes the image of the cl.

Clarsach Society
22 Durham Rd South, Edinburgh EH15 3PD
Tel: 0131 669 8972 *Fax:* 0131 468 1223
Email: arco@globalnet.co.uk

Alistair Cockburn, admin.
Promotes the teaching and playing of the celtic harp; organises the Edinburgh Harp Festival and publishes mus for celtic harp.
9 area branches throughout the UK. A full mus catalogue is now available.

Committee of Principals of Conservatoires
c/o Birmingham Conservatoire, Paradise Circus, Birmingham B3 3HG
Tel: 0121 331 5910 *Fax:* 0121 331 5906

George Caird, sec (from Aug 1998); Janet Ritterman, sec (to Jul 1998).
The association has a membership of the major independent conservatoires of mus in the UK. Before Aug 1998 enquiries should be addressed to Janet Ritterman, c/o Royal College of Music, Prince Consort Rd, South Kensington, London SW7 2BS.

Community and Education Project
Sadler's Wells, Rosebery Av, London EC1R 4TN
Tel: 0171 278 6563

Sheryl Aitcheson, community and educ mgr.
Arranges tours, talks, w/shops, m/classes and outreach projects with educ and community groups.

Community Education Development Centre (CEDC)
The Woodway Park School, Wigstone Rd, Coventry CV2 2RH
Tel: 01203 655700 *Fax:* 01203 655701

Phil Street, dir; Kathy Deeth, centre mgr.

Composers' Guild of Great Britain
The Penthouse, 4 Brook St, Mayfair, London W1Y 1AA
Tel: 0171 629 0886 *Fax:* 0171 629 0993

Naomi Moskovic, gen sec.
Represents mainly classical mus composers and provides guidance on commission fees and publishing.
Publications include *Composer News* and *First Performances*. Member of the Alliance of Composer Organisations.

Contemporary Music-Making for Amateurs (COMA)
13 Wellington Way, Bow, London E3 4NE
Tel: 0181 980 1527
Email: coma@compuserve.com

Chris Shurety, dir.
Provides opportunities for amateurs of all abilities to take part in contemporary mus-making.
Also developing a high-quality contemporary repertoire for amateur ens through commissions and research.

Cornet and Trumpet Society (CATS)
Dept of Music, University of Huddersfield, Queensgate, Huddersfield HD1 3DH
Tel: 01484 472007 *Fax:* 01484 472656

Corps of Drums Society
62 Gally Hill Rd, Church Crookham, Hants GU13 0RU
Tel: 01252 614852

Reg Davis, hon sec.
Promotes and preserves the concept and traditions of drum and fife mus, and assists in achieving and maintaining standards of efficiency.

Curwen Institute
5 Bigbury Close, Coventry CV3 5AJ
Tel: 01203 413010 *also fax*

John Dowding, dir.
Promotes the New Curwen Method which encourages children to listen attentively to mus, to recognise pitch, rhythm and phrasing, develop

a musical memory, and sing at sight with confidence.

Dalcroze Society
41a Woodmansterne Rd, Coulsdon, Surrey CR5 2DJ
Tel: 0181 645 0714 *also fax*

P Piqué, sec.
Mus education through movement. Rhythmics, improvisation, ear training and therapy for all age groups.
Summer course 27-31 Jul 1998 at Christ Church College, Canterbury.

Early Music Network
Sutton House, 2-4 Homerton High St, London E9 6JQ
Tel: 0181 533 2921 *Fax:* 0181 533 2922

Alison Blunt, admin.
To generate the development of early mus through the promotion of live performances, education and the dissemination of information.

Educational Centres Association (ECA)
Fareham Adult Education Centre, Wickham Rd, Fareham, Hants PO16 7DA
Tel: 01329 315753 *Fax:* 01329 826915

Susan S Dickinson, gen sec.
National adult education network concerned with

furthering the development of adult education locally, nationally and internationally.

Educational Institute of Scotland
46 Moray Pl, Edinburgh EH3 6BH
Tel: 0131 225 6244 *Fax:* 0131 220 3151

Ronald A Smith, gen sec.
Scottish teachers' union. Publishes *Scottish Educational Journal*, minimum 6 pa, free to members.

English Folk Dance and Song Society
Cecil Sharp House, 2 Regents Park Rd, London NW1 7AY
Tel: 0171 485 2206 *Fax:* 0171 284 0534

Diana Jewitt, teacher training mgr.
Information service; school supply catalogue, project packs; library including tapes and videos.

English Poetry and Song Society
76 Lower Oldfield Pk, Bath, Somerset BA2 3HP
Tel: 01225 313531

Richard Carder, chmn; Joyce Phillips, treasurer.
EPSS is dedicated to the performance, publication and recording of English Art Songs; newsletter and song lists by living composers; competitions.

English Regional Arts Boards
5 City Rd, Winchester, Hants SO23 8SD
Tel: 01962 851063 *Fax:* 01962 842033

Email: info.erab@artsfb.org.uk
Website: www.arts.org.uk

Christopher Gordon, chief exec; Carolyn Nixson, assistant
Information, co-ordination and liaison services for the ten Regional Arts Boards in England and national and international representation of their interests.

Enterprise Music Scotland
Westburn House, Westburn Pk, Aberdeen AB25 3DE
Tel: 01224 620025 *Fax:* 01224 620027

Ronnie Rae, exec dir.
Established to take over from the Scottish Arts Council the administration of funding, tours co-ordination and development of mus clubs and arts guilds in Scotland.

Ernest Read Music Association (ERMA)
9 Cotsford Av, New Malden, Surrey KT3 5EU
Tel: 0181 942 0318

Noel Long, dir.
Organises and promotes concerts for children, training orch and summer courses.

European Association of Teachers (EAT/AEDE)
20 Brookfield, Highgate West Hill, London N6 6AS
Tel: 0181 340 9136

Mary Duce, hon sec (UK section).
As the UK branch of a European organisation, works to promote and examine cross-curricular European knowledge in schools and colleges through FCAA approved tests.

European Guitar Teacher's Association (UK) Ltd (EGTA)
29 Longfield Rd, Tring, Herts HP23 4DG

Sarah Clark, sec; John Williams, president.
Aims to improve the standard of gui education and the inst's place in the mainstream musical world.

European Piano Teachers' Association (UK) Ltd (EPTA)
1 Wildgoose Dr, Horsham RH12 1TU
Tel: 01403 267761 *also fax*

Frances Bryan, admin; Carola Grindea, founder; Kendall Taylor CBE, president; Frank Martin, chmn.
Founded in 1978 to promote excellence in piano playing and teaching in the UK.

European String Teachers Association (ESTA)
247 Hay Green La, Bournville, Birmingham B30 1SH
Tel: 0121 475 3345 *also fax*

Olive Goodborn, admin.
Aims to raise the standard of str playing and teaching, provide an international forum for the exchange of ideas, promote w/shops, lectures, discussions and sponsor publications.

Faculty of Church Music
27 Sutton Pk, Blunsdon, Swindon SN2 4BB
Tel: 0181 675 0180

Rev G Gleed, registrar.
Promotion of high standards in Church mus through graded exams. Tuition provided in theoretical subjects and for external mus degrees.

Federation Internationale des Jeunesses Musicales *see* Youth and Music

Federation of Music Services
Wheatley House, 12 Lucas Rd, High Wycombe, Bucks HP13 6QE
Tel: 01494 439572 *also fax*

Richard Hichman, chief exec; Michael Wearne, chmn.
The Federation aims to offer support and advice to mus services in the provision and development of high quality specialist mus education to schools and the wider community; to help mus services to maintain and develop access and opportunity; and to promote the work of mus services.

Fellowship of Makers and Researchers of Historical Instruments
171 Iffley Rd, Oxford OX4 1EL
Email: jeremy.montagu@music.oxford.ac.uk

Jeremy Montagu, hon sec.
Promotes authenticity in the reconstruction and use of historical insts.

Flutewise
9 Beaconsfield Rd, Portslade, E Sussex BN41 1XA
Tel: 01273 702367 *Fax:* 01273 888864
Email: flutewise@i-gadgets.com
Website: www.ndirect.co.uk/~flutewise

James Galway, president; Liz Goodwin, ed.
Organisation for all flautists, especially the young. Quarterly magazine with competitions and prizes. Regular events.

Galpin Society
2 Quinton Rise, Oadby, Leicester LE2 5PN
Tel: 0116 271 1808 *also fax*

P Holden, sec and admin.
Founded in 1946 for the publication of original research into the history, construction, development and use of mus insts.

Girls' Public Day School Trust
100 Rochester Row, London SW1P 1JP
Tel: 0171 393 6666 *Fax:* 0171 393 6789

M Oakley, sec.

Girls' Schools Association
130 Regent Rd, Leicester LE1 7PG
Tel: 0116 254 1619 *Fax:* 0116 255 3792
Email: gsa@dial.pipex.com

Ms S Cooper, gen sec; Mrs W Khan, admin.

Handbell Ringers of Great Britain
87 The Woodfields, Sanderstead, South Croydon, Surrey CR2 0HJ
Tel: 0181 651 2663 *also fax*

Sandra Winter, hon sec.
National association for handbell, handchime and belleplate tune ringers.

Headmasters' and Headmistresses Conference
130 Regent Rd, Leicester LE1 7PG
Tel: 0116 285 4810 *Fax:* 0116 247 1167

Vivian Anthony, sec.
Association of heads of independent boys and co-educational schools, with 242 members. Publishes a private members bulletin. Divided into 7 areas, each area meeting regularly to exchange ideas and concerns.

Headteachers Association of Scotland
University of Strathclyde, Jordanhill Campus, Southbrae Dr, Glasgow G13 1PP
Tel: 0141 950 3298 *Fax:* 0141 950 3434
Email: head.teachers@strath.ac.uk

James B O McNair, sec.
Exists to promote education, particularly secondary education in Scotland and to safeguard and promote the interests of headteachers, deputy heads and assistant heads.

House of Commons Culture, Media and Sport Committee
Committee Office, 7 Millbank, London SW1P 3JA
Tel: 0171 219 6120/5739/6188 *Fax:* 0171 219 6606
Email: cmscom@parliament.uk
Website: www.parliament.uk

Colin Lee, clerk of the committee.
The committee examines the work of the Department of Culture, Media and Sport and of associated public bodies.

House of Commons Education and Employment Committee
Committee Office, House of Commons, London SW1A 0AA
Tel: 0171 219 5774/6243/6181/0653 *Fax:* 0171 219 6606
Email: educempcom@parliament.uk
Website: www.parliament.uk/commons/selcom/edemhome.htm

Matthew Hamlyn, clerk of the committee; Kenneth Fox, second clerk.
Monitors activities of DFEE and associated public bodies.

Hymn Society of Great Britain and Ireland
7 Paganel Rd, Minehead, Somerset TA24 5ET
Tel: 01643 703530

Rev Geoffrey Wrayford, sec.
Society for those interested in the study and application of hymnody.

Incorporated Association of Organists
11 Stonehill Dr, Bromyard, Herefordshire HR7 4XB
Tel: 01885 483155 *Fax:* 01885 488609

Richard Popple MBE, hon gen sec.
Dedicated to improving org playing at all levels; has over 6000 members worldwide. Publishes *Organists' Review* quarterly.

Incorporated Association of Preparatory Schools
11 Waterloo Pl, Leamington Spa, Warwicks CV32 5LA
Tel: 01926 887833 *Fax:* 01926 888014
Email: hq@iaps.org.uk

J H Morris, gen sec.
The main professional association for headteachers of independent preparatory and junior schools throughout the British Isles and overseas.

Incorporated Society of Musicians
10 Stratford Pl, London W1N 9AE
Tel: 0171 629 4413 *Fax:* 0171 408 1538
Email: membership@ism.org
Website: www.ism.org

Neil Hoyle, chief exec.
Professional body for all musicians. Legal, financial and professional services; conferences, seminars and publications. Full, associate, student and corporate categories.

Incorporated Society of Organ Builders
Petersfield, Hants GU32 3AT
Tel: 01730 262151 *also fax*

D M van Heck, sec.
Pipe org builders association.

Independent Schools Association
Boys' British School, East St, Saffron Walden, Essex CB10 1LS

Tel: 01799 523619 *Fax:* 01799 524892
Email: isa@dial.pipex.com

T M Ham, gen sec.

Independent Schools Careers Organisation
12a Princess Way, Camberley, Surrey GU15 3SP
Tel: 01276 21188 *Fax:* 01276 691833
Email: info@isco.org.uk

G W Searle, national dir.
Provides advice to boys and girls concerning all aspects of higher education and careers. Support and training is provided for school staff.

Independent Schools Information Service (ISIS)
56 Buckingham Gate, London SW1E 6AG
Tel: 0171 630 8793 *Fax:* 0171 630 5013
Email: national@isis.org.uk
Website: www.isis.org.uk

D J Woodhead, dir.
Information for parents about independent schools, including specialist mus and choir schools and mus scholarships.

Institute of Contemporary Arts
The Mall, London SW1Y 5AH
Tel: 0171 930 0493 *Fax:* 0171 873 0051
Email: lois@ica.org.uk
Website: www.newmediacentre.com

Christine Atha, dir, live arts.

Institute of Leisure and Amenity Management (ILAM)
Ilam House, Lower Basildon, Reading, Berks RG8 9NE
Tel: 01491 874800 *Fax:* 01491 874801
Email: info@ilam.co.uk
Website: www.ilam.co.uk

Alan Smith, dir.
Professional body representing over 7000 managers throughout the leisure industry. ILAM represents its members both nationally and regionally, offering its own qualification system and a wide range of benefits to members, including education and training seminars, dissemination of information, publications and conferences.

Institute of Musical Instrument Technology
8 Chester Ct, Albany St, London NW1 4BU
Tel: 0171 935 8682 *Fax:* 0171 224 0957

Julian Markson, hon sec.
Promotes the professional status of members engaged in mus inst design, manufacture and repair.

International Association for the Study of Popular Music
Graduate Research Centre in Culture and Communication, University of Sussex, Falmer, Brighton BN1 9QT
Tel: 01273 606755 *Fax:* 01273 678644
Email: culcom@sussex.ac.uk

Sarah Thornton, chair; Dave Hesmondhalgh, sec and treasurer.
The association brings together scholars of popular mus from 36 different countries; it includes sociologists, musicologists, anthropologists, educationalists and others.

International Association of Music Libraries
Archives and Documentation Centres, c/o County Library Headquarters, Walton St, Aylesbury, Bucks HP20 1UU
Tel: 01296 382266 *Fax:* 01296 382274

Margaret Roll, gen sec.
Careers information and special students subscriptions available to those working in, or with interest in, mus librarianship.

International Piano Teachers' Consultants (IPTEC)
29 Beaumont Rd, Chiswick, London W4 5AL
Tel: 0181 994 4288

Meriel Jefferson, hon sec.
1-day courses. Consultations available in specialist subjects.

International Shakuhachi Society
Lorien, Wadhurst, Sussex TN5 6PN
Tel: 01892 782045

Dan E Mayers, president; Clive Bell, sec and treasurer.
The society provides information on teachers, methods and recordings to devotees of Shakuhachi worldwide. Also provides Shakuhachi insts and bamboo blanks. Periodically publishes hardback volume, *Annals of the International Shakuhachi Society*, sent free to members.

International Society for Contemporary Music (ISCM)
British Section, c/o SPNM, Francis House, Francis St, London SW1P 1DE
Tel: 0171 828 9696 *Fax:* 0171 931 9928
Email: spnm@spnm.org.uk

Gill Graham, admin.
The ISCM British section organises talks, concerts and exhibitions and provides information on the activities of the International Society for Contemporary Music. The ISCM world mus days will be held in Manchester 17-26 Apr 1998.

International Society for Music Education (ISME)

International Centre for Research in Music Education, University of Reading, Bulmershe Ct, Reading RG6 1HY
Tel: 0118 931 8846 *also fax; Fax:* 0118 935 2080
Email: e.smith@reading.ac.uk
Website: www.isme.org

Elizabeth Smith, admin.
Aims to promote mus education throughout the world as an integral part of general education through conferences, publications, etc. Membership information and details of the next world conference are available from the above address.

International Society for the Study of Tension in Performance

School of Music, Kingston University, c/o 28 Emperor's Gate, London SW7 4HS
Tel: 0171 373 7307 *Fax:* 0171 373 5440

Carola Grindea, chmn; Gordana Petrovic, sec.
Charitable organisation committed to helping musicians afflicted by physical and psychological problems at ISSTIP/London College of Music 'Performing Arts Clinic'.
Publishes ISSTIP journal.

International Viola Society (British Chapter)

36 Seeleys, Harlow, Essex CM17 0AD
Tel: 01279 422567

John White, president and organising sec.
Association for the promotion of va performance and research. Affiliated to the Lionel Tertis International Viola Competition held every 3 yrs at Port Erin, Isle of Man (next competition 2000). The 1998 International Viola Congress will be held at the RSAMD, Glasgow on 16-19 Jul (*Tel:* 0141 334 4867 for further details).

Irish Contemporary Music Centre

95 Lower Baggot St, Dublin 2, Republic of Ireland
Tel: 00 353 1 661 2105 *Fax:* 00 353 1 676 2639
Email: info@cmc.ie
Website: www.cmc.ie

Eve O'Kelly, dir.
Promotes and documents Irish contemporary mus.

Jazz Services Ltd

Room 518, Africa House, 64 Kingsway, London WC2B 6BD
Tel: 0171 405 0737/47/57 *Fax:* 0171 405 0828
Email: jazz@dial.pipex.com
Website: ds.dial.pipex.com/town/square/ad663/

Chris Hodgkins, dir; Celia Wood, information.
Jazz Services promotes the growth and

ASSOCIATIONS

development of jazz within the UK by providing services in marketing, communications, touring, information, education and jazz newspapers.

Kato Havas Association For The New Approach (KHANA)
3 Beacon View, Marple, Stockport SK6 6PX
Tel: 0161 449 7347

Gloria Bakhshayesh, admin and treasurer.
Kato Havas vn teaching method. KHANA holds w/shops on the alleviation and prevention of physical tensions and anxiety in str playing. 2 journals pa.

Klavar Music Foundation of Great Britain
171 Yarborough Rd, Lincoln LN1 3NQ
Tel: 01522 523117

Michael Magnus Osborn, dir.
Educ Trust. Klavar system correspondence courses for pno, org, gui and pno-accordion. Klavar notation printed mus supplies.

The Kodály Institute of Britain
133 Queen's Gate, London SW7 5LE
Tel: 0171 823 7371 Fax: 0171 584 7691

Mary Skone-Roberts, admin; Cecilia Vajda, dir.
Adult education; 1-yr p/t courses in musicianship. W/end courses on early childhood mus education, primary and secondary education. Annual Aug international summer school in London. Publications include books, video and audio cassettes.

Library Association
7 Ridgmount St, London WC1E 7AE
Tel: 0171 636 7543 Fax: 0171 436 7218
Email: info@la-hq.org.uk
Website: www.la-hq.org.uk

Ross Shimmon, chief exec.
Professional body for library and information managers with 25,000 members UK and overseas.

London Suzuki Group
96 Farm La, London SW6 1QH
Tel: 0171 386 8006
Email: lsg@pullinger.prestel.co.uk

Christine Livingstone, mus dir; Nicholas Pullinger, admin.
Charitable organisation of teachers, parents and children committed to the Suzuki approach to mus education for children aged 3-18.

Lute Society
Southside Cottage, Brook Hill, Albury, Guildford GU5 9DJ
Tel: 01483 202159 Fax: 01483 203088
Email: lutesoc@aol.com
Website: ds.dial.pipex.com/silvius/lute/

Christopher Goodwin, sec.
Holds 4 meetings pa in central London with lectures and recitals on all aspects of the lute and related insts and their repertoire. Publishes annual journal The Lute, quarterly newsletter Lute News, performing editions, working drawings of lutes. Holds occasional 1 day w/shops. Lutes available for hire.

Mechanical-Copyright Protection Society Ltd (MCPS)
Elgar House, 41 Streatham High Rd, London SW16 1ER
Tel: 0181 664 4400 Fax: 0181 769 8792
Email: webmaster@mcps.co.uk
Website: www.mcps.co.uk

Simon Lindsay, customer services adviser.
Membership organisation that acts as a centralised licensing and collection agency for mechanical royalties, whenever its members' musical works are recorded.

Metier
Glyde House, Glydegate, Bradford, W Yorks BD5 0BQ
Tel: 01274 738800 Fax: 01274 391566

Claire Pickard, info offr.
Metier is the industry lead body developing standards of competence for a wide range of occupations in the arts and entertainment sector, many of which will underpin new National and Scottish Vocational Qualifications. (NVQ already available in Music Performance at Level 4.) It is an approved Industry Training Organisation acting as a focal point for training matters and representing the interests of employers in the sector to TECs, LECs and government.

Music Education Council
54 Elm Rd, Hale, Altrincham, Cheshire WA15 9QP
Tel: 0161 928 3085 Fax: 0161 929 9648
Email: ahassan@easynet.co.uk

Anna Hassan, admin.
The major forum for those involved in mus education and training in the UK.

Music for Youth
102 Point Pleasant, London SW18 1PP
Tel: 0181 870 9624 Fax: 0181 870 9935
Website: www.pjpubs.co.uk/mfy

Larry Westland CBE, exec dir.
Charity dedicated to providing regional and national platforms for young musicians.

627

ASSOCIATIONS

Music Masters' and Mistresses' Association (MMA)
Three Ways, Chicks La, Kilndown, Cranbrook, Kent TN17 2RS
Tel: 01892 890537 *also fax*

Victoria Aldous-Ball, admin.
Furthers all aspects of mus in schools. Membership open to those teaching mus in schools, and those wishing to support the development of mus in schools. Regular regional meetings, courses and an annual conference are held. Termly journal and annual mus scholarship guide.

Music, Mind and Movement
28 Glebe Place, London SW3 5LD
Tel: 0171 352 1666 *also fax*

Lucinda Mackworth-Young, Nicola Gaines, Karin Greenhead, dirs.
An association devoted to enhancing the performance and teaching of mus and dance through an integrated multi-arts approach. Courses run for performers, teachers and students in the practical application of psychology, eurhythmics, dance through the ages and other disciplines to performance, teaching and learning of mus and dance. Courses may be validated by Trinity College of Music as bearing credit to the ATCL and LTCL (Music Education) or certificate in mus education.

Music Publishers' Association Ltd
3rd Floor, Strandgate, 18-20 York Buildings, London WC2N 6JU
Tel: 0171 839 7779 *Fax:* 0171 839 7776
Email: mpa@mcps.co.uk

Sarah Faulder, chief exec; Peter Dadswell, exec adviser.
Trade organisation representing mus publishers in the UK, advising and assisting members in the promotion and protection of mus copyright.

Musicians Benevolent Fund
16 Ogle St, London W1P 8JB
Tel: 0171 636 4481 *Fax:* 0171 637 4307
Email: helen.faulkner@mbf.sprint.com

Philip Jones CBE, chmn; Helen Faulkner, sec.
Largest charity in the UK helping professional musicians and their dependants in need.

Musicians Benevolent Fund, Friends of the
16 Ogle St, London W1P 8JB
Tel: 0171 636 4481 *Fax:* 0171 637 4307
Email: hilary.pentycross@mbf.sprint.com.uk
Website: www.mbf.org.uk

Hilary Pentycross, co-ord.
The Friends support the Musicians Benevolent Fund which is the largest musical charity in the UK helping professional musicians and their dependants in need.

Musicians' Union
60-62 Clapham Rd, London SW9 0JJ
Tel: 0171 582 5566 *Fax:* 0171 582 9805
Email: info@musiciansunion.org.uk
Website: www.musiciansunion.org.uk

Dennis Scard, gen sec.

NATFHE - The University and College Lecturers' Union
27 Britannia St, London WC1X 9JP
Tel: 0171 837 3636 *Fax:* 0171 837 4403
Email: natfhe-hq@geo2.poptel.org.uk

Represents lecturers in post-16 educ. Campaigns for high quality education opportunities as well as decent pay and conditions for staff. Active mus section.

National Association for Gifted Children
Elder House, Milton Keynes MK9 1LR
Tel: 01908 673677 *Fax:* 01908 673679
Email: nagc@rmplc.co.uk

Peter Carey, dir; Michal Hambourg, mus counsellor.
A national charity helping able and talented children to achieve fulfilment and advising those involved in their upbringing and education.

National Association for Music Staff in Higher Education
Royal Northern College of Music, 124 Oxford Rd, Manchester M13 9RD
Tel: 0161 273 6283 *Fax:* 0161 273 7611
Email: c.r.timms@bham.ac.uk; colin@fs1.rncm.ac.uk

Colin Timms, chmn.
Professional subject association for mus staff in higher educ. Membership is arranged through mus depts. It is a forum for debate and exchange of information about teaching methodology and admin matters.

National Association for Primary Education (NAPE)
University of Leicester, Barrack Rd, Northampton NN2 6AF
Tel: 01604 636326 *Fax:* 01604 636328
Email: nationaloffice@nape.org.uk
Website: www.nape.org.uk

Jacqui Middlewood, hon gen sec.
Membership includes parents, teachers, governors, school communities and others who share concern for children's education from 0-13. Festival of voices held annually in London.

National Association for Special Education Needs
NASEN House, 4-5 Amber Business Village, Amber Close, Amington, Tamworth B77 4RP
Tel: 01827 311500 *Fax:* 01827 313005
Email: welcome@nasen.org.uk

Promotes the development of children and

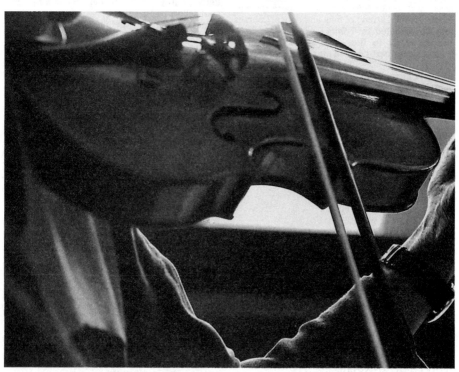

young people with special educational needs, wherever they are located, offering support to those who work with them.

National Association of Advisory Officers for Special Education
32a Pleasant Valley, Saffron Walden, Essex CB11 4AP
Tel: 01799 521257 *also fax*

Links inspectors and advisers with responsibility for special educational provision both in mainstream and special schools and those involved in OFSTED inspections with an SEN brief.

National Association of Careers and Guidance Teachers
Portland House, 4 Bridge St, Usk, Gwent NP5 1BG
Tel: 01291 672985 *Fax:* 01291 672090
Website: www.careersoft.co.uk/nacgt

Mrs J G Cook, gen sec.
Professional association for careers teachers and others involved in careers education and guidance.

National Association of Choirs
21 Charmouth Rd, Lower Weston, Bath BA1 3LJ
Tel: 01225 426713

John Robbins, gen sec.
NAC caters exclusively for choirs, providing a wide range of services such as liaison with festivals, insurance, charitable status applications, mus discount, mus loan scheme. Choirs benefit from being placed in groups for local and combined choir activities.

National Association of Head Teachers
1 Heath Sq, Boltro Rd, Haywards Heath, W Sussex RH16 1BL
Tel: 01444 472472 *Fax:* 01444 472473

David Hart OBE, gen sec.
NAHT membership is open to heads and deputies of schools of all types serving the education of pupils aged 3-19.

National Association of Music Educators
52 Hall Orchard La, Frisby-on-the-Wreake, Melton Mowbray, Leics LE14 2NH
Tel: 01664 434379 *Fax:* 01664 434137
Email: musiceducation@name.org.uk

Jane Easton, professional offr.
Professional support for those in mus education - class and instrumental teachers, advisers, inspectors, consultants and administrators. Subject support for those in teaching and inspection. Professional development for members. National and regional conferences. Publications and regular newsletters. Membership: £40 annually.

National Association of Musical Instrument Repairers
2 Arthur Cottages, Frimley Rd, Ash Vale, Surrey GU12 5PD
Tel: 01252 518098
Email: glissmus@aol.com

Richard Dawson.
Individual repairers dedicated to maintaining standards of quality in a particular inst. Enables enquirers to contact a local repairer of the appropriate specialism.

National Association of Percussion Teachers
138 Springbank Rd, London SE13 6SU
Tel: 0181 698 7885 *Fax:* 0181 461 5910
Email: christine.skinner@lineone.net

Christeen Skinner, sec.
To further the knowledge of perc playing and teaching and ensuring the highest standards are maintained.

National Association of Schoolmasters' Union and Women Teachers (NASUWT)
Hillscourt Education Centre, Rose Hill, Rednal, Birmingham B45 8RS
Tel: 0121 453 6150

Nigel de Gruchy, gen sec.

National Association of Youth Orchestras
Ainslie House, 11 St Colme St, Edinburgh EH3 6AG
Tel: 0131 539 1087 *Fax:* 0131 539 1069
Email: admin@nayo.org.uk
Website: www.nayo.org.uk

Carol Main, dir; Jenny Brockie, admin.
National association for youth orchs throughout UK. Activities include annual Festival of British Youth Orchestras in Edinburgh and Glasgow, Anglo-German Youth Music Week, British Reserve Insurance Conducting Prize (biennial), British Reserve Insurance Youth Orchestra Awards (annual).
Newsletter *Full Orchestra* 3 pa, free to members. Marion Semple Weir library of chmbr mus, no hire charges to members.

National Early Music Association
18 High St, Caythorpe, Grantham, Lincs NG32 3BS
Tel: 01400 273795
Website: www.brainlink.com/~starmus/unison/nema/nema.html

Elspeth Fraser-Darling, admin.
NEMA publishes the *Early Music Yearbook* incorporating the Register of Early Music and the bi-annual journal *Leading Notes*.

National Federation of Music Societies

Francis House, Francis St, London SW1P 1DE
Tel: 0171 828 7320 *Fax:* 0171 828 5504
Email: nfms@nfms.demon.co.uk

Rubin Osterley, chief exec.
Provides legal, financial, artistic, training, advocacy and lobbying services for 2000 voluntary member mus societies.

National Harmonica League

Rivendell, High St, Shirrell Heath, Nr Southampton, Hants SO32 2JN
Tel: 01329 832178 *Fax:* 01329 832178
Email: 100571.132@compuserve.com

Colin Mort, chmn.
For harmonica enthusiasts; newsletter and events.

National Institute for Careers Education and Counselling

Sheraton House, Castle Pk, Cambridge CB3 0AX
Tel: 01223 460277 *Fax:* 01223 311708
Email: nicec@crac.org.uk

A G Watts, dir.
Carries out applied research and development work related to careers guidance in educational settings and in work and community settings.

National Institute of Adult Continuing Education

21 De Montfort St, Leicester LE1 7GE
Tel: 0116 255 1451 *Fax:* 0116 285 4514
Email: niace@niace.org.uk
Website: www.niace.org.uk

Louise McGill, snr info offr.
Twice yearly, Jan/Aug, publishes *Time to Learn* at £4.25, detailing a wide range of w/end and 1-wk residential courses held at various centres throughout the UK.

National Junior Music Club of Great Britain

23 Hitchin St, Biggleswade, Beds SG18 8AX
Tel: 01767 316521 *Fax:* 01767 317221

Douglas Coombes, mus dir; Rose Miles, membership sec; Carole Lindsay-Douglas, ed.
Termly resource magazine for primary and middle school teachers. Membership includes right to photocopy for use within own school, and preferential fees for courses and summer school organised by the club.

National Music Council

Francis House, Francis St, London SW1P 1DE
Tel: 0181 347 8618 *also fax*

Russell Jones, chmn; Mark Isherwood, deputy chmn; Jennifer Goodwin, admin.
Forum for mus organisations concerned to

further the interests of mus and musicians in the UK.

National Operatic and Dramatic Association (NODA)
NODA House, 1 Crestfield St, London WC1H 8AU
Tel: 0171 837 5655 *Fax:* 0171 833 0609

Mark Thorburn, chief exec.
Umbrella body for the Amateur Theatre. Services include discounted sales of mus, scripts, make-up, insurance, etc. Also summer school and conferences.

National Piano Centre
5 Summerfield Rd, London W5 1ND
Tel: 0181 997 1793 *also fax*

Jonathan Ranger, dir.
Working collection of the history and development of the pno. Courses and training. Resource centre and forum for mus professionals, teachers, students, arts organisations, schools, colleges and individuals. Membership includes meetings, visits, publications, discounts, information and advice.

National Sound Archive (British Library)
96 Euston Rd, London NW1 2DB
Tel: 0171 412 7440 *Fax:* 0171 412 7441
Email: nsa@bl.uk
Website: www.bl.uk/collections.sound-archive

A Crispin Jewitt, dir.
Largest reference collection of sound recordings in the UK open to the public, full reference library of associated literature. Information on commercial discs, broadcasting, history of recording. Free listening service; groups from schools, universities and colleges welcome to listen by prior arrangement. Free newsletter.

National Union of Students
461 Holloway Rd, London N7 6LJ
Tel: 0171 737 2944 *Fax:* 0171 924 0890
Email: waves@mite.co.uk

National Union of Teachers
Hamilton House, Mabledon Pl, London WC1H 9BD
Tel: 0171 388 6191 *Fax:* 0171 387 8458
Website: www.teachers.org.uk

Doug McAvoy, gen sec; Steve Sinnott, dep gen sec.

National Youth Jazz Association
11 Victor Rd, Harrow, Middx HA2 6PT
Tel: 0181 863 2717 *Fax:* 0181 863 8685
Email: bill.ashton@virgin.net
Website: www.classical-artists.com/nyjo

William Ashton, chmn.
NYJA organises two Sat clinics by the National Youth

Jazz Orchestra and w/shops throughout Britain usually in conjunction with a concert by NYJO.

Northumbrian Pipers' Society
Morpeth Chantry Bagpipe Museum, Bridge St, Morpeth, Northumberland NE61 1PJ
Tel: 01670 519466 *Fax:* 01670 511326

J Richmond, hon sec.
Supports the playing and making of Northumbrian pipes, and the composition of traditional Northumbrian mus.

Opera and Music Theatre Forum
c/o Association of British Orchestras, Francis House, Francis St, London SW1P 1DE
Tel: 0171 828 8023 *Fax:* 0171 931 9959
Email: abo@orchestranet.co.uk

Jean Nicholson, mgr; Judith Ackrill, chmn.
Represents small and medium-scale opera companies in UK and international links. Information centre for related activities and serves to advance the ideals of its member companies.

Orff Society (UK)
7 Rothesay Av, Richmond, Surrey TW10 5EB
Tel: 0181 876 1944
Website: www.catan.demon.co.uk/orff/

Margaret Murray, hon sec.
Through teachers' courses it promotes Orff's creative approach to mus education, stressing improvisation and using voices, movement and perc insts.

Performing Right Society (PRS)
29-33 Berners St, London W1P 4AA
Tel: 0171 580 5544 *Fax:* 0171 306 4050
Email: pubrel@prs.co.uk
Website: prs.co.uk

John Hutchinson, chief exec.
Protects, promotes and administers the public performance and broadcasting rights of its composer, songwriter and mus publisher members.

Pianoforte Tuners' Association
10 Reculver Rd, Herne Bay, Kent CT6 6LD
Tel: 01227 368808
Website: www.pianotuner.org.uk

Mrs V M Addis, sec.
The association has countrywide membership. An examination is required for entry.

The Pianola Institute
6 Southbourne, Hayes, Bromley, Kent BR2 7NJ

Denis Hall, chmn; C L'Enfant, sec.
Journal, concerts, library of rolls, roll and information archive.

633

Piobaireachd Society

20 Otago St, Glasgow G12 8JH
Tel: 0141 334 3587 *Fax:* 0141 337 3024

Dugald MacNeill, sec.

Pipers' Guild

121 Hallam Way, West Hallam, Derbys DE7 6LP
Tel: 0115 930 8323
Email: margent@rmplc.co.uk
Website: www.quantine.co.uk/~piper/pgpage.htm

Stephanie Payne, sec; Mary Argent, chmn; Betty Roe, president.
Organisation for the making, playing and decorating of bamboo pipes (insts similar to Renaissance rcdrs).

Pro Corda Trust (National School for Young Chamber Music Players)

Leiston Abbey House, Theberton Rd, Leiston, Suffolk IP16 4TB
Tel: 01728 831354 *Fax:* 01728 832500

Pamela Spofforth MBE, artistic dir emeritus; Mererid Crump, admin.
Courses held during school holidays for young str players and pianists under the direction of distinguished musicians see **Summer Schools and Short Courses**.

Professional Association of Teachers

2 St James' Ct, Friar Gate, Derby DE1 1BT
Tel: 01332 372337 *Fax:* 01332 290310/292431

David Jones, acting gen sec; Richard Fraser, communications offr.
Independent trade union and professional association with around 40,000 members from all parts of the UK in both the maintained and independent sectors, teaching at all levels from nursery to further and higher education. PAT is non-party political and is not affiliated to the TUC. A publications list is available.

Qualifications and Curriculum Authority (QCA)

222 Euston Rd, London NW1 2BZ
Tel: 0171 229 1234; 0171 243 9250 (media)
Fax: 0171 221 2368

Sir William Stubbs, chmn; Sir Dominic Cadbury, dep chmn; Nicholas Tate, chief exec.
A public body brought into being on 1 Oct 1997 by the Education Act 1997. The act gave QCA a core remit to promote quality and coherence in education and training. QCA brings together the work of the National Council for Vocational Qualifications (NCVQ) and the School Curriculum and Assessment Authority (SCAA) with additional powers and duties. Its remit ranges from the under-fives to higher level vocational qualifications. It is responsible for ensuring that the curriculum and qualifications available to young people and adults are of a high quality,
coherent and flexible. As a body committed to enhancing quality in education, ACA aims to help raise national standards of achievement. This includes promoting greater access to and participation in education and training, enhancing lifelong learning opportunities, creating ways of giving credible national recognition for all learners, and developing ways of increasing achievements in literacy, numeracy and key skills generally.

Reed Organ Society (UK branch)

York House, Bluntisham Rd, Colne, Huntingdon, Cambs PE17 3LY
Tel: 01487 842722 *Fax:* 01223 330388
Email: brian.styles@mrc-bsu.cam.ac.uk

Brian C Styles, regional counsellor.
International society with headquarters in the USA. Publishes quarterly journal with historical, restoration and performance articles.

Royal College of Organists

7 St Andrew St, London EC4A 3LQ
Tel: 0171 936 3606 *Fax:* 0171 353 8244

Gordon Clarke, registrar; Alan Dear, snr exec; Robin Langley, librarian.
Educational charity of 3000 members for promotion of org playing and choir training. Exams for Associateship, Fellowship diplomas, choir training and org teaching diplomas and preliminary certificate. Library and programme of lectures, seminars, short courses, overseas tours, m/classes. Also jnr section.

Royal Musical Association

Dept of Music, University of Leeds, Leeds LS2 9JT
Tel: 0113 233 2579 *Fax:* 0113 233 2586
Email: j.g.rushton@leeds.ac.uk
Website: www.soton.ac.uk/~stilwell/rma.html

Julian Rushton, president.
The RMA holds meetings for the presentation of musicological papers and publishes a scholarly journal, a research chronicle and a series of monographs. It hosts one-day meetings, an annual conference (Apr) and a conference for research students.

Royal School of Church Music

Cleveland Lodge, Westhumble, Dorking RH5 6BW
Tel: 01306 877676 *Fax:* 01306 887260

Harry Bramma, dir.
Training and advisory organisation for the development of church mus. Membership open to all churches, with or without choirs, and to individuals.

Royal Scottish Country Dance Society
12 Coates Cres, Edinburgh EH3 7AF
Tel: 0131 225 3854 *Fax:* 0131 225 7783

Miss G S Parker, sec.
Aims to preserve and further the practice of traditional Scottish country dances and to provide education and instruction to this end. Has 162 branches throughout the world and more than 500 affiliated groups. Founded 1923.

Royal Scottish Pipe Band Association
45 Washington St, Glasgow G3 8AZ
Tel: 0141 221 5414 *Fax:* 0141 221 1561

J Mitchell Hutcheson, exec offr.
Association of amateur pipe bands. 12 branches running education classes. Organises contests and championships. Publishes bi-monthly magazine, *The Pipe Band.* Annual Summer School in last week of Jul at above address.

Royal Scottish Pipers' Society
127 Rose St, South La, Edinburgh EH2 4BB
Tel: 0131 225 4123 *Fax:* 01620 842146

M J B Lowe, sec.

Royal Society of Musicians of Great Britain
10 Stratford Pl, London W1N 9AE
Tel: 0171 629 6137 *also fax*

Maggie Gibb, sec.
The Society exists to provide help for professional musicians and their families in need as a result of illness, accident or old age.

RVW Trust
7th Floor, Manfield House, 1 Southampton St, London WC2R 0LR
Tel: 0171 379 6547 *Fax:* 0171 240 6333

Bernard Benoliel, admin.
Assists young British composers with premieres and second performances and promotes works by neglected British composers of the past. The Trust also considers applications from the smaller mus festivals who programme mus by young British composers. Does not accept applications towards the cost of recordings, mus insts, degree or summer courses.

Schools Music Association of Great Britain (SMA)
71 Margaret Rd, New Barnet, Herts EN4 9NT
Tel: 0181 440 6919 *also fax*

Maxwell Pryce, hon sec and chief exec.
Promotes the mus education of school pupils and students by encouraging and supporting all who work with them.

Scottish Amateur Music Association
18 Craigton Cres, Alva, Clackmannanshire FK12 5DS
Tel: 01259 760249

Margaret W Simpson, hon sec.
Provides national training courses to help and encourage amateur mus-making in Scotland.

Scottish Community Education Council
Rosebery House, 9 Haymarket Terrace, Edinburgh EH12 5EZ
Tel: 0131 313 2488 *Fax:* 0131 313 6800
Email: scec@scec.dircon.co.uk
Website: www.scec.net

Charlie McConnell, chief exec.
The council helps those active in community education to meet the learning needs of people in communities. This is achieved through influencing public policy and awareness, promoting effective strategies and best practice, and providing information, publications and other services.

Scottish Music Education Forum
School of Music, Dept of Aesthetic Education, Northern College, Hilton Pl, Aberdeen AB24 4FA
Tel: 01224 283558 *Fax:* 01224 283900
Email: j.p.stephens@norcol.ac.uk

Jonathan Stephens, dir of mus, head of aesthetic educ.
Acts as co-ordinating body, providing a point of contact for those involved in mus and mus education courses, associations and societies. Membership consists of reps from wide range of mus interests: school, higher education, commerce, industry and special interest groups including Scottish traditional mus. Aims to promote diversity of mus in Scotland, maintain particular strengths, collate and disseminate information, and identify and promote good practice.

Scottish Music Information Centre
1 Bowmont Gardens, Glasgow G12 9LR
Tel: 0141 334 6393 *Fax:* 0141 337 1161
Email: smic@glasgow.almac.co.uk
Website: www.music.gla.ac.uk/htmlfolder/resources/smic/homepage

Kirsteen McCue, gen mgr; Alasdair Pettinger, information offr.
Resource and information centre for mus (especially contemporary) by Scottish and Scottish-based composers. Reference, hire and audio libraries; photocopying service, promotional activities.

Scottish Secondary Teachers' Association

15 Dundas St, Edinburgh EH3 6QG
Tel: 0131 556 5919 *Fax:* 0131 556 1419
Email: sstateach@aol.com

David Eaglesham, gen sec.
Professional association for secondary teachers in Scotland. Recognised at the Scottish Office Education Dept and represented on the Scottish Joint Negotiating Committee for Teaching Staff in School Education. Publishes bulletins (6 pa) and *Secondary Teacher* (4 pa) for members only.

Secondary Heads Association

130 Regent Rd, Leicester LE1 7PG
Tel: 0116 299 1122 *Fax:* 0116 299 1123

John Sutton, gen sec.
Professional association which caters specifically for principals, heads and deputies in secondary schools and colleges.

Society for Music Analysis

Dept of Music, University of Nottingham, University Pk, Nottingham NG7 2RD
Tel: 0115 951 4755 *Fax:* 0115 951 4756
Email: sally.britten@nottingham.ac.uk
Website: www.blackwellpublishers.co.uk/

S Britten, admin; R Pascall, president.
Society for the development of all aspects of mus analysis, especially research and teaching. Open to lecturers, students and all who are interested in analysis.

Society for Research in the Psychology of Music and Music Education

c/o Dept of Music, The University of Sheffield, Western Bank, Sheffield S10 2TN
Website: www.shef.ac.uk/uni/academic/l-m/mus/staff/wlw/srpmme.html

Annette Davison, membership sec.
Aims to encourage the exchange of ideas and to disseminate research findings in the fields of psychology of mus and in mus education.

Society for the Promotion of New Music (SPNM)

Francis House, Francis St, London SW1P 1DE
Tel: 0171 828 9696 *Fax:* 0171 931 9928
Email: spnm@spnm.org.uk

Gill Graham, exec dir; Peter Craik, admin; Sarah Gibbon, educ offr.
SPNM promotes concerts and w/shops nationwide with new works by new composers. Education work with young people and their teachers. Also publishes *new notes* monthly concert listings magazine.

ASSOCIATIONS

Society of Assistants Teaching in Preparatory Schools
Cherry Trees, Stebbing, Great Dunmow, Essex CM6 3ST
Tel: 01371 856369
Email: satips@ford.anglia.ac.uk
Website: www.rmplc.co.uk/orgs/satips/index.html

Bob Carter, mus sec.
The mus group of an organisation covering all subjects taught in prep schools. It publishes termly broadsheets for members and organises occasional conferences.

Society of Headmasters and Headmistresses of Independent Schools
Celedston, Rhosesmor Rd, Halkyn, Holywell CH8 8DL
Tel: 01352 781102 *also fax*

I D Cleland, gen sec.
An association of 75 heads of independent secondary schools with VI forms. Most of the schools have boarders and almost all are wholly or partly co-educational. The society represents the smaller independent school offering a balanced education to pupils of widely varying interests and abilities; also included are two of the specialist mus schools and a ballet school.

Society of Recorder Players
15 Palliser Rd, London W14 9EB
Tel: 0171 385 7321
Email: secretary@srp.org.uk

A Read, sec.
A national society with international membership offering rcdr players in the UK the opportunity to meet regularly and play in conducted ens. Over 50 groups meet nationwide, mostly on a monthly basis. Members also receive *The Recorder Magazine* quarterly. The Society issues its own certificate to confirm a candidate's ability to conduct and direct rcdr groups and an annual festival, w/shops and other events take place throughout the year.

Society of Schoolmasters and Schoolmistresses
Doltons Farm, Newport Rd, Woburn MK17 9HX
Tel: 01525 290093

Mrs B Skipper, sec.
Gives assistance to necessitous masters and mistresses of all recognised schools, independent or maintained and their dependents, provided such persons have been continuously engaged in teaching for not less than 10 years.

Society of Teachers of the Alexander Technique (STAT)
20 London House, 266 Fulham Rd, London SW10 9EL
Tel: 0171 351 0828 *Fax:* 0171 352 1556

Email: stat@pavilion.co.uk
Website: www.pavilion.co.uk/stat/welcome.html

Angela Price, admin.
The society can provide a list of members who teach in the UK and members of affiliated societies throughout the world (please enclose an A5 sae) and information on the technique.

Sonic Arts Network *formerly* EMAS
London House, 271-273 King St, London W6 9LZ
Tel: 0181 741 7422 *Fax:* 0181 741 7433
Email: samantha@sonicart.demon.co.uk

Samantha Seaborne, exec dir; Paul Wright, educ dir; Rachel Spencer, admin.
National association of composers, performers and teachers and others interested in the creative uses of technology in the composition and performance of mus. Campaigns for a national centre for sonic art and initiates education projects bringing together composers, school pupils and teachers. Also INSET on ways of integrating new technology with other classroom resources.

Sound Sense, The National Community Music Association
Riverside House, Rattlesden, Bury St Edmunds, Suffolk IP30 0SF
Tel: 01449 736287 *Fax:* 01449 737649
Email: 100256.30@compuserve.com
Website: ourworld.compuserve.com/homepages/soundsense

Kathryn Deane, dir; Gloria Hall, admin.
Sound Sense is the development agency for participatory, creative mus-making, offering support, advice and training to community musicians and groups as well as other arts and educational organisations. Information services include publications, mus and disability advice and a Lottery help scheme for members.

Steel Band Adviser
60 Greenford Gardens, Greenford, Middx UB6 9LZ
Tel: 0181 578 6485; 0850 650401 *Fax:* 0181 578 6485
Email: terry.noel@btinternet.com

Terry Noel, chmn.
Provides advice on all aspects of steel bands, getting insts, tuition, upkeep of insts.

Traditional Music and Song Association of Scotland
17 Calton Rd, Edinburgh EH8 8DL
Tel: 0131 557 8484 *Fax:* 0131 557 6519

Elspeth Cowie, national organiser.
National organisation promoting the performance and awareness of traditional Scottish mus and song, story-telling and dance. Organises w/shops,

639

m/classes and school curriculum enrichment visits.

Ulster Society of Organists and Choirmasters
1b Beverley Hills, Bangor, N Ireland BT20 4NA
Tel: 01247 465222

Rodney Bambrick, hon sec.
Provides a forum for church musicians of all denominations; lectures, discussions, recitals, w/shops, org visits, etc.

Universities and Colleges Admissions Service (UCAS)
Fulton House, Jessop Av, Cheltenham, Glos GL50 3SH
Tel: 01242 227788 (enquiries); 01242 222444
Fax: 01242 221622
Email: enq@ucas.ac.uk

M A Higgins, chief exec; A P McClaren, deputy chief exec.
UCAS is the central agency through which applicants apply for all f/t u/grad first degrees and most DipHE and HND courses at universities and colleges in the UK.

Universities Association for Continuing Education
School of Continuing Education, University of Leeds, Leeds LS2 9JT
Tel: 0113 233 3184 *Fax:* 0113 233 3246
Email: j.brownridge@leeds.ac.uk
Website: www.stir.ac.uk/epd/uace/

Richard Taylor, sec.
The association promotes and represents the interests of continuing education within higher education, acts as a forum for the discussion of policy issues, promotes and conducts research and disseminates the results to the general public and interested organisations.

Viola d'Amore Society of Great Britain
4 Constable Rd, Felixstowe, Suffolk IP11 7HH
Tel: 01394 285584

Ian White, Annelise Tinlin; Nicholas Neale, dirs; Ian James, sec.
Aims to promote the viola d'amore, and to use it in performance with other insts. Also publishes original works from the 18th C and supplies them on demand. Tuition available along with advice over proper set-ups of insts and stringing. Also repairs to insts and bows.

Viola da Gamba Society
56 Hunters Way, Dringhouses, York YO2 2JJ
Tel: 01904 706959 *also fax*

Caroline Wood, admin.
Publishes annual journal and quarterly newsletter *Music for Viols.* Meetings and conferences. Viols for hire.

The Voices Foundation
21 Earls Court Sq, London SW5 9BY
Tel: 0171 370 1944 *Fax:* 0171 370 1874

Susan Digby, principal; Michael Stocks, dir of curriculum and training.
Educational charity specialising in mus curriculum development in primary schools and the professional development of primary teachers. 1-day w/shops for parents and teachers.

Walton (William) Trust
12 Central Chambers, Wood St, Stratford-upon-Avon CV37 6JQ
Tel: 01789 261573 *Fax:* 01789 266467
Email: sw_artists@msn.com

Stephannie Williams, artistic dir.
The Trust was created to establish the property 'La Mortella' as a study centre for gifted young musicians under the guidance of the world's leading teachers; to organise and administrate education projects in schools, and to aid research projects related to the life and work of William Walton and closely allied subjects.

Welsh Amateur Music Federation
9 Museum Pl, Cardiff CF1 3NX
Tel: 01222 394711 *Fax:* 01222 221447

Keith Griffin, dir.
The Federation offers financial assistance, advice and training to amateur mus organisations in Wales. It founded and now administers the National Youth Brass Band of Wales and the National Youth Choir of Wales.

Welsh Association of Ladies' Choirs
11 The Firs, Newton Burrows, Porthcawl, Mid Glamorgan CF36 5AX
Tel: 01656 782970

J L Walker, sec; V Grenfell, chmn.
Works to develop an appreciation of female choral singing within a wider audience; provides a forum for shared experience and increases the co-operation between individuals and choirs by arranging massed events.

Welsh Association of Male Choirs
98 Glannant Way, Cimla Neath, West Glamorgan, SA11 3YN
Tel: 01639 767884; 01639 637932 *also fax*

J J Watkins, organising sec; J Layton Watkins, admin sec.
Offers a legal advice service and mus and insurance at a discount to members. Also organises festival.

Welsh Folk Dance Society
Ffynnonlwyd, Trelech, Caerfyrddin, Sir Gaerfyrddin SA33 6QZ
Tel: 01994 484496

Dafydd M Evans, sec.
Formed in 1949 to promote Welsh folk dancing and dance mus.

Welsh Folk Song Society
Hafan, Cricieth, Gwynedd
Tel: 0176652 2096

Buddug Lloyd Roberts, sec.

Welsh Jazz Society Ltd
26 The Balcony, Castle Arcade, Cardiff CF1 2BY
Tel: 01222 340591 *Fax:* 01222 665160
Email: jazzwale@compuserve.com

Brian Hennessey, mgr dir.
An educational charity devoted to the promotion, education and presentation of jazz in all its varied forms.

Welsh Music Information Centre
46 Richmond Rd, Reath, Cardiff CF2 3AS

Operations of the WMIC have been temporarily suspended. Address any enquiries to Peter Reynolds at the address above.

White (Ernest George) Society
106 Gladstone Rd, South Willesborough, Ashford, Kent TN24 0DD
Tel: 01233 629921

Dorothy Douse, sec.
An educational charity to promote White's voice teaching on the principles described as Sinus Tone Production.

Workers' Educational Association
17 Victoria Park Sq, London E2 9PB
Tel: 0181 983 1515 *Fax:* 0181 983 4840
Email: wea-uk@mcrl.poptel.org.uk

Robert Lochrie, gen sec.

Adult education charity with 14 districts and over 700 branches in the UK.

Workers' Music Association
240 Perry Rise, Forest Hill, London SE23 2QT
Tel: 0181 699 2250

A F Schuman, hon sec; M Cook, chair.
The association believes that mus has a bearing on social life and is a means of attaining a brighter and better society; publishes mus, annual summer school of mus; London-based choir.

Young Concert Artists Trust
23 Garrick St, London WC2E 9AX
Tel: 0171 379 8477 *Fax:* 0171 379 8467

Rosemary Pickering, chief exec.
A charity offering career management for young musicians. Annual auditions. Apply to YCAT for application forms and eligibility.

Young Persons Concert Foundation
95 Wellington Rd, Enfield, Middx EN1 2PW
Tel: 0181 360 7390; 01923 859388 *Fax:* 0181 364 0185
Website: www.webcasting.com/stamps/found.htm

William A J Starling, artistic dir; Sally Needleman, special projects co-ord.
Presents w/shops and concerts (from individual str, w/wind, br and perc sections to full orch) by young professional players from the Foundation Philharmonic Orchestra; free to schoolchildren where sponsorship is available.

Youth and Music
28 Charing Cross Rd, London WC2H 0DB
Tel: 0171 379 6722 *Fax:* 0171 497 0345
Email: stagepass@dial.pipex.com

Alan Fluck, artistic dir; Katharine Meadows, admin dir.
Operates *Stagepass,* a nationwide ticket concessionary scheme for young people. British representative of Jeunesses Musicales. Also World Orchestra, World Choir, international mus camps, etc.

Music and Disability

Sound Sense (address below) has taken over services formerly provided by the National Music and Disability Service, and will provide additional information concerning all aspects of music for and on behalf of people with disabilities.

Organisations

All Clear Designs Ltd
3rd Floor, Cooper House, 2 Michael Rd, London SW6 2AD
Tel: 0171 384 2950/1 *Fax:* 0171 384 2951
Email: allclear@easynet.co.uk

James Holme-Siedle, dir.
Specialises in access design and disability equality training, following a format of detailed audits on existing buildings or advice on new designs which produce working documents for the architect and designer. The disability equality training offers customised courses, run by disabled trainers, for design professionals and staff within a range of organisations.

Arts Council of England
14 Great Peter St, London SW1P 3NQ
Tel: 0171 333 0100
Website: www.artscouncil.org.uk

Mary Holland, policy officer.
The Arts Council publishes a directory of arts and disability contacts, available from the Information Department, price £10. Enquiries about the funding of mus-related projects should be made to the mus dept.

Arts for Health
Manchester Metropolitan University, All Saints, Manchester M15 6BY
Tel: 0161 236 8916 *Fax:* 0161 247 6390
Email: p.senior@mmu.ac.uk

Peter Senior MBE, dir.
National centre providing practical consultancy, advice and information to all those interested in using any art form as a complimentary aspect of health care.

Artsline
54 Chalton St, Camden, London NW1 1HS
Tel: 0171 388 2227 *Fax:* 0171 383 2653
Email: artsline@dircon.co.uk
Website: www.dircon.co.uk/artsline

Pauline Guthrie, development offr.
Minicom available. Information and advice service for disabled people on access to arts and entertainments, including participation in the arts, in London. Open for enquiries Mon-Fri 9.30am-5.30pm. *Play*, a booklet with details of activities available to disabled children. Also produces other access guides, including those for theatres, cinemas, mus venues and tourist attractions. Also runs a multi-cultural project for disabled people from ethnic minority communities with a mobile library service and an access guide to venues with a multicultural focus.

Association of Professional Music Therapists
38 Pierce La, Fulbourn, Cambs CB1 5DL
Tel: 01223 880377 *Fax:* 01223 881679

Diana Asbridge, admin.
Deals with the needs of professional mus therapists in relation to standards of practice, employment, career structure, training, etc.

Beethoven Fund for Deaf Children
PO Box 16975, London NW8 6ZL
Tel: 0171 586 8107 *Fax:* 0171 722 7981

Ann Rachlin MBE, founder, chmn and trustee; Kevin Maddison, hon treasurer and trustee; Max Ziff, vice-chmn and trustee.
Charity providing specially-designed instruments to help profoundly deaf children to speak. Funds musical speech therapy centres throughout UK for deaf children.

British Dyslexia Association
98 London Rd, Reading, Berks RG1 5AU
Tel: 0118 966 8271 (helpline); 0118 966 2677
Fax: 0118 935 1927
Email: info@dyslexiahelp-bda.demon.co.uk
Website: www.bda-dyslexia.org.uk/

Provides information and advice relating to the effect of dyslexia on reading and writing mus. Also deals with individual enquiries regarding mus difficulties arising from dyslexia.

British Society for Music Therapy
25 Rosslyn Av, E Barnet, Herts EN4 8DH
Tel: 0181 368 8879 *also fax*

Helen Tyler, chair.
The BSMT promotes the use and development of mus therapy in the treatment, education and rehabilitation of children and adults suffering from emotional, physical or mental handicap.

Membership is open to all interested in mus therapy. The Society holds meetings, w/shops and conferences. Publishes a journal (jointly with the Association of Professional Music Therapists) and a bulletin for members.

British Wireless for the Blind Fund
Gabriel House, 34 New Rd, Chatham, Kent ME4 4QR
Tel: 01634 832501 *Fax:* 01634 817485
Email: margaret@blind.org.uk
Website: www.blind.org.uk

Mrs M R Grainger, chief exec; Mrs C Ford, fundraiser.
Provides radios and radio cassette recorders on a free permanent loan basis to registered blind people in need in the UK.

The Chantry Trust
1a King's Mews, London WC1N 2JA
Tel: 0171 242 8586 *Fax:* 0171 831 7914

Rex Montgomery, founder and admin.
Organisation researching therapeutic benefits of mus in education for autistic and handicapped children. Grants not available at present, but occasional gifts of books and manuscript material made to established bodies in similar fields.

Community Music Wales
2 Leckwith Pl, Canton, Cardiff CF1 8PA
Tel: 01222 387620 *also fax*
Email: cmw@mcr1.poptel.org.uk

Steve Garrett, development offr; Sarah Harman, development offr; Biddy Wells, youth development worker.
Community Music Wales is inspired by the belief that everyone can derive pleasure and satisfaction from playing mus, and that mus projects provide a rich learning environment in which a host of other important skills can be acquired. Resources and expertise in a wide range of mus forms, including mus technology, are made available to people who are typically excluded from opportunities for creative self-expression and personal development for reasons of disability or disadvantage. Also professional training course for community musicians.

Council for Music in Hospitals
74 Queens Rd, Hersham, Surrey KT12 5LW
Tel: 01932 252809 *Fax:* 01932 252966

Susan Alcock, dir; Diana Greenman, admin.
Over 3000 performances pa given by professional musicians in hospitals, homes and hospices throughout the UK.

Council for Music in Hospitals (Scotland)
10 Forth St, Edinburgh EH1 3LD
Tel: 0131 556 5848 *Fax:* 0131 556 0225

Alison Frazer, dir.
Concerts of live mus given by professional musicians selected for their communication skills. Participation encouraged. Venues include hospitals, hospices, homes for elderly people and day centres.

Disability Scotland
5 Shandwick Pl, Edinburgh EH2 4RG
Tel: 0131 229 8632 *Fax:* 0131 229 5168

Robert Pickles, social issues offr.
Works with Scottish cultural agencies and institutions to ensure that opportunities are created for people with a disability to become involved in cultural activities.

Drake Music Project
Christchurch Forum, Trafalgar Rd, London SE10 9EQ
Tel: 0181 305 0580 *Fax:* 0181 305 0583
Email: drake@dircon.co.uk

Adèle Drake, project dir; Brent Barraclough, development dir; Tim Anderson, technology mgr.
The Drake Music Project, in collaboration with the mus technology dept of York University, is involved in research including specialist software development. Enables people with severe disabilities to explore the world of mus through w/shops, and trains professionals in related fields. Also London, Scotland, Midlands, Ireland and Northern England co-ordinators.

Healing Arts: Isle of Wight
St Mary's, Parkhurst Rd, Newport, Isle of Wight PO30 5TG
Tel: 01983 524081 ext 4253 *Fax:* 01983 525157

Guy Eades, arts dir.
Co-ordinates an arts programme across the spectrum of health services on the Isle of Wight.

Hospice Arts
Forbes House, 9 Artillery La, London E1 7LP
Tel: 0171 377 8484 *Fax:* 0171 377 0032

David Frampton, acting dir.
National charity established to develop creative and therapeutic arts activities for hospice patients throughout the UK.

London Disability Arts Forum
34 Osnaburgh St, London NW1 3ND
Tel: 0171 916 5484 *Fax:* 0171 916 5396

Diane Pungartnik, co-ord.
Set up to define and promote disability arts, to provide a forum for disabled artists and performers and to further participation and representation of disabled people in the arts. Publishes an annual directory of disabled

performers, which includes many musicians and produces a yearly musical performance programme.

Music for Disabled People
Kirkstyle, The Creek, Lower Sunbury, Middx TW16 6BY
Tel: 01932 765885 *also fax*

Ophra Goetz, dir of mus.
Takes live mus to people who cannot get to concert halls.

MusicSpace Trust
St Matthias Campus, UWE (Oldbury), Court Rd,
Fishponds, Bristol BS16 1UP
Tel: 0117 976 2634 *Fax:* 0117 976 2635

Leslie Bunt, dir.
Provides mus therapy sessions for people of all ages, also w/shops and training sessions, including a p/t mus therapy training course in conjunction with Bristol University.

National Association for Special Educational Needs (NASEN)
NASEN House, 4-5 Amber Business Village, Amber Close, Amington, Tamworth B77 4RP
Tel: 01827 311500 *Fax:* 01827 313005
Email: welcome@nasen.org.uk
Website: www.nasen.org.uk

C Gallow, exec office admin.
Promotes the interests of children and young people with special educational needs and supports those who work with them.

National Disability Arts Forum
Mea House, Ellison Pl, Newcastle NE1 8XS
Tel: 0191 261 1628 *Fax:* 0191 222 0573
Email: 100575.3633@compuserve.com
Website: www.disabilitynet.co.uk.groups/ndaf

Geoff Armstrong, dir; Sian Williams, information worker.
Organisation established by disabled people to promote equality of opportunity for disabled people in all aspects of the arts. It is particularly concerned with supporting the development of disability arts locally, nationally and internationally.

Nordoff-Robbins Music Therapy Centre
2 Lissenden Gardens, London NW5 1PP
Tel: 0171 267 4496 *Fax:* 0171 267 4369

Pauline Etkin, dir.
Centre houses a clinic which children and adults with a variety of needs can attend for mus therapy. Offers a 2-yr Master of Music Therapy training validated by City University. Library holds collection of material including documentation of the work of Dr Nordoff and Dr Robbins.

Northern Ireland Music Therapy Trust
Graham House, Knockbracken Healthcare Pk, Saintfield Rd, Belfast BT8 8BH
Tel: 01232 705854 *also fax*

David Browne, business mgr.
Promotes interest in and the application of mus therapy throughout Northern Ireland.

Nottinghamshire Arts Support Service
Eastbourne Centre, Station Rd, Sutton in Ashfield, Notts NG17 5FF
Tel: 01623 556804 *Fax:* 01623 517529

John Childs, regional arts co-ord (special needs). Developing the use of mus and a variety of creative work within schools for children with learning difficulties.

Research Centre for the Education of the Visually Handicapped
School of Education, University of Birmingham, Edgbaston, Birmingham B15 2TT
Tel: 0121 414 6733 *Fax:* 0121 414 4865

The centre produces programs for very young and less able children and for adults wishing to convert braille into text; also programs to enable totally blind adults to have the freedom of using word processors.

Royal Association for Disability and Rehabilitation (RADAR)
12 City Forum, 250 City Rd, London EC1V 8AF
Tel: 0171 250 3222; 0171 250 4119 (minicom)
Fax: 0171 250 0212

A national campaigning and information organisation working with and for physically disabled people with an information dept for general enquiries.

Royal National Institute for the Blind
Music Education Advisory Service, National Education Services, Garrow House, 190 Kensal Rd, London W10 5BT
Tel: 0181 968 8600 *Fax:* 0181 960 3593
Email: szimmermann@rnib.org.uk

Sally-Anne Zimmermann, mus educ adviser.
Offers advice and information on all matters concerning the mus education of visually impaired children and adults.

Shape London
c/o The London Voluntary Sector Resource Centre, 356 Holloway Rd, London N7 6PA
Tel: 0171 700 0100 *Fax:* 0171 700 8143

Maggie Woolley, dir.
Arts development agency working with disabled people for greater access and involvement in all aspects of the arts.

Sound Sense
National Music and Disability Information Service,
Riverside House, Rattlesden, Bury St Edmunds, Suffolk
IP30 0SF
Tel: 01449 736287 *Fax:* 01449 737649
Email: 100256.30@compuserve.com
Website: ourworld.compuserve.com/homepages/soundsense

Roni Armstrong, NMDIS adviser.
The National Music and Disability Information
Service, run by Sound Sense, gives information
and advice on most aspects of mus and disability

issues. Publications and a quarterly journal are
available.

**Yorkshire and Humberside Association for
Music in Special Education**
46 Nunroyd Rd, Leeds LS17 6PF
Tel: 0113 268 4198

Mavis West, sec.
Open to anyone interested in exploring the role
of mus with people with special needs for
pleasure, education and communication through
courses, seminars, w/shops and concerts.

Professional Training

The courses listed below are mainly designed for able-bodied people who wish to work with
people with disabilities.

Anglia Polytechnic University
Division of Music and Performing Arts, East Rd,
Cambridge CB1 1PT
Tel: 01223 363271

Helen Odell-Miller, admissions tutor and course dir.
MA and Professional Diploma in Music Therapy
cover both university work and placements.
Applicants should normally possess a degree or
graduate diploma in mus but graduates of other
disciplines with an appropriate level of
musicianship will be considered. Some practical
experience needed, working with people with
learning disabilities and/or mental illness. 15 places
on course. 38 weeks f/t from Sep-Aug. Fees: £3880.

Bristol University
Dept for Continuing Education, 8-10 Berkeley Sq, Clifton,
Bristol BS8 1HH
Tel: 0117 928 7135; 0117 928 7140 *Fax:* 0117 925 4975
Email: john.pickard@bristol.ac.uk

John Pickard, lecturer and course organiser in mus.
2-yr p/t diploma in mus therapy. Applicants
should possess a mus degree or diploma and be
age 25 or above. 15 places on course. Next
course Jan 2000.

Centre for Music Therapy and Related Practices
Northern College, Hilton Pl, Aberdeen AB24 4FA
Tel: 01224 283500 ext 3510 *Fax:* 01224 283900
Email: j.w.robertson@norcol.ac.uk

James Robertson, co-ord of mus therapy practices.
The centre seeks to provide BEd Hons mus
students with an insight into the nature and
value of mus therapy practices. Central to this
will be the opportunity for children with a wide
range of needs to receive mus therapy provision.
It is also envisaged that this work will be
developed on a modular basis for existing
teachers and related professionals.

City University
Music Dept, Northampton Sq, London EC1V 0HB
Tel: 0171 477 8284 *Fax:* 0171 477 8576

Denis Smalley, head of dept.
Offers one research fellowship in mus therapy
for graduate mus therapists wishing to pursue
theoretical and academic studies in relation to
practical clinical work.

Colchester Institute
Music Dept, Sheepen Rd, Colchester, Essex CO3 3LL
Tel: 01206 718000 *Fax:* 01206 763041

Christopher Turner, module leader.
In the final yr of the mus BA/BA Hons, there is
special honours study entitled Health and
Educational Studies for Musicians.

Goldsmiths, University of London
Dept of Professional and Community Education,
Lewisham Way, London SE14 6NW
Tel: 0171 919 7229

Rachel Darnley-Smith, James D'Angelo, course
tutors.
Termly introduction to the ways in which various
forms of mus and vocal sound phenomena can
be used to promote physical and mental health
in both clinically diagnosed cases and people
who want to reduce stress and release energy
blockages. Very suitable for those considering a
career in mus therapy or in conducting sound
health w/shops.

Guildhall School of Music and Drama
Silk St, Barbican, London EC2Y 8DT
Tel: 0171 628 2571 *Fax:* 0171 256 9438

Sarah Hoskyns, head of mus therapy dept; Jackie
Robarts, mus therapy lecturer; Elaine Streeter,
mus therapy tutor.

Publishers to the performing arts

RHINEGOLD PUBLISHING

YEARBOOKS

British & International Music Yearbook
Britain's most comprehensive and accurate directory of the classical music industry
Published each November £23.95

British Performing Arts Yearbook
The guide to performing companies, venues, suppliers, services, festivals, education and support organisations
Published each January £23.95

Music Education Yearbook
A guide for parents, teachers, students and musicians
Published each June £16.50

OTHER PUBLICATONS

The Musician's Handbook
A compendium of advice for the music profession
£14.95 (hardback)

Healthy Practice for Musicians
An expertly written self-help guide covering the whole spectrum of a musician's physical and mental well-being
£16.95 (hardback)

Arts Marketing
The definitive guide to audience-building through effective marketing
£18.95 (hardback)

Analysis Matters
A students' revision guide to the Group 1 London Examinations' Advanced Level Musical History and Analysis Papers for 1998 and 1999
£10.00

Kein Angst Baby
A singer's guide to German operatic auditions in the 1990s
£9.95

The Art of Conducting
A guide to essential skills
£12.95

MAGAZINES

Classical Music
The magazine of the classical music profession
Fortnightly £2.95
Annual UK Subscription £56.00

Music Teacher
Respected and enjoyed by music teachers for more than 85 years
Monthly £2.95
Annual UK Subscription £34.00

The Singer
For amateur and professional singers of every persuasion – from cabaret to grand opera
Bi-monthly £2.40
Annual UK Subscription £14.40

Piano
The magazine for performers and enthusiasts of classical, jazz and blues piano
Bi-monthly £2.40
Annual UK Subscription £14.40

Early Music Today
Britain's brightest early music news magazine
Bi-monthly £2.40
Annual UK Subscription £14.40

Opera Now
The international magazine for opera professionals
Bi-monthly £4.95
Annual UK Subscription £29.70

Music Scholar
A guide to scholarships for young musicians
Published each November £3.00

Rhinegold Publishing Limited
241 Shaftesbury Avenue
London WC2H 8EH
Tel 0171 333 1721 Fax 0171 333 1769
E-mail book.sales@rhinegold.co.uk

Diploma in Music Therapy. 1-yr p/grad mus therapy course validated by the University of York and recognised by the Dept of Health. Applicants must normally have had 3 yrs of f/t higher education. Applications from mature professional musicians are also welcomed. Some experience with disabled, mentally or physically ill or hospitalised people necessary, as is personal therapy prior to or during the course.

Nordoff-Robbins Music Therapy Centre
2 Lissenden Gardens, London NW5 1PP
Tel: 0171 267 4496 *Fax:* 0171 267 4369

Pauline Etkin, dir and head of training.
Offers a 2-yr Master of Music Therapy training validated by City University. Fees: £4400. Places: max 6 pa. Also one-day conferences for those interested in mus therapy for children and adults and 10-week evening class on Nordoff-Robbins approach to mus therapy.

Roehampton Institute, London
Dept of Music, Southlands College, 80 Roehampton La, London SW15 5SL
Tel: 0181 392 3432 *Fax:* 0181 392 3435
Email: music@roehampton.ac.uk

John Woodcock, Kay Sobey, mus therapy programme conveners.
Introduction to Music Therapy. A short course in the spring term for those in related professions

or who are considering training. Graduate Diploma in Music Therapy (1 f/t; 2-3 p/t, recognised by the Association of Professional Music Therapists) is designed to train musicians as therapists with the ability and flexibility to practise professionally with a wide range of clients within the NHS, education, social services or private sector. Also a research MA. Fees: Graduate Diploma in Mus Therapy, £3328 (1 yr f/t, home fee), £1352 (p/t yr 1), £1976 (p/t, yr 2); MA Mus Therapy, £1104.

Royal Academy of Music
Marylebone Rd, London NW1 5HT
Tel: 0171 873 7373

Graeme Humphrey, course dir.
Optional information and performance opportunities for all f/t students who wish to develop their performing and communication skills for the benefit of schools audiences.

Royal National College for the Blind
College Rd, Hereford HR1 1EB
Tel: 01432 265725 *Fax:* 01432 353478

Greg Barker, head of creative arts.
A course in Braille mus and psychology of teaching the visually impaired (offered to overseas students who are expected to return to their own countries to teach).

Activities and Courses for People with Disabilities

Artsreach
Jacksons Lane Community Centre, 269a Archway Rd, London N6 5AA
Tel: 0181 340 5226 *Fax:* 0181 348 2424

Patricia Place, co-ord.
Offers arts-based w/shops (including mus) to special schools and units, integration work in mainstream schools, primarily in the London Boroughs of Barnet, Camden, Islington and Haringay.

The Bull
68 High St, Barnet EN5 5SJ
Tel: 0181 449 0048 *Fax:* 0181 364 9037

Runs occasional art w/shops for adults with learning difficulties. Regular programme of mus events, including rock, funk, jazz and Klezmer.

Carousel
Community Base, 113-117 Queen's Rd, Brighton BN1 3XG
Tel: 01273 234734

Sal Robarts, admin.
Works to promote the active involvement and

participation of people with learning difficulties in the arts (including mus) through w/shops, residencies and special events, performances, exhibitions, and training courses run for volunteers and staff.

Community Music East Ltd
70 King St, Norwich NR1 1PG
Tel: 01603 628367 *Fax:* 01603 767863

CME has developed a substantial programme of work with a range of special needs clients in East Anglia, establishing long-term educational w/shop programmes.

Council for Music in Hospitals
74 Queens Rd, Hersham, Surrey KT12 5LW
Tel: 01932 252809/252811 *Fax:* 01932 252966

Susan Alcock, dir; Diana Greenman, admin.
Over 3000 performances pa given by professional musicians for patients in hospitals, homes and hospices throughout the UK.

Council for Music in Hospitals (Scotland)
10 Forth St, Edinburgh EH1 3LD
Tel: 0131 556 5848 *Fax:* 0131 556 0225

Alison Frazer, dir.
Concerts of live mus given by professional musicians selected for their communication skills. Participation encouraged. Venues include hospitals, hospices, homes for elderly people and day centres.

Creative Young People Together (CRYPT Foundation)
Forum Workspace, Stirling Rd, Chichester, W Sussex PO19 2EN
Tel: 01243 786064

Residencies in the community arranged for young people (age 18-30) with disabilities to further their arts skills, including all aspects of mus.

Drake Music Project
Christchurch Forum, Trafalgar Rd, London SE10 9EQ
Tel: 0181 305 0580 *Fax:* 0181 305 0583
Email: drake@dircon.co.uk

Adèle Drake, project dir; Brent Barraclough, development dir; Tim Anderson, technology mgr. Weekly mus w/shops to enable children and adults with physical disabilities to produce and play mus by use of computers and electronic technology. Training of teachers, carers and musicians through seminars and in-service training days. Summer courses and residencies are held in London, Yorkshire, Scotland, Midlands, Ireland and Sarajevo.

Ebony Steelband Trust
Acklam Playcentre and Adventure, 6 Acklam Rd, London W10 5QZ
Tel: 0181 960 6424 *Fax:* 0181 964 4624

Darren Francis, project dir; Pepe Francis, mgr. Classes and w/shops throughout London to provide relief and personal development through the provision of mus therapy. One to one sessions are also available. Steelpan tutors are available for all educational establishments.

English Touring Opera
W121 Westminster Business Sq, Durham St, London SE11 5JH
Tel: 0171 820 1131/1141 (minicom and voice) *Fax:* 0171 735 7008

Paul Reeve, educ mgr; Nicholas Skilbeck, artistic consultant.
ETO run an extensive programme of work for people with disabilities including w/shops and signed performances for people who are deaf or hard of hearing, w/shops for visually impaired people and creative opera projects with adults and young people with disabilities. Also projects and recital programmes in hospitals and hospices.

Firebird Trust
27 Newport, Lincoln LN1 3DN
Tel: 01522 522995 *also fax*

Sibyl Burgess, dir.
The trust carries out a large number of w/shops, residencies, research and training projects.

Glamorgan Summer School
University of Glamorgan, Pontypridd CF37 1DL
Tel: 01443 482828 *Fax:* 01443 480558

Gill Giles, summer school admin.
Combined arts w/shop for people with and without learning difficulties, combining elements of mus, dance, movement, visual arts and drama (1 week each, 27 Jul-7 Aug 1998).

Heart'n'Soul
c/o Albany Empire, Douglas Way, Deptford, London SE9 4AG
Tel: 0181 694 1632; 0181 694 2988
Email: heartnsoul@compuserve.com
Website: www.heartnsoul.co.uk

Mark Williams, dir; Alix Parker, co-dir; Yvette Thelemmont, tour mgr.
Theatrical mus company for people with learning disabilities, touring shows and mus and organised by members within the UK and abroad. Also runs two 1-yr accredited theatre courses for people with learning disabilities. Course entitled Music, Theatre and Workshop Skills and Technical Theatre Skills.

Leeds College of Music
3 Quarry Hill, Leeds LS2 7PD
Tel: 0113 222 3400 *also fax*
Website: www.netlink.co.uk/users/zappa/clcm/clcm.html

Kate Holdsworth.
Mus-making lessons for disabled people and those with learning difficulties.

Lewisham Academy of Music
77 Watson's St, Deptford, London SE8 4AU
Tel: 0181 691 0307 *also fax*

Keith Swales, exec co-ord.
A range of w/shops for people with special needs.

Live Music Now!
4 Lower Belgrave St, London SW1W 0LJ
Tel: 0171 730 2205 *Fax:* 0171 730 3641

Virginia Renshaw, dir; Katherine Potter, asst dir.
Brings live mus performances by selected young professional musicians into community venues, especially those for disadvantaged and disabled people.

Morley College
61 Westminster Bridge Rd, London SE1 7HT
Tel: 0171 928 8501 ext 238 *Fax:* 0171 928 4074

Robert Hanson, dir of mus.
Offers two specific courses, Music for People with Learning Difficulties and Music for People with Physical Disabilities. Also aims to integrate disabled people into other classes.

Music and the Deaf
Kirklees Media Centre, 7 Northumberland St, Huddersfield HD1 1RL
Tel: 01484 425551 *Fax:* 01484 425560

Paul Whittaker, artistic dir.
An organisation to help hearing-impaired people of all ages to explore the world of mus and to develop their own mus skills and interests in all its forms. W/shops, lectures, residencies, signed song. Various publications available.

Northampton Footlights Group
c/o 20 Duncan Ct, Wellingborough NN8 2BP
Tel: 01933 229512

Eileen Smith, sec.
Amateur operatic company of disabled and able-bodied people.

Richard Attenborough Centre for Disability and the Arts
University of Leicester, PO Box 138, University Rd, Leicester LE1 9HN
Tel: 0116 252 2455 *Fax:* 0116 252 5165
Email: racentre@le.ac.uk
Website: www.le.ac.uk/racentre

E Hartley, dir.
Organises taught courses and opportunities to participate in creative arts activities, including mus w/shops. Priority is given to people with disabilities.

Royal National College for the Blind
College Rd, Hereford HR1 1EB
Tel: 01432 265725 *Fax:* 01432 353478

Greg Barker, head of creative arts.
F/t pno tuning and repair course for the visually impaired; course to prepare students for teachers and performers diplomas at mus colleges; BTEC First Diploma Performing Arts; f/t and short courses in mus technology.

SHARE Music
15 Deramore Dr, Belfast BT9 5JQ
Tel: 01232 669042 *also fax*

Michael Swallow, admin.
Promotes residential courses in mus and drama with special facilities for people with physical disabilities or sensory impairments.

SITE at the City Lit
Stukeley St, London WC2B 5LJ
Tel: 0171 831 6908

Janet Wyatt MBE, head of section.
Programme of w/shops and classes for people with learning difficulties. Training course for teachers, musicians and others in Independence Through Education (mus and other arts).

Stackpole Centre
Home Farm, Stackpole, Pembroke, Dyfed SA71 5DQ
Tel: 01646 661425 *Fax:* 01646 661456

Alison Rees, Adrian Lewis.
Stackpole Centre Theatre. Newly opened theatre with mus and art w/shop spaces. Fully accessible facilities. Courses, w/shops and events including live mus programme (jazz, world, classical and folk). Opportunities for musicians, mus teachers and mus therapists to run courses.

Strathcona Theatre Company
Unit 13 The Leather Market, Weston St, London SE1 3ER
Tel: 0171 403 9316 *Fax:* 0171 403 9587
Email: stc@strathco.demon.co.uk

Ann Cleary, dir; Roger Farrell, admin.
Theatre company of people with learning difficulties who devise their own productions.

Wedgwood Memorial College
Barlaston, Stoke-on-Trent, Staffs ST12 9DG
Tel: 01782 372105 *Fax:* 01782 372393
Email: wedgwood.college@staffordshire.gov.uk
Website: www.aredu.demon.co.uk/wedgwoodcollege

Derek Tatton, principal.
Residential adult education college which organises regular mus courses for visually impaired people including one on 'Creative Arts'.

Wheelchair Dance Association
43 Thurlby Rd, Wembley, Middx HA0 4RT
Tel: 0181 902 5102

Michael Massey, national sec and tutor.
National body promoting wheelchair dancing. Assistance given and starter packs available.

Wingfield Trust
4 Mortlock Ct, 63 Whitta Rd, Manor Park, London E12 5DU

Ms C Woods, gen sec.
Mus activities to assist children and adults with physical or minor learning handicaps to overcome disabilities by learning to play mus insts. The Wingfield Orchestra, made up of able-bodied and disabled people, gives concerts in and around the outskirts of London.

Manufacturers and Retailers

Acorn (Percussion) Ltd
Unit 33, Abbey Business Centre, Ingate Pl, London SW8 3NS
Tel: 0171 720 2243 (24 hrs) *Fax:* 0171 627 8883

Richard Benson, dir; Marguerite Vetter, dir of sales. Manufacturer and supplier of a variety of multi-cultural and mainstream perc insts for special needs education and hospitals. Also insts for general school use.

Echo City
7 Mornington Terrace, Camden, London NW1 7RR
Tel: 0171 387 7962

Paul Shearsmith, member.
Designs, builds and installs sound playgrounds and organises inst building and mus w/shops. Office hours 10am-4pm Mon-Thu.

Music Education Supplies
101 Banstead Rd South, Sutton, Surrey SM2 5LH
Tel: 0181 770 3866 *Fax:* 0181 770 3554

Ray Mason, dir.
Agents of Sonor school perc and suppliers of Suzuki handchimes and perc, Nordoff-Robbins reed horns, Aulos recorders, books, insts, etc.

Partially Sighted Society
PO Box 322, Doncaster, S Yorks DN1 2XA
Tel: 01302 323132 *Fax:* 01302 368998

Provides wide-spaced, heavily lined manuscript and a service for enlarging mus.

REMAP (Technical Equipment for Disabled People)
Hazeldene, Ightham, Sevenoaks, Kent TN15 9AD
Tel: 01732 883818 *Fax:* 01732 886238

John Wright, dir.
Registered charity which designs, manufactures and supplies 'one-off' aids and adaptions that are not commercially available.

Individual Tuition

Musicians' Union Offices

Musicians' Union
National Office, 60-62 Clapham Rd, London SW9 0JJ
Tel: 0171 582 5566 *Fax:* 0171 582 9805
Email: info@musicians.org.uk
Website: www.musiciansunion.org.uk

Dennis Scard, gen sec; Bob Wearn, mus educ offr. The Musicians' Union is taking an increasingly active role in mus education, and publishes a National Directory of Instrumental Teachers, copies of which are distributed to mus shops. The regional organisers are well equipped to deal with local enquiries about those of its members who give private tuition, and these are shown below together with a list of places within the area where there are Union branches. Enquirers may be referred to the local branch secretary, but the regional organiser is the best contact.

Central London Branch Office
60-62 Clapham Rd, London SW9 0JJ
Tel: 0171 582 5566

Horace Trubridge, London district organiser and Central London branch sec.
Central London; E London; N London; S London; S E London; S W London; W London.

Midlands Office
Musicians' Union, Benson House, Lombard St, Birmingham B12 0QN
Tel: 0121 622 3870 *Fax:* 0121 622 5361

Bob Bennett, district organiser, jazz section organiser, br band liason.
Birmingham; Coventry and Rugby; Derby; Leamington Spa; Leicester; Northampton; Nottingham; Stoke-on-Trent.

North and North East Office
327 Roundhay Rd, Leeds LS8 4HT
Tel: 0113 248 1335 *Fax:* 0113 248 1292
Website: www.musiciansunion.org.uk

Bob Wearn, educ offr.
Barnsley; Bradford; Bridlington; Darlington; Doncaster; Durham; Hoghton-le-Spring; Hull and Grimsby; Leeds; Lincoln; Maryport; Middlesbrough; Newcastle upon Tyne; Rotherham; Scarborough; Sheffield; South Tyne; Sunderland; York.

North-West Office
40 Canal St, Manchester M1 3WD
Tel: 0161 236 1764 *Fax:* 0161 236 0159

Bill Kerr, district organiser.
Barrow; Blackpool; Isle of Man; Liverpool; Manchester; N Wales coast; Preston; Southport; Stockport.

Scottish Office
11 Sandyford Pl, Glasgow G3 7NB
Tel: 0141 248 3723 *Fax:* 0141 204 3510

Ian Smith, Scottish organiser; Francesca Howell, asst.
Aberdeen; Alloa and Stirling; Edinburgh; Falkirk; Glasgow; Highlands and Islands; Perth; South West Scotland; Tayside.

South-East Office
60-62 Clapham Rd, London SW9 0JJ
Tel: 0171 582 5566 *Fax:* 0171 582 9805

Alfred Clarke, district organiser.
Aldershot; Bognor Regis; Bournemouth; Brighton; E Kent; Eastbourne; Folkestone; Hastings; Medway; Milton Keynes; Oxford; Portsmouth and IoW; Reading; Southampton.

South-West Office
Musicians Union, 131 St Georges Rd, Bristol BS1 5UW
Tel: 0117 926 5438 *Fax:* 0117 925 3729

Paul Westwell, district organiser.
Avon; Cardiff; Channel Islands; Cornwall; Exeter; Llanelli and Dyfed; Mid-Glamorgan; Newport; Plymouth; Salisbury; Swindon; Taunton; Torbay; Wessex; W Glamorgan.

Incorporated Society of Musicians

Incorporated Society of Musicians
10 Stratford Pl, London W1N 9AE
Tel: 0171 629 4413 *Fax:* 0171 408 1538
Email: membership@ism.org
Website: www.ism.org

Neil Hoyle, chief exec; Elizabeth Poulsen, head of professional policy.
The Incorporated Society of Musicians, the UK's professional association for musicians, enables private teachers with recognised qualifications and suitable experience to be represented as specialists in inst, vocal and other teaching. Members of the ISM Private Teachers' Section are approved for listing in the ISM Register of Professional Private Music Teachers, after their qualifications and experience have been vetted by the ISM. All teachers listed in the Register are

653

required to observe a code of ethics and are provided with a code of practice. The Register is published annually and issued throughout the UK to public and mus libraries, retailers, local authorities, mus colleges, schools and many other outlets. Copies are on sale from the ISM offices. Private teachers in the ISM are encouraged to attend courses and seminars on professional development. The Diploma in Music Teaching in Private Practice, run by the University of Reading in collaboration with the ISM, is a course of continuing professional education for all mus teachers in private practice holding inst or singing qualifications.

Other Registers

Educamus Music Education Consultancy and Employment Agency
71 Margaret Rd, New Barnet, Herts EN4 9NT
Tel: 0181 440 6919 *also fax*

Maxwell Pryce.
Consultancy and register of music teachers.

Periodicals

Some of the music resource centres, listed under **Resource Centres**, also publish their own in-house magazines. Journals of societies dedicated to instruments will be found in the **Associations** section. A more extensive list of music periodicals can be found in the *British Music Yearbook*.

British Journal of Music Education
Cambridge University Press, Edinburgh Building, Shaftesbury Rd, Cambridge CB2 2RU
Tel: 01223 312393 *Fax:* 01223 315052

John Paynter; Keith Swanwick, eds.
Institutions £52 annual sub (3 issues); individuals £31; students £24.

Choir and Organ
Orpheus Publications Ltd, 7 St John's Rd, Harrow, Middx HA1 2EE
Tel: 0181 863 2020 *Fax:* 0181 863 2444

Basil Ramsey, ed; Matthew Power, assistant ed; Shirley Ratcliffe, choral ed.
Bi-monthly publication devoted to the organ and choral world. Articles on choral and organ music. Insights into the careers of leading organists and choral conductors, examination of important new insts and comprehensive reviews of new publications and recordings. £2.95 per issue; £17.70 annual sub.

Classical Music
Rhinegold Publishing Ltd, 241 Shaftesbury Av, London WC2H 8EH
Tel: 0171 333 1742 (ed); 0171 333 1733 (advertising)
Fax: 0171 333 1769
Email: classical.music@rhinegold.co.uk

Keith Clarke, ed; Rebecca Agnew, deputy ed; Sara Cunningham, asst ed.
Fortnightly news magazine with reports on educational activities. £2.95 per issue; £56 annual UK sub.

Double Bassist
Orpheus Publications, 7 St John's Rd, Harrow, Middx HA1 2EE
Tel: 0181 863 2020 *Fax:* 0181 862 2444
Email: bassist@the strad.demon.co.uk

Paul Cutts, ed; Marcus Netherwood, publisher; Jonathan Everitt, ad exec.
The only independent internationl db magazine. News, interviews, profiles of db players past and present, composers and teachers; CD, sheet mus, new product and book reviews. Coverage of classical and jazz scene. Future plans also include folk and country features.

Early Music
Oxford University Press, 70 Baker St, London W1M 1DJ
Tel: 0171 616 5902 *Fax:* 0171 616 5901
Email: jnl.early-music@oup.co.uk

Tess Knighton, ed; David Roberts, asst ed.
Includes articles on performance practice and all aspects of medieval, renaissance and baroque music; for scholars, performers and listeners. Quarterly (£10 per issue; £40 annual sub; £68 institutions; £25 students). Subs: OUP Journals Dept, Gt Clarendon St, Oxford OX2 6DB *Tel:* 01865 267907.

Early Music Today
Rhinegold Publishing Ltd, 241 Shaftesbury Av, London WC2H 8EH
Tel: 0171 333 1744 (ed); 0171 333 1733 (advertising)
Fax: 0171 333 1769
Email: emt@rhinegold.co.uk

Lucien Jenkins, ed; Sara Cunningham, editorial asst.
Profiles of performers, insts, composer and repertoire guides; news, regular articles of interest to musicians, inst makers, students and amateurs. Book, mus, CD and concert reviews, listings of classes, courses, concerts, w/shops and broadcasting. Bi-monthly £2.40; £14.40 annual sub.

Educational Computing and Technology
Training Information Network, Jubilee House, The Oaks, Ruislip, Middlesex HA4 7LF
Tel: 01895 622112 *Fax:* 01895 621582

Phil Martin, ed.
Bi-monthly £3.50; £20 annual sub. Regularly includes articles on mus technology and features of interest to primary and secondary mus teachers and specialists.

Harpsichord and Fortepiano
Peacock Press, Scout Bottom Farm, Mytholmroyd, Hebden Bridge, W Yorks HX7 5JS
Tel: 01422 882751 *Fax:* 01422 886157

Alison Holloway, Peter Holloway, eds (Europe); Dave Gayman, ed (America).
£12 annual sub (2 issues).

International Journal of Music Education
ISME, International Centre for Research in Music Education, University of Reading, Bulmershe Ct, Reading RG6 1HY
Tel: 0118 931 8846 *also fax; Fax:* 0118 935 2080
Email: e.smith@reading.ac.uk
Website: www.isme.org
Jack Dobbs, Anthony Kemp, eds.
The journal of the International Society for Music Education with articles on various aspects of research in world musics in mus education. £15 for 2 issues (May and Nov).

Isstip Journal
c/o 28 Emperor's Gate, London SW7 4HS
Tel: 0171 373 7307 *Fax:* 0171 373 5440
Carola Grindea, Suzanna Widmer, eds.
£3.50. Free to members.

The Mix
Future Publishing, 30 Monmouth St, Bath BA1 2BW
Tel: 01225 442244 *Fax:* 01225 462986
Email: themix@futurenet.co.uk
Chris Kempster, ed.
12 issues pa. Mus production magazine with reviews of equipment and interviews with artists, producers and engineers. Free CD containing samples, mus and software. £3.50; £29.95 annual sub.

Music in the Curriculum
In Harmony, CIHE, The Avenue, Southampton SO17 1BG
Tel: 01703 216207 *Fax:* 01703 230944
Tim Cain.
For those with an interest in primary mus teaching. Information, articles, photocopiable activities and reviews of resources. 3 issues pa; £10 pa (£7.50 for students).

Music Journal
Incorporated Society of Musicians, 10 Stratford Pl, London W1N 9AE
Tel: 0171 629 4413; 0171 278 3686 (ad sales) *Fax:* 0171 408 1538
Email: membership@ism.org
Website: www.ism.org
Neil Hoyle, chief exec and ed; Kim Davenport Gee, production.
Monthly magazine of the Incorporated Society of Musicians, available to non-members on sub. News, views and features on every aspect of the mus profession. £2.50 per issue; £25 annual sub.

Music Makers
In Harmony, CIHE, The Avenue, Southampton SO17 1BG
Tel: 01703 216207 *Fax:* 01703 230944
Nicholas Barlow.
For those with an interest in secondary mus teaching. Information, articles, units of work, photocopiable resources and reviews. 3 issues pa. £11.50 pa (£7.50 for students).

Music Teacher
Rhinegold Publishing Ltd, 241 Shaftesbury Av, London WC2H 8EH
Tel: 0171 333 1747 (ed); 0171 333 1733 (advertising)
Fax: 0171 333 1769
Email: music.teacher@rhinegold.co.uk
Lucien Jenkins, ed; Sara Cunningham, asst ed.
For everyone involved in mus education. Regular articles on mus technology, conservatoires, specialist mus schools, NC, mus in primary schools, dance, contemporary mus, jazz, composing, improvisation, teaching adults and late starters, exam boards, the DFEE and outreach work of orchs. Also reviews of new mus, books and teaching resource materials, analyses of exam set works, teaching notes on graded pno and vn exams available to subscribers only. Monthly £2.95 per issue; £34 annual sub.

The Musical Times
63b Jamestown Rd, London NW1 7DB
Tel: 0171 482 5697 (ed); 0171 613 0717 (ad) *Fax:* 0171 613 1108 (ad)
Antony Bye, ed; Brian R Hook, ad mgr.
Monthly musical journal carrying articles of general and academic interest plus book, record, mus and occasional concert reviews. £2.50.

Musician
Musicians' Union, 60-62 Clapham Rd, London SW9 0JJ
Tel: 0171 582 5566 *Fax:* 0171 582 9805
Brian Blain, Tristan Evans, eds.
Official journal of the Musicians' Union, quarterly.

National Junior Music Club of Great Britain
23 Hitchin St, Biggleswade, Beds SG18 8AX
Tel: 01767 316521 *Fax:* 01767 317221
Carole Lindsay-Douglas, ed.
National Junior Music Club Magazine published termly, 3 issues pa. Annual membership including magazine £8.50.

Opera Now
Rhinegold Publishing Ltd, 241 Shaftesbury Av, London WC2H 8EH
Tel: 0171 333 1740 (ed); 0171 333 1733 (advertising)
Fax: 0171 333 1769
Email: opera.now@rhinegold.co.uk
Ashutosh Khandekar, ed-in-chief; Antonia Couling, deputy ed; Matthew Peacock, asst ed.
For opera lovers, providing personal profiles, historical research, reviews, international listings and news from the world of opera. Bi-monthly £4.95; £29.70 annual UK sub.

The Piano
Rhinegold Publishing Ltd, 241 Shaftesbury Av, London WC2H 8EH
Tel: 0171 333 1724 (ed); 0171 333 1733 (advertising)
Fax: 0171 333 1769

Jeremy Siepmann, ed.
Reports on pianists, pianos, summer schools, courses, competitions and all aspects of piano-playing and studying from classics to the blues. For professionals, students and amateurs. Bi-monthly £2.40; £14.40 annual sub.

Piano Journal
European Piano Teachers Association, 28 Emperor's Gate, London SW7 4HS
Tel: 0171 259 2379

Malcolm Troup, ed; Carola Grindea, consultant ed.
Journal of EPTA UK; the only European journal devoted exclusively to the pno in all its aspects. 3 issues pa; £8 annual sub.

Primary Music Today
Peacock Press, Scout Bottom Farm, Mytholmroyd, Hebden Bridge, W Yorks HX7 5JS
Tel: 01422 882751 *Fax:* 01422 886157

Jo Glover, Susan Young, eds.
Aimed at the non-specialist mus teacher in all UK primary schools. 3 issues pa; £13 annual sub.

Recorder Magazine
Peacock Press, Scout Bottom Farm, Mytholmroyd, Hebden Bridge, W Yorks HX7 5JS
Tel: 01422 882751 *Fax:* 01422 886157
Email: ruxbury@delphi.com

Andrew Mayes, ed.
Quarterly rcdr magazine with regular schools mus supplement. Also general articles, features, reviews, lists of recreational and w/end courses. £13 annual sub.

The Register of Musicians in Education
ISM, 10 Stratford Pl, London W1N 9AE
Tel: 0171 629 4413; 0171 278 3686 (ad sales)
Fax: 0171 408 1538

Email: membership@ism.org
Website: www.ism.org
Elizabeth Poulsen, ed; Kim Davenport Gee, production.
Annual directory of specialists in every aspect of mus education with classified listings of primary, secondary, FE, HE, consultants, etc. £10.

The Singer
Rhinegold Publishing Ltd, 241 Shaftesbury Av, London WC2H 8EH
Tel: 0171 333 1746 (ed); 0171 333 1733 (advertising)
Fax: 0171 333 1769
Email: the.singer@rhinegold.co.uk

Antonia Couling, ed.
Provides information on courses, w/shops, m/classes and conferences for singers of all musical styles, and carries regular columns and features on teaching, training, vocal health and career development. Bi-monthly £2.40; £14.40 annual sub.

Sound-On-Sound
SOS Publications Ltd, Media House, Trafalgar Way, Bar Hill, Cambs CB3 8SQ
Tel: 01954 789888 *Fax:* 01954 789895
Email: feedback@sospubs.co.uk
Website: www.sospubs.co.uk

Paul White, ed; Ian Gilby, publisher.
Hi-tech mus recording magazine for professionals and beginners alike. Monthly £3.25; £35 annual UK sub.

Times Educational Supplement
Admiral House, 66-68 East Smithfield, London E1 9XY
Tel: 0171 782 3000 *Fax:* 0171 782 3200
Email: chat@tesl.demon.co.uk

Heather Neill, arts and literary ed.
Surveys, reports and features on current topics of interest in education. Weekly £1.

YES Magazine
CODA Music Centre, Christchurch, Dorset BH23 5QL
Email: 100534.476@compuserve.com

David Walters, ed.
Yamaha Educational Supplement, distributed to schools twice a year. Free.

Libraries

The following list is limited to major collections of musical interest with some special collections in larger libraries. An asterisk (*) indicates membership of the International Association of Music Libraries, Archives and Document Centre, c/o County Library Headquarters, Walton St, Aylesbury, Bucks HP20 1UU *Tel:* 01296 382266 *Fax:* 01296 382274.

National Copyright Libraries

These libraries are available for reference only. Application for a reader's ticket is essential.

Aberystwyth

National Library of Wales
Aberystwyth, Ceredigion SY23 3BU
Tel: 01970 632800 *Fax:* 01970 615709
Email: rhidian.griffiths@llgc.org.uk

Ms dept rich in 19th C Welsh mus; large coll of printed Welsh mus; Welsh mus catalogue.

Cambridge

Cambridge University Library
West Rd, Cambridge CB3 9DR
Tel: 01223 333000/72 *Fax:* 01223 333160
Email: rma@ula.cam.ac.uk

Includes Hedli Anderson coll, F T Arnold coll, F A Booth coll, Edith Coates and Harry Powell Lloyd coll, Marion Scott coll, Alfredo Campoli coll, Peter Warlock autograph mss, R J S Stevens diaries and memoires, W H Weiss papers and diaries, Hans Keller papers, James Hook autograph mss.

Edinburgh

National Library of Scotland
George IV Bridge, Edinburgh EH1 1EW
Tel: 0131 226 4531 *Fax:* 0131 220 6662
Email: enquiries@nls.uk
Website: www.nls.uk

Special colls including Balfour-Handel, Hopkinson-Berlioz, Hopkinson-Verdi; also Scottish mus colls and Grainger mss.

London

British Library
Music Library, 96 Euston Rd, London NW1 2DB
Tel: 0171 412 7772 *Fax:* 0171 412 7751
Email: music-library@bl.uk

Music Library has over one million items of printed mus received by copyright deposit, purchase or gift. Special colls include Hirsch Music Library, Royal Music Library (including Handel autographs). Dept of Manuscripts has large coll of mus mss including autographs of Bach, Haydn, Mozart, Beethoven, Elgar, Vaughan Williams, Holst, Britten, Tippett, etc; medieval and modern vocal and inst mus, Stefan Zweig coll, Royal Philharmonic coll (on loan).

Oxford

Bodleian Library, Music Section *
Oxford OX1 3BG
Tel: 01865 277063 *Fax:* 01865 277182
Email: music@bodley.ox.ac.uk

Including 10th-20th C mss; former Music School coll, Deneke-Mendelssohn coll, Wight Bequest, Bourne Bequest, Harding coll, former St Michael's College, Tenbury coll.

British Library Document Supply Centre

British Library Document Supply Centre
Boston Spa, Wetherby, W Yorks LS23 7BQ
Tel: 01937 546060 *Fax:* 01937 546333
Email: dsc-customer-services@bl.uk

The British Library Document Supply Centre acts as a clearing house for all inter-library loans, both nationally and internationally, with a system of 'back-up' libraries, including the National Copyright Libraries and the major regional libraries (see below). In addition it has an extensive stock of its own, including a substantial and comprehensive collection of mus scores (excluding vocal and orch sets). The BLDSC does not lend directly to individuals, but through a network of borrowers comprised of public libraries, university and college libraries, and institutions. Any organisation may apply to join, details from the above address.

Major Regional Public Libraries

These libraries have major music collections, and also act as regional and national centres for lending. Personal or institutional borrowers are welcome.

Birmingham

Central Music Library *
Chamberlain Sq, Birmingham B3 3HQ
Tel: 0121 235 2482 Fax: 0121 233 9702

Including coll of British Institute of Organ Studies, material surrounding Birmingham Triennial Festivals including ms score of Mendelssohn's 'Elijah', letters by Elgar, Gounod, Bruch etc.

Liverpool

Central Library (Music)
William Brown St, Liverpool L3 8EW
Tel: 0151 225 5463

Including Carl Rosa opera library.

London

Barbican Music Library
Barbican Centre, London EC2Y 8DS
Tel: 0171 638 0672 Fax: 0171 638 2249

Includes The Music Performance Research Centre.

Westminster Music Library
160 Buckingham Palace Rd, London SW1W 9UD
Tel: 0171 798 2192 Fax: 0171 798 2181

Colls include Oriana Madrigal Soc.

Manchester

Henry Watson Music Library *
Central Library, St Peter's Sq, Manchester M2 5PD
Tel: 0161 234 1976 Fax: 0161 234 1963
Email: artsgroup@mcr1.poptel.org.uk

Including 2000 items of early printed mus and 500 mss and Newman Flower Handel Collection.

Wakefield

Wakefield Library HQ *
Balne La, Wakefield, W Yorks WF2 0DQ
Tel: 01924 302229 Fax: 01924 302245

Yorkshire Libraries Joint Music and Drama Collection: large coll of choral and orch sets.

Regional Public Libraries

These libraries hold a significant stock of scores, sheet music, books, audio/visual material and collections of local interest. Unless specified otherwise material is available nationally via the inter-library loan system.

London

Barnet Libraries Arts and Museums *
Hendon Music Library, The Burroughs, London NW4 4BQ
Tel: 0181 359 2882

Includes colls of recordings of Chopin, Liszt, stage musicals and Japanese ethnic mus.

London Borough of Enfield Central Music Library *
Cecil Rd, Enfield, London EN2 6TW
Tel: 0181 967 9367

Audio specialisation includes JS Bach.

Fulham Music Library *
598 Fulham Rd, London SW6 5NX
Tel: 0181 576 5253 Fax: 0171 736 3741
Email: info@haflibs.org.uk
Website: www.ftech.net/~haflibs

For details of collections see Hammersmith Music Library.

London Borough of Greenwich Libraries
Support Services, Plumstead Library, 232 Plumstead High St, London SE18 1JL
Tel: 0181 317 4466 Fax: 0181 317 4868

Special audio colls of Ravel, Schumann, English folk mus, jazz performers.

Hammersmith Music Library *
Shepherds Bush Rd, London W6 7AT
Tel: 0181 576 5054 Fax: 0181 576 5022
Email: info@haflibs.org.uk
Website: www.ftech.net/~haflibs

Cassettes, CDs, videos, LPs, mus books, scores and magazines. Audio specialisation: Mendelssohn, Vaughan Williams, jazz artists HP-JEF, folk music of Iran, Iraq, Jordan, Lebanon and Syria, British poetry.

659

London Borough of Islington Libraries *

Central Library, 2 Fieldway Cres, London N5 1PF
Tel: 0171 619 6954 *Fax:* 0171 619 6902

Audio specialisation of classical composers GM-KH (excluding Handel and J Haydn), jazz musicians, folk mus of SE Europe and recordings of obsolete mus insts. Loans within Greater London to personal borrowers only.

London Borough of Southwark Libraries *

Dulwich Library, 368 Lordship La, London SE22 8NB
Tel: 0181 693 5171 *Fax:* 0181 693 5135

Sutton Central Library *

St Nicholas Way, Sutton, Surrey SM1 1EA
Tel: 0181 770 4765 *Fax:* 0181 770 4777

Sets of vocal scores, small coll of orch parts available on loan. Audio specialisation includes recordings of Bruckner, choral recitals, jazz artists GIM-HARD, ethnic folk mus of the USA. Music Master/Gramophone cats on CD-Rom, song index, MPA cat on CD-Rom.

Wandsworth Music Libraries

Balham Music Library, Ramsden Rd, London SW12 8QY
Tel: 0181 871 7195 *Fax:* 0181 675 4015

Encompasses Battersea, Balham and Putney mus libraries. Comprehensive stocks of CDs, cassettes, videos (also LPs at Balham), scores and books. Vocal score sets collection at Putney. GLASS collection (Greater London Audio Specialisation Scheme) at Putney. Wandsworth collection in this scheme comprises Prokofiev, Rachmaninoff, film soundtracks, jazz artists and Scottish folk mus.

Aylesbury

Buckinghamshire County Library *

County Library Headquarters, Walton St, Aylesbury, Bucks HP20 1UU
Tel: 01296 382266 *Fax:* 01296 382274

Vocal sets, sheet mus.

Ballynahinch

South Eastern Education and Library Board *

Library Headquarters, Reference and Information Service, Windmill Hill, Ballynahinch, Co Down BT24 8DH
Tel: 01238 566400 *Fax:* 01238 565072

Coll of cassettes, CDs and mus scores covering all types of mus.

Blackburn

Blackburn Music Library

Blackburn Central Library, Town Hall St, Blackburn BB2 1AG
Tel: 01254 661221 *Fax:* 01254 690539

Includes multimedia, a/v, extensive jazz collection.

Bournemouth

Bournemouth Music Library

Meyrick Rd, Lansdowne, Bournemouth BH1 3DJ
Tel: 01202 553781 *Fax:* 01202 291781

Camm coll of (mainly 19th C) full scores, miniature scores, chmbr and inst mus. Wide range of printed mus, books, CDs and videos. Sets of choral and orch works available.

Brighton

Brighton Music Library

115 Church St, Brighton, E Sussex BN1 1UD
Tel: 01273 296961 *Fax:* 01273 296965/296951

General range of scores, books, CDs, cassettes, records and video.

Bristol

Bristol Music Library *

Central Library College Green, Bristol BS1 5TL
Tel: 0117 929 9149 *Fax:* 0117 922 6775

Russell coll of Victorian and Edwardian songs. Coll of books, mus and recordings by Bristol authors and musicians. Comprehensive coll of books, journals, scores, sets of choral/orch parts and recordings.

Cambridge

Cambridge City Area Libraries

Central Library, 7 Lion Yard, Cambridge CB2 3QD
Tel: 01223 712000 *Fax:* 01223 712018
Email: cambridge.central.library@camcnty.gov.uk
Website: www.camcnty.gov.uk/library/lib1/libs.htm

Cardiff

Cardiff County Library Service: Cardiff Central Library *

St David's Link, Frederick St, Cardiff CF1 4DT
Tel: 01222 382116 *Fax:* 01222 238642
Email: robboddy@cardlib.demon.co.uk

Mackworth and Aylward colls of 17th and 18th C mss and printed mus; currently on long-term loan to University College Cardiff Music Library.

Chesterfield

Chesterfield Library *
County Music and Drama Library, New Beetwell St,
Chesterfield, Derbyshire S40 1QN
Tel: 01246 209292 *Fax:* 01246 209304

General colls of single copy material, vocal sets, orch sets and playsets. Coke-Steele coll of books, scores and some mss (not yet catalogued but available for consultation by prior arrangement).

Colchester

Colchester Central Library *
Trinity Sq, Colchester, Essex CO1 1JB
Tel: 01206 562243 *Fax:* 01206 562413

Large coll of sets of vocal and orch mus, county mus coll.

Cork

Cork City Library
Grand Parade, Cork, Eire, Republic of Ireland
Tel: 00 353 21 277110 *Fax:* 00 353 21 275684
Email: cork.citylibrary@indigo.ie

General stock including classical, inst, vocal, choral and orch, pop and rock, jazz, blues, light opera, musicals, films, br and military band, Irish traditional and world mus, children's mus. Large coll of audio material and listening facilities.

Devizes

Wiltshire County Music and Drama Library *
Sheep St, Devizes, Wilts SN10 1DL
Tel: 01380 722633 *Fax:* 01380 722161

Reference books, mus scores, vocal and orch sets, records, cassettes and Cds.

Dorking

Surrey Performing Arts Library *
Vaughan Williams House, West St, Dorking, Surrey RH4 1BY
Tel: 01306 887509; 01306 875453 (enquiries)
Fax: 01306 875074
Email: p.arts@dial.pipex.com

Large range of printed and a/v mus reference, information and lending materials. Major regional coll of choral and orch performance material. Charges for the loan of choral and orch sets.

Dudley

Dudley Library *
St James's Rd, Dudley, W Mids DY1 1HR
Tel: 01384 815554 *Fax:* 01384 815543
Email: dudlib@dudley.gov.uk

Ealing

Ealing Public Libraries *
Library Support Centre, Ealing Central Sports Ground,
Horsenden La South, Greenford UB6 8AP
Tel: 0181 810 7664 *Fax:* 0181 810 7651

Eastbourne

Eastbourne Music Library
Grove Rd, Eastbourne, E Sussex BN21 4TL
Tel: 01323 434224 *Fax:* 01323 649174

Nearly 10,000 sound recordings on record, cassettes and CD covering all types of mus both classical and popular. Scores, books, *MusicMaster/Gramophone* on CD-Rom, and song index.

Edinburgh

Edinburgh City Libraries *
Music Library, George IV Bridge, Edinburgh EH1 1EG
Tel: 0131 225 5584 *Fax:* 0131 225 8783

Books, scores, cassettes and CDs for borrowing. Reference material includes periodicals. Scottish mus from all periods is strongly represented. Information files are maintained covering local mus teachers, societies and organisations.

Gloucester

Gloucester Music and Drama Library *
Greyfriars, Gloucester GL1 1TS
Tel: 01452 426982 *Fax:* 01452 506241

Mus sets, printed mus, books, CDs, cassettes, videos. Inter-library loan. Personal borrowers only. CD-Roms for reference.

Hatfield

Hertfordshire County Music Library *
Central Resources Library, New Barnfield, Travellers La,
Hatfield, Herts AL10 8XG
Tel: 01707 281533 *Fax:* 01707 281514
Email: fmo34@viscount.org.uk

Fairly large general coll, including sets of vocal scores and orch material primarily for local use, although will consider inter-library loan.

661

Lincoln

Lincolnshire County Libraries *
Lincoln Central Library, Free School La, Lincoln LN1 1EZ
Tel: 01522 549160 Fax: 01522 575011

General public library mus coll with books, scores, sets of vocal and orch mus, CDs.

Luton

Luton Central Music Library *
St George's Sq, Luton, Beds LU2 1NG
Tel: 01582 730161 Fax: 01582 724638

Scores, books, CDs, cassettes. Archive of Luton Girls' Choir material.

Newcastle upon Tyne

Newcastle Libraries and Information Services *
City Library, Princess Sq, Newcastle upon Tyne NE99 1DX
Tel: 0191 261 0691 Fax: 0191 261 1435
Email: nlis.human@dial.pipex.com

Scores, books, small coll of vocal sets. Catalogue of printed mus and comprehensive directory coverage. Loan coll of CDs and audio cassettes.

Nottingham

Nottingham Central Library *
Angel Row, Nottingham NG1 6HP
Tel: 0115 947 3591 Fax: 0115 950 4207
Email: cenlib@notlib.demon.co.uk

Eric Coates coll. Inter-library loan system.

Plymouth

Plymouth Music and Drama Library *
Central Library, Drake Circus, Plymouth, Devon PL4 8AL
Tel: 01752 385914 also fax

Vocal and orch sets. Rev Sabine Baring-Gould coll of folk song mss. Mus scores, playscripts, playsets and books on mus and theatre for loan. Cassettes, CDs, videos. Comprehensive reference stock, including *Music Master/Gramophone* on CD-Rom, song index.

Preston

Lancashire County Library *
County Library Headquarters, 143 Corporation St, Preston, Lancs PR1 2UQ
Tel: 01772 264051 Fax: 01772 264880
Email: maninf@library.org.uk

Kathleen Ferrier coll includes some mss and autographed scores. J A Fuller-Maitland coll (*The Times* mus critic 1889-1911) includes books, scores, periodicals and mss with special emphasis on English folk mus, Bach and Purcell.

Reading

Music and Drama Library *
Reading Central Library, Abbey Sq, Reading RG1 3BQ
Tel: 0118 950 9244

Vocal and drama set colls. Books, scores, videos, cassettes and CDs.

Ruthin

Denbighshire Library and Information Service
c/o Ruthin Library, Record St, Ruthin, Denbighshire LL15 1DS
Tel: 01824 705274/706767 Fax: 01824 702580

Special coll of Welsh mus.

St Austell

Cornwall County Music and Drama Library *
2 Carlyon Rd, St Austell, Cornwall PL25 4LD
Tel: 01726 61702 Fax: 01726 71214

Large general coll of mus scores, including performance sets (vocal and orch); Cornish mus (folk, dance, carols); classical CDs, books on all aspects of mus for lending and reference.

Shrewsbury

Shropshire Music and Drama Library *
Lending Library, Castle Gates, Shrewsbury, Shropshire SY1 2AS
Tel: 01743 255341 Fax: 01743 255309
Email: lp97@dial.pipex.com

General colls including classical, popular, folk and world mus. Inter-library loan.

Warwick

Warwickshire County Council *
Barrack St, Warwick CV34 4TH
Tel: 01926 412168 Fax: 01926 412471
Email: warcolib@dial.pipex.com

16,000 mus scores, including vocal sets and sets of part-songs. Books on mus and some orch sets in the schools mus library.

Worcester

Hereford and Worcester County Libraries *
County Hall, Spetchley Rd, Worcester WR5 2NP
Tel: 01905 763763 Fax: 01905 766244
Email: mmessenger@hereford-worcester.gov.uk
Website: www.hereford-worcester.gov.uk/homepage

Choral sets, vocal scores, etc, at Worcester City Library. Sound recordings at all branch libraries; some single scores at larger branches.

Wrekin

Wrekin Music Library
Wellington Library, Walker St, Wellington TF1 1DB,
Wrekin
Tel: 01952 244013 *Fax:* 01952 256960

General collections including classical, popular, folk and world mus. Inter library loan.

Yeovil

Somerset County Library *
County Music and Drama Library, King George St, Yeovil,
Somerset BA20 1PY
Tel: 01935 472020 *Fax:* 01935 431847
Email: rdtaylor@nildram.co.uk

Church and Cathedral Libraries

These libraries are private but are usually open to bona fide scholars. Applications for admission are advisable.

London

Lambeth Palace Library
London SE1 7JU
Tel: 0171 928 6222

A few mss (including early 16th C choir books) and some printed books including church mus.

St Paul's Cathedral Library
London EC4M 8AE
Tel: 0171 246 8325; 0171 236 4128 *Fax:* 0171 248 3104

17th-18th C ms part-books; a number of autograph scores of services and anthems, some by former organists, mainly 19th and 20th C.

Westminster Abbey Library
East Cloister, London SW1P 3PA
Tel: 0171 222 5152 *Fax:* 0171 222 6391

Includes 16th-19th C mss and printed mus.

Rest of Great Britain

Bristol

Baptist College Library
Woodland Rd, Bristol BS8 1UN
Tel: 0117 926 0248 *Fax:* 0117 927 7070

Special coll of Baptist hymn books (mostly words only).

Methodist Church Music Society Library
Wesley College, Henbury Rd, Westbury on Trym, Bristol
BS10 7QD
Tel: 0117 959 1200 *Fax:* 0117 950 1277

Coll of hymn books, psalters, etc, and books with special emphasis on hymnody and church mus, 17th-20th C.

Canterbury

Cathedral Archives
The Precincts, Canterbury CT1 2EH
Tel: 01227 463510 *Fax:* 01227 762897

Medieval mus mss, 17th-18th C choir mus mss; printed choir mus.

Cathedral Library
The Precincts, Canterbury CT1 2EH

Tel: 01227 458950 *Fax:* 01227 762897
Email: s.m.hingley@ukc.ac.uk

18th-19th C printed choral mus. Ms and printed vocal and orch mus of Canterbury Catch Club 18th-19th C. Ms and printed mus of Canterbury Amateur Harmonic Society 18-19th C.

Durham

Dean and Chapter Library
The College, Durham DH1 3EH
Tel: 0191 386 2489
Email: r.c.norris@durham.ac.uk

17th-19th C cathedral choir and organists mss; 17th-19th C printed mus from Bamburgh Castle; Philip Falle coll of 17th C printed mus. 2 wks notice needed to visit. Open Mon-Fri 9am-1pm, 2.15-5pm only, closed Aug.

Hereford

Cathedral Library
Hereford HR1 2NG
Tel: 01432 359880 *Fax:* 01432 355929

Chained library. 18th-20th C printed and mss

mus, including Roger North, Wesley and Elgar mss. Hereford Breviary, with mus, c1270.

Lichfield

Cathedral Library
14 The Close, Lichfield, Staffs
Tel: 01543 256120

Catalogue of 18th-early 19th C mss. Catalogue of 17th to mid-19th C printed mus in preparation.

Lincoln

Cathedral Library
Lincoln LN2 1PZ
Tel: 01522 544544 *Fax:* 01522 511307

Including medieval mss and early printed mus. 17th-19th C ms part books.

Ripon

Cathedral Library
Ripon, N Yorks HG4 1QT
Tel: 01765 602072 *Fax:* 01765 603462

16th C liturgical printed books; Higgin bequest (now on deposit at Brotherton Library, Leeds University).

Wimborne

Minster Church of St Cuthburga Library
High St, Wimborne, Dorset BH21 1HT
Tel: 01202 884753

Chained library of early mus.

Winchester

Cathedral Library
5 The Close, Winchester, Hants SO23 9LS
Tel: 01962 853137 *Fax:* 01962 841519
Email: winchester.cathedral.office@dial.pipex.com

Coll of 18th and 19th C printed church mus.

Windsor

St George's Chapel Chapter Library
Windsor Castle, Windsor, Berks SL4 1NJ
Tel: 01753 865538 *Fax:* 01753 620165

Including mss of Tallis and William Child.

Worcester

Cathedral Music Library
Worcester WR1 2LH
Tel: 01905 28854 *Fax:* 01905 611139

17th-18th C part books, mss and printed church mus.

York

York Minster Library
Dean's Pk, York YO1 2JD
Tel: 01904 625308/611118 *Fax:* 01904 611119

Including 16th-20th C mss and printed mus.

University and College Libraries

Primarily available to staff and students of the institution, but visiting scholars may also be admitted. Applications in writing are advisable.

London

Goldsmiths College Library *
New Cross, London SE14 6NW
Tel: 0171 919 7168 *Fax:* 0171 919 7165
Email: lbs0lpm@gold.ac.uk

Includes the A L Lloyd coll (scores, books and offprints of folk and traditional mus, especially Eastern Europe) and the Ewan MacColl/Peggy Seeger coll (books and scores, especially English and Scottish folksong).

Guildhall School of Music and Drama *
Barbican, London EC2Y 8DT

Tel: 0171 382 7178 *Fax:* 0171 786 9378
Email: gsmd_library@gsmd.ac.uk
Website: www.gsmd.ac.uk

Includes Appleby gui coll, Alkan Society coll and Goossens ob mus coll.

Imperial College of Science, Technology and Medicine *
Haldane Music Library, London SW7 2AZ
Tel: 0171 594 8812 *Fax:* 0171 584 3763
Email: j.m.smith@ic.ac.uk
Website: www.lib.ic.ac.uk/

Haldane mus coll. Recordings, scores, books.

King's College London Library
Strand, London WC2R 2LS
Tel: 0171 873 2394 *Fax:* 0171 872 0207
Email: evelyn.cornell@kcl.ac.uk
Website: www.kcl.ac.uk/kis/support/lib/top.html

London College of Music and Media
Thames Valley University LRC, St Mary's Rd, London W5 5RF
Tel: 0181 231 2648 *Fax:* 0181 231 2631
Email: colin.steele@tvu.ac.uk
Website: www.tvu.ac.uk

Scores, books, journals, LPs, CDs, listening facilities, CD-Rom multimedia.

London School of Economics
Shaw Library, Houghton St, London WC2A 2AE
Tel: 0171 955 7171 (pm only)

Books, scores, periodicals and recordings.

Morley College Library
61 Westminster Bridge Rd, London SE1 7HT
Tel: 0171 928 8501 *Fax:* 0171 928 4074

Scores, sheet mus, books, records, CDs.

Royal Academy of Music Library
Marylebone Rd, London NW1 5HT
Tel: 0171 873 7323 *Fax:* 0181 873 7322
Email: library@ram.ac.uk

Including Sir Henry Wood library of orch mus, Sir Arthur Sullivan archives, English Bach Society Library, R J S Stevens Library, David Munrow Library.

Royal College of Music Library *
Prince Consort Rd, London SW7 2BS
Tel: 0171 591 4325 *Fax:* 0171 589 7740
Email: pthompson@rcm.ac.uk
Website: www.rcm.ac.uk

Includes libraries of Sacred Harmonic Society, Concerts of Ancient Music, Heron-Allen coll.

Royal College of Organists
7 St Andrews St, London EC4A 3LQ
Tel: 0171 936 3606; 0171 936 4321 *Fax:* 0171 353 8244; 0171 936 3966
Email: admin-rco@btinternet.com

Mainly org mus and books on the org, primarily for reference during college opening hrs.

School of Oriental and African Studies Library
University of London, Thornhaugh St, Russell Sq, London WC1H 0XG
Tel: 0171 323 6105 *Fax:* 0171 436 3844
Email: yyl@soas.ac.uk
Website: www.soas.ac.uk/library/guides/recordings.html

Books, sound recordings (and video) of Oriental and African mus.

Trinity College of Music
The Library, Academic Studies Centre, 10-11 Bulstrode Pl, London W1M 5FW
Tel: 0171 935 5773 *Fax:* 0171 224 6278
Email: library@tcm.ac.uk

Including 16th-17th C printed mus.

University of London Library Music Collection *
Senate House, Malet St, London WC1E 7HU
Tel: 0171 636 8000 ext 5038 *Fax:* 0171 436 1494
Email: ull@ull.ac.uk
Website: www.ull.ac.uk

Including library of Royal Musical Association; Tudor Church Music coll, Littleton coll.

Aberdeen

Aberdeen University Library *
Queen Mother Library, Meston Walk, Aberdeen AB24 3UE
Tel: 01224 272592 *Fax:* 01224 487048
Email: r.turbet@abdn.ac.uk

Including libraries of Gavin Greig and Forbes Leith; Stationers' Hall coll (18th-19th C printed mus obtained under copyright).

Aberystwyth

University of Wales (Hugh Owen Library)
Aberystwyth, Dyfed SY23 3DZ
Tel: 01970 622391 *Fax:* 01970 622404
Email: library@aber.ac.uk

Including David de Lloyd mss; Mendelssohn letters and autographs; George Powell bequest (19th C scores and some 18th-19th C mss).

Belfast

Queen's University *
Belfast BT7 1NN
Tel: 01232 335020 *Fax:* 01232 323340
Email: nrussell@qub.ac.uk
Website: www.qub.ac.uk/

Including Bunting mss of Irish folk mus; Hamilton Harty library.

Birmingham

Barber Music Library *
University of Birmingham, Edgbaston, Birmingham B15 2TS
Tel: 0121 414 5852 *Fax:* 0121 414 5853
Email: a.greig@bham.ac.uk
Website: www.bham.ac.uk/isg/

Including Granville Bantock, Gloria Rose and Shaw-Hellier colls, Elgar diaries.

Birmingham Conservatoire *
Information Services' Library, Paradise Pl, Birmingham B3 3HG
Tel: 0121 331 5914/5 *Fax:* 0121 331 5906
Email: mu.library@uce.ac.uk
Website: www.uce.ac.uk/

Birmingham Flute Society coll.

Bristol

University Library
Tyndall Av, Bristol BS8 1TJ
Tel: 0117 928 9000 *Fax:* 0117 925 5334
Email: library@bris.ac.uk
Website: www.bris.ac.uk/depts/library

Cambridge

Anglia Polytechnic University Library *
East Rd, Cambridge CB1 1PT
Tel: 01223 363271 ext 2302 *Fax:* 01223 363271
Website: www.anglia.ac.uk/fes/library/home.htm

Cambridge University Library *see* National Copyright Libraries

Cambridge University Musical Society
c/o University Music School, West Rd, Cambridge CB3 9DP
Tel: 01223 335180/3

Including approx 400 sets of orch parts.

Clare College
Cambridge CB3 9AJ
Tel: 01223 333202/333228 *Fax:* 01223 357664

Including mss of Cecil Sharp's folksong colls; mss of W C Denis-Browne; mss of F P Haines.

Gonville and Caius College
Cambridge CB2 1TA
Tel: 01223 332419 *Fax:* 01223 332430
Email: glh22@cus.cam.ac.uk
Website: www.cai.cam.ac.uk/library/

Including mss and fragments of mus from the 10th-18th C (mostly 11th-14th C); also papers and materials relating to Charles Wood (1866-1926).

King's College
Rowe Music Library, Cambridge CB2 1ST
Tel: 01223 331252

Including libraries of L T Rowe, A H Mann and A H King; also E J Dent papers.

Magdalene College
Cambridge CB3 0AG
Tel: 01223 332100 *Fax:* 01223 332187

Pepys Library (personal library of Samuel Pepys (1633-1703): mss, ballads, printed mus); library open chiefly during term-time (appointment necessary). Catalogued in R C Latham, ed The Pepys Library at Magdalene College, Cambridge *(11 vols)*, IV.

Pembroke College
Cambridge CB2 1RF
Tel: 01223 338100 *Fax:* 01223 338163
Email: lib@pem.cam.ac.uk

Including 17th C ms part-mus; 18th C chmbr mus.

Pendlebury Library of Music
University Music School, West Rd, Cambridge CB3 9DP
Tel: 01223 335182 *Fax:* 01223 335067

Library of the university mus faculty.

Peterhouse
Trumpington St, Cambridge CB2 1RD
Tel: 01223 338200 *Fax:* 01223 337578

Including 16th-17th C part-books (permanently deposited at University Library).

St John's College
Cambridge CB2 1TP
Tel: 01223 338662 *Fax:* 01223 337035
Email: library@joh.cam.ac.uk

Samuel Butler coll, Rootham compositions.

Trinity College
Cambridge CB2 1TQ
Tel: 01223 338488 *Fax:* 01223 338532
Email: trin-lib@lists.cam.ac.uk
Website: www.trin.cam.ac.uk

Including roll of 15th C English carols, two 15th C Greek mss with mus, lute tablatures of Bacheler, Greaves, Johnson and Taylor, autographs of Gray, Parry and Stanford; early printed mus of Byrd, Mace, Playford and Purcell.

Cardiff

University of Wales College of Cardiff *
Music Dept, Corbett Rd, Cardiff CF1 3EB
Tel: 01222 874000 ext 4387
Email: musicliby@cardiff.ac.uk
Website: www.cf.ac.uk/uwcc/liby/music.html#finding

Mackworth coll: early 18th C printed and mss scores. Aylward coll: printed editions of 18th and 19th C scores.

Welsh College of Music and Drama Library *
Castle Grounds, Cathays Pk, Cardiff CF1 3ER
Tel: 01222 342854 *Fax:* 01222 237639
Email: agusjm@wcmd.ac.uk

Colchester

Colchester Institute Library *
Sheepen Rd, Colchester, Essex CO3 3LL
Tel: 01206 718641/718644 *Fax:* 01206 718643

Liturgical mus, wind band and jazz band scores, collected works.

Durham

University Library
Palace Green Section, Durham DH1 3RN
Tel: 0191 374 3001

Britten correspondence and related mss, Dame Ethel Smyth mss, medieval liturgical mss, Prott Green Collection of hymn books and hymnology.

Edinburgh

Edinburgh University Library: Main Library
George Sq, Edinburgh EH8 9LJ
Tel: 0131 650 3384 *Fax:* 0131 667 9780
Email: library@ed.ac.uk
Website: www.lib.ed.ac.uk

General and special book colls include books of Scottish song; special colls include early Scottish mss (surviving leaves of 14th C Inchcolm Antiphoner, and colls of lute and pipe-tunes, etc); English madrigal books; Marjorie Kennedy-Fraser coll of Hebridean folk-song recordings and books on Highland mus and dance; archives of the Scottish Students' Song Book Committee (1901-1991) and Edinburgh Royal Choral Union (1857-). Main mus colls are held in the Reid Music Library *(see below)*.

Edinburgh University Library: Reid Music Library *
Alison House, 12 Nicolson Sq, Edinburgh EH8 9DF
Tel: 0131 650 2436 *Fax:* 0131 650 2425
Email: reid.music.library@ed.ac.uk
Website: www.lib.ed.ac.uk/

Mus section of Edinburgh University Library. Colls of scores, books and periodicals on Western mus. Special colls include Sir Donald Tovey archive; Niecks bequest of books on the theory of mus; Weiss coll of Beethoven literature; Kenneth Leighton mss; Dallapiccola complete scores.

New College Library
Mound Pl, Edinburgh EH1 2LU
Tel: 0131 650 8957 *Fax:* 0131 650 6579

The Divinity section of Edinburgh University Library. Special colls including James Thin Hymnology Collection.

School of Scottish Studies
University of Edinburgh, 27 George Sq, Edinburgh EH8 9LD
Tel: 0131 650 3060/4159

Book colls include Scots and Gaelic song since the 18th C, folk mus and ethnomusicology of Ireland, England, N America and the world. Archives include traditional and national Scottish mus field recordings, the John Levy coll of ethnomusicological recordings (mostly oriental), the Peter Cooke coll of African mus recordings, the Will Forret coll of Scottish national, popular, folk revival mus, and smaller colls (Chilean, Irish, Indian).

Egham

Royal Holloway, University of London, Music Library *
Egham Hill, Egham, Surrey TW20 0EX
Tel: 01784 443560/443759 *Fax:* 01784 439441
Email: c.grogan@rhbnc.ac.uk
Website: www.lb.rhbnc.ac.uk

Includes library of Dom Anselm Hughes.

Exeter

University Library *
Stocker Rd, Exeter, Devon EX4 4PT
Tel: 01392 263860 *Fax:* 01392 263871
Email: j.a.crawley@exeter.ac.uk

Including special coll of American mus.

Glasgow

Royal Scottish Academy of Music and Drama *
100 Renfrew St, Glasgow G2 3DB
Tel: 0141 332 4101 *Fax:* 0141 332 5924
Email: ibs01pm@gold.ac.uk

University Library *
Hillhead St, Glasgow G12 8QE
Tel: 0141 330 6797 *Fax:* 0141 330 4952
Email: library@gla.ac.uk (general); m.sillito@lib.gla.ac.uk (music)
Website: www.lib.gla.ac.uk

Includes Euing Music coll; Drysdale, Farmer, Lamond, McEwen, MacCunn, Zavertal colls. Incorporates Trinity College library and Mearns coll of hymnology.

Guildford

George Edwards Library
University of Surrey, Guildford, Surrey GU2 5XH
Tel: 01483 300800 ext 3322 *Fax:* 01483 259500

Hull

Brynmor Jones Library
The University of Hull, Cottingham Rd, Hull, N
Humberside HU6 7RX
Tel: 01482 465274 *Fax:* 01482 466205
Email: library@lib.hull.ac.uk

Lancaster

University Library *
Bailrigg, Lancaster LA1 4YH
Tel: 01524 65201 *Fax:* 01524 63806

Including libraries of H F Redlich, Edward
Lockspeiser.

Leeds

Brotherton Library
University of Leeds, Leeds LS2 9JT
Tel: 0113 233 5513 *Fax:* 0113 233 5561
Email: library@library.leeds.ac.uk

Including mss and correspondence of
Mendelssohn, Charles Dibdin mss, Novello (mus
publishers) mss and correspondence,
correspondence of Herbert Thompson (mus
critic).

Leeds College of Music
3 Quarry Hill, Leeds LS2 7PD
Tel: 0113 222 3400 *Fax:* 0113 243 8798
Website: www.netlink.co.uk/users/zappa/clcm/clcm.html

Scores, books, journals, recordings. Jazz archive
available by appointment for reference.

Leicester

University Library
PO Box 248, University Rd, Leics LE1 9QD
Tel: 0116 252 2042 *Fax:* 0116 252 2066
Email: library@uk.ac.leicester

General mus section of university library.

Liverpool

The University of Liverpool Music Library
82 Bedford St South, PO Box 147, Liverpool L69 3BX
Tel: 0151 794 3105/2684 *Fax:* 0151 794 2681
Email: qlis05@liv.ac.uk

Russian mus, German mus 1830-1945, French mus
1860-1945, facsimile editions.

Manchester

John Rylands University Library *
Oxford Rd, Manchester M13 9PP

Tel: 0161 275 4985 (mus library) *Fax:* 0161 273 7488
Website: rylibweb.man.ac.uk/

Includes 9th-15th C liturgical mss; 15th-20th C
printed mus.

Royal Northern College of Music Library *
124 Oxford Rd, Manchester M13 9RD
Tel: 0161 907 5243 *Fax:* 0161 273 7611

Including Rawsthorne mss; Horenstein coll;
Brodskyana (memorabilia of Adolph Brodsky);
Newmania (memorabilia of Philip Newman);
Rothwell coll of wind mus; Dame Eva Turner coll;
John Ogden archive; Ida Carroll archive; RNCM
collection of historical mus insts.

Norwich

University of East Anglia Library
Norwich NR4 7TJ
Tel: 01603 592434 *Fax:* 01603 259490

Nottingham

Music Library *
The Arts Centre, University of Nottingham, University Pk,
Nottingham NG7 2RD
Tel: 0115 951 4596 *Fax:* 0115 951 4756
Email: robin.phillips@nottingham.ac.uk
Website: www.nottingham.ac.uk/library/

Approximately 20,000 books and scores, including
many collected editions of composers and national
mus collections. Also sheet mus and miniature
scores. Over 30 current periodical subscriptions.

Oxford

Bodleian Library *see* **National Copyright
Libraries** *

Brasenose College Library
Oxford OX1 4AJ
Tel: 01865 277827 *Fax:* 01865 277831

Includes Heberden bequest of books about mus
in Ancient Greece and Rome.

Christ Church Library
Oxford OX1 1DP
Tel: 01865 276169
Email: library@christ-church.ox.ac.uk

Includes Henry Aldrich bequest and Richard
Goodson bequest.

Oriel College Library
Oxford OX1 4EW
Tel: 01865 276558

Includes Lord Leigh of Stoneleigh coll of
17th-18th C printed mus.

University Faculty of Music Library *
St Aldate's, Oxford OX1 1DB
Tel: 01865 276146/8 *Fax:* 01865 286260
Email: john.wagstaff@music.ox.ac.uk

Open Mon-Fri 9.30am-5.30pm (term-time) 10am-4.30pm (vacations). General u/grad and research mus coll, including sound and video recordings.

Reading

International Centre for Research in Music Education
University of Reading, Bulmershe Ct, Earley, Reading RH6 1HY
Tel: 0118 931 8821 *Fax:* 0118 935 2080
Email: e.smith@reading.ac.uk

Comprehensive coll of publications and materials for primary and secondary class teaching.

University Music Library *
35 Upper Redlands Rd, Reading, Berks RG1 5JE
Tel: 0118 931 8413 *Fax:* 0118 931 8412

Finzi coll.

St Andrews

University Library
North St, St Andrews, Fife KY16 9TR
Tel: 01334 476161 *Fax:* 01334 462282
Email: nfd@st-and.ac.uk

Includes Finzi coll of 18th C mus.

Sheffield

University of Sheffield Music Library
38 Taptonville Rd, Sheffield, S Yorks S10 5BR
Tel: 0114 222 7330 *Fax:* 0114 266 8053
Email: t.mccanna@sheffield.ac.uk

Southampton

Hartley Library
University of Southampton, University Rd, Highfield, Southampton SO17 1BJ
Tel: 01703 595000 ext 2372 *Fax:* 01703 593007
Email: ng@soton.ac.uk
Website: www.soton.ac.uk/~library

Scores, books, periodicals.

Totnes

Dartington College of Arts Library
Totnes, Devon TQ9 6EJ
Tel: 01803 861651 *Fax:* 01803 863569
Email: library@dartington.ac.uk
Website: www.dartington.ac.uk

York

University Library *
Heslington, York YO1 5DD
Tel: 01904 433865 *Fax:* 01904 433866
Email: libr1@york.ac.uk
Website: www.york.ac.uk

Copland coll and Delius coll.

Libraries of Societies and Institutions

These libraries are for the use of members and staff, but reference facilities are extended to visitors. Applications in writing are advisable.

London

Arts Council of England Reference Library and Enquiry Service
14 Gt Peter St, London SW1P 3NQ
Tel: 0171 333 0100; 0171 973 6517 *Fax:* 0171 973 6590
Website: www.artscouncil.org.uk

Material on arts policy and admin, subsidy and funding of the arts in UK and overseas. Enquiries from 10am-1pm and 2-5pm, Mon-Fri; visits by appointment only with library staff.

The BBC Music Library *
Broadcasting House, Portland Pl, London W1A 1AA
Tel: 0171 765 3724 *Fax:* 0171 765 5304

Largest collection of performing material and commercial and private gramophone records. Loans of mus materials for non-broadcast use are made only if no other source exists and are subject to copyright restrictions; the sound recordings collection is for BBC programme purposes only.

British Film Institute National Library
21 Stephen St, London W1P 2LN
Tel: 0171 255 1444 *Fax:* 0171 436 2338
Website: www.bfi.org.uk/

Includes information about film and TV mus and composers. Small coll of film scores.

British Institute of Recorded Sound
see British Library National Sound Archive *under*

Specialised Gramophone Record and Tape Libraries.

British Music Information Centre
10 Stratford Pl, London W1N 9AE
Tel: 0171 499 8567 *Fax:* 0171 499 4795
Email: bmic@bmic.co.uk
Website: www.bmic.co.uk

Reference coll: 20th C mus by British composers; visitors welcome (Mon-Fri noon-5pm). Reading and listening facilities, free of charge.

Commonwealth Institute
Commonwealth Resource Centre, Kensington High St, London W8 6NQ
Tel: 0171 603 4535 ext 210 *Fax:* 0171 603 2807
Website: www.commonwealth.org.uk/

Coll includes mus from most commonwealth countries; loan service for teachers throughout Britain.

English Folk Dance and Song Society *
Vaughan Williams Memorial Library, Cecil Sharp House, 2 Regent's Park Rd, London NW1 7AY
Tel: 0171 284 0523 *also fax*

Includes Cecil Sharp bequest; original recordings by many leading folksong collectors.

Gerald Coke Handel Collection
40 Brunswick Sq, London WC1N 1AZ

Handel coll. A privately owned library, until further notice written application essential to Gerald Coke Foundation at above address.

Jewish Music Information Centre
The Manor House, 80 East End Rd, London N3 2SY
Tel: 0181 349 4731

Library of reform liturgical mus. Resource library of many tapes and volumes not generally available.

Jewish Music Resource Centre
City University, Northampton Sq, London EC1V 0HB
Tel: 0171 477 8284 *Fax:* 0171 477 8576
Email: jewishmusic@jmht.org
Website: www.city.ac.uk/music/

Books, recordings and sheet mus. Harry Rosencweig Collection.

The Prokofiev Archive *
Goldsmiths College, University of London, London SE14 6NW
Tel: 0171 919 7558 *Fax:* 0171 919 7255
Email: mua01nm@gold.ac.uk
Website: musicinfo.gold.ac.uk/music/prokofiev.html

Property of the Serge Prokofiev Foundation. The archive holds copies of published works, microfilms of ms, books, articles and reviews; sound recordings, letters, photos, documents. Also houses the Stravinsky collection.

Society for Co-operation in Russian and Soviet Studies
320 Brixton Rd, London SW9 6AB
Tel: 0171 274 2282 *Fax:* 0171 274 3230

Reference library of mus scores, encyclopaedias and recordings appertaining to Russian and Soviet mus and composers. Fees available on request.

Aldeburgh

Britten-Pears Library *
Red House, Aldeburgh, Suffolk IP15 5PZ
Tel: 01728 452615 *Fax:* 01728 453076
Email: bpl@uea.ac.uk
Website: www.lib.uea.ac.uk/libinfo/localcol/britwelc/britwelc.ht

Mss of Britten and other composers including Bridge, Holst, Tippett, Armstrong Gibbs, Alwyn, Shostakovich. Also special material on English song and English Opera Group Archive, books, printed mus, correspondence, sound recordings, ephemera and photographs. Open for research, by appointment only.

Cambridge

Dept of Manuscripts and Printed Books
Fitzwilliam Museum, Trumpington St, Cambridge CB2 1RB
Tel: 01223 332900 *Fax:* 01223 332923

Coll includes Fitzwilliam Virginal Book, composers' autographs, 16th-20th C especially Handel.

Cardiff

Welsh Music Information Centre
c/o ASS Library, University of Wales, College of Cardiff, Corbett Rd, Cardiff CF1 1XL

Mus of Welsh composers, published and unpublished. Open week days 9.30am-1pm or afternoons by appointment.

Crowthorne

British Institute of Jazz Studies
17 The Chase, Crowthorne, Berks RG45 6HT
Tel: 01344 775669 *Fax:* 01344 780947

Library of jazz and blues material: books, periodicals, ephemera, etc; visits by appointment.

Ely

ESM International Music Information
PO Box 1, Ely, Cambridge CB6 3DJ
Tel: 01353 663020 *Fax:* 01353 667798

Recordings and biographical notes of musicians,

singers, composers, bands, ens, groups, orchestras, etc from all over the world.

Eton

College Library
Eton College, Windsor, Berks SL4 6DB
Tel: 01753 671221 *Fax:* 01753 671244

Includes the Eton Choir Book (c1500), 18th C ms org books, minor mss of works by Parry, Butterworth, Quilter, Warlock, Hoddinott, etc.

Glasgow

Scottish Music Information Centre *
1 Bowmont Gardens, Glasgow G12 9LR
Tel: 0141 334 6393 *Fax:* 0141 337 1161
Email: smic@glasgow.almac.co.uk
Website: www.music.gla.ac.uk/htmlfolder/resources/smic/ homepage

Information and documentation centre for Scottish composers and Scottish mus. Scores, recordings, rare books and mss, some available for sale or hire.

Loughton

National Jazz Foundation Archive
Loughton Central Library, Traps Hill, Loughton, Essex IG10 1HD
Tel: 0181 502 0181 *Fax:* 0181 508 5041

Archive of printed material for research into jazz. Books, periodicals, concert brochures, photographs, posters, etc.

Manchester

Chetham's Library
Long Millgate, Manchester M3 1SB
Tel: 0161 834 7961 *Fax:* 0161 839 5797

Halliwell-Phillipps coll of proclamations, broadsides, ballads and poems. For reference only.

Preston

Library of Light-Orchestral Music
Lancaster Farm, Chipping La, Longridge, Preston, Lancs PR3 2NB
Tel: 01772 783646 *Fax:* 01772 786026

Standard published sets, ms arrangements, parts from film, recording, TV, radio, theatrical productions; hire and sale.

Stockport

National Library for the Blind
Far Cromwell Rd, Bredbury, Stockport, Cheshire SK6 2SG
Tel: 0161 355 2000 *Fax:* 0161 355 2098
Email: nlbuk@compuserve.com

Large coll of braille mus on free loan (print and braille catalogue available); UK source for Library of Congress braille and large-print mus; enlarging service.

Stratford upon Avon

Shakespeare Centre Library
Henley St, Stratford upon Avon, Warwicks CV37 6QW
Tel: 01789 201813 *Fax:* 01789 296083
Email: library@shakespeare.org.uk

Mus connected with Shakespeare and RSC productions, including Vaughan Williams mus.

Westhumble

Royal School of Church Music
Cleveland Lodge, Westhumble, Dorking RH5 6BW
Tel: 01306 877676 *Fax:* 01306 877260
Email: jhender@rscm.u-net.com

Colles Library, church mus and books. Please enquire for details of access.

Specialised Gramophone Record and Tape Libraries

This list does not include the record collections available at many public libraries.

London

BBC Music Library *see* Libraries of Societies and Institutions *

British Library National Sound Archive
The British Library, 96 Euston Rd, London NW1 2DB
Tel: 0171 412 7440 *Fax:* 0171 412 7441
Email: nsa@bl.uk
Website: www.bl.uk/collections/sound-archive

Largest reference collection of sound recordings in the UK open to the public, full reference library of associated literature. Information on commercial discs and location of recordings around the UK. All facilities free; groups from schools, universities, colleges welcome to listen by prior arrangement; w/shops, talks and seminars also offered by arrangement.

BTW Production Music Library
106 Westpole Av, Cockfosters, Herts EN4 0BB
Tel: 0181 449 6110 *also fax*

Mus for TV, radio and a/v productions.

MCPS Ltd *
Elgar House, 41 Streatham High Rd, London SW16 1ER
Tel: 0181 769 4400

Comprehensive computerised database of commercially recorded material in the UK, including items now deleted from the catalogue.

Music Performance Research Centre
Barbican Library, Barbican Centre, Silk St, London EC2Y 8DS
Tel: 01932 860472 *also fax;*
Website: www.musicpreserved.org

A/v archive concerned with preservation, rights protection and research of public mus performances by international artists. Also records and houses interviews with performers.

National Sound Archive
see British Library National Sound Archive.

School of Oriental and African Studies Library
University of London, Thornhaugh St, London WC1H 0XG
Tel: 0171 637 2388 ext 2305 *Fax:* 0171 436 3844

Email: yyl@soas.ac.uk
Website: www.soas.ac.uk/library/guides/recordings.html

Video and sound recordings of Oriental and African mus.

Cambridge

Cambridge Anthropology Sound Archive
Dept of Social Anthropology, Free School La, Cambridge CB2 3RF
Tel: 01223 334599/334402

Coll of commercial and field recordings of traditional and other mus from all countries.

Gloucester

The Traditions Library
16 Brunswick Sq, Gloucester GL1 1UG
Tel: 01452 415110
Email: folktrax@demon.co.uk

International traditional mus and customs in print and on studio tape, cassette, film and video.

St Annes-on-Sea

Long Playing Record Library Ltd
Squires Gate Music Centre, Rear 13 St Andrews Rd South, St Annes-on-Sea, Lancs FY8 1SX
Tel: 01253 782588 *Fax:* 01253 782985

Commercial lending library for CDs; also specialist suppliers of CDs and tapes to libraries, broadcasting stations, individuals worldwide, specialising in classical mus.

Museums and Other Collections

Hours of opening may vary considerably, and should be checked before a visit is organised. Some collections may be viewed only after written application to the curator.

London

Fenton House
Hampstead Grove, London NW3 6RT
Tel: 0171 435 3471

Early keyboard insts.

The Handel House Trust Ltd
10 Stratford Pl, London W1N 9AE
Tel: 0171 495 1685 *Fax:* 0171 495 1759
Email: handel.house@virgin.net

Charity engaged in establishing a museum to Handel in his home at 25 Brook St, Mayfair, London W1.

Horniman Museum and Gardens
100 London Rd, London SE23 3PQ

Tel: 0181 699 1872 *Fax:* 0181 291 5506
Email: palmer@horniman.demon.co.uk;
allen@horniman.demon.co.uk

Large coll of mus insts from all over world (6000 insts, 1500 on display) including Adam Carse coll, Percy A Bull coll, L Wayne coll of concertinas, Alice Schulmann Frank coll of world mus insts and Dolmetsch coll. Library includes sections on mus insts. Also education service.

Museum of London
London Wall, London EC2Y 5HN
Tel: 0171 600 3699 *Fax:* 0171 600 1058

Str, keyboard and wind insts; small coll only, 1950s fittings from Dobell's Jazz shop, printed ephemera on theatres and mus in London, (closed Mon). Small number of paper rolls, vinyl discs, cylinders, c1900-70s.

Musical Museum (Charitable Trust)
368 High St, Brentford, Middx TW8 0BD
Tel: 0181 560 8108

Keyboards, automatic mus insts, player-pnos, orchestrions, Wurlitzer Fotoplayer, Welte Philharmonic Reproducing Pipe Organ, Aeolian Residence Duo-Art Pipe Organ, etc. Open w/ends Apr-Oct 2pm-5pm, Weds Jul-Aug 2-4pm.

Royal College of Music
Prince Consort Rd, London SW7 2BS
Tel: 0171 589 3643; 0171 591 4346 *Fax:* 0171 589 7740; 0171 591 4340
Email: ewells@rcm.ac.uk

Museum of insts (keyboard, str, wind), including Tagore, Donaldson, Hipkins, Ridley and Hartley colls; 600 insts (500 European, 100 Asian and African). Dept of Portraits and Performance History: paintings, prints, photographs, concert programmes, etc.

Theatre Museum
Tavistock St, Covent Garden, London EC2E 7PA
Tel: 0171 836 7891 *Fax:* 0171 836 5148

National mus of performing arts including theatre, mus, pop, melodrama, ballet and opera. Public research facilities.

Victoria and Albert Museum
Cromwell Rd, South Kensington, London SW7 2RL
Tel: 0171 938 8500/8287 *Fax:* 0171 938 8283

Comprehensive exhibition coll of decorative mus insts; mus insts and mus iconography included in National Art Library at the V & A.

Belfast

Ulster Museum
Botanic Gardens, Belfast BT9 5AB
Tel: 01232 383000 *Fax:* 01232 383013

Small coll of ancient and modern mus insts. Ethnographic mus insts includes 2 sets of Chimu pottery pan pipes, 2 Bronze Age horns, 3 pairs of Uillean pipes, 4 harps, 2 fifes, 4 Lambeg drums.

Birmingham

Museum of Science and Industry
Newhall St, Birmingham B3 1RZ
Tel: 0121 235 1661 *Fax:* 0121 233 9210

Museum closed, access for research purposes only and by appointment. Mechanical mus insts; coll of mus boxes.

Bradford

Bolling Hall Museum
Bowling Hall Rd, Bradford, W Yorks BD4 7LP
Tel: 01274 723057 *Fax:* 01274 726220
Email: abickley@legend.co.uk

Coll of mus insts dispersed among various museums in Bradford Metropolitan area. Mostly at Cliffe Castle Museum.

Cambridge

Fitzwilliam Museum
Trumpington St, Cambridge CB2 1RB
Tel: 01223 332900 *Fax:* 01223 332923

A few guis, lutes and keyboard insts and a pitch pipe.

University Museum of Archaeology and Anthropology
Downing St, Cambridge CB2 3DZ
Tel: 01223 333516 *Fax:* 01223 333503

Coll of insts of anthropological interest.

Cardiff

Museum of Welsh Life (National Museums and Galleries of Wales)
St Fagans, Nr Cardiff CF5 6XB
Tel: 01222 573500 *Fax:* 01222 573490
Website: www.cardiff.ac.uk/nmgw/stfagans.html

Str, keyboard and wind insts.

Carlisle

City Museum and Art Gallery
Tullie House, Castle St, Carlisle, Cumbria CA3 8TP
Tel: 01228 34781 *Fax:* 01288 810249

Str and wind insts, including Andrea Amati vn of 1564 and str insts by Forster family.

Cheltenham

Holst Birthplace Museum
4 Clarence Rd, Pittville, Cheltenham, Glos GL52 2AY
Tel: 01242 524846 *Fax:* 01242 262334

Unique coll of Holst material including printed mus, pictures, concert programmes, books, personal possessions. Open to public all yr (closed Sun-Mon), small admission charge, enquiries to information offr, Cheltenham Art Gallery, Clarence St, Cheltenham *Tel:* 01242 237431.

Chester

Grosvenor Museum
27 Grosvenor St, Chester CH1 2DD
Tel: 01244 402008 *Fax:* 01244 347587

Unique set of Bressan rcdrs (recording available).

Douglas

Manx National Heritage
Manx Museum and National Trust, Douglas, Isle of Man IM1 3LY
Tel: 01624 648000 *Fax:* 01624 648001

Str, keyboard and wind insts.

Edinburgh

Edinburgh University
Collection of Historic Musical Instruments, Reid Concert Hall, Bristo Sq, Edinburgh EH8 9AG
Tel: 0131 650 2423/2 *Fax:* 0131 650 2425
Email: a.myers@ed.ac.uk
Website: www.music.ed.ac.uk/euchmi/

University coll of over 2000 historic mus insts spanning 400 yrs. Open Wed pm, Sat am, (Mon-Fri throughout Edinburgh Festival). Admission free.

National Museums of Scotland
Chambers St, Edinburgh EH1 1JF
Tel: 0131 225 7534 *Fax:* 0131 220 4819
Website: www.nms.ac.uk

International and Scottish collections of str, keyboard and wind insts, including Glen and Ross bagpipe coll, coll of pipe-making tools. Jean Jenkins coll of sound recordings (ethnomusicological), also photographic slides and mus insts.

St Cecilia's Hall (Edinburgh University)
Niddry St, Cowgate, Edinburgh EH1 1LJ
Tel: 0131 650 2805 *Fax:* 0131 650 2812
Email: russell.collection@music.ed.co.uk
Website: www.music.ed.ac.uk/russell/index.html

Russell Coll of Early Keyboard Insts: hpds, virginals, spinets, clvds, early pnos and chmbr orgs from 1586-1840.

Scottish United Services Museum
The Castle, Edinburgh EH1 2NG
Tel: 0131 225 7534 *Fax:* 0131 225 3848

Military wind and perc insts from 18th C. Sound archives on tape of European and N American military mus (appointment necessary).

Glasgow

Art Gallery and Museum
Kelvingrove, Glasgow G3 8AG
Tel: 0141 221 9600 *Fax:* 0141 287 2690

Coll of historical mus insts.

Goudhurst

Finchcocks Living Museum of Music
Finchcocks, Goudhurst, Kent TH17 1HH
Tel: 01580 211702 *Fax:* 01580 211007

Richard Burnett coll of historic keyboard insts. Open Sun and Bank Holidays Easter-Sep; Wed and Thu in Aug; other times by prior arrangement. Musical tours whenever open.

Hailsham

Michelham Priory
Upper Dicker, Hailsham, E Sussex BN27 3QS
Tel: 01323 844224 *Fax:* 01323 844030

Includes Alice Schulmann Frank coll of world mus insts (formerly Mummery coll).

Halifax

Shibden Hall
Listers Rd, Halifax, W Yorks HX3 6XG
Tel: 01422 352246 *Fax:* 01422 348440

General coll of mus insts, particularly 18th C chmbr. Also 19th C scores.

Holdenby

Holdenby House
Holdenby, Northants NN6 8DJ
Tel: 01604 770074 *Fax:* 01604 770962

Non-player pno exhibition, old pnos from 1790. 11 pnos from British Piano Museum. House parties by appointment, min 25.

Huddersfield

Tolson Memorial Museum
Ravensknowle Pk, Wakefield Rd, Huddersfield HD5 8DJ
Tel: 01484 223830 *Fax:* 01484 223843

Br, wind and str insts.

Ipswich

Christchurch Mansion
Christchurch Pk, Ipswich IP4 2BE
Tel: 01473 253246 *Fax:* 01473 210328

Str, wind and keyboard insts. Enquiries and correspondence to Ipswich Museum, *see below.*

Ipswich Museum
High St, Ipswich IP1 3QH
Tel: 01473 213761 *Fax:* 01473 281274

Ethnographic insts.

Keighley

Cliffe Castle Art Gallery and Museum
Keighley, W Yorks BD20 6LH
Tel: 01535 618230 *Fax:* 01535 610536

General coll of mus insts.

Liverpool

Liverpool Museum
William Brown St, Liverpool L3 8EN
Tel: 0151 478 4399 *Fax:* 0151 478 4390

Coll of 17th-19th C insts including former Rushworth and Dreaper coll.

Maidstone

Museum and Art Gallery
Maidstone, Kent ME14 1LH
Tel: 01622 754497 *Fax:* 01622 602193

Str, keyboard and wind insts, includes Handel's portable clvd.

Manchester

Royal Northern College of Music
124 Oxford Rd, Manchester M13 9RD
Tel: 0161 907 5243 *Fax:* 0161 273 7611

RNCM coll of historic and ethnic insts.

Merthyr Tydfil

Cyfarthfa Castle Art Gallery and Museum
Merthyr Tydfil, Merthyr Tydfil County Borough CF47 8RE
Tel: 01685 723112 *also fax; Fax:* 01685 722146

Mid 19th C coll of insts, ms mus, photographs and ephemera relating to the Cyfarthfa Band; also ethnographic inst coll.

Northleach

Keith Harding's World of Mechanical Music
Oak House, High St, Northleach, Glos GL54 3ET
Tel: 01451 860181 *Fax:* 01451 861133
Website: www.leisurehunt.com/womm.htm

Demonstrations of antique clocks, musical boxes, automata, reproducing pnos and mechanical mus insts presented as live entertainment. Restoration work done.

Norwich

St Peter Hungate Museum (Norfolk Museums Service)
Princes St, Norwich NR3 1AE
Tel: 01603 667231

Str, keyboard and wind insts formerly used in churches.

Strangers' Hall Museum (Norfolk Museums Service)
Charing Cross, Norwich NR2 4AL
Tel: 01603 667229

Str, keyboard, perc and mechanical wind insts. Gramophones, printed and ms mus in store. Viewing by arrangement.

Oxford

Ashmolean Museum
Beaumont St, Oxford OX1 2PH
Tel: 01865 278000 *Fax:* 01865 278042

Hill coll of str insts and bows (photographs and measured drawings of str insts available for research).

Bate Collection of Musical Instruments
Oxford University Faculty of Music, St Aldate's, Oxford OX1 1DB
Tel: 01865 276139 *Fax:* 01865 276128
Email: bate.collection@music.oxford.ac.uk

W/wind, br, early keyboards and bow makers w/shop. Open Mon-Fri 2-5pm, admission free. Open Sat during University full term, 10am-12pm.

University of Oxford, Pitt Rivers Museum
South Parks Rd, Oxford OX1 3PP
Tel: 01865 270927 *Fax:* 01865 274725
Email: pitt@ermine.ox.ac.uk

Important worldwide coll of more than 6000 mus insts. New gallery Music Makers in the Balfour Building, 60 Banbury Rd, Oxford *Tel:* 01865 274726, including a sound guide and a/v booth.

St Albans

Organ Museum
320 Camp Rd, St Albans, Herts AL1 5PB
Tel: 01727 851557 *also fax*

Mechanical insts and theatre orgs; open Sun 2.15-4.30pm. Other times by arrangement. Correspondence and enquiries to the Secretary, c/o 326 Camp Rd, St Albans, Herts AL1 5PB.

Shipley

Victorian Reed Organ and Harmonium Museum
Victoria Hall, Victoria Rd, Saltaire Village, Shipley,
W Yorks
Tel: 01274 585601 (after 5pm)

Private collection of 95 reed orgs. Players encouraged to play. Also mechanical reed orgs. Open to the public Sun-Thu 11am-4pm.

Worcester

The Elgar Birthplace Museum
Crown East La, Lower Broadheath, Worcester WR2 6RH
Tel: 01905 333224 *also fax*

Unique coll of Elgarian material including scores, books, photographs, insts and personal possessions.

York

York Castle Museum
York YO1 1RY
Tel: 01904 653611 *Fax:* 01904 671078

Social history museum of everyday life. General coll of mus insts, with good w/wind, keyboard and mechanical sections (some on display).

Useful Book List

All the books listed below should be available in public libraries. News and reviews concerning new publications on music and education are frequently carried in the *British Music Education Journal* published by Cambridge University Press, *Music Teacher* magazine published by Rhinegold Publishing, *International Journal of Music Education* published by Reading University, *The Times Educational Supplement* and *The Times Higher Educational Supplement*. A list of articles carried over the last year in *Music Teacher*, *British Journal of Music Education* and the *International Journal of Music Education* can be found in the **Resources Published in 1997** section.

A Basis for Music Education
Routledge, 11 New Fetter La, London EC4P 4EE
Keith Swanwick. £12.99.

The Art of Conducting
Rhinegold Publishing Ltd, 241 Shaftesbury Av, London WC2H 8EH
Tel: 0171 333 1721 *Fax:* 0171 333 1769
Email: sales@rhinegold.co.uk
£10 plus £2.50 postage.

Awards for First Degree Study at Commonwealth Universities
Publications Dept, Association of Commonwealth Universities, John Foster House, 36 Gordon Sq, London WC1H 0PF
Tel: 0171 387 8572 *Fax:* 0171 387 2655
Email: info@acu.ac.uk
Website: www.acu.acac.uk
Sue Kirkland, head of mkt development. Biennial (odd years).

Awards for Postgraduate Study at Commonwealth Universities
Publications Dept, Association of Commonwealth Universities, John Foster House, 36 Gordon Sq, London WC1H 0PF
Tel: 0171 387 8572 *Fax:* 0171 387 2655
Email: info@acu.ac.uk
Website: www.acu.ac.uk
Sue Kirkland, head of mkt development. Biennial (odd years).

Awards for University Administrators and Librarians
Publications Dept, Association of Commonwealth Universities, John Foster House, 36 Gordon Sq, London WC1H 0PF
Tel: 0171 387 8572 *Fax:* 0171 387 2655
Email: pubinf@acu.ac.uk
Sue Kirkland, head of mkt development. Biennial (even years).

Awards for University Teachers and Research Workers
Publications Dept, Association of Commonwealth Universities, John Foster House, 36 Gordon Sq, London WC1H 0PF
Tel: 0171 387 8572 *Fax:* 0171 387 2655
Email: pubinf@acu.ac.uk
Sue Kirkland, head of mkt development. Biennial (even years).

Boarding Schools and Colleges 1997
John Catt Educational Ltd, Great Glemham, Saxmundham, Suffolk IP17 2DH
Tel: 01728 663666 *Fax:* 01728 663415
Email: office@johncatt.co.uk
Website: www.johncatt.co.uk
Derek Bingham, editor in chief.

British and International Music Yearbook
Rhinegold Publishing Ltd, 241 Shaftesbury Av, London WC2H 8EH
Tel: 0171 333 1721 *Fax:* 0171 333 1769
Email: sales@rhinegold.co.uk
£23.95 post free.

British Performing Arts Yearbook
Rhinegold Publishing Ltd, 241 Shaftesbury Av, London WC2H 8EH
Tel: 0171 333 1721 *Fax:* 0171 333 1769
Email: sales@rhinegold.co.uk
£23.95 post free.

British Qualifications
Kogan Page, 120 Pentonville Rd, London N1 9JN
Tel: 0171 278 0433 *Fax:* 0171 837 6348
Email: kpinfo@kogan-page.co.uk
Ann McCarthy, mkt exec. A complete guide to educational, technical, professional and academic qualifications in Britain. £45 (hardback), £29.99 (paperback).

Careers in Music

Heinemann Publishers Oxford, Halley Court, Jordan Hill, Oxford OX2 8EJ
Tel: 01865 314320 *Fax:* 01865 314091
Email: bhukorders@repp.co.uk

John Westcombe. £10.50.

Choosing Your Independent School

ISIS, 56 Buckingham Gate, London SW1E 6AG
Tel: 0171 630 8793/4 *Fax:* 0171 630 5013
Email: national@isis.org.uk
Website: www.isis.org.uk

Mrs Parrish, admin. Annual. £8.50 plus £2 postage.

The Complete Degree Course Offers for Entry into Higher Education 1999

Bailey Distribution Ltd, Unit 1, Learoyd Rd, Mountfield Road Industrial Estate, New Romney, Kent TN28 8XU
Tel: 01797 369961 *Fax:* 01797 366638
Email: tracy@trotman.co.uk
Website: www.trotmanpublishing.co.uk

Published by Trotman & Co Ltd. Comprehensive coverage of entry requirements for every degree course in the UK. £17.99 plus £1 UK postage, £2 overseas postage.

CRAC Degree Course Guides 1998/99

Hobsons Publishing plc, Bateman St, Cambridge CB2 1LZ
Tel: 01223 354551 *Fax:* 01223 323154
Website: www.hobsons.co.uk

Fiona Jenkins, mkt manager. £4.99 each plus £1 postage.

CRAC Directory of Further Education

Hobsons Publishing plc, Bateman St, Cambridge CB2 1LZ
Tel: 01223 354551 *Fax:* 01223 323154
Website: www.hobsons.co.uk

Fiona Jenkins, mkt manager Annual directory. £69.50.

CRAC Which Degree Series 1999

Hobsons Publishing plc, Bateman St, Cambridge CB2 1LZ
Tel: 01223 354551 *Fax:* 01223 323154
Website: www.hobsons.co.uk

Fiona Jenkins, mkt manager 4 vols: Arts Humanities and Languages; Engineering, Technology and Geography; Sciences, Medicine and Mathematics; Social Sciences, Business, Education and Law, £19.99 each on CD-Rom.

CRAC Which University

Hobsons Publishing plc, Bateman St, Cambridge CB2 1LZ
Tel: 01223 354551 *Fax:* 01223 323154
Website: www.hobsons.co.uk

Fiona Jenkins, mkt manager £58.

Curriculum Confidential 6

Courseware Publications, 4 Apple Barn Ct, Old Church La, Westley, Bury St Edmunds, Suffolk IP33 3TJ
Tel: 01284 703300 *also fax*

Jim Sweetman's guide to the National Curriculum. £11.20 including postage.

Education Authorities' Directory and Annual

School Government Publishing Co, Darby House, Bletchingly Rd, Merstham, Redhill RH1 3DN
Tel: 01737 642223 *Fax:* 01737 644283

£72 (hardcase), £60 (paperback). Free postage.

Education Yearbook

Financial Times Management Dept CS, Financial Times Professional Distribution Centre, Sloudburn Crescent, Fylde Rd, Southport, Merseyside PR9 9YF
Tel: 01704 508080 *Fax:* 01704 506685

£89.

The European Choice

Department for Education and Employment, Publications PO Box 5050, Sudbury, Suffolk Co10 6ZQ
Tel: 0845 6022260

Free.

The Gabbitas Guide to Independent Schools

Kogan Page Ltd, 120 Pentonville Rd, London N1 9JN
Tel: 0171 278 0433 *Fax:* 0171 837 6348
Email: kpinfo@kogan-page.co.uk

Ann McCarthy, mkt exec. £9.99.

Getting Into Music, Drama & Dance

Bailey Distribution Ltd, Unit 1, Learoyd Rd, Mountfield Road Industrial Estate, New Romney, Kent TN28 8XU
Tel: 01797 369961 *Fax:* 01797 366638
Email: tracy@trotman.co.uk
Website: www.trotmanpublishing.co.uk

Published by Trotman & Co Ltd. Gives advice on how students can maximise their chances of entering these professions and the relevant university or college courses. £7.99 plus £1 UK postage, £2 overseas postage.

Getting into USA Universities and Colleges

Bailey Distribution Ltd, Unit 1, Learoyd Rd, Mountfield Road Industrial Estate, New Romney, Kent TN28 8XU
Tel: 01797 369961 *Fax:* 01797 366638
Email: tracy@trotman.co.uk
Website: www.trotmanpublishing.co.uk

Published by Trotman & Co Ltd. £7.99 plus £1 UK postage, £2 overseas postage.

Good Schools Guide
Ebury Press, Random Century House, 20 Vauxhall Bridge Rd,
London SW1V 2SA
Tel: 0171 973 9690 *Fax:* 0171 233 7398

Syd Moore. £10.99.

Graduate Careers Information Booklet: Performing Arts and Arts Administration
CSU Ltd Despatch Department, 1st Floor, Armstrong
House, Oxford Rd, Manchester M1 7ED
Tel: 0161 236 9816 *Fax:* 0161 236 8541
Website: www.prospects.csu.ac.uk

Mary Findon, AgCAS liaison offr and despatch
manager. £2.25.

Fees, Grants and Loans to Students
Dept of Education for Northern Ireland, Rathgael House,
Balloo Rd, Bangor, Co Down BT19 7PR
Tel: 01247 279417

Copies may be obtained from the student
support branch at the above address or from the
educational library boards. Free of charge.

Handbook of Music Awards and Scholarships
Musicians' Benevolent Fund, 16 Ogle St, London W1P 7JB
Tel: 0171 636 4481

Valerie Beale, ed. £3.50.

Higher Education in the European Community
Kogan Page, 120 Pentonville Rd, London N1 9JN
Tel: 0171 278 0433 *Fax:* 0171 837 6348
Email: kpinfo@kogan-page.co.uk

Ann McCarthy, mkt exec.

How To Choose Your Degree Course
Bailey Distribution Ltd, Unit 1, Learoyd Rd, Mountfield
Road Industrial Estate, New Romney, Kent TN28 8XU
Tel: 01797 369961 *Fax:* 01797 366638
Email: tracy@trotman.co.uk
Website: www.trotmanpublishing.co.uk

Published by Trotman & Co Ltd. Reference
source to all major UK university and college
courses. £14.99 plus £1 UK postage, £2 overseas
postage.

How to Complete Your UCAS Form 1999
Bailey Distribution Ltd, Unit 1, Learoyd Rd, Mountfield
Road Industrial Estate, New Romney, Kent TN28 8XU
Tel: 01797 369961 *Fax:* 01797 366638
Email: tracy@trotman.co.uk
Website: www.trotmanpublishing.co.uk

Published by Trotman & Co Ltd. Tony Higgins,
ed. £7.99 plus £1 UK postage and £2 overseas
postage.

Independent Schools Yearbook
A & C Black, PO Box 19, Huntingdon, Cambs PE19 3SF
Tel: 01480 212666 *Fax:* 01480 405014

Hilary While, educ sales co-ord. £25 plus £3.60
postage.

It's Your Choice
Department for Education and Employment, PO Box 6927,
London E3 3NZ
Tel: 0171 510 0150 *Fax:* 0171 510 0196

A guide to choosing at 16.

Making Music with the Young Child with Special Needs
Jessica Kingsley Publishers, 116 Pentonville Rd, London
N1 9JB
Tel: 0171 833 2307 *Fax:* 0171 837 2917
Email: post@jtp.com
Website: www.jtp.com

Amanda Little, mkt assistant Elaine Streeter. £7.99.

The Mature Students Guide to Higher Education
UCAS, Fulton House, Jessop Av, Cheltenham, Glos GL50 3SH
Tel: 01242 222444 *Fax:* 01242 255725

Tony Charlton, student support facilitator. Guide
for adults of all ages who may be interested in
considering entry to higher education, offering
advice on becoming a student, life as a student,
choosing a subject/course, choosing a
university/college, the application process and
sources of advice. Free of charge, orders to the
UCAS distribution dept.

Music and People with Developmental Disabilities
Jessica Kingsley Publishers, 116 Pentonville Rd, London N1 9JB
Tel: 0171 833 2307 *Fax:* 0171 837 2917
Email: post@jtp.com
Website: www.jtp.com

F W Schalkwijk. £14.95.

Music Education in Theory and Practice
Falmer Press, Rankine Rd, Basingstoke, Hampshire
RG24 8PR
Tel: 01256 813000 *Fax:* 01256 479438
Email: book.orders@tandf.co.uk
Website: www.tandf.co.uk

Luke Hacker, mkt assistant Charles Plummeridge. £12.

Music for Life: Aspects of Creative Music Therapy with Adult Clients
Jessica Kingsley Publishers, 116 Pentonville Rd, London N1 9JB
Tel: 0171 833 2307 *Fax:* 0171 837 2917
Email: post@jtp.com
Website: www.jtp.com

Gary Ansdell. £14.95.

Music Lessons for Children with Special Needs
Jessica Kingsley Publishers, 116 Pentonville Rd, London N1 9JB
Tel: 0171 833 2307 *Fax:* 0171 837 2917
Email: post@jtp.com
Website: www.jtp.com

T M Perry. £12.95.

Music, Mind and Education
Routledge, 11 New Fetter La, London EC4P 4EE

Keith Swanwick. £11.99.

Music of Our Time: The Catalogue
Schott & Co Ltd, Brunswick Rd, Ashford, Kent TN23 1EH
Tel: 01233 628987 *Fax:* 01233 610232
Website: www.schott-music.com

Judith Webb, head of sales and market. A catalogue of 20th C mus, listing composers with their works, index by inst categories and list of anniversaries. £15.

Music Therapy in Health and Education
Jessica Kingsley Publishers, 116 Pentonville Rd, London N1 9JB
Tel: 0171 833 2307 *Fax:* 0171 837 2917
Email: post@jtp.com
Website: www.jtp.com

Margaret Heal, Tony Wigram (eds). £19.95.

Music Therapy Research and Practice in Medicine: From Out of the Silence
Jessica Kingsley Publishers, 116 Pentonville Rd, London N1 9JB
Tel: 0171 833 2307 *Fax:* 0171 837 2917
Email: post@jtp.com
Website: www.jtp.com

David Aldridge. £18.95.

The Musician's Handbook
Rhinegold Publishing Ltd, 241 Shaftesbury Av, London WC2H 8EH
Tel: 0171 333 1721 *Fax:* 0171 333 1769

£12.95 plus £2.00 postage.

NAFTHE Handbook of Initial Teacher Training
Linneys, ESL, Newgate La, Mansfield, Notts NG18 2PA
Tel: 01623 450450 *Fax:* 01623 450451

John Taylor, sales co-ord. £12, free postage within UK, overseas plus £2 postage per book.

The NatWest Student Book 1999 Entry
Bailey Distribution Ltd, Unit 1, Learoyd Rd, Mountfield Road Industrial Estate, New Romney, Kent TN28 8XU
Tel: 01797 369961 *Fax:* 01797 366638
Email: tracy@trotman.co.uk
Website: www.trotmanpublishing.co.uk

Published by Trotman & Co Ltd. Klaus Boehm and Jenny Lees-Spalding ed. Guide for applicants to UK universities and colleges. £10.99 plus £1 UK postage, £2 overseas postage.

The Parents' Guide to Higher Education
UCAS, Fulton House, Jessop Av, Cheltenham, Glos GL50 3SH
Tel: 01242 222444 *Fax:* 01242 255725

Tony Charlton, student support. The guide is for parents of school and college students, offering advice on making the right choices in higher education, the application process, financial considerations and life as a student. Free.

Potter Guide to Higher Education: 1999 Entry
Dalebank Books, Arden Lodge, Savile Pk Rd, Halifax HX1 2XR
Tel: 01422 349111 *Fax:* 01422 351275

Sheila Potter, mgr ed.
£16.75 (bookshops), £14.50 plus £3.95 postage direct from Dalebank Books.

The Primary Education Directory
School Government Publishing Co, Darby House, Bletchingly Rd, Merstham, Redhill RH1 3DN
Tel: 01737 642223 *Fax:* 01737 644283
Website: www.schoolgovernment.co.uk

£45. Free postage.

Questions & Answers series: Music
Bailey Distribution Ltd, Unit 1, learoyd Rd, Mountfield Road Industrial Estate, New Romney, Kent TN28 8XU
Tel: 01797 369961 *Fax:* 01797 366638
Email: tracy@trotman.co.uk
Website: www.trotmanpublishing.co.uk

Published by Trotman & Co ltd. £3.99 plus £1 UK postage, £2 overseas postage.

SOCRATES - ERASMUS - The UK Guide 1998
ISCO Publications, 12a Princess Way, Camberley, Surrey GU15 3SP
Tel: 01276 21188 *Fax:* 01276 691833

Sylvia Pool, publications co-ord. £10.90 plus £1.70 postage (no postage charged on orders of 2 or more copies).

The Special Education Directory
School Government Publishing Co, Darby House, Bletchingly Rd, Merstham, Redhill RH1 3DN
Tel: 01737 642223 *Fax:* 01737 644283
Website: www.schoolgovernment.co.uk

£30 (paperback). Free postage.

Student Grants and Loans: A Brief Guide 1997-8
Department for Education and Employment, Publications PO Box 5050, Sudbury, Suffolk CO10 6ZQ
Tel: 0845 6022260

Free.

Student Support in Scotland - A Guide to Undergraduate Allowances
Students Awards Agency for Scotland, Gyleview House, 3 Redheughs Rigg, South Gyle, Edinburgh EH12 9HH
Tel: 0131 244 5823 *Fax:* 0131 244 5887

Linda McCandless, policy mgr.

Students' Money Matters
Bailey Distribution Ltd, Unit 1, Learoyd Rd, Mountfield Road Industrial Estate, New Romney, Kent TN28 8XU
Tel: 01797 369961 *Fax:* 01797 366638
Email: tracy@trotman.co.uk
Website: www.trotmanpublishing.co.uk

Published by Trotman & Co Ltd. £8.99 plus £1 UK postage, £2 overseas postage.

Teaching Music in the Primary School
Cassell plc, Wellington House, 125 Strand, London WC2R 0BB
Tel: 0171 420 5555 *Fax:* 0171 240 7261

Huw Neill, academic promotions exec. Joanna Glover, Stephen Ward, eds. £13.99.

The Times Good University Guide
Times Books, HarperCollins Publishers, 77-85 Fulham Palace Rd, London W6 8JB
Tel: 0181 741 7070 *Fax:* 0181 307 4813

Abigail Dawson, mkt manager. £8.99.

University and College Entrance: The Official UCAS Guide to University and College Entrance 1998
Sheed & Ward Ltd, 14 Coopers Row, London EC3N 2BH
Tel: 0171 702 9799 *Fax:* 0171 702 3583

Annual. Published by UCAS, but available from Sheed & Ward Ltd at the above address. £18.95.

Welsh Language Booklet on Student Grants and Loans
Welsh Office Education Dept, Cathays Park, Cardiff CF1 3NQ
Tel: 01222 825831 *Fax:* 01222 825823

The World of Learning
Europa Publications, 18 Bedford Sq, London WC1B 3JN
Tel: 0171 580 8236 *Fax:* 0171 637 0922
Email: sales@europapublications.co.uk

Peter Jackson, sales director. £225 including postage.

Alphabetical Index of Advertisers

Alphabetical Index of Subjects

For your *free* editorial entry in the

Music Education Yearbook 1999/2000

complete this form and return to:

The Editor, Music Education Yearbook,
Rhinegold Publishing Ltd, 241 Shaftesbury Avenue,
London WC2H 8EH *Tel:* 0171 333 1761

ORGANISATION/INSTITUTION. . . . .
SECTION OF BOOK . . . .
ADDRESS. . . . .
. . . .
. . . .
. . . . POSTCODE. . . . .
TEL NO · FAX NO . . . .
EMAIL · WEBSITE. . . . .
CONTACT NAME · POSITION . . . .
ADDITIONAL PERSONNEL (WITH TITLES). . . . .
. . . .
COMPREHENSIVE DETAILS

(Please refer to relevant section of book to see the type of information required)
. . . .
. . . .
. . . .
. . . .
. . . .
. . . .
. . . .

Please attach any additional details to support your entry. All
editorial entries are *free,* but are included at the discretion of the Editor.
Entries may be shortened for publication.